WHEN
GHOST MEETS GHOST

BY

WILLIAM DE MORGAN
AUTHOR OF "JOSEPH VANCE," "ALICE-FOR-SHORT," ETC.

NEW YORK
HENRY HOLT AND COMPANY
1914

Dedicated to
The Spirit of Fiction

CONTENTS

PART I

vii

CONTENTS

PART II

WHEN GHOST MEETS GHOST

PART I

WHEN GHOST MEETS GHOST

CHAPTER O

A CONNECTING-LINK BETWEEN THE WRITER AND THE STORY, AMOUNT-
ING TO VERY LITTLE. THERE WAS A COURT SOME FIFTY YEARS
SINCE IN LONDON, SOMEWHERE, THAT IS NOW NOWHERE. THAT'S
ALL !

SOME fifty years ago there still remained, in a street reachable
after inquiry by turning to the left out of Tottenham Court
Road, a rather picturesque Court with an archway; which I, the
writer of this story, could not find when I tried to locate it the
other day. I hunted for it a good deal, and ended by coming
away in despair and going for rest and refreshment to a new-born
teashop, where a number of young ladies had lost their individuality, and the one who brought my tea was callous to me and
mine because you pay at the desk. But she had an orderly soul,
for she turned over the lump of sugar that had a little butter
on it, so as to lie on the buttery side and look more tidy-like.
If the tea had been China tea, fresh-made, it might have
helped me to recollecting the name of that Court, which I am
sorry to say I have forgotten. But it was Ceylon and had stood.
However, it was hot. Only you will never convince me that it
was fresh-made, not even if you have me dragged asunder by
wild horses. Its upshot was, for the purpose of this story, that
it did not help me to recollect the name of that Court.
I have to confess with shame that I have written the whole
of what follows under a false pretence; having called it out of its
name, to the best of my belief, throughout. I know it had a
name. It does not matter; the story can do without accuracy—
commonplace matter of fact !
But do what I will, I keep on recollecting new names for it,
and each seems more plausible than the other. Coltsfoot Court,
Barretts Court, Chesterfield Court, Sapps Court ! Any one of
these, if I add seventeen-hundred-and-much, or eighteen-hundred-
and-nothing-to-speak-of, seems to fit this Court to a nicety. Suppose we make it Sapps Court, and let it go at that !

3

Oh, the little old corners of the world that were homes and are gone! Years hence the Court we will call Sapps will still dwell in some old mind that knew its every brick, and be portrayed to credulous hearers yet unborn as an unpretentious Eden, by some *laudator* of its *tempus actum*—some forgotten soul waiting for emancipation in an infirmary or almshouse.

Anyhow, *I* can remember this Court, and can tell a tale it plays a part in, only not very quick.

Anybody might have passed down the main street and never noticed it, because its arched entry didn't give on the street, but on a bay or *cul-de-sac* just long enough for a hansom to drive into but not to turn round in. There was nothing to arrest the attention of the passer-by, self-absorbed or professionally engaged; simultaneous possibilities, in his case.

But if the passer-by forgot himself and neglected his proper function in life at the moment that he came abreast of this *cul-de-sac,* he may have thereby come to the knowledge of Sapps Court; and, if a Londoner, may have wondered why he never knew of it before. For there was nothing in the external appearance of its arched entry to induce him to face the difficulties incidental to entering it. He may even have nursed intentions of saying to a friend who prided himself on his knowledge of town:—" I say, Old Cock, you think yourself mighty clever and all that, but I bet you can't tell me where Sapps Court is." If, however, he never went down Sapps Court at all—merely looked at his inscription and, recollecting his own place in nature, passed on—I shouldn't be surprised.

It went downhill under the archway when you did go in, and you came to a step. If you did not tumble owing to the suddenness and depth of this step, you came to another; and were stupefied by reaching the ground four inches sooner than you expected, and made conscious that your skeleton had been driven an equal distance upwards through your system. Then you could see Sapps Court, but under provocation, from its entry. When you recovered your temper you admitted that it was a better Court than you had anticipated.

All the residences were in a row on the left, and there was a dead wall on the right with an inscription on a stone in it that said the ground twelve inches beyond belonged to somebody else. This wall was in the confidence of the main street, lending itself to a fiction that the houses therein had gardens or yards behind them. They hadn't; but the tenants believed they had, and hung out chemises and nightgowns and shirts to dry in the areas they built up their faith on; and really, if they were properly wrung out afore hung up there was nothing to complain of, because the blacks didn't hold on, not to crock, but got shook off or blew away of theirselves. We put this in the language of our informant.

However, the story has no business on the other side of this wall. What concerns it is the row of houses on the left.

If ever a row of houses bore upon them the stamp of having been overtaken and surrounded by an unexpected city, these did. The wooden palings that still skirted the breathing-room in front of them almost said aloud to every newcomer:—"Where is the strip of land gone that we could see beyond, day by day; that belonged to God-knows-who; whose further boundary was the road the haycarts brought their loads on, drawn by deliberate horses that had bells?" The persistent sunflowers that still struggled into being behind them told tales of how big they were in youth, years ago, when they could turn to the sun and hope to catch his eye. The stray wallflowers murmured to all who had ears to hear:—"This is how we smelt in days gone by—but oh!—so much stronger!" The wooden shutters, outside the ground-floors that really stood upon the ground, told, if you chose to listen, of how they kept the houses safe from thieves in moonlit nights a century ago; and the doors between them—for each house was three windows wide—opened straight into the kitchen. So they were, or had been, cottages. But the miscreant in possession twenty years ago, instigated by a jerry-builder, had added a storey and removed the tiled roofs whose garrets were every bit as good as the jerry-built rooms that took their place. Sapp himself may have done it—one knows nothing of his principles—and at the same time in a burst of overweening vanity called his cottages his Court. But one rather likes to think that Sapp was with his forbears when this came about, when the wall was built up opposite, and the cottages could no longer throw their dust everywhere, but had to resort to a common dustbin at the end of the Court, which smelt so you could smell it quite plain across the wall when the lid was off. That dustbin was the outward and visible sign of the decadence of Sapp.

CHAPTER I

OF DAVE AND DOLLY WARDLE AND THEIR UNCLE MOSES, WHO HAD
BEEN A PRIZEFIGHTER, AND THEIR AUNT M'RIAR, WHO KEPT AN
EYE ON THEM. OF DAVE'S SERVICES TO THE PUBLIC, AND OF AN-
OTHER PUBLIC THAT NEARLY MADE UNCLE MO BANKRUPT. OF HIS
PAST BATTLES, NOTABLY ONE WITH A SWEEP. OF MRS. PRICHARD
AND MRS. BURR, WHO LIVED UPSTAIRS. OF A BAD ACCIDENT THAT
BEFELL DAVE, AND OF SIMEON STYLITES. HOW UNCLE MO STRAPPED
UP DAVE'S HEAD WITH DIACHYLUM BOUGHT BY A VERY BAD BOY,
MICHAEL RAGSTROAR, THE LIKE OF WHOM YOU NEVER! OF THE
JUDGEMENT OF SOLOMON, AND DAVE'S CAT

IN the last house down the Court, the one that was so handy
to the dustbin, lived a very small boy and a still smaller sister.
There were other members of the household—to wit, their Uncle
Moses and their Aunt M'riar, who were not husband and wife,
but respectively brother and sister of Dave's father and mother.
Uncle Moses' name was Wardle, Aunt M'riar's that of a deceased
or vanished husband. But Sapps Court was never prepared to
say offhand what this name was, and "Aunt M'riar" was universal. So indeed was "Uncle Mo"; but, as No. 7 had been
spoken of as "Wardle's" since his brother took the lower half
of the house for himself and his first wife, with whom he had
lived there fifteen years, the name Wardle had come to be the
name of the house. This brother had been some ten years younger
than Moses, and had had apparently more than his fair share
of the family weddings; as "old Mo," if he ever was married,
had kept the lady secret; from his brother's family certainly, and
presumably from the rest of the world.

Our little boy was the sort of boy you were sorry was ever going
to be eleven, because at five years and ten months he was that
square and compact, that chunky and yet that tender, that no
right-minded person could desire him to be changed to an im-
pident young scaramouch like young Michael Ragstroar four doors
higher up, who was eleven and a regular handful.

His name was Dave Wardle, after his father; and his sister's
Dorothea, after her mother. Both names appeared on a tomb-
stone in the parish churchyard, and you might have thought
they was anybody, said Public Opinion; which showed that Dave

and his sister were orphans. Both had recollections of their father, but the funeral he indulged in three years since had elbowed other memories out of court. Of their mother they only knew by hearsay, as Dave was only three years old when his sister committed matricide, quite unconsciously, and you could hear her all the way up the Court. Pardon the story's way of introducing attestations to some fact of interest or importance in the language in which its compiler has received it.

They were good children to do with, said their Aunt M'riar, so long as you kep' an eye. And a good job they were, because who was to do her work if she was every minute prancing round after a couple of young monkeys? This was a strained way of indicating the case; but there can be no doubt of its substantial truth. So Aunt M'riar felt at rest so long as Dave was content to set up atop of the dustbin-lid and shout till he was hoarse; all the while using a shovel, that was public property, as a gong.

Perhaps Dave took his sister Dolly into his confidence about the nature of the trust he conceived himself to hold in connection with this dustbin. To others of the inhabitants he was reticent, merely referring to an emolument he was entitled to. " The man on the lid," he said, " has a farden." He said this with such conviction that few had the heart to deny the justice of the claim outright, resorting to subterfuges to evade a cash settlement. One had left his change on the piano; another was looking forward to an early liquidation of small liabilities on the return of his ship to port; another would see about it next time Sunday come of a Friday, and so on. But only his Uncle Moses ever gave him an actual farthing, and Dave deposited it in a cat on the mantelshelf, who was hollow by nature, and provided by art with a slot in the dorsal vertebræ. It could be shook out if you wanted it, and Dave occasionally took it out of deposit in connection with a course of experiments he was interested in. He wished to determine how far he could spit it out.

This inquiry was a resource against *ennui* on rainy days and foggy days and days that were going to clear up later. All these sorts were devised by the malignity of Providence for the confusion of small boys yearning to be on active service, redistributing property, obstructing traffic, or calling attention to personal peculiarities of harmless passers-by. But it was not so inexhaustible but that cases occurred when those children got that unsettled and masterful there was no abiding their racket; and as for Dolly, her brother was making her every bit as bad as himself. At such times a great resource was to induce Uncle

Moses to tell some experiences of a glorious past, his own. For he had been a member of the Prize Ring, and had been slapped on the back by Dukes, and had even been privileged to grasp a Royal hand. He was now an unwieldy giant, able to get about with a stick when the day was fine, but every six months less inclined for the effort.

Uncle Moses, when he retired from public life, had put all his winnings, which were considerable, into a long lease of a pot-house near Golden Square, where he was well-known and very popular. If, however, there had been a rock on the premises and he had had all the powers of his namesake, four-half would have had to run as fast from it as ever did water from the rock in Horeb, to keep down the thirst of Golden Square. For Uncle Moses not only refused to take money from old friends who dwelt in his memory, but weakly gave way to constructive allegations of long years of comradeship in a happy past, which his powers of recollection did not enable him to contradict. " Wot, old Moses!—you'll never come for to go for to say you've forgot old Swipey Sam, jist along in the Old Kent Road—Easy Shavin' one 'apenny or an arrangement come to by the week! " Or merely, " Seein' you's as good as old times come alive again, mate." Suchlike appeals were almost invariable from any cus- tomer who got fair speech of Uncle Moses in his own bar. In his absence these claims were snuffed out roughly by a prosaic barman—even the most pathetic ones, such as that of an extinct thimblerigger for whom three small thimbles and one little pea had ceased for ever, years ago, when he got his fingers in a sausage- machine. But Uncle Moses was so much his own barman that this generosity told heavily against his credit; and he would certainly have been left a pauper but for the earnest counsels of an old friend known in his circle of Society as Affability Bob, although his real name was Jeremiah Alibone. By him he was persuaded to dispose of the lease of the " Marquess of Montrose " while it still had some value, and to retire on a pound a week. This might have been more had he invested all the proceeds in an annuity. " But, put it I do! " said he. " I don't see my way to no advantage for David and Dorothy, and this here young newcome, if I was to hop the twig." For this was at the time of the birth of little Dave, nearly six years before the date of this story.

Affability Bob applauded his friend's course of action in view of its motive. " But," said he, " I tell you this, Moses. If you'd 'a' gone on standin' Sam to every narrycove round about Soho

much longer, 'No effects' would have been *your* vardict, sir."
To which Uncle Moses replied, "Right you are, old friend," and
changed the subject.

However, there you have plenty to show what a rich mine of
past experience Uncle Moses had to dig in. The wonder was
that Dave and Dolly refused to avail themselves of its wealth,
always preferring a monotonous repetition of an encounter their
uncle had had with a Sweep. He could butt, this Sweep could,
like a battering-ram, ketching hold upon you symultaneous
round the gaiters. He was irresistible by ordinary means, his
head being unimpressionable by direct impact. But Uncle Moses
had been one'too many for him, having put a lot of thinking into
the right way of dealing with his system.

He had perceived that the hardest head, struck evenly on both
sides at the same moment, must suffer approximately as much
as if jammed against the door-post and catched full with a fair
round swing. Whereas had these blows followed one another
on a yielding head, the injury it inflicted as a battering-ram
might have outweighed the damage it received in inflicting it.
As it was, Peter—so Uncle Moses called the Sweep—was for one
moment defenceless, being preoccupied in seizing his opponent
by the ankles; and although his cranium had no sinuses, and
was so thick it could crush a quart-pot like an opera-hat, it did
not court a fourth double concussion, and this time he was
destined to disappoint his backers.

His opponent, who in those days was known as the Hanley
Linnet, suffered very little in the encounter. No doubt you
know that a man in fine training can take an amazing number
of back-falls on fair ground, clear of snags and brickbats; and,
of course, the Linnet's seconds made a special point of this,
examining careful and keeping an eye to prevent the introduction of broke-up rubbish inside the ropes by parties having an
interest, or viciously disposed.

"There you are again, Uncle Mo, a-tellin' and a-tellin' and
a-tellin'!" So Aunt M'riar would say when she heard this narrative going over well-known ground for the thousandth time.
"And them children not lettin' you turn round in bed, *I* call
it!" This was in reference to Dave and Dolly's severity about
the text. The smallest departure from the earlier version led
to both them children pouncing at once. Dave would exclaim
reproachfully:—"You *did* say a Sweep with one blind eye, Uncle
Mo!" and Dolly would confirm his words with as much emphasis
as her powers of speech allowed. "Essoodid, a 'Weep with one

b'ind eye!"—also reproachfully. Then Uncle Moses would supply a corrected version of whatever was defective, in this case
an eye not quite blind, but nearly, owing to a young nipper,
no older than Dave, aiming a broken bottle at him as the orficers was conducting of him to the Station, after a fight Wands-
worth way, the other party being took off to the Horspital for
dead.

The Jews, I am told, won't stand any nonsense when they
have their sacred writings copied, always destroying every inaccurate MS. the moment an error is spotted in it. Dave and
Dolly were not the Jews, but they were as intolerant of variation in the text of this almost sacred legend of the Sweep.
"S'ow me how you punched him, wiv Dave's head," Dolly would
say; and she would be most exacting over the dramatic rendering
of this ancient fight. "Percisely this way like I'm showing you—
only harder," was Uncle Moses' voucher for his own accuracy.
"Muss harder?" inquired Dolly. "Well—a tidy bit harder!"
said the veteran with truth. The head of the Sweep's understudy, Dave, was not equal to a full-dress rehearsal. So Dolly
had to be content with the promise of a closer reading of the
part when her brother was growed up.

But it was rather like Aunt M'riar said, for Uncle Moses.
Those two young Turks didn't allow their uncle no latitude, in
the manner of speaking. He couldn't turn round in bed.

These rainy days, when the children could not possibly be
allowed out, taxed their guardians' patience just to the point
of making them—suppose we say—not ungrateful to Providence
when old Mrs. Prichard upstairs giv' leave for the children to
come and play up in her room. She was the only other in-
dweller in the house, living in the front and back attics with Mrs.
Burr, who took jobs out in the dressmaking, and very moderate
charges. When Mrs. Burr worked at home, Mrs. Prichard
enjoyed her society and knitted, while Mrs. Burr cut out and
basted. Very few remarks were passed; for though Mrs. Burr
was snappish now and again, company was company, and Mrs.
Prichard she put up with a little temper at times, because we
all had our trials; and Mrs. Burr was considered good at heart,
though short with you now and again. Hence when loneliness
became irksome, Mrs. Prichard found Dave and Dolly a satisfaction, so long as nothing was broke. It was a pleasant extension of the experience of their early youth to play at monarchs,
military celebrities, professional assassins, and so on, in old Mrs.
Prichard's room upstairs. And sometimes nothing *was* broke.

Otherwise one day at No. 7, Sapps Court, was much the same as another.

Uncle Mo's residence in Sapps Court dated many years before the coming of Aunt M'riar; in fact, as far back as the time he was deprived of his anchorage in Soho. He was then taken in by his brother, recently a widower; and no question had ever arisen of his quitting the haven he had been, as it were, towed into as a derelict; until, some years later, David announced that he was thinking of Dolly Tarver at Ealing. Moses smoked through a pipe in silence, so as to give full consideration; then said, like an easy-going old boy as he was:—"You might do worse, Dave. I can clear out, any minute. You've only got to sing out." To which his brother had replied:—"Don't you talk of clearing out, not till Miss Tarver she tells you." Moses' answer was:—"I'm agreeable, Dave"; and the matter dropped until some time after, when he had made Dolly Tarver's acquaintance. She, on hearing that her union with David would send Mo again adrift, had threatened to declare off if such a thing was so much as spoke of. So Moses had remained on, in the character of a permanency saturated with temporariness; and, when the little boy Dave began to take his place in Society, proceeded to appropriate—so said the child's parents—more than an uncle's fair share of him.

Then came the tragedy of his mother's death, causing the Court to go into mourning, and leaving Dave with a sister, too young to be conscious of responsibility for it. Not too young, however, to make her case heard—the case all living things have against the Power that creates them without so much as asking leave. The riot she made being interpreted by both father and uncle as protest against Mrs. Twiggins, a midwife who made herself disagreeable—or, strictly speaking, more disagreeable; being normally unpleasant, and apt to snap when spoke to, however civil—it was thought desirable to call in the help of her Aunt M'riar, who was living with her family at Ealing as a widow without incumbrance. Dolly junior appeared to calm down under Aunt M'riar's auspices, though every now and then her natural indignation got the better of her self-restraint. Dave junior was disgusted with his sister at first, but softened gradually towards her as she matured.

His father did not long survive the death of his young wife. Even an omnibus-driver is not exempt from inflammation of the lungs, although the complaint is not so fatal among persons exposed to all weathers as among leaders of indoor lives. A violent double pneumonia carried off Uncle Mo's brother, six months after he became a widower, and about three years before the date of this story.

Whether in some other class of life a marriageable uncle and aunt—sixty and forty respectively—would have accepted their condominium of the household that was left, it is not for the story to discuss. Uncle Moses refused to give up the two babies, and Aunt M'riar refused to leave them, and—as was remarked by both—there you were! It was an *impasse.* The only effect it had on the position was that Uncle Mo's temporariness got a little boastful, and slighted his permanency. The latter, however, paid absolutely no attention to the insult, and the only change that took place in the three following years at No. 7, Sapps Court, had nothing to do with the downstairs tenants. Some months before the first date of the story, a variation came about in the occupancy upstairs, Mrs. Prichard and Mrs. Burr taking the place of some parties who, if the truth was told, were rather a riddance. The fact is merely recorded as received; nothing further has transpired regarding these persons.

Mrs. Prichard was a very old lady who seldom showed herself outside of her own room—so the Court testified—but who, when she did so, impressed the downstairs tenants as of unfathomable antiquity and a certain pictorial appearance, causing Uncle Mo to speak of her as an old picter, and Dave to misapprehend her name. For he always spoke of her as old Mrs. Picture. Mrs. Burr dawned upon the Court as a civil-spoken person who was away most part of the day, and who did not develope her identity vigorously during the first year of her tenancy. One is terribly handicapped by one's own absence, as a member of any Society.

As time went on, Dave and Dolly, who began life with an idea that Sapps Court was the Universe, became curious about what was going on outside. They grew less contented with the dustbin, and ambition dictated to Dave an enthronement on an iron post at the entrance, under the archway. The delight of sitting on this post was so great that Dave willingly faced the fact that he could not get down, and whenever he could persuade anyone to put him up ran a risk of remaining there *sine die.* When he could not induce a native of the Court to do this, he endeavoured to influence the outer public, not without success. For when it came to understand—that public—that the grubby little tenant of Dave's grubby little shirt and trousers was not asking the time nor for a hoyp'ny, but was murmuring shyly:—"I soy, mawster, put me up atop," at the same time slapping the post on either side with two grubby little fat hands, it would unbend and comply, telling Dave to hold on tight, and never asking no questions how ever the child was to be got off of it when the time came. Because people are that selfish and inconsiderate.

The difficulty of getting down off of it all by himself, without a friendly supporting hand in the waistband of his trousers, was connected with the form of this post's head. It was not a disused twenty-four pounder with a shot in its muzzle, as so many posts are, but a real architectural post, cast from a pattern at the foundry. Its capital expanded at the top, and its projecting rim made its negotiation difficult to climbers, if small; hard to get round from below, and perilous to leave hold of all of a sudden-like, in order to grasp the shaft in descent. But then, it was this very expansion that provided a seat for Dave, which the other sort of post would hardly have afforded.

How did Simeon Stylites manage to scrat on? One prefers to think that an angel put him on his column, carrying him somewhat as one carries a cat; and called for him to be taken down at convenient intervals by appointment. The mind revolts at the idea that he really never came down, quite never! But then, when the starving man is on at the Aquarium, we—that is to say, the humane public—are apt to give way to mere maudlin sentimentalism, and hope he is cheating. And when a person at a Music Hall folds backwards and looks through his legs at us forwards, we always hope he feels no strain—nothing but a great and justifiable professional pride. It is not a pleasant feeling that any of these good people are suffering on our behalf. However, in the case of Simeon Stylites there was a mixture of motives, no doubt.

Dave Wardle was too young to have motives, and had none. unless the desire to surprise and impress Dolly had weight with him. But he had the longing on him which that young gentleman in the poem expressed by writing the Latin for *taller* on a flag.; and to gratify it had scaled the dustbin as the merest infant. It was an Alpine record. But the iron post was no mere Matterhorn. It was like Peter Bot's Mountain; and once you was up, there you were, and no getting down!

The occasional phrases for which I am indebted to Aunt M'riar which have crept into the text recently—not, as I think, to its detriment—were used by her after a mishap which befell her nephew owing to the child's impatience. If he'd only a had the sense to set still a half a minute longer, she would have done them frills and could have run up the Court a'most as soon as look at you. But she hoped what had happened would prove a warning, not only to Dave, but to all little boys in a driving hurry to get off posts. And not only to them either, but to Youth generally, to pay attention to what was said to it by Age and Experience, neither of which ever climb up posts without some safe guarantee of being able to climb down again.

What had happened was that Dave had cut his head on the ornate plinth of that cast-iron post, his hands missing their grip as his legs caught the shaft, so that he turned over backwards and his occiput suffered. He showed a splendid spirit— quite Spartan, in fact—bearing in mind his uncle's frequent homilies on the subject of crying; a thing no little boy, however young, should dream of. Dolly was under no such obligation, according to Uncle Moses, being a female or the rudiment of one, and on this occasion she roared for herself and her brother, too. Aunt M'riar was in favour of taking the child to Mr. Ekins, the apothecary, for skilled surgery to deal with the case, but Uncle Moses scouted the idea.

" Twopenn'orth o' stroppin' and a basin o' warm water," said he, " and I'll patch him up equal to Guy's Hospital. . . . Got no diacklum? Then send one of those young varmints outside for it. . . . You've no call to go yourself." For a various crowd of various ages under twelve had come from nowhere to enjoy the tragic incident.

" Twopenn'orth of diaculum plaster off of Mr. Ekings the 'poarthecary? " said that young Michael Ragstroar, thrusting himself forward and others backward; because, you see, he was such a cheeky, precocious young vagabond. " Mean to say I can't buy twopenn'orth of diaculum plaster off of Mr. Ekings the 'poarthecary? Mean to say my aunt that orkupies a 'ouse in Chiswick clost to high-water mark don't send me to the 'poarthecaries just as often as not? For the mixture to be taken regular . . . Ah!—where's the twopence? 'And over! "

Whereupon, such is the power of self-confidence over everyone else, that Aunt M'riar entrusted twopence to this youth, quite forgetting that he was only eleven. Yet her faith in him was not ill-founded, for he returned like an echo as to promptitude. Only, unlike the echo, he came back louder than he went, and more positive.

" There's the quorntity and no cheatin'," said he. " You can medger it up with a rule if you like. It'll medger, you find if it don't! Like I told you! And a 'apenny returned on the transaction." The tension of the situation did not admit of the measuring test—nor indeed had Aunt M'riar data to go upon—and as for the halfpenny, it stood over.

Uncle Moses had not laid false claim to surgical skill, and was able to strap the wound a'most as if he'd been brought up to it. By the time it was done Dave's courage was on the wane, and he wasn't sorry to lie his head down and shut to his eyes. Because the lids thereof were like the lids of plate-chests.

However, before he went off very sound asleep—so sound you might have took him for a image—he heard what passed between Uncle Moses and Michael, whose name has been spelt herein so that you should think of it as Sapps Court did; but its correct form is Rackstraw.

" Now, young potato-peelin's, how much money did the doctor hand you back for that diacklum? "

" Penny. Said he'd charge it up to the next Dook that come to his shop."

Thereupon Aunt M'riar taxed the speaker with perfidy. " Why, you little untrue, lyin', deceitful story," she said. " To think you should say it was only a ha'penny! "

" I never said no such a thing. S'elp me! "

" ' 'Apenny returned on the transaction ' was the very identical selfsame words." Thus Aunt M'riar testified. " And what is more," she added inconsecutively, " I do not believe you've any such an aunt, nor yet ever been to Chiswick."

But young potato-peelings, so called from his father's vocation of costermonger, defended himself with indignation. " Warn't that square? " said he. " He never said I warn't to keep it all, didn't that doctor! " Then he took a high position as of injured virtue. " There's your 'apenny! There's both your 'apennies! Mean to say I 'aven't kep' 'em safe for yer? " Uncle Moses allowed the position of bailee, but disposed of the penny as Solomon suggested in the case of the baby, giving one halfpenny to Michael, and putting the other in Dave's cat on the mantel-shelf.

He justified this course afterwards on the ground that the doctor's refund was made to the actual negotiator, and that Aunt M'riar had in any case received full value for her money. Who could say that the doctor, if referred to, would not have repudiated Aunt M'riar's claim *in toto?*

Warnings, cautions, and moral lessons derived from this incident had due weight with Dave for several days; in fact, until his cut healed over. Then he forgot them and became as bad as ever.

CHAPTER II

HOW DAVE FAILED TO PROFIT BY HIS EXPERIENCE. OF PAOLO TOSCANELLI AND CHRISTOPHER COLUMBUS. OF A NEW SHORE DAVE AND DOLLY REACHED BY EXPLORATION, ROUND THE CORNER; AND OF OTHER NAVIGATORS WHO HAD, IN THIS CASE, MADE IT FOR THEMSELVES. OF THE PUBLIC SPIRIT OF DAVE AND DOLLY, AND THE CONSTRUCTION OF A *BARRAGE*. HOW MRS. TAPPING AND MRS. RILEY HEARD THE ENGINES. OF A SHORTAGE OF MUD, AND A GREAT RESOLVE OF DAVE'S. WHY NOT SOME NEW MUD FROM THE NEW SHORE?

THE interest of Dave's accident told in the last chapter is merely collateral. It shows how narrow an escape the story that follows had not only of never being finished, but even of never being written. For if its events had never happened, it goes near to certainty that they would never have been narrated. Near, but not quite. For even if Dave had profited by these warnings, cautions, and moral lessons to the extent of averting what now appears to have been Destiny, some imaginative author might have woven a history showing exactly what might have happened to him if he had not been a good boy. And that history, in the hands of a master—one who had the organ of the conditional præterpluperfect tense very large—might have worked out the same as this.

The story may be thankful that no such task has fallen to its author's lot. It is so much easier to tell something that actually did happen than to make up as you go.

Dave was soon as bad as ever—no doubt of it. Only he kept clear of that post. The burnt child dreads the fire, and the chances are that admonitions not to climb up on posts had less to do with his abstention from this one than the lesson the post itself had hammered into the back of his head. Exploration of the outer world—of the regions imperfectly known beyond that post—had so far produced no fatal consequences; so that Aunt M'riar's and Uncle Mo's warnings to the children to keep within bounds had not the same convincing character.

But a time was at hand for the passion of exploration to seize upon these two very young people, and to become an excitement as absorbing to them as the discovery of America to Paolo

Toscanelli and Christopher Columbus. At first it was satisfied by the *cul-de-sac* recess on which Sapps Court opened. But this palled, and no wonder! How could it compete with the public highway out of which it branched, especially when there was a new shore—that is to say, sewer—in course of construction?

To stand on the edge of a chasm which certainly reached to the bowels of the earth, and to see them shovelled up from plat-form to platform by agencies that spat upon their hands for some professional reason whenever there came a lull in the supply from below, was to find life worth living indeed. These agencies conversed continually about an injury that had been inflicted on them by the Will of God, the selfish caprice of their employers, or the cupidity of the rich. They appeared to be capable of shovelling in any space, however narrow, almost to the extent of surrendering one dimension and occupying only a plane surface. But it hadn't come to that yet. The battens that kept the trench-sides vertical were wider apart than what you'd have thought, when you come to try 'em with a two-fut rule. And the short lengths of quartering that kep' 'em apart were not really intersecting the diggers' anatomies as the weaver's shuttle passes through the warp. That was only the impression of the unconcerned spectator as he walked above them over the plank bridge that acknowledged his right of way across the road. His sympathies remained unentangled. If people navigated, it was their own look out. You see, these people were navvies, or navigators, although it strains one's sense of language to describe them so.

The best of it was to come. For in time the lowest navvy was threatened with death by misadventure, unless he come up time enough to avoid the water. The small pump the job had been making shift with was obliged to acknowledge itself beaten, and to make way for one with two handles, each with room for two pumpers; and this in turn was discarded in favour of a noisy affair with a donkey-engine, which brought up the yellow stream as fast as ever a gutter of nine-inch plank, nailed up to a **V**, would carry it away. And it really was a most extraordinary thing that of all those navigators there was not one that had not predicted in detail exactly the course of events that had come about. Mr. Bloxam, the foreman, had told the governor that there would be no harm in having the pump handy, seeing they would go below the clay. And each of the others had—so they themselves said—spoken in the same sense, in some cases using a most inappropriate adjective to qualify the expected flood. Why, even Sleepy Joe had seen that! Sleepy Joe was this same foreman, and he lived in a wooden hutch on the job, called The Office.

But the watershed of any engine—whatever may be its donkey-power, and whatever that name implies—slops back where a closed spout changes suddenly to an open gutter, and sets up independent lakes and rivers. This one sent its overflow towards Sapps Court, the incline favouring its distribution along the gutter of the *cul-de-sac,* which lay a little lower than the main street it opened out of. Its rich, ochrous rivulets—containing no visible trace of hæmorrhage, in spite of that abuse of an adjective—were creeping slowly along the interstices of cobblestone paving that still outlived the incoming of Macadam, when Dave and Dolly Wardle ventured out of their archway to renew a survey, begun the previous day, of the fascinating excavation in the main street.

Here was an opportunity for active and useful service not to be lost. Dave immediately cast about to scrape up and collect such mud as came ready to hand, and with it began to build up an intercépting embankment to stop the foremost current, that was winding slowly, like Vesuvian lava, on the line of least resistance. Dolly followed his example, filling a garment she called her pinafore with whatever mould or *débris* was attainable, and bringing it with much gravity and some pride to help on the structure of the dyke. A fiction, rather felt than spoken, got in the air that Sapps Court and its inhabitants would be overwhelmed as by Noah's flood, except for the exertions of Dave and his sister. It appealed to some friends of the same age, also inhabitants of the Court, and with their assistance and sympathy it really seemed—in this fiction—that a catastrophe might be averted. You may imagine what a drove of little grubs those children looked in the course of half an hour. Not that any of them were particularly spruce to begin with.

However, there was the embankment holding back the dirty yellow water; and now the pump was running on steady-like, there didn't so much come slopping over to add to the deluge that threatened Sapps Court. The policeman—the only one supposed to exist, although in form he varied slightly—made an inquiry as to what was going on, to be beforehand with Anarchy. He said:—"What are you young customers about, taking the Company's water?" That seemed to embody an indictment without committing the accuser to particulars. But he took no active steps, and a very old man with a fur cap, and

no teeth, and big bones in his cheeks, said:—"It don't make no
odds to we, I take it." He was a prehistoric navvy, who had
become a watchman, and was responsible for red lanterns hooked
to posts on the edge of chasms to warn carts off. He was going
to sleep in half a tent, soothed or otherwise by the unflagging
piston of that donkey-engine, which had made up its mind to
go till further notice.

The men were knocking off work, and it was getting on for
time for those children to have their suppers and be put to bed.
But as Aunt M'riar had some trimming to finish, and it was a
very fine evening, there was no harm in leaving them alone a
few minutes longer. As for any attractive influences of supper,
those children never come in of theirselves, and always had to be
fetched.

An early lamplighter—for this was in September, 1853—
passed along the street with a ladder, dropping stars as he went.
There are no lamplighters now, no real ones that run up ladders.
Their ladders vanished first, leaving them with a magic wand
that lighted the gas as soon as you got the tap turned; only that
was ever so long, as often as not. Perhaps things are better
now that lamps light themselves instinctively at the official
hour of sunset. At any rate, one has the satisfaction of occasionally seeing one that won't go out, but burns on into the daylight to spite the Authorities.

They were cold stars, almost green, that this lamplighter
dropped; but this was because the sun had left a flood of orange-
gold behind it, enough to make the tune from "Rigoletto" an
organ was playing think it was being composed in Italy again.
The world was a peaceful world, because Opulence, inflated and
moderate, had gone out of town: the former to its country-house,
or a foreign hotel; the latter to lodgings at the seaside to bathe
out of machines and prey on shrimps. The lull that reigned in
and about Sapps Court was no doubt a sort of recoil or backwater from other neighbourhoods, with high salaries or real and
personal estate, whose dwellings were closed and not being
properly ventilated by their caretakers. It reacted on business
there, every bit as much as in Oxford Street; and that was how
Tapping's the tallow-chandler's—where you got tallow candles
and dips, as well as composites; for in those days they still
chandled tallow—didn't have a single customer in for ten whole
minutes by the clock. In that interval Mrs. Tapping seized the
opportunity to come out in the street and breathe the air. So
did Mrs. Riley next door, and they stood conversing on the topics

of the day, looking at the sunset over the roofs of the *cul-de-sac* this story has reference to. For Mrs. Tapping's shop was in the main road, opposite to where the embankment operations were in hand.

"Ye never will be tellin' me now, Mrs. Tapping, that ye've not hur-r-rd thim calling 'Fire!' in the sthrate behind? Fy-urr, fy-urr, fy-urr!" This is hard to write as Mrs. Riley spoke it, so great was her command of the letter *r*.

"Now you name it, Mrs. Riley, deny it I can't. But to the point of taking notice to bear in mind—why no! It was on my ears, but only to be let slip that minute. Small amounts and accommodations frequent, owing to reductions on quantity took, distrack attention. I was a-sayin' to my stepdaughter only the other day that hearin' is one thing and listenin' is another. And she says to me, she says, I was talking like a book, she says. Her very expression and far from respectful! So I says to her, not to be put upon, 'Lethear,' I says, 'books ain't similar all through but to seleck from, and I go accordin'. . . .'" Mrs. Tapping, whose system was always to turn the conversation to some incident in which she had been prominent, might have developed this one further, but Mrs. Riley interrupted her with Celtic *naïveté*.

"D'ye mane to say, me dyurr, that ye can't hearr 'em now? Kape your tongue silent and listen!" A good, full brogue permits speech that would offend in colourless Saxon; and Mrs. Tapping made no protest, but listened. Sure enough the rousing, maddening "Fire, fire, fire, fire, fire!" was on its way at speed somewhere close at hand. It grew and lessened and died. And Mrs. Riley was triumphant. "That's a larrudge fire, shure!" said she, transposing her impression of the enthusiasm of the engine to the area of the conflagration. Cold logic perceives that an engine may be just as keen to pump on a cottage as on a palace, before it knows which. Mrs. Riley had come from Tipperary, and had brought a sympathetic imagination with her, leaving any logic she possessed behind.

A few minutes before the lamplighter passed—saying to the old watchman:—" Goin' to bed, Sam?" and on receiving the reply, "Time enough yet!" rejoining sarcastically:—" Time enough for a quart!"—the labourers at the dyke had recognised the fact that unless new material could be obtained, the pent-up waters would burst the curb and bound, rejoicing to be free, and rush headlong to the nearest drain. All the work would be lost unless a fresh supply could be obtained; the ruling fiction of a new

Noachian deluge might prove a deadly reality instead of, as now, a theoretical contingency under conditions which engineering skill might avert. The Sappers and Miners who were roused from their beds to make good a dynamited embankment and block the relentless Thames did not work with a more untiring zeal to baffle a real enemy than did Dave and Dolly to keep out a fictitious one, and hypothetically save Uncle Moses and Aunt M'riar from drowning. But all efforts would be useless if there was to be a shortage of mud.

The faces of our little friends, and their little friends, were earnestness itself as they concentrated on the great work in the glow of the sunset. They had no eyes for its glories. The lamplighter even, dropping jewels as he went, passed them by unheeded. The organ interpreted Donizetti in vain. Despair seemed imminent when Dolly, who, though small, was as keen as the keenest of the diggers, came back after a special effort with no more than the merest handful of gutter-scrapings, saying with a most pathetic wail:—" I tan't det no more! "

Then it was that a great resolve took shape in the heart of Dave. It found utterance in the words:—" Oy wants some of the New Mud the Men spoyded up with their spoyds," and pointed to an ambitious scheme for securing some of the fine rich clay that lay in a tempting heap beyond the wooden bridge across the sewer-trench. The bridge that Dave had never even stood upon, much less crossed!

The daring, reckless courage of the enterprise! Dolly gasped with awe and terror. She was too small to find at a moment's notice any terms in which she could dissuade Dave from so venturesome a project. Besides, her faith in her brother amounted to superstition. Dave *must* know what was practicable and righteous. Was he not nearly six years old? She stood speechless and motionless, her heart in her mouth as she watched him go furtively across that awful bridge of planks and get nearer and nearer to his prize.

There were lions in his path, as there used to be in the path of knights-errant when they came near the castles of necromancers who held beautiful princesses captive—to say nothing of full-blown dragons and alluring syrens. These lions took in one case, the form of a butcher-boy, who said untruthfully:—" Now, young hobstacle, clear out o' this! Boys ain't allowed on bridges; " and in another that of Michael Ragstroar, who said, " Don't you let the Company see you carryin' off their property. They'll rip you open as soon as look at you. You'll be took afore the Beak." Dave was not yet old enough to see what a very perverted view of legal process these words contained, but his blue eyes looked mistrustfully at the speaker as he watched him pass up the street towards the Wheatsheaf, swinging a yellow jug with ridges round its neck and a full corporation. Michael had been sent to fetch the beer.

If the blue eyes had not remained fixed on that yellow jug and its bearer till both vanished through the swing-door of the Wheatsheaf—if their owner's mistrust of his informant had been strong enough to cancel the misgivings that crossed his baby mind, only a few seconds sooner, would things have gone otherwise with Dave? Would he have used that beautiful lump of clay, as big as a man of his age could carry, on the works that were to avert Noah's flood from Sapps Court? Would he and Dolly not probably have been caught at their escapade by an indignant Aunt M'riar, corrected, duly washed and fed, and sent to bed sadder and wiser babies? So few seconds might have made the whole difference.

Or, if that heap of clay had been thrown on the other side of the trench, on the pavement instead of towards the traffic— why then the children might have taken all they could carry, and Old Sam would have countenanced them, in reason, as like as not. But how little one gains by thinking what might have been! The tale is to tell, and tells that these things were not otherwise, but thus.

Uncle Moses was in the room on the right of the door, called the parlour, smoking a pipe with the old friend whose advice had probably kept him from coming on the parish.

" Aunt M'riar! " said he, tapping his pipe out on the hob, and taking care the ashes didn't get in the inflammable stove-ornament, " I don't hear them young customers outside. What's got 'em? "

" Don't you begin to fret and werrit till I tell you to it, Moses. The children's safe and not in any mischief—no more than usual. Mr. Alibone seen 'em." For although the world called this friend Affability Bob and Uncle Moses gave him his christened name, Aunt M'riar always spoke of him, quite civil-like, thus.

" You see the young nippers, Jerry? " said the old prizefighter; who always got narvous, as you might say, though scarcely alarmed, when they got out of sight and hearing; even if it was for no more time than what an egg takes.

" Jist a step beyond the archway, Mosey," said Mr. Alibone.

"Paddlin' and sloppin' about with the water off o' the shore-pump. It's all clean water, Mrs. Catchpole, only for a little clay."
Aunt M'riar, whose surname was an intrinsic improbability in the eyes of Public Opinion, and who was scarcely ever called by it, except by Mr. Jerry, expressed doubts. So he continued:—
"You see, they're sinking for a new shore clear of the old one. So nothing's been opened into."
"Well," said Aunt M'riar, "I certainly did think the flaviour was being kep' under wonderful. But now you put it so, I understand. What I say is—if dirt, then clean dirt; and above all no chemicals! . . . What's that you're saying, Uncle Mo?"
"Why, I was a-thinking," said Uncle Moses, who seemed rest-less, "I was a-thinking, Bob, that you and me might have our pipes outside, being dry underfoot." For Uncle Moses, being gouty, was ill-shod for wet weather. He was slippered, though not lean. And though Mrs. Burr, coming in just then, added her testimony that the children were quite safe and happy, only making a great mess, Uncle Moses would not be content to remain indoors, but must needs be going out. "These here young juveniles," said he, outside in the Court, "where was it you took stock of 'em, did you say?"
"Close to hand," said Affability Bob. "One step out of the archway. There you'll find 'em, old man. Don't you fret your kidneys. They're all right. Hear the engines?"
"Whereabouts is the fire?"
"Somewhere down by Walworth. I saw the smoke, crossing Hungerford Bridge. This engine's coming down our road out-side."
"I reckon she may be, by the sound. She'll be half-way to Blackfriars before we're out of this here Court. If she gets by where the road's up! Maybe she'll have to go back."
"There she stops! What's the popilation shoutin' at?" For the tramp of the engine's horses, heard plain enough on the main road, came to an end abruptly, and sounds ensued—men's shouts, women's cries—not reconcilable with the mere stoppage of a fire-engine by unexpected narrows or an irregular coal-cart.
"Couldn't say, I'm sure. They're a nizy lot in these parts." So said Uncle Moses, and walked slowly up the Court, stopping for breath half-way.

CHAPTER III

WHY THAT ENGINE STOPPED.   BUT THE WHEELS HAD NOT GONE OVER
DAVE.   HOW PETER JACKSON CARRIED HIM AWAY TO THE HOSPITAL.
OF DOLLY'S DESPAIR AT THE COLLAPSE OF THE *BARRAGE*, AND OF
AN OLD COCK, NAMED SAM.   MRS. TAPPING'S EXPERIENCES, AND
HER DAUGHTER, ALETHEA.   OF THE VICISSITUDES OF THE PUBLIC,
AND ITS AMAZING RECUPERATIVE POWERS.   HOW UNCLE MOSES AND
MR. ALIBONE WENT TO THE HOSPITAL

So few seconds would have made the whole difference. But so
engrossing had Dave found the contemplation of Michael Ragstroar and his yellow jug, so exciting particularly was its disappearance into the swing-door of the Wheatsheaf, that he
forgot even the new mud that the men had spaded up with their
spades. And these seconds slipped by never to return. Then
when Michael had vanished, the little man stooped to secure his
cargo. It was slippery and yet tenacious; had been detachable
with difficulty from the spade that wrenched it from the virgin
soil of its immemorial home, and was now difficult to carry.
But Dave grappled bravely with it and turned to go back across
the bridge.

A coming whirlwind, surely, in the distance of the street—
somewhere now where all the gas-lamps' cold green stars are
merged in one—now nearer, nearer still; and with it, bringing
folk to doors and windows to see them pass, the war-cry of the
men that fight the flames. Charioteers behind blood-horses
bathed in foam; heads helmeted in flashing splendour; eyes all
intent upon the track ahead, keen to anticipate the risks of
headlong speed and warn the dilatory straggler from its path.
Nearer and nearer—in a moment it will pass and take some road
unknown to us, to say to fires that even now are climbing up
through roof and floor, clasping each timber in a sly embrace
fatal as the caress of Death itself :—" Thus far shalt thou go and
no farther ! " Close upon us now, to be stayed with a sudden cry
—something in the path ! Too late !

Too late, though the strong hand that held the reins brought
back the foaming steeds upon their haunches, with startled eyes
and quivering nostrils all agape. Too late, though the helmeted
men on the engine's flank were down, almost before its swerve

had ceased, to drag at every risk from beneath the plunging hoofs the insensible body of the child that had slipped from a clay heap by the roadside, on which it stood to gaze upon the coming wonder, and gone headlong down quite suddenly upon the open road.

You who read this, has it ever fallen to your lot to guide two swift horses at a daring speed through the narrow ways, the ill-driven vehicles, the careless crowds and frequent drunkards of the slum of a great city? If so, you have earned some right to sit in judgment on the fire-engine that ran our little friend down. But you will be the last of all men to condemn that fire-engine.

"Dead, mate?" One of the helmeted men asks this of the other as they escape from the plunging hoofs. They are used to this sort of thing—to every sort of thing.

"Insensible," says the other, who holds in his arms the rescued child, a mere scrap of dust and clay and pallor and a little blood.

A fire-engine calculates its rights to pause in fractions of a minute. The unused portion of twenty seconds the above conversation leaves, serves for a glance round in search of some claimant of the child, or a responsible police-officer to take over the case. Nothing presents itself but Mrs. Tapping, too much upset to be coherent, and not able to identify the child; Mrs. Riley, little better, but asking:—"Did the whales go overr it, thin?" The old man Sam, the watchman, is working round from his half-tent, where he sleeps in the traffic, but cannot possibly negotiate the full extent of trench and bridge for fifty seconds more. Time cannot be lavished waiting for him. The man at the reins, with seeming authority, clinches the matter.

"You stop, Peter Jackson. *Hospital!* Don't you let the child out of your hands before you get there. Understand?—All clear in front?" Two men, who have taken the horses' heads, to soothe their shaken nerves with slaps and suitable exclamations, now give them back to their owners, leaving them free to rear high once or twice to relieve feeling; while they themselves go back, each to his own place on the engine. A word of remonstrance from the driver about that rearing, and they are off again, the renewed fire-cry scarcely audible in the distance by the time Old Sam gets across the wooden bridge.

To him, as to a responsible person, says Peter Jackson:—"Know where he belongs?"—and to Mrs. Riley, as to one not responsible, but deserving of sympathy:—"No—the wheels haven't been over him."

"Down yonder Court, I take it. Couldn't say for sartin."
So says Sam; and Mrs. Tapping discerns with pious fervour the
Mercy of God in this occurrence, He not having flattened the
child out on the road outright.

But Peter Jackson's question implied no intention to communicate with the little victim's family. To do so would be a
clear dereliction of duty; an offence against discipline. He has
his instructions, and in pursuance of them strides away to the
Hospital without another word, bearing in his arms a light
burden so motionless that it is hard to credit it with life. So
quickly has the whole thing passed, that the drift of idlers
hard on his heels is a fraction of what a couple more minutes
would have made it. It will have grown before they reach the
Middlesex, short as the distance is. Then a police-sergeant,
who joins them half-way, will take notes and probably go to
find the child's parents; while Peter Jackson, chagrined at this
hitch in his day's fire-eating, will go off Walworth way at the best
speed he may, after handing over his charge to an indisputable
House-Surgeon.

One can picture to oneself how the whole thing might pass
as it did, between the abrupt check of the engine's career, heard
by Uncle Moses and his friend, and the two or three minutes later
when they emerged through the archway to find Dolly in despair;
not from any knowledge of the accident to Dave, for intense preoccupation and a rampart of clay had kept her in happy ignorance of it, but because the water had broken bounds and Noah's
flood had come with a vengeance. Questioned as to Dave's
whereabouts, she embarked on a lengthy stuttered explanation
of how Dave had dode round there—pointing to the clay heap—
to det some of the new mud the men had spoyded up with their
spoyds. She reproduced his words, of course. Uncle Moses was
trying to detect her meaning without much success, when he
became aware that the old man in the fur cap who had shouted
more than once, "I say, master!" was addressing him.

"Is that old cock singing out to one of we, Jerry?" said Uncle
Moses. And then replied to the old cock:—"Say what you've
got to say, mate! Come a bit nigher."

Thereupon Old Sam crossed the bridge, slowly, as Uncle Moses
moved to meet him. "Might you happen to know anything of this
little boy?" said old Sam.

Uncle Moses caught the sound of disaster in his accent, before
his words came to an end. "What's the little boy?" said he.
"Where have you got him?" And Dolly, startled by the strange

sound in her uncle's voice, forgot Noah's flood, and stood dumb and terrified with outstretched muddy hands.

" I may be in the wrong of it, master "—thus Old Sam in his slow way, a trial to impatience—" but maybe this little maid's brother. They've took him across to the Hospital." Old Sam did not like to have to say this. He softened it as much as he could. Do you not see how? Omit the word " across," and see how relentless it makes the message. Do you ask why? Impossible to say—but it *does!*

Then Uncle Moses shouted out hoarsely, not like himself : " The Hospital—the Hospital—hear that, Bob! Our boy Dave in the Hospital! " and, catching his friend's arm, " Ask him—ask more! " His voice dropped and his breath caught. He was a bad subject for sudden emotions.

" Tell it out, friend—any word that comes first! " says Mr. Alibone. And then Old Sam, tongue-freed, gives the facts as known to him. He ends with:—" Th' young child could never have been there above a minute, all told, before the engine come along, and might have took no warning at twice his age for the vairy sudden coming of it." He dwells upon the shortness of the time Dave had been on the spot as though this minimised the evil. " I shouldn't care to fix the blame, for my own part," says he, shaking his head in venerable refusal of judicial functions not assigned to him so far.

" Is the child killed, man? Say what you know! " Thus Mr. Alibone brusquely. For he has caught a question Uncle Moses just found voice for:—" Killed or not? "

The old watchman is beginning slowly:—" That I would not undertake to say, sir . . ." when he is cut off short by Mrs. Riley, anxious to attest any pleasant thing, truly if possible; but if otherwise, anyhow!—" Kilt is it? No, shure thin! Insinsible." And then adds an absolutely gratuitous statement from sheer optimism :—" Shure, I hur-r-d thim say so mesilf, and I wouldn't mislade ye, me dyurr. Will I go and till his mother so for ye down the Court? To till her not to alarrum hersilf! "

But by this time Uncle Moses had rallied. The momentary qualm had been purely physical, connected with something that a year since had caused a medical examination of his heart with a stethoscope. He had been too great an adept in the art of rallying after knock-down blows in his youth to go off in a faint over this. He had felt queer, for all that. Still, he declined Mrs. Riley's kindly meant offer. " Maybe I'll make the best job of it myself," said he. " Thanking you very kindly all the same, ma'am!" After which he and his friend vanished back into Sapps Court, deciding as they went that it would be best to persuade Aunt M'riar to remain at home, while they themselves went to the Hospital, to learn the worst. It would never do to leave Dolly alone, or even in charge of neighbours.

Mrs. Riley's optimism lasted till Uncle Moses and Mr. Alibone disappeared, taking with them Dolly, aware of something terrible afoot; too small to understand the truth, whatever it was; panic-stricken and wailing provisionally to be even with the worst. Then, all reason for well-meaning falsehood being at an end, the Irishwoman looked facts in the face with the resolution that never flinches before the mishaps of one's fellow-man, especially when he is a total stranger.

"The power man!" said she. "He'll have sane the last of his little boy alive, only shure one hasn't the harrut to say the worrd. Throubles make thimsilves fast enough without the tilling of thim, and there'll be manes and to spare for the power payple to come to the knowledge without a worrd from you or me, Mrs. Tapping."

Then said Mrs. Tapping, on the watch for an opening through which she could thrust herself into the conversation; as a topic, you understand:—"Now there, Mrs. Riley, you name the very reason why I always stand by like, not to introduce my word. Not but that I will confess to the temptation undergone this very time to say that by God's will the child was took away from us, undeniable. Against that temptation I kep' my lips shut. Only I will say this much, and no concealment, that if my husband had been spared, being now a widow fourteen years, and heard me keep silence many a time, he might have said it again and again, like he said it a hundred times if he said it once when alive and able to it:—'Mary Ann Tapping, you do yourself no justice settin' still and list'nin', with your tongue in your mouth God gave you, and you there to use it!' And I says to Tapping, fifty times if I said it once, 'Tapping,' says I, 'you better know things twiced before you say 'em for every onced you say 'em before you know 'em.' Then Tapping, he says, was that to point at 'Lethear? And I says yes, though the girl was then young and so excusable. But she may learn better, I says, and made allowance though mistaken. . . ." This is just as good a point for Mrs. Tapping to cease at as any other in the story. In reality Heaven only knows when she ceased.

A very miscellaneous public gathered round and formed false ideas of what had happened from misinformants. The most popular erroneous report ran towards connecting it somehow with the sewer-trench, influencing people to look down into its depths and watch for the reappearance of something supposed to be expected back. So much so that more than one inoffensive person asked the man in charge of the pumping engine—which went honourably on without a pause—whether "it" was down there. He was a morose and embittered man—had been crossed in love, perhaps—for he met all inquiries by another:—"Who are you a-speaking to?" and, on being told, added:—"Then why couldn't you say so?" Humble apology had then to be content with, "No, it ain't down there and never has been, if you ask me,"—in answer to the previous question.

Old Sam endeavoured more than once to point out that the accident need not necessarily end fatally. He invented tales of goods-trains that had passed over him early in life, and the surgical skill that had left him whole and sound. Trains were really unknown in his boyhood, but there was no one to contradict him. The public, stimulated to hopefulness, produced analogous experiences. It had had a hay-cart over it, with a harvest-home on the top, such as we see in pictures. It had had the Bangor coach over it, going down hill, and got caught in the skid. It had been under an artillery corps and field-guns at a gallop, when the Queen revoo'd the troops in Hyde Park. And look at it now! Horse-kicks and wheel-crushing really had a bracing tendency; gave the constitution tone, and seldom left any ill effects.

Only their consequences must be took in time. Well!—hadn't the child gone to the Hospital? Dissentients who endeavoured to suggest that broken bones and dislocations were unknown before the invention of surgeons, were rebuked by the citation of instances of neglected compound fractures whose crippled owners became athletes after their bones had been scientifically reset, having previously been rebroken in the largest number of places the narrator thought he could get credence for. Hope told her flattering tale very quickly, for when Dave's uncle and Jerry Alibone reappeared on their way to find the truth at the Hospital, her hearers were ready with encouragement, whether they knew anything about the matter or not. "I don't believe they do," said Uncle Moses, and Mr. Alibone replied—"Not they, bless your heart!" But it was refreshing for all that.

They met the police-sergeant on the way, coming from the Hospital to bring the report and make inquiry about the child's belongings. They credited him with superhuman insight when he addressed them with:—" Either of you the father of a child knocked down by Fire-engine 67A in this street—taken into accident ward?" He spoke just as though Engine 68B had knocked another child down in the next street, and so on all over London.

But his sharpness was merely human. For scarcely a soul had passed but paused to look round after them, wondering at the set jaw and pallid face of the huge man who limped on a stick, seeming put to it to keep the speed. Uncle Moses, you see, was a fine man in his own way of the prizefighter type; and now, in his old age, worked out a little like Dr. Samuel Johnson.

The report, as originally received by the police-officer, was that the child was not killed but still unconscious. A good string of injuries were credited to the poor little man, including a dislocated femur and concussion of the brain. Quite enough, alone!— for the patient, his friends and relations. The House-Surgeon, speaking professionally, spoke also hopefully of undetected complications in the background. We might pull him through for all that. This report was materially softened for the child's family. Better not say too much to the parents at present, either way!

CHAPTER IV

HOW UNCLE MO AND HIS FRIEND COULD NOT GET MUCH ENCOURAGE-
MENT. DOLLY'S ATTITUDE. ACHILLES AND THE TORTOISE, AND
DOLLY'S PUDDING. HOW UNCLE MO'S SPIRITS WENT DOWN INTO
HIS BOOTS. HOW PETER JACKSON THE FIREMAN INTERVIEWED
MICHAEL RAGSTROAR, UPSIDE DOWN, AND BROUGHT AUNT M'RIAR'S
HEART INTO HER MOUTH. HOW DAVE CAME HOME IN A CAB, AND
MICHAEL RAGSTROAR GOT A RIDE FOR NOTHING. OF SISTER NORA,
WHO GOT ON THE COURT'S VISITING LIST BEFORE IT CAME OUT THAT
SHE WAS MIXED UP WITH ARISTOCRATS

THE present writer, half a century since—he was then neither *we* nor a writer—trod upon a tiny sapling in the garden of the house then occupied by his kith and kin. It was broken off an inch from the ground, and he distinctly remembers living a disgraced life thereafter because of the beautiful tree that sapling might have become but for his inconsiderate awkwardness. If the censorious spirit that he aroused could have foreseen the tree that was to grow from the forgotten residuum of the accident, the root that it left in the ground, it would not perhaps have passed such a sweeping judgment. Any chance wayfarer in St. John's Wood may see that tree now—from the end of the street, for that matter.

So perhaps the old prizefighter might have mustered more hope in response to Aunt M'riar's plucky rally against despair. The tiny, white, motionless figure on the bed in the accident ward, that had uttered no sound since he saw it on first arriving at the Hospital, might have been destined to become that of a young engineer on a Dreadnought, or an unfledged dragoon, for any authenticated standard of Impossibility.

The House-Surgeon and his Senior, one of the heads of the Institution,—interviewed by Uncle Moses and Aunt M'riar when they came late by special permission and appointment, hoping to hear the child's voice once more, and found him still insensible and white—testified that the action of the heart was good. The little man had no intention of dying if he could live. But both his medical attendants knew that the tremulous inquiry whether there was any hope of a recovery—within a reasonable time understood, of course—was really a petition for a favourable verdict at any cost. And they could not give one, for all they would have been glad to do so. They have to damn so many hopes in a day's work, these Accident Warders!

"It's no use asking us," said they, somehow conjointly. "There's not a surgeon in all England that could tell you whether it will be life or death. We can only say the patient is making a good fight for it." They seemed very much interested in the case, though, and in the queer old broken-hearted giant that sobbed over the half-killed baby that could not hear nor answer, speak to it as he might.

"What did you say your name was?" said the Senior Surgeon to Uncle Moses.

"Moses Wardle of Hanley, called the Linnet. Ye see, I was a Member of the Prize Ring, many years. Fighting Man, you might say."

"I had an idea I knew the name, too. When I was a youngster thirty odd years ago I took an interest in that sort of thing. You fought Bob Brettle, and the umpires couldn't agree."

"That was it, master. Well, I had many a turn up—turn up and turn down, either way as might be. But I had a good name. I never sold a backer. I did my best by them that put their money on me." For the moneychanger, the wagermonger, creeps in and degrades the noble science of damaging one's fellow-man effectively; even as in old years he brought discredit on cock-fighting, in which at least—you cannot deny it—the bird cuts a better figure than he does in his native farmyard.

" Come round after twelve to-morrow, and we may know more," said the House-Surgeon. " It's not regular—but ask for me." And then the older Surgeon shook Uncle Moses by the hand, quite respectful-like—so Mr. Jerry said to Aunt M'riar later—and the two went back, sad and discouraged, to Sapps Court.

What made it all harder to bear was the difficulty of dealing with Dolly. Dolly knew, of course, that Dave had been took to the Horsetickle—that was the nearest she could get to the word, after frequent repetitions—and that he was to be made well, humanly speaking, past a doubt. The little maid had to be content with assurances to this effect, inserting into the treaty a stipulation as to time.

" Dave's doin' to tum home after dinner," said she, when that meal seemed near at hand. And Uncle Moses never had the heart to say no.

Then when no Dave had come, and Dolly had wept for him in vain, and a cloth laid announced supper, Dolly said—moved only by that landmark of passing time—" Dave *is* a-doin' to tum home after supper; he *is* a-doin', Uncle Mo, he *is* a-doin'! " And what could her aunt and uncle do but renew the bill, as it were; the promise to pay that could only be fulfilled by the production of Dave, whole and sound.

She refused food except on condition that an exactly similar helping should be conveyed to Dave in the Horsetickle. She withdrew the condition that Uncle Moses and herself should forthwith convey Dave's share of the repast to him, in consideration of a verbal guarantee that little girls were not allowed in such Institutions. Why she accepted this so readily is a mystery. Possibly the common form of instruction to little girls, dwelling on their exclusion by statute or usage from advantages enjoyed by little boys, may have had its weight. Little girls, *exempli gratia,* may not lie on their backs and kick their legs up. Little boys are at liberty to do so, subject to unimportant reservations, limiting the area at their disposal for the practice. It is needless—and might be thought indelicate—to instance the numerous expressions that no little girl should use under any circumstances, which are regarded as venial sin in little boys, except of course on Sunday. Society does not absolutely countenance the practices of spitting and sniffing in little boys, but it closes its eyes and passes hypocritically by on the other side of the road; while, on the other hand, little girls indulging in these vices would either be cast out into the wilderness, or have to accept the *rôle* of penitent Magdalens. Therefore when Dolly was told that little girls were not allowed in Hospitals, it may only have presented itself to her as another item in a code of limitations already familiar.

The adhibition in visible form of a pendant to her own allowance of pudding or bread-and-milk, to be carried to the Horsetickle by Uncle Moses on his next visit, had a sedative effect, and she was contented with it, without insisting on seeing the pledge carried out. Her imagination was satisfied, as a child's usually is, with any objective transaction. Moreover, a dexterous manipulation of the position improved matters. The portion allotted to Dave was removed, ostensibly to keep it warm for him, but reproduced to do duty as a second helping for Dolly. Of course, it had to be halved again for Dave's sake, and an ancient puzzle solved itself in practice. The third halving was not worth sending to the Hospital. Even so a step too small to take was left for Achilles when the tortoise had only just started. " Solvitur ambulando," said Philosophy, and *a priori* reasoning took a back place.

Her constant inquiries about the date of Dave's cure and return were an added and grievous pain to her aunt and uncle. It was easy for the moment to procrastinate, but how if the time should come for telling her that Dave would never come back— no, never?

But the time was not to come yet. For a few days Life showed indecision, and Uncle Mo and Aunt M'riar had a thumping heart apiece each time they stood by the little, still, white figure on the bed and thought the breath was surely gone. They were allowed in the ward every day, contrary to visitor-rule, apparently because of Uncle Mo's professional eminence in years gone by—an odd reason when one thinks of it! It was along of that good gentleman, God bless him!—said Aunt M'riar— that knew Uncle Mo's name in the Ring. In fact, the good gentleman had said to the House-Surgeon in private converse: " You see, there's no doubt the old chap ended sixteen rounds with Brettle in a draw, and Jem Mace had a near touch with Brettle. No, no—we must let him see the case day by day." So Uncle Mo saw the case each day, and each day went away to transact such business with Hope as might be practicable. And each day, on his return, there was a voice heard in Sapps Court, Dolly weeping for her elder brother, and would not be comforted. "Oo *did* said oo would fess Dave back from the Horsetickle, oo know oo did, Uncle Mo"; and similar reproaches, mixed themselves with her sobs. But for many days she got no consolation beyond assurance that Dave would come to-morrow, discharged cured.

Then, one windy morning, a punctual equinoctial gale, gathering up its energies to keep inoffensive persons awake all night and, if possible, knock some chimney-stacks down, blew Uncle Mo's pipelight out, and caused him to make use of an expression. And Aunt M'riar reproved that expression, saying:—"Not with that blessed boy lying there in the Hospital should you say such language, Moses, more like profane swearing, I call it, than a Christian household."

"He's an old Heathen, ma'am, is Moses," said Mr. Alibone, who was succeeding in lighting his own pipe, in spite of the wind in at the street door. Because, as we have seen, in this Court— unlike the Courts of Law or Her Majesty's Court of St. James's —the kitchens opened right on the street. Not but what, for all that, there was the number where you would expect, on a shiny boss you could rub clean and give an appearance. Aunt M'riar said so, and must have known.

Uncle Moses shook his head gravely over his own delinquency, as if he truly felt it just as much as anybody. But when he got his pipe lighted, instead of being cheerful and making the most of what the doctor had said that very day, his spirits went down into his boots, which was a way they had.

"'Tain't any good to make believe," said he. "Supposin' our boy never comes back, M'riar!"

"There, now!" said Aunt M'riar. "To hear you talk, Mo, wouldn't anybody think! And after what Dr. Prime said only this afternoon! I should be ashamed."

"What was it Dr. Prime said, Mo?" asked Mr. Alibone, quite cheerful-like. "Tell us again, old man." For you see, Uncle Moses he'd brought back quite an encouraging report, whatever anyone see fit to say, when he come back from the Hospital. Dr. Prime was the House-Surgeon.

"I don't take much account of him," said Uncle Mo. "A well-meanin' man, but too easy by half. One o' your good-natured beggars. Says a thing to stuff you up like! For all I could see, my boy was as white as that bit of trimmin' in your hand, M'riar."

" But won't you tell us what the doctor *said,* Mo?" said Mr. Alibone. " I haven't above half heard the evening's noose." He'd just come in to put a little heart into Moses. " Said the little child had a better colour. But I don't set any store by that." And then what does Uncle Moses do but reg'lar give away and go off sobbing like a baby. " Oh, M'riar, M'riar, we shall never have our boy back—no, never!"

And then Aunt M'riar, who was a good woman if ever Mr. Alibone come across one—this is what that gentleman could and did tell a friend after, incorporated verbatim in the text—she up and she says :—" For shame of yourself, Mo, for to go and forget yourself like that before Mr. Alibone! I tell you I believe we shall have the boy back in a week, all along o' what Dr. Prime said." On which, and a further representation that he would wake Dolly if he went on like that, Uncle Mo he pulled himself together and smoked quiet. Whereupon Aunt M'riar dwelt upon the depressing effect a high wind in autumn has on the spirits, with the singular result referred to above, of their retractation into their owner's boots, like quicksilver in a thermometer discouraged by the cold. After which professional experience was allowed some weight, and calmer counsels prevailed.

About this time an individual in a sort of undress uniform, beginning at the top in an equivocal Tam-o'-Shanter hat, sauntered into the *cul-de-sac* to which Sapps Court was an appendix. He appeared to be unconcerned in human affairs, and indeed independent of Time, Space, and Circumstance. He addressed a creature that was hanging upside down on some railings, apparently by choice.

" What sort of a name does this here archway go by?" said he, without acute curiosity.

" That's Sappses Court," said the creature, remaining inverted. " Say it ain't?" He appeared to identify the uniform he was addressing, and added :—" There ain't a fire down that Court, 'cos I knows and I'm a telling of yer. You'd best hook it." The uniform hooked nothing. Then, in spite of the creature—who proved, right-side-up, to be Michael Ragstroar—shouting after him —" You ain't wanted down that Court!" he entered it deliberately, whistling a song then popular, whose singer wished he was with Nancy, he did, he did, in a second floor, with a small back-door, to live and die with Nancy.

Having identified Sapps, he seemed to know quite well which house he wanted, for he went straight to the end and knocked at No. 7.

" Sakes alive! " said Aunt M'riar, responsive to the knock. " There's no fire here."

" I'm off duty," said the fireman briefly. " I've come to tell you about your young customer at the Hospital."

Aunt M'riar behaved heroically. There was only, to her thinking, one chance in ten that this strange, inexplicable messenger should have brought any other news to their house than that of its darling's death; but that one chance was enough to make her choke back a scream, lest Uncle Mo should have one moment of needless despair. And else—it shot across her mind in a second—might not a sudden escape from despair even be fatal to that weak heart of his? So Aunt M'riar pulled to the door behind her to say, with an effort:—" Is he dead?" The universe swam about outside while she stood still, and something hummed in her head. But through it she heard the fireman say:—" Not he!" as of one endowed with a great vitality, one who would take a deal of killing. When he added:—" He's spoke," though she believed her ears certainly, for she ran back into the kitchen crying out:—" He's spoke, Mo, he's spoke!" she did it with a misgiving that the only interpretation she could see her way to *must* be wrong—was altogether too good to be true.

Uncle Mo fairly shouted with joy, and this time woke Dolly, who thought it was a calamity, and wept. Fully five minutes of incoherent rejoicing followed, and then details might be rounded off. The fireman had to stand by his engine on the night-shift in an hour's time, but he saw his way to a pipe, and lit it.

" They're always interested to hear the ending-up of things at the Station," said he, to account for himself and his presence, " and I made it convenient to call round at the Ward. The party that took the child from me happened to be there, and knew me again." He, of course—but you would guess this— was Peter Jackson of Engine 67A. He continued:—" The party was so obliging as to take me into the Ward to the bedside. And it was while I was there the little chap began talking. The party asked me to step in and mention it to you, ma'am, or his uncle, seeing it was in my road to the Station." Then Peter Jackson seemed to feel his words needed extenuation or revision. " Not but I would have gone a bit out of the way, for that matter!" said he.

" 'Twouldn't be any use my looking round now, I suppose?" said Uncle Mo. Because he always was that restless and fidgety.

" Wait till to-morrow, they said, the party and the nurse. By reason the child might talk a bit and then get some healthy sleep. What he's had these few days latterly don't seem to count." Thus Peter Jackson, and Uncle Moses said he had seen the like. And then all three of them made the place smokier and smokier you could hardly make out across the room.

"Mo's an impatient old cock, you see!" said Mr. Alibone, who seemed to understand Peter Jackson, and *vice versa*. And Uncle Mo said:—"I suppose I shall have to mark time." To which the others replied that was about it.

"Only whatever did the young child say, mister?" said Aunt M'riar; like a woman's curiosity, to know. But those other two, they was curious underneath-like; only denied it.

"I couldn't charge my memory for certain, ma'am," said Peter Jackson, "and might very easy be wrong." He appeared to shrink from the responsibility of making a report, but all his hearers were agreed that there was no call to cut things so very fine as all that. A rough outline would meet the case.

"If it ran to nonsense in a child," said Uncle Mo—"after all, what odds?" And Aunt M'riar said:—"Meanin' slips through the words sometimes, and no fault to find." She had not read "Rabbi Ben Ezra," so this was original.

Peter Jackson endeavoured to charge his memory, or perhaps more properly, to discharge it. Dave had said first thing when he opened his eyes:—"The worty will be all over the hedge. Let me go to stop the worty." Of course, this had been quite un-intelligible to his hearers. However, Mr. Alibone and Uncle Mo were *au fait* enough of the engineering scheme that had led to the accident, to supply the explanation. Dave's responsibility as head engineer had been on his conscience all through his spell of insensibility, and had been the earliest roused matter of thought when the light began to break.

Besides, it so chanced that testimony was forthcoming to sup-port this view and confirm Dave's sanity. Dolly, who had been awakened by the noise, had heard enough to convey to her small mind that something pleasant had transpired in relation to Dave. Though young, she had a certain decision of character. Her be-haviour was lawless, but not unnatural. She climbed out of her wooden crib in Aunt M'riar's bedroom, and slipping furtively down the stair which led direct to the kitchen, succeeded in bound-ing on to the lap of her uncle; from which, once established, she knew it would be difficult for her aunt to dislodge her. She crowed with delight at the success of this escapade, and had the satisfaction of being, as it were, confirmed in her delinquency by her aunt wrapping a shawl round her. This was partly on the score of the cold draughts in such a high wind, partly as a measure of public decency. She was in time to endorse her uncle's explanation of Dave's speech intelligibly enough, with a due allowance of interpretation.

Closely reported, the substance of her commentary ran as follows:—" Dave tooktited the mud when I fessed him the mud in my flock "—this was illustrated in a way that threatened to outrage a sensitive propriety, the speaker's aunt's—" and spooshed up the worty and spooshed up the worty "—this repetition had great value —" and spooshtited the worty back, and then there wasn't no more mud . . . it was all fessed away in my flock . . . All dorn!—ass, it was—*all* dorn! "—this was in a minor key, and thrilled with pathos—" and Dave dode to fess more where the new mud was, and was took to the Horsetickle and never come back no more . . ." At this point it seemed best to lay stress upon the probable return of Dave, much to Dolly's satisfaction; though she would have been better pleased if a date had been fixed.

Our own belief is that Dolly thought the Horsetickle was an institution for the relief of sufferers from accidents occasioned by horses, and that no subsequent experience ever entirely dissipated this impression. The chances are that nine or ten of the small people one sees daily and thinks of as " the children," are laying up, even at this moment, some similar fancy that will last a lifetime. But this is neither here nor there.

What is more to the purpose is that a fortnight later Dave was brought home in a cab—the only cab that is recorded in History as having ever deliberately stood at the entrance to Sapps Court, with intent. Cabs may have stood there in connection with other doorways in the *cul-de-sac,* but ignoring proudly the archway with the iron post. Dave was carried down the Court by his uncle with great joy, and Michael Ragstroar seized the opportunity to tie himself somehow round the axle of the cab's backwheels, and get driven some distance free of charge.

Dave, as seen by Dolly on his return, was still painfully white, and could not walk. And Dolly might not come banging and smashing down on him like a little elephant, because it would hurt him; so she had to be good. The elephant simile was due to a lady—no doubt well-meaning—who accompanied Dave from the Hospital, and came more than once to see him afterwards. But it was taking a good deal on herself to decide what Dolly ought or ought not to do to Dave.

In those days slumming proper had not set in, and the East End was only known geographically, except, no doubt, to a few enthusi-asts—the sort that antedates first discovery after the fact, and takes a vicious pleasure in precursing its successors. But unas-suming benefactresses occurred at intervals whom outsiders knew broadly as Sisters of Charity. Such a one was this lady, between whom and Aunt M'riar a sympathetic friendship grew up before the latter discovered that Dave's hospital friend was an Earl's niece, which not unnaturally made her rather standoffish for a time. However, a remark of Mr. Alibone's—who seemed to know—that the lady's uncle was a belted Earl, and no mistake, palliated the Earldom and abated class prejudice. The Earl naturally went up in the esteem of the old prizefighter when it transpired that he was belted. What more could the most exacting ask?

But it was in the days when this lady was only "that party from the Hospital," that she took root at No. 7, Sapps Court. No. 7 was content that she should remain nameless; but when she said, in some affair of a message to be given at the Hospital, that its bearer was to ask for Sister Nora, it became impossible to ignore the name, although certainly it was a name that compli-cated matters. She remained, however, plain Sister Nora, without suspicion of any doubtful connections, until a scheme of a daring character took form—nothing less than that Dave should be taken into the country for change of air.

Uncle Mo was uneasy at the idea of Dave going away. Besides, he had always cherished the idea that the air of Sapps Court was equal to that of San Moritz, for instance. Look at what it was only a few years before Dave's father and mother first moved in, when it was all fields along the New Road—which has since been absurdly named Euston and Marylebone Road! Nothing ever come to change the air in Sapps Court that Uncle Mo knew of. And look at the wallflowers growing out in front the same as ever!

Uncle Mo, however, was not the man to allow his old-fashioned prejudices to stand in the way of the patient's convalescence, and an arrangement was made by Sister Nora that Dave should be taken charge of, for a while, by an old and trustworthy inhabitant of the Rocestershire village of which her uncle, the belted Earl, was the feudal lord and master, or slave and servant, according as you look at it. It was during the arrangement of this plan that his Earldom leaked out, creating serious misgivings in the minds of Uncle Mo and Aunt M'riar that they would be ill-advised if they allowed themselves to get mixed up with that sort of people.

CHAPTER V

THEY were sad days in Sapps Court after Sister Nora bore Dave away to Chorlton-under-Bradbury; particularly for Dolly, whose tears bathed her pillow at night, and diluted her bread-and-milk in the morning. There was something very touching about this little maid's weeping in her sleep, causing Aunt M'riar to give her a cracknell biscuit—to consume if possible; to hold in her sleeping hand as a rapture of possession, anyhow. Dolly accepted it, and contrived to enjoy it slowly without waking. What is more, she stopped crying; and my belief is, if you ask me, that sleep having deprived her of the power of drawing fine distinctions, she mistook this biscuit for Dave. Its *caput mortuum* was still clasped to her bosom when, deep unconsciousness merging all distinctions in unqualified existence, she was having her sleep out next day.

Dolly may have felt indignant and hurt at the audacious false promises of her uncle and aunt as to Dave's return. He had come home, certainly, but badly damaged. It was a sad disappointment; the little woman's first experience of perfidy. Her betrayers made a very poor show of their attempts at compensation—toys and suchlike. There was a great dignity in Dolly's attitude towards these contemptible offerings of a penitent conscience. She accepted them, certainly, but put them away in her bots to keep for Dave. Her box—if one has to spell it right—was an overgrown cardboard box with " Silk Twill " written on one end, and blue paper doors to fold over inside. It had been used as a boat, but condemned as unseaworthy as soon as Dolly could not sit in it to be pushed about, the gunwale having split open amidships. Let us hope this is right, nautically.

Considered as a safe for the storage of valuables, Dolly's box would have acquitted itself better if fair play had been shown to it. Its lid should have been left on long enough to produce an impression, and not pulled off at frequent intervals to exhibit its contents. No sooner was an addition made to these than Dolly would say, for instance, that she must s'ow Mrs. Picture upstairs the most recent acquisitions. Then she would insist on trying to carry it upstairs, but was not long enough in the arms, and Aunt M'riar had to do it for her in the end. Not, however, unwillingly, because it enabled her to give her mind to pinking or gauffering, or whatever other craft was then engaging her attention. We do not ourself know what pinking is, or gauffering; we have only heard them referred to. A vague impression haunts us that they fray out if not done careful. But this is probably valueless.

No doubt Dolly's visits upstairs in connection with this box were answerable for Aunt M'riar's having come to know a good deal about old Mrs. Prichard's—or, according to Dave and Dolly, Picture's—antecedents. A good deal, that is, when it came to be put together and liberally helped by inferences; but made up of very small deals—disjointed deals—in the form in which they were received by Aunt M'riar. As, for instance, on the occasion just referred to, shortly after Dave had gone on a visit to the tenant of the belted Earl, Uncle Mo having gone away for an hour, to spend it in the parlour of The Rising Sun, a truly respectable house where there were Skittles, and Knurr and Spell. He might, you see, be more than an hour: there was no saying for certain.

"I do take it most kind of you, ma'am," said Aunt M'riar for the fiftieth time, with departure in sight, "to keep an eye on the child. Some children nourishes a kind of ap'thy, not due to themselves, but constitutional in their systems, and one can leave alone without fear by reason of it. But Dolly is that busy and attentive, and will be up and doing, so one may easy spoil a tuck or stand down an iron too hot if called away sudden to see after the child."

The old woman seemed to Aunt M'riar to respond vaguely. She loved to have the little thing anigh her, and hear her clacket. "All my own family are dead and gone, barring one son," said she. And then added, without any consciousness of jarring ideas:— "He would be forty-five." Aunt M'riar tried in vain to think of some way of sympathizing, but was relieved from her self-imposed duty by the speaker continuing—"He was my youngest. Born at Macquarie Harbour in the old days. The boy was born up-country—yes, forty-five years agone."

"Not in England now, ma'am, I suppose," said Aunt M'riar, who could not see her way to anything else. The thought crossed her mind that, so far as she knew, no male visitor for the old tenant of the attics had so far entered the house.

The old woman shook her head slowly. "I could not say," she said. "I cannot tell you now if he be alive or dead." Then she became drowsy, as old age does when it has talked enough; so, as Aunt M'riar had plenty to see to, she took her leave, Dolly remaining in charge as per contract. .

Aunt M'riar passed on these stray fragments of old Mrs. Prichard's autobiography to Uncle Mo when he came in from The Rising Sun. The old boy seemed roused to interest by the mention of Van Diemen's Land. "I call to mind," said he, "when I was a youngster, hearing tell of the convicts out in those parts, and how no decent man could live in the place. Hell on Earth, they did say, those that knew." Thereupon old Mrs. Prichard straightway became a problem to Aunt M'riar. If there were none but con-victs in Van Diemen's Land, and all Mrs. Prichard's boys were born there, the only chance of the old woman not having been the mother of a convict's children lay in her having been possibly the wife of a gaoler, at the best. And yet—she was such a nice, pretty old thing! Was it conceivable?

Then in subsequent similar interviews Aunt M'riar, inquisitive-like, tried to get further information. But very little was forth-coming beyond the fact that Mrs. Prichard's husband was dead. What supported the convict theory was that his widow never referred to any relatives of his or her own. Mrs. Burr, her com-panion or concomitant—or at least fellow-lodger—was not uncom-municative, but knew "less than you might expect" about her. Aunt M'riar cultivated this good woman with an eye to informa-tion, holding her up—as the phrase is now—at the stairfoot and inveigling her to tea and gossip. She was a garrulous party when you come to know her, was Mrs. Burr; and indeed, short of inti-macy, she might have produced the same impression on any person well within hearing.

"Times and again," said she in the course of one such conver-sation, which had turned on the mystery of Mrs. Prichard's antecedents, "have I thought she was going to let on about her belongings, and never so much as a word! Times and again have I felt my tongue in the roof of my mouth, for curiosity to think what she would say next. And there, will you believe me, missis? —it was no better than so much silence all said and done! Nor it wasn't for want of words, like one sits meanin' a great deal and when it comes to the describin' of it just nowhere! She was by way of keeping something back, and there was I sat waiting for it, and guess-working round like, speculating, you might say, to think what it might be when it come. Thank you, ma'am—not another cup!"

"There's more in the pot, ma'am," said Aunt M'riar, looking

into it to see, near the paraffin lamp which smelt: they all did in those days. But Mrs. Burr had had three; and three does, mostly. If these excellent women's little inflections of speech, introduced thus casually, are puzzling, please supply inverted commas. Aunt M'riar organized the tea-tray to take away and wash up at the sink, after emptying saucer-superfluities into the slop-basin. Mrs. Burr referred to the advantages we enjoy as compared with our forbears, instancing especially our exemption from the worship of wooden images, Egyptian Idles—a spelling accommodated to meet an impression Mrs. Burr had derived from a Japanese Buddha—and suchlike, and Tea.

"However they did without it I cannot think," said she. "On'y, of course, not having to stitch, stitch, stitch from half-past six in the morning till bedtime made a difference." Her ideas of our ancestors were strongly affected by a copper-plate engraving in a print-shop window in Soho, even as idolatry had been presented to her by a Tea-Man and Grocer in Tottenham Court Road. It was Stothard's "Canterbury Pilgrims"—*you* know!—and consequently her *moyen age* had a falcon on its wrist, and a jester in attendance, invariably. "They was a good deal in the open air, and it tells," was her tribute to the memory of this plate. She developed the subject further, incidentally. "Tryin' on is a change, of course, but liable to temper, and vexatious when the party insists on letting out and no allowance of turn-over. The same if too short in front. What was I a-sayin'? . . . Oh, Mrs. Prichard—yes! You was inquiring, ma'am, about the length of time I had known her. Just four years this Christmas, now I think of it. Time enough and to spare to tell anything she liked—if she'd have liked. But you may take it from me, ma'am, on'y to go no further on any account, that Mrs. Prichard is not, as they say, free-spoke about her family, but on the contrary the contrairy." Mrs. Burr was unconsciously extending the powers of the English tongue, in varying one word's force by different accents.

Uncle Moses he cut in, being at home that time:—"Was you saying, ma'am, that the old widder-lady's husband had been a convict in Australia?"

Oh no!—Mrs. Burr had never got that far. So she testified. Aunt M'riar, speaking from the sink, where she was extracting out the tea-leaves from the pot, was for calling Uncle Moses over the coals. Anybody might soon be afraid to say anything, to have been running away with an idea like that. No one had ever said any such a thing. Indeed, the convict was entirely inferential, and had no foundation except in the fact that the old woman's son had been born at Macquarie Harbour. Uncle Mo's impression that Van Diemen's Land was a sort of plague-spot on the planet—the *bacilli* of the plague being convicted criminals— was no doubt too well grounded. But it was only a hearsay of youth, and even elderly men may now fail to grasp the way folk spoke and thought of those remote horrors, the Penal Settlements, in the early days of last century—a century with whose years those of Uncle Moses, after babyhood, ran nearly neck and neck. That fellow-creatures, turned t'other way up, were in Hell at the Antipodes, and that it was so far off it didn't matter—that was the way the thing presented itself, and supplied the excuse for forgetting all about it. Uncle Mo had " heard tell " of their existence; but then they belonged to the criminal classes, and he didn't. If people belonged to the criminal classes it was their own look out, and they must take the consequences.

So that when the old boy referred to this inferential convict as a presumptive fact, the meaning of his own words had little force for himself. Even if the old lady's husband had been a convicted felon, it was now long enough ago to enable him to think of him as he thought of the chain-gangs eight thousand miles off as the crow flies—or would fly if he could go straight; the nearest way round mounts up to twelve. Anyhow, there was no more in the story than would clothe the widowhood of the upstairs tenant with a dramatic interest.

So, as it appeared that Mrs. Prichard's few words to Aunt M'riar were more illuminating than anything Mrs. Burr had to tell, and *they* really amounted to very little when all was said and done, there was at least nothing in the convict story to cause misgivings of the fitness of the upstairs attic to supply a haven of security for Dolly, while her aunt went out foraging for provisions; or when, as we have seen sometimes happened, Dolly became troublesome from want of change, and kep' up a continual fidget for this or that, distrackin' your—that is, Aunt M'riar's—attention.

CHAPTER VI

PHŒBE AND THE SQUIRE'S SON. HER RUNAWAY MARRIAGE WITH HIM.
HOW HE DABBLED IN FORGERY AND BURNED HIS FINGERS. OF A
JUDGE WHO TOOK AFTER THE PSALMIST. VAN DIEMEN'S LAND, AND
HOW PHOEBE GOT OUT THERE. HOW BOTH TWINS WERE PROVED DEAD
BY IRRESISTIBLE EVIDENCE, EACH TO EACH. HOW THORNTON FORGO_
THAT PHOEBE COULD NEVER BE LEGALLY HIS WIDOW. HOW HIS SON
ACTED WELL UP TO HIS FATHER'S STANDARD OF IMMORALITY. MAR-
RIAGE A MEANS TO AN END, BUT ONLY ONCE. AN ILL-STARRED
BURGLARY. NORFOLK ISLAND. WHY BOTH MRS. DAVERILLS CHANGED
THEIR NAMES

IF this story should ever be retold by a skilful teller, his power
of consecutive narrative and redisposition of crude facts in a better order will be sure to add an interest it can scarcely command
in its present form. But it is best to make no pretence to niceties
of construction, when a mere presentation of events is the object
in view. The following circumstances in the life of old Mrs. Prichard constitute a case in point. The story might, so to speak, ask
its reader's forgiveness for so sudden a break into the narrative.
Consider that it has done so, and amend the tale should you ever
retell it.

Maisie Runciman, born in the seventies of the previous century,
and close upon eighty years of age at the time of this story,
was the daughter of an Essex miller, who became a widower when
she and her twin sister Phœbe were still quite children. His only
other child, a son many years their senior, died not long after
his mother, leaving them to the sole companionship of their father.
He seems to have been a quarrelsome man, who had estranged
himself from both his wife's relatives and his own. He also had
that most unfortunate quality of holding his head high, as it
is called; so high, in fact, that his twin girls found it difficult
to associate with their village neighbours, and were driven back
very much on their own resources for society. Their father's
morose isolation was of his own choosing. He was, however,
affectionate in a rough way to them, and their small household
was peaceful and contented enough. The sisters, wrapped up in
one another, as twins so often are, had no experience of any other
condition of life, and thought it all right and the thing that
should be.

All went well enough—without discord anyhow, however monotonously—until Maisie and Phœbe began to look a little like women; which happened, to say the truth, at least a year before their father consented to recognise the fact, and permit them to appear in the robes of maturity. About that time the young males of the neighbourhood became aware, each in his private heart, of an adoration cherished for one or other of the beautiful twins from early boyhood. Would-be lovers began to buzz about like flies when fruit ripens. If any one of these youths had any doubt about the intensity and immutability of his passion, it vanished when the girls announced official womanhood by appearing at church in the costume of their seniors. Some students of the mysterious phenomena of Love have held that man is the slave of millinery, and that women are to all intents and purposes their skirts. It is too delicate a question for hurried discussion in a narrative which is neither speculative nor philosophical, but historical. All that concerns its writer is that no sooner did the costume of the miller's daughters suggest that they would be eligible for the altar, than they grew so dear, so dear, that everything masculine and unattached was ambitious to be the jewel that trembled at their ear, or the girdle about their dainty, dainty waist.

The worst of it for these girls was that their likeness to one another outwent that of ordinary twinship. It resembled that of the stage where the same actor personates both Dromios; and their life was one perpetual Comedy of Errors. Current jest said that they themselves did not know which was which. But they did know, perfectly well, and had no misgivings whatever about becoming permanently confused; even when, having been dressed in different colours to facilitate distinction, they changed dresses and produced a climax of complication. Even this was not so bad as when Phœbe had a tiff with Maisie—a rare thing between twins—and Maisie avenged herself by pretending to be Phœbe, affecting that all the latter's protests of identity were malicious misrepresentation. Who could decide when they themselves were not of a tale? What settled the matter in the end was that Phœbe cried bitterly at being misrepresented, while Maisie was so ill-advised as not to do the same, and even made some parade of triumph. "Yow are Maisie. I heerd yow a-crowun'," said an old stone-dresser, who, with other mill-hands, was referred to for an opinion.

This was when they were quite young, before slight variations of experience had altered appearance and character to the point of making them distinguishable when seen side by side. Not, however, to the point of rendering impossible a trick each had played more than once on too importunate male acquaintances. What could be more disconcerting to the protestations of a rustic admirer than " Happen you fancy you are speaking to my sister Phœbe, sir?" from Maisie, or *vice versa?* It was absolutely impossible to nail either of these girls to her own identity, in the face of her denial of it in her sister's absence. Perhaps the only real confidence on the point that ever existed was their mother's, who knew the two babies apart—so she said—because one smelt of roses, the other of marjoram.

It may easily have been that the power of duping youth and shrewdness, as to which sister she really was, weighed too heavily with each of these girls in their assessment of the value of lovers' vows. And still more easily that—some three years later than the girlish jest related a page since—when Maisie, playing off this trick on a wild young son of the Squire's, was met by an indignant reproach for her attempted deception, she should have been touched by his earnestness and seeming insight into her inner soul, and that the incident should have become the cornerstone of a fatal passion for a damned scoundrel. " Oh, Maisie— Maisie! "—thus ran his protestation—" Dearest, best, sweetest of girls, how can you think to dupe me when your voice goes to my heart as no other voice ever can—ever will? How, when I know you for mine—mine alone—by touch, by sight, by hearing?" The poor child's innocent little fraud had been tried on a past-master in deception, and her own arrow glanced back to wound her, beyond cure perhaps. His duplicity was proved afterwards by the confession of his elder brother Ralph, a young man little better than himself, that the two girls had been the subject of a wager between them, which he had lost. This wager turned on which of the two should be first " successful " with one of the beautiful twins; and whether it showed only doubtful taste or infamous bad feeling depended on what interpretation was put on the word " success " by its perpetrators. A lenient one was possible so long as no worse came of it than that Thornton Daverill, the younger brother, became the accepted suitor of Maisie, and Ralph, the elder, the rejected one of Phœbe. Thornton's success was no doubt due in a great measure to Maisie's failure to mislead him about her identity, and Ralph's rejection possibly to the poor figure he cut when Phœbe played fast and loose with hers. That there was no truth or honour in Thornton's protestations to Maisie, or even honest loss of self-control under strong feeling, is evident from the fact that he told his brother as a good joke that his power of distinguishing between the girls was due to nothing more profound than that Maisie always gave him her hand to shake and Phœbe only her fingers. Possibly this test would only have held good in the case of men outside the family. It was connected with some minute sensitiveness of feeling towards that class, not perceptible by any other.

But in whatever sense Thornton and Maisie were trothplight, her father opposed their marriage, although it would no doubt have been a social elevation for the miller's daughter. It must be admitted that for once the inexorable parent may have been in the right. Tales had reached him, unhappily too late to prevent the formation of an acquaintance between the young squires and his daughters, of the profligacies—dissoluteness with women and at the gaming-table—of both these young men. And it is little wonder that he resolutely opposed the union of Thornton and Maisie—she a girl of nineteen!—at least until there was some sign of reform in the youth, some turning from his evil ways.

It was a sad thing for Maisie that her father's exclusiveness had created so many obstacles to the associations of his daughters with older women. No one had ever taken the place of a mother to them. It is rare enough for even a mother to speak explicitly to her daughter of what folk mean when they tell of the risks a girl runs who weds with a man like Thornton Daverill. But she may do so in such a way as to excite suspicion of the reality, and it is hard on motherless girls that they should not have this slender chance. A father can do nothing, and old fulminations of well-worn Scriptural jargon—hers was an adept in texts—had not even the force of their brutal plain speech. For to these girls the speech was not plain—it was only what Parson read in Church. That described and exhausted it.

The rest of the story follows naturally—too naturally—from the position shown in the above hasty sketch. Old Isaac Runciman's ill-temper, combined with an almost ludicrous want of tact, took the form of forbidding Thornton Daverill the house. The student of the art of dragging lovers asunder cannot be too mindful of the fact that the more they see of each other, the sooner they will be ripe for separation. If Maisie had been difficult to influence when her father contented himself with saying that he forbade the marriage *ex cathedra paternæ auctoritatis*, she became absolutely intractable when, some time after, this authority went the length of interdicting communications. Secret interviews, about double the length of the public ones they supplanted, gave the indignant parent an excuse for locking the girl into her own room. All worked well for the purpose of a thoroughly unprincipled scoundrel. Thornton, who would probably have married Maisie if nothing but legal possession had been open to him, saw his way to the same advantages without the responsibilities of marriage, and jumped at them. Do not blame Maisie overmuch for her share of what came about. The step she consented to was one of which the *full* meaning could only be half known to a girl of her age and experience. And the man into whose hands it threw her past recovery was in her eyes the soul of honour and chivalry—ill-judging, if at all, from the influence of a too passionate adoration for herself. Conception of the degree and nature of his wicke'dness was probably impossible to her; and, indeed, may have been so still—however strange it may seem —to the very old lady whom, under the name of Mrs. Prichard, Dolly Wardle used to visit in Sapps Court, " Mrs. Picture in the topackest" being the nearest shot she was able to make at her description.

Whether it was so or not, this old, old woman was the very selfsame Maisie that sixty odd years before lent a too willing ear to the importunities of a traitor, masquerading with a purpose; and ultimately consented to a runaway marriage with him, he being alone responsible for the arrangement of it and the legality of the wedding. The most flimsy *mise en scène* of a mock ceremony was sufficient to dupe a simplicity like hers; and therein was enacted the wicked old tragedy possible only in a world like ours, which ignores the pledge of the strong to the weak, however clearly that pledge may be attested, unless the wording of it jumps with the formularies of a sanctioned legalism. A grievous wrong was perpetrated, which only the dishonesty of Themis permits; for an honest lawgiver's aim should be to find means of enforcing a sham marriage, all the more relentlessly in proportion to the victim's innocence and the audacity of the imposture.

The story of Maisie's after-life need hardly have been so terrible, on the supposition that the prayer " God, have mercy upon us! " is ever granted. Surely some of the stabs in store for her need not have gone to the knife-hilt. Much information is lacking to make the tale complete, but what follows is enough. Listen to it and fill in the blanks if you can—with surmise of alleviation, with interstices of hypothetical happiness—however little warrant the known facts of the case may carry with them.

Thornton Daverill was destined to bring down Nemesis on his head by touching Themis on a sensitive point—monetary integrity. Within five years, a curious skill which he possessed of simulating the handwriting of others, combined with a pressing want of ready money, led him to the commission of an act which turned out a great error in tactics, whatever place we assign it in morality. Morally, the forgery of a signature, especially if it be to bring about a diminution of cash in a well-filled pocket, is a mere peccadillo compared with the malversation of a young girl's life. Legally it is felony, and he who commits it may get as long a term of penal servitude as the murderer of whose guilt the jury is not confident up to hanging point.

The severity of the penal laws in the reign of George III. was due no doubt to a vindictiveness against the culprit which—in theory at any rate—is nowadays obsolete, legislation having for its object rather the discouragement of crime on the *tapis* than the meting out of their deserts to malefactors. In those days the indignation of a jury would rise to boiling-point in dealing with an offence against sacred Property, while its blood-heat would remain normal over the deception and ruin of a mere woman. Therefore the jury that tried Thornton Daverill for forging the signature of Isaac Runciman on the back of a promissory note found the accused guilty, and the judge inflicted the severest penalty but one that Law allows. For Thornton might have been hanged.

But neither judge nor jury seemed much interested in the convict's behaviour to the daughter of the man he had tried to swindle out of money. On the contrary, they jumped to the conclusion that his wife was morally his accomplice; and, indeed, if it had not been for her great beauty she would very likely have gone to the galleys too. There was, however, this difference between their positions, that the prosecution was dependent on her father's affidavit to prove that the signature was a forgery, and so long as only the man he hated was legally involved, he was to be relied on to adhere to his first disclaimer of it. Had Maisie been placed beside her husband in the dock, how easily her father might have procured the liberation of both by accepting his liability—changing his mind about the signature and discharging the amount claimed! If the continuance of the prosecution had depended on either payer or payee, this would have been the end of it. What the creditor—a usurer—wanted was his money, not revenge. Indeed, Thornton would never have been made the subject of a criminal indictment at his instance, except to put pressure on Isaac Runciman for payment for his daughter's sake.

The bringing of the case into Court created a new position. An accommodation that would have been easy enough at first —an excusable compounding of a felony—became impossible under

the eyes of the Bench. And this more especially because one of
the Judges of Assize who tried the case acquired an interest in
Maisie analogous to the one King David took in the wife of Uriah
the Hittite, and perceived the advantages he would derive if this
forger and gambler was packed off to a life far worse than the
death the astute monarch schemed for the great-hearted soldier
who was serving ·him. Whether the two were lawfully man and
wife made no difference to this Judge. Maisie's devotion to her
scoundrel was the point his lordship's legal acumen was alive to,
and he himself was scarcely King of Israel. One wonders sometimes—at least, the present writer has done so—what Bathsheba's
feelings were on the occasion referred to. We can only surmise,
and can do little more in the case of Maisie. The materials for
the retelling of this story are very slight. Their source may be
referred to later. For the moment it must be content with the
bare facts.

This Bathsheba was able to say "Hands off!" to her King
David, and also able—but Heaven knows how!—to keep up a correspondence with the worthless parallel of the Hittite throughout
the period of his detention in an English gaol, or, it may be,
on the river hulks, until his deportation in a convict ship to Sydney, from which place occasional letters reached her, which were
probably as frequent as his opportunities of sending them, until,
a considerable time later—perhaps as much as five years; dates
are not easy to fix—one came saying that he expected shortly to
be transferred to the new penal settlement in Van Diemen's
Land.

At the beginning of last century the black hulks on the Thames
and elsewhere were known and spoken of truly as "floating Hells."
Any penal colony was in one point worse; he who went there left
Hope behind, so far as his hopes were centred in his native land.
For to return was Death.

After his transfer to Van Diemen's Land, no letter reached her
for some months. Then came news that Thornton had benefited
by the extraordinary fulness of the powers granted to the Gov-
ernors of these penal settlements, who practically received the
convicts on lease for the term of their service. They were, in
fact, slaves. But this told well for Maisie's husband, whose father
had been at school with the then supreme authority at Macquarie
Harbour. This got him almost on his arrival a ticket-of-leave, by
virtue of which he was free within the island during good behaviour. He soon contrived, by his superior education and manners, to get a foothold in a rough community, and saw his way

to rising in the world, even to prosperity. In a very short time, said a later letter, he would save enough to pay Maisie's passage out, and then she could join him. The only redeeming trait the story shows of this man is his strange confidence that this girl, whom he had cruelly betrayed, would face all the terrors of a three-months' sea-voyage and travel, alone in a strange land, to become the slave and helpless dependent of a convict on ticket-of-leave.

She had returned to her father's house a year after the trial, her sister having threatened to leave it unless her father permitted her to do so, taking with her her two children; a very delicate little boy, born in the first year of her marriage, and a girl baby only four months old, which had come into the world eight months after its wretched parent's conviction. During this life at her father's the little boy died. He had been christened, after his father and uncle, Phœbe's rejected suitor—Ralph Thornton Daverill. The little girl she had baptized by the name of Ruth. This little Ruth she took with her, when, on Phœbe's marriage two years later, she went to live at the house of the new-married couple; and one would have said that the twins lived in even closer union than before, and that nothing could part them again.

It would have been a mistake. Within three years Maisie received a letter enclosing a draft on a London bank for more than her passage-money, naming an agent who would arrange for her in everything, and ending with a postscript:—" Come out at once." Shortly after, no change having been noticeable in her deportment, except, perhaps, an increased tenderness to her child and her sister, she vanished suddenly; leaving only a letter to Phœbe, full of contrition for her behaviour, but saying that her first duty was towards her husband. She had not dared to take with her her child, and it had been a bitter grief to her to forsake it, but she knew well that it would have been as great a bitterness to Phœbe to lose it, as she was herself childless at the time; and, indeed, her only consolation was that Phœbe would still continue to be, as it were, a second mother to " their child," which was the light in which each had always looked upon it.

Both of them seemed to have been under an impression that only one of two twins can ever become a mother. Whether there is any foundation for this, or whether it is a version of a not uncommon belief that twins are always childless, the story need not stop to inquire. It was falsified in this case by the birth of a son to Phœbe, *en secondes noces*, many years later. But this hardly touches the story, as this son died in his childhood. All that is needed to be known at present is that, as the result of Maisie's sudden disappearance, Phœbe was left in sole possession of her four-year-old daughter, to whose young mind it was a matter of indifference which of two almost indistinguishable identities she called by the name of mother. With a little encouragement she accepted the plenary title for the then childless woman to whom the name gave pleasure, and gradually forgot the mother who had deserted her; who, in the course of very little time, became the shadow of a name. All she knew then was that this mother had gone away in a ship; and, indeed, for months after little more was known to her aunt.

However, a brief letter did come from the ship, just starting for Sydney, and the next long-delayed one announced her arrival there, and how she had been met at the port by an agent who would make all arrangements for her further voyage. How this agency managed to get her through to Hobart Town in those days is a mystery, for there was no free immigration to the island till many years after, only transports from New South Wales being permitted to enter the port. She got there certainly, and was met by her husband at the ship. And well for her that it was so, for in those days no woman was safe by herself for an hour in that country.

It may seem wonderful that so vile a man should have set himself to consult the happiness of a woman towards whom he was under no obligation. But her letters to her sister showed that he did so; and those who have any experience of womanless lands men have to dwell in, whether or no, know that in such lands the market-value of a good sample is so far above rubies, that he who has one, and could not afford another if he lost the first, will be quite kind and nice and considerate to his treasure, in case King Solomon should come round, with all the crown-jewels to back him and his mother's valuation to encourage a high bid. Phœbe had for four or five years the satisfaction of receiving letters assuring her of her sister's happiness and of the extraordinary good fortune that had come to the reformed gambler and forger, whose prison-life had given him a distaste for crimes actively condemned by Society.

Among the items of news that these letters contained were the births of two boys. The elder was called Isaac after his grandfather at the urgent request of Maisie; but on condition that if another boy came he should be called Ralph Thornton, a repetition of the name of her first baby, which died in England. This is done commonly enough with a single name, but the duplication is exceptional. Whether the name was actually used for the younger child Phœbe never knew. Probably a letter was lost containing the information.

When Isaac Runciman died Phœbe wrote the news of his death to Maisie and received no reply from her. In its stead—that is to say, at about the time it would have been due—came a letter from Thornton Daverill announcing her sister's death in Australia. It was a brief, unsatisfying letter. Still, she hoped to receive more details, especially as she had followed her first letter, telling of her father's death, with another a fortnight later, giving fuller particulars of the occurrence. In due course came a second letter from her brother-in-law, professing contrition for the abruptness of his first, but excusing it on the ground that he was prostrated with grief at the time, and quite unable to write. He added very full and even dramatic particulars of her sister's death, giving her last message to her English relatives, and so forth.

But that sister was *not* dead. And herein follow the facts that have come to light of the means her husband employed to make her seem so, and of his motives for employing them.

To see these clearly you must keep in mind that Thornton was tied for life within the limits of the penal settlements. Maisie was free to go; with her it was merely a question of money. As time went on, her yearning to see her child and her twin-sister again grew and grew, and her appeals to her husband to allow her sometime to revisit England in accordance with his promise became every year more and more urgent. He would be quite a rich man soon—why should she not? Well—simply that she might not come back! That was his view, and we have to bear in mind that it would have been impossible for him to replace her, except from among female convicts assigned to settlers; nominally as servants, but actually as mates on hire—suppose we call them. One need not say much of this unhappy class; it is only mentioned to show that Thornton could have found no woman to take the place of the beautiful and devoted helpmeet whose constancy to him had survived every trial. No wonder he was ill at ease with the idea of her adventuring back to England alone. But it took a mind as wicked as his to conceive and execute the means by which he prevented it. It seems to have been suggested by the fact that the distribution of letters in his district had been assigned to him by the Governor. This made it easy to deliver them or keep them back, when it was in his interest to do so, without fear of detection. The letters coming from England were few indeed, so he was able to examine them at leisure.

At first he was content to withhold Phœbe's letters, hoping that

Maisie would be satisfied with negative evidence of her death, which he himself suggested as the probable cause of their suspension. But when this only increased her anxiety to return to her native land, he cast about for something he could present as direct proof. The death of her father supplied the opportunity. A black-edged sheet came, thickly written with Phœbe's account of his last illness, in ink which, as the event showed, did not defy obliteration. Probably Thornton had learned, among malefactors convicted of his own offence, secrets of forgery that would seem incredible to you or me. He contrived to obliterate this sheet all but the date-stamps outside, and then—the more readily that he had been informed that only fraud for gain made forgery felony —elaborated as a palimpsest a most careful letter in the handwriting of the father announcing Phœbe's own death, and also that of the daughter whom Maisie had bequeathed to her care. He must have been inspired and upborne in this difficult task by the spirit of a true artist. No doubt all *faussure,* to any person with an accommodating moral sense, is an unmixed delight. This letter remains, and has been seen by the present writer and others. The dexterity of the thing almost passes belief, only a few scarcly perceptible traces of the old writing being visible, the length of the new words being so chosen as to hide most of the old ones. What is even more incredible is that the original letter from Phœbe was deciphered at the British Museum by the courtesy of the gentlemen engaged in the deciphering and explanation of obscure inscriptions.

The elaborate fiction the forger devised may have been in part due to a true artist's pleasure in the use of a splendid opportunity, such as might never occur again. But on close examination one sees that it was little more than a skilful recognition of the exigencies of the case. The object of the letter was to remove once and for ever all temptation to Maisie to return to her native land. Now, so long as either her sister or her little girl were living in England the old inducement would be always at work. Why not kill them both, while he had the choice? It would be more troublesome to produce proof of the death of either, later. But he mistrusted his skill in dealing with fatal illness. A blunder might destroy everything. Stop!—he knew something better than that. Had not the transport that brought him out passed a drowned body afloat, and wreckage, even in the English Channel? Shipwreck was the thing! He decided on sending Nicholas Cropredy, his wife's brother-in-law, across the Channel on business—to Antwerp, say—and making Phœbe and little Ruth go out to nurse him through a fever. Their ship could go to the bottom, with a stroke of his pen. Only, while he was about it, why not clear away the brother-in-law—send them all out in the same ship? No—*that* would not do! Where would the motive be, for all those three to leave England? A commercial mission for the man alone would be quite another thing. Very perplexing! . . . Yes—no—yes! . . . There—he had got it! Let them go out and nurse him through a fever, and all be drowned together, returning to England.

That was a triumph. And the finishing touch to the narrative he based on it was really genius. Little hope was entertained of the recovery of the remains, but it was not impossible. The writer's daughter might rest assured that if any came to the surface, and were identified, they should be interred in the family grave where her mother reposed in the Lord, in the sure and certain hope of a joyful resurrection.

Was it to be wondered at that so skilful a contrivance duped an unsuspicious mind like Maisie's? The only thing that could have excited suspicion was that the letter had been delayed a post—time, you see, was needed for the delicate work of forgery —and the date of despatch from London was in consequence some two months too old. But then the letter was of the same date; indeed, the forgery was a repeat of the letter it effaced, wherever this was possible. Besides, the delay of a letter from England could never occasion surprise.

She took the sealed paper from her husband, breaking the seals with feverish haste, and destroying the only proof that it had been opened on the way. For the wax, of course, broke, as her husband had foreseen, on its old fractures, where he had parted them carefully and reattached them with some similar wax dissolved in spirit. He watched her reading the letter, not without an artist's pride at her absolute unsuspicion, and then had to undergo a pang of fear lest the news should kill her. For she fell insensible, only to remain for a long time prostrate with grief, after a slow and painful revival.

There was little need for Thornton to reply to Phœbe's letter that he had effaced. Nevertheless, he did so; partly, perhaps, from the pleasure he naturally took in playing out the false *rôle* he had assigned himself. Yes—he was a widower. But the poignancy of his grief had prevented him writing all the particulars of his wife's death. He now gave the story of the death of a woman on a farm near, with changed names and some clever addenda, the composition of which amused his leisure and gratified a spirit of falsehood which might, more fortunately employed, have found an outlet in literary fiction. The effect of this letter on Phœbe was to satisfy her so completely of her sister's death that, had it ever been called in question, she would have been the hardest to convert to a belief in the contrary. On the other hand, Maisie's belief in *her* death was equally assured, and her quasi-husband rested secure in his confidence that nothing would now induce her to leave him. Should he ever wish to be rid of her, he had only to confess his deception, and pack her off to seek her sister. That no news ever came of her father's death was not a matter of great surprise to Maisie. She had no surviving correspondent in England who would have written about it. Her husband may have practised some *finesse* later to convince her of it, but its details are not known to the writer of the story.

They, however, were never parted until, twenty years later, his death left Maisie a widow, as she believed. It would have been well for her had it been so, for he died after making that very common testamentary mistake—a too ingenious will. It left to "my third son Ralph Thornton Daverill," on coming of age, all his property after "my wife Maisie, *née* Runciman," had received the share she was "legally entitled to." But she was unable to produce proof of her marriage when called on to do so, and was, of course, legally entitled to nothing. Thornton had been so well off that "widow's thirds" would have placed her in comfortable circumstances. As it was, the whole of his property went to her only surviving son, a youth who had inherited, with some of his father's good looks, all his bad principles; and in addition a taint—we may suppose—of the penal atmosphere in which he was born. But there was not a shadow of doubt about his being the person named in the will. Perhaps, if it had been worded "my lawful son," Themis would have jibbed.

The young man, on coming of age, acquired control of the whole of his father's property, and soon started on a career of extravagance and debauchery. His mother, however, retained some influence over him, and persuaded him, a year later, before he had had time to dissipate the whole of his inheritance, to return with her to England, hoping that the moral effect of a change from the gaol-bird atmosphere of felony that hung over the whole land of his birth would develop whatever germ of honour or right feeling he possessed.

She was not very sanguine, for his boyhood had been a cruel affliction to her. And the results showed that whatever hopes she had entertained were ill-founded. Arrived in London, with

money still at command, he plunged at once into all the dissipa-
tions of the town, and it became evident that in the course of a
year or so he would run through the remainder of his patrimony.

About this time he met with an experience which now and then
happens to men of his class. He fell violently in love—or in what
he called love—with a girl who had very distinct ideas on the
subject of marriage. One was that the first arrangement of their
relations which suggested themselves to her lover were not to be
entertained, and therefore she refused to entertain them. He
tried ridicule, indignation, and protestation—all in vain! She
appeared not to object to persecution—rather liked it. But she
held out no hopes except legitimate ones. At last, when the young
man was in a sense desperate—not in a very noble sense, but
desperate for all that—she intimated to him that, unless he was
prepared to accept her scheme of life, she knew a very respectable
young man who was; a young man in Smithfield Market with
whom she had walked out, and you could never have told. Which
means that this young man disguised himself so subtly on Sunday
to go into Society, that none would have guessed that he passed
the week in contact with grease and blood, and dared to twist
the tails of bullocks in revolt against their fate, shrinking naturally from the axe. His intentions were, nevertheless, honourable,
and Polly, the barmaid at the One Tun Inn, honoured them, while
her affections were disposed towards her Australian suitor whose
intentions were not. The young reprobate, however, had to climb
down; but he made his surrender conditional on one thing—that
his marriage with Polly should remain a secret. No doubt parallel
enterprises would have been interrupted by its publication. Anyhow, his mother never knew of his marriage, nor set eyes on her
daughter-in-law.

His marriage was, in fact, merely a means to an end, and was
a most reluctant concession to circumstances on his part. It
was true he deprived himself of all chance of offering the same
terms again for the same goods, unless, indeed, he ran the risks
of a bigamist. But what can a man do under such circumstances? He is what he is, and it does seem a pity sometimes
that he was made in the image of God, whether for God's sake
or his own. Young Daverill's end attained, he flung away his
prize almost without a term of intermediate neglect to save his
face. She, poor soul, who had lived under the impression that
all men were "like that" but that honourable marriage "reformed" them, was desperate at first when she found her mistake. Her "lawful husband," having attained his end, announced

his weariness of lawful marriage with a candour even coarser than
that of Browning's less lawful possessor of Love—he who "half
sighed a smile in a yawn, as 'twere." He replied to all Polly's
passionate claims to him as a legal right, and hints that she could
and would enforce her position:—" Try it on, Poll—you and your
lawyers!" And, indeed, we have never been able to learn how
the strong arm of the Law enforces marital obligations; barring
mere cash payments, of which Polly's attitude was quite oblivious.
Moreover, he was at that time prepared with money, and did actually maintain his wife up to the point of every possible legal
compulsion until the end of his solvency, not a very long period.

For his life-drama, or the first act of it, was soon played out.
It was substantially his father's over again. He ran through
what was left of his money in a little over a year—so splendid
were the gambler's opportunities in these days; for the Georgian
era had still a short lease of years to run, and folly dies hard.
His attempts to reinstate himself at the expense of a Bank, by
a simple process of burglary, in partnership with a professional
hand whose acquaintance he had made at "The Tun," led to
disastrous failure and the summary conviction of both partners.

None of this came to the knowledge of his wife, as how should
it? He wrote no news of it to her, and their relation was known
to very few. Moreover, the burglary was in Bristol and Polly
was at a farmhouse in Lincolnshire, awaiting a birth which only
added another grief to her life, for her child was born dead. She
recovered from a long illness which swallowed up the remains
of the money her husband had given her, to find herself destitute
and minus most of the good looks which had obtained for her
her previous situation. She succeeded thereafter in maintaining
herself by needlework—she was an adept in that—and so avoided
becoming an incumbrance on her family, which she could no longer
help now as she had done in her prosperity. But of her worthless
husband's fate she never knew anything, the trial having taken
place during an illness which nearly ended all her miseries for
her. By the time she was on the way to recovery it would have
been difficult to trace her husband, even had she had any motive
for doing so.

As for him—a convict and the son of a convict—his period of
detention in the hulks on the Thames was followed by the usual
voyage to the Antipodes; but this time the vessel into which he
was transhipped at Sydney sailed for Norfolk Island, not Hobart
Town nor Macquarie Harbour. Maisie's son was not destined to
revisit the land of his birth. The early deliverance from actual

bondage to a condition free in all but the name, which had led to his father's successful later career, was impossible in an island half the size of the Isle of Wight, and the man grew to his surroundings. A soul ready to accept the impress of every stamp of depravity in the mint of vice was soon well beyond the reach of any possible redemption in contact with the moral vileness of the prisons on what was, but for their contamination, one of the loveliest islands in the Pacific.

After his departure his mother may have been influenced by a wish to obliterate her whole past, and this wish may have been the cause of her adoption of a name not her own. Some lingering reluctance to make her severance from her own belongings absolute may have dictated the choice of the name of Prichard, which was that of an old nurse of her childhood, who had stood by her mother's dying bed. It would serve every reasonable purpose of disguise without grating on memories of bygone times. A shred of identity was left to cling to. It is less clear why the quasi-daughter whom she had never seen should have repudiated her married name. Polly was under no obligation not to call herself Mrs. Daverill, unless it were compliance with her promise to keep the marriage secret. She, however, acquiesced in the Mrs., and supplied a name as a passport to a respectable widowhood. But she did not dress the part very vigorously, and report soon accepted the husband as a bad lot and a riddance. Nothing very uncommon in that!

CHAPTER VII

OF DAVE WARDLE'S CONVALESCENCE. OF MRS. RUTH THRALE, WIDOW AND OGRESS, WHO APPRECIATED HIM. HIS ACCOUNT OF HIS HOSPITAL EXPERIENCE. HOW HE MADE THE ACQUAINTANCE OF A COUNTESS, AND TOLD HER ABOUT WIDOW THRALE'S GRANDFATHER'S WATER-MILL. CONCERNING JUNO LUCINA. THESEUS AND ARIADNE. HOW DAVE DETECTED A FAMILY LIKENESS, AND NEARLY RUBBED HIS EYES OUT. HOW GRANNY MARRABLE SHOWED HIM THE MILL AT WORK AND MR. MUGGERIDGE

IF the daylight were not so short in October at Chorlton-under-Bradbury, in Rocestershire, that month would quite do for summer in as many autumns as not. As it is, from ten till five, the sun that comes to say goodbye to the apples, that will all be plucked by the end of the month, is so strong that forest trees are duped, and are ready to do their part towards a green Yule if only the midday warmth will linger on to those deadly small hours of the morning, when hoarfrost gets the thin end of its wedge into the almanack, and sleepers go the length of coming out of bed for something to put over their feet, and end by putting it over most of their total. From ten till five, at least, the last swallows seem to be reconsidering their departure, and the skylarks to be taking heart, and thinking they can go on ever so much longer. Then, not unfrequently, day falls in love with night for the sake of the moonrise, and dies of its passion in a blaze of golden splendour. But the memory of her does not live long into the heart of the night, as it did in the long summer twilights. Love cools and the dews fall, and the winds sing dirges in the elms through the leaves they will so soon scatter about the world without remorse; and then one morning the grass is crisp with frost beneath the early riser's feet, and he finds the leaves of the ash all fallen since the dawn, a green, still heap below their old boughs stript and cold. And he goes home and has all sorts of things for breakfast, being in England.

But no early riser had had this experience at Chorlton-under-Bradbury on that October afternoon when Dave Wardle, personally conducted by Sister Nora, and very tired with travelling from a distant railway-station—the local line was not there in the fifties—descended from the coach or omnibus at the garden gate of Widow Thrale, the good woman who was going to feed him, sleep him, and enjoy his society during convalescence.

The coach or omnibus touched its hat and accepted something from Sister Nora, and went on to the Six Bells in High Street, where the something took the form of something else to drink, which got into its head. The High Street was very wide, and had more water-troughs for horses than recommended themselves to the understanding. But they might have succeeded in doing so before the railway came in these parts, turning everything to the rightabout, as Trufitt phrased it at the Bells. There were six such troughs within a hundred yards; and, as their contents never got into the horses' heads, what odds if there were? When the world was reasonable and four or five horns were heard blowing at once, often enough, in the high road, no one ever complained, that old Trufitt ever heard tell of. So presumably there were no odds.

Widow Thrale lived with an old lady of eighty, who was also

a widow; or, one might have said, even more so, seeing that her widowhood was a double one, her surname, Marrable, being the third she had borne. She was, however, never called Widow Marrable, but always Granny Marrable; and Dave's hostess, who was to take charge of him, was not her daughter, as might have seemed most probable, but a niece who had filled the place of a daughter to her and was always so spoken of. What an active and vigorous octogenarian she was may be judged from the fact that, at the moment of the story, she was taking on herself the task of ushering into the world her first great-grandchild, the son or daughter—as might turn out—of her granddaughter, Maisie Costrell, the only daughter of Widow Thrale. For this young woman had ordained that " Granny " should officiate as high-priestess on this occasion, and we know it is just as well to give way to ladies under such circumstances.

So when Dave and Sister Nora were deposited by the coach at Strides Cottage, it was Widow Thrale who received them. She did not produce on the lady the effect of a *bona-fide* widow of fifty-five—this description had been given of her—not so much because of the non-viduity of her costume, for that was temperate and negative, as because Time seemed to have let his ravages stand over for the present. Very few casual observers would have guessed that she was over forty-five. Ruth Thrale—that was her name in full—had two sons surviving of her own family, both at sea, and one daughter, Maisie Costrell aforesaid. So she was practically now without incumbrances, and terribly wanting some to kiss, had hit upon the expedient of taking charge of invalid children and fostering them up to kissing-point. They were often poor, wasted little articles enough at the first go off, but Mrs. Ruth usually succeeded in making them succulent in a month or so. It was exasperating, though, to have them go away just as they were beginning to pay for fattening. The case was analogous to that of an ogress balked of her meal, after going to no end of expense in humanised cream and such-like.

All the ogress rose in her heart when she saw our little friend Dave Wardle. But she was very careful about his stiff leg. Her eyes gleamed at the opportunities he would present for injudicious overfeeding—or suppose we say stuffing at once and have done with it. A banquet was ready prepared for him, to which he was adapted in a chair of suitable height, and which he began absorbing into his system without apparently registering any date of completion. You must not imagine he had been stinted of food on the journey: indeed, he may be said to have been taking refreshment more or less all the way from London. But he was one of the sort that can go steadily on, converting helpings into small boy, apparently without intermediate scientific events—gastric juice and blood-corpuscles, and so forth. He was able to converse affably the while, accepting suggestions as to method in the spirit in which they were given. In reporting his remarks the spelling cannot be too phonetical; if unintelligible at first, read them literally aloud to a hearer who does not see the letterpress. The conversation had turned on Dave's accident.

"Oy sawed the firing gin coming, and oy said to stoarp, and the firing gin didn't stoarpt, and it said whoy—whoy—whoy!" This was an attempt to render the expressive cry of the brigade; now replaced, we believe, by a tame bell. "Oy sawed free men shoyning like scandles, and Dolly sawed nuffink—no, nuffink!" The little man's voice got quite sad here. Think what he had seen and Dolly had missed!

Mrs. Ruth was harrowed by what the child must have suffered. She expressed her feelings to Sister Nora. Not, however, without Dave catching their meaning. He was very sharp.

"It hurted at the Hospital," said he. That is, the accident itself had been too sudden and overwhelming to admit of any estimate of the pain it caused; the suffering came with the return of consciousness. Then he added, rather inexplicably:—"It didn't hurted Dolly."

Sister Nora, looking with an amused, puzzled face at the small absurdity, assimilating suitable nourishment and wrestling with his mother-tongue at its outset, said:—"Why didn't it hurted Dolly, I wonder?" and then illuminated:—"Oh—I see! It balances Dolly's account. Dolly was the loser by not seeing the fire-engine, but she escaped the accident. Of course!" Whereupon the ogress said with gravity, after due reflection: "I think you are right, ma'am." She then pointed out to Dave that well-regulated circles sit still at their suppers, whereas he had allowed his feelings, on hearing his intelligibility confirmed, to break out in his legs and kick those of the table. He appeared to believe his informant, and to determine to frame his behaviour for the future on the practices of those circles. But he should have taken his spoon out of his mouth while forming this resolution.

He then, as one wishing to entertain in Society, went on to detail his experiences in the Hospital, giving first—as it is always well to begin at the beginning—the names of the staff as he had mastered them. There was Dr. Dabtinkle, or it might have been Damned Tinker, a doubtful name; and Drs. Inkstraw, Jarbottle, and Toby. His hearers were able to identify the names of Dalrymple, Inglethorpe, and Harborough. They were at work on Toby, who defied detection, when it became evident that sleep was overwhelming their informant. He was half roused to be put in a clean nightgown that smelt of lavender, and then curled round his hands and forgot the whole Universe.

"What a nice little man he is!" said Sister Nora. "He's quite a baby still, though he's more than six. Some of the London children are so old. But this child's people seem nice and old-fashioned, although his uncle was a prizefighter."

"Laws-a-me!" said Mrs. Ruth. "To think of that now! A prizefighter!" And she had to turn back to Dave's crib, which they were just leaving, to see whether this degraded profession had set its stamp on her prey. . . . No, it was all right! She could gloat over that sleeping creature without misgiving.

"I've just thought who Toby is," said Sister Nora. "Of course, it's Dr. Trowbridge, the head surgeon. I fancy, now I come to think of it, the juniors are apt to speak of him without any Dr. I don't know why. I shall tell Dr. Damned Tinker his name. . . . Oh no—he won't be offended."

Sister Nora was driven away to the mansion of her noble relative, three miles off, in a magnificent carriage that was sent for her, in which she must have felt insignificant. Perhaps she got there in time to dress for dinner, perhaps not. Wearers of uniforms wash and brush up: they don't dress.

She reappeared at Mrs. Marrable's cottage two days later, in the same vehicle, accompanied by the Countess her aunt, who remained therein. Dave was brought out to make her acquaintance, but not to be taken for a long drive—only a very short one, just up and down and round, because Sister Nora wouldn't be more than five minutes. He was relieved when he found himself safe inside the carriage with her, out of the way of her haughty and overdressed serving-men, whom he mistrusted. The coachman, Blencorn, was too high up in the air for human intercourse. Dave found the lady in the carriage more his sort, and told her, in Sister Nora's absence—she having vanished into the house—many interesting experiences of country life. The ogress had taken off his clean shirt, which he had felt proud of, and looked forward to a long acquaintance with; substituting another, equally good, perhaps, but premature. She had fed him well; he gave close particulars of the diet, laying especial stress on the fact that he had requisitioned the outside piece, presumably of the loaf, but possibly of some cake. Her ladyship seemed to think its provenance less important than its destination. She was able to identity from her own experience a liquid called scream, of which Dave had bespoken a large jug full, to be taken to Dolly on his return home. He went on to relate how he had been shown bees, a calf, and a fool with long legs; about which last the lady was for a moment at fault, having pictured to herself a Shakespearean one with a bauble. It proved to be a young horse, a very young one, whose greedy habits Dave described with a simple but effective directness. But he was destined to puzzle his audience by his keen interest in something that was on the mankleshelf, his description of which seemed to relate to nothing this lady's recollection of Strides interior supplied.

"What on earth does the little man mean by a water-cart on the mantelshelf, Mrs. Thrale?" said the Countess on leavetaking. The widow had come out to reclaim her young charge, who seemed not exactly indignant but perceptibly disappointed, at her ladyship's slowness of apprehension. He plunged afresh into his elucidation of the subject. There *was* a water-cart with four horses, to grind the flour to make the bread, behind a glast on the chimley-shelf. He knew he was right, and appealed to Europe for confirmation, more to reinstate his character for veracity than to bring the details of the topic into prominence.

"That is entirely right, my lady," said Widow Thrale, apologetic for contradiction from her duty to conscience on the one hand, and her reluctance to correct her superiors on the other, but under compulsion from the former. "Quite correct. He's chattering about my grandfather's model of his mill. He doesn't mean water-cart. He means water-mill. Only there's a cart with horses in the yard. It's a hundred years old. It's quite got between the child's mind and his reason, and he wants to see it work like I've told him."

"Yes," said Dave emphatically, "with water in the cistern." He stopped suddenly—you may believe it or not—because of a misgiving crossing his mind that he was using some of Sister Nora's name too freely. Find out where for yourself.

However, nothing of the sort seemed to cross anyone else's mind, so Dave hoped he was mistaken. His hostess proceeded to explain why she could not gratify his anxiety to see this contrivance at work. "I could show it to him perfectly well," she said, "only to humour a fancy of Granny's. She never would have anyone touch it but herself, so we shall have to have patience, some of us." Dave wondered who the other spectators would be when the time came—would the Countess be one of them? And would she get down and come into the house, or have it brought out for her to see in the carriage?

Mrs. Thrale continued:—" I should say it hadn't been set a-going now for twenty years. . . . No, more! It was for the pleasuring and amusement of my little half-brother Robert she made it work, and we buried him more years ago than that." And then they talked about something else, which Dave did not closely follow, because he was so sorry for Mrs. Thrale. He could not resist the conviction that her little half-brother Robert was dead. Because, if not, they surely never would have buried him. He was unable to work this out to a satisfactory conclusion, because Sister Nora was waiting to resume her place in the carriage, and he had no sooner surrendered it to her than the lateness of the hour was recognised, and the distinguished visitors drove away in a hurry.

Although Mrs. Marrable had gone away from home ostensibly to welcome into the world a great-grandchild, the announcement that one had arrived preceded her return nearly a week. Other instances might be adduced of very old matriarchs who have imagined themselves Juno, as she certainly did. Juno, one may reasonably suppose, did not feel free to depart until matters had been put on a comfortable footing. Of course, the goddess had advantages; omnipresence, for instance, or at least presence at choice. One official visit did not monopolize her. Old Mrs. Marrable—Granny Marrable *par excellence*—had but one available personality, and had to be either here or there, never everywhere! So Dave and another convalescent had Strides Cottage all to themselves and their ogress, for awhile.

The country air did wonders for the London child. This is always the case, and contains the truth that only strong children outlive their babyhood in London, and these become normal when they are removed to normal human conditions. Dave began becoming the robust little character Nature had intended him to be, and evidently would soon throw off the ill-effects of his accident, with perhaps a doubt about how long the leg would be stiff.

So by the time Granny Marrable returned into residence she was not confronted with an invalid still plausibly convalescent, but an eatable little boy, from the ogress point of view, who used a crutch when reminded of his undertaking to do so. Otherwise he preferred to neglect it, leaving it on chairs or on the settle by the fireplace, like Ariadne on Naxos; evidently feeling, when he was recalled to his duty towards it, as Theseus might have felt if remonstrated with by Minos for his desertion of his daugh-

ter. In reinstating it he would be acting for the crutch's sake.
And why should he trouble to do this, when the other little boy,
Marmaduke, who had nothing whatever the matter with *his* leg,
was always ambitious to use this crutch, or scrutch. He was the
Dionysos of the metaphor.

However, the crutch was not in question when Dave first set
eyes on Granny Marrable. It was at half-past seven o'clock on
a cold morning, when the last swallow had departed, and the
skylarks were flagging, and the tragedy of the ash-leaves was close
at hand, that Dave awoke reluctantly from a remote dream-world
with Dolly in it, and Uncle Mo, and Aunt M'riar, and Mrs. Picture upstairs, to hear a voice, that at first seemed Mrs. Picture's in
the dream, saying: "Well, my little gentleman, you *do* sleep
sound!"

But it wasn't Mrs. Prichard's, or Picture's, voice; it was Granny
Marrable's. For all her eighty years, she had walked from Costrell's farm, her great-grandson's birthplace, three miles off, or
thereabouts; and had arrived at her own door, ten minutes since,
quite fresh after an hour's walk. She was that sort of old woman.

Dave was almost as disconcerted as when he woke at the
Hospital and saw no signs of his home, and no old familiar faces.
He sat up in bed and wrestled with his difficulties, his eyelids
being among the chief. If he rubbed them hard enough, no doubt
the figure before him would cease to be Mrs. Picture, even as
the other figure the dream had left had ceased to be Aunt M'riar,
and had become Widow Thrale. Not but that he would have
accepted her as Mrs. Picture, being prepared for almost anything
since his accident, if it had not been for the expression, "My
little gentleman," which quarrelled with her seeming identity. Oh
no!—if he rubbed away hard enough at those eyes with his night-
gown-sleeve, this little matter would right itself. Of course, Mrs.
Picture would have called him Doyvy, or the name he gave that
inflection to.

"Child!—you'll rub your pretty eyes out that fashion," said
Granny Marrable. And she uncrumpled Dave's small nightgown-
sleeve the eyes were in collision with, and disentangled their owner
from the recesses of his bedclothes. Then Dave was quite convinced it was not Mrs. Picture, who was not so nearly strong as
this dream-image. or waking reality.

"He'll come awake directly," said the younger widow. "He
do sleep, Granny!" For Widow Thrale often called her aunt
"Granny" as a tribute to her own offspring. Otherwise she
thought of her as "Mother." Her own mother was only a half-

forgotten fact, a sort of duplicate mother, who vanished when she was almost a baby. She continued:—" He goes nigh to eating up his pillow he does. There never was a little boy sounder; all night long not a move! Such a little slugabed I never!" And then this ogress—for she really was no better—was heartless enough to tickle Dave and kiss him, with an affectation of devouring him. And he, being tickled, had to laugh; and then was quite awake, for all the world as if he could never go to sleep again.

"I fought," said he, feeling some apology was due for his mis-apprehension, "I fought it was old Mrs. Picture on the top-landing in the hackicks."

"He's asleep still," said the ogress. "Come along, and I'll wash your sleep out, young man!" And she paid no attention at all to Dave's attempted explanations of his reference to old Mrs. Picture or Prichard. He may be said to have lectured on the subject throughout his ablutions, and really Widow Thrale was not to blame, properly speaking, when he got the soap in his mouth.

Dave lost no time in mooting the subject of the water-mill, and it was decided that as soon as he had finished dictating a letter he had begun to Dolly, Granny Marrable—whom he ad-dressed as "Granny Marrowbone"—would exhibit this ingenious contrivance.

He stuck to his letter conscientiously; and it was creditable to him, because it took a long time. Yet the ground gone over was not extensive. He expressed his affection for Dolly herself, for Uncle Mo and Aunt M'riar, and subordinately for Mrs. Picture, and even Mrs. Burr. He added that there was ducks in the pond. That was all; but it was not till late in the morning that the letter was completed. Then Dave claimed his promise. He was to see the wheel go round, and the sacks go up into the granary above the millstones. It was a pledge even an old lady of eighty could not go back on.

Nor had she any such treacherous intention. So soon as ever the dinner-things were cleared away, Granny Marrable with her own hands lifted down the model off of the mantelshelf, and removing the glass from the front of the case, brought the contents out on the oak table the cloth no longer covered, so that you might see all round. Then the cistern—which after all had noth-ing to do with Sister Nora—was carefully filled with water so that none should spill and make marks, neither on the table nor yet on the mill itself, and then it was wound up like a clock till you couldn't wind no further and it went click. And then the water in the cistern was let run, and the wheels went round; and Dave knew exactly what a water-mill was like, and was assured—only this was a pious fiction—that the water made the wheels go round. The truth was that the clockwork worked the wheels and made them pump back the water as fast as ever it came down. And this is much better than in real mills, because the same water does over and over again, and the power never fails. But you have to wind it up. You can't expect everything!

Granny Marrable gave a brief description of the model. Her brother, who died young, made it because he was lame of one leg; which meant that enforced inactivity had found a sedentary employment in mechanisms, not that all lame folk make mills. Those two horses were Mr. Pitt and Mr. Fox. That was her father standing at the window, with his pipe in his mouth, a miracle of delicate workmanship. And that was the carman, Mr. Muggeridge, who used to see to loading up the cart.

Children are very perverse in their perception of the relative importance of things they are told, and Dave was enormously impressed with Mr. Muggeridge. Silent analysis of the model was visible on his face for awhile, and then he broke out into catechism:—" Whoy doesn't the wheel-sacks come down emptied out?" said hĕ. He had not got the expression " wheat-sacks " right.

" Well, my dear," said Granny Marrable, who felt perhaps that this question attacked a weak point, " if it was the mill itself, they would. But now it's only done in small, we have to pretend." Dave lent himself willingly to the admission of a transparent fiction, and it was creditable to his liberality that he did so. For though the sacks were ingeniously taken into the mill-roof under a projecting hood, they reappeared instantly to go up again through a hole under the cart. Any other arrangement would have been too complex; and, indeed, a pretence that they took grain up and brought flour down might have seemed affectation. A conventional treatment was necessary. It had one great advantage, too: it liberated the carman for active service elsewhere. It was entirely his own fault, or his employer's, that he stood bolt upright, raising one hand up and down in time with the movement of the wheels. The miller did not seem to mind; for he only kept on looking out of window, smoking.

But the miller and the carman were not the only portraitures this model showed. Two very little girls were watching the rising grain-sacks, each with her arm round the other. The miller may have been looking at them affectionately from the window; but really he was so very unimpressive—quite inscrutable! Dave inquired about these little girls, after professing a satisfaction he only partly felt about the arrangements for receiving the raw material and delivering it ground.

"Whoy was they bofe of a size?" said he, for indeed they were exactly alike.

"Because, my dear, that is the size God made them. Both at the same time!"

"Who worze they?" asked Dave, clinching the matter abruptly —much too interested for circumlocution.

"Myself, my dear, and my little sister, born the same time. With our lilac frocks on and white bonnets to shade the sun off our eyes. And each a nosegay of garden flowers." There was no more sorrow in the old woman's voice than belongs to any old voice speaking thoughtfully and gently. Her old hand caressed the crisp locks of the little, interested boy, and felt his chin appreciatively, as she added:—"Three or four years older than yourself, my dear! Seventy years ago!" with just the ring of sadness—no more—that always sounds when great age speaks of its days long past.

The other convalescent boy here struck in, raising a vital question. "Which is you, and which is her?" said he. He had come in as a new spectator; surrendering Dave's crutch, borrowed as needless to its owner, in compliance with a strange fascination, now waning in charm as the working model asserted its powers. Dionysos had deserted Ariadne again.

"This is me," said Granny Marrable. "And this is Maisie." And now you who read probably know, as clearly as he who writes, who she was, this octogenarian with such a good prospect of making up the hundred. She was Phœbe, the sister of old Mrs. Prichard, whose story was told in the last chapter. But most likely you guessed that pages ago.

I, who write, have no aim in telling this story beyond that of repeating as clearly and briefly as may be the bare facts that make it up—of communicating them to whoever has a few hours to spare for the purpose, with the smallest trouble to himself in its perusal. I feel often that my lack of skill is spoiling what might be a good story. That I cannot help; and I write with the firm conviction that any effort on my part to arrange these facts in such order that the tale should show dramatic force, or startle him with unexpected issues of event, would only procure derision for its writer, and might even obscure the only end he has at heart, that of giving a complete grasp of the facts, as nearly as may be in the order of their occurrence.

There is one feature in the story which the most skilful narrator might easily fail to present as probable—the separation of these twin sisters throughout a long lifetime, a separation contrary to nature; so much so, indeed, that tales are told of twins living apart, the death or illness of one of whom has brought about the death or similar illness of the other. One would at least say that neither could die without knowledge of the other; might even infer that either would go on thinking the other living, without some direct evidence of death, some seeming communication from the departed. But the separation of Phœbe from Maisie did not come under these conditions; each was the victim of a wicked fraud, carried out with a subtlety that might have deceived Scotland Yard. There can be no doubt that it would have had the force to obscure any phenomenon of a so-called telepathic nature, however vivid, as proof that either twin was still alive; as the percipient, in the belief that her sister's death was established beyond a doubt, would unhesitatingly conclude that the departed had revisited earth, or had made her presence felt by some process hard to understand from our side.

To see the story in its right light we must always keep in view the extraordinary isolation of the penal settlement. All convict life is cut off from the world, but in Van Diemen's Land even the freest of men out on ticket-of-leave—free sometimes so long that the renewal of their licence at its expiration became the merest form—was separated from the land of his birth, even from the mainland of Australia, by a barrier for him almost as impassable as the atmosphere that lies between us and the visible land of the moon. Keep in mind the hundred-and-odd miles of sea—are you sure you thought of it as so much?—that parts Tasmania from the nearest point of New South Wales, and picture to yourself the few slow sailing-ships upon their voyages from Sydney, five times as distant. To go and come on such a journey was little else to the stay-at-home in those days, than that he should venture beyond the grave and return.

No!—the wonder to my mind is not that the two sisters should have been parted so utterly, and each been so completely duped about the other's death, but that Maisie should have returned less than five-and-twenty years later, and that, so returning, she should not have come to the knowledge that her sister was still living.

CHAPTER VIII

MICHAEL RAGSTROAR'S SLIDE, AND THE MILK. CONCERNING DAVE'S RE-
TURN TO SAPPS COURT, WHICH HAD SHRUNK IN HIS ABSENCE. OF
THE PHYSICAL IMPOSSIBILITY OF A WIDOW'S GRANDMOTHER. DAVE'S
TALE OF THE WATER-MILL. SISTER NORA'S EXACTING FATHER. HOW
DAVE WENT TO SCHOOL, AND UNCLE MO SOUGHT CONSOLATION IN
SOCIETY, WHILE DOLLY TOOK STRUVVEL PETER TO VISIT MRS. PRICH-
ARD. HOW THAT OLD LADY KNITTED A COMFORTER, AND TOLD AUNT
M'RIAR OF HER CONVICT LOVER'S DEPARTURE

THE heart of the ancient prizefighter in Sapps Court swelled
with joy when the day of Dave's return was officially announced.
He was, said Aunt M'riar, in and out all the afternoon, fidgeting-
like, when it actually came. And the frost was that hard that
ashes out of the dustbin had to be strewed over the paving to
prevent your slipping. It might not have been any so bad though,
only for that young Michael Ragstroar's having risen from his
couch at an early hour, and with diabolical foresight made a
slide right down the middle of the Court. He had chosen this
hour so early, that he was actually before the Milk, which was
always agreeable to serve the Court when the tenantry could do
—taken collectively—with eightpennyworth. It often mounted
up to thrice that amount, as a matter of fact. On this occasion
it sat down abruptly, the Milk did, and gave a piece of its mind
to Michael's family later, pointing out that it was no mere question of physical pain or ill-convenience to itself, but that its
principal constituent might easily have been spilled, and would
have had to be charged for all the same. The incident led to a
collision between Michael and his father, the coster; who, however, remitted one-half of his son's deserts and let him off easy
on condition of his reinstating the footway. Michael would have
left all intact, he said, had he only been told that his thoughtfulness would provoke the Court's ingratitude. " Why couldn't they
say aforehand they didn't want no slide? " said he. " I could just
as easy have left it alone." It was rather difficult to be quite even
with Michael Ragstroar.

However, the ground was all steady underfoot when Dave, in
charge of Sister Nora, reappeared, looking quite rosy again, and
only limping very slightly. He had deserted Ariadne altogether

by now, and Dionysos may have done so, too, for anything the story knows. Anyhow, the instability of the planet that had resulted from local*frost did not affect Dave at all, now that Michael had spilt them hashes over the ground. Dave was bubbling over with valuable information about the provinces, which had never reached the Metropolis before, and he was in such a hurry to tell about a recent family of kittens, that he scamped his greetings to his own family in order to get on to the description of it.

But neither this, nor public indignation against the turpitude of slide-makers generally and that young Micky in particular, could avert his relatives' acknowledgments of their gratitude—what a plague thanks are!—from a benefactress who was merely consulting a personal dilettantism in her attitude towards her species, and who regarded Dave as her most remunerative investment for some time past.

" We shall never know how to be grateful enough, ma'am, for your kindness to Dave," said Aunt M'riar. " No—never! "

" Not if we was to live for ever," said Uncle Mo. And he seemed to mean it, for he went on:—" It's a poor way of thanks to be redooced to at the best, just to be grateful and stop it off at that. But 'tis in the right of it as far as it goes. You take me, missis? I'm a bad hand to speak my mind; but you'll count it up for hearty thanks, anyhow."

" Of course I will, Mr. Wardle," said Sister Nora. " But, oh dear!—what a fuss one does make about nothing! Why, he's such a ducky little chap, anybody would be glad to."

Dave struck into the conversation perceiving an opportunity to say something appropriate: " There was sisk duskses in the pong in the field, and one of the duskses was a droyk with green like ribbings, and Mrs. Thrale she said a little boy stumbled in the pong and was took out green, and some day I should show Dolly the droyk and I should show Uncle Mo the droyk and I should show Aunt M'riar the droyk. And there was a bool." At which point the speaker suddenly became shyly silent, perhaps feeling that he was premature in referring thus early to a visit of his family to Chorlton-under-Bradbury. It would have been better taste to wait, he thought.

However, no offence seemed to be taken. Uncle Mo said: " Oh, that was it—was it? I hope the bull had a ring on his nose." Dave appeared doubtful, with a wish to assent. Then Aunt M'riar, who—however good she was—certainly had a commonplace mind, must needs say she hoped Dave had been a very good little boy. The banality of it!

Dave felt that an effort should be made to save the conversation. The bull's nose and its ring suggested a line to go on. " The lady," said he decisively, " had rings on hèr fingers. Dimings and pearls and scrapphires "—he took this very striking word by storm—" and she giv' 'em me for to hold one at a time. . . . Yorce she did! " He felt sure of his facts, and that the lady's rings on her fingers made her a legitimate and natural corollary to a bull with one on its nose.

" The lady would be my Cousin Philippa," said Sister Nora. " She's always figged up to the nines. Dave took her for a drive in the carriage—didn't you, Dave? " There was misrepresentation in this, but a way grown-up people have of understanding each other over the heads of little boys prevented the growth of false impressions. Uncle Mo and Aunt M'riar quite understood, somehow, that it was the lady that had taken Dave for a drive. Dave allowed this convention to pass without notice, merely nodding. He reserved criticism for the days to come, when he should have a wider vocabulary at command.

Then Sister Nora had gone, and Dave was having his first experience of the shattered ideal. Sapps Court was neither so large nor so distinguished as the conception of it that he had carried away into the country with him; with the details of which he had endeavoured to impress Granny Marrable and the ogress. Dolly was not so large as he had expected to find her; but then he had had that expectation owing to a message, which had reached him in his absence, that she was growing out of all knowledge. His visit was inside three months; so this was absurd. One really should be careful what one says to six-year-olds. The image of Dolly that Dave brought back from the provinces nearly filled up the Sapps Court memory supplied. It was just the same shape as Dolly, but on a much larger scale. The reality he came back to was small and compact, but not so influential.

Dolly's happiness at his return was great and unfeigned, but its expression was handicapped by her desire that a doll Sister Nora brought her should be allowed to sleep off the effects of an exhausting journey. Only Shakespearean dramatic power could have ascribed sleep to this doll, who was a similitude of Struvvel Peter in the collected poems of that name just published. Still, Dolly gave all of herself that this matronly preoccupation could spare to Dave. She very soon suggested that they should make a joint visit to old Mrs. Picture upstairs. She could carry Struvvel Peter in her arms all the time, so that his sleep should not be disturbed.

This was only restless love of change on Dolly's part, and Uncle Mo protested. Was his boy to be carried off from him when only just this minute he got him back? Who was Mrs. Prichard that such an exaggerated consideration should be shown to her? Dave expressed himself in the same sense, but with a less critical view of Mrs. Prichard's pretensions.

Aunt M'riar pointed out that there was no call to be in a driving hurry. Presently, when Mr. Alibone come in for a pipe, like he said he would, then Dave and Dolly might go up and knock at Mrs. Prichard's door, and if they were good they might be let in. Aunt M'riar seized so many opportunities to influence the young towards purity and holiness that her injunctions lost force through the frequency of their recurrence, always dangling rewards and punishments before their eyes. In the present case her suggestions worked in with the general feeling, and Dave and Dolly sat one on each knee of Uncle Mo, and made intelligent remarks. At least, Dave did; Dolly's were sometimes confused, and very frequently uncompleted.

Uncle Mo asked questions about Dave's sojourn with Widow Thrale. Who was there lived in the house over and above the Widow? Well—said Dave—there was her Granny. Uncle Mo derided the idea of a Widow's Granny. Such a thing was against Nature. Her mother was possible but uncommon. But as for her Granny!—draw it mild, said Uncle Mo.

"But my dear Mo," said Aunt M'riar. "Just you give consideration. You're always for sayin' such a many things. Why, there was our upstairs old lady she says to me she was plenty old enough to be my grandmother. Only this very morning, if you'll believe me, she said that very selfsame thing. 'I'm plenty old enough to be your grandmother,' she says."

"As for the being old enough, M'riar," said Uncle Mo, "there's enough and to spare old enough for most anything if you come to that. But this partick'lar sort don't come off. Just you ask anybody. Why, I'll give ye all England to hunt 'em up. Can't say about foreigners, they're a queer lot; but England's a Christian country, and you may rely upon it, and so I tell you, you won't light on any one or two widders' Grannies in the whole show. You try it!" Uncle Moses was not the first nor the only person in the world that ever proposed an impracticable test to be carried out at other people's expense, or by their exertions. It was, however, a mere *façon de parler,* and Aunt M'riar did not show any disposition to start on a search for widows' grandmothers.

The discussion was altogether too deep for Dave. So after a

moment of grave perplexity he started a new topic, dashing into it without apology, as was his practice. "Granny Marrowbone's box on the chimley-piece is got glast you can see in, and she's got two horses in a wagging, and the wheels goes round and round and round like a clock, and there was her daddy stood at the window and there was saskses was took up froo a hole, and come back froo a hole, and there was Muggeridge that see to loading up the cart, and there was her and her sister bofe alike of one size, and there was the water run over . . ." Here Dave flagged a little after so much eloquence, and no wonder. But he managed to wind up:—"And then Granny Marrowbone put it back on the mankleshelf for next time."

This narrative was, of course, quite unintelligible to its hearers; but we understand it, and its mention of the carman's name. A child that has to repeat a story will often confuse incidents limitlessly, and nevertheless hold on with the tenacity of a bull-pup to some saving phrase heard distinctly once and for ever. Even so, Dave held on to Muggeridge, that see to loading up the cart, as a great fact rooted in History.

"H'm!" said Uncle Mo. "I don't make all that out. Who's Muggeridge in it?"

"He see to the sacks," said Dave.

"Counting of 'em out, I reckon." Uncle Mo was thinking of coal-sacks, and the suggestions of a suspicious Company. Dave said nothing. Probably Uncle Mo knew. But he was all wrong, perhaps because the association of holes with coals misled him.

"Was it Mrs. Marrable and her sister?" asked Aunt M'riar. "Why was they both of a size?"

Dave jumped at the opportunity of showing that he had profited by *résumés* of this subject with his hostess. "Because they were the soyme oyge," said he. "Loyke me and Dolly. We aren't the soyme oyge, me and Dolly." That is to say, he and Dolly were an example of persons whose relative ages came into court. Their classification differed, but that was a detail.

Aunt M'riar was alive to the possibility that the sister of Granny Marrable was her twin, and said so. But Uncle Mo took her up short for this opinion. "What!" said he, "the same as the old party two pair up? No, no!—you won't convince me there's two old parties at once with twin sisters. One at a time's plenty on the way-bill." Because, you see, Aunt M'riar had had a good many conversations with Mrs. Prichard lately, and had repeated words of hers to Uncle Moses. "I was a twin myself," she had

said; and added that she had lost her sister near upon fifty
years ago.

The truth was too strange to occur to even the most observant
bystander; *videlicet,* on the whole, Mr. Alibone; who, coming in
and talking over the matter anew, only said it struck him as a
queer start. This expression has somehow a sort of flavour of
its user's intention to conduct inquiry no farther. Anyhow, the
subject simply dropped for that time being, out of sight and out
of mind.

It was very unfair to Dave, who was, after all, a model of
veracity, that he should be treated as a romancer, and never
confronted with witnesses to confirm or contradict his statements.
Even Uncle Mo, who took him most seriously, continued to doubt
the existence of widows' grandmothers, and to accept with too
many reservations his account of the mill-model. Sister Nora,
as it chanced, did not revisit Sapps Court for a very long time,
for she was called away to Scotland by the sudden illness of her
father, who showed an equivocal affection for her by refusing to
let anyone else nurse him.

So it came about that Dave, rather mortified at having doubt
thrown on narratives he knew to be true, discontinued his attempts
to establish them. And that the two old sisters, so long parted,
still lived on apart; each in the firm belief that the other was
dead a lifetime since. How near each had been to the knowledge
that the other lived! Surely if Dave had described that mill-
model to old Mrs. Picture, suspicions would have been excited.
But Dave said little or nothing about it.

It is nowise strange to think that the bitter, simultaneous grief
in the heart of either twin, now nearly fifty years ago, still survived in two hearts that were not too old to love; for even those
who think that love can die, and be as though it had never been,
may make concession to its permanency in the case of twins—may
even think concession scientific. But it is strange—strange beyond expression—that at the time of this story each should have
had love in her heart for the same object, our little Dave Wardle;
that Master Dave's very kissable countenance had supplied the
lips of each with a message of solace to a tired soul. And most
of all that the tears of each, and the causes of them, had provoked the inquisitiveness of the same pair of blue eyes and set
their owner questioning, and that through all this time the child
had in his secret consciousness a few words that would have fired
the train. Never was a spark so near to fuel, never an untold
tale so near its hearer, never a draught so near to lips athirst.

But Dave's account of the mill was for the time forgotten. It happened that old Mrs. Prichard was not receiving just at the time of his return, so his visits upstairs had to be suspended. By the time they were renewed the strange life in the country village had become a thing of the past, and important events nearer home had absorbed the mill on the mantelshelf, and the ducks in the pond and Widow Thrale and Granny Marrable alike. One of the important events was that Dave was to be took to school after Christmas.

It was in this interim that old Mrs. Prichard became a very great resource to Aunt M'riar, and when the time came for Dave to enter on his curriculum of scholarship, the visiting upstairs had become a recognised institution. Aunt M'riar being frequently forsaken by Uncle Mo, who marked his objection to the scholastic innovation by showing himself more in public, notably at The Rising Sun, whose proprietor set great store by the patronage of so respectable a representative of an Institution not so well thought of now as formerly, but whose traditions were still cherished in the confidential interior of many an ancient pot-house of a like type—Aunt M'riar, so forsaken, made these absences of her brother-in-law a reason for conferring her own society and Dolly's on the upstairs lodger, whenever the work she was engaged on permitted it. She felt, perhaps, as Uncle Mo felt, that the house warn't like itself without our boy; but if she shared his feeling that it was a waste of early life to spend it in learning to read slowly, write illegibly, and cypher incorrectly, she did so secretly. She deferred to the popular prejudice, which may have had an inflated opinion of the advantages of education; but she acknowledged its growth and the worldly wisdom of giving way to it.

Old Mrs. Prichard and Aunt M'riar naturally exchanged confidences more and more; and in the end the old lady began to speak without reserve about her past. It came about thus. After Christmas, Dave being culture-bound, and work of a profitable nature for the moment at a low ebb, Aunt M'riar had fallen back on some arrears of stocking-darning. Dolly was engaged on the object to which she gave lifelong attention, that of keeping her doll asleep. I do not fancy that Dolly was very inventive; but then, you may be, at three-and-a-half, seductive without being inventive. Besides, this monotonous fiction of the need of her doll for sleep was only a *scenario* for another incident—the fear of disturbance by a pleace'n with two heads, a very terrible possibility.

Old Mrs. Prichard, whom I call by that name because she was known by no other in Sapps Court, was knitting a comforter for Dave. It went very slowly, this comforter, but was invaluable as an expression of love and goodwill. She couldn't get up and downstairs because of her back, and she couldn't read, only a very little, because of her eyes, and she couldn't hear—not to say *hear* —when read aloud to. This last may have been no more than what many of us have experienced, for she heard very plain when spoke to. That is Aunt M'riar's testimony. My impression is that, as compared with her twin sister Phœbe, Maisie was at this date a mere invalid. But she looked very like Phœbe for all that, when you didn't see her hands. The veins were too blue, and their delicacy was made more delicate by the aggressive scarlet she had chosen for the comforter.

" It makes a rest to do a little darning now and again." Aunt M'riar said this, choosing a worsted carefully, so it shouldn't quarrel with its surroundings. " I take a pleasure in it more than not. On'y as for knowing when to stop—there! "

" I mind what it was in my early days up-country," said the old woman. " 'Twas not above once in the year any trade would reach us, and suchlike things as woollen socks were got at by the moth or the ants. They would sell us things at a high price from the factory as a favour, but my husband could not abide the sight of them. It was small wonder it was so, Mrs. Wardle." That was the name that Aunt M'riar had come to be called by, although it was not her own real name. Confusion of this sort is not uncommon in the class she belonged to. Sapps Court was aware that she was not Mrs. Wardle, but she had to be accounted for somehow, and the name she bore was too serious a tax on the brain-power of its inhabitants.

She repeated Mrs. Prichard's words: " From the factory, ma'am? I see." Because she did not understand them.

" It was always called the factory," said Mrs. Prichard. But this made Aunt M'riar none the wiser. *What* was called the factory? The way in which she again said that she *saw* amounted to a request for enlightenment. Mrs. Prichard gave it. " It was the Government quarters with the Residence, and the prisons where the convicts were detained on their arrival. They would not be there long, being told off to work in gangs up-country, or assigned to the settlers as servants. But I've never told you any of all this before, Mrs. Wardle." No more she had. She had broached Van Diemen's Land suddenly, having gone no farther before than the mere fact of her son's birth at Port Macquarie.

Aunt M'riar couldn't make up her mind as to what was expected of her, whether sympathy or mere interest or silent acquiescence. She decided on a weak expression of the first, saying:— " To think of that now—all that time ago! "

" Fifty long years ago! But I knew of it before that, four years or more," said the old lady. It did not seem to move her much—probably felt to her like a previous state of existence. She went on talking about the Convict Settlement, which she had outlived. Her hearer only half understood most of it, not being a prompt enough catechist to ask the right question at the right time.

For Aunt M'riar, though good, was a slowcoach, backward in cross-examination, and Mrs. Prichard's first depositions remained unqualified, for discussion later with Uncle Mo. However, one inquiry came to her tongue. " Was you born in those parts yourself, ma'am? " said she. Then she felt a little sorry she had asked it, for a sound like annoyance came in the answer.

" Who—I? No, no—not I—dear me, no! My father was an Essex man. Darenth, his place was called." Aunt M'riar repeated the name wrongly:—" Durrant? " She ought to have asked something concerning his status and employment. Who knows but Mrs. Prichard might have talked of that mill and supplied a clue to speculation?—not Aunt M'riar's; speculation was not her line. Others might have compared notes on her report, literally given, with Dave's sporting account of the mill-model. And yet—why should they? With no strong leading incident in common, each story might have been discussed without any suspicion that the flour-mill was the same in both.

So that Mrs. Prichard's tale so far supplies nothing to link her with old Granny Marrable, as unsuspicious as herself. What Aunt M'riar found her talking of, half to herself, when her attention recovered from a momentary fear that she might have hurt the old lady's feelings, was even less likely to connect the two lives.

" I followed my husband out. My child died—my eldest—here in England. I went again to live at home. Then I followed him out. He wrote to me and said that he was free. Free on the island, but not to come home. We had been over four years parted then." She said nothing of the child she left behind in England. Too much to explain perhaps?

Aunt M'riar was struck by a painful thought; the same that had crossed her mind before, and that she had discarded as somehow inconsistent with this old woman. The convicts—the convicts? She had grasped the fact that this couple had lived in Van

Diemen's Land, and inferred that children were born to them there. But—was the husband himself a convict? She repeated the words, "Free on the island, but not to come home?" as a question.

She was quite taken aback with the reply, given with no visible emotion. "Why should I not tell you? How will it hurt me that you should know? My husband was convicted of forgery and transported."

"God's mercy on us!" said Aunt M'riar, dropping her work dumfoundered. Then it half entered her thought that the old woman was wandering, and she nearly said :—"Are you sure?"

The old woman answered the thought as though it had been audible. "Why not?" she said. "I am all myself. Fifty years ago! Why should I begin to doubt it because of the long time?" She had ceased her knitting and sat gazing on the fire, looking very old. Her interlaced thin fingers on the strain could grow no older now surely, come what might of time and trouble. Both had done their worst. She went on speaking low, as one talks to oneself when alone. "Yes, I saw him go that morning on the river. They rowed me out at dawn—a pair of oars, from Chatham. For I had learned the day he would go, and there was a sure time for the leaving of the hulks; if not night, then in the early dawn before folk were on the move. This was in the summer."

"And did you see him?" said Aunt M'riar, hoping to hear more, and taking much for granted that she did not understand, lest she should be the loser by interruption.

"I saw him. I saw him. I did not know then that _he_ saw _me_. They dared not row me near the wicked longboat that was under the hulk's side waiting—waiting to take my heart away. They dared not for the officers. There was ten men packed in the stern of the boat, and he was in. among them. And, as they sat, each one's hand was handcuffed to his neighbour. I saw him, but he could not raise his hand; and he dared not call to me for the officers. I could not have known him in his prison dress—it was too far—but I could read his number, 213M. I know it still— 213M. . . . How did I know it? Because he got a letter to me." She then told how a man had followed her in the street, when she was waiting in London for this chance of seeing her husband, and how she had been afraid of this man and taken refuge in a shop. Then how the shopkeeper had gone out to speak to him and come back, saying :—"He's a bad man to look at, but he means no harm. He says he wants to give you a letter, miss." How she then spoke with the man and received the letter, giving him a guinea for the rolled-up pencil scrawl, and he said:—"It's worth more than that for the risk I ran to bring it ye. But for my luck I might be on the ship still." Whereupon she gave him her watch. That was how she came to know 213M.

"But did you see your husband again?" asked Aunt M'riar, listening as Dave might have done; and, like him, wanting each instalment of the tale rounded off.

"Yes. Climbing up the side of the great ship half-way to the Nore. It was a four-hours' pull for the galley—six oars—each man wristlocked to his oar; and each officer with a musket. But we had a little sail and kept the pace, though the wind was easterly. Then, when we reached the ship where she lay, we went as near as ever my men dared. And we saw each one of them—the ten—unhandcuffed to climb the side, and a cord over the side made fast to him to give him no chance of death in the waters —no chance! And then I saw my husband and knew he saw me."

"Did he speak?"

"He tried to call out. But the ship's officer struck him a cruel blow upon the mouth, and he was dragged to the upper deck and hidden from me. We saw them all aboard, all the ten. It was the last boat-load from the hulk, and all the yards were manned by now, and the white sails growing on them. Oh, but she was beautiful, the great ship in the sunshine!" The old woman, who had spoken tearlessly, as from a dead, tearless heart, of the worst essentials of her tragedy, was caught by a sob at something in this memory of the ship at the Nore—why, Heaven knows!—and her voice broke over it. To Aunt M'riar, cockney to the core, a ship was only a convention, necessary for character, in an offing with an orange-chrome sunset claiming your attention rather noisily in the background. There were pavement-artists in those days as now. This ship the old lady told of was a new experience for her—this ship with hundreds of souls on board, men and women who had all had a fair trial and been represented by counsel, so had nothing to complain of even if innocent. But all souls in Hell, for all that!

The old voice seemed quite roused to animation—a sort of heart-broken animation—by the recollection of this ship. "Oh, but she was beautiful!" she said again. "I've dreamed of her many's the time since then, with her three masts straight up against the blue; you could see them in the water upside down. I could not find the heart to let my men row away and leave her there. I had come to see her go, and it was a long wait we had. . . . Yes, it was on towards evening before the breeze came to move her; and all those hours we waited. It was money to my men, and they had a good will to it." She stopped, and Aunt M'riar waited for her to speak again, feeling that she too had a right to see this ship's image move. Presently she looked up from her darning and got a response. "Yes, she did move in the end. I saw the sails flap, and there was the clink of the anchor-chain. I've dreamt it again many and many a time, and seen her take the wind and move, till she was all a mile away and more. We watched her away with all aboard of her. And when the wind rose in the night I was mad to think of her out on the great sea, and how I should never see him again. But the time went by, and I did."

This was the first time old Mrs. Prichard spoke so freely about her former life to Aunt M'riar. It was quite spontaneous on the old lady's part, and she stopped her tale as suddenly as it had begun. The fragmentary revelations in which she disclosed much more of her story, as already summarised, came at intervals; always dwelling on her Australian experiences, never on her girlhood—never on her subsequent life in England. The reason of this is not clear; one has to accept the fact. The point to notice is that nothing she said could possibly associate her with old Mrs. Marrable, as told about by Dave. There had been mention of Australia certainly. Yet why should Granny Marrable's sister having died there forty-odd years ago connect her with an old woman of a different name, now living? Besides, Dave was not intelligible on this point.

Whatever she told to Aunt M'riar was repeated to Uncle Mo— be sure of that! Still, fragmentary stories, unless dressed up and garnished by their retailer, do not remain vividly in the mind of their hearer, and Uncle Mo's impressions of the upstairs tenant's history continued very mixed. For Aunt M'riar's style was unpolished, and she did not marshall her ideas in an impressive or lucid manner.

CHAPTER IX

OF A WATERSIDE PUBLIC-HOUSE, AT CHISWICK, AND TWO MEN IN ITS
BACK GARDEN. HOW THE RIVER POLICE TOOK AN INTEREST IN THEM.
A TROUBLESOME LANDING AND A BAD SPILL. HOW FOUR MEN WENT
UNDER WATER, AND TWO WERE NOT DROWNED. OF THE INQUEST ONE
OF THE OTHERS TOOK THE STAR PART IN. A MODEL WITNESS, AND
HIS GREAT-AUNT

JUST off the Lower Mall at Hammersmith there still remains
a scrap of the waterside neighbourhood that, fifty years ago, believed itself eternal; that still clung to the belief forty years ago;
that had misgivings thirty years ago; and that has suffered such
inroads from eligible residences, during the last quarter of a century, that its residuum, in spite of a superficial appearance of duration, is really only awaiting the expiration of leases to be given
over to housebreakers, to make way for flats.

Fifty years ago this corner of the world was so self-reliant that
it was content—more than content—to be unpatrolled by police;
in fact, felt rather resentful when an occasional officer passed
through, as was inevitable from time to time. It would have been
happier if its law-abiding tendencies had always been taken for
granted. Then you could have drunk your half a pint, your
quart, or your measurable fraction of a hogshead, in peace and
quiet at the bar of the microscopic pub called The Pigeons, without fear of one of those enemies of Society—*your* Society—coming
spying and prying round after you or any chance acquaintance
you might pick up, to help you towards making that fraction a
respectable one. If it was summer-time, and you sat in the little
back-garden that had a ladder down to the river, you might feel
a moment's uneasiness when the river-police rowed by, as sometimes happened; only, on the other hand, you might feel soothed
by their appearance of unconcern in riparian matters, almost
amounting to affectation. If any human beings took no interest in your antecedents, surely it would be these two leisurely
rowers and the superior person in the starn, with the oilskin
cape?

It was not summer-time—far from it—on the day that concerns
this story, when two men in the garden of The Pigeons looked out
over the river, and one said to the other:—"Right away over

yonder it lies, halfway to Barn Elms." They were so busy over the locating of it, whatever it was, that they did not notice the police-wherry, oarless in the swift-running tide, as it slipped down close inshore, and was abreast of them before they knew it. Perhaps it was the fact that it was not summer, and that these men must have left a warm fire in the parlour of The Pigeons, to come out into a driving north-east wind bringing with it needle-pricks of microscopic snow, hard and cold and dry, that made the rowers drop their oars and hold back against the stream, to look at them.

Or was it that the man in the stern had an interest in one of them. An abrupt exclamation that he uttered at this moment seemed, to the man rowing stroke, who heard more than his mate, to apply to the thicker and taller man of the two. This one, who seemed to treat his pal as an inferior or subordinate, met his gaze, not flinching. His companion seemed less at his ease, and to him the big man said, scarcely moving his lips to say it:—"Steady, fool!—if you shy, we're done." On which the other remained motionless. What they said was heard by a boy close at hand; but for whose version, given afterwards, this story would have been in the dark about it.

The two rowers kept the boat stationary, backing water. The steersman's left hand played with the tiller-rope, and the boat edged slowly to the shore. There was a grating thrown out over the water from the parapet of the river-wall, to the side of which was attached a boat-ladder, now slung up, for no boat's crew ever stopped here at this season. The boat was nearing this—all but close—when the bigger man spoke, on a sudden. But he only said it was a rough night, sergeant!

It was a rough night, or meant to be one in an hour or so. But it was impossible for an Official to accept another person's opinion without loss of dignity. Therefore the sergeant, always working the boat edgewise towards the ladder, only responded, "Roughish!" qualifying the night, and implying a wider experience of rough nights than his hearer's. If impressions derived from appearance are to be relied on, his experience must have been a wide one. For one thing, he himself seemed a dozen years at least the younger of the two. He added, as the boat touched the ladder, bringing each in full view of the other, and making speech easy between them:—" A man don't make the voyage out to Sydney without seeing some rough weather."

A very attentive observer might have said that he watched the man he addressed more closely than the talk warranted, and certainly would have seen that the latter started. He half began "Who the Hell . . . ?" but flagged on the last word—just stopped short of Sheol—and the growl that accompanied it turned into "I've never been in those parts, master."

"Never said you had. *I* have, though." One might have thought, by his tone, that this officer chuckled secretly over something. He was pleased, at least. But he gave no clue to his thoughts. He seemed disconcerted at the height above the water of the projecting grating and slung-up ladder. An active man, unencumbered, might easily enough have landed himself on it from the boat. Yet a boy might have made it impossible, standing on the grating. A resolute kick on the first hand-grip, or in the face of the climber, would have met the case, and given him a back-fall into the boat or the water. A chilly thought that, on a day like this. But why should such a thought cross the mind of this man, now? It did, probably, and he gave up the idea of landing.

Instead, he felt in his pocket, and drew out a spirit-flask. "Maybe," said he, "your mate would oblige so far as to ask the young lady at the bar to fill this up with Kinahan's LL? *She* won't make any bones about it if he says it's for me, Sergeant Ibbetson—*she'll* know." He inverted it to see that it was empty, and the man who had not spoken accepted the mission at a nod from his companion, whose social headship the speech of the policeman seemed somehow to have taken for granted.

The sergeant watched him out of sight; then, the moment he had vanished, said:—"Now I come to think of it, Cissy Tuttle that was here has married a postman, and the young lady that's took it over may not know my name." His speech had not the appearance of a sudden thought, and the less so that he began to get rid of his oilskin incumbrance almost before he had uttered it.

The understanding of what then happened needs a clear picture of the exact position of things at this moment. The boat, held back by the dipped oars, but steadied now and again by the hand of the sergeant on the grating or ladder, lay uneasily between the wind and the current. The man on the grating showed some unwillingness to lend the hand-up that was asked for; and took exception, it seemed, to the safety of the landing on any terms. "Maybe you want a dip in the river, master?" said he. "It's no concern of mine. Only I don't care to take your weight on this greasy bit of old iron. I'm best out of the water."

The sergeant paused, looked at the grating, which certainly

sloped outwards, then at the boat and at the ladder. " Catch hold! "
said he.

But the other held back. " Why can't your mate there hand
me the end of that painter, and slue her round? That's easy!
Won't take above a half a minute, and save somebody a wet shirt.
Tie her nose to the ring yonder!—just bring you up oppos*ite* to
where I'm standing! Think it out, master."

The sergeant, however, seemed to have made up his mind in
spite of the reasonableness of this suggestion. For when the man
rowing bow stooped back and reached out for the painter—the
course seemed the obvious and natural one—he was stopped by
his chief, who said rather tartly:—" You take your orders from
me, Cookson! " and then held out his hand as before, saying:—
" You're a tidy weight, my lad. *I* shan't pull you overboard."

He did, nevertheless, and it came about thus. The two men
at the oars saw the whole thing, and were clear in their account
of it after. Ibbetson, their sergeant, did *not* take the hand that
was proffered him, but seized its wrist. It seemed to them that
he made no attempt to lift himself up from the boat; and the
nearer one, pulling stroke, would have it that Ibbetson even hooked
the seat with his foot, as though to get a purchase on the man's
wrist that he held. Anyhow, the result was the same. The man
lost his footing under the strain, and pitehed sheer forward on
his assailant; for the aggressive intention of the latter may be
taken as established beyond a doubt. As he fell, he struck out
with his left hand, landing on Ibbetson's mouth, and cutting off
his last words, an order, shouted to the rowers:—" Sheer off, and
row for the bridge . . . I can . . ." Both of them believed he
would have said:—" I can manage him by myself."

But nothing further passed. For the boat, not built to keep
an even keel with two strong men struggling together in the
stern, lurched over, shipping water the whole length of the counter.
The rowers tried to obey orders, the more readily—so they said
after—that their chief seemed quite a match for his man. There
was a worse danger ahead, a barge moored in the path, and they
had to clear, one side or the other. The best chance was outside,
and they would have succeeded but for the cable that held her.
It just caught the bow oar, and the boat swung round, the stroke
being knocked down between the seats in his effort to back water
and keep her clear. Half-crippled already and at least one-third
full of water, she was in no trim to dodge the underdraw of the
sloping bows of an empty barge, at the worst hour of ebb-tide.
The boy in the garden, next door to The Pigeons, whom curiosity

had kept on the watch, saw the swerve off-shore; the men struggling in the stern; the collision with the moorings; and the final wreck of the boat. Then she vanished behind the barge, and was next seen, bottom-up, by children on the bridge over the little creek three minutes lower down the stream, whose cries roused those in hearing and brought help. When the man came back with the whisky-flask, his mate had vanished, and the boat with its crew. If he guessed what had passed, it was from the running and shouting on the bank, and the boats that were putting off in haste; and then, well over towards Hammersmith Bridge, that they reached their quarry and were trying to right her on the water, possibly thinking to find some former occupant shut in beneath. He did not wait to see the upshot; but, pocketing the flask, got away unnoticed by anyone, all eyes being intent upon the incident on the river.

The sergeant, Ibbetson, was drowned, and the facts narrated are taken literally, or inferred, from what came out at the inquest. The theory that recommended itself to account for his conduct was that he had recognised a culprit whom he had known formerly, for whose apprehension a reward had been offered, and had, without hesitation, formed a plan of separating him from his companion—or companions, for who could say they were alone?—and securing him in the boat, when no escape would have been possible, as they could have made straight for the floating station at Westminster. It was a daring idea, and might have succeeded but for that mooring-cable.

The body of the sergeant showed marks of the severity of the struggle in which he had been engaged. The two upper front teeth were loosened, probably by the blow he received at the outset, and there were finger-nail dents on the throat as from the grasp of a strangling hand. That his opponent should have disengaged himself from his clutch was matter of extreme surprise to all who had experienced submersion, and knew its meaning. Even to those who have never been under water against their will, the phrase " the grip of a drowning man " has a terribly convincing sound. That this opponent rose to the surface alive, and escaped, was barely entertained as a surmise, only to be dismissed as incredible; and this improbability became even greater when his companion was captured alone, a month later, in the commission of a burglary at Castelnau, which—so it was supposed—the two had been discussing just before the police-boat appeared. The two rowers were rescued, one, a powerful swimmer, having kept the other afloat till the arrival of help. At the inquest neither of these men seemed as much concerned at Ibbetson's death as might have been expected, and both condemned afterwards that officer's treacherous grip of the hand extended to help him. Whatever he knew to his proposed prisoner's disadvantage, there are niceties of honour in these matters—little chivalries all should observe.

The only evidence towards establishing the identity of the man who had disappeared was that of the stroke-oar, Simeon Rowe, the rescuer of his companion. This man's version of Ibbetson's exclamation was "Thorney Davenant!—I know you, my man!" At the time of the inquest, no identification was made with any name whose owner was being sought by the Police, so no one caught the clue it furnished. There may have been slowness or laxity of investigation, but a sufficient excuse may lie in the fact that Ibbetson certainly spoke the name wrong, or that his hearer caught it wrong. The name was not Davenant, but Daverill. He was the son of old Mrs. Prichard, of Sapps Court, called after his father, and inheriting all his worst qualities. If Sergeant Ibbetson spoke truly when he said "I know you!" to him, he was certainly entitled to a suspension of opinion by those who condemned his *ruse* for this man's capture.

Still, a code of honour is always respectable, and these two policemen may have supposed that their mate knew no worse of this convict than that he had redistributed some property—was what the first holder of that property would have called a thief. One prefers to think that Ibbetson knew of some less equivocal wickedness.

Perhaps this man, supposed to be drowned, would not have reappeared in this story had it not been for one of the witnesses at the inquest, the boy who overheard the conversation between him and his mate, before the arrival of the police-boat.

"This boy," said the Coroner's clerk, who seemed to have an impression that this was a State Prosecution, and that he represented the Crown, "can give evidence as to a conversation between the "—he wanted to say "the accused"; it would have sounded so well, but he stopped himself in time—"between the man whose body has not been found, and "—here he would have liked to say "an accomplice "—" and another person who has eluded the . . . that is to say, whom the police have, so far, failed to identify . . ."

"That's all right," said the Coroner. "That'll do. Boy's got something he can tell us. What's your name, my man?"

"Wot use are you a-going to make of it?" said the boy. He did not appear to be over twelve years old, but his assurance could

not have been greater had he been twelve score. A reporter put
a dot on his paper, which meant " Laughter, in which the Coroner
joined, in a parenthesis."

An old woman who had accompanied the boy, as tutelary genius,
held up a warning finger at him. " Now, you Micky," said she,
" you speak civil to the gentleman and answer his questions accordin'." She then said to the Coroner, as one qualified to explain
the position :—" It's only his manners, sir, and the boy has not
a rebellious spirit being my grandnephew." She utilised a lax
structure of speech to introduce her relationship to the witness.
She was evidently proud of being related to one, having probably
met with few opportunities of distinction hitherto.

The witness, under the pressure at once of family influence and
constituted authority, appeared to give up the point. " 'Ave it
your own way! " said he. " Michael Ragstroar."

" How am I to spell it? " said the clerk, without taking his pen
out of the ink, as though it would dry in the air.

" This ain't school! " said our young friend from Sapps Court,
whom you probably remember. Michael had absconded from his
home, and sought that of his great-aunt; the only person, said
contemporary opinion, that had a hounce of influence with him.
It was not clear why such a confirmed reprobate should quail
before the moral force of a small old woman in a mysteriously
clean print-dress, and tortoise-shell spectacles she would gladly
have kept on while charing, only they always come off in the
pail. But he did, and when reproached by her for his needlessly
defiant attitude, took up a more conciliatory tone. " Carn't recollect, or p'r'aps I'd tell yer," said he.

" Never mind the spelling! " said the Coroner, who had to pre-
side at another inquest at Kew very shortly. " Let's get the young
man's evidence." But Michael objected to giving evidence. Whereupon the Coroner, perceiving his mistake, said: " Well, then, suppose we let it alone for to-day. You may go home, Micky, and
find out how your name's spelt, against next time it's wanted.
Where's the other boy that heard what the men were saying? Call
him."

" There warn't any other boy within half a mile," exclaimed
Michael indignantly. " I should have seen him. Think I've got
no eyes? There warn't another blooming bloke in sight."

" Didn't the other boy see several other men in the back-garden
of the ale-house? " said the Coroner. And the Inspector of Police
had the effrontery to reply: " Oh yes, three or four! " And then
both of them looked at Michael, and waited.

Michael's indignation passed all bounds, and betrayed him into the use of language of which his great-aunt would have deemed him incapable. She was that shocked, she never! The expressions were not Michael's own vocabulary at all, but corruptions that had crept into his phraseology from associations with other boys, chance acquaintances, who had evolved them among themselves, nourishing them from the corruption of their own hearts. As soon as Michael—deceived by the mendacious dialogue of the Coroner and the Inspector, and under the impression that the particulars he was giving, whether true or false, were not evidence —had told with some colouring about the two men in the garden and what they said, the old lady made a powerful effort to detain the Coroner to give him particulars of Michael's parentage and education, and to exculpate herself from any possible charge of neglecting her grandnephew, to whom she was a second parent. In fact, had her niece Ann never married Daniel Rackstraw, she and her—Ann, that is—would have done much better by Michael and his sisters. Which left a false impression on her hearers' minds, that Michael was an illegitimate son; whereas really she was only dealing with his existence as rooted in the nature of things, and certain to have come about without the intrusion of a male parent in the family.

As for the details of his testimony, surrendered unconsciously as mere facts, not evidence, there was little in them that has not been already told. The conversation of the two men, as given in the text, was taken from Michael's version, and he was the only hearer. But he only saw their backs, except that when the struggle came off he caught sight of the ex-convict's face for a moment. He would know him again if he saw him any day of the week. Some days, he seemed to imply, were worse for his powers of identification than others. It was unimportant, as both the survivors of the accident had noted the man's face carefully enough, considering that he was to them at first nothing beyond a chance bystander. He wasn't a bad-looking man; that was clear. But he was possibly not in very good drawing, as they agreed that he had a peculiarity—his two halves didn't square. This no doubt referred to the same thing Michael described by calling him " a sideways beggar."

The Coroner's Jury had some trouble to agree upon a verdict. " Death by Misadventure " seemed wrong somehow. How could drowning with the finger-nails of an adversary in his throat be accounted misadventure? No doubt Abel died by misadventure, in a sense. But no other verdict seemed possible, except Manslaughter by the person whom Ibbetson supposed this man to be when he laid hands on him. And how if he was mistaken? " Manslaughter against some person unknown " sounded well. Only if the person was unknown, why Manslaughter? If Brown is ever so much justified in dragging Smith under water by the honest belief that he is Jones, is Smith guilty of anything but self-defence when he does his best to get out of Brown's clutches? Moreover, the annals of life-saving from drowning show that the only chance of success for the rescuer often depends on whether the drowning man can be made insensible or overpowered. Otherwise, death for both. If this unknown man was *not* the object of Police interest he was supposed to have been taken for, he might only have been doing his best to save the lives of both. In that case, had the inquest been on both, the verdict must have been one that would ascribe Justifiable Homicide to him and Manslaughter to Ibbetson. For surely if the police-sergeant had been the survivor, and the other man's body had been found to be that of some inoffensive citizen, Ibbetson would have been tried for manslaughter. In the end a verdict was agreed upon of Death by Drowning, which everybody knew as soon as it was certain that Life was extinct.

Somewhat later Ibbetson was supposed to have taken him for a returned convict, whose name was variously given, but who had been advertised for as Thornton, one of his aliases; and in consequence of this discovery the vigilance of the Police for the apprehension of the missing man, under this name, was increased and the reward doubled. And this, in spite of a universal inference that he was dead, and that his body was flavouring whitebait below bridge. This did not interfere with a belief on the part of the crew of the patrolling boat—known to Michael—owing to a popular chant of boys of his own age—as " two blackbeetles and one water-rat," that his corpse would float up one day near the place of his disappearance. But their eyes looked for it in vain; and though the companion with whom he was discussing the burglary to be executed at Barn Elms was caught *in flagrante delicto* and sent to Portland Island, nothing was heard of him or known of his whereabouts.

Michael ended his stay with his great-aunt shortly afterwards, returning home with a budget of legends founded on his waterside experience. As he had a reputation for audacious falsehood without foundation, it is no matter of surprise that the whole story of the water-rat's death and the inquest were looked upon as exaggerations too outrageous for belief even by the most credulous. Probably his version of the incidents, owing to its rich substratum of the marvellous yet true, was much more accurate than was usual with him when the marvellous depended on his ingenuity to provide it. It was, however, roundly discredited in his own circle, and nothing in it could have evoked recognition in Sapps Court even if the name of the convict had reached the ears that knew it. For it was not only wrongly reported but was still further distorted by Michael for purposes of astonishment.

CHAPTER X

OF THE EARLDOM OF ANCESTER, AND ITS EARL'S COUNTESS'S OPINION OF HIM. HOW HER SECOND DAUGHTER CAME OUT IN THE GARDEN. HOW SHE SAW A TRESPASSER, WITH SUCH A NICE DOG! HE MUSTN'T BE SHOT, *COUTE QUE COUTE!* A LITTLE STONE BRIDGE. A SLIT IN A DOG'S COLLAR. OLD MICHAEL'S OBSTINACY. HOW GWENDOLEN RAN AWAY TO DRESS, AND WAS UNSOCIABLE AT DINNER. THE VOICE OF A DOG IN TROUBLE. ACHILLES, AND HIS RECOGNITION. HOW THEY FOLLOWED ACHILLES, AT HIS OWN REQUEST, AND WHAT HE SHOWED THE WAY TO. BUT THE MAN WAS NOT DEAD

IF a stranger from America or Australia could have been shown at a glance all that went to make up the Earldom of Ancester, he would have been deeply impressed. All the leagues of parkland, woodland, moorland, farmland that were its inheritance would have impressed him, not because of their area—because Americans and Australians are accustomed to mere crude area in their own departments of the planet—but because of the amazing amount of old-world History transacted within its limits; the way the antecedent Earls meddled in it; their magnificent record of treachery and bloodshed and murder; wholesale in battle, retail in less showy, but perhaps even more interesting, private assassination; fascinating cruelties and horrors unspeakable! They might have been impressed also, though, of course, in a less degree, by the Earldom's very creditable show of forbears who, at the risk of being uninteresting, behaved with common decency, and did their duty in the station to which God or Debrett had called them; not drawing the sword to decide a dispute until they had tried one or two of the less popular expedients, and slighting their obligations to the Melodrama of the future. Which rightly looks for its supplies of copy to persons of high birth and low principles.

The present Earl took after his less mediæval ancestry; and though he received the sanction of his wife, and of persons who knew about things, it was always conceded to him with a certain tone of allowance made for a simple and pastoral nature. In the vulgarest tongue it might have been said that he would never cut a dash. In his wife's it was said that really the Earl was one of the most admirable of men, only never intended by Providence for the Lord-Lieutenancy of a County. He was scarcely to blame, therefore, for his shortcomings in that position. It could not rank as one to which God had called him, without imputing instability, or an oversight, to his summoner. As a summons from Debrett, there is no doubt he was not so attentive to it as he ought to have been.

His own opinion about the intentions of Providence was that they had been frustrated—by Debrett chiefly. If they had fructified he would have been the Librarian of the Bodleian. Providence also had in view for him a marvellous collection of violins, unlimited Chinese porcelain, and some very choice samples of Italian majolica. But he would have been left to the undisturbed enjoyment of his treasures. He could have passed a peaceful life gloating over Pynsons and Caxtons, and Wynkyn de Wordes, and Grolier binding, and Stradivarius, and Guarnerius, and Ming, and Maestro Giorgio of Gubbio. But Debrett got wind of the intentions of Providence, and clapped a coronet upon the head of their intended *bénéficiaire* without so much as with your leave or by your leave, and there he was—an Earl! He had all that mere possessions could bestow, but always with a sense that Debrett, round the corner, was keeping an eye on him. He had to assuage that gentleman—or principle, or lexicon, or analysis, whatever he is! —and he did it, though rather grudgingly, to please his Countess, and from a general sense that when a duty is a bore, it ought to be complied with. His Countess was the handsome lady with the rings whom Dave Wardle had taken for a drive in her own carriage.

This sidelight on the Earl is as much illumination as the story wants, for the moment. The sidelight on the terrace of Ancester Towers, at the end of a day in July following the winter of Dave's accident, was no more than the Towers thought their due after standing out all day against a grey sky, in a drift of warm, small rain that made oilskins and mackintoshes an inevitable Purgatory inside; and beds of lakes, when horizontal, outside. It was a rainbow-making gleam at the end of thirty-six depressing hours, bursting through a cloud-rift in the South with the exclamation—

the Poet might have imagined—"Make the most of me while you can; I shan't last."

To make the most of it was the clear duty of the owner of a golden head of hair like that of Lady Gwendolen, the Earl's second daughter. So she brought the head out into the rainbow dazzle, with the hair on it, almost before the rain stopped; and, indeed, braved a shower of jewels the rosebush at the terrace window drenched her with, coming out. What did it matter?—when it was so hot in spite of the rain. Besides, India muslin dries so quick. It isn't like woollen stuff.

If you could look back half a century and see Gwendolen on the terrace then, you would not be grateful to any contemporary malicious enough to murmur in your ear:—"Old Lady Blank, the octogenarian, who died last week, was this girl then. So reflect upon what the conventions are quite in earnest—for once—in calling your latter end." You would probably dodge the subject, replying—for instance—"How funny! Why, it must have taken twelve yards to make a skirt like that!" For these were the days of crinolines; of hair in cabbage-nets, packed round rubber-inflations; of what may be called proto-croquet, with hoops so large that no one ever failed to get through, except you and me; the days when *Ah che la morte* was the last new tune, and Landseer and Mulready the last words in Art. They were the days when there had been but one Great Exhibition—think of it!—and the British Fleet could still get under canvas. We, being an old fogy, would so much like to go back to those days—to think of daguerreo-types as a stupendous triumph of Science, balloons as indigenous to Cremorne, and table-turning as a nine-days' wonder; in a word, to feel our biceps with satisfaction in an epoch when wheels went slow, folk played tunes, and nobody had appendicitis. But we can't!

However, it is those very days into which the story looks back and sees this girl with the golden hair, who has been waiting in that rainbow-glory fifty years ago for it to go on and say what it may of what followed. She comes out on the terrace through the high middle-window that opens on it, and now she stands in the blinding gleam, shading her eyes with her hand. It is late in July, and one may listen for a blackbird's note in vain. That song in the ash that drips a diamond-shower on the soaked lawn, whenever the wind breathes, may still be a thrush; his last song, perhaps, about his second family, before he retires for the season. The year we thought would last us out so well, for all we wished to do in it, will fail us at our need, and we shall find that the

summer we thought was Spring's success will be Autumn, much
too soon, as usual. Over half a century of years have passed since
then, and each has played off its trick upon us. Each Spring has
said to us:—"Now is your time for life. Live!" and each Summer has jilted us and left us to be consoled by Autumn, a Job's
comforter who only says:—"Make the best of me while you can,
for close upon my heels is Winter."

You can still see the terrace much as this young woman, Lady
Gwendolen Rivers—that was her name—saw it on that July evening, provided always that you choose one with such another rainbow. There is not much garden between it and the Park, which
goes on for miles, and begins at the sunk fence over yonder. They
are long miles too, and no stint; and it is an hour's walk from
the great gate to the house, unless you run; so says the host of
the Rivers Arms, which is ten minutes from the gate. You can
lose yourself in this park, and there are red-deer as well as fallow-
deer; and what is more, wild cattle who are dangerous, and who
have lived on as a race from the days of Welsh Home Rule, and
know nothing about London or English History. Even so in the
Transvaal it is said that some English scouts came upon a peaceful valley with a settlement of Dutch farmers therein, who had
to be told about the War to check their embarrassing hospitality.
The parallel fails, however, for the wild white cattle of Ancester
Park paw the earth up and charge, when they see strangers. The
railway had to go round another way to keep their little scrap of
ancient forest intact; for the family at the Castle has always taken
the part of the bulls against all comers. Little does Urus know
how superficial, how skin-deep, his loneliness has become—that
he is really under tutelage unawares, and even surreptitiously
helped to supplies of forage in seasons of dearth! Will his race
linger on and outlive the race of Man when that biped has shelled
and torpedoed and dynamited himself out of existence? And will
they then fill the newest New Forest that will have covered the
smokeless land, with the descendants of the herds that Cæsar's
troops found in the Hercynian wilds? They are a fascinating subject for a wandering pen, but the one that writes this must not
be led away from Lady Gwendolen on the terrace that looks across
this cramped inheritance of beech and bracken. If she could
always look like what the level sun makes her now, in the heart
of a rainbow, few things the world can show would outbid her
right to a record, or make the penning of it harder. For just at
this moment she looks simply beautiful beyond belief. It is not
all the doing of the sunrays, for she is a fine sample of nineteen,

of a type which has kindled enthusiasm since the comparatively recent incursion of William the Norman, and will continue to do so till finally dynamited out of existence, *ut supra.*

She is looking out under her hand—to make sight possible against the blaze—at a man who is plodding across the nearest opening in the woodland. How drenched he must be! What can possess him, to choose a day like this to go afoot through an undergrowth of bracken a day's raindrift has left water-charged? She knows well what a deluge meets him at every step, and watches him, pressing through it as one who has felt the worst pure water can do, and is reckless. She watches him into a clear glade, with a sense of relief on his behalf. She does not feel officially called upon to resent a stranger with a dog—in a territory sacred to game!—for the half-overgrown track he seems to have followed is a world of fallow-deer and pheasants. She is the daughter of the house, and trespassers are the concern of Stephen Solmes the head gamekeeper.

The trespasser seems at a loss which way to go, and wavers this way and that. His dog stands at his feet looking up at him, wagging a slow tail; deferentially offering no suggestion, but ready with advice if called upon. The young lady's thought is:—" Why can't he let that sweet dog settle it for him? *He* would find the way." Because she is sure of the sweetness of that collie, even at this distance. Ultimately the trespasser leaves the matter to the dog, who appears gratified and starts straight for where she stands. Dogs always do, says she to herself. But there is the haw-haw fence between them.

The dog stops. Not because of the obstacle—what does he care for obstacles?—but because of the courtesies of life. The man that made this sunk fence did it to intercept any stray collie in the parkland from scouring across into the terraced garden, even to inaugurate communications between a strange young lady and the noblest of God's creatures, his owner. That is the dog's view. So he stands where the fence has stopped him, a beseeching explanatory look in his pathetic eyes; and a silky tail, that is nearly dry already, marking time slowly. A movement of permission would bring him across into the garden; but then—is he not too wet? Young Lady Gwendolen says " No, dear!" regretfully, and shakes her head as though he would understand the negative. Perhaps he does, for he trots back to his master, who, however—it must be admitted—has whistled for him.

The pedestrian turns to go, but sees the lady well, though not very near her yet. She knows he sees her, as he raises his hat.

She has an impression of his personality from the action; which, it may be, guides her conduct in what follows.

He seems to have made up his mind to avoid the house, taking a visible path which skirts it, and possibly to strike away from it into the wider parkland, over yonder where the great oaks are. He is soon lost in a hazel coppice.

Then she thinks. That dog will be shot if Solmes catches sight of it. She knows old Stephen. Oh, for but one word with the dog's master! It might just make the whole difference.

She does not think long; in fact, there is no time to lose. The man and the dog must pass over Arthur's Bridge if they follow the path. She can intercept them there by taking a short cut through the Trings; a name with a forgotten origin, which hugs the spot unaccountably. " I wonder what a tring was, and when " says Gwendolen to herself, between those unsolved riddles and the bridge.

The bridge is a little stone bridge, just wide enough for a chaise to go through gently. Gwendolen has soaked her shoes to reach it. Still, she *must* save that dog from the Ranger's gun at any cost. A fig for the wet! She has to dress for dinner—indeed, her maid is waiting for her now—and dry stockings will be a negligible factor in that great total. There comes the pedestrian round by Swayne's Oak—another name whose origin no man knows.

The dog catches sight of her, and is off like a shot, his master trying vainly to whistle him back. The young lady is quite at ease —*she* is not afraid of dogs! She even laughs at this one's demonstrative salute, which leaves a paw-mark on either shoulder. For dogs do not scruple to kiss those they love, without making compliments.

His master is apologetic, coming up with a quickened pace. At a rebuke from him the collie becomes apologetic too; would be glad to explain, but is handicapped by language. He is, however, all repentance, and falls back behind his master, leaving matters in his hands. At the least—though the way of doing it may have been crude—he has brought about an introduction, of a sort.

There is no intrusive wish on the man's part to take undue advantage of it. His speech, " Achilles means well; it is only his cordiality," seems to express the speaker's feeling that somehow he is certain to be understood. His addendum—" I am really as sorry as I can be, all the same "—may be credited to ceremonial courtesy, flavoured with contrition. His wind-up has a sort of laugh behind it:—"Particularly because I have no business in this part of the Park at all. I can only remedy that by my absence."

"You will promise me one thing, if you please . . ."

"Yes—whatever you wish."

"Lead your dog till you are outside the Park. If he is seen he may be shot. I could not bear that that dog should be shot." Something in the man's tone and manner has made it safe for the girl to overstep the boundaries of chance speech to an utter stranger.

He has no right—that he feels—to presume upon this semi-confidence of an impulsive girl, whoever she is. True, her beauty in that last glory of the sunset puts resolution to the test. But he *has* no right, and there's an end on't! "I will tie Achilles up," he says. "I should not like him to be shot."

"Oh!—is he Achilles?"

"His mother was Thetis."

"Then, of course, he is Achilles." At this point the boundaries of strangership seem insistent. After all, this man may be Tom or Dick or Harry. "You will excuse my speaking to you," says the young lady. "I had no one to send, and I saw you from the terrace. It was for the dog's sake."

In his chivalrous determination not to overdraw the blank cheque she has signed for him unawares, the stranger conceives that a few words of dry apology will meet the case, and leave him to go on his way. So, though powerfully ignoring the fact that that outcome will be an unwelcome one, he replies:—"I quite understand, and I am sincerely grateful for your caution." He gets at a dog-chain in the pocket of his waterproof overcoat, and at the click of it Achilles comes to be tied up. As he fastens the clasp to its collar, he adds:—"I should not have let him run loose like this, only that I am so sure of him. He is town-bred and a stranger to the chase. He can collect sheep, owing to his ancestry; but he never does it now, because he has been forbidden." While he speaks these last words he is examining something in the dog's leather collar. "It will hold, I think," says he. "A cut in the strap—it looks like." Then this oddly befallen colloquy ends and each gives the other a dry good-evening. The young lady's last sight of that acquaintance of five minutes shows him endeavouring to persuade the dog not to drag on his chain. For Achilles, for some dog-reason man will never know, is no sooner leashed than he makes restraint necessary by pulling against it with all his might.

"I hope that collar won't break," says the young lady as she goes back to dress for dinner. The sun's gleam is dead, and the black cloud-bank that hides it now is the rain that is coming soon. See!—it has begun already.

.   .   .   .   .

Old Mrs. Solmes at the Ranger's Lodge, a mile distant, said to her old husband:—"Thou'rt a bad ma-an, Stephen, to leave thy goon about lwoaded, and the vary yoong boy handy to any mischief. Can'st thou not bide till there coom time for the lwoadin' of it?"

Said old Stephen sharply, "Gwun, wench? There be no *gwun*. 'Tis a roifle! And as fower the little Seth, yander staaple where it hangs is well up beyond the reach of un. Let a' be, Granny!"

The old woman, in whom grandmotherhood had overweighted all other qualities, by reason of little Seth's numerous first cousins, made no reply, but looked uneasily at the rifle on the wall. Little Seth—her appropriated grandchild, both his parents being dead—was too small at present to do any great harm to anyone but himself; but the time might come. He was credited with having swallowed an inch-brad, without visible inconvenience; and there was a threatening appearance in his eye as of one who would very soon climb up everywhere, fall off everything, appropriate the forbidden, break the frangible, and, in short, behave as—according to his grandmother—his father had done before him.

His old grandfather, who had a combative though not unamiable disposition, took down the rifle as an act of self-assertion, and walked out into the twilight with it on his shoulder. It was simply a contradictious action, as there was no warranty for it in vert and venison. But he had to garnish his action with an appearance of plausibility, and nothing suggested itself. The only course open to him was to get away out of sight, with implication of a purpose vaguely involving fire-arms. A short turn in the oak-wood—as far, perhaps, as Drews Thurrock—would fortify his position, without committing him to details: he could make secrecy about them a point of discipline. He walked away over the grassland, a fine, upright old figure; in whose broad shoulders, seen from behind, an insight short of clairvoyance might have detected what is called *temper*—meaning a want of it. He vanished into the oak-wood, where the Druid's Stone attests the place of sacrifice, human or otherwise.

Some few minutes later the echoes of a rifle-shot, unmistakable alike for that of shot-gun or revolver, circled the belt of hills that looks on Ancester Towers, and died at Grantley Thorpe. Old Stephen, when he reappeared at the Lodge half an hour later, could explain his share in this with only a mixed satisfaction. For though his need of his rifle—whether real or not—had justified its readiness for use, he had failed as a marksman; the stray dog he fired at, after vanishing in a copse for a few minutes, having scoured away in a long detour; as he judged, making for the Castle.

"And a rare good hap for thee, husband!" said the old woman when she heard this. "Whatever has gotten thy wits, ma'an, to win out and draa' trigger on a pet tyke of some visitor lady at the Too'ers?"

"Will ye be tellun me this, and tellun me that, Keziah? I tell 'ee one thing, wench, it be no consarn o' mine whose dog be run loose in th' Park. Be they the Queen's own, my orders say shoot un! Do'ant thee know next month be August?" Nevertheless, the old man was not altogether sorry that he had missed. He might have been called over the coals for killing a dog-visitor to the Towers. He chose to affect regret for discipline's sake, and alleged that the dog had escaped into the wood only because he had no second cartridge. This was absurd. In these days of quick-shooters it might have been otherwise. In those, the only abominations of the sort were Colonel Colt's revolvers; and *they* were a great novelty, opening up a new era in murder.

The truth was that this view of the culprit's identity had dawned on him as soon as he got a second view of the dog visibly making for the Castle—almost too far in any case for a shot at anything smaller than a doe—and he would probably have held his hand for both reasons even if a reload had been possible.

Lady Gwendolen, treasuring in her heart a tale of adventure—however trivial—to tell at the dinner-table in the evening, submitted herself to be prepared for that function. She seemed absent in mind; and Lutwyche her maid, observing this, skipped intermediate reasonings and straightway hoped that the cause of this absence of mind had come over with the Conqueror and had sixty thousand a year. Meanwhile she wanted to know which dress, my lady, this evening?—and got no answer. Her ladyship was listening to something at a distance; or, rather, having heard something at a distance, was listening for a repetition of it. "I wonder what that can have been?" said she. For fire-arms in July are torpid mostly, and this was a gunshot somewhere.

"They are firing at the Butts at Stamford Norton, my lady," said Lutwyche; who always knew things, sometimes rightly—sometimes wrongly. This time, the latter.

"Then the wind must have gone round. Besides, it would come again. Listen!" Thus her ladyship, and both listened. But nothing came again.

Lady Gwendolen was as beautiful as usual that evening, but contrary to custom silent and *distraite*. She did not tell the story of the Man in the Park and his dog. She kept it to herself. She was unresponsive to the visible devotion of a Duke's eldest son, who came up to Lutwyche's standard in all particulars. She did not even rise to the enthusiasm of a very old family friend, the great surgeon Sir Coupland Merridew, about the view from his window across the Park, although each had seen the same sunset effect. She only said:—"Oh—have they put you in the Traveller's Room, Sir Coupland? Yes—the view is very fine!" and became absent again. She retired early, asking to be excused on the score of fatigue; not, however, seriously resenting her mother's passing reference to a nursery rhyme about Sleepy-head, whose friends kept late hours, nor her "Why, child, you've had nothing to tire you!" She was asleep in time to avoid the sound of a dog whining, wailing, protesting vainly, with a great wrong on his soul, not to be told for want of language.

She woke with a start very early, to identify this disturbance with something she lost in a dream, past recovery, owing to this sudden awakening. She had her hand on the bell-rope at her bed's head, and had all but pulled it before she identified the blaze of light in her room as the exordium of the new day. The joy of the swallows at the dawn was musical in the ivy round her window, open through the warm night; and the turtle-doves had much to say, and were saying it, in the world of leafage out beyond. But there was no joy in the persistent voice of that dog, and no surmise of its hearer explained it.

She found her feet, and shoes to put them in, before she was clear about her own intentions; then in all haste got herself into as much clothing as would cover the risks of meeting the few early risers possible at such an hour—it could but be some chance groom or that young gardener—and, opening her door with thief-like stealth, stole out through the stillness night had left behind, past the doors of sleepers who were losing the sweetest of the day. So she thought—so we all think—when some chance gives us precious hours that others are wasting in stupid sleep. But even *she* would not have risen but for that plaintive intermittent wail and a growing construction of a cause for it—all fanciful perhaps —that her uneasy mind would still be at work upon. She *must* find out the story of it. More sleep now was absurd.

Two bolts and a chain—not insuperable obstacles—and she was free of the side-garden. An early riser—the one she had foreseen, a young gardener she knew—with an empty basket to hold flowers for the still sleeping household to refresh the house with in an hour, and its bed-bound sluggards in two or three, was astir and touched a respectful cap with some inner misgiving that this unwonted vision was a ghost. But he showed a fine discipline, and called it " My lady " with presence of mind. Ghost or no, that was safe! " What *is* that dog, Oliver? " said the vision.

The question made all clear. The answer was speculative. " Happen it might be his lordship's dog that came yesterday—feeling strange in a strange place belike? "

" No dog came yesterday. Lord Cumberworld hasn't a dog. I *must* know. Where is it? "

Oliver was not actor enough not to show that he was concealing wonderment at the young lady's vehemence. His eyes remained wide open in token thereof.

" In the stables, by the sound of it, my lady," was his answer.

His lady turned without a word, going straight for the stables; and he followed when, recollecting him, she looked back to say, " Yes—come! "

Grooms are early risers in a well-kept stable. There is always something to be done, involving pails, or straps, or cloths, or barrows, or brushes, even at five in the morning in July. When the young gardener, running on ahead, jangled at the side-gate yard-bell, more than one pair of feet was on the move within; and there was the cry of the dog, sure enough, almost articulate with keen distress about some unknown wrong.

" What *is* the dog, Archibald?—what *is* the dog? " The speaker was too anxious for the answer to frame her question squarely. But the old Scotch groom understood. " Wha can tell that? " says he. " He's just stra'ad away from his home, or lost the track of a new maister. They do, ye ken, even the collies on the hillsides. Will your ladyship see him? "

" Yes—yes! That is what I came for. Let me." A younger groom, awaiting this instruction, goes for the dog, whose clamour has increased tenfold, becoming almost frenzy when he sees his friend of the day before; for he is Achilles beyond a doubt. Achilles, mad with joy—or is it unendurable distress?—or both?

" Your leddyship will have seen him before, doubtless," says old Archibald. He does not say, but means:—" We are puzzled, but submissive, and look forward to enlightenment."

" Let him go—yes, *I* know him!—don't hold him. Oh, Achilles,

you darling dog—it *is* you! . . . Yes—yes—let him go—he'll be
all right. . . . Yes, dear, you *shall* kiss me as much as you like."
This was in response to a tremendous accolade, after which the
dog crouched humbly at his idol's feet; whimpering a little still,
beneath his breath, about something he could not say. She for her
part caressed and soothed the frightened creature, asking the
while for information about the manner of his appearance the
night before.

It seemed that on the previous evening about eight o'clock he
had been found in the Park just outside the door of the walled
garden south of the Castle, as though he was seeking to follow
someone who had passed through. That at least was the impression of Margery, a kitchen-maid, whom inquiry showed to have
been the source of the first person plural in the narrative of Tom
Kettering, the young groom, who had come upon the dog crouched
against this door; and, judging him to be in danger in the open
Park, had brought him home to the stables for security.

How had the collie behaved when brought up to the stable?
Well—he had been fair quiet—only that he was always for going
out after any who were leaving, and always "wakeriff, panting,
and watching like," till he, Tom Kettering, tied him up for the
night. And then he started crying and kept on at it till they
turned out, maybe half an hour since.

"He has not got his own collar," said the young lady suddenly.
"Where is his own collar?"

"He had ne'er a one on his neck when I coom upon him," says
Tom. "So we putten this one on for a makeshift."

"It's mair than leekly, my lady,"—thus old Archibald—"that
he will have slipped from out his ain by reason of eempairfect
workmanship of the clasp. Ye'll ken there's a many cheap collars
sold. . . ." The old boy is embarking on a lecture on collar-
structure, which, however, he is not allowed to finish. The young
lady interrupts.

"I saw his collar," says she, "and it was *not* a collar like this"
—that is, a metal one with a hasp—"it was a strap with a buckle,
and his master said there was a cut in it. That was why it broke."
Then, seeing the curiosity on the faces of her hearers, who would
have thought it rather presumptuous to ask for an explanation,
she volunteers a short one ending with:—"The question is now,
how can we get him back to his master?" It never crossed her
mind that any evil hap had come about. After all, the dog's excitement and distress were no more than his separation from his
owner and his strange surroundings might have brought about in

any case. The whole thing was natural enough without assuming disaster, especially as seen by the light of that cut in the strap. The dog was a town-bred dog, and once out of his master's sight, might get demoralised and all astray.

No active step for restoring Achilles to his owner seeming practicable, nothing was left but to await the action that gentleman was sure to adopt to make his loss known. Obviously the only course open to us now was to take good care of the wanderer, and keep an ear on the alert for news of his owner's identity. All seemed to agree to this, except Achilles.

During the brief consultation the young lady had taken a seat on a clean truss of hay, partly from an impulse most of us share, to sit or lie on fresh hay whenever practicable; partly to promote communion with the dog, who crouched at her feet worshipping, not quite with the open-mouthed, loose-tongued joy one knows so well in a perfectly contented dog, but now and again half-uttering a stifled sound—a sound that might have ended in a wail. When, the point seeming established that no further step could be taken at present, Lady Gwendolen rose to depart, a sudden frenzy seized Achilles. There is nothing more pathetic than a dog's effort to communicate his meaning—clear to him as to a man—and his inability to do it for want of speech.

" You darling dog! " said Gwendolen. " What can it be he wants? Leave him alone and let us see. . . . No—don't touch his chain! " For Achilles, crouched one moment at her feet, the next leaping suddenly away, seemed like to go mad with distress.

The young groom Tom said something with bated breath, as not presuming to advise too loud. His mistress caught his meaning, if not his words. " What! "—she spoke suddenly—" knows where he is—his master? " The thought struck a cold chill to her heart. It could only mean some mishap to the man of yesterday. What sort of mishap?

Some understanding seems to pass between the four men—Archibald, the two young grooms, and the gardener—something they will not speak of direct to her ladyship. " What?—what's that? " says she, impatient of their scrupulousness towards her sheltered inexperience of calamity. " Tell me straight out! "

Old Archibald takes upon himself, as senior, to answer her question. " I wouldna' set up to judge, my lady, for my ain part. But the lads are all of one mind—just to follow on the dog's lead, for what may come o't." Then he is going on " Ye ken maybe the mon might fall and be ill able to move . . ." when he is caught up sharp by the girl's " Or be killed. Yes—follow the dog." Why should she be kept from the hearing of a mishap to this stranger, even of his death?

Old Stephen at the Lodge saw the party and came out in haste. He had his story to tell, and told it as one who had no blame for his own share in it. Why should he have any? He had only carried out his orders. Yes—that was the dog he drew trigger on. He could not be mistaken on that point.

"And you fired on the dog to kill it," says the young lady, flashing out into anger.

The old man stands his ground. "I had my orders, my lady," says he. "If I caught sight of e'er a dog unled—to shoot un."

"The man he belonged to—did you not see him?"

"No ma'an coom in my sight. Had I seen a ma'an, I would have wa'arned and cautioned him to keep to the high road, not to bring his dog inside o' the parkland. No—no—there was ne'er a ma'an, my lady." He goes on, very slightly exaggerating the time that passed between his shot at the dog and its reappearance, apparently going back to the Castle. He rather makes a merit of not having fired again from a misgiving that the dog's owner might be there on a visit. Drews Thurrock, he says, is where he lost sight of the dog, and that is where Achilles seems bent on going.

Drews Thurrock is a long half-mile beyond the Keeper's Lodge in Ancester Park, and the Lodge is a long half-mile from the Towers. Still, if it was reasonable to follow the dog at all, where would be the sense of holding back or flagging till he should waver in what seemed assurance of his purpose. No—no! What he was making for might be five miles off, for all that the party that followed him knew. But trust in the creature's instinct grew stronger each time he turned and waited for their approach, then scoured on as soon as it amounted to a pledge that he would not be deserted. There was no faltering on his part.

The river, little more than a brook at Arthur's Bridge, is wide enough here to deserve its name. The grove of oaks which one sees from the Ranger's Lodge hides the water from view. But Gwendolen has it in her mind, and with it a fear that the dog's owner will be found drowned. It was there that her brother Frank died four years since, and was found in the deep pool above the stepping-stones, caught in a tangle of weed and hidden, after two days' search for him far and wide. If that is to be the story we shall know, this time, by the dog's stopping there. Therefore none would hint at an abandonment of the search having come thus far, even were he of the mind to run counter to the wish of the young lady from the Castle. None dares to do this, and the party follows her across the stretch of gorse and bracken called the Warren to the wood beyond. There the dog has stopped, waiting eagerly, showing by half-starts and returns that he knows he would be lost to sight if he were too quick afoot. For the wood is dark in front of him and the boughs hang low.

"Nigh enough to where I set my eye on him at the first of it, last evening," says old Stephen. He makes no reference to the affair of the gunshot. Better forgotten perhaps!

But he is to remember that gunshot, many a wakeful night. For the forecast of a mishap in that fatal pool is soon to be dissipated. As the party draws nearer the dog runs back in his eagerness, then forward again. And then Lady Gwendolen follows him into the wood, and the men follow her in silence. Each has some anticipation in his mind—a thing to be silent about.

There is a dip in the ground ahead, behind which Achilles disappears. Another moment and he is back again, crying wildly with excitement. The girl quickens a pace that has flagged on the rising ground; for they have come quickly. And now she stands on the edge of a buttress-wall that was once the boundary —so says tradition—of an amphitheatre of sacrifice. Twenty yards on yonder is the Druids' altar, or the top of it. For the ground has climbed up stone and wall for fifteen hundred years, and the moss is deep on both; rich with a green no dye can rival, for the soaking of yesterday's rain is on it still. But she can see nothing for the moment, for the dog has leapt the wall and vanished.

"'Tis down below, my lady—beneath the wall." It is the young gardener who speaks. The others have seen what he sees, but are shy of speech. He has more claim than they to the position of a friend, after so many conferences with her ladyship over roots and bulbs this year and last. He repeats his speech lest she should not have understood him.

"Then quick!" says she. And all make for the nearest way down the wall and through the fern and bramble.

What the young gardener spoke of is a man's body, seeming dead. No doubt of his identity, for the dog sits by him motionless, waiting. *His* part is finished.

Now that the thing is known and may be faced without disguise the men are all activity. Knives are out cutting away rebellious thorny stems that will not keep down for trampling, and a lane is made through the bush that keeps us from the body, while minutes that seem hours elapse. That will do now. Bring him out, gently.

Shot through the head—is that it? Is there to be no hope? The girl's heart stands still as old Stephen stoops down to examine the head, where the blood is that has clotted all the hair and beard and run to a pool in the bracken and leaked away—who can say how plentifully?—into a cleft in the loose stones fallen from the wall. The old keeper is in no trim for his task—one that calls for a cool eye and a steady finger-touch. For it is he that has done this, and the white face and lifeless eye are saying to him that he has slain a man. He has too much at stake for us to accept his statement that the wound on the temple is no bullet-hole in the skull, but good for profuse loss of blood for all that. He has seen such a wound before, he says. But then his wish for a wound still holding out some hope of life may have fathered this thought, and even a false memory of his experience. Perhaps he is right, though, in one thing. If the body is lifted and carried, even up to the lodge, the blood may break out again. Leave him where he is till the doctor comes.

For, at the first sight of the body, the young groom was off like a shot to harness up the grey in the dog-cart, a combination favouring speed, and drive his hardest to Grantley Thorpe for Dr. Nash, the nearest medical resource. He is gone before the young lady, who knows of one still nearer, can be alive to his action, or to anything but the white face and lifeless hand Achilles licks in vain.

Then, a moment later, she is aware of what has been done, and exclaims:—" Oh dear!—why did you send him? Dr. Merridew is at the Castle." For she knew Sir Coupland before he had his knighthood. Thereon the other groom is starting to summon him, but she stops him. She will go herself; then the great man will be sure to come at once.

Sir Coupland Ellicott Merridew, F.R.S., F.R.C.S., F.R.C.P., etc.—a whole alphabet of them—was enjoying this moment of the first unalloyed holiday he had had for two years, by lying in bed till nine o'clock. If it made him too late for the collective breakfast in the new dining-room—late Jacobean—he had only to ring for a private subsection for himself. He had had a small cup of coffee at eight, and was congratulating himself on it, and was now absolutely in a position not to give any consideration to anything whatever.

But cruel Destiny said No!—he was not to round off his long night's rest with a neat peroration. He was interrupted in the middle of it by what seemed, in his dream-world, just reached, the loud crack of a bone that disintegrated under pressure; but that when he woke was clearly a stone flung at his window. What a capital instance of dream-celerity, thought he! Fancy the first half of that sound having conjured up the operating-theatre at University College Hospital, fifteen years ago, and a room full of intent faces he knew well, and enough of the second half being available for him to identify it as—probably—the *poltergeist* that infested that part of the house. Perhaps, if he took no notice, the *poltergeist* would be discouraged and subside. Anyhow, he wouldn't encourage it.

But the sound came again, and the voice surely of Gwendolen, his very great friend, with panic in it, and breathlessness as of a voice-reft runner. He was out of bed in twenty, dressing-gowned in forty, at the window in fifty, seconds. Not a minute lost!

"What's all that? . . . A man shot! All right, I'll come."

"Oh, do! It's so dreadful. Stephen Solmes shot him by mistake for a dog . . . at least, I'll tell you directly."

"All right. I'll come now." And in less than half an hour the speaker is kneeling by the body on the grass; and those who found it, with others who have gathered round even in this solitude, are waiting for the first authoritative word of possible hope. Not despair, with a look like that on the face of a Fellow of the Royal College of Surgeons.

"There is a little blood coming still. Wait till I have stopped it and I'll tell you." He stops it somehow with the aid of a miraculous little morocco affair, scarcely bigger than a card-case. He never leaves home without it. Then he looks up at the anxious, beautiful face of the girl who stoops close by, holding a dog back. "He is not dead," says he. "That is all I can say. He must be moved as little as possible, but got to a bed—somewhere. Is that his dog?"

"Yes. This is Achilles."

"How do you know it is Achilles?"

"I'll tell you directly. *He* told me his name yesterday." She nods towards the motionless figure on the turf. It is not a corpse yet; that is all that can be said, so far.

CHAPTER XI

THE HON. PERCIVAL PELLEW AND MISS CONSTANCE SMITH-DICKENSON,
WHOSE BLOOM HAD GONE OFF. OLD MAIDS WERE TWENTY-EIGHT,
THENADAYS. HOW THE TRAGEDY CAME OUT, AND MR. PELLEW TALKED
IT OVER WITH MISS SMITH-DICKENSON, ALTHOUGH HER BLOOM RE-
MAINED OFF. WHO THE SHOT MAN WAS. OF MR. PELLEW'S CAUTION,
AND A DARK GREEN FRITILLARY. WHAT YOU CAN DO AND CAN'T DO,
WHEN YOU ARE A LADY AND GENTLEMAN

At the Towers, in those days, there was always breakfast, but
very few people came down to it. In saying this the story accepts
the phraseology of the household, which must have known. Norbury the butler, for instance, who used the expression to the Hon.
Percival Pellew, a guest who at half-past nine o'clock that morning
expressed surprise at finding himself the only respondent to The
Bell. It was the Mr. Pellew mentioned before, a Member of Parliament whose humorous speeches always commanded a hearing,
even when he knew nothing about the subject under discussion;
which, indeed, was very frequently the case.

Perhaps it was to keep his hand in that he adopted a tone of
serious chaff to Mr. Norbury, such as some people think a well-
chosen one towards children, to their great embarrassment. He
replied to that most responsible of butlers with some pomposity
of manner. "The question before the house," said he—and paused
to enjoy a perversion of speech—"the question before the house
comes down to breakfast I take to be this:—Is it breakfast at all
till somebody has eaten it?"

"I could not say, sir." Mr. Norbury's manner is dignified, def-
erential, and dry. More serious than need be perhaps.

The Hon. Percival is not good at insight, and sees nothing
of this. "It certainly appears to me," he says, taking his time
over it, "that until breakfast has broken someone's fast, or someone has broken his own at the expense of breakfast . . . What's
that?"

"One of the ladies coming down, sir." Mr. Norbury would not,
in the ordinary way of business, have mentioned this fact, but it
had given him a resource against a pleasantry he found distasteful. Of course, *he* knew the event of the morning. Yet he could
not say to the gentleman:—"A truce to jocularity. A man was

shot dead half a mile off last night, and the body has been taken to the Keeper's Lodge."

The lady coming downstairs was Miss Constance Smith-Dickenson, also uninformed about the tragedy. She had made her first appearance yesterday afternoon, and had looked rather well in a pink-figured muslin at dinner. The interchanges between this lady and the Hon. Percival, referring chiefly to the fact that no one else was down, seemed to have no interest for Mr. Norbury; who, however, noted that no new topic had dawned upon the conversation when he returned from a revision of the breakfast-table. The fact was that the Hon. Percival had detected in Miss Dickenson a fossil, and was feeling ashamed of a transient interest in her last night, when she had shown insight, under the guidance—suppose we say—of champagne. Her bloom had gone off, too, in a strange way, and bloom was a *sine qua non* to this gentleman. She for her part was conscious of a chill having come between them, she having retired to rest the evening before with a refreshing sensation that all was not over—could not be—when so agreeable a man could show her such marked attention. That was all she would endorse of a very temperate Vanity's suggestions, mentally crossing out an *s* at the end of " attention." If you have studied the niceties of the subject, you will know how much that letter would have meant.

A single lady of a particular type gets used to this sort of thing. But her proper pride has to be kept under steam, like a salvage-tug in harbour when there is a full gale in the Channel. However, she is better off than her great-great-aunts, who were exposed to what was described as *satire*. Nowadays, presumably, Man is not the treasure he was, for a good many women seem to scrat on cheerfully enough without him. Or is it that in those days he was the only person employed on his own valuation?

In the period of this story—that is to say, when our present veterans were schoolboys—the air was clearing a little. But the smell of the recent Georgian era hung about. There was still a fixed period in women's lives when they suddenly assumed a new identity—became old maids and were expected to dress the part. It was twenty-eight, to the best of our recollection. Therefore Miss Smith-Dickenson, who was thirty-eight if she was a minute, became a convicted impostor in the eyes of the Hon. Percival, when, about ten hours after he had said to himself that she was not a bad figure of a woman and that some of her remarks were racy, he perceived that she was going off; that her complexion didn't bear the daylight; that she wouldn't wash; that she was probably a favourite with her own sex, and, broadly speaking, an Intelligent Person. "Never do at all!" said the Hon. Percival to himself. And Space may have asked "What for?" But nobody answered.

On the other hand, the lady perceived, in time, that the gentleman looked ten years older by daylight; that no one could call him corpulent exactly; that he might be heavy on hand, only perhaps he wanted his breakfast—men did; that the Pall Mall and Piccadilly type of man very soon palled, and that, in short, that steam-tug would be quite unnecessary this time.

Therefore, when Lady Gwendolen appeared, *point-device* for breakfast as to dress, but looking dazed and preoccupied, she found this lady and gentleman being well-bred, as shown by scanty, feelingless remarks about the absence of morning papers as well as morning people. Her advent opened a new era for them, in which they could cultivate ignorance of one another on the bosom of a newcomer common to both.

"Only you two!" said the newcomer; which Miss Dickenson thought scarcely delicate, considering the respective sexes of the persons addressed. "I knew I was late, but I couldn't help it. Good-morning, Aunt Constance." She gave and got a kiss. The Hon. Percival would have liked the former for himself. Why need he have slightly flouted its receiver by a mental note that he would not have cared about its *riposte?* It had not been offered.

"How well you *are* looking, dear!" said Aunt Constance, holding her honorary niece at arms' length to visualise her robustness. She was not a real Aunt at all, only an old friend of the family.

"I'm not," said Gwendolen. "Norbury, is breakfast ready? Shall we go in? . . . Oh no, nothing! Please don't talk to me about it. I mean I'm all right. Ask Sir Coupland to tell you." For the great surgeon had come into the room, and was talking in an undertone to the old butler. Lady Gwendolen added an apology which she kept in stereotype for the non-appearance of her mother at breakfast. The Earl's absence was a usage, taken for granted. Some said he had a cup of coffee in his own room at eight, and starved till lunch.

Other guests appeared, and the usual English country-house breakfast followed: a haphazard banquet, a decorous scrimmage for a surfeit of eggs, and fish, and bacon, and tongue, and tea, and coffee, and porridge, and even Heaven itself hardly knows what. Less than usual vanished to become a vested interest of digestion; more than usual went back to the kitchen for appreciation elsewhere. For Sir Coupland, appealed to, had given a brief

intelligent report of the occurrence of the morning. Then followed undertones of conversation apart between him and the Hon.
Percival, who had not the heart for a pleasantry, and groups of
two or three aside. Lady Gwen alone was silent, leaving the narration entirely to her medical friend, to whom she had told the
incident of last evening—her interview with the man now lying
between life and death, and the way his body was found by following the dog. She left the room as early as courtesy allowed, and
Sir Coupland did not remain long. He had to go and tell the
matter to the Earl, he said. Gwendolen, no doubt, had to do the
same to her mother the Countess. It was an awful business.

Said Miss Smith-Dickenson to the Hon. Percival, on the shady
terrace, a quarter of an hour afterwards, " He *did* tell you who
the man is, though? Or perhaps I oughtn't to ask? " Other guests
were scattered otherwhere, talking of the trâgedy. Not a smile
to be seen; still, the victim of the mishap was a stranger. It was
a cloud under which a man might enjoy a cigar, *quand même*.

The Hon. Percival knocked an instalment of *caput mortuum* off
his; an inch of ash which had begun on the terrace; so the interview was some minutes old. " Yes," said he. " Yes, he knows who
it is. That's the worst of it."

" The worst of it? "

" I don't know of any reason myself why I should not tell you
his name. Sir Coupland only said he wanted it kept quiet till he
could see his father, whom he knows, of course. I understand that
the family belongs to this county—lives about twenty miles off."
The lady felt so confident that she would be told the name that she
seized the opportunity to show how discreet she was, and kept
silence. *She* was quite incapable of mere vulgar inquisitiveness,
you see. Her inmost core had the satisfaction of feeling that its
visible outer husk, Miss Constance Smith-Dickenson, was killing
two birds with one stone. The way in which the gentleman continued justified it. " Besides, I know I may rely upon *you* to say
nothing about it." Clearly the effect of her visible, almost palpable, discretion! For really—said the core—this good gentleman
never set eyes on my husk till yesterday evening. And he *is* a
Man of the World and all that sort of thing.

Miss Smith-Dickenson knew perfectly well how her sister Lilian
—the one with the rolling, liquid eyes, now Baroness Porchammer—
would have responded. But she herself mistrusting her powers of
gushing right, did not feel equal to " Oh, but how nice of you to
say so, dear Mr. Pellew! " And she felt that she was not cut out for
a satirical puss neither, like her sister Georgie, now Mrs. Amphlett

Starfax, to whom a mental review of possible responses assigned, "Oh dear, how complimentary we are, all of a sudden!"—with possibly a heavy blow on the gentleman's fore-arm with a fan, if she had one. So she decided on "Pray go on. You may rely on my discretion." It was simple, and made her feel like Elizabeth in "Pride and Prejudice"—a safe model, if a little old-fashioned.

The gentleman pulled at his cigar in a considerative way, and said in a perfunctory one:—"I am sure I may." Nevertheless, he postponed his answer through a mouthful of smoke, dismissing it into the atmosphere finally, to allow of speech determined on during its detention: "I'm afraid it's Adrian Torrens—there can't be two of the name who write poetry. Besides—the dog!"

The lady said "Good Heavens!" in a frightened underbreath, and was visibly shocked. For it is usually someone of whom one knows nothing at all that gets shot accidentally. Now, Adrian Torrens was the name of a man recently distinguished as the author of some remarkable verse. A man of very good family too. So—altogether! . . . This was the expression used by Miss Smith-Dickenson's core, almost unrebuked. "Of course, I remember the poem about the collie-dog," she added aloud.

"Can you remember the name of the dog? Wasn't it Æneas?"

"No—Achilles."

"I meant Achilles. Well—his dog's Achilles."

"I thought you said there was no name on the collar."

"No more there was. But I understand that Gwen met him yesterday evening—down by Arthur's Bridge, I believe—and had some conversation with him, I gather."

"Oh!"

"But why? Why 'Oh!'—I mean?"

"I didn't mean anything. Only that she was looking so scared and unhappy at breakfast, and that would account for it."

"Surely . . ."

"Surely what?"

"Well—does it want accounting for? A man shot dead almost in sight of the house, and by your own gamekeeper! Isn't that enough?"

"Enough in all conscience. But it makes a difference. All the difference. I can't exactly describe . . . It is not as if she had never met him in her life before. *Now* do you see? . . ."

"Never met him in her life before? . . ." The Hon. Percival stands waiting for more, one-third of his cigar in abeyance between his finger-tips. Getting no more, he continues:—"Why—you don't mean to say? . . ."

" What ? "

" Well—it's something like this, if I can put the case. Take
somebody you've just met and spoken to . . ." But Mr. Pellew's
prudence became suddenly aware of a direction in which the conversation might drift, and he pulled up short. If he pushed on
rashly, how avoid an entanglement of himself in a personal discussion? If his introduction to this lady had been days old, instead
of merely hours, there would have been no quicksands ahead. He
felt proud of his astuteness in dealing with a wily sex.

Only he shouldn't have been so transparent. All that the lady
had to do was to change the subject of the conversation with
venomous decision, and she did it. " What a beautiful dark green
fritillary ! " said she. " I hope you care for butterflies, Mr. Pellew. I simply dote on them." She was conscious of indebtedness
for this to her sister Lilian. Never mind!—Lilian was married
now, and had no further occasion to be enchanting. A sister
might borrow a cast-off. Its effect was to make the gentleman
clearly alive to the fact that she knew exactly why he had stopped
short.

But Miss Smith-Dickenson did *not* say to Mr. Pellew :—" I am
perfectly well aware that you, sir, see danger ahead—danger of a
delicate discussion of the difference *our* short acquaintance would
have made to me if I had heard this morning that *you* were shot
overnight. Pray understand that I discern in this nothing but
restless male vanity, always on the alert to save its owner—or
slave—from capture or entanglement by dangerous single women
with no property. You would have been perfectly safe in my
hands, even if your recommendations as an Adonis had been less
equivocal." She said no such thing. But something or other—
can it have been the jump to that butterfly?—made Mr. Pellew
conscious that if she *had* worded a thought of the kind, it would
have been just like a female of her sort. Because he wasn't going
to end up that she wouldn't have been so very far wrong.

A name ought to be invented for these little ripples of human
intercourse, that are hardly to be called embarrassments, seeing
that their *monde* denies their existence. We do not believe it is
only nervous and imaginative folk that are affected by them. The
most prosaic of mankind keeps a sort of internal or subjective
diary of contemporary history, many of whose entries run on such
events, and are so very unlike what their author said at the time.

The dark green fritillary did not stay long enough to make any
conversation worth the name, having an appointment with a friend
in the air. Mr. Pellew hummed *Non piu andrai farfallon amoroso,*

producing on the mind of Miss Dickenson vague impressions of the Opera, Her Majesty's—not displaced by a Hotel in those days —tinctured with a consciousness of Club-houses and Men of the World. This gentleman, with his whiskers and monocular wrinkle responding to his right-eye-glass-grip, who had as good as admitted last night that his uncle was intimate with the late Prince Regent, was surely an example of this singular class; which is really scarcely admissible on the domestic hearth, owing to the purity of the latter. Possibly, however, these impressions had nothing to do with the lady's discovery that perhaps she ought to go in and find out what "they" were thinking of doing this morning. It may be that it was only due to her consciousness that you cannot—when female and single—stand alone with a live single gentleman on a terrace, both speechless. You can walk up and down with him, conversing vivaciously, but you mustn't come to an anchor beside him in silence. There would be a suspicion about it of each valuing the other's presence for its own sake, which would never do.

"Goin' in？" said the Hon. Percival. "Well—it's been very jolly out here."

"Very pleasant, I am sure," said Miss Constance Smith-Dickenson. If either made a diary entry out of this, it was of the slightest. She moved away across the lawn, her skirt brushing it audibly, as the cage-borne skirt of those days did, suggesting the advantages of Jack-in-the-Green's costume. For Jack could leave his green on the ground and move freely inside it. He did not stick out at the top. Mr. Pellew remained on the shady terrace, to end up his cigar. He was a little disquieted by the recollection of his very last words, which remembered themselves on his tongue-tip as a key remembers itself in one's hand, when one has forgotten if one really locked that box. Why, though, should he not say to a maiden lady of a certain age—these are the words he thought in—that it was very nice on this terrace？ Why not indeed？ But that wasn't exactly the question. What he had really said was that it *had been* very nice on this terrace. All the difference!

Miss Dickenson was soon aware what the "they" she had referred to was going to do, and offered to accompany it. The Countess and her daughter and others were the owners of the voices she could hear outside the drawing-room door when at liberty to expand, after a crush in half a French window that opened on the terrace. Her ladyship the Countess was as completely upset as her husband's ancestry permitted—quite white and almost crying, only not prepared to admit it. "Oh, Constance dear," said she. "Are you there? You are always so sensible. But isn't this awful?"

Aunt Constance perceived the necessity for a sympathetic spurt. She had been taking it too easily, evidently. She was equal to the occasion, responding with effusion that it was "so dreadful that she could think of nothing else!" Which wasn't true, for the moment before she had been collating the Hon. Percival's remarks and analysing the last one. Not that she was an unfeeling person—only more like everyone else than everyone else may be inclined to admit.

CHAPTER XII

HOW THE COUNTESS AND HER DAUGHTER WALKED OVER TO THE VERDERER'S HALL. HOW ACHILLES KNEW BETTER THAN THE DOCTORS. THE ACCIDENT WAS NOT A FATAL ACCIDENT. AN OLD GENERAL WHO MADE A POOR FIGURE AS A CORPSE. HOW THE WOUNDED MAN'S FATHER AND SISTER CAME, AND HOW HE HIMSELF WAS TO BE CARRIED TO THE TOWERS

THERE was no need for a reason why Lady Gwendolen and her mother should take the first opportunity of walking over to the Lodge, where this man lay either dead or dying; but one presented itself to the Countess, as an addendum to others less defined. "We ought to go," said she, "if only for poor old Stephen's sake. The old man will be quite off his head with grief. And it was such an absolute accident."

This was on the way, walking over the grassland. Aunt Constance felt a little unconvinced. He who sends a bullet abroad at random may hear later that it had its billet all along, though it was so silent about it. As for the girl, she was in a fever of excitement; to reach the scene of disaster, anyhow—to hear some news of respite, possibly. No one had vouched for Death so far.

Sir Coupland was already on the spot, having only stayed long enough to give particulars of the catastrophe to the Earl; but he was not by the bedside. He was outside the cottage, speaking with Dr. Nash, the local doctor from Grantley Thorpe, who had passed most of the night there. There was a sort of conclusiveness about their conference, even as seen from a distance, which promised ill. As the three ladies approached, he came to meet them.

"Is there a chance?" said the Countess, as he came within hearing.

Only a shake of the head in reply. It quenches all the eagerness to hear in the three faces, each in its own degree. Aunt Constance's gives place to "Oh dear!" and solicitude. Lady Ancester's to a gasp like sudden pain, and "Oh, Sir Coupland! are you quite, *quite* sure?" Her daughter's to a sharp cry, or the first of one cut short, and "Oh, mamma!" Then a bitten lip, and a face shrinking from the others' view as she turns and looks out across the Park. That is Arthur's Bridge over yonder, where last evening she spoke with this man that now lies dead, and took some note of his great dark eyes in the living glory of the sunset.

As the world and sky swim about her for a moment, even she herself wonders why she should be so hard hit. A perfect stranger! A man she had never before in her life spoken to. And then, for such a moment! But the great dark eyes of the man now dead are upon her, and she does not at first hear that her mother is speaking to her.

"Gwen dear! . . . Gwen darling!—you hear what Sir Coupland says? We can do no good." She has to touch her daughter's arm to get her attention.

"Well!" The girl turns, and her tears are as plain on her face as its beauty. "That means go home?" says she; and then gives a sort of heart-broken sigh. "Oh dear!" Her lack of claim to grieve for this man cuts like a knife.

"We can do no good," her mother repeats. "Now, can we?"

"No, I see. Suppose we go." She turns as though to go, but either her intention hangs fire, or she only wishes her face unseen for the moment; for she pauses, saying to her mother: "There is old Stephen. Ought we not to see him—one of us?"

"Yes!" says her ladyship, decisive on reflection. "I had forgotten about old Stephen. But *I* can go to him. You go back! . . . Yes, dear, you had better go back . . . What?"

"I am not going back. I want to see the body—this man's body. I want to see his face. . . . No; I am not a child, mamma. Let me have my way."

"If you must, darling, you must. But I cannot see what use it can be. See—here is Aunt Constance! *She* does not want to see it. . . ." A confirmatory head-shake from Miss Dickenson. "Why should *you?*"

"Aunt Constance never spoke to him. I did. And he spoke to me. Let me go, mamma dear. Don't oppose me." Indeed, the girl seems almost feverishly anxious, quite on a sudden, to have this wish. No need for her mother to accompany her, she adds. To which her mother replies:—"I would if you wished it, dear Gwen"; whereupon Aunt Constance, perceiving in her heart an opportunity for public service tending to distinction, says so would she. Further, in view of a verdict from somebody somewhere later on, that she showed a very nice feeling on this occasion, she takes an opportunity before they reach the cottage to say to Lady Gwendolen in an important aside:—"You won't let your mother go into the room, dear. Anything of this sort tells so on her system." To which the reply is rather abrupt:—"You needn't come, either of you." So that is settled.

The body had not been carried into a room of the cottage, but into what goes by the name of the Verderer's Hall, some fifty yards off. That much carriage was spared by doing so. It now lies on the "Lord's table," so called not from any reference to sacramental usage, but because the Lord of the Manor sat at it on the occasions of the Manorial Courts. Three centuries have passed since the last Court Baron; the last landlord who sat in real council with his tenantry under its roof having been Roger Earl of Ancester, who was killed in the Civil War. But old customs die hard, and every Michaelmas Day—except it fall on a Sunday—the Earl or his Steward at twelve o'clock receives from the person who enjoys a right of free-warren over certain acres that have long since har- boured neither hare nor rabbit, an annual tribute which a chronicle as old as Chaucer speaks of as "iiij tusshes of a wild bore." If no boars' tusks are forthcoming, he has to be content with some equivalent devised to meet their scarcity nowadays. Otherwise, the old Hall grows to be more and more a museum of curios con- nected with the Park and outlying woodlands, the remains of the old forest that covered the land when even Earls were upstarts. A record pair of antlers on the wall is still incredulously meas- ured tip to tip by visitors unconvinced by local testimony, and a respectable approach to Roman Antiquities is at rest after a learned description by Archæology. The place smells sweet of an old age that is so slow—that the centuries have handled so ten- derly—that one's heart thinks of it rather as spontaneous preserva- tion than decay. It will see to its own survival through some lifetimes yet, if no man restores it or converts it into a Studio.

Is his rating "Death" or not, whose body is so still on its extemporised couch—just a mattress from the keeper's cottage close at hand? Was the doctor's wording warranted when he said just now under his breath:—"It is in here"? Could he not have said

"He"? What does the dog think, that waits and watches immovable at *its* feet? If this is death, what is he watching for? What does the old keeper himself think, who lingers by this man whom he may have slain—this man who *may* live, yet? He has scarcely taken his eyes off that white face and its strapped-up wound from the first moment of his sight of it. He does not note the subdued entry of Lady Gwendolen and the two doctors, and when touched on the shoulder to call his attention to the presence of a ladyship from the Castle, defers looking round until a fancy of his restless hope dies down—a fancy that the mouth was closing of itself. He has had such fancies by scores for the last few hours, and said farewell to each with a groan.

"My mother is at the cottage, Stephen," says Gwen. "She would like to see you, I know." Thereon the old man turns to go. He looks ten years older than his rather contentious self of yesterday. The young lady says no word either way of his responsibility for this disaster. She cannot blame, but she cannot quite absolve him yet, without a grudge. Her mother can; and will, somehow.

The dog has run to her side for a moment—has uttered an undertone of bewildered complaint; then has gone back patiently to his old post, and is again watching. The great surgeon and the girl stand side by side, watching also. The humbler medico stands back a little, his eyes rather on his senior than on the body.

"It is absolutely certain—this?" says Lady Gwen; questioning, not affirming. She is wonderfully courageous—so Sir Coupland thinks—in the presence of Death. But she is ashy white.

He utters the barest syllable of doubt; then half-turns for courtesy to his junior, who echoes it. Then each shakes his head, looking at the other.

"Is there no sound—nothing to show?" Gwen has some hazy idea that there ought to be, if there is not, some official note of death due from the dying, a rattle in the throat at least.

Sir Coupland sees her meaning. "In a case of this sort," says he, "sheer loss of blood, the breath may cease so gradually that sound is impossible. All one can say is that there *is* no breath, and no action of the heart—so far as one can tell." He speaks in a business-like way that is a sort of compliment to his hearer; no accommodation of facts as to a child; then raises the lifeless hand slightly and lets it fall, saying:—"See!"

To his surprise the girl, without any comment, also raises the hand in hers, and stands holding it. "Yes—it will fall," says he, as though she had spoken questioning it. But still she holds it, and never shrinks from the horror of its mortality, somewhat to the wonder of her only spectator. For the other doctor has withdrawn, to speak to someone outside.

Of a sudden the dog Achilles starts barking. A short, sharp, startled bark—once, twice—and is silent. The girl lays the dead hand gently down, not dropping it, but replacing it where it first lay. She does not speak for a moment—cannot, perhaps. Then it comes with a cry, neither of pain nor joy—mere tension. " Oh, Dr. Merridew . . . the fingers closed . . . They closed on mine . . . the fingers *closed.* . . . I know it. I know it . . . The fingers *closed!* . . ." She says it again and again as though in terror that her word might be doubted. He sees as she turns to him that all her pride of self-control has given way. She is fighting against an outburst of tears, and her breath comes and goes at will, or at the will of some power that drives it. Sir Coupland may be contemplating speech—something it is correct to say, something the cooler judgment will endorse—but whatever it is he keeps it to himself. He is not one of those cheap sages that has *hysteria* on his tongue's tip to account for everything. It *may* be that; but it may be . . . Well—he has seen some odd cases in his time.

So, without speaking to the agitated young lady, he simply calls his colleague back; and, after a word or two aside with him, says to her:—" You had better leave him to us. Go now." It gives her confidence that he does not soothe or cajole, but speaks as he would to a man. She goes, and as she walks across to the Keeper's Lodge makes a little peace for her heart out of small material. Sir Coupland said " him " this time—look you!—not " it " as before.

The daughter finds the mother, five minutes later, trying a well-meant word to the old keeper; to put a little heart in him, if possible. It was no fault of his; he only carried out his orders, and so on. Gwen is silent about her experience; she will not raise false hopes. Besides, she is only half grieved for the old chap— has only a languid sympathy in her heart for him who, tampering with implements of Death, becomes Cain unawares. If she is right, he will know in time. Meanwhile it will be a lesson to him to avoid triggers, and will thus minimise the exigencies of Hell. Also, she has recovered her self-command; and will not show, even to her mother, how keen her interest has been in this man in the balance betwixt life and death.

As to the older lady, who has fought shy of seeing the body, the affair is no more than a casualty, very little coloured by the fact that its victim is a " gentleman." This sort of thing may impress the groundlings, while a real Earl or Duke remains untouched. A coronet has a very levelling effect on the plains below. Your mere baronet is but a hillock, after all. Possibly, however, this is a proletariate view, which always snubs rank, and her ladyship the Countess may never have given a thought to this side of the case. Certainly she is honestly grieved on behalf of her old friend Stephen, whom she has known for thirty years past. In fact, of the two, as they walk back to the Towers, the mother shows more than the daughter the reaction of emotion.

Says her daughter to her as they walk back—the three as they came—" I believe he will recover, for all that. I believe Dr. Merridew believes it, too. I am certain the fingers moved." Her manner lays stress on her own equanimity. It is more self-contained than need be, all things considered.

" The eyesight is easily deceived," says Miss Dickenson, prompt with the views of experience. She always holds a brief for common sense, and is considered an authority. " Even experts are misled—sometimes—in such cases. . . ."

Gwen interrupts:—" It had nothing to do with eyesight. I *felt* the fingers move." Whereupon her mother, roused by her sudden emphasis, says:—" But we are so glad that it *should* be so, Gwen darling." And then, when the girl stops in her walk and says:— " Of course you are—but why not?" she has a half-smile as for petulance forgiven, as she says:—" Because you fired up so about it, darling; that's all. We did not understand that you had hold of the hand. Was it stiff?" This in a semi-whisper of protest against the horror of the subject.

" Not the least. Cold!—oh, how cold!" She shudders of set purpose to show how cold. " But not *stiff*."

The two other ladies go into a partnership of seniority, glancing at each other; and each contributes to a duet about the duty of being hopeful, and we shall soon know, and at any rate, the case could not be in better hands, and so on. But whereas the elder lady was only working for reassurance—puzzled somewhat at a certain flushed emphasis in this beautiful daughter of hers— Miss Smith-Dickenson was taking mental notes, and looking intuitive. She was still looking intuitive when she joined the numerous party at lunch, an hour later. She had more than one inquiry addressed to her about " this unfortunate accident," but she reserved her information, with mystery, acquiring thereby a more defined importance. A river behind a *barrage* is much more impressive than a pump.

Sir Coupland Merridew's place at table was still empty when the first storm of comparison of notes set in over the events and deeds of the morning. A conscious reservation was in the air about the disaster of last night, causing talk to run on every other subject, but betrayed by more interest in the door and its openings than lunch generally shows. Presently it would open for the overdue guest, and he would have news worth hearing, said Hope. For stinted versions of event had leaked out, and had outlived the reservations and corrections of those who knew.

Lunch was conscious of Sir Coupland's arrival in the house before he entered, and its factors nodded to each other and said: "That's him!" Nice customs of Grammar bow before big mouthfuls. However, Miss Smith-Dickenson did certainly say: "I believe that *is* Sir Coupland."

It was, and in his face was secret content and reserve. In response to a volley of What?—Well?—Tell us!—and so forth, he only said:—" Shan't tell you anything till I've had something to eat!" But he glanced across at Lady Gwen and nodded slightly —a nod for her exclusive use.

Lunch, liberated by what amounted to certainty that the man was not killed, ran riot; almost all its factors taking a little more, thank you! It was brought up on its haunches by being suddenly made aware that Sir Coupland—having had something to eat— had spoken. He had to repeat his words to reach the far end of the long table.

"Yes—I said . . . only of course if you make such a row you can't hear. . . . I said that this gentleman cannot be said to have recovered consciousness"—here he paused for a mistaken exclamation of disappointment to get nipped in the bud, and then continued—"yet a while. However, I am glad to say I—both of us, Dr. Nash and myself, I should say—were completely mistaken about the case. It has turned out contrary to every expectation that . . ." Nobody noticed that a pause here was due to Lady Gwen having made "No!" with her lips, and looked a protest at the speaker. He went on:—" Well . . . in short . . . I would have sworn the man was dead . . . and he isn't! That's all I have to say about it at present. It might be over-sanguine to say he is alive—meaning that he will succeed in keeping so—but he is certainly not *dead.*" Miss Dickenson lodged her claim to a mild form of omniscience by saying with presence of mind:—" Exactly!" but without presumption, so that only her near neighbours heard her. Self-respect called for no more.

Had the insensible man spoken?—the Earl asked pertinently. Oh dear, no! Nothing so satisfactory as that, so far. The vitality was almost *nil.* The Earl retired on his question to listen to what a Peninsular veteran was saying to Gwen. This ancient warrior was one who talked but little, and then only to two sorts, old men like himself, with old memories of India and the Napoleonic wars, and young women like Gwen. As this was his way, it did not seem strange that he should address her all but exclusively, with only a chance side-word now and then to his host, for mere courtesy.

"When I was in Madras in eighteen-two—no—eighteen-three," he said, "I was in the Nineteenth Dragoon's under Maxwell—he was killed, you know—in that affair with the Mahrattas . . ."

"I know. I've read about the Battle of Assaye, and how General Wellesley had two horses shot under him. . . ."

"That was it. Scindia, you know—that affair! They had some very good artillery for those days, and our men had to charge up to the guns. I was cut down in Maxwell's cavalry charge, and went near bleeding to death. He was a fine fellow that did it . . ."

"Never mind him! You were going to tell me about yourself."

"Why—I was given up for dead. It was a good job I escaped decent interment. But the surgeon gave me the benefit of the doubt, and stood me over for a day or two. Then, as I didn't decay properly . . ."

"Oh, General—don't be so horrible!" This from Miss Smith-Dickenson close at hand. But Gwen is too eager to hear, to care about delicacies of speech, and strikes in:—

"Do go on, General! Never mind Aunt Constance. She is so fussy. Go on—'didn't decay properly' . . ."

"Well—I was behindhand! Not up to my duties, considered as a corpse! The doctor stood me over another twenty-four hours, and I came to. I was very much run down, certainly, but I *did* come to, or I shouldn't be here now to tell you about it, my dear. I should have been sorry."

A matter-of-fact gentleman "pointed out" that had General Rawnsley died of his wounds, he would not have been in a position to feel either joy or sorrow, or to be conscious that he was not dining at Ancester. The General fished up a wandering eyeglass to look at him, and said:—"Quite correct!" Miss Smith-Dickenson remarked upon the dangers attendant on over-literal interpretations. The Hon. Mr. Pellew perceived in this that Miss Dickenson had a sort of dry humour.

"But you *did* come to, General, and you *are* telling me about it," said Lady Gwen. "Now, how long was it before you rejoined your regiment?"

"H'm—well! I wasn't good for much two months later, or I should have come in for the fag-end of the campaign. All right in three months, I should say. But then—I was a young fellah!—in those days. How old's your man?"

"This gentleman who has been shot?" says Gwen, with some stiffness. "I have not the slightest idea." But Sir Coupland answered the question for her. "At a guess, General, twenty-five or twenty-six. He ought to do well if he gets through the next day or two. He may have a good constitution. I can't say yet. Yours must have been remarkable."

"I had such a good appetite, you know," says the General. "Such a devil of a twist! If I had had my way, I should have been at Argaum two months later. But, good Lard!—they wouldn't let me out of Hospital." The old soldier, roused by the recollection of a fifty-year-old grievance, still rankling, launched into a denunciation of the effeminacy and timidity of Authorities and Seniors, of all sorts and conditions. His youth was back upon him with its memories, and he had forgotten that he too was now a Senior. His torrent of thinly disguised execrations was of service to Lady Gwen; as the original subject of the conversation, just shot, was naturally forgotten. She had got all the enlightenment she wanted about him, and was cultivating an artificial lack of interest in his accident.

She was, however, a little dissatisfied with her own success in this branch of horticulture. Her anxiety had felt itself fully justified till now by the bare facts of the case. Her longing that this man should not die was so safe while it seemed certain that he could not live, that she felt under no obligation to account to herself for it. Analysis·of niceties of feeling in the presence of Death were uncalled for, surely. But now, with at least a chance of his recovery, she felt that she ought to be able to think of something else. So she talked of Sardanapalus and Charles Keane at the Princesses' Theatre—the first a play, the second a player—and the General, declining more than monosyllables to the matter-o'-fact gentleman, subsided into wrathful recollection of an exasperated young Dragoon chafing under canvas beneath an Indian sun, and panting for news of his regiment in the north, fifty years before.

But such intermittent conversation could not prevent her seeing that Norbury the butler had handed a visiting-card, pencilled on the back, to her father, and had whispered a message to him with a sense of its gravity, and that her father had replied:—"Yes, say I will be there presently." Nor that—in response to remote inquiry from his Countess at the end of an avenue of finger-glasses —he had thrown the words " Hamilton Torrens and the daughter— mother too ill to come—won't come up to the house until he's fit to move! " all the length of the table. That her mother had said:— " Oh yes—you know them," perhaps because of an apologetic manner in her husband for being the recipient of the message. Also that curiosity and information were mutual in the avenue, and that next-door neighbours but one were saying:—" What's that? " and getting no answer.

However, the Intelligence Department did itself credit in the end, and everyone knew that, immediately on the receipt of sanction from headquarters, Tom Kettering the young groom had mounted the grey mare—a celebrity in these parts—and made a foxhunter's short cut across a stiff country to carry the news of the disaster to Pensham Steynes, Sir Hamilton Torrens's house twenty miles off, and that that baronet and his daughter Irene Torrens had come at once. " I hope he hasn't killed the mare," said the Earl apprehensively. But his wife summoned Norbury to a secret confidence, saying after it:—" No—it's all right—he came on the box—didn't ride." From which the Earl knew—if the avenue didn't—that Tom Kettering the groom, after an incredible break across country, stabled the mare at Pensham Steynes, and rode back with the carriage. The whole thing had been negotiated in less than three hours.

All these things Gwendolen comes to be aware of somehow. But all of us know how a chance word in a confused conversation stays by the hearer, who is forced to listen to what is no elucidation of it, and is discontented. Such a word had struck this young lady; and she watched for her father, as lunch died away, to get the elucidation overdue. She was able to intercept him at the end of a long colloquy with Sir Coupland. " What did you mean, papa dearest, just now? . . ."

"What did I mean, dear? . . . When? "

" By ' until he's fit to move '? "

" I meant until Sir Coupland says he can be safely brought up to the house."

" *This* house, my dear? " It is not Gwen who speaks, but her mother, who has joined the conversation.

" Certainly, my love," says the Earl, with a kind of appealing diffidence. " If you have no very strong objection. He can be carried, Sir Coupland says, as soon as the wound is safe from inflammation. Of course he must not be left at the Hall."

" Of course not. But there are beds at the Lodge. . . ." However, the Earl says with a meek self-assertion :—" I think I would rather he were brought here. His father and George were at Christ Church together. . . ." Before which her ladyship concedes the point. His lordship then says he shall go at once to the Hall to see Sir Hamilton, and Gwen suggests that she shall accompany him. She may persuade Miss Torrens to come up to the Towers.

This assumption that the wounded man could be moved, after conversation between the Earl and Sir Coupland, was so reassuring, that Gwendolen felt it more than ever due to herself to cultivate that indifference about his recovery. However, she could not easily be too affectionate and hospitable to his sister under the circumstances.

By-the-by, it was rather singular that she had never seen this Irene Torrens, when they were almost neighbours—only eighteen miles by road between them. And Irene's father had been her Uncle George's great friend at Oxford; both at Christ Church! This uncle, who, like his friend Torrens, had gone into the army, was killed in action at Rangoon, long before Gwendolen's day.

It all takes so long to tell. The omission of half would shorten the tale and spare the reader so much. What a very small book the History of the World would be if all the events were left out!

CHAPTER XIII

BACK IN SAPPS COURT. MICHAEL RAGSTROAR'S SECULARISM. HIS EX-
TENDED KNOWLEDGE OF LIFE. YET A GAOL-BIRD PROPER WAS OUT-
SIDE IT. ONE IN QUEST OF A WIDOW. THE DEAD BEETLE IN DOLLY'S
CAKE. HOW UNCLE MO DID NOT LIKE THE MAN'S LOOKS. THERE
WAS NO WIDOW DAVERILL AND NEITHER BURR NOR PRICHARD WOULD
DO. HOW AUNT M'RIAR HAD BEEN AT CHAPEL. THE SONS OF LEVI.
MICHAEL'S NOBLE LOYALTY TOWARDS OUTLAWS

IT was a fine Sunday morning in Sapps Court, and our young friend Michael Rackstraw was not attending public worship. Not that it was his custom to do so. Nevertheless, the way he replied to a question by a chance loiterer into the Court seemed to imply the contrary. The question was, what the Devil he was doing that for?—and referred to the fact that he was walking on his hands. His answer was, that it was because he wasn't at Church. Not that all absentees from religious rites went about upside down;

but that, had he been at Church, the narrow exclusiveness of its ritual would have kept him right side up.

The speaker's appearance was disreputable, and his manner morose, sullen, and unconciliatory. Michael, even while still upside down, fancied he could identify a certain twist in his face that seemed not unfamiliar; but thought this might be due to his own drawbacks on correct observation. Upright again, his identification was confirmed and he knew quite well whose question he was answering by the time he felt his feet. It was the man he had seen in the clutches of the water-rat at Hammersmith, when both were capsized into the river six months ago. This put him on his guard, and he prepared to meet further questions with evasion or defiance. But he would flavour them with substantial facts. It would confuse issues and make it more difficult to convict him of mendacity.

"You don't look an unlikely young beggar," said the man. "What name are you called?"

Michael thought a moment and settled that it might be impolitic to disclose his name. So he answered simply:—"Ikey." Now, this name was not contrary to any statute or usage. The man appeared to accept it in good faith, and Michael decided in his heart that he was softer than what he'd took him for.

He recovered some credit, however, by his next inquiry which seemed to place baptismal names among negligibles: "Ah, that's it, is it? But Ikey what? What do they call your father, if you've got one?"

Three courses occurred to Michael; improbable fiction, evasive or defiant; plausible fiction; and the undisguised truth. As the first, the Duke of Wellington's name recommended itself. He had, however, decided mentally that this man was a queer customer, and might be an awkward customer. So he discarded the Duke—satire might irritate—and chose the second course to avoid the third. But he was betrayed by Realism, which suggested that a study from Nature would carry conviction. He decided on assuming the name of his friend the apothecary round the corner, up the street facing over against the Wheatsheaf. He replied that his father's name was Heeking's. It was easier to do this than to invent a name, which might have turned out an insult to the human understanding. He was disgusted to be met with incredulity.

"Don't believe you," said the man. "You're a young liar. Where's your father now—now this very minute?"

"Abed."

" What's he doing there ? "

" Sleeping of it off. It was Saturday with him last night. He had to be fetched from the King's Arms very careful. Perkins's Entire. Barclay Perkins. Fetched him myself! Mean to say I didn't ? " But this part of the tale was probable and no comment seemed necessary.

" Where's your mother ? "

" Cookin' 'im a bloater over the fire. It does the temper good. Can't yer smell it ? " A flavour of cooking confirmed Michael's words, but he seemed to require a more formal admission of his veracity than a mere nostril set ajar and a glance at an open window. " Say, if you don't! On'y there's no charge for the smelling of it. She'll tell yer just the same like me, word in and word out. You can arks for yourself. I can 'oller 'er up less time than talkin' about it. You've only to say ! "

But this man, the twist of whose face had not been improved by his recognition of the bloater, seemed to wish to confine his communications to Michael, rather decisively. Indeed, there was a sound of veiled intimidation in his voice as he said:—" You leave your mother to see to the herrings, young 'un, and just you listen to me. You be done with your kidding and listen to me. *You* can tell me as much as I want to know. Sharp young beggar! —you know what's good for you." An intimidation of a possible *douceur* perhaps ?

Now Master Michael, though absolutely deficient in education— his class, a sort of aristocracy of guttersnipes, was so in the pre-Board-School fifties,—was as sharp as a razor already even in the days of Dave Wardle's early accident, and had added a world of experience to his stock in the last few months. He had, in fact, been seeing the Metropolis, as an exponent or auxiliary of his father's vocation as a costermonger; and had made himself extremely useful, said Mr. Rackstraw, in the manner of speaking. Only the manner of speaking, strictly reported, did not use the expression *extremely,* but another one which we need not dwell upon except to make reference to its inappropriateness. Mr. Rackstraw was not a man of many words, so he had to fall back upon the same very often or hold his tongue: a course uncongenial to him. This word was a *pièce de résistance*—a kind of sheet-anchor.

In the course of these last few months of active costermongery, of transactions in early peas and new potatoes, spring-cabbage and ripe strawberries, he had acquired not only an insight into commerce but apparently an intimate knowledge of every street in London, and a very fair acquaintance with its celebrities; meaning thereby its real celebrities—its sportsmen, patrons of the Prize Ring, cricketers, rowing-men, billiard-players, jockeys—what not? Its less important representative men, statesmen, bishops, writers, artists, lawyers; soldiers and sailors even, though here concession was rife, had to take a second place. But there was one class— a class whose members may have belonged to any one of these— of which Michael's experience was very limited. It was the class of gaol-birds. This type, the most puzzling to eyes that see it for the first time, the most unmistakable by those well read in it, was the type that was now setting this juvenile coster's wits to work upon its classification, on this May morning in Sapps Court. Michael's previous record of him was an interrupted sight of his face in the river-garden at Hammersmith, and a reference to his felonious antecedents at the inquest. He was, by the time the conversation assumed the interest due to a hint of emolument, able to say to himself that he should know the Old Bailey again by the cut of its jib next time he came across it.

In reply, he scorned circumlocution, saying briefly:—" Wot'll it come to? Wot are you good for? That's the p'int."

" You tell me no lies and you'll see. There's an old widow-lady down this Court. Don't you go and say there ain't!"

" There's any number. Which old widder?"

" Name of Daverill. Old enough to be your father's granny."

" No sich a name! There's one a sight older than that though— last house down the Court—top bell."

" How old do you make her out?"

" Two 'underd next birthday!" But Michael perceived in his questioner's eye a possible withdrawal of his offer of a consideration, and amended his statement:—" Ninety-nine, p'raps!—couldn't say to arf a minute."

" House at the end where the old cock in a blue shirt's smoking a pipe—is that it?"

" Ah!—up two flights of stairs. But she can't see you, nor yet hear you, to speak of."

" Who's the old cock?"

" This little boy's uncle. He b'longs to the Fancy. 'Eavyweight he was, wunst upon a time." And Dave Wardle, who had joined the colloquy, gave confirmatory evidence: " He's moy Uncle Moses, he is. And he's moy sister Dolly's Uncle Moses, he is. And moy sister Dolly she had a piece of koyk with a beadle in it. She *had.* A dead beadle!" But this evidence was ruled out of court by general consent; or rather, perhaps, it should be said that the witness remained in the box giving evidence of the same nature for his own satisfaction, while the court's attention wandered. "Oh—he was a heavyweight, was he? An ugly customer, I should reckon." The stranger said this more to himself than to the boys. But he spoke direct to Michael with the question, "What was it you said was the old lady's name, nów?"

The boy, shrewd as he was, was but a boy after all. Was it wonderful that he should accept the implication that he had given the name? Thrown off his guard he answered:—"Name of Richards." Whereupon Dave, who was still stuttering on melodiously about the dead monster in Dolly's cake, endeavoured to correct his friend without complete success.

"Pitcher, is it?" said the stranger. Michael, disgusted to find that he had been betrayed into giving a name, though he was far from clear why it should have been reserved, was glad of Dave's perverted version, as replacing matters on their former footing. But the repetition of the name, by voices the stimulus of definition had emphasized, caught the attention of Uncle Moses, who thereon moved up the Court to find out who this stranger could be, who was so evidently inquiring about the upstairs tenant. As he reached close inspection-point his face did not look as though the visitor pleased him. The latter said good-morning first; but, simple as his words were, the gaol-bird manner of guarded suspicion crept into them and stamped the speaker.

"Don't like the looks of you, mister!" said Uncle Mo to himself. But aloud he said:—"Good-morning to *you*, sir. I understood you to be inquiring for Mrs. Prichard."

"No—Daverill. No such a name, this young shaver says."

"Not down this Court. It wasn't Burr by any chance now, was it?"

"No—Daverill."

"Because there *is* a party by the name of Burr if you could have seen your way." This was only the natural civility which sometimes runs riot with an informant's judgment, making him anxious to meet the inquirer at any cost, whatever inalienable stipulations the latter may have committed himself to. In this case it seemed that nothing short of Daverill, crisp and well defined, would satisfy the conditions. The stranger shook his head with as much decision as reciprocal civility permitted—rather as though he regretted his inability to accept Burr—and replied that the name had "got to be" Daverill and no other. But he seemed reluctant to leave the widows down this Court unsifted, saying:—"You're sure there ain't any other old party now?" To which

Uncle Moses responded: "Ne'er a one, master, to *my* knowledge. Widow Daverill she's somewheres else. Not down *this* Court!" He said it in a valedictory way as though he had no wish to open a new subject, and considered this one closed. He had profited by his inspection of the stranger, and had formed a low opinion of him.

But the stranger's reluctance continued. "You couldn't say, I suppose," said he, in a cautious hesitating way, "you couldn't say what countrywoman she was, now?" His manner might easily have been—so Uncle Mo thought at least—that of indigence trying to get a foothold with an eye to begging in the end. It really was the furtive suspiciousness that hangs alike upon the miscreant and the mere rebel against law into whose bones the fetter has rusted. The guilt of the former, if he can cheat both the gaol and the gallows, may merge in the demeanour of a free man; that of the latter, after a decade of prison-service you or I might have remitted, will hang by him till death.

Uncle Mo may have detected, through the mere blood-poisoning of the prison, the inherent baseness of the man, or may have re-coiled from the type. Anyway, his instinct was to get rid of him. And evidently the less he said about anyone in Sapps Court the better. So he replied, surlily enough considering his really amiable disposition:—"No—I could *not* say what countrywoman she is, master." Then he thought a small trifle of fiction thrown in might contribute to the detachment of this man's curiosity from Mrs. Prichard, and added carelessly:—"Some sort of a foringer I take it." Which accounted, too, for his knowing nothing about her. No true Englishman knows anything about that benighted class.

Now the boy Michael, all eyes and ears, had somehow come to an imperfect knowledge that Mrs. Prichard had been in Australia once on a time. The imperfection of this knowledge had affected the name of the place, and when he officiously struck in to supply it, he did so inaccurately. "Horstrian she is!" He added:—"Rode in a circus, she did." But this was only the reaction of misinterpretation on a too inventive brain.

"Then she ain't any use to me. Austrian, is she?" Thus the stranger; who then, after a slow glare up and down the Court, in search of further widows perhaps, turned to go, saying merely:— "I'll wish you a good-morning, guv'nor. Good-morning!" Uncle Mo watched him as he lurched up the Court, noting the oddity of his walk. This man, you see, had been chained to another like himself, and his bias went to one side like a horse that has gone in harness. This gait is known in the class he belonged to as the "darby-roll," from the name by which fetters are often spoken of.

"How long has that charackter been makin' the Court stink, young Carrots?" said Uncle Moses to Michael.

"Afore you come up, Mr. Moses."

"Afore I come up. How long afore I come up?"

Michael appeared to pass through a paroxysm of acute calcula-tion, ending in a lucid calm with particulars. "Seven minute and a half," said he resolutely. "Wanted my name, he did!"

"What did you tell him?"

"I told 'im a name. Orl correct it was. Only it warn't mine. I was too fly for him."

"What name did you tell him?"

"Mr. Eking's at the doctor's shop. He'll find that all right. He can read it over the door. He's got eyes in his head." No doubt sticklers for conscience will quarrel with the view that the demands of Truth can be satisfied by an authentic name applied to the wrong person.

It did not seem to grate on Uncle Moses, who only said:— "Sharp boy! But don't you tell no more lies than's wanted. Only now and again to shame the Devil, as the sayin' is. And you, little Dave, don't you tell nothing but the truth, 'cos your Aunt M'riar she says not to it." Dave promised to oblige.

Aunt M'riar, returning home with Dolly from a place known as "Chapel"—a place generally understood to be good, and an antidote to The Rising Sun, which represented Satan and was bad—only missed meeting this visitor to Sapps by a couple of minutes. She might have just come face to face with him the very minute he left the Court, if she had not delayed a little at the baker's, where she had prevailed on Sharmanses—the promoter of some latent heat in the bowels of the earth which came through to the pavement, making it nice and dry and warm to set upon in damp, cold weather—to keep the family Sunday dinner back just enough to guarantee it brown all through, and the potatoes crackly all over. Sharmanses was that obliging he would have kep' it in—it was a shoulder of mutton—any time you named, but he declined to be responsible that the gravy should not dry up. So Dolly carried her aunt's prayer-book, feeling like the priests, the Sons of Levi, which bare the Ark of the Covenant; and Aunt M'riar carried the Tin of the Shoulder of Mutton, and took great care not to spill any of the Gravy. The office of the Sons of Levi was a sinecure by comparison.

Why did our astute young friend Michael keep his counsel

about the identity of the bloke that come down the Court that Sunday morning? Well—it was not mere astuteness or vulgar cunning on the watch for an honorarium. It was really a noble chivalry akin to that of the schoolboy who will be flogged till the blood comes, rather than tell upon his schoolfellow, even though he loathes the misdemeanour of the latter. It was enough for Michael that this man was wanted by Scotland Yard, to make silence seem a duty—silence, at any rate, until interrogated. He was certainly not going to volunteer information—was, in fact, in the position of the Humanitarian who declined to say which way the fox had gone when the scent was at fault; only with this difference—that the hounds were not in sight. Neither was he threatened with the hunting-whip of an irate M.F.H. "Give the beggar his chance!"—that was how Michael looked at it. He who knows the traditions of the class this boy was born in will understand and excuse the feeling.

Michael was—said his *entourage*—that sharp at twelve that he could understand a'most anything. He had certainly understood that the man whom he saw in the grip of the police-officer overturned in the Thames was wanted by Scotland Yard, to pay an old score, with possible additions to it due to that officer's death. He had understood, too, that the attempt to capture the man had been treacherous according to his ideas of fair play, while he had no information about his original crime. He did not like his looks, certainly, but then looks warn't much to go by. His conclusion was—silence for the present, without prejudice to future speech if applied for. When that time came, he would tell no more lies than were wanted.

CHAPTER XIV

OF A VISIT MICHAEL PAID HIS AUNT, AND OF A FISH HE NEARLY CAUGHT. THE PIGEONS, NEXT DOOR, AND A PINT OF HALF-AND-HALF. MISS JULIA HAWKINS AND HER PARALYTIC FATHER. HOW A MAN IN THE BAR BROKE HIS PIPE. OF A VISIT MICHAEL'S GREAT-AUNT PAID MISS HAWKINS. TWO STRANGE POLICEMEN. HOW MR. DAVERILL MIGHT HAVE ESCAPED HAD HE NOT BEEN A SMOKER. A MIRACULOUS RECOVERY, SPOILED BY A STRAIGHT SHOT

MICHAEL RAGSTROAR's mysterious attraction to his great-aunt at Hammersmith was not discountenanced or neutralised by his family in Sapps Court, but rather the reverse: in fact, his visits to her received as much indirect encouragement as his parents considered might be safely given without rousing his natural combativeness, and predisposing him against the ounce of influence which she alone exercised over his rebellious instincts. Any suspicion of moral culture might have been fatal, holy influences of every sort being eschewed by Michael on principle.

So when Michael's mother, some weeks later than the foregoing incident, remarked that it was getting on for time that her branch of the family should send a quartern of shelled peas and two pound of cooking-cherries to Aunt Elizabeth Jane as a seasonable gift, her lord and master had replied that he wasn't going within eleven mile of Hammersmith till to-morrow fortnight, but that he would entrust peas and cherries, as specified, to " Old Saturday Night," a fellow-coster, so named in derision of his adoption of teetotalism, his name being really Knight. He was also called Temperance Tommy, without irony, his name being really Thomas. He, a resident in Chiswick, would see that Aunt Elizabeth Jane got the consignment safely.

Michael's father did this in furtherance of a subtle scheme which succeeded. His son immediately said:—" Just you give *him* 'em, and see if he don't sneak 'em. See if he don't bile the peas and make a blooming pudd'n of the cherries. You see if he don't! That's all I say, if you arsk me." A few interchanges on these lines ended in Michael undertaking to deliver the goods personally as a favour, time enough Sunday morning for Aunt Elizabeth Jane herself to make a pudding of the cherries, blooming or otherwise.

As a sequel, Michael arrived at his aunt's so early on the following Sunday that the peas and the cherries had to wait for hours to be cooked, while Aunt Elizabeth Jane talked with matrons round in the alley, and he himself took part in a short fishing expedition, nearly catching a roach, who got away. The Humanitarian—is that quite the correct word, by-the-by?—must rejoice at the frequency of this result in angling.

" The 'ook giv'," said Michael, returning disappointed. " Wot can you expect with inferior tarkle? " He then undertook to get a brown Toby jug filled at The Pigeons; though, being church-time—the time at which the Heathen avail themselves of their opportunity of stopping away from church—the purchase of one pint full up, and no cheating, was a statutable offence on the part of the seller.

But when a public has a little back-garden with rusticated wood-work seats, painful to those rash enough to avail themselves of them, and a negotiable wall you and your jug can climb over and descend from by the table no one ever gets his legs under owing to this same rusticity of structure, then you can do as Michael did, and make your presence felt by whistling through the keyhole, without fear of incriminating the Egeria of the beer-fountain in the locked and shuttered bar, near at hand.

Egeria was not far off, for her voice came saying:—"Say your name through the keyhole; the key's took out. . . . No, you ain't Mrs. Treadwell next door! You're a boy."

"Ain't a party-next-door's grandnephew a boy?" exclaimed Michael indignantly. "She's sent me with her own jug for a pint of arfnarf! Here's the coppers, all square. You won't have nothing to complain of, Miss 'Orkins."

Miss Hawkins, the daughter of The Pigeons, or at least of their proprietor, opened the door and admitted Michael Ragstroar. Her father had drawn his last quart for a customer many long years ago, and his right-hand half was passing the last days of its life in a bedroom· upstairs. A nonagenarian paralysed all down one side may be described as we have described Mr. Hawkins. He was still able to see dimly, with one eye, the glorious series of sporting prints that lined the walls of his room; and such pulses as he had left were stirred with momentary enthusiasm when the Pytchley Hunt reached the surviving half of his understanding. The other half of him had lived, and seemed to have died, years ago. The two halves may have taken too much when they were able to move about together and get at it—too much brandy, rum, whisky; too many short nips and long nips—too cordial cordials. Perhaps his daughter took the right quantity of all these to a nicety, but appearances were against her. She was a woman of the type that must have been recognised in its girlhood as stunning, or ripping, by the then frequenters of the bar of The Pigeons, and which now was reluctant to admit that its powers to rip or stun were on the wane at forty. It was that of an inflamed blonde putting on flesh, which meant to have business relations with dropsy later on, unless—which seemed unlikely—its owner should discontinue her present one with those nips and cordials. She had no misgivings, so far, on this point; nor any, apparently, about the seductive roll of a really fine pair of blue eyes. While as for her hair, the bulk and number of the curl-papers it was still screwed up in spoke volumes of what its release would reveal to an astonished Sunday afternoon when its hour should come—not far off now.

There was a man in the darkened bar, smoking a long clay.

Michael felt as if he knew him as soon as he set eyes on him,. but it was not till the pipe was out of his mouth that he saw who he was. He had been ascribing to the weight or pressure of the pipe the face-twist which, when it was removed, showed as a slight distortion. It was the man he had seen twice, once in the garden he had just left, and once at Sapps Court. Michael considered that he was entitled to a gratuity from this man, having interpreted his language as a promise to that effect, and having received nothing so far.

He was not a diffident or timid character, as we know. " Seen you afore, guv'nor! " was his greeting.

The man gave a start, breaking his pipe in three pieces, but getting no farther than the first letter of an oath of irritation at the accident. " What boy's this? " he cried out, with an earnestness nothing visible warranted.

" Lard's mercy, Mr. Wix! " exclaimed the mistress of the house,. turning round from the compounding of the half-and-half. " What a turn you giv'! And along of nothing but little Micky from Mrs. Treadwell next door! Which most, Micky? Ale or stout? "

" Most of whichever costis most," answered Michael, with simplicity. Thereon he felt himself taken by the arm, and turning, saw the man's face looking close at him. It was the sort of face that makes the end of a dream a discomfort to the awakener.

" Now, you young beggar!—*where* have you seen me afore? I ain't going to hurt you. You tell up straight and tell the truth."

" Not onlest you leave hold of my arm! "

" You do like he says, Mr. Wix. . . . Now you tell Mr. Wix, Micky. *He* won't hurt you." Thus Miss Julia, procuring liberty for the hand to receive the half-and-half she was balancing its foam on.

Michael rubbed the arm with his free hand as he took the brown jug, to express resentment in moderation. But he answered his questioner:—" Round in Sappses Court beyont the Dials acrost Oxford Street keepin' to your left off Tottenham Court Road. You come to see for a widder, and there warn't no widder for yer. Mean to say there was? "

" Where I sent you, Mr. Wix," said Miss Julia. " To Sapps Court, where Mrs. Treadwell directed me—where her nephew lives. That's this boy's father. You'll find that right."

" Your Mrs. Treadmill, *she's* all right. Sapps Court's all right of itself. But it ain't the Court I was tracking out. If it was, they'd have known the name of Daverill. Why—the place ain't

no bigger than a prison yard! About the length of down your
back-garden to the water's edge. It's the wrong Court, and there
you have it in a word. She's in Capps Court or Gapps Court—
some * * * of a Court or other—not Sapps." A metaphor has
to be omitted here, as it might give offence. It was not really
a well-chosen or appropriate one, and is no loss to the text. "What's
this boy's name, and no lies?" he added after muttering to himself
on the same lines volcanically.

"How often do you want to be told *that,* Mr. Wix? This boy's
Micky Rackstraw, lives with his grandmother next door. . . .
Well—her sister then! It's all as one. Ain't you, Micky?"

"Ah! Don't live there, though. Comes easy-like, now and
again. Like the noospapers."

"He's a young liar, then. Told me his name was Ikey." Miss
Hawkins pointed out that Ikey and Micky were substantially
identical. But she was unable to make the same claim for Rackstraw and Ekins, when told that Micky had laid claim to the
latter. She waived the point and conducted the beer-bearer back
the way he came, handing him the brown jug over the wall, not
to spill it.

But she suggested, in consideration of the high quality of the
half-and-half, that her next-door neighbour might oblige by stepping in by the private entrance, to speak concerning Sapps Court
and its inhabitants; all known to her more or less, no doubt.
Which Aunt Elizabeth was glad to do, seeing that the cherry-tart
was only just put in the oven, and she could spare that few minutes without risk.

Now, this old lady, though she was but a charwoman depending
for professional engagements rather on the goodwill—for auld
lang syne—of one or two families in Chiswick, of prodigious opulence in her eyes, yet was regarded by Sapps Court, when she
visited her niece, Mrs. Rackstraw, or Ragstroar, Michael's mother,
as distinctly superior. Aunt M'riar especially had been so much
impressed with a grey shawl with fringes and a ready cule—spelt
thus by repute—which she carried when she come of a Sunday,
that she had not only asked her to tea, but had taken her to pay
a visit to Mrs. Prichard upstairs. She had also in conversation
taken Aunt Elizabeth Jane largely into her confidence about Mrs.
Prichard, repeating, indeed, all she knew of her except what
related to her convict husband. About that she kept an honourable silence.

It was creditable to Miss Juliarawkins, whose name—written
as pronounced—gives us what we contend is an innocent pleasure,

that she should have suspected the truth about Wix or Daverill's want of shrewdness when he visited Sapps Court. She had been bliassed towards this suspicion by the fact that the man, when he first referred to Sapps Court, had spoken the name as though sure of it; and it was to test its validity that she invited Aunt Elizabeth Jane round by the private door, and introduced her to the darkened bar, where the ex-convict was lighting another pipe. She had heard Mrs. Treadwell speak of Aunt M'riar; and now, having formed a true enough image of the area of the Court, had come to the conclusion that all its inhabitants would be acquainted, and would talk over each other's affairs.

"Who the Hell's that?" Mr. Wix started as if a wasp had stung him, as the old charwoman's knock came at the private entrance alongside of the bar. He seemed very sensitive, always on the watch for surprises.

"Only old Treadwell from next door. *She* ain't going to hurt you, Tom. You be easy." Miss Hawkins spoke with another manner as well as another name now that she and this man were alone. She may never possibly have known his own proper name, he having been introduced to her as Thomas Wix twenty years ago. An introduction with a sequel which scarcely comes into the story.

His answer was beginning:—"It's easy to say be easy . . ." when the woman left the room to admit Aunt Elizabeth Jane. Who came in finishing the drying of hands, suddenly washed, on a clean Sunday apron. "Lawsy me, Miss Hawkins!" said she. "I didn't know you had anybody here."

It was not difficult to *entamer* the conversation. After a short interlude about the weather, to which the man's contribution was a grunt at most, the old lady had been started on the subject of her nephew and Sapps Court, and to this he gave attention. If she had had her tortoiseshell glasses she might have been frightened by the way he knitted his brows to listen. But she had left them behind in her hurry, and he kept back in a dark corner.

"About this same aged widow body," said he, fixing the conversation to the point that interested him. "What sort of an age now should you give her? Eighty—ninety—ninety-five—ninety-nine?" He stopped short of a hundred. Nobody one knows is a hundred. Centenarians are only in newspapers.

"I can tell you her age from her lips, mister. Eighty-one next birthday. And her name, Maisie Prichard."

Mr. Wix's attention deepened, and his scowl with it. "Now, can you make that safe to go upon?" he said with a harsh stress on a voice already harsh. "How came the old lady to say her own christened name? I'll pound it I might talk to you most of the day and never know your first name. Old folks they half forget 'em as often as not."

Miss Hawkins struck in:—"Now you're talking silly, Mr. Wix. How many young folk tell you their christened names right off?" But she had got on weak ground. She got off it again discreetly. "Anyhow, Mrs. Treadwell she's inventing nothing, having no call to." She turned to Aunt Elizabeth Jane with the question:—"How come she to happen to mention the name, ma'am?"

"Just as you or I might, Miss Julia. Mrs. Wardle she said, 'I was remarking of it to Mrs. Treadwell,' she said, 'only just afore we come upstairs, ma'am,' she said, 'that you was one of twins, ma'am,' she said. And then old Mrs. Prichard she says, 'Ay, to be sure,' she says, 'twins we were—Maisie and Phœbe. Forty-five years ago she died, Phœbe did,' she says. 'And I've never forgotten Phœbe,' she says. 'Nor yet I shan't forget Phœbe not if I live to be a hundred!'"

"Goard blind my soul!" Mr. Wix muttered this to himself, and though Aunt Elizabeth Jane failed to catch the words, she shuddered at the manner of them. She did not like this Mr. Wix, and wished she had not forgotten her tortoiseshell spectacles, so as to see better what he was like. The words she heard him say next had nothing in them to cause a shudder, though the manner of them showed vexation:—"If that ain't tryin' to a man's temper! There she was all the time!" It is true he qualified this last substantive by the adjective the story so often has to leave out, but it was not very uncommon in those days along the riverside between Fulham and Kew.

"I thought you said the name was Daverill," said Miss Hawkins, taking the opportunity to release a curl-paper at a looking-glass behind bottles. It was just upon time to open, and the barmaid had got her Sunday out.

"Why the Hell shouldn't the name be Daverill? In course I did! Ask your pardon for swearing, missis. . . ." This was to the visitor, who had begun to want to go. "You'll excuse my naming to you all my reasons, but I'll just mention this one, not to be misunderstood. This here old lady's a sort of old friend of mine, and when I came back from abroad I says to myself I'd like to look up old Mrs. Daverill. So I make inquiry, you see, and my man he tells me—he was an old mate of mine, you see—she's gone to live at Sevenoaks—do you see?—at Sevenoaks. . . ."

"Ah, I see! I've been at Sevenoaks."

"Well—there she had been and gone away to town again. Then says I, 'What's her address?' So they told me they didn't know, it was so long agone. But the old woman—*her* name was Killick, or Forbes was it?—no, Killick—remembered directing on a letter to Mrs. Daverill, Sapps Court. And Juliar here she said she'd heard tell of Sapps Court. So I hunted the place up and found it. Then your Mrs. Wardle's husband—I take it he was Moses Wardle the heavyweight in my young days—he put me off the scent because of the name. The only way to make Prichard of her I can see is—she married again. Well—did no one ever hear of an old fool that got married again?"

"That's nothing," said Miss Hawkins. "They'll marry again with the rattle in their throats."

That tart was in the oven, and had to be remembered. Or else Aunt Elizabeth Jane wanted to see no more of Mr. Wix. "I must be running back to my cooking," said she. "But if this gentleman goes again to find out Sappses, he's only got to ask for my niece at Number One, or Mrs. Wardle at Number Seven, and he'll find Mrs. Prichard easy." She did not speak directly to the man, and he for his part noticed her departure very slightly, giving it a fraction of a grunt he wanted the rest of later.

Nor did Aunt Elizabeth Jane seem in a great hurry to get away when Miss Hawkins had seen her to the door. She lingered a moment to refer to Aunt's M'riar's talk of Widow Prichard. Certainly Mrs. Wardle at Number Seven *she* said nothing of any second marriage, and thought Prichard was the name of the old lady's first husband, who had died in Van Diemen's Land. Miss Julia paid very little attention. What business of hers was Widow Prichard? She was much more interested in a couple of policemen walking along the lane. Not a very common spectacle in that retired thoroughfare! Also, instead of following on along the riverside road it opened into, they both wheeled right-about-face and came back.

Miss Julia, taking down a shutter to reinstate The Pigeons as a tavern open to customers, noted that the faces of these two were strange to her. Also that they passed her with the barest good-morning, forbiddingly. The police generally cultivate intercourse with public-house keepers of every sort, but when one happens to be a lady with ringlets especially so; even should her complexion be partly due to correctives, to amalgamate a blotchiness. These officers overdid their indifference, and it attracted Miss Julia's attention.

Aunt Elizabeth Jane thought at the time she might have mistaken what she heard one of them say to the other. For, of course, she passed them close. The words she heard seemed to be:—" That will be Hawkins." Something in them rang false with her concept of the situation. But there was the cherry-tart to be seen to, and some peas to boil. Only not the whole lot at once for only her and Michael! As for that boy, she had sent him off to the baker's, the minute he came back, to wait till the bit of the best end of the neck was sure to be quite done, and bring it away directly minute.

That day there was an unusually high spring-tide on the river, and presumably elsewhere; only that did not concern Hammersmith, which ascribed the tides to local impulses inherent in the Thames. Just after midday the water was all but up to the necks of the piers of Hammersmith Bridge, and the island at Chiswick was nearly submerged. Willows standing in lakes were recording the existence of towing-paths no longer able to speak for themselves, and the insolent plash of ripples over wharves that had always thought themselves above that sort of thing seemed to say:—" Thus far will I come, and a little farther for that matter." Father Thames never quite touched the landing of the boat-ladder, at the end of the garden at The Pigeons, but he went within six inches of it.

" The water wasn't like you see it now, that day," said a man in the stern of a boat that was hanging about off the garden. " All of five foot lower down, I should figure it. *He* didn't want no help to get up—not he! "

" It was a tidy jump up, any way you put it," said the stroke oar.

" Well—he could have done it! But he was aiming to help his man to a seat in the boat, not to get a lift up for himself. I've not a word to say against Toby Ibbetson, mind you! He took an advantage some wouldn't, maybe. And then it's how you look at it, when all's done. You know what Daverill was wanted for? " Oh yes—both oars knew that. " I call to mind the place—knew it well enough. Out near Waltham Abbey. Lonely sort of spot. . . . Yes—the girl died. Not before she'd had time to swear to the twist in his face. He had been seen and identified none so far off an hour before. Quite a young girl. Father cut his throat. So would you. Thought he ought to have seen the girl safe home. So he ought. Ain't that our man's whistle? " The boat, slowly worked in towards The Pigeons, lays to a few strokes off on the slack water. The tide's mandate to stop has come. The sergeant is waiting for a second whistle to act.

Inside the tavern the woman has closed the street-door abruptly—

has given the alarm. "There's two in the lane!" she gasps. "Be sharp, Tom!"

"Through the garden?" he says. "Run out to see."

She is back almost before the door she opens has swung to. "It's all up, Tom," she cries. "There's the boat!"

"Stand clear, Juli-ar!" he says. "I'll have a look at your roof. Needn't say I'm at home. Where's the key?"

"I'll give it you. You go up!" She forgets something, though, in her hurry. His pipe remains on the table where he left it smoking, lying across the unemptied pewter. *He* forgets it, too, though he follows her deliberately enough. Recollection and emergency rarely shake hands.

She meets him on the stairs coming down from the room where the paralysed man lies, hearing but little, seeing only the walls and the ceiling. "It's on the corner of the chimney-piece," she says. "*He's* asleep." Daverill passes her, and just as he reaches the door remembers the pipe. It would be fatal to call out with that single knock at the house-door below. Too late!

She still forgets that pipe, and only waits to be sure he is through, to open the door to the knocker. By the time she does so he has found the key and passed through the dormer door that gives on the leads. The paralysed man has not moved. Moreover, he cannot see the short ladder that leads to the exit. It is on his dead side.

"You've a party here that's wanted, missis. Name of Wix or Daverill. Man about five-and-forty. Dark hair and light eyes. Side-draw on the mouth. Goes with a lurch. Two upper front eye-teeth missing. Carries a gold hunting-watch on a steel chain. Wears opal ring of apparent value. Stammers slightly." So the police-officer reads from his warrant or instructions, which he offers to show to Miss Hawkins, who scarcely glances at it.

Who so surprised and plausible as she? Why—her father is the only man in the house, and him on his back this fifteen years or more! What's more, he doesn't wear an opal ring. Nor any ring at all, for that matter! But come in and see. Look all over the house if desired. *She* won't stand in the way.

"Our instruction is to search," says the officer. He looks like a sub-inspector, and is evidently what a malefactor would consider a "bad man" to have anything to do with. Miss Hawkins knows that her right of sanctuary, if any, is a feeble claim, probably overruled by some police regulation; and invites the officers into the house, almost too demonstratively. Just then she suddenly recollects that pipe.

"You can find your way in, mister," she says; and goes through to the bar. The moment she does so the officer shows alacrity.

"Keep an eye to that cellar-flap, Jacomb," he says to his mate, and follows the lady of the house. He is only just in time. "Is that your father's pipe?" he asks. In another moment she would have hidden it.

"Which pipe?—oh, this pipe?—*this* pipe ain't nothing. Left stood overnight, I suppose." And she paused to think of the best means of getting the pipe suppressed. There was no open grate in the bar to throw it behind. She was a poor liar, too, and was losing her head.

"Give me hold a quarter of a minute," says the officer. She cannot refuse to give the pipe up. "Someone's had a whiff off this pipe since closing-time last night," he continues, touching the still warm bowl; for all this had passed very quickly. And he actually puts the pipe to his lips, and in two or three draws works up its lingering spark. "A good mouthful of smoke," says he, blowing it out in a cloud.

"You can look where you like," mutters the woman sullenly. "There's no man for you. Only you won't want to disturb my father. He's only just fell asleep."

"He'll be sleeping pretty sound after fifteen year." Thus the officer, and the unhappy woman felt she had indeed made a complete mess of the case. "Which is his room now, ma'am? We'll go there first."

Up the stairs and past a window looking on the garden. The day is hot beneath the July sun, and the two men in uniform who are coming up the so-called garden, or rather gravelled yard, behind The Pigeons, are mopping the sweat from their brows. They might have been customers from the river, but Miss Hawkins knows the look of them too well for that. The house is surrounded—watched back and front. Escape is hopeless, successful concealment the only chance.

"Been on his back like that for fifteen years, has he?" So says the officer looking at the prostrate figure of the old man on the couch. He is not asleep now—far from it. His mouth begins to move, uttering jargon. His one living eye has light in it. There is something he wants to say and struggles for in vain. "Can't make much out of that," is the verdict of his male hearer. His daughter can say that he is asking his visitor's name and what he wants. He can understand when spoken to, she says. But the intruder is pointing at the door leading to the roof. "Where does that go to?" he asks.

"Out on the tiles. I'll see for the key and let you through, if you'll stop a minute." It is the only good bit of acting she has done. Perhaps despair gives histrionic power. She sees a chance of deferring the breaking-down of that door, and who knows what may hang on a few minutes of successful delay? Before she goes she suggests again that the paralysed man will understand what is said to him if spoke to plain. Clearly, he who speaks plain to him will do a good-natured act.

Whether the officer's motives are Samaritan or otherwise, he takes the hint. As the woman gets out of hearing, he says:—"You are the master of this house, I take it?" And his hearer's crippled mouth half succeeds in its struggle for an emphatic assent. He continues:—"In course you are. I'm Sub-Inspector Cardwell, N Division. There's a man concealed in your house I'm after. He's wanted. . . . Who is he?"—a right guess of an unintelligible question—"You mean what name does he go by? Well—his name's Daverill, but he's called Thornton or Wix as may be. P'r'aps you know him, sir?" Whether or no, the name has had effect electrically on its hearer, who struggles frantically—painfully—hopelessly for speech. The officer says commiseratingly:—"Poor devil!—he's quite off his jaw"; and then, going to the open window, calls out to his mates of the river-service, below in the garden:—"Keep an eye on the roof, boys."

Then he goes out on the stair-landing. That woman is too long away—it is out of all reason. As he passes the paralytic man, he notes that he seems to be struggling violently for something—either to speak or to rise. He cannot tell which, and he does best to hasten the return of the woman who can.

Out on the landing, Miss Hawkins, who has not been looking for keys, but supplying her first Sunday customers in their own jugs, protests that she has fairly turned the house over in her key-hunt—all in vain! Her interest seems vivid that these police shall not be kept off her roof. She suggests that a builder's yard in the Kew Road will furnish a ladder long enough to reach the roof. "Shut on Sunday!" says Sub-Inspector Cardwell conclusively. Then let someone who knows how be summoned to pick the lock. By all means, if such a person is at hand. But no trade will come out Sunday, except the turn-cock, obviously useless. That is the verdict. "You'll never be for breaking down the door, Mr. Inspector, with my father there ill in the room!"—is the woman's appeal. "Not till we've looked everywhere else," is the reply. "I'll say that much. I'll see through the cupboards in the room, though. *That* won't hurt him."

Little did either of them anticipate what met their eyes as the door opened. There on the couch, no longer on his back, but sitting up and gasping for clearer speech, which he seemed to have achieved in part, was the paralysis-stricken man. The left hand, powerless no longer, was still uncertain of its purpose, and wavered in its ill-directed motion; the right, needed to raise him from his pillow, grasped the level moulding of the couch-back. Its fingers still showed a better colour than those of its fellow, which trembled and closed and reopened, as though to make trial of their new-found power. His eyes were fixed on this hand rather than on his daughter or the stranger. His knees jerked against the light bondage of a close dressing-gown, and his right foot was striving to lift or help the other down to the floor. Probably life was slower to return to it than to the hand, as the blood returns soonest to the finger-tips after frost. Only the face was quite changed from its seeming of but ten minutes back. The voice choked and stammered still, but speech came in the end, breaking out with a shout-burst:—" Stop—stop—stop! "

" Easy so—easy so! " says the police-officer, as the woman gives way to a fit of hysterical crying, more the breaking-point of nerve-tension than either joy or pain. " Easy so, master!—easy does it. Don't you be frightened. Plenty of time and to spare! "

The old man gets his foot to the floor, and his daughter, under no impulse of reason—mere nerve-paroxysm—runs to his side crying out:—" No, dear father! No, dear father! Lie down—lie down! " She is trying to force him back to his pillow, while he chokes out something he finds it harder to say than " Stop—stop! " which still comes at intervals.

" I should make it easy for him, Miss Hawkins, if I was in your place. Let the old gentleman please himself." Thus the officer, whose sedateness of manner acts beneficially. She accepts the suggestion, standing back from her father with a stupid, bewildered gaze, between him and the exit to the roof. " Give him time," says Sub-Inspector Cardwell.

He takes the time, and his speech dies down. But he can move that hand better now—may make its action serve for speech. Slowly he raises it and points—points straight at his daughter. He wants her help—is that it? She thinks so, but when she acts on the impulse he repels her, feebly shouting out: " No—no—no! "

" Come out from between him and the clock, missis," says the officer, thinking he has caught a word right, and that a clock near the door is what the old man points at. " He thinks it's six o'clock."

But the word was not *six*. The daughter moves aside, and yet the finger points. "It's nowhere near six, father dear!" she says. "Not one o'clock yet!" But still the finger points. And now a wave of clearer articulation overcomes a sibilant that has been the worst enemy of speech, and leaves the tongue free. "Wix!" That's the word.

"Got it!" exclaims the officer, and the woman with a shriek falls insensible. He takes little notice of her, but whistles for his mate below—a peculiar whistle. It brings the man who was keeping watch in the lane. "Got him all right," says his principal. "Out here on the tiles. That's your meaning, I take it, Mr. Hawkins?" The old man nods repeatedly. "And he's took the key out with him and locked to the door. That's it, is it?" More nods, and then the officer mounts the short ladder and knocks hard upon the door. He speaks to the silence on the other side. "You've been seen, Mr. Wix. It's a pity to spoil a good lock. You've got the key. We can wait a bit. Don't hurry!"

Footsteps on the roof, and a shout from the garden below! He is seen now—no doubt of it—whatever he was before. What is that they are calling from the garden? "He's got a loose tile. Look out!"

"Don't give him a chance to aim with it," says Jacomb below to his chief on the ladder. Who replies:—"He's bound to get half a chance. Keep your eyes open!" A thing to be done, certainly, with that key sounding in the lock.

The officer Cardwell only waited to hear it turn to throw his full weight on the door, which opened outwards. He scarcely waited for the back-click to show that the door, which had no hasp or clutch beyond the key-service, was free on its hinges. Nevertheless, he was not so quick but that the man beyond was quicker, springing back sharp on the turn of his own hand. Cardwell stumbled as the door gave, unexpectedly easily, and nearly fell his length on the leads.

Jacomb, on the second rung of the step-ladder, feels the wind of a missile that all but touches his head. He does not look round to see what it strikes, but he hears a cry; man or woman, or both. In front of him is his principal, on his legs again, grasping the wrist of the right hand that threw the tile, while his own is on its owner's throat.

"All right—all right!" says Mr. Wix. "You can stow it now. I could have given you that tile under your left ear. But the right man's got the benefit. You may just as well keep the snitchers for when I'm down. There's no such * * * hurry." Nevertheless, the eyes of both officers are keen upon him as he, descends the ladder under sufferance.

On the floor below, beside the bed he lay on through so many weary years, lies Miss Julia's old father, stunned or dead. Her own insensibility has passed, but has left her in bewilderment, dizzy and confused, as she kneels over him and tries for a sign of life in vain. At the ladder-foot the officers have fitted their prisoner with handcuffs; and then Cardwell, leaving him, goes to lift the old man back to his couch. But first he calls from the window:—" Got him all right! Fetch the nearest doctor."

Through the short interval between this and Daverill's removal, words came from him which may bring the story home or explain it if events have not done so already. " The old * * * has got his allowance. *He* won't ask for no more. Who was he, to be meddling? You was old enough in all conscience, July-ar!" His pronunciation of her name has a hint of a sneer in it—a sneer at the woman he victimised, some time in the interval between his desertion of his wife and his final error of judgment—dabbling in burglary. She might have been spared insult; for whatever her other faults were, want of affection for her betrayer was not among them, or she would not have run the risks of concealing him from the police.

Her paralytic father's sudden reanimation under stress of excitement was, of course, an exceptionally well-marked instance of a phenomenon well enough known to pathologists. It had come within his power to avenge the wrong done to his daughter, and never forgiven by him. Whether the officers would have broken down the door, if he had not seized his opportunity, may be uncertain, but there can be no doubt that the operative cause of Daverill's capture was his recovery of vital force under the stimulus of excitement at the amazing chance offered him of bringing it about.

The affair made so little noise that only a very few Sunday loiterers witnessed what was visible of it in the lane, which was indeed little more than the unusual presence of two policemen. Then, after a surgeon had been found and had attended to the injured man, it leaked out that a malefactor had been apprehended at The Pigeons and taken away in the police-boat to the Station lower down the river.

That singular couple, Michael Ragstroar and his great-aunt, had got to the cherry-tart before a passing neighbour, looking in at their window, acquainted them what had happened. If after Michael come from the bake-'us with the meat, which kep' hot stood under its cover in the sun all of five minutes and no one any the worse, while the old lady boiled a potato—if Michael had not been preoccupied with a puppy in this interim, he might easy have seen the culprit took away in the boat. He regretted his loss; but his aunt, from whom we borrow a word now and then, pointed out to him that we must not expect everything in this world. Also the many blessings that had been vouchsafed to him by a Creator who had his best interests at heart. Had he not vouchsafed him a puppy?—on lease certainly; but he would find that puppy here next time he visited Hammersmith, possibly firmer in his gait and nothing like so round over the stomach. And there was the cherry-tart, and the crust had rose beautiful.

Michael got home very late, and was professionally engaged all the week with his father. He saw town, but nothing of his neighbours, returning always towards midnight intensely ready for bed. By the time he chanced across our friend Dave on the following Saturday, other scenes of London Life had obscured his memory of that interview at The Pigeons and its sequel. So, as it happened, Sapps Court heard nothing about either.

The death of Miss Hawkins's father, a month later, did not add a contemptible manslaughter to Thornton Daverill's black list of crimes. For the surgeon who attended him—while admitting to her privately that, of course, it was the blow on the temple that brought about the cause of death—denied that it was itself the cause; a nice distinction. But it seemed needless to add to the score of a criminal with enough to his credit to hang him twice over; especially when an Inquest could be avoided by accommodation with Medical Jurisprudence. So the surgeon, at the earnest request of the dead man's daughter, made out a certificate of death from something that sounded plausible, and might just as well have been cessation of life. It was nobody's business to criticize it, and nobody did.

CHAPTER XV

THE BEER AT THE KING'S ARMS. HOW UNCLE MO READ THE *STAR*, LIKE
A CHALDEAN, AND BROKE HIS SPECTACLES. HOW THE *STAR* TOLD
OF A CONVICT'S ESCAPE FROM A JUG. HOW AUNT M'RIAR OVERHEARD
THE NAME "DAVERILL," AND WAS QUITE UPSET-LIKE. HER DEGREES
AND DATES OF INFORMATION ABOUT THIS MAN AND HIS ANTECEDENTS.
UNCLE MO'S IGNORANCE ABOUT HERS. HOW SHE DID NOT GIVE THE
STAR TO MRS. BURR INTACT

THE unwelcome visitor who, in the phrase of Uncle Mo, had made
Sapps Court stink—a thing outside the experience of its inhabitants—bade fair to be forgotten altogether. Michael, the only
connecting link between the two, had all memory of the Hammersmith arrest quite knocked out of his head a few days later
by a greater incident—his father having been arrested and fined
for an assault on a competitor in business, with an empty sack.
It was entirely owing to the quality of the beer at the King's
Arms that Mr. Rackstraw lost his temper.

But Daverill's corruption of the Court's pure air was not destined to oblivion. It was revived by the merest accident; the merest, that is, up to that date. There have been many merer ones
since, unless the phrase has been incorrectly used in recent
literature.

One day in July, when Uncle Moses was enjoying his afternoon
pipe with his old friend Affability Bob, or Jerry Alibone, and reading one of the new penny papers—it was the one called the *Morning
Star,* now no more—he let his spectacles fall when polishing them;
and, rashly searching for them, broke both glasses past all redemption. He was much annoyed, seeing that he was in the middle
of a sensational account of the escape of a prisoner from Coldbath
Fields house of detention; a gaol commonly known the "The Jug."
It was a daring business, and Uncle Mo had just been at the full
of his enjoyment of it when the accident happened.

"Have you never another pair, Mo?" said Mr. Alibone. And
Uncle Mo called out to Aunt M'riar:—"M'riar!—just take a look
round and see for them old glasses upstairs. I've stood down on
mine, and as good as spiled 'em. Look alive!" For, you see,
he was all on end to know how this prisoner, who had been put in

irons for violence, and somehow got free and overpowered a gaoler who came alone into his cell, had contrived his final escape from the prison.

Mr. Alibone was always ready to deserve his name of Affability Bob. "Give me hold of the paper, Mo," said he. "Where was you? . . . Oh yes—here we are! . . . 'almost unparalleled audacity.' . . . I'll go on there." For Uncle Mo had read some aloud, and Mr. Alibone he wanted to know too, to say the truth. And he really was a lot better scollard than Mo—when it came to readin' out loud—and tackled "unparalleled" as if it was just nothing at all; it being the word that brought Moses up short; and, indeed, Aunt M'riar, whom we quote, had heard him wrestling with it through the door, and considered it responsible for the accident. Anyhow, Mr. Jerry was equal to it, and read the remainder of the paragraph so you could hear every word.

"What I don't make out," said Uncle Mo, "is why he didn't try the same game without getting the leg-irons on him. He hadn't any call to be violent—that I see—barring ill-temper."

"That was all part of the game, Mo. Don't you see the game? It was putting reliance on the irons led to this here warder making so free. You go to the Zoarlogical Gardens in the Regency Park, and see if the keeper likes walking into the den when the Bengal tiger's loose in it. These chaps get like that, and they have to get the clinkers on 'em."

"Don't quite take your idear, Jerry. Wrap it up new."

"Don't you see, old Mo? He shammed savage to get the irons on his legs, knowing how he might come by a file—which I don't, and it hasn't come out, that I see. Then he spends the inside o' the night getting through 'em, and rigs himself up like a picter, just so as if they was on. So the officer was took in, with him going on like a lamb. Then up he jumps and smashes his man's skull—makes no compliments about it, you see. Then he closes to the door and locks it to enjoy a little leisure. And then he changes their sootes of cloze across, and out he walks for change of air. And he's got it!"

Uncle Mo reflected and said:—"P'r'aps!" Then Aunt M'riar, who had hunted up the glasses without waking the children, reappeared, bringing them; and Uncle Mo found they wouldn't do, and only prevented his seeing anything at all. So he was bound to have a new pair and pay by the week. A cheap pair, that would see him out, come to threepence a week for three months.

The discovery of this painful fact threw the escaped prisoner into the shade, and the *Morning Star* would have been lost sight of—because it was only Monday's paper, after all!—unless Aunt M'riar she'd put it by for upstairs to have their turn of it, and Mrs. Burr could always read some aloud to Mrs. Prichard, failing studious energy on the part of the old lady. She reproduced it in compliance with the current of events.

For Uncle Moses, settling down to a fresh pipe after supper, said to his friend, similarly occupied:—"What, now, was the name of that charackter—him as got out at the Jug?"

"Something like Mackerel," said Mr. Alibone.

"Wrong you are, for once, Jerry! 'Twarn't no more Mackerel than it was Camberwell."

Said Mr. Jerry:—"Take an even tizzy on it, Mo?" He twisted the paper about to recover the paragraph, and found it. "Here we are! 'Ralph Daverill, *alias* Thornton, *alias* Wix, *alias!*' . . ."

"Never mind his ale-houses, Jerry. That's the name I'm consarned with—Daverill . . . What's the matter with M'riar?"

Uncle Mo had not finished his sentence owing to an interruption. For Aunt M'riar, replacing some table-gear she was shifting, had sat down suddenly on the nearest chair.

"Never you mind me, you two. Just you go on talking." So said Aunt M'riar. Only she looked that scared it might have been a ghost. So Mrs. Burr said after, who came in that very minute from a prolonged trying on.

"Take a little something, M'riar," said Uncle Mo. He got up and went to the cupboard close at hand, to get the something, which would almost certainly have taken the form of brandy. But Aunt M'riar she said never mind *her!*—she would be all right in a minute. And in a metaphorical minute she pulled herself together, and went on clearing off the supper-table. Suggestions of remedies or assistance seemed alike distasteful to her, whether from Mrs. Burr or the two men, and there was no doubt she was in earnest in preferring to be left to herself. So Mrs. Burr she went up to her own supper, with thanks in advance for the newspaper when quite done with, according to the previous intention of Aunt M'riar.

The two smokers picked life up at the point of interruption, while Aunt M'riar made a finish of her operations in the kitchen. Uncle Mo said:—"Good job for you I didn't take your wager, Jerry. Camberwell isn't in it. Mackerel goes near enough to landing—as near as Davenant, which is what young Carrots called him."

This was the case—for Michael, though he had been silent at the time about the Inquest, had been unable to resist the temptation to correct Uncle Moses when the old boy asked: "*Wot* did he say was the blooming name of the party he was after—Daverill —Daffodil?" His answer was:—"No it warn't! Davenant was what *he* said." His acumen had gone the length of perceiving in the stranger's name a resemblance to the version of it heard more plainly in the Court at Hammersmith. This correction had gratified and augmented his secret sense of importance, without leading to any inquiries. Uncle Mo accepted Davenant as more intrinsically probable than Daffodil or Daverill, and forgot both names promptly. For a subsequent mention of him as Devilskin, when he referred to the incident later in the day, can scarcely be set down to a recollection of the name. It was quite as much an appreciation of the owner.

"But what's your consarn with any of 'em, Mo?" said Mr. Jerry.

Uncle Moses took his pipe out of his mouth to say, almost oratorically:—"Don't you *re*-member, Jerry, me telling you—Sunday six weeks it was—about a loafing wagabond who came into this Court to hunt up a widder named Daverill or Daffodil, or some such a name?" Uncle Moses paused a moment. A plate had fallen in the kitchen. Nothing was broke, Aunt M'riar testified, and closed the door. Uncle Mo continued:—"I told you Davenant, because of young Radishes. But I'll pound it I was right and he was wrong. Don't you call to mind, Jeremiah?" For Uncle Mo often addressed his friend thus, for a greater impressiveness. Jeremiah recalled the incident on reflection. "There you are, you see," continued Uncle Mo. "Now you bear in mind what I tell you, sir;"—this mode of address was also to gain force—"He's him! That man's *him*—the very identical beggar! And this widder woman he was for hunting up, she's his mother or his aunt."

"Or his sister—no!—sister-in-law."

"Not if she's a widder's usual age, Jerry." Uncle Mo always figured to himself sisters, and even sisters-in-law, as essentially short of middle life. You may remember also his peculiar view that married twins could not survive their husbands.

"What sort of man did you make him out to be, Mo?"

"A bad sort in a turn-up with no rules. Might be handy with a knife on occasion. Foxy sort of wiper!"

"Not your sort, Mo?"

"Too much ill-will about him. Some of the Fancy may have run into bad feeling in my time, but mostly when they shook hands inside the ropes they meant it. How's yourself, M'riar?"

Here Aunt M'riar came in after washing up, having apparently overheard none of the conversation.

"I'm nicely, Mo, thankee! Have you done with the paper, Mr. Alibone? . . . Thanks—I'll give it to 'em upstairs. . . . Oh yes! I'm to rights. It was nothing but a swimming in the head! Goodnight!" And off went Aunt M'riar, leaving the friends to begin and end about two more pipes; to talk over bygones of the Ring and the Turf, and to part after midnight.

Observe, please, that until Mr. Jerry read aloud from the *Star* Mr. Wix's *aliases,* Aunt M'riar had had no report of this escaped convict, except under the name of Davenant; and, indeed, very little under that, because Uncle Mo, in narrating to her the man's visit to Sapps Court, though he gave the name of his inquiry as Davenant, spoke of the man himself almost exclusively as Devilskin. And really she had paid very little attention to the story, or the names given. At the time of the man's appearance in the Court nothing transpired to make her associate him with any past experience of her own. He was talked about at dinner on that Sunday certainly; but then, consider the responsibilities of the carving and distribution of that shoulder of mutton.

Aunt M'riar did not give the newspaper to Mrs. Burr, to read to Mrs. Prichard, till next day. Perhaps it was too late, at near eleven o'clock. When she did, it was with a reservation. Said she to Mrs. Burr:—"You won't mind losing the bit I cut out, just to keep for the address?—the cheapest shoes I ever did!—and an easy walk just out of Oxford Street." She added that Dave was very badly off in this respect. But she said nothing about what was on the other side of the shoe-shop advertisement. Was she bound to do so? Surely one side of a newspaper-cutting justifies the scissors. If Aunt M'riar could want one side, ever so little, was she under any obligation to know anything about the other side?

Anyhow, the result was that old Mrs. Prichard lost this opportunity of knowing that her son was at large. And even if the paragraph had not been removed, its small type might have kept her old eyes at bay. Indeed, Mrs. Burr's testimony went to show that the old lady's inspection of the paper scarcely amounted to solid perusal. Said she, accepting the *Star* from Aunt M'riar next morning, apropos of the withdrawn paragraph: "That won't be any denial to Mrs. Prichard, ma'am. There's a-many always wants to read the bit that's tore off, showin' a contradictious temper like. But she ain't that sort, being more by way of looking at the paper than studying of its contents." Mrs. Burr then preached a short homily on the waste of time involved in a close analysis of the daily press, such as would enable the reader to discriminate between each day's issue and the next. For her part the news ran similar one day with another, without, however, blunting her interest in human affairs. She imputed an analogous attitude of mind to old Mrs. Prichard, the easier of maintenance that the old lady's failing sight left more interpretations of the text open to her imagination.

Mrs. Burr, moreover, went on to say that Mrs. Prichard had been that upset by hearing about the builders, that she wasn't herself. This odd result could not but interfere with the reading of even the lightest literature. Its cause calls for explanation. Circumstances had arisen which, had they occurred in the winter-time, would have been a serious embarrassment to the attic tenants in Sapps Court. As it chanced, the weather was warm and dry; otherwise old Mrs. Prichard and Mrs. Burr would just have had to turn out, to allow the builder in, to attend to the front wall. For there was no doubt that it was bulging and ought to have been seen to, æons ago. And it was some days since the landlord's attention had been called, and Bartletts the builders had waked all the dwellers in Sapps Court who still slept at six o'clock, by taking out a half a brick or two to make a bearing for as many putlogs—pronounced pudlocks—as were needed for a little bit of scaffold. For there was more than you could do off a ladder, if you was God A'mighty Himself. Thus Mr. Bartlett, and Aunt M'riar condemned his impiety freely. Before the children! Closely examined, his speech was reverential, and an acknowledgment of the powers of the Constructor of the Universe as against the octave-stretch forlorn of our limitations. But it was Anthropomorphism, no doubt.

CHAPTER XVI

OF LONDON BUILDERS, AND THEIR GREAT SKILL. OF THE HUMILIATING POSITION OF A SHAMEFACED BAT. HOW MR. BARTLETT MADE ALL GOOD. A PEEP INTO MRS. PRICHARD'S MIND, LEFT ALONE WITH HER PAST. MR. BARTLETT'S TRUCK, AND DAVE WARDLE'S ANNEXATION OF IT. MRS. TAPPING'S IMPRESSIONABILITY. AN ITALIAN MUSICIAN'S MONKEY. A CLEAN FINISH. THE BULL AND THE DUCKPOND. OF MRS. PRICHARD'S JEALOUSY OF MRS. MARROWBONE. CANON LAW. HOW DAVE DESCRIBED HER RIVAL. HER SISTER PHOEBE. BUT—WHY DAVERILL, OF ALL NAMES IN THE WORLD? FOURPENNYWORTH OF CRUMPETS

IF you have ever given attention to buildings in the course of erection in London, you must have been struck with their marvellous stability. The mere fact that they should remain standing for five minutes after the removal of the scaffold must have seemed to you to reflect credit on the skill of the builder; but that they should do so for a lifetime—even for a century!—a thing absolutely incredible. Especially you must have been impressed by the nine-inch wall, in which every other course at least consists of bats and closures. You will have marvelled that so large a percentage of bricks can appear to have been delivered broken; but this you would have been able to account for had you watched the builder at work, noting his vicious practice of halving a sound brick whenever he wants a bat. It is an instinct, deep-rooted in bricklayers, against which unprofessional remonstrance is useless —an instinct that he fights against with difficulty whenever popular prejudice calls for full bricks on the face. So when the wall is not to be rendered in compo or plaster, he just shoves a few in, on the courses of stretchers, leaving every course of headers to a lifetime of effrontery. What does it matter to him? But it must be most painful to a conscientious bat to be taken for a full brick by every passer-by, and to be unable to contradict it.

Now the real reason why the top wall of No. 7, Sapps Court was bulging was one that never could surprise anyone conversant to this extent with nine-inch walls. For there is a weakest point in every such wall, where the plate is laid to receive the joists, or jystes; which may be pronounced either way, but should always be nine-inch. For if they are six-inch you have to shove 'em in nearer together, and that weakens your wall, put it how you may. You work it out and see if it don't come out so. So said the builder, Mr. Bartlett, at No. 7, Sapps Court, when having laid bare the ends of the top-floor joists in Mrs. Prichard's front attic it turned out just like he said it would—six-inch jystes with no hold to 'em, and onto that all perished at the ends! Why ever they couldn't go to a new floor when they done the new roof Mr. Bartlett could not conceive. They had not, and what was worse they had carried up the wall on the top of the old brickwork, adding to the dead weight; and it only fit to pull down, as you might say.

However, the weather was fine and warm all the time Mr. Bartlett rebuilt two foot of wall by sections; which he did careful, a bit at a time. And all along, till they took away the scaffolding and made good them two or three pudlock-holes off of a ladder, they was no annoyance at all to Mrs. Prichard, nor yet to Mrs. Burr, excepting a little of that sort of flaviour that goes with old brickwork, and a little of another that comes with new, and a bit of plasterers' work inside to make good. Testimony was current in and about the house to this effect, and may be given broadly in the terms in which it reached Uncle Moses. His comment was that the building trade was a bad lot, mostly; you had only to take your eye off it half a minute, and it was round at the nearest bar trying the four-half. Mr. Jerry's experience had been the same.

Mrs. Burr was out all day, most of the time; so it didn't matter to her. But it was another thing for the old woman, sometimes alone for hours together; alone with her past. At such times her sleeping or waking dreams mixed with the talk of the bricklayers outside, or the sound of a piano from one of the superior houses that back-wall screened the Court from—though they had no call to give theirselves airs that the Court could see—a piano on which talent was playing scales with both hands, but which wanted tuning. Old Mrs. Prichard was not sensitive about a little discord now and again. As she sat there alone, knitting worsteds or dozing, it brought back old times to her, before her troubles began. She and her sister could both play easy tunes, such as the " Harmonious Blacksmith " and the " Evening Hymn," on the square piano she still remembered so well at the Mill. And this modern piano— heard through open windows in the warm summer air, and mixing with the indistinguishable sounds of distant traffic—had something of the effect of that instrument of seventy years ago, breaking the steady monotone of rushing waters under the wheel that scarcely ever paused, except on Sunday. What had become of the old square piano she and Phœbe learned to play scales on? What becomes of all the old furnishings of the rooms of our childhood? Did any man ever identify the bed he slept in, the table he ate at, half a century ago, in the chance-medley of second-hand—third-hand—furniture his father's insolvency or his own consigned it to? Would she know the old square piano again now, with all its resonances dead—a poor, faint jargon only in some few scattered wires, far apart? Yes—she would know it among a hundred, by the inlaid bay-leaves on the lid that you could lift up to look inside. But that was accounted lawless, and forbidden by authority.

She dreamed herself back into the old time, and could see it all. The sound of the piano became mixed, as she sat half dozing, with the smell of the lilies of the valley which—according to a pleasing fiction of Dolly Wardle—that little person's doll had brought upstairs for her, keeping wide awake until she see 'em safe on the table in a mug. But the sound and the smell were of the essence of the mill, and were sweet to the old heart that was dying slowly down—would soon die outright. Both merged in a real dream with her sister's voice in it, saying inexplicably: "In the pocket of your shot silk, dear." Then she woke with a start, sorry to lose the dream; specially annoyed that she had not heard what the carman—outside with her father—had begun to say about the thing Phœbe was speaking of. She forgot what that was, and it was very stupid of her.

That was Mr. Bartlett outside, laying bricks; not the carman at all. What was that he was saying?

"B'longed to a Punch's show, he did. Couldn't stand it no longer, he couldn't. The tune it got on his narves, it did! If it hadn't 'a been for a sort o' reel ease he got takin' of it quick and slow—like the Hoarperer—he'd have gave in afore; so there was no pretence. It's all werry fine to say temp'ry insanity, but I tell you it's the contrairy when a beggar comes to his senses and drownds hisself. Wot'd the Pope do if he had to play the same tune over and over and over and over? . . . Mortar, John! And 'and me up a nice clean cutter. That's your quorlity, my son." And the Court rang musically to the destruction of a good brick.

John—who was only Mr. Bartlett's son for purposes of rhetoric —slapped his cold unwholesome mortar-pudding with a spade; and ceded an instalment, presumably. Then his voice came: "Wot didn't he start on a new toon for, for a wariation?"

Mr. Bartlett was doing something very nice and exact with the three-quarter he had just evolved, so his reply came in fragments as from a mind preoccupied. "Tried it on he had—that game—

more times than once. . . . But the boys they took it up, and
aimed stones. . . . And the public kep' its money in its pocket
—not to encourage noo Frenchified notions—not like when they
was a boy. So the poor beggar had to jump in off of the end of
Southend Pier, and go out with the tide." He added, as essential,
that Southend Pier was better than two mile long; so there was
water to drownd a man when the tide was in.

The attention of very old people may be caught by a familiar
word, though such talk as this ripples by unheeded. The sad tale
of the Punch's showman—the exoteric one, evidently—roused no
response in the mind of old Mrs. Prichard, until it ended with
the tragedy at Southend. The name brought back that terrible
early experience of the sailing of the convict-ship—of her despairing effort at a farewell to be somehow heard or seen by the man
whom she almost thought of as in a grave, buried alive! She
was back again in the boat in the Medway, keeping the black spot
ahead in view—the accursed galley that was bearing away her
life, her very life; the man no sin could change from what he was
to her; the treasure of her being. She could hear again the monotonous beat of her rowers' pair of oars, ill-matched against the
four sweeps of the convicts, ever gaining—gaining. . . .

Surely she would be too late for that last chance, that seemed
to her the one thing left to live for. And then the upspringing
of that blessed breeze off the land that saved it for her. She could
recall her terror lest the flagging of their speed for the hoisting of
the sail should undo them; the reassuring voice of a hopeful boat-
man—" You be easy, missis; we'll catch 'em up! "—the less confident one of his mate—" Have a try at it, anyhow! " Then her joy
when the sail filled and the plashing of her way spoke Hope beneath her bulwark as she caught the wind. Then her dread that the
Devil's craft ahead would make sail too, and overreach them after
all, and the blessing in her heart for her hopeful oarsman, whose
view was that the officer in charge would not spare his convicts
any work he could inflict. " He'll see to it they arn their breaf-
fastis, missis. He ain't going to unlock their wristis off of the
oars for to catch a ha'porth o' blow. You may put your money
on him for that." And then the sweet ship upon the water, and
her last sight of the man she loved as he was dragged aboard into
the Hell within—scarcely a man now—only " 213 M " !

Then the long hours that followed, there in the open boat beneath the sun, whose setting found her still gazing in her dumb
despair on what was to be his floating home for months. Such a
home! Scraps of her own men's talk were with her still—the

names of passing craft—the discontent in the fleet—the names of
landmarks on either coast. Among these Southend—the word that
caught her ear and set her a-thinking. But there was no pier two
miles long there then. She was sure of that.

What was it Mr. Bartlett was talking about now? A grievance
this time! But grievances are the breath of life to the Human
Race. The source of this one seemed to be Sapps proprietor, who
was responsible for the restrictions on Mr. Bartlett's enthusiasm,
which might else have pulled the house down and rebuilt it. "Wot
couldn't he do like I told him for?"—thus ran the indictment—
"Goard A'mighty don't know, nor yet anybody else! Why—*he*
don't know, hisself! I says to him, I says, just you clear out them
lodgers, I says, and give me the run of the premises, I says, and
it shan't cost you a fi'-pun note more in the end, I says. Then
if he don't go and tie me down to a price for to make good front
wall and all dy-lapidations. And onlest he says wot he means by
good, who's to know? . . . Mortar, John!" John supplied mortar
with a slamp—a sound like the fall of a pasty Titan on loose
boards. The grievance was resumed, but with a consolation. "Got
'im there, accordin' as I think of it! Wot's his idear of *good?*—
that's wot *I* want to know. Things is as you see 'em . . ." Mr.
Bartlett would have said the *esse* of things was *percipi,* had he
been a Philosopher, and would have felt as if he knew something.
Not being one, he subsided—with truisms—into silence, content
with the weakness of Sapps owner's entrenchments.

Mr. Bartlett completed his contract, according to his interpretation of the word "good"; and it seems to have passed muster,
and been settled for on the nail. Which meant, in this case, as
soon as a surveyor had condemned it on inspection, and accepted
a guinea from Mr. Bartlett to overlook its shortcomings; two operations which, taken jointly, constituted a survey, and were paid
for on another nail later. The new bit of brickwork didn't look
any so bad, to the eye of impartiality, now it was pointed up; only
it would have looked a lot better—mind you!—if Mr. Bartlett had
been allowed to do a bit more pointing up on the surrounding
brickwork afore he struck his scaffold. But Sapps landlord was
a narrer-minded party—a Conservative party—who wouldn't go
to a sixpence more than he was drove, though an economy in the
long-run. The remarks of the Court and its friends are embodied
in these statements, made after Mr. Bartlett had got his traps
away on a truck, which couldn't come down the Court by reason
of the jam. It was, however, a source of satisfaction to Dave
Wardle, whose friends climbed into it while he sat on the handle,

outweighing him and lifting him into the air. Only, of course, this joy lasted no longer than till they started loading of it up.

It lasted long enough, for all that, to give quite a turn to Mrs. Tapping, whom you may remember as a witness of Dave's accident —the bad one—nine months ago. Ever since then—if Mrs. Riley, to whom she addressed her remarks, would believe her—Mrs. Tapping's heart had been in her mouth whenever she had lighted her eye on young children a-playing in the gutters. As children were plentiful, and preferred playing wherever the chances of being run over seemed greatest, this must have been a tax on Mrs. Tapping's constitution. She had, however, borne up wonderfully, showing no sign of loss of flesh; nor could her flowing hair have been thinned —to judge by the tubular curls that flanked her brows, which were neither blinkers nor cornucopias precisely; but which, opened like a scroll, would have resembled the one; and, spirally prolonged, the other. It was the careful culture of these which distracted the nose of Mrs. Tapping's *monde,* preoccupied by a flavour of chandled tallow, to a halo of pomatum. Mrs. Riley was also unchanged; she, however, had no alarming cardiac symptoms to record.

But as to that turn Dave Wardle giv' Mrs. Tapping. It really sent your flesh through your bones, all on edge like, to see a child fly up in the air like that. So she testified, embellishing her other physiological experience with a new horror unknown to Pathologists. Mrs. Riley, less impressionable, kept an even mind in view of the natural invulnerability of childhood and the special guardianship of Divine Omnipotence. If these two between them could not secure small boys of seven or eight from disaster, what could? The unbiassed observer—if he had been passing at the time—might have thought that Dave's chubby but vigorous handgrip and his legs curled tight round the truck-handle were the immediate and visible reasons why he was not shot across the truck into space. Anyhow, he held on quite tight, shouting loudly the next item of the programme—" Now all the other boys to jump out when oy comes to free. One, two, *free!* " In view of the risk of broken bones the other boys were prompt, and Dave came down triumphantly. Mrs. Riley's confidence had been well founded.

" Ye'll always be too thinder-harruted about the young spalpeens, me dyurr," she said. " Thrust them to kape their skins safe! Was not me son Phalim all as bad or wurruss. And now to say his family of childher! "

Mrs. Tapping perceived her opportunity, and jumped at it. " That is the truth, ma'am, what you say, and calls to mind the very words my poor husband used frequent. So frequent, you might say, that as often as not they was never out of his mouth. ' Mary Ann Tapping, you are too tender-hearted for to carry on at all; bein', as we are, subjick.' And I says back to him : ' Tapping '—I says—' no more than my duty as a Christian woman should. Read your Bible and you will find,' I says. And Tapping he would say :—' Right you are, Mary Ann, and viewin' all things as a Gospel dispensation. But what I look at, Mary Ann '—he says—' is the effect on your system. You are that 'igh-strung and delicate organized that what is no account to an 'arder fibre tells. So bear in mind what I say, Mary Ann Tapping '—he says—' and crost across the way like the Good Samaritan, keepin' in view that nowadays whatever we are we are no longer Heathens, and cases receive attention from properly constitooted Authorities, or are took in at the Infirmary.' Referring, Mrs. Riley, ma'am, to an Italian organ-boy bit by his own monkey, which though small was vicious, and open to suspicion of poison. . . .'' Mrs. Tapping dwelt upon her past experience and her meritorious attitude in trying circumstances, for some time. As, in this instance, she had offered refreshment to the victim, which had been requisitioned by his monkey, who escaped and gave way to his appetite on the top of a street-lamp, but was recaptured when the lamplighter came with his ladder.

" Shure there'll be nothing lift of the barrow soon barring the bare fragmints of it," said Mrs. Riley, who had been giving more attention to the boys and the truck than to the Italian and the monkey. And really the repetition of the pleasing performance with the handle pointed to gradual disintegration of Mr. Bartlett's property.

However, salvage was at hand. A herald òf Mr. Bartlett himself, or of his representatives, protruded slowly from Sapps archway, announcing that his scaffold-poles were going back to the sphere from which they had emanated on hire. It came slowly, and gave a margin for a stampede of Dave and his accomplices, leaving the truck very much aslant with the handle in the air; whereas we all know that a respectable hand-barrer, that has trusted its owner out of sight, awaits his return with the quiet confidence of horizontality; or at least with the handle on the ground. Mr. Bartlett's comment was that nowadays it warn't safe to take one's eyes off of anything for half-a-quarter of a minute, and there would have to be something done about it. He who analyses this remark may find it hard to account for its having been so intelligible at first hearing.

But Mrs. Tapping and Mrs. Riley—who were present—were not analytical, and when Mr. Bartlett inquired suspiciously if any of them boys belonged to either of you ladies, one of the latter replied with a counter-inquiry:—"What harrum have the young boys done ye, thin, misther? Shure it's been a playzin' little enjoyment forr thim afther school-hours!" Which revealed the worst part of Mr. Bartlett's character and his satellite John's, a sullen spirit of revenge, more marked perhaps in the man than in the master; for while the former merely referred to the fact that he would know them again if he saw them, and would then give them something to recollect him by, the latter said he would half-skin some of 'em alive if he could just lay hands on 'em. But the subject dropped, and Mr. Bartlett loaded up his truck and departed. And was presently in collision with the authorities for leaving it standing outside the Wheatsheaf, while he and John consumed a half-a-pint in at the bar.

When the coast was quite clear, the offenders felt their way back, not disguising their satisfaction at their transgression. Mrs. Riley seemed to think that she ought to express the feeling the Bench would have had, had it been present. For she said: " You'll be laying yourselves open to pinalties, me boys, if ye don't kape your hands off other payple's thrucks, and things that don't consurrun ye. So lave thim be, and attind to your schooling, till you're riddy for bid." Dave's blue eyes dwelt doubtfully on the speaker, expressing their owner's uncertainty whether she was in earnest or not. Indeed, her sympathy with the offenders disqualified her for judicial impressiveness. Anyhow, Dave remained unimpressed, to judge by his voice as he vanished down the Court to narrate this pleasant experience to Uncle Moses. It was on Saturday afternoon that this took place. Have you ever noticed the strange fatality which winds up all building jobs on Saturday? Only not *this* Saturday—always next Saturday. It is called by some " making a clean finish."

Old Mrs. Prichard lent herself to the fiction that she would rejoice when the builders had made this clean finish. But she only did so to meet expectation half-way. She had no such eagerness for a quiet Sunday as was imputed to her. Very old people, with hearing at a low ebb, are often like this. The old lady during the ten days Mr. Bartlett had contrived to extend his job over— for his contract left all question of extras open—had become accustomed to the sound of the men outside, and was sorry when they died away in the distance, after breeding dissension with poles in the middle distance; that is to say, the Court below. She had felt alive to the proximity of human creatures; for Mr. Bartlett and John still came under that designation, though builders by trade. If it had not been Saturday, with a prospect of Dave and Dolly Wardle when they had done their dinners, she would have had no alleviation in view, and would have had to divide the time between knitting and dozing till Mrs. Burr came in—as she might or might not—and tea eventuated: the vital moment of her day.

However, this was Saturday, and Dave and Dolly came up in full force as the afternoon mellowed; and Aunt M'riar accompanied them, and Mrs. Burr she got back early off her job, and there was fourpennyworth of crumpets. Only that was three-quarters of an hour later.

But Dave was eloquent about his adventure with the truck, judging the old lady of over eighty quite a fit and qualified person to sympathize with the raptures of sitting on a handle, and being jerked violently into the air by a counterpoise of confederates. And no doubt she was; but not to the extent imputed to her by Dave, of a great sense of privation from inability to go through the experience herself. Nevertheless there was that in his blue eyes, and the disjointed rapidity of his exposition of his own satisfaction, that could bridge for her the gulf of two-thirds of a century between the sad old *now*—the vanishing time—and the merry *then* of a growing life, and all the wonder of the things to be. The dim illumination of her smile spread a little to her eyes as she made believe to enter into the glorious details of the exploit; though indeed she was far from clear about many of them. And as for Dave, no suspicion crossed his mind that the old lady's professions of regret were feigned. He condemned Aunt M'riar's attitude, as that of an interloper between two kindred souls.

"There, child, that'll do for about Mr. Bartlett's truct." So the good woman had said, showing her lack of *geist*—her Philistinism. "Now you go and play at The Hospital with Dolly, and don't make no more noise than you can help." This referred to a game very popular with the children since Dave's experience as a patient. It promised soon to be the only record of his injuries, as witness his gymnastics of this morning.

But he was getting to be such a big boy now—seven, last birthday—that playing at games was becoming a mere concession to Dolly's tender youth. Old Mrs. Prichard's thin soprano had an appeal to this effect in it—on Dave's behalf—as she said: "Oh, but the dear child may tell me, please, all about the truck and some more things, too, before he goes to play with Dolly. He has always such a many things to tell, has this little man! Hasn't he now, Mrs. Wardle?"

Aunt M'riar—good woman as she was—had a vice. She always would improve occasions. This time she must needs say:—"There, Davy, now! Hear what Mrs. Prichard says—so kind! You tell Mrs. Prichard all about Mrs. Marrowbone and the bull in the duckpond. You tell her!"

Dave, with absolute belief in the boon he was conferring on his venerable hearer, started at once on a complicated statement, as one who accepted the instruction in the spirit in which it was given. But first he had to correct a misapprehension. "The bool wasn't in the duckpong. The bool was in Farmer Jones's field, and the field was in the duckpong on the other side. And the dusk was in the pong where there wasn't no green." Evidently an oasis of black juice in the weed, which ducks enjoy. Dave thought no explanation necessary, and went on:—"Then Farmer Jones he was a horseback, and he rodid acrost the field, he did. And he undooed the gate with his whip to go froo, and it stumbled and let the bool froo, and Farmer Jones he rodid off to get the boy that understoodid the bool. He fetched him back behind his saddle, he did. And then the boy he got the bool's nose under control, and leaded him back easy, and they shet to the gate." One or two words—"control," for instance—treasured as essential and conscientiously repeated, gave Dave some trouble; but he got through them triumphantly.

"Is that all the story, Dave?" said Mrs. Prichard, who was affecting deep interest; although it was by now painfully evident that Dave had involved himself in a narrative without much plot. He nodded decisively to convey that it was substantially complete, but added to round it off:—"Mr. Marrowbone the Smith from Crincham he come next day and mended up the gate, only the bool he was tied to a post, and the boy whistled him a tune, or he would have tostid Mr. Marrowbone the Smith."

Said Aunt M'riar irrelevantly:—"What was the tune he whistled, Dave? You tell Mrs. Prichard what tune it was he whistled!" To which Dave answered with reserve:—"A long tune." Probably the whistler's stock was limited, and he repeated the piece, whatever it was, *da capo ad libitum*. This legend—the thin plot of Dave's story—will not strike some who have the misfortune to own bulls as strange. In some parts of the country boys are always requisitioned to attend on bulls, who especially hate men, perhaps resenting their monopoly of the term *manhood*.

This conversation would scarcely have called for record but for what it led to.

Old Mrs. Prichard, like Aunt M'riar, had a vice. It was jealousy. Her eighty years' experience of a bitter world had left her—for all that she would sit quiet for hours and say never a word—still longing for the music of the tide that had gone out for her for ever. The love of this little man—which had not yet learned its value, and was at the service of age and youth alike—was to her even as a return of the sea-waves to some unhappy mollusc left stranded to dry at leisure in the sun. But her heart was in a certain sense athirst for the monopoly of his blue eyes. She did not grudge him to any legitimate claimant—to Uncle Mo or to Aunt M'riar, nor even to Mrs. Burr; though that good woman scarcely challenged jealousy. Indeed, Mrs. Burr regarded Dave and Dolly as mere cake-consumers—a public hungering for sweet-stuffs, and only to be bought off by occasional concessions. It was otherwise with unknown objects of Dave's affection, whose claims on him resembled Mrs. Prichard's own. Especially the old grand-mother at the Convalescent Home, or whatever it was, where the child had recovered from his terrible accident. She grudged old Mrs. Marrowbone her place in Dave's affections, and naturally lost no opportunity of probing into and analysing them.

Said the old lady to Dave, when the bull was disposed of: "Was Mr. Marrowbone the Smith old Mrs. Marrowbone's grandson?" Dave shook his head rather solemnly and regretfully. It is always pleasanter to say *yes* than *no;* but in this case Truth was com-pulsory. "He wasn't *anyfink* of Granny Marrowbone's. No, he wasn't!" said he, and continued shaking his head to rub the fact in.

"Now you're making of it up, Dave," said Aunt M'riar. "You be a good little boy, and say Mr. Marrowbone the Smith was old Mrs. Marrowbone's grandson. Because you know he was—now don't you, Davy? You tell Mrs. Prichard he was old Mrs. Mar-rowbone's grandson!" Dave, however, shook his head obdurately. No concession!

"Perhaps he was her son," said Mrs. Prichard. But this sur-mise only prolonged the headshake; which promised to become chronic, to pause only when some ground of agreement could be discovered.

"The child don't above half know what he's talking about, not to say *know!*" Thus Aunt M'riar in a semi-aside to the old lady. It was gratuitous insult to add:—"He don't reely know what's a grandson, ma'am."

Dave's blue eyes flashed indignation. "Yorse I *does* know!" cried he, loud enough to lay himself open to remonstrance. He continued under due restraint:—" I'm going to be old Mrs. Marrowbone's grangson." He then remembered that the treaty was conditional, and added a proviso:—" So long as I'm a good boy!"

"Won't you be my grandson, too, Davy darling?" said old Mrs. Prichard. And, if you can conceive it, there was pain in her voice —real pain—as well as the treble of old age. She was jealous, you see; jealous of this old Mrs. Marrowbone, who seemed to come between her and her little new-found waterspring in the desert.

But Dave was embarrassed, and she took his embarrassment for reluctance to grant her the same status as old Mrs. Marrowbone. It was nothing of the sort. It was merely his doubt whether such an arrangement would be permissible under canon law. It was bigamy, however much you chose to prevaricate. The old lady's appealing voice racked Dave's feelings. " I carn't!" he exclaimed, harrowed. " I've spromussed to be Mrs. Marrowbone's grangson— I have." And thereupon old Mrs. Prichard, perceiving that he was really distressed, hastened to set his mind at ease. Of course he couldn't be her grandson, if he was already Mrs. Marrowbone's. She overlooked or ignored the possible compromise offered by the fact that two grandmothers are the common lot of all mankind. But it would be unjust—this was clear to her—that Dave should suffer in any way from her jealous disposition. So she put her little grievance away in her inmost heart—where indeed there was scarcely room for it, so preoccupied had the places been —and then, as an active step towards forgetting it, went on to talk to Dave about old Mrs. Marrowbone, although she was not Mr. Marrowbone the Smith's grandmother.

" Tell us, Dave dear, about old Mrs. Marrowbone. Is she very old? Is she as old as me?" To which Aunt M'riar as a sort of Greek chorus added:—" There, Davy, now, you be a good boy, and tell how old Mrs. Marrowbone is."

Dave considered. " She's not the soyme oyge," said he. " She can walk to chutch and back, Sunday morning." But this was a judgment from physical vigour, possibly a fallible guide. Dave, being prompted, attempted description. Old Mrs. Marrowbone's hair was the only point he could seize on. A cat, asleep on the hearthrug, supplied a standard of comparison. " Granny Marrowbone's head's the colour of this," said Dave, with decision, selecting a pale grey stripe. And Widow Thrale's was like that— one with a deeper tone of brown, with scarcely any perceptible grey.

"And which on Pussy is most like mine, Dave?" said Mrs. Prichard. There was no hesitation in the answer to this. It was "that sort";—that is, the colour of Pussy's stomach, unequivocal white. And which did Dave like best—an unfair question which deserved and got a Parliamentary answer. "All free," said Dave.

But this was merely colour of hair, a superficial distinction. How about Granny Marrowbone's nose. "It's the soyme soyze," was the verdict, given without hesitation. What colour were her eyes? "Soyme as yours." But Dave was destined to incur public censure—Aunt M'riar representing the public—for a private adventure into description. "She's more teef than you," said he candidly.

"Well, now, I do declare if ever any little boy was so rude! I never did! Whatever your Uncle Moses would say if he was told, I can't think." Thus Aunt M'riar. But her attitude was artificial, for appearance sake, and she knew perfectly well that Uncle Moses would only laugh and encourage the boy. The culprit did not seem impressed, though ready to make concessions. Yet he did not really better matters by saying:—"She's got *some* teef, she has"; leaving it to be inferred that old Mrs. Prichard had none, which was very nearly true. The old lady did not seem the least hurt. Nor was she hurt even when Dave—seeking merely to supply accurate detail—added, in connection with the old hand that wandered caressingly over his locks and brows:—"Her hands is thicker than yours is, a lot!"

"I often think, Mrs. Wardle," said she, taking no advantage of the new topic offered, "what we might be spared if only our teeth was less untrustworthy. Mine stood me out till over fifty, and since then they've been going—going. Never was two such rows of teeth as I took with me to the Colony. Over fifty years ago, Mrs. Wardle!"

"To think of that!" said Aunt M'riar. It was the time—not the teeth—that seemed so wonderful. Naturally old Mrs. Prichard's teeth went with her. But fifty years! And their owner quite bright still, when once she got talking.

She was more talkative than usual this afternoon, and continued: —"No, I do not believe, Mrs. Wardle, there was ever a girl with suchlike teeth as mine were then." And then this memory brought back its companion memory of the long past, but with no new sadness to her voice: "Only my dear sister Phœbe's, Mrs. Wardle, I've told you about. She was my twin sister . . . I've told you . . . you recollect? . . ."

"Yes, indeed, ma'am, and died when you was in the Colony!"

"I've never seen another more beautiful than Phœbe." She spoke with such supreme unconsciousness of the twinship that Aunt M'riar forgot it, too, until her next words came. "I was never free to say it of her in those days, for they would have made sport of me for saying it. There was none could tell us apart then. It does not matter now." She seemed to fall away into an absent-minded dream, always caressing Dave's sunny locks, which wanted cutting.

Aunt M'riar did not instantly perceive why a twin could not praise her twin's beauty; at least, it needed reflection. She was clear on the point, however, by the time Dave, merely watchful till now, suddenly asked a question:—"What are stwins?" He had long been anxious for enlightenment on this point, and now saw his opportunity. His inquiry was checked—if his curiosity was not satisfied—by a statement that when a little boy had a brother the same age that was twins, incorrectly stwins. He had to affect satisfaction.

The old woman, roused by Dave's question, attested the general truth of his informant's statements; then went back to the memory of her sister. "But I never saw her again," said she.

"No, ma'am," said Aunt M'riar. "So I understood. It was in England she died?"

"No—no! Out at sea. She was drowned at sea. Fifty years ago . . . Yes!—well on to fifty years ago." She fell back a little into her dreamy mood; then roused herself to say:—"I often wonder, Mrs. Wardle, suppose my sister had lived to be my age, should we have kept on alike?"

Aunt M'riar was not a stimulus to conversation as far as perspicuity went. A general tone of sympathy had to make up for it. "We should have seen, ma'am," said she.

"Supposing it had all gone on like as it was then, and we had just grown old together! Supposing we had neither married, and no man had come into it, should we all our lives have been mistaken for one another, so you could not tell us apart?"

Aunt M'riar said "Ah!" and shook her head. She was not imaginative enough to contribute to a conversation so hypothetical.

There was nothing of pathos, to a bystander, in the old woman's musical voice, beyond its mere age—its reedy tone—which would have shown in it just as clearly had she been speaking of any topic of the day. Conceive yourself speaking about long forgotten events of your childhood to a friend born thirty—forty—fifty years later, and say if such speech would not be to you what old Mrs. Prichard's was to herself and her hearer, much like revival of the past history of someone else. It was far too long ago now—if it had ever been real; for sometimes indeed it seemed all a dream—to lacerate her heart in recollecting it. The memories that could do that belonged to a later time; some very much later—the worst of them. Not but that the early memories could sting, too, when dragged from their graves by some remorseless resurrectionist—some sound, like that piano; some smell, like those lilies of the valley. Measure her case against your own experience, if its span of time is long enough to supply a parallel.

Her speech became soliloquy—was it because of a certain want of pliancy in Aunt M'riar?—and seemed to dwell in a disjointed way on the possibility that her sister might have changed with time otherwise than herself, and might even have been hard to recognise had they met again later. It would be different with two girls of different ages, each of whom would after a long parting have no guide to the appearance of her sister; while twins might keep alike; the image of either, seen in the glass, forecasting the image of the other.

Aunt M'riar made a poor listener to this, losing clues and forging false constructions. But her obliging disposition made her seem to understand when she did not, and did duty for intelligence. Probably Dave—on the watch for everything within human ken—understood nearly as much as Aunt M'riar. Something was on the way, though, to rouse her, and when it came she started as from a blow. What was that the old lady had just said? How came that name in her mouth? . . .

"What I said just now, Mrs. Wardle? . . . Let me see! . . . About what my husband used to say—that Phœbe's memory would go to sleep, not like mine, and I was a fool to fret so about her. I would not know her again, maybe, if I saw her, nor she me. . . . Yes—he said all that. . . . What?"

"What was the *name* you said just now? Ralph . . . something! Ralph what?"

"Oh—yes—I know! What Phœbe would have been if she had married my husband's brother—Mrs. Ralph Daverill. . . ."

"Good Lord!" exclaimed Aunt M'riar.

"Ah, there now!" said the old lady. "To think I should never have told you his name!" She missed the full strength of Aunt M'riar's exclamation; accounted it mere surprise at what was either a reference to a former husband or an admission of a pseudonym. Aunt M'riar was glad to accept matters as they stood, merely disclaiming excessive astonishment and suggesting that she might easy have guessed that Mrs. Prichard had been married

more than once. She was not—she said—one of the prying sort.
But she was silent about the cause of her amazement; putting the
name in a safe corner of her memory, to grapple with it later.
The old woman, however, seemed to have no wish for concealments, saying at once:—" I never had but one husband, Mrs. Wardle; but I'll tell you. I've always gone by the name of Prichard
ever since my son. . . . But I never told you of him neither!
It is he I would forget. . . ." This disturbed her—made her
take the caressing hand restlessly from Dave's head, to hold and
be held by the other. She had to be silent a moment; then said
hurriedly:—" He was Ralph Thornton, after his father and uncle.
His father was Thornton—Thornton Daverill. . . . I'll tell you
another time." Thereupon Aunt M'riar held her tongue, and Mrs.
Burr came in with the fourpennyworth of crumpets.

An unskilful chronicler throws unfair burdens on his reader.
The latter need not read the chronicle certainly; there is always
that resource! If, however, he reads this one, let him keep in
mind that Aunt M'riar did *not* know that the escaped prisoner
of her newspaper-cutting had been asking for a widow of the
name of Daverill, whom he had somehow traced to Sapps Court,
any more than she knew—at that date—that old Mrs. Prichard
should really have been called old Mrs. Daverill. She only knew
that *his* name was Daverill. So it was not in order to prevent
Mrs. Prichard seeing it that she cut that paragraph out of the
Morning Star. She must have had some other reason.

CHAPTER XVII

A LADY AND GENTLEMAN, WHO HUNG FIRE. NATURAL HISTORY, AND
ARTIFICIAL CHRONOLOGY. NEITHER WAS TWENTY YEARS YOUNGER.
CONFIDENCES ABOUT ANOTHER LADY AND GENTLEMAN, SOME YEARS
SINCE. HOW THE FIRST GENTLEMAN FINISHED HIS SECOND CIGAR.
DR. LIVINGSTONE AND SEKELETU. MR. NORBURY'S QUORUM. WHY
ADRIAN TORRENS WOKE UP, AND WHOSE VOICE PROMISED NOT TO MEN-
TION HIS EYES. FEUDAL BEEF-TEA, AND MRS. BAILEY. AN EARLY
VISIT, FROM AN EARL. AN EXPERIMENT THAT DISCLOSED A PAINFUL
FACT

IT is three weeks later at the Castle; three weeks later, that is,
than the story's last sight of it. It is the hottest night we have

had this year, says general opinion. Most of the many guests are scattered in the gardens after dinner, enjoying the night-air and the golden moon, which means to climb high in the cirrus-dappled blue in an hour or so. And then it will be a fine moonlight night.

On such a night there is always music somewhere, and this evening someone must be staying indoors to make it, as it comes from the windows of the great drawing-room that opens on the garden. Someone is playing a Beethoven sonata one knows well enough to pretend about with one's fingers, theoretically. Only one can't think which it is. So says Miss Smith-Dickenson, in the Shrubbery, to her companion, who is smoking a Havana large enough to play a tune on if properly perforated. But she wishes Miss Torrens would stop, and let Gwen and the Signore sing some Don Juan. That is Miss Dickenson's way. She always takes exception to this and to that, and wants t'other. It does not strike the Hon. Percival Pellew, the smoker of the big cigar, as a defect in her character, but rather as an indication of its illumination— a set-off to her appearance, which is, of course, at its best in the half-dark of a Shrubbery by moonlight, but is *passée* for all that. Can't help that, now, can we? But Mr. Pellew can make retrospective concession; she must have told well enough, properly dressed, fifteen years ago. She don't exactly bear the light now, and one can't expect it.

The Hon. Percival complimented himself internally on a greater spirituality, which can overlook such points—mere clay?—and discern a peculiar essence of soul in this lady which, had they met in her more palatable days, might have been not uncongenial to his own. Rather a pity!

Miss Dickenson could identify a glow-worm and correct the ascription of its light to any fellow's cigar-end thrown away. She made the best figure that was compatible with being indubitably *passée* when she went down on one knee in connection with this identification. Mr. Pellew felt rather relieved. Her outlines seemed somehow to warrant or confirm the intelligence he had pledged himself to. He remarked, without knowing anything about it, that he thought glow-worms didn't show up till September.

"Try again, Mr. Pellew. It's partridge-shooting that doesn't begin till September. That's what you're thinking of."

"Well—August, then!"

"No—that's grouse, not glow-worms. You see, you are reduced to July, and it's July still. Do take my advice, Mr. Pellew, and leave Natural History alone. Nobody will ever know you know nothing about it, if you hold your tongue."

The Hon. Percival was silent. He was not thinking about his shortcomings as a Natural Historian. The reflection in his mind was:—" What a pity this woman isn't twenty years younger! " He could discriminate—so he imagined—between mere flippancy and spontaneous humour. The latter would have sat so well on the girl in her teens, and he would then have accepted the former as juvenile impertinence with so much less misgiving that he was being successfully made game of. He could not quite shake free of that suspicion. Anyhow, it was a pity Miss Smith-Dickenson was thirty-seven. That was the age her friend Lady Ancester had assessed her at, in private conversation with Mr. Pellew. " Though what the deuce my cousin Philippa "—thus ran a very rapid thought through his mind—" could think I wanted to know the young woman's age for, I can't imagine."

" There it is! " said the lady, stooping over the glow-worm. " Little hairy thing! I won't disturb it." She got on her feet again, saying:—" Thank you—I'm all right! " in requital of a slight excursion towards unnecessary help, which took the form of a jerk cut short and an apologetic tone. " But don't talk Zoölogy or Botany, please," she continued. " Because there's something I want you to tell me about."

" Anything consistent with previous engagements. Can't break any promises."

" Have you made any promises about the man upstairs? "

" Not the ghost of a one! But he isn't ' the man upstairs ' to me. He's the man in the room at the end of my passage. That's how I came to see him."

" You did see him? "

" Oh yes—talked to him till the nurse stopped it. I found we knew each other. Met him in the Tyrol—at Meran—ten years ago. He was quite a boy then. But he remembered me quite well. It was this morning."

" Did he recognise you, or you him? "

" Why—neither exactly. We found out about Meran by talking. No—poor chap!—he can't recognise anybody, by sight at least. He won't do that yet awhile."

The lady said " Oh? " in a puzzled voice, as though she heard something for the first time; then continued: " Do you know, I have never quite realised that . . . that the eyes were so serious. I knew all along that there was *something,* but . . . but I understood it was only weakness."

" They have been keeping it dark—quite reasonably and properly, you know—but there is it! He can't see—simply can't see.

His eyes *look* all right, but they won't work. His sister knows, of course, but he has bound her over to secrecy. He made me promise to say nothing, and I've broken my promise, I suppose. But—somehow—I thought you knew."

"Only that there was *something*—no idea that he was blind. But I won't betray your confidence."

"Thank you. It's only a matter of time, as I gather. But a bad job for him till he gets his sight again."

"He will, I suppose, in the end?"

"Oh yes—in the end. Sir Coupland is cautious, of course. But I don't fancy he's really uneasy. His sight might come back suddenly, he said, at any moment. Of course, *he* believes his eyesight will come back. Only meanwhile he wants—it was a phrase of his own—to keep all the excruciation for his own private enjoyment. That's what he said!"

"I see. Of course, that makes a difference. And you think Sir Coupland thinks he will get all right again?"

Mr. Pellew says he does think so, reassuringly. "It has always struck me as peculiar," says he, "that Tim's family . . . I beg pardon—I should have said the Earl's. But you see I remember him as a kid—we are cousins, you know—and his sisters always called him Tim. . . . Well, I mean the family here, you know, seem to know so little of the Torrenses. Lady Gwen doesn't seem to have recognised this chap in the Park."

"I believe she has never seen him. He has been a great deal abroad, you know."

"Yes, he's been at German Universities, and games of that sort."

"Is that your third cigar, Mr. Pellew?"

"No—second. Come, I say, Miss Dickenson, two's not much. . . ."

But her remark was less a tobacco-crusade than a protest against too abrupt a production of family history by a family friend. Mr. Pellew felt confident it would come, though; and it did, at about the third whiff of the new cigar.

"I suppose you know the story?"

"Couldn't say, without hearing it first to know."

"About Philippa and Sir Hamilton Torrens?"

"Can't say I have. But then I'm the sort of fellah nobody ever tells things to."

"I suppose I oughtn't to have mentioned it."

"I shall not tell anyone you did so. You may rely on that." Mr. Pellew gave his cigar a half-holiday to say this seriously, and Miss Dickenson felt that his type, though too tailor-made, was always to be relied on; you had only to scratch it to find a Gentle-man underneath. No audience ever fails to applaud the discovery on the stage. Evidently there was no reserve needed—a relation of the Earl, too! Still, she felt satisfied at this passing recognition of Prudence on her part. Preliminaries had been done justice to.

She proceeded to tell what she knew of the episode of her friend's early engagement to the father of the gentleman who had been shot. It was really a very flat story; so like a thousand others of its sort as scarcely to claim narration-space. Youth, beauty, high spirits, the London season, first love—warranted the genuine article—parental opposition to the union of Romeo and Juliet, on the vulgar, unpoetical ground of Romeo having no particular in-come and vague expectations; the natural impatience of eighteen and five-and-twenty when they don't get their own way in every-thing; misunderstandings, ups-and-downs, reconciliations and new misunderstandings; finally one rather more serious than its prede-cessors, and judicious non-interference of bystanders—under-handed bystanders who were secretly favouring another suitor, who wasn't so handsome and showy as Romeo certainly, but who was of sterling worth and all that sort of thing. Besides, he was very nearly an Earl, and Hamilton Torrens was three-doors off his fa-ther's Baronetcy and Pensham Steynes. This may have had its weight with Juliet. Miss Dickenson candidly admitted that she herself would have been influenced; but then, no doubt she was a worldling. Mr. Pellew admired the candour, discerning in it ex-aggeration to avoid any suspicion of false pretence. He did not suspect himself of any undue leniency to this lady. She was alto-gether too *passée* to admit of any such idea.

The upshot of the flat episode, of course, was that Philippa "became engaged" to her new suitor, and did *not* fall out with him. They were married within the year, and three months later her former *fiancé's* father died, rather unexpectedly. His eldest son, coming home from Burmah on sick-leave, died on the voyage, of dysentery; and his second brother, a naval officer, was in the autumn of the same year killed by a splinter at the Battle of Navarino. So by a succession of fatalities Romeo found himself the owner of his father's estate, and a not very distant neighbour of Juliet and his successful rival.

It appeared that he had consoled himself by marrying a Miss Abercrombie, Miss Dickenson believed. These Romeos always marry a Miss Something; who, owing to the way she comes into the story, is always on the top-rung of the ladder of insipidity. Nobody cares for her; she appears too late to interest us. No doubt there were several Miss Abercrombies on draught, and he selected the tallest or the cleverest or the most musical, avoiding, of course, the dowdiest.

However, there was Lady Ancester's romance, told to account for the languid intercourse between the Castle and Pensham Steynes, and the non-recognition of one another by Gwen and the Man in the Park. Miss Dickenson added a rider to the effect that she could quite understand the position. It would be a matter of mutual tacit consent, tempered down by formal calls enough to allay local gossip. " I think Miss Torrens has stopped," said she collaterally; you know how one speaks collaterally? " Shall we walk towards the house? "

Then the Hon. Percival made a speech he half repented of later; *videlicet,* when he woke next morning. It became the fulcrum, as it were, of an inexplicable misgiving that Miss Dickenson would be bearing the light worse than ever when he saw her at breakfast. The speech was:—" It's very nice out here. One can hear the Don at Covent Garden. Besides . . . one can hear out here just as well." This must have been taken to mean that two could. For the lady's truncated reply was:—" Till you've finished your cigar, then! "

Combustion was lip-close when the cigar-end was thrown away. The reader of this story may be able to understand a thing its writer can only record without understanding—the fact that this gentleman felt grateful to the fine moonlight night, now nearly a *fait-accompli,* for enhancing this lady's white silk, which favoured a pretence that she was only reasonably *passée,* and enabled him to reflect upon the contour of her throat without interruption from its skin. For it had a contour by moonlight. Well!— sufficient to the day is the evil thereof; daylight might have its say to-morrow. Consider the clock put back a dozen years!

" Oh yes, he's asleep still, but I've seen him—looked in on my way down. Do you know, I really believe he will be quite fit for the journey to-morrow. He's getting such a much better colour, and last night he seemed so much stronger." Thus the last comer to the morning-rally of breakfast claimants, in its ante-room, awaiting its herald. Miss Irene Torrens is a robust beauty with her brother's eyes. She has been with him constantly since she came with her father three weeks ago, and the two of them watched his every breath through the terrible day and night that followed.

" Then perhaps he will let us see him," says Lady Gwen. " At last! "

"You must not expect too much," says Miss Torrens. She does not like saying it, but facts are overpowering. Her brother has exacted a pledge from her to say nothing, even now, about his blindness—merely to treat him as weak-eyed temporarily. He will pass muster, he says—will squeak through somehow. "I can't have that glorious girl made miserable," were the words he had used to her, half an hour since. This Irene will be all on tenter-hooks till the interview is safely over. Meanwhile it is only prudent not to sound too hopeful a note. It is as well to keep a margin in reserve in case the performance should fall through.

Irene's response to her brother's words had been, "She is a glorious girl," and she was on the way to "You should have seen her eyes last night over that Beethoven!" But she broke down on the word *eyes*. How else could it have been? Then the blind man had laughed, in the courage of his heart, as big a laugh as his pitiable weakness could sustain, and had made light of his affliction. He had never given way from the first hour of his revival, when he had asked to have the shutters open, and had been told they were already wide open, and the July sun streaming into the room.

It was the Countess who answered Irene's caution, as accompaniment to her morning salute. "We are not to expect *anything, my dear.* That is quite understood. It would be unreasonable. And we won't stop long and tire him. But this girl of mine will never be happy if he goes away without our—well!—becoming acquainted, I might almost say. Because really we are perfect strangers. And when one has shot a man, even by accident. . . ." Her ladyship did not finish, but went on to hope the eyesight was recovering.

"Oh yes!" said Irene audaciously. "We are quite hopeful about it now. It will be all right with rest and feeding up. Only, if I let you in to see him you *will* promise me, won't you—not to say a word about his eyes? It only frightens him, and does no one any good." Of course, Miss Torrens got her promise. It was an easy one to make, because reference to the eyes only seemed a means towards embarrassment. Much easier to say nothing about them. Gwen and Miss Torrens, very *liées* already, went out by the garden window to talk, but would keep within hearing because breakfast was imminent.

More guests, and the newspapers; as great an event in the early fifties as now, but with only a fraction of the twentieth century's allowance of news. Old General Rawnsley, guilty of his usual rudeness in capturing the *Times* from all comers, had to surrender it to the Hon. Percival because none but a dog-in-the-manger could read a letter from Sir C. Napier of Scinde, and about Dr. Livingstone and Sekeletu and the Leeambye all at the same time. All comers, or several male comers at least, essayed to pinion the successful captor of the *Times,* thirsting for information about their own special subjects of interest. No—the Hon. Percival did *not* see anything, so far, about the new Arctic expedition that was to unearth, or dis-ice, the *Erebus* and *Terror;* but the inquirer, a vague young man, shall have the paper directly. Neither has he come on anything, as yet, about a mutiny in the camp at Chobham. But the paper shall be at the disposal of this inquirer, too, as soon as the eye in possession has been run down to the bottom of this column. In due course both inquirers get hold of corners at the moment of surrender, and then have paroxysms of polite concession which neither means in earnest, during which the bone of contention becomes the prey of a passing wolf. Less poetically, someone else gets hold of the paper and keeps it.

The Hon. Percival really surrendered the paper, not because his interest in Lord Palmerston's speech had flagged, but because he had heard Miss Dickenson come in, and that consideration about her endurance of the daylight weighed upon him. On the whole, she is standing the glare of day better than he expected, and her bodice seems very nicely cut. It may have been an accident that she looked so dowdy yesterday morning. He and she exchange morning greetings, passionlessly but with civility. The lady may be accounting a *tête-à-tête* by moonlight with a gentleman, an hour long, an escapade, and he may be resolving on caution for the future. By-the-by, *can* a lady have a *tête-à-tête* with another lady by moonlight? Scarcely!

Mr. Norbury, the butler, always feels the likeness of the breakfast rally to fish in a drop-net. If he acts promptly, he will land his usual congregation. He must look in at the door to see if there is a quorum. A quarum would do. A cujus is a great rarity; though even that happens after late dances, or when influenza is endemic. Mr. Norbury looked in at the rally and recognised its psychological moment. More briefly, he announced that breakfast was ready, while a gong rang up distant sheep astray most convincingly.

Adrian Torrens, too weak still to show alacrity in waking, hears the sound and is convinced. How he would rejoice to join the party below! He knows *that,* in his sleep; and resolves as soon as he can speak to tell Mrs. Bailey the nurse he could perfectly well have got up for breakfast. Yet he knows he is glad to be kept lying down, for all that.

He wakes cherishing his determination to say this to his tyrant, and is conscious of the sun by the warmth, and the unanimity of the birds. He knows, too, that the casement is open, by the sound of voices in the garden below. His sister's voice and another, whose owner's image was the last thing human he had seen, with the eyes that he dared not think had looked their last upon the visible world when the crash came from Heaven-knows-where and shut it out. He could identify it beyond a doubt; could swear to it, now that he had come to understand the real story of his terrible mishap, as the first sound that mixed with his returning life, back from a painless darkness which was a Heaven compared to the torture of his reviving consciousness. It was strange to be told now that at that moment the medical verdict had been given that he was dead. But he could swear to the voice—even to the words! What was it saying now?

"You may rely on me—indeed you may—to say nothing about the eyes. He will be just able to see us, I suppose?"

"He will hardly recognise you. How long was it altogether, do you think?"

"At Arthur's Bridge? Five minutes—perhaps less."

"He took a good look at you?"

"I suppose so. I think he did, as soon as he had got the dog chained. Oh yes—I should say certainly! I fancied he might have seen me before, but it seems not."

"He says not. But you were not out when he went to Konigsberg."

"Oh no—I had quite a long innings after that. . . . Well!—it *does* sound like cricket, doesn't it? Go on."

"Oh—I see what you mean. What a ridiculous girl you are! What was I saying! . . . Oh, I recollect! That was just after he graduated at Oxford. Then he went to South America with Engelhardt. He really has been very little at home for three years—over three years—past."

"We shall see if he knows me. I won't say anything to guide him." Then he heard his sister's voice reply to the speaker with words she had used before:—"You know you must not expect too much." To which Lady Gwendolen reiterated: "Oh, you may trust me. I shall say nothing to him about it. . . . Oh, you darling!" This was to Achilles, manifestly. He had become restless at the sound of conversation below, and had been looking round the door-jamb to see if by any chance a dog could get out. The entry of the nurse a moment since, with a proto-stimulant on a tray, had let him out to tear down the stairs to the garden, rudely thrusting aside the noble owner of the house, out of bounds in a dressing-gown and able to defy Society.

No lack of sight can quench the image in its victim's brain of Achilles' greeting to the owners of the two voices. His sister has her fair share of it—no more!—but her friend gets an accolade of a piece with the one she received that morning by Arthur's Bridge, three weeks since. So his owner's brain-image says, confirmed by sounds from without. He is conscious of the absurdity of building so vivid and substantial a superstructure on so little foundation, and would like to protest against it.

"Good-morning, Nurse. I'm better. What is it?—beef-tea. Earls' cooks make capital beef-tea. On the whole I am in favour of Feudalism. Nothing can be sweeter or neater or completer— or more nourishing—than its beef-tea. Don't put any salt in till I tell you. . . . Oh no—*I'm* not going to spill it!" This is preliminary; the protest follows. "Who's talking to my sister under the window? . . . that's her voice." Of course, he knew perfectly well all the time.

The nurse listens a moment. "That's her ladyship," says she, meaning the Countess. Gwen's voice is not unlike her mother's, only fuller. "They are just going in to breakfast. The gong went a minute ago."

Now is his time to condemn the tyranny which keeps him in bed in the morning and lying down all day. "I *could* have got up and gone downstairs, Mrs. Bailey, you know I could."

Mrs. Bailey pointed out that had this scheme been carried out a life would have been sacrificed. She explained to a newcomer, no less a person than the Earl himself, that Mr. Torrens would kill himself in five minutes if she did not keep the eyes of a lynx on him all the blessed day. She is always telling him so without effect, he never being any the wiser, even when she talks her head off. Patients never are, being an unmanageable class at the best. A nurse with her head on ought to be a rarity, according to Mrs. Bailey.

The image of the Earl in the blind man's mind is very little helped by recollection of the few occasions, some years ago, on which he has seen him. It becomes now, after a short daily chat with him each morning since he gained strength for interviews, that of an elderly gentleman with a hesitating manner anxious to accommodate difficulties, soothing an unreasonable race with a benevolent optimism, pouring oil on the troubled waters of local religion and politics, taking no real interest in the vortices into which it has pleased God to drag him, all with one distinct object in view—that of adding to his collections undisturbed. That is the impression he has produced on Mr. Adrian Torrens in a dozen of his visits to his bedside. His lordship has made it a practice to look in at his victim—for that is the way he thinks of him, will he nill he!—as early every day as possible, and as late. He has suffered agonies from constant longings to talk about his Amatis or his Elzevirs or his Petitots, checked at every impulse by the memory of the patient's blindness. He is always beginning to say how he would like to show him this or that, and collapsing. This also is an inference of Mr. Torrens, drawn in the dark, from sudden hesitations and changes of subject.

"How are we this morning, Nurse?" On the mend, it seems, being more refractory than ever; always a good sign with patients. But we must be kept in bed, till midday at any rate, for some days yet. Or weeks or months or years according to the degree of our intractability. The Earl accepts this as common form, and goes to the bedside saying sum-upwardly:—"No worse, at any rate!"

"Tremendously better, Lord Ancester! *Tremendously* better, thanks to you and Mrs. Bailey. . . . Catch hold of the cup, Nurse . . . Yes, I've drained it to the dregs. . . . I know what you are going to say, my lord. . . ."

"I was going to say that Mrs. Bailey and I are not on the same footing. Mrs. Bailey didn't shoot you. . . . Yes, now grip hard! That's right! Better since yesterday certainly—no doubt of it!"

"Mrs. Bailey didn't shoot me in the mere vulgar literal sense. But she was contributory, if not an accessory after the fact. It was written in the Book of Fate that Mrs. Bailey would bring me beef-tea this very day. If she had accepted another engagement the incident would have had to be rewritten; which is impossible by hypothesis. Moreover, so far as I can be said to have been shot, it was as a trespasser, not as a man. . . . Is there a close season for trespassers? If there is, I admit that you may be technically right. *Qui facit per alium facit per se.* . . . By-the-by, I hope poor Alius is happier in his mind. . . ."

"Poor who?" says the Earl. He is not giving close attention to the convalescent's disconnected chatter. He has been one himself, and knows how returning life sets loose the tongue.

"The *alius* you facitted per. The poor chap that had the bad luck to shoot me. Old Stephen—isn't he? Poor old chap! *What a mischance!*"

"Oh yes—old Stephen! I see—he's *alius,* of course. He comes over two or three times a day to see how you are going on. They think him rather a nuisance in the house, I believe. I have tried to comfort him as well as I could. He will be glad of to-day's report. But he can't help being dispirited, naturally."

"He's so unaccustomed to homicide, poor old chap! People should be educated to it, in case of accidents. They might be allowed to kill a few women and children for practice—should never be left to the mercy of their consciences, all raw and susceptible. Poor old Stephen! I really think he might be allowed to come and see me now. I'm so very much improved that a visit from my assassin would be a pleasant experience—a wholesome stimulus. Wouldn't throw me back at all! Poor old Stephen!" He seemed seriously concerned about the old boy; would not be content without a promise that he and his wife should pay him an early visit.

He had been immensely better after that M.P. paid him a visit yesterday morning. Mrs. Bailey confirmed this, testifying to the difficulty with which the patient had been persuaded to remain in bed. But she had the whip-hand of him there, because he couldn't find his clothes without her help. This gives the Earl an idea of the condition of the patient's eyesight beyond his previous concept of its infirmities. He has been misled by its apparent soundness—for no one would have guessed the truth from outward seeming—and the nurse's accident of speech rouses his curiosity.

"Ah, by-the-by," he says, "I was just going to ask." Which is not strictly true, but apology to himself for his own neglect, "How *are* the eyes?"

"Oh, the eyes are right enough," says the patient. He goes on to explain that they are no inconvenience whatever so long as he keeps them shut. It is only when he opens them that he notices their defect; which is, briefly, that he can't see with them. His lordship seems to feel that eyes so conditioned are hardly satisfactory. It is really new knowledge to him, and he accepts it restlessly. He spreads his fingers out before the deceptive orbs that look so clear, showing indeed no defect but a kind of uncertainty; or rather perhaps a too great stillness as though always content with the object in front of them. "What do you see now?" he asks in a nervous voice.

"Something dark between me and the light."

"Is that all? Can't you see what it is?"

"A book." A mere guess based on the known predilections of the questioner.

"Oh dear!" says the Earl. "It was my hand." He sees that the nurse is signalling with headshakes and soundless lip-words, but has not presence of mind to catch her meaning.

The other seems to feel his speech apologetically, as though it were his own fault. "I see better later in the day," he says. Which may be true or not.

The nurse's signalling tells, and the questioner runs into an opposite extreme. "One is like that in the morning sometimes," says he absurdly, but meaning well. He is not an Earl who would be of much use in a hospital for the treatment of nervous disorders. However, having grasped the situation he shows tact, changing the conversation to the heat of the weather and the probable earliness of the crops. No one should ever *show* tact. He will only be caught *flagrante delicto*. Mr. Torrens is perfectly well aware of what is occurring; and, when he lies still and unresponsive with his eyes closed, is not really resting after exertion, which is the nurse's interpretation of the action, but trying to think out something he wants to say to the Earl, and how to say it. It is not so easy as light jesting.

The nurse telegraphs silently lipwise that the patient will doze now for a quarter of an hour till breakfast; and the visitor, alive to the call of discretion, has gone out gently before the patient knows he has left the bedside.

Things that creak watch their opportunity whenever they hear silence. So the Earl's gentle exit ends in a musical and penetrating *arpeggio* of a door-hinge, equal to the betrayal of Masonic secrecy if delivered at the right moment. "Is Mrs. Bailey gone?" says the patient, ascribing the wrong cause to it.

"His lordship has gone, Mr. Torrens. He thought you were dropping off."

"Stop him—stop him! Say I have something particular to say. Do stop him!" It must be something very particular, Nurse thinks. But in any case the patient's demand would have to be complied with. So the Earl is recaptured and brought back.

"Is it anything I can do for you, Mr. Torrens? I am quite at your service."

"Yes—something of importance to me. Is Mrs. Bailey there?"

"She is just going." She had not intended to do so. But this was a hint clearly. It was accepted.

"All clear!" says the Earl. "And the door closed."

" My sister has promised to ask the Countess and your daughter
—Lady Gwen, is it not?"

" That is my daughter's name, Gwendolen. 'Has promised to
ask them ' . . . what?"

" To give me an opportunity before I go of thanking them both
for all the great kindness they have shown me, and of apologizing
for my wish to defer the interview."

" Yes—but why me? . . . I mean that that is all quite in order,
but how do I come in?" As the speaker's voice smiles as well as
his face, his hearer's blindness does not matter.

" Only this way. You know the doctors say my eyesight is not
incurable—probably will come all to rights of itself. . . ."

" Yes—and then?"

" I want them—her ladyship and . . ."

" My wife and daughter. I understand."

". . . I want them to know as little about it as possible; to
know *nothing* about it *if* possible. You knew very little about it
yourself till just now."

" I was misled—kindly, I know—but misled for all that. And
the appearance is so extraordinary. Nobody could guess. . . ."

" Exactly. Because the eyes are really unaffected and are sure
to come right. See now what I am asking you to do for me. Help
me to deceive them about it. They will not test my eyesight as
you did just now. . . ."

" How do you know that?"

" Because I heard Irene and your daughter talking in the garden a few minutes ago—just after the breakfast-bell rang—talking
about me, and I eavesdropped as hard as I could. Lady Gwendolen
has promised Irene to say nothing about my eyesight for my sake.
She will keep her promise. . . ."

" How do you know that?"

" By the sound of her voice."

" She is only a human girl."

" I am convinced that she will keep it; though, I grant you,
circumstances are against her. And neither she nor her mother
will try to find out, if they believe I see them dimly. That is
where *you* come in. Only make them believe that. Don't let them
suppose I am all in the dark. Say nothing of your crucial experiment just now. Irene—dear girl—has been a good sister to me,
and has told many good round lies for my sake. But she will
explain to God. I cannot ask you, Lord Ancester, to tell stories
on my behalf. My petition is only for a modest prevarication—
the cultivation of a reasonable misapprehension to attain a justi-

fiable end. Consider the position analogous to that of one of Her
Majesty's Ministers catechized by an impertinent demagogue. No
fibs, you know—only what a truthful person tells instead of a fib!
For my sake!"
"I am not thinking of my character for veracity," says the Earl
thoughtfully. "You should be welcome to a sacrifice of that under the circumstances. I was thinking what form of false representation would be most likely to gain the end, and safest. Do
you know, I am inclined to favour the policy of saying as little
as possible? My dear wife is in the habit of imputing to me a
certain slowness and defective observation of surrounding event.
It is a common wifely attitude. You need not fear my being asked
any questions. In any case, I fully understand your wishes, and
you may rely on my doing my best. Here is your breakfast coming.
I hope you will not be knocked up with all this talk."

CHAPTER XVIII

BLIND MEN CAN'T SMOKE. CAN'T THEY? HOW THE COUNTESS AND HER
DAUGHTER AT LAST INTERVIEWED THEIR GUEST. HIS SUBTLE AR-
RANGEMENTS FOR SEEMING TO SEE THEM. A BLUNDER OVER A
HANDSHAKE, AND ALL THE FAT IN THE FIRE, NEARLY! AN ELECTRIC
SHOCK. THE EXCELLENCE OF ACHILLES' HEART. HOW MR. TORRENS
SPOILED IT ALL! BLUE NANKIN IS NOT CROWN DERBY. GWEN'S GREAT
SCHEME. HOW SHE CARRIED IT OUT

THE morning passed, with intermittent visitors, one at a time.
Each one, coming away from the bedside, confirmed the report
of his predecessor as to the visible improvement of the convalescent. Each one in turn, when questioned about the eyesight,
gave a sanguine report—an echo of the patient's own confidence,
real or affected, in its ultimate restoration. He would be all right
again in a week or so.
Underhand ways were resorted to of cheating despair and getting at the pocket of Hope. Said one gentleman to the Earl—who
was keeping his counsel religiously—" He can't read small print."
Whereto the Earl replied—" Not yet awhile, but one could hardly
expect that "; and felt that he was carrying out his promise with
a minimum of falsehood. Yet his conscience wavered, because
an eyesight may be unable to read small print, and yet unable to
read large print, or any print at all. Perhaps he had better have

left the first broad indisputable truth to impose on its hearer unassisted.

Another visitor scored a success on behalf of Optimism by reporting that the patient had smoked a cigar in defiance of medical prohibitions. "Can't be much wrong with his eyes," said this one, "if he can smoke. You shut your eyes, and try!" Put to the proof, this dictum received more confirmation than it deserved, solely to secure an audience for the flattering tales of Hope.

Much of the afternoon passed too, but without visitors. Because it would never do, said Irene, for her brother not to be at his best when Gwen and her mother came to pay their visit, resolved on this morning, at what was usually the best moment of his day—about five o'clock. Besides, he was to be got up and really dressed—not merely huddled into clothes—and this was a fatiguing operation, never carried out in dire earnest before. Doctor and Nurse had assented, on condition that Mr. Torrens should be content to remain in his room, and not insist on going downstairs. Where was the use of his doing so, with such a journey before him to-morrow? Better surely to husband the last grain of strength—the last inch-milligramme of power—for an eighteen-mile ride, even with all the tonics in the world to back it! Mr. Torrens consented to this reservation, and promised not to be rebellious.

So—in time—the hour was at hand when he would see. . . . No!—*not* see—there was the sting of it! . . . that girl he had spoken with at Arthur's Bridge. The vision of her in the sunset was upon him still. He had pleaded with his sister that, come what might, she should not come to him in his darkness, in the hope that this darkness might pass away and leave her image open to him as before. For this hope had mixed itself with that strong desire of his heart that his own disaster should weigh upon her as little as possible. He had kept this meeting back almost till the eleventh hour, hoping against hope that light would break; longing each day for a gleam of the dawn that was to give him his life once more, and make the whole sad story a matter of the past. And now the time had come; and here he stood awaiting the ordeal he had to pass successfully, or face his failure as he might.

If he could but rig up an hour's colourable pretext of vision, however imperfect, the reality might return in its own good time —if that was the will of Allah—and that time might be soon enough. She might never know the terrible anticipations his underthought had had to fight against.

"You look better in the blue Mandarin silk than you would in your tailor's abominations," said Irene, referring to a dressing-gown costume she had insisted on. "Only your hair wants cutting, dear boy! I won't deceive you."

"That's serious!" He lets it pass nevertheless. "Look here, 'Rene, I want you to tell me. . . . Where are you?—oh, here!—all right. . . . Now tell me—should you say I saw you, by the look of my eyes?"

"Indeed I should. Indeed, indeed, *nobody* could tell. Your eyes look as strong as—as that hooky bird's that sits in the sun at the Zoölogical and nictitates . . . isn't that the word? . . . Goes twicky-twick with a membrane. . . ."

"Fish eagle, I expect."

"Shouldn't wonder! Only, look here! . . . You mustn't claw hold of Gwen like that. How can you tell, without?"

"Where they are, do you mean? Oh, I know by the voice. You go somewhere else and speak." Whereupon Irene goes furtively behind him, and says suddenly:—"Now look at me!" It is a success, for the blind man faces round, looking full at her.

She claps her hands. "Oh, Adrian!" she cries, "are you sure you don't see—aren't you cheating?" A memory, in this, of old games of blindman's-buff. "You always did cheat, darling, you know, when we played on Christmas Eve. How do I know I can trust you?" She goes close to him again caressing his face. "Oh, *do* say, dear boy, you can see a little!" But it is no use. He can say nothing.

There are a few moments of distressing silence, and then the brother says:—"Never mind, dear! It will be all right. They say so. Take me to the window that I may look out!" They stand together at the open casement, listening to the voices of the birds. The shrewdest observer might fail to detect the flaw in those two full clear eyes that seem to look out at the leagues of park-land, the spotted deer in the distance, the long avenue-road soon indistinguishable in the trees. The sister sees those eyes, no other than she has always known them, but knows that they see nothing.

"When I was here first," says the brother, "the thrushes were still singing. They are off duty by now, the very last of them." He stops listening. "That's a yellow-hammer. And that's a linnet. *You* can't tell one from the other."

"I know. I'm shockingly ignorant. . . . What, dear? What is it you want?" Her brother has been exploring the window-frame with a restless hand, as though in search of some latch or blind-cord. He cannot find what he wants.

"I want to come to a clearness about the position of this blessed window," he says. "Which direction is the bed in now? Well—describe it this way, suppose! Say I'm looking north now, with my shoulder against the window. Where's the bed? South-west—south-east—due south?"

"South-west by south. Perhaps that's not nautical, but you know what I mean."

"All right! Now, look here! As I stand here—looking out slantwise—where's the sunset? I mean, where would it be?—where does it mean to be?"

"You would be looking straight at it. Of course, you are not really looking north. . . . There—now you are!" She had taken her hands from the shoulder they were folded on and turned his head to the right. "But, I say, Adrian dear! . . ." She hesitates.

"What, for instance?"

"Don't try to humbug too much. Don't try to do it, darling boy. You'll only make a hash of it."

"All right, goosey-woosey! I'll fry my own fish. Don't you be uneasy!" And then they talk of other things: the journey home to-morrow, and how it shall be as good as lying in bed to Adrian, in the big carriage with an infinity of cushions; the new friends they have made here at the Towers, with something of wonderment that this chance has been so long postponed; the kindness they have had from them, and the ill-requital Adrian made for it yesterday by breaking that beautiful blue china tea-cup—any trifle that comes foremost—anything but the great grief that underlies the whole.

For Irene would have her brother at his best, that the visit to him of her new-made friend Gwen may go off well, and steer clear of the ambushes that beset it. Better that that visit should never come off, than that her friend should be left to share their fears for the future. Each is hiding from the other a weakening confidence in the renewal of suspended eyesight, weaker at the outset than either had been prepared to admit to the other.

"Look here, 'Rene," says Adrian, an hour later, during which his sister has read aloud to him, lying by the open window. "Never mind Becky Sharp; she'll keep till the evening. Can we see Arthur's Bridge from this window, where I saw your friend Lady Gwen? It was Arthur's, wasn't it? What Arthur? King Arthur?"

"Yes, if you like. Only don't go and call it Asses' Bridge, as you did the other day—not when the family's here. It sounds disrespectful."

"Not a bit. It only looks as if Euclid had been round. But answer my question. . . . Oh, we *can* see it! Very well, then; show me which way it lies. Is it visible—the actual bridge itself, I mean—not the place it's in?"

Irene got up and looked out of the window from behind her brother's chair. "Yes," she said. "One sees the stone arch plain. How can I show you?" She took his head in her hands again to guide it to a true line of sight.

"Between us and the sunset?"

"Thereabouts. Rather on the left."

"Very good. Now we can go on with Becky Sharp."

"That's it, my lord, is it? Where was I?—oh, Sir Pitt Crawley. . . ." And then the reading was continued, till tea portended, and Irene went away to capture her visitors.

All the sting of his darkness came upon him in its fulness as he heard that voice on the stairs. Oh, could he but see her for one moment—only one moment—to be sure that that dazzling image of three weeks since was not a mere imagination! He knew well the enchantment of the rainbow gleam on sea and earth and sky—the glory that makes Aladdin's palace of the merest hovel. He could scarcely have said to a nicety why a self-deception on this score seemed to him fraught with such evil. If it was a terror on Gwen's behalf, that a false image cherished through a period of reviving eyesight should in the end prove an injustice to her, and cast a chill over his own passionate admiration—for it was that at least that a chance of five minutes had enthralled him with—he banished that terror artificially from his mind. What could it matter to *her,* if he *was* taken aback and disappointed at her not turning out what his excited fancy had made her that evening at Arthur's Bridge? What was he to *her* that any chance man might not have been, after so scanty an interchange of words?

That was his dominant feeling, or underlying it, as her voice neared the door of his room, saying:—"Fancy your carrying him away without our seeing him—so much as thinking of it! I call you a wicked, unprincipled sister." To which another voice, a maternal sort of voice, said what must have been: "Don't speak so loud!"—or its equivalent. For the girl's voice dropped, her last words being:—"*He* won't hear, at this distance."

Then, she was actually coming in at the door! He could hear the prodigious skirt-rustle that is now a thing of womanhood's past—though we adored every comely example, mind you, we oldsters in those days, for all that she carried a milliner's shop on her back—and as it climaxed towards entry had to remember by force how slight indeed had been his interchange of words with the visitor he wished to see—to see by hearing, and to touch the hand of twice. For he had counted his coming privileges in his heart already, even if his reason had made light of its arithmetic. He would be on the safe side now—so he said to himself—and think of the elder lady as the player of the leading *rôle*. No disparagement to her subordinate; the merest deference to convention!

There was no mishap about the first meeting; only a narrow escape of one. The man in the dark reckoned it safest to extend his hand and leave it, to await the first claimant. He took for granted this would be the mother, and as his hand closed on a lady's, not small enough to call his assumption in question, said half interrogatively:—" Lady Ancester? "

" That's Gwen," said his sister's voice. And at the word an electric shock of a sort passed up his arm, the hand that still held his showing no marked alacrity to release it.

" Yes, this is *me*," says the voice of its owner, " *that's* mamma."

Lady Ancester, standing close to her, meets his outstretched hand and shakes it cordially. Then follows pleasantry about mistaking the mother for the daughter, with assumption of imperfect or dim vision only to account for it, and a declaration from Adrian that he had been cautioned not to confuse the one with the other. There *is* a likeness, as a matter of fact, and Irene has talked to him of it. The whole thing is slighter than the telling of it.

Then the three ladies and the one man have grouped—composed themselves—for reasonable chat. He is in his invalid chair by special edict, at the window, and the two visitors face him half-flanking it. His sister leans over him behind on the chair-back. She has kept very close to him, guiding him under pretence that he wants support, which is scarcely the case now, so rapid has been his progress in this last week. She is very anxious lest her brother should venture too rashly on fictitious proofs of eyesight that does not exist. But it can all be put down to uneasiness about his strength.

The platitudes of mere chat ensue, the Countess being prolocutrix. But she can be sincerely earnest in speaking of her own concern about the accident, and her family's. Also to the full about the rejoicing of everyone when it was " certain that all would turn out well." She has been bound over to say nothing about the eyesight, and keeps pledges; almost too transparently, perhaps. A word or two about it as a thing of temporary abeyance might have been more plausible.

Gwen has become very silent since that first warmth of her greeting. She is leaving the conversation to her mother, which puzzles Irene, who had framed a different picture of the interview, and is disappointed so far. Achilles, the dog, too, may be disappointed—may be feeling that something more demonstrative is due to the position. Irene imputes this view to him, inferring it from his restless appeals to Gwen, as he leans against her skirts, throwing back a pathetic gaze of remonstrance for something too complex for his powers of language. Her comment:—" He is always like that,"—seems to convey an image of his whereabouts to his master, confirmed perhaps by expressive dog-substitutes for speech.

" You mustn't let my bow-wow worry you, Lady Gwendolen. He presumes till he's checked, on principle. Send him to lie down over here. Here, Ply, Ply, Ply! . . . Oh, won't he come?" Probably Achilles knows that his master, who speaks, is only being civil.

" No—because I'm holding him. I want him here. He's a darling!" So says Gwen; and then continues:—" Oh yes, *I* know why he's Ply—short for Pelides. I think he thinks I think it was his fault, and wants forgiveness."

" Possibly. But it is also possible that he sees his way by cajolery to all the sweet biscuits with a little crown on them that come about with tea. He wants none of us to have any. Pray do not think any the worse of him. How is he to know that a well-bred person hungers for little crown biscuits? We are so affected that there is nothing for him to go by."

" And he's a dear, candid darling! Of course he is. He shall have everything he wants." Achilles appears to accept the concession as deserved, but to be ready to requite it with undying love.

" It is all the excellence of his heart, I am aware, and a certain simplicity and directness," says Adrian. " But all the same he mustn't spoil ladies' dresses—beyond a certain point, of course. I have been very curious to know, Lady Gwendolen, whether his paws came off—the marks of them, I mean—on that lovely India muslin I saw you in three weeks ago, just before this unfortunate affair which has given so much trouble to everybody at—at . . . Arthur's Bridge, of course! Couldn't think of the name at the moment. At Arthur's Bridge. I'm afraid he didn't do that dress any good."

"It wasn't a new dress," says Gwen, "as far as I remember." A point her maid would know more about, clearly.

Lady Ancester seems to think a little *ex post facto* chaperonage would not be inappropriate. "Gwen was out of bounds, I understand," she says; which means absolutely nothing, but sounds well.

The remark seems somehow to focus the conversation, and become a stepping-stone to a review of the recent events. Evidently the principal actor in them takes that view. "I had no idea whom I was speaking to," he says, "still less that Lady Gwendolen had taken the trouble to come away from the house with so kind a motive. Of course, I have heard all about it from my sister."

Gwen perfectly understands. "And then you walked over to Drews Thurrock, and Achilles' collar broke, and he got away." She speaks as one who waits for more.

"He did, and I am sorry to say he forgot himself. The old Adam broke out in him in connection with the sudden springing of a hare, just under his nose. It was almost the moment after his collar broke, and it is quite possible he thought I meant to let him go. But after all, Achilles is human, and really I could not blame him in any case. Try to see the thing from his point of view. Fancy discovering an unused faculty lying dormant— art, song, eloquence—and an unprecedented opportunity for its use! Do you know, I don't believe Achilles had ever so much as seen a hare before?—not a live one! He smelt one once at a poulterer's—a dead one that was starting for the Antipodes with its legs crossed. The poulterer lost his temper, very absurdly. . . ."

"Well—did he catch the hare? I mean the first hare."

"That I can't say. Both vanished, and I suspect the hare got away. I'm sure of one thing, that if Achilles did catch him he didn't know what to do with him. He has not the sporting spirit. Cats interest him in his native town, but when they show fight he comes and complains to me that they are out of order. He overhauled a kitten three weeks old once, that had come out to see the world, and it defied him to mortal combat. Achilles talked to me all the way down the street about that kitten."

"I want to know what happened next." From Gwen.

"Yes—silly old chatterbox!—keep to the point." Thus Irene; and Lady Ancester, who has been accepting the hare and the cats with dignity, even condescension, adds:—"We were just at the

most interesting part of the story." This was practically her ladyship's first sight of the son of the man she had gone so near to
marrying over five-and-twenty years ago. The search to discover
a *modus vivendi* between a past and present at war may have
thrown her a little out of her usual demeanour. Gwen wondered
why mamma need be so ceremonious.

Adrian was perfectly unconscious of it, even if Irene was not.
He ran on :—" Oh—the story! Yes—Achilles forgot himself, and
was off after the hare like a whirlwind. . . . I don't know, Lady
Ancester, whether you have ever blown a whistle in the middle of
an otherwise unoccupied landscape, with no visible motive ? "

Her ladyship had not apparently. Irene found fault with the
narrator's style, suggesting a more prosaic one. But Gwen said:
" Oh, Irene dear, what a perfect *sister* you are! Why can't you
let Mr. Torrens tell his tale his own way ? "

So Mr. Torrens went on :—" It doesn't matter. If you had ever
done so, I believe you would confirm my experience of the position.
If Orpheus had whistled, instead of singing to a lute, Eurydice
would have stopped with Pluto, and Orpheus would have cut a
very poor figure. I began to perceive that Achilles wasn't going
to respond, and I knew the hare wouldn't, all along. So I walked
on and got to a wood of oaks with an interesting appearance.
The interesting appearance was inviting, so I went inside. Achilles
was sure to turn up, I thought. Poor dear!—I didn't see him for
some days after that, when I came to and heard all about it. He
had been very uneasy about me, I'm afraid."

" But inside the wood with the interesting appearance—what
happened then ? " Gwen would not tolerate digression.

" Well, I came to the edge of a wall with a little sunk glade
beyond, and was looking across some blackberry bushes when I
heard a rifle-shot, and the whirr of a bullet. I had just time to
notice that the whirr came *with* the gunshot—if it had been in
the opposite direction it would have followed it—when I was struck
on the head and fell. It was the fall that knocked me insensible,
but it was the gunshot that was responsible for all that bleeding. . . . Do you know, I can't tell you how sorry I am for that
old boy that fired the shot ? I can't imagine anything more miserable than shooting a man by accident."

It was then that an uneasy feeling about those eyes, that looked
so clear and might be so deceiving, took hold of Gwen's mind, and
would not be ignored on any terms. The speaker's " you "—was
it addressed in this case to her or to her mother ? The line of his
vision seemed to pass between them. If he could see at all, ever

so dimly, he could look towards the person he addressed. One does not always do so; true enough! But one does not stare to right or to left of him. And she felt sure these words had been spoken to herself.

So while her mother was joining in commiseration of old Stephen, towards whom she herself felt rather brutal, she was casting about for some means of coming at the truth. Irene was no good, however altruistic her motives might be for story-telling. . . . No!—his eyes looked at her in quite another fashion that evening at Arthur's Bridge, in the light of the sunset. She *must* get at the truth, come what might!

She left her mother to express sympathy for old Stephen, remaining rather obdurately silent; checking a wish to say that it served the old man right for meddling with loaded guns. She waited for the subject to die down, and then recurred to its predecessor. Did Mr. Torrens walk straight from Arthur's Bridge to the Thurrock or go roundabout? She did not really want to know —merely wanted to get him to talk about himself again. He might say something about his sight, by accident.

He replied:—" I did not go absolutely straight. I went first to where a couple of stones—a respectable married couple, I should say—were standing close together in the fern, with big initials cut on them. Their own, I presume." Gwen said she knew them; they were parish boundaries. " Well—probably that hare was trying what it felt like to be in two parishes at once, for he jumped from behind that stone and started for the Thurrock—that's right, isn't it? "

" Drews Thurrock? Yes."

" It was unfortunately just then that the collar broke. I whistled until I felt undignified, and then went straight for the said Thurrock, rather dreading that I should find Achilles awaiting applause for an achievement in—in leporicide, I suppose. . . ."

" I'm sure you didn't."

" I did not. So I waited a little, and was thinking what I had better do next, when the shot came. You can almost see the place from this window." He got up from his chair, standing exactly where he had stood when his sister made his hand point out Arthur's Bridge in blind show. He made a certain amount of pretence that he could see; and, indeed, seemed to do so. No stranger to the circumstances could have detected it. " I couldn't be sure about the place of the stones, though," said he, carefully avoiding direct verbal falsehood; at least, so Irene thought, trembling at his rashness. He went on:—" Oh dear, how doddery one

does feel on one's legs after a turn out of this kind!" and fell
back in his chair, his sister alone noticing how he touched it with
his hand first to locate it. "I shall be better after a cup of tea,"
said he. And the whole thing was so natural that although he had
not said in so many words that he could see anything, the impression that he could was so strong that Gwen could have laughed
aloud for joy. "He really does see *something!*" she exclaimed to
herself.

If he could only have been content with this much of success!
But he must needs think he could improve upon it—reinforce it.
His remark about the cup of tea had half-reference to its appearance on the horizon; or, rather on the little carved-oak table near
the window, whose flaps were being accommodated for its reception
as he spoke. The dwellers in this part of the country considered
five o'clock tea at this time an invention of their own, and were
rather vain of it. Another decade made it a national institution.

"If there is one thing I enjoy more than another," he said,
"it is a copper urn that boils furiously by magic of its own accord.
When I was a kid our old cook Ursley used to allow me to come
into the kitchen and see the red-hot iron taken out of the fire and
dropped into the inner soul of ours, which was glorious." This was
all perfectly safe, because there was the urn in audible evidence.
Indeed, the speaker might have stopped there and scored. Why
need he go on? "And these blue Nankin cups are lovely. I never
could go crockery-mad as some people do. But good Nankin blue
goes to my heart." And he really thought, poor fellow, that he had
done well, and been most convincing.

Alas for his flimsy house of cards! Down it came. For there
had only been four left of that blue tea-service, and he had broken
one. The urn was hissing and making its lid jump in the middle
of a Crown Derby tea-set, so polychromatic, so self-assertive in
its red and blue and gold, that no ghost of a chance was left of
catching at the skirts of colour-blindness to find a golden bridge
of escape from the blunder. The most colour-blind eyes in the
world never confuse monochrome and polychrome.

There is a sudden terror-struck misgiving on the beautiful face
of Gwen, and an uneasy note of doubt in her mother's voice,
seeking by vague speech to elude and slur over the difficulty.
"The patterns are quite alike," she says weakly. The blind man
feels he has made a mistake, and is driven to safe silence. He
understands his slip more clearly when the servant, speaking
half-aside, but audibly, to the Countess, says:—"Mrs. Masham
said the blue was spoiled for four, my lady, and to bring four of

the China." Crown Derby is more distinctly China in English vernacular than Nankin blue.

Please understand that the story is giving at great length incidents that passed in fractions of a minute—incidents Time recorded *currente calamo* for Memory to rearrange at leisure. The incident of the tea-cups was easily slurred over and forgotten. Adrian Torrens saw the risks of attempting too much, and gave up pretending that he could see. Irene and the Countess let the subject go; the former most willingly, the latter with only slight reluctance. Gwen alone dwelt upon it, or rather it dwelt upon her; her memory could not shake it off. Do what she would the thought came back to her: "He cannot see *at all*. I must know—I *must* know!" She could not join in the chit-chat which went on under the benevolent influence of the tea-leaf, the great untier of tongues. She could only sit looking beautiful, gazing at the deceptive eyes she felt so sure were blind to her beauty, devising some means of extracting confession from their owner, and thereby knowing the worst, if it was to come. It was interesting to her, of course, to hear Mr. Torrens talk of the German Universities, with which he seemed very familiar; and of South America, the area of which, he said, had stood in the way of his becoming equally familiar with it. He had been about the world a good deal for a man of five-and-twenty.

"Gwen thought you were more," said Irene. "At Arthur's Bridge, you know! She thought you were twenty-seven."

"Because I was so wet through. Naturally. I was soaked and streaky. Are you sure it wasn't thirty-seven, Lady Gwendolen?"

It has been mentioned that Lady Ancester had a matter-of-fact side to her character. But was it this that made her say thoughtfully:—"Twenty-five perhaps—certainly not more!" Probably her mind had run back nearly thirty years, and she was calculating from the date of this man's father's marriage, which she knew; or from that of his eldest brother's birth, which she also knew. She was not so clear about Irene. At the time of that young lady's first birthday—her only one, in fact—her close observation of her old flame's family dates was flagging. But she was clear that this Adrian's birth had followed near upon that of her own son Frank, drowned a few years since so near the very place of this gunshot accident. The coincidence may have made her identifications keener. Or Adrian's reckless chat, so like his father's in old days that she had more than once gone near to comment on it, may have roused old memories and set her a-fixing dates.

Adrian laughed at the way his age seemed to be treated as an open question. " We have the Registrar on our side, at any rate, Lady Ancester. I can answer for that. By-the-by, wasn't my father . . . did not my father? . . ." He wanted to say: " Was not my father a friend of your brother in old days? " But it sounded as if the friendship, whatever it was, had lessened in newer days, and he knew of nothing to warrant the assumption. He knew nothing of his father's early love passages, of course. Fathers don't tell their sons what narrow escapes they have had of being somebody else, or somebody else being they—an awkward expression!

Her ladyship thought over a phrase or two before she decided on :—" Your father used to come to Clarges Street in my mother's time." She was pleased with the selection; but less so with a second, one of several she tried to herself and rejected. " We have really scarcely met since those days. I thought him wonderfully little changed."

Has a parent of yours, you who read—or of ours, for that matter—ever spoken to one or other of us, I wonder, of some fancy of his or her bygone days; one whose greeting, company manners apart, was an embrace; whose letters were opened greedily; whose smile was rapture, and whose frown a sleepless night? If he or she did so, was the outcome better than the Countess's?

She wanted to run away, but could not just yet. She made believe to talk over antecedents—making a conversation of indescribable baldness, and setting Irene's shrewd wits to work to find out why. It was not *her* brother, but her husband's, who had been Sir Hamilton's college-friend. Yes, her father was well acquainted with Mr. Canning, and so on. This was her contribution to general chat, until such time had elapsed as would warrant departure and round the visit plausibly off.

It was Clarges Street that had done it. Irene was sure of that! She, the daughter of the Miss Abercrombie her father had married, sitting there and coming to conclusions!

However, the Countess meant to go—no doubt of it. " You have paid my brother such a short visit, after all," said Irene. " Please don't go away because you fancy you are tiring him." But it was no use. Her ladyship meant to go, and went. Regrets of all sorts, of course; explanatory insincerities about stringent obligations elsewhere; even specific allegations of expected guests; false imputation of exacting claims to the Earl. All with one upshot—departure.

Gwen had taken little or no notice of what was passing, since that betraying incident of the Crown Derby set. Her mind was at work on schemes for discovery of the truth about those eyes. She got on the track of a good one. If she could only contrive to be alone with him for one moment. Yes—it *was* worth trying?

It was her mother's inexplicable alacrity to be gone that gave the opportunity. Her ladyship said good-bye to Mr. Torrens; was sorry she had to go, but the Earl was so fussy about anything the least like an appointment—some concession to conscience in the phrasing of this—in short, go she must! Having committed herself thus, to wait for her daughter would have been the merest self-stultification. She went out multiplying apologies, and Irene naturally accompanied her along the lobby, assisted and sanctioned by Achilles. Gwendolen was alone with the man who was still credited with sight enough to see *something*—provided that it was a palpable something. Now—if she could only play her part right!

"Mamma is always in such a fuss to go somewhere and do something else," she said, rather affecting the drawl of a fashionable young lady; for she could hide anxiety better, she felt, that way. "Do you know, Mr. Torrens, I don't believe a word of all that about people coming. Nobody's coming. If there is, they've been there ever so long. I did so want to talk to you about one of your poems. I mustn't stop now, I suppose, or I shall be in a scrape." But all the while that she was saying this she was standing with her right hand outstretched, as though to say good-bye. Only the word remained unspoken.

"Which of my poems was it?" He was to all seeming looking full at her, yet his hand did not come out to meet hers. There was hope still. How could he ratify an adieu with a handshake, on the top of a question that called for an answer?

Gwen had not arranged the point in her mind—had not thought of any particular poem in fact. She took the first that occurred to her. "It's the one called 'A Vigil in Darkness,'" she said. And then she would have been so glad to withdraw it and substitute another. That was not possible—she had to finish:—"I wanted to know if any other English poet has ever used 'starren' for stars."

Adrian laughed. "I remember," said he; then quoted: "'The daughters of the dream witch come and go,' don't they? 'The black bat hide the *starren* of the night.' That's it, isn't it? . . . No—so far as I know! But they are a queer lot. Nobody ever knows what they'll be at next in the way of jargon. It's some rubbish I wrote when I was a boy. I put it with the others to please 'Re." This was his shortest for Irene.

If he would only have toned down his blank ignorance of the beautiful white hand stretched out so appealingly to him—made the least concession! If he had but held in readiness an open-fingered palm, with intent, there would have been hope. But alas! —no such thing. When, instead, he thrust both hands into the pockets of the blue Mandarin-silk dressing-gown, Gwen felt exactly as if a knife had cut her heart. And there were his two beautiful eyes looking—looking—straight at her! Need Fate have worded an inexorable decree so cruelly?

Hope caught at a straw, *more suo*. What was more likely than that darkness was intermittent? Many things—most things for that matter! Any improbability to outwit despair. Anything rather than final surrender. Therefore, said Gwen to herself, her hand outstretched should await his, however sick at heart its owner felt, till the last pretext of belief had flagged and died— belief in the impossibility of so terrible a doom, consistently with any decent leniency of the Creator towards His creatures.

"Oh—to please Irene, was it?" said Gwen, talking chancewise; not meaning much, but hungering all the while for the slightest aliment for starving Hope. "Who were 'the daughters of the Dream Witch?'" And then she was sorry again. Better that a poem about darkness should have been forgotten! She kept her hand outstretched, mind you!—even though Adrian made matters worse by folding his hands round his arms on a high chair-back, and leaning on it. "I wonder who she is," was the girl's thought, as she looked at a ring.

"Let me see!" said he. "How does it go?" Then he quoted, running the lines into one: "'In the night-watches in the garden of Night ever the watchman sorrowing for the light waiteth in silence for the silent Dawn. Dead sleep is on the city far below.' Then the daughters of the Dream Witch came and went as per contract. No—I haven't the slightest idea who they were. They didn't leave their names."

"You will never be serious, Mr. Torrens." She felt too heart-sick to answer his laugh. She never moved her hand, watching greedily for a sign that never came. There was Irene coming back, having disposed of her ladyship! "I *must* go," said Gwen, "because of mamma. She's the Dream Witch, I suppose. I *must* go. Good-bye, Mr. Torrens! But I can leave *my* name—Gwen or Gwendolen. Choose which you prefer." She had to contrive a laugh, but it caught in her throat.

"Gwen, I think." It was such a luxury to call her by her name, holding her hand in his—for, the moment she spoke "good-bye," his hand had come to meet hers like a shot—that he seemed in no hurry to relinquish it. Nor did she seem concerned to have it back at the cost of dragging. "Did you ever live abroad?" said he. "In Italy they always kiss hands—it's rather rude not to. Let's pretend it's Italy."

She was not offended; might have been pleased, in fact—for Gwen was no precisian, no drawer of hard-and-fast lines in flirtation—if it had not been for the black cloud that in the last few minutes had been stifling her heart. As it was, Adrian's trivial presumption counted for nothing, unless, indeed, it was as the resolution of a difficulty. It was good so far. Even so two pugilists are glad of a way out of a close grip sometimes. It ended a handshake neither could withdraw from gracefully. "Good-bye, Mr. Torrens," she said, and contrived another laugh. "I'll come again to talk about the poetry. I *must* go now." She passed Irene, coming in from a moment's speech with the nurse outside, with a hurried farewell, and ran on to her mother's room breathless.

CHAPTER XIX

GWEN'S PESSIMISM. IT WAS ALL OUR FAULT! HOW SHE KNEW THAT
    ADRIAN TORRENS WAS FIANCE, AND HOW HER MOTHER TOOK KINDLY
    TO THE IDEA. PEOPLE ONLY KNOW WHAT THE WILL OF GOD IS, NOT
    WHAT IT ISN'T. BUT ADRIAN TORRENS DID *NOT* COME TO TABLE.
    LONELINESS, AND NIGHT—ALL BUT SLEEPLESS. WANT OF COMMON
    SENSE. THE FATE OF A FEATHER. COUNTING A THOUSAND. LOOK
    ING MATTERS CALMLY IN THE FACE. A GREAT DECISION, AND WHAT
    GWEN SAW IN A MIRROR

LADY ANCESTER, not sorry to get away from a position which involved the consideration that she was unreasonable in feeling reluctance to remain in it, endeavoured on arriving in her own room to congratulate herself on her own share in an embarrassing interview.

She had got through it very well certainly, but not so well as she had been led to expect by her meeting with his father three weeks since. She had had her misgivings before that interview, and had been pleasantly surprised to find how thoroughly the inexorable present had ridden rough-shod over the half-forgotten past. Their old identities had vanished, and it was possible to be civil and courteous, and that sort of thing; even to send messages of sympathy, quite in earnest, to the lady who up till now had been little more than the Miss Abercrombie Hamilton Torrens married. Being thus set at ease about what seemed rocks of embarrassment ahead, in the father's case, Lady Ancester had looked forward with perfect equanimity to making the acquaintance of the son—had, in fact, only connected him in her mind with this deplorable accident, which, however, she quite understood to be going to be a thing of the past. All in good time. Her equanimity had, however, been disturbed by the young man's inherited manner, which his father had so completely lost; above all things by his rapid nonsense, one of his father's leading characteristics in youth. She condemned it as more nonsensical, which probably only meant that she herself was older. But the manner—the manner of it! How it brought back Clarges Street and her mother, and the family earthquake over her resolution to marry a young Dragoon, with three good lives between him and his inheritance! She was taken aback to find herself still so sensitive about that old story.

She had not succeeded in ridding herself of her disquieting memories when her daughter followed her, choking back tense excitement until she had fairly closed the door behind her. Then her words came with a rush, for all that she kept her voice in check to say them.

"He cannot *see*, mamma—he cannot see *at all!* He is dead stone-blind—for life—for life! And *we* have done it—*we* have done it!" Then she broke down utterly, throwing herself on a sofa to hide in its cushions the torrent of tears she could no longer keep back. "*We* have done it—*we* have done it!" she kept on crying. "*We* have ruined his life, and the guilt is ours—ours—*all!*"

The Countess, good woman, tried to mix consolation with protest against such outrageous pessimism. She pointed out that there was no medical authority for such an extreme view as Gwen's. On the contrary, Sir Coupland had spoken most hopefully. And, after all, if Mr. Torrens could see Arthur's Bridge he could not be absolutely blind.

"He could not see Arthur's Bridge *at all*," said Gwen, sitting up and wiping her tears, self-possessed again for the moment from the stimulus of contradiction, always a great help. "I stood facing him for five minutes holding out my hand for him to shake, and he never—*never*—saw it!"

"Perhaps he doesn't like shaking hands," said her mother weakly. "Some people don't."

"They do mine," said Gwen. "Besides, he did in the end, and . . ."

"And what?"

"And nothing." At which point Gwen broke down again, crying out as before that he was blind, and she knew it. The doctors were only talking against hope, and *they* knew it. "Oh, mother, mother," she cried out, addressing her mother as she would often do when in trouble or excited, "how shall we bear it, years from now, to know that he can see nothing—*nothing!*—and to know that the guilt of his darkness lies with us—is ours—is yours and mine? Have we ever either of us said a word of protest against that wicked dog-shooting order? It was in the attempt to commit a crime that we sanctioned, that old Stephen tried to shoot that darling Achilles. Oh, I know it was no fault of old Stephen's!" She became a little calmer from indulgence of speech that had fought for hearing. "Oh no, mother dear, it's no use talking. If Mr. Torrens never recovers his eyesight he has only us to thank for it." She paused a moment, and then added:—"And how I shall look that girl in the face I don't know!"

. "What girl?".

"Oh, didn't you see? The girl he's got that engaged ring on his finger about. You didn't see? You never *do* see, mamma dear!"

"I didn't notice any particular ring, dear." Her ladyship may have felt a relief about something, to judge by her manner. "Has Irene said anything to you?" she asked.

Gwen considered a little. "Irene talks a good deal about a Miss Gertrude Abercrombie, a cousin. But she has never *said* anything."

"Oh!—it's Miss Gertrude Abercrombie? . . ."

"*I* know nothing about it. I was only guessing. She may be Miss Gertrude Anybody. Whoever she is, it's the same thing. *Think* what she's lost!"

"She has, indeed, my dear," says the elder lady, who is not going to give up this acceptable Miss Gertrude Anybody, even at the risk of talking some nonsense about her. "And we must all feel for the cruelty of her position. But if she is—as I have no doubt she is—truly attached to Mr. Torrens, she will find her consolation in the thought that it is given to her to . . . to . . ." But the Countess was not rhetorician enough to know that choice words should be kept for perorations. She had quite taken the edge off her best arrow-head. She could not wind up "to be a consolation to her husband" with any convincingness. So when Gwen interrupted her with:—"I see what you mean, but it's nonsense,"

she fell back upon the strong entrenchment of seniors, who know
the Will of God. They really do, don't you know? "At least,"
she said, "this Miss Abercrombie must admit that no blame can
fairly be laid at our door for what was so manifestly ordained by
the Almighty. Sir Hamilton Torrens himself was the first to ex-
onerate your father. His own keeper is instructed to shoot all
dogs except poodles."

"It was not the Will of God at all . . ."

"My dear!—how *can* you know that?"

"Well—not more than everything else is! It was old Stephen's
not hitting his mark. And he would have killed Achilles, then.
Oh dear, how I do sometimes wish God could be kept out of it! . . .
No, mamma, it's no use looking shocked. Whatever makes out
that it was not our fault is wrong, and Sir Hamilton Torrens
didn't mean that when he said it."

"My dear, it is his own son."

"Very well, then, all the more! Oh, you know what I mean. . . .
No, mamma," said she as she left the room, "it isn't any use. I
am utterly miserable about it."

And she was, though she herself scarcely knew yet how miserable.
So long as she had someone else to speak to, the whole deadly
truth lingered on the threshold of her mind and would not enter.
She ascribed weight to opinions she would have disregarded had
she had no stake on the chance of their correctness.

She caught at the narration of her maid Lutwyche, prolonging
her hair-combing for talk's sake. Lutwyche had the peculiarity
of always accommodating her pronunciation to the class she was
speaking with, elaborating it for the benefit of those socially above
her. So her inquiry how the gentleman was getting on was accounted for by her having seen him from the guardian. Speaking
with an equal, she would have said garden. She had seen him
therefrom, and been struck by his appearance of recovered vigour,
especially by his visible enjoyment of the land escape. She would
have said landscape to Cook. Pronounced anyhow, her words were
a comfort to her young mistress, defending her a very little against
the black thoughts that assailed her. Similarly, Miss Lutwyche's
understanding that Mr. Torrens would come to table this evening
was a flattering unction to her distressed soul, and she never questioned her omniscient handmaid's accuracy. On the contrary, she
utilised a memory of some chance words of her mother to Irene,
suggesting that her brother might be "up to coming down" that
evening, as a warrant for replying:—"I believe so."

Nevertheless, she had no hope of seeing him make his appearance in the brilliantly illuminated Early Jacobean drawing-room, where at least two of the upstairs servants had to light wax tapers for quite ten minutes at dusk, to be even with a weakness of the Earl's for wax-candlelight and no other. And when Irene appeared without him, her " Oh dear!—your brother wasn't up to coming down, then ? " was spiritless and perfunctory. Nor did she believe her friend's " No—we thought it best to be on the safe side." For she knew now why it was that this absence from the evening banquet—" family dinner-table " is too modest a phrase—had been so strenuously insisted on. There was no earthly reason why Irene's brother should not have dressed and sat at table. Were there no sofas in the Early Jacobean drawing-room ? There was no reason against his presence at all except that his absolute blindness must needs have been manifest to every observer. She could see it all now.

"You know, dear," said Irene, " if Adrian were a reasonable being, there would be no harm in his dining down, as Lutwyche calls it. He could sit up to dinner perfectly, but no earthly persuasion would get him up to bed till midnight. And as for lying down on sofas in the drawing-room after dinner, you could as soon get a mad bull to lie down on a sofa as Adrian, if there was what Lutwyche calls company."

So that evening the beauty of the Earl's daughter—whose name among the countryfolk, by-the-by, was " Gwen o' the Towers "—was less destructive than usual to the one or two new bachelors who helped the variation of the party. For monumental beauty kills only poets and dreamers, and these young gentlemen were Squires. The verdict of one of them about her tells its tale:—" A stunner to look at, but too standoffish for my money ! " She was nothing of the sort; and would gladly, to oblige, have shot a smile or an eye-flash at either of them if her heart had not been so heavy. But she wanted terribly to be alone and cry all the evening, and was of no use as a beauty. Perhaps it was as well that it was so, for these unattached males.

When the time came for the loneliness of night she was frightened of it, and let Irene go at her own door with reluctance. In answer to whom she said at parting:—"No—no, dear! I'm perfectly well, and nothing's the matter." Irene spoke back after leaving her:—" You know I'm not the least afraid about him. It will be all right." Then Gwen mustered a poor laugh, and with " Of course it will, dear! " vanished into her bedroom.

She got to sleep and slept awhile; then awoke to the worst solitude a vexed soul knows—those terrible " small hours " of the morning. Then, every mere insect of evil omen that daylight has

kept in bounds grows to the size of an elephant, and what was
the whirring of his wings becomes discordant thunder. Then pal-
liatives lose their market-value, and every clever self-deception that
stands between us and acknowledged ill bursts, bubblewise, and
leaves the soul naked and unarmed against despair.

Gwen waked without provocation at about three in the morning;
waked Heaven knew why!—for there was all the raw material
of a good night's rest; the candidate for the sleepership; a prodigiously comfortable bed; dead silence, not so much as an owl
in the still night she looked out into during an excursion warranted to promote sleep—but never sleep itself! She had been
dragged reluctantly from a dreamless Nirvana into the presence
of a waking nightmare—two great beautiful eyes that looked at
her and saw nothing; and this coercion, she somehow felt, was
really due to an unaccountable absence of mind on her part.
Surely she could have kept asleep with a little more common sense.
She would go back from that excursion reinforced, and bid defiance to that nightmare. Sleep would come to her, she knew, if
she could find a *modus vivendi* with a loose flood of golden hair,
and could just get hold of a feather-quill that was impatient of
imprisonment and wanted to see the world. She searched for it
with the tenderest of finger-tips because she knew—as all the
feather-bed world knows—that if one is too rough with it, it goes
in, and comes out again just when one is dropping off. . . .

There!—it was caught and pulled out. She would not burn
it. It would smell horribly and make her think of Lutwyche's
remedy for fainting fits, burned feathers held to the nostrils.
No!—she would put it through the casement into the night-air,
and it would float away and think of its days on the breast of an
Imbergoose, and believe them back again. Oh, the difference
between the great seas and winds, and the inside of that stuffy
ticking! Poor little breast-feather of a foolish bird! Yes—now
she could go to sleep! She knew it quite well—she had only to
contrive a particular attitude. . . . There, that was right! Now
she had only to put worrying thoughts out of her head and count
a thousand . . . and then—oblivion!

Alas, no such thing! In five minutes the particular attitude was
a thing of the past, and the worrying thoughts were back upon
her with a vengeance. Or, rather, the worrying thought; for her
plural number was hypocrisy. She was in for a deadly wakeful
night, a night of growing fever, with those sightless eyes expelling
every other image from her brain. She was left alone with the
darkness and a question she dared not try to answer. Suppose that

when those eyes looked upon her that evening at Arthur's Bridge for the first time—suppose it was also the last? What then? How could she know it, and know how the thing came about, and whom she held answerable for it, and go on living? . . .

No—her life would end with that. Nothing would again be as it had been for her. Her childhood had ended when she first saw Death; when her brother's corpse was carried home dripping from within a stone's throw of this new tragedy. But was not that what bills of lading call the " Act of God "—fair play, as it were, on the part of Fate? What was this? . . . Come—this would never do, with a pulse like that!

No one should ever feel his pulse, or hers, at night. Gwen was none the better for doing it. Nor did she benefit by an operation which her mind called looking matters calmly in the face. It consisted in imaginary forecasts of a *status quo* that was to come about. She had to skip some years as too horrible even to dream of; years needed to live down the worst raw sense of guilt, and become hardened to inevitable life. Then she filled in her *scenario* with Sir Adrian Torrens, the blind Squire of Pensham Steynes, and his beautiful and accomplished wife, a dummy with no great vitality, constructed entirely out of a ring on Mr. Torrens's finger and an allusion of Irene's to the Miss Gertrude Abercrombie, whose skill in needlework surpassed Arachne's. Gwen did not supply this lady with a sufficiently well-marked human heart. Perhaps the temptation to make her clever and shrewd but not sympathetic, not quite up to her husband's deserts, was irresistible. It allowed of an unprejudiced consciousness of what she, Gwen, would have been in this dummy's situation. It allowed latitude to a fancy that portrayed Lady Gwendolen Whatever-she-had-become—because, of course, *she* would have to marry some fool—as the staunch and constant friend of the family at Pensham. Her devotion to the dummy when in trouble—and, indeed, she piled up calamities for the unhappy lady—was monumental; an example to her sex. And when, to the bitter grief of her devoted husband, the dummy died—all parties being then, at a rough estimate, forty—and she herself, his dearest friend, stood by the dummy's grave with him, and, generally speaking, sustained him in his tribulation, a disposition to get the fool out of the way grew strong enough to make its victim doubt her own vouchers for her own absolute disinterestedness. She turned angrily upon her fancies, tore them to tatters, flung them to the winds. One does this, and then the pieces join themselves together and reappear intact.

She was no nearer sleep after looking matters calmly in the

face, that way, for a full hour. Similar trials to dramatize a probable future all ended on the same lines, and each time Gwen was indignant with herself for her own folly. What was this man to her, whom she had seen twice? Little enough!—she pledged herself to it in the Court of Conscience! What was she to him, who had spoken with her twice certainly; but *seen* her— oh, how little! Why, *she* had seen *him* more, of the two, if one came to close quarters with Time. See how long he was stooping over that unfortunate dog-chain!

Sitting up in bed in the dim July dawn, wild-eyed in an un- shepherded flock of golden locks, this young lady was certainly surpassingly beautiful. She was revolving in her poor, aching head a contingency she had not fully allowed for. Suppose— merely to look other things in the face, you see!—suppose there were *no* dummy! What chance would the poor fellow have then of winning the love of any woman, with those blind eyes in his head? Gwen got up restlessly and went to the casement, meeting a stream of level sunlight that the swallows outside in the ivy were making the subject of comment, and stood looking out over the leagues of the ancient domain of her forefathers. "Gwen o' the Towers"—that was her name. It seemed to join chorus with her own answer to the last question, to her satisfaction.

To offer the consolation of her love, to give all she had to give, to this man as compensation for the great curse that had fallen on him through the fault of her belongings, seemed to her in her excited state easy and nowise strange—mere difficulty of the nego- tiation apart. She elected to shut her eyes to a fact we and the story can guess—we are so shrewd, you see!—and to make a parade in her own eyes of a self-renunciation approaching that of Marcus Curtius. If only the gulf would open to receive her she would fling herself in. She ignored the dissimilarities of detail in the two cases, especially the conceivable promised land at the bottom of *her* gulf. The Roman Eques had nothing but death and dark- ness to look forward to.

The difficulties of the scheme shot across her fevered conception of it. How if, though he was not affianced to the dummy, or any other lay figure she might provide, his was a widowed heart left barren by the hand of Death? How if some other disappointment had marred his life?—some passion for a woman who had rashly accepted somebody else before meeting him? This happens we know; so did Gwen, and was sorry. How if some minx—Lut- wyche's expression—had bewitched him and slighted him? He might nurse a false ideal of her till Doomsday. Men did some-

times, *cæteris paribus*. But how could she—how *could* she? . . .
Anyhow, Gwen might have seen her way through that difficulty
with a fair chance. But—to be invisible!

The morning sun had been at variance with some flames, hard
to believe clouds, and had just dispersed them so successfully
that their place in the heavens knew them no more. His rays,
unveiled, bore hard upon the blue eyes, sore with watching, of
the girl a hundred million miles off, and drove her from her casement. Gwen of the Towers fell back into the room, all the flowing lawn of the most luxurious *robe-de-nuit* France could provide
turned to gold by the touch of Phœbus. She paused a moment
before a mirror, to glance at her pallor in it, and to wonder at
the sunlight in the wealth of its setting of ungroomed, uncontrollable locks. It was not vanity exactly that provoked the despairing thought:—" But he will never see me—never! " A girl
would have been a hypocrite indeed who could shut her eyes to
what Gwen saw in that looking-glass. She knew all about it—had
done so from babyhood.

Some relaxation of the mind gave Morpheus an opportunity,
and he took such advantage of a willing victim that Lutwyche,
coming three hours later, scarcely knew how to deal with the case,
and might have been uneasy at such an intensive cultivation of
sleep if she had been a nervous person. But she was prosaic and
phlegmatic, and held to the general opinion that nothing unusual
ever happened. So she was content to make a little extra noise;
and, when nothing came of it, to go away till rung for. That was
how Gwen came to be so late at breakfast that morning.

CHAPTER XX

HOW THE HON. PERCIVAL GAVE MISS DICKENSON HIS ACCOUNT OF THE
BLIND MAN. HOW THAT ANY YOUNG MAN SOEVER IS GLAD THAT ANY
YOUNG LADY SOEVER ISN'T *FIANCEE*, EXCEPT SHE BE UGLY. MISS
DICKENSON'S EFFRONTERY. HOW MR. PELLEW SAID " POOH ! "
IRENE'S ABSENCE, VISITING. EVERYONE'S ELSE ABSENCE, EXCEPT THE
BLIND MAN'S, GWEN'S, AND MRS. BAILEY'S, WHO HAD A LETTER TO
WRITE

THE Hon. Percival Pellew had not been at the Towers continuously throughout the whole three weeks following the accident.
The best club in London could not have spared him as long as

that. He had returned to his place in the House a day or two later, had voted on the Expenses at Elections Bill, and had then gone to a by-election in Cornwall to help his candidate to keep his expenses at a minimum. His way back to the club did not lie near Ancester Towers, but he reconciled a renewal of his visit there to his conscience by the consideration that an unusually late Session was predicted. A little more country air would do him no harm, and the Towers was the best club in the country. He had had absolutely no motive whatever for going there, outside what this implies. Unless, indeed, something else was implied by his pledging his honour to himself that this was the case. Self-deception is an art that Man gives a great deal of attention to, and Woman nearly as much.

The Countess said to him, on the evening of his reappearance in time to dress for dinner:—" Everybody's gone, Percy—I mean everybody of your lot a fortnight ago." Whereto he replied:—" How about the wounded man？" and her ladyship said:—" Mr. Torrens？ Oh yes, Mr. Torrens is here still and his sister—they'll be here a few days longer. . . . There's nobody else. Yes, there's Constance Dickenson. Norbury, teli them to keep dinner back a little because of Mr. Pellew." This was all in one sentence, chiefly to the butler. She ended:—" All the rest are new," and the gentleman departed to dress in ten minutes—long ones probably. This was two or three evenings before Miss Dickenson saw that glow-worm in the garden. Perhaps three, because two are needed to account for the lady's attitude about that cigar, and twelve hours for a coolness occasioned by her ladyship's saying in her inconsiderate way:—" Oh, you are quite old friends, you two, of course—I forgot." Only fancy saying that a single lady and gentleman were " quite old friends "! Both parties exhibited mature courtesy, enriched with smiles in moderation. But for all that their relations painfully resembled civility for the rest of that evening.

However, whatever they were then, they were reinstated by now; that is to say, by the morning after Gwen's bad night. Eavesdrop, please, and overhear what you can in the arbutus walk, half-way through the Hon. Percival's first cigar.

The gentleman is accounting for something he has just said. " What made me think so was his being so curious about our friend Cumberworld. As for Gwen, I wouldn't trust her not to be romantic. Girls are."

The lady speaks discreetly:—" Certainly no such construction would have occurred to me. One has to be on one's guard against romantic ideas. She might easily be—a—*éprise,* to some extent—as girls are. . . ."

"But spooney, no! Well—perhaps you're right."

"I don't know whether I ought to say even that. I shouldn't, only to you. Because I know I can rely on your discretion. . . ."

"Rather. Only you must admit that when she appeared this morning—and last night—she was looking . . ."

"Looking what?"

"Well . . . rather too statuesque for jollity."

"Perhaps the heat. I know she complains of the heat; it gives her a headache."

"Come, Miss Dickenson, that's not fair. You know it was what *you* said began it."

"Began what?"

"Madam, what I am saying arises naturally from . . ."

"There!—do stop being Parliamentary and be reasonable. What you mean is—have those two fallen head over ears in love, or haven't they?" Discussions of this subject of Love are greatly lubricated by exaggeration of style. It is almost as good as a foreign tongue. She continued more seriously:—"Tell me a little more of what Mr. Torrens said."

"When I saw him this morning?" Mr. Pellew looked thoughtfully at what was left of his cigar, as if it would remind him if he looked long enough, and then threw it abruptly away as though he gave it up as a bad job. "No," he said, falling back on his own memory. "It wasn't what he said. It was the way of saying it. Manner is incommunicable. And he said so little about her. He talked a good deal about Philippa in a chaffy sort of way—said she was exactly his idea of a Countess—why had one such firm convictions about Countesses and Duchesses and Baronets and so on? It led to great injustice, causing us to condemn nine samples out of ten as Pretenders, not real Countesses or Duchesses or Baronets at all. He was convinced his own dear dad was a tin Baronet; or, at best, Britannia-metal. Alfred Tennyson had spoken of two sorts—little lily-handed ones and great broad-shouldered brawny Englishmen. Neither would eat the sugar nor go to sleep in an armchair with the *Times* over his head. *His* father did both. I admitted the force of his criticism, but could not follow his distinction between Countesses and Duchesses. Duchesses were squarer than Countesses, just as Dukes were squarer than Earls."

"I think they are," said Miss Dickenson. She shut her eyes a moment for reflection, and then decided:—"Oh yes—certainly squarer—not a doubt of it!" Mr. Pellew formed an image in his mind, of this lady fifteen years ago, with its eyes shut. He did not the least know why he did so.

"Torrens goes on like that," he continued. "Makes you laugh sometimes! But what I was going to say was this. When he had disposed of Philippa and chaffed Tim a little—not disrespectfully you know—he became suddenly serious, and talked about Gwen— spoke with a hesitating deference, almost ceremoniously. Said he had had some conversation with Lady Gwendolen, and been impressed with her intelligence and wit. Most young ladies of her age were so frivolous. He was the more impressed that her beauty was undeniable. The brief glimpse he had had of her had greatly affected him artistically—it was an Æsthetic impression entirely. He overdid this."

Miss Dickenson nodded slightly in confidence with herself. *Her* insight jotted down a brief memorandum about Mr. Pellew's, and the credit it did him. That settled, she recalled a something he had left unfinished earlier. "You were asking about Lord Cumberworld, Mr. Pellew?"

"Whether there was anything afoot in that quarter? Yes, he asked that, and wanted to know if Mrs. Bailey, who had been retailing current gossip, was rightly informed when she said that there was, and that it was going to come off. He was very anxious to show how detached he was personally. Made jokes about its 'coming off' like a boot. . . ."

"Stop a minute to see if I understand. . . . Oh yes—I see. 'If there was anything afoot.' Of course. Go on."

"It was a poor quip, and failed of its purpose. His relief was too palpable when I disallowed Mrs. Bailey. . . . By-the-by, that's a rum thing, Miss Dickenson,—that way young men have. I believe if I did it once when I was a young fillah I did it fifty times."

"Did what?"

"Well—breathed free on hearing that a girl wasn't engaged. Doesn't matter how doosid little they know of her—only seen her in the Park on horseback, p'r'aps—they'll eat a lot more lunch if they're told she's still in the market. Fact!"

Miss Dickenson said that no doubt Mr. Pellew knew best, and that it was gratifying to think how many young men's lunches her earlier days might have intensified without her knowing anything about it. The gentleman felt himself bound to reassure and confirm, for was not the lady *passée?* "Rather!" said he; this favourite expression this time implying that the name of these lunches was no doubt Legion. An awkward sincerity of the lady caused her to say:—"I didn't mean that." And then she had to account for it. She was intrepid enough to venture on: "What I meant was, never being engaged," but not cool enough to keep of one colour exactly. It didn't rise to the height of embarrassment, but something rippled for all that.

A cigar Mr. Pellew was lighting required unusual and special attention. It had a mission, that cigar. It had to gloss over a slight flush on its smoker's cheeks, and to take the edge off the abruptness with which he said,—"Oh, gammon!" as he threw a Vesuvian away.

He picked up the lost thread at the point of his own indiscreet excursion into young-manthropology—his own word when he apologized for it. "Anyhow," said he, "it struck me that our friend upstairs was very hard hit. He made such a parade of his complete independence. Of course, I'm not much of a judge of such matters. Not my line. I understand that he has been prorogued— I mean his departure has. He's to try his luck at coming downstairs this evening after feeding-time. He funks finding the way to his mouth in public. Don't wonder—poor chap!"

Then this lady had a fit of contrition about the way in which she had been gossiping, and tried to back out. She had the loathsome meanness to pretend that she herself had been entirely passive, a mere listener to an indiscreet and fanciful companion. "What gossips you men are!" said she, rushing the position boldly. "Fancy cooking up a romance about this Mr. Torrens and Gwen, when they've hardly so much as," she had nearly said, "set eyes on each other"; but revised it in time for press. It worked out "when she has really only just set eyes on him, and chatted half an hour."

Mr. Pellew's indignation found its way through a stammer which expressed the struggle of courtesy against denunciation. "Come—hang it all!" said he. "It wasn't *my* romance. . . . Oh, well, perhaps it wasn't yours either. Only—play fair, Miss Dickenson. Six of the one and half a dozen of the other! Confess up!"

The lady assumed the tone of Tranquillity soothing Petulance. "Never mind, Mr. Pellew!" she said. "You needn't lie awake about it. It doesn't really matter, you know. . . . *Have* you got the right time? Because I have to be ready at half-past eleven to drive with Philippa. I promised. . . . What!—a quarter past? I must run." She looked back to reassure possible perturbation. "It really does *not* matter between *us*," said she, and vanished down the avenue.

The Hon. Percival Pellew walked slowly in the opposite direction in a brown study, leaving his thumbs in his armholes, and playing *la ci darem* with his fingers on his waistcoat. He played it twice or thrice before he stopped to knock a phenomenal ash off his cigar. Then he spoke, and what he said was "Pooh!"

The story does not know why he said "Pooh!" It merely notes, apropos of Miss Dickenson's last words, that the first person plural pronoun, used as a dual by a lady to a gentleman, sometimes makes hay of the thirdness of their respective persons singular. But if it had done so, this time, "Pooh!" was a weak counter-blast against its influence.

Irene's friend Gretchen von Trendelenstein had written that morning that she was coming to stay with the Mackworth Clarkes at Toft, only a couple of miles off. She would only have two days, and could not hope to get as far as Pensham, but couldn't Irene come to *her?* She was, you see, Irene's bosom friend. The letter had gone to Pensham and been forwarded, losing time. This was the last day of visiting-possibility at Toft. So Irene asked to be taken there; and, if she stayed, would find her way back somehow. Mr. Norbury, however, after referring to Archibald, the head of the stables, made *dernier ressorts* needless, and Irene was driven away behind a spirited horse by the young groom, Tom Kettering.

Her brother would have devolved entirely on Mrs. Bailey and chance visitors, if he had not struck vigorously against confinement to his room, after a recovery of strength sufficient to warrant his removal to his home eighteen miles away. If he was strong enough for that, he was strong enough for an easy flight of stairs, down and up, with tea between. Mrs. Bailey, the only obstacle, was overruled. Indeed, that good woman was an anachronism by now, her only remaining function being such succour as a newly blinded man wants till he gets used to his blindness. Tonics and stimulants were coming to an end, and her professional extinction was to follow. Nevertheless, Mr. Torrens held fast to dining in solitude until he recovered his eyesight, or at least until he had become more dexterous without it.

Now, it happened that on this day of all others three attractive events came all at once—the Flower Show at Brainley Thorpe, the Sadleigh Races, and a big Agricultural Meeting at King's Grantham, where the County Members were to address constituents. The Countess had promised to open the first, and the absence of the Earl from the second would have been looked upon as a calamity. All the male non-coroneted members of the company of mature years were committed to Agriculture or Bookmaking, and the younger ones to attendance on Beauty at the Flower Show. Poor Adrian Torrens!—there was no doubt he had been forgotten. But he was not going to admit the slightest concern about that. "Go away to your Von, darling Stupid!" said he. "And turn head over heels in her and wallow. Do you want to be the death of me? Do you want to throw me back when I'm such a credit to Mrs. Bailey and Dr. Nash?" Irene had her doubts—but there! —wasn't Gretchen going to marry an Herr Professor and be a Frau when she went back to Berlin, and would she ever see her again? Moreover, Gwen said to her:—"He won't be alone if he's downstairs in the drawing-room. Some of the women are sure to stop. It's too hot for old Lady Cumberworld to go out. I heard her say so."

"*She'll* be no consolation for him," said Irene.

"No—that she won't! But unless there's someone else there she'll have Inez—you've seen the Spanish *dame-de-compagnie?*— and *she'll* enjoy a flirtation with your brother. He'll speak Spanish to her, and she'll sing Spanish songs. *He* won't hurt for a few hours."

So Tom Kettering drove Irene away in the gig, and Adrian was guided downstairs to an empty hall by Mrs. Bailey at four o'clock, so as to get a little used to the room before anyone should return. Prophecy depicted Normal Society coming back to tea, and believed in itself. Achilles sanctioned his master's new departure by his presence, accompanying him to the drawing-room. This dog was not only tolerated but encouraged everywhere. Dogs are, when their eyes are pathetic, their coats faultless, and their compliance with household superstitions unhesitating.

"Anybody in sight, Mrs. Bailey?"

"Nobody yet, Mr. Torrens."

"*Speriamo!* Perhaps there's a piano in the room, Mrs. Bailey?"

"There's two. One's stood up against the wall shut. The other's on three legs in the middle of the room." That one was to play upon, she supposed, the other to sing to.

"If you will be truly obliging—you always are, you know—and conduct me to the one on three legs in the middle of the room, I will play you an air from Gluck's ' Orfeo,' which I am sure you will enjoy. . . . Oh yes—I can do without any music-books because I have played it before, not infrequently. . . ."

"I meant to set upon." In fact, Mrs. Bailey regarded this as the primary purpose of music-books; and so it was, at the home of her niece, who could play quite nicely. There was only two and they "just did." She referred to this while Mr. Torrens was spinning the music-stool to a suitable height for himself. He responded with perfect gravity—not a fraction of a smile—that books were apt to be too high or too low. It was the fault of the composers clearly, because the binders had to accept the scores as they found them. If the binders were to begin rearranging music to make volumes thicker or thinner, you wouldn't be able to play straight on. Mrs. Bailey concurred, saying that she had always said to her niece not to offer to play a tune till she could play it right through from beginning to end. Mr. Torrens said that was undoubtedly the view of all true musicians, and struck a chord, remarking that the piano had been left open. "How ever could you tell *that* now, Mr. Torrens?" said Mrs. Bailey, and felt that she was in the presence of an Artist.

Nevertheless, she seemed to be lukewarm about *Che faro,* merely remarking after hearing it that it was more like the slow tunes her niece played than the quick ones. The player said with unmoved gravity this was *andante.* Mrs. Bailey said that her niece, on the contrary, had been christened Selina. She could play the Polka. So could Mr. Torrens, rather to the good woman's surprise and, indeed, delight. He was so good-humoured that he played it again, and also the *Schottische;* and would have stood Gluck over to meet her taste indefinitely, but that voices came outside, and the selection was interrupted.

The voice of Lady Ancester was one, saying despairingly:— "My dear, if you're not ready we must go without you. I *must* be there in time." Miss Dickenson's was another, attesting that if the person addressed did not come, sundry specified individuals would be in an awful rage.

"Well, then, you must go without me. Flower shows always bore me to death." This was a voice that had not died out of the blind man's ears since yesterday; Lady Gwendolen's, 'of course. It added that its owner must finish her letter, or it would miss the six o'clock post and not catch the mail; which would have, somehow, some disastrous result. Then said her mother's voice, she should have written it before. Then justification and refutation, and each voice said its say with a difference—more of expounding, explaining—with a result like in Master Hugues of Saxe-Gotha's mountainous fugue, that one of them, Gwen's, stood out all the stiffer hence. No doubt you know your Browning. Gwen asserted herself victor all along the line, and remonstrance died a natural death. But what was she going to do all the afternoon? A wealth of employments awaited her, she testified. Rarely had so many arrears remained unpaid. Last and least she must try through that song, because she had to send the music back to the Signore. So the Countess supposed she must go her own way, and presently Adrian Torrens was conscious that her ladyship had gone hers, by the curt resurrection of sounds in abeyance some-while since; sounds of eight hoofs and four wheels; suddenly self-assertive, soon evanescent.

Was Gwen really going to come to sing at this piano? *That* was something worth living for, at least. But no!—conclusions must not be jumped in that fashion. Perhaps she had a piano in her own room. Nothing more likely.

Achilles had stepped out, hearing sounds as of a departure; and now returned, having seen that all was in satisfactory order. He sighed over his onerous responsibilities, and settled down to repose —well-earned repose, his manner suggested.

"I suppose I shall have to clear out when her young ladyship comes in to practise," said Mrs. Bailey. Mr. Torrens revolted inwardly against ostracising the good woman on social grounds; but then, *did* he want her to remain if Gwen appeared? Just fancy—to have that newcomer all to himself for perhaps an hour, as he had her for five minutes yesterday! Too good to be true! He compromised with his conscience about Mrs. Bailey. "Don't go away till she does, anyhow," said he. And then he sang Irish Melodies with Tom Moore's words, and rather shocked his hearer by the message the legatee of the singer received about his heart. She preferred the Polka.

It chanced that Mrs. Bailey also had weighty correspondence on hand, relating to an engagement with a new patient; and, with her, correspondence was no light matter. Pride had always stood between Mrs. Bailey and culture, ever since she got her schooling done. Otherwise she might have acquired style and a fluent caligraphy. As it was, her style was uncertain and her method slow. Knowing this—without admitting it—she was influenced by hearing a six o'clock post referred to, having previously thought her letters went an hour later. So she developed an intention of completing her letter, of which short instalments had been turned out at intervals already, as soon as ever the advent of a guest or visitor gave her an excuse for desertion. Of course a member of the household was better than either; so she abdicated without misgiving when—as she put it—she heard her young ladyship a-coming.

Her young ladyship was audible outside long enough for Mrs. Bailey to abdicate before she entered the room. They met on the stairs and spoke. Was that Mr. Torrens at the piano?—asked

Gwen. Because if it was she mustn't stop him. She would cry
off and try her song another time.

But Mrs. Bailey reassured her, saying:—" He won't go on long,
my lady. You'll get your turn in five minutes," in an undertone.
She added:—" He won't see your music-paper. Trust him for
that." These words must have had a new hope in them for the
young lady, for she said quickly: " You think he *does* see *something*, then?" The answer was ambiguous. " Nothing to go by."
Gwen had to be content with it.

Is there any strain of music known to man more harrowingly
pathetic than the one popularly known as *Erin go bragh?* Does
it not make hearers without a drop of Erse blood in their veins
thrill and glow with a patriotism that complete ignorance of the
history of Ireland never interferes with in the least? Do not their
hearts pant for the blood of the Saxon on the spot, even though
their father's name be Baker and their mother's Smith? Ours
does.

Adrian Torrens, though his finger-tips felt strange on the keys
in the dark, and his hands were weak beyond his own suspicion of
their weakness, could still play the Polka for Mrs. Bailey. When
his audience no longer claimed repetition of that exciting air, he
struck a chord or two of some Beethoven, but shook his head with
a sigh and gave it up. However, less ambitious attempts were open
to him, and he had happened on Irish minstrelsy; so, left to himself, he sang *Savourneen Dheelish* through.

Gwen, entering unheard, was glad she could dry her eyes undetected by those sightless ones that she knew showed nothing to
the singer—nothing but a black void. The pathos of the air backed
by the pathos of a voice that went straight to her heart, made of
it a lament over the blackness of this void—over the glorious bygone sunlight, never a ray of it to be shed again for him! There
was no one in the room, and it was a relief to her to have this
right to unseen tears. The feverish excitement of her sleepless night had subsided,
but the memory of a strange resolve clung to her, a resolution to
do a thing that then seemed practicable, reasonable, right; that
had seemed since, more than once, insurmountable—yes! Insane—
yes! But *wrong*—no! Now, hard hit by *Savourneen Dheelish,*
the strength to think she might cross the barriers revived, and
the insanity of the scheme shrank as its rightness grew and grew.
After all, did she not belong to herself? To whom else, except
her parents? Well—her duty to her parents was clear; to ransom

their consciences for them; to enable them to say " We destroyed this man's eyesight for him, but we gave him Gwen." If only this pianist could just manage to love her on the strength of Arthur's Bridge and that rainbow gleam! But how to find out? She could see herself in a mirror near by as she thought it, and the resplendent beauty that she could not handle was ä bitterness to her; she gazed at it as a warrior might gaze at his sword with his hands lopped off at the wrists. Still, he *had* seen her; that was something! She would not have acknowledged later, perhaps, that at this moment her mind was running on a foolish thought:— " Did I, or did I not, look my best at that moment? "

She never noticed the curious *naïveté* which left unquestioned her readiness to play the part she was casting for herself—the *rôle* of an eyeless man's mate for life—yet never taxed her with loving him. Perhaps it was the very fact that the circumstances of the case released her from confessing her love, that paved the way for her to action that would else have been impossible. " By this light," said Beatrice to Benedick, " I take thee for pure pity." It was a vast consolation to Beatrice to say this, no doubt.

Achilles stopped *Savourneen Dheelish* by his welcome to the newcomer. To whom Gwen said:—" Oh, you darling! " But to his master she said:—" Go on, it's me, Mr. Torrens. Gwen."

" I know—' Gwen or Gwendolen.' " How easy it would have been for this quotation from yesterday's postscript to seem impertinent! This man had just the right laugh to put everything in its right place, and this time it disclaimed audacious Christian naming. He went on:—" I mustn't monopolize your ladyship's piano," and accommodated this mode of address to the previous one by another laugh, exactly the right protest against misinterpretation.

" My ladyship doesn't want her piano," said Gwen. " She wants to hear you go on playing. I had no idea you were so musical. Say good-evening, and play some more."

He went his nearest to meeting her hand, and his guesswork was not much at fault. A galvanic thrill again shot through him at her touch, and again neither of them showed any great alacrity to disconnect. " You are sorry for me," said he.

" Indeed I am. I cannot tell you how much so." She seemed to keep his hand in hers to say this, and the action and the word were mated, to his mind. She could not have done this but for my misfortune, thought he to himself. But oh!—what leagues apart it placed them, that this semi-familiarity should have become possible on so short an acquaintance! Society reserves would have kept him back still in the ranks of men. This placed him among cripples, a disqualified ruin.

His heart sank, for he knew now that she had no belief that this awful darkness would end. So be it! But, for now, there was the pure joy of holding that hand for a moment! Forget it all—forget everything!—think only of this little stolen delirium I can cheat the cruelty of God out of, before I am the forsaken prey of Chaos and black Night. That was his thought. He said not a word, and she continued:—"How much can you play? I mean, can you do the fingering in spite of your eyes? Try some more." She had barely withdrawn her hand even then.

"I only make a very poor business of it at present," he said. "I shall have to practise under the new circumstances. When the music jumps half a mile along the piano I hit the wrong note. Anything that runs easy I can play." He played the preliminary notes of the accompaniment of *Deh vieni alla finestra.* "Anything like that. But I can't tackle anything extensive. My hands haven't quite got strong again, I suppose. Now you come!"

He was beginning a hesitating move from the music-stool with a sense of the uncertainty before him when his anchorage was forsaken, but postponed it as a reply to his companion's remark:— "I'm not coming yet. I'll play presently. . . . You were accompanying yourself just now. I was listening to you at the end of the piano."

"Anybody can accompany himself; he's in his own confidence." He struck a chord or two, of a duet, this time, and she said:— "Yes—sing that. I can recollect it without the music. I've sung it with the Signore no end of times." They sang it together, and Gwen kept her voice down. She was not singing with the tenor known all over Europe, this time; nor was the room at any time, big as it was, more than large enough for this young lady *à pleine voix.* Besides, Mr. Torrens was not in force, on that score. In fact, at the end of this one song he dropped his fingers on his knees from the keyboard, and said in a tone that professed amusement at his own exhaustion: "That's all I'm good for. Funny, isn't it?"

CHAPTER XXI

BOTHER MRS. BAILEY! A GOOD CREATURE. MARCUS CURTIUS AND UN-
MAIDENLINESS. THE DREAM WITCH AND HER DAUGHTERS. HOW
GWEN TOLD OF HER TRICK, AND MR. TORRENS OF HOW HE WAKED
UP TO HIS OWN BLINDNESS. THE PECULIARITIES OF DOWAGER-
DUCHESSES. CAN GRIGS READ DIAMOND TYPE? THE HYPOTHESIS
MR. TORRENS WAS AFFIANCED TO. ADONIS, AND THAT DETESTABLE
VENUS. EARNESTNESS AND A CLIMAX. AN EARTHQUAKE, OR HEART-
QUAKE

THE Philosopher may see absurdity in the fact that, when two
persons make concordant consecutive noises for ten minutes, the
effect upon their relativities is one that without them might not
have come about in ten weeks. We are not prepared to condemn
the Philosopher, for once. He is prosy, as usual; but what he says
refers to an indisputable truth. Nothing turns diversity into du-
ality quicker than Music.

Gwen did not think the breakdown of the tenor at all funny,
and was rather frightened, suggesting Mrs. Bailey. "Bother Mrs.
Bailey!" said Adrian. "Only it's very ungrateful of me to bother
Mrs. Bailey." Said Gwen:—"She really is a good creature." He
replied:—"That's what she is precisely. A good creature!" Gwen
interpreted this as disposing of Mrs. Bailey. Acting as her agent,
she piloted the blind man through the perils of the furniture to
a satisfactory sofa, but could not prevail on him to lie down
on it. He seemed determined to assert his claim to a discharge
cured; allowing a small discount, of course, in respect of this
plaguy eye-affection. In defence of his position that it was a
temporary inconvenience, sure to vanish with returning vigour,
he simply nailed his colours to the mast—would hear of no
surrender.

Tea was negotiated, as customary at the Towers, and he made
a parade of his independence over it. No great risks were involved, the little malachite table placed as a cup-haven being too
heavy to knock over easily. He was able, too, to make a creditable
show of eyesight over the concession of little brown biscuits to
Achilles; only really Achilles did all the seeing. A certain pretence of vision was possible too, in the distinguishing of those
biscuits which were hard from a softer sort; which Achilles ac-

cepted, under protest always, with an implication that he did it to oblige the donor. He had sacrificed his sleep—that was his suggestion—and he did not deserve to be put off with shoddy goods.

"He always has a nap during music now," said his master. "He used to insist on singing too, if he condescended to listen. I had some trouble to convince him that he couldn't sing—hadn't been taught to produce his voice . . ."

"Dear creature!—his voice produced itself like mine. M. Sanson—you know the great training man?—wanted me to sing in one of my thoraxes or glottises or œsophaguses. I believe I have several, but I don't know which is which. He said my voice would last better. But I said I would have both helpings at once; a recollection of nursery dinner, you know . . ."

"1 understand—Achilles's view. There, you see!" This was a claim that an audible tail-flap on the ground was applause. It really was nothing but its owner's courteous recognition of his own name, to which he was always alive.

Gwen continued:—"Luckily I met the Signore, who told me Sanson's view was very natural. What would become of all the trainers if people produced their own voices?"

"What, indeed? But you did get some sort of drill?"

"Of course. The dear old Signore gave me some lessons. He told me an infallible rule for people with souls. I was to sing as if the composer was listening. I might sing scales and exercises if I liked. They had a use. They prevented one's spoiling the great composers by hacking them over and over before one could sing."

Adrian felt that chat of this sort was the best after all, to keep safe for him his *modus vivendi* with this girl, in a world she was suddenly lighting up for him in defiance of his darkness. He *could* have friendship, and he was not prepared to admit that estrangement might be the more livable *modus* of the two. So he shut his mental eyes as close as his physical ones, and chatted. He told a story of how a great poet, being asked a question in a lady's album:—"What is your favourite employment?" wrote in reply:— "Cursing the schoolmaster who made me hate Horace in my boyhood." It was a pity to spoil "Ah vous dirai-je, maman?" for the young pianist, but *pluies de perles* taught nobody anything.

Gwen for her part was becoming painfully alive to the difficulties of her Quixotic undertaking. Marcus Curtius's self-immolation was easy by comparison, with all the cheers of assembled Rome crowding the Forum to back him. If only the horse her metaphor had mounted would take the bit in his teeth and bolt, tropically, how useful a phantasy it would be! She became terribly afraid her heroic resolve might die a natural death during intelligent conversation. Bother *pluies de perles* and the young pianist! This dry alternation of responses quashed all serious conversation. And if this Adrian Torrens went away, to-morrow or next day, what chance would there be in the uncertain future to compare with this one? When could she be sure of being alone with him for an hour, at his father's house or elsewhere? She must—she would—at least find from him whether some other parallel of the Roman Knight had bespoken the plunge for herself. She could manage that surely without being "unmaidenly," whatever that meant. If she couldn't, she would just cut the matter short and *be* unmaidenly. But know she *must!*

There is a time before the sun commits himself to setting—as he has done every day till now, and we all take it for granted he will do to-morrow—when the raw afternoon relents and the shadows lengthen over the land; an hour that is not sunset yet, but has begun to know what sunset means to do for roof and tree-top, and the high hills when a forecast of the night creeps round their bases; and also for the good looks of man and wench and beast, and even ugly girls. This hour had come, and with it the conviction that everybody was sure to be very late to-night, before Gwen, sitting beside the blind man on the sofa he had flouted as a couch, got a chance to turn the conversation her way—to groom the steed, so to speak, of Marcus Curtius for that appointment in the Forum. It came in a lull, consequent on the momentary dispersion of subject-matter by the recognition of Society's absence and its probable late recurrence.

"I was so sorry yesterday, Mr. Torrens." A modulation of Gwen's tone was not done intentionally. It came with her wish to change the subject.

"What for, then?" said Mr. Torrens, affecting a slight Irish accent with a purpose not quite clear to himself. It might have given his words their degree on a seriometer, granted the instrument.

"Don't laugh at me, because I'm in earnest. I mean for being so unfeeling. . . ."

"Unfeeling?"

"Yes. I don't think talking about it again can make it any worse. But I do want you to know that I only said it because I got caught—you know how words get their own way sometimes. . . ."

"But what?—why?—when? What words got their way this time?"

"I'm almost sorry I've spoken, if you didn't notice it. Because then I'm such a fool for raking it up again. . . . Why, of course, when I pitched on those lines of yours. And any others would have done just as well. . . ."

"Lord 'a massy me!—as Mrs. Bailey says. 'The daughters of the Dream Witch'? What's the matter with *them?* *They're* all right."

"Oh yes—they're all right, no doubt. But I was thinking of . . . Oh, I can't bear to talk about it! . . . Oh dear!—I wish I hadn't mentioned it. . . ."

"Yes, but *do* mention it. Mention it again. Mention it lots of times. Besides, I know what you mean. . . ."

"What?"

"The 'watchman sorrowing for the light,' of course! It seemed like me. Do you know it never crossed my mind in that con- nection?"

"Is that really true? But, then, what an idiot I was for saying anything about it! Only I couldn't help myself. I was so miser- able! It laid me awake all night to think of it." This was not absolutely true, because Gwen had really lain awake on the main question, the responsibility of her family for that shot of old Stephen's. But, to our thinking, she was justified in using any means that came to hand. She went on:—"I'm not sure that it would not have come to nearly the same thing in any case—the sleepless night, I mean. I did not know till yesterday how . . . b-bad your eyes were"—for she had nearly said the word *blind*— "because they kept on making the best of it for our sakes, Irene and Mrs. Bailey did . . ."

Adrian cut her speech across with an ebullition of sound sense —a protest against extremes—a counterblast to hysterical judg- ments. Obviously his duty! He succeeded in saying with a suffi- cient infusion of the correct bounce:—"My dear Lady Gwendolen, indeed you are distressing yourself about me altogether beyond anything that this unlucky mishap warrants. In a case of this sort we must submit to be guided by medical opinion; and nothing that either Sir Coupland Merridew or Dr. Nash has said amounts to more than that recovery will be a matter of time. We must have patience. In the meantime I am really the gainer by the accident, for I shall always look upon my involuntary intrusion on your hospitality as one of the most fortunate events of my life. . . ."

" ' Believe me to remain very sincerely yours, Adrian Torrens.' ''
She struck in with a ringing laugh, and finished up what really
would have been a very civil letter from him. " Now, dear Mr.
Torrens, do stop being artificial. Say you're sorry, and you won't
do so any more."

" Please, I'm sorry and I won't do so any more. . . . But I did
do it very well, now didn't I? You must allow that."

" You did indeed, and Heaven knows how glad I should be to
be able to be taken in by it and believe every word the doctors
say. But when one has been hocus-pocussed about anything one
. . . one feels very strongly about, one gets suspicious of everybody. . . . Oh yes—indeed, I think very likely the doctors are
right, and if Dr. Merridew had only said that you couldn't see
at all now, but that the sight was sure to come back, I should have
felt quite happy yesterday when . . ." She stopped, hesitating,
brought up short by suddenly suspecting that she was driving home
the fact of his blindness, instead of helping him to keep up heart
against it. But how could she get to her point without doing so?
How could Marcus Curtius saddle up for his terrible leap, and
keep the words of the Oracle a secret?

At any rate, he could not see her confusion at her own *malapropos*
—that was something! She recovered from it to find him saying:—
" But what I want to know is—*what* happened yesterday? I mean,
how came you to know anything you did not know before? Was
it anything *I* did? I thought I got through it so capitally." He
spoke more dejectedly than hitherto, palpably because his efforts
at pretence of vision had failed. The calamity itself was all but
forgotten.

Gwen saw nothing ahead but confession. Well—it might be
the best way to the haven she wanted to steer for. " It was not
what you *did*," said she. " You made believe quite beautifully all
the time we were sitting there, talking talk. It was when I was
just going. You remember when mamma had gone away with
'Rene, and I put my foot in it over those verses? "

" Yes, indeed I do. Only, you know, that wasn't because of the
Watchman. I never mixed him in—not with my affairs. A sort
of Oriental character! "

" Well—that was my mistake. You remember when, anyhow?
Now, do you know, all the time I was standing there talking about
the Watchman, I was holding out my hand to you to say good-
night, and you never offered to take it, and put your hands in
your pockets? It must have gone on for quite two minutes. And
I was determined not to give a hint, and there was no one else

there. . . ." Gwen thought she could understand the gesture that made her pause, a sudden movement of the blind man's right hand as though it had been stung by the discovery of its own backwardness.

He dropped it immediately in a sort of despairing way, then threw it up impatiently. "All no use!" he said. "No use—no use—no use!" The sound of his despair was in his voice as he let the hand fall again upon his knee. He gave a heart-broken sigh:—"Oh dear!" and then sat on silent.

Gwen was afraid to speak. For all she knew, her first word might be choked by a sob. After a few moments he spoke again:— "And there was I—thinking—thinking . . ." and stopped short.

"Thinking what?" said Gwen timidly.

"I will tell you some time," he said. "Not now!" And then he drew a long breath and spoke straight on, as though some obstacle to speech had gone. "It has been a terrible time, Lady Gwendolen—this first knowledge of . . . of what I have lost. Put recovery aside for a moment—let the chance of it lie by, until it is on the horizon. Think only what the black side of the shield means—the appalling darkness in the miserable time to come— the old age when folk will call me the blind Mr. Torrens; will say of me:—'You know, he was not born blind—it was an accident— a gunshot wound—a long while back now.' And all that long while back will have been a long vacuity to me, and Heaven knows what burden to others. . . . I have known it all from the first. I knew it when I waked to my senses in the room upstairs—to all my senses but one. I knew it when I heard them speak hopefully of the case; hope means fear, and I knew what the fear was they were hoping against. That early morning when stupor came to an end, and my consciousness came back, I remembered all. But I thought the darkness was only the sweet, wholesome darkness of night, and my heart beat for the coming of the day. The day came, sure enough, but I knew nothing of it. The first voice I heard was Mrs. Bailey's, singing pæans over my recovery. She had been lying in wait for it, in a chair beside the bed which I picture to myself as a chair of vast scope and pretensions. I did not use my tongue, when I found it, to ask where I was—because I knew I was somewhere and the bed was very comfortable. I asked what o'clock it was, and was told it was near nine. Then, said I, why not open the shutters and let in the light?"

"What did Mrs. Bailey say?"

"Mrs. Bailey said Lord have mercy, gracious-goodness-her, and I at once perceived that I was in the hands of a good creature.

I must have done so, because I exhorted her to act in her official
capacity. When she said:—'Why ever now, when the sun's
a-shining fit to brile the house up!' I said to her—to remove ambiguity, you see—'Do be a good creature and tell me, *is* the room
light or dark? She replied in a form of affidavit:—'So help me,
Mr. Torrens, if this was the last Bible word I was to speak, this
room is light, not dark, nor yet it won't be, not till this blessed
evening when there come candles or the lamp, as preferred.' I had
a sickening perplexity for a while whether I was sane or mad,
awake or dreaming, lying there with my heart adding to my embarrassment needlessly by beating in a hurry. Then I remember
how it came to me all at once—the whole meaning of it. Till
now, blind men had been other people. Now I was to be one
myself. . . . Say something! . . . I don't like my own voice
speaking alone. . . . there *is* no one else in the room, is there?"

" Not a soul. And nobody will come. The dowager-duchess is
having tea in her own room, and all the others will be late."

Something in this caused Mr. Torrens to say, with ridiculous
inconsecutiveness:—" Then you're not engaged to Lord Cumberworld?"

" I certainly am *not* engaged to Lord Cumberworld," said Gwen
with cold emphasis. " Why did you think I was?"

" Mrs. Bailey."

" Mrs. Bailey! And why did you think I wasn't?"

" That requires thought. I don't quite see, now I come to think
of it, why a lady shouldn't be engaged to a party and speak about
his grandma as . . ."

" As I spoke of his just now? Why not, indeed? She *is* a
dowager-duchess."

" I admit it. But there are ways and ways of calling people
dowager-duchesses. It struck me that your way suggested that
there was something ridiculous about . . . about *dowadging*."

" So there is—to me. I believe it arose from the newspaper
saying, when we had a ball in London for me to come out, that
the Dowager Lady Scamander had a magnificent diamond
stomacher. Perhaps you don't happen to know the shape of
that good lady? . . . Never mind. Anyhow, I am *not* engaged
to this one's grandson; and she's safe in the west wing, where the
ghost never goes. We've got it all to ourselves. Go on!"

" My first idea was how to prevent Europe and Asia finding
it out and frightening my family, at least until my eyes had had
time to turn round. The next voice I heard was the doctor's,
summoned, I suppose, by Mrs. Bailey. It was cheerful, and said

that was good hearing, and now we should do. He said:—'You lie quiet, Mr. Torrens, and I'll tell you what it all was; because I daresay you don't know, and would like to.' I said yes—very much. So he told me the story in a comfortable optimist way—said it was a loss of blood from the occipital artery that had made such a wreck of me, but that a contusion of the head had been the cause of the insensibility, which had nearly stopped the action of the heart, else I might have bled to death. . . ."

"Oh, how white you were when we found you!" Gwen exclaimed—"So terribly white! But I half think I can see how it happened. Your heart stopped pumping the blood out, because you were stunned, and that gave the artery a chance to pull itself together. That's the sort of idea Dr. Merridew gave me, with the long words left out."

"What a very funny thing!" said Adrian thoughtfully, "to have one's life saved by being nearly killed by something else. *Similia similibus curantur.* However, all's fish that comes to one's net. Well—when Sir Coupland had told me his story, he said casually:—'What's all this Mrs. Bailey was telling me about your finding the room so dark?'" I humbugged a little over it, and said my eyesight was very dim. Whatever he thought, he said very little to me about it. Indeed, he only said that he was not surprised. A shock to the head and loss of blood might easily react on the optic nerve. It would gradually right itself with rest. I said I supposed he could try tests—lenses and games—to find out if the eyes were injured. He said he would try the lenses and games later, if it seemed necessary. For the present I had better stay quiet and not think about it. It would improve. Then my father and 'Rene came, and were jolly glad to hear my voice again. For I had only been half-conscious for days, and only less than half audible, if, indeed, I ever said anything. But I was on my guard, and my father went away home without knowing, and I don't believe 'Rene quite knows now. It was your father who spotted the thing first. Had he told you, to put you up to the hand-shaking device?"

"He never said a word. The handshaking was my own brilliant idea. When I found—what I did find out—I went away and had a good cry in mamma's room." This speech was an effort on Gwen's part to get a little nearer—ever so little—to Marcus Curtius; nearer, that is, to her metaphorical parallel of his heroism. Marcus had got weaker as an imitable prototype during the conversation, and it had seemed to Gwen that he might slip through her fingers altogether, if no help came. Her "good cry" reinforced

Marcus, and quite blamelessly; for who could find fault with her for that much of concern for so fearful a calamity? What had she said that she might not have said to a friend's husband, cruelly and suddenly stricken blind? Indeed, could she as a friend have said less? Was her human pity to be limited to women and children and cases of special licence, or pass current merely under *chaperonage?* No—she was safe so far certainly.

"Oh, Lady Gwendolen, I can't stand this," was Adrian's exclamation in a tone of real distress. "Why—why—should I make you miserable and lay you awake o' nights? I couldn't help your finding out, perhaps. But what a selfish beast I am to go on grizzling about my own misfortune. . . . Well—I *have* been grizzling! And all the while, as like as not, the medicos are right, and in six weeks I shall be reading diamond type as merry as a grig. . . ."

"Do grigs read diamond type?"

"*I* may be doing so, anyhow, grigs or no!" He paused an instant, his absurdity getting the better of him. "I may have employed the expression 'grigs' rashly. I do not really know how small type they can read. I withdraw the grigs. Besides, there's another point of view. . . ."

"What's that?" Gwen is a little impatient and absent. Marcus Curtius has waned again perceptibly.

"Why—suppose I had been knocked over two miles off, carried in, for instance, at the Mackworth Clarkes', where 'Rene's gone . . . !"

"But you weren't!"

"Lady Gwendolen, you don't understand the nature of an hypothesis"—his absurdity gets the upper hand again—"the nature of an hypothesis is that its maker is always in the right. I am, this time. If I had been nursed round at the Mackworth Clarkes', you would have known nothing about me except as a mere accident—a person in the papers—a person one inquires after. . . ."

Gwen interrupts him with determination. "Stop, Mr. Torrens," she says, "and listen to me. If you had been struck by a bullet fired by my father's order, by his servant, on his land, it would not have mattered what house you were taken to, nor who nursed you round. I should have felt that the guilt—yes, the guilt!— the *sin* of it was on the conscience of us all; every one of us that had had a hand, a finger, in it, directly or indirectly. How could I have borne to look your sister in the face . . . ?"

"You wouldn't have known her! Come, Lady Gwen!"

"Very well, then, give her up. Suppose, instead, the girl you are engaged to had been a friend of mine, how could I have borne to look *her* in the face?"

"*She's* a hypothesis. There's no such interesting damsel—that I know of . . ."

"Oh, isn't there? . . . Well—she's a hypothesis, and I've a right to as many hypothesisses as you have."

"I can't deny it."

"Then how should I look her in the face? Answer my question, and don't prevaricate."

"What a severe—Turk you are! But I won't prevaricate. You wouldn't be called on to look the hypothesis in the face. She would have broken me off, like a sensible hypothesis that knew what was due to itself and its family. . . ."

"Do be serious. Indeed *I* am serious. It was in my mind all last night—such a dreadful haunting thought!—what would this girl's feelings be to me and mine? I made several girls I know stand for the part. You know how one overdoes things when one is left to oneself and the darkness? . . ."

"Yes—that I do! No doubt of it!" The stress of a meaning he could not help forced its way into his words, in spite of himself. Surely you need not have shown it, said an inner voice to him. He made no reply. But he did not see how.

Almost before he had time to repent she had cried out:—"Oh, there now! See what I have done again! I did not mean it. Do forgive me!" Neither saw a way to patching up this lapse, and it was ruled out by tacit consent. Gwen resumed:—"You know, I mean, how one dreams a thousand things in a minute, and everything is as big as a house, even when it's only strong coffee. This was worse than strong coffee. There were plenty of them, these hypothesisses. . . . Oh yes!—we know plenty of girls you do. I could count you up a dozen. . . ."

"—One's enough!—that means that one's the allowance, not that it's one too many. . . ."

"Well—there were a many reproachful dream-faces, and every one of them said to me:—' See what you have made of my life that might have been so happy. See how you have con . . .'" Gwen had very nearly said *condemned,* but stopped in time. She could not refer to the demands of an eyeless mate for constant help in little things, and all the irksomeness of a home.

Adrian, pretending not to hear " con," spoke at once. " But did none of these charming girls—I'm sure I should have loved heaps of them—did none of them remind you that they were hypothetical?"

"Dear Mr. Torrens, I can't tell you how good and brave you seem to me for laughing so much, and turning everything to a joke. But I *was* in earnest."

"So was I."

"*Then* I did not understand."

"What did you think I meant?"

"I thought you were playing fast and loose with the nonsense about the hypothesis. I did indeed."

"Well, I was serious underneath. Listen, and I'll tell you. This *fiancée* of mine that you seem so cocksure about has no existence. I give you my honour that it is so, and that I am glad of it. . . . Yes—glad of it! How could I bear to think I was inflicting myself on a woman I loved, and making her life a misery to her?"

Gwen thought of beginning:—"If she loved you," and giving a little sketch of a perfect wife under the circumstances. It never saw the light, owing to a recrudescence of Marcus Curtius, who stood to win nothing by his venture—was certainly not in love with Erebus. An act of pure self-sacrifice on principle! Nothing could be farther from her thoughts, be so good as to observe, than that she *loved* this man!

He went on uninterrupted:—"No, indeed I am heartily glad of it. It would be a terrible embarrassment at the best. I should want to let her off, and she would feel in honour bound to hold on, and really of all the things I can't abide self-sacrifice is. . . . Well, Lady Gwendolen, only consider the feelings of the chap on the altar! Hasn't he a right to a little unselfishness for his own personal satisfaction?" This was a sad wet blanket for Marcus Curtius.

Gwen did not believe that Adrian's disclaimer of any preoccupation of his affections was genuine. According to her theory of life—and there is much to be said for it—a full-blown Adonis, that is to say, a lovable man, refusing to love any woman on any terms, was a sort of monstrosity. The original Adonis of Art and Song was merely an *homme incompris,* according to this young lady. He hated Venus—odious woman!—and no wonder. *She* to claim the rank of a goddess! Besides, Gwen suspected that Adrian was only prevaricating. Trothplight was one thing, official betrothal another. It was almost too poor a shuffle to accuse him of, but she was always flying at the throat of equivocation, even when she knew she might be outclassed by it. "You are playing with words, Mr. Torrens," said she. "You mean that you and this young lady are not 'engaged to be married'? Perhaps not, but that has nothing to do with the matter. I cannot feel it in my bones—as Mrs. Bailey says—that any woman you could care for would back out of it because you . . . because of this dreadful accident." Her voice was irresolute in referring to it, and some wandering wave of that electricity that her finger-tips were sq full of made a cross-circuit and quickened the beating of her hearer's heart. The vessel it struck in mid-ocean had no time to right itself before another followed. "Surely—if she were worth a straw—if she were worth the name of a woman at all—she would feel it her greatest happiness to make it up to you for such. . . ." She was going to say "a privation," but she always shied off designating the calamity. In her hurry to escape from "privation" she landed her speech in a phrase she had not taken the full measure of—"Well—perhaps I oughtn't to say that! I may be taking the young woman's name in vain. I only mean that that is what *I* should feel in her position."

It had come as a chance speech before she saw its bearings. There was not the ghost of an *arrière pensée* behind the simple fact that she had no choice but to judge another woman's mind by her own; a natural thought! Her first instinct was to spoil the force she had not meant it to have, by dragging the red herring of some foolish joke across the trail.

But—to think of it! Here had she been hatching such a brave scheme of making her own life, and all the devotion she somehow believed she could give, a compensation for a great wrong, and here she was now affrighted at the smell of powder! Pride stepped in, and the memory of Quintus Curtius. No—she would not say a single word to undo the effect of her heedlessness. Let the worst stand! They had left her in the place of that hypothesis whom she had herself discarded. It was no fault of hers that had involved her personally. Was she bound to back out? She bit her lip to check her own impulse to utter some cheap corrective.

Until that rather scornful disclaimer of the Duke's son, Mrs. Bailey's piece of fashionable intelligence had served—whether Adrian believed it or not—as a sort of chaperon's ægis extended over this interview. It had protected him against himself—against his impulse to break through a silence that his three weeks' memory of this girl's image had made painful. Recollect that her radiant beauty, in that setting sun-gleam, was the last thing human his eyes had rested on before the night came on him—the night that might be endless. It was not so easy, now that an imaginary *fiancée* had been curtly swept away, to fight against a temptation he conceived himself bound in honour not to give way to. Not so easy because *something,* that he hoped was not his vanity, was telling him that this girl beside him, her very self that he had seen once, whose image was to last for ever, was at least not placing obstacles in his way. For anything that *she* was doing to prevent it, he might drive a coach-and-six through the social code that blocks a declaration of passion to a girl under age without the consent of her parents. He was conscious of this code, and his general acceptance of it. But he was not so law-abiding but that he must needs get on the box—of the coach-and-six—and flick the leaders with his whip.

For he asked abruptly:—"How do you know that?" driving home the nail of personality to the head.

"Perhaps I am wrong," said Gwen, dropping her flag an inch. "But I was thinking so all last night. I was in a sort of fever, you see, because I felt so guilty, and it grew worse and worse. . . ."

"You were thinking that . . . ?"

"Well—you know—it was before I had any idea she was a hypothesis. I thought she was real because of the ring."

"My ring! Fancy! . . . But I'll tell you about my ring presently. Tell me what you were thinking. . . ."

"Why—what I said before!"

"But what *was* it?"

"Do you know, I think it was only a sort of attempt to get a little sleep. You were so fearfully on my conscience, and it made it so much easier to bear. . . . Only it worried me to think that perhaps she might turn round and say:—'This was no fault of mine. Why should I bear for life the burden of other people's sins?' . . . If she was a perfect beast—*beast,* you know! . . ."

"The hypothesis would not have been a perfect beast. She would have been a perfect lady, and Mrs. Bailey would have attested it. She would have pointed out the desirability of a sister's love—at reasonable intervals; visits and so on—for a man with his eyes poked out. She might even have gone the length of insinuating that the finger of Providence did it. . . ."

"Now you are talking nonsense again. Do be serious!"

"Well—let's be serious! Suppose you tell me what it was you were thinking that made the existence of that very dry and unsatisfying hypothesis such a consolation!"

"I should like to tell you—only I know I shall say it wrong, and you will think me an odd girl; or unfeeling; which is worse."

"I should do nothing of the sort. But I'll tell you what I should think—what I have thought all this time I have been hearing your voice—I merely mention it as a thing of pathological interest. . . ."

" Go on."

" I should think it didn't matter what you said so long as you went on speaking. Because whenever I hear your voice I can shut my eyes and forget that I am blind."

" Is that empty compliment, or are you in earnest ? "

" I was jesting a minute ago, but now I am in earnest. I mean what I say. Your voice takes the load off my heart and the darkness off my brain, and we are standing again by that stone bridge over yonder—Arthur's Bridge—and I see you in all your beauty—oh! such beauty—as I look up from Ply's cut collar against the sunset sky. That was my last hour of vision, and its memory will go with me to the grave. And now when I hear your voice, it all comes back to me, and the terrible darkness has vanished—or the sense of it anyhow! . . ."

" If that is so you shall hear it until your sight comes back—it will—it must ! "

" How if it never comes back? How if I remain as I am now for life ? "

" I shall not lose my voice."

How it came about neither could ever say; but each knew that it happened then, just at that turn in the conversation, and that no one came rushing into the drawing-room as they easily might have done—this lax structure of language was employed later in reference to it—nor did any of the thousand interruptions occur that might have occurred. Mrs. Bailey might have come to Mr. Torrens to know how many g's there were in agreeable, or a tea-collector might have prowled in to add relics to her collection, or even the sound of the carriage afar—inaudible by man—might have caused Achilles to requisition the opening of the drawing-room door, that he might rush away to sanction its arrival. Two guardian angels—the story thinks—stopped any of these things happening. What did happen was that Gwen and Adrian, who a moment before were nominally a lady and gentleman chatting on a sofa near the piano, whose separation involved no consequences definable for either, were standing speechless in each other's arms—speechless but waiting for the power to speak. For nobody can articulate whose heart is thumping out of all reason. He has to wait—or she, as may be. One of each is needed to develope an earthquake of this particular kind.

It was just as well that the Hon. Percival Pellew and Aunt Constance Smith-Dickenson, who had started to walk from the flower-show with a couple of young monkeys whose object in life was to spare everybody else their company from selfish motives, did *not* come rushing into the drawing-room just then, but a quarter of an hour later. For even if the parties had caught the sound of their arrival in time, the peculiarity of Mr. Torrens' blindness would have stood in the way of any successful pretence that he and Lady Gwendolen had been keeping their distance up to Society point. We know how easy it is for normal people, when caught, to pretend they are looking at dear Sarah's interesting watercolours together, or anything of that sort. And even if the blind man had been able to strike a bar or two carelessly on the piano, to advertise his isolation, their faces would have betrayed them. Not that the tears of either could have been identified on the face of the other. It was a matter of expression. Every situation in this world has a stamp of its own for the human face, and no stamp is more easily identified than that on the face of lovers who have just found each other out.

Anyhow this story cannot go on, until the absurd tempest that has passed over these two allows them to speak. Then they do so on an absolutely new footing, and the man calls the girl his dearest and his own, and Heaven knows what else. There one sees the difference between the B.C. and A.D. of the Nativity of Love. It is a new Era. Call it the Hegira, if you like.

"I saw you once, dear love,"—he is saying—"I saw you once, and it was you—you—you! The worst that Fate has in store for me cannot kill the memory of that moment. And if blindness was to be the price of this—of this—why, I would sooner be blind, and have it, than have all the eyes of Argus and . . . and starve."

"You wouldn't know you were starving," says Gwen, who is becoming normal—resuming the equanimities. "Besides, you would be such a Guy. No—please don't! Somebody's coming!"

"Nobody's coming. It's all right. I tell you, Gwen, or Gwendolen—do you know I all but called you that, when you came in, before we sang . . . ?"

"Why didn't you quite? However, I'm not sorry you didn't on the whole. It might have seemed paternal, and I should have felt squashed. And then it might never have happened at all, and I should just have been a young lady in Society, and you a gentleman that had had an accident."

"It would have happened just the same, *I* believe. Because why? I had *seen* you. At least, it *might* have."

"It *has* happened, and must be looked in the face. Now whatever you do, for Heaven's sake, don't go talking to papa and being penitent, till I give you leave."

"What should I be able to say to him? *I* don't know. I can't justify my actions—as the World goes. . . ."

"Why not?"

"Nobody would hold a man blameless, in my circumstances, who made an offer of marriage to a young lady under . . ."

"It's invidious to talk about people's ages."

"I wasn't going to say twenty-one. I was going to say under her father's roof. . . ."

"Nobody ever makes offers of marriage on the top of anybody's father's roof. Besides, you never made any offer, strictly speaking. You said . . ."

"I said that if I had my choice I would have chosen it all as it now is, only to hear your voice in the dark, rather than to be without it and have all the eyes of . . . didn't I say Argus?"

"Yes—you said Argus. But that was a *façon-de-parler;* at least I hope so, for the sake of the Hypothesis. . . . Oh dear!— what nonsense we two are talking. . . ." Some silence; otherwise the *status quo* remained unchanged. Then he said:—"*I* wonder if it's all a dream and we shall wake." And she replied: "Not both—that's absurd!" But she made it more so by adding:— "Promise you'll tell me your dream when we wake, and I'll tell you mine." He assented:—"All right!—but don't let's wake yet."

By now the sun was sinking in a flame of gold, and every little rabbit's shadow in the fern was as long as the tallest man's two hours since, and longer. The level glare was piercing the sheltered secrets of the beechwoods, and choosing from them ancient tree-trunks capriciously, to turn to sudden fires against the depths of hidden purple beyond—the fringe of the mantle the vanguard of night was weaving for the hills. Not a dappled fallow-deer in the coolest shade but had its chance of a robe of glory for a little moment—not a bird so sober in its plumage but became, if only it flew near enough to Heaven, a spark against the blue. And the long, unhesitating rays were not so busy with the world without, but that one of them could pry in at the five-light window at the west end of the Jacobean drawing-room at the Towers, and reach the marble Ceres the Earl's grandfather brought from Athens. And on the way it paused and dwelt a moment on a man's hand caressing the stray locks of a flood of golden hair he could not see —might never see at all. Or who might live on—such things have been—to find it grey to a half-illuminated sight in the dusk of life. So invisible to him now; so vivid in his memory of what seemed

to him no more than a few days since! For half the time, remember, had been to him oblivion—a mere blank. And now, in
the splendid intoxication of this new discovery, he could well afford to forget for the moment the black cloud that overhung the
future, and the desperation that might well lie hidden in its heart,
waiting for the day when he should know that Hope was dead.
That day might come.

"Shall I tell you now, my dearest, my heart, my life"—this is
what he is saying, and every word he says is a mere truth to him;
a sort of scientific fact—"shall I tell you what I was going to say
an hour ago? . . ."

"It's more than an hour, but I know when. About me sticking
my hand out?"

"Just exactly then. I was thinking all the while that in another moment I should have your hand in mine, and keep it as
long as I dared. Eyes were nothing—sight was nothing—life itself
was nothing—nothing was anything but that one moment just
ahead. It would not last, but it would fill the earth and the
heavens with light and music, and keep death and the fiend that
had been eating up my soul at bay—as long as it lasted. Dear
love, I am not exaggerating . . ."

"Do you expect me to believe that? Now be quiet, and perhaps I'll tell you what I was thinking when I found out you
couldn't see—have been thinking ever since. I thought it well
over in the night, and when I came into this room I meant it. I
did, indeed."

"Meant what?"

"Meant to get at the truth about that ring of yours. I had
got it on the brain, you see. I meant to find out whether she
was anybody or nobody. And if she was nobody I was going
to . . ." She comes to a standstill; for, even now—even after
such a revelation, with one of his arms about her waist, and his
free hand caressing her hair—Marcus Curtius sticks in her throat
a little.

"What were you going to?" said Adrian, really a little puzzled.
Because even poets don't understand some women.

"Well—if it wasn't you I wouldn't tell. I . . . I had made up
my mind to apply for the vacant place." This came with a rush,
and might not have come at all had she felt his eyes could see
her; knowing, as she did, the way the blood would quite unreasonably mount up to her face the moment she had uttered it. "It
all seemed such plain sailing in the middle of the night, and it
turned out not quite so easy as I thought it would be. You

know. . . . Be quiet and let me talk now! . . . it was the guilt
—my share in it—that was so hard to bear. I wanted to do
something to make it up to you. And what could I do? A woman
is in such a fix. Oh, how glad I was when you opened fire on
your own account! Only *frightened*, you know." He was beginning to say something, but she stopped him with:—" I know what
you are going to say, but that's just where the difficulty came in.
If only I hadn't cared twopence about you it would have been so
easy! . . . Did you say how? Foolish man!—can't you see that
if I hadn't loved you one scrap, or only half across your lips as
we used to say when we were children, it would have been quite
a let-off to be met with offers of a brother's love . . . and that
sort of thing. . . . Isn't that them?" This was colloquial. No
doubt Gwen was exceptional, and all the other young ladies in the
Red Book would have said:—" Are not these they?"

This story does not believe that Gwen's statement of her recent
embarrassment covered the facts. Probably a woman in her position would be less held at bay by the chance of a rebuff, than by
a deadly fear of kisses chilled by a spirit of self-sacrifice. . . .
Ugh!—the hideous suspicion! The present writer, from information received, believes that little girls like to think that they are
made of sugar and spice and all that's nice, and that their lover's
synthesis of slugs and snails and puppy-dogs' tails doesn't matter
a rap so long as they are ravenous. But they mustn't snap, however large a percentage of puppy-dogs they contain.

Anyhow, Marcus Curtius never came off. He was really impossible; and, as we all know, what's impossible very seldom comes
to pass. And this case was not among the exceptions.

It wasn't them. But a revision of the relativities was necessary.
When Miss Dickenson and the Hon. Percival did come in, Gwen
was at the piano, and Adrian at the right distance for hearing.
Nothing could have been more irreproachable. The newcomers,
having been audibly noisy on the stairs, showed as hypocritical by
an uncalled-for assumption of preternatural susceptibility to the
absence of other members of their party acknowledging their necessity to make up a Grundy quorum. There is safety in number
when persons are of opposite sexes, which they generally are.

" Can't imagine what's become of them!" said Mr. Pellew, rounding off some subject with a dexterous implication of its nature.
" By Jove!—that's good, though! Mr. Torrens down at last!"
Greetings and civilities, and a good pretence by the blind man of
seeing the hands he meets half-way.

" That young Lieutenant What's-his-name and the second Accrington girl, Gwen dear. They must have missed us and gone round by Furze Heath. I shall be in a fearful scrape with Lady Accrington, I know. Why didn't you come to the flower-show?" Thus Miss Dickenson, laying unnecessary stress on the absentees.

"I had a headache," says Gwen, "and Gloire de Dijon roses always make my headaches worse. . . . Yes, it's very funny. Mr. Torrens and I have been boring one another half the afternoon. But I've written some letters. Do you know this in the new Opera—Verdi's?" She played a phrase or two of the *Trovatore*. For it was the new Opera that year, and we were boys . . . *eheu fugaces!*

"I really think I ought to walk back a little and see about those young people," says Aunt Constance fatuously. Thereupon Gwen finds she would like a little walk in the cool, and will accompany Aunt Constance. But just after they have left the room Achilles, whose behaviour has really been perfect all along, is seized with a paroxysm of interest in an inaudible sound, and storms past them on the stairs to meet the carriage and keep an eye on things. So they only take a short turn on the terrace in the late glow of the sunset, and go up to dress.

Adrian and the Hon. Percival spend five minutes in the growing twilight, actively ignoring all personal relations during the afternoon. They discuss flower-shows on their merits, and recent Operas on theirs. They censure the fashions in dress—the preposterous crinolines and the bonnets almost hanging down on the back like a knapsack—touch politics slightly: Louis Napoleon, Palmerston, Russian Nicholas. But they follow male precedents, dropping trivialities as soon as womankind is out of hearing, and preserve a discreet silence—two discreet silences—about their respective recencies. They depart to their rooms, Adrian risking his credit for a limited vision by committing himself to Mr. Pellew's arm and a banister.

CHAPTER XXII

THEOPHILUS GOTOBED. HOW A TENOR AND A SOPRANO VANISHED. HOW
GWEN ANNOUNCED HER INTENDED MARRIAGE. PRACTICAL ENCOUR-
AGEMENT. AUNT CONSTANCE AND MR. PELLEW, AND HOW THEY WERE
OLDER THAN ROMEO, JULIET, GWEN, AND MR. TORRENS. HOW THEY
STAYED OUT FIVE MINUTES LONGER, AND MISS DICKENSON CAME
ACROSS THE EARL WITH A CANDLE-LAMP. HOW GWEN'S FATHER
KNEW ALL ABOUT IT. NEVERTHELESS THE EARL DID NOT KNOW
BROWNING. BUT HE SUSPECTED GWEN OF QUIXOTISM, FOR ALL THAT.
ONE'S TONGUE, AND THE CHOICE BETWEEN BITING IT OFF OR HOLD-
ING IT. HOW GWEN HAD BORROWED LORD CUMBERWORLD'S PENCIL.
MRS. BAILEY AND PARISIAN PROFLIGACY

THE galaxy of wax lights had illuminated the Jacobean drawing-
room long enough to have become impatient, if only they had had
human souls, before the first conscientious previous person turned
up dressed for dinner, and felt ashamed and looked at a book. He
affected superiority to things, saying to the subsequent conscientious person :—" Seen this ?—' The Self-Renunciation of Theophilus
Gotobed ? '—R'viewers sayts 'musing; " and handing him Vol. I.,
which he was obliged to take. He just looked inside, and laid it
on the table. " Looks intristin'! " he said.

It was bad enough, said Mr. Norbury to Cook sympathetically
in confidence, to put back three-quarters of an hour, without her
ladyship making his lordship behindhander still. This was because
news travelled to the kitchen—mind you never say anything whatever in the hearing of a servant!—that their two respective ships
were in collision in the Lib'ary; *harguing* was the exact expression.
It was the heads of the household who were late. Lady Gwendolen
apologized for them, saying she was afraid it was her fault. It
was. But she didn't look penitent. She looked resplendent.

The two couples who had parted company, being anxious to
advertise their honourable conduct, executed a quartet-without-
music in extenuation of what appeared organized treachery. The
soprano and tenor had lost sight of the alto and basso just on
the other side of Clocketts Croft, where you came to a stile. They
had from sheer good-faith retraced their steps to this stile and
sat on it reluctantly, in bewilderment of spirit, praying for the
spontaneous reappearance of the wanderers. These latter testified
unanimously that they had seen the tenor assist the soprano over

this stile, and that then the couple had disappeared to the right through the plantation of young larches, and they had followed them along a path of enormous length with impenetrable arboriculture on either hand, without seeing any more of them, and expected to find them on arriving. The tenor and soprano gave close particulars of their return along this self-same path. All the evidence went to show that a suspension of natural laws had taken place, the simultaneous presence of all four at that stile seeming a mathematical certainty from which escape was impossible.

Guilty conscience—so Gwen thought at least—was discernible in every phrase of the composition. This was all very fine for Lieutenant Tatham and Di Accrington, the two young monkeys. But why Aunt Constance and her middle-aged M.P.? If they wanted to, why couldn't they, without any nonsense? That was the truncated inquiry Gwen's mind made.

She herself was radiant, dazzling, in the highest spirits. But her mother was silent and pre-occupied, and rather impatient with her more than once during the evening. The Earl was the same, minus the impatience.

This was because of two very short colloquies under pressure, between Gwen's departure upstairs and the Countess's overdue appearance at dinner. The first began in the lobby outside Gwen's room, where her mother overtook her on her way to her own. Here it is in full:

" Oh—there you are, child! What a silly you were not to come! How's your headache? . . . I do wish your father would have those stairs altered. It's like the ascent of Mount Parnassus." Buckstone was presenting a burlesque of that name just then, and her ladyship may have had it running in her head.

" It wasn't a real headache—only pretence. Come in here, mamma. I've something to say. . . . No—I haven't rung for Lutwyche yet. *She's* all right. Come in and shut the door."

" Why, girl, what's the matter? Why are you . . . ? "

" Why am I what? "

" Well—twinkling and—breathing and—and altogether! " Her ladyship's descriptive power is fairly good as far as it goes, but it has its limits.

" I don't believe I'm either twinkling or breathing or altogether . . . Well, then—I'm whatever you like—all three! Only listen to me, mamma dear, because there's not much time. I'm going to marry Adrian Torrens. There! "

" Oh—my dear! " It is too much for the Countess after those

stairs! She sinks on a chair clutching her fingers tight, with wide eyes on her daughter. It is too terrible to believe. But even in that moment Gwen's beauty has such force that the words "A blind man!—never to see it!" are articulate in her mind. For her child never looked more beautiful—one half queenly effrontery, her disordered locks against the window-light making a halo of rough gold round a slight flush its wearer would resent the name of shame for; the other half, the visible flinching from confession she would resent still more for justifying it.

"Why—do you know anything against him?"

"Darling!—you might marry anybody, and you know it."

"Oh yes; I know all about it. I prefer this one. But *do* you know anything against him?"

"Only . . . only his *eyes!* . . . Oh dear! You know you said so yourself yesterday—that the sight was destroyed . . ."

"Who destroyed his sight? Tell me that!"

"If you are going to take that tone, Gwendolen, I really cannot talk about it. You and your father must settle it between you somehow. It was an accident—a very terrible accident, I know—but I must go away to dress. It's eight. . . . Anyhow, *one* thing, dear! You haven't given him any encouragement—at least, I *hope* not . . ."

"Given him any what?"

"Any practical encouragement . . . any . . ."

"Oh yes—any quantity." She has to quash that flinching and brazen it out. One way is as good as another. "I didn't tell him to pull my hair down, though. I didn't mind. But if he had been able to see I should have been much more strict."

"Gwen dear—you are perfectly . . . *shameless!* . . . Well—you are a very odd girl . . ." This is concession; oddity is not shamelessness.

"Come, mamma, be reasonable! If you can't see anybody and you mayn't touch them, it comes down to making remarks at a respectful distance, and then it's no better than acquaintance—visiting and leaving cards and that sort of thing. . . . Come in!" Lutwyche interrupted with hot water, her expression saying distinctly:—"I am a young woman of unimpeachable character, who can come into a room where a titled lady and her daughter are at loggerheads, no doubt about a love-affair, and can shut my eyes to the visible and my ears to the audible. Go it!"

Nevertheless, the disputants seemed to prefer suspension of their discussion, and the elder lady departed, saying they would both be late for dinner.

This was the first short colloquy. The second was in the Earl's dressing-room, from which he was emerging when his wife, looking scared, met him coming out in *grande tenue* through the district common to both, the room Earls and Countesses had occupied from time immemorial. He saw there was some excitement afoot, but was content to await the information he knew would come in the end. Tacit reciprocities of misunderstanding ensuing, he felt it safest to say:—"Nothing wrong, I hope?" This is what followed:

"I think you might show more interest. I have been very much startled and annoyed. . . . But I must tell you later. There's no time now."

"I think," says his lordship deferentially, "that, having mentioned it, it might be better to . . ."

"I suppose you mean I oughtn't to have mentioned it. . . . Starfield, I cannot possible wear that thick dress to-night. It's suffocating. Get something thinner. . . . Oh, well—if I must tell you I must tell you! Go back in your room a minute while Starfield finds that dress. . . . Oh no—*she's* not listening . . . never mind *her!* There, the door's shut!"

"Well—what *is* it?"

"It's Gwen. However, I dare say it's only a flash in the pan, and she'll be off after somebody else. If only my advice had been taken he never would have come into the house. . . ."

"But who *is* he, and what is *it?*"

"My dear, I'll tell you if you'll not be so impatient. It's this young Torrens. . . . Yes—now you're shocked. So was I." For no further explanations are necessary. When one hears that "it" is John and Jane, one knows.

"But, Philippa, are you sure? It seems to me perfectly incredible."

"Speak to her yourself."

"She's barely seen him; and as for him, poor fellow, he has never seen *her* at all." The rapidity of events seems out of all reason to a constitutionally cautious Earl.

"My dear, how unreasonable you are! If he could *see* her, of course, she wouldn't think of him for one moment. At least, I suppose not."

"I *cannot* understand," says the bewildered Earl. And then he begins repeating her ladyship's words "If—he—could . . ." as though inviting a more intelligible repetition. This is exasperating —a clear insinuation of unintelligibility.

"Oh dear, how slow men are!" The lady passes through a short phase of collapse from despair over man's faculties, then returns to a difficult task crisply and incisively. " Well, at any rate, you can see *this?* The girl's got it into her head that the accident was *our* fault, and that it's *her* duty to make it up to him."

" But, then, she's not really in love with him, if it's a self-denying ordinance."

The Countess is getting used to despair, so she only shrugs a submissive shoulder and remarks with forbearance:—" It is *no* use trying to make you understand. Of course, it's *because* she is in love with him that she is going in for . . . what did you call it? . . ."

" A self-denying ordinance."

" *I* call it heroics. If she wasn't in love with him, do you suppose she would want to fling herself away?"

" Then it isn't a self-denying ordinance at all. I confess I *don't* understand. I must talk to Gwen herself."

" Oh, talk to her by all means. But don't expect to make any impression on her. I know what she is when she gets the bit in her teeth. Certainly talk to her. I really must go and dress now . . ."

" Stop one minute, Philippa. . . ."

" Well—what?"

" Apart from the blindness—poor fellow!—is there anything about this young man to object to? There's nothing about his family. Why!—his father's Hamilton Torrens, that was George's great friend at Christ Church. And his mother was an Abercrombie. . . ."

" I can't go into that now." Her ladyship cuts Adrian's family very short. Consider her memories of bygones! No wonder she became acutely alive to her duties as a hostess. She had created a precedent in this matter, though really her husband scarcely knew anything about her *affaire de cœur* with Adrian's father thirty years ago. It was not a hanging matter, but she could not object to the young man's family after such a definite attitude towards his father.

Here ends the second short colloquy, which was the one that caused the Earl to be so more than usually absent that evening. It had the opposite effect on her ladyship, who felt better after it; braced up again to company-manners after the first one. Gwen, as mentioned before, was dazzling; superb; what is apt to be called a cynosure, owing to something Milton said. Nevertheless, the Shrewd Observer, who happened in this case to be Aunt Constance, noticed that at intervals the young lady let her right-hand neighbour talk, and died away into preoccupation, with a vital undercurrent of rippled lip and thoughtful eye. Another of her shrewd observations was that when the Hon. Percival, referring to Mr. Torrens, still an absentee by choice, said:—"I tried again to persuade him to come down at feeding-time, but it was no go," Gwen came suddenly out of one dream of this sort to say from her end of the table, miles off:—"He really prefers dining by himself, I know," and went in again.

It was this that Aunt Constance referred to in conversation with Mr. Pellew, at about half-past ten o'clock in that same shrubbery walk. They had cultivated each other's absence carefully in the drawing-room, and had convinced themselves that neither was necessary to the other. That clause having been carried nem. con., they were entitled to five minutes' chat, without prejudice. Neither remembered, perhaps, the convert to temperance who decided that passing a public-house door à contre-cœur entitled him to half-a-pint.

"How did you get on with little Di Accrington?" the lady had said. And the gentleman had answered:—"First-rate. Talked to her about *your* partner all the time. How did you hit it off with him?" A sympathetic laugh over the response: "Capitally— he talked about *her,* of course!" quite undid the fiction woven with so much pains indoors, and also as it were lighted a little collateral fire they might warm their fingers at, or burn them. However, a parade of their well-worn seniority, their old experience of life, would keep them safe from *that.* Only it wouldn't do to neglect it.

Mr. Pellew recognised the obligation first. "Offly amusin'!— young people," said he, claiming, as the countryman of Shakespeare, his share of insight into Romeo and Juliet.

"Same old story, over and over again!" said Aunt Constance. They posed as types of elderliness that had no personal concern in love-affairs, and could afford to smile at juvenile flirtations. Mr. Pellew felt interested in Miss Dickenson's bygone romances, implied in the slight shade of sentiment in her voice—wondered in fact how the doose this woman had missed her market; this was the expression his internal soliloquy used. She for her part was on the whole glad that an intensely Platonic friendship didn't admit of catechism, as she was better pleased to leave the customers in that market to the uninformed imagination of others, than to be compelled to draw upon her own.

The fact was that, in spite of its thinness and slightness, this Platonic friendship with a mature bachelor whose past—while she acquitted him of atrocities—she felt was safest kept out of sight, had already gone quite as near to becoming a love-affair as anything her memory could discover among her own rather barren antecedents. So there was a certain sort of affectation in Aunt Constance's suggestion of familiarity with Romeo and Juliet. She wished, without telling lies, to convey the idea that the spinsterhood four very married sisters did not scruple to taunt her with, was either of her own choosing or due to some tragic event of early life. She did not relish the opposite pole of human experience to her companion's. Of course, he was a bachelor nominally unattached—she appreciated that—just as she was a spinster very actually unattached. But all men of his type she had understood were alike; only some—this one certainly—were much better than others. Honestly she was quite unconscious of any personal reason for assigning to him a first-class record.

Attempts to sift the human mind throw very little light upon it, and the dust gets in the eyes of the story. Perhaps that is why it cannot give Miss Dickenson's reason for not following up her last remark with:—" And will go on so, I suppose, to the end of time!" as she had half-intended to do, philosophically. Possibly she thought it would complicate the topic she was hankering after. It would be better to keep that provisionally clear of subjects made to the hand of writers of plays. She would not go beyond hypnotic suggestion at present. She approached it with the air of one who dismisses a triviality.

" It seems Mr. Adrian Torrens is a musician as well as a poet."

" Had they been playing the piano? "

" Really, Mr. Pellew, how absurd you are! Where does 'they' come in? "

" Oh—well—a—of course—I thought you were referring to . . ."

" Whom did you suppose I was referring to? " Aggressive equanimity here that can wait weeks, if necessary.

" Torrens and my cousin Gwen! Be hanged if I can see why I shouldn't refer to them! "

" Do so by all means. I wasn't, myself; but it doesn't matter. It was Nurse Bailey told Lutwyche, whom I borrow from Gwen sometimes, that Mr. Torrens was a great musician."

" How does Nurse Bailey know? "

" He was playing to her quite beautiful in the drawing-room just before her young ladyship came in. And then Mrs. Bailey went upstairs to write a letter because there was plenty of time before the post."

" Can't say I believe Nurse Bailey's much of a dab at music." Mr. Pellew was reflecting on the humorous background of Miss

Dickenson's character, clear to his insight in her last speech. "But it was just post-time when we got back from the flower-show. . . . What then? Why, her young ladyship must have been there long enough for Mrs. Bailey to write a letter."

"Is that the way you gossip at your Club, Mr. Pellew?"

"Come, I say, Miss Dickenson, that's too bad! I merely remark that a lady and gentleman must have had plenty of time for music, and you call it 'gossip.'"

"Precisely."

"Well, I say it's a jolly shame! . . . You don't suppose there *is* anything there, do you?" This came with a sudden efflux of seriousness.

Aunt Constance had landed her fish and was blameless. Nobody could say she had been indiscreet. She, too, could afford to be suddenly serious. "I don't mind saying so to you, Mr. Pellew," she said, "because I know I can rely upon you. But did you notice at dinner-time, when you said you had tried to persuade Mr. Torrens to come down, that Gwen took upon herself to answer for him all the way down the table?"

"By Jove—so she did! I didn't notice it at the time. At least, I mean I did notice it at the time, but I didn't take much notice of it. Well—you know what I mean!" As Miss Dickenson knows perfectly well, she tolerates technical flaws of speech with a nod, and allows Mr. Pellew to go on:—"But, I say, this will be an awful smash for the family. A blind man!" Then he becomes aware that a conclusion has been jumped at, and experiences relief. "But it may be all a mistake, you know." Aunt Constance's silence has the force of speech, and calls for further support of this surmise. "They haven't had the time. She has only known him since yesterday. At least he had never seen her but once—he told me so—that time just before the accident."

"Gwen is a very peculiar girl," says the lady. "A spark will fire a train. Did you notice nothing when we came in from the flower-show?"

"Nothing whatever. Did you?"

"Little things. However, as you say, it may be all a mistake. I don't think anything of the time, though. Some young people are volcanic. Gwen might be."

"I saw no sign of an eruption in him—no lunacy. He chatted quite reasonably about the division on Thursday, and the crops and the weather. Never mentioned Gwen!"

"My dear Mr. Pellew, you really are quite pastoral. Of course, Gwen is exactly what he would *not* mention."

Mr. Pellew seems to concede that he is an outsider. "You think it was Love at first sight, and that sort of thing," he says. "Well—I hope it will wash. It don't always, you know."

"Indeed it does not." The speaker cannot resist the temptation to flavour philosophy with a suggestion of tender regrets—a hint of a life-drama in her own past. No questions need be answered, and will scarcely be asked. But it is candid and courageous to say as little as may be about it, and to favour a cheerful outlook on Life. She is bound to say that many of the happiest marriages she has known have been marriages of second—third—fourth—fifth —nth Love. She had better have let it stand at that if she wanted her indistinct admirer to screw up his courage then and there to sticking point. For the Hon. Percival had at least seen in her words a road of approach to a reasonably tender elderly avowal. But she must needs spoil it by adding—really quite unconsciously —that many such marriages had been between persons in quite mature years. Somehow this changed the nascent purpose kindled by a suggestion of nth love in Autumn to a sudden consciousness that the conversation was sailing very near the wind—some wind undefined—and made Mr. Pellew run away pusillanimously.

"By-the-by, did you ever see the Macganister More man that died the other day? Married the Earl's half-sister?"

"Never. Of course, I know Clotilda perfectly well."

"Let's see—oh yes!—she's Sister Nora. Oh yes, of course I know Clotilda. She's his heiress, I fancy—comes into all the property—no male heir. She'll go over to Rome, I suppose."

"Why?"

"Always do—with a lot of independent property. Unless some fillah cuts in and snaps her up."

"Do tell me, Mr. Pellew, why it is men can never credit any woman with an identity of her own?"

"Well, I only go by what I see. If they don't marry they go over to Rome—when there's property—dessay I'm wrong. . . . What o'clock's that?—ten, I suppose. No?—well, I suppose it must be eleven, when one comes to think of it. But it's a shame to go in—night like this!" And then this weak-minded couple impaired the effect of their little declaration of independence of the united state—the phrase sounds familiar somehow!—by staying out five or six minutes longer, and going in half an hour later; two things only the merest pedant would declare incompatible. But it kept the servants up, and Miss Dickenson had to apologise to Mr. Norbury.

How many of us living in this present century can keep alive to the fact that the occupants of country-mansions, now resplendent with an electric glare which is destroying their eyesight and going out suddenly at intervals, were sixty years ago dependent on candles and moderator lamps, which ran down and had to be wound up, and then ran down again, when there was no oil. There was no gas at the Towers; though there might have been, granting seven miles of piping, from which the gas would have escaped into the roots of the beeches and killed them.

Even if there had been, it does not follow that Miss Dickenson, in full flight to her own couch, would not have come upon the Earl in the lobby near Mr. Torrens's quarters, with a candle-lamp in his hand, which he carried about in nocturnal excursions to make sure that a great conflagration was not raging somewhere on the premises. He seemed, Miss Dickenson thought, to be gazing reproachfully at it. It was burning all right, nevertheless. She wished his lordship good-night, and fancied it was very late. The Earl appeared sure of it. So did a clock with clear ideas on the subject, striking midnight somewhere, ponderously. The lady passed on; not, however, failing to notice that the lamp stopped at a door on the way, and that its bearer was twice going to knock thereat and didn't. Then a dog within intimated that he should bark presently, unless attention was given to an occurrence he could vouch for, which his master told him to hold his tongue about; calling out " Come in! " nevertheless, to cover contingencies.

The passer-by connected this with Gwen's behaviour at dinner, and other little things she had noticed, and meant to lie awake on the chance of hearing his lordship say good-night to Mr. Torrens, perhaps illuminating the situation. But resolutions to lie awake are the veriest gossamer, blown away by the breath that puts the bedside candle out. Miss Dickenson and Oblivion had joined hands some time when his lordship said good-night to Mr. Torrens.

He had found him standing at his window, as though the warm night-air was a luxury to him, in the blue silk dressing-gown he had affected since his convalescence. There was no light in the room; indeed, light would have been of no service to him in his state. He did not move, but said: " I suppose I ought to be thinking of turning in now, Mrs. Bailey? "

" It isn't Mrs. Bailey," said the Earl. " It's me. Gwen's father."

" God bless my soul! " exclaimed Adrian, starting back from the window. " I thought it was the good. creature. I had given you up, Lord Ancester—it got so late." For his lordship had made a visit of inquiry and a short chat with this involuntary guest an invariable finish to his daily programme, since the latter recovered consciousness. "I'm afraid there's no light in the room," said Adrian. "I told 'Rene to blow the candles out. I can move about very fairly, you see, but I never feel safe about knocking things down. I might set something on fire." If he had had his choice, he would rather not have had another interview with his host until he was at liberty to confess all and say *peccavi*. Even " Gwen's father's " announcement of himself did not warrant his breaking his promise.

"There is no light," said the visitor, "except mine that I have brought with me. I expected to find you in the dark—indeed, I was afraid I might wake you out of your first sleep. I came because of Gwen—because I felt I *must* see you before I went to bed myself." He paused a moment, Adrian remaining silent, still at a loss; then continued:—" This has been very sudden, so sudden that it has quite. . . ."

Then Adrian broke out:—" Oh, how you must be blaming me! Oh, what a *brute* I've been! . . ."

" No—no, no—*no!* Not that, not that *at all!* Not a word of blame for anybody! None for you—none for Gwen. But it has been so—so sudden. . . ." Indeed, Gwen's father seems as though all the breath, morally speaking, had been knocked out of his body by this escapade of his daughter's. For, knowing from past experience the frequent tempestuous suddenness of her impulses, and convinced that Adrian in his position neither could nor would have shown definitely the aspirations of a lover, his image of their interview made Gwen almost the first instigator in the affair. " Why, you—you have hardly *seen* her——" he says, referring only to the shortness of their acquaintance, not to eyesight.

Adrian accepts the latter meaning without blaming him. "Yes," he says, "but see her I *did*, though it was but a glimpse. I tell you this, Lord Ancester—and it is no rhapsody; just bald truth— that if this day had never come about. . . . I mean if it had come about otherwise; I might have gone away this morning, for instance . . . and if I had had to learn, as I yet may, that this black cloud I live in was to. be my life for good, and all that image I saw for a moment of Gwen—Gwen in her glory in the light of the sunset, for one moment—one moment! . . ." He breaks down over it.

The Earl's voice is not in good form for encouragement, but he does his best. " Come—come! It's not so bad as all that yet. See what Merridew said. Couldn't say anything for certain for another three months. Indeed he said it might be more, and yet you might have your sight back again without a flaw in either eye. He really said so!"

"Well—he's a jolly good fellow. But what I mean is, what I was going to say was that my recollection of her in that one moment would have been the one precious thing left for me to treasure through the pitch-darkness. . . . You remember—or perhaps not—that about a hand's breadth of it—the desert, you know —shining alone in the salt leagues round about. . . ."

"N-no. I don't think I do. Is it . . . a . . . Coleridge ? "

"No—Robert Browning. He'd be new to you. You would hardly know him. However, I should try to forget the rest of the desert this time."

The Earl did not follow, naturally, and changed the subject. "It is very late," he said, "and I have only time to say what I came to say. You may rely on my not standing arbitrarily in the way of my daughter's wishes when the time comes—and it has not come yet—for looking at that side of the subject. It can only come when it is absolutely certain that she knows her own mind. She is too young to be allowed to take the most important step in life under the influence of a romantic—it may be Quixotic—impulse. I have just had a long talk with her mother about it, and I am forced to the conclusion that Gwen's motives are not so unmixed as a girl's should be, to justify bystanders in allowing her to act upon them—bystanders I mean who would have any right of interference. . . . I am afraid I am not very clear, but I shrink from saying what may seem unfeeling. . . ."

"Probably you would not hurt me, and I should deserve it, if you did."

"What I mean is that Gwen's impulse is . . . is derived from . . . from, in short, your unhappy accident. I would not go so far as to say that she has schemed a compensation for this cruel disaster . . . which we need hardly be so gloomy about yet awhile, it seems to me. But this I do say "—here the Earl seemed to pick up heart and find his words easier—"that if Gwen has got that idea I thoroughly sympathize with her. I give you my word, Mr. Torrens, that not an hour passes, for me, without a thought of the same kind. I mean that I should jump at any chance of making it up to you, for mere ease of mind. But I have nothing to give that would meet the case. Gwen has a treasure—herself! It is another matter whether she should be allowed to dispose of it her own way, for her own sake. Her mother and I may both feel it our duty to oppose it."

Adrian said in an undertone, most dejectedly: "You would be right. How could I complain?" Then it seemed to him that his words struck a false note, and he tried to qualify them. "I mean—how could I say a word of any sort? Could I complain of any parents, for trying to stop their girl linking her life to mine? And such a life as hers! And yet if it were all to do again, how could I act otherwise than as I did a few hours since. Is there a man so strong anywhere that he could put a curb on his heart and choke down his speech to convention-point, if he thought that a girl like Gwen . . . I don't know how to say what I want. All speech goes wrong, do what I will."

"If he thought that a girl like Gwen was waiting for him to speak out? Is that it? . . . Oh—well—not exactly that! But something of the sort, suppose we say?" For Adrian's manner had entered a protest. "Anyhow I assure you I quite understand my Gwen is—very attractive. But nobody is blaming anybody. After all, what would the alternative have been? Just some hypocritical beating about the bush to keep square with the regulations—to level matters down to—what did you call it?—convention-point! Nothing gained in the end! Let's put all that on one side. What *we* have to look at is this—meaning, of course, by 'we,' my wife and myself:—Is Gwen really an independent agent? Is she not in a sense the slave of her own imagination, beyond and above the usual enthralment that one accepts as part of the disorder. I myself believe that she is, and that the whole root and essence of the business may be her pity for yourself, and also I should say an exaggerated idea of her own share in the guilt. . . ."

"There *was* none," Adrian struck in decisively. "But I understand your meaning exactly. Listen a minute to this. If I had thought what you think possible—well, I would have bitten my tongue off rather than speak. Why, think of it! To ask a girl like that to sacrifice herself to a cripple—a half-cripple, at least. . . ."

"Without good grounds for supposing she was waiting to be asked," said the Earl; adding, to anticipate protest:—"Come now! —that's what we mean. Let's say so and have done with it," to which Adrian gave tacit assent. His lordship continued:—"I quite believe you; at least, I believe you would rather have held your tongue than bitten it off. I certainly should. But—pardon my saying so—I cannot understand . . . I'm not finding fault or doubting you . . . I *cannot* understand how you came to be so— so . . . I won't say cocksure—let's call it sanguine. If there had been time I could have understood it. But I cannot see where the time came in."

Adrian fidgetted uneasily, and felt his cheeks flush. " I can answer for when it began, with me. I walked across that glade from Arthur's Bridge quite turned into somebody else, with Gwen stamped on my brain like a Queen's head on a shilling, and her voice in my ears as plain as the lark's overhead. But whether we started neck and neck, I know not. I do know this, though, that I shall never believe that if I had been first seen by her in my character as a corpse, either she or I would ever have been a penny the wiser."

" You are the wiser?—quite sure? " The Earl seemed to have his doubts.

" Quite sure. Do you recollect how ' the Duke grew suddenly brave and wise '? He was only the ' fine empty sheath of a man ' before. But it's no use quoting Browning to you."

" Not the slightest. I suppose he was referring to a case of love at first sight—is that it? . . . It is a time-honoured phenomenon, only it hardly comes into practical politics, because young persons are so secretive about it. I can't recollect any lady but Rosalind who mentioned it at the time—or any gentleman but Romeo, for that matter. Gwen has certainly kept her own counsel for three weeks past."

" Dear Lord Ancester, you are laughing at me. . . ."

" No—no! No, I wouldn't do that. Perhaps I was laughing a little at human nature. That's excusable. However, I understand that you *are* cocksure—or sanguine—about the similarity of Romeo's case. I won't press Gwen about Rosalind's. Of course, if she volunteers information, I shall have to dismiss the commiseration theory—you understand me?—and suppose that she is healthily in love. By healthily I mean selfishly. If no information is forthcoming, all I can say is—the doubt remains; the doubt whether she is not making herself the family scapegoat, carrying away the sins of the congregation into the wilderness."

" You know I think that all sheer nonsense, whatever Gwen thinks? She may think the sins of the congregation are as scarlet. To me they are white as wool."

" The whole question turns on what Gwen thinks. Believing, as I do, that my child may be sacrificing herself to expiate a sin of mine, I have no course but to do my best to prevent her, or, at least to postpone irrevocable action until it is certain that she is animated by no such motive. I might advocate that you and she should not meet, for—suppose we say—a twelvemonth, but that I have so often noticed that absence not only 'makes the heart grow fonder,' as the song says, but also makes it very turbulent and unruly. So I shall leave matters entirely alone—leave her to settle it with her mother. . . . Your sister knows of this, I suppose?"

"Oh yes! Gwen told her of it across the table at dinner-time."

"Across the table at dinner-time? *Imp*-ossible!"

"Well—look at this!" Adrian produces from his dressing-gown pocket a piece of paper, much crumpled, with a gilt frill all round, and holds it out for the Earl to take. While the latter deciphers it at his candle-lamp, he goes on to give its history. Irene had been back very late from the Mackworth Clarkes, and had missed the soup. She had not spoken with Gwen at all, and as soon as dessert had effloresced into little *confetti*, had been told by that young lady to catch, the thing thrown being the wrapper of one of these, rolled up and scribbled on. "She brought it up for me to see," says Adrian, without thought of cruel fact. Blind people often speak thus.

The Earl cannot help laughing at what he reads aloud. "'I am going to marry your brother'—that's all!" he says. "That's what she borrowed Lord Cumberworld's pencil for. Really Gwen *is* . . . !" But this wild daughter of his is beyond words to describe, and he gives her up.

If the Duke's son had not been honourable, he might have peeped and known his own fate. For he had been entrusted with this missive, to hand across the table to Irene lower down. Lady Gwendolen ought to have given it to Mr. Norbury, to hand to Miss Torrens on a tray. That was Mr. Norbury's opinion.

When the Earl looked up from deciphering the pencil-scrawl, he saw that Adrian's powers were visibly flagging; and no wonder, convalescence considered, and such a day of strain and excitement. He rose to go, saying:—"You see what I want—nothing in a hurry."

Adrian's words were slipping away from him as he replied, or tried to reply:—"I see. If I were to get my eyes back, Gwen might change her mind." But he failed over the last two letters. Mrs. Bailey, still in charge, lived on the other side of a door, at which the Earl tapped, causing a scuttling and a prompt appearance of the good creature, who seemed to have an ambush of grog ready to spring on her patient. It was what was wanted.

"Remember this, Mr. Torrens," said his lordship, when a rally encouraged him to add a postscript, "that in spite of what you say, I feel just as Gwen does, that the blame of your mishap lies with me and mine—with me chiefly. . . ."

"All nonsense, my lord! Excuse my contradicting you flatly. Your instruction, not expressed but implied, to old Stephen, was clearly *not* to miss his mark. If he had killed Achilles you *would* have been responsible, as Apollo was responsible for the arrow of Paris. . . . Yes, my dear, we were talking about you." This was to the collie, who woke up from deep sleep at the sound of his name, and felt he could mix with a society that recognised him. But not without shaking himself violently and scratching his head, until appealed to to stop.

The Earl let further protest stand over, and said good-night, rather relieved at the beneficial effect of the good creature's ministrations. The excellent woman herself, when the grog was disposed of, facilitated her charge's dispositions for the night, and retired to rest with an ill-digested idea that she had interrupted a conversation about the corrupt gaieties of a vicious foreign capital, inhabited chiefly by atheists and idolaters.

The Countess's long talk with her husband, wedged in between an early abdication of the drawing-room and the sound of Gwen laughing audaciously with Miss Torrens on the staircase, and more temperate good-nights below, had tended towards a form of party government in which the Earl was the Liberal and her ladyship the Conservative party. The Bill before the House was never exactly read aloud, its contents being taken for granted. When the Countess had said, in their previous interview, first that it was Gwen, and then that it was this young Torrens, she had really exhausted the subject.

Nevertheless she seemed now to claim for herself credit for a clear exposition of the contents of this Bill, in spite of constant interruptions from a factious Opposition. "I hope," she said, "that, now that I have succeeded in making you understand, you will speak to Gwen yourself. I suppose she's not going to stop downstairs all night."

The Earl also supposed not. But even in that very improbable event the resources of human ingenuity would not be exhausted. He could, for instance, go downstairs to speak to her. But other considerations intervened. Was her ladyship's information unimpeachable? Was it absolutely impossible that she should have been misled in any particular? Could he, in fact, consider his information official?

The Countess showed unexampled forbearance under extreme

trial. "My dear," she said, "how perfectly absurd you are! How can there be any doubt of the matter? Listen to me for one moment and think. When a girl insists on talking to her mother when both are late for dinner, and have hardly five minutes to dress, and says flatly, 'Mamma dear, I am going to marry So-and-so, or So-and-so'—because it's exactly the same thing, whoever it is—how can there be any possibility of a mistake?"

"Very little, certainly," says the Earl reflectively. He seemed to consider the point slowly. "But it can hardly be said to be exactly the same thing in all cases. This case is peculiar—is peculiar."

"I can't see where the peculiarity comes in. You mean his eyes. But a girl either is, or is not, in love with a man, whether he has eyes in his head or not."

"Indisputably. But it complicates the case. You must admit, my dear, that it complicates the case."

"You mean that I am unfeeling? Wouldn't it be better to say so instead of beating about the bush? But I am nothing of the sort."

"My dear, am I likely to say so? Have you ever heard me hint such a thing? But one may be sincerely sorry for the victim of such an awful misfortune, and yet feel that his blindness complicates matters. Because it does."

"I'm not sure that I understand what you are driving at. Perhaps we are talking about different things." This is not entirely without forbearance—may show a trace of uncalled-for patience, as towards an undeserved conundrum-monger.

"Perhaps we are, my dear. But as to what I'm driving at. Can you recall what Gwen said about his eyes?"

"I think so. Let me see. . . . Yes—she said did I know anything against him. I said—nothing except his eyes. And then she said—I recollect it quite plainly—'Who destroyed his sight? Tell me that!'"

"What did you answer to that?"

"I refused to talk any longer, and said you and she must settle it your own way."

"Nothing else?"

"Oh—well—nothing—nothing to speak of! Lutwyche came worrying in with hot water."

The Earl sat cogitating until her ladyship roused him by saying "Well!" rather tartly. Then he echoed back:—"Well, Philippa, I think possibly you are right."

"Only possibly!"

"Probably then. Yes—certainly probably!"

"What about?"

"I thought I understood you to say that, in your opinion, Gwen had got it into her head that . . ."

"Oh dear! . . . There—never mind!—go on." She considered her husband a prolix Earl, sometimes.

". . . That the accident was *our* fault, and that it was *her* duty to make it up to him."

"Of course she has. What did you suppose?"

"I supposed she might have—a—fallen in love with him. I thought you thought so, too, from what you said."

"My dear Alexander, shall I never make you understand?" Her ladyship only used the long inconvenient name to emphasize rhetoric, which she did also in this instance by making every note *staccato.* "Gwen, has, fallen, in, love, with, Mr. Torrens, because, we, *did it? Now* do you see?"

"She has a—mixture of motives, in fact?"

"Absolutely none whatever! She's over head and ears in love with him *because* his eyes are out. No other reason in life! What earthly good do you think the child thinks she could do him if she *didn't* love him? Men will never understand girls if they live till Doomsday."

The Earl did not grapple with the problems this suggested; but reflected, while her ladyship waited explicitly. At last he said:— "It certainly appears to me that if Gwen's . . . predilection for this man depends in any degree on a mistaken conviction of duty, the only course open to us is to—to temporise—to deprecate rash actions and undertakings. Under the circumstances it would be impossible to condemn or find fault with either. It is perfectly inconceivable that poor Torrens—should have—should have taken any initiative. . . ."

"Oh, my dear, what nonsense! Of course, Gwen did that. She proposed to him when I was away at the flower-show. . . ."

"Philippa—how *can* you? How would such a thing be *possible?* Really—*really! . . .*"

"Well, *really really* as much as you like, but any woman could propose to a blind man—a little way off, certainly—only I don't know that Gwen . . ." However, the Countess stopped short of her daughter's reference to a respectful distance and card-leaving.

It was at this point that Gwen and Irene were audible on the stairs, suggesting the lateness of the hour. The Earl said:—"I think I shall go and see Torrens as soon as there's quiet. I have gone to him every evening till now. I may speak to him about this." To which her ladyship replied:—" Now mind you put your foot down. What I am always afraid of with you is indecision." He made no answer, but listened, waiting for the last disappearance couchwards. Then he went to his room for his hand-lamp, as described, and after satisfying himself about that conflagration's non-existence, was just in time to cross Miss Dickenson, a waif overdue, and wonder what on earth had made that very spirit and image of all conformity guilty of such a lapse.

Then followed his interview with Mr. Torrens already detailed. Perhaps the foregoing should have come first. If ever you retell the tale you can make it do so. But whatever you do be careful to insist on that point of not talking before the servants. Dwell on the fact that Miss Lutwyche went straight to the Servants' Hall, after putting a finishing touch on her young ladyship, and said to the housekeeper:—" You'll be very careful, Mrs. Masham, to say nothing whatever about her young ladyship and Mr. Torrenson "; it being one of her peculiarities to alter the names of visitors on the strength of alleged secret information, to prove that she was in the confidence of the family. To which Mrs. Masham replied:—" Why not be outspoken, Anne Lutwyche? " provoking, or licensing, further illumination on the subject; with the result that in half an hour the household was observing discreet silence about it, and exacting solemn promises of equal discretion from acquaintances as discreet as itself. But there were words between Mrs. Starfield, the Countess's abettor in dressing, and Miss Lutwyche; the former having found herself forestalled in her theory of the argument in the Lib'ary, which she had reported as the cause of delay, by the latter's prompt expression of cautious reserve, and having accused her of throwing out hints and nothing to go upon. Whereupon the young woman had indignantly repudiated the idea that a frank nature like hers could be capable of an underhand *insinuendo,* and had felt a great and just satisfaction with her powers of handling her mother-tongue.

CHAPTER XXIII

PSYCHOLOGIES ABOUT THE COUNTESS. HOW GWEN WOULDN'T GO TO
ATHENS, OR ROME, OR TO STONE GRANGE. BUT SHE WOULD GO WITH
HER COUSIN CLO TO CAVENDISH SQUARE. HOW THEY DROVE OVER TO
GRANNY MARRABLE'S, AND DAVE'S LETTER WAS TALKED ABOUT. HIS
AMANUENSIS. OH, BUT HOW STRANGE THAT PHŒBE SHOULD READ
MAISIE'S WRITING AGAIN! AN ODIOUS LITTLE GIRL, WITH A STYE
IN HER EYE. AN IMPRESSIONIST PICTURE. HOW MICHAEL'S FRIENDS
SHOULD BE ESCHEWED, IF NOT HIMSELF. HOW GRANNY MARRABLE
AND HER SISTER HAD MADE SLIDES ON ICE THAT THAWED SEVENTY
YEARS AGO. HOW A LADY AND GENTLEMAN JUMPED FARTHER OFF

THE Countess of Ancester was mistaken when she said to Gwen's
mother that that young lady was sure to cool down, as other young
ladies, noteworthily her own mother's daughter, had done under
like circumstances. The story prefers this elaborate way of referring to what that august lady said to herself, to more literal and
commonplace formulas of speech; because it emphasizes the official,
personal, and historical character of the speaker, the hearer, and
the instance she cited, respectively. She spoke as a Countess, a
Woman of the World, one who knew what her duty was to herself
and her daughter, and had made up her mind to perform it, and
not be influenced by sentimental nonsense. She listened as a
parent, really very fond of this beautiful creature for which she
was responsible, and painfully conscious of a bias towards sentimental nonsense, which taxed her respect for her official adviser.
She referred to her historical precedent—her own early experience
—with a confidence akin to that of the passenger in sight of Calais,
who dares to walk about the deck because he knows how soon it
will be safe to say he was always a very good sailor.

But just as that very good sailor is never quite free from painful
memories of moments on the voyage, over which he might have
had to draw a veil, so this lady had to be constantly on her guard
against recurrent images of her historical precedent, during her
periods of wavering between her two suitors. Could she not remember—could she ever forget rather?—Romeo's passionate
epistles and Juliet's passionate answers, during that period of
enforced separation; when the latter had not begun to cool down,
and was still able to speak of Gwen's father—undeveloped then

in that capacity—as a tedious, middle-aged prig whom her ridiculous aunt wanted to force upon her? Was it a sufficient set-off against all this fiery correspondence that she had burned one preposterous—and red-hot—effusion, and started seriously on cooling, because a friend brought her news that Romeo was not pining at all, but had, on the contrary, danced three waltzes with a fascinating cousin of hers? Of course it was, said the Countess officially, and she had behaved like a good historical precedent, which Gwen would follow in due course. Give her time.

Nevertheless her unofficial self was grave and reflective more than once over the likeness of this young Adrian to Hamilton, his father, especially in his faculty for talking nonsense. Some people seemed to think his verses good. Perhaps the two things were not incompatible. Hamilton had never written verses, as far as she knew. No doubt that Miss Abercrombie his father married was responsible for the poetry. If he had married another Miss Abercrombie it might have been quite different. She found it convenient to utilise a second example of the same name; some suppositions are more convenient than others. She shirked one which would have cancelled Gwen, as an impossibility. One *must* look accomplished facts in the face.

The cooling down did not start with the alacrity which her ladyship had anticipated. She had expected a fall of at least one degree in the thermometer within a couple of months. Time seems long or short to us in proportion as we are, so to speak, brought up against it. Only the unwatched pot boils over; and, broadly speaking, pudding never cools, and blowing really does very little good. This lady would have *blown* her daughter metaphorically— perhaps thrown cold water on her passion would be a better metaphor—if her husband had not earnestly dissuaded her from doing so. It would only make matters worse. If Gwen was to marry a blind man, at least do not let her do it in order to contradict her parents. Fights and Love Affairs alike are grateful to bystanders who do not interfere; but interference is admissible in the former, to assist waverers up to the scratch. In the latter, the sooner time is called, the better for all parties. But if time is called too soon, ten to one the next round will last twice as long.

The Earl also interposed upon his wife's attempt to stipulate for a formal declaration of reciprocal banishment. " Very well, my dear Philippa! " said he. " Forbid their meeting, if you like! You can do it, because Adrian is bound in honour to forward it if we insist. But in my opinion you will by doing so destroy the last chance of the thing dying a natural death." Said Philippa:—

"I don't believe you want it to"—a construction denounced, we believe, by sensitive grammarians. The Earl let it pass, replying:—"I do not wish it to die a violent death." Her ladyship dropped the portcullis of her mind against a crowd of useless reflections. One was, whether her own relation with this young man's father had died a violent death; and, if so, was she any the worse? The rest were a motley crowd, with "might have been!" tattooed upon their brows and woven into the patterns of the garments. Among them, two images—a potential Adrian and a potential Gwen—each with one variation of parentage, but quite out of court for St. George's, Hanover Square. Are the Countess's thoughts obscure to you? They were, to her. So she refused to entertain them.

In the Earl's mind there was an element bred of his short daily visits to the young man, whose disaster had been a constant source of self-reproach to him. If only its victim had been repugnant to him, he would have been greatly helped in the continual verdicts of the Court of his own conscience, which frequently discharged him without a stain on his character. How came it, then, that he so soon found himself back in the dock, or re-arguing the case as counsel for the prisoner? Probably his sentiments towards the young man himself were responsible for some of his discontent with his own impartial justice, however emphatically he rejected the idea. There is nothing like a course of short attendances at the bedside of a patient to generate an affection for its occupant, and in this case everything was in its favour. All question of responsibility for Adrian's accident apart, there was enough in his personality to get at the Earl's soft corners, especially the one that constantly reminded its owner that he was now without a son and heir. For, since his son Frank was drowned, he was the father of daughters only. It was not surprising that he should enter some protest against any but a spontaneous cancelling of Gwen's trothplight. It was only fair that spontaneity should have a chance. He did not much believe that the cooling down process would be materially assisted by a spell of separation; but if Philippa would not be content without it, try it, by all means! If she could persuade her daughter to go with her to Paris, Rome, Athens—New York, for that matter!—why, go! But the Earl's shrug as he said this meant that her young ladyship had still to be reckoned with, and that pig-headed young beauties in love were kittle cattle to shoe behind. Those were the words his brain toyed with, over the case, for a moment.

The reckoning bristled with difficulties, and every unit was dis-

puted. Paris was not fit to be visited, with the present government; and was not safe, for that matter. Cholera was raging in
Rome. Athens was a mass of ruins from the recent earthquakes.
Gwen wavered a moment over New York, not seriously suggested.
It was so absurd as to be worth a thought. This seems strange
to us, nowadays; but it was then nearly as far a cry to Broadway
as it is now to Tokio.

Appeals to Gwen to go abroad with her mother failed. She
also made difficulties—good big ones—about going with her parents
to Scotland. Her scheme was transparent, though she indignantly
disclaimed it. How could anything be more absurd than to accuse
her of conspiring with Irene towards a visit to that young lady
at Pensham Steynes? Had she not promised to live without seeing
Adrian for six months, and was she not to be trusted to keep her
word?

She really wished to convince her father of the reality of her
attachment, apart from compensation due to loss of sight. So
she agreed to accompany Cousin Clotilda to London, and to stay
with her at the town-mansion of the Macganister More, who had
just departed this life, leaving the whole of his property to the
said Cousin, his only daughter and heiress. She rather looked
forward to a sojourn in the great house in Cavendish Square, a
mysterious survival of the Early Georges, which had not been really
tenanted for years, though Sister Nora had camped in it on an
upstairs floor you could see Hampstead Heath from. It would
be fun to lead a gypsy life there, building castles in the air with
Sister Nora's great inheritance, and sometimes peeping into the
great unoccupied rooms, all packed-up mirrors and chandeliers and
consoles and echoes and rats—a very rough inventory, did you say?
But admit that you know the house! Its individuality is unimportant here, except in so far as it supplied an attraction to London for a love-sick young lady. Its fascination and mystery were
strong. So were the philanthropies that Sister Nora was returning
to, refreshed by a twelve-month of total abstinence, with more
power to her elbow from a huge balance at her banker's, specially
contrived to span the period needed for the putting of affairs in
order.

So when Miss Grahame—that was the family name—went on
to London, after a month's stay at the Towers, Gwen was to accompany her. That was the arrangement agreed upon. But before
they departed, they paid a visit to Granny Marrable at Chorlton,
who was delighted at the reappearance of Sister Nora, and was
guilty of some very transparent insincerity in her professions of

heartfelt sorrow for the Macganister More. He, however, was very soon dismissed from the conversation, to make way for Dave Wardle.

Her young ladyship from the Castle hardly knew anything about Dave. In fact, his fame reached her for the first time as they drove past the little church at Chorlton on their way to Strides Cottage, Mrs. Marrable's residence. Sister Nora was suddenly afraid she had "forgotten Dave's letter after all." But she found it, in her bag; and rejoiced, for had she not promised to return it to Granny Marrable, to whom—not to herself—it was addressed, after Dave's return last year to his parents. Lady Gwendolen was, or professed to be, greatly interested; reading the epistle carefully to herself while her cousin and Granny Marrable talked over its writer. But she was fain to ask for an occasional explanation of some obscurity in the text.

It was manifestly a dictated letter, written in a shaky hand as of an old person, but not an uneducated one by any means; the misspellings being really intelligent renderings of the pronunciation of the dictator. As, for instance, the opening:—"Dear Granny Marrowbone," which caused the reader to remark:—"I suppose that doesn't mean that the writer thinks you spell your name that way, Mrs. Marrable, only that the child *says* Marrowbone." The owner of the name assented, saying:—"That would be so, my lady, yes." And her ladyship proceeded: "I like you. I like Widow Thrale. I like Master Marmaduke!"—This was the other small convalescent, he who had an unnatural passion for Dave's crutch, likened to Ariadne—"I like Sister Nora. I like the Lady. I like Farmer Jones, but not much. I am going to scrool on Monday, and shall know how to read and write with a peng my own self." "Quite a love-letter," said Gwen, after explanations of the persons referred to—as that "the lady" was the mother of her own personal ladyship; that is, the Countess herself. Gwen continued, identifying one of the characters:—"But that was hypocrisy about Farmer Jones. He didn't like Farmer Jones at all. I don't. . . . That's not all. What's this?" She went on, reading aloud:— "'Writited for me by Mrs. Picture upstairs on her decks with hink.' I see he has signed it himself, rather large. I wonder who is Mrs. Picture, who writes for him."

"We heard a great deal about Mrs. Picture, my lady." Sister Nora thought her name might be Mrs. Pitcher, though odd. "I could hardly say myself," said Granny Marrable diffidently.

Gwen speculated. "Pilcher, or Pilchard, perhaps! It couldn't be Picture. What did he tell you about her?"

"Oh dear—a many things! Mrs. Picture had been out to sea, in a ship. But she will be very old, too, Mrs. Picture. I call to mind now, that the dear child couldn't tell *me* from Mrs. Picture when he first came, by reason of the white hair. So she may be nigh my own age."

Gwen was looking puzzled over something in the letter. "'Out to sea in a ship!'" she repeated. "I wonder, has 'decks' anything to do with that? . . . N-n-no!—it must be 'desk.' It can't be anything else." It was, of course, Mrs. Prichard's literal accept- ance of Dave's pronunciation. But it had a nautical air for the moment, and seemed somehow in keeping with that old lady's marine experience.

Widow Thrale then came in, bearing an armful of purchases from the village. With her were two convalescents; who must have nearly done convalescing, they shouted so. The ogress abated them when she found her granny had august company, and re- moved them to sup apart with an anæmic eight-year-old little girl; in none of whom Sister Nora showed more than a lukewarm in- terest, comparing them all disparagingly with Dave. In fact, she was downright unkind to the anæmic sample, likening her to knuckle of veal. It was true that this little girl had a stye in her eye, and two corkscrew ringlets, and lacked complete training in the use of the pocket-handkerchief. All the ogress seemed to die out of Widow Thrale in her presence, and the visitors avoided contact with her studiously. She seemed malignant, too, driving her chin like a knife into the *nuque* of one of the small boys, who kicked her shins justifiably. However, they all went away to con- valesce elsewhere, as soon as their guardian the ogress had trans- planted from a side-table a complete tea-possibility; a tray that might be likened to Minerva, springing fully armed from the head of Jove. "Your ladyship will take tea," said Granny Marrable, in a voice that betrayed a doubt whether the Norman Conquest could consistently take tea with Gurth the Swineherd.

Her ladyship had no such misgiving. But an aristocratic preju- dice dictated a reservation:—"Only it must be poured straight off before it gets like ink. . . . Oh, stop!—it's too black already. A little hot water, thank you!" And then Mrs. Thrale, in cold blood, actually stood her Rockingham teapot on the hob; to be- come an embittered deadly poison, a slayer of the sleep of all human creatures above a certain standard of education. When all other class distinctions are abolished, this one will remain, like the bones of the Apteryx.

"We'll pay a visit to Dave," said Sister Nora. "Perhaps he'll introduce us to Mrs. Picture." Nothing hung on the conversation, and Mrs. Picture, always under that name—there being indeed none to correct it—cropped up and vanished as often as Dave was referred to. One knows how readily the distortions of speech of some lovable little man or maid will displace proper names, whose owners usually surrender them without protest. That Granny Marrowbone and Mrs. Picture were thereafter accepted as the working designations of the old twins was entirely owing to Dave Wardle.

"Mrs. Picture lives upstairs, it seems," said Gwen, referring to the letter. "I wonder you saw nothing of her, Cousin Chloe."

"Why should I, dear? I never went upstairs. I heard of her because the little sister-poppet wanted to take the doll I gave her to show to a person the old prizefighter spoke of as the old party two-pair-up. But I thought the name was Bird."

"A prizefighter!" said Gwen. "How interesting! We *must* pay a visit to the Wardle family. Is it a very awful place they live in?" This question was asked in the hope of an affirmative answer, Gwen having been promised exciting and terrible experiences of London slums.

"Sapps Court?" said Miss Grahame, speaking from experience. "Oh no!—quite a respectable place. Not like places I could show you out of Drury Lane. I'll show you the place where Jo was, in this last Dickens." Which would fix the date of this story, if nothing else did.

Granny Marrowbone looked awestruck at this lady's impressive knowledge of the wicked metropolis, and was, moreover, uneasy about Dave's surroundings. She had had several other letters from Dave; the latter ones to some extent in his own caligraphy, which often rendered them obscure. But the breadth of style which distinguished his early dictated correspondence was always in evidence, and such passages as lent themselves to interpretation sometimes contained suggestions of influences at work which made her uneasy about his future. These were often reinforced by hieroglyphs, and one of these in particular appeared to refer to persons or associations she shrank from picturing to herself as making part of the child's life. She handed the letter which contained it to Sister Nora, and watched her face anxiously as she examined it.

Sister Nora interpreted it promptly. "A culprit running away from the Police, evidently. His legs are stiff, but the action is brisk. I should say he would get away. The police seem to threaten, but not to be acting promptly. What do you think, Gwen ? "

" Unquestionably! " said Gwen. " The Police are very impressive with their batons. But what on earth is this thing underneath the malefactor? " Sister Nora went behind her chair, and they puzzled over it, together. It was inscrutable.

At last Sister Nora said slowly, as though still labouring with perplexity :—" Is it possible?—but no, it's impossible—possible he means that? . . ."

" Possible he means what? "

" My idea was—but I think it's quite out of the question—— Well!—you know there is a prison called ' The Jug,' in that sort of class? "

" I didn't know it. It looks very like a jug, though—the thing does. . . . Yes—he's a prisoner that's got out of prison. He must have had the Jug all to himself, though, it's so small! "

" I do believe that's what it is, upon my word. There was an escape from Coldbath Fields—which is called the Stone Jug— some time back, that was in the papers. It made a talk. That's it, I do believe! " Sister Nora was pleased at the solution of the riddle; it was a feather in Dave's cap.

Said Gwen :—" He did escape, though! I'm glad. He must have been a cheerful little culprit. I should have been sorry for him to get into the hands of those wooden police." Her accept- ance of Dave's Impressionist Art as a presentment of facts was a tribute to the force of his genius. Some explanatory lettering, of mixed founts of type, had to be left undeciphered.

The ogress came back from the convalescents; having assigned them their teas, and enjoined peace. " You should ask her lady- ship to read what's on the back, Granny," she said; not to presume overmuch by direct speech to the young lady from the Towers. The old lady said acquiescingly :—" Yes, child, that would be best. If you please, my lady! "

" This writing here? " said Gwen, turning the paper. " Oh yes —this is Mrs. Picture again. ' Dave says I am to write for him what this is he has drawed for Granny Marrowbone to see. The lady may see it, too.' . . . That's not me; he doesn't know me. . . . Oh, I see!—it's my mother. . . ."

" Yes—that's Cousin Philippa. Go on."

Gwen went on :—" ' It is the Man in High Park at the Turpen- tine Micky '—some illegible name—' knew and that is Michael in the corner larfing at the Spolice. The Man has got out of sprizzing and the Spolice will not cop him.' There was no room for Michael

Somebody, and he hasn't worked out well," said Gwen, turning the image of Michael several ways up, to determine its components. But it was too Impressionist. " I suppose ' cop ' means capture ? " said she.

" That's it," said Sister Nora. " I think I know who Michael is. He's Michael Rackstraw, a boy. Dave's Uncle had a bad impression of him—said he would live to be hanged at an early date. He wouldn't be surprised to hear that that young Micky had been pinched, any minute. ' Pinched ' is the same as ' copped.' Uncle Moses' slang is out-of-date."

She looked again at the undeciphered inscription. " I think ' Michael ' explains this lot of big and little letters," she said; and read them out as: " ' m, i, K, e, y, S, f, r, e, N, g.' Mickey's friend, evidently ! "

" Oh, dearie me ! " said the old lady. " To think now that that dear child should be among such dreadful ways. I do wonder now —and, indeed, my lady and Miss Nora, I've been thinking a deal about him, with his blue eyes and curly brown hair, and him but just turned of seven. . . . I have been thinking, my lady, only perhaps it's hardly for me to say . . . I *have* been a wondering whether this . . . elderly person . . . only God forgive me if I do her wrong ! . . . whether this Mrs. Picture. . . ." Granny Marrable wavered in her indictment—hoped perhaps that one of the ladies would catch her meaning and word her interpretation.

Sister Nora understood, and was quite ready with one. " Oh yes, I see what you mean, Mrs. Marrable—whether the old woman is the right sort of old woman for Dave. And it's very natural and quite right of you to wonder. *I* should if I hadn't seen the boy's parents—his uncle and aunt. . . . Oh yes, of course, they are not his parents in the vulgar sense ! Don't be commonplace, Gwen ! . . . nice, quiet, old-fashioned sort of folk, devoted to the children. As for the prizefighting, I don't think anything of that. I'm sure he fought fair; and it was the same for both anyhow ! He's an old darling, *I* think. I'll show him to you, Gwen, down his native court. Really, dear Granny Marrable, I don't think you need be the least uneasy. We'll go and see Dave the moment we get up to London—won't we, Gwen ? "

" We'll go there first," said Gwen. But for all this reassurance the old lady was clearly uneasy. " With regard to the boy Michael," said she hesitatingly, " did you happen, ma'am, to *see* the boy Michael. . . . I mean, did he ? . . ."

" Did he turn up when I was there, you mean ? Well—no, he didn't ! But after all, what does the boy Michael come to in it ?

He'd made a slide down the middle of the Court, and Uncle Moses prophesied his death on the gallows! But, dear me, all children make slides—girls as well as boys. I used to make slides, all by myself, in Scotland."

Granny Marrable's mind ran back seventy years or so. "Yes, indeed, that is true; and so did I." She nodded towards the chimneyshelf, where the mill-model stood—Dave's model. "There's the mill where I had my childhood, and it's there to this day, they tell me, and working. And the backwater above the dam, it's there, too, I lay, where my sister Maisie and I made a many slides when it froze over in the winter weather. And there's me and Maisie in our lilac frocks and white sun-bonnets. Five-and-forty years ago she died, out in Australia. But I've not forgotten Maisie."

She could mention Maisie more serenely than Mrs. Prichard, *per contra*, could mention Phœbe. But, then, think how differently the forty-five years had been filled out in either case. Maisie had been forced to *ricordarsi del tempo felice* through so many years of *miseria*. Phœbe's journey across the desert of Life had paused at many an oasis, and their images remained in her mind to blunt the tooth of Memory. The two ladies at least heard nothing in the old woman's voice that one does not hear in any human voice when it speaks of events very long past.

Gwen showed an interest in the mill. "You and your sister were very much alike," she said.

"We were twins," said Granny Marrable. But, as it chanced, Gwen at this moment looked at her watch, and found it had stopped. She missed the old woman's last words. When she had satisfied herself that the watch was still going she found that Granny Marrable's speech had lost its slight trace of sadness. She had become a mere recorder, *viva voce*. "Maisie married and went abroad—oh dear, near sixty years ago! She died out there just after our father—yes, quite forty-five—forty-six years ago!" Her only conscious suppression was in slurring over the gap between Maisie's departure and her husband's; for both ladies took her meaning to be that her sister married to go abroad, and did not return.

It was more conversation-making than curiosity that made Gwen ask:—"Where was 'abroad'? I mean, where did your sister go?" The old lady repeated:—"To where she met her death, in Australia. Five-and-forty years ago. But I have never forgotten Maisie." Gwen, looking more closely at the mill-model as one bound to show interest, said:—"And this is where you used to slide on the ice with her, on the mill-dam, all that time ago. Just fancy!" The reference to Maisie was the merest chat by the way; and the conversation, at this mention of the ice, harked back to Sapps Court.

"Of course you made slides, Granny Marrable," said Sister Nora; "and very likely somebody else tumbled down on the slides. But you have never been hanged, and Michael won't be hanged. It was only Uncle Moses's fun. And as for old Mrs. Picture, I daresay if the truth were known, Mrs. Picture's a very nice old lady? I like her for taking such pains with Dave's letter-writing. But we'll see Mrs. Picture, and find out all about it. Won't we, Gwen?" Gwen assented con amore, to reassure the Granny, who, however, was evidently only silenced, not convinced, about this elderly person in London, that sink of iniquities.

Gwen resumed her seat and took another cup of tea, really to please her hosts, as the tea was too strong for anything. Then Feudalism asserted itself as it so often does when County magnates foregather with village minimates—is that the right word? Landmarks, too, indisputable to need recognition were ignored altogether, and all the hearsays of the countryside were reviewed. The grim severance between class and class that up-to-date legislation makes every day more and more well-defined and bitter had no existence in fifty-four at Chorlton-under-Bradbury. Granny Marrable and the ogress, for instance, could and did seek to know how the gentleman was that met with the accident in July. Of course, *they* knew the story of the gentleman's relation with "Gwen o' the Towers," and both visitors knew they knew it; but that naturally did not come into court. It underlay the pleasure with which they heard that Mr. Adrian Torrens was all but well again, and that the doctors said his eyesight would not be permanently affected. Gwen herself volunteered this lie, with Sir Coupland's assurance in her mind that, if Adrian's sight returned, it would probably do so outright, as a salve to her conscience.

"There now!" said Widow Thrale. "There will be good hearing for Keziah when she comes nigh by us next, maybe this very day. For old Stephen he's just gone near to breaking his heart over it, taking all the fault to himself." Keziah was Keziah Solmes, Stephen Solmes's old wife, whose sentimentalism would have saved Adrian Torrens's eyesight if she had not had such an obstinate husband. Stephen was a connection of the departed saddler, the speaker's husband.

Said Sister Nora as they rose to rejoin the carriage:—"Now remember!—you're not to fuss over Dave, Mrs. Thrale. *We'll* see that he comes to no harm." The ogress did not seem so uneasy about the child, saying:—" It's the picture of the man running from the Police Granny goes by, and 'tis no more than any boy might draw." Whereat Sister Nora said, laughing: "You needn't get scared about Mickey, if that's it. He's just a young monkey." But the old woman seemed still to be concealing disquiet, saying only:—" I had no thought of the boy." She had formed some misapprehension of Dave's surrounding influences, which seemed hard to clear up.

Riding home Gwen turned suddenly to her cousin, after reflective silence, saying:—" What makes the old Goody so ferocious against the little boy's Mrs. Picture?" To which the reply was:— "Jealousy, I suppose. What a beautiful sunset! That means wind." But Sister Nora was talking rather at random, and there may have been no jealousy of old Maisie in the heart of old Phœbe.

Moreover, Gwen's was not an inquiry-question demanding an answer. It was interrogative chat. She was thinking all the while how amused Adrian would have been with Dave's letter and the escaped prisoner. Then her thought was derailed by one of the sudden jerks that crossed the line so often in these days. Chat with herself must needs turn on the mistakes she had made in not borrowing that letter to enclose with her next one to Adrian, for him to . . . to *what?* There came the jerk! What could he see? Indeed, one of the sorest trials of this separation from him was the way her correspondence—for she had insisted on freedom in this respect—was handicapped by his inability to read it. How could she allow all she longed to say to pass under the eyes even of Irene, dear friend though she had become? She would have given worlds for an automaton that could read aloud, whose speech would repeat all its eyes saw, without passing the meaning of it through an impertinent mind.

Sister Nora was quite in her confidence about her love-affair; in fact, she had seen Adrian for a moment, her arrival at the Towers on her way from Scotland after her father's death having overlapped his departure—which had been delayed a few days by pretexts of a shallow nature—just long enough to admit of the introduction. She inclined to partisanship with the Countess. Why—see how mad the whole thing was! The girl had fancied herself in love with him after seeing him barely once, for five minutes. It never could last. She was, however, quite prepared to back Gwen if it did show signs of being, or becoming, a *grande passion.* Meanwhile, evidently the kindest thing was to turn her mind in another direction, and the inoculation of an Earl's daughter with the virus of an enthusiasm which has been since called *slumming* presented itself to her in the light of an effort-worthy end. Sister Nora was far ahead of her time; it should have fallen twenty years later.

But she was not going to imperil her chances of success by using too strong a *virus* at the first injection. Caution was everything. This projected visit to Sapps Court was a perfect stepping-stone to a stronger regimen, such as an incursion into the purlieus of Drury Lane. Tom-all-alone's might overtax the nervous system of a neophyte. The full-blown horrors which civilisation creates wholesale, and remedies retail, were not to be grappled with by untrained hands. A time might come for that; meanwhile—Sapps Court, clearly!

The two ladies had a quiet drive back to the Towers. How very quiet the latter end of a drive often is, as far as talk goes! Does the Ozymandian silence on the box react upon the rank and file of the expedition, or is it the hypnotic effect of hoof-monotony? Lady Gwen and Miss Grahame scarcely exchanged a word until, within a mile of the house, they identified two pedestrians. Of whom their conversation was precisely what follows, not one word more or less:—

" There they are, Cousin Chloe, exactly as I prophesied."

" Well—why shouldn't they be ? "

" I didn't say anything about shoulds and shouldn't. I merely referred to facts. . . . Come—*say* you think it ridiculous ! "

" I can't see why. Their demeanour appears to me unexceptionable, and perfectly dignified. Everything one would expect, knowing the parties. . . ."

" Are they going to walk about like that to all eternity, being unexceptionable ? That's what I want to know ? "

" You are too impatient, dear ! "

" They have been going on for months like that; at least, it *seems* months. And never getting any nearer ! And then when you talk to them about each other, they speak of each other *respectfully !* They really do. He says she is a shrewd observer of human nature, and she says he appears to have had most interesting experiences. Indeed, I'm not exaggerating."

" My dear Gwen, what *do* you expect ? "

" Oh—*you* know ! You're only making believe. Why, when I said to him that she had been a strikingly pretty girl in her young days, and had refused no end of offers of marriage, he . . . *What* do you say ? "

"I said 'not no end.'"

"Well—of course not! But I thought it as well to say so."

"And what did he say to that?"

"He got his eyeglass right to look at her, as if he had never seen her before, and came to a critical decision:—' Ye-es, yes, yes—so I should have imagined. Quite so!' It amounted to acquiescing in her having gone off, and was distinctly rude. She's better than that when I speak to her about him certainly. This morning she said he smoked too many cigars."

"How absurd you are, Gwen! Why was that better?"

"H'm—it's a little difficult to say! But it *is* better, distinctly. There—they've heard us coming!"

"Why?"

"Because they both jumped farther off. They were far enough already, goodness knows! . . . Good evening, Percy! Good evening, Aunt Constance! We've had such a lovely drive home from Chorlton. I suppose the others are on in front." And so forth. Every *modus vivendi*, at arm's length, between any and every single lady and gentleman, was to be fooled to the top of its bent, in their service.

The carriage was aware it was *de trop*, but was also alive to the necessity of pretending it was not. So it interested itself for a moment in some palpable falsehoods about the cause of the pedestrians figuring as derelicts; and then, representing itself as hungering for the society of their vanguard, started professedly to overtake it. It was really absolutely indifferent on the subject.

"I suppose," said Miss Grahame enigmatically, as soon as inaudibility became a certainty, "I suppose that's why you wanted Miss Smith-Dickenson to come to Cavendish Square?"

Gwen did not treat this as a riddle; but said, equally inexplicably:—"He could call." And very little light was thrown on the mystery by the reply:—"Very well, Gwen dear, go your own way." Perhaps a little more, though not much, by Gwen's marginal comment:—"You know Aunt Constance lives at an outlandish place in the country?"

"Do you know, Gwen dear," said Miss Grahame, after reflection, "I really think we ought to have offered them a lift up to the house. Stop, Blencorn!" Blencorn stopped, without emotion. Gwen said:—"What nonsense, Cousin Chloe! They're perfectly happy. Do leave them alone. Go on, Blencorn!" Who, utterly unmoved, went on. But Sister Nora said:—"No, Gwen dear, we really ought! Because I know Mr. Pellew has to catch his train, and he'll be late. Don't go on, Blencorn!" Gwen appearing to

assent reluctantly, the arrangement stood; as did the horses, gently
conversing with each other's noses about the caprices of the
carriage.

CHAPTER XXIV

HOW IT CAME ABOUT THAT THE LADY AND GENTLEMAN COULD JUMP
FARTHER OFF. WHAT MISS DICKENSON WANTED TO SAY AND DIDN'T,
AND THE REPLY MR. PELLEW DIDN'T MAKE, IN FULL. OF A SPLIT
PATHWAY, AND THE SHREWDNESS OF RABBITS. BUT THERE WAS NO
RABBIT, AND WHEN BLENCORN STOPPED AGAIN, THEY OVERTOOK THE
CARRIAGE. THEIR FAREWELL, AND HOW MR. PELLEW RAN AGAINST
THE EARL

THE Hon. Percival was called away to town that evening, and
was to catch the late train at Grantley Thorpe, where it stopped
by signal. There was no need to hurry, as he belonged to the class
of persons that catch trains. This class, when it spends a holiday
at a country-house, dares to leave its packing-up, when it comes
away, to its valet or lady's-maid *pro tem.*, and knows to a nicety
how low it is both liberal and righteous to assess their services.

If this gentleman had not belonged to this class, it is, of course,
possible that he would still have joined the party that had walked
over, that afternoon, to see the Roman Villa at Ticksey, the ancient
Coenobantium, in company with sundry Antiquaries who had
lunched at the Towers, and had all talked at once in the most
interesting possible way on the most interesting possible subjects.
It was the presence of these gentlemen that, by implication, supplied a reason why Gwen and Sister Nora should prefer the others,
on in front, to the less pretentious stragglers whom they had overtaken.

Archaic Research has an interest short of the welfare of Romeo
and Juliet; or, perhaps, murders. But neither of these topics lend
themselves, at least until they too become ancient history, to discussion by a Society, or entry on its minutes. Perhaps it was the
accidental occurrence of the former one, just as the party started
to walk back to the Towers, that had caused Mr. Percival and Aunt
Constance to lag so far behind it, and substitute their own interest
in a contemporary drama for the one they had been professing, not
very sincerely, in hypocausts and mosaics and terra-cottas.

For this lady had then remarked that, for her part, she thought
the Ancient Romans were too far removed from our own daily

life for any but Antiquarians to enter sympathetically into theirs. She herself doted on History, but was inclined to draw the line at Queen Ann. It would be mere affectation in her to pretend to sympathize with Oliver Cromwell or the Stuarts, and as for Henry the Eighth he was simply impossible. But the Recent Past touched a chord. Give her the four Georges. This was just as she and the Hon. Percival began to let the others go on in front, and the others began to use their opportunity to do so.

Three months ago the gentleman might have decided that the lady was talking rot. Her position now struck him as original, forcible, and new. But he was so keenly alive to the fact that he was not in the least in love with her, that it is very difficult to account for his leniency towards this rot. It showed itself as even more than leniency, if he meant what he said in reply:—" By Jove, Miss Dickenson, I shouldn't wonder if you were right. I never thought of it that way before!"

" I'm not quite sure I ever did," she answered; telling the truth; and not seeming any the worse, in personality, for doing so. " At least, until I got rather bored by having to listen. I really hate speeches and lectures and papers and things. But what I said is rather true, for all that. I'm sure I shall be more interested in the house the Prince Regent was drunk in, where I'm going to stay in town, than in any number of atriums. It *does* go home to one more—now, doesn't it?"

Mr. Pellew did not answer the question. He got his eyeglass right, and looked round—he had contracted a habit of doing this— to see if Aunt Constance was justifying the tradition of her youth, reported by her adopted niece. He admitted that she was. Stimulated by this conviction, he decided on:—" Are you going to stay in town? Where?"

" At Clotilda's—Sister Nora, you know. In Cavendish Square. I hope it's like what she says. Scarcely anything has been moved since her mother died, when she was a baby, and for years before that the drawing-rooms were shut up. Why did you ask?" This was a perfectly natural question, arising out of the subject before the house.

Nevertheless it frightened the gentleman into modifying what he meant to say next, which was:—" May I call on you there?" He gave it up, as too warm on the whole, considering the context, and said instead:—" I could leave your book." Something depended on the lady's answer to this. So she paused, and worded it:—" By all means bring it, if you prefer doing so," instead of:—" You needn't take any trouble about returning the book."

Only the closest analysis can be even with the contingencies of some stages in the relativities of grown-ups, however easily one sees through the common human girl and boy. Miss Dickenson's selected answer just saved the situation by the skin of its teeth. For there certainly was a situation of a sort. Nobody was falling in love with anybody, that saw itself; but for all that a fatality dictated that Mr. Pellew and Aunt Constance were in each other's pockets more often than not. Neither had any wish to come out, and popular observation supplied the language the story has borrowed to describe the fact.

The occupant of Mr. Pellew's pocket was, however, dissatisfied with her answer about the book. Her tenancy might easily become precarious. She felt that the maintenance of Cavendish Square, as a subject of conversation, would soften asperities and dispel misunderstandings, if any. So, instead of truncating the subject of the book-return, she interwove it with the interesting mansion of Sister Nora's family, referring especially to the causes of her own visit to it. "Gwen and Cousin Clo, as she calls her, very kindly asked me to go there if I came to London; and I suppose I shall, if my sister Georgie and her husband are not at Roehampton. Anyway, even if I am not there, I am sure they will be delighted to see you. . . . Oh no!—Roehampton's much too far to come with it, and I can easily call for it." This was most ingenious, for it requested Mr. Pellew to make his call a definite visit, while depersonalising that visit by a hint at her own possible absence. This uncertainty also gave latitude of speech, her hypothetical presence warranting an attitude which would almost have implied too warm a welcome from a certainty. She even could go so far as to add:—"However, I should like to show you the Prince's drawing-room—they call it so because he got drunk there; it's such an honour, you see!—so I hope I shall be there."

"Doosid int'ristin'—shall certainly come! Gwen's to go to London to get poor Torrens out of her head—that's the game, isn't it?"

"That sort of thing, I believe. Change of scene and so on." Miss Dickenson spoke as one saturated with experience of refractory lovers, not without a suggestion of having in her youth played a leading part in some such drama.

"Well—I'm on his side. P'r'aps that's not the right way to put it; I suppose I ought to say *their* side. Meaning, the young people's, of course! Yes, exactly."

"One always takes part against the stern parent." The humour of this received a tributary laugh. "But do you really think

Philippa wrong, Mr. Pellew? I must say she seems to me only reasonable. The whole thing was so absurdly sudden."

Mr. Pellew was selecting a cigar—why does one prefer smoking the best one first?—and was too absorbed to think of anything but "Dessay!" as an answer. His choice completed, he could and did postpone actually striking a match to ask briefly:—"Think anything'll come of it?"

Miss Dickenson, being a lady and non-smoker, could converse consecutively, as usual. "Come of what, Mr. Pellew? Do you mean come of sending Gwen to London to be out of the young man's way, or come of . . . come of the . . . the love-affair?"

"Well—whichever you like! Either—both!" The cigar, being lighted, drew well, and the smoker was able to give serious attention. "What do you suppose will be the upshot?"

"Impossible to say! Just look at all the circumstances. She sees him first of all for five minutes in the Park, and then he gets shot. Then she sees him when he's supposed to be dead, just long enough to find out that he's alive. Then she doesn't see him for a fortnight—or was it three weeks? Then she sees him and finds out that his eyesight is destroyed. . . ."

"That's not certain."

"Perhaps not. We'll hope not. She finds out—what she finds out, suppose we say! Then they get left alone at the piano the whole of the afternoon, and . . ."

"And all the fat was in the fire?"

"What a coarse and unfeeling way of putting it, Mr. Pellew!"

"Well—*I* saw it was, the moment I came into the room. So did you, Miss Dickenson! Don't deny it."

"I certainly had an impression they had been precipitate."

"Exactly. Cut along!"

"And then, you know, he was to have gone home next day, and didn't. He was really here four days after that; and, of course, all that time it got worse."

"*They* got worse?"

"I was referring to their infatuation. It comes to the same thing. Anyhow, there was plenty of time for it, or for them—which ever one calls it—to get up to fever-heat. Four days is plenty, at their time of life. But the question is, will it last?"

"I should say no! . . . Well, no—I should say yes!"

"Which?"

"H'm—well, perhaps *no!* Yes—*no!* At the same time, the parties are peculiar. He'll last—there's no doubt of that! . . .

And I don't see any changed conditions ahead. . . . Unless. . . ."

" Unless what ? "

" Unless he gets his eyesight again."

" Do you mean that Gwen will put him off, if he sees her ? "

" No—come now—I say, Miss Dickenson—hang it all ! "

" Well, I didn't know ! How was I to ? "

Some mysterious change in the conditions of the conversation came about unaccountably, causing a laugh both joined in with undisguised cordiality; they might almost be said to have hob-nobbed over a unanimous appreciation of Gwen. Its effect was towards a mellower familiarity—an expurgation of starch, which might even hold good until one of them wrote an order for some more. For this lady and gentleman, however much an interview might soften them, had always hitherto restiffened for the next one. At this exact moment, Mr. Pellew entered on an explanation of his meaning in a lower key, for seriousness; and walked per-ceptibly nearer the lady. Because a dropped voice called for proximity.

" What I meant to say was, that pity for the poor chap's mis-fortune may have more to do with Gwen's feelings towards him —you understand?—than she herself thinks."

" I quite understand. Go on."

" If he were to recover his sight outright there would be noth-ing left to pity him for. Is it not conceivable that she might change altogether ? "

" She would not admit it, even to herself."

" That is very likely—pride and *amour propre,* and that sort of thing ! But suppose that he suspected a change ? "

" I see what you mean."

" These affairs are so confoundedly . . . ticklish. Heaven only knows sometimes which way the cat is going to jump ! It cer-tainly seems to me, though, that the peculiar conditions of this case supply an element of insecurity, of possible disintegration, that does not exist in ordinary everyday life. You must admit that the circumstances are . . . are abnormal."

" Very. But don't you think, Mr. Pellew, that circumstances very often *are* abnormal?—more often than not, I should have said. Perhaps that's the wrong way of putting it, but you know what I mean." Mr. Pellew didn't. But he said he did. He recog-nised this way of looking at the unusual as profound and per-spicuous. She continued, reinforced by his approval:—" What I was driving at was that when two young folks are very—as the phrase goes—spooney, they won't admit that peculiar conditions have anything to do with it. They have always been destined for one another by Fate."

"How does that apply to Gwen and Torrens?"

"Merely that when Mr. Torrens's sight comes back. . . . What?"

"Nothing. I only said I was glad to hear you say *when,* not *if.* Go on."

"When his sight comes back—unless it comes back very quickly —they will be so convinced they were intended for one another from the beginning of Time, that they won't credit the accident with any share in the business."

"Except as an Agent of Destiny. I think that quite likely. It supplies a reason, though, for not getting his sight back in too great a hurry. How long should you say would be safe?"

"I should imagine that in six months, if it is not broken off, it will have become chronic. At present they are rather . . . rather . . ."

"Rather underdone. I see. Well—I don't understand that any-one wants to take them off the hob. . . ."

"I think her mother does."

"Not exactly. She only wishes them to stand on separate hobs for three months. They will hear each other simmer. My own belief is that they will be worked up to a sort of frenzy, compared to which those two parties in Dante . . . you know which I mean? . . ."

"Paolo and Francesca?"

Mr. Pellew thought to himself how well enformed Miss Dickenson was. He said aloud:—"Yes, them. Paolo and Francesca would be quite lukewarm—sort of negus!—compared to our young friends. Correspondence is the doose. Not so bad in this case, p'r'aps, because he can't read her letters himself. . . . I don't know, though—that might make it worse. . . . Couldn't say!" And he seemed to find that cigar very good, and, indeed, to be enjoying himself thoroughly.

Had Aunt Constance any sub-intent in her next remark? Had it any hinterland of discussion of the ethics of Love, provocative of practical application to the lives of old maids and old backelors —if the one, then the other, in this case—strolling in a leisurely way through bracken and beechmast, fancy-free, no doubt? If she had, and her companion suspected it, he was not seriously alarmed, this time. But then he was off to London in a couple of hours.

Her remark was:—"You seem to be quite an authority on the subject, Mr. Pellew."

"No—you don't mean that? Does me a lot of credit, though! Guessin', I am, all through. No experience—honour bright!"

"You don't expect me to believe that, Mr. Pellew?"

"Needn't believe it, unless you like, Miss Dickenson. But it's true, for all that. Never was in love in my life!"

"You must have found life very dull, Mr. Pellew. How a man can contrive to exist without. . . . Isn't that wheels?" It didn't matter whether it was or not, but the lady's speech had stumbled into a pitfall—she was exploring a district full of them—and she thought the wheels might rescue her.

But the gentleman was not going to let her off, though he was ready to suppose the wheels were the carriage coming back. "It won't catch us up for ever so long, you'll see! Such a quiet evening as this, one hears miles off. . . ." He interrupted his own speech by a variation of tone, repeating the pitfall words:— "'Contrive to exist without'"—and then supplied as sequel:— "'womankind somehow or other.' That's what you mean to say, isn't it?"

"Yes." No qualification!—more pitfalls, perhaps.

"Only I never said anything of the sort! Never meant it, anyhow. What I meant was that I had never caught the disorder like my blind friend. He went off at score like Orlando in 'Winter's Tale.'"

"In 'As You Like It.'"

"I meant 'As You Like It.' I suppose it was because he happened to come across thingummybob—Rosalind."

"It always is."

"P'r'aps I never came across Rosalind. Anyhow, I give you my honour I never had any experience to make me an authority on the subject. I expect you are a much better one than I."

"Why?" Miss Dickenson's share of the conversation had become very dry and monosyllabic.

What was passing in her mind, and reducing her to monosyllables, was the thought that she was a woman, and, as such, handicapped in speech with a man; while he could say all he pleased about himself, and expect her to listen to it with interest. They had been gradually becoming intimate friends, and this intimacy had ripened sensibly even during this short chat, the sequel of the separation from the Archæological Congress, which it suited them to believe only just out of sight and hearing: quite within shot considered as *chaperons*. Their familiarity had got to such a pitch that the Hon. Percival had contrived to take her into his confidence about his own life, and she had to remain tongue-tied about hers, being a woman.

How could she say to him:—"I have never had the ghost of a love-affair in the whole of my colourless, but irreproachable, life. A mystic usage of my family of four sisters, a nervous invalid mother, and an absent-minded father, determined my status in early girlhood. I was to show a respectful interest in the love-affairs of my sisters, who were handsome and pretty and charming and attractive and *piquantes*, while I was relatively plain and backward, besides having an outcrop on one cheek which has since been successfully removed. I was not to presume upon my position as a sister to express opinions about these said love-affairs, because I was not supposed to know anything about such matters. They were not in my department. My *rôle* was a domestic one, and I had a high moral standpoint; which I would gladly have dispensed with, but the force of family tradition overpowered me. It has been a poor consolation to me to carry about this standpoint like a campstool to the houses of the friends I visit at intervals, now that my sisters are all married, and my mother has departed this life, and my father has married a Mrs. Dubosc, with whom I don't agree. I lead a life of constant resentment against unattached mankind, who decide, after critical inspection, that they won't, when I have really never asked them to. You and I have been more companionable—more like keeping company, as Lutwyche would say—than any man I ever came across, and I should like to be able to say to you that, even as you never met with Rosalind, even so I never met with Orlando, but without any phase of my career to correspond with the one you so delicately hinted at just now, in your own. For I fancied I read between your lines that your scheme of life had not been precisely that of an anchorite. Pray understand that I have never supposed it was so, and that I rather honour your attempt to indicate the fact to me without outraging my maidenly—old maidish, if you will—susceptibilities"?

It was because Miss Constance Dickenson, however improbable it may seem, had wanted to say all this and a great deal more, and could not see her way to any of it, that she had become dry and monosyllabic. It was because of this compulsory silence that she felt that even her brief:—"Why?" in answer to Mr. Pellew's suggestion that an Orlando must have come on her stage though no Rosalind had come on his, struck her after it had passed her lips as a false step.

He in his turn was at a loss to get something worded so as not to overstep his familiarity-licence. Rough-hewn, it might have run thus:—" Because no girl, as pretty as you must have been, fifteen or twenty years ago, ever goes without a lover *in posse*, though he may never work out as a husband *in esse*, nor even a *fiancé*." He did not see his way to polishing and finishing it so that it would be safe. He could manage nothing better than " Obviously!" He said it twice certainly, and threw away the end of his cigar to repeat it. But he might not have done this if he had not been so near departure.

Somehow, it left them both silent. Sauntering along on the new-fallen beechmast, struck by the gleams of a sunset that seemed to be giving satisfaction to the ringdoves overhead, it could not be necessary to prosecute the conversation. All the same, if it had paused on a different note, an incredibly slight incident that counted for something quite measurable in the judgment of each, might have had no importance whatever.

But really it was so slight an incident that the story is almost ashamed to mention it. It was this. An island of bracken, with briars in its confidence, not negotiable by skirts—especially in those days—must needs split a path of turf-velvet wide enough for acquaintances, into two paths narrow enough for lovers. Practically, the choice between walking in one of these at the risk of some little rabbit misinterpreting their relations, and going round the island, lay with the gentleman. The Hon. Percival did not mince the matter, as he might have done last week, but diminished his distance from his companion in order that one narrow pathway should accommodate both. It was just after they had passed the island that Miss Dickenson exclaimed:—" There's the carriage," and Gwen perceived their consciousness of its proximity. The last episode of the story comes abreast of the present one.

The story is ashamed of its own prolixity. But how is justice to be done to the gradual evolution of a situation if hard-and-fast laws are to be laid down, restricting the number of words that its chronicler shall employ? Condemn him by all means, but admit at least that every smallest incident of the foregoing narrative had its share of influence on the future of its actors.

It is true that nothing very crucial followed. For when, after the carriage had pulled up and interrupted the current of conversation, and gone on again leaving it doubtful how it should be resumed, it again stopped for the pedestrians to overtake it, it became morally incumbent on them to do so, and also prudent to accept its statement that it was nearly half-past six, and to take advantage of a lift that it offered. For Mr. Pellew must not miss that train. The carriage may have noticed that it never overtook the Archæological Congress, which must have walked very quick, unless indeed the two stragglers walked very slow.

Miss Dickenson must have dressed for dinner much quicker than they walked along the avenue. For when Mr. Pellew, after a short snack, on his way to put himself in the gig beside his traps, looked in at the drawing-room to see if there was anyone he had failed to say good-bye to, he found that lady very success-fully groomed in spite of her alacrity, and suggesting surprise at its success. Fancy her being down before everyone else after all! Here is the conversation:

" Well, good-bye! I'll remember the book. I've enjoyed my visit enormously."

" It has been quite delightful. We've had such wonderful weather. Don't put yourself out of the way to bring the book, though. I don't want it back yet a while."

" All right. Thursday morning you leave here, didn't I hear you say? I shall have read it by then. I could drop round Thursday evening. Just suit me!"

" That will do perfectly. Only not if it's the least troublesome to bring it."

" Oh no; not the very slightest! Nine?—half-past?"

" Nine—any time. I would say come to dinner, only I haven't mentioned it to Miss Grahame, and I don't know her arrange-ments. . . ."

" Bless me, no—the idea! I'll drop round after dinner at the Club. Nine or half-past."

" We shall expect you. Good-bye!"

" Good-bye!" But Mr. Pellew, turning to go and leaving his eyes behind him, collided with the Earl, who was adhering to a conscientious rule of always being punctual for dinner.

" Oh—Percy! You'll lose your train. Stop a minute!—there was something I wanted to say. What *was* it? . . . Oh, I know. Gwen's address in London—have you got it? She's going to stay with her cousin, you know—hundred-and-two, Cavendish Square. She'll be glad to see you if you call, I know." This was founded on a misapprehension, which the family resented, that it was not able to take care of itself in his absence. The Countess would have said:—" Fancy Gwen wanting to be provided with visitors!"

This estimable nobleman was destined to suspect he had put his foot in it, this time, from the way in which his suggestion was received. An inexplicable *nuance* of manner pervaded his two guests, somewhat such as the Confessional might produce in a penitent with a sense of humour, who had committed a funny crime. It was, you see, difficult to assign a plausible reason why Mr. Pellew and Miss Dickenson should have already signed a treaty on the subject.

Perhaps it was not altogether disinterested in the gentleman to look at his watch, and accept its warning that nothing short of hysterical haste would catch his train for him. However, the grey mare said, through her official representative in the gig behind her, that we should do it if the train was a minute or so behind. So possibly he was quite sincere.

CHAPTER XXV

CONCERNING CAVENDISH SQUARE, AND ITS WHEREABOUTS IN THE EARLY FIFTIES. MRS. FITZHERBERT AND PRINCESS CAROLINE. TWO LONG-FORGOTTEN CARD-PACKS. DUMMY, AND HOW MR. PELLEW TOOK HIS HAND. GWEN'S PERVERTED WHIST-SENSE. THE DUST OF AGES, AT ITS FINEST. HOW IT TURNED THE TALK, AND MOULDED EVENT. HOW GWEN'S PEN SCRATCHED ON INTO THE NIGHT

ÆSTHETIC TOPOGRAPHY is an interesting study. Seen by its light, at the date of this story, Oxford Street was certainly at one and the same time the South of the North of London, and the North of the South. For whereas Hanover Square, which is only a stone's throw to the south of it, is, so to speak, saturated with Piccadilly—and when you are there you may just as well be in Westminster at once—it is undeniable that Cavendish Square is in the zone of influence of Regent's Park, and that Harley and Wimpole Streets, which run side by side north from it, never pause to breathe until they all but touch its palings. Once in Regent's Park, how can Topography—the geometric fallacy apart—ignore St. John's Wood? And once St. John's Wood is admitted, how is it possible to turn a cold shoulder to Primrose Hill? Cross Primrose Hill, and you may just as well be out in the country at once.

But there!—our impressions may be but memories of fifty years ago, and our reader may wonder why Cavendish Square suggests them.

He himself, probably very much our junior—a bad habit other people acquire as Time goes on—may consider Harley Street and

Wimpole Street just as much town as Hanover Square, and St. John's Wood—even Primrose Hill!—as on all fours with both. We forgive him. One, or possibly we ought to say several, should learn to be tolerant of the new-fangled opinions of hot-headed youth. We were like that oursélf, when a boy. But let him have his own way. These streets shall be unmitigated Town now, to please him, in spite of the walks Dr. Johnson had in Marylebone Fields. To be sure, Marylebone Fields soon became Gardens thenabouts, like Ranelagh, and you drove along Harley Street to a musical entertainment there, with music by Pergolesi and Galuppi.

The time of this story is post-Johnsonian, but it is older than its readers; unless, indeed, a chance oldster now and then opens it to see if it is a proper book to have in the house. The world in the early fifties was very unlike what it is in the present century, and *that* isn't yet in its teens. It was also very unlike what it had been in the days when the family mansion in Cavendish Square, that had not had a family in it then for forty years, was as good as new. It was so, no doubt, for a good while after George the Third ceased to be King, because the thorough griming it has had since had hardly begun, and fields were sweet at Paddington, and the Regent could be bacchanalian in that big drawing-room on the first floor without any consciousness that he had a Park in the neighbourhood. Oh dear—how near the country Cavendish Square was in those days!

By the time Queen Victoria was on the throne the grime had set in in earnest, and was hard at work long before the fifty-one Exhibition reported progress—progress in bedevilment, says the Pessimist? Never mind him! Let him sulk in a corner while the Optimist dwells on the marvellous developments of which fifty-one was only symptomatic—the quick-firing guns and smokeless powder; the mighty ships, a dozen of them big enough to take all the Athenians of the days of Pericles to the bottom at once; the machines that turn out books so cheap that their contents may be forgotten in six months, and no one be a penny the worse; the millionaires who have so much money they can't spend it— heaps and heaps of wonders up-to-date that no one ever feels surprised at nowadays. The Optimist will tell you all about them. For the moment, let's pretend that none of them have come to pass, and get back to Cavendish Square at the date of the story, and the suite of rooms on the second floor that had been Sister Nora's town anchorage when she first made Dave Wardle's acquaintance as an unconscious Hospital patient, and that had been renovated since her father's death to serve as a *pied-à-terre* until she could be sure of her arrangements in the days to come.

Her friends were not the least too tired, thank you, after the journey, to be shown the great drawing-room, on which the touching incident in the life of a Royal Personage had conferred an historical dignity. "I think—" said she "—only I haven't quite made up my mind yet—that I shall call this ward Mrs. Fitzherbert, and the next room Princess Caroline. Or the other way round. Which do you think?" For one of her schemes was to turn the old family mansion into a Hospital.

"Let me see!" said Gwen. "I've forgotten my history. Mrs. Fitzherbert was his wife, wasn't she?"

Miss Dickenson was always to be relied on for general information. "Unquestionably," said she. "But he repudiated her for political reasons, a course open to him as heir to the throne. Legally, Princess Caroline of Brunswick was his lawful wife. . . ."

"And, lawfully," said Gwen, "Mrs. Fitzherbert was his legal wife. Nothing can be clearer. Yes—I should say certainly call the big room Mrs. Fitzherbert. Whom shall you call the other rooms after, Clo?"

"All the others. There's any number! Mrs. Robinson, Lady Jersey, Lady Conyngham . . . one for every room in the house, and several over. Just fancy!—the room has never been altered, since those days. It was polished up for my poor mother—whom no doubt I saw in my youth, but took no notice of. You see, I wasn't of an age to take notice, when she departed to Kingdom-come, and my father exiled himself to Scotland. . . ."

"And he kept it packed up like this—how long?"

"Well—you know how old I am. Twenty-seven."

Aunt Constance corrected dates. "George the Fourth," said she chronologically, "ascended the throne in 1820. Consequently he cannot have become intoxicated in this room. . . ."

Sister Nora interrupted. Of course he couldn't—not in her father's time. The cards and dice were going in her great-uncle's time, who drank himself to death forty years ago. "There used to be some packs of cards," said she, "in one of these drawers. I know I saw some there, only it's a long time back—almost the only time I ever came into the room. I'll look. . . . Take care of the dust!"

It was lucky that the cabinet-maker who framed that inlaid table knew his business—they did, in his day—or the rounded front might have called for a jerk, instead of giving easily to the pull it had awaited so patiently, through decades. "There they are!" said Gwen, "with nobody to deal them. Poor cards—locked up in the dark all these years! Do let's have them out and play dummy to-night."

A spirit of Conservatism suggested that it would be impious to disturb a *status quo* connected with Royalty. But Gwen said, touching a visible ace:—"Just think, Clo, if *you* were an ace, and had a chance of being trumps, how would you like to be shut up in a drawer again?" This appeal to our common humanity had its effect, and a couple of packs were brought out for use. No language could describe the penetrating powers of the dust that accompanied their return to active duties. It ended the visit *en passant* of these three ladies, who were not sorry to find themselves in an upstairs suite of rooms with a kitchen and a miniature household, just established regardless of expense. Because three hundred a year was what Miss Grahame was "going to" live upon, as soon as she had "had time to turn round," and for the moment it was absurd to draw hard and fast lines. Just wait and give her time, to get a little settled!

The fatigue of the journey was enough to negative any idea of going out anywhere, and indeed there was nothing in the way of theatre or concert that was at all tempting. But it was not enough to cause collapse, and whist became plausible within half an hour after dinner. There was something delightful in the place, too, with its windows opening on the tree-tops of the Square, and the air of a warm autumn evening bringing in the sound of a woebegone brass band from afar, mixed with the endless hum of wheels with hoof-beats in the heart of it, like currants in a cake. The air was all the sweeter that a whiff of chimney-smoke broke into it now and again, and emphasized its quality. When the band left off the "Bohemian Girl" and rested, and imagination was picturing the trombone in half, at odds with condensation, a barrel-organ was able to make itself heard, with *Il Pescatore,* till the band began again with The Sicilian Bride, and drowned it.

Miss Dickenson had been discreet about her expectation of a visitor. She maintained her discretion even when the sound of a hansom's lids, followed by "Yes—this house!" and a double knock below, turned out not to be a mistake, but the Hon. Percival Pellew, Carlton Club. She nevertheless roused the interested suspicion of Gwen and her hostess, who looked at each other, and said respectively:—" Oh, it's my cousin Percy," and "Oh, Mr. Pellew"; the former adding:—"He can take Dummy's hand"; the latter,—"Oh, of course, ask him to come up, Maggie! Don't let him go away on any account." But neither of these ladies expressed any surprise at the rather prompt recrudescence of Mr. Pellew, last seen at the Towers two days since.

The only flaw in a pretext that Mr. Pellew had come to leave Tennyson's " Princess," with his card in it, and run away as if the book-owner would bite him, was perhaps the ostentation with which that lady left his detention to her hostess. It would have been at once more candid and more skilful to say, " Oh yes, it's my book. But I didn't want Mr. Pellew about bringing it back," with a judicious infusion of enthusiasm that the visitor's efforts to get away should fail. However, the flaw was slight, and no one cared about the transparency of the pretext. Moreover, Maggie, a new importation from the Highlands, thought that her young ladyship, whose beauty had overwhelmed her, was at the bottom of it—not Aunt Constance.

" Now you *are* here, Percy, you had better make yourself useful. Sit as we are. I'm not sorry you're come, because I hate playing dummy." This was Gwen, naturally.

The impersonality of Dummy furnished a topic to tide over the assimilation of things, and help the social *fengshui* to plausibility. There was a fillah—said Mr. Pellew—at the Club, who wouldn't take Dummy unless that fiction was accommodated with a real chair. And there was another fillah who couldn't play unless the vacant chair was taken away. Something had happened to this fillah when he was a boy, and anything like a ghost was uncongenial to him. You shouldn't lock up children in the dark or make grimaces at them if you wanted them not to be nervous in after-life . . . and so forth.

Gwen was a bad whist-player, sometimes taking a very perverted view of the game. As, for instance, when, after Mr. Pellew had dealt, she asked her partner how many trumps she held. " Because, Clo," said she, " I've only got two, and unless you've got at least four, I don't see the use of going on." Public opinion condemned this attitude as unsportsmanlike, and demanded another deal. Gwen welcomed the suggestion, having only a Knave and a Queen in all the rest of her hand.

Her partner expressed disgust. " I think," she said, " you might have held your tongue, Gwen, and played it out. But I shan't tell you why."

" Oh, I know, of course, without your telling me. You're made of trumps. I'm so sorry, dear! There—see!—I've led." She played Knave.

" This," said Mr. Pellew, with shocked gravity, " is not whist."

" Well," said Gwen, " I can *not* see why one shouldn't say how many cards one has of any suit. Everyone knows, so it must be fair. Everyone sees Dummy's hand."

" I see your point. But it's not whist."

" Am I to play, or not? " said Aunt Constance. She looked across at her partner, as a serious player rather amused at the childish behaviour of their opponents. A sympathetic bond was thereby established—solid seriousness against frivolity.

" Fire away! " said Gwen. " Second player plays lowest." Miss Dickenson played the Queen. " That's not whist, aunty," said Gwen triumphantly. Her partner played the King. " There now, you see! " said Gwen. She belonged to the class of players who rejoice aloud, or show depression, after success or failure.

This time her exultation was premature. Mr. Pellew, without emotion, pushed the turn-up card, a two, into the trick, saying to his partner:—" Your Queen was all right. Quite correct! " The story does not vouch for this. It may have been wrong.

" Do you mean to say, Cousin Percy "—thus Gwen, with indignant emphasis—" that you've not got a club in your hand, at the very first round. You cannot expect us to believe that! " Mr. Pellew pointed out that if he revoked he would lose three tricks. " Very well," said Gwen. " I shall keep a very sharp look out." But no revoke came, and she had to console herself as a loser with the reflection that it was only the odd trick, after all—one by cards and honours divided.

This is a fair sample of the way this game went on establishing a position of moral superiority for Mr. Pellew and his partner, who looked down on the irregularities of their opponents from a pinnacle of True Whist. Their position as superior beings tended towards mutual understandings. A transition state from their relations in that easy-going life at the Towers to the more sober obligations of the metropolis was at least acceptable; and this isolation by a better understanding of tricks and trumps, a higher and holier view of ruffing and finessing, appeared to provide such a state. There was partnership of souls in it, over and above mere vulgar scoring.

Nothing of interest occurred until, in the course of the second rubber, Gwen made a misdeal. Probably she did so because she was trying at the same time to prove that having four by honours was absurd in itself—an affront to natural laws. It was the merest accident, she maintained, when all the court-cards were dealt to one side—no merit at all of the players. Her objection to whist was that it was a mixture of skill and chance. She was inclined to favour games that were either quite the one or quite the other.

Roulette was a good game. So was chess. But whist was neither fish nor flesh nor good red herring. . . . Misdeal! The analysis of games stopped with a jerk, the dealer being left without a turn-up card.

"But what a shame!" said Gwen. "Is it fair I should lose my deal when the last card's an ace? How would any of you like it?" The appeal was too touching to resist, though Mr. Pellew again said this wasn't whist. A count of the hands showed that Aunt Constance held one card too few and Gwen one too many. A question arose. If a card were drawn from the dealer's hand, was the trump to remain on the table? Controversy ensued. Why should not the drawer have her choice of thirteen cards, as in every analogous case? On the other hand, said Gwen, that ace of hearts was indisputably the last card in the pack; and therefore the trump-card, by predestination.

Mr. Pellew pointed out that it mattered less than Miss Dickenson thought, as if she pitched on this very ace to make up her own thirteen, its teeth would be drawn. It would be no longer a turn-up card, and some new choice of trumps would have to be made, somehow; by *sortes Virgilianœ*, or what not. Better have another deal. Gwen gave up the point, under protest, and Miss Dickenson dealt. Spades were trumps, this time.

It chanced that Gwen, in this deal, held the Knave and Queen of hearts. She led the Knave, and only waiting for the next card, to be sure that it was a low one, said deliberately to her partner:— "Don't play your King, Cousin Clo; Percy's got the ace," in defiance of all rule and order.

"Can't help it," said Cousin Clo. "Got nothing else!" Out came the King, and down came the ace upon it, naturally.

"There now, see what I've done," said Gwen. "Got your King squashed!" But she was consoled when Mr. Pellew pointed out that if Miss Grahame had played a small card her King would almost certainly have fallen to a trump later. "It was quite the right play," said he, "because now your Queen makes. You couldn't have made with both."

"I believe you've been cheating, and looking at my hand," said Gwen. "How do you know I've got the Queen?"

"How did you know I had got the ace?" said Mr. Pellew. And really this was a reasonable question.

"By the mark on the back. I noticed it when I turned it up, when hearts were trumps, last deal. I don't consider that cheating. All the same, I enjoy cheating, and always cheat whenever I can. Card games are so very dull, when there's no cheating."

"But, Gwen dear, I don't see any mark." This was Miss Grahame, examining the last trick. She put the ace, face down, before this capricious whist-player, who, however, adhered to her statement, saying incorrigibly:—"Well, look at it!"

"I only see a shadow," said Mr. Pellew. But it wasn't a shadow. A shadow moves.

Explanation came, on revision of the ace's antecedents. It had lain in that drawer five-and-twenty years at least, with another card half-covering it. In the noiseless air-tight darkness where it lay, saying perhaps to itself:—"Shall I ever take a trick again?" there was still dust, dust of thought-baffling fineness! And it had fallen, fallen steadily, with immeasurable slowness and absolute impartiality, on all the card above had left unsheltered. There was the top-card's silhouette, quite recognisable as soon as the shadow was disestablished.

"It will come out with India-rubber," said Miss Grahame. "I shouldn't mess it about, if I were you," said Gwen. "I know India-rubber. It grimes everything in, and makes black streaks." Which was true enough in those days. The material called bottle-rubber was notable for its power of defiling clean paper, and the sophisticated sort for becoming indurated if not cherished in one's trouser-pockets. The present epoch in the World's history can rub out quite clean for a penny, but then its *dramatis personæ* have to spend their lives dodging motor-cars and biplanes, and holding their ears for fear of gramophones. Still, it's *something!*

Mr. Pellew suggested that the best way to deal with the soiled card would be for whoever got it to exhibit it, as one does sometimes when a card's face is seen for a moment, to make sure everyone knows. We were certainly not playing very strictly. This was accepted *nem. con.*

But the chance that had left that card half-covered was to have its influence on things, still. Who can say events would have run in the same grooves had it not directed the conversation to dust, and caused Mr. Pellew to recollect a story told by one of those Archæological fillahs, at the Towers three days ago? It was that of the tomb which, being opened, showed a forgotten monarch of some prehistoric race, robed, crowned, and sceptred as of old; a little shrunk, perhaps, a bit discoloured, but still to be seen by his own ghost, if earth-bound and at all interested. Still to be seen, even by Cook's tourists, had he but had a little more staying-power. But he was never seen, as a matter of fact, by any man but the desecrator of his tomb. For one whiff of fresh air brought

him down, a crumbling heap of dust with a few imperishable orna-
ments buried in it. His own ghost would not have known him
again; and, in less time than it takes to tell, the wind blew him
about, and he had to take his chance with the dust of the desert.

"I suppose it isn't true," said Gwen incredulously. "Things of
that sort are generally fibs."

"Don't know about this one," said Mr. Pellew, sorting his cards.
"Funny coincidence! It was in the *Quarterly Review*—very first
thing I opened at—Egyptian Researches. . . . That's our trick,
isn't it?"

"Yes—my ten. I'll lead. . . . Yes!—I think I'll lead a diamond.
I always envy you men your Clubs. It must be so nice to have
all the newspapers and reviews. . . ." Aunt Constance said this,
of course.

"It wasn't at the Club. Man left it at my chambers three
months ago—readin' it by accident yesterday evening—funny coincidence—talkin' about it same morning! Knave takes. No—
you can't trump. You haven't got a trump."

"Now, however did you know that?" said Gwen.

"Very simple. All the trumps are out but two, and I've got
them here in my hand. See?"

"Yes, I see. But I prefer real cheating, to taking advantages
of things, like that. . . . What are you putting your cards down
for, Cousin Percy?"

"Because that's game. Game and the rubber. We only want
two by cards, and there they are!"

When rubbers end at past ten o'clock at night, well-bred people
wait for their host to suggest beginning another. Ill-bred ones,
that don't want one, say suddenly that it must be getting late—
as if Time had slapped them—and get at their watches. Those
that do, say that that clock is fast. In the present case no disposition existed, after a good deal of travelling, to play cards till
midnight. But there was no occasion to hustle the visitor downstairs.

Said Miss Dickenson, to concede a short breathing pause:—
"Pray, Mr. Pellew, when a gentleman accidentally leaves a book
at your rooms, do you make no effort to return it to him?"

"Well!" said Mr. Pellew, tacitly admitting the implied im-
peachment. "It *is* rather a jolly shame, when you come to think of
it. I'll take it round to him to-morrow. Gloucester Place, is it—
or York Place—end of Baker Street? . . . Can't remember the
fillah's name to save my life. Married a Miss Bergstein—rich
bankers. Got his card at home, I expect. However, that's where

he lives—York Place. He's a Sir Somebody Something. . . .
What were you going to say?"

"Oh—nothing. . . . Only that it would have been very interesting to read that account. However, Sir Somebody Something
must be wanting his *Quarterly Review*. . . . Never mind!"

Gwen said:—"What nonsense! He's bought another copy by
this time. He can afford it, if he's married a Miss Bergstein.
Bring it round to-morrow, Percy, to keep Aunt Constance quiet.
We shan't take her with us to see Clo's little boy. We should
make too many." Then, in order to minimise his visit next day,
Mr. Pellew sketched a brief halt in Cavendish Square at half-past
three precisely to-morrow afternoon, when Miss Dickenson could
"run her eye" through the disintegration of that Egyptian King,
without interfering materially with its subsequent delivery at Sir
Somebody Something's. It was an elaborate piece of humbug, welcomed with perfect gravity as the solution of a perplexing and
difficult problem. Which being so happily solved, Mr. Pellew could
take his leave, and did so.

"Didn't I do that capitally, Clo?"

"Do which, dear?"

"Why—making her stop here to see him. Or giving her leave
to stop; it's the same thing, only she would rather do it against
her will. I mean saying we should make too many at Scraps
Court, or whatever it is."

"Oh yes—quite a stroke of genius! Gwen dear, what an invet-
erate matchmaker you are!"

"Nonsense, Clo! I never . . ." Here Gwen hung fire for a
moment, confronted by an intractability of language. She took
the position by storm, *more suo:*—"I never *mutchmoke* in my
life. . . . What?—Well, you may laugh, Clo, but I never *did!*
Only when two fools irritate one by not flying into each other's
arms, and wanting to all the time. . . . Oh, it's exasperating,
and I've no patience!"

"You are quite sure they do . . . want to?"

"Oh yes—I think so. At least, I'm quite sure Percy does."

"Why not Aunt Constance?"

"Because I can't imagine anyone wanting to rush into any of
my cousins' arms—my he-cousins. It's a peculiarity of cousins,
I suppose. If any of mine had been palatable, he would have
caught on, and it would have come off. Because they all want
me, always."

"That's an old story, Gwen dear." The two ladies looked ruefully at one another, with a slight shoulder-shrug apiece over a

hopeless case. Then Miss Grahame said:—" Then you consider
Constance Dickenson is still palatable? " She laughed on the
word a little—a sort of protest. " At nearly forty? "

" Oh dear, yes! Not that she's forty, nor anything like it. She's
thirty-six. Besides, it has nothing to do with age. Or very little.
Why—how old is that dear old lady at Chorlton that was jealous
of your little boy's old woman in London? "

" Old Goody Marrable? Over eighty. But the other old lady
is older still, and Dave speaks well of her, anyhow! We shall see
her to-morrow. We must insist on that."

" Well—I could kiss old Goody Marrable. I should be sorry
for her bones, of course. But they're not her fault, after all! She's
quite an old darling. I hope Aunt Connie and Percy will manage a little common sense to-morrow. They'll have the house to
themselves, anyhow. Ta bye-bye, Chloe dear! "

Miss Grahame looked in on her way to her own room to see
that Miss Dickenson had been provided with all the accessories
of a good night—a margin of pillows and blankets *à choix,* and
so on. Hot-water-bottle time had scarcely come yet, but hospitality might refer to it. There was, however, a word to say touching the evening just ended. What did Miss Grahame think of
Gwen? Aunt Constance's *parti pris* in life was a benevolent interest in the affairs of everybody else.

Miss Grahame thought Gwen was all right. The amount of
nonsense she had talked to-night showed she was a little excited.
A sort of ostentatious absurdity, like a spoiled child! Well—
she has been a spoiled child. But she—the speaker—always had
believed, did still believe, that Gwen was a fine character underneath, and that all her nonsense was on the surface.

" Will she hold to it, do you think? "

" How can I tell? I should say yes. But one never knows.
She's writing him a long letter now. She's in the next room to
me, and I heard her scratching five minutes after she said good-
night. I hope she won't scribble all night and keep me awake.
My belief is she would be better for some counter-excitement. A
small earthquake! Anything of that sort. Good-night! It's very
late." But it came out next day that Gwen's pen was still scratching when this lady got to sleep an hour after.

CHAPTER XXVI

A PROFESSIONAL CONSULTATION ACROSS A COUNTER, AND HOW THE STORY
OF THE MAN IN HYDE PARK WAS TOLD BY DOLLY.   HOW AUNT
M'RIAR KNEW THE NAME WAS NOT "DARRABLE."   HOW SHE TOLD
UNCLE MO WHOSE WIFE SHE WAS AND WHOSE MOTHER MRS. PRITCH-
ARD WAS.   HOW POLLY DAVERILL JUNIOR HAD DIED UNBAPTIZED, AND
ATTEMPTS TO BULLY THE DEVIL ARE FUTILE.   HOW HER MOTHER
WAS   FORMERLY   BARMAID   AT   THE   ONE   TUN,   BUT   BECAME
AUNT M'RIAR LATER, AND HOW THE TALLOW CANDLE JUST LASTED
OUT.   HOW DOLLY, VERY SOUND ASLEEP, WAS GOOD FOR HER AUNT

"I SHOULDN'T take any violent exercise, if I was you, Mr. Wardle," said Mr. Ekings, the Apothecary, whose name you may remember Michael Ragstroar had borrowed and been obliged to
relinquish.   "I should be very careful what I ate, avoiding especially pork and richly cooked food.   A diet of fowls and fish—
preferably boiled. . . ."

"Can't abide 'em!" said Uncle Moses, who was talking over
his symptoms with Mr. Ekings at his shop, with Dolly on his
knee.   "And whose a-going to stand Sam for me, livin' on this
and livin' on that?   Roasted chicking's very pretty eating, for
the sake of the soarsages, when you're a Lord Mayor; but for them
as don't easy run to half-crowns for mouthfuls, a line has to be
drawed.   Down our Court a shilling has to go a long way, Dr.
Ekings."

The medical adviser shook his head weakly.   "You're an intractable patient, Mr. Moses," he said.   He knew that Uncle
Moses's circumstances were what is called moderate.   So are a
church mouse's; and, in both cases, the dietary is compulsory.   Mr.
Ekings tried for a common ground of agreement.   "Fish doesn't
mount up to much, by the pound," he said, vaguely.

"Fishes don't go home like butcher's meat," said Uncle Moses.

"You can't expect 'em to do that," said Mr. Ekings, glad of
an indisputable truth.   "But there's a vast amount of nourishment
in 'em, anyway you put it."

"So there is, Dr. Ekings.   In a vast amount of 'em.   But you
have to eat it all up.   Similar, grass and cows.   Only there's no
bones in the grass.   Now, you know, what I'm wanting is a pick-
me-up—something with a nice clean edge in the smell of it,

like a bottle o' salts with holes in the stopper. And tasting of
lemons. I ain't speaking of the sort that has to be shook when
took. Nor yet with peppermint. It's a clear sort to see through,
up against the light, what I want."

Mr. Ekings, a humble practitioner in a poor neighbourhood,
supplied more mixtures in response to suggestions like Uncle
Mo's, than to legitimate prescriptions. So he at once undertook
to fill out the order, saying in reply to an inquiry, that it would
come to threepence, but that Uncle Mo must bring or send back
the bottle. He then added a few drops of chloric ether and am-
monia, and some lemon to a real square bottleful of aq. pur.
haust., and put a label on it with superhuman evenness, on which
was written "The Mixture—one tablespoonful three times a day."
Uncle Moses watched the preparation of this *elixir vitæ* with the
extremest satisfaction. He foresaw its beneficial effect on his
system, which he had understood was to blame for his occasional
attacks of faintness, which had latterly been rather more frequent.
Anything in such a clean phial, with such a new cork, would be
sure to do his system good.

Mrs. Riley came in for a bottle which was consciously awaiting
her in front of the leeches, and identified it as "the liniment,"
before Mr. Ekings could call to mind where he'd stood it. She
remarked, while calculating coppers to cover the outlay, that she
understood it was to be well r-r-r-rhubbed in with the parrum of
her hand, and that she was to be thr-rusted not to lit the patiint
get any of it near his mouth, she having been borrun in Limerick
morr' than a wake ago. She remarked to Uncle Mo that his boy
was looking his bist, and none the wurruss for his accidint. Uncle
Mo felt braced by the Celtic atmosphere, and thanked Mrs. Riley
cordially, for himself and Dave.

"Shouldn't do that, if I was you, Mr. Wardle," said Mr. Ekings
the Apothecary, as Uncle Mo hoisted Dolly on his shoulder to carry
her home.

"No more shouldn't I, if you was me, Dr. Ekings," was the intractable patient's reply. "Why, Lard bless you, man alive, Dolly's
so light it's as good as a lift-up, only to have her on your shoulders! Didn't you never hear tell of gravitation? Well—that's it!"
But Uncle Mo was out of his depth.

"It'll do ye a powerful dale of good, Mr. Wardle," said Mrs.
Riley. "Niver you mind the docther!" And Uncle Mo departed,
braced again, with his *elixir vitæ* in his left hand, and Dolly on
his right shoulder, conversing on a topic suggested by Dr. Ekings's
remarks about diet.

"When Dave tooktid Micky to see the fisses corched in the Turpentine, there was a jenklum corched a fiss up out of the water, and another jenklum corched another fiss up out of the water. . . ." Dolly was pursuing the subject in the style of the Patriarchs, who took their readers' leisure for granted, and never grudged a repetition, when Uncle Mo interrupted her to point out that it was not Dave who took Michael Ragstroar to Hy' Park, but *vice versa*. Also that the whole proceeding had been a disgraceful breach of discipline, causing serious alarm to himself and Aunt M'riar, who had nearly lost their reason in consequence—the exact expression being "fritted out of their wits." If that young Micky ever did such a thing again, Uncle Mo said, the result would be a pretty how-do-you-do, involving possibly fatal consequences to Michael, and certainly local flagellation of unheard-of severity.

Dolly did not consider this was to the point, and pursued her narrative without taking notice of it. "There was a jenklum corched a long fiss, and there was another jenklum corched a short fiss, and there was another jenklum corched a short fiss. . . ." This seemed to bear frequent repetition, but came to an end as soon as history ceased to supply the facts. Then another phase came, that of the fishers who didn't corch no fiss, whose name appeared to be Legion. They lasted as far as the arch into Sapps Court, and Uncle Mo seemed rather to relish the monotony than otherwise. He would have made a good Scribe in the days of the Pharaohs.

But Dolly came to the end of even the unsuccessful fishermen. Just as they reached home, however, she produced her convincing incident, all that preceded it having evidently been introduction pure and simple. "And there was a man saided fings to Micky, and saided fings to Dave, and saided fings to . . ." Here Dolly stuttered, became confused, and ended up weakly: "No, he didn't saided no fings, to no one else."

A little *finesse* was necessary to land the *elixir vitæ* on the parlour chimney-piece, and Dolly on the hearthrug. Then Uncle Mo sat down in his own chair to recover breath, saying in the course of a moment:—"And what did the man say to Dave, and what did he say to young Sparrowgrass?" He did not suppose that "the man" was a person capable of identification; he was an unknown unit, but good to talk about.

"He saided Mrs. Picture." Dolly placed the subject she proposed to treat broadly before her audience, with a view to its careful analysis at leisure.

"What on 'arth did he say Mrs. Picture for? *He* don't know Mrs. Picture." The present tense used here acknowledged the man's authenticity, and encouraged the little maid—three and three-quarters, you know!—to further testimony. It came fairly fluently, considering the witness's recent acquisition of the English language.

"He doos know Mrs. Picture, ass he doos, and he saided Mrs. Picture to Micky, ass he did." This was plenty for a time, and during that time the witness could go on nodding with her eyes wide open, to present the subject lapsing, for she had found out already how slippery grown-up people are in argument. Great force was added by her curls, which lent themselves to flapping backwards and forwards as she nodded.

It was impossible to resist such evidence, outwardly at least, and Uncle Mo appeared to accept it. "Then the man said Mrs. Picture to Dave," said he. "And Dave told it on to you, was that it?" He added, for the general good of morality:—"*You're* a nice lot of young Pickles!"

But this stopped the nodding, which changed suddenly to a negative shake, of great decision. "The man never saided nuffint to Dave, no he didn't."

"Thought you said he did. You're a good 'un for a witness-box! Come up and sit on your old uncle. The man said Mrs. Picture to young Sparrowgrass—was that it?" Dolly nodded violently. "And young Sparrowgrass he passed it on to Dave?" But it appeared not, and Dolly had to wrestle with an explanation. It was too much involved for letterpress, but Uncle Mo thought he could gather that Dave had been treated as a mere bystander, supposed to be absorbed in angling, during a conversation between Michael Ragstroar and the Man. "Dave he came home and told you what the Man said to Micky—was that it?" So Uncle Mo surmised aloud, not at all clear that Dolly would understand him. But, as it turned out, he was right, and Dolly was glad to be able to attest his version of the facts. She resumed the nodding, but slower, as though so much emphasis had ceased to be necessary. "Micky toldited Dave," she said. She then became immensely amused at a way of looking at the event suggested by her uncle. The Man had told Micky; Micky had told Dave; Dave had told Dolly; and Dolly had told Uncle Mo, who now intensified the interest of the event by saying he should tell Aunt M'riar. Dolly became vividly anxious for this climax, and felt that this was life indeed, when Uncle Mo called out to Aunt M'riar:—"Come along here, M'riar, and see what sort of head

and tail you can make of this here little Dolly!" Whereupon
Aunt M'riar came in front out at the back, and listened to a
repetition of Dolly's tale while she dried her arms, which had been
in a wash-tub.

"Well, Mo," she said, when Dolly had repeated it, more or less
chaotically, "if you ask me, what I say is—you make our Dave
speak out and tell you, when he's back from school, and say
you won't have no nonsense. For the child is that secretive
it's all one's time is worth to be even with him. . . . What's
the Doctor's stuff for you've been spending your money on at
Ekingses?"

"Only a stimulatin' mixture for to give tone to the system.
Dr. Ekings says it'll do it a world o' good. Never known it fail,
he hasn't."

"Have you been having any more alarming symptoms, Mo, and
never told me?"

"Never been better in my life, M'riar. But I thought it was
getting on for time I should have a bottle o' stuff, one sort or
other. Don't do to go too long without a dose, nowadays." Whereupon Aunt M'riar looked incredulous, and read the label, and smelt
the bottle, and put it back on the mantelshelf. And Uncle Mo
asked for the wineglass broke off short, out of the cupboard; because it was always best to be beforehand, whether you had anything the matter or not.

Whatever Aunt M'riar said, Dave was not secretive. Probably
she meant communicative, and was referring to the fact that Dave,
whenever he was called on for information, though always prompt
to oblige, invariably made reply to his questioner in an undertone, in recognition of a mutual confidence, and exclusion from
it of the Universe. He had a soul above the vulgarities of publication. Aunt M'riar merely used a word that sounded well, irre-
spective of its meaning—a common literary practice.

Therefore Dave, when applied to by Uncle Mo for particulars
of what "the Man" said, made a statement of which only portions
reached the general public. This was the usual public after supper; for Mr. Alibone's companionship in an evening pipe was an
almost invariable incident at that hour.

"What's the child a-sayin' of, Mo?" said Aunt M'riar.

"Easy a bit, old Urry Scurry!" said Uncle Mo, drawing on
his imagination for an epithet. "Let me do a bit of listening. . . .
What was it the party said again, Davy—just *precisely*? . . ."
Dave was even less audible than before in his response to this,
and Uncle Mo evidently softened it for repetition:—"Said if

Micky told him any—etceterer—lies he'd rip his heart out? Was that it, Dave?"

"Yorce," said Dave, aloud and emphatically. *"This* time!" Which seemed to imply that the speaker had refrained from doing so, to his credit, on some previous occasion. Dave laid great stress on this point.

Aunt M'riar seemed rather panic struck at the nature of this revelation. "Well now, Mo," said she, "I do wonder at you, letting the child tell such words! And before Mr. Alibone, too!"

Mr. Jerry's expression twinkled, as though he protested against being credited with a Pharisaical purity, susceptible to shocks. Uncle Mo said, with less than usual of his easy-going manner:— "I'm a going, M'riar, to get to the bottom of this here start. So you keep outside o' the ropes!" and then after a little by-play with Dave and Dolly, which made the hair of both rougher than ever, he said suddenly to Dave:—"Well, and wasn't you frightened?"

"Micky wasn't frightened," said Dave, discreetly evasive. He objected to pursuing the subject, and raised a new issue. The sketch that followed of the interview between Micky and the Man was a good deal blurred by constant India-rubber, but its original could be inferred from it—probably as follows, any omissions to conciliate public censorship being indicated by stars. Micky speaks first:

"Who'll you rip up? You lay 'ands upon me, that's all! You do, and I'll blind your eyesight, s'elp me! Why, I'd summing a Police Orficer, and have you took to the Station, just as soon as look at you. . . ." It may be imagined here that Michael's voice rose to a half-shriek, following some movement of the Man towards him. "I would, by Goard! You try it on, that's all!"

"Shut up with your * * row, you * * young * * . . . No, master, I ain't molestin' of the boy; only just frightening him for a bit of a spree! *I* don't look like the sort to hurt boys, do I, guv'nor?" This was addressed to a bystander, named in Dave's report as "the gentleman." Who was accompanied by another, described as "the lady." The latter may have said to the former:—"I think he looks a very kind-hearted man, my dear, and you are making a fuss about nothing." The latter certainly said "Hggrromph!" or something like it, which the reporter found difficult to render. Then the man assumed a hypocritical and plausible manner, saying to Michael:—"I'm your friend, my boy, and there's a new shilling for you, good for two * * tanners any day of the week." Micky seemed to have been softened

by this, and entered into a colloquy with the donor, either not heard
or not understood by Dave, whose narrative seemed to point to
his having been sent to a distance, with a doubt about inapplicable
epithets bestowed on him by the Man, calling for asterisks in a
close report. Some of these were probably only half-understood,
even by Micky; being, so to speak, the chirps of a gaol-bird. But
Dave's report seemed to point to " Now, is that * * young * * to
be trusted not to split ? " although he made little attempt to render
the asterisky parts of speech.

Uncle Mo and Mr. Jerry glanced at one another, seeming to
understand a phrase that had puzzled Aunt M'riar.

" That was it, Mo," said Mr. Jerry, exactly as if Uncle Mo
had spoken, " *spit upon* meant *split upon.*" Dave in his innocence
had supposed that a profligacy he was himself sometimes guilty
of had been referred to. He felt that his uncle's knee was for
the moment the stool of repentance, but was relieved when a new
reading was suggested. There could be no disgrace in splitting,
though it might be painful.

" And, of course," said Uncle Mo, ruffling Dave's locks, " of
course, you kept your mouth tight shut—hay ? " Dave, bewildered, assented. He connected this *bouche cousue* with his own
decorous abstention, not without credit to himself. Who shall
trace the inner workings of a small boy's brain ? " Instead of
telling of it all, straight off, to your poor old uncle ! " There was
no serious indignation in Uncle Mo's tone, but the boy was too
new for nice distinctions. The suggestion of disloyalty wounded
him deeply, and he rushed into explanation. " Becorze—becorze—
becorze—becorze," said he—" becorze Micky said *not* to ! " He arrived at his climax like a squib that attains its ideal.

" Micky's an owdacious young varmint," said Uncle Mo.
" Small boys that listened to owdacious young varmints never
used to come to much good, not in *my* time ! " Dave looked
shocked at Uncle Mo's experience. But he had reservations to
offer as to Micky, which distinguished him from vulgar listeners
to incantations. " Micky said not to, and Micky said Uncle Mo
didn't want to hear tell of no Man out in Hoy' Park, and me to
keep my mouth shut till I was tolded to speak."

" And you told him to speak, and he spoke ! " said Mr. Jerry,
charitably helping Dave. " You couldn't expect any fairer than
that, old Mo." Public opinion sanctioned a concession in this
sense, and Dave came off the stool of repentance.

" Very good, then ! " said Uncle Mo. " That's all squared, and
we can cross it off. But what I'm trying after is, how did this

here . . . bad-languagee "—he halted a minute to make this word—
" come to know anything about Goody Prichard upstairs ? "

" Did he ? " said Mr. Jerry, who of course had only heard Dave
on the subject.

" This young party said so," said Uncle Mo, crumpling Dolly
to identify her, " at the very first go off. Didn't you, little ginger-
pop, hay ? " This new epithet was a passing recognition of the
suddenness with which Dolly had broken out as an informant. It
gratified her vanity, and made her chuckle.

Dave meanwhile had been gathering for an oratorical effort,
and now culminated. " I never told Dolly nuffint *about* Mrs. Picture upstairs. What *I* said was ' old widder lady.' "

" Dolly translated it, Mo, don't you see ? " said Mr. Jerry. Then,
to illuminate possible obscurity, he added :—" Off o' one slate onto
the other! Twig ? "

" I twig you, Jerry." Uncle Mo winked at his friend to show
that he was alive to surroundings and tickled Dave suddenly from
a motive of policy. " How come this cove to know anything
about any widder lady—hay ? That's a sort of p'int we've got to
consider of." Dave was impressed by his uncle's appearance of
profound thought, and was anxious not to lag behind in the
solution of stiff problems. He threw his whole soul into his
answer. " Because he was *The Man*." Nathan the prophet can
scarcely have been more impressive. Perhaps, on the occasion
Dave's answer recalls, someone said :—" Hullo ! " in Hebrew, and
gave a short whistle. That was what Mr. Jerry did, this time.

Uncle Mo enjoined self-restraint, telegraphically; and said,
verbally :—" What man, young Legs ? Steady a minute, and tell
us who he was." Which will be quite intelligible to anyone whose
experience has included a small boy in thick boots sitting on his
knee, and becoming excited by a current topic.

Dave restrained his boots, and concentrated his mind on a statement. It came with pauses and repetitions, which may be omitted.
" He worze the same Man as when you and me and Micky, only
not Dolly, see him come along down the Court Sunday morning.
Munce ago ! " This was emphatic, to express the date's remoteness. " He wanted for to be told about old Widow Darrable who
lived down this Court, and Micky he said no such name, nor yet
anywhere's about this neighbourhood, he said. And the Man
he said Micky was a young liar. And Micky he said who are you
a-callin' liar ? . . ."

" *What* name did he say ? " Uncle Mo interrupted, with growing interest. Dave repeated his misapprehension of it, which incor-

porated an idea that similar widows would have similar surnames. If one was Marrable, it was only natural that another should be Darrable.

Aunt M'riar, whose interest also had been some time growing, struck in incisively. "The name was Daverill. He's mixed it up with the old lady in the country he calls his granny." She was the more certain this was so owing to a recent controversy with Dave about this name, ending in his surrender of the pronunciation "Marrowbone" as untenable, but introducing a new element of confusion owing to Marylebone Church, a familiar landmark.

There was something in Aunt M'riar's manner that made Uncle Mo say:—"Anything disagreed, M'riar?" Because, observe, his interest in this mysterious man in the Park turned entirely on Mrs. Prichard's relations with him, and he had never imputed any knowledge of him to Aunt M'riar. Why should he? Indeed, why should we, except from the putting of two and two together? Of which two twos, Uncle Mo might have known either the one or the other—according to which was which—but not both. This story has to confess occasional uncertainty about some of its facts. There may have been more behind Uncle Mo's bit of rudeness about Aunt M'riar's disquiet than showed on the surface. However, he never asked any questions.

Those who have ever had the experience of keeping their own counsel for a long term of years know that every year makes it harder to take others into confidence. A concealed troth-plight, marriage, widowhood—to name the big concealments involving no disgrace—gets less and less easy to publish as time slips by, even as the hinges rust of doors that no man opens. There may be nothing to blush about in that cellar, but the key may be lost and the door-frame may have gripped the door above, or the footstone jammed it from below, and such fungus-growth as the darkness has bred has a claim to freedom from the light. Let it all rest—that is its owner's word to his own soul—let it rest and be forgotten! All the more when the cellar is full of garbage, and he knows it.

There was no garbage in Aunt M'riar's cellar that she was guilty of, but for all that she would have jumped at any excuse to leave that door tight shut. The difficulty was not so much in what she had to tell—for her conscience was clear—as in rousing an unprepared mind to the hearing of it. Uncle Mo, quite the reverse of apathetic to anything that concerned the well-being of any of his surroundings, probably accounted Aunt M'riar's as second to none but the children's. Nevertheless, the difficulty of rousing him to an active interest in this hidden embarrassment of hers, of which he had no suspicion, was so palpable to Aunt M'riar, that she was sorely put to it to decide on a course of action. And the necessity for action was not imaginary. Keep in mind that all Uncle Mo's knowledge of Aunt M'riar's antecedents was summed up in the fact of her widowhood, which he took for granted—although he had never received it *totidem verbis* when she first came to supplant Mrs. Twiggins—and which had been confirmed as Time went on, and no husband appeared to claim her. Even if he could have suspected that her husband was still living, there was nothing in the world to connect him with this escaped convict. No wonder Uncle Mo's complete unconsciousness seemed to present an impassable barrier to a revelation. Aunt M'riar had not the advantages of the Roman confessional, with its suggestive *guichet*. Had some penitent, deprived of that resource, been driven back on the analogous arrangement of a railway booking-office, the difficulty of introducing the subject could scarcely have been greater.

However, Aunt M'riar was not going to be left absolutely without assistance. That evening—the evening, that is, of the day when Dave told the tale of the Man in the Park—Uncle Moses showed an unusual restlessness, following on a period of thoughtfulness and silence. After supper he said suddenly:—" I'm a-going to take a turn out, M'riar. Any objection?"

"None o' my making, Mo. Only Mr. Jerry, he'll be round. What's to be told him?"

"Ah—I'll tell you. Just you say to Jerry—just you tell him . . ."

"What'll I tell him?" For Uncle Mo appeared to waver.

"Just you tell him to drop in at The Sun, and bide till I come. They've a sing-song going on to-night, with the pianner. He'll make hisself happy for an hour. I'll be round in an hour's time, tell him."

"And where are you off for all of an hour, Mo?"

"That's part of the p'int, M'riar. Don't you be too inquis-eye-tive. . . . No—I don't mind tellin' of ye, if it's partic'lar. I'm going to drop round to the Station to shake hands with young Simmun Rowe—they've made him Inspector there—he's my old pal Jerky Rowe's son I knew from a boy. Man under forty, as I judge. But he won't let me swaller up *his* time, trust him! Tell Jerry I'll jine him at half-after nine, the very latest."

"I'll acquaint him what you say, Mo. And you bear in mind what Mr. Jeffcoat at The Sun had to say about yourself, Mo."

"What was it, M'riar? Don't you bottle it up."

"Why, Mr. Jeffcoat he said, after passing the time of day, round in Clove Street, 'I look to Mr. Wardle to keep up the character of The Sun,' he said. So you bear in mind, Mo."

Whereupon Uncle Mo departed, and Aunt M'riar was left to her own reflections, the children being abed and asleep by now; Dolly certainly, probably Dave.

Presently the door to the street was pushed open, and Mr. Jerry appeared. "I don't see no Moses?" said he.

Aunt M'riar gave her message, over her shoulder. To justify this she should have been engaged on some particular task of the needle, easiest performed when seated. Mr. Alibone, to whom her voice sounded unusual, looked round to see. He only saw that her hands were in her lap, and no sign was visible of their employment. This was unlike his experience of Aunt M'riar. "Find the weather trying, Mrs. Wardle?"

"It don't do me any harm."

"Ah—some feels the heat more than others."

Aunt M'riar roused herself to reply:—"If you're meaning me, Mr. Alibone, it don't touch me so much as many. Only my bones are not so young as they were—that's how it came I was sitting down. Now, supposin' you'd happened in five minutes later, you might have found me tidin' up. I've plenty to do yet awhile." But this was not convincing, although the speaker wished to make it so; probably it would have been better had less effort gone to the utterance of it. For Aunt M'riar's was too obvious.

Mr. Jerry laughed cheerfully, for consolation. "Come now, Aunt M'riar," said he, "*you* ain't the one to talk as if you was forty, and be making mention of your bones. Just you let them alone for another fifteen year. That'll be time." Mr. Jerry had been like one of the family, so pleasantry of this sort was warranted.

It was not unwelcome to Aunt M'riar. "I'm forty-six, Mr. Jerry," she said. "And forty-six is six-and-forty."

"And fifty-six is six-and-fifty, which is what I am, this very next Michaelmas. Now I call that a coincidence, Mrs. Wardle."

Aunt M'riar reflected. "I should have said it was an accident, Mr. Jerry. Like anythin' else, as the sayin' is. You mention to Mo, not to be late, no more than need be. Not to throw away good bedtime!" Mr. Jerry promised to impress the advantages of early hours, and went his way. But his reflections on his short interview with Aunt M'riar took the form of asking himself what had got her, and finding no answer to the question. Something evidently had, from her manner, for there was nothing in what she said.

He asked the same question of Uncle Mo, coming away from The Sun, where they did not wait for the very last tune on the piano, to the disgust of Mr. Jeffcoat, the proprietor. "What's got Aunt M'riar?" said Uncle Mo, repeating his words. "Nothin's got Aunt M'riar. She'd up and tell me fast enough if there was anything wrong. What's put you on that lay, Jerry?"

"I couldn't name any one thing, Mo. But going by the looks of it, I should judge there was a screw loose in somebody's wheel-barrow. P'r'aps I'm mistook. P'r'aps I ain't. S'posing you was to ask her, Mo!—asking don't cost much."

Uncle Moses seemed to weigh the outlay. "No," he said. "Asking wouldn't send me to the work'us." And when he had taken leave of his friend at their sundering-point, he spent the rest of his short walk home in speculation as to what had set Jerry off about Aunt M'riar. It was with no misgiving of hearing of anything seriously amiss that he said to her, as he sat in the little parlour recovering his breath, after walking rather fast, while she cultured the flame of a candle whose wick had been cut off short:—"Everything all right, M'riar?" He was under the impression that he asked in a nonchalant, easy-going manner, and he was quite mistaken. It was only perfectly palpable that he meant it to be so, and he who parades his indifference is apt to overreach himself.

Aunt M'riar had been making up her mind that she must tell Mo what she knew about this man Daverill, at whatever cost to herself. It would have been much easier had she known much less. Face to face with an opportunity of telling it, her resolution wavered and her mind, imperfectly made up, favoured post-ponement. To-morrow would do. "Ho yes," said she. "Everything's all right, Mo. Now you just get to bed. Time enough, I say, just on to midnight!" But her manner was defective and her line of argument ill-chosen. Its result was to produce in her hearer a determination to discover what had got her. Because it was evident that Jerry was right, and that *something* had. "One of the kids a-sickenin' for measles! Out with it, M'riar! Which is it—Dave?"

"No, it ain't any such a thing. Nor yet Dolly. . . . Anyone ever see such a candle?"

"Then it's scarlatinar, or mumps. One or other on 'em!"

"Neither one nor t'other, Mo. 'Tain't neither Dave nor Dolly, this time." But something or other was somebody or something, that was clear! Aunt M'riar may have meant this, and yet not seen how very clear she made it. She recurred to that candle, and a suggestion of Uncle Mo's. "It's easy sayin', 'Run the toller off,' Mo; but who's to do it with such a little flame?"

Presently the candle, carefully fostered, picked up heart, and the tension of doubt about its future was relieved. "She'll do now," said Uncle Mo, assigning it a gender it had no claim to. "But what's gone wrong, M'riar?"

The appeal for information was too simple and direct to allow of keeping it back; without, at least, increasing its implied importance. Aunt M'riar only intensified this when she answered:— "Nothing at all! At least, nothing to nobody but me. Tell you to-morrow, Mo! It's time we was all abed. Mind you don't wake up Dave!" For Dave was becoming his uncle's bedfellow, and Dolly her aunt's; exchanges to vary monotony growing less frequent as the children grew older.

But Uncle Mo did not rise to depart. He received the candle, adolescent at last, and sat holding it and thinking. He had become quite alive now to what had impressed Mr. Jerry in Aunt M'riar's appearance and manner, and was harking back over recent events to find something that would account for it. The candle's secondary education gave him an excuse. Its maturity would have left him no choice but to go to bed.

A light that flashed through his mind anticipated it. "It's never that beggar," said he, and then, seeing that his description was insufficient:—"Which one? Why, the one we was a-talking of only this morning. Him I've been rounding off with Inspector Rowe—our boy's man he saw in the Park. You've not been alarmin' yourself about *him?*" For Uncle Mo thought he could see his way to alarm for a woman, even a plucky one, in the mere proximity of such a ruffian. He would have gone on to say that the convict was, by now, probably again in the hands of the police, but he saw as the candle flared that Aunt M'riar's usually fresh complexion had gone grey-white, and that she was nodding in confirmation of something half-spoken that she could not articulate.

He was on his feet at his quickest, but stopped at the sound of her voice, reviving. "What—what's that, M'riar?" he cried. "Say it again, old girl!" So strange and incredible had the words seemed that he thought he heard, that he could not believe in his own voice as he repeated them:—"*Your* husband!" He was not clear about it even then; for, after a pause long enough for the candle to burn up, and show him, as he fell back in his seat, Aunt M'riar, tremulous but relieved at having spoken, he repeated them again:—"Your *husband!* Are ye sure you're saying what you mean, M'riar?"

That it was a relief to have said it was clear in her reply:— "Ay, Mo, that's all right—right as I said it. My husband. You've known I had a husband, Mo." His astonishment left him speechless, but he just managed to say:—"I thought him dead;" and a few moments passed. Then she added, as though deprecatingly:—"You'll not be angry with me, Mo, when I tell you the whole story?"

Then he found his voice. "Angry!—why, God bless the wench! —what call have I to be angry?—let alone it's no concern of mine to be meddlin' in. Angry! No, no, M'riar, if it's so as you say, and you haven't gone dotty on the brain!"

"I'm not dotty, Mo. You'll find it all right, just like I tell you. . . ."

"Well, then, I'm mortal sorry for you, and there you have it, in a word. Poor old M'riar!" His voice went up to say:—"But you shan't come to no harm through that character, if that's what's in it. I'll promise ye that." It fell again. "No—I won't wake the children. . . . I ain't quite on the shelf yet, nor yet in the dustbin. There's my hand on it, M'riar."

"I know you're good, Mo." She caught at the hand he held out to give her, and kept it. "I know you're good, and you'll do like you say. Only I hope he won't come this way no more. I hope he don't know I'm here." She seemed to shudder at the thought of him.

"Don't he know you're here? That's rum, too. But it's rum, all round. Things *are* rum, sometimes. Now, just you take it easy, M'riar, and if there's anything you'll be for telling me— because I'm an old friend like, d'ye see?—why, just you tell me as much as comes easy, and no more. Or just tell me nothing at all, if it sootes you better, and I'll set here and give an ear to it." Uncle Mo resumed his former seat, and Aunt M'riar put back the hand he released in her apron, its usual place when not on active service.

"There's nothing in it I wouldn't tell, Mo—not to you—and it won't use much of the candle to tell it. I'd be the easier for you to know, only I'm not so quick as some at the telling of things." She seemed puzzled how to begin.

Uncle Moses helped. "How long is it since you set eyes on him?"

" Twenty-five years—all of twenty-five years."
Uncle Mo was greatly relieved at hearing this. " Well, but,
M'riar—twenty-five years! You're shet of the beggar—clean shet
of him! You are *that,* old girl, legally and factually. But then,"
said he, " when was you married to him? "
" I've got my lines to show for that, Mo. July six, eighteen
twenty-nine."
Uncle Mo repeated the date slowly after her, and then seemed
to plunge into a perplexing calculation, very distorting to the
natural repose of his face. Touching his finger-tips appeared to
make his task easier. After some effort, which ended without
clear results, he said:—" What I'm trying to make out is, how
long was you and him keeping house? Because it don't figure up.
How long should you say? "
" We were together six weeks—no more."
" And you—you never seen him since? "
" Never since. Twenty-five years agone, this last July! " **At**
which Uncle Mo was so confounded that words failed him. His
only resource was a long whistle. Aunt M'riar, on the contrary,
seemed to acquire narrative powers from hearing her own voice,
and continued:—" I hadn't known him a twelvemonth, and I
should have been wiser than to listen to him—at my age, over one-
and-twenty! "
" But you made him marry you, M'riar? "
" I did that, Mo. And I have the lines and my ring, to show
it. But I never told a soul, not even mother. I wouldn't have
told her, to be stopped—so bad I was! . . . What!—Dolly—
Dolly's mother? Why, she was just a young child, Dave's age! . . .
How did I come to know him? It was one day in the bar—he
came in with Tom Spring, and ordered him a quart of old Ken-
nett. He was dressed like a gentleman, and free with his
money. . . ."
" I knew old Tom Spring—he's only dead this two years past.
I s'pose that was The Tun, near by Piccadilly, I've heard you
speak on."
". . . That was where I see him, Mo, worse luck for the day!
The One Tun Inn. They called him the gentleman from Australia. He was for me and him to go to Brighton by the coach,
and find the Parson there. But I stopped him at that, and we
was married in London, quite regular, and we went to Brighton,
and then he took me to Doncaster, to be at the races. There's
where he left me, at the Crown Inn we went to, saying he'd be
back afore the week was out. But he never came—only letters

came with money—I'll say that for him. Only no address of
where he was, nor scarcely a word to say how much he was sending. But I kep' my faith towards him; and the promise I made,
I kep' all along. And I've never borne his name nor said one
word to a living soul beyond one or two of my own folk, who were
bound to be quiet, for their sake and mine. Dolly's mother, she
came to know in time. But the Court's called me Aunt M'riar all
along."

A perplexity flitted through Uncle Mo's reasoning powers, and
vanished unsolved. Why had he accepted "Aunt M'riar" as a
sufficient style and title, almost to the extent of forgetting the
married name he had heard assigned to its owner five years since?
He would probably have forgotten it outright, if the post had not,
now and then—but very rarely—brought letters directed to "Mrs.
Catchpole," which he had passed on, if he saw them first, with
the comment:—"I expect that's meant for you, Aunt M'riar";
treating the disposition of some person unknown to use that name
as a pardonable idiosyncrasy. When catechized about her, he had
been known to answer:—"She ain't a widder, not to my thinking,
but her husband he's as dead as a door-nail. Name of Scratchley;
or Simmons—some such a name!" As for the designation of
"Mrs. Wardle" used as a ceremonial title, it was probably a
vague attempt to bring the household into tone. Whoever knows
the class she moved in will have no trouble in recalling some case
of a similar uncertainty.

This is by way of apology for Uncle Mo's so easily letting that
perplexity go, and catching at another point. "What did he make
you promise him, M'riar? Not to let on, I'll pound it! He
wanted you to keep it snug—wasn't that the way of it?"

"Ah, that was it, Mo. To keep it all private, and never say
a word." Then Aunt M'riar's answer became bewildering, inexplicable. "Else his family would have known, and then I should
have seen his mother. Seein' I never did, it's no wonder I didn't
know her again. I might have, for all it's so many years." It
was more the manner of saying this than the actual words, that
showed that she was referring to a recent meeting with her husband's mother.

Uncle Mo sat a moment literally open-mouthed with astonishment. At length he said:—"Why, when and where, woman alive,
did you see his mother?"

"There now, Mo, see what I said—what a bad one I am at
telling of things! Of course, Mrs. Prichard upstairs, she's Ralph
Daverill's mother, and he's the man who got out of prison in

the *Mornin' Star* and killed the gaoler. And he's the same man came down the Court that Sunday and Dave see in the Park. That's Ralph Thornton Daverill, and he's my husband! "

Uncle Mo gave up the idea of answering. The oppression of his bewilderment was too great. It seemed to come in gusts, checked off at intervals by suppressed exclamations and knee-slaps. It was a knockdown blow, with no one to call time. But then, there were no rules, so when a new inquiry presented itself, abrupt utterance followed:—" Wasn't there any? . . . wasn't there any? . . ." followed by a pause and a difficulty of word-choice. Then in a lowered voice, an adjustment of its terms, due to delicacy:—" Wasn't there any consequences—such as one might expect, ye know? "

Aunt M'riar did not seem conscious of any need for delicacies. " My baby was born dead," she said. " That's what you meant, Mo, I take it? " Then only getting in reply:—" That was it, M'riar," she went on:—" None knew about it but mother, when it was all over and done with, later by a year and more. I would have called the child Polly, being a girl, if it had lived to be christened. . . . Why would I?—because that was the name he knew me by at The Tun."

Uncle Mo began to say:—" If the Devil lets him off easy, I'll . . ." and stopped short. It may have been because he reflected on the limitations of poor Humanity, and the futility of bluster in this connection, or because he had a question to ask. It related to Aunt M'riar's unaccountable ignorance throughout of Daverill's transportation to Norfolk Island, and the particular felony that led to it. " If you was not by way of seeing the police-reports, where was all your friends, to say never a word? "

" No one said nothing to me," said Aunt M'riar. She seemed hazy as to the reason at first; then a light broke:—" They never knew his name, ye see, Mo." He replied on reflection:—" Course they didn't—right you are! " and then she added:—" I only told mother that; and she's no reader."

A mystery hung over one part of the story—how did she account for herself to her family? Was she known to have been married, or had popular interpretation of her absence inclined towards charitable silence about its causes—asked no questions, in fact, giving up barmaids as past praying for? She seemed to think it sufficient light on the subject to say:—" It was some length of time before I went back home, Mo," and he had to press for particulars.

His conclusion, put briefly, was that this deserted wife, reappearing at home with a wedding-ring after two years' absence, had decided that she would fulfil her promise of silence best by giving a false married name. She had engineered her mother's inspection of her marriage-lines, so as to leave that good woman—a poor scholar—under the impression that Daverill's name was Thornton; not a very difficult task. The name she had chosen was Catchpole; and it still survived as an identifying force, if called on. But it was seldom in evidence, " Aunt M'riar " quashing its unwelcome individuality. The general feeling had been that " Mrs. Catchpole " might be anybody, and did not recommend herself to the understanding. There was some sort o' sense in " Aunt M'riar."

The eliciting of these points, hazily, was all Uncle Mo was equal to after so long a colloquy, and Aunt M'riar was not in a condition to tell more. She relit another half-candle that she had blown out for economy when the talk set in, and called Uncle Mo's attention to the moribund condition of his own:— " There's not another end in the house, Mo," said she. So Uncle Mo had to use that one, or get to bed in the dark.

He had been already moved to heartfelt anger that day against this very Daverill, having heard from his friend the Police-Inspector the story of his arrest at The Pigeons, at Hammersmith; and, of course, of the atrocious crime which had been his latest success with the opposite sex. This Police-Inspector must have been Simeon Rowe, whom you may remember as stroke-oar of the boat that was capsized there in the winter, when Sergeant Ibbetson of the river-police met his death in the attempt to capture Daverill. Uncle Mo's motive in visiting the police-station had not been only to shake hands with the son of an old acquaintance. He had carried what information he had of the escaped convict to those who were responsible for his recapture.

If you turn back to the brief account the story gave of Maisie Daverill's—or Prichard's—return to England, and her son's marriage, and succeed in detecting in Polly the barmaid at the One Tun any trace of the Aunt M'riar with whom you were already slightly acquainted, it will be to the discredit of the narrator. For never did a greater change pass over human identity than the one which converted the *beauté de diable* of the young wench just of age, who was serving out stimulants to the Ring, and the Turf, and the men-about-town of the late twenties, to that of the careworn, washtub-worn, and needle-worn manipulator of fine linen and broidery, who had been in charge of Dolly and Dave

Wardle since their mother's death three years before. Never was there a more striking testimony to the power of Man to make a desolation of the life of Woman, nor a shrewder protest against his right to do so. For Polly the Barmaid, look you, had done nothing that is condemned by the orthodox moralities; she had not even flown in the face of her legal duty to her parents. Was she not twenty-one, and does not that magic numeral pay all scores?

The Australian gentleman had one card in his pack that was Ace of Trumps in the game of Betrayal. He only played it when nothing lower would take the trick. And Polly got little enough advantage from the sanction of the Altar, her marriage-lines and her wedding-ring, in so far as she held to the condition precedent of those warrants of respectability, that she should observe silence about their existence. The only duplicity of which she had been guilty was the assumption of a false married name, and that had really seemed to her the only possible compromise between a definite breach of faith and passive acceptance of undeserved ill-fame. And when the hideous explanation of Daverill's long disappearance came about, and *éclaircissement* seemed inevitable, she saw the strange discovery she had made of his relation to Mrs. Prichard, as an aggravation to the embarrassment of acknowledging his past relation to herself.

There was one feeling only that one might imagine she might have felt, yet was entirely a stranger to. Might she not have experienced a longing—a curiosity, at any rate—to set eyes again on the husband who had deserted her all those long years ago? And this especially in view of her uncertainty as to how long his absence had been compulsory? As a matter of fact, her only feeling about this terrible resurrection was one of shrinking as from a veritable carrion, disinterred from a grave she had earned her right to forget. Why need this gruesome memory be raked up to plague her?

The only consolation she could take with her to a probably sleepless pillow was the last charge of the old prizefighter to her not to fret. " You be easy, M'riar. He shan't come a-nigh *you*. I'll square *him* fast enough, if he shows up down this Court—you see if I don't! " But when she reached it, there was still balm in Gilead. For was not Dolly there, so many fathoms deep in sleep that she might be kissed with impunity, long enough to bring a relieving force of tears to help the nightmare-haunted woman in her battle with the past?

As for Mo, his threat towards this convicted miscreant had no connection with his recent interview with his police-officer friend

—no hint of appeal to Law and Order. The anger that burnt in his heart and sent the blood to his head was as unsullied, as pure, as any that ever Primeval Man sharpened flints to satisfy before Law and Order were invented.

CHAPTER XXVII

HOW UNCLE MO MADE THE DOOR-CHAIN SECURE, AND A SUNFLOWER LOOKED ON THE WHILE. HOW AUNT M'RIAR STOPPED HER EARS. A BIT OF UNCLE MO'S MIND. HOW DOLLY KISSED HIM THROUGH THE DOOR-CRACK, BUT NOT MRS. BURR. CONCERNING RATS, TO WHICH UNCLE MO TOOK THE OPPOSITE VIEW. OF ONE, OR SOME, WHICH TRAVELLED OUT TO AUSTRALIA WITH OLD MRS. PRICHARD. HOW DAVE MET THREE LADIES IN A CARRIAGE, NONE OF WHOM KISSED HIM. HOW UNCLE MO WENT UPSTAIRS WITH THE CHILDREN, IN CONNECTION WITH THE RATS HE HAD DISCREDITED, AND STAYED UP QUITE A TIME. HOW HE INTERVIEWED MR. BARTLETT ABOUT THEM

"You're never fidgeting about *him?*" said Aunt M'riar to Uncle Mo, one morning shortly after she had told him the story of her marriage. "He's safe out of the way by now. You may rely on your police-inspectin' friend to inspect *him*. Didn't he as good as say he was took, Mo?"

"That warn't precisely the exact expression used, M'riar," said Uncle Mo, who was doing something with a tool-box at the door that opened on the front-garden that opened on the Court. Dolly was holding his tools, by permission—only not chisels or gouges, or gimlets, or bradawls, or anything with an edge to it—and the sunflower outside was watching them. Uncle Mo was extracting a screw with difficulty, in spite of the fact that it was all but out already. He now elucidated the cause of this difficulty, and left the Police Inspector alone. " 'Tain't stuck, if you ask me. I should say there never had been no holt to this screw from the beginning. But by reason there's no life in the thread, it goes round and round rayther than come out. . . . Got it!—wanted a little coaxin', it did." That is to say, a few back-turns with very light pressure brought the screw-head free enough for a finger-grip, and the rest was easy. "It warn't of any real service," said Uncle Mo. "One size bigger would ketch and hold in. This here one's only so much horse-tentation. Now I can't get a bigger one

through the plate, and I can't rimer out the hole for want of a
tool—not so much as a small round file. . . . Here's a long 'un,
of a thread with the first. He'll ketch in if there's wood-backin'
enough. . . . That's got him! Now it'll take a Hemperor, to get
that out." Uncle Mo paused to enjoy a moment's triumph, then
harked back:—" No—the precise expression made use of was, they
might put their finger on him any minute."

" Which don't mean the same thing," said Aunt M'riar.

" No more it don't, M'riar, now you mention it. But he won't
trust his nose down this Court. If he does, and I ain't here, just
you do like I tell you. . . ."

Aunt M'riar interrupted. " I couldn't find it in me to give him
up, Mo. Not for all I'm worth!" She spoke in a quick undertone, with a stress in her voice that terrified Dolly, who nearly
let go a hammer she had been allowed to hold, as harmless.

" Not if you knew what he's wanted for, this·time? "

" Don't you tell me, Mo. I'd soonest know nothing. . . No—
no—don't you tell me a word about it! " And Aunt M'riar clapped
her hands on her ears, leaving an iron, that she had been trying
to abate to a professional heat, to make a brown island on its
flannel zone of influence. All her colour—she had a fair share
of it—had gone from her cheeks, and Dolly was in two minds
whether she should drop the hammer and weep.

Uncle Mo's reassuring voice decided her to do neither, this time.
" Don't you be frightened, M'riar," said he. " I wasn't for telling
you his last game. Nor it wouldn't be any satisfaction to tell.
I was only going to say that if he was to turn up in these parts,
just you put the chain down—it's all square and sound now—and
tell him he'll find me at The Sun." He closed the door and put
the chain he had been revising on its mettle; adding as he did so,
in defiance of Astronomy:—" 'Tain't any so far off, The Sun."
Dolly's amusement at the function of the chain, and its efficacy,
was so great as to cause her aunt to rule, as a point of Law, that
six times was plenty for any little girl, and that she must leave
her uncle a minute's peace.

Dolly granting this, Aunt M'riar took advantage of it, to ask
what course Uncle Mo would pursue, if she complied with his
instructions. " If you gave him up to the Police, Mo," she
said, " and I'd sent him to you, it would be all one as if I'd
done it."

" I'll promise not to give him to the Police, if he comes to me
off of your sending, M'riar. In course, if he's only himself to·
thank for coming my way, that's another pair of shoes."

" But if it was me, what'll you do, Mo? " Aunt M'riar wasn't getting on with those cuffs.

" What'll I do? Maybe I'll give him . . . a bit of my mind."

" No—what'll you do, Mo? " There was a new apprehension in her voice as she dropped it to say:—" He's a younger man than you, by nigh twenty years."

The anticipation of that bit of Uncle Mo's mind had gripped his jaw and knitted his brow for an instant. It vanished, and left both free as he answered:—" You be easy, old girl! I won't give him a chance to do *me* no harm." Aunt M'riar bent a suspicious gaze on him for a moment, but it ended as an even more than usually genial smile spread over the old prizefighter's face, and he gave way to Dolly's request to be sut out only dest this once more; which ended in a Pyramus and Thisbe accommodation of kisses through as much thoroughfare as the chain permitted. They were painful and dangerous exploits; but it was not on either of those accounts that Mrs. Burr, coming home rather early, declined to avail herself of Dolly's suggestion that she also should take advantage of this rare opportunity for uncomfortable endearments; but rather in deference to public custom, whose rules about kissing Dolly thought ridiculous.

The door having to be really shut to release the chain, its reopening seemed to inaugurate a new chapter, at liberty to ignore Dolly's flagrant suggestions at the end of the previous one. Besides, it was possible for Uncle Mo to affect ignorance; as, after all, Dolly was outside. Mrs. Burr did not tax him with insincerity, and the subject dropped, superseded by less interesting matter.

" I looked in to see," said Aunt M'riar, replying to a question of Mrs. Burr's. " The old lady was awake and knitting, last time. First time she'd the paper on her knee, open. Next time she was gone off sound."

" That's her way, ma'am. Off and on—on and off. But she takes mostly to the knitting. And it ain't anything to wonder at, I say, that she drops off reading. I'm sure I can't hold my eyes open five minutes over the newspaper. And books would be worse, when you come to read what's wrote in them, if it wasn't for having to turn over the leaves. Because you're bound to see where, and not turn two at once, or it don't follow on." Aunt M'riar and Uncle Mo confirmed this view from their own experience. It was agreed further that small type—Parliamentary debates and the like—was more soporific than large, besides spinning out the length and deferring the relaxation of turning over, when in book-form. Short accidents, and not too prolix criminal

proceedings were on the whole the most palatable forms of literature. It was not to be wondered at that old Mrs. Prichard should
go to sleep over the newspaper at her age, seeing that none but
the profoundest scholars could keep awake for five minutes while
perusing it. The minute Dave came in from school he should take
Dolly upstairs to pay the old lady a visit, and brighten her up
a bit.

"Very like she's been extra to-day"—thus Mrs. Burr continue:
—"by reason of rats last night, and getting no sleep."

"There ain't any rats in your room, missis," said Uncle Mo.
"We should hear 'em down below if there was."

"What it is if it ain't rats passes me then, Mr. Wardle. I do
assure you there was a loud crash like a gun going off, and we
neither of us hardly got any sleep after."

"Queer, anyhow!" said Uncle Mo. But he evidently doubted
the statement, or at least thought it exaggerated.

"I'll be glad to tell her you take the opposite view to rats,
Mr. Moses," said Mrs. Burr. "For it sets her on fretting when
she gets thinking back. And now she'll never be tired of telling
about the rats on the ship when she was took out to Australia.
Running over her face, and starting her awake in the night! It
gives the creeps only to hear."

"There, Dolly, now you listen to how the rats run about on
Mrs. Picture when she was on board of the ship." Thus Aunt
M'riar, always with that haunting vice of perverting Art, Literature, Morals, and Philosophy to the oppressive improvement of
the young. She seldom scored a success, and this time she was
hoisted with her own petard. For Dolly jumped with delight at
the prospect of a romance of fascinating character, combining
Zoölogy and Travel. She applied for a place to hear it, on the
knee of Mrs. Burr, who, however, would have had to sit down
to supply it. So she was forced to be content with a bald version
of the tale, as Mrs. Burr had to see to getting their suppers
upstairs. She was rather disappointed at the size and number
of the rats. She enquired:—"Was they large rats, or small?"
and would have preferred to hear that they were about the size
of small cats—not larger, for fear of inconveniencing old Mrs.
Picture. And a circumstance throwing doubt on their number
was unwelcome to her. For it appeared that old Mrs. Picture
slept with her fellow-passengers in a dark cabin, and no one
might light a match all night for fear of the Captain. And rats
ran over those passengers' faces! But it may have been all the
same rat, and to Dolly that seemed much less satisfactory than

troops. She was rather cast down about it, but there was no need to discourage Dave. She could invent some extra rats, when he came back from school.

Lay down the book, you who read, and give but a moment's thought to the strangeness of these two episodes, over half a century apart. One, in the black darkness of an emigrant's sleeping-quarters on a ship outward-bound, all its tenants huddled close in the stifling air; child and woman, weak and strong, sick and healthy even, penned in alike to sleep their best on ranks of shelves, a mere packed storage of human goods, to be delivered after long months of battle with the seas, ten thousand miles from home. Or, if you shrink from the thought that Maisie's luck on her first voyage was so cruel as that, conceive her interview with those rodent fellow-passengers as having taken place in the best quarters money could buy on such a ship—and what would *they* be, against a good steerage-berth nowadays?—and give her, at least, a couch to herself. Picture her, if you will, at liberty to start from it in terror and scramble up a companion ladder to an open deck, and pick her way through shrouds and a bare headway of restless sprits above, and Heaven knows what of coiled cordage and inexplicable bulkhead underfoot, to some haven where a merciful old mariner, alone upon his watch, shuts his eyes to his duty and tolerates the beautiful girl on deck, when he is told by her that she cannot sleep for the rats. Make the weather fair, to keep the picture at its best, and let her pass the hours till the coming of the dawn, watching the mainmast-truck sway to and fro against the Southern Cross, as the breeze falls and rises, and the bulwark-plash is soft or loud upon the waters.

And then—all has vanished! That was half a century ago, and more. And a very little girl with very blue eyes and a disgracefully rough shock of golden curls has just been told of those rats, and has resolved to add to their number—having power to do so, like a Committee—when she comes to retell the tale to her elder brother; and then they will both—and this is the strangest of all!—they will both go and make a noisy and excited application to an authority to have it confirmed or contradicted. And this authority will be that girl who sat on that deck beneath the stars, and listened to the bells sounding the hours through the night, to keep the ship's time for a forgotten crew, on a ship that may have gone to the bottom many a year ago, on its return voyage home perhaps—who knows?

Before Dave heard Dolly's version of the rats, he had a tale of his own to tell, coming in just after Mrs. Burr had departed. As he was excited by the event he was yearning to narrate, he did not put it so lucidly as he might have done. He said:—" Oy saw the lady, and another lady, and another lady, all in one carriage. And they see me. And the lady "—he still pronounced this word *loydy*—" she see me on the poyvement, and 'Stop' she says. And then she says, 'You're Doyvy, oyn't you, that had the ax-nent?' I says these was my books I took to scrool. . . ."

" Didn't you *say* you was Davy? " said Uncle Mo. And Aunt M'riar she actually said:—" Well, I never!—not to tell the lady who you was! "

Dave was perplexed, looking with blue-eyed gravity from one to the other. " The loydy said I *was* Doyvy," said he, in a slightly injured tone. He did not at all like the suggestion that he had been guilty of discourtesy.

" In course the lady knew, and knew correct," said Uncle Mo, drawing a distinction which is too often overlooked. " Cut along and tell us some more. What more did the lady say? "

Dave concentrated his intelligence powerfully on accuracy:— " The loydy said to the yuther loydy—the be-yhooterful loydy . . ."

" Oh, there was a beautiful lady, was there? "

Dave nodded excessively, and continued:—" Said here's a friend of mine, Doyvy Wardle, and they was coming to poy a visit to, to-morrow afternoon."

" And what did the other lady say? "

Dave gathered himself together for an effort of intense fidelity:— " She said—she said—' He's much too dirty to kiss in the open street '—she said, ' and better not to touch.' Yorce! " He seemed magnanimous towards Gwen, in spite of her finical delicacy.

Aunt M'riar turned his face to the light, by the chin. " What's the child been at? " said she.

" The boys had some corks," was Dave's explanation. Nothing further seemed to be required; Uncle Mo merely remarking: " It'll come off with soap." However, there was some doubt about the identity of these carriage ladies. Was one of them the original lady of the rings; who had taken Dave for a drive or *vice versa*. " Not her! " said Dave; and went on shaking his head so long to give his statement weight, that Aunt M'riar abruptly requested him to stop, as her nervous system could not bear the strain. It was enough, she said, to make her eyes come out by the roots.

" She must have been somebody else. She couldn't have been nobody," said Uncle Mo cogently. " Spit it out, old chap, Who was she? "

It was easy to say who she was; the strain of attestation had turned on who she wasn't. Dave became fluent:—" Whoy, the loydy what was a cistern, and took me in the roylwoy troyne and in the horse-coach to Granny Marrowbone." For he had never quite dissociated Sister Nora from ball-taps and plumbings. He added after reflection:—" Only not dressed up like then ! "

At this point Dolly, whose preoccupation about those rats had stood between her and a reasonable interest in Dave's adventure, struck in noisily and rudely with disjointed particulars about them, showing a poor capacity for narrative, and provoking Uncle Mo to tickling her with a view to their suppression. Aunt M'riar seized the opportunity to capture Dave and subject him to soap and water at the sink.

As soon as the boys' corks, or the effect of using them after ignition as face-pigments, had become a thing of the past, Dave and Dolly were ready to pay their promised visit to Mrs. Prichard. Uncle Mo suggested that he might act as their convoy as far as the top-landing. This was a departure from precedent, as stair-climbing was never very welcome to Uncle Mo. But Aunt M'riar consented, the more readily that she was all behind with her work. Uncle Mo not only went up with the children, but stayed up quite a time with the old lady and Mrs. Burr. When he came down he did not refer to his conversation with them, but went back to Dave's encounter with his aristocratic friends in the street.

" The lady that sighted our boy out," said he, " she'll be Miss What's-her-name that come on at the Hospital—her with the clean white tucker. . . ." This referred to a vaguely recollected item of the costume in which Sister Nora was dressed up at the time of Dave's accident. It had lapsed, as inappropriate, during her nursing of her father in Scotland, and had not been resumed.

" That's her," said Aunt M'riar. " Sister of Charity—that's what *she* is. The others are ladyships, one or both. They all belong." The tone of remoteness might have been adopted in speaking of inhabitants of Mars and Venus.

" I thought her the right sort, herself," said Uncle Mo, implying that others of her *monde* might be safely assumed to be the wrong sort, pending proof of the contrary. " Anyways, she's coming to pay Dave a visit, and I'll be glad of a sight of her, for one ! "

" Oh, I've no fault to find, Mo, if that's what you mean." Aunt M'riar was absorbed in her mystery, doing justice to what was probably a lady's nightgear, of imperial splendour. So she probably had spoken rather at random; and, indeed, seemed to think apology necessary. She took advantage of the end of an episode to say, while contemplating the perfection of two unimpeachable cuffs:—" So long as the others don't give theirselves no airs." Isolated certainly, as to structure; but, after all, has speech any use except to communicate ideas?

Uncle Mo presumably understood, as he accepted the form of speech, saying:—" And so long as we do ourselves credit, M'riar."

" Well, Mo, you never see me do anything but behave."

" That I never did, M'riar. Right you are! " Which ended a little colloquy that contained or implied a protest against the compulsory association of classes, expressed to a certain extent by special leniency towards an exceptional approach from without. Having entered his own share of the protest, Uncle Mo announced his intention of seeking Mr. Bartlett the builder, to speak to him about them rats. This saying Aunt M'riar did not even condemn as enigmatical, so completely did all that relates to buildings lie outside her jurisdiction.

" I've got my 'ands so full just now," said Mr. Bartlett, when Uncle Mo had explained the object of his visit, " or I'd step round to cast an eye on that bressumer. Only you may make your mind easy, and say I told you to it. If we was all of us to get into a perspiration whenever a board creaked or a bit of loose parging come down a chimley, we shouldn't have a minute's peace of our lives. Some parties is convinced of Ghosts the very first crack! Hysterical females in partic'lar." Mr. Bartlett did not seem busy, externally; but he contrived to give an impression that he was attending to a job at Buckingham Palace.

Uncle Mo felt abashed at his implied rebuke. It was not deserved, for he was guiltless of superstition. However, he had accepted the position of delegate of the top-floor, which, of course, was an hysterical floor, owing to the sex of its tenants. For Mr. Bartlett's meaning was the conventional one, that all women were hysterical, not some more than others. Uncle Mo felt that his position was insecure; and that he had better retire from it. Noises, he conceded, was usually nothing at all; but he had thought he would mention them, in this case.

Mr. Bartlett professed himself sincerely obliged to all persons who would mention noises, in spite of their equivocal claims to existence. It might save a lot of trouble in the end, and you never knew. As soon as he had a half an hour to spare he would give attention. Till Tuesday he was pretty well took up. No one need fidget himself about the noises he mentioned; least of all need the landlord be communicated with, as he was not a Practical

Man, but in Independent Circumstances. Moreover, he lived at Brixton.

CHAPTER XXVIII

OF A RAID ON DOLLY'S GARDEN. THAT YOUNG DRUITT'S BEHAVIOUR TO HIS SISTER. MR. RAGSTROAR'S ACCIDENT, AND HIS MOKE. HOW THE TWO LADIES CAME AT LAST. LADY GWENDOLEN RIVERS, AND HOW DOLLY GOT ON HER LAP. HOW DAVE WENT UPSTAIRS TO GET HIS LETTER. HOW MRS. PRICHARD HAD TAKEN MRS. MARROWBONE TO HEART, AND *VICE VERSA*. HOW DOLLY GOT A LOCK OF GWEN'S HAIR, AND *VICE VERSA*. HOW DAVE DELAYED AND DOLLY AND GWEN WENT TO FETCH HIM. A REMARKABLE SOUND. THEN GOD-KNOWS-WHAT, OUTSIDE!

An effort of horticulture was afoot in the front-garden of No. 7, Sapps Court. Dave Wardle and Dolly were engaged in an attempt to remedy a disaster that had befallen the Sunflower. There was but one—the one that had been present when Uncle Mo was adjusting that door-chain.

Its career had been cut short prematurely. For a boy had climbed up over the end wall of those gardens acrost the Court, right opposite to where it growed; and had all but cut through the stem, when he was cotched in the very act by Michael Ragstroar. That young coster's vigorous assertion of the rights of property did a man's heart good to see, nowadays. The man was Uncle Mo, who got out of the house plenty of time to stop Michael half-murdering the marauder, as soon as he considered the latter had had enough, he being powerfully outclassed by the coster-monger boy. Why, he was only one of them young Druitts, when all was said and done! Michael felt no stern joy in him—a foeman not worth licking, on his merits. But the knife that he left behind, with a buckhorn handle, was a fizzing knife, and was prized in after-years by Michael.

The Wardle household had gone into mourning for the Sun-flower. Was it not the same Sunflower as last year, reincarnated? Dolly sat under it, shedding tears. Uncle Mo showed ignorance of gardening, saying it might grow itself on again if you giv' it a chance; not if you kep' on at it like that. Dave disagreed with this view, but respectfully. His Hospital experience had taught him the use of ligatures; and he kept on at it, obtaining from Mrs. Burr a length of her wide toyp to tie it in position.

If limbs healed up under treatment, why not vegetation? The operator was quite satisfied with his handiwork.

In fact, Dave and Dolly both foresaw a long and prosperous life for the flower. They rejected Aunt M'riar's suggestion, that it should be cut clear off and stood in water, as a timid compromise—a stake not worth playing for. And Michael Ragstroar endorsed the flattering tales Hope told, citing instances in support of them derived from his own experience, which appeared to have been exceptional. As, for instance, that over-supplies of fruit at Covent Garden were took back and stuck on the stems again, as often as not. "I seen 'em go myself," said he. " 'Ole cartloads!"

"Hark at that unblushing young story!" said Aunt M'riar, busy in the kitchen, Michael being audible without, lying freely. "He'll go on like that till one day it'll surprise me if the ground don't open and swallow him up."

But Uncle Mo had committed himself to an expression of opinion on the vitality of vegetables. He might condemn exaggeration, but he could scarcely repudiate a principle he had himself almost affirmed. He took refuge in obscurity. " 'Tain't for the likes of us, M'riar," said he, shaking his head profoundly, " to be sayin' how queer starts there mayn't be. My jiminy!—the things they says in lecters, when they gets the steam up!" He shook his head a little quicker, to recover credit for a healthy incredulity, and arranged a newspaper he was reading against difficulties, to gain advantages of position and a better discrimination of its columns.

"If it was the freckly one with the red head," said Aunt M'riar, referring back to the fracas of the morning, "all I can say is, I'm sorry you took Micky off him." From which it appeared that this culprit was not unknown. Indeed, Aunt M'riar was able to add that Widow Druitt his mother couldn't call her soul her own for that boy's goings on.

"He'd got a tidy good punishing afore I got hold of the scruff of my man's trousers," said Uncle Mo, who seemed well contented with the culprit's retribution; and, of course, he knew. "Besides," he added, "he had to get away over them bottles." That is to say, the wall-top, bristling with broken glass. Humanity had paved the way for the enemy's retreat. Uncle Mo added inquiry as to how the freckly one's behaviour to his family had come to the knowledge of Sapps Court.

"You can see acrost from Mrs. Prichard's. He do lead 'em all a life, that boy! Mrs. Burr she saw him pour something down his sister's back when she was playing scales. Ink, she says, by the look. But, of course, it's a way off from here, over to Mrs. Druitt's."

"Oh—she's the one that plays the pyanner. Same tune all through—first up, then down! Good sort of tune to go to sleep to!"

" 'Tain't a tune, Mo. It's *scales*. She's being learned how. One day soon she'll have a tune to play. An easy tune. Mrs. Prichard says *she* could play several tunes before she was that girl's age. Then she hadn't no brother to werrit her. I lay that made a difference." Aunt M'riar went on to mention other atrocities ascribed by Mrs. Burr to the freckly brother. His behaviour to his musical sister had, indeed, been a matter of serious concern to the upstairs tenants, whose window looked directly upon the back of Mrs. Druitt's, who took in lodgers in the main street where Dave had met with his accident.

The boy Michael was suffering from enforced leisure on the day of this occurrence, as his father's cart had met with an accident, and was under repair. Its owner had gone to claim compensation personally from the butcher whose representative had ridden him down; not, he alleged, by misadventure, but from a deep-rooted malignity against all poor but honest men struggling for a livelihood. No butcher, observe, answers this description. Butchers are a class apart, whose motives are extortion, grease, and blood. They wallow in the last with joy, and practise the first with impunity. If they can get a chance to run over you, they'll do it! Trust them for that! Nevertheless, so hopeless would this butcher's case be if his victim went to a lawyer, that it was worth having a try at it afore he done that—so Mr. Rackstraw put it, later. Therefore, he had this afternoon gone to High Street, Clapham, to apply for seven pun' thirteen, and not take a penny less. Hence his son's ability to give attention to local matters, and a temporary respite to his donkey's labours in a paddock at Notting Hill. As for Dave, and for that matter the freckly boy, it was not term-time with them, for some reason. Dave was certainly at home, and was bidden to pay a visit to Mrs. Prichard in the course of the afternoon, if those lady-friends of his whom he met in the street yesterday did not come to pay *him* a visit. It was not very likely they would, but you never could tell. Not to place reliance!

Uncle Mo kept looking at his watch, and saying that if this here lady meant to turn up, she had better look alive. Being reproved for impatience by Aunt M'riar, he said very good, then— he'd stop on to the hour. Only it was no use runnin' through the day like this, and nothing coming of it, as you might say. This was only the way he preferred of expressing impatience for the visit. It is a very common one, and has the advantages of concealing that impatience, putting whomsoever one expects in the position of an importunate seeker of one's society, and suggesting that one is foregoing an appointment in the City to gratify him. Uncle Mo did unwisely to tie himself to the hour, as he became thereby pledged to depart, he having no particular wish to do so, and no object at all in view.

But he was not to be subjected to the indignity of a recantation. As the long hand of his watch approached twelve, and he was beginning to feel on the edge of an embarrassment, Dave left off watering the Sunflower, and ran indoors with the news that there were two ladies coming down the Court, one of whom was Sister Nora, and the other " the other lady." Dave's conscience led him into a long and confused discrimination between this other lady and the other other lady, who had shared with her the back-seat in that carriage yesterday. It was quite unimportant which of the two had come, both being unknown to Dave's family. Moreover, there was no time for the inventory of their respective attributes Dave wished to supply. He was still struggling with a detail, in an undertone lest it should transpire in general society, when he found himself embraced from behind, and kissed with appreciation. He had not yet arrived at the age when one is surprised at finding oneself suddenly kissed over one's shoulder by a lady. Besides, this was his old acquaintance, whom he was delighted to welcome, but who made the tactical mistake of introducing " the other lady " as Lady Gwendolen Rivers. Stiffness might have resulted, if it had not been for the conduct of that young lady, which would have thawed an iceberg. It was not always thus with her; but, when the whim was upon her, she was irresistible.

" I know what Dave was saying to you when we came in, Mr. Wardle," said she, after capturing Dolly to sit on her knee, and coming to an anchor. " He was telling you exactly what his friend had said to him about me. He was Micky. I've heard all about Micky. This chick's going to tell me what Micky said about me. Aren't you, Dolly?" She put Dolly at different distances, ending with a hug and a kiss, of which Dolly reciprocated the latter.

Dolly would have embarked at once on a full report, if left to herself. But that unfortunate disposition of Aunt M'riar's to godmother or countersign the utterances of the young, very nearly nipped her statement in the bud. " There now, Dolly dear," said the excellent woman, "see what the lady says!—you're to tell her just exactly what Micky said, only this very minute in the garden." Which naturally excited Dolly's suspicion, and made her impute motives. She retired within herself—a self which, however, twinkled with a consciousness of hidden knowledge and a resolution not to disclose it.

Gwen's tact saved the position. "Don't you tell *them,* you know—only me! You whisper it in my ear. . . . Yes—quite close up, like that." Dolly entered into this with zest, the possession of a secret in common with this new and refulgent lady obviously conferring distinction.

Sister Nora—not otherwise known to Sapps Court—was resuming history during the past year for the benefit of Uncle Mo. She had seen nothing of Dave, or, indeed, of London, since October; till, yesterday, when she got back from Scotland, whom should she see before she had been five minutes out of the station but Dave himself! Only she hardly knew him, his face was so black. Here Uncle Mo and Aunt M'riar shook penitential heads over his depravity. Sister Nora paid a passing tribute to the Usages of Society, which rightly discourage the use of burnt cork on the countenance, and proceeded. She had heard of him, though, having paid a visit to Widow Thrale in the country, where he got well after the Hospital.

This was a signal for Dave to find his voice, and he embarked with animation on a variegated treatment of subjects connected with his visit to the country. A comparison of his affection for Widow Thrale and Granny Marrable, with an undisguised leaning to the latter; a reference to the lady with the rings, her equipage, and its driver's nose; Farmer Jones's bull, and its untrustworthy temper; the rich qualities of duckweed; the mill-model on the mantelshelf, and individualities of his fellow-convalescents. This took time, although some points were only touched lightly.

Possibly Uncle Moses thought it might prove prolix, as he said:—"If I was a young shaver now, and ladies was to come to see me, I should get a letter I was writing, to show 'em." The delicacy and tact with which this suggestion was offered was a little impaired by Aunt M'riar's:—"Yes, now you be a good boy, Dave, and . . ." and so forth.

Many little boys would not have been so magnanimous as Dave, and would have demurred or offered passive resistance. Dave merely removed Sister Nora's arm rather abruptly from his neck, saying:—"Storp a minute!" and ran up the stairs that opened on the kitchen where they were sitting. There was more room there than in the little parlour.

Uncle Moses explained:—"You see, ladies,· this here young Dave, for all he's getting quite a scholar now, and can write any word he can spell, yet he don't take to doing it quite on his own hook just yet a while. So he gets round the old lady upstairs, for to let him set and write at her table. Then she can tip him a wink now and again, when he gets a bit fogged."

"That's Mrs. Picture," said Gwen, interested. But she did not speak loud enough to invite correction of her pronunciation of the name, and Sister Nora merely said:—"That's her!" and nodded. Dolly at once launched into a vague narrative of a misadventure that had befallen her putative offspring, the doll that Sister Nora had given her last year. Struvvel Peter had met with an accident, his shock head having got in a candle-flame in Mrs. Picture's room upstairs, so that he was quite smooth before he could be rescued. The interest of this superseded other matter.

"Davy he's a great favourite with the ladies," said Uncle Mo, as Struvvel Peter subsided. "He ain't partic'lar to any age. Likes 'em a bit elderly, if anythin', I should say." He added, merely to generalise the conversation, and make talk:—"Now this here old lady in the country she's maybe ten years younger than our Mrs. Prichard, but she's what you might call getting on in years."

"Prichard," said Gwen, for Sister Nora's ear. "I thought it couldn't be Picture."

"Prichard, of course! How funny we didn't think of it—so obvious!"

"Very—when one knows! I think I like Picture best."

Aunt M'riar, not to be out of the conversation, took a formal exception to Uncle Mo's remark:—"The ladies they know how old Old Mrs. Marrable in the country is, without your telling of 'em, Mo."

"Right you are, M'riar! But they don't know nothing about old Mrs. Prichard." Uncle Mo had spoken at a guess of Mrs. Marrowbone's age, of which he knew nothing. It was a sort of emulation that had made him assess *his* old lady as the senior. He felt vulnerable, and changed the conversation. "That young Squire's taking his time, M'riar. Supposin' now I was just to sing out to him?"

But both ladies exclaimed against Dave being hurried away from his old lady. Besides, they wanted to know some more about her—what sort of classification hers would be, and so on. There were stumbling-blocks in this path. Better keep clear of classes— stick to generalities, and hope for lucky chances!

"What made Dave think the old souls so much alike, Mrs. Wardle?" said Sister Nora. "Children are generally so sharp to see differences."

"It was a kind of contradictiousness, ma'am, no better I do think, merely for to set one of 'em alongside the other, and look at." Aunt M'riar did not really mean contradictiousness, and can hardly have meant *contradistinction,* as that word was not in her vocabulary. We incline to look for its origin in the first six letters, which it enjoys in common with contrariwise and con-trast. This, however, is Philology, and doesn't matter. Let Aunt M'riar go on.

"Now just you think how alike old persons do get, by reason of change. 'Tain't any fault of their own. Mrs. Prichard she's often by way of inquiring about Mrs. Marrowbone, and I should say she rather takes her to heart."

"How's that, Mrs. Wardle? Why 'takes her to heart'?" A joint question of the ladies.

"Well—now you ask me—I should say Mrs. Prichard she wants the child all to herself." Aunt M'riar's assumption that this inquiry had been made without suggestion on her own part was unwarranted.

"*I'll* tell you, ladies," said Uncle Mo, rolling with laughter. "The old granny's just as jealous as any schoolgirl! She's *that,* and you may take my word for it." He seemed afraid this might be interpreted to Mrs. Prichard's disadvantage; for he added, recovering gravity:—"Not that I blame her for it, mind you!"

"Do you hear *that,* Gwen?" said Sister Nora. "Mrs. Picture's jealous of Granny Marrowbone. . . . I must tell you about that, Mrs. Wardle. It's really as much as one's place is worth to men-tion Mrs. Prichard to Mrs. Marrable. I assure you the old lady believes I-don't-know-what about her—thinks she's a wicked old witch who will make the child as bad as herself! She does, in-deed! But then, to be sure, Goody Marrable thinks everyone is wicked in London. . . . What's that, Gwen?"

"We want a pair of scissors, Dolly and I do. Do give us a pair of scissors, Aunt Maria. . . . Yes, go on, Clo. I hear every word you say. How very amusing! . . . Thank you, Aunt Maria!" For Gwen and Dolly had just negotiated an exchange of locks of hair, which had distracted the full attention of the former from the conversation. She had, however, heard enough to confirm a half-made resolution not to leave the house without seeing Mrs. Prichard.

" Ass! Vis piece off vat piece," says Dolly, making a selection from the mass of available gold, which Gwen snips off ruthlessly.

" Well! " says Aunt M'riar, with her usual record of inexperience of childhood. " I never, never did, in all my christened days! "

" Quip off a bid, bid piece with the fiddlers," says Dolly, delighted at the proceeding. " A bid piece off me at the vethy top." The ideal in her mind is analogous to the snuffing of a candle. A lock of a browner gold than the one she gives it for is secured— big enough, but not what she had dreamed of.

Uncle Mo was seriously concerned at Dave's prolonged absence. Not that he anticipated any mishap!—it was only a question of courtesy to visitors. Supposing Aunt M'riar was to go up and collar Dave and fetch him down, drastically! Uncle Mo always shirked stair-climbing, partly perhaps because he so nearly filled the stairway. He overweighted the part, æsthetically.

Gwen perceived her opportunity. " Please do nothing of the sort, Aunt Maria," said she. " Look here! Dolly and I are going up to fetch him. Aren't we, Dolly? "

It would have needed presence of mind to invent obstacles to prevent this, and neither Uncle Mo nor Aunt M'riar showed it, each perhaps expecting Action on the other's part. Moreover, Dolly's approval took such a tempestuous form that opposition seemed useless. Besides, there was that fatal assurance about Gwen that belongs to young ladies who have always had their own way in everything. It cannot be developed in its fulness late in life.

Aunt M'riar's protest was feeble in the extreme. " Well, I should be ashamed to let a lady carry me! That I should! " If Aunt M'riar had known the resources of the Latin tongue, she might have introduced the expression *ceteris paribus*. No English can compass that amount of slickness; so her speech was left crude.

Uncle Mo really saw no substantial reason why this beautiful vision should not sweep Dolly upstairs, if it pleased her. He may have felt that a formal protest would be graceful, but he could not think of the right words. And Aunt M'riar had fallen through. Moreover, his memory was confident that he had left his bedroom-door shut. As to miscarriage of the expedition into Mrs. Prichard's territory, he had no misgiving.

Miss Grahame was convinced that the incursion would have better results if she left it to its originator, than if she encumbered it with her own presence. After all, the room could be no larger than the one she sat in, and might be smaller. Anyhow, they could get on very well without her for half an hour. And she wanted a chat with Dave's guardians; she did not really know them intimately.

" The two little ones must be almost like your own children to you, Mr. Wardle," said she, to broach the conversation.

" Never had any, ma'am," said Uncle Mo, literal-minded from constitutional good-faith.

" If you *had* had any was what I meant." Perhaps the reason Miss Grahame's eye wandered after Aunt M'riar, who had followed Gwen and Dolly—to " see that things were straight," she said—was that she felt insecure on a social point. Uncle Mo's eye followed hers.

" Nor yet M'riar," said he, seeing a precaution necessary. " Or perhaps I should say *one.*' Not good for much, though! Born dead, I believe—years before ever my brother married her sister. Never set eyes on M'riar's husband! Name of Catchpole, I believe. . . . That's her coming down." He raised his voice, dropped to say this, as she came within hearing :—" Yes—me and M'riar we share 'em up, the two young characters, but we ain't neither of us their legal parents. Not strickly as the Law goes, but we've fed upon 'em like, in a manner of speaking, from the beginning, or nigh upon it. Little Dave, he's sort of kept me a-going from the early days, afore we buried his poor father— my brother David, you see. He died down this same Court, four year back, afore little Dolly was good for much, to look at. . . . They all right, M'riar? "

" They're making a nice racket," said Aunt M'riar. " So I lay there ain't much wrong with *them.*" She picked up a piece of work to go on with, and explored a box for a button to meet its views. Evidently a garment of Dolly's. Probably this was a slack season for the higher needlework, and the getting up of fine linen was below par.

Uncle Mo resumed :—" So perhaps you're right to put it they are like my own children, and M'riar's." He was so chivalrously anxious not to exclude his co-guardian from her rights that he might have laid himself open to be misunderstood by a stranger. Miss Grahame understood him, however. So she did, thoroughly, when he went on :—" I don't take at all kindly, though, to their growing older. Can't be helped, I suppose. There's a many pecu-

liar starts in this here world, and him as don't like 'em just
has to lump 'em. As I look at it, changes are things one has to
put up with. If we had been handy when we was first made, we
might have got our idears attended to, to oblige. Things are
fixtures, now."

Miss Grahame laughed, and abstained consciously from referring to the inscrutable decrees of Providence which called aloud
for recognition. "Of course, children shouldn't grow," she said.
"I should like them to remain three, especially the backs of their
necks." Uncle Mo's benevolent countenance shone with an unholy cannibalism, as he nodded a mute approval. There was
something very funny to his hearer in this old man's love of children, and his professional engagements of former years, looked
at together.

Aunt M'riar took the subject *au serieux*. "Now you're talking
silly, Mo," she said. "If the children never grew, where would
the girls be? And a nice complainin' you men would make then!"

Miss Grahame made an effort to get away from abstract Philosophy. "I'm afraid it can't be helped now, anyhow," said she.
"Dave *is* growing, and means to be a man. Oh dear—he'll be a
man before we know it. He'll be able to read and write in a few
months."

Uncle Mo's face showed a cloud. "Do ye really think that,
ma'am?" he said. "Well—I'm afeared you may be right." He
looked so dreadfully downcast at this, that Miss Grahame was
driven to the conclusion that the subject was dangerous.

She could not, however, resist saying:—"He *must* know *some*
time, you know, Mr. Wardle. Surely you would never have Dave
grow up uneducated?"

"Not so sure about that, ma'am!" said Uncle Mo, shaking a
dubious head. "There's more good men spiled by schoolmasters
than we hear tell of in the noospapers." What conspiracy of
silence in the Press this pointed at did not appear. But it was
clear from the tone of the speaker that he thought interested
motives were at the bottom of it.

Now Miss Grahame was said by critical friends—not enemies;
at least, they said not—to be over-anxious to confer benefits of
her own selection on the Human Race. Her finger-tips, they
hinted, were itching to set everyone else's house in order. Naturally, she had a strong bias towards Education, that most formidable inroad on ignorance of what we want to know nothing
about. Uncle Mo regarded the human mind, if not as a strong-
hold against knowledge, at least as a household with an inalienable

right to choose its ·guests. Miss Grahame was in favour of invitations issued by the State, and *visé'd* by the Church. Everything was to be correct, and sanctioned. But it was quite clear to her that these views would not be welcome to the old prizefighter, and she was fain to be content with the slight protest against Obscurantism just recorded. In short, Miss Grahame found nothing to say, and the subject had to drop.

She could, however, lighten the air, and did so. "What on earth are they about upstairs?" said she. "I really think I might go up and see." And she was just about to do so, with the assent of Aunt M'riar, when the latter said suddenly:—"My sakes and gracious! What's that?" rather as though taken aback by something unaccountable than alarmed by it.

Uncle Mo listened a moment, undisturbed; then said, placidly:— "Water-pipes, *I* should say." For in a London house no sound, even one like the jerk of a stopped skid on a half-buried boulder, is quite beyond the possible caprice of a choked supply-pipe.

Miss Grahame would have accepted the sound as normal, with some reservation as to the strangeness of everyday noises in this house, but for Aunt M'riar's exclamation, which made her say:— "Isn't that right?"

It was not, and the only human reply to the question was a further exclamation from Aunt M'riar—one of real alarm this time—at a disintegrating cracking sound, fraught with an inexplicable sense of insecurity. "*That* ain't water-pipes," said Uncle Mo.

Then something—something terrifying—happened in the Court outside. Something that came with a rush and roar, and ended in a crash of snapping timber and breaking glass. Something that sent a cloud of dust through the shivered window-panes into the room it darkened. Something that left behind it no sound but a sharp cry for help and moaning cries of pain, and was followed by shouts of panic and alarm, and the tramp of running feet—a swift flight to the spot of helpers who could see it without, the thing that had to be guessed by us within. Something that had half-beaten in the door that Uncle Mo, as soon as sight was possible, could be seen wrenching open, shouting loudly, inexplicably:—"They are underneath—they are underneath!"

Who were underneath? The children? And underneath what? A few seconds of dumb terror seemed an age to both women. Then, Gwen on the stairs, and her voice, with relief in its ring of resolution. "Don't talk, but come up *at once!* The old lady

must be got down, *somehow!* Come up!" A consciousness of
Dolly crying somewhere, and of Dave on the landing above, shouting:—" Oy say, oy say!" more, Miss Grahame thought, as a small
boy excited than one afraid; and then, light through the dust-
cloud. For Uncle Mo, with a giant's force, had released the
jammed door, and a cataract of brick rubbish, falling inwards,
left a gleam of clear sky to show Gwen, beckoning them up, none
the less beautiful for the tension of the moment, and the traces
of a rough baptism of dust.

What was it that had happened?

CHAPTER XXIX

OF A LADY AND GENTLEMAN ON THE EDGE OF A LONG VOYAGE TOGETHER.
SHALL THEY TAKE THE TICKETS? HOW MR. PELLEW HEARD SEV-
ERAL CLOCKS STRIKE ONE. HOW HE CALLED NEXT DAY, AND HEARD
ABOUT THE CHOBEY FAMILY. THE PROFANITY OF POETS, WHEN
PROFANE. HOW MR. PELLEW SOMETIMES WENT TO CHURCH. THE
POPULAR SUBJECT OF LOVE, IN THE END. MRS. AMPHLETT STAR-
FAX'S VIEWS. KISSING FROM A NEW STANDPOINT. HOW MR. PEL-
LEW FORGOT, OR RECOLLECTED, HIMSELF. BONES, BELOW, AND HIS
BAD GUESSING. HOW THE CARRIAGE CAME BACK WITH A FRIEND
IT HAD PICKED UP, WHOM MR. PELLEW CARRIED UPSTAIRS. UN-
EQUIVOCAL SIGNS OF AN ATTACHMENT WHICH

HAD Gwen really been able to see to the bottom of her cousin's,
the Hon. Percival's mind, she might not have felt quite so certain
about his predispositions towards her adopted aunt. The description of these two as wanting to rush into each other's arms was
exaggerated. It would have been fairer to say that Aunt Constance was fully prepared to consider an offer, and that Mr. Pellew was beginning to see his way to making one.

The most promising feature in the lady's state of mind was
that she was formulating consolations, dormant now, but actively
available if by chance the gentleman did not see his way. She
was saying to herself that if another flower attracted this bee,
she herself would thereby only lose an admirer with a disposition
—only a slight one perhaps, but still undeniable—to become corpulent in the course of the next few years. She could subordinate her dislike of smoking so long as she could suppose him
ever so little in earnest; but; if he did waver by any chance,

what a satisfaction it would be to dwell on her escape from—
here a mixed metaphor came in—the arms of a tobacco shop!
She could shut her eyes, if she was satisfied of the sincerity of a
redeeming attachment to herself, to all the contingencies of the
previous life of a middle-aged bachelor about town; but they
would no doubt supply a set-off to his disaffection, if that was
written on the next page of her book of Fate. In short, she
would be prepared in that case to accept the conviction that she
was well rid of him. But all this was subcutaneous. Given only
the one great essential, that he was not merely philandering, and
then neither his escapades in the past, nor his cigars, nor even
his suggestions towards a corporation, would stand in the way
of a whole-hearted acceptance of a companion for life who had
somehow managed to be such a pleasant companion during that
visit at the Towers. At least, she would be better off than her
four sisters. For this lady had a wholesome aversion for her
brothers-in-law, tending to support the creed which teaches that
the sacrament of marriage makes of its votaries, or victims, not
only parties to a contract, but one flesh, and opens up undreamed-of
possibilities of real fraternal dissension.

The gentleman, on the other hand, was in what we may suppose
to be a corresponding stage of uncertainty. He too was able to
perceive, or affect a perception, that, after all, if he came to the
scratch and the scratch eventuated—as scratches do sometimes—
in a paralysis of astonishment on the lady's part that such an
idea should ever have entered into the applicant's calculations, it
wouldn't be a thing to break his heart about exactly. He would
have made rather an ass of himself, certainly. But he was quite
prepared not to be any the worse.

This was, however, not subcutaneous, with him. He said it
to himself, quite openly. His concealment of himself from himself turned on a sort of passive resistance he was offering to a
growing reluctance to hear a negative to his application. He was,
despite himself, entertaining the question:—Was this woman
whom he had been assessing and wavering over, *more masculino,*
conceivably likely to reject him on his merits? Might she not
say to him:—" I have seen your drift, and found you too pleasant
an acquaintance to condemn offhand. But now that you force
me to ask myself the question, ' Can I love you?' you leave me
no choice but to answer, ' I can't.' " And he was beginning to
have a misgiving that he would very much rather that that scratch,
if ever he came to it, should end on very different lines from this.
All this, mind you, was under the skin of his reflections.

As he walked away slowly in the moonlight, with the appointment fresh in his mind to return next day on a shallow archæological pretext, he may have been himself at a loss for his reason
for completing a tour of the square, and pausing to look up at
the house before making a definite start for his Club, or his rooms
in Brook Street. Was any reason necessary, beyond the fineness
of the night? He had an indisputable right to walk round Cavendish Square without a reason, and he exercised it. He rather
resented the policeman on his beat saying goodnight to him,
as though he were abnormal, and walked away in the opposite
direction from that officer, who was searchlighting areas for want
of something to do, with an implication of profound purpose. He
decided on loneliness and a walk exactly the length of a cigar,
throwing its last effort to burn his fingers away on his doorstep.
He carried the animation of his thoughts on his face upstairs
to bed with him, for it lasted through a meditation at an open
window, through a chorus of cats about their private affairs, and
the usual controversy about the hour among all the town-clocks,
which becomes embittered when there is only one hour to talk
about, and compromise is impossible. Mr. Pellew heard the last
opinion and retired for the night at nine minutes past. But he
first made sure that that *Quarterly Review* was in evidence, and
glanced at the Egyptian article to confirm his impression of the
contents. They were still there. He believed all his actions were
sane and well balanced, but this was credulity. One stretches a
point sometimes, to believe oneself reasonable.

It was a model September afternoon—and what can one say
more of weather?—when at half-past three precisely Mr. Pellew's
hansom overshot the door of 102, Cavendish Square, and firmly
but amiably insisted on turning round to deposit its fare according
to the exact terms of its contract. Its proprietor said what he
could in extenuation of its maladroitness. They shouldn't build
these here houses at the corners of streets; it was misguiding to
the most penetrating intellect. He addressed his fare as Captain,
asking him to make it another sixpence. He had been put to a
lot of expense last month, along of the strike, and looked to the
public to make it up to him. For the cabbies had struck, some
weeks since, against sixpence a mile instead of eightpence. Mr.
Pellew's heart was touched, and he conceded the other sixpence.

There at the door was Miss Grahame's open landaulet, and there
were she and Gwen in it, just starting to see the former's little
boy. That was how Dave was spoken of, at the risk of creating
a scandal. They immediately lent themselves to a gratuitous

farce, having for its object the liberation of Mr. Pellew and Miss Dickenson from external influence.

"Constance *was* back, wasn't she?" Thus Miss Grahame; and Gwen had the effrontery to say she was almost certain, but couldn't be quite sure. If she wasn't there, she would have to go without that pulverised Pharaoh, as Sir Somebody Something's just yearnings for his *Quarterly* were not to be made light of. "Don't you let Maggie take the book up to her, Percy. You go up in the sitting-room—you know, where we were playing last night?—and if she doesn't turn up in five minutes don't you wait for her!" Then the two ladies talked telegraphically, to the exclusion of Mr. Pellew, to the effect that Aunt Constance had only gone to buy a pair of gloves in Oxford Street, and was pledged to an early return. The curtain fell on the farce, and a very brief interview with Mary at the door ended in Mr. Pellew being shown upstairs, without reservation. So he and Aunt Constance had the house to themselves.

To do them justice, the attention shown to the covering fiction of the book-loan was of the very smallest. It could not be ignored altogether; so Miss Dickenson looked at the article. She did not read a word of it, but she looked at it. She went further, and said it was interesting. Then it was allowed to lie on the table. When the last possible book has been printed—for even Literature must come to an end some time, if Time itself does not collapse— that will be the last privilege accorded to it. It will lie on the table, while all but a few of its predecessors will stand on a bookshelf.

"It's quite warm out of doors," said Mr. Pellew.

"Warmer than yesterday, I think," said Miss Dickenson. And then talk went on, stiffly, each of its contribuents execrating its stiffness, but seeing no way to relaxation.

"Sort of weather that generally ends in a thunderstorm."

"Does it? Well—perhaps it does."

"Don't you think it does?"

"I thought it felt very like thunder an hour ago."

"Rather more than an hour ago, wasn't it?"

"Just after lunch—about two o'clock."

"Dessay you're right. I should have said a quarter to." Now, if this sort of thing had continued, it must have ended in a joint laugh, and recognition of its absurdity. Aunt Constance may have foreseen this, inwardly, and not been prepared to go so fast. For she accommodated the conversation with a foothold, partly ethical, partly scientific.

" Some people feèl the effect of thunder much more than others. No doubt it is due to the electrical condition of the atmosphere. Before this was understood, it was ascribed to all sorts of causes." " I expect it's nerves. Haven't any myself! Rather like tropical storms than otherwise."

Here was an opportunity to thaw the surface ice. The lady could have done it in an instant, by talking to the gentleman about himself. That is the " Open Sesame! " of human intercourse. She preferred to say that in their village—her clan's, that is—in Dorsetshire, there was a sept named Chobey that always went into an underground cellar and stopped its ears, whenever there was a thunderstorm.

Mr. Pellew said weakly:—" It runs in families." He had to accept this one as authentic, but he would have questioned its existence if anonymous. He could not say:—" How do you know? " to an informant who could vouch for Chobey. Smith or Brown would have left him much freer. The foothold of the conversation was giving way, and a resolute effort was called for to give it stability. Mr. Pellew thought he saw his way. He said:—" How jolly it must be down at the Towers—day like this! "

" Perfectly delicious! " was the answer. Then, in consideration of the remoteness of mere landscape from personalities, it was safe to particularise. " I really think that walk in the shrubbery, where the gentian grew in such quantity, is one of the sweetest places of the kind I ever was in."

" I know I enjoyed my . . ." Mr. Pellew had started to say that he enjoyed himself there. He got alarmed at his own temerity and backed out . . . " my cigars there," said he. A transparent fraud, for the possessive pronoun does not always sound alike. " My," is one thing before " self," another before " cigars." Try it on both, and see. Mr. Pellew felt he was detected. He could slur over his blunder by going straight on; any topic would do. He decided on:—" By-the-by, did you see any more of the dog? "

" Achilles? He went away, you know, with Mr. Torrens and his sister, a few days after."

" I meant that. Didn't you say something about seeing him with the assassin—the old gamekeeper—what was his name? "

" Old Stephen Solmes? Yes. I saw them walking together, apparently on the most friendly terms. Gwen told me afterwards. They were walking towards his cottage, and I believe Achilles saw him safe home, and came back."

" Just so. Torrens told me about the dog when old Solmes came

to say good-bye to him, and do a little more penance in sackcloth
and ashes. I am using Torrens's words. The old chap made a
scene—went down on his knees and burst out crying—and the
dog tried to console him. Torrens seemed quite clear about what
was passing in the dog's mind."

"What did he say the dog meant? Can you remember?" Miss
Dickenson was settling down to chat, perceptibly.

"Pretty well. Achilles had wished to say that he personally,
so far from finding fault with Mr. Solmes for trying to shoot
him, fully recognised that he drew trigger under a contract to do
so, given circumstances which had actually come about. He
would not endeavour to extenuate his own conduct, but submitted
that he was entitled to a lenient judgment, on the ground that
a hare, the pursuit of which was the indirect cause of the whole
mishap, had jumped up from behind a stone. . . . Well—I suppose I oughtn't to repeat all a profane poet thinks fit to say. . . ."

"Please do! Never mind the profanity!" It really was a
stimulus to the lady's curiosity.

Mr. Pellew repeated the apology which the collie's master had
ascribed to him. Achilles had only acted in obedience to Instincts
which had been Implanted in him in circumstances for which
he was not responsible, and which might, for anything he knew,
have been conceived in a spirit of mischief by the Author of all
Good. This levity was stopped by a shocked expression on the
lady's face. "Well," said the gentleman, "you mustn't blow *me*
up, Miss Dickenson. I am only repeating, as desired, the words
of a profane poet. He had apologized, he told me, for what he
said, when his sister boxed his ears."

"Serve him right. But what was his apology?"

"That he owed it to Achilles, who was unable to speak for
himself, to lay stress on what he conceived to be the dog's
Manichæan views, which he had been most unwillingly forced to
infer from his practice of suddenly barking indignantly at the
Universe, in what certainly seemed an unprayerful spirit."

"It was only Mr. Torrens's nonsense. He wanted to blaspheme
a little, and jumped at the opportunity. They are all alike, Poets.
Look at Byron and Shelley!"

Mr. Pellew, for his own purposes no doubt, managed here to
insinuate that he himself was not without a reverent side to his
character. These fillahs were no doubt the victims of their own
genius, and presumably Mr. Torrens was a bird of the same
feather. He himself was a stupid old-fashioned sort of fillah,
and couldn't always follow this sort of thing. It was as delicate

a claim as he could make to sometimes going to Church on Sunday, as was absolutely consistent with Truth.

To his great relief, Miss Dickenson did not catechize him closely about his religious views. She only remarked, reflectively and vaguely :—" One hardly knows what to think. Anyone would have said my father was a religious man, and what does he do but marry a widow, less than three years after my mother's death! "

Certainly the coherency of this speech was not on its surface. But Mr. Pellew accepted it contentedly enough. At least, it clothed him with some portion of the garb of a family friend; say shoes or gloves, not the whole suit. Whichever it was, he pulled them on, and felt they fitted. He began to speak, and stopped; was asked what he was going to say, and went on, encouraged :—" I was going to say, only I pulled up because it felt impertinent. . . ."

" Not to me! Please tell me exactly! "

" I was going to ask, how old is your father? Is he older than me? "

" Why, of course he is! I'm thirty-six. How old are you? Tell the truth! " At this exact moment a funny thing happened. The *passée* elderly young lady vanished—she who had been so often weighed, found wanting, and been put back in the balance for reconsideration. She vanished, and a desirable *alter ego*— Mr. Pellew's, as he hoped—was looking across at him from the sofa by the window, swinging the tassel of the red blind that kept the sun in check, and hushed it down to a fiery glow on the sofa's occupant waiting to know how old he was.

" I thought I had told you. Nearly forty-six."

" Very well, then! My father is five-and-twenty years your senior."

" If you had to say exactly *why* you dislike your father's having married again, do you think you could? "

" Oh dear, no! I'm quite sure I couldn't. But I think it detestable for all that."

" I'm not sure that you're right. You may be, though! Are you sure it hasn't something to do with the . . . with the party he's married? "

" Not at all sure." Dryly.

" Can't understand objecting to a match on its own account. It's always something to do with the outsider that comes in— the one one knows least of."

" You wouldn't like this one." It may seem inexplicable, that these words should be the cause of the person addressed taking the nearest chair to the speaker, having previously been a nomad with his thumbs in the armholes of his waistcoat. Close analysis may connect the action with an extension of the family-friendship wardrobe, which it may have recognised—a neckcloth, perhaps—and may be able to explain why it seemed doubtful form to the Hon. Percival to keep his thumbs in those waistcoat-loops. To us, it is perfectly easy to understand—without any analysis at all —why, at this juncture, Miss Dickenson said:—"I suppose you know you may smoke a cigarette, if you like?"

In those days you might have looked in tobacconist's shop-windows all day and never seen a cigarette. It was a foreign fashion at which sound smokers looked askance. Mossoos might smoke it, but good, solid John Bull suspected it of being a kick-shaw not unconnected with Atheism. He stuck to his pipe chiefly. Nevertheless, it was always open to skill to fabricate its own cigarettes, and Mr. Pellew's aptitude in the art was known to Miss Dickenson. The one he screwed up on receipt of this licence was epoch-making. The interview had been one that was going to last a quarter of an hour. This cigarette made its duration indeterminate. Because a cigarette is not a cigar. The latter is like a chapter in a book, the former like a paragraph. At the chapter's end vacant space insists on a pause for thought, for approval or condemnation of its contents. But every paragraph is as it were kindled from the last sentence of its predecessor; as soon as each ends the next is ready. The reader aloud is on all fours with the cigarette-smoker. He doesn't always enjoy himself so much, but that is neither here nor there.

It was not during the first cigarette that Mr. Pellew said to Aunt Constance:—"Where is it they have gone to-day, do you know?" That first one heard, if it listened, all about the lady's home in Dorsetshire and her obnoxious stepmother. It may have wondered, if it was an observant cigarette, at the unreserve with which the narrator took its smoker into the bosom of her confidence, and the lively interest her story provoked. If it had—which is not likely, considering the extent of its experience—a shrewd perception of the philosophy of reciprocity, probably it wondered less. It heard to the end of the topic, and Mr. Pellew asked the question above stated, as he screwed up its successor, and exacted the death-duty of an ignition from it.

"They ought to be coming back soon," was the answer. "I told them I wouldn't have tea till they came. They're gone to see a *protégée* of Clotilda's, who lives down a Court. It's not very far off; under a mile, I should think. We saw him in the street, coming from the railway-station. He looked a nice boy. That is to say, he would have looked nice, only he and his friends had all been blacking their faces with burnt cork." " What a lark! Why didn't you go to the Court? . . . I'm jolly glad you didn't, you know, but you might have. . . ." This was just warm enough for the position. With its slight extenuation of slang, it might rank as mere emphasized civility.

It was Miss Dickenson's turn to word something ambiguous to cover all contingencies. " Yes, I should have been very sorry if you had come to bring the book, and not found me here." This was clever, backed by a smile. She went on:—" They thought two would be quite enough, considering the size of the Court."

A spirit of accommodation prevailed. Oh yes—Mr. Pellew quite saw that. Very sensible! " It don't do," said he, " to make too much of a descent on this sort of people. They never know what to make of it, and the thing don't wash!" But he was only saying what came to hand; because he was extremely glad Miss Dickenson had not gone with the expedition. How far he perceived that his own visit underlay its arrangements, who can say? His perception fell short of being ignorant that he was aware of it. Suppose we leave it at that!

Still, regrets—scarcely Jeremiads—that she had not been included would be becoming, all things considered. They could not be misinterpreted. " I was sorry not to go," she said. " His father was a prizefighter and seems interesting, according to Clotilda. Her idea is to get Gwen enthusiastic about people of this sort, or any of her charitable schemes, rather than dragging her off to Switzerland or Italy. Besides, she won't go! "

" That's a smasher! The idea, I suppose, is to get her away and let the Torrens business die a natural death. Well—it won't! "

" You think not? "

" No thinking about it! Sure of it! I've known my cousin Gwen from a child—so have you, for that matter!—and I know it's useless. If she will, she will, you may depend on't; and if she won't she won't, and there's an end on't. You'll see, she'll consent to go fiddling about for three months or six months to Wiesbaden or Ems or anywhere, but she'll end by fixing the day and ordering her trousseau, quite as a matter of course! As for *his* changing—pooh! " Mr. Pellew laughed aloud. Miss Dickenson looked a very hesitating concurrence, which he felt would bear refreshing. He continued:—" Why, just look at the case! A man loses his eyesight and is half killed five minutes after seeing—for the first time, mind you, for the first time!—my cousin

Gwen Rivers, under specially favourable circumstances. When he comes to himself he finds out in double quick time that she loves him? *He* change? Not he!"

"Do tell me, Mr. Pellew. . . . I'm only asking, you know; not expressing any opinion myself. . . . Do tell me, don't you think it possible that it might be better for both of them—for Gwen certainly, if it . . . if it never . . ."

"If it never came off? If you ask me, all I can say is, that I haven't an opinion. It is so absolutely their affair and nobody else's. That's my excuse for not having an opinion, and you see I jump at it."

"Of course it is entirely their affair, and one knows. But one can't help thinking. Just fancy Gwen the wife of a blind country Squire. It is heartbreaking to think of—now isn't it?"

But Mr. Pellew was not to be moved from his position. "It's their own look out," said he. "Nobody else's!" He suddenly perceived that this might be taken as censorious. "Not finding fault, you know! You're all right. Naturally, you think of Gwen."

"Whom ought I to think of? Oh, I see what you mean. It's true I don't know Mr. Torrens—have hardly seen him!"

"I saw him a fairish number of times—one time with another. He's a sort of fillah . . . a sort of fillah you can't exactly describe. Very unusual sort of fillah!" Mr. Pellew held his cigarette a little way off to look at it thoughtfully, as though it were the usual sort of fellow, and he was considering how he could distinguish Mr. Torrens from it.

"You mean he's unusually clever?"

"Yes, he's that. But that's not exactly what I meant, either. He's clever, of course. Only he doesn't give you a chance of knowing it, because he turns everything to nonsense. What I wanted to say was, that whatever he says, one fancies one would have said it oneself, if one had had the time to think it out."

Miss Dickenson didn't really identify this as a practicable shade of character, but she pretended she did. In fact she said:— "Oh, I know exactly what you mean. I've known people like that," merely to lubricate the conversation. Then she asked: "Did you ever talk to the Earl about him?"

"Tim? Yes, a little. He doesn't disguise his liking for him, personally. He's rather . . . rather besotted about him, I should say."

"*She* isn't." How Mr. Pellew knew who was meant is not clear, but he did.

"Her mother, you mean," said he. "Do you know, I doubt if Philippa dislikes him? I shouldn't put it that way. But I think she would be glad for the thing to die a natural death for all that. Eyes apart, you know." When people begin to make so very few words serve their purpose it shows that their circumferences have intersected—no mere tangents now. A portion of the area of each is common to both. Forgive geometry this intrusion on the story, and accept the metaphor.

"Yes, that's what it is," said Aunt Constance. And then in answer to a glance that, so to speak, asked for a confirmation of a telegram:—"Oh yes, I know we both mean the same thing. You were thinking of that old story—the old love-affair. I quite understand." She might have added "this time," because the last time she knew what Mr. Pellew meant she was stretching a point, and he was subconscious of it.

"That's the idea," said he. "I fancy Philippa's feelings must be rather difficult to define. So must his papa's, I should think."

"I can't fancy anything more embarrassing."

"Of course Tim has a mighty easy time of it, by comparison."

"Does he necessarily know anything about it?"

"He must have heard of it. It wasn't a secret, though it wasn't announced in the papers. These things get talked about. Besides, she would tell him."

"Tell him? Of course she would! She would tell him that that young Torrens was a 'great admirer' of hers."

"Yes—I suppose she *would* make use of some expression of that sort. Capital things, expressions!"

Aunt Constance seemed to think this phrase called for some sort of elucidation. "I always feel grateful," said she, "to that Frenchman—Voltaire or Talleyrand or Rochefoucauld or somebody—who said language was invented to conceal our thoughts. That was what you meant, wasn't it?"

"Precisely. I suppose Sir Torrens—this chap's papa—told the lady he married . . ."

"She was a Miss Abercrombie, I believe."

"Yes—I believe she was. . . . Told her he was a great admirer of her ladyship once on a time—a boyish freak—that sort of thing! Pretends all the gilt is off the gingerbread now. Wish I had been there when Sir Hamilton turned up at the Towers, after the accident."

"I *was* there."

"Well! And then?"

"Nothing and then. They were—just like anybody else. When

I saw them was after his son had begun to pull round. Till then
I fancy neither he nor the sister . . ."

" Irene. ' 'Rene,' he calls her. Jolly sort of girl, and very
handsome."

" Neither Irene nor her father came downstairs much. It was
after you went away."

" And what did they say?—him and Philippa, I mean."

" Oh—say? What *did* they say? Really I can't remember.
Said what a long time it was since they met. Because I don't
believe they *had* met—not to shake hands—for five-and-twenty
years!"

" What a rum sort of experience! Do you know? . . . only of
course one can't say for certain about anything of this sort . . ."

" Do I know? Go on."

" I was going to say that if I had been them, I should have
burst out laughing and said what a couple of young asses we
were!" The Hon. Percival was very colloquial, but syntax was
not of the essence of the contract, if any existed.

Aunt Constance was not in the mood to pooh-pooh the *tendresses*
of a youthful passion. She was, if you will have it so, sentimental. "Let me think if I should," said she, with a momentary
action of closing her eyes, to keep inward thought free of the
outer world. In a moment they were open again, and she was
saying:—" No, I should not have done anything of the sort. One
laughs at young people, I know, when they are so very inflam-
matory. But what do we think of them when they are not?"
She became quite warm and excited about it, or perhaps—so
thought Mr. Pellew as he threw his last cigarette-end away through
that open window—the blaze of a sun that was forecasting its
afterglow made her seem so. Mr. Pellew having thrown away
that cigarette-end conscientiously, and made a pretence of seeing
it safe into the front area, was hardly bound to go back to his
chair. He dropped on the sofa, beside Miss Dickenson, with one
hand over the back. He loomed over her, but she did not shy
or flinch.

" What indeed!" said he seriously, answering her last words.
" A young man that does not fall in love seldom comes to any
good." He was really thinking to himself:—" Oh, the mistakes
I should have been saved in life, if only this had happened to
me in my twenties!" He was not making close calculation of
what the lady's age would have been in those days.

She was dwelling on the abstract question:—" You know, say
what one may, the whole of their lives is at stake. And we never

think them young geese when the thing comes off, and they become couples."

"No. True enough. It's only when it goes off and they don't."

"And what is so creepy about it is that we never know whether
the couple is the right couple."

"Never know anything at all about anything beforehand!"
Mr. Pellew was really talking at random. Even the value of this
trite remark was spoiled. For he added:—"Nor afterwards, for
that matter!"

Miss Dickenson admitted that we could not lay too much stress
on our own limitations. But she was not in the humour for platitudes. Her mind was running on a problem that might have
worried Juliet Capulet had she never wedded her Romeo and
taken a dose of hellebore, but lived on to find that County Paris
had in him the makings of a lovable mate. Quite possible, you
know! It was striking her that if a trothplight were nothing but
a sort of civil contract—civil in the sense of courteous, polite,
urbane, accommodating—an exchange of letters through a callous
Post Office—a woman might be engaged a dozen times and meet
the males implicated in after-life, without turning a hair. But
even a hand-clasp, left to enjoy itself by its parents—not nipped
in the bud—might poison their palms and recrudesce a little in
Society, long years after! While, as for lips. . . .

Something crossed her reflections, just on the crux of them—
their most critical point of all. "There!" said she. "Did you
hear that? I knew we should have thunder."

But Mr. Pellew had heard nothing and was incredulous. He
verified his incredulity, going to the window to look out. "Blue
sky all round!" said he. "Must have been a cart!" He went
back to his seat, and the explanation passed muster.

Miss Dickenson picked up her problem, with that last perplexity hanging to it. No, it was no use!—that equable deportment
of Sir Hamilton and Philippa remained a mystery to her. She,
however—mere single Miss Dickenson—could not of course guess
how these two would see themselves, looking back, with all the
years between of a growing Gwen and Adrian; to her, it was just
the lapse of so much time, nothing more—a year or so over the
time she had known Philippa. For Romeo and Juliet were meta-
phors out of date when she came on the scene, and Philippa was
a Countess.

She was irritated by the inability she felt to comment freely
on these views of the position. It would have been easier—she
saw this—to do so had Mr. Pellew gone back to his chair, instead

of sitting down again beside her on the sofa. It was her own fault perhaps, because she could not have sworn this time that she had not seemed to make room. That unhappy sex—the female one—lives under orders to bristle with incessant safeguards against misinterpretation. Heaven only knows—or should we not rather say, Hell only knows?—what latitudes have claimed "encourage-ment" as their excuse! That lady in Browning's poem never should have looked at the gentleman so, had she meant he should not love her. So *he* said! But suppose she saw a fly on his nose—how then?

Therefore it would never have done for Miss Dickenson to go into close analysis of the problems suggested by the meeting of two undoubted *fiancés* of years long past, and the inexplicable self-command with which they looked the present in the face. She had to be content with saying:—" Of course we know nothing of the intentions of Providence. But it's no use pretending that it would not feel very—queer." She had to clothe this word with a special emphasis, and backed it with an implied contortion due to teeth set on edge. She added:—" All I know is, I'm very glad it wasn't *me.*" After which she was clearly not responsible if the topic continued.

Mr. Pellew took the responsibility on himself of saying with deep-seated intuition:—" I know precisely what you mean. You're perfectly right. Perfectly!"

" A hundred little things," said the lady. The dragging in of ninety-nine of these, with the transparent object of slurring over the hundredth, which each knew the other was thinking of, merely added to its vividness. Aunt Constance might just as well have let it alone, and suddenly talked of something else. For instance, of the Sun God's abnormal radiance, now eloquent of what he meant to do for the metropolis when he got a few degrees lower, and went in for setting, in earnest. Or if she shrank from that, as not prosaic enough to dilute the conversation down to mere chat-point, the Ethiopian Serenaders who had just begun to be inexplicable in the Square below. But she left the first to assert its claim to authorship of the flush of rose colour that certainly made her tell to advantage, and the last to account for the ani-mation which helped it. For the enigmatic character of South Carolina never interferes with a certain brisk exhilaration in its bones. . She repeated in a vague way:—" A hundred things!" and shut her lips on particularisation.

" I don't know exactly how many," said Mr. Pellew gravely. He sat drawing one whisker through the hand whose elbow was on

the sofa-back, with his eyes very much on the flush and the animation. "I was thinking of one in particular."

"Perhaps *I* was. I don't know."

"I was thinking of the kissin'."

"Well—so was I, perhaps. I don't see any use in mincing matters." She had been the mincer-in-chief, however.

"Don't do the slightest good! When it gets to kissin'-point,
it's all up. If I had been a lady, and broken a fillah off, I think
I should have been rather grateful to him for getting out of the
gangway. Should have made a point of getting out, myself."

The subject had got comfortably landed, and could be philosophically discussed. "I dare say everyone does not feel the point
as strongly as I do," said Miss Dickenson. "I know my sister
Georgie—Mrs. Amphlett Starfax—looks at it quite differently, and
thinks me rather a . . . prig. Or perhaps *prig* isn't exactly the
word. I don't know how to put it. . . ."

"Never mind. I know exactly what you mean."

"You see, the circumstances are so different. Georgie had been
engaged six times before Octavius came on the scene. But, oh
dear, how I *am* telling tales out of school! . . ."

"Never mind Georgie and Octavius. They're not your sort.
You were saying how you felt about it, and that's more interesting. Interests me more!" Conceive that at this point the lady
glanced at the speaker ever so slightly. Upon which he followed
a slight pause with:—"Yes, why are you a *prig,* as she thought
fit to put it?"

"Because I told her that if ever I found a young man who
suited me—and *vice versa*—and it got to . . . to what you called
just now 'kissing-point,' I should not be so ready as she had been
to pull him off like an old glove and throw him away. That was
when I was very young, you know. It was just after she jilted
Ludwig, who afterwards married my sister Lilian—Baroness
Porchammer; my eldest sister. . . ."

"Oh, *she* jilted Ludwig, and *he* married your sister Lilian, was
that it?" Mr. Pellew, still stroking that right whisker thoughtfully, was preoccupied by something that diverted interest from
this family history.

Aunt Constance did not seem to notice his abstraction, but
talked on. "Yes—and what is so funny about Georgie with
Julius is that they don't seem to mind kissing now from a new
standpoint. Georgie particularly. In fact, I've seen her kiss
him on both sides and call him an old stupid. However, as you
say, the cases are not alike. Perhaps if Philippa's old love had

married her sister—Lady Clancarrock of Garter, you know—instead of Uncle Cosmo, as they call him, they could have got used to it, by now. Only one must look at these things from one's own point of view, and by the light of one's experience." A ring on her right hand might have been one of the things, and the sun-ray through the blind-slip the light of her experience, as she sat accommodating the flash-light of the first to the gleam of the second.

If everyone knew to a nicety his or her seeming at the precise point of utterance of any speech, slight or weighty, nine-tenths of our wit or profundity would remain unspoken. Man always credits woman with knowing exactly what she looks like, and engineering speech and seeming towards the one desired end of impressing him—important Him! He acquits himself of studying the subject! Probably he and she are, as a matter of fact, six of the one and half a dozen of the other. Of this one thing the story feels certain, that had Miss Dickenson been conscious of her neighbour's incorporation into a unit of magnetism—he being its victim—of her mere outward show in the evening light with the subject-matter of her discourse, this little lecture on the ethics of kissing would never have seen the light. But let her finish it. Consider that she gives a pause to the ring-gleam, then goes on, quite in earnest.

"It's very funny that it should be so, I know—but there it is! If I had ever been engaged, or on the edge of it—I never have, really and truly!—and the infatuated youth had . . . had complicated matters to that extent, I never should have been able to wipe it off. That's an expression of a small niece of mine—three-and-a-quarter. . . . Oh dear—but I never *said* you might! . . ."

For the gentleman's conduct had been extraordinary! unwarranted, perhaps, according to some. According to others, he may only have behaved as a many in his position would have behaved half an hour sooner. "I am," said he, "the infatuated youth. Forgive me, Aunt Constance!" For he had deliberately taken that lady in his arms and kissed her.

The foregoing is an attempt to follow through an interview the development of events which led to its climax—a persistent and tenacious attempt, more concerned with its purpose than with inquiring into the interest this or that reader may feel who may chance to light upon this narrative. No very close analysis of the sublatent impulses and motives of its actors is professed or attempted; only a fringe of guesswork at the best. But let a protest be recorded against the inevitable vernacular judgment in disfavour of the lady. "Of course—the minx! As if she didn't know what she was about the whole time. As if she wasn't leading him on!" Because that is the attitude of mind of the correct human person in such a case made and provided. That is, if an inevitable automatic action can be called an attitude of mind. Is rotation on its axis an attitude of a wheel's mind? To be sure, though, a wheel may turn either of two ways. A ratchet-wheel is needed for this metaphor.

However, the correct human person may be expressing a universal opinion. This is only the protest of the story, which thinks otherwise. But even if it were so, was not Miss Dickenson well within her rights? The story claims that, anyhow. At the same time, it records its belief that four-fifths of the *dénouement* was due to Helios. The magic golden radiance intoxicated Mr. Pellew, and made him forget—or remember—himself. The latter, the story thinks. That ring perhaps had its finger in the pie—but this may be to inquire too curiously.

One thing looks as though Miss Dickenson had not been working out a well-laid scheme. Sudden success does not stop the heart with a jerk, or cause speechlessness, even for a moment. Both had happened to her by the time she had uttered her *pro forma* remonstrance. Her breath lasted it out. Then she found it easiest to remain passive. She was not certain it would not be correct form to make a show of disengaging herself from the arms that still held her. But—she didn't want to!

This may have justified Mr. Pellew's next words:—"You do forgive me, don't you?" more as assertion than inquiry.

She got back breath enough to gasp out:—"Oh yes—only don't talk! Let me think!" And then presently:—"Yes, I forgive you in any case. Only—I'll tell you directly. Let's look out of the window. I want to feel the air blow. . . . You startled me rather, that's all!'

Said Mr. Pellew, at the window, as he reinstated an arm dispossessed during the transit:—"I did it to . . . to *clinch* the matter, don't you see? I thought I should make a mess of it if I went in for eloquence."

"It was as good as any way. I wasn't the least angry. Only . . ."

"Only what?"

"Only by letting you go on like this"—half a laugh came in here—"I don't consider that I stand committed to anything."

"I consider that *I* stand committed to everything." The arm may have slightly emphasized this.

"No—that's impossible. It *must* be the same for both."

"Dearest woman! Just as you like. But I know what I mean." Indeed, Mr. Pellew did seem remarkably clear about it. Where, by-the-by, was that *passée* young lady, and that middle-aged haunter of Clubs? Had they ever existed?

Bones was audible from below, as they stood looking out at the west, where some cirro-stratus clouds were waiting to see the sun down beyond the horizon, and keep his memory golden for half an hour. Bones was affecting ability to answer conundrums, asked by an unexplained person with a banjo, who treated him with distinction, calling him "Mr. Bones." Both were affecting an air of high courtesy, as of persons familiar with the Thrones and Chancelleries of Europe. The particulars of these conundrums were inaudible, from distance, but the scheme was clear. Bones offered several solutions, of a fine quality of wit, but wrong. He then produced a sharp click or snap, after his kind, and gave it up. His friend or patron then gave the true solution, whose transcendent humour was duly recognised by Europe, and moved Bones to an unearthly dance, dryly but decisively accompanied on his instrument. A sudden outburst of rhythmic banjo-thuds and song followed, about Old Joe, who kicked up behind and before, and a yellow girl, who kicked up behind Old Joe. Then the Company stopped abruptly and went home to possible soap and water. Silence was left for the lady and gentleman at No. 102 to speak to one another in undertones, and to wonder what o'clock it was.

"They ought to be back by now," says she. "I wonder they are so late. They are making quite a visitation of it."

Says he:—"Gwen is fascinated with the old prizefighter. Just like her! I don't care how long they stop; do you?"

"I don't think it matters," says she, "to a quarter of an hour. The sunset is going to be lovely." This is to depersonalise the position. A feeble attempt, under the circumstances.

It must have been past the end of that quarter of an hour, when—normal relations having been resumed, of course—Miss Dickenson interrupted a sub-vocal review of the growth of their acquaintance to say, "Come in!" The tap that was told to come in was Maggie. Was she to be making the tea? Was she to lay it? On the whole she might do both, as the delay of the absentees longer was in the nature of things impossible.

But, subject to the disposition of Mr. Pellew's elbows on the window-sill, they might go on looking out at the sunset and feel *réglés*. Short of endearments, Maggie didn't matter.

The self-assertion of Helios was amazing. He made nothing
of what one had thought would prove a cloud-veil—tore it up,
brushed it aside. He made nothing, too, of the powers of eyesight of those whose gaze dwelt on him over boldly.

"It *is* them," said Miss Dickenson, referring to a half-recognised
barouche that had turned the corner below. "But who on earth
have they got with them? I can't see for my eyes."

"Only some friend they've picked up," said Mr. Pellew. But
he rubbed his own eyes, to get rid of the sun. Recovered sight
made him exclaim:—"But what are the people stopping for? . . .
I say, something's up! Come along!" For, over and above a
mysterious impression of the unusual that could hardly be set
down to the bird's-eye view as its sole cause, it was clear that
every passer-by was stopping, to look at the carriage. Moreover,
there was confusion of voices—Gwen's dominant. Mr. Pellew
did not wait to distinguish speech. He only repeated:—"Come
along!" and was off downstairs as fast as he could go. Aunt
Constance kept close behind him.

She was too bewildered to be quite sure, offhand, why Gwen
looked so more than dishevelled, as she met them at the stair-
foot, earnest with excitement. Not panic-struck at all—that was
not her way—but at highest tension of word and look, as she
made the decision of her voice heard:—"Oh, there you are, Mr.
Pellew. Make yourself useful. Go out and bring her in. Never
mind who! Make haste. And Maggie's to fetch the doctor."
Mr. Pellew went promptly out, and Miss Dickenson was beginning:—"Why—what? . . ." But she had to stand inquiry over.
For nothing was possible against Gwen's:—"Now, Aunt Connie
dear, don't ask questions. You shall be told the whole story, all
in good time! Let's get her upstairs and get the doctor." They
both followed Mr. Pellew into the street, where a perceptible crowd,
sprung from nowhere, was already offering services it was not
qualified to give, in ignorance of the nature of the emergency that
had to be met, and in defiance of a policeman.

Mr. Pellew had taken his instructions so quickly from Miss
Grahame, still in the carriage, that he was already carrying the
doctor's patient, whoever and whatever she was, but carefully
as directed, into the house. At any rate it was not Miss Grahame
herself, for that lady's voice was saying, collectedly:—"I don't
think it's any use Maggie going, Gwen, because she doesn't know
London. James must fetch him, in the carriage. Dr. Dalrymple,
65, Weymouth Street, James! Tell him he *must* come, at once!
Say *I* said so." It was then that Aunt Constance perceived in

the clear light of the street, that not only was the person Mr. Pellew was carrying into the house—whom she could only identify otherwise as having snow-white hair—covered with dust and soiled, but that Gwen and Miss Grahame were in a like plight, the latter in addition being embarrassed by a rent skirt, which she was fain to hold together as she crossed the doorstep. Once in the house she made short work of it, finishing the rip, and acquiescing in the publicity of a petticoat. It added to Aunt Constance's perplexity that the carriage and James appeared in as trim order as when they left the door three hours since. These hours had been eventful to her, and she was really feeling as if the whole thing must be a strange dream.

She got no explanation worth the name at the time of the incident. For Gwen's scattered information after the old snow-white head was safe on her own pillow—she insisted on this—and its owner had been guaranteed by Dr. Dalrymple, was really good for very little. The old lady was Cousin Clo's little boy's old Mrs. Picture, and she was the dearest old thing. There had been an accident at the house while they were there, and a man and a woman had been hurt, but no fatality. The man had not been taken to the Hospital, as his family had opposed his going on the ground of his invulnerability. The old prizefighter was uninjured, as well as those two nice children. They might have been killed. But as to the nature of the accident, it remained obscure, or perhaps the ever-present consciousness of her own experience prevented Aunt Constance getting a full grasp of its details. The communication, moreover, was crossed by that lady's exclamation:—" Oh dear, the events of this afternoon! " just at the point where the particulars of the mishap were due, to make things intelligible.

At which exclamation Gwen, suddenly alive to a restless conscious manner of Aunt Constance's, pointed at her as one she could convict without appeal, saying remorselessly:—" Mr. Pellew has proposed and you have accepted him while we were away, Aunt Connie! Don't deny it. You're engaged! "

" My dear Gwen," said Miss Dickenson, " if what you suggest were true, I should not dream for one moment of concealing it from you. But as for any engagement between us, I assure you there is no such thing. Beyond showing unequivocal signs of an attachment which . . ."

Gwen clapped the beautiful hands, still soiled with the dirt of Sapps Court, and shook its visible dust from her sleeve. Her laugh rang all through the House. " That's all right! " she cried.

"He's shown unequivocal signs of an attachment which. Well—what more do you want? Oh, Aunt Connie, I'm *so* glad!"

All that followed had for Miss Dickenson the same dream-world character, but of a dream in which she retained presence of mind. It was needed to maintain the pretext of unruffled custom in her communications with her male visitor; the claim to be, before all things, normal, on the part of both, in the presence of at least one friend who certainly knew all about it, and another who may have known. Because there was no trusting Gwen. However, she got through it very well.

Regrets were expressed that Sir Somebody Something had not got his *Quarterly* after all; but it would do another time. Hence consolation. After Mr. Pellew had taken a farewell, which may easily have been a tender one, as nobody saw it, she heard particulars of the accident, which shall be told here also, in due course.

Some embarrassment resulted from Gwen's headstrong action in bringing the old lady away from the scene of this accident. She might have been provided for otherwise, but Gwen's beauty and positiveness, and her visible taking for granted that her every behest would be obeyed, had swept all obstacles away. As for her Cousin Clotilda, she was secretly chuckling all the while at the wayward young lady's reckless incurring of responsibilities towards Sapps Court.

CHAPTER XXX

THE LETTER GWEN WROTE TO MR. TORRENS, TO TELL OF IT. MATILDA, WHO PLAYED SCALES, BUT NOT "THE HARMONIOUS BLACKSMITH." THE OLD LADY'S JEALOUSY OF GRANNY MARROWBONE, AND DAVE'S FIDELITY TO BOTH. HOW BEHEMOTH HICCUPPED, AND DAVE WENT TO SEE WHAT WAS BROKEN. THE EARTHQUAKE AT PISA. IT WAS OWING TO THE REPAIRS. HOW PETER JACKSON APPEARED BY MAGIC. HOW MR. BARTLETT SHORED NO. 7 UP TEMPORY, AND THE TENANTS HAD TO MAKE THE BEST OF WHAT WAS LEFT OF IT. UNCLE MO'S ENFORCED BACHELOR LIFE

IF love-letters were not so full of their writers' mutual satisfaction with their position, what a resource amatory correspondence would be to history!

In the letters to her lover with which Gwen at this time filled every available minute, the amatory passages were kept in check by the hard condition that they had to be read aloud to their blind recipient. So much so that the account which she wrote to him of her visit to Sapps Court will be very little the shorter for their complete omission.

It begins with a suggestion of suppressed dithyrambics, the suppression to be laid to the door of Irene. But with sympathy for her, too—for how can she help it? It then gets to business. She is going to tell "the thing"—spoken of thus for the first time— in her own way, and to take her own time about it. It is not even to be read fast, but in a leisurely way; and, above all, Irene is not to look on ahead to see what is coming; or, at least, if she does she is not to tell. Quite enough for the present that he should know that she, Gwen, has escaped without a scratch, though dusty. She addresses her lover, most unfairly, as "Mr. Impatience," in a portion of the letter that seems devised expressly to excite its reader's curiosity to the utmost. The fact is that this young beauty, with all her inherent stability and strength of character, was apt to be run away with by impish proclivities, that any good, serious schoolgirl would have been ashamed of. This letter offered her a rare opportunity for indulging them. Let it tell its own tale, even though we begin on the fifth page.

"I must pause now to see what sort of a bed Lutwyche has managed to arrange for me, and ring Maggie up if it isn't comfortable. Not but what I am ready to rough it a little, rather than that the old lady should be moved. She is the dearest old thing that ever was seen, with the loveliest silver hair, and must have been surpassingly beautiful, I should say. She keeps on reminding me of someone, and I can't tell who. It may be Daphne Palliser's grandmother-in-law, or it may be old Madame Edelweissenstein, who's a *chanoinesse*. But the nice old lady on the farm I told you of keeps mixing herself up in it—and really all old ladies are very much alike. By-the-by, I haven't explained her yet. Don't be in such a hurry! . . . There now!—my bed's all right, and I needn't fidget. Clo says so. The old lady is asleep with a stayed pulse, says Dr. Dalrymple, who has just gone. And anything more beautiful than that silver hair in the moonlight I never saw. Now I really must begin at the beginning.

" Clo and I started on our pilgrimage to Sapps Court at half-past three, without the barest suspicion of anything pending, least of all what I'm going to tell. Go on. We left Mr. Percival Pellew on the doorstep, pretending he was going to leave a book for Aunt Constance, and go away. Such fun! He went upstairs and stopped two hours, and I do believe they've got to some sort of decorous trothplight. Only A. C. when accused, only says he has shown unmistakable evidence of something or other, I forget what. Why on earth need people be such fools? There they both *are,* and what more *can* they want? She admits, however, that there is 'no engagement'! When anybody says *that,* it means they've been kissing. You ask Irene if it doesn't. Any female, I mean. Now go on.

"A more secluded little corner of the world than Sapps Court I never saw! Clo's barouche shot us out at the head of the street it turns out of, and went to leave a letter at St. John's Wood and be back in half an hour. We had no idea of a visitation, then. Besides, Clo had to be at Down Street at half-past five. There is an arch you go in by, and we nearly stuck and could go neither way. I was sorry to find the houses looked so respectable, but Clo tells me she can take me to some much better ones near Drury Lane. Dave, the boy, and his Uncle and Aunt, and a little sister, Dolly, whom I nearly ate, live in the last house down the Court. When we arrived Dolly was watering a sunflower, almost religiously, in the front-garden eight feet deep. It would die vethy thoon, she said, if neglected. She told us a long screed, about Heaven knows what—I think it related to the sunflower, which a naughty boy had chopped froo wiv a knife, and Dave had tighted on, successfully.

"The old prizefighter is just like Dr. Johnson, and I thought he was going to hug Clo, he was so delighted to see her, and so affectionate. So was Aunt Maria, a good woman who has lost her looks, but who must have had some, twenty years ago. I got Dolly on my knee, and *we* did the hugging, Dolly telling me secrets deliciously, and tickling. She is four next birthday, a fact which Aunt Maria thought should have produced a sort of what the *Maestro* calls *precisione.* I preferred Dolly as she was, and we exchanged locks of hair.

"We had only been there a very short time when Uncle Moses suggested that Dave should fetch a letter he was writing, from 'Old Mrs. Prichard's Room' upstairs, and Dave—who is a dear little chap of six or seven or eight—rushed upstairs to get it. I forgot how much I told you about the family, but I know I said something in yesterday's letter. Anyhow, 'old Mrs. Prichard' was not new to me, and I was very curious to see her. So when more than five minutes had passed and no Dave reappeared, I proposed that Dolly and I should go up to look for him, and we went, Aunt Maria following in our wake, to cover contingencies. She went back, after introducing me to the very sweet old lady in a high-backed chair, who comes in as the explanation of the beginning of this illegible scrawl. How funny children are! I do believe Uncle Moses was right when he said that Dave, if anything, preferred his loves to be 'a bit elderly.' I am sure these babies see straight through wrinkles and decay and toothless gums to the burning soul the old shell imprisons, and love it. Do you recollect that picture in the Louvre we both had seen, and thought the same about?—the old man with the sweet face and the appalling excrescence on the nose, and the little boy's unflinching love as he looks up at him. Oh, that nose!!! However, there is nothing of that in old Mrs. Picture, as Dave called her, according to her own spelling. *Her* face is simply perfect. . . . There!—I went in to look at it again by the moonlight, and I was quite right. And as for her wonderful old white hair! . . . I could write for ever about her.

"I think our incursion must have frightened the old soul, because she had lived up there by herself, except for her woman-friend who is out all day, and Aunt Maria and the children now and then, since she came to the house; so that a perfect stranger rushing in lawlessly—well, can't you fancy? However, she really stood it very well, considering.

"'I have heard of you, ma'am, from Dave. He's told me all about your rings. Where is the boy? . . . Haven't you, Dave—told me all about the lady's rings?'

"Dave came from some absorbing interest at the window, to say:—'It wasn't her,' with a sweet, impressive candour. He went back immediately. Something was going on outside. I explained, as I was sharp enough to guess, that my mother was the lady with the rings. I got into conversation with the old lady, and we soon became friends. She was very curious about 'old Mrs. Marrable' in the country. Indeed, I believe Uncle Mo was not far wrong when he said she was as jealous as any schoolgirl. It is most amusing, the idea of these two octogenarians falling out over this small bone of contention!

"While we talked, Dave and Dolly looked out of the window, Dave constantly supplying bulletins of the something that was going on without. I could not make it out at first, and his interjections of 'Now she's took it off'—'Now she's put it on again'—made me think he was inspecting some lady who was 'trying on' in the opposite house. It appeared, however, that the thing that was taken off and put on was not a dress, but some sort of plaister or liniment applied to the face of a boy, the miscreant who had made a raid on Dave's garden that morning, and spoiled his sunflower (see *ante*). It was because Dave had become so engrossed in this that he had not come downstairs again with his letter.

"The old lady, I am happy to say, was most amiable, and took to me immensely. I couldn't undertake to say now exactly how we got on such good terms so quickly. We agreed about the wickedness of that boy, especially when Dave reported ingratitude on his part towards the sister, who was tending him, whom he smacked and whose hair he pulled. To think of his smacking that dear girl that played the piano so nicely all day! And pulling her backtails so she called out when she was actually succouring his lacerated face. I gathered that her name may have been Matilda, and that she wore plaits.

"'I think her such a nice, dear girl,' said old Mrs. Picture— I like that name for her—'because she plays the piano all day long, and I sit here and listen, and think of old times.' I asked a question. 'Why, no, my dear!—I can't say she knows any tunes. But she plays her scales all day, very nicely, and makes me think of when my sister and I played scales—oh, so many years ago! But we played tunes too. I sometimes think I could teach her " The Harmonious Blacksmith," if only we was a bit nearer.' I could see in her old face that she was back in the Past, listening to a memory. How I wished I had a piano to play 'The Harmonious Blacksmith' for her again!

"I got her somehow to talk of herself and her antecedents, but rather stingily. She married young and went abroad, but she seemed not to want to talk about this. I could not press her. She had come back home—from wherever she was—many years after her husband's death, with an only son, the survivor of a family of four children. He was a man, not a boy; at least, he married a year or so after. She 'could not say that he was dead.' Otherwise, she knew of no living relative. Her means of livelihood was an annuity 'bought by my poor son before . . .'—before something she either forgot to tell, or fought shy of—the last, I think. 'I'm very happy up here,' she said. 'Only I might not be, if I was one of those that wanted gaiety. Mrs. Burr she lives with me, and it costs her no rent, and she sees to me. And my children —I call 'em mine—come for company, 'most every day. Don't you, Dave?'

"Dave tore himself away from the pleasing spectacle of his enemy in hospital, and came to confirm this. 'Yorce!' said he, with emphasis. 'Me and Dolly!' He recited rapidly all the days of the week, an appointment being imputed to each. But he weakened the force of his rhetoric by adding:—'Only not some of 'em always!' Mrs. Picture then said:—'But you love your old granny in the country better than you do me, don't you, Davy dear?' Whereupon Dave shouted with all his voice:—'I *doesn't!*' and flushed quite red, indignantly.

"The old lady then said, most unfairly:—'Then which do you love best, dear child? Because you must love *one* best, you know!' I thought Dave's answer ingenious:—'I loves whichever it *is,* best.' If only all young men were as candid about their loves, wouldn't they say the same?

"Dolly had picked up the recitation of the days of the week for her own private use, and was repeating it *ad libitum* in a melodious undertone, always becoming louder on Flyday, Tackyday, Tunday. She was hanging over the window-sill watching the surgical case opposite. How glad I am now when I recollect my impulse to catch the little maid and keep her on my knee! Dolly's good Angel prompted this, and had a hand in my inspiration to tell the story of Cinderella, with occasional refrains of song which I do believe old Mrs. Picture enjoyed as much as the two smalls. I shudder as I think what it would have been if they had still been at the window when IT came—the thing I have been so long postponing.

"It came without any warning that it would have been possible to act upon. We might certainly have shouted to those below to stand clear, *if we had ourselves understood.* But how *could* we? You can have no idea how bewildering it was.

"When something you can't explain portends Heavens-know-what, what on earth can you do? Pretend it's ghosts, and very curious and interesting? I think I might have done so this time, when an alarming noise set all our nerves on the jar. It was not a noise capable of description—something like Behemoth hiccuping goes nearest. Only I didn't want to frighten the babies, so I said nothing about the ghosts. Dolly said it wasn't her—an obvious truth. Old Mrs. Picture, said it must have been her chair—an obvious fallacy. She then deserted her theory and suggested that Dave should 'go down and see if anything was broken,' which Dave immediately started to do, much excited.

"I felt very uncomfortable and creepy, for it recalled the shock of earthquake Papa and I were in at Pisa two years ago—it is a feeling one never gets over, that *terremotitis,* as Papa called it. I believe I was more alarmed than Dolly, and as for Dave, I am sure that so far he thought the whole thing the best fun imaginable. Picture to yourself, as he slams the door behind him and shouts his message to the world below, that I remain seated facing the light, while Dolly on my knee listens to a postscript of Cinderella. My eyes are fixed on the beauty of the old side-face I see against the light. Get this image clear, and then I will tell you what followed.

"Even as I sat looking at the old lady, that noise came again, and plaster came tumbling down from the ceiling, obscuring the window behind. As I fixed my eyes upon it, falling, I saw beyond it what really made me think at first that I was taking leave of my senses. The houses opposite seemed to shoot straight up into the air, as though they were reflections in a mirror which had fallen forward. An instant after, I saw what had happened. It was the window that was moving, not the houses.

"It was so odd! I had time to see all this and change my mind, before the great crash came to explain what had happened. For until the roar of a cataract of disintegrated brickwork, followed by a cloud of choking dust, showed that the wall of the room had fallen outwards, leaving the world clear cut and visible under a glorious afternoon sky until that dust-cloud came and veiled it, I could not have said what the thing was, or why. There seemed to be time—good solid time!—between the sudden day-blaze and the crash below, and I took advantage of it to wonder what on earth was happening.

"Then I knew it all in an instant, and saw in another instant that the ceiling was sagging down; for aught I knew, under the weight of a falling roof.

"Old Mrs. Picture was not frightened at all. 'You get this little Dolly safe, my dear,' said she to me. 'I can get myself as far as the landing. But don't you fret about me. I'm near my time.' She seemed quite alive to the fact that the house was falling, but at eighty, what did that matter? She added quite quietly:—'It's owing to the repairs.' Dolly suddenly began to weep, panic-struck.

"I saw that Mrs. Picture could not rise from her chair, though she tried. But what could I do? Any attempt of mine to pick her up and carry her would only have led to delay. I saw it would be quicker to get help, and ran for it, overtaking Dave on the stairs.

"Below was chaos. The kitchen where I had left my cousin talking with Uncle Mo and Aunt Maria was all but darkened, and the place was a cloud of dust. I could see that Uncle Mo was wrenching open the street-door, which seemed to have stuck, and then that it opened, letting in an avalanche of rubbish, and some light. Cries came from outside, and Aunt Maria called out that it was Mrs. Burr. Thereon Uncle Mo, crying 'Stand clear, all!' began flinging the rubbish back into the room with marvellous alacrity for a man of his years, and no consideration at all for glass or crockery. I felt sick, you may fancy, when it came home to me that someone was crying aloud with pain, buried under that heap of fallen brickwork.

" But we could be of no use yet a while, so I told Clo and Aunt Maria to come upstairs and help to get the old lady down. They did as they were bid, being, in fact, terrified out of their wits, and quite unable to make suggestions. A male voice came from within the room where I had just left Mrs. Picture by herself. I took it quite as a matter of course.

" 'You keep out on that landing, some of you, till I tell you to come in. This here floor won't carry more than my weight.' This was what I heard a man say, speaking from where the window had been, mysteriously. I was aware that he had stepped from some ladder on to the floor of the room, jumping on it recklessly as though to test its bearing power. Then that he had gathered up my old new acquaintance in a bundle, carefully made in a few seconds, and had said:—' Come along down!' to all whom it might concern. He shepherded us, all three women and the two children, into a back-bedroom below, and went away, leaving his bundle on the bed; saying, after glancing round at the cornice:—' You'll be safe enough here for a bit, just till we can see our way.' He had a peculiar hat or cap, and I saw that he was a fireman. I did not know that firemen held any intercourse with human creatures. It appears that they do occasionally, under reserves.

" Then it was that I became alarmed about my old lady. Her face had lost what colour it had, and her finger-tips had become blue and lifeless. But she spoke, faintly enough, although quite clearly, always urging us to go to a safer place, and leave her to her luck. This was, of course, nonsense. Nor was there any safer place to go to, so far as I understood the position. Aunt Maria went down to find brandy, if possible, in the heart of the confusion below. She found half a wineglassful somewhere, and brought back with it a report of progress. They had to be cautious in removing the rubbish, so that no worse should come to the sufferer it had half buried. We kept it from the old lady that this was her fellow-lodger, Mrs. Burr, and made her take some brandy, whether she liked it or no. I then went down to see for myself, and Clo came too.

" The police had taken prompt possession of the Court, and only a limited force of volunteers were allowed to share in the removal of the rubbish. Uncle Mo and the fireman, who seemed to be a personal friend, were attacking the ruin from within, throwing the loose bricks back into the kitchen, and working for the dear life.

"As we came in they halted, in obedience to, 'Easy a minute, you inside there. Gently does it,' from the spontaneous leading mind, whoever he was, without. Uncle Mo, streaming with perspiration, and forgetful of social niceties, turned to me saying:— 'You go back, my dear, you go back! 'Tain't for you to see. You go back!' I replied:—'Nonsense, Mr. Wardle! What do you take me for?' For had I not stood beside *you,* my darling, when you lay dead in the Park?

"I could see what had taken place. The woman had been just about to knock at the door when the wall fell from above. Nothing had struck her direct, else she would almost surely have been killed. The ruin had fallen far enough from the house to avoid this, but the recoil of its disintegration (I'm so proud of that expression) had jammed her against the wall and choked the door. . . . I'm so sleepy I can't write another word."

No doubt the sequel described how Mrs. Burr, rescued alive, but insensible, was borne away on a stretcher to the Hospital, and how the party were released from the house, whose complete collapse must have presented itself to their excited imaginations as more than a possibility. No doubt also obscure points were made plain; as, for instance, the one which is prominent in the short newspaper report, which runs as follows:—"A singular fall of brickwork, the consequences of which might easily have proved fatal, occurred on Thursday last at Sapps Court, Marylebone, when the greater part of the front-wall of No. 7 fell forward into the street, blocking the main entrance and causing for a time the greatest alarm to the inhabitants, who, however, were all ultimately rescued uninjured. A remarkable circumstance was that the cloud of dust raised by the shower of loose brickwork was taken for smoke and was sufficient to cause an alarm of fire; as a matter of fact, two engines had arrived before the circumstances were explained. The mistake was not altogether unfortunate, as an escape ladder which was passing at the time was of use in reaching the upper floors, whose tenants were at one time in considerable danger. A sempstress, Mrs. Susan Burr, living upstairs, was returning home at the moment of the calamity, and was severely injured by the falling brickwork, but no serious result is anticipated. A costermonger of the name of Rackstraw also received some severe contusions, but if we may trust the report of his son, an intelligent lad of thirteen, he is very little the worse by his misadventure."

Although "no serious result was anticipated" in Mrs. Burr's case—in the newspaper sense of the words, which referred to the Coroner—the results were serious enough to Mrs. Burr. She was disabled from work indefinitely, and was too much damaged to hope to leave the Hospital, for weeks at any rate. A relative was found, ready to take charge of her when that time should arrive, but apparently not ready to disclose her own name. For, so far as can be ascertained, she was never spoken of at Sapps Court otherwise than as " Mrs. Burr's married niece."

Mr. Bartlett was on the spot, within an hour, taking measures for the immediate safety of the inmates, and his own ultimate pecuniary advantage. He pointed out it was quite unnecessary for anyone to turn out of the rooms below, although he admitted that the open air had got through the top story. His immediate resources were quite equal to a temporary arrangement practicable in a couple of hours or so. A contrivance of inconceivable slightness, involving no drawbacks whatever to families occupying the premises it was engendered in, was necessary to hold the roof up up tempory, for fear it should come with a run. It was really a'most nothing in the manner of speaking. You just shoved a len'th of quartering into each room, all down the house to the bottom, with a short scaffold-board top and bottom to distribute out the weight, and tapped 'em across with a 'ammer, and there you were! The top one ketched the roof coming down, and you had no need to be apprehensive, because it would take a tidy weight—double what Mr. Bartlett was going to put upon it.

This was a security against a complete collapse of the roof and upper floor, but if it come on heavy rain, what would keep Aunt M'riar's room dry? She and Dolly could not sleep in a puddle. Mr. Bartlett, however, pledged himself to make all that good with a few yards of tarpauling, and Aunt M'riar and Dolly went to bed, with sore misgivings as to whether they would wake alive next day. Dolly woke in the night and screamed with terror at what she conceived was a spectre from the grave, but which was really nothing but a short length of scaffold-pole standing upright at the foot of her bed.

This was bad enough, but it further appeared next day that a new floor would be de rigueur overhead in Mrs. Prichard's room.

Not only were sundry timber balks shoved up against the house outside so they couldn't constitoot a hindrance to anyone—so Mr. Bartlett said when he giv' in a price for the job—but the street-door wouldn't above half shet to, and all the windows had to be seen to. Add to this afflictions from tarpaulings that would keep you bone-dry even if there come a thunderstorm—or perhaps, properly speaking, that would have done so only they were just a trifle wore at critical points—and smells of damp plaster that quite took away the relish from your food, and you will form some idea what remaining in the house during the repairs meant to Uncle Mo and his belongings.

Not that Dolly and Dave took their sufferings to heart much. The novelties of the position went far to compensate them for its drawbacks. One supreme grief there was for them, certainly. The avalanche of brickwork had destroyed, utterly and irrevocably, that cherished sunflower. They had clung to a lingering hope that, as soon as the claims of humanity had been discharged by the rescue of the victims of the catastrophe, the attention of the rescuers would be directed to carefully removing the *débris* from above their buried treasure. They were shocked at the callous indifference shown to its fate. It was an early revelation of the heartlessness of mankind. Nevertheless, the shattered sunflower was recovered in the end, and Dolly took it to bed with her, and cried herself to sleep over it.

So it seemed impossible for Dave and Dolly, and their uncle and aunt, all to remain on in the half-wrecked house. But then —where had they to go to? It was clear that Dolly and her aunt would have to turn out, and the only resource seemed to be that they should go away for a while to her grandmother's, an old lady at Ealing, who existed, but went no further. She had never entered Sapps Court, but her daughters, Aunt M'riar and Dolly's mother, had paid her dutiful visits. There was no ill-feeling— none whatever! So to Ealing Aunt M'riar went, two or three days later, and Dave went too, although he was convinced Uncle Mo couldn't do without him.

The old boy himself remained in residence, being fed by The Rising Sun; which sounds like poetry, but relates to chops and sausages and a half-a-pint, a monotonous dietary on which he subsisted until his family returned a month later to a reinstated mansion. He lived a good deal at The Sun during this period, relying on the society of his host and his friend Jerry. His retrospective chats with the latter recorded his impressions of the event which had deprived him of his household, and left him a childless wanderer on the surface of Marylebone.

"Red-nosed Tommy," said he, referring to Mr. Bartlett, "he wouldn't have put in that bit of bressemer to ketch up those rotten joists over M'riar's room if I hadn't told him. We should just have had the floor come through and p'r'aps my little maid and M'riar squashed dead right off. You see, they would have took it all atop, and no mistake. Pore Susan got it bad enough, but it wasn't a dead squelch in her case. It come sideways." Uncle Mo emptied his pipe on the table, and thoughtfully made the ash do duty first for Mrs. Burr, and then for Aunt M'riar and Dolly, by means of a side-push and a top-squash with his finger. He looked at the last result sadly as he refilled his pipe—a hypothetically bereaved man. Dolly might have been as flat as that!

"How's Susan Burr getting on?" asked Mr. Alibone.

"That's according to how much money you're inclined to put on the doctors. Going by looks only—what M'riar says—she don't give the idea of coming to time. Only then, there's Sister Nora —Miss Grahame they call her now; very nice lady—she's on the doctor's side, and says Mrs. Burr means to pull round. Hope so!"

"How's Carrots—Carrots senior—young Radishes' dad?"

"Oh—him? He's all right. He ain't the sort to take to bein' doctored. He's getting about again."

"I thought a bit of wall came down on him."

"Came down bodily, he says. But it don't foller that it did, because he says so. Anyhow, he got a hard corner of his nut against it. He ain't delicate. He says he'll have it out of the landlord—action for damages—wilful neglect—'sorlt and battery— that kind o' thing!"

"Won't Mrs. Burr?"

"Couldn't say—don't know if a woman counts. But it don't matter. Sister Nora, she'll see to her. Goes to see her every day. She or the other one. I say, Jerry! . . ."

"What say, old Mo?"

"You haven't seen the other one."

"Oh, that's it, is it?" Mr. Jerry spoke perceptively, appreciatively. For Uncle Mo, by partly closing one eye, and slightly varying the expression of his lips, had contrived somehow to convey the idea that he was speaking of dazzling beauty, not by any means unadorned.

"I tell you this, Jerry, and you can believe me or not, as you like. If I was a young feller, I'd hang about Hy' Park all day long only to get a squint at her. My word!—there's nothing to

come anigh her—ever I saw! And there she was, a-kissing our
little Dolly, like e'er a one of us! "
" What do you make out her name to be? " said Mr. Jerry.
" Sister Nora called her *Gwen,*" replied Mo, speaking the name
mechanically but firmly. " But what the long for that may be,
I couldn't say. 'Tain't Gwenjamin, anyhow." He stopped to
light his pipe.
" It was this young ladyship that carried off old Prichard in
a two-horse carriage, I take it."
Uncle Mo nodded. " Round to Sister Nora's—in Cavendish
Square—with a black Statute stood upright—behind palin's.
M'riar she's been round to see the old lady there, being told to.
And seemin'ly this here young Countess "—Uncle Mo seemed to
object to using this word—" she's a-going to carry the old lady
off to the Towels, where she lives when she's at home. . . ."
" The Towels? Are you sure it isn't *Towers?* Much more
likely! "
Uncle Mo made a mental note about Jerry, that he was tainted
with John Bull's love of a lord. How could anything but a reverent study of Debrett have given such an insight into the names
of Nobs' houses? " It don't make any odds, that I can see! "
was his comment. The correction, however, resulted in an incumbrance to his speech, as he was only half prepared to concede
the point. He continued:—" She's a-going, as I understand from
M'riar, to pack off Mrs. Prichard to this here Towels, or Towers,
accordin' as we call it. And, as I make it out, she'll keep her
there till so be as Mr. Bartlett gets through the repairs. Or she'll
send her back to a lodgin'; or not, as may be. Either, or eye-ther."
Having thus, as it were, saturated his speech with freedom of
alternative, Uncle Mo dismissed the subject, in favour of Gwen's
beauty. " But—to look at her! " said he. The old man was quite
in love.
Mr. Jerry disturbed his contemplation of the image Gwen had
left him. " How long does Bartlett mean to be over the job? "
he asked.
" He means to complete in a month. If you trust his word. I
can't say I do."
" When *will* he complete, Mo? That's the question. What's
the answer? "
" The Lord alone knows." Uncle Mo shook his head solemnly.
But he recalled his words. " No—He don't! Even the Devil
don't know. I tell you this, Jerry—there never was a buildin'
job finished at any time spoke of aforehand. It's always *after*

any such a time. And if you jump on for to catch it up, it's *afterer.*"

" Best to hold one's tongue about it, eh? Anyway, the old lady's got a berth for a time. Rum story! She'd have been put to it if it hadn't been for the turn things took. When's she to go?"

" To these here Towels, or Towers, whichever you call 'em? M'riar didn't spot that. When she's took back, I suppose. When the young lady goes."

" What'll your young customer say to Mrs. Prichard being gone, when his aunt brings him back?"

Uncle Mo seemed to cogitate over this. He had not perhaps been fully alive to the disappointment in store for Dave when he came back and found no Mrs. Picture at Sapps Court. Poor little man! The old prizefighter's tender heart was touched on his boy's behalf. But after all there would be worse trials than this on the rough road of life for Dave. " He'll have to lump it, I expect, Jerry," said he. " Besides, Mrs. P., she'll come back as soon as the new plaster's dry. She's not going to stop at the Towels—Towers—whatever they are!—for a thousand years."

CHAPTER XXXI

HOW GWEN GOT AT MRS. PRICHARD'S HISTORY, OR SOME OF IT. ONE CRIME MORE OF HER SON'S. THE WALLS OF TROY, AND THOSE OF SAPPS COURT. AUNT M'RIAR'S VISIT OF INSPECTION. HOW SHE CALLED ON MRS. RAGSTROAR, WHO SENT HER SECRETIVE SON ROUND. HIS MESSAGE FROM MR. WIX. WHO WAS COMING TO SEE HIS MOTHER, UNLESS SHE WAS SOMEBODY ELSE. A MESSAGE TO MR. WIX, UNDERTAKEN BY MICHAEL. UNCLE MO'S JOY AT THE PROSPECT OF DAVE AND DOLLY

How very improbable the Actual would sometimes feel, were it not for our knowledge of the events which led up to it! Nothing could have been more improbable *per se* than that old Mrs. Prichard, upstairs at No. 7, down Sapps Court, should become the guest of the Earl and Countess of Ancester, at The Towers in Rocestershire. But a number of improbable antecedent events combined to make it possible, and once its possibility was established, it only needed one more good substantial improbability to make it actual. Gwen's individuality was more than

enough to supply this. But just think what a succession of coincidences and strange events had preceded the demand for it!
To our thinking the New Mud wanted for Dave's *barrage* was
responsible for the whole of it. But for that New Mud, Dave
would not have gone to the Hospital. But for the Hospital, he
would never have excited a tender passion in the breast of Sister
Nora; would never have visited Granny Marrowbone; would never
have been sought for by The Aristocracy at his residence in Sapps
Court. Some may say that at this point nothing else would have
occurred but for the collapse of Mr. Bartlett's brickwork, and that
therefore the rarity of sound bricks in that conglomerate was the
vera causa of the events that followed. But why not equally the
imperfection of old Stephen's aim at Achilles? If he had killed
Achilles, it is ten to one Gwen would have gone abroad with her
mother, instead of being spirited away to Cavendish Square by her
cousin in order that she should thereby become entangled in slums.
Or for that matter, why not the death of the Macganister More?
Had he been living still, Cousin Clo would never have visited
Ancester Towers at all.

No—no! Depend upon it, it was the New Mud. But then,
Predestination would have been dreadfully put out of temper
if, instead of imperious impulsive Gwen, ruling the roast and the
boiled, and the turbot with *mayonnaise,* and everything else for
that matter, some young woman who could be pulverised by a
reproof for Quixotism had been her understudy for the part, and
she herself had had mumps or bubonic plague at the time of the
accident. In that case Predestination would hardly have known
which way to turn, to get at some sort of compromise or accommodation that would square matters. For there can be no reasonable doubt that what did take place was quite in order, and
that—broadly speaking—everyone had signed his name over the
pencil marks, and filled in his witness's name and residence, in
the Book of Fate. If Gwen's understudy had been called on, there
would have been—to borrow a favourite expression of Uncle Mo's
—a pretty how-do-you-do, on the part of Predestination.

Fortunately no such thing occurred, and Predestination's powers of evasion were not put to the test. The Decrees of Fate were
fulfilled as usual, and History travelled on the line of least resistance, to the great gratification of The Thoughtful Observer. In
the case of lines of compliance with the will of Gwen, there was
no resistance at all. Is there ever any, when a spoiled young
beauty is ready to kiss the Arbiters of Destiny as a bribe, rather
than give way about a whim, reasonable or unreasonable?

And, after all, so many improbabilities having converged towards creating the situation, there was nothing so very unreasonable in Gwen's whim that old Mrs. Picture should go back with her to the Towers. It was only the natural solution of a difficulty in a conjunction of circumstances which could not have varied materially, unless Gwen and her cousin had devolved the charge of the old lady on some Institution—say the Workhouse Infirmary —or a neighbour, or had forsaken her altogether. They preferred carrying her off, as the story has seen, in a semi-insensible state from the shock, to their haven in Cavendish Square. Next day an arrangement was made which restored to Gwen—who had slept on a sofa, when she was not writing the letter quoted in the foregoing text—the couch she had insisted on dedicating to " Old Mrs. Picture," as she continued to call her.

It was very singular that Gwen, who had seen the old twin sister—as *we* know her to have been—should have fallen so in love with the one whose acquaintance she last made. The story can only accept the fact that it was so, without speculating on its possible connection with the growth of a something that is not the body. It may appear—or may not—to many, that, in old Maisie's life, a warp of supreme love, shuttle-struck by a weft of supreme pain, had clothed her soul, as it were, in a garment unlike her sister's; a garment some eyes might have the gift of seeing, to which others might be blind. Old Granny Marrable had had her share of trouble, no doubt; but Fate had shown her fair play. Just simple everyday Death!—maternity troubles lived through in shelter; nursing galore, certainly—who escapes it? Of purse troubles, debts and sordid plagues, a certain measure no doubt, for who escapes *them?* But to that life of hers the scorching fires that had worked so hard to slay her sister's heart, and failed so signally, had never penetrated. Indeed, the only really acute grief of her placid life had been the supposed death of this very sister, now so near her, unknown. Still, Gwen might, of course, have taken just as strongly to Granny Marrable if some slight chance of their introduction had happened otherwise.

The old lady remained at Cavendish Square three weeks, living chiefly in an extra little room, which had been roughly equipped for service, to cover the contingency. As Miss Lutwyche seemed to fight shy of the task, Maggie, the Scotch servant, took her in hand, grooming her carefully and exhibiting her as a sort of sweet old curiosity picked up out of a dustheap, and now become the possession of a Museum. Aunt Constance, who kept an eye of culture on Maggie's dialect, reported that she had said of the old lady, that she was a "douce auld luckie": and that she stood in need of no "bonny-wawlies and whigmaleeries," which, Miss Grahame said, meant that she had no need of artificial decoration. She was very happy by herself, reading any easy book with big enough print. And though she was probably not so long without the society of grown people as she had often been at Sapps Court, she certainly missed Dave and Dolly. But she seemed pleased and gratified on being told that Dave was not gone, and was at present not going, anywhere near old Mrs. Marrable in the country.

The young lady broached her little scheme to her venerable friend, or *protégée,* as soon as it became clear that a return to the desolation to which Mr. Bartlett had converted Sapps Court might be a serious detriment to her health. Mr. Bartlett himself admitted the facts, but disputed the inferences to be drawn from them. Yes—there was, and there would be, a trifle of myesture hanging round; nothing in itself, but what you might call traces of ewaporation. You saw similar phenomena in sinks, and at the back of cesterns. But you never come across anyone the worse for 'em. He himself benefited by a hatmosphere, as parties called it nowadays, such as warn't uncommon in basements of unoccupied premises, and in morasses. But you were unable to account for other people's constitutions not being identical in all respects with your own. Providence was inscrutable, and you had to look at the symptoms. These were the only guides vouchsafed to us. He would, however, wager that as soon as the paperhanger was out of the house and the plaster giv' a chance to 'arden, all the advantages of a bone-dry residence would be enjoyed by an incoming tenant.

Portions of this opinion leaked out during a visit of Aunt M'riar to Mrs. Prichard, at Cavendish Square, she having come from Ealing by the 'bus to overhaul the position with Uncle Mo, and settle whether she and Dave and Dolly could return next week with safety. They had decided in the negative, and Mr. Bartlett had said it was open to them to soote themselves. Uncle Mo's sleeping-room had, of course, been spared by the accident, so he only suffered from a clammy and depressing flavour that wouldn't hang about above a day or two. At least, Mr. Bartlett said so.

Gwen treated the idea that Mrs. Prichard should so much as talk about returning to her quarters, with absolute derision. "I'm going to keep you here and see you properly looked after, Mrs. Picture, till I go to the Towers. And then I shall just take you with me." For she had installed the name Picture as the

old lady's working designation with such decision that everyone
else accepted it, though one or two used it in inverted commas.
" I always have my own way," she added with a full, rich laugh
that Lord William Bentinck might have heard on his black ped-
estal in the Square below.

Aunt M'riar departed, not to be too late for her 'bus, and Gwen
stayed for a chat. She often spent half an hour with the old lady,
trying sometimes to get at more of her past history, always feeling that she was met by reticence, never liking to press roughly
for information.

The two thin old palms that had once been a beautiful young
girl's closed on the hand that was even now scarcely in its fullest
glory of life, as its owner's eyes looked down into the old eyes that
had never lost their sweetness. The old voice spoke first. " Why
—oh why," it said, " are you so kind to me? My dear! "

" Is it strange that I should be kind to you? " said Gwen, speaking somewhat to herself. Then louder, as though she had been
betrayed into a claim to benevolence, and was ashamed:—" The
kindness comes to very little, when all's said and done. Besides,
you can . . ." She paused a moment, taking in the pause a seat
beside the arm-chair, without loosing the hand she held; then made
her speech complete:—" Besides, you can pay it all back, you
know! "

" I pay! How can I pay it back? "

" You can. I'm quite in earnest. You can pay me back every-
thing I can do for you—everything and more—by telling me. . . .
Now, you mustn't be put out, you know, if I tell you what it is."
Gwen was rather frightened at her own temerity.

" My dear—just fancy! Why should I want you not to know—
anything I can tell, if I can remember it to tell you? What is
it? "

" How you come to be living in Sapps Court. And why you are
so poor. Because you are poor."

" No, I have a pound a week still. I have been better off—yes!
I have been well off."

" But how came you to live in Sapps Court? "

" How came I? . . . Let me see! . . . I came there from Skillicks, at Sevenoaks, where I was last. Six shillings was too much
for me alone. It is only seven-and-sixpence at Sapps for both
of us. It was through poor Susan Burr that I came there. To
think of her in the Hospital! "

" She's going on very nicely to-day. I went to see her with my
cousin. Go on. It was through her? . . ."

"Through her I came to Sapps. She wanted to be in town for her work, and found Sapps. She had no furniture, or just a bed. And I had been able to keep mine. Then, you see, I wanted a helping hand now and again, and she had her sight, and could make shift to keep order in the place. I had every comfort, be sure!" This was spoken with roused emphasis, as though to dissipate uneasiness about herself.

"I saw you had some nice furniture," said Gwen. "I was on the look out for your desk, where Dave's letters were written."

"Yes, it's mahogany. I was frightened about it, for fear it should be scratched. But Davy's Aunt Maria was saying Mr. Bartlett's men had been very civil and careful, and all the furniture was safe in the bedroom at the back, and the door locked."

"But where did the furniture come from?"

"From the house."

"The house where you lived with your husband?"

The old woman started. "Oh no! Oh no—no! All that was long—long ago." She shrank from disinterring all but the most recent past.

But it was the deeper stratum of oblivion that had to be reached, without dynamite if possible. "I see," Gwen said. "Your own house after his death?"

Memory was restive, evidently—rather resented the inquiry. Still, a false inference could not be left uncorrected. "Neither my husband's nor mine," was the answer. "It was my son's house, after my husband's death." Its tone meant plainly:—"I tell you this, for truth's sake. But, please, no more questions!"

Gwen's idea honestly was to drop the curtain, and her half-dozen words were meant for the merest epilogue. When she said:— "And he is dead, too?" she only wanted to round off the conversation. She was shocked when the two delicate old hands hers lay between closed upon it almost convulsively, and could hardly believe she heard rightly the articulate sob, rather than speech, that came from the old lady's lips.

"Oh, I hope so—I hope so!"

"Dear Mrs. Picture, you hope so?" For Gwen could not reconcile this with the ideal she had formed of the speaker. At least, she could not be happy now without an explanation.

Then she saw that it would come, given time and a sympathetic listener. "Yes, my dear, I hope so. For what is his life to him—my son—if he is alive? The best I can think of for him, is that he is long dead."

"Was he mad or bad?"

"Both, I hope. Perhaps only mad. Then he would be neither bad nor good. But he was lost for me, and we were well apart: before he was "—she hesitated—" sent away. . . ."

" Sent away! Yes—where? "

" I ought not to tell you this . . . but will you promise me? . . ."

" To tell no one? Yes—I promise."

" I know you will keep your promise." The old lady kept on looking into the beautiful eyes fixed on hers, still caressing the hand she held, and said, after a few moments' silence :—" He was sent to penal servitude, not under his own name. They said his name was . . . some short name . . . at the trial. That was at Bristol." Then, after another pause, as though she had read Gwen's thoughts in her scared, speechless face :—" It was all right. He deserved his sentence."

" Oh, I am so glad! " Gwen was quite relieved. " I was afraid he was innocent. I thought he could not be guilty, because of you. But was he really wicked—*bad,* I mean—as well as legally guilty? "

" I like to hope that he was mad. The offence that sent him to Norfolk Island was scarcely a wicked one. It was only burglary, and it was a Bank." The old face looked forgiving over this, but set itself in lines of fixed anger as she added :—" It was not like the thing that parted us."

" You wish not to tell me that? "

" My dear, it is not a thing for you to hear." The gentleness of the speaker averted the storm of indignation and contempt which similar expressions of the correctitudes had more than once excited in this rebellious young lady.

But Gwen felt at liberty to laugh a little at them, or could not resist the temptation to do so. " Oh dear! " she cried. ' " Am I a new-born baby, to be kept packed in cotton-wool, and not allowed to hear this and hear that? Do, dear Mrs. Picture—you don't mind my calling you by Dave's name?—do tell me what it was that parted you and your son. *I* shall understand you. I'm not Mary that had a little lamb."

" Well, my dear, when I was about your age, before I was married, I'm not at all sure that *I* should have understood. Perhaps that is really the reason why I took the girl's part. . . ."

" Why you took the girl's part? " said Gwen, who had *not* understood, so far, and was puzzled at the expression.

" Yes. I believed her story. They tried to throw the blame on her; he did, himself. My dear, it was his cowardice and treachery that made me hate him. You are shocked at that? "

"No—at least, I mean, I don't believe you meant it."
"I meant it at the time, my dear. And I counted him as dead,
and tried to forget him. But it is hard for a mother to forget
her son."
"I should have thought so." Gwen was not quite happy about
old Mrs. Picture's inner soul. How about a possible cruel corner
in it?
The old lady seemed to suspect this question's existence, unex-
pressed. Apology in her voice hinted at need of forgiveness—
pleaded against condemnation. "But," she said, after a faltered
word or two, short of speech, "you do not know, my dear, how
bad a man can be. How should you?"
Perhaps the tone of her voice threw a light on some obscurity
accepted ambiguities had left. For Gwen said, rather suddenly:
"You need not tell me any more. You have told me plenty and
I understand it." And so she did, for working purposes, though
perhaps some latitudes in the sea of this Ralph Daverill's iniquities were by her unexplored and unexplorable.
This particular atrocity of his has no interest for the story, beyond the fact that it was the one that led to his separation from
his mother, and that it accounts for the very slight knowledge that
she seems to have had of the details of his conviction and deportation. It must have happened between his desertion of his lawful wife, Dave's Aunt M'riar, and his ill-advised attempt at
burglary. Whether his offence against "the girl" whose part his
mother took was made the subject of a criminal indictment is
not certain, but if it was he must have escaped with a slight pun-
ishment, to be able to give his attention to the strong room of
that Bank so soon after. Those who are inclined to think that his
mother was unforgiving towards her own son, to the extent of
vindictiveness, may find an excuse for her in a surmise which some
facts connected with the case made plausible, that he adduced
some childish levities on this girl's part as a warrant for his
atrocious behaviour towards her, and so escaped legal penalty.
Those who know with what alacrity male jurymen will accept
evasions of this sort, will admit that this is at least possible.
This is conjecture, by the way, as Gwen asked to know no more
of the incident, seeming to shrink from further knowledge of it
in fact. She allowed it to pass out of the conversation, retaining
the pleasant and wholesome attempt to redistribute the Bank's
property as at least fit for discussion, and even pardonable—an
act due to a mistaken economic theory—redistribution of prop-

erty by a free lance, not wearing the uniform of a School of Political Thought.

"But how long was his term of service?" she asked, coming back into the fresher air of mere housebreaking.

"I am afraid it was for fourteen years. But I have never known. I can hardly believe it now, but I know it is true for all that, that he was convicted and transported without the trial coming to my ears at the time. I only knew that he had disappeared, and thought it was by his own choice. And what means had I of finding him, if I had wanted to? *That* I never did."

"Because of . . . because of the girl?"

"Because of the girl Emma. . . . Oh yes! I was his mother, but . . ." She stopped short. Her meaning was clear; some sons would cripple the strongest mother's love.

"Then you had to give up the house," said Gwen, to help her away from the memory that stung her, vividly.

"I gave it up and sold the furniture, all but one or two bits I kept by me—Dave Wardle's desk, and the arm-chair. I went to a lodging at Sidcup—a pretty place with honeysuckles round my window. I lived there a many years, and had friends. Then the railway came, and they pulled the cottage down—Mrs. Hutchinson's. And all the folk I knew were driven away—went to America, many of them; all the Hutchinsons went. I remember that time well. But oh dear—the many moves I had after that! I cannot tell them all one from another. . . ."

"It tires you to talk. Never mind now. Tell me another time."

"No—I'm not tired. I can talk. Where was I? Oh—the lodgings! I moved many times—the last time to Sapps Court, not so very long ago. I made friends with Mrs. Burr at Skillicks, as I told you."

"And that is what made you so poor?"

"Yes. I have only a few hundred pounds of my own, an annuity —it comes to sixty pounds a year. I have learned how to make it quite enough for me." Nevertheless, thought Gwen to herself, the good living in her temporary home in Cavendish Square had begun to tell favourably. Enough is seldom as good as a feast on sixty pounds a year. The old lady seemed, however, to dismiss the subject, going on with something antecedent to it:—"You see now, my dear, why I said 'I hope.' What could the unhappy boy be to me, or I to him? But I shall never know where he died, nor when."

Gwen tried to get at more about her past; but, at some point antecedent to this parting from her son, she seemed to become

more reserved, or possibly she had overtasked her strength by
so much talk. Gwen noticed that, in all she had told her, she had
not mentioned a single name of a person. Some slight reference
to Australia, which she had hoped would lead naturally to more
disclosure, seemed rather, on second thoughts, to furnish a landmark or limit, with the inscription: " Thus far and no farther."
You—whoever you are, reading this—may wonder why Gwen, who
had so lately heard of Australia, and Mrs. Marrable's sister who
went there over half-a-century ago, did not forthwith put two and
two together, and speculate towards discovery of the truth. It may
be strange to you to be told that she *was* reminded of old Mrs.
Marrable's utterance of the word " Australia " when old Mrs.
Prichard spoke it, and simply let the recollection drop idly, *because*
it was so unlikely the two two's would add up. To be sure, she
had quite forgotten, at the moment, *what* the old Granny at Chorlton had said about the Antipodes. It is only in books that people
remember all through, quite to the end.

Bear this in mind, that this sisterhood of Maisie and Phœbe
was entrenched in its own improbability, and that one antecedent
belief of another mind at least would have been needed to establish
it. A hint, a suggestion, might have capitalised a dozen claims
to having said so all along. But all was primeval silence. There
was not a murmur in Space to connect the two.

Mr. Bartlett, the builder, after inspecting the collapse of the
wall, lost no time in drawing up a contract to reinstate same
and make good roof, replacing all defective work with new where
necessary; only in his haste to come to his impressive climax—
" the work to be done to the satisfaction of yourself or your Surveyor for the sum of £99 . 8 . 4 (ninety-nine pounds eight shillings
and fourpence),"—he spelt this last word *nesseracy*. He called on
the landlord, the gentleman of independent means at Brixton,
with this document in his pocket and a strong conviction of his
own honesty in his face, and pointed out that what he said all
along had come to pass. As his position had been that unless
the house was rebuilt—by him—at great expense, it was pretty
sure to come tumbling down, as these here old houses mostly did,
it was difficult for the gentleman of independent means to gain-
say him, especially as the latter's wife became a convert to Mr.
Bartlett on the spot. It was his responsible and practical manner
that did it. She directed her husband—a feeble sample of the
manhood of Brixton—not to set up his judgment against that of
professional experience, but to affix his signature forthwith to the

document made and provided. He said weakly:—"I suppose I must." The lady said:—"Oh dear, no!—he must do as he liked." He naturally surrendered at discretion, and an almost holy expression of contentment stole over Mr. Bartlett's countenance, superseding his complexion, which otherwise was apt to remain on the memory after its outlines were forgotten.

To return once more to the drying of the premises after their reconstruction. The accepted view seemed to be that as soon as Mr. Bartlett and his abettors cleared out and died away, the walls would begin to dry, and would make up for lost time. Everyone seemed inclined to palliate this backwardness in the walls, and to feel that they, themselves, had they been in a like position, could not have done much drying—with all them workmen in and out all day; just think!

But now a new era had dawned, and what with letting the air through, and setting alight to a bit of fire now and again, and the season keeping mild and favourable, with only light frostis in the early morning—only what could you expect just on to Christmas? —there seemed grounds for the confidence that these walls would do themselves credit, and yield up their chemically uncombined water by evaporation. HO_2, who existed in those days, was welcome to stay where he was.

However, these walls refused to come to the scratch on any terms. Homer is silent as to how long the walls of Ilium took to dry; they must have been wet if they were built by Neptune. But one may be excused for doubting if they took as long as wet new plaster does, in premises parties are waiting to come into, and getting impatient, in London. Ascribe this laxity of style to the historian's fidelity to his sources of information.

Not that it would be a fair comparison, in any case. For the walls of Troy were peculiar, having become a meadow with almost indecent haste during the boyhood of Ascanius, who was born before Achilles lost his temper; and before the decease of Anchises, who was old enough to be unable to walk at the sacking of the city. But no doubt you will say that that is all Virgil, and Virgil doesn't count.

The point we have to do with is that the walls at No. 7 did *not* dry. And you must bear in mind that it was not only Mrs. Prichard's apartment that was replastered, but that there was a lot done to the ceiling of Aunt M'riar's room as well, and a bit of the cornice tore away where the wall gave; so that the surveyor he ordered, when he come to see it, all the brickwork to come down as far as flush with the window, which had to be allowed extra for on the contract. Hence the decision—and even that was coming on to November—that the children should stop with their granny at Ealing while their aunt come up to get things a little in order, and the place well aired.

Aunt M'riar's return for this purpose drags the story on two or three weeks, but may just as well be told now as later.

When she made this second journey up to London, she found Mr. Bartlett's ministrations practically ended, his only representatives being a man, a boy, and a composite smell, whereof one of the components was the smell of the man. Another, at the moment of her arrival, putty, was going shortly to be a smell of vivid green paint, so soon as ever he had got these two or three panes made good. For he was then going to put a finishing coat on all woodwork previously painted, and leave his pots in the way till he thought fit to send for them, which is a house-painter's prerogative. He seemed to be able to absorb lead into his system without consequences.

" There's been a young sarsebox making inquiry arter you, missis," said this artist, striving with a lump of putty that no incorporation could ever persuade to become equal to new. He was making it last out, not to get another half-a-pound just yet a while. " Couldn't say his name, but I rather fancy he belongs in at the end house."

Aunt M'riar identified the description, and went up to her room wondering why that young Micky had been asking for her. Uncle Moses was away, presumably at The Sun. She busied herself in endeavours to reinstate her sleeping-quarters. Disheartening work!—we all know it, this circumventing of Chaos. Aunt M'riar worked away at it, scrubbed the floor and made the bed, taking the dryness of the sheets for granted because it was only her and not Dolly to-night, and she could give them a good airing in the kitchen to-morrow. The painter-and-glazier, without, painted and glazed; maintaining a morose silence except when he imposed its observance also on a boy who was learning the trade from him very gradually, and suffering from *ennui* very acutely. He said to this boy at intervals:—" You stow that drumming, young Ebenezer, and 'and me up the turps "—or some other desideratum. Which suspended the drumming in favour of active service, after which it was furtively resumed.

Uncle Mo evidently meant to be back late. The fact was, his home had no attraction for him in the absence of his family, and the comfort of The Sun parlour was seductive. Aunt M'riar's visit was unexpected, as she had not written in advance. So when the painter-and-glazier began to prepare to leave his tins and pots and brushes and graining-tools behind him till he could make it convenient to call round and fetch them, Aunt M'riar felt threatened by loneliness. And when he finally took his leave, with an assurance that by to-morrow morning any person so disposed might rub his Sunday coat up against *his* day's work, and never be a penny the worse, Aunt M'riar felt so forsaken that she just stepped up the Court to hear what she might of its news from Mrs. Ragstroar, who was momentarily expecting the return of her son and husband to domestic dulness, after a commercial career out Islington way. They had only got to stable up their moke, whose home was in a backyard about a half a mile off, and then they would seek their Penates, who were no doubt helping to stew something that smelt much nicer than all that filthy paint and putty.

" That I could not say, ma'am," said Mrs. Ragstroar, in answer to an inquiry about the object of Micky's visit. " Not if you was to offer five pounds. That boy is Secrecy Itself! What he do know, and what he do not know, is 'id in his 'art; and what is more, he don't commoonicate it to neither me nor his father. Only his great-aunt! But I can send him round, as easy as not."

Accordingly, about half an hour later, when Aunt M'riar was beginning to wonder at the non-appearance of Uncle Mo, Master Micky knocked at her door, and was admitted.

" 'Cos I've got a message for you, missis," said he. He accepted the obvious need of his visit for explanation, without incorporating it in words. " It come from that party—party with a side-twist in the mug—party as come this way of a Sunday morning, askin' for old Mother Prichard—party I see in Hy' Park along of young Dave. . . ."

Aunt M'riar was taken aback. " How ever come you to see more of *him?* " said she. For really this was, for the moment, a greater puzzle to her than why, being seen, he should send *her* a message.

Micky let the message stand over, to account for it. " 'Cos I did see him, and I ain't a liar. I see him next door to my great-aunt, as ever is. Keep along the 'Ammersmith Road past the Plough and Harrow, and so soon as ever you strike the Amp'shrog, you bear away to the left, and anybody'll tell you The Pidgings, as soon as look at you. Small 'ouse, by the river. Kep' by Miss Horkings, now her father's kicked. Female party." This was due to a vague habit of the speaker's mind, which divided the opposite sex into two genders, feminine and neuter; the latter

including all those samples, unfortunate enough—or fortunate
enough, according as one looks at it—to present no attractions to
masculine impulses. Micky would never have described his great-
aunt as a female party. She was, though worthy, neuter beyond
a doubt.

Aunt M'riar accepted Miss Hawkins, without further analysis.
"*She* don't know me, anyways," said she. "Nor yet your Hyde
Park man, as far as I see. How come he to know my name?
Didn't he never tell you?" She was incredulous about that
message.

"He don't know nobody's name, as I knows on. Wot he said
to me was a message to the person of the house at the end o'
the Court. Same like you, missis!"

"And what was the message?"

"I'll tell you that, missis, straight away and no lies." Micky
gathered himself up, and concentrated on a flawless delivery of
the message:—" He said he was a-coming to see his mother; that's
what *he* said—his *mother,* the old lady upstairs. Providin' she
wasn't nobody else! He didn't say no names. On'y he said if she
didn't come from Skillick's she *was* somebody else."

"Mrs. Prichard, she came from Skillick's, I know. Because
she said so. That's over three years ago." Aunt M'riar was of a
transparent, truthful nature. If she had been more politic, she
would have kept this back. "Didn't he say nothing else?" she
asked.

"Yes, he did, and this here is what it was:—'Tell the person of
the house,' he says, 'to mention my name,' he says. 'Name o'
Darvill,' he says. So I was a-lyin', missis, you see, by a sort o'
chance like, when I said he said no names. 'Cos he *did.* He said
his own. Not but what he goes by the name of Wix."

"What does he want of old Mrs. Prichard now?"

"A screw. Sov'rings, if he can get 'em. Otherwise bobs, if he
can't do no better."

"Mrs. Prichard has no money."

"He says she has and he giv' it her. And he's going to have
it out of her, he says."

"Did he say that to you?"

"Not he! But he said it to Miss Horkings. Under his nose,
like." No doubt this expression, Michael's own, was a derivative
of "under the rose." It owed something to *sotto voce,* and something to the way the finger is sometimes laid on the nose to de-
note acumen.

"Look you here, Micky! You're a good boy, ain't you?"

"Middlin'. Accordin'." An uncertain sound. It conveyed a doubt of the desirability of goodness.

"You don't bear no ill-will neither to me, nor yet to old Mrs. Prichard?"

"Bones alive, no!" This also may have been coined at home. "That was the idear, don't you twig, missis? I never did 'old with windictiveness, among friends."

"Then you do like I tell you. When are you going next to your aunt at Hammersmith?"

Micky considered a minute, as if the number of his booked engagements made thought necessary, and then said decisively: "To-morrow mornin', to oblige."

"Very well, then! You go and find out this gentleman . . ."

"He ain't a gentleman. He's a varmint."

"You find him out, and say old Mrs. Prichard she's gone in the country, and you can't say where. No more you can't, and I ain't going to tell you. So just you say that!"

"I'm your man, missis. On'y I shan't see him, like as not. He don't stop in one place. The orficers are after him—the police."

Then Aunt M'riar showed her weak and womanish character. Let her excuse be the memory of those six rapturous weeks, twenty-five years ago, when she was a bride, and all her life was rosy till she found herself deserted—left to deal as she best might with Time and her loneliness. You see, this man actually *was* her husband. Micky could not understand why her voice should change as she said:—"The police are after him—yes! But you be a good boy, and leave the catching of him to them. 'Tain't any concern of yours. Don't you say nothing to them, and they won't say nothing to you!"

The boy paused a moment, as though in doubt; then said with insight:—"I'll send 'em the wrong way." He thought explanation due, adding:—"I'm fly to the game, missis." Aunt M'riar had wished not to be transparent, but she was not good at this sort of thing. True, she had kept her counsel all those years, and no one had seen through her, but that was mere opacity in silence.

She left Micky's apprehension to fructify, and told him to go back and get his supper. As he opened the door to go Uncle Mo appeared, coming along the Court. The sight of him was welcome to Aunt M'riar, who was feeling very lonesome. And as for the old boy himself, he was quite exhilarated. "Now we shall have those two young pagins back!" he said.

CHAPTER XXXII

Mr. PERCIVAL PELLEW and Miss Constance Smith-Dickenson
had passed, under the refining influence of Love, into a new phase,
that of not being formally engaged. It was to be distinctly understood that there was to be nothing precipitate. This condition
has its advantages; very particularly that it postpones, or averts,
family introductions. Yet it cannot be enjoyed to the full without downright immorality, and it always does seem to us a pity
that people should be forced into Evil Courses, in order to shun
the terrors of Respectability. Why should not some compromise
be possible? The life some couples above suspicion contrive to
lead, each in the other's pocket as soon as the eyes of Europe
wander elsewhere, certainly seems to suggest a basis of negotiation.
No doubt you know that little poem of Browning about the lady
and gentleman who watched the Seine, and saw Guizot receive
Montalembert, who rhymed to "flare"? Of course, the case was
hardly on all fours with that of our two irreproachables, but we
suspect a point in common. We feel sure that those lawless
loiterers in a dissolute capital were joyous at heart at having
escaped the fangs of the brothers of the one, and the sisters of
the other, respectively, although at the cost of having the World's
bad names applied to both. In this case there were no brothers
on the lady's part, and only one sister on the gentleman's. But
Aunt Constance was not sorry for a breathing-pause before being
subjected to an inspection through glasses by the Hon. Mrs. Bem-
bridge Corlett, which was the name of the unique sister-sample,
and herself subjecting Mr. Pellew to a similar overhauling by her
own numerous relatives. She had misgivings about the *accolade*
he might receive from Mrs. Amphlett Starfax, and also about the

soul-communion which her sister Lilian, who had a sensitive nature, demanded as the price of recognition in public a second time of all persons introduced to her notice.

Mr. Pellew's description of the Hon. Mrs. Corlett had impressed her with the necessity of being ready to stand at bay when the presentation came off.

"Dishy will look at you along the top of her nose, with her chin in the air," said he. "But you mustn't be alarmed at that. She only does it because her glasses—we're all short-sighted—slip off her nose at ordinary levels. And when you come to think of it, how can she hold them on with her fingers when she looks at you. Like taking interest in a specimen!"

"I am a little alarmed at your sister Boadicea, Percy, for all that," said Miss Dickenson, and changed the conversation. This was only a day or two after the Sapps Court accident, and the phase of not being formally engaged had begun lasting as long as possible, being found satisfactory. So old Mrs. Prichard was a natural topic to change to. "Isn't it funny, this whim of Gwen's, about the old lady you carried upstairs?"

"What whim of Gwen's?"

"Oh, don't you know. Of course you don't! Gwen's fallen in love with her, and means to take her to the Towers with her when she goes back."

"Very nice for the old girl. What's she doing that for?"

"It's an idea of hers. However, there is some reason in it. The old lady's apartments must be dry before she goes back to them, and that may be weeks."

"Why can't she stop where she is?"

"All by herself? At least, only the cook! When Miss Grahame goes to Devonshire, Maggie goes with her, to lady's-maid her."

"I thought we were going to be pastoral, and only spend three hundred a year on housekeeping."

"So we are—how absurdly you do put things, Percy!—when we make a fair start. But just till we begin in earnest, there's no need for such strictness. Anyhow, if Maggie doesn't go to Devonshire, she'll go back to her parents at Invercandlish. So the old lady can't stop. And Gwen will go back to the Towers, of course. I don't the least believe they'll hold out six months, those two . . . What little ducks Kinkajous are! Give me a biscuit. . . . No—one of the soft ones!"

For, you see, they were at the Zoölogical Gardens. They had felt that these Gardens, besides being near at hand, were the kind of Gardens in which the eyes of Europe would find plenty to occupy them, without staring impertinently at a lady and gentleman who were not formally engaged. Who would care to study them and *their* ways when he could see a Thibetan Bear bite the nails of his hind-foot, or observe the habits of Apes, or sympathize with a Tiger about his lunch? Our two visitors to the Gardens had spent an hour on these and similar attractions, noting occasionally the flavour that accompanies them, and had felt after a visit to the Pythons, that they could rest a while out of doors and think about the Wonders of Creation, and the draw-backs they appear to suffer from. But a friendly interest in a Python had lived and recrudesced as the Kinkajou endeavoured to get at some soft biscuit, in spite of a cruel wire screen no one bigger than a rat could get his little claw through.

"I don't believe that fillah *was* moving. He was breathing. But he wasn't moving. I know that chap perfectly well. He never moves when anyone is looking at him, out of spite. He hears vis-itors hope he'll move, and keeps quite still to disappoint them." It was Mr. Pellew who said this. Miss Dickenson shook her head incredulously.

"He *was* moving, you foolish man. You should use your eyes. That long straight middle piece of him on the shelf moved; in a very dignified way, considering. The move moved along him, and went slowly all the way to his tail. When I took my eyes off I thought the place was moving, which is a proof I'm right. . . . Oh, you little darling, you've dropped it! I'm so sorry. I must have another, because this has been in the mud, and you won't like it." This was, of course, to the Kinkajou.

Mr. Pellew supplied a biscuit, but improved the occasion:— "Now if this little character could only keep his paws off the Public, he wouldn't want a wire netting. Couldn't you give him a hint?"

"I could, but he wouldn't take it. He's a little darling, but he's pig-headed. . . ." A pause, and then a quick explanatory side-note:—"Do you know, I think that's Sir Coupland Merri-dew coming along that path. I hope he isn't coming this way. . . . I'm afraid he is, though. You know who I mean? He was at the Towers. . . ."

"I know. Yes, it's him. He's coming this way. If he sees it's us, he'll go off down the side-path. But he won't see—he's too short-sighted. Can't be helped!"

"Oh dear—what a plague people are! Let's be absorbed in the Kinkajou. He'll pass us."

But the great surgeon did nothing of the sort. On the contrary he said:—" I saw it was you, Miss Dickenson." Then he reflected about her companion, and said he was Mr. Pellew, he thought, and further:—" Met you at Ancester in July." It was a great relief that he did *not* say:—" You are a lady and gentleman, and can perhaps explain yourselves. *I* can't!" He appeared to decide on silence about *them,* as irrelevant, and went on to something more to the purpose—" Perhaps you know if the family are in town—any of them?" Miss Dickenson testified to the whereabouts of Lady Gwendolen Rivers, and Sir Coupland wrote it in a notebook. There seemed at this point to be an opportunity to say how delightful the Gardens were this time of the year, so Miss Dickenson seized it.

" I didn't come to enjoy the gardens," said the F.R.C.S. " I wish I had time. I came to see to a broken scapula. Keeper in the Ostrich House—bird pecked him from behind. Did it from love, apparently. Said to be much attached to keeper. Two-hundred-and-two, Cavendish Square, is right, isn't it?"

" Two-hundred-and-two; corner house. . . . Must you go on? Sorry!—you could have told us such interesting things." The effect of this one word " us," indiscreetly used, was that Sir Coupland, walking away to his carriage outside the turnstiles, wondered whether it would come off, and if it did, would there be a family? Which shows how very careful you have to be, when you are a lady and gentleman.

The former, in this case, remained unconscious of her *lapsus linguæ;* saying, in fact:—" I think we did that very well! I wonder whether he will go and see Gwen!"

" I hope he will. Do you know, I couldn't help suspecting that he had something to say about Torrens's eyesight—something good. Perhaps it was only the way one has of catching at straws. Still, unless he has, why should he want to see Gwen? He couldn't want to tell her there was no hope—to rub it in!"

" I see what you mean. But I'm afraid he only put down the address for us to tell her he did so—just to get the credit of a call without the trouble."

" When did you take to Cynicism, madam? . . . No—come. I say—that's not fair! It's only my second cigar since I came to the Gardens. . . ." The byplay needed to make this intelligible may be imagined, without description.

Does not the foregoing lay further stress on the curious fact that the *passée* young lady and the oscillator between Pall Mall and that Club at St. Stephen's—this describes the earlier seeming of these two—have really vanished from the story? Is it not a profitable commentary on the mistakes people make in the handling of their own lives?

Sir Coupland Merridew was not actuated by the contemptible motive Aunt Constance had ascribed to him. Moreover, the straw Mr. Pellew caught at was an actual straw, though it may have had no buoyancy to save a swimmer. It must have had *some* though, or Sir Coupland would never have thrown it to Gwen, struggling against despair about her lover's eyesight. Of course he did not profess to do so of set purpose; that would have pledged him to an expression of confidence in that straw which he could hardly have felt.

When he called at Cavendish Square two days later at an un-earthly hour, and found Gwen at breakfast, he accounted for his sudden intrusion by producing a letter recently received from Miss Irene Torrens, of which he said that, owing to the peculi-arity of the handwriting, he had scarcely been able to make out anything beyond that it related to her brother's blindness. Prob-ably Lady Gwendolen knew her handwriting better than he did. At any rate, she might have a shot at trying to make it out. But presently, when she had time! He, however, would take a cup of coffee, and would then go on and remove a portion of a diseased thigh-bone from a Royal leg—that of Prince Hohenslebenschlangenspielersgeiststein—only he never could get the name right.

The story surmises that, having carefully read every word of the letter, he chose this way of letting Gwen know of a fluctuation in Adrian's eye-symptoms; which, he had inferred, would not reach her otherwise. But he did not wish false hopes to be built on it. The deciphering of the illegibilities by Gwen, under correctives from himself, would exactly meet the case.

"I can *not* see that 'Rene's writing is so very illegible," said Gwen. "Now be quiet and let me read it." She settled down to perusal, while Sir Coupland sipped his coffee, and watched her colour heighten as she read. That meant, said he to himself, that he must be ready to throw more cold water on this letter than he had at first intended.

Said Gwen, when she had finished:—"Well, that seems to me very plain and straightforward. And as for illegibility, I know many worse hands than 'Re's."

"What's that word three lines down? . . . Yes, that one!"

"Dreaming.'"

"I thought it was 'drinking.'"

"It certainly is 'dreaming' plain enough!"

"What do you make of it? Don't read it all through. Tell me the upshot."

"I don't mind reading it. But I'll tell it short, as you're in a hurry. Adrian dropped asleep on the sofa, and woke with a start, saying:—'What's become of Septimius Severus on the bookshelf?' It was a bust, it seems. 'Re said:—'How did you know it had been moved?' and he seemed quite puzzled and said:—'I can't tell. I forgot I was blind, and saw the whole room.' Then 'Re said, he must have been dreaming. 'But,' said he, 'you say it *has* been moved.' So what does 'Re do but say he *must* have heard somehow that it was moved, *because* it was impossible that he should have been able to see only just that much and no more. . . . Oh dear!" said Gwen, breaking off suddenly. "What a pleasure people do seem to take in being silly!"

Sir Coupland proceeded to show deference to correct form. "It is far more likely," said he, "that Mr. Torrens had heard someone say the bust was moved, and had forgotten it till he woke up out of a dream, than that he should have a sudden flash of vision." A more cautious method than Irene's, of assuming the point at issue.

Gwen paid no attention to this, putting it aside to apologize to Irene. "However, 'Re had the sense to write straight to you about it. I'll say that for her." Then she read the letter again while Sir Coupland spun out his cup of coffee. She was still dwelling on it when he looked at his watch suddenly and said: "I must be off. Consider Prince Hohenschlangen's necrosis!" Then said Gwen, pinning him to truth with the splendour of her eyes:—"You are perfectly and absolutely certain, Dr. Merridew, that a momentary gleam of true vision in such a case would be *impossible?*"

"I never said *that,*" said Sir Coupland.

"What *did* you say?" said Gwen.

"As improbable as you please, short of impossible. Now I'm off. Impossible's a long word, you know, and very hard to spell." Sir Coupland went off in a hurry, leaving Irene's letter in Gwen's possession, which was dishonourable; because he had really read the injunction it contained, on no account to show it to Gwen in case she should build false hopes on it. But then Gwen had not read this passage aloud to him, so he did not know it officially.

Lunch was the next conclave of the small household, and although Mr. Pellew was there—it was extraordinary how seldom he was anywhere else!—Irene's letter was freely handed round the table and made the subject of comment.

"It won't do to build upon it," said Cousin Clo.

"Why not?" said Gwen.

"It never does to be led away," said Miss Dickenson. Her reputation for sagacity had to be maintained.

"Doesn't it?" said Gwen.

Mr. Pellew was bound, in consideration of his company, to dwell upon the desirableness of keeping an even mind. Having done full justice to this side of the subject, he added a rider. He had always said the chances were ten to one Torrens would recover his eyesight, and this sort of thing looked uncommonly like it. Now didn't it? Whereupon Gwen, who shook hands with him across the table to show her approval, said that anyhow she must hear Adrian's own account of this occurrence from his own mouth forthwith, and she should go back to-morrow to the Towers, and insist upon driving over to Pensham Steynes, whether or no!

Miss Grahame remonstrated with her later, when Aunt Constance and her swain had departed to some dissipation—the story is not sure it was not Madame Tussaud's—and pointed out that she really had solemnly promised not to see Mr. Torrens for six months. She admitted this, but counterpointed out that she could just see him for half an hour to hear his own account of the incident, and then they could begin fair. She was a girl of her word, and meant to keep it. Only, no date had been fixed. As for her pledges to assist her cousin's schemes for benefiting Sapps Court and its analogues, in Drury Lane or elsewhere, was she not going to carry off the old fairy godmother she had discovered and give her such a dose of fresh air and good living as she had not had for twenty years past? Could any Patron Saint of Philanthropy ask more?

Gwen, of course, had her way. She did not cut her visit to Cavendish Square needlessly short. She remained there long enough to give some colour to the pretext that she was exploring slums with philanthropy in view, and actually to make a visit with her cousin to the reconstructed home of the Wardles in Sapps Court. But no response came to knocking at door or window, and it was evident that Aunt M'riar had not returned. Michael Ragstroar, the making of whose acquaintance on this occasion gratified both ladies, offered to go to The Sun for Uncle Mo and bring him round; but his offer was declined, as their time was limited. This must have been a few days before the return of Aunt M'riar and the children, and in the interim her young ladyship had taken flight to the home of her ancestors, contriving somehow to convey away with her her new-made old friend, and to provide her with comfortable lodgment in the housekeeper's quarters, making Mrs. Masham, the housekeeper, responsible for her comforts.

As for the old lady herself, she was very far from being sure that she was not dreaming.

END OF PART I

WHEN GHOST MEETS GHOST

PART II

CHAPTER I

MICKY'S AUNT, WHO HAD A COLD. MASCHIL THE CHIEF MUSICIAN, AND DOEG THE EDOMITE. A SUNDAY-RAPTURE. THE BEER. HOW MISS JULIA HAWKINS THOUGHT THE GLASS A FRAUD. HOW MICKY DELIVERED HIS MESSAGE. A CONDITIONAL OFFER OF MARRIAGE. JANUS HIS BASKET. ALETHEA'S AUNT TREBILCOCK. A SHREWD AND HOOKY KITTEN WHO GOT OUT. HER MAJESTY'S HORSE-SLAUGHTERER. OF A LEAN LITTLE GIRL. HER BROTHER'S NOSE. HOW MR. WIX KNOCKED AT AUNT M'RIAR'S DOOR. THE CHAIN. HOW AUNT M'RIAR IMPRESSED MR. WIX AS AN IDIOT. WHO WAS THE WOMAN? HOW SHE OPENED THE DOOR FOR MICKY'S SAKE, AND LOOKED HARD AT HER HUSBAND. HIS LAWFUL WIFE! SCRIPTURE READINGS IN HELL. HOW SHE WENT TO FETCH ALL THE MONEY SHE HAD IN THE HOUSE. HOW MR. WIX CAPTURED UNCLE MO'S OLD WATCH. HOW AUNT M'RIAR TRIPPED UNCLE MO UP

THE return of the two young pagans to Sapps Court, and the complete re-establishment of Uncle Mo's household, had to be deferred yet one or two more days, to his great disappointment. On the morning following Aunt M'riar's provisional return, the weather set in wet, and the old boy was obliged to allow that there ought to be a fire in the grate of Aunt M'riar's wrecked bedroom for at least a couple of days before Dolly returned to sleep in it. He attempted a weak protest, saying that his niece was a dry sort of little party that moisture could not injure. But he conceded the point, to be on the safe side.

Aunt M'riar said never a word to him about the message she had received from the convict through the boy Micky, and the answer she had returned. She had not forgotten Uncle Mo's communications with that Police Inspector, and felt confident that her reception of a message from Mr. Wix at his old haunt would soon be known to the latter if she did not keep her counsel about it. The words she used in her heart about it were nearly identical with Hotspur's. Uncle Moses would not utter what he did not know. She had not a thought of blame for Mo, for she knew that her disposition to shield this man was idiosyncrasy—could not in the nature of things be shared, even by old and tried friends.

389

There was a fine chivalric element about this defensive silence of hers. The man was now nothing to her—dust and ashes, dead and done with! This last phrase was the one her heart used about him—not borrowed from Browning any more than its other speech from Shakespeare. "I've done with *him* for good and all," said she to herself. "But the Law shall not catch him along o' me." He was vile—vile to her and to all women—but she could bear her own wrong, and she was not bound to fight the battles of others. He was a miscreant and a felon, the mere blood on those hands was not his worst moral stain. He was foul from the terms of his heritage of life, with the superadded foulness of the galleys. But she *had* loved him once, and he was her husband.

Micky kept his word, going over to his great-aunt the following Sunday; to oblige, as he said. Mrs. Treadwell had a cold, and was confined to the house; but the boy was a welcome visitor. "There now, Michael," said she, "I was only just this minute thinking to myself, if Micky was here he could go on reading me the Psalms, where I am, instead of me putting my eyes out. For the sight is that sore and inflamed, and my glasses getting that wore out from being seen through so much, that I can't hardly make out a word."

Micky's only misgivings on his visits to Aunt Elizabeth Jane were connected with a Family Bible to which his old relative was devoted, and with her disposition to make him read the Psalms aloud. Neither of them attached any particular meaning to the text; she being contented with its religious *aura* and fitness for Sunday, and he absorbed in the detection of correct pronunciation by spelling, a syllable at a time. So early an allusion to this affliction disheartened Micky on this occasion, and made him feel that his long walk from Sapps Court had been wasted, so far as his own enjoyment of it was concerned.

"Oh, 'ookey, Arntey," said he dejectedly, "I say now—look here! Shan't I make it Baron Munch Hawson, only just this once?" For his aunt possessed, as well as the Holy Scriptures, a copy of Baron Munchausen's Travels and a Pilgrim's Progress. Conjointly, they were an Institution, and were known as Her Books.

But she resisted the secular spirit. "On Sunday morning, my dear!" she exclaimed, shocked. "How ever you *can!* Now if on'y your father was to take you to Chapel, instead of such a bad example, see what good it would do you both."

The ounce of influence that Aunt Elizabeth Jane alone possessed told on Michael's stubborn spirit, and he did not contest the point. "Give us the 'Oly Bible!" said he briefly. "Where's where you was?"

"That's a good boy! Now you just set down and read on where I was. 'To, the, chief, musician,' and the next word's a hard word and you'll have to spell it." For, you see, Aunt Elizabeth Jane's method was to go steadily on with a text, and not distinguish titles and stage directions.

So her nephew, being docile, tackled the fifty-second Psalm, and did not flinch from *m, a, s,* mass—*c, h, i, l,* chill; total, Mass-Chill—nor from *d, o,* do; *e, g,* hegg; total, Do-Hegg. But when he came to Ahimelech, he gave him up, and had to be told. However, he laboured on through several verses, and the old charwoman listened in what might be called a Sunday-rapture, conscious of religion, but not attaching any definite meaning to the words. As for Micky, he only perceived that David and Saul, Doeg the Edomite, and Ahimelech the Priest, were religious, and therefore bores. He had a general idea that the Psalmist could not keep his hair on. He might have enjoyed the picturesque savagery of the story if Aunt Elizabeth Jane had known it well enough to tell him. But when you read for flavour, and ignore import, the plot has to go to the wall.

Aunt Elizabeth Jane kept her nephew to his unwelcome devotional enterprise until the second "Selah"—a word which always seemed to exasperate him—provoked his restiveness beyond his powers of restraint. "I say, Aunt Betsy," said he, "shan't I see about gettin' in the beer?" This touched a delicate point, for his visit being unexpected, rations were likely to be short.

Some reproof was necessary. "There now, ain't you a tiresome boy, speaking in the middle!" But this was followed by: "Well, my dear, I can't take anything myself, the cold's that heavy on me. But that's no reason against a glass for you, after your walk. On'y I tell you, you'll have to make your dinner off potatoes and a herring, that you will, by reason there's nothing else for you. And all the early shops are shut an hour ago."

Then Michael showed how great his foresight and resource had been. "Bought a mutting line-chop coming along, off of our butcher. Fivepence 'a'pen'y. Plenty for two if you know how to cook it right, and don't cut it to waste." In this he showed a thoughtfulness beyond his years, for the knowledge that the amount of flesh on any bone, may be doubled—even quadrupled— by the skill of its carver, is rarely found except in veterans.

Aunt Elizabeth Jane paid a tribute of admiration. "My word!" said she, "who ever would have said a boy could! Now you shall cook that chop while I tell you how." So the fifty-second Psalm lapsed, and Michael was at liberty to forget Doeg the Edomite.

But the glass of beer claimed attention first, because it would never do to leave that chop to get cold while he went for it next door. Aunt Elizabeth Jane allowed Michael to take the largest glass, as he had read so good and bought his own chop, and with it he crossed the wall into the garden of The Pigeons, as the story has seen him do before.

Miss Juliarawkins, summoned by a whistle through the keyhole, looked a good deal better in sackcloth and ashes than she had done in several discordant colours. She was going to stop as long as ever she could in mourning for her father, so as to get the wear out of the stuff, and make it of some use. Some connection might die, by good luck. She was one of those that held with making the same sackcloth and ashes do for two.

She looked critically at the rather large tumbler Micky had brought for his beer, and made difficulties about filling of it right up, even with the top. For this was a supply under contract. A glass full was to be paid for as a short half-pint. But as Miss Hawkins truly said, no glass had any call to be half as big as Saint Paul's. Her customer, however, was not to be put off in this way. A glass was a glass, and a half-pint was a half a pint. There was no extry reduction when the glass was undersized. You took the good with the bad.

A voice Micky knew growled from a recess:—" Give the young beggar full measure, Juli*ar*. What he means is, you go by a blooming average."

Miss Hawkins filled up the glass this once, but said:—" You tell your Aunt Treadwell she'll have to keep below the average till Christmas. *I* never see such a glass!"

Micky was not sorry to find that he could deliver his message direct. He had not hoped to come upon the man himself. He paid for his beer on contract terms, and said confidentially:—" I say, missis, I got a message for him in there."

" Mrs. Treadwell's nephew Michael from next door says he's got a message for you, and you can say if you'll see him. Or not." This was spoken snappishly, as though a coolness were afoot.

The man replied with mock amiability, meant to irritate. " You can send him in here, Juliar. You're open to." But when in compliance with the woman's curt:—" You hear—you can go in," the boy entered the little back-parlour, he turned on him sud-

denly and fiercely, saying:—"You're the * * * young nark of
some damned teck—some * * * copper, by Goard!"
If the boy had flinched before this accusation, which meant that
he was a police-spy employed by a detective, he might have repented it. But Micky was no coward, and stood his ground; all
the more firmly that he fully grasped the man's precarious position, in the very house where he had been once before captured.
He answered resolutely:—"I could snitch upon you this minute,
master, if I was to choose. But you aren't no concern of mine,
further than I've got a message for you."

"The boy's all safe," said ·Miss Hawkins briefly, outside.
Whereupon the man, after a subsiding growl or two, said:—"You
gave the party my message? What had she got to say back again?
You may mouth it out and cut your lucky."

Micky gave his message in a plain and business-like manner.
"Mrs. Wardle she's back after the accident, and Mrs. Prichard
she's in the country, and she don't know where."

"Who don't know where? Mrs. Prichard?"

"Mrs. Wardle. I said you was a-coming to see your mother,
onlest 'the old lady wasn't your mother. Then you shouldn't
come."

"What did she say about Skillicks?"

"Said Mrs. Prichard come from Skillickses. Three year agone."

"You hear that, Miss Hawkins?" Mr. Wix seemed pleased,
as one who had scored, adding:—"I knew it was the old
woman. . . . Anything else she said?"

Micky appeared to consider his answer; then replied:—"Said
I wasn't to split upon you."

"What the Hell does she say that for? She don't know who
I am."

Micky considered again, and astutely decided, perceiving his
mistake, to say as little as possible about Aunt M'riar's seeming
interest in Mr. Wix's safety from the Law. Then he said:—
"She don't know nothing about you, but when I says to her the
Police was after you, she cuts in sharp, and says, she does, that
was no concern o' mine, and I was to say nothing to them, and they
wouldn't say nothing to me."

Mr. Wix said, "Rum!" and Miss Hawkins, who had been keeping her ears open close at hand, looked in through the bar-
casement to say:—"You go there, Wix, and back to gaol you
go! I only tell you." And retired, leaving the convict knitting
tighter the perplexed scowl on his face. He called after her:—
"Come back here, you Juliar!"

"I can hear you."

"What the Devil do you mean?"

"Can't you see for yourself? This woman don't want the boy to get fifty pound. If I was in her shoes, I shouldn't neither." Micky only heard this imperfectly.

"You wouldn't do anything under a hundred, you wouldn't. Good job for me they don't double the amount. . . . Easy does it, Juliar—only a bit of my fun!" For Miss Hawkins, even as a woman stung by a cruel insult, had shown her flashing eyes, heightened colour, and panting bosom at the bar-opening as before. Mr. Wix seemed gratified. "Pity you don't flare up oftener, Juliar," said he. "You've no idea what a much better woman you look. Damn it, but you *do!*"

The woman made an effort, and choked her anger. "God forgive you, Wix!," said she, and fell back out of sight. Michael thought he heard her sob. He was not too young to understand this little drama, which took less time to act than to tell.

The convict had lost the thread of his examination, and had to hark back. *Why* was it, Mrs. Prichard had gone away into the country? . . . Oh, the house had fallen down, had it? But, then, how came Mrs. Wardle to be living in it still? Because, said Michael, it was only the wall fell off of the front, and now Mr. Bartlett he'd made all that good, and Mrs. Prichard was only kep' out by the damp. Did Mrs. Wardle *really* not know where Mrs. Prichard was? She had not told Michael, that was all he could say. Old Mo he'd never slept out of the house, only the family. And they was coming back soon now. Was old Mo an invalid, who never went out? "No fear!" said Michael. "He's all to rights, only a bit oldish, like. He spends the arternoons round at The Sun, and then goes home to supper." The interview ended with a present of half-a-bull to Micky from the convict, which the boy seemed to stickle at accepting. But he took it, and it strengthened his resolution not to turn informer, which was probably Mr. Wix's object.

He came away with an impression that Miss Hawkins had said:—"The boy's lying. How could the front-wall of a house fall down?" But he had heard no more and was glad to come away. He went back to his Aunt Betsy and cooked his chop under her tutelage. What a time he had been away, said she!

If Micky had remembered word for word the whole of this interview, he might have had misgivings of the effect of one thing he had said unawares. It was his reference to Uncle Mo's absence at The Sun during the late afternoon. Manifestly, it left the

house in Mr. Wix's imagination untenanted, during some two
hours of the day, except by Aunt M'riar, and the children perhaps. And what did *they* matter?

"You're mighty wise, Juliar, about the party of the house and
the fifty-pun' reward." So said the convict when the woman came
back, after seeing that Micky had crossed the wall unmolested by
authority. "Folk ain't in any such a hurry to get a man hanged
when they know what'll happen if they fail of doing it. Not even
for fifty pound!"

"What *will* happen?"

"Couldn't say to a nicety. But she would stand a tidy chance
of getting ripped up, next opportunity." He seemed pleased at
his expression of this fact, as he took the first pulls at a fresh
pipe, on the window-seat with his boots against the shutter and
a grip of interlaced fingers behind his close-cut head for support.
Why in Heaven's name does the released gaol-bird crop his hair?
One would have thought the first instinct of regained freedom
would have been to let it grow.

Miss Hawkins looked at him without admiration. "I often
wonder," said she, "at the 'many risks I run to shelter you, for
you're a bloody-minded knave, and that's the truth. It was a
near touch but I might have lost my licence, last time."

"The Beaks were took with your good looks, Juliar. They're
good judges of a fine woman. An orphan you was, too, and the
mourning sooted you, prime!" He looked lazily at her, puffing—
not without admiration, of a sort. Her resentment seemed to
gratify him more than any subserviency. He continued:—"Well,
nobody can say I haven't offered to make an honest woman of *you,*
Juliar."

"Much it was worth, your offer! As if you was free! And
me to sell The Pigeons and go with you to New York! No—
no! I'm better off as I am, than that."

"I'm free, accordin' to Law. Never seen the girl, nor heard
from her—over twenty years now—twenty-three at least. Scot-
free of *her,* anyhow! Don't want none of her, cutting in to spoil
my new start in life. Re-spectable man—justice of peace, p'r'aps."
He puffed at his pipe, pleased with the prospect. Then he sounded
the keynote of his thought, adding:—"Why—how much could
you get for the freehold of this little tiddleywink?"

If Miss Julia had been ever so well disposed towards being
made technically an honest woman by her betrayer of auld lang
syne, this declaration of his motives might easily have hardened
her heart against him. What fatuity of affection could have

survived it? Yet his candour was probably his only redeeming feature. He was scarcely an invariable hypocrite; he was merely heartless, sensual, and cruel to the full extent of man's possibilities. Nevertheless, he could and would have lied black white with a purpose. He was, this time, thrown off his guard, as it were, and truthful by accident. Whether the way in which the woman silently repelled his offer was due to her disgust at its terms, or whether she had her doubts of the soundness of his jurisprudence, the story can only guess. Probably the latter. She merely said:—" I'm going to open the house," and left his inquiry unanswered. This was notice to him that his free run of the lower apartments was ended. He went upstairs to some place of concealment.

" What was you and young Carrots so busy about below here? " said Uncle Mo next day, coming down the stairs to breakfast in the kitchen an hour later than Aunt M'riar.

" Telling me of his Aunt Betsy yesterday. Mind your shirt-sleeve. It's going in the butter."

" What's Aunt Betsy's little game? . . . No, it's all right—the butter's too hard to hurt. . . . Down 'Chiswick way, ain't she? "

" Hammersmith." Aunt M'riar wasn't talkative; but then, this morning, it was bloaters. They should only just hot through, or they dry.

" Who was the bloke he was talking about? Somebody he called *him*." Uncle Mo's ears had been too sharp.

" There!—I've no time to be telling what a boy says. No one any good, I'll go bail! " Whereupon, as Uncle Mo's curiosity was not really keenly excited, the subject dropped.

But, as a matter of fact, Michael had contrived in a short time to give an account of his experience of yesterday. And he had left Aunt M'riar in a state of disquiet and apprehension which had to be concealed, somehow. For she was quite clear that she would not take Mo into her confidence. She saw she had to choose between risking an interview with this convict husband of hers, and giving him up to the Law, probably to the gallows.

The man would come again to seek out his old mother, to extort money from her; that was beyond a doubt. But would he of necessity recognise the wife of twenty-three years ago in the very middle-aged person Aunt M'riar saw in the half of a looking-glass that Mr. Bartlett's careful myrmidons had not broken? Would she recognise him? Need either see the other? Well— no! Communications might be restricted to speech through a door with the chain up.

She took the boy Michael freely into her confidence about her
unwillingness to see this man. But that she could do on the
strength of his bad character; her own relation to him of course
remained concealed. She puzzled her confidant not a little by her
seeming inconsistency—so repugnant was she to the miscreant
himself, yet so anxious that he should not fall into the hands
of the Police. Micky kept his perplexity to himself, justifying
his mother's estimate of his character.

But this much was clearly understood between them, that should
the convict be seen by Micky on his way to the house, he should
forthwith take one of two courses. If Uncle Mo was absent at
the time, he was to warn Aunt M'riar of Mr. Wix's approach.
If otherwise, he was to warn the unwelcome visitor of the risk
he would run if he persisted in his attempt to procure an interview. Of course the chances were that Micky would be away on
business, selling apples, potatoes, and turnips.

As it turned out, however, he was able to observe one of the
conditions of this compact.

It was on the Tuesday following the boy's visit to his great-
aunt that Mrs. Tapping had words with her daughter Alethea.
They arose out of Alethea's young man, an upstart. At least, he
was so designated by Mrs. Tapping, for aspiring to the hand of
this young lady; who, though plain by comparison with her mother
at the same age, and no more figure than what you see, was that
sharp with her tongue when provoked, it made your flesh curdle
within you to hear her expressions. We need hardly say that we
have to rely on her mother for these facts. It was, however, the
extraction of Alethea that determined the presumptuousness of
her young man's aspirations. He was marrying into two families,
the Tappings and the Davises, which, though neither of them
lordly, had always held their heads high and their behaviour according. Whereas this young Tom was metaphorically nobody,
though actually in a shoe-shop and giving satisfaction to his
employers, with twenty-one shillings a week certain and a rise
at Christmas. You cannot do that unless you are a physical entity,
but when your grandmother is in an almshouse and your father
met his death in an inferior capacity at a Works, you have no
call to give yourself airs, and the less you say the better.

This brief sketch of the *status quo* was given to Mrs. Riley by
Mrs. Tapping, in her woollen shawl for the first time, because of
the sharp edge in the wind, with a basket on her arm that Janus
would have found useful, owing to its two lids, one each side the

handle. They were at the entrance to Mrs. Riley's shop, and that good woman was bare-armed and bonnetless in the cold north wind. She had not lost her Irish accent.

"It is mesilf agrays with you intoirely," said she sympathetically.

"Not but what I do freely admit," said Mrs. Tapping, pursuing her topic in a spirit of magnanimity, "that young Rundle himself never makes bold, and is always civil spoke, which we might expect, seeing what is called for, measuring soles. For I always do say that the temptation to forget theirself is far more than human, especially flattenin' down the toe to get the len'th, though of course the situation would be sacrificed, and no character." This was an allusion to the delicacy of the position of one who adjusts a sliding spanner to the foot of Beauty, to determine its length to a nicety. The subject suggests curious questions. Suppose—to look at its romantic side, as easier of discussion— that you, young lady, were passionately adored by the young man at your shoe-shop, and he were to kiss your foot as Vivien did Merlin's, could you—would you—complain at the desk and lose him his situation? And how about the Pope? Is his Holiness never measured—*sal a reverentia!*—for his shoes? Or does the Œcumenical Council guess, and strike an average? However, the current of the story need not be interrupted to settle that.

"He intinds will," said Mrs. Riley. This was merely a vague compliment to Alethea's suitor. "Ye see, me dyurr, it's taking the young spalpeen's part she'll be, for shure! It is the nature of thim." That is to say, lovers.

"But never to the point of calling tyrant, Mrs. Riley. Nor ojus vulgarity. Nor epithets I will not repeat, relating to family connections. Concerning which, *I* say, God forgive Alethear! For the accommodation at a nominal rent of persons in reduced circumstances is not an almshouse, say what she may. And her Aunt Trebilcock is not a charitable object, nor yet a deserving person, having mixed with the best. And in so young a girl texts are not becoming, to a parent."

"Which was the tixt, thin?" said Mrs. Riley, interested. "I'm bel'avin' ye, me dyurr!" This was to encourage Mrs. Tapping, and disclaim incredulity.

"Since you're asking me, Mrs. Riley ma'am, I will not conceal from you the Scripture text used only this morning by my own daughter, to my face. 'Pride goeth before destruction, and a haughty spirit before a fall.' Whereupon I says to Alethear, 'Alethear,' I says, 'be truthful, and admit that old Mrs. Rundle

and your Aunt Trebilcock are on a dissimular footing, one being
distinctly a Foundation in the Whitechapel Road, and the other
Residences, each taking their own Milk.'" Some further particulars came in here, relating to the bone of that mornin's contention, which had turned on Mrs. Tapping's objections to her daughter's demeaning, or bemeaning, herself, by marrying into a lower
rank of life than her own.

All this conversation of these two ladies has nothing to do with
the story. The only reason for referring to it is that it took
place at this time, just opposite Mrs. Riley's shop, and led her
to remark:—"You lave the young payple alone, Mrs. Tapping,
and they'll fall out. You'll only kape thim on, by takin' order
with thim. Thrust me. Whativer have ye got in the basket?"

Mrs. Tapping explained that she was using it to convey a kitten,
born in her establishment, to Miss Druitt at thirty-four opposite,
who had expressed anxiety to possess it. It was this kitten's expression of impatience with its position that had excited Mrs.
Riley's curiosity. "Why don't ye carry the little sowl across in
your hands, me dyurr?" said she; not unreasonably, for it was
only a stone's-throw. Mrs. Tapping added that this was no common kitten, but one of preternatural activity, and possessed of
diabolical tentacular powers of entanglement. "I would not undertake," said she, "to get it across the road, ma'am, only catching
hold. Nor if I got it safe across, to onhook it, without tearing."
Mrs. Riley was obliged to admit the wisdom of the Janus basket.
She knew how difficult it is to be even with a kitten.

This one was destined to illustrate the resources of its kind.
For as Mrs. Tapping endeavoured to conduct the conversation
back to her domestic difficulties, she was aware that the Janus
basket grew suddenly lighter. Mrs. Riley exclaimed at the same
moment:—"Shure, and the little baste's in the middle of the
road!" So it was, hissing like a steam-escape, and every hair on
its body bristling with wrath at a large black dog, who was smelling it in a puzzled, thoughtful way, *sans rancune*. A cart, with
an inscription on it that said its owner was "Horse-Slaughterer
to Her Majesty," came thundering down the street, shaking three
drovers seriously. The dog, illuminated by some new idea, started
back to bark in a sudden panic-stricken way. Who could tell
what new scourge this was that dogdom had to contend
with?

Her Majesty's Horse-Slaughterer pulled his cart up just in time.
It would else have run over a man who was picking the kitten up.
All the males concerned exchanged execrations, and then the cart

went on. The dog's anxiety to smell the phenomenon survived, till the man kicked him and told him to go to Hell.

"Now who does this here little beggar belong to?" said the man, whom Mrs. Riley did not like the looks of. Mrs. Tapping claimed the cat, and expressed wonder as to how it had got out of the basket. Heaven only knew! It is only superhuman knowledge, divine or diabolical, that knows how cats get out of baskets; or indeed steel safes, or anything.

"As I do not think, mister," said Mrs. Tapping—deciding at the last moment not to say "my good man"—"it would be any use to try getting of it inside of this basket out here in the street, let alone its aptitude for getting out when got in, I might trouble you to be so kind as to fetch it into my shop next door here, by the scruff of its neck preferable. . . . Thank you, mister!" She had had some idea of making it "Sir," but thought better of it.

The kitten, deposited on the counter, concerned itself with a blue-bottle fly. The man remarked that it was coming on to rain. Mrs. Tapping had not took notice of any rain, but believed the statement. Why is it that one accepts as true any statement made by a visibly disreputable male? Mrs. Tapping did not even look out at the door, for confirmation or contradiction. She was so convinced of this rain that she suggested that the man should wait a few minutes to see if it didn't hold up, because he had no umbrella. His reply was:—"Well, since you're so obliging, Missis, I don't mind if I do. My mate I'm waiting for, he'll be along directly." He declined a chair or stool, and waited, looking out at the door into the *cul de sac* street that led to Sapps Court, opposite. Mrs. Tapping absented herself in the direction of a remote wrangle underground, explaining her motive. She desired that her daughter, whose eyesight was better than her own, should thread a piece of pack-thread through a rip in the base of the Janus basket, which had to account for the kitten's appearance in public. She did not seem apprehensive about leaving the shop ungarrisoned.

But had she been a shrewder person, she might have felt misgivings about this man's character, even if she had acquitted him of such petty theft as running away with congested tallow candles. For no reasonable theory could be framed of a mate in abeyance, who would emerge from anywhere down opposite. A mate of a man who seemed to be of no employment, to belong to no recognised class, to wear description-baffling clothes—not an ostler's, nor an undertaker's, certainly; but some suspicion of one or other,

Heaven knew why!—and never to look straight in front of him. Without some light on his vocation, imagination could provide no mate. And this man looked neither up nor down the street, but remained watching the *cul de sac* from one corner of his eye. It was not coming on to rain as alleged, and he might have had a better outlook nearer the door. But he seemed to prefer retirement.

The wrangle underground fluctuated slightly, went into another key, and then resumed the theme. A lean little girl came in, who tapped on the counter with a coin. She called out "'A'p'orth o' dips!" taking a tress of her hair from between her teeth to say it, and putting it back to await the result. She had a little brother with her, who was old enough to walk when pulled, but not old enough to discipline his own nose, being dependent on his sister's good offices, and her pocket-handkerchief. He offered a sucked peardrop to the kitten, who would not hear of it.

There certainly was no rain, or Mrs. Riley would never have remained outside, with those bare arms and all. There she was, saying good-evening to someone who had just come from Sapps Court. The man in the shop listened, closely and curiously.

"Good-avening, Mr. Moses, thin! Whin will we see the blessed chilther back? Shure it's wakes and wakes and wakes!" Which written, looks odd; but, spoken, only conveyed regretful reference to the time Dave and Dolly had been away, without taxing the hearer's understanding. "They till me your good lady's been sane, down the Court."

Uncle Mo had just come out, on his way to a short visit to The Sun. He was looking cheerful. "Ay, missis! Their aunt's bringin' of 'em back to-morrow from Ealing. *I'*ll be glad enough to see 'em, for one."

"And the owld sowl upstairs. Not that I iver set my eyes on her, and that's the thrruth."

"Old Mother Prichard? Why—that's none so easy to say. So soon as her swell friends get sick of her, I suppose. She's being cared for, I take it, at this here country place."

"'Tis a nobleman's sate in the Norruth, they sid. Can ye till the name of it, to rimimber?" Mrs. Riley had an impression shared by many, that noblemen's seats are, broadly speaking, in the North. She had no definite information.

Uncle Mo caught at the chance of warping the name, uncorrected. "It's the Towels in Rocestershire," said he with effrontery. "Some sort of a Dook's, good Lard!" Then to change the subject:—"She won't have no place to come back to, not till Mrs. Burr's out and about again."

"The axidint, at the Hospital. No, indade! And how's the poor woman, hersilf? It was the blissin' of God she wasn't kilt on the spot!"

"It warn't a bad bit of luck. She'll be out of hospital next week, I'm told. They're taking their time about it, anyhow! Good-night to ye, missis! The rain's holdin' off." And Uncle Mo departed. Aunt M'riar had insisted on his not discontinuing any of his lapses into bachelorhood proper; which implies pub or club, according to man's degree.

Just a few minutes ago—speaking abreast of the story—Aunt M'riar, getting ready at last to do a little work after so much tidying up, had to go to the door to answer a knock. Its responsible agent was Michael, excited. "It's *him!*" said he. "I seen him myself. Over at Tappingses. And Mr. Moses, he's a-conversing with Missis Riley next door." He went on to offer to make an affidavit, as was his practice, not only on the Testament, but on most any book you could name.

It was not necessary: Aunt M'riar believed him. "You tell him," she replied, "that Mrs. Prichard's gone away, and no time fixed for coming back. Then he'll go. If he don't go, and comes along, just you say to him Mr. Wardle he'll be back in a minute. He'll be only a short time at The Sun."

"I'll say wotsumever you please, Missis Wardle. Only that won't carry no weight, not if I says it ever so. He's a sly customer. Here he is a-coming. Jist past the post!" That is, the one Dave broke his head off.

Aunt M'riar's heart thumped, and she felt sick. "*You* say there's no one in the house then," said she. This was panic, and loss of judgment. For the interview was palpable to anyone approaching down the Court. Micky must have felt this, but he only said:—"I'll square him how I can, missis," and withdrew from the door. Mr. Wix's lurching footstep, with the memory of its fetters on it, approached at its leisure. He stopped and looked round, and saw the boy, who acknowledged his stare. "I see you a-coming," said Michael.

Mr. Wix said:—"Young Ikey." He appeared to consider a course of action. "Now do you want another half-a-bull?"

"Ah!" Micky was clear about that.

"Then you do sentry-go outside o' this, in the street, and if

you see a copper turning in here, you run ahead and give the
word. Understand? This is Wardle's, ain't it?"
"That's Wardle's. But there ain't nobody there."
"You young liar. I saw you talking through the door, only this
minute."
"That warn't anybody, only Aunt M'riar. Party you wants is
away—gone away for a change. Mr. Moses ain't there, but he'll
be back afore you can reckon him up. You may knock at that
door till you 'ammer in the button, and never find a soul in the
house, only Aunt M'riar. You try! 'Ammer away!" There
was a *faux air* of self-justification in this, which did not bear
analysis. Possibly Micky thought so himself, for he vanished
up the Court. He would at least be able to bring a false alarm
if any critical juncture arose.

The ex-convict watched him out of sight, and then knocked at
the door, and waited. The woman inside had been listening to
his voice with a quaking heart—had known it for 'that of her
truant husband of twenty years ago, through all the changes time
had made, and in spite of such colour of its own as the prison
taint had left in it. And he stood there unsuspecting; not a
thought in his mind of who she was, this Aunt M'riar! Why
indeed should he have had any?

She could not trust her voice yet, with a heart thumping like
that. She might take a moment's grace, at least, for its violence
to subside. She sat down, close to the door, for she felt sick and
the room went round. She wanted not to faint, though it was
not clear that syncope would make matters any the worse. But
the longer he paused before knocking again, the better for Aunt
M'riar.

The knock came, a *crescendo* on the previous one. She *had* to
respond some time. Make an effort and get it over!

"That * * * young guttersnipe's given me a bad character,"
muttered Wix, as he heard the chain slipped into its sheath. Then
the door opened, and a tremulous voice came from within.

"What is it . . . you want?" it said. Its trepidation was out
of all proportion to the needs of the case. So thought Mr. Wix,
and decided that this Aunt M'riar was some poor nervous hysteric,
perhaps an idiot outright.

"Does an old lady by the name of Prichard live here, mistress?"
He hid his impatience with this idiot, assuming a genial or conciliatory tone—a thing he perfectly well knew how to do, on
occasion. "An old lady by the name of Prichard. . . . You've
got nothing to be frightened of, you know. I'm not going to do

her any harm, nor yet you." He spoke as to the idiot, in a reassuring tone. For the hysterical voice had tried again for speech, and failed.

Aunt M'riar mustered a little more strength. " Old Mrs. Prichard's away in the country," she said almost firmly. " She's not likely to be back yet awhile. Can I take any message ? "

" Are *you* going in the country ? "

" For when she comes back, I should have said."

" Ah—but when will that be ? Next come strawberry-time, perhaps ! I'll write to her."

" I can't give her address." Aunt M'riar had an impression that the omission of " you " after " give " just saved her telling a lie here. Her words might have meant: " I am not at liberty to give her address to anyone." It was less like saying she did not know it.

His next words startled her. " *I* know her address. Got it written down here. Some swell's house in Rocestershire." He made a pretence of searching among papers.

Aunt M'riar was so taken by surprise at this that she had said " Yes—Ancester Towers " before she knew it. She was not a person to entrust secrets to.

" Right you are, mistress ! Ancester Towers it is." He was making a pretence, entirely for his own satisfaction, of confirming this from a memorandum. Mr. Wix had got what he wanted, but he enjoyed the success of his ruse. Of course, he had only used what he had just overheard from Uncle Moses.

The thought then crossed Aunt M'riar's mind that unless she inquired of him who he was, or why he wanted Mrs. Prichard, he would guess that she knew already. It was the reaction of her concealed knowledge—a sort of innocent guilty conscience. It was not a reasonable thought, but a vivid one for all that—vivid enough to make her say :—" Who shall I say asked for her ? "

" Any name you like. It don't matter to me. I shall write to her myself."

Guilty consciences—even innocent ones—can never leave well alone. The murderer who has buried his victim must needs hang about the spot to be sure no one is digging him up. One looks back into the room one lit a match in, to see that it is not on fire. A diseased wish to clear herself from any suspicion of knowing anything about her visitor, impelled Aunt M'riar to say :—" Of course I don't know the name you go by." Obviously she would have done well to let it alone.

A person who had never borne an *alias* would have thought

nothing of Aunt M'riar's phrase. The convict instantly detected the speaker's knowledge of himself. Another thought crossed his mind:—How about that caution this woman had given to Micky? Why was she so concerned that the boy should not "split upon" him? "Who the devil are you?" said he suddenly, half to himself. It was not the form in which he would have put the question had he reflected.

The exclamation produced a new outcrop of terror or panic in Aunt M'riar. She found voice to say:—"I've told you all I can, master." Then she shut the door between them, and sank down white and breathless on the chair close at hand, and waited, longing to hear his footsteps go. She seemed to wait for hours.

Probably it was little over a minute when the man outside knocked again—a loud, sepulchral, single knock, with determination in it. Its resonance in the empty house was awful to the lonely hearer.

But Aunt M'riar's capacity for mere dread was full to the brim. She was on the brink of the reaction of fear, which is despair— or, rather, desperation. Was she to wait for another appalling knock, like that, to set her heartstrings vibrating anew? To what end? No—settle it now, under the sting of this one.

She again opened the door as before. "I've told you all I know about Mrs. Prichard, and it's true. You must just wait till she comes back. I can't tell you no more."

"I don't want any more about Mrs. Prichard. I want to see side of this door. Take that * * * chain off, and speak fair. I sent you a civil message through that young boy. He gave it you?"

"He told me what you said."

"What did he say I said? If he told you any * * * lies, I'll half murder him! What did he say?"

"He said you was coming to see your mother, and Mrs. Prichard she must be your mother if she comes from Skillicks. So I told him she come from Skillicks, three year agone. Then he said you wanted money of Mrs. Prichard. . . ."

"How the devil did he know that?"

"He said it. And I told him the old lady had no money. It's little enough, if she has."

"And that was all?"

"All about Mrs. Prichard."

"Anything else?"

"He told me your name."

"What name?"

" Thornton Daverill." The moment Aunt M'riar had said this
she was sorry for it. For she remembered, plainly enough considering the tension of her mind, that Micky had only given
her the surname. Her oversight had come of her own bitter
familiarity with the name. Think how easy for her tongue to
trip!

" Anything else? "

" No—nothing else."

" You swear to Goard? "

" I have told you everything."

" Then look you here, mistress! I can tell you this one thing.
That young boy never told you Thornton. I've never named the
name to a soul since I set foot in England. How the devil come
you to know it? "

Aunt M'riar was silent. She had given herself away, and had
no one but herself to thank for it.

" How the devil come you to know it? " The man raised his
voice harshly to repeat the question, adding, more to himself:—
" You're some * * * jade that knows me. Who the devil *are*
you? "

The woman remained dumb, but on the very edge of desperation.

" Open this damned door! You hear me? Open this door—
or, look you, I tell you what I'll do! Here's that * * * young
boy coming. I'll twist his neck for him, by Goard, and leave
him on your doorstep. You put me ,to it, and I'll do it. I'm
good for my word." A change of tone, from savage anger to
sullen intent, conveyed the strength of a controlled resolve, that
might mean more than threat. At whatever cost, Aunt M'riar
could not but shield Micky. It was in her service that he had
provoked this man's wrath.

She wavered a little, closed the door, and slipped the chain-
hook up to its limit. Even then she hesitated to withdraw it
from its socket. The man outside made with his tongue the click
of acceleration with which one urges a horse, saying, " Look
alive! " She could see no choice but to throw the door open and
face him. The moment that passed before she could muster the
resolution needed seemed a long one.

That she was helped to it by an agonising thirst, almost, of
curiosity to see his face once more, there can be no doubt. But
could she have said, during that moment, whether she most desired that he should have utterly forgotten her, or that he should
remember her and claim her as his wife? Probably she would

not have hesitated to say that worse than either would be that
he should recognise her only to slight her, and make a jest, maybe,
of the memories that were his and hers alike.

She had not long to wait. It needed just a moment's pause—
no more—to be sure no sequel of recognition would follow the
blank stare that met her gaze as she threw back the door, and
looked this husband of hers full in the face. None came, and her
heart throbbed slower and slower. It would be down to self-command in a few beats. Meanwhile, how about that chance slip of
her tongue? " Thornton " had to be accounted for.

The man's stare was indeed blank, for any sign of recognition
that it showed. It was none the less as intent and curious as
was the scrutiny that met it, looking in vain for a false lover
long since fled, not a retrievable one, but a memory of a sojourn
in a garden and a collapse in a desert. So little was left, to
explain the past, in the face some violence had twisted askew,
close-shaved and scarred, one white scar on the temple warping
the grip in which its contractions held a cold green orb that
surely never was the eye that was a girl-fool's *ignis fatuus,* twenty
odd years ago. So little of the flawless teeth, which surely those
fangs never were!—fangs that told a tale of the place in which
they had been left to decay; for such was prison-life three-quarters
of a century since. It was strange, but Aunt M'riar, though she
knew that it was he, felt sick at heart that he should be so unlike
himself.

He was the first to speak. " You'll know me again, mistress,"
he said. He took his eyes off her to look attentively round the
room. Uncle Mo's sporting prints, prized records of ancient battles, caught his eye. " Ho—that's it, is it? " said he, with a short
nod of illumination, as though he had made a point as a cross-
examiner. " That's where we are—Figg and Broughton—Corbet—
Spring? . . . That's your game, is it? Now the question is,
where the devil do I come in? How come you to know my name's
Thornton? That's the point! "

Now nothing would have been easier for Aunt M'riar than to
say that Mrs. Prichard had told her that her only surviving son
bore this name. But the fact is that the old lady, quite a recent
experience, had for the moment utterly vanished from her thoughts,
and the man before her had wrenched her mind back into the
past. She could only think of him as the cruel betrayer of her
girlhood, none the less cruel that he had failed in his worst plot
against her, and used a legitimate means to cripple her life. She
could scarcely have recalled anything Mrs. Prichard had said, for

the life of her. She was face to face with the past, yet standing at bay to conceal her identity.

Think how hard pressed she was, and forgive her for resorting to an excusable fiction. It was risky, but what could she do? "I knew your wife," said she briefly. "Twenty-two years agone."

"You mean the girl I married?" He had had to marry one of them, but could only marry one. That was how he classed her. "What became of that girl, I wonder? Maybe you know? Is she alive or dead?"

"I couldn't say, at this len'th of time." Then she remembered a servant, at the house where her child was born, and saw safety for her own fiction in assuming this girl's identity. Invention was stimulated by despair. "She was confined of a girl, where I was in service. She gave me letters to post to her husband. R. Thornton Daverill." That was safe, anyhow. For she remembered giving letters, so directed, to this girl.

The convict sat down on the table, looking at her no longer, which she found a relief. "Did that kid live or die?" said he. "Blest if I recollect!"

"Born dead. She had a bad time of it. She came back to London, and I never see any more of her." Aunt M'riar should have commented on this oblivion of his own child. She was letting her knowledge of the story influence her, and endangering her version of it.

The man stopped and thought a little. Then he turned upon her suddenly. "How came you to remember that name for twenty-two years?" said he.

A thing she recollected of this servant-girl helped her at a pinch. "She asked me to direct a letter when she hurt her hand," she said. "When you've wrote a name, you bear it in mind."

"What did she call the child?"

"It was born dead."

"What did she mean to call it?"

The answer should have been "She didn't tell me." But Aunt M'riar was a poor fiction-monger after all. For what must she say but "Polly, after herself"?

"Not Mary?"

Then Aunt M'riar forgot herself completely. "No—Polly. After the name you called her, at The Tun." She saw her mistake, too late.

Daverill turned his gaze on her again, slowly. "You seem to remember a fat lot about this and that!" said he. He got down off the table, and stepped between Aunt M'riar and the door, say-

ing:—"Come you here, mistress!" The harshness of his voice
was hideous to her. He caught her wrist, and pulled her to the
window. The only gas-lamp the Court possessed shone through
it on her white face. "Now—what's your * * * married name?"
Aunt M'riar could not utter a word.

"I can tell you. You're that * * * young Polly, and your name's
Daverill. You're my lawful wife—d'ye hear?" He gave a horrible laugh. "Why, I thought you was buried years ago!"

She began gasping hysterically:—"Leave me—leave me—you
are nothing to me now!" and struggled to free herself. Yet, inex-
pressibly dreadful as the fact seemed to her, she knew that her
struggle was not against the grasp of a stranger. Think of that
bygone time! The thought took all the spirit out of her resistance.

He returned to his seat upon the table, drawing her down beside him. "Yes, Polly Daverill," said he, "I thought you dead
and buried, years ago. I've had a rough time of it, since then,
across the water." He paused a moment; then said quite clearly,
almost passionlessly:—"God curse them all!" He repeated the
words, even more equably the second time; then with a rough bear-
hug of the arm that gripped her waist:—"What have *you* got to
say about it, hay? Who's your * * * husband now? Who's your
prizefighter?"

The terrified woman just found voice for:—"He's not my husband." She could not add a word of explanation.

The convict laughed unwholesomely, beneath his breath. "*That's*
what you've come to, is it? Pretty Polly! Mary the Maid of
the Inn! The man you've got is not your husband. Sounds like
the parson—Holy Scripture, somewhere! I've seen him. He's at
the lush-ken down the road. Now you tell the truth. When's he
due back here?"

She had only just breath for the word seven, which was true.
It was past the half-hour, and he would not have believed her
had she said sooner. But it was as though she told him that she
knew she was helplessly in his power for twenty-five minutes.
Helplessly, that is, strong resolution and desperation apart!

"Then he won't be here till half-past. Time and to spare!
Now you listen to me, and I'll learn you a thing or two you don't
know. You are my—lawful—wife, so just you listen to me! Ah,
would you? . . ." This was because he had supposed that a look
of hers askant had rested on a knife upon the table within reach.
It was a pointed knife, known as "the bread knife," which Dolly
was never allowed to touch. He pulled her away from it, caught
at it, and flung it away across the room. "It's a narsty, dan-

gerous thing," he said, "safest out of the way!" Then he went on:—"You—are—my—lawful—wife, and what St. Paul says mayhap you know? 'Wives, submit yourselves to your husbands, as it is fit in the Lord.' . . . What!—me not know my * * * Testament! Why!—it's the only * * * book you get a word of when you're nursing for Botany Bay fever. God curse 'em all! Why—the place was Hell—Hell on earth!"

Aunt M'riar now saw too late that she should not have opened that door, at any cost. But how about Micky? Surely, however, that was a mere threat. What had this man to gain by carrying it out? Why had she not seen that he would never run needless risk, to gain no end?

The worst thorn in her heart was that, changed as he was from the dissolute, engaging youth that she had dreamed of reforming, she still knew him for himself. He was, as he said, her husband. And, for all that she shrank from him and his criminality with horror, she was obliged to acknowledge—oh, how bitterly!—that she wanted help against herself as much as against him. She was obliged to acknowledge the grisly force of Nature, that dictated the reimposition of the yoke that she had through all these years conceived that she had shaken off. And she knew that she might look in vain for help to Law, human or theological. For each in its own way, and for its own purposes, gives countenance to the only consignment of one human creature to the power of another that the slow evolution of Justice has left in civilised society. Each says to the girl trapped into unholy matrimony, from whom the right to look inside the trap has been cunningly withheld:—"Back to your lord and master! Go to him, he is your husband—kiss him—take his hand in thine!" Neither is ashamed to enforce a contract to demise the self-ownership of one human being to another, when that human being is a woman. And yet Nature is so inexorable that the victim of a cruel marriage often needs help sorely—help against herself, to enable her, on her own behalf, to shake off the Devil some mysterious instinct impels her to cling to. Such an instinct was stirring in Aunt M'riar's chaos of thought and feeling, even through her terror and her consciousness of the vileness of the man and the vileness of his claim over her. The idea of using the power that her knowledge of his position gave her never crossed her mind. Say rather that the fear that a call for help would consign him to a just retribution for his crimes was the chief cause of her silence.

A dread that she might be compelled to do so was lessened by his next speech. "You've no call to look so scared, Polly Daverill.

You do what I tell you, and be sharp about it. What are you good for?—that's the question! Got any money in the house?"

She felt relieved. Now he would take his arm away. That arm was all the worse from the fact that her shrinking from it was one-sided. "A little," she answered. "It's upstairs. Let me get it."

He relaxed the arm. "Go ahead!" he said. "I'll follow up." She cried out with sudden emphasis:—"No—I will not. I will not." And then with subdued earnestness:—"Indeed I will bring it down. Indeed I will."

"You won't stick up there, by any chance, till your man that's not your husband happens round?"

She addressed him by name for the first time. "Thornton, did I ever tell you a lie?"

"I never caught you in one, that I know of. Cut along!"

She went like a bird released. Once in her room, and clear of him, she could lock her door and cry for help. She turned the key, and had actually thrown up the window-sash, when her own words crossed her mind—her claim to veracity. No—she would keep a clear conscience, come what might. She glanced up the Court, and saw Micky coming through the arch; then closed the window, and took an old leather purse from the drawer of the looking-glass Mr. Bartlett's men had not broken. It contained the whole of her small savings.

After she left the room, Daverill had glanced round for valuables. An old silver watch of Uncle Mo's, that always stopped unless allowed to lie on its back, was ticking on the dresser. The convict slipped it into his pocket, and looked round for more, opening drawers, looking under dish-covers. Finding nothing, he sat again on the table, with his hands in the pockets of his velveteen corduroy coat. His face-twist grew more marked as he wrinkled the setting of a calculating eye. "I should have to square it with Miss Juliar," said he, in soliloquy. He was evidently clear about his meaning, whatever it was.

The boy came running down the Court, and entering the front-yard, whose claim to be a garden was now *nil*, tapped at the window excitedly. Daverill went to the door and opened it.

"Mister Moses coming along. Stopping to speak to Tappingses. You'd best step it sharp, Mister Wix!"

"Polly Daverill, look alive!" The convict shouted at the foot of the stairs, and Aunt M'riar came running down. "Where's the * * * cash?" said he.

"It's all I've got," said poor Aunt M'riar. She handed the

purse to him, and he caught it and slipped it in a breast-pocket, and was out in the Court in a moment, running, without another word. He vanished into the darkness.

Five minutes later, Uncle Mo, escaping from Mrs. Tapping, came down the Court, and found the front-door open and no light in the house. He nearly tumbled over Aunt M'riar, in a swoon, or something very like it, in the chair by the door.

CHAPTER II

HOW ADRIAN TORRENS COULD SING WITHOUT WINCING. FIGARO. DICTA-TION OF LETTERS. HOW ADRIAN BROKE DOWN. THE LERNAEAN HYDRA'S EYE-PEEPS. HOW ADRIAN COULD SEE NOTHING IN ANY NUMBER OF LOOKING-GLASSES. HOW GWEN, IN SPITE OF APPEAR-ANCES, HELD TO THE SOLEMN COMPACT. SIR MERRIDEW'S TREACH-ERY. SEPTIMIUS SEVERUS. HOW GWEN HAD BEEN TO LOOK AT ARTHUR'S BRIDGE. A KINKAJOU IS NOT A CARCAJOU. OF THE PECU-LIARITIES OF FIRST-CLASS SERVANTS. MRS. PICTURE'S STORY DI-VULGED BY GWEN. HOW DAVE'S RIVAL GRANNIES WERE SAFEST APART

OLD folk and candles burn out slowly at the end. But before that end comes they flicker up, once, twice, and again. The candle says:—"Think of me at my best. Remember me when I shone out thus, and thus; and never guttered, nor wanted snuffing. Think of me when you needed no other light than mine, to look in Bradshaw and decide that you had better go early and ask at the Station." Thus says the candle.

And the old man says to the old woman, and she says it back to him:—"Think of me in the glorious days when we were dawn-ing on each other; of that most glorious day of all when we found each other out, and had a tiff in a week and a reconciliation in a fortnight!" Then each is dumb for a while, and life ebbs slowly, till some chance memory stirs among the embers, and a bright spark flickers for a moment in the dark. The candle dies at last, and smells, and mixes with the elements. And some say you and I will do the very same—die and go out. Possibly! Just as you like! Have it your own way.

It is even so with the Old Year in his last hours. Is ever an October so chill that he may not bid you suddenly at midday to come out in the garden and recall, with him, what it was

like in those Spring days when the first birds sang; those Summer
days when the hay-scent was in Cheapside, and a great many
roses had not been eaten by blights, and it was too hot to mow
the lawn? Is ever a November so self-centred as to refuse to help
the Old Year to a memory of the gleams of April, and the nightingale's first song about the laggard ash-buds? Is icy December's
self so remorseless, even when the holly-berries are making a
parade of their value as Christmas decorations?—even when it's
not much use pretending, because the Waits came last night,
and you thought, when you heard them, what a long time ago
it was that a little boy or girl, who must have been yourself,
was waked by them to wonder at the mysteries of Night? But
nothing is of any use in December, because January will come,
and this year will be dead and risen from its tomb, and the
metaphorically disposed will be hoping that Resurrection is not
so uncomfortable as all that comes to.

That time was eight weeks ahead one morning at Pensham
Steynes, which has to be borne in mind, as the residence of Sir
Hamilton Torrens, Bart., when the blind man, his son, was dictating to his sister Irene one of the long missives he was given
to sending to his *fiancée* in London. It was just such a late
October day as the one indirectly referred to above; in fact, it
would quite have done for a Spring day, if only you could have
walked across the lawn without getting your feet soaked. The
chance primroses that the mild weather had deluded into budding
must have felt ashamed of their stupidity, and disgusted at the
sight of the stripped trees, although they may have reaped some
encouragement from a missel-thrush that had just begun again
after the holiday, and been grateful to the elms and oaks that
had kept some decent clothing on them. Irene had found one
such primrose in a morning walk, and a confirmation of it in the
morning's *Times*.

"Why didn't you say the ground was covered with them, 'Re?
I could have believed in any number on your authority. Surely,
a chap with his eyes out is entitled to the advantages which seeing
nothing confers on him. Do please perjure yourself about violets
and crocuses on my behalf. It is quite a mistake to suppose I
shall be jealous. You've no idea what a magnanimous elder
brother you've got." So Adrian had said when they came in, and
had felt his way to the piano—it was extraordinary how he had
learned to feel his way about—and had played the air of "Sumer
is ycumin in, lhude sing cucu," with the courage of a giant. Not
only that, but actually sang it, and never flinched from:—"Grow-

eth seed and bloweth meed and springeth wood anew." And his heart was saying to him all the while that he might never again see the springing of the young corn, and the daisies in the grass, and the new buds waiting for the bidding of the sun.

Irene, quite alive to her brother's intrepidity, but abstaining resolutely from spoken acknowledgment—for would not that have been an admission of the need for courage?—had gone through a dramatic effort on her own behalf, a kind of rehearsal of the part she had to play. She had arranged writing materials for action, and affected the attitude of a patient scribe, longing for dictation. She had assumed a hardened tone, to say:—"When you're ready!" Then Adrian had deserted the piano, and addressed himself to dictation. "Where were we?" said he. For the letter was half written, having been interrupted by visitors the day before.

"When the Parysfort women came in?" said Irene. "We had got to the old woman. After the old woman—what next?"

Adrian repeated, "After the old woman—after the old woman." Then he said suddenly:—"Bother the old woman. I tell you what, 'Re, we must tear this letter up, and start fair. Those people coming in spoiled it." His tone was vexed and restless. The weariness of his blindness galled him. This fearful inability to write was one of his worst trials. He fought hard against his longing to cry out—to lighten his heart, ever so little, by expression of his misery; but then, the only one thing he could do in requital of the unflagging patience of this dear amanuensis, was to lighten the weight of her sorrow for him. And this he could only do by showing unflinching resolution to bear his own burden. One worst unkindest cut of all was that any word of exasperation against the cruelty of a cancelled pen might seem an imputation on her of ineffective service, almost a reproach. It was perhaps because the visitors of yesterday were so evidently to blame for the miscarriage of this letter, that Adrian felt, in a certain sense, free to grieve aloud. It was a relief to him to say:—"The Devil fly away with the Honourable Misses Parysforts!"

"Suppose we have a clean slate, darling, and I'll tear the letter up, old woman and all. Or shall I read back a little, to start you?"

"Oh no—please! On no account read anything again. . . . Suppose I confess up! Make some stars, and go on like this:— 'These are not Astronomy, but to convey the idea that I have forgotten where I was, and that we have to make it a rule never to re-read, for fear I should tear it up. I believe I was trying to find a new roundabout way of saying how much more to me you were than anything in Heaven or Earth.'" The dictation paused. "Go on," said the amanuensis. "After 'Heaven and Earth'?" She paused with an expectant pen, her eyes on the paper. Then she looked up, to see that her brother's face was in his hands, dropped down on the side-cushion of the sofa. She waited for him to speak, knowing he would only think she did not see him. But she had to wait overlong for the lasting powers of this excuse; so she let it lapse, and went to sit beside him, and coaxed his hands from his face, kissing away something very like a tear. "But why now, darling?" said she. "You know what I mean. What was it in the letter?"

"Why—I was going to say," replied Adrian, recovering himself, "I was going on to 'the thing that makes day of my darkness' or something of that sort—some poetical game, you know —and then I thought what a many things I could write if I could write them myself, and shut them in the envelope for Gwen alone, that I can't say now, though the dearest sister ever man had yet writes them for me. I *can* say to *her,* darling, that if I were offered my eyesight back, by some irritating fairy godmother—that kind of thing—in exchange for the Gwen that is mine, I would not accept her boon upon the terms. I should, on the contrary, wish I were the Lernæan Hydra, that I might give the balance of seven pairs of eyes rather than . . ."

"Rather than lose Gwen." Irene spoke, because he had hesitated.

"Exactly. But I got stuck a moment by the reflection that Gwen's sentiments might not have remained altogether unchanged, in that case. In fact, she might have run away, at Arthur's Bridge. It is an obscure and difficult subject, and the supply of parallel cases is not all one could wish."

"I don't see why we shouldn't put all or any of that in the letter." For Irene always favoured her brother's incurable whimsicality as a resource against the powers of Erebus and dark Night, and humoured any approach to extravagance, to disperse the cloud that had gathered. This one pleased him.

"How shall we put it? . . . somehow like this. . . . By-the-by, do you know how to spell Lernæan? . . ." He paused abruptly, and seemed to listen. "Sh—sh a minute! What's that outside? I thought I heard somebody coming." Irene listened too.

"Ply hears somebody," she said. And then she had all but said "Look at him!" in an unguarded moment.

An instant later the dog had started up and scoured from the room as if life and death depended on his presence elsewhere. Adrian heard something his sister did not, and exclaimed " What's that ? "

" Nothing," said Irene.   " Only someone at the front-door. Ply's always like that."

" I didn't mean Ply.   Listen !   Be quiet."   The room they were in was remote from the front-door of the house, and the voice they heard was no more than a musical modulation of silence.   It had a power in it, for all that, to rouse the blind man to excitement.   He had to put a restraint on himself to say quietly :—" Suppose you go and see !   Do you mind ? "   Irene left the room.

Anyone who had seen Adrian then for the first time, and watched him standing motionless with his hands on a chairback and the eyes that saw nothing gazing straight in front of him, but not towards the door, would have wondered to see a man of his type apparently so interested in his own image, repeated by the mirror before him as often as eyesight could trace its give-and-take with the one that faced it on the wall behind him. He was the wrong man for a Narcissus.   The strength of his framework was wrong throughout.   Narcissus had no bone-distances, as artists say, and his hair was in crisp curls, good for the sculptor.   No one ever needed to get a pair of scissors to snip it. But though anyone might have marvelled at Adrian Torrens's seeming Narcissus-like intentness on his own manifold image, he could never have surmised that cruel blindness was its apology. He could never have guessed, from anything in their seeming, that the long perspective of gazing orbs, vanishing into nothingness, were not more sightless than their originals.

He only listened for a moment.   For, distant as she was, Irene's cry of surprise on meeting some new-comer was decisive as to that new-comer's identity.   It could be no one but Gwen.   Irene's welcome settled that.

The blind man was feeling his way to the door when Gwen opened it.   Then she was in his arms, and what cared he for anything else in the heavens above or the earth beneath ?   His exultation had to die down, like the resonant chords in the music he had played an hour since, before he could come to the level of speech.   Then he said prosaically :—" This is very irregular ! How about the solemn compact ?   How are we going to look our mamma in the face ? "

" Did it yesterday evening ! " said Gwen.   " We had an explosion. . . .   Well, I won't say that—suppose we call it a warm discussion, leading to a more reasonable attitude on the part of . . . of the people who were in the wrong. The other people, that is to say!"

"Precisely. They always are. I vote we sit on the sofa, and you take your bonnet off. I know it's on by the ribbons under your chin—not otherwise."

"What a clever man he is—drawing inferences! However, bonnets *have* got very much out of sight, I admit. Hands off, please! . . . There!—now I can give particulars."

Irene, who—considerately, perhaps—had not followed closely, here came in, saying:—"Stop a minute! I haven't heard anything yet. . . . There!—now go on."

She found a seat, and Gwen proceeded.

"I came home yesterday, with an old woman I've picked up, who certainly is the dearest old woman. . . ."

"Never mind the old woman. Why did you come?"

"I came home because I chose. I came here because I wanted to. . . . Well, I'll tell you directly. What I wish to mention now is that I have not driven a coach-and-six through the solemn compact. I assented to a separation for six months, but no date was fixed. I assure you it wasn't. I was looking out all the time, and took good care."

"Wasn't it fixed by implication?" This was Irene.

"Maybe it was. But *I* wasn't. We can put the six months off, and start fair presently. Papa quite agreed."

"Mamma didn't?" This was Adrian.

"Of course not. That was the basis of the . . . warm discussion which followed on my declaration that I was coming to see you to-day. However, we parted friends, and I slept sound, with a clear conscience. I got up early, to avoid complications, and made Tom Kettering drive me here in the dog-cart. It took an hour and a half because the road's bad. It's like a morass, all the way. I like the sound of the horse's hoofs when I drive, not mud-pie thuds."

"We didn't hear any sound at all, except Ply. . . . Yes, dear! —of course *you* heard. I apologize." Irene said this to Achilles, who, catching his name, took up a more active position in the conversation, which he conceived to be about himself. Some indeterminate chat went on until Gwen said suddenly:—"Now I want to talk about what I came here for."

"Go it!" said Adrian.

"I want to know all about what 'Re said to Dr. Merridew in her letter. . . . Well, what's the matter?"

Amazement on Irene's fact had caused this. "And that man calls himself an F.R.C.S.!" said she.

Adrian, uninformed, naturally asked why not. Gwen supplied a clue for guessing. "He said he couldn't read your handwriting, and gave me your letter to make out."

"What nonsense! I write perfectly plainly."

"So I told him. But he maintained he had hardly been able to make out a word of it. Of course I read it. Your caution to him not to tell me was a little obscure, but otherwise I found it easy enough. Anyhow, I read all about it. And now I know."

"Well—I'll never trust a man with letters after his name again. Of course he was pretending."

"But what for?"

"Because he wanted to tell you, and didn't want to get in a scrape for betraying my confidence."

Adrian struck in. Might he ask what the rumpus was about? Why Sir Merridew, and why letters?

Irene supplied the explanation. "I wrote to him about you and Septimius Severus. . . . Don't you recollect? And I cautioned him particularly not to tell Gwen. . . . Why not? Why—of course not! It was sheer, inexcusable dishonesty, and I shall tell him so next time I see him."

Gwen appeared uninterested in the point of honour. "I wonder," she said, "whether he thought telling me of it this way would prevent my building too much on it, and being disappointed. That would be so exactly like Dr. Merridew."

"I think," said Adrian deliberately, "that I appreciate the position. Septimius Severus figures in it as a bust, or as an indirect way of describing a circumstance; preferably the latter, I should say, for it must be most uncomfortable to be a bust. As an Emperor he is inadmissible. I remember the incident—but I suspect it was only a dream." His voice fell into real seriousness as he said this; then went back to mock seriousness, after a pause. "However, I am bound to say that 'inexcusable dishonesty' is a strong expression. I should suggest 'pliable conscience,' always keeping in view the motive of . . . Yes, Pelides dear, but I have at present nothing for you in the form of cake or sugar. Explain yourself somehow, to the best of your ability." For Achilles had suddenly placed an outstretched paw, impressively, on the speaker's knee.

"I see what it was," said Gwen. "You said 'pliable conscience'—just now."

"Well?"

"He thought he was the first syllable. Never mind *him!* I want you to tell me about Septimius Severus. He's what I came about. What was it that happened, exactly?" Thereupon Adrian gave the experience which the story knows already, in greater detail.

In the middle, a casual housekeeper was fain to speak to Miss Torrens, for a minute. Who therefore left the room and became a voice, housekeeping, in the distance.

Then Gwen made Adrian tell the story again, cross-examining him as one cross-examines obduracy in the hope of admissions that will at least countenance a belief in the truth that we want to be true. If Adrian had seen his way to a concession that would have made matters pleasant, he would have jumped at the chance of making it. But false hope was so much worse than false despair. Better, surely, a spurious growth of the latter, with dis-illusionment to come, than a stinted instalment of the former with a chance of real despair ahead. Adrian took the view that Sir Coupland was really a weak, good-natured chap who had wanted Gwen to have every excuse for hope that could be constructed, even with unsound materials; but who also wanted the responsibilities of the jerry-builder to rest on other shoulders than his own. Gwen discredited this view of the great surgeon's character in her inner consciousness, but hardly had courage to raise her voice against it, because of the danger of fostering false hopes in her lover's mind. Nevertheless she could not be off fanning a little flame of comfort to warm her heart, from the conviction that so respon-sible an F.R.C.S. would never have gone out of his way to show her the letter if he had not thought there was some chance, how-ever small, of a break in the cloud.

After Sir Coupland's letter and its subject had been allowed to lapse, Gwen said:—"So now you see what I came for, and that's all about it. What do you think I did, dearest, yesterday as soon as I had seen my old lady comfortably settled? She was dreadfully tired, you know. But she was very plucky and wouldn't admit it."

"Who the dickens *is* your old lady?"

"Don't be impatient. I'll tell you all in good time. First I want to tell you where I went yesterday afternoon. I went across the garden through the rose-forest . . . you know?—what you said must be a rose-forest to smell like that. . . ."

"I know. And you went through the gate you came through,"— even so a Greek might have spoken to Aphrodite of "the sea-foam you sprang from"—"and along the field-path to the little bridge fat men get stuck on. . . ." This was an exaggeration of an overstatement of a disputed fact.

"Yes, my dearest, and I was there by myself. And I stood and looked over to Swayne's Oak and thought to myself if only it all could happen again, and a dog might come with a rush and kiss me, and paw me with his dirty paws! And then if you— *you—you* were to come out of the little coppice, and come to the rescue, all wet through and dripping, how I would take you in my arms, and keep you, and not let you go to be shot. I *would.* And I would say to you:—' I have found you in time, my darling, I have found you, in time to save you. And now that I have found you, I will keep you, like this. And you would look at me, and see that it was not a forward girl, but me myself, your very own, come for you. . . . I wonder what you would have said."

"I wonder what I should have said. I think I know, though. I should have said that although a perfect stranger, I should like, please, to remain in Heaven as long—I am quoting Mrs. Bailey— as it was no inconvenience. I might have said, while in Heaven, that we were both under a misapprehension, having taken for granted occurrences, to the development of which our subsequent experiences were essential. But I should have indulged the misapprehension. . . ."

"Of course you would. Any man in his senses would. . . ."

"I agree with you."

"Unless he was married or engaged or something."

"That might complicate matters. Morality is an unknown quantity. . . . But, darling, let's drop talking nonsense. . . ."

"No—don't let's! It's such sensible nonsense. Indeed, dearest. I saw it all plain, as I stood there yesterday at Arthur's Bridge. I saw what it had all meant. I did not know *at the time,* but I should have done so if I had not been a fool. I did not see then why I stood watching you till you were out of sight. But I do see now."

Adrian answered seriously, thoughtfully, as one who would fain get to the heart of a mystery. "I knew quite well then— I am convinced of it—why I turned, when I thought I was out of sight, to see if you were still there. I turned because my heart was on fire—because my world was suddenly filled with a girl I had exchanged fifty words with. I was not unhappy before you dawned—only tranquil."

"What were you thinking of, just before you saw me, when you were wading through the wet fern? I think *I* was only thinking how wet the ferns must have been. How little I thought then who the man was, with the dog! You were only 'the man' then."

"And then—I got shot! I'm so glad. Just think, dearest, what a difference it would have made to me if that ounce of lead had gone an inch wrong. . . ."

"And you had been killed outright!"

"I didn't mean that. I meant the other way. Suppose it had missed, and I had finished my walk with my eyes in my head, and come back here and got an introduction to the girl I saw in the Park, and not known what to say to her when I got it!"

"I should have known you at once."

"Dearest love, some tenses of verbs are kittle-cattle to shoe behind. 'Should have' is one of the kittlest of the whole lot. You would have thought me an interesting author, and I should have sent you a copy of my next book. And then we should have married somebody else."

"Where is the organ of nonsense in Poets' heads, I wonder. It must be this big one, on the top."

"No—that's veneration. My strong point. It shows itself in the readiness with which I recognise the Finger of Providence. I discern in the nicety with which old Stephen's bullet did its pre-destined work a special intervention on my behalf. A little more and I should have been sleeping with my fathers, or have joined the Choir of Angels, or anyhow been acting up to my epitaph to the best of my poor ability. A little less, and I should have gone my way rejoicing, ascribing my escape from that bullet to the happy-go-lucky character of the Divine disposition of human affairs. I should never have claimed the attentions due to a slovenly, unwholesome corpse. . . ."

"You shall *not* talk like that. Blaspheme as much as you like. I don't mind blasphemy."

Adrian kissed the palm of the hand that stopped his mouth, and continued speech, under drawbacks. "An intelligent analysis will show that my remarks are reverential, not blasphemous. You will at least admit that there would have been no Mrs. Bailey."

Gwen removed her hand. "None whatever! Yes, you may talk about Mrs. Bailey. There would have been no Mrs. Bailey, and I should never have lain awake all night with your eyes on my con-science. . . . Yes—the night after mamma and I had tea with you. . . ."

"My eyes on your conscience! Oh—my eyes be hanged! Would I have my eyes back now?—to lose *you!* Oh, Gwen, Gwen!—sometimes the thought comes to me that if it were not for my privation, my happiness would be too great to be borne—that I should scarcely dare to live for it, had the price I paid for it been less. What is the loss of sight for life to set against . . ."

"Are you aware, good man, that you are talking nonsense? Be a reasonable Poet, at least!"

She was drawing her hand caressingly over his, and just as she said this, lifted it suddenly, with a start. "Your ring scratches," said she.

"Does it?" said he, feeling it. "Oh yes—it does. I've found where. I'll have it seen to. . . . I wonder now why I never noticed that before."

"It's a good ring that won't scratch its wearer. I suppose I was unpopular with it. It didn't hurt. Perhaps it was only in fun. Or perhaps it was to call attention to the fact that you have never told me about it. You haven't, and you said you would."

"So I did, when we had The Scene." He meant the occasion on which, according to Gwen's mamma, she had made him an offer of her affections in the Jacobean drawing-room. "It's a ring with magic powers—nothing to do with any young lady, as you thought. It turns pale at the approach of poison."

"Let's get some poison, and try. Isn't there some poison in the house?"

"I dare say there is, in the kitchen. You might touch the bell and ask."

"I shall do nothing of the sort. I mean private poison—doctor's bottles—blue ones with embossed letters. . . . *You* know?"

"*I* know. My maternal parent has any number. But all empty, I'm afraid. She always finishes them. Besides—don't let's bring her in! She has such high principles. However, I've got some poison—what an Irish suicide would consider the rale cratur—only I won't get it out even for this experiment, because I may want it. . . ."

"You *may want it!*"

. "Of course." He suddenly deserted paradox and levity, and became serious. "My dearest, think of this! Suppose I were to lose you, here in the dark! . . . Oh, I know all that about duty —*I* know! I would not kill myself at once, because it would be unkind to Irene. But suppose I lost Irene too?"

"I can't reason it out. But I can't believe it would ever be right to destroy oneself."

"Possibly not, but once one was effectually destroyed. . . ."

"That sounds like rat-paste." Gwen wanted to joke her way out of this region of horrible surmise.

But Adrian was keen on his line of thought. "Exactly!" said he. "Vermin destroyer. *I* should be the vermin. But once destroyed, what contrition should I have to endure? Remorse is a game that takes two selves to play at it—a criminal and a conscientious person! Suppose the rat-paste had destroyed them both!"

"But would it?"

"Absolute ignorance, whether or no, means an even chance of either. I would risk it, for the sake of that chance of rich, full-blown Non-Entity. Oh, think of it!—after loneliness in the dark!—loneliness that once was full of life. . . ."

"But suppose the other chance—how then?"

"Suppose I worked out as a disembodied spirit—and I quite admit it's as likely as not, neither more nor less—it does not necessarily follow that Malignity against Freethinkers is the only attribute of the Creator. When one contemplates the extraordinary variety and magnitude of His achievements, one is tempted to imagine that He occasionally rises above mere personal feeling. It certainly does seem to me that damning inoffensive Suicides would be an unwarrantable abuse of Omnipotence. The fact is, I have a much better opinion of the Most High than many of His admirers."

"But, nonsense apart. . . . Yes—it *is* nonsense! . . . do you mean that you would kill yourself about me?"

"Yes."

"I'm so glad, because I shan't give you the chance. But dear, silly man—dearest, silliest man!—I do wish you would give me up that bottle. I'll promise to give it back if ever I want to jilt you. Honour bright!"

"I dare say. With the good, efficacious poison emptied away; and tea, or rum, or Rowland's Macassar instead! I cannot conceive a more equivocal position than that of a suicide who has taken the wrong poison under the impression that he has launched himself into Eternity."

"Oh no—I could never do that! It would be such a cruel hoax. Now, dearest love, do let me have that bottle to take care of. Indeed, if ever I jilt you, you shall have it back. Engaged girls—honourable ones!—always give presents back on jilting. *Do* let me have it!"

Adrian laughed at her earnestness. "*I'm* not going to poison myself," said he. "Unless you jilt me! So it comes to exactly the same thing, either way. There—be easy now! I've promised. Besides, the Warroo or Guarano Indian who gave it me—out on the Essequibo; it was when I went to Demerara—told me it wouldn't keep. So I wouldn't trust it. Much better stick to nice, wholesome, old-fashioned Prussic Acid." He had quite dropped his serious tone, and resumed his incorrigible levity.

"Did you really have it from a wild Indian? Where did he get it? Did he make it?"

"No—that's the beauty of it. The Warroos of Guiana are great dabs at making poisons. They make the celebrated Wourali poison, the smallest quantity of which in a vein always kills. It has never disappointed its backers. But he didn't make this. He brought it from the World of Spirits, beyond the grave. It is intended for internal use only, being quite inoperative when injected into a vein. Irene unpacked my valise when I came back, and touched the bottle. And an hour afterwards she saw that her white cornelian had turned red."

"Nonsense! It was a coincidence. Stones do change."

"I grant you it was a coincidence. Sunrise and daybreak are coincidences. But one is because of t'other. Irene believed my poison turned her stone red, or she would never have refused to wear it a minute longer, from an unreasonable dislike of the Evil One, whose influence she discerned in this simple, natural phenomenon. I considered myself justified in boning the ring for my own use, so I had it enlarged to go on my finger, and there it is, on! I shall never see it again, unless Septimius Severus turns up trumps. What colour should you say it was now?"

Gwen took the hand with the mystic ring on it, turning it this way and that, to see the light reflected. "Pale pink," she said. "Yes—certainly pale pink." She appeared amused, and unconvinced. "I had no idea 'Re was superstitious. You are excusable, dearest, because, after all, you are only a man. One expects a woman to have a little commonsense. Now if . . ." She appeared to be wavering over something—disposed towards concessions.

"Now if what?"

"If the ring had had a character from its last place—if it had distinguished itself before. . . ."

"Oh, I thought I told you about that. I forgot. It was a ring with a story, that came somehow to my great-great-grandfather, when he was in Paris. It had done itself great credit—gained quite a reputation—at the Court of Louis Quatorze, on the fingers I believe of the Marchioness de Brinvilliers and Louise de la Vallière. . . . Yes, I think both, but close particulars have always been wanting. 'Re only consented to wear it on condition she should be allowed to disbelieve in it, and then when this little strámash occurred through my bringing home the Warroo poison, her powers of belief at choice seem to have proved insufficient. . . . Isn't that her, coming back?"

It was; and when she came into the room a moment later, Gwen said:—"We've been talking about your ring, and a horrible little bottle of Red Indian poison this silly obstinate man has got hidden away and won't give me."

"I know," said Irene. "He's incorrigible. But don't you believe him, Gwen, when he justifies suicide. It's only his nonsense." Irene had come back quite sick and tired of housekeeping, and was provoked by the informal *status quo* of the young lady and gentleman on the sofa into remarking to the latter:—"Now you're happy."

"Or ought to be," said Gwen.

"Now, go on exactly where you were," said Irene.

"I will," said Adrian. "I was just expressing a hope that Gwen had been regular in her attendance at church while in London." He did not seem vitally interested in this, for he changed almost immediately to another subject. "How about your old lady, Gwen? She's your old lady, I suppose, whose house tumbled down?"

"Yes, only not quite. We got her out safe. The woman who lived with her, Mrs. Burr. . . . However, I wrote all that in my letter, didn't I?"

"Yes—you wrote about Mrs. Burr, and how she was a commonplace person. We thought you unfeeling about Mrs. Burr."

"I was, quite! I can't tell you how it has been on our consciences, Clo's and mine, that we have been unable to take an interest in Mrs. Burr. We tried to make up for it, by one of us going every day to see her in the hospital. I must say for her that she asked about Mrs. Prichard as soon as she was able to speak—asked if she was being got out, and said she supposed it was the repairs. She is not an imaginative or demonstrative person, you see. When I suggested to her that she should come to look after Mrs. Prichard in the country, till the house was rebuilt, she only said she was going to her married niece's at Clapham. I don't know why, but her married niece at Clapham seemed to me indisputable, like an Act of Parliament. I said 'Oh yes!' in a convinced sort of way, as if I knew this niece, and acknowledged Clapham."

"Then you have got the old lady at the Towers?"

"Yes—yesterday. I don't know how it's going to answer."

Adrian said: "Why shouldn't it answer?"

Irene was sharper. "Because of the servants, I suppose," said she.

Gwen said:—"Ye-es, because of the household."

"I thought," said Adrian, "that she was such a charming old lady." This took plenty of omissions for granted.

"So she is," said Gwen. "At least, *I* think her most sweet and fascinating. But really—the British servant!"

"*I* know," said Irene.

"Especially the women," said Gwen. "I could manage the men, easily enough."

"You *could*," said Adrian, with expressive emphasis. And all three laughed. Indeed, it is difficult to describe the subserviency of her male retinue to "Gwen o' the Towers." To say that they were ready to kiss the hem of her garment is but a feeble expression of the truth. Say, rather, that they were ready to fight for the privilege of doing so!

"I can't say," Gwen resumed, "precisely what I found my misgivings on. Little things I can't lay hold of. I can't find any *fault* with Lutwyche when she was attending on the dear old soul in Cavendish Square. But I couldn't help thinking . . ."

"What?"

"Well—I thought she showed a slightly fiendish readiness to defer to my minutest directions, and perhaps, I should say, a fell determination not to presume." Telegraphies of slight perceptive nods and raised eyebrows, in touch with shoulder shrugs not insisted on, expressed mutual understanding between the two young ladies. "Of course, I may be wrong," said Gwen. "But when I interviewed Mrs. Masham last thing last night, it was borne in upon me, Heaven knows how, that she had been in collision with Lutwyche about the old lady."

"What is it you call her?" said Irene. "Old Mrs. Picture? There's nothing against her, is there?"

Adrian had seemed to be considering a point. "Did you not say something—last letter but one, I think—about the old lady's husband having been convicted and transported?"

"Oh *yes!*—but that's not to be talked about, you know! Besides, it was her son, not her husband, that I wrote about. I only found out about the husband a day or two ago. Only you must be very careful, dearest, and remember it's a dead secret. I promise not to tell things, and then of course I forget, when it's you. Old Mrs. Picture would quite understand, though, if I told her."

Adrian said that he really must have some more of the secret to keep, or it would not be worth keeping.

So Gwen told them then and there all that old Mrs. Picture had told her of her terrible life-story. It may have contained things this present narrative has missed, or *vice versa*, but the essential points were the same in both.

"What a queer story!" said Adrian. "Did the old body cry when she told it?"

"Scarcely, if at all. She looked very beautiful—you've no idea how lovely she is sometimes—and told it all quite quietly, just as if she had been speaking of someone else."

"I have always had a theory," said Adrian, "that one gets less and less identical as Time goes on. . . ."

"What do you mean by that?" said Gwen.

"Haven't the slightest idea!" Adrian had been speaking seriously, but at this point his whimsical mood seized him. He went on:—"You don't mean to say, I hope, that you are going to make meaning a *sine qua non* in theories? It would be the death-knell of speculation."

"You don't know what a goose you are engaged to, Gwen," said Irene parenthetically.

"Yes, I do. But he meant something this time. He *does*, you know, now and again, in spite of appearances to the contrary. What *did* you mean, please?"

"I can only conjecture," said Adrian incorrigibly. Then, more in earnest:—"I think it was something like this. I know that I am the same man that I was last week so long as I remember what happened last week. Suppose I forget half—which I do, in practice—I still remain the same man, according to my notion of identity. But it is an academical notion, of no use in everyday life. A conjurer who forgets how to lay eggs in defiance of natural law, or how to find canaries in pocket-handkerchiefs, is not the same conjurer, in practical politics. And yet he is the same man. Dock and crop his qualities and attributes as you will, he keeps the same man, academically. But not for working purposes. By the time you can say nothing about him, that was true of him last week, he may just as well be somebody else."

"Mind you recollect all that, and it will do in a book," said his sister. "But what has it to do with Gwen's old woman?"

"Yes—what has it to do with my old woman?" said Gwen.

"Didn't you say," Adrian asked, "that the old lady told all about her past quite quietly, just as if she had been speaking of somebody else? Your very expression, ma'am! You see, she was to all intents and purposes somebody else then, or has become somebody else now. I always wonder, whether, if one had left oneself—one of one's selves—behind in the past, like old Mrs. Picture, and some strange navigation on the sea of life were to land one in a long-forgotten port, where the memory still hung on, in a mind or two, of the self one had left behind—would the self one had grown to be bring conviction to the mind or two? Wouldn't the chance survivors who admitted that you were Jack or Jim or Polly be discouraged if they found that Jack or Jim or Polly had forgotten the old pier that was swept away, or the old pub which the new hotel was, once. Wouldn't they discredit you? Wouldn't they decide that, for all your bald, uninteresting identity—mere mechanical sameness—you wouldn't wash?"

"Rip van Winkle washed," said Gwen.

"Because Washington Irving chose. I sometimes imagine Rip isn't really true. Anyhow, his case doesn't apply. *He* remembered everything as if it was yesterday. For him, it *was* yesterday. So he was the same man, both in theory and practice. Jack and Jim and Polly were to forget, by hypothesis."

"Does old Mrs. Picture?" asked Irene.

"I should say—very little," said Gwen. "Less now than when I took her first to Cavendish Square. She'll get very communicative, I've no doubt, if she's fed up, in the country air. I shall see to that myself. So Mrs. Masham had better look out."

"There's mamma!" said Irene suddenly. "I'll go and see that she gets her writing things. . . . No—don't you move! She won't come in here. She wants to write important letters. You sit still." And Irene went off to intercept the Miss Abercrombie her father had married all those years ago instead of Gwen's mother. She does not come much into this story, but its reader may be interested to know that she was an enthusiastic Abolitionist, and a friend of the Duchess of Sutherland. There was only one thing in those days that called for abolition—negro slavery in America; so everyone who recollects the fifties will know what an Abolitionist was. Nevertheless, though Lady Torrens happens to keep outside the story, it would have been quite another story without her.

Adrian was a good son, and loved his mother duly. She returned his affection, but could not stand his poetical effusions, which she thought showed an irreverent spirit. We are not quite sure they did not.

CHAPTER III

HOW AN OLD LADY WAS TAKEN FOR A DRIVE, AND SAW JONES'S BULL,
ALL IN A DREAM. STRIDES COTTAGE AND A STRANGE CONTIGUITY.
AFTER SIXTY YEARS! HOW TOBY SMASHED A PANE OF GLASS WITH
A HORSE-CHESTNUT, AND NEARLY HAD NO SUGAR IN HIS BREAD-AND-
MILK. HOW THE OLD BODY CURTSIED AND THE OLD SOUL DIDN'T
GO TO SLEEP. HOW GWEN NEARLY FORGOT TO INTRODUCE THEM.
HOW MRS. PICTURE KNOCKED UP AND RAN DOWN,—BUT WOULD NOT
HAVE MUTTON BROTH. BUT NEITHER KNEW! HOW MRS. PICTURE
THOUGHT MRS. MARRABLE A NICE PERSON. HOW GWEN LUNCHED
WITH HER PARENTS. "REALLY, OUR DAUGHTER!" HOW LOOKING
AMUSED DOES NO GOOD. WAS GWEN JONES'S BULL, OR HOW? NOR-
BURY AS AN ORACLE. HOW THE EARL WENT ROUND TO SEE THE
FAIRY GODMOTHER

It had all come on the old woman like a bewildering dream.
It began with the sudden appearance, as she dozed in her chair
at Sapps Court, all the memories of her past world creeping spark-
like through its half-burned scroll, a dream of Gwen in her glory,
heralded by Dave; depositing Dolly, very rough-headed, on the
floor, and explaining her intrusion with some difficulty owing to
those children wanting to explain too. This was dreamlike enough,
but it had become more so with the then inexplicable crash that
followed a discomfort in the floor; more so with that strange half-
conscious drive through the London streets in the glow of the
sunset; more so yet, when, after an interval of real dreams, she
woke to the luxury of Sister Nora's temporary arrangements,
pending the organization of the Simple Life; more dreamlike
still when she woke again later, to wonder at the leaves of the
creeper that framed her lattice at the Towers, ruby in the dawn
of a cloudless autumn day, and jewelled with its dew. She had
to look, wonderingly, at her old unchanged hands, to be quite
sure she was not in Heaven. Then she caught a confirmatory
glimpse of her old white head in a mirror, and that settled it.
Besides, her old limbs ached; not savagely, but quite perceptibly,
and that was discordant with her idea of Heaven.

Her acquiescence was complete in all that had happened. Not
that it was clearly what she would have chosen, even if she could
have foreseen all its outcomings, and pictured to herself what

she would have been refusing, had refusal been practicable. Her actual choice, putting aside newly kindled love for this mysterious and beautiful agency, half daughter and half Guardian Angel, that had been sprung upon her life so near its close, might easily have been to face the risks of some half-dried plaster, and go back to her old chair by the fire in Sapps Court, and her day-dreams of the huge cruel world she had all but seen the last of; to watch through the hours for what was now the great relaxation of her life, the coming of Dave and Dolly, and to listen through the murmur of the traffic that grew and grew in the silence of the house, for the welcome voices of the children on the stairs. But how meet Gwen's impulsive decisions with anything but acquiescence? It was not, with her, mere ready deference to the will of a superior; she might have stickled at that, and found words to express a wish for her old haunts and old habits of life. It was much more nearly the feeling a mother might have had for a daughter, strangely restored to her, after long separation that had made her a memory of a name. It was mixed with the ready compliance one imputes to the fortunate owner of a Guardian Angel, who is deserving of his luck. No doubt also with the fact that no living creature, great or small, ever said nay to Gwen. But, for whatever reason, she complied, and wondered.

Remember, too, the enforced associations of her previous experience. Think how soon the conditions of her early youth—which, if they afforded no high culture, were at least those of a respected middle class in English provincial life—came to an end, and what they gave place to! Then, on her return to England, how little chance her antecedents and her son's vicious inherited disposition gave her of resuming the position she would have been entitled to had her exile, and its circumstances, not made the one she had to submit to abnormal! Aunt M'riar and Mrs. Burr were good women, but those who study class-niceties would surely refuse to *ranger* either with Granny Marrable. And even that old lady is scarcely a fair illustration; for, had her sister's bridegroom been what the bride believed him, the social outcome of the marriage would have been all but the same as of her own, had she wedded his elder brother.

It is little wonder that old Mrs. Picture, who once was Maisie, should succumb to the influences of this dazzling creature with all the world at her feet. And less that these influences grew upon her, when there was none to see, and hamper free speech with conventions. For when they were alone, it came about that either unpacked her heart to the other, and Gwen gave all the tale of the shadow on her own love in exchange for that of the blacker shadows of the galleys—of the convict's cheated wife, and the terrible inheritance of his son.

The story is sorry to have to admit that Gwen's bad faith to the old lady, in the matter of her pledge of secrecy, did not show itself only in her repetition of the story to her lover and his sister. She told her father, a nobleman with all sorts of old-fashioned prejudices, among others that of disliking confidences entrusted to him in disregard of solemn oaths of secrecy. His protest intercepted his daughter's revelation at the outset. " Un-principled young monkey! " he exclaimed. " You mustn't tell me when you've promised not to. Didn't you, now? "

" Of course I did! But *you* don't count. Papas don't, when trustworthy. Besides, the more people of the right sort know a secret, the better it will be kept." Gwen had to release her lips from two paternal fingers to say this. She followed it up by using them—she was near enough—to run a trill of kisslets across the paternal forehead.

" Very good! " said the Earl. " Fire away! " It has been mentioned that Gwen always got her will, somehow. This *how* was the one she used with her father. She told the whole tale without reserves; except, perhaps, slight ones in respect of the son's misdeeds. They were not things to be spoken of to a good, innocent father, like hers.

She answered an expression on his face, when she had finished, with:—" As for any chance of the story not being true, that's impossible."

" Then it must be true," was the answer. Not an illogical one! " Don't agree meekly," says Gwen. " Meek agreement is contradiction. . . . What makes you think it fibs? "

" I don't think it fibs, my darling. Because I attach a good deal of weight to the impression it has produced upon you. But other people might, who did not know you."

" Other people are not to be told, so they are out of it. . . . Well, perhaps that *has* very little to do with the matter."

" Not very much. But tell me!—does the old lady give no names at all? "

" N-no!—I can remember none. Her real name is not Picture, of course . . . I should have said Prichard."

" I understand. But couldn't you get at her husband's name, to verify the story? "

" I don't want it verified. Where's the use? . . . No, she hasn't told me a single surname of any of the people. . . . Oh yes—stop a minute! Of course she told me Prichard was a name in her family—some old nurse's. But it's such a common name."

"Did she not say where she came from—where her family belonged?"

"Yes—Essex. But Essex is like Rutlandshire. Nobody has ever been to either, or knows anyone that is there by nature."

"I didn't know that was the case, but I have no interest in proving the contrary. Suppose you try to get at her husband's name—her real married name. I could tell my man in Lincoln's Inn to hunt up the trial. Or even if you could get the exact date it might be enough. There cannot have been so very many fathers-in-laws' signatures forged in one year."

But Gwen did not like to press the old lady for information she was reluctant to give, and the names of the family in Essex and the delinquent remained untold; or, if told to Gwen, were concealed more effectually by her than the narrative they were required to fill out. And as the confidants to whom she had repeated that narrative were more loyal to her than she herself had been to its first narrator, it remained altogether unknown to the household at the Towers; and, indeed, to anyone who could by repeating it have excited suspicion of the twinship of the farmer's widow at Chorlton-under-Bradbury and the old lady whom her young ladyship's eccentricities had brought from London.

Apart from their close contiguity, nothing occurred for some time to make mutual recognition more probable than it had been at any moment since Dave's visit to Chorlton had disclosed to each the bare fact of the other's existence. They were within five miles of one another, and neither knew it; nor had either a thought of the other but as a memory of long ago; still cherished, as a sepulchral stone cherishes what Time leaves legible, while his slow hand makes each letter fainter day by day.

And yet—how near they went on one occasion to what must have led to recognition, had the period of their separation been less cruelly long, and its strange conditions less baffling! How near, for instance, three or four days after old Maisie's arrival at the Towers, when Gwen the omnipotent decided that she would take Mrs. Picture for a long drive in the best part of the day— the longest drive that would not tire her to death!

Whether the old soul that her young ladyship had taken such a fancy to—that was how Blencorn the coachman and Benjamin the coachboy thought of her—really enjoyed the strange experience of gliding over smooth roads flanked by matchless woodlands or primeval moorland; cropless Autumn fields or pastures of con-

tented cattle; through villages of the same mind about the un-
desirableness of change that had been their creed for centuries,
with churches unconscious of judicious restoration and an un-
flawed record of curfews; by farms with all the usual besetting
sins of farms, black duck-slush and uncaptivating dung-heaps;
cattle no persuasion weighs with; the same hen that never stops
the same dissertation on the same egg, the same cock ʹthat has
some of the vices of his betters, our male selves to wit—whether
the said old soul really enjoyed all this, who can say? She may
have been pretending to satisfy her young ladyship. If so, she
succeeded very well, considering her years. But it was all part
of a dream to her.

In that dream, she waked at intervals to small realities. One
of these was Farmer Jones's Bull. Not that she had more than
a timid hope of seeing that celebrated quadruped himself. She
was, however, undisguisedly anxious to do so; inquiring after
him; the chance of his proximity; the possibility of cultivating his
intimate acquaintance. No other bull would serve her purpose,
which was to take back to Dave, who filled much of her thoughts,
an authentic report of Farmer Jones's.

" Dave must be a very nice little boy," said Gwen. " Anyhow,
he's pretty. And Dolly's a darling." This may have been partly
due to the way in which Dolly had overwhelmed the young lady
—the equivalent, as it were, of a kind of cannibalism, or perhaps
octopus-greed—which had stood in the way of a maturer friendship with her brother. However, there had really been very little
time.

" You see, my dear," said the old lady, " if I was to see Farmer
Jones's Bull, I could tell the dear child about him in London.
Isn't that a Bull?" But it wasn't, though possibly a relation he
would not have acknowledged.

" I think Blencorn might make a point of Farmer Jones's Bull,"
said Gwen. " Blencorn!"

" Yes, my lady."

" I want to stop at Strides Cottage, coming back. You know—
Mrs. Marrable's!"

" Yes, my lady."

" Well—isn't that Farmer Jones's farm, on the left, before we
get there? Close to the Spinney." Now Mr. Blencorn knew perfectly well. But he was not going to admit that he knew, because
farms were human affairs, and he was on the box. He referred
to his satellite, the coachboy, whose information enabled him to
say:—" Yes, my lady, on the left." Gwen then said:—" Very

good, then, Blencorn, stop at the gate, and Benjamin can go in and say we've come to see the Bull. Go on!"

"I wonder," said old Mrs. Prichard, with roused interest, "if that is Davy's granny I wrote to for him. Such a lot he has to say about her! But it was Mrs. . . . Mrs. Thrale Dave went to stop with."

"Mrs. Marrable—Granny Marrable—is Mrs. Thrale's mother. A nice old lady. Rather younger than you, and awfully strong. She can walk nine miles." In Rumour's diary, the exact number of a pedestrian's miles is vouched for, as well as the exact round number of thousands Park-Laners have *per annum*. "I dare say we shall see her," Gwen continued. "I hope so, because I promised my cousin Clo to give her this parcel with my own hands. Only she may be out. . . . Aren't you getting very tired, dear Mrs. Picture?"

Mrs. Picture was getting tired, and admitted it. "But I must see the Bull," said she. She closed her eyes and leaned back, and Gwen said:—"You can drive a little quicker, Blencorn." There had been plenty of talk through a longish drive, and Gwen was getting afraid of overdoing it.

This was the gate of the farm, my lady. Should Benjamin go across to the house, and express her ladyship's wishes? Benjamin was trembling for the flawless blacking of his beautiful boots, and the unsoiled felt of his leggings. Yes, he might go, and get somebody to come out and speak to her ladyship, or herself, as convenient. But while Benjamin was away on this mission, the unexpected came to pass in the form of a boy. We all know how rarely human creatures occur in fields and villages, in England. This sporadic example, in answer to a question "Are you Farmer Jones's boy?" replied guardedly:—"Ees, a be woon."

"Very well then," said Gwen. "Find Farmer Jones, to show us his Bull."

The boy shook his head. "Oo'r Bull can't abide he," said he. "A better tarry indowers, fa'ather had, and leave oy to ha'andle un. A be a foine Bull, oo'r Bull!"

"You mean, you can manage your Bull, and father can't. Is that it?" Assent given. "And how can you manage your Bull?"

"Oy can whistle un a tewun."

"Is he out in the field, or here in his stable or house, or whatever it's called?"

"That's him nigh handy, a-roomblin'." It then appeared that this youth was prepared, for a reasonable consideration, to lead this formidable brute out into the farmyard, under the influence of musical cajolery. He met a suggestion that his superiors might disapprove of his doing so, by pointing out that they would all keep " yower side o' th' gayut " until the Bull—whose name, strange to say, seemed to be Zephyr—was safe in bounds, chained by his nose-ring to a sufficient wall-staple.

Said old Mrs. Picture, roused from an impending nap by the interest of the event:—" This must be the boy Davy told about, who whistled to the Bull. Why—the child can never tire of telling that story." It certainly was the very selfsame boy, and he was as good as his word, exhibiting the Bull with pride, and soothing his morose temper as he had promised, by monotonous whistling. Whether he was more intoxicated with his success or with a shilling Gwen gave him as recompense, it would have been hard to say.

The old lady was infinitely more excited and interested about this Bull, on Dave's account, than about any of the hundred-and-one things Gwen had shown her during her five-mile drive. When Gwen gave the direction:—" Go on to Strides Cottage, Blencorn," and Blencorn, who had scarcely condescended to look at the Bull, answered:—" Yes, my lady," her interest on Dave's account was maintained, but on a rather different line. She was, however, becoming rapidly too fatigued to entertain any feelings of resentment against her rival, and none mixed with the languid interest the prospect of seeing her aroused during the three-minutes' drive from Farmer Jones's to Strides Cottage.

This story despairs of showing to the full the utter strangeness of the position that was created by this meeting of old Maisie and old Phœbe, each of whom for nearly half a century had thought the other dead. It is forced to appeal to its reader to make an effort to help its feeble presentations by its own powers of imagery.

Conceive that suddenly a voice that imposed belief on its hearers had said to each of them:—" This is your sister of those long bygone years—slain, for you, by a cunning lie; living on, and mourning for a death that never was; dreaming, as you dreamed, of a slowly vanishing past, vanishing so slowly that its characters might still be visible at the end of the longest scroll of recorded life. Look upon her, and recognise in that shrunken face the lips you kissed, the cheeks you pressed to yours, the eye that laughed and gave back love or mockery! Try to hear in that frail old voice the music of its speech in the years gone by; ask for the song it knew so well the trick of. Try to caress in those grey, thin old tresses the mass of gold from whose redundance you cut the treasured locks you almost weep afresh to see and handle, even now." Then try to imagine to yourself the outward seeming of its hearers, always supposing them to understand. It is a large supposition, but the dramatist would have to accept it, with the ladies in the stalls getting up to go.

Are *you* prepared to accept, off the stage, a snapshot recognition of each other by the two old twins, and curtain? It is hard to conceive that mere eyesight, and the hearing of a changed voice, could have provoked such a result. However, it is not for the story to decide that in every case it would be impossible. It can only record events as they happened, however much interest might be gained by the interpolation of a little skilful fiction.

That morning, at Strides Cottage, a regrettable event had disturbed Granny Marrable's equanimity. A small convalescent, named Toby, who was really old enough to know better, had made a collection of beautiful, clean, new horse-chestnuts from under the tree in the field behind the house. Never was the heart of man more embittered by this sort being no use for cooking than in the case of these flawless, glossy rotundities. Each one was a handful for a convalescent, and that was why Toby so often had his hands in his pockets. He was, in fact, fondling his ammunition, like Mr. Dooley. For that was, according to Toby, the purpose of Creation in the production of the horse-chestnut tree. He had awaited his opportunity, and here it was:—he was unwatched in the large room that was neither kitchen nor living-room, but more both than neither, and he seized it to show his obedience to a frequent injunction not to throw stones. He was an honourable convalescent, and he proved it in the choice of a missile. His first horse-chestnut only gave him the range; his second smashed the glass it was aimed at. And that glass was the door or lid of the automatic watermill on the chimney-piece!

The Granny was quite upset, and Widow Thrale was downright angry, and called Toby an undeserving little piece, if ever there was one. It was a harsh censure, and caused Toby to weep; in fact, to roar. Roaring, however, did nothing towards repairing the mischief done, and nearly led to a well-deserved penalty for Toby, to be put to his bed and very likely have no sugar in his bread-and-milk—such being the exact wording of the sentence. It was not carried out, as it was found that the watermill and horses, the two little girls in sun-bonnets, and the miller smoking at the window, were all intact; only the glass being broken. There was no glazier in the village, which broke few windows, and was content to wait the coming round of a peripatetic plumber, who came at irregular intervals, like Easter, but without astronomical checks. So, as a temporary expedient to keep the dust out, Widow Thrale pasted a piece of paper over the breakage, and the mill was hidden from the human eye. Toby showed penitence, and had sugar in his bread-and-milk, but the balance of his projectiles was confiscated.

Consequently, old Mrs. Marrable was not in her best form when her young ladyship arrived, and Benjamin the coachboy came up the garden pathway as her harbinger to see if she should descend from the carriage to interview the old lady. She did not want to do so, as she felt she ought to get Mrs. Prichard home as soon as possible; but wanted, all the same, to fulfil her promise of delivering Sister Nora's parcel with her own hands. She was glad to remain in the carriage, on hearing from Benjamin that both Granny Marrable and her daughter were on the spot; and would, said he, be out in a minute.

"They'll curtsey," said Gwen. "Do, dear Mrs. Picture, keep awake one minute more. I want you so much to see Dave's other Granny. She's such a nice old body!" Can any student of language say why these two old women should be respectively classed as an old soul and an old body, and why the cap should fit in either case?

"I won't go to sleep," said Mrs. Prichard, making a great effort. "That must be Dave's duck-pond, across the road." The duck-pond had no alloy. She did not feel that her curiosity about Dave's other Granny was quite without discomfort.

"Oh—had Dave a duck-pond? It looks very black and juicy. . . . Here come the two Goodies! I've brought you a present from Sister Nora, Granny Marrable. It's in here. I know what it is because I've seen it—it's nice and warm for the winter. Take it in and look at it inside. I mustn't stop because of Mrs. . . . There now!—I was quite forgetting. . . ." It shows how slightly Gwen was thinking of the whole transaction that she should all but tell Blencorn to drive home at this point, with the scantiest farewell to the Goodies, who had curtsied duly as foretold. She collected herself, and continued:—"You remember the small boy, Mrs. Marrable, when I came with Sister Nora, whose letter we read about the thieves and the policeman?"

"Ah, dear, indeed I do! That dear child!—why, what would we not give, Ruth and me, to see him again?"

"Well, this is Mrs. Picture, who wrote his letter for him. This

is Granny Marrable, that Dave told you all about. She says she
wants him back."

And then Maisie and Phœbe looked each other in the face again
after half a century of separation. Surely, if there is any truth
in the belief that the souls of twins are linked by some unseen
thread of sympathy, each should have been stirred by the presence
of the other. If either was, she had no clue to the cause of her
perturbation. They looked each other in the face; and each made
some suitable recognition of her unknown sister. Phœbe hoped
the dear boy was well, and Maisie heard that he was, but had not
seen him now nigh a month. Phœbe had had a letter from him
yesterday, but could not quite make it out. Ruth would go in
and get it, for her ladyship to see. Granny Marrable made little
direct concession to the equivocal old woman who might be anything, for all she was in her ladyship's carriage.

"I suppose," said Gwen, "the boy has tried to describe the
accident, and made a hash of it. Is that it?"

"Indeed, my lady, he does tell something of an accident. Only
I took it for just only telling—story-book like! . . . Ah, yes,
that will be the letter. Give it to her ladyship."

Gwen took the letter from Widow Thrale, but did not unfold
it. "Mayn't I take it away," she said, "for me and Mrs. Picture
to read at home? I want to get her back and give her some food.
She's knocking up."

Immediately Granny Marrable's heart and Widow Thrale's
overflowed. What did the doubts that hung over this old person
matter, whatever she was, if she was running down visibly within
the zone of influence of perceptible mutton-broth; which was confirming, through the door, what the wood-smoke from the chimney
had to say about it to the Universe? Let Ruth bring out a cup
of it at once for Mrs. Picture. It was quite good and strong
by now. Granny Marrable could answer for that.

But it was one thing to be generous to a rival, another to accept
a benevolence from one. Mrs. Picture quite roused herself to
acknowledge the generosity, but she wouldn't have the broth on
any terms, evidently. Gwen thought she could read the history
of this between the lines. As we have seen, she was aware of
the sort of jealousy subsisting between these two old Grannies
about their adopted grandson. She thought it best to favour immediate departure, and Blencorn jumped at the first symptom of
a word to that effect. The carriage rolled away, waving farewells
to the cottage, and the tenants of the latter went slowly back to
the mutton-broth.

And neither of the two old women had the dimmest idea whose face it was that she had looked at in the broad full light of a glorious autumn day; not passingly, as one glances at a stranger on the road, who comes one knows not whence, to vanish away one knows not whither; but inquiringly, as when a first interview shows us the outward seeming of one known by hearsay—one whom our mind has dwelt on curiously, making conjectural images at random, and wondering which was nearest to the truth. And to neither of those who saw this meeting, for all they felt interest to note what each would think of the other, did the thought come of any very strong resemblance between them. They were two old women—that was all!

And yet, in the days of their girlhood, these old women had been so much alike that they were not allowed to dress in the same colour, for mere mercy to the puzzled bystanders. So much alike that when, for a frolic, each put on the other's clothes, and answered to the other's name, the fraud went on for days, undetected!

It seems strange, but gets less strange as all the facts are sorted out, and weighed in the scale. First and foremost the whole position was so impossible *per se*—one always knows what is and is not possible!—that any true version of the antecedents of the two old women would have seemed mere madness. Had either spectator noted that the bones of the two old faces were the same, she would have condemned her own powers of observation rather than doubt the infallibility of instinctive disbelief, which is the attitude of the vernacular mind not only to what it wishes to be false, but to anything that runs counter to the octave-stretch forlorn—as Elizabeth Browning put it—of its limited experience. Had either noted that the eyes of the two were the same, she would have attached no meaning to the similarity. So many eyes are the same! How many shades of colour does the maker of false eyes stock, all told? Guess them at a thousand, and escape the conclusion that in a world of a thousand million, a million of eyes are alike, if you can. If they had compared the hair still covering the heads of both, they would have found Dave's comparison of it with Pussy's various tints a good and intelligent one. Maisie was silvery white, Phœbe merely grey. But the greatest difference was in the relative uprightness and strength of the old countrywoman, helped—and greatly helped—by the entire difference in dress.

No!—it was not surprising that bystanders should not suspect offhand that something they would have counted impossible was actually there before them in the daylight. Was it not even less so that Maisie and Phœbe, who remembered Phœbe and Maisie last in the glory and beauty of early womanhood, should each be unsuspicious, when suspicion would have gone near to meaning a thought in the mind of each that the other had risen from the grave? It is none the less strange that two souls, nourished unborn by the same mother, should have all but touched, and that neither should have guessed the presence of the other, through the outer shell it dwelt in.

How painfully we souls are dependent on the evidence of our existence—eyes and noses and things!

To get back to the thread of the story. Mrs. Picture, on her part, seemed—so far as her fatigue allowed her to narrate her impressions—to take a more favourable view of her rival than the latter of herself. She went so far as to speak of her as " a nice person." But she was in a position to be liberal; being, as it were, in possession of the bone of contention—unconscious Dave, equally devoted to both his two Grannies! Would she not go back to him, and would not he and Dolly come up and keep her company, and Dolly bring her doll? Would not Sapps Court rise, metaphorically speaking, out of its ashes, and the rebuilt wall of that Troy get bone-dry, and the window be stood open on summer evenings by Mrs. Burr, for to hear Miss Druitt play her scales? It was much easier for Maisie to forgive Phœbe her claim on Dave's affection than *vice versa*.

She was, however, so thoroughly knocked up by this long drive that she spoke very little to Gwen about Strides Cottage or anything else, at the time. Gwen saw her on the way to resuscitation, and left her rather reluctantly to Mrs. Masham and Lutwyche; who would, she knew, take very good care that her visitor wanted for nothing, however much she suspected that those two first-class servants were secretly in revolt against the duty they were called on to execute. They would not enter their protest against any whim of her young ladyship, however mad they might think it, by any act of neglect that could be made the basis of an indictment against them.

She herself was overdue at the rather late lunch which her august parents were enjoying in solitude. They were leaving for London in the course of an hour or so, having said farewell in the morning to such guests as still remained at the Towers; and intended, after a short stay in town, to part company—the Earl going to Bath, where it was his practice each year to go through a course of bathing, by which means he contended his life might

HOW THE TWINS SAW EACH OTHER   441

be indefinitely prolonged—to return in time for Christmas, which they would probably celebrate—or, as the Earl said, undergo—at Ancester Towers, according to their usual custom.

"What on earth have you been doing, Gwen, to make you so late?" said the Countess. "We couldn't wait."

"It doesn't matter," was her daughter's answer. "I can gobble to make up for lost time. Don't bring any arrears, Norbury. I can go on where they are. What's this—grouse? Not if it's grousey, thank you! .•. . Oh—well—perhaps I can endure it . . . What have I been doing? Why, taking a drive! . . . Yes—hock. Only not in a tall glass. I hate tall glasses. They hit one's nose. Besides, you get less. . . . I took my old lady out for a drive—all round by Chorlton, and showed her things. We saw Farmer Jones's Bull."

"Is that the Bull that killed the man?" This was the Earl. His eyes were devouring his beautiful daughter, as they were liable to do, even at lunch, or in church.

"I believe he did. It was a man that beat his wife. So it was a good job. He's a dear Bull, but his eyes are red. He had a little boy . . . Nonsense, mamma!—why don't you wait till I've done? He had a little boy to whistle to him and keep his nerves quiet. The potatoes could have waited, Norbury." The story hopes that its economies of space by omitting explanations will not be found puzzling.

The Countess's mien indicated despair of her daughter's manners or sanity, or both. Also that attempts to remedy either would be futile. Her husband laughed slightly to her across the table, with a sub-shrug—the word asks pardon—of his shoulders. She answered it by another, and "Well!" It was as though they had said:—"Really—our daughter!"

"And where else did you go?" said the Earl, to re-rail the conversation. "And what else did you see?"

"Mrs. Picture was knocking up," said Gwen. "So we didn't see so much as we might have done. We left a parcel from Cousin Clo at Goody Marrable's, and then came home as fast as we could pelt. You know Goody Marrable, mamma?"

"Oh dear, yes! I went there with Clo, and she gave us her strong tea."

Gwen nodded several times. "Same experience," said she. "Why is it they *will?*" The story fancies it referred, a long time since, to this vice of Goody Marrable's. No doubt Gurth the Swineherd would have made tea on the same lines, had he had any to make.

The Countess lost interest in the tea question, and evidently had something to say. Therefore Gwen said:—"Yes, mamma! What?" and got for answer:—"It's only a suggestion."

"But *what* is a suggestion?" said the Earl.

"No attention will be paid to it, so it's no use," said her ladyship.

"But what *is* it?" said the Earl. "No harm in knowing *what* it is, that I can see!"

"My dear," said the Countess, "you are always unreasonable. But Gwen may see some sense in what I say. It's no use your looking amused, because that doesn't do any good." After which little preliminary skirmish she came to the point, speaking to Gwen in a half-aside, as to a fellow-citizen in contradistinction to an outcast, her father. "Why should not your old woman be put up at Mrs. Marrable's? They do this sort of thing there. However, perhaps Mrs. Marrable is full up."

"I didn't see anybody there but the two Goodies. I didn't go in, though. But why is Mrs. Picture not to stop where she is?"

"Just as you please, my dear." Her ladyship abdicated with the promptitude of a malicious monarch, who seeks to throw the Constitution into disorder. "How long do you want to stop here yourself?"

"I haven't made up my mind. But *why* is Mrs. Picture not to stop where she is?" This was put incisively.

Her ladyship deprecated truculence. "My dear Gwen!—really! *Are* you Farmer Jones's Bull, or who?" Then, during a lull in the servants, for the moment out of hearing, she added in an undertone:—"You can ask Norbury, and see what *he* thinks. Only wait till Thomas is out of the room." To which Gwen replied substantially that she was still in possession of her senses.

Now Norbury stood in a very peculiar relation to this noble Family. Perhaps it is best described as that of an Unacknowledged Deity, tolerating Atheism from a respect for the Aristocracy. He was not allowed altars or incense, which might have made him vain; but it is difficult to say what questions he was not consulted on, by the Family. Its members had a general feeling that opinions so respectful as his *must* be right, even when they did not bear analysis.

Gwen let the door close on Thomas before she approached the Shrine of the Oracle. It must be admitted that she did so somewhat as Farmer Jones's Bull might have done. "*You've* heard all about old Mrs. Picture, Norbury?" said she.

Why should it have been that Mr. Norbury's "Oh *dear*, yes,

my lady!" immediately caused inferences in his hearers' minds—
one of which, in the Countess's, caused her to say to Gwen, under
her voice:—"I told you so!"?

But Gwen was consulting the Oracle; what did it matter to
her what forecasts of its decisions the Public had made? "But
you haven't *seen* her?" said she. No—Mr. Norbury had *not*
seen her; perfect candour must admit that. She was only known
to him by report, gathered from conversations in which he himself was not joining. How could he be induced to disclose that
part of them that was responsible for a peculiar emphasis in his
reply to her ladyship's previous question?

Not by the Countess's—"She is being well attended to, I suppose?" spoken as by one floating at a great height above human
affairs, but to a certain extent responsible if they miscarried. For
this only produced a cordial testimonial from the Oracle to the
assiduity, care, and skill with which every want of the old lady
was being supplied. Gwen's method was likely to be much more
effective, helped as it was by her absolute licence to be and to do
whatever she liked, and to suffer nothing counter to her wishes,
though, indeed, she always gained them by omnipotent persuasion. She had also, as we have seen, a happy faculty of going
straight to the point. So had Farmer Jones's Bull, no doubt,
on occasion shown.

"Which is it, Lutwyche or Mrs. Masham?" said she. What
it was that was either remained indeterminate.

Mr. Norbury set himself to say which, without injustice to anyone concerned. He dropped his voice to show how unreservedly
he was telling the truth, yet how reluctant he was that his words
should be overheard at the other end of the Castle. "No blame
attaches," said he, to clear the air. "But, if I might make so
bold, the arrangement would work more satisfactory if put upon
a footing."

The Countess said:—"You see, Gwen. I told you what it would
be." The Earl exchanged understandings with Norbury, which
partly took the form of inaudible speech. The fact was that
Gwen had sprung the old lady on the household without doing
anything towards what Mr. Norbury called putting matters on
a footing.

CHAPTER IV

OLD MEMORIES, AGAIN. THE VOYAGE OUT, FIFTY YEARS SINCE. SAPPS
COURT, AND BREAD-AND-BUTTER SPREAD ON THE LOAF. HOW GWEN
CAME INTO THE DREAM SUDDENLY. HOW THEY READ DAVE'S LET-
TER, AND MUGGERIDGE WAS UNDECIPHERABLE. HOW IT WASN'T THE
MIDDLE AGES, BUT JEALOUSIES BRED RUCTIONS. SO GWEN DINED
ALONE, BUT WENT BACK. A CONTEMPTIBLE HOT-WATER BOTTLE.
MISS LUTWYCHE'S SKETCH OF THE RUCTIONS, AND HER MAGNA-
NIMITY. NAPOLÉON DE SOUCHY. HIS VANITY. BUT MAISIE AND
PHŒBE REMAINED UNCONSCIOUS, AS WHY SHOULD THEY NOT? IN-
DEED, WHY NOT POSTPONE THE DISCOVERY UNTIL AFTER THE GREAT
INTERRUPTION, DEATH?

THE problem of where the anomalous old lady was to be lodged
might have been solved by what is called an accommodating disposition, but not by the disposition incidental to the *esprit de corps*
of a large staff of domestic servants. To control them is notoriously the deuce's own delight, and old Nick's relish for it must
grow in proportion as they become more and more corporate. As
Mr. Norbury said—and we do not feel that we can add to the
force of his words—her young ladyship had not took proper account of tempers. Two of these qualities, tendencies, attributes,
or vices—or indeed virtues, if you like—had developed, or germinated, or accrued, or suppurated, as may be, in the respective
bosoms of Miss Lutwyche and Mrs. Masham. It was not a fortunate circumstance that the dispositions of these two ladies, so
far from being accommodating, were murderous. That is, they
would have been so had it happened to be the Middle Ages, just
then. But it wasn't. Tempers had ceased to find expression in
the stiletto and the poison-cup, and had been curbed and stunted
down to taking the other party up short, showing a proper spirit,
and so on.

"What was that you were saying to Norbury, papa dear?"
Gwen asked this question of her father in his own room, half an
hour later, having followed him thither for a farewell chat.

"Saying at lunch?" asked the Earl, partly to avoid distraction
from the mild Havana he was lighting, partly to consider his
answer.

"Saying at lunch. Yes."

"Oh, Norbury! Well!—we were speaking of the same thing as you and your mother, I believe. Only it was not so very clear what that was. You didn't precisely . . . formulate."

"Dear good papa! As if everything was an Act of Parliament! What did Norbury say?"

"I only remember the upshot. Miss Lutwyche has a rather uncertain temper, and Mrs. Masham has been accustomed to be consulted."

"Well—and then?"

"That's all I can recollect. It's a very extraordinary thing that it should be so, but I have certainly somehow formed an image in my mind of all my much too numerous retinue of servants taking sides with Masham and Miss Lutwyche respectively, in connection with this old lady of yours, who must be a great curiosity, and whom, by the way, I haven't seen yet." He compared his watch with a clock on the chimney-piece, whose slow pendulum said—so he alleged—"I, am, right, you, are, wrong!" all day.

"Suppose you were to come round and see her now!"

"Should I have time? Yes, I think I should. Just time to smoke this in peace and quiet, and then we'll pay her a visit. Mustn't be a long one."

*   *   *   *   *   *   *

The day had lost its beauty, and the wind in the trees and the chimneys was inconsolable about the loss, when Gwen said to the old woman:—"Here's my father, come to pay you a visit, Mrs. Picture." Thereon the Earl said:—"Don't wake her up, Gwennie." But to this she said:—"She isn't really asleep. She goes off like this." And he said:—"Old people do."

Her soft hand roused the old lady as gently as anything effectual could. And then Mrs. Picture said:—"I heard you come in, my dear." And, when Gwen repeated that her father had come, became alive to the necessity of acknowledging him, and had to give up the effort, being told to sit still.

"You had such a long drive, you see," said Gwen. "It has quite worn you out. It was my fault, and I'm sorry." Then, relying on inaudibility:—"It makes her seem so old. She was quite young when we started off this morning."

"Young folks," said his lordship, "never believe in old bones, until they feel them inside, and then they are not young folks any longer. Why—where did we drive to, to knock ourselves up so? What's her name—Picture?" He was incredulous, evidently, about such a name being possible. But there was a sort of graciousness, or goodwill, about his oblique speech in the first person plural, that more than outweighed abruptness in his question about her.

She rallied under her visitor's geniality—or his emphasis, as might be. "Maisie Prichard, my lord," said she, quite clearly. Her designation for him showed she was broad awake now, and took in the position. She could answer his question, repeated:— "And where *did* we drive?" by saying:—"A beautiful drive, but I've a poor head now for names." She tried recollection, failed, and gave it up.

"Chorlton-under-Bradbury?" said the Earl.

"We went there too. I know Chorlton quite well, of course. The other one!—where the clock was." Gwen supplied the name, a singular one, Chernoweth; and the Earl said:—"Oh yes— Chernoweth. A pretty place. But why 'Chorlton quite well, of course'?"

Gwen explained. "Because of the small boy, Dave. Don't you know, papa?—I told you Mrs. Picture has directed no end of letters to Chorlton, for Dave." The Earl was not very clear. "Don't you remember?—to old Mrs. Marrable, at Strides Cottage?" Still not very clear, he pretended he was, to save trouble. Then he weakened his pretence, by saying:—"But I remember Mrs. Marrable, and Strides Cottage, near forty years ago, when your Uncle George and I were two young fellows. Fine, handsome woman she was—didn't look her age—she had just married Farmer Marrable—was a widow from Sussex, I think. Can't think what her name had been . . . knew it once, too!"

"She's a fine-looking old lady now," said Gwen. "Isn't she, Mrs. Picture?"

"I am sure she is that too, my dear, or you would not say so. Only my eyesight won't always serve me nowadays as it did, not for seeing near up." The reserves about Dave's other Granny were always there, however little insisted on. Old Maisie was exaggerating about her eyesight. She had seen her rival quite clearly enough to have an opinion about her looks.

"Did you see the inside of the cottage, and the old chimney-corners? And the well out at the back?" Thus the Earl.

"We didn't go in. I wanted to get home. But what a lot you recollect of it, papa dear!"

"I ought to recollect something about it. It was Strides Cottage where your Uncle George was taken when he broke his leg, riding."

"Oh, was it there? Yes, I've heard of that. His horse threw him on a heap of stones, and bolted, and pitched into Dunsters Gap, and had to be shot." "Yes, he shouldn't have ridden that horse. But he was always at that sort of thing, George." A sound came in here that had the same relation to a sigh that a sip has to a draught. "Well!— Mrs. Marrable nursed him up at Strides Cottage till he was fit to move—they were afraid about his back at first—and I used to ride over every morning. We used to chaff poor Georgy about his beautiful nurse. . . . Oh yes!—she was young enough for that. Woman well under forty, I should say."

Gwen made calculations and attested possibilities. Oh dear, yes!—Granny Marrable must have been under forty then. She surprised his lordship, first by gently smoothing aside the silver hair on the old woman's forehead, then by stooping down and kissing it. "Why, how old are you now, dear?" she said, as though she were speaking to a child. He for his part was only surprised, not dumfounded. He just felt a little glad his Countess was elsewhere; and was not sorry, on looking round, to see that no domestic was present. What a wild, ungovernable daughter it was, this one of his, and how he loved it!

So did old Mrs. Picture, to judge by the illumination of the eyes she turned up to the girl's young face above her. "How old am I now, my dear?" said she. "Eighty-one this Christmas." Thereupon said Gwen:—"You see, papa! Old Mrs. Marrable must have been quite a young woman in Uncle George's time. She's heaps younger than Mrs. Picture." She again smoothed the beautiful silver hair, adding:—"It's not unfeelingness, because Uncle George died years before I was born."

"Killed at Rangoon in twenty-four," said the Earl, with another semi-sigh. "Poor Georgy!" And then his visit was cut as short as—even shorter than—his forecast of its duration, for his next words were:—"I hear someone coming to fetch me. Your mamma is sure to start an hour before the time. Good-bye, Mrs. . . . Picture. I hope you are being well fed and properly attended to." To which the old lady replied:—"I thank your lordship, indeed I am," in an old-fashioned way that went well with the silver hair. And Gwen said:—"Dear old parent! Do you think *I* shan't see to that?" and followed him out of the room.

"She's a nice old soul," said he, in the passage. "I wanted to see what she was like. But I thought it best to say nothing about the convict."

"Of course not. I'll follow you round before you go, to say good-bye. You won't start for half an hour." And Gwen returned to the old soul, who presently said to her—to account to her for knowing how to say "my lord" and "your lordship"—"When I first married, my husband's great friend was Lord Pouralot. But I very soon called him Jack." This was a reminiscence of her interim between her victimisation and loneliness, which of course her innocence thought of as marriage. But was this early lordship's really a ladyship, if such a one appeared, we wonder? Very likely she was only another dupe, like Maisie. Possibly less fortunate, in one way. For, owing to the high price of women, in the land of Maisie's destiny, she—poor girl—never knew she was not a good one, until she found she was not a widow, although her worthless love of a lifetime was dead.

Oh, the difference Law's sanctions make! For a woman shall be the same in thought and word and deed through all her sojourn on Earth, yet vary as saint and sinner with the hall-mark of Lincoln's Inn.

Gwen followed the Earl very shortly, and left old Maisie to dream away the time until, somewhile after the final departure of her parents, she was free to return. When she did so she found the old woman sitting where she had left her, to all seeming quite contented. The day had died a sudden death intestate, and the flickering firelight meant to have its say unmolested, till candletime. The intrusion of artificial light was intercepted by Gwen, who liked to sit and talk to Mrs. Picture in the twilight, thank you, Mrs. Masham! Take it away!

Where had the old mind wandered in that two hours' interval? Had the actual meeting with her sister—utterly incredible even had she known its claims to belief—taken any hold on it that bore comparison with that of Farmer Jones's Bull, for instance, or the visit of a real live Earl? Certainly not the former, while as for the latter it was at best a half-way grip between the two; perhaps farther, if anything, from the supreme Bull, the great enthralling interest that was to be vested in her letter to Dave, to be written at the next favourable climax of strength, nourished by repose. Some time in the morning—to-day she was far too tired to think of it.

How she dwelt upon that appalling quadruped, and his savage breast—have bulls breasts?—soothed by the charms of music! How she phrased the various best ways of describing the mountain he was pleased to call his neck, with its half-hundredweight of dewlap; the merciless strength of his horns; the blast of steam from his nostrils into the chill of the October day; the deep-seated objection to everybody in his lurid eyes, attesting the un-clubableness of his disposition! How she hesitated between this way and that of expressing to the full his murderousness and the beautiful pliancy of his soul, if got at the right way; showing, as the pseudo-Browning has it, that "we never should think good impossible"!

One thing she made up her mind to. She would not tell that dear boy, that this bull—which was in a sense *his* bull, or Sapps Court's, according as you look at it—had ever had to succumb on a fair field of battle. For Gwen had told her, as they rode home, and she had roused herself to hear it, how one summer morning, so early that even rangers were still abed and asleep, they were waked by terrific bellowings from a distant glade in the park-lands, and, sallying out to find the cause, were only just in time to save the valued life of this same bull—even Jones's. For he had broken down a gate and vanished overnight, and wandered into the sacred precincts of the *villosi terga bisontes,* the still-wild denizens of the last league of the British woodlands Cæsar found; and *Bos Taurus* had risen in his wrath, and showed that an ancient race was not to be trifled with, with impunity. Even Jones's Bull went down in the end—though, mind you, evidence went to show that he made an hour's stand!—before the overwhelming rush and the terrible horns of the forest monarch. And the victor only gave back before a wall of brandished torch and blazing ferns, that the unsportsmanlike spirit of the keepers did not scru-ple to resort to. No—she would not admit that Dave's bull had ever met his match. She would say how he had killed a man, which Gwen had told her also; but to save the boy from too much commiseration for this man, she would lay stress upon the bru-tality of the latter to his wife, and even point out that Farmer Jones's Bull might be honestly unconscious of the consequences that too often result when one gores or tramples on an object of one's righteous indignation.

Strides Cottage played a very small part in the memories of the day. Some interest certainly attached to the older woman who had emerged from it to interview the carriage, but it was an interest apt to die down when once its object had been ascertained to resemble any other handsome old village octogenarian. Any peculiarity or deformity might have intensified it, or at least kept it alive; mere good looks and upright carriage, and strict conformity with the part of an ancient dependent of a great local

potentate, neither fed nor quenched the mild fires of her rival
granny's jealousy. Old Mrs. Picture had looked upon Granny
Marrable, and was none the wiser. That Granny had at least
seen her way to moralising on the way appearances might dupe
us, and how sad it would be if, after all, such a respectable-looking
old person should be an associate of thieves, a misleader of youth,
and a fraud. But Mrs. Picture found little to say to herself,
and nothing to say to anybody else, about Strides Cottage.

Rather, she fell back, as soon as Jones's Bull flagged, on her
long record of an unforgotten past. That wind that was growing
with the nightfall no longer moaned for her in the chimney, five
centuries old, of the strange great house strange Fate had brought
her to, but through the shrouds of a ship on the watch for what
the light of sunrise might show at any moment. She could hear
the rush and ripple of the cloven waters under the prow, just as
a girl who leaned upon the gunwale, intent for the first sight of
land, heard it in the dawn over fifty years ago. She could seem
to look back at the girl—who was, if you please, herself—and a
man who leaned on the same timber, some few feet away, intent
on the horizon or his neighbour, as might be; for he stood aft,
and her face was turned away from him. And she could seem
to hear his words too, for all the time that came between:—" Say
the word, mistress, and I'll be yours for life. I would give all
I have to give, and all I may live to get, but to call you mine for
an hour." And how his petition seemed empty sound, that she
could answer with a curt denial, so bent was her heart on another
man in the land she hoped to see so soon. Yet he was a nice
fellow, too, thought old Mrs. Prichard as she sat before Mrs.
Masham's fire at the Towers; and she forgave him the lawlessness
of his impulse for its warmth, bred in the narrow limits of a ship
on the seas for three long months!—how could he help it? Such
a common story on shipboard, and . . . such an uncommon ending! Ask the captains of passenger ships what *they* think, even
now that ships steam twenty knots an hour. One's fellow-
creatures are so human, you see.

Then a terrible dream of a second voyage, from Sydney to Port
Macquarie, that almost made her wish she had accepted this
man's offer to see her safe into the arms of her lawful owner,
out on leave and growing prosperous in Van Diemen's Land. Need
she have said him nay so firmly? Could she not have trusted
to his chivalry? Or was the question she asked herself not rather,
could she have trusted her own heart, if that chivalry had stood as
gold in the furnace.

Back again to the throbbing wheel, and the ceaseless flow of the little river at the Essex mill, and childhood! Why should her waking dream hark back to the dear old time? The natural thing would have been to dream on into the years she spent out there with the man she loved, who at least, to all outward seeming, gave her back love for love, while he played the sly devil against her for his own ends. But she knew nothing of this: and, till his death revealed the non-legal character of their union, she could leave him on his pinnacle. So it was not because her mind shrank from these memories of her married life that it conjured back again the scent of the honeysuckles on the house-porch that looked on the garden with the sundial on the wall above it, its welcome to that of the June roses; its dissension with the flavour of the damp weeds that clung to the time-worn timbers of the water-wheel, or that of the grinding flour when the wind blew from the mill, and carried with it from the ventilators some of the cloud that could not help forward the whitening of the roof. She might almost have been breathing again the air that carried all these scents; and then, with them, the old mill itself was suddenly upon her; and she and Phœbe were there, in the shortest waists ever frockmaker dreamed of, and the deepest sunbonnets possible, with the largest possible ribbons, very pale yellow to harmonize—as canons then ruled—with the lilac of their dresses. They were there, they two, watching the inexhaustible resource of interest to their childish lives; the consignment of grain to storage in the loft above the whirling stones, and the dapple-grey horse that was called Mr. Pitt, and the dark one with the white mane that was Mr. Fox. She could remember *their* names well; but by some chance all those years of utter change had effaced that of the carman who slung the sacks on the fall-rope, which by some mysterious agency bore them up to a landing they vanished from into a doorway half-way to Heaven. What on earth was that man's name? Her mind became obsessed with the name Tattenhall, which was entirely wrong, and, moreover, stood terribly in the way of Muggeridge, which—you may remember?—was the name Dave had carried away so clearly from his inspection of the mill on Granny Marrable's chimney-piece.

Her memories of her old home had died away, and she was back in Sapps Court again, sympathizing with Dolly over an accident to Shockheaded Peter, the articulation of whose knee-joint had given way, causing his leg to come off promptly, from lack of integuments and tendons. She had pointed out to Dolly that it was still open to her, as The Authority, to hush Peter to sleep as before, his leg being carefully replaced in position, although without ligatures. Dolly had carried out this instruction in perfect good faith; but it had not led to a satisfactory result. It failed owing to the patient's restlessness. " He *will* tit in his s'eep, and he tums undone," said the little lady, hard to console. Oh dear—how soon Dolly would be four, and begin to lose her early versions of consonants!

Poor Susan Burr had then flashed across her recollection, provoked by the bread-and-butter Dolly baptized with the bitter tears she shed over Peter's leg. That naturally led to the household loaf, which was buttered before the slice was cut; sometimes the whole round, according to how many at tea. This led to a controversy of long standing between Dave and Dolly, as to which half should be took first; Dave having a preference for the underside, with the black left on. Students of the half-quartern household loaf will appreciate the niceties involved. In this connection, Susan Burr had come in naturally, like the officiating priest at Mass. Poor Susan! Suppose, after all, that Europe had been mistaken in what seemed to be its estimate of married nieces at Clapham! Suppose Susan was being neglected—how then? But marriage and Clapham, between them, soothed and reassured misgivings a mere unqualified niece might easily generate. By this time the waking dreamer was on the borderland of sleep, and Mrs. Burr's image crossed it with her and became a real dream, and whistled the tune the boy had whistled to Farmer Jones's Bull. And into that dream came, suddenly and unprovoked, her sister Phœbe of old, beautiful and fresh as violets in April, and ended a tale of how she would have none of Ralph Daverill, come what might, by saying, " Why, you are all in the dark, and the fire's going out! "

This resurrection of Phœbe, at this moment, may have been mere coincidence—a reflex action of Gwen's sudden reappearance; her first words creating, in her hearer's sleep-waking mind, the readiest image of a youth and beauty to match her own. As soon as the dream died, the dreamer was aware of the speaker's identity. " Oh, my dear! " she said, " I've been asleep almost ever since you went away."

" Mrs. Masham was quite right, for once, not to let them disturb you. Now they'll bring tea—it's never too late for tea— and then we can read your little friend's letter." Thus Gwen, and the old woman brightened up under a living interest.

" There now! " said she. " The many times I've told my boy

that one day he would write my letters for me, instead of me for him! To think of his managing all by himself, spelling and all!"

"Well, we shall see what sort of a job the young man's made of it. Put the candles behind Mrs. Picture, Lupin, so as not to glare her eyes." Lupin obeyed, with a studied absence of protest on her face against having to wait upon an anomaly. Who could be sure this venerable person—from Sapps Court, think of it!—had never waited on anyone herself? It was the ambiguity that was so disgusting.

"Please may I see it, to look at?" said Mrs. Picture. "I may not be able to read it, quite, but you shall have it back, to read." She was eager to see the young scribe's progress, but was baffled by obscurities, as she anticipated. She was equal to:—"Dear Granny Marrable." No more!

"Hand it over!" said Gwen. "'Dear Granny Marrable.' That's all plain sailing; now what's this? 'This crorce is for Dolly's love.' There's a great big black cross to show it, and everything is spelt just as I say it. 'I give you my love itself!' Really, he's full of the most excellent differences, as Shakespeare says. I'll go on. 'Arnt M'riar she's took. . . .' Oh dear! this *is* a word to make out! Whatever can it be? Let's see what comes after. . . . Oh, it goes on:—'because she is not here.' Really it looks as if Aunt Maria had gone to Kingdom Come. Is there anything she *would* have taken because she was 'not there,' that you know of? Is your tea all right?"

"It's very nice indeed, my dear. I think perhaps it might be the omnibus, because Aunt M'riar *did* take the omnibus that day she came to see me. She was to come again, without the children, to see all straight."

"H'm!—it may be the omnibus, spelt with an H. Suppose we accept *homliburst,* and see how it works out! '. . . because she is not here. She is going'—he's put a W in the middle of going—'to see Mrs.'—I know this word is Mrs., but he's put the S in the middle and the R at the end—'to see Mrs. Spicture tookted away by Dolly's lady to Towel.' That wants a little think-ing out." Gwen stopped to think it over, and wondrous lovely she looked, thinking.

"Perhaps," said the old lady diffidently, "I can guess what it means, because I know Dave. Suppose Aunt M'riar came the day we came away, and found us gone! If she came up to say good-bye? . . ."

"No, that won't do! Because we came on Wednesday. This was written on Thursday. It's dated 'On Firsday.' Did he mean that Aunt Maria had come up to Sapps Court, but would not come to Cavendish Square because she knew you had come here? It's quite possible. I don't wonder Mrs. Marrable couldn't make it out." The old lady seemed to think the interpretation plausible, and Gwen read on:—"'I say we had an axdnt'—that really is beautifully spelt—'because the house forled over, and Mrs. Ber underneath and Me and Dolly are sory.'" Gwen stopped a moment to consider the first two words of this sentence, and decided that "I say" was an apostrophe. "I see," said she, "that the next sentence has your name in it again, only he's left out the U, and made you look something between Spider and Spectre."

"The dear boy! What does he say next about me?" The old lady was looking intensely happy; a reflex action of Dave.

"There's a dreadful hard word comes next. . . . Oh—I see what it is! 'Supposing.' Only he's made it 'sorsppposing'—such a lot of P's! I think it is only to show how diffidently he makes the suggestion. It doesn't matter. Let's get on. 'Supposing you was to show'—something I really cannot make head or tail of—'to Mrs. Spictre who is my other graney?' I wonder what on earth it can be!"

"I don't think it's any use my looking, my dear. What letters does it look most like?"

"Why!—here's an M, and a U, and a C, and an E, and an R, and an I, and a J. That's a word by itself. 'Mucerij.' But what word can he mean? It can't be *mucilage;* that's impossible! I thought it might be *museum* at first, as it was to be shown. But it's written too plain, in a big round hand—all in capitals. What *can* it be?" And Gwen sat there puzzling, turning the word this way and that, looking all the lovelier for the ripple of amusement on her face at the absurd penmanship of the neophyte.

Poor dear Dave! With the clearest possible perception of the name Muggeridge, when spoken, he could go no nearer to correct writing of it than this! He could hardly have known of the two G's, from the sound; but the omission of the cross-bar from the one that was *de rigueur* was certainly a *lapsus calami,* and a serious one. The last syllable was merely phonetic, and unrecognisable; but the G that looked like a C was fatal.

It was an odd chance indeed that brought this name, or its distortion, to challenge recognition at this moment, when the thought of its owner had just passed off the mind that might have recognised it, helped by a slight emendation. The story

dwells on it from a kind of fascination, due to the almost incredible strangeness of these two sisters' utter unconsciousness
of one another, and yet so near together! It was almost as though
a mine were laid beneath their feet, and this memory of a name
floated over it as a spark, and drifted away on a wind of chance
to be lost in a space of oblivion. However, sparks drift back, now
and again.

This conversation over Dave's letter had no peculiar interest
for either speaker, over and above its mere face-value, which was
of course far greater for the elder of the two. Gwen deciphered
it to the end, laughing at the writer's conscientious efforts towards
orthography. But when the end came, with an attestation of
affectionate grandsonship that roused suspicions of help from
seniors, so orthodox was the spelling, she consigned the missive
to its envelope after very slight revision of points of interest.
But she would talk a little about Dave too, in deference to his
other granny's solicitude about him. That was the source of her
own interest in what was otherwise a mere recollection of an
attractive *gamin* with an even more attractive sister.

It was part of the embarrassment consequent on her own headstrong creation of an anomalous social position, that Gwen could
not decide, nominally omnipotent as she was in her parents'
absence, on telling the servants to serve her dinner in the room
Mrs. Picture occupied. Had it not been for her suspicion of a
hornet's nest at hand, she might have dared to ordain that Mrs.
Picture should be her sole guest in her own section of the Towers,
or at least that she herself should become the table-guest of the
old lady in Francis Quarles; "might have," not "would have,"
because Mrs. Picture's own feelings had to be reckoned with.
Might she not be embarrassed, and overweighted by too emphatic a change of circumstances? Indeed, had Gwen known
it, she was only tranquil and contented with things as they were
in the sense in which one who passes through a dream is tranquil
and contented. It was the quietude of bewilderment, alive to
gratitude.

Uncertainty on this point co-operated with the possible hornet's nest, and sent Gwen away to a lonely evening meal in her
own rooms; for nothing short of a suite of apartments was allotted
to any inmate of importance at the Towers. She had to submit to
a banquet of a kind, if only as a measure of conciliation to the
household. But, the banquet ended, she was free to return and
take coffee with her *protégée*. She had no objection to talking
about her lover to Mrs. Picture, rather welcoming the luxury of

speaking of her marriage with him as a thing already guaranteed by Fate.

"When we are married," said she, "I mean to have that delicious old house we saw on the hill. That's why I wanted to show it to you. It's all nonsense about the ghost. I dare say the Roundheads murdered the ghost there—I mean the woman the ghost's the ghost of—but she wouldn't appear to me. Ghosts never do. Did you ever see one?... But you wouldn't be in the house. You would be at a sweet little cottage just close, which is simply one mass of roses. You and Dolly. And Mrs. Burr." Mrs. Burr was thrown into attend to the *ménage*.

Old Mrs. Picture did not quite know what to say. She had found out instinctively that perpetual gratitude had its drawbacks for the receiver as well as the giver. So she said, diffidently:—"Wouldn't it cost a great deal of money?"

"Cost nothing," said Gwen. "The place belongs to my father. It's all very well for people, that mind ghosts, not to live in it. But I don't see why that should apply to Mr. Torrens and me."

"Doesn't he mind ghosts?"

"Not the least." She was going to say more, but was stopped, by danger ahead. The chances of his seeing, or not seeing, a ghost, could hardly be discussed. The old lady probably felt this too, for she seemed to keep something back.

Her next words showed what it had been, in an odd way. "Is he not to see?" she said, speaking almost as if afraid of the sound of her own words.

Gwen's answer came in a hurried undertone:—"Oh, I dare not think so. He *will* see! He *must* see!" Her distress was in her fingers, that she could not keep still, as well as in her voice. She rose suddenly, crossed the room to the window, and stood looking out on the darkness.

Presently she turned round, esteeming herself mistress of her strength again, and hoping for the serenity of her companion's old face, and its still white hair, to help her. Old Maisie could not shed a tear now on her own behalf. But ... to think of the appalling sorrow of this glorious girl! Gwen did not return to her seat; but preferred a footstool, at the feet of the dear old lady, whose voice was heart-broken.

"Oh, my dear—my dear! That he should never see *you!* ... never! ... never!" The golden head with all its wealth was in her lap, and the silver of her own was white against it as she spoke. No such tears had yet fallen from Gwen's eyes as these that mixed with this old woman's, the convict's relict—the convict's mother—from Sapps Court.

An effort against herself, to choke them back, and an ignominious failure! A short breakdown, another effort, and a success! Gwen rose above herself, morally triumphant. The beautiful young face, when it looked up, assorted well with the words:—
" This is all cowardice, dear Mrs. Picture. He *has* seen, though it was only a few seconds. The sight is there. And look what Dr. Merridew said. His eyes might be as strong as they had ever been in his life."

Then followed reflections on the pusillanimity of despair, the duty of hoping, and an attempt on Gwen's part to forestall a possible shock to the old lady should she ever come to the knowledge of Adrian's free opinions. She wanted her to think well of her lover. But she could not conscientiously give him a character for orthodoxy. She took refuge in a position which is often a great resource in like cases, ascribing to him an intrinsic devoutness, a hidden substantial sanctity compatible with the utmost latitudes of heterodoxy; a bedrock of devout gneiss or porphyry hidden under a mere alluvium of modern freethinking; a reality— if the truth were known—of St. Francis of Assisi behind a mask of Voltaire. Her hearer only half followed her reasoning, but that mattered little, as she was brimming with assent to anything Gwen advanced, with such beautiful and earnest eyes to back it.

" It's a great deal too far to drive you over to see him," said Gwen. " It would knock you to pieces—eighteen miles each way! It's over two hours and a half in the carriage, even when the roads are not muddy. The mare got me there in an hour and three-quarters the other day, but you couldn't stand that sort of thing. I'm going again in the gig to-morrow. . . . Oh no!— not till eleven o'clock. I shall come and sit with you and see all comfortable before I go. I shall get there at lunch. How do you get on with Masham?" This was asked with a pretence of absence of misgiving, and the response to it was a testimonial to Mrs. Masham, rather overdone. Gwen extenuated Mrs. Masham. She had known Masham all her life, and she really was a very good woman, in spite of her caps. As for her expanse, it was not her fault, but the hand of Nature; and her black jet ringlets were, Gwen believed, congenital.

But the next clock was going to say ten, however inaccurately. In fact, a little one, in a hurry, got its word in first, and was condemned by a reference to Gwen's repeater, which refused to go farther than nine. She, however, rang up Masham, of whose voice, *inter alias*, she had been half-conscious in the distance for some time past; and who gave the impression of having recently shown a proper spirit.

"She'll be better in bed, I think, Masham. She's had such a tiring day. It was my fault. I was rather afraid at the time. I suppose she'll be all right. She gets everything she wants, I suppose?"

"I beg your ladyship's pardon!"

"She gets everything she wants?"

"So far as comes to my knowledge, my lady. Touching wishes not expressed, I could not undertake to say." Mrs. Masham bridled somewhat, and showed signs of having a right to feel injured. "If your ladyship would make inquiry, and satisfy yourself. . . ." Then something would be revealed in the service of Truth. Only she did not finish the sentence.

It was Gwen's way to accept every challenge. "Is her bed nice and warm?" said she, going straight to a point—the nearest in sight, for this took place within view of the bed in question, seen through a half-open door. Prudence would have waived investigation, but Gwen's prudence was never at home when wanted. She ought not to have accepted the housekeeper's suggestion that she could satisfy herself by an autopsy. The comfort of this couch, warm or cold, was already leagues above its occupant's wildest conception of luxury. What must her ladyship do but say:—"Yes, thank you, Masham, I'll feel for myself." And there, if that young hussy, Lupin, hadn't sent the hot bottle right down to the end!

This version of the incident, gathered from a subsequent communication of the housekeeper, will be at once intelligible to all but the very few to whom the hot bottle is a stranger. *They* have not had the experience so many of us are familiar with, of being too short to reach down all that way, and having either to wallow under the coverlids like a Kobold, or untuck the bed, and get at the remote bottle like a paper-knife.

Probably this bottle's prominence in the unpleasantness that germinated among the servants who remained at the Towers after the departure of the Earl and Countess was due to the extreme impalpability of other grievances. It was something you could lay hold of; and was laid hold of, for instance, by Miss Lutwyche, to flagellate Mrs. Masham. "At any rate," said that severe critic, "what I took charge of, that I would act up to. When I undertook the old party in Cavendish Square, she was kept warm, and no playing fast and loose with bottles. And she didn't give offence, that I see, but seemed "—here her love of new expressions came in, tending to wards superiority—" but seemed of an accommodating habit." This expression was far from unfortunate, and it was owing to the disposition so described that old Maisie, as soon as she was fully aware that she had been the unintentional cause of strained relations in the household, became very uncomfortable; and, much as she loved the beautiful but headstrong creature that had taken such a fancy to her, felt more than ever that the sooner she returned to her own proper surroundings the better.

Gwen returned to her own quarters after a certain amount of good-humoured fault-finding, having listened to and made light of many expressions of contrition from the old lady that she should have occasioned what Miss Lutwyche afterwards spoke of as just so much uncalled-for hot water. Gwen's youth and high spirits, and her supreme contempt for the petty animosities of the domestics, made it less easy for her to understand the feelings of her old guest, and the rather anomalous position in which she had placed her. She thought she had said all she need about it when she warned Mrs. Picture not to be put out by Mrs. Masham and Lutwyche's nonsense. Servants were always like that. Bother Mrs. Masham and Lutwyche!

The latter, however, when assisting her young mistress to retire for the night—an operation which takes two when a young lady of position is cast for the leading part—was eloquent about the hot water, which she said no doubt prevailed, but appeared to her entirely unwarranted. Her account of the position redounded to her own credit. Hers had been the part of a peacemaker. She had made the crooked straight, and the rough places plain. The substratum of everybody else's character was also excellent, but human weakness, to which all but the speaker were liable, stepped in and distorted the best intentions. If only Mrs. Masham did not give away to the sharpness of her tongue, a better heart did not exist. Mr. Norbury might frequently avoid misunderstandings if an acute sense of duty and an almost startling integrity of motive were the only things wanted to procure peace with honour in a disturbed household. But that was where it was. You must have Authority, and a vacillating disposition did not contribute to its exercise. In Mr. Norbury a fatal indecision in action and a too great sensitiveness of moral fibre paralysed latent energies of a high order which might otherwise have made him a leader among men. As for the girls, the dove-like innocence of inexperience, so far as it could exist among a lot of young monkeys, was responsible for *their* contribution to the hot water. A negligible quantity of a trivial ingredient! Young persons were young persons, and would always remain so—an enigmatical saying. As for the French Cook, Napoléon de Souchy, he was in bed and knew nothing about it. Besides, he went next day. He had, in fact, gone by the same train as the Earl, travelling first-class, and had been taken for his lordship at Euston, which hurt his vanity.

To this revelation Gwen listened with interest, hoping to hear more precisely what the row was about. Why hot water at all, if uncalled for? As she had not expected to hear much, she was very little surprised to hear nothing. She pictured the attitude in action of Miss Lutwyche, whom she knew well enough to know that she would coax history in her own favour. The best of lady's-maids cannot be at once a Tartar and an Angel. Gwen surmised that in the region of the servants' common-room and the kitchen Miss Lutwyche would show so much of the former as had been truly ascribed to her, whereas she herself would only see the latter. The worst of it was that her old lady, being within hearing, would know or suspect the dissensions she was the innocent cause of, and would be uncomfortable. She must say or do something, consolatory or reassuring, to-morrow. She fretted a little, till she fell asleep, over this matter, which was really a trifle. Think of the thing she had seen that day, that she was so profoundly unconscious of—the two sisters whose lips met last a lifetime ago; whose grief, each for each, had nearly died of time!—think of the two of them, then and there, face to face in the daylight! But they too slept, that night, old Maisie and old Phœbe, as calm as Gwen; and as safe, to all seeming, in their ignorance.

Would it not be better—thought thinks, involuntarily—that they should remain in this ignorance, through the little span of Time still left them, in a state which is at best decay? Would it not be best that the few hours left should run their course, and that the two should either pass away to nothingness and peace, as may be, or—as may be too, just as like as not—wake to a wonder none can comprehend, an inconceivable surprise, a sudden knowledge what the whole thing meant that must seem, if they come to comprehend it now, a needless cruelty? If they—and you and I, in our turn—are to be nothing, mere items of the past lost in Oblivion, why not spare them the hideous revelation of the many, many years of might-have-been, when the same sun shone unmoved on each, even marked the hours for them alike, each unseen by the other, each beyond the sound of the other's speech, the touch of the other's hand? Why should either now, at the eleventh hour, come to know of the audacious fraud that made them strangers? But why—why anything, for that matter? Why the smallest pain, the greatest joy? What end does either serve, but to pass and be forgotten. What is left for us but the bald consolation of imaging a form for the Supreme Power—one like ourselves by preference—and a concession to it. . . . *Fiat. voluntas tua!* It doesn't really matter *what* form, you see! The phantasmata vary, but the invisible what?—or who?—remains the same. Gloria in excelsis Deo, nomine quocunque!

CHAPTER V

HOW MRS. PICTURE SPOILED OLD PHOEBE'S DREAM, BUT WAS A NICE OLD SOUL, TO LOOK AT. PARSON DUNAGE'S MOTHER. A CLOCK THAT STRUCK, BETWEEN TWO TWINS. HOW TOBY DID NOT WAKE, AND KEZIAH SOLMES CAME NEXT DAY FOR HIM. THE WICKED MAN WHO DID IT AGAIN, AND HIS RESEMBLANCE TO TOBY. THE COATINGS OF THE LATTER'S STOMACH. MRS. LAMPREY. COLONEL WARRENDER AND THE PHEASANTS. HOW WIDOW THRALE AND KEZIAH WENT TO SEE AN OLD SOUL NEXT DAY. A RETROSPECULATION. SUPPOSE WIDOW THRALE HAD BEEN TOLD! ON IMPROBABILITY, IMPOSSIBILITY, INCREDIBILITY, AND MAISIE'S PILGRIMAGE TO A GRAVE SHE NEVER FOUND. MATTHEW, MARK, LUKE, JOHN, AND THEIR IRRELEVANCE

" 'Tis pity she could not stop!" said Granny Marrable in the course of evening chat with the niece, who was scarcely thought of as anything but a daughter, by even the oldest village gossips. Indeed, when we reflect that little Ruth Daverill, now Widow Thrale, was under four when her mother tore herself from her to rejoin her husband, it is little wonder that she should take the same view of her own parentage. For one thing, there was the twinship between the mother and aunt. The child under four can have seen little difference between them.

The pen almost shrinks from writing Widow Ruth's reply to old Phœbe, so plainly did it word her ignorance of who this was that she had seen two hours since. "Who, mother? Oh, the old person! Ay, but she has a kind heart, has Gwen." This was not disrespectful familiarity. All the villagers in those parts, talking among themselves, gave their christened names to the Earl's family. The moment an outsider came in, " The Family " consisted entirely of lordships and ladyships.

But how strange, that such a speech—actually the naming of a mother by a daughter—should be so slightly spoken, in an ignorance so complete!

Granny Marrable's thought, of the two, dwelt more on " the old person "; whose identity, as Dave's other Granny, had made its impression on her. Otherwise, for all she had seen of her, it might have passed from her mind. Also, she was grieved about that mutton-broth. The poor old soul had just looked worn to death, and all that way to drive! If she had only just swallowed half a cup, it would have made such a difference. It added to Granny Marrable's regret, that the mutton-broth had proved so good. The old soul had passed on unrefreshed even while Strides Cottage was endorsing that mutton-broth.

The Granny quite fretted over it, not even the beautiful fur tippet Sister Nora had sent her having power to expel it from her mind. And, quite late, nigh on to midnight, she woke with a start from a dream she had had; it set her off talking again about old Mrs. Picture. For it was one of this old lady's vices that she would sit up late and waste a deal of good sleep out of bed in that venerable arm-chair of hers.

" There now, Ruth," said she, " I was asleep again and dreaming." For she never would admit that this practice was an invariable one.

" What about, mother? " said Widow Thrale.

" That breaking of the glass set me a-dreaming over our old mill, and your mother, child, that died across the seas. We was both there, girls like, all over again. Only Dave's Mrs. Picture, she come across the dream, and spoilt it."

It was not necessary for Mrs. Ruth to take her attention off the pillow-lace she was at work upon. She remarked:—" I thought her a nice old soul, to look at." This was not quite uncoloured by the vague indictment against Mrs. Picture about Dave, who had, somehow, qualified for the receipt of forgiveness. Which implies some offence to condone.

Shadowy as the offence was, Granny Marrable could not ignore it altogether. " Good looks are skin-deep—so they say! But it's not for me to be setting up for judge. At her time of life, and she a-looking so worn out, too! " The memory of the mutton-broth rankled. Forgiveness was setting in.

" At her time of life, mother? Why, she's none so much older

than you. What should you take her to be?" The subject was
just worth spare attention not wanted for the lace-spools.

"Why, now—there's Parson Dunage's mother at the Rectory.
She's ninety-four this Christmas. This old soul she might be
half-way on, between me and Parson Dunage's mother at the
Rectory."

Mrs. Ruth dropped the spools, to think arithmetically, with her
fingers. "Eighty-six, eighty-seven, eighty-eight," she said,
"Eighty-seven! . . . This one's nearer your own age than that,
mother." She went on with her work.

"There now, Ruth, is not that just like you, all over? You
will always be making me out older than I am. I am not turned
of eighty-one, child, not till next year. My birthday comes the
first day of the year."

"I thought you and my mother were both born at Christmas."

"Well, my dear, we always called it Christmas, for to have a
birthday together on New Year's Eve. But the church-clock
got time to strike the hour betwixt and between the two of us,
so Maisie was my elder sister by just that, and no more. She
would say . . . Ah dearie me!—poor Maisie! . . . she would say
by rights *she* should marry first, being the elder. And then I
would tell her the clock was fast, and we were both of an age.
'Twas a many years sooner she married, as God would have it.
All of three years before ever I met poor Nicholas." And then the
old woman, who had hitherto kept back the story of her sister's
marriage, made a slip of the tongue. "Maybe I was wrong, but
I was a bit scared of men and marriage in those days."

It was no wonder Ruth connected this with the father she had
never seen. "Why *did* my father go to Australia?" said she.
It was asked entirely as a matter of history, for did it not happen
before the speaker was born? The passive acceptance through
a lifetime of such a fact can only be understood by persons who
have experienced a similar sealed antecedent. Non-inquiry into
such a one may be infused into a mother's milk.

Granny Marrable could be insensible to pressure after a lifetime of silence. She had never thrown light on the mystery and
she would not, now. Her answer even suggested a false solution.
"He grew to be rich after your mother died. But I lost touch
of him then, and when and where he came by his death is more
than I can tell ye, child!" There was implication in this of a
prosperous colonist, completely impatriated in the land of his
wealth.

Ruth's father's vanished history was of less importance than the clock's statement that it was midnight. Her "Now, mother, we're later and later. It's striking to-morrow, now!" referred to present life and present bedtime, and her rapid adjustment of the spools meant business.

The old Granny showed no sense of having escaped an embarrassment. She did not shy off to another subject. On the contrary, she went back to the topic it had hinged on. "Eighty-one come January!" said she, lighting her own candle. "And please God I may see ninety, and only be the worse by the price of a new pair of glasses to read my Testament. Parson Dunage's mother at the Rectory, she's gone stone-deaf, and one may shout oneself hoarse. But everyone else than you, child, *I* can hear plain enough. There's naught to complain of in *my* hearing, yet a while."

Granny Marrable's conscience stung her yet again about Mrs. Picture's departure unrefreshed. "I would have been the happier for knowing that that old soul was none the worse," said she. But all the answer she got was:—"Be quiet, mother, you'll wake up Toby."

She harped on the same string next day, the immediate provocation to the subject being a visit from Keziah Solmes, the old keeper's wife—you remember her connection Keziah; she who remonstrated with her husband about the use of fire-arms, and nearly saved Adrian Torrens's eyesight?—who had been driven over, in a carrier's cart that kept up a daily communication between the Towers and Chorlton, in pursuance of an arrangement suggested one day by Gwen. Why should not Widow Thrale's convalescents, when good, enjoy the coveted advantages of a visit to the Towers? Mrs. Keziah Solmes had welcomed the opportunity for her grandson Seth. Seth was young, but with well-marked proclivities and aspirations, one of which was a desire for male companionship, preferably of boys older than himself, whom he could incite to acts of lawlessness and destruction he was still too small to commit effectually. He despised little girls. He had been pleased with the account given of the convalescent Toby, and had consented to receive him on stated terms, having reference to the inequitable distribution of cake in his own favour. Hence this visit of his grandmamma to Strides Cottage, with the end in view that she should return with Toby, who for his part had undertaken to be good, with secret reservations in his own mind as to special opportunities to be bad, created by temporary withdrawals of control.

"He can be a very bad little boy indeed," said Widow Thrale, shaking her head solemnly, "when he's forgotten himself. Who was it broke a pane of glass Thursday morning before his breakfast, and very nearly had no sugar?"

Toby said, "Me!" and did not show a contrite heart; seemed too much like the wicked man that did it again.

Granny Marrable entered into undertakings for Toby's future conduct. "He's going to be a wonderful good little boy this time," said she, "and do just exactly whatever he's told, and nothing else." Toby looked very doubtful, but allowed the matter to drop.

"He's vary hearty to look at now, Aunt Phœbe," said Mrs. Keziah—Granny Marrable was always Aunt Phœbe to her husband's relations—when this youth had gone away to conduct himself unexceptionably elsewhere, on his own recognisances. "What has the little ma'an been ailing with?" Widow Thrale gave particulars of Toby's disaster, which had let him in for a long convalescence, the moral of which was that no little boy should drink lotions intended for external use only, however inquiring his disposition might be. Toby had nearly destroyed the coatings of his stomach, and his life had only been preserved by a miracle; which, however, *had* happened, so it didn't matter.

Mrs. Solmes was to await the return of the carrier's cart in a couple of hours, hence it was possible to review and report upon the little local world, deliberately. Granny Marrable began near home. How was the visitor's husband?

"He doan't get any yoonger, Aunt Phœbe," said Keziah. "But he has but a vary little to complain of, at his time of life. If and only he could just be off fretting! He's never been the same in heart since he went so nigh to killing Mr. Torrens o' Pensham, him that yoong Lady Gwen is ta'aking oop with. But a can't say a didn't forewarn him o' what cooms of a lwoaded gwun. And he *doan't*—so I'll do him fair justice."

"Young Torrens of Pensham, *he* can't complain," said a sharp, youngish woman who had come into the room just soon enough to catch the thread of the conversation. She was the housekeeper at Dr. Nash's, who supplied what he prescribed, and was always very obliging about sending. She came with a bottle.

"Why can't he complain, Mrs. Lamprey?" Widow Thrale asked this first, so the others only thought it.

"Where would he have been, Mrs. Thrale, but for the accident? *Accident* you may call it! A rare bit o' luck some'll think! Why—who would the young gentleman have got for a wife, if nobody had shot him? Answer me that! Some girl, I suppose!"

Yes, indeed! To marry Gwen o' the Towers! But how about the poor gentleman's eyesight? This crux was conjointly propounded. "Think what eyesight is to a man!" said Widow Thrale gravely and convincingly.

Mrs. Lamprey echoed back:—"His eyesight?" with a pounce on the first syllable. But seemed to reflect, saying with an abated emphasis:—"Only of course you wouldn't know *that*." Know what?—said inquiry. "Why—about his eyesight! And perhaps I've no call to tell you, seeing I had it in confidence, as you might say."

This was purely formal, in order to register a breach of confidence as an allotropic form of good faith. All pointed out their perfect trustworthiness; and Mrs. Lamprey, with very little further protest, narrated how she had been present when her master, Dr. Nash—whom you will remember as having attended Adrian after the accident—told how his colleague at Pensham Steynes had written to him an account of the curious momentary revival of Adrian's eyesight, or perhaps dream. But Dr. Nash had thrown doubt on the dream, and had predicted to his wife that other incidents of the same sort would follow, would become more frequent, and end in complete recovery.

A general expression of rejoicing—most emphatic on the part of Keziah, who had a strong personal interest at stake—was followed by a reaction. It was hardly possible to concede Gwen o' the Towers to any consort short of a monarch on his throne, or a coroneted lord of thousands of acres at least, except by virtue of some great sacrifice on the part of the fortunate man, that would average his lot with that of common humanity. It wasn't fair. Let Fate be reasonable! Adrian, blind for life, was one thing; but to call such a peerless creature wife, and have eyes to see her! A line must be drawn, somewhere!

"We must hope," said Granny Marrable, as soon as a working eyesight was fairly installed in each one's image of Mr. Torrens, "that he may prove himself worthy."

Said Widow Thrale:—"'Tis no ways hard to guess which her ladyship would choose. I would not have been happy to wed with a blind husband. Nor yourself, Cousin Keziah!"

Said Mrs. Keziah:—"I'm a-looking forward to the telling of my good man. But I lay he'll be for sayun' next, that he'll be all to blame if the wedding turn out ill."

"How can ye put that down to him, to lay it at his door? The fault is none of his, Cousin Keziah." Thus Widow Thrale. "Truly the fault be none of his. But thou doesna knaw Ste'aphen Solmes as I do. He'll be for sayun'—if that g'woon had a been unlwoaded, Master Torrens had gone his way, and no harm done, nouther to him nor yet to Gwen. But who can say for certain that 'tis not God's will all along?"

Mrs. Lamprey interrupted. There was the child's medicine, to be taken regular, three times a day as directed on the bottle, and she had to take Farmer Jones his gout mixture. "But what I told you, that's all correct," said she, departing. "The gentleman will get his eyesight again, and Dr. Nash says so."

Keziah waited for Mrs. Lamprey to depart, and then went on:— "They do say marriages are made in Heaven, and 'tis not unlike to be true. 'Tis all one there whether we be high or low." This was a tribute to Omnipotence, acknowledging its independence of County Families. So august a family as the Earl's might wed as it would, without suffering disparagement. Anyway, there was her young ladyship driving off this very morning to Pensham, so there was every sign at present that the decrees of Providence would hold good. She, Keziah, had heard from her nephew, Tom Kettering, where he was to drive, the carrier's cart having called at the Towers after picking her up at the cottage. Moreover, she—having alighted to interchange greetings with the household—had chanced to overhear her young ladyship say where she was going and when she would be back. She was talking with an old person, a stranger, in black, with silver-white hair.

"That would be Dave's old Mrs. Picture, Ruth," said Granny Marrable, with apparent interest. She was not at all sorry to hear something of her having arrived safely at the Towers, none the worse for her long drive yesterday. Mrs. Keziah, however, showed a disposition to qualify her report, saying:—"Th' o'ald la'ady was ma'akin' but a power show, at that. She'll be a great age, shower-ly! Only they do say, creaking dowers ha'ang longest."

Said Widow Thrale then, explanatorily:—"Mother will be fretting by reason that the old soul would take no refreshment. But reckon you can't with Wills and Won'ts, do what you may! They just drove away, sharp, they did! I tell mother she took no harm, and if she did, t'was no fault of hers, or mine, I lay!"

Two days later, Widow Thrale went over by arrangement to Mrs. Solmes's cottage to recover her convalescent, Toby. She also travelled by the carrier's cart, accepting the hospitality of her cousin for the night, and returning next day with Toby. Granny Marrable was not going to be left alone at the cottage, as she was bidden to spend a day or two with her granddaughter, or more strictly grandniece, Maisie Costrell, to make up for her inability, owing to a bad cold six weeks since, to accompany Widow Thrale to the first celebration of the birthday of the latter's grandchild, at whose entry into the world you may remember the old lady was officiating when Dave visited Strides Cottage a year ago.

Said she, parting at the door from Widow Thrale:—"You'll keep it in mind what I said, Ruth."

Said Ruth, in reply,—"Touching the two yards of calico, or young Davy's London Granny?" For she had more than one mission to Keziah.

"If you name her so, child." This rather stiffly. "Anywise, her young ladyship's old soul that come in the carriage. 'Tis small concern of mine or none at all to be asking. But I would be the easier to be assured that all went well with her, looking so dazed as she did. At her time of life too! More like than not Keziah will be for taking you over to the Castle, and maybe you'll see Mrs.—Picture. . . ."

"Picture's not her real name, only young Davy he's made it for her."

"Well, child, 'tis the same person bears it, whatever the name be! Maybe you'll see Mrs. Picture, and maybe she'll have something to tell of little Davy. I would have made some inquiry of him from her myself, but the time was not to spare." This Granny had not been at all disposed to admit that another Granny could give her any information about Dave. But curiosity rankled, and inquiry through an agent was another matter.

"Lawsey me, mother," said Widow Thrale. "I'll get Keziah to take me round, and I'll get some gossip with the old soul. I'll warrant she hasn't lost her tongue, even be she old as Parson Dunage's mother at the Rectory. Good-bye, mother dear! Take care of yourself on the road to Maisie's. Put on Sister Nora's fur tippet in the open cart, for the wind blows cold at sundown." Granny Marrable disallowed the fur tippet, with some scorn for the luxury of the Age.

If Brantock the carrier, who drove away with Widow Thrale, promising that she should be in time for sooper at Soalmes's, and a bit thrown in, had been told whose mother she would speak with next day, and when she saw her last, he would probably have said nothing—for carriers don't talk; they carry—but his manner would have betrayed his incredulity. And Brantock was no more of a Sadducee than his betters. Who could have believed that that afternoon Widow Thrale and Granny Marrable went away in opposite directions, the former to her own mother, the latter to Mrs. Picture's grandchild, amid the utter ignorance of all concerned? Yet the facts of the case were just as we have stated them, and no one of the incidents that brought them about was in itself incredible.

Brantock was not told anything at all about anything, and did not himself originate a single remark, except that the rain was holding off. It may have been. His horse appeared to have read the directions on all the parcels, choosing without instruction the most time-saving routes to their different destinations, and going on the moment they were paid for. In fact, Mr. Brantock had frequently to resume his seat on a cart in motion, at the risk of his life. When they arrived at the passenger's destination, the horse looked round to make quite sure she was safe on the ground, and then started promptly. His master showed his superiority to the mere brute creation, at this point, by saying, " Good-night, mistress! " The horse said nothing.

Widow Thrale had only expected to hear a mixed report of the success of her convalescent's visit, so she was not disappointed. It gradually came out that Seth and Toby had at first glared suspiciously at one another; the former, as the host, refusing to shake hands; the latter denying his identity, saying to him explicitly:—" *You* ain't the woman's little boy! " They had then dissimulated their hostility, in order to mislead their introducers. They had even gone the length of affecting readiness to play together, in order that they might take advantage of the absence of authority to arrange a duel without seconds. This was interrupted, not because the unrestrained principals could injure each other—they were much too small and soft to do that—but in order to do justice to civilised usage, which defines the relations of host and guest; crossing fisticuffs, even pacifisticuffs, off their programme altogether, and only countenancing religion and politics with reservations. Being separated, each laid claim to having licked the other. In which they followed the time-honoured usage of embattled hosts, or at least of their respective war correspondents. They then became fast friends till death. Widow Thrale was grieved and shocked at the behaviour of a little boy to whom she had ascribed superhuman goodness. A fallen idol!

However, as both were too young to be troubled with consciences, and nothing appeared to overtax their powers of digestion, the visit was considered a great success. In fact, it competed with a previous visit last year, of our Dave Wardle, to the disadvantage of the latter; as Dave and Seth had been too far apart in age, and the only point in which Dave's visit scored was that he was big enough to carry Seth on his shoulders, and even this had been prohibited owing to his recent surgical experiences. The making of the comparison naturally led to the connection of Dave, whatever it was, with the old woman at the Towers, whom Lady Gwen had nigh lost her wits about—so folks said. "But tha knowas what o'or Gwen be!" said Mrs. Keziah. Gwen's reputation with all the countryside was that of waywardness and wilfulness carried to excess, but always with an unerring nobility of object.

Old Stephen had something to say about this, and preferred to put it as a contradiction to Keziah. "Na-ay, na-ay, wife! O'or Gwen can guess a lady, by tokens, as well as thou or I. Tha-at be the story of it. Some la-ady that's coom by ill-luck in her o'ald age, and no friend to hand. She'm gotten a friend now, and a good one!" The old boy did not seem nearly so depressed as his wife's account of him had led Strides Cottage to believe. But then, to be sure, the first thing she had told him when she reached home with the boy yesterday, was Mrs. Lamprey's story of Mr. Torrens's probable restoration of sight. Hope was Hope, and the cloud had lifted. His speculation about Mrs. Picture's possible social status was quite a talkative effort, for him.

Somehow it did not seem convincing to his hearers. Keziah shook her head in slow doubt. "If that were the right of it, husband, the housekeeper's rooms would be no place for her. Gwen would not put it on her to bide with Mrs. Masham."

Old Stephen did not acquiesce. "May happen the old soul would shrink shy of the great folk at the Towers," said he.

"Ay, but there be none!" said his wife. She went on to say that there was scarce a living soul now at the Castle, beyond Gwen and sundry domestics, making ready for the Colonel on Monday. This was a gentleman who scarcely comes into the story, a much younger brother of the Countess, who was allowed to bring friends down for the shooting every autumn to the Towers, and took full advantage of the permission. This year had been an exceptionally good year for the pheasants; in *their* sense, not the sportsman's. For all the Colonel's friends were in the Crimea, and the October shooting had been sadly neglected except by the poachers. He was now back from the Crimea, but was not good for much shooting or fox-hunting, having been himself shot through the lungs in September at the Battle of the Alma, and invalided home. But he was already equal to the duties of host to a shooting-party, and though he could kill nothing himself, he could hear others do so, and could smell the nice powder. The Earl hated this sort of thing, and was glad to get out of the way till the worst of it was over.

Widow Thrale kept modestly outside this review of the Castle's economies, but when they were exhausted referred again to her wish to get a sight of old Mrs. Picture, putting her anxiety to do so entirely on the shoulders of the Granny, of whose wish to know that the old woman had borne the rest of her journey she made the most. She was not prepared to confess to her own curiosity, so she used this device to absolve her of confession. Cousin Keziah also was really a little inquisitive, so an arrangement was easily made that these two should walk over to the Towers on the afternoon of next day, pledging old Stephen to the keeping of a careful eye on the pranks of the two young conspirators against the peace and well-being of maturity, whose business it is to know the exact amount of licence permissible to youth, and at what point the restraint of a firm enunciation of high moral principles becomes a necessity.

If Widow Thrale had been seized with a sudden mania for the improbable, and had set her wits to work their hardest on a carefully chosen typical example, could she have lighted on one that would have imposed a greater strain on human powers of belief than the presence, a mile off, of her mother, dead fifty years since? How improbable it would have seemed to her that her aunt and her kith and kin of that date should fall so easily dupes to a fraud! How improbable that folk should be so content without inquiry, on either side of the globe; that her own mother should remain so for years, and should even lack curiosity, when she returned to England, to seek out her sister's grave; an instinctive tribute, one would have said, almost certain to be paid by so loving a survivor! How improbable that no two lines of life of folk concerned should ever intersect thereafter, through nearly fifty years! And then, how about her father?—how about possible half-brothers and sisters of hers?—how improbable that they should remain quiescent and never seek to know anything about their own flesh and blood, surviving in England! What a tissue of improbabilities!

But then, supposing all facts known, would not old Maisie's daughter have admitted their possibility, even made concession as to probability? Had the tale been told to her then and there, at the Ranger's Lodge in the Park, the two forged letters shown her, and all the devil's cunning of their trickery, would it have seemed so strange that her simple old aunt should be caught in the snare, or others less concerned in the detection of the fraud? And had she then come to know this—that when her mother in the end, twenty years later, came back to her native land, her first act was to seek out the grave where she knew her father was buried, and to find his name alone upon it; that she was then misled by a confused statement of a witness speaking from hearsay; and that she went away thereupon, having kept a strict lock on her tongue as to her own name, and the marriage she now knew to have been no marriage—had Ruth Thrale been told all this, would it not have gone far to soften the harshness of the tale's incredibility?

That story was a strange one, nevertheless, of Maisie's visit to the little graveyard in Essex, where she thought to find the epitaph of Phœbe and of Phœbe's husband probably, and her father's to a certainty. For wherever her brother-in-law and his wife were interred, her father's remains must have been placed beside her mother's, in the grave she had known from her childhood. But nothing had been added to the inscription of her early recollections, except her father's name and appropriate Scriptural citations; with a date, as it chanced, near enough to the one she expected, to rouse no suspicion of the deceptions her husband had practised on her.

Her consciousness of her equivocal position had weighed upon her so strongly that she hesitated to make herself known to any of the older inhabitants of the village—indeed, she would have been at a loss whom to choose—and least of all to any of her husband's relatives, though it would have been easy to find them. No doubt also it made her speech obscure to the only person of whom she made any inquiry. This person, who may have been the parish clerk, saw her apparently looking for a particular grave, and asked if he could give any information. Instead of giving her sister's name, or her own, she answered:—" I am looking for my sister's grave. We were the daughters of Isaac Runciman." His reply:—" She went away. I could not tell you where " was evidently a confused idea, involving a recollection by a man well under forty of Maisie's own disappearance during a period of his boyhood just too early for vital interest in two young women in their twenties. He had taken her for Phœbe. But he must have felt the shakiness of his answer afterwards. For nothing can make it a coherent one, as a speech to Phœbe. On the other hand, it did not seem incoherent to Maisie. She connected it with the false story of her sister's departure to nurse her husband in Belgium, and the wreck of the steamer in which they recrossed the Channel. Her tentative question:—"Did you know of the shipwreck?" only confirmed this. His reply was:—"I was not here at the time, so I only knew that she was going abroad to her husband." *He* was speaking of Maisie's own voyage to Australia, and took her speech to mean that the ship *she* sailed in was wrecked. *She* was thinking of the forged letter.

Have you, who read this, ever chanced to have an experience of how vain it is to try to put oneself in touch with events of twenty or thirty years ago? How came Matthew, Mark, Luke, and John to be so near of a tale if, as some fancy, they never put stylus to papyrus till Paul pointed out their duty to them? Did they compare notes? But if they did, why did they leave any work to be done by harmonizers?

However, this story has nothing to do with Matthew, Mark, Luke, or John. Reflections suggest themselves, for all that, with unconscious Mrs. Ruth Thrale in charge of her cousin by marriage, Keziah Solmes, making her way by the road—because the short cut through the Park is too wet—to the great old Castle, with a room in it where an old, old woman with a sweet face and silver-white hair is watching the cold November sun that has done its best for the day and must die, and waiting patiently for the coming of a Guardian Angel with a golden head and a voice that rings like music. For that is what Gwen o' the Towers is to old Mrs. Prichard of Sapps Court, who came there from Skillicks.

What is that comely countrywoman on the road to old Mrs. Prichard? What was old Mrs. Prichard to her, fifty-odd years ago, before she drew breath? What, when that strong hand, a baby's then, tugged at those silver locks, then golden?

CHAPTER VI

OLD Maisie had a difficulty in walking, owing to rheumatism. But this had improved since her promotion from the diet of Sapps Court to that of Cavendish Square; and later, of the Towers. So much so, that she would often walk about the room, for change; and had even gone cautiously on the garden-terrace, keeping near the house; which was possible, as Francis Quarles had lodged on a ground-floor when he gave his name to the room she occupied.

So, this afternoon, after wondering for some time whose voices those were she heard, variously, in the several passages and ante-chambers of the servants' quarters, and deciding that one broad provincial accent was a native's, and the other, a softer and sweeter one, that of one of the inhabitants of Strides Cottage, she could not be sure which, she got up slowly from her chair by the fire, and made her way to the window, to see the better the little that was left of the sunlight.

Was that cold red disk, going oval in the colder grey of the mist that rose from the darkening land, the selfsame remorseless sun that, one Christmas Day that she remembered well, blazed so over Macquarie that the awkward well-handle, the work of a convict on ticket-of-leave, who had started a forge near by, grew so hot it all but singed the sheep's wool she wrapped round it to protect her hands? So hot that her husband, even when the sun was as low as this, could light his pipe with a burning-glass—a telescope lens whose tube had gone astray, to lead a useless life elsewhere. She remembered that shoeing-smith well; a good fellow, sentenced for life for a crime akin to Wat Tyler's, mercifully reprieved from death by King George in consideration of his provocation; for was he not, like Wat Tyler, the girl's father? She remembered what she accounted that man's only weakness—his dwelling with joy on the sound of the hammer-stroke of his swift, retributive justice—the concussion of the remorseless wrought iron on the split skull of a human beast. She remembered his words with a shudder:—" Ay, mistress, I can shut my eyes and listen for it now. And many was the time it gave me peace to think upon it. Ay!—in the worst of my twenty years, the nights in the cursed river-boat they called the hulks, I could bear them I was shut up with in the dark, and the vermin that crawled about us, and a'most laugh to be able to hear it again, and bless God that it sent him to Hell without time for a prayer!" The words came back to her mind like the hideous incident of a dream we cannot for shame repeat aloud, and made her flesh creep. But then, sup-pose the girl had been her Dolly Wardle, grown big, or her own little maid, whom she never saw again, who died near fifty years ago! Why—the sleeping face of that baby was fresh on her lips still; had never lost its freshness since she tore herself away to reach, at any cost, the man she loved!

Could not the sun have been content to set, without becoming a link with a past she shrank from, so many were the evil memo-ries that clung about it? She was glad that someone should come into the room, to break through this one. There was nothing in this good-humoured villager—surely Pomona's self in a cotton print, somewhat older than is usual with that goddess—nothing but what served to banish these nightmares of her lonely recol-lection. Only, mind you, Sam Rendall—that was Wat Tyler's name, this time—was a good man, who deserved to have had that daughter's children on his knee. She, Maisie, had deserted hers.

" May happen you'll call me to mind, ma'am, me and my old mother, at the door of Strides Cottage, two days agone. I made bold to look in, hoping to see you better." Thus Pomona, and old Maisie was grateful for the wholesome voice. Still, she was puzzled, being unconscious that she had seemed so ill. Pomona thought her introduction of herself had not been clear, and re-peated:—" Strides Cottage, just this side Chorlton, betwixt Farmer Jones and the Reedcroft—where her young ladyship bid stop the carriage. . . ." She paused to let the old lady think. Perhaps she was going too fast.

But no—it was not that at all. Old Maisie was quite clear about the incident, and its whereabouts. " Oh yes!" said she. " I knew it was Strides Cottage, because I had the name from my

little Davy, for the envelopes of his letters. And I knew Farmer
Jones, because of his Bull. It was only a bit of fatigue, with the
long ride." Then as the bald disclaimer of any need for solicitude
seemed a chill return for Pomona's cordiality, old Maisie hastened
to add a corollary:—"I did not find the time to thank your mother
as I would have liked to do; but I get old and slow, and the
coachman was a bit quick of his whip. I should be sorry for you
to think me ungrateful, or your good mother."

It was as well that she added this, for there was a shade of
wavering in Ruth Thrale's heart as to whether the interview was
welcome. A trace of that jealousy about Dave just hung in
Maisie's manner. And she rather stood committed, by not having
accepted the mutton-broth. That corollary may have been Heaven-
sent, to keep the mother and daughter in touch, in the dark—just
for a chance of light!

And yet it only just served its turn. For the daughter's half-
hesitating reply:—"But I thought I would look in," if expanded to
explanation-point, would have been worded:—"I came to show
good-will, more than from any grounded misgivings about your
health, ma'am; and now, having shown it, it is time to go." And
she might have departed, easily.

But Fate also showed good-will, and would not permit it. Old
Mrs. Picture became suddenly alive to the presence of a well-
wisher, and to her own reluctance to drive her away. "Oh, but
you need not go yet," said she. "Or perhaps they want you?"

Oh dear no!—nobody wanted *her*. Her friend she came with,
her Cousin Keziah, was talking to Mrs. Masham. The pleasant
presence would remain, its owner said, and take a seat near the
fire. The old lady was glad, for she had had but little talk with
anyone that day. Her morning interview with Gwen had been a
short one, for that young lady was longing to get away for a
second visit to her lover.

Old Maisie, to encourage possible diffidence to believe that a
quiet chat would really be welcome to her, made reference to
the disappointment such a short allowance of her young ladyship had been, and resuming her high-backed chair, put on her
spectacles to get a better view of her visitor—oh, how unconsciously!

Think of the last kiss she gave a sleeping baby, half a century
ago!

There was, of course, a topic they could speak of—little Dave
Wardle, dear to both. Widow Thrale, fond as she had been of
the child, had not Granny Marrable's bias towards monopolizing

him. *That* was the result of a *grande passion*, generated perhaps
by the encouragement the young man had given to a second
Granny, so very equivalent to his first. Moreover, there was that
obscure reference in his letters to an accident—for *axdnt* was a
mere clerical error. She worded an inquiry after Dave, tentatively.
" I have not seen the dear child for four weeks," said old Maisie.
" Oh dear me, yes—four weeks and more! Let me see, when was
the accident? . . . Oh dear!—how the time does slip away! . . ."
" Was that the accident Dave speaks of in his letter? We
could not quite make out Dave's letter. Sometimes 'tis a little
to seek, what the child means."

Old Maisie nodded assent. " But he'll soon be quite a scholar
and write his own letters all through. I think her ladyship took
this one to send it back. I can tell you about the accident. It
was owing to the repairs." The old lady pursued the subject in
the true spirit of a narrator, beginning at a wrong end, by preference one unintelligible to her hearer. In consequence, the actual
fall of the house-wall was postponed, in favour of a description
of its cause, which dealt specially with the blamelessness of Mr.
Bartlett, and incidentally with the dishonesty of some colleagues
of his, of whom he had spoken as " they," without particulars.
Her leniency to Mr. Bartlett was entirely founded on the fact that
she had conversed with him once on the subject, and had been
mysteriously impressed with his simplicity and manliness. How
did Mr. Bartlett manage it? A faint percentage of beer, like
foreign matter in analyses, is not alone enough to establish integrity. Nor a flavour of clothes.

The wall fell in the end, and Widow Thrale saw a light on the
story, after expressing more admiration and sympathy for Mr.
Bartlett than was human, under the circumstances. She was much
impressed. " And by the mercy of God you were all saved, ma'am,"
said she. " Her young ladyship and little Dave, and his sister, and
yourself! " It really seemed quite a stroke of business, this, on
the part of a Superior Power, which had left building materials
and gravitation, after creating them, to their own wayward
impulses.

Old Maisie admitted the beneficence of Providence, but rather
as an act of courtesy. " For," said she, " we were never in any
real danger, owing to the piece of timber Mr. Bartlett had thrown
across to catch the floor-joists." She was of course repeating Mr.
Bartlett's own words, without close analysis of their actual meaning. Her mind only just avoided associations of cricket. But
poor Susan Burr—oh dear!—that was much worse. " She has

done wonderfully well, though," continued the old lady, "and her case gave the greatest satisfaction to the Doctors at the Hospital. She has written to me herself since leaving. And she must be really better, because she has gone to her married niece at Clapham." It seemed a sort of destiny that this niece's wifehood should always be emphasized. It was almost implied that a less complete recovery would have resulted in a journey to a single niece, at Clapham; or possibly, only at Battersea. Widow Thrale was interested in the accident, but she wanted to get back to Dave Wardle. "Then no one could live in the house, ma'am," she said, "after it had fallen down?"

"Not in my rooms upstairs, nor his Aunt M'riar's underneath. Only his uncle stopped in, to keep the place. *His* room was all safe. It was like the front of two rooms, all down in the street as if it was an earthquake. And no forewarning, above a crack or two! But the children safe, God be thanked, and her young ladyship! Also her cousin, Miss Grahame, down below with Aunt M'riar."

"That lady we call Sister Nora?"

"That lady. But I was so stunned and dazed with the start it gave me, and the noise, that I had no measure of anything. They took me home with them. I can just call to mind moving in the carriage, and the lamplighter." Old Maisie recollected seeing the lamplighter, but she had forgotten how she was got into that carriage.

"Then you hardly saw the children?"

"I was all mazed. I heard my Dolly cry, poor little soul! Her ladyship says Dave took Dolly up very short for being such a coward. But he kissed her, for comfort, and to keep her in heart."

"*He* didn't cry!"

"Davy?—not he. Davy makes it a point to be afraid of nothing. His uncle has taught him so. He was "—here some hesitation—"he belonged to what they called the Prize Ring. A professional boxer." It sounded better than "prizefighter"—more restrained.

"Oh dear!" said Widow Thrale. "Yes. I had heard that."

"But he is a good man," said old Maisie, warming to the defence of Uncle Mo. "He is indeed! He won't let Dave fight, only a little now and then. But Dave says he told him, Uncle Mo did, that if ever he saw a boy hit a little girl, he was to hit that boy at once, without stopping to think how big he was. And he told him where! Is not that a good man?"

" Oh dear! " said Widow Thrale again, uneasily. " Won't Dave hit some boy that's too strong for him, and get hurt? "

" I think he may, ma'am. But then . . . someone *may* take his part! I should pray." She went on to repeat an adventure of Dave's, when he behaved as directed to a young monster who was stuffing some abomination into a little girl's mouth. But it ended with the words:—" The boy ran away." Perhaps Uncle Mo had judged rightly of the class of boy that he had in mind, as almost sure to run away.

The Pomona in Widow Thrale had gone behind a cloud during her misgivings about Uncle Mo. The cloud passed, as the image of this boy fled from Nemesis. He was a London boy, evidently, and up to date. The Feudal System, as surviving at Chorlton, countenanced no such boys. The voice of Pomona was cheerful again as she resumed Dave:—" Where, then, is the boy, till he goes back home? "

" His aunt has got him at her mother's, at Ealing. His real grandmother's." Pomona had a subconsciousness that this made three; an outrageous allowance of grandmothers for any boy! But she would not say so, as this old lady might be sensitive about her own claims, which might be called in question if Dave's list was revised.

Ealing recalled an obscure passage in his letter, which was really an insertion, in the text, of the address of his haven of refuge. It read, transcribed literally:—" My grandMother is hEALing," and the recollection of it reinforced the laugh with which Pomona pleaded to misinterpretation. " Mother and I both thought she had cut herself," said she.

Old Maisie, amused at Dave, made answer:—" No!—it's where he is. Number Two, Penkover Terrace, Ealing. Penkover is very hard to recollect. So do write it down. Write it now. I shall very likely forget it directly; because when I get tired with talking, I swim, and the room goes round. . . . Oh no—I'm not tired yet, and you do me good to talk to."

But the old lady had' talked to the full extent of her tether. But even in this short conversation the impression made upon her by this new acquaintance was so favourable that she felt loth to let her depart; to leave her, perhaps, to some memory of the past as painful as the one she had interrupted. If she had spoken her exact mind she would have said:—" No, don't go yet. I can't talk much, but it makes me happy to sit here in the growing dusk and hear about Dave. It brings the child back to me, and does my heart good." That was the upshot of her thought, but she felt that their acquaintance was too short to warrant it. She was bound to make an effort, if not to entertain, at least to bear her share of the conversation.

"Tell me more about Davy, when you had him at the Cottage. Did he talk about me?" This followed her declaration that she was "not tired yet" in a voice that lost force audibly. Her visitor chose a wiser course than to make a parade of her readiness to take a hint and begone. She chatted on about Dave's stay with her a year since, about little things the story knows already, while the old lady vouched at intervals—quite truly—that she heard every word, and that her closed eyes did not mean sleep. The incident of Dave's having persisted—when he awaked and found "mother" looking at him, the day after his first arrival— that it was old Mrs. Picture upstairs, and how they thought the child was still dreaming, was really worth the telling. Old Maisie showed her amusement, and felt bound to rouse herself to say:— "The name is not really Picture, but it doesn't matter. I like Dave's name—Mrs. Picture!" It was an effort, and when she added:—"The name is really Prichard," her voice lost strength, and her hearer lost the name. Fate seemed against Dave's pronunciation being corrected.

You know the game we used to call Magic Music—we oldsters, when we were children? You know how, from your seat at the piano, you watched your listener striving to take the hints you strove to give, and wandering aimlessly away from the fire-irons he should have shouldered—the book he should have read upside down—the little sister he should have kissed or tickled—what not? You remember the obdurate pertinacity with which he missed fire, and balked the triumphant outburst that should have greeted his success? Surely, if some well-wisher among the choir of Angels, harping with their harps, had been at Chorlton then and there, under contract to guide Destiny, by playing loud and soft—not giving unfair hints—to the reuniting of the long-lost sisters, that Angel would have been hard tried to see how near the spark went to fire the train, yet flickered down and died; how many a false scent crossed the true one, and threw the tracker out!

Old Maisie's powers of sustained attention were, of course, much less than she supposed, and her visitor's pleasant voice, rippling on in the growing dusk, was more an anodyne than a stimulant. She did not go to sleep—people don't! But something that very nearly resembled sleep must have come to her. Whatever it was, she got clear of it to find, with surprise, that Mrs. Thrale, with

her bonnet off, was making toast at the glowing wood-embers; and
that candles were burning and that, somehow tea had germinated.
"I thought I would make you some toast, more our sort. . . .
Oh yes! What the young lady has brought is very nice, but
this will be hotter." The real Pomona never looked about fifty—
she was a goddess, you see!—but if she had, and had made toast,
she must have resembled Ruth Thrale.
    Then old Maisie became more vividly alive to her visitor, helped
by the fact that she had been unconscious in her presence. That
was human nature. The establishment of a common sympathy
about Lupin, the tea-purveyor, was social nature. Pomona had
called Miss Lupin "the young lady." This had placed Miss Lupin;
she belonged to a superior class, and her ministrations were a
condescension. It was strange indeed that such trivialities should
have a force to span the huge gulf years had dug between these
two, and yet never show a rift in the black cloud of their fraud-
begotten ignorance. They *did* draw them nearer together, beyond
a doubt; especially that recognition of Miss Lupin's position. Old
Maisie had never felt comfortable with the household, while
always oppressed with gratitude for its benevolences. She had
felt that she had expressed it very imperfectly to her young ladyship, to cause her to say:—"They will get all you want, I dare
say. But how *do* they behave? That's the point! Are they
giving themselves airs, or being pretty to you?" For this downright young beauty never minced matters. But naturally old
Maisie had felt that she could do nothing but show gratitude for
the attention of the household, especially as she could not for the
life of her define the sources of her discomfort in her relations
with it.
    This saddler's widow from Chorlton, with all her village life
upon her, and her utter ignorance of the monstrous world of
Maisie's own past experience, came like a breath of fresh air.
Was it Pomona though?—or was it the tea? Reserve gave way to
an impulse of informal speech:—"My dear, you have had babies
of your own?"
    Pomona's open-eyed smile seemed to spread to her very finger-
tips. "Babies? *Me?*" she exclaimed. "Yes, indeed! But not
so very many, if you count them. Five, all told! Two of my little girls I lost—'tis a many years agone now. My two boys are
aboard ship, one in the Black Sea, one in the Baltic. My eldest
on the *Agamemnon*. My second—he's but sixteen—on the *Ti-
thonus*. But he's seen service—he was at Bomarsund in August.
Please God, when the war is over, they'll come back with a many

tales for their mother and their granny! I lie awake and pray for them, nights."

The old lady kept her thoughts to herself—even spoke with unwarranted confidence of these boys' return. She shied off the subject, nevertheless. How about the other little girl, the one that still remained undescribed?

"My married daughter? She is my youngest. She's married to John Costrell's son at Denby's farm. Maisie. Her first little boy is just over a year old."

Old Maisie brightened, interested, at the name. A young Maisie, so near at hand! "My own name!" she said. "To think of that!" Yet, after all, the name was a common one.

"Called after her grandmother," said Ruth Thrale, equably—chattily. "Mother has gone over to-day to make up for not going on his birthday." Of course the "grandmother" alluded to was her own proper mother, the young mother on whose head that old silver hair she was watching so unconsciously had been golden brown, fifty years ago. For all that, Ruth spoke of her aunt as "mother," automatically. What wonder that old Maisie accepted Granny Marrable's Christian name as the same as her own. "My name is the same as your mother's, then!" seemed worth saying, on the whole, though it put nothing very uncommon on record.

How near the spark was to the tinder!—how loud that Angel would have had to play! For Ruth Thrale might easily have chanced to say:—"Yes, the same that my mother's was." And that past tense might have spoken a volume.

But Destiny was at fault, and the Angel would have had to play *pianissimo*. Miss Lupin came in, bearing a log that had taken twenty years to grow and one to dry. The glowing embers were getting spent, and the open hearth called for reimbursement. It seemed a shame those sweet fresh lichens should burn; but then, it would never do to let the fire out! Miss Lupin contrived to indicate condescension in her attitude, while dealing with its reconstruction. No conversation could have survived such an inroad, and by the time Miss Lupin had asked if she should remove the tea etceteras, the review of Pomona's family was forgotten, and Destiny was baffled.

Another floating spark went even nearer to the tinder, when, going back to Dave and Dolly, old Maisie talked of the pleasure of having the little girl at home, now that Dave was so much away at school. She was getting dim in thought and irresponsible when she gave Widow Thrale this chance insight into her early days. It was a sort of slip of the mind that betrayed her into saying:—" Ah, my dear, the little one makes me think of my own little child I left behind me, that died—oh, such a many years ago! . . ." Her voice broke into such audible distress that her hearer could not pry behind her meaning; could only murmur a sympathetic nothing. The old lady's words that followed seemed to revoke her lapse:—" Long and long ago, before ever you were born, I should say. But she was my only little girl, and I keep her in mind, even now." Had not Widow Thrale hesitated, it might have come out that *her* mother had fled from her at the very time, and that her own name was Ruth. How could suspicion have passed tiptoe over such a running stream of possible surmise, and landed dryfoot?

But nothing came of it. There was nothing in a child that died before she was born, to provoke comparison of her own dim impressions of her mother's departure—for old Phœbe had kept much of the tale in abeyance—and her comments hung fire in a sympathetic murmur. She felt, though, that the way she had appeased her thirst for infancy might be told, appropriately; dwelling particularly on the pleasures of nourishing convalescents up to kissing-point, as the ogress we have compared her to might have done up to readiness for the table. Old Maisie was quite ready to endorse all her views and experiences, enjoying especially the account of Dave's rapid recovery, and his neglected Ariadne.

A conclusive sound crept into the conversation of Mrs. Solmes and the housekeeper, always audible without. " I think I hear my Cousin Keziah going," said Mrs. Thrale. " I must not keep her."

" Thank you, my dear! I mean—thank you for coming to see me!" It was the second time old Maisie had said " my dear " to this acquaintance of an hour. But then, her face, that youth's comeliness still clung to, invited it.

" 'Tis I should be the one to thank, ma'am, both for the pleasure, and for the hearing tell of little Davy. Mother will be very content to get a little news of the child. Oh, I can tell you she grudges her share of Dave to anyone! If mother should take it into her head to come over and hear some more, for herself, you will not take it amiss? It will be for love of the child." Then, as a correction to what might have seemed a stint of courtesy:—" And for the pleasure of a visit to you, ma'am." Said old Maisie absently:—" I hope she will." And then Widow Thrale saw that all this talking had been quite enough, and took her leave.

This was the second time these two had parted, in half a century. They shook hands, this time, and there was no glimmer in the mind of either, of who or what the other was. Each remained as unconscious of the other's identity as that sleeping child in her crib had been, fifty years ago, of her mother's heart-broken beauty as she tore herself away, with the kiss on her lips that dwelt there still.

They shook hands, with affectionate cordiality, and the old lady, hoping again that the visitor's "mother" would pay her a visit, settled back to watching the fire creep along the lichens, one by one, on that beechen log the squirrels had to themselves a year ago.

Unconscious Widow Thrale had much to say of the pretty old lady as she and Mrs. Solmes walked back to the Ranger's Cottage through the nightfall. Fancy mother taking it into her head that Dave would be the worse by such a nice old extra Granny as that! She must be very much alone in the world though, to judge by what little she had told of her life in Sapps Court. No single hint of kith and kin! Had Keziah not heard a word about her antecedents? Well—nothing to ma'ak a stowery on't! Housekeeper Masham had expressed herself ambiguously, saying that her yoong la'adyship had lighted down upon the old lady in stra'ange coompany; concerning which she, Masham, not being called upon to deliver judgment, preferred to keep her mowuth shoot. Keziah contrived to convey that this shutting of Mrs. Masham's mouth had carried all the weight of speech, all tending to throw doubt on Mrs. Picture, without any clue to the special causes of offence against her.

Whatever misgivings about the old lady Widow Thrale allowed to re-enter her mind were dispersed on arriving at the Cottage. For Toby and Seth, being sought for to wash themselves and have their suppers, were not forthcoming. They had vanished. They were found in the Verderer's Hall, where they had concealed themselves with ingenuity, unnoticed by old Stephen, whom they had followed in and allowed to depart, locking the door after him and so locking them in. It was sheer original sin on their part—the corruption of Man's heart. The joy of occasioning so much anxiety more than compensated for delayed supper; and penalties lapsed, owing to the satisfaction of finding that they had not both tumbled into a well two hundred feet deep. Old Stephen's remark that, had he been guilty of such conduct in his early youth, he would have been all over wales, had an historical interest, but nothing further. They seemed flattered by his opinion that they were a promussin' yoong couple. However, the turmoil they created drove the previous events of the day out of Widow Thrale's head. She slept very sound and—forgot all about her interview with the old visitor at the Towers!

Old Maisie, alone in Francis Quarles as she had been so often in the garret at Sapps Court, became again the mere silver-headed relic of the past, waiting patiently, one would have said, for Death; content to live, content to die; ready to love still; not strong enough to hate, and ill-provided with an object now. Not for the former—no, indeed! Were there not her Dave and her Dolly to go back to? She had not lost them much, for they, too, were away from poor, half-ruined Sapps Court. She would go back soon. But then, how about her Guardian Angel? She would lose her—*must* lose her, some time! Why not now?

What had she, old Maisie, done to deserve such a guardian-ship?—*friendship* was hardly the word to use. An overpresump-tion in one so humble! Who could have foreseen all this bewilder-ment of Chance six weeks ago, when her great event of the day was a visit of the two children. She resented a half-thought she could not help, that called her gain in question. Was not Sapps Court her proper place? Was she not too much out of keeping with her surroundings? Could she even find comfort, when she re-turned to her old quarters, in wearing these clothes her young ladyship had had made for her; so unlike her own old wardrobe, scarcely a rag of it newer than Skillicks? She fought against the ungenerous thought—the malice of some passing imp, surely! —and welcomed another that had strength to banish it, the image of her visitor of to-day.

There she was again—at least, all that memory supplied! What was her dress? Old Maisie could not recall this. The image sup-plied a greeny-blue sort of plaid, but memory wavered over that. Her testimony was clear about the hair; plenty of it, packed close with a ripple on the suspicion of grey over the forehead, that seemed to have halted there, unconfirmed. At any rate, there would be no more inside those knot-twists behind, that still showed an autumnal golden brown, Pomona-like. Yes, she had had abundance in the summer of her life, and that was not so long ago. How old was she?—old Maisie asked herself. Scarcely fifty yet, seemed a reasonable answer. She had forgotten to ask her christened name, but she could make a guess at it—could fit her with one to her liking. Margaret—Mary?—No, not exactly. Try Bertha. . . . Yes—Bertha might do. . . . But she could think about her so much better in the half-dark. She rose and blew the candles out, then went back to her chair and the line of thought that had pleased her.

How fortunate this good woman had been to hit upon the convalescent idea! She, herself, when her worst loneliness clouded her horizon, might have devised some such *modus vivendi*—as between herself and her enemy, Solitude; not as mere means to live. But, indeed, Solitude had intruded upon her first, disguised as a friend. The irksomeness of life had come upon her later, when the sting of her son's wickedness began to die away. Moreover, her delicacy of health had disqualified her for active responsibilities. This Mrs. Marrable's antecedents had made no inroads on *her* constitution, evidently.

See where the fire had crept over these lichens and devoured them! The log would soon be black, when once the heat got a fair hold of it. Now, the pent-up steam from some secret core, that had kept its moisture through the warmth of a summer, hissed out in an angry jet, stung by the conquering flame. There, see!—from some concealment in the bark, mysteriously safe till now, a six-legged beetle, panic-struck and doomed. Cosmic fires were at work upon his world—that world he thought so safe! It was the end of the Universe for him—*his* Universe! Old Maisie would gladly have played the part of a merciful Divinity, and worked a miraculous salvation. But alas!—the poor little fugitive was too swift to his own combustion in the deadly fires below. Would it be like that for us, when our world comes to an end? Old Maisie was sorry for that little beetle, and would have liked to save him.

She sat on, watching the tongues of flame creep up and up on the log that seemed to defy ignition. The little beetle's fate had taken her mind off her retrospect; off Dave and Dolly, and the pleasant image of Pomona. She was glad of any sign of life, and the voices that reached her from the kitchen or the servants' hall were welcome; and perhaps . . . *perhaps* they were not quarrelling. But appearances were against them. Nevertheless, the lull that followed made her sorry for the silence. A wrangle toned down by distance and intervening doors is soothingly suggestive of company—soothingly, because it fosters the distant hearer's satisfaction at not being concerned in it. Old Maisie hoped they would go on again soon, because she had blown those lights out rashly, without being sure she could relight them. She could tear a piece off the newspaper and light it at the fire of course. But—the idea of tearing a newspaper! This, you see, was in fifty-four, and tearing a number of the *Times* was like tearing a book. No spills offered themselves. She made an excursion into her bedroom for the matchbox and felt her way to it. But it was empty! The futility of an empty matchbox is as the effrontery of the celebrated misplaced milestone. Expeditions for scraps of waste-paper in the dark, with her eyesight, might end in burning somebody's will, or a cheque for pounds. That was her feeling, at least. Never mind!—she could wait. She had been told always to ring the bell when she wanted anything, but she had never presumed on the permission. A lordly act, not for a denizen of Sapps Court! Roxalana or Dejanira might pull bells. Very likely the log would blaze directly, and she would come on a scrap of real waste-paper.

Stop! . . . Was not that someone coming along the passage, from the kitchen. Perhaps someone she could ask? She would not go back to her chair till she heard who it was. She set the door " on the jar " timidly, and listened. Yes—she knew the voices. It was Miss Lutwyche and one of the housemaids. Not Lupin—the other one, Mary Anne, who seldom came this way, and whom she hardly knew by sight. But what was it that they were saying?

Said Miss Lutwyche:—" Well, I call her a plaguy old cat. . . . No, I don't care if she does hear me." However, she lowered her voice to finish her speech, and much that followed was inaudible to old Maisie. Who of course supposed she was the plaguy old cat!

Then Mary Anne became audible again, confirming this view:— " Is that her room? " For the subject of the conversation had changed in that inaudible phase—changed from Mrs. Masham to the queer old soul her young ladyship had pitchforked down in the middle of the household.

" That's her room now. Old Mashey has been turned out. She's next door. She's supposed to look after her and see she wants for nothing. . . . I don't know. Perhaps she does. I wash my hands." At this point the poor old listener heard no more. What she had heard was a great shock to her; really almost as great a shock as the crash at Sapps Court. She found her way back to her chair and sat and cried, in the darkened room. She was a plaguy old cat, and Miss Lutwyche, with whom she had been on very good terms in Cavendish Square, had washed her hands of her! Then, when the servants here were attentive to her—and they were all right, as far as that went—it was mere deceptiousness, and they were wishing her at Jericho.

She was conscious that the lady's-maid and Mary Anne came

back, still talking. But she had closed the door, and was glad she could not hear what they were saying. A few minutes after, Mrs. Masham appeared from her own room close by, having apparently recovered her temper. But, said old Maisie to herself, all this was sheer hypocrisy; a mere timeserver's assumption of civility towards a plaguy old cat!

"You'll be feeling ready for your bit of supper, Mrs. Pilcher," said the housekeeper; who, having been snubbed by Miss Lutwyche for saying "Pilchard," had made compromise. She could not be expected to accept "Picture." The bit of supper was behind her on a tray, borne by Lupin. "Why—you're all in the dark!" She rebuked the servant-girl because there were no matches, and on production of a box from the latter's pocket, magnanimously lit the candles with her own hands, continuing the while to reproach her subordinate for neglect of the guest entrusted to her charge. That guest's thought being, meanwhile, what a shocking hypocrite this woman was. Probably Mrs. Masham was no more a hypocrite than old Maisie was an old cat. That is to say, if the latter designation meant a termagant or scold. There must be now and again, in Nature, a person without a hall-mark of either Heaven or Hell, and Mrs. Masham may have had none. In that recent encounter in the kitchen which old Maisie had been conscious of, she had lost her temper with Miss Lutwyche; but so might anyone, if you came to that. Cook had come to that, after Miss Lutwyche left the room, and her designation of that young lady as a provocation, and a hussy, had done much to pacify Mrs. Masham.

Anyhow, Mrs. Masham was on even terms with herself, if not in a treacle-jar, when she sat down by the fire to do—as she thought—her duty by her young ladyship's *protégée*. She was that taken up, she said, every minute of the day, that she did not get the opportunities her heart longed for of cultivating the acquaintance of her guest. But she was thankful to hear that Mrs. Pilcher had not been any the worse for her talk with her visitor an hour since. Widow Thrale, living like she did over at Chorlton, was a sort of stranger at the Towers. But only a subacute stranger, as her husband, when living, was frequently in evidence there, in connection with the stables.

Old Maisie was interested to hear anything about her pleasant visitor. What sort of aged woman did Mrs. Masham take her to be? Her voice, said the old lady, was that of a much younger person than she seemed, to look at.

"How old would she be?" said the housekeeper. "Well—she

might be a child of twelve or thirteen when her mother came to
Strides Cottage, and married Farmer Marrable there. . . ."
" Then her name was never Marrable at all," said old Maisie.
" No. Granny Marrable, she'd been married before, in Sussex.
Now what *was* her first husband's name? . . . Well—I ought to
be able to recollect *that!* Ruth—Ruth—Ruth what?" She was
trying to remember the name by which she had known Widow
Thrale in her childhood. Her effort to do so, had it succeeded,
would have made a complete disclosure almost inevitable, owing
to the peculiarity of Granny Marrable's first husband's name. " I
ought to be able to recollect, but there!—I can't. I suppose it
would be because we always heard her spoken of as Mrs. Marrable's Ruth. I saw but very little of her; only when I was a
child. . . ." She paused a moment, arrested by old Maisie's expression, and then said:—" Yes . . . why? " . . . and stopped.
" Because if I had known she was Ruth I would have told her
that my little girl that died was Ruth. Just a fanciful idea! "
But the speaker's supper was getting cold. The housekeeper departed, telling Lupin to get some scrapwood to make a blaze
under that log, and make it show what a real capacity it had as
fuel, if only justice was done to its combustibility.

This chance passage of conversation between old Maisie and
the housekeeper ran near to sounding the one note needed to force
the truth of an incredible tale on the blank unsuspicion of its
actors. A many other little things may have gone as near. If
so, none left any one of its audience, or witnesses, more absolutely in the dark about it than the solitary old woman who that
evening watched that log, stimulated by the scrapwood during
her very perfunctory supper; first till it became a roaring flame
that laughed at those two candles, then till the flame died down
and left it all aglow; then till the fire reached its heart and broke
it, and it fell, and flickered up again and died, and slowly resolved
itself into a hillock of red ember and creeping incandescence, a
treasury still of memories of the woodlands and the coming of the
spring, and the growth of the leaves that perished.

At about nine o'clock, Lupin, acting officially, came to offer
her services to see the old lady to bed. No!—if she might do
so she would rather sit up till her ladyship came in. She could
shift for herself; in fact, like most old people who have never been
waited on, she greatly preferred it. Only, of course, she did not
say so. But Lupin *was* sitting up for her ladyship, with Miss
Lutwyche, and would purvey hot water then, in place of this,
which would be cold. She brought a couple of young loglets to

keep a little life in the fire, and went away to contribute to an everlasting wrangle in the servants' hall.

The wind roared in the chimney and made old Maisie's thoughts go back to the awful sea. Think of the wrecks this wind would cause! Of course she was all wrong; one always is, indoors, with a huge chimney which is a treasure-house of sound. Gwen was just saying at that moment, to Adrian and his sister, what a delicious night it was to be out of doors! And the grey mare, in a hurry to go, was undertaking through an interpreter to be back in an hour and three-quarters easy. And then they were off, Gwen laughing to scorn Irene's reproaches to her for not staying the night. All that was part of Gwen's minimisation of her guilt in this postponement of the separation test. The stars seemed to flash the clearer in the heavens for such laughter as hers, in such a voice. But all the while old Maisie was haunted with images of a chaise blown into ditches and over bridges, and colliding with blown-down elms, in league for mischief with blown-out lamps. Be advised, and *never* fidget about the absent!

She would rather have gone on doing so than that the recollection should come back to her of Lutwyche's odious designation that she had taken to herself, so warrantably to all appearance. A *plaguy old cat!* What had she ever done or said to Miss Lutwyche, or any of them, to deserve such a name? And then that girl who was with her had seemed to accept it so easily—certainly without any protest. She was ready to admit, though, that her vituperators had concealed their animus well, the hypocrites that they were! Look how amiable Mrs. Masham had made believe to be, an hour ago ! A shade of graciousness—an infinitesimal condescension—certainly nothing worse than that! But the hypocrisy of it! She had never been quite comfortable in her ill-assigned position of guest undefined—dear, beautiful Gwen's fault! Never, since the housekeeper on first introduction had jumped at her reluctance to taint the servants' hall with Sapps Court, interpreting it as a personal desire to be alone. But she had never suspected that she was a plaguy old cat, and did not feel like her idea of one.

Conceive the position of a lonely octogenarian, injudiciously thrust into a community where she was not welcome—by a Guardian Angel surely, but one who had never known the meaning of the word " obstacle." Conceive that her poverty had never meant pauperisation, and that graciousness and condescension are always tainted with benevolence, to the indigent. She had done nothing to deserve having anything bestowed on her, and the wing of a chicken she had supped upon would have stuck in her throat with that qualification. Understand, too, that when this thought crossed her mind, she recoiled from it and cried out upon her petty pride that would call anything in question that had been *visé* and endorsed by that dear Guardian Angel. Use these helps towards a glimpse into her heart as she watched the new wood go the way of the old, and say if you wonder that she cried silently over it. Now if only that nice person that came to-day could have stayed on, to pass the time with her until the welcome sound should come of the chaise's homeward wheels and the grey mare's splendid pace, bringing her what she knew would come if Gwen was in it, a happy fare- well interview with her idol before she went to bed. Yes—how nice it would have been to have her here! Ruth Thrale—yes, Ruth—her own little daughter's name of long ago! This Ruth *was* her own daughter. But how to know it!

CHAPTER VII

HOW GWEN CAME BACK, AND FOUND THE "OLD CAT" ASLEEP. AND TOOK OFF HER SABLES. A CANDLE-LIGHT JOURNEY THROUGH AN ANCIENT HOUSE, AND A TELEGRAPHIC SUMMONS. HOW GWEN RUSHED AWAY BY A NIGHT-TRAIN, BECAUSE HER COUSIN CLOTILDA SAID DON'T COME. HOW SHE LEFT A LETTER FOR WIDOW THRALE AT THE RANGER'S LODGE

JUST as the watched pot never boils, so the thing one waits for never comes, so long as one waits *hard*. The harder one waits the longer it is postponed. When one sits up to open the door to the latchkeyless, there is only one sure way of bringing about his return, and that is to drop asleep *à contre cœur,* and sleep too sound for furious knocks and rings, gravel thrown at windows, and intemperate language, to arouse you. Then he will come back, and be obliged to say he has only knocked once, and you will say you had only just closed your eyes.

Old Maisie was quite sure she had just closed hers, when of a sudden the voice she longed for filled Heaven and Earth, and said:—" Oh, what a shame to come and wake you out of such a beautiful sleep! But you mustn't sleep all night in the arm-chair. Poor dear old Mrs. Picture! What would Dave say! What would Mrs. Burr say!" And then old Maisie waked from a dream about unmanageable shrimps, to utter the correct formula with a conviction of its truth, this time. She *had* only just closed her eyes. Only just!

Miss Lutwyche, in attendance, ventured on sympathetic familiarity. Mrs. Picture would not get any beauty-sleep to-night, that was certain. For it is well known that only sleep in bed deserves the name, and a clock was putting its convictions about midnight on record, dogmatically.

Gwen's laugh rang out soon enough to quash its last *ipse dixits.* " Then the mischief's done, Lutwyche, and another five minutes doesn't matter. Mrs. Picture's going to tell me all her news. Here—get this thing off! Then you can go till I ring." The thing, or most of it, was an unanswerable challenge to the coldest wind of night—the cast-off raiment of full fifty little sables, that scoured the Russian woods in times gone by. Surely the breezes had drenched it with the very soul of the night air in that ride beneath the stars, and the foam of them was shaken out of it as it released its owner.

Then old Maisie was fully aware of her Guardian Angel, back again—no dream, like those shrimps! And her voice was saying:— " So you had company, Mrs. Picture dear. Lutwyche told me. The widow-woman from Chorlton, wasn't it? How did you find her? Nice? "

Yes, the widow-woman was very nice. She had stayed quite a long time, and had tea. " I liked her very much," said old Maisie. " She was easy." Then—said inference—somebody is difficult. Maisie did not catch this remark, made by one of the most inaudible of speakers. " Yes," she said, " she stayed quite a long time, and had tea. She is a very good young woman "— for, naturally, eighty sees fifty-odd as youth, especially when fifty-odd seems ten years less—" and we could talk about Dave. It was like being home again." She used, without a trace of *arrière pensée,* a phrase she could not have bettered had she tried to convey to Gwen her distress at hearing she was a plaguy old cat. Then she suddenly saw its possible import, and would have liked to withdraw it. " Only I would not seek to be home again, my dear, when I am near you." She trembled in her eagerness to get this said, and not to say it wrong.

Gwen saw in an instant all she had overlooked, and indeed she *had* overlooked many things. It was, however, much too late at night to go into the subject. She could only soothe it away now, but with intention to amend matters next day; or, rather, next daylight. So she said:—" The plaster will very soon be dry now in Sapps Court, dear Mrs. Picture, and then you shall

go back to Dave and Dolly, and I will come and see you there.
You must go to bed now. So must I—I suppose? I will come to
you to-morrow morning, and you will tell me a great deal more.
Now good-night!" That was what she said aloud. To herself
she thought a thought without words, that could only have been
rendered, to do it justice:—"The Devil fly away with Mrs.
Masham, that she couldn't contrive to make this dear old soul
comfortable for a few weeks, just long enough for some plaster
to dry." She went near adding:—"And myself, too, not to have
foreseen what would happen!" But she bit this into her underlip,
and cancelled it.

She rang the bell for Lutwyche, now the sole survivor in the
kitchen region. Who appeared, bearing hot water—some for the
plaguy old cat. Gwen said good-night again, kissing the old lady
affectionately when Lutwyche was not looking. Mistress and maid
then, when the cat at her own request was left to get herself
into sleeping trim, started on the long journey through corridors
and state-rooms through which her young ladyship's own quarters
had to be reached. Corridors on whose floors one walked up and
down hill; great chambers full of memories, and here and there
indulging in a ghost. Tudor rooms with Holbeins between the
windows, invisible to man; Jacobean rooms with Van Dycks,
nearly as regrettably invisible; Lelys and Knellers, much more
regrettably visible. Across the landing the great staircase, where
the Reynolds hangs, which your *cicerone* of this twentieth century will tell you was the famous beauty of her time, and the
grandmother of another famous Victorian beauty, dead not a
decade since. And on this staircase Gwen, half pausing to glance
at her departed prototype, started suddenly, and exclaimed:—
" What's that?"

For a bell had broken the silence of the night—a bell that had
enjoyed doing so, and was slow to stop. Now a bell after midnight in a house that stands alone in a great Park, two miles
from the nearest village, has to be accounted for, somehow. Not
by Miss Lutwyche, who merely noted that the household would
hear and answer the summons.

Her young ladyship was not so indifferent to human affairs as
her attendant. She said:—"I must know what that is. They
won't send to tell me. Come back!" She had said it, and started,
before that bell gave in and retired from public life.

Past the Knellers and Lelys, among the Van Dycks, a scared
figure, bearing a missive. Miss Lupin, and no ghost—as she might
have been—in the farther door as her ladyship passes into the

room. She has run quickly with it, and is out of breath. "A telegraph for your ladyship!" is all she can manage. She would have said "telegram" a few years later.

A rapid vision, in Gwen's mind, of her father's remains, crushed by a locomotive, itself pulverised by another—for these days were rich in railway accidents—then a hope! It may be the fall of Sebastopol; a military cousin had promised she should know it as soon as the Queen. Give her the paper and end the doubt! . . . It is neither.

It is serious, for all that. Who brought this?—that's the first question, from Gwen. Lúpin gives a hurried account. It is Mr. Sandys, the station-master at Grantley Thorpe, who has galloped over himself to make sure of delivery. Is he gone? No—he has taken his horse round to Archibald at the Stables to refit for a quieter ride back. Very well. Gwen must see him, and Tom Kettering must be stopped going to bed, and must be ready to drive her over to Grantley, if there is still a chance to catch the up-train for Euston. Lutwyche may get things ready at once, on the chance, and not lose a minute. Lupin is off, hotfoot, to the Stables, to catch Mr. Sandys, and bring him round.

White and determined, after reading the message, Gwen retraces her steps. Outside old Mrs. Picture's door comes a moment of irresolution, but she quashes it and goes on. Old Maisie is not in bed yet—has not really left that tempting fireside. She becomes conscious of a stir in the house, following on a bell that she had supposed to be only a belated absentee. She opens her door furtively and listens.

That is Gwen's voice surely, beyond the servants' quarter, speaking with a respectful man. The scraps of speech that reach the listener's ear go to show that he assents to do something out of the common, to oblige her ladyship. Something is to happen at three-fifteen, which he will abet, and be responsible for. Only it must be three-fifteen sharp, because something—probably a train —is liable to punctuality.

Then a sound of an interview wound up, a completed compact. And that is Gwen, returning. Old Maisie will not intrude on the event, whatever it be. She must wait to hear to-morrow. So she closes her door, furtively, as she opened it; and listens still, for the silences of the night to reassert themselves. No more words are audible, but she is conscious that voices continue, and that her Guardian Angel's is one. Then footsteps, and a hand on the door. Then Gwen, white and determined still, but speaking gently, to forestall alarm, and reassure misgiving.

" Dear Mrs. Picture, it's nothing—nothing to be alarmed about.
But I have to go up to London by the night train. See!—I will
tell you what it is. I have had this telegraphic message. Is it
not wonderful that this should be sent from London, a hundred
miles off, two hours ago, and that I should have it here to read
now? It is from my cousin, Miss Grahame. I am afraid she is
dangerously ill, and I must go to her because she is alone. . . .
Yes—Maggie is very good, and so is Dr. Dalrymple. But some
friend should be with her or near her. So I must go." She did
not read the message, or show it.

" But my dear—my dear—is it right for you to go alone, in the
dark. . . .   Oh, if I were only young! . . ."

" I shall be all right. I shall have Lutwyche, you know. Don't
trouble about me. It is you I am thinking of—leaving you here.
I am afraid I may be away some days, and you may not be comfortable. . . .   No—I can't possibly take you with me. I have
to get ready to go at once. The trap will only just take me and
Lutwyche, and our boxes. It must be Tom Kettering and the
trap. The carriage could not do it in the time. The Scotch express passes Grantley Thorpe at three-fifteen—the station-master
can stop it for me. . . .   What!—go beside the driver! Dear
old Mrs. Picture, the boxes have to go beside the driver, and Lutwyche and I have to hold tight behind. . . .   No, no!—you must
stay here a day or two—at least till we know the plaster's dry
in Sapps Court. As soon as I have been to see myself, one of the
maids shall bring you back, and you shall have Dave and Dolly—
there! Now go to bed, that's an old dear, and don't fret about
me. I shall be all right. Now, go I must! Good-bye!" She was
hurrying from the room, leaving the old lady in a great bewilderment, when she paused a moment to say:—" Stop a minute!—I've
an idea. . . .   No, I haven't. . . .   Yes, I have. . . .   All right!—
nothing—never mind!" Then she was gone, and old Maisie felt
dreadfully alone.

Arrived in her own room, where Lutwyche, rather gratified with
her own importance in this new freak of Circumstance, was endeavouring to make a portmanteau hold double its contents, Gwen
immediately sat down to write a letter. It required five minutes
for thought and eight minutes to write; so that in thirteen minutes it was ready for its envelope. Gwen re-read it, considered
it, crossed a *t* and dotted an *i*, folded it, directed it, took it out to
re-re-read, said thoughtfully:—" Can't do any possible harm," concluded it past recall, and added " By bearer " on the outside. It
ran thus:

"WIDOW THRALE,

"I want you to do something for me, and I know you will do it. To-morrow morning go to my old Mrs. Picture whom you saw to-day, and make her go back with you and your boy to Strides Cottage, and keep her there and take great care of her, till you hear from me. She is a dear old thing and will give no trouble at all. Ask anyone for anything you want for her—money or things—and I will settle all the bills. Show this letter. She knows my address in London. I am going there by the night express.

"GWENDOLEN RIVERS."

She slipped this letter into her pocket, and made a descent on Miss Lutwyche for her packing, which she criticized severely. But packing, unlike controversy, always ends; and in less than half an hour, both were in their places behind Tom Kettering and the grey mare, who had accepted the prospect of another fifteen miles without emotion; and Mrs. Masham and Lupin were watching them off, and thinking how nice it would be when they could get to bed.

"Now you think the mare can do it, Tom Kettering?"

"Twice and again, my lady, and a little over. And never be any the worse to-morrow!" Thus Tom Kettering, with immovable confidence. The mare as good as endorsed his words, swinging her head round to see, and striking the crust of the earth a heavy blow with her off hind-hoof.

"And we shall have time for you to get down at your Aunt Solmes's to leave my letter?"

"I count upon it, my lady, quite easy. We'll be at the Thorpe by three, all told, without stepping out." And then the mare is on the road again, doing her forty-first mile, quite happily.

They stopped at the bridle-path to the Ranger's Cottage, and Tom walked across with the letter—an unearthly hour for a visit! —and came back within ten minutes. All right! Her ladyship's wishes should be attended to! Then on through the starlight night, with the cold crisp air growing colder and crisper towards morning. Then the railway-station where Feudal tradition could still stop a train by signal, but only one or two in the day ever stopped of their own accord, in the fifties. *Now*, as you know, every train stops, and Spiers and Pond are there, and you can lunch and have Bovril and Oxo. Then, the shoddy-mills were undreamed of, where your old clothes are carefully sterilised before they are turned into new wool; and the small-arms factory, where Cain buys an outfit cheap; and the colour-works, that makes aniline dyes that last, if you settle monthly, until you pay for them.

Nothing was there then, and the train that stopped by signal came through a smokeless night, with red eyes and green that gazed up or down the line to please the Company; and started surlily, in protest at the stoppage, but picked its spirits slowly up, and got quite exhilarated before it was out of hearing, perhaps because it was carrying Gwen to London.

The dejection of its first start might have persevered and made its full-fledged rapidity joyless, had it known the errand of its beautiful first-class passenger. For the telegram Gwen had received, that had sent her off on this wild journey to London in the small hours of the morning, was this that follows, neither more nor less:

" On no account come. Why run risks? You will not be admitted. Never mind what Dr. Dalrymple says.—CLOTILDA."

Just conceive this young lady off in such a mad way when it was perfectly clear what had happened! She might at least have waited until she received the letter this message had so manifestly outraced; Dr. Dalrymple's letter, certain to come by the first post in the morning. And she would have waited, no doubt, if she had not been Gwen. Being Gwen, her first instinct was to get away before that letter came, enjoining caution, and deprecating panic, and laying stress on this, that, and the other—a parcel of nonsense all with one object, to counsel pusillanimousness, to inspire trepidation. She knew that would be the upshot. She knew also that Dr. Dalrymple would play double, frightening her from coming, while assuring the patient that he had vouched for the entire absence of danger and the mildness of the type of the disorder, whatever it was. It would never do for Clotilda to know that she—Gwen—was being kept away, for safety's sake. That was the sum and substance of her reflections. And the inference was clear:—Push her way on to Cavendish Square, and push her way in, if necessary!

A thought crossed her mind as the train whirled away from Grantley Station. Suppose it was smallpox, and she should catch it and have her beauty spoiled! Well—in that case an ill wind would blow *somebody* good! Her darling blind man would never see it. Let us be grateful for middle-sized mercies!

CHAPTER VIII

HOW THAT WIDOW GOT THE "OLD CAT" AWAY TO STRIDES COTTAGE. MR. BRANTOCK'S HORSE. ELIZABETH-NEXT-DOOR, AND THE BIT OF FIRE SHE MADE. HOW TOFT THE GIPSY SPOTTED A LIKENESS, AND REPAIRED THE GLASS TOBY HAD AIMED AT. HOW OLD MAISIE'S ACQUAINTANCE WITH HER DAUGHTER GREW TO FRIENDSHIP. AND HER DAUGHTER SHOWED HER GRANDFATHER'S MILL. HOW COULD THIS MILL BE YOUR GRANDFATHER'S, WHEN IT WAS MY FATHER'S? BUT SEE HOW SMALL IT WAS! TWO ARMS LONG, FIFTY YEARS AGO! AND NOW! . . . A RESTLESS WAKING AND A DARING EXCURSION. ONLY THE HOUSE-DOG ABOUT! ON THE FENDER! SEE THERE—AN ARM AND A HALF LONG ONLY—IN FACT, LESS!

OLD Maisie waked late, and no wonder! Or, more properly, she slept late, and had to be waked. Mrs. Masham did it, saying at the same time to a person in her company:—"Oh no, Mrs. Thrale—*she's* all right!—we've no call to be frightened yet a while." She added, as signs of life began to return:—"She'll be talking directly, you'll see."

Then the sleeper became conscious, and roused herself, to the point of exclaiming:—"Oh dear, what is it?" A second effort made her aware that her agreeable visitor of yesterday was at her bed's foot, and that her awakener was saying at her side:—"Now you tell her. She'll hear you now." Mrs. Masham seemed to assume official rights as a go-between, with special powers of interpretation.

Widow Thrale looked more Pomona-like than ever in the bright sunshine that was just getting the better of the hoar-frost. She held in her hand a letter, to which she seemed to cling as a credential—a sort of letter of marque, so to speak. "'Tis a bidding from her young ladyship," said the interpreter collaterally. She herself said, in the soothing voice of yesterday:—"From her young ladyship, who has gone to away London unforetold, last night. She will have me get you to my mother's, to make a stay with us for a while. And my mother will make you kindly welcome, for the little boy Dave's sake, and for her ladyship's satisfaction." She read the letter of marque, as far as "take great care of her, till you hear from me."

"I will get up and go," said the old lady. Then she appeared

disconcerted at her own alacrity, saying to the housekeeper:—
"But you have been so kind to me!"

"What her young ladyship decides," said Mrs. Masham, "it is
for us to abide by." She referred to this as a sort of superseding
truth, to which all personal feelings—gratitude, ingratitude, resentment, forgiveness—should be subordinated. It left open a
claim to magnanimity, on her part, somehow. Further, she said
she would tell Lupin to bring some breakfast for Mrs. Pilcher.

The task of getting the old lady up to take it seemed to devolve
naturally on Widow Thrale, who accepted it discreetly and skil-
fully, explaining that Mr. Brantock's cart would wait an hour to
oblige, and would go very easy along the road, not to shake. Old
Maisie did not seem alarmed, on that score.

She had lain awake in the night in some terror of the day to
come, alone with a household which appeared to have decided,
though without open declaration, that she was a plaguy old cat.
She had been roused from a final deep sleep to find that her
Guardian Angel's last benediction to her had been to make the
very arrangement she would have chosen for herself had she been
put to it to make choice. That her mind had never mooted
the point was a detail, which retrospect corrected. She was
ashamed to find she was so glad to fly from Mrs. Masham and
Company, and already began to be uneasy lest she had misjudged
them. But then—a plaguy old cat!

However, the decision of this at present did not arise from the
circumstances. What did was that, in less than the hour Mr.
Brantock's cart could concede, she was seated therein, comfortably
wrapped up, beside this really very nice and congenial saddler's
relict, having been somehow dressed, breakfasted, and generally
adjusted by hands which no doubt had acquired the sort of skill
a hospital nurse gets—without the trenchant official demeanour
which makes the patient shake in his shoes, if any—by her considerable experience of convalescents of all sorts and the smaller
sizes.

Mr. Brantock's cart jogged steadily on by cross-cuts and by-
roads at the dictation of parcels whose destinations Mr. Brantock's horse bore in mind, and chose the nearest way to, allowing
his so-called driver to deliver them on condition that the con-
signees paid cash. His harness stood in the way of his doing so
himself. Think what it was that was concealed from old Maisie
and Widow Thrale respectively, as they travelled in Mr. Brantock's cart. The intensity of this mother's and daughter's ignorance of one another outwent the powers of mere language to tell.

To the mother the daughter was the very nice young—relatively young—woman who had taken such good care of Dave last year, who was now so very kind and civil as to take charge of an old encumbrance at the bidding of a glorious Guardian Angel, who had dawned on these last days suddenly, inexplicably! An encumbrance at least, and no doubt plaguy, or she never would have been called an old cat.

To the daughter the mother was a good old soul, to be made much of and fostered; nursed if ill, entertained if well; borne with if, as might be, she developed into a trial—turned peevish, irritable, what not! Had not Gwen o' the Towers spoken, and was not the taint of Feudalism still strong in Rocestershire half a century back? Gwen o' the Towers had spoken, and that ended the matter.

Otherwise they were no more conscious of each other's blood in their own veins than was the convalescent Toby, who enlivened the dulness of the journey by dwelling on the *menus* he preferred for breakfast, dinner, and supper respectively. He elicited information about Dave, and was anxious to be informed which would lick. He put the question in this ungarnished form, not supplying detailed conditions. When told that Dave would, certainly, being nearly two years older, he threw doubt on the good faith of his informant.

But the journey came to an end, and though Widow Thrale had locked up the Cottage when she came away yesterday, she had left the key with Elizabeth-next-door—whoever she was; it does not matter—asking her to look in about eleven and light a bit of fire against her, Widow Thrale's, return. So next-door was applied to for the key, and the bit of fire—a very large bit of a small fire, or a small bit of a very large one—was found blazing on the hearth, and the cloth laid for dinner and everything.

According to Elizabeth-next-door, absolutely nothing had happened since Mrs. Marrable went away yesterday. Routine does not happen; it flows in a steady current which Event, the fidget, may interrupt for a while, but seldom dams outright. Elizabeth's memory, however, admitted on reconsideration that Toft the glazier had come to see for a job, and that she had sought for broken windows in Strides Cottage and found none. Toft was quite willing to mend any pane on his own responsibility, neither appealing to the County Court to obtain payment, nor smashing the pane in default of a cash settlement; a practice congenial to his gipsy blood, although he was the loser by the price of the glass. Toft had greatly desired to repair the glass front of the little case or cabinet on the mantelshelf, but Elizabeth had not dared to sanction interference with an heirloom. That was quite right, said Widow Thrale. What would mother have said if any harm had been done to her model? Besides, it did not matter! Because Toft would look in again to-day or to-morrow, when he had finished on the conservatories at the Vicarage.

None of this conversation reached old Maisie's ears at the time; only as facts referred to afterwards. As soon as the key was produced by Elizabeth-next-door, the old lady, treated as an invalid in the face of her own remonstrance, was inducted through the big kitchen or sitting-room, which she was sorry not to stop in, to a bedroom beyond, and made to lie down and rest and drink fresh milk. When she got up to join Widow Thrale's and Toby's midday meal, all reference to glass-mending was at an end, and Toby was making such a noise about the relative merits of brown potatoes in their skins, and potatoes *per se* potatoes, that you could not hear yourself speak.

In spite of her separation from her beautiful new Guardian Angel, and her uneasiness about the nature of that dangerous illness—for were not people dying of cholera every day?—she felt happier at Strides Cottage than in the ancient quarters Francis Quarles had occupied, where her position had been too anomalous to be endurable. Gwen's scheme had been that Mrs. Masham should play the part Widow Thrale seemed to fill so easily. It had failed. The fact is that nothing but sympathy with vulgarity gives what is called tact, and in this case the Guardian Angel's scorn of the stupid reservations and distinctions of the servantry at the Towers had quite prevented her stocking the article.

Perhaps Mrs. Thrale fell so easily into the task of making old Maisie happy and at ease because she was furnished with a means of explaining her and accounting for her, by the popularity Dave Wardle had achieved with the neighbours a year ago. Thus she had said to Elizabeth-next-door:—" You'll call to mind our little Davy Wardle, a twelvemonth back?—he that was nigh to being killed by the fire-engine? Well—there then!—this old soul belongs with him. 'Tis she he called his London Granny, and old Mrs. Picture. I would not speak to her exact name, never having been told it—'tis something like Picture. Her young ladyship at the Towers has given me the charge of her. She's a gentle old soul, and sweet-spoken, to my thinking." So that when Elizabeth-next-door came to converse with old Maisie, they had a topic in common. Dave's blue eyes and courteous demeanour having left a strong impression on next-door, and on all who came within his radius. Perhaps if such a lubricant had existed at the Towers, the social machinery would have worked easier, and heated bearings would have been avoided.

It was the same with one or two others of the neighbours, who really came in to learn something of the aged person with such silvery-white hair, whom Widow Thrale had brought to the Cottage. Little memories of Dave were a passport to her heart. What strikes us, who know the facts, as strange, is that no one of these good women—all familiar with the face of Granny Marrable—were alive to the resemblance between the two sisters. And the more strange, that this likeness was actually detected even in the half-dark, by an incomer much less habituated to her face than many of them.

This casual incomer was Toft, the vagrant glazier, and—so said chance report, lacking confirmation—larcenous vagrant. His Assyrian appearance may have been responsible for this. It gave rise to the belief that he was either Hebrew or Egyptian. And, of course, no jew or gipsy could be an honest man. That saw itself, in a primitive English village.

Toft had made his appearance at Strides Cottage just after dusk, earnestly entreating to be allowed to replace the glass Toby's chestnut-shot had broken, for nothing—yes, for nothing!—if Widow Thrale was not inclined to go to fourpence for it. The reply was:—" 'Tis not the matter of the money, Master Toft. 'Tis because I grudge the touching of a thing my mother sets store by, when she is not here herself to overlook it." Now this was just after old Maisie had quitted the room, to lie down and rest again before supper, having been led into much talk about Dave. Toft had seen her. His answer to Widow Thrale was:—" Will not the old wife come back, if I bide a bit for her coming?" His mistake being explained to him, his comment was:—" Zookers! I'm all in the wrong. But I tell ye true, mistress, I did think her hair was gone white, against what I see on her head three months agone. And I was of the mind she'd fell away a bit." Widow Thrale in the end consented to allow the damage to be made good, she herself carefully removing the precious treasure from its case, and locking it into a cupboard while Toft replaced the broken glass. This done, under her unflagging supervision, the model was replaced; fourpence changed hands, and the glazier went his way, saying, as he made his exit:—" That *was* a chouse, mistress."

But Toft was the only person who saw the likeness; or, at any rate, who confessed to seeing it. It is, of course, not at loggerheads with human nature, that others saw it too, but kept the discovery to themselves. It was so out of the question that the resemblance *should* exist, that the fact that it *did* stood condemned on its merits. Therefore, silence! Another possibility is that the intensely white hair, and the seeming greater age, of old Maisie, had more than their due weight in heading off speculation. Old Phœbe's teeth, too, made a much better show than her sister's.

One thing is certain, that the person most concerned, Ruth Thrale herself, remained absolutely blind to a fact which might have struck her had she not been intensely familiar with her reputed mother's face. The features of every day were things *per se*, not capable of comparison with casual extramural samples. They never are, within family walls.

That this was no mere inertness of observation, but a good strong opacity of vision, was clear when, after leaving the convalescent Toby to dreams of indulgence in the pleasures of the table, and victorious encounters, she roused her old visitor to bring her into supper.

" There now!—it *is* strange that I should have company tonight. I never thought to have the luck, yesterday, when you were giving me *my* tea, Mrs. . . ." She stopped on the name, and supplied a cup thereof—supper was a mixed meal at Strides Cottage—then continued:—" That brings to mind to ask you, whether little Davy is in the right of it when he writes your name ' Picture '? . . . Is he not, mayhap, calling you out of your name, childlike? "

" But of course he is, bless his little heart! My name is Prichard. P-r-i-c-h—Prich." She spelt the first syllable, to make sure no *t* got in. " The Lady, Gwen, has taken it of him, to humour him and Dolly, just as their young mouths speak it—Picture! But it isn't Picture; it's Prichard." Old Maisie felt quite mendacious. She seldom had to state so roundly that her assumed name was authentic. Widow Thrale made no comment, only saying:—" I thought the child had made ' Picture ' out of his own head." The talk scarcely turned on the name for more than a minute, as she went on to say:—" Now you must eat some supper, Mrs. Prichard, because you hardly took anything for dinner. And see what a ride you had! " She went on to make appeals on behalf of bacon, eggs, bloaters, cold mutton and so on, with only a very small response from the old lady, who seemed to live on nothing. A compromise was effected, the latter promising to take some gruel just before going to bed.

Two influences were at work to keep the antecedents of either out of the conversation. Old Maisie fought shy of inquiries, which might have produced counter-inquiry she could scarcely have met by silence; and Mrs. Thrale shrank, with a true instinctive delicacy, from prying into a record which had the word *poverty* so legible on its title-page, and signs of a former well-being so visible on its subject. Besides, how about Sapps Court and Dave's uncle, the prizefighter?

She felt curiosity, all the same. However, information might come, unsought, as the ground thawed. A springlike mildness was in the atmosphere of their acquaintance, and it began to tell on the ice, very markedly, as they sat enjoying the firelight; candles blown out, and the flicker of the wood-blaze making sport with visibility on the walls and dresser—on the dominant willow-pattern of the latter, with its occurrences of polished metal, and precious incidents of Worcester or Bristol porcelain; or the pictorial wealth of the former, the portrait of Lord Nelson, and the British Lion, and all the flags of all the world in one frame; to say nothing of some rather woebegone Bible prints, doing full justice to the beards of Susannah's elders, and the biceps of Samson. On all these, and prominently on the sampler worked by Hephzibah Marrable, 1672, a ship-of-war in full sail, with cannons firing off wool in the same direction, and defeating the Dutch Fleet, presumably. Perhaps the Duke of York's flagship.

The two had talked of many things. Of the great bull-dog who was such a safeguard against thieves that they never felt insecure at night, and were very careless in consequence about bolts and bars; and who had investigated the visitor very carefully on her first arrival, suspiciously, but seemed now to have given her his complete sanction. Of the cat on the hearth and the Family at the Towers—small things and large; but with a great satisfaction for old Maisie, when the statement was made with absolute confidence that Mr. Torrens, who was said to be the man of her young ladyship's choice, would recover his eyesight. Mrs. Lamprey's version of Dr. Nash's pronouncement was conclusive, and was conscientiously repeated, without exaggeration; causing heartfelt joy to old Maisie, with a tendency to consider how far Mr. Torrens deserved his good fortune, the moment his image was endowed with eyesight. That, you remember, was the effect of Mrs. Lamprey's first communication yesterday. Then Widow Thrale had read a letter from her son on the *Agamemnon,* in the Black Sea, cheerfully forecasting an early collapse of Russia before the prowess of the Allies, and an early triumphant return of the Fleet with unlimited prize-money. Old Maisie had to envy perforce this mother's pride in this son, his daring and his chivalry, his invincibility by foes, his generosity to the poor and weak. Her envy was forced from her—how could it have been otherwise?—but her love came with it. All her heart went out to the sweet, proud, contented face as the firelight played on it, and made the treasured letter visible to its reader. Then she had listened to particulars of the other son, in the Baltic, of whom his mother was temperately proud, not rising to her previous enthusiasm. He had, however, been in action; that was his strong point, at present. By that time Mrs. Thrale's domestic record only needed a word or two about her daughter, Mrs. Costrell, to be complete for its purpose, a tentative enlightenment of its hearer, which might induce counter-revelation. But the old lady did not respond, clinging rather to inquiry about her informant's affairs. For which the latter did not blame her, for who could say what reasons she might have for her reticence. At any rate, *she* would not try to break through it.

All this talk, by the comfortable fireside, was nourishment to the growing germ of old Maisie's affection for this chance acquaintance of a day. Her faith in all her surroundings—her Guardian Angel apart—had been sadly shaken by the expression " plaguy old cat." This woman could be relied upon, she was sure. She could not be disappointed in her—how could she doubt it? Whether their unknown kinship was a mysterious help to this confidence is a question easy to ask. The story makes no attempt to answer it.

A bad disappointment was pending, however. After some chance references to " mother," her great vigour in spite of her eighty years, the distances she could walk, and so on—and some notes about neighbours—Farmer Jones's Bull, mentioned as a local celebrity, naturally led back to Dave.

" The dear boy was never tired of telling about that Bull," said old Maisie. " I thought perhaps he made up a little as he went, for children will. Was it all true he told me about how he wasn't afraid to go up close, and the Bull was good and quiet? "

" Quite true," answered Mrs. Thrale. " Only we would never have given permission, me and mother, only we knew the animal by his character. He cannot abide grown men, and he's not to be trusted with women and little girls. But little boys may pat him, and no offence given. It was all quite true."

" Well, now!—that is very nice to know. Was it true, too, all about the horses and the wheelsacks, and the water-cart? "

" Of course!—oh yes, of course it was! That was our model.

Only it should not have been wheelsacks. *Wheat* sacks! And water-cart!—he meant *water-wheel*. Bless the child!—he'd got it all topsy-turned. There's the model on the mantel-shelf, with the cloth over it. I'll take it off to show you. That won't do any harm. I only covered it so that no one should touch the glass. Because Ben Toft said the putty would be soft for a few days." A small bead-worked tablecloth, thick and protective, had been wrapped round the model.

Widow Thrale relighted the candles, which had been out of employment. They did not give a very good light. The old lady was just beginning to feel exhausted with so much talk. But she was bound to see this—Dave's model, his presentment of which had been a source of speculation in Sapps Court! Just fancy! Widow Thrale lifted it bodily from the chimney-shelf, and placed it on the table.

"Mother ought to tell you about it," said she, disengaging the covering, "because she knows so much more about it than I do. You see, when the water is poured in at the top and the clock-work is wound up, the mill works and the sacks go up and down, and one has to pretend they are taking grist up into the loft. It was working quite beautiful when mother put the water in for Dave to see. And it doesn't go out of order by standing; for, the last time before that, when mother set it going, was for the sake of little Robert that we lost when he was little older than Dave. Such a many years it seems since then! . . . What?"

For as she chatted on about what she conceived would be her visitor's interest in the model—Dave's interest, to wit—she had failed to hear her question, asked in a tremulous and almost inaudible voice:—"Where was it, the mill? . . . Whose mill?" A repetition of it, made with an effort, caused her to look round.

And then she saw that old Maisie's breath was coming fast, and that her words caught in it and became gasps. Her conclusion was immediate, disconnecting this agitation entirely from the subject of her speech. The old lady had got upset with so much excitement, that was all. Just think of all that perturbation last night, and the journey to-day! At her time of life! Besides, she had eaten nothing.

Evidently the proper course now was to induce her to go to bed, and get her that gruel, which she had promised to take. "I am sure you would be better in bed, Mrs. Prichard," said Mrs. Thrale. "Suppose you was to go now, and I'll get you your gruel."

Old Maisie gave way at once to the guidance of a persuasive hand, but held to her question. "Whose mill was it?"
"My grandfather's. Take care of the little step . . . you shall see it again to-morrow by daylight. Bed's the place for you, dear Mrs. Prichard. Why—see!—you are shaking all over."

So she was, but not to such an extent as to retard operations. The old white head was soon on its pillow, but the old white face was unusually flushed. And the voice was quite tremulous that said, inexplicably:—"How came *your* grandfather to be the owner of that mill?"

Even a younger and stronger person than old Maisie might have lost head to the extent of not seeing that the best thing to say was:—"I have seen this model before. I knew it in my childhood." But so dumfoundered was she by what had been so suddenly sprung upon her that she could not have thought of any right thing to say, to save her life.

And how could Widow Thrale discern anything in what she *did* say but the effect of fatigue, excitement, and underfeeding on an octogenarian; probably older, and certainly weaker, than her mother? How came *her* grandfather to be the owner of Darenth Mill, indeed! Well!—she could get Dr. Nash round at half an hour's notice; that was one consolation. Meanwhile, could she seriously answer such an inquiry? Indeed she scarcely recognised that it *was* an inquiry. It was a symptom.

She spoke to the old head on the pillow, with eyes closed now. "Would you dislike it very much, ma'am, if I was to put one spoonful of brandy in the gruel? There is brandy without sending for it, because of invalids."

"Thank you, I think no brandy. It isn't good for me. . . . But I like to have the gruel, you know." She would not unsay the gruel, because she was sure this kind-hearted woman would take pleasure in getting it for her. Not that she wanted it.

Widow Thrale went back to the kitchen to see to the gruel. She was absolutely free from any thought of the model, in relation to the old lady's indisposition, or collapse, whichever it was. Lord Nelson himself, on the wall, was not more completely detached from it. While the gruel was arriving at maturity, she wrapped the covering again carefully over the mill and the wheel-sacks and the water-cart, and Muggeridge, and replaced it on the chimney-shelf.

Left alone, old Maisie, no longer seeing the model before her, began to waver about the reality of the whole occurrence. Might it not have been a dream, a delusion; at least, an exaggeration?

There was a model, with horses, and a waggon—yes! But was she quite sure it was *her* old mill—her father's? How could she be sure of anything, when it was all so long ago? Especially when her pulse was thumping, like this. Besides, there was a distinct fact that told against the identity of this model and the one it was so bewilderingly like; to wit—the size of it. That old model of sixty years ago was twice the size of this. She knew that, because she could remember her own hand on it, flat at the top. Her hand and Phœbe's together!—she remembered the incident plainly.

Here was Mrs. Thrale back with the gruel. How dear and kind she was! But a horrible thought kept creeping into old Maisie's mind. Was she—a liar? Had she not said that it was her grandfather's mill? Now that could *not* be true. If she had said great-uncle. . . . Well!—would that have made it any better? On reflection, certainly not! For *her* father had had neither brother nor sister. It was a relief to put speculation aside and accept the gruel.

She made one or two slight attempts to recur to the mill. But her hostess made no response; merely discouraged conversation on every topic. Mrs. Prichard had better not talk any more. The thing for her to do was to take her gruel and go to sleep. Perhaps it was. A reaction of fatigue added powerful arguments on the same side, and she was fain to surrender at discretion.

She must have slept for over six hours, for when the sudden sound of an early bird awakened her the dawn was creeping into the house. The window of her own room was shuttered and curtained, but she saw a line of daylight under the door. No one was moving yet. She instantly remembered all the events she had gone to sleep upon; the recollection of the mill-model in particular rushing at her aggressively, almost producing physical pain, like a blow. She knew there was another pain to come behind it, as soon as her ideas became collected. Yes—there it was! This dear lovable woman whom she had been so glad of, after the duplicity of those servants at the Towers, was as untrustworthy as they, and the whole world was a cheat! How else could it be, when she had heard her with her own ears say that that mill had belonged to her grandfather?

'She lay and chafed, a helpless nervous system dominated by a cruel idea. Was there no way out? Only one—that she herself had been duped by her own imagination. But then, how was that possible? Unless, indeed, she was taking leave of her senses. Because, even supposing that she could fancy that another model of another mill could deceive her by a chance likeness; how about those two tiny figures of little girls in white bonnets and lilac frocks? Oh, that she could but prove them phantoms of an imagination stimulated by the first seeming identity of the building and the water-wheel! After all, all water-mills were much alike. Yes, the chances were large that she had cheated herself. But certainty—certainty—*that* was what she wanted. She felt sick with the intensity of her longing for firm ground.

Was it absolutely impossible that she should see for herself now—*now?* She sat up in bed, looking longingly at the growing light of the doorslip. After all, the model was but six paces beyond it, at the very most. She would be back in bed in three minutes, and no harm done. No need for a candle, with the light.

The bird outside said again the thing he had said before, and it seemed to her like: " Yes—do it." She got out of bed and found her slippers easily; then a warm overall of Gwen's providing. Never since her impoverishment had she worn such good clothes.

Her feet might fail her—they had done so before now. But she would soon find out, and would keep near the bed till she felt confidence. . . . Oh yes—*they* would be all right!

The door-hasp shrieked like a mandrake—as door-hasps do, in silence—but waked no one, apparently. There was the kitchen-door at the end of the brick-paved lobby, letting through dawn's first decision about the beginning of the day. Old Maisie went cautiously over the herring-boned pavement, with a hand against the wall for steadiness. This door before her had an old-fashioned latch. It would not shriek, but it might clicket.

Only a very little more, and then she was in the kitchen! There was more light than she had expected, for one of the windows was not only shutterless, but without either blind or curtain. She was not surprised, for she remembered what her hostess had said about the housedog, and security from thieves. That was a source of alarm, for one short moment. Might he not hear her, and bark? Then a touch of a cold nose, exploring her feet, answered the question. He *had* heard her, and he would not bark. He seemed to decide that there was no cause for active intervention, and returned to his quarters, wherever they were.

But where was the sought-for model? Not on the table where she saw it yesterday; the table was blank, but for the chrysanthemums in a pot of water in the middle. On the chimney-piece then, back in its place, rather high up—there it was, to be sure! But such a disappointment! She could have *seen* it there, though it was rather out of reach for her eyesight. But alas!—it was wrapped up again in that cloth. It was a grievous disappointment.

Perhaps she might contrive to see a little behind it, by pulling it aside. Yes—there!—she could *reach* it, at any rate. But to pull it aside was quite another matter. Its texture was prohibitive. Fancy a strip of cocoanut matting, with an uncompromising selvage, wrapped round a box of its own width, with its free end under the box! Then compare the rigidity of beadwork and cocoanut matting. The position was hopeless. It was quite beyond her strength to reach it down, and she would have been afraid to do so in the most favourable circumstances imaginable.

Quite hopeless! But there was one thing she might satisfy herself of—the relative sizes of her own hand and the case. Yes—by just standing on the secure steel fender to gain the requisite four inches, she could lay her two hands over the top, length for length, and the finger-tips would not meet, any more than hers met Phœbe's when their frock-cuffs were flush with the edge of her father's old model, all those years and years ago. Because her mind was striving to discredit the authenticity of this one.

Slowly and cautiously, for rheumatism had its say in the matter, she got a safe foothold on the fender and her hands up to the top, measuring. See there! Exactly as she had foretold—half the size! She knew she could not be mistaken about the frock-cuffs, and so far from the finger-tips meeting, with the two middle fingers bickering a little about their rights, there was an overlap as far as the second joint. The hands had grown a little since those days, no doubt, but not to that extent. She tried them both ways to make sure, left on right, and right on left, lest she should be deceiving herself. She was quite unnerved with self-mistrust, but so taken up with avoiding a mismeasurement now, that she could not sift that question of the hands' growth.

Probably everyone has detected outrageous errors in his own answers to his own question:—How old was I when this, that, or the other happened?—errors always in the direction of exaggeration of age. The idea in old Maisie's mind, that she and Phœbe were at least grown girls, was an utter delusion. Mere six-year-olds at the best! The two hands, that she remembered, were the hands of babies, and the incident had happened over seventy years ago.

CHAPTER IX

A QUIET RAILWAY-STATION. ONE PASSENGER, AND A SHAKEDOWN AT
MOORE'S. THE CONVICT DAVERILL'S SEARCH FOR HIS MOTHER.
GRANNY MARRABLE'S READING OF " PILGRIM'S PROGRESS." A MAN ON
A STILE. SOME MEMORIES OF NORFOLK ISLAND. A FINGER-JOINT.
AN OATH ADMINISTERED BY AN AMATEUR, WITHOUT A TESTAMENT.
HOW DAVERILL SPOKE HIS NAME TWICE, AND THE FIRST TIME UN-
DID THE SECOND. OFF THROUGH A HEDGE, FOLLOWED BY A RE-
SPECTABLE MAN. HOW OLD PHŒBE FOUND AN ENIGMA IN HER
POCKET

IN those days the great main lines of railway were liable to long
silences in the night. At the smaller stations particularly, after
the last train up and the last train down had passed without killing somebody at a level crossing, or leaving you behind because
you thought it was sure to be late, and presumed upon that certainty, an almost holy calm would reign for hours, and those
really ill-used things, the sleepers, seemed to have a chance at
last. For after being baffled all day by intermittent rushing fiends,
and unwarrantable shuntings to and fro, and droppings of sudden
red-hot clinkers on their counterpanes, an inexplicable click or two
—apparently due to fidgety bull's-eyes desirous of change—could
scarcely be accounted a disturbance.

No station in the world was more primevally still than Grantley
Thorpe, after the down three-thirty express—the train that crossed
the three-fifteen that carried Gwen to London—had stopped, that
the word of Bradshaw should be fulfilled; had deposited the smallest conceivable number of passengers, and wondered, perhaps,
why remaindermen in the carriages always put their heads out
to ask what station this was. On this particular occasion, Bradshaw scored, for the down train entered the station three minutes
after the up train departed, twelve minutes behind. Then the little station turned off lights, locked up doors of offices and lids
of boxes, and went to bed. All but a signalman, in a box on a
pole.

There was one passenger, not a prepossessing one, who seemed
morose. His only luggage was a small handbag, and that was
against him. It is not an indictable offence to have no luggage,
but if a referendum were taken from railway-porters, it *would*

be. However, this man was, after all, a third-class passenger, so perhaps he was excusable for carrying that bag.

"I suppose," said he, surrendering his ticket, "it's no part of your duty to tell a cove where he can get a sleep for half a night. You ain't paid for it." Whether this was churlishness, or a sort of humour, was not clear, from the tone.

Sandys, the station-master, one of the most good-humoured of mortals, preferred the latter interpretation. "It don't add to our salary, but it ought to. Very obliging we are, in these parts! How much do you look to pay?"

The man drew from his pocket, presumably, the fund he had to rely upon, and appeared to count it, with dissatisfaction. "Two and a kick!" said he. "I'll go to the tizzy, for sheets." This meant he would lay out the tizzy, or kick, provided that his bed was furnished with sheets. He added, with a growl, that he was not going to be put off with a horserug, this time. The adjective he used to qualify the previous rug showed that his experiences had been peculiar, and disagreeable.

"You might ask at Moore's, along on your left where you see yonder light. Show your money first, and offer to pay in advance. Cash first, sleep afterwards. There's someone sitting up, or they wouldn't show a light. . . . Here, Tommy, you're going that way. You p'int him out Moore's." Thus the station-master, who then departed along a gravel path, through a wicket-gate. It led to his private residence, which was keeping up its spirits behind a small grove of sunflowers which were not keeping up theirs. They had been once the admiration of passing trains, with a bank of greensward below them with "Grantley Thorpe" on it in flints, in very large caps.; and now they were on the brink of their graves in the earth so chilly, and didn't seem resigned.

Tommy the porter did not relish his companion, evidently, as he walked on, a pace ahead, along the road that led to the village. He never said a word, and seemed justified in outstripping that slow, lurching, indescribable pace, which was not lameness, in order to stimulate it by example.

"Yarnder's Mower's," said Tommy, nodding towards a small pothouse down a blind alley. "You wo'ant find nowat to steal there, at Mower's."

"What the Hell do you mean by that?"

"What do I me'an—is that what you're asking?" Raised voice.

"Ah—what do you mean by 'steal'?"

"Just what a sa'ay! What do they me'an in London?"

"London's a large place—too large for this time o' night. You come along there one o' these days, and you'll find out what they mean." He sketched the behaviour of Londoners towards rustic visitors untruthfully—if our experience can be relied on—and in terms open to censure; ending up:—" You'll find what they'll do, fast enough! Just you show up there, one o' these fine days." He had only warped the subject thus in order to introduce the idea of a humiliating and degrading chastisement, as an insult to his hearer.

He vanishes from the story at this point, in a discharge of Parthian shafts by Tommy the young railwayman, not very energetically returned, as if he thought the contest not worth prolonging. Vanishes, that is to say, unless he was the same man who spoke with Mrs. Keziah Solmes at about eleven o'clock the next morning, in the road close by the Ranger's Cottage, close to where the grey mare started on her forty-first mile, yesterday. If this person spoke truth when he said he had come from a station much farther off than Grantley Thorpe, he was *not* the same man. Otherwise, the witnesses agreed in their description of him.

Mrs. Solmes's testimony was that a man in rough grey suit —frieze or homespun—addressed her while she was looking out for the mail-cart, with possible letters, and asked to be directed to Ancester Towers; which is, at this point, invisible from the road. She suspected him at first of being a vagrant of some new sort—then of mere eccentricity. For plenty of eccentrics came to get a sight of the Towers. She had surmised that his object was to do so, and had told him, that as the family were away, strangers could be admitted by orders obtainable of Kiffin and Clewby, his lordship the Earl's agents at Grantley. He then told her that he had walked over from Bridgport, where the Earl had no agent. He did not wish to go over the Towers, but to inquire for a party he was anxious to see; an old party by the name of Prichard. That was, he said, his own name, and she was a relation of his—in fact, his mother. He had not seen her for many a long year, and his coming would be a bit of a surprise. He had been away in the Colonies, and had not been able to play the part of a dutiful son, but by no choice of his own. Coming back to England, his first thought had been to seek out the old lady, " at the old address." But there he found the house had fallen down, and she was gone away temporary, only she could be heard of at Ancester Towers in Rocestershire.

Mrs. Keziah was so touched by this tale of filial affection, that she nipped in the bud a sprouting conviction that the man was no better than he—and others—should be. She interested herself

at once. "You wo'ant need to ask at the Towers, master," said
she. "I can tell you all they can, up there. And very like a
bit more. The old dame she's gone away with my cousin, maybe
an hour ago—may be more. She'll ta'ak she to her mother's at
Chorlton, and if ye keep along the straight road for Grantley till
ye come to sign-po'ast, sayun' 'To Dessington and Chorlton,'
then another three-qua'arters of an 'oor 'll ta'ak ye there, easy."

The dutiful son looked disappointed, but did not lose his equable
and not unpleasant manner. "I thought I was nigher my journey's end than that, marm," said he. "I *was* looking forward
to the old lady giving me a snack of breakfast. . . . But don't
you mind me! I'll do all right. I got a bit of bread coming along
from Gridgport. . . . Ah!—Bridgport I should have said." For
he had begun to say Grantley.

Even if Mrs. Solmes had not been on the point of offering rest
and refreshment, this disclaimer of the need of it would have suggested that she should do so. After all, was he not the son of
that nice old soul her cousin Ruth Thrale had taken such a fancy
to? If she came across the old lady herself, how should she look
her in the face, after letting her toil-worn son add five miles to
seven, on an all but empty stomach. Of course, she immediately
asked him in, going on ahead of him to explain him to her husband, who looked rather narrowly at the newcomer, but could not
interpose upon a slice of cold beef and a glass of ale, especially
as it seemed to be unasked for, however welcome.

"'Tis a tidy step afoot from Bridgport Ra'aby, afower breakfast," said old Stephen, keeping his eye, nevertheless, on the man's
face, with only a half-welcome on his own. "But come ye in,
and the missus 'll cast an eye round the larder for ye. You be a
stra-anger in these parts, I take it."

The beef and ale seemed very welcome, and the man was talkative. Did his hosts know Mrs. Prichard personally? Only just seen
her—was that it? She must be gone very grey by now; why—she
was going that way when he saw her last, years ago. He never
said how many years. He couldn't say her age to a nicety, but
she must be well on towards eighty. However did she come to
be at the country seat of the great Earl of Ancester?—that was
what puzzled him.

Mrs. Solmes could not tell him everything, but she had a good
deal to tell. The old lady she had seen was very grey certainly,
but had seemed to her cousin Ruth Thrale, who had tea with
her yesterday, quite in possession of her faculties, and—oh dear
yes!—able to get about, but suffering from rheumatism. But then

just think—nearly eighty! As for how she came to be at the
Towers, all that Mrs. Solmes knew was that it was through a
sort of fancy of her young ladyship, Lady Gwen Rivers, reputed
one of the most beautiful young ladies in England, who had
brought her from London after the accident already referred to,
and who had gone away by the night-train, leaving a request
to her cousin Ruth to take charge of her till her return. She
could have repeated all she had heard from Mrs. Thrale, but
scarcely felt authorised to do so.

One untoward incident happened. The infant Seth, summoned
to show himself, stood in a corner and pouted, turned red, and
became *intransigeant;* finally, when peremptorily told to go and
speak to the gentleman, shrank from and glared at him; only
allowed his hand to be taken under compulsion, and rushed away
when released, roaring with anger or terror, or both, and wiping
the touch of the stranger off his offended hand. This was entirely
unlike Seth, whose defects of character, disobedience to Law and
Order, and love of destruction for its own sake, were qualified
by an impassioned affection for the human race, causing him to
attach himself to that race, as a sort of rock-limpet, and even
to supersede kisses by licks. His aversion to this man was a new
departure.

He, for his part, expressed his surprise at Seth's attitude.
He was noted in his part of the world for his tenderness towards
young children. His circle of acquaintances suffered the little
ones to come unto him contrary to what you might have thought,
he being but an ugly customer to look at. But his heart was
good—a rough diamond! When he had expressed his gratitude
and tramped away down the road, after carefully writing down
the address " Strides Cottage, Chorlton " and the names of its
occupants, old Stephen and Keziah looked each at the other, as
though seeking help towards a good opinion of this man, and
seemed to get none.

Old Granny Marrable always found a difficulty in getting away
from her granddaughter Maisie's, because her presence there was
so very much appreciated. Her great-grandson also, whose charms
were developing more rapidly than is ever the case in after-life,
was becoming a strong attraction to her. Moreover, a very old
friend of hers, Mrs. Naunton, residing a short mile away, at Dessington, had just pulled through rheumatic fever, and was getting
well enough to be read to out of " Pilgrim's Progress."

This afternoon, however, Mrs. Naunton did not prove well

enough to keep awake when read to, even for Mr. Greatheart to slay Giant Despair. In fact, Mrs. Marrable caught her snoring, and read the rest to herself. It was too good to lose. When the Giant was disposed of past all recrudescence, she departed for her return journey instead of waiting for her granddaughter's brother-in-law, a schoolboy with a holiday, to come and see her home. She knew he would come by the short cut, across the fields, so she took that way to intercept him, in spite of the stiles. As a rule she preferred the highroad.

The fields were very lonely, but what did that matter? How little one feels the loneliness of an old familiar pathway! No one ever *had* been murdered in these fields, and no one ever would be. Granny Marrable walked on with confidence. Nevertheless, had she had her choice, she would have preferred the loneliness unalloyed by the presence of the man on the stile, at the end of Farmer Naunton's twelve-acre pasture, if only because she anticipated having to ask him to let her pass. For he seemed to have made up his mind to wait to be asked; if approached from behind, at any rate. She could not see his face or hands, only his outline against the cold, purple distance, with a red ball that had been the sun all day. "Might I trouble you, master?" she said.

The man turned his head just as far as was necessary for his eyes, under tension, to see the speaker; then got down, more deliberately than courteously, on his own side of the stile. "Come along, missus," he said. "Never mind legs. Yours ain't my sort. Over you go!"

Safe in the next field, Granny Marrable turned to thank him. But not before she had put three or four yards between them. Not that she anticipated violence, but from mere dislike of what she would have called sauciness in a boy, but which was, in a man of his time of life, sheer brutal rudeness. "Thank you very kindly, master!" said she. "Sorry to disturb you!"

He ought to have said that she was kindly welcome, or that he was very happy, but he said neither, only looking steadily at her. So she simply turned to go away.

She walked as far as the middle of the next field, not sorry to be out of this man's reach; and rather glad that, when she was within it, she was not a young girl, unprotected. That shows the impression he had given her. Also that his steady look was concentrating to a glare as she lost sight of his face, and that she would be glad when she was sure she had seen the last of it. She walked a little quicker as soon as she thought her doing so would attract no notice.

" Hi—missus ! " She quickened her pace as the words—a hoarse call—caught her up. She even hoped she might be mistaken—had made a false interpretation of some entirely different sound; not the cawing of one of those rooks—that was against reason. But it might have been a dog's bark at a distance, warped by imagination. She had known that to happen. If so, it would come again. She stood and waited quietly.

It came again, distinctly. " Hi—missus ! " No dog's bark that, but that man's voice, to a certainty, nearer. Then again " Hi—missus ! " nearer still—almost close—and the sound of his feet. A halting, dot-and-go-one pace; not lame, but irregular.

She was a courageous old woman, was old Granny Marrable. But the place was a very lonely one, and . . . Well—she did not mind about her money ! It was her treasured old gold watch, that her first husband gave her, that she was thinking of. . . .

There !—what a fool she was, to get into such a taking when, ten to one, she had only dropped something, and he was running after her to restore it. She faced about, and looked full at him.

" Ah ! " said he. " Take a good look ! You've seen me afore. No hurry—easy does it ! " His voice showed such entire conviction, and at the same time such a complete freedom from anything threatening or aggressive, that all her fear left her at once. It was a mistake—nothing worse !

But was she absolutely sure, without her glasses ? All she could see was that the face was that of a hard man, close-cropped and close-shaved, square and firm in the jaw. Not an ugly face, but certainly not an attractive one. " I think, sir," she said conciliatorily, " you have mistook me for someone else. I am sure."

" Maybe, mother," said he, " you'll know me through your glasses. Got 'em on you ? . . . Ah—that's right ! Fish 'em out of your pocket ! Now ! " As the old lady fitted on her spectacles, which she only used for near objects and reading, the man removed his hat and stood facing her, and repeated the word " Now ! "

So absolutely convinced was she that he was merely under a misconception, that she was really only putting on her glasses to humour him, and give him time to find out his mistake. The fact that he had addressed her as " mother " counted for absolutely nothing. Any man in the village would address her as " mother," as often as not. It was affectionate, respectful, conciliatory, but by no means a claim of kinship. The word, moreover, had a distinct tendency to remove her dislike of the speaker, which had not vanished with her fear of him, now quite in abeyance.

" Indeed, sir," said she, after looking carefully at his face,

"I cannot call you to mind. I cannot doubt but you have taken me for some other person." Then she fancied that something the man said, half to himself, was:—"That cock won't fight."

But he seemed, she thought, to waver a little, too. And his voice had not its first confidence, as it said:—"Do you mean to say, mother, that you've forgotten my face? *My face!*"

The familiar word "mother" still meant nothing to her—a mere epithet! Just consider the discrepancies whose reconciliation alone would have made it applicable! When she answered, some renewal of trepidation in her voice was due to the man's earnestness, not to any apprehension of his claim. "I am telling God's own truth, master," she said. "I have never set eyes upon ye in my life, and if I had, I would have known it. There be some mistake, indeed." Then timorously:—"Whom—whom—might ye take me for?"

The man raised his voice, more excitably than angrily. "What did I say just now?—*mother!*—that's English, ain't it?" But his words had no meaning to her; there was nothing in their structure to change her acceptation of the word "mother," as an apostrophe. Then, in response to the blank unrecognition of her face, he continued:—"What—still? I'm not kidding myself, by God, am I? . . . No—don't you try it on! I ain't going to have you running away. Not yet a while. . . . Ah—would you!"

He caught her by the wrist to check her half-shown tendency to turn and run; not, as she thought, from a malefactor, but a madman. A cry for help was stopped by a change in his tone—possibly even by the way his hand caught her wrist; for, though strong, it was not rough or ungentle. Little enough force was needed to detain her, and no more was used. He was mad, clearly, but not ferocious. "I'm not going to hurt ye, mother," said he. "But you leave your eyes on me a minute, and see if I'm a liar." He remained with his own fixed on hers, as one who waits impatiently for what he knows must come.

But no recognition followed. In vain did the old lady attempt —and perfectly honestly—to detect some reminder of some face seen and hitherto forgotten, in the hard cold eyes and thick-set jaw, the mouth-disfiguring twist which flawed features, which, handsome enough in themselves, would have otherwise gone near to compensate a repellent countenance. The effort was the more hopeless from the fact that it was a face that, once seen, might have been hard to forget. After complying to the full with his suggestion of a thorough examination, she was forced to acknowledge failure. "Indeed and indeed, sir," she said, "my mem-

ory is all лt fault. If ever I saw ye in my life, 'tis so long ago
I've forgotten it."

"Ah—you may say long ago!" The madman—for to her he
was one; some lunatic at large—seemed to choke a moment over
what he had to say, and then it came. " Twenty years and more—
ay!—twenty years, and five over—and most of the time in Hell!
Ah—run away, if you like—run away from your own son!" He
released her arm; but though the terror had come back twofold,
she would not run; for the most terrible maniac is pitiful as well
as terrible, and her pity for him put her thoughts on calming and
conciliating him. He went on, his speech breaking through something that choked it back and made it half a cry in the end.
" Fourteen years of quod—fourteen years of prison-food—fourteen
years of such a life that * * * prayers, Sundays, and the * * *
parson that read 'em was as good as a holiday! Why—I tell you!
It was so bad the lifers would try it on again and again, to kill
themselves, and were only kept off of doing it by the cat, if they
missed their tip." This was all the jargon of delirium to the
terror-stricken old woman; it may be clear enough to the ordinary
reader, with what followed. " I tell you I saw the man that got
away over the cliff, and shattered every bone in his body. I saw
him carried out o' hospital and tied up and flogged, for a caution,
till the blood run down and the doctor gave the word stop." He
went on in a voluble and disjointed way to tell how this man was
" still there! There where your son, mother, spent fourteen out
of these twenty-five long years past!"

But the more he said, the more clear was it to Granny Marrable
that he was an escaped lunatic. There was, however, in all this
sheer raving—as she counted it—an entire absence of any note
of personal danger to herself. Her horror of him, and the condition of mind that his words made plain, remained; her apprehension of violence, or intimidation to make her surrender valuables, had given place to pity for his miserable condition. His repeated use of the word " mother " had a reassuring effect almost,
while she accounted that of the word " son " as sheer distem-
perature of the brain. But why should she not make use of it to
divert his mind from the terrible current of thought, whether delusion or memory, into which he had fallen? " I never had but
one son, sir," she said, " and he has been dead twenty-three years
this Christmas, and lies buried beside his father in Chorlton
church."

The fugitive convict—for the story need not see him any longer
from old Phœbe's point of view only—face to face with such a

quiet and forcible disclaimer of identity, could not but be staggered, for all that this old woman's face was his mother's; or rather,
was the face he had imaged to himself as hers, all due allowance
being made—so he thought—for change from sixty-five to eighty.
Probably, had he seen the two old sisters side by side, he would
have chosen this one as his mother. Her eighty was much nearer
to her sixty than old Maisie's. She was no beautiful old shadow,
with that strange plenty of perfectly white hair. Time's hand had
left hers merely grey, as a set off against the lesser quantity he had
spared her. As Dave Wardle had noticed, her teeth had suffered
much less than his London Granny's. Altogether, she was mar-
vellously close to what the convict's preconception of " Mrs. Prichard " had been.

It is easy to see how this meeting came about. After he left
the hospitable cottage of the Solmes's, he had walked on in a leisurely way, stopping at " The Old Truepenny, J. Hancock," to add
another half-pint to the rather short allowance he had consumed
at the cottage. This was a long half-pint, and took an hour;
so that it was well on towards the early November sunset before
he started again for Chorlton. J. Hancock had warned him not
to go rowund by t' roo'ad, but to avail himself of the cross-cut
over the fields to Dessington. When old Phœbe overtook him, he
was beginning to wonder, as he sat on the stile, how he should
introduce himself at Strides Cottage. There might be men there.
Then, of a sudden, he had seen that the old woman who had disturbed his cogitations, must be his mother! How could there be
another old woman so like her, so close at hand?

Her placid, resolute, convincing denial checkmated his powers
of thought. As is often the case, details achieved what mere
bald asseveration of fact would have failed in. The circumstan-
tial statement that her son lay buried beside his father in Chorlton
Churchyard corroborated the denial past reasonable dispute. But
nothing could convince his eyesight, while his reason stood aghast
at the way it was deceiving him.

" Give me hold of your fin, missus," he said. " I won't call you
' mother.' Left-hand. . . . No—I'm not going for to hurt you.
Don't you be frightened! " He took the hand that, not without
renewed trepidation and misgiving, was stretched out to him, and
did *not* do with it what its owner expected. For her mind, following his action, was assigning it to some craze of Cheiromancy
—what she would have called Fortune-telling. It was no such
thing.

He did not take his eyes from her face, but holding her hand in his, without roughness, felt over the fingers one by one, resting chiefly on the middle finger. He took his time, saying nothing. At last he relinquished the hand abruptly, and spoke. " No— missus—you're about right. You're *not* my mother." Then he said:—" You'll excuse me—half a minute more! Same hand, please!" Then went again through the same operation of feeling, and dropped it. He seemed bewildered, and saner in bewilderment than in assurance.

Old Phœbe was greatly relieved at his recognition of his mistake. "Was it something in the hand ye knew by, master?" she said timidly. For she did not feel quite safe yet. She began walking on, tentatively.

He followed, but a pace behind—not close at her side. "Something in the hand," said he. "That was it. Belike you may have seen, one time or other, a finger cut through to the bone?"

"Yes, indeed," said she, "and the more's the pity for it! My young grandson shut his finger into his new knife. But he's in the Crimea now."

"Did the finger heal up linable, or a crotch in it?"

"It's a bit crooked still. Only they say it won't last on to old age, being so young a boy at the time."

"Ah!—that's where it was. My mother was well on to fifty when I gave her that chop, and *she* got her hooky finger for life. All the ten years I knew it, it never gave out." Old Phœbe said nothing. Why the man should be so satisfied with this finger evidence she did not see. But she was not going to revive his doubts. She kept moving on, gradually to reach the road, but not to run from him. He kept near her, but always hanging in the rear; so that she could not go quick without seeming to do so.

If she showed willingness to talk with him, he might follow quicker, and they would reach the road sooner. "I'm rarely puzzled, master," she said, "to think how you should take me for another person. But I would not be prying to know. . . ."

"You would like to know who I mistook ye for, mayhap? Well —I'll tell you as soon as not. I took you for my mother—just what I told you! She's somewhere down in these parts—goes by the name of Prichard." Old Phœbe wanted to know why she "went by" the name—was it not hers?—but she checked a mere curiosity. "Maybe you can tell me where 'Strides Cottage' is? That's where she got took in. So I understand."

"Oh no!—you have the name wrong, for certain. My house where I live is called Strides Cottage. There be no Mrs. Prichard there, to my knowledge."

" That's the name told to me, anyhow. Mrs. Prich-ard, of Sapps
Court, London."

" Now who ever told ye such a tale as that? I know now who
ye mean, master. But she's not at Strides Cottage. She's up at
the Towers "—rather a hushed voice here—" by the wish and permission of her young ladyship, Lady Gwendolen, and well cared
for. Ye will only be losing your time, master, to be looking for
her at Strides."

The convict looked at her fixedly. " Now which on ye is telling
the truth?—you or t'other old goody? That's the point." He
spoke half to himself, but then raised his voice, speaking direct
to her. " I was there a few hours back, nigh midday, afore I
come on here. She ain't there—so they told me."

" At the Towers—the Castle? "

" I saw no Castle. My sort ain't welcome in Castles. The party
at the house off the road—name of Keziah—she said Mrs. Prichard had been took off to Chorlton by her cousin, Widow—Widow
Thrale."

" Yes, that is my daughter. Then Keziah Solmes knew? "

" She talked like it. She said her cousin and Mrs. Prichard
had gone away better than two hours, in the carrier's cart. So
it was no use me inquiring for her at the Towers." He then produced the scrap of paper on which he had scribbled the address.
A little more talk showed Granny Marrable all the story knows—
that this sudden translation of her old rival in the affections of
Dave Wardle, from the Towers to her own home, had been
prompted by the sudden departure of her young ladyship for
London. The fact that the whole thing had come about at the
bidding of " Gwen o' the Towers " was absolute, final, decisive
as to its entire rectitude and expediency. But she could see that
this strange son who had not seen his mother for so long had
identified her in the first plausible octogenarian whom he chanced
upon as soon as he was sure he was getting close to the object
of his search, and that he was not known to her ladyship at all,
while his proximity was probably unsuspected by " old Mrs. Picture " herself. Besides, her faith in her daughter's judgment was
all-sufficient. She was quite satisfied about what she would find
on her return home. Nevertheless, this man was of unsound
mind. But he might be harmless. They often were, in spite of
a terrifying manner.

His manner, however, had ceased to be terrifying by the time
a short interchange of explanations and inquiries had made Granny
Marrable cognisant of the facts. She was not the least alarmed

THE DUTIFUL SON 523

that she should have that curious rolling gait alongside of her.
She was uneasy, for all that, as to how a sudden visit of this
man to Strides Cottage would work, and cast about in her mind
how she should best dissuade him from making his presence known
to his mother before she herself had had an opportunity of sounding a note of preparation. She had not intended to go home for
a day or two, but she could get her son-in-law to drive her over,
and return the same day. His insanity, or what she had taken
for insanity, had given her such a shock that she was anxious to
spare her daughter a like experience.

"I think, sir," she began diffidently, "that if I might make so
bold as to say so. . . ."

"Cut along, missis! If you was to make so bold as to say
what?"

"It did come across my mind that your good mother—not being hearty like myself, but a bit frail and delicate—might easy
feel your coming as an upset. Now a word beforehand. . . ."

"What sort of a word?" said he, taking her meaning at once.
"What'll you say? No palavering won't make it any better.
She'll do best to see me first, and square me up after. What'll
you make of the job?"

Now the fact was that the offer to prepare the way for his
proposed visit which she had been on the point of making had
been quite as much in her daughter's interest as in his mother's.
She found his question difficult. All she could answer was:—"I
could try."

He shook his head doubtfully, walking beside her in silence.
Then an idea seemed to occur to him, and he said:—"Hold hard
a minute!" causing her to stop, as she took him literally. He also
paused. "Strike a bargain!" said he. "You do me a good turn,
and I'll say yes. You give me your word—your word afore God
and the Bible—not to split upon me to one other soul but the old
woman herself, and I'll give you a free ticket to say whatever
you please to her when no one else is eavesdropping. Afore God
and the Bible!"

Granny Marrable's fear of him began to revive. He might
be mad after all, with that manner on him, although his tale
about Mrs. Prichard might be correct. But there could be no reason for withholding a promise to keep silence about things said
to her under a false impression that she was his mother. Her
doubt would rather have been as to whether she had any right
to repeat them under any circumstances. "I will promise you,

sir, as you wish it, to say nothing of this only to Mrs. Prichard herself. I promise."

"Afore God and the Bible? The same as if there was a Bible handy?"

"Surely, indeed! I would not tell a falsehood."

"Atop of a Testament, like enough! But how when there's none, and no Parson?" He looked at her with ugly suspicion on his face. And then an idea seemed to strike him. "Look ye here, missus!" said he. "You say Jesus Christ!"

"Say what?—Oh why?" For blind obedience seemed to her irreverent.

"No—you don't get out that way, by God! I hold you to that. You say Jesus Christ!" He seemed to congratulate himself on his idea.

Old Phœbe could not refuse. "Before Jesus Christ," she said reverently, at the same time bending slightly, as she would have done in Chorlton Church.

The convict seemed gratified. He had got his security. "That warn't bad!" said he. "The bob in partic'lar. Now I reckon you're made safe."

"Indeed, you may rely on me. But would you kindly do one thing—just this one! Give me your name and address, and wait to hear from me before you come to the Cottage. 'Tis only for a short time—a day or two at most."

"Supposin' you don't write—how then? . . . Ah, well!—you look sharp about it, and I'll be good for a day or two. Give you three days, if you want 'em."

"I want your mother's leave. . . ."

"Leave for me to come? · If she don't send it, it'll be took. Just you tell her that! Now here's my name di-rected on this envelope. You can tell me of a quiet pub where I can find a gaff, and you send me word there. See? Quiet pub, a bit outside the village! Or stop a bit!—I'll go to J. Hancock—the Old True-penny, on the road I come here by. Rather better than a mile along." Of course the old lady knew the Old Truepenny. Every-one did, in those parts. She took the envelope with the name, and as the twilight was now closing in to darkness, made no attempt to read it, but slipped it carefully in her pocket. Then a thought occurred to her, and she hesitated visibly on an inquiry. He an-ticipated it, saying:—"Hay?—what's that?"

"If Mrs. Prichard should seem not to know—not to recog-nise. . . ." She meant, suppose that Mrs. Prichard denies your claim to be her son, what proof shall I produce? For any man could assume any name.

The convict probably saw the need for some clear token of his identity. " If the old woman kicks," said he, "just you remember this one or two little things from me to tell her, to fetch her round. Tell her, I'm her son Ralph, got away from Australia, where he's been on a visit these twenty-five years past. Tell her. . . . Yes, you may tell her the girl's name was Drax—Emma Drax. Got it?"

" I can remember Emma Drax."

" She'll remember Emma Drax, and something to spare. She was a little devil we had some words about. *She'll* remember her, and she'll know me by her. Then you can tell her, just to top up—only she won't want any more—that her name ain't Prichard at all, but Daverill. . . What!—Well, of course I meant making allowance for marrying again. Right you are, missus! How the Hell should I have known, out there?" For he had mistaken Granny Marrable's natural start at the too well-remembered name she had scarcely heard for fifty years, for a prompt recognition of his own rashness in assuming it had been intentionally discarded.

She, for her part, although her hearing was good considering her age, could not have been sure she had heard the name right, and was on the edge of asking him to repeat it when his unfortunate allusion to Hell—the merest colloquialism with him—struck her recovered equanimity amidships, and made her hesitate. Only, however, for a moment, for her curiosity about that name was uncontrollable. She found voice against a beating heart to say:— " Would you, sir, say the name again for me? My hearing is a bit old."

" Her name, same as mine, Daver-hill." He made the mistake, fatal to clear speech, of overdoing articulation. All the more that it caused a false aspirate; not a frequent error with him, in spite of his long association with defective speakers. It relieved her mind. Clearly a surname and a prefix. She had not got it right yet, though. She forgot she had it written down, already.

" I did not hear the first name clear, sir. Would you mind saying it again?"

He did not answer at once. He was looking fixedly ahead, as though something had caught his attention in the coppice they were approaching. A moment later, without looking round, he answered rapidly;—" Same name as mine—you've got it written down, on the paper I gave you." And then, without another word, he turned and ran. He was so quick afoot, in spite of the halting gait he had shown in walking, that he was through the hedge he made for, across the grassland, and half-way over the stubble-field that lay between it and a plantation, before she knew the cause of his sudden scare. Then voices came from the coppice ahead—a godsend to the poor old lady, whose courage had been sorely tried by the interview—and she quickened her pace to meet them. She did not see the fugitive vanish, but pressed on.

Yes—just as she thought! One of the voices was that of Harry Costrell, her grandson-in-law; another that of a stranger to her, a respectable-looking man she was too upset to receive any other impression of, at the moment; and the third that of her grand-daughter. Such a relief it was, to hear the cheerful ring of her greeting.

"Why, Granny, we thought you strayed and we would have to look for ye in Chorlton Pound. . . . Why, Granny darling, what-ever is the matter? There—I declare you're shaking all over!"

Old Phœbe showed splendid discipline. It was impossible to conceal her agitation, but she could make light of it. She had a motive. Remember that that great grandchild of hers had been born over a twelvemonth ago! "My dear," she said, "I've been just fritted out of my five wits by a man with a limp, that took me for his mother and I never saw him in my life." It did not seem to her that this was "splitting upon" the man. After all, she would have to account for him somehow, and it was safest to ascribe insanity to him.

But the respectable-looking man had suddenly become an energy with a purpose. "Which way's the man with the limp gone?" said he; adding to himself, in the moment required for indicating accurately the fugitive's vanishing-point in the plantation:—"He's my man!" Granny Marrable's pointing finger sent him off in pursuit before either of the others could ask a question or say a word. Harry, the grandson, wavered a moment between grand-filial duty and the pleasures of the chase, and chose the latter, utilising public spirit as an excuse for doing so.

Maisie junior was not going to allow her grandmother to stay to see the matter out, nor indeed did the old lady feel that her own strength could bear any further trial. On the way home to the cottage at Dessington she gave a reserved version of her strange interview, always laying stress on the insanity she con-fidently ascribed to her terrifying companion. As soon as he had died out of the immediate present, she began to find commisera-tion for him.

But then, how about the mission of the respectable man, who

had, it appeared, represented himself as a police-officer on the track of an atrocious criminal, about the charges against whom he had almost kept silence, merely saying that he was a returned convict, and liable to arrest on that ground alone, but that he was " wanted " on several accounts? He had followed his quarry to Grantley Thorpe, arriving by an early train, to find that a man answering to his description had started on foot a couple of hours previously, having asked his way to Ancester Towers. He had followed him there in a hired gig; and, of course, found the connecting clue at Solmes's cottage, and followed him on to Dessington, calling at " T. Hancock's Old Truepenny " by the way, and being guided by T. Hancock's information to run the gig round by the road and intercept his man at the end of the short cut. The younger Maisie and her young brother-in-law, coming by in search of her overdue grandmother, had entered into conversation with him; and he had accompanied them as far as the other side of the coppice wood, and given them the particulars of his errand above stated.

It was all very exciting, and rather horrible. But old Phœbe kept back all her horrors, and even the man's claim to be the son of an old person who had gone to Strides Cottage. Mrs. Prichard she said never a word of, much as she longed to tell the whole story. But she was greatly consoled for this by the succulence of her year-old great-grandson, whose grip, even during sleep, was so powerful as to elicit a forecast of a distinguished future for him, as a thieftaker.

She never got that envelope out of her pocket, conceiving it to be included in her pledge of secrecy. She would look at it before she went to bed. But was it any wonder that she did not, and that her granddaughter had to undress her and put her to bed like a tired child? The last sound of which she was conscious was the voice of Harry Costrell, returning after a long and futile chase, immensely excited and pleased, and quite ready to submit to any sort of fragmentary supper.

Then deep, deep sleep. Then an awakening to daylight, and all the memories of yestereven crowding in upon her—among them an address and a name in the pocket of the gown by the bed-side. She could reach it easily.

There it was. She lay back in bed uncrumpling it, expecting nothing. . . .

This was the fag-end of a dream, surely! But no—there the words were, staring her in the face:—" Ralph Thornton Daverill! " And her mind staggered back fifty years.

CHAPTER X

A WORD FOR TYPHUS. DR. DALRYMPLE'S PECULIAR INTEREST IN THE
CASE. THE NURSE'S FRONT TOOTH. AN INVALID WHO MEANT BUSI-
NESS. SAPPS COURT AGAIN. HOW DAVE AND DOLLY LEFT THINGS
BE IN MRS. PRICHARD'S ROOM. DOLLY JUNIOR'S LEGS. QUEEN VIC-
TORIA AND PRINCE ALBERT. MRS. BURR'S RETURN. BUT SHE COULD
GIVE AUNT M'RIAR A LIFT, IN SPITE OF HER INSTEP. HOW THE
WRITING-TABLE HAD LOST A LEG. WHAT IT WOULD COME TO TO
MAKE A SOUND JOB OF IT. BUT ONLY BY EMPTYING OUT THE THINGS
INSIDE OF THE DRAWER. WHO WOULD ACT AS BAILEE? HOW A
VISION VOLUNTEERED. HOW THE LOCK CAME OPEN QUITE EASY, AND
MRS. BURR MADE A NEAT PACKET OF WHAT IT RELEASED, TO BE TOOK
CHARGE OF BY THE VISION

IT had got wind in Cavendish Square that Typhus had broken
out at Number One-hundred-and-two. That was the first form
rumour gave to the result of a challenge to gaol-fever, recklessly
delivered by Miss Grahame in a top-attic in Drury Lane. It was
unfair to Typhus, who, if not disqualified from saying a word on
his own behalf, might have replied:—" I am within my rights. I
know my place, I hope. I never break out in the homes of the
Well-to-do. But if the Well-to-do come fussing round in the
homes of the Ill-to-be, they must just take their chance of catching
me. I wash my hands of all responsibility."

And no doubt the excuse would have been allowed by all fair-
minded Nosologists. For although Typhus—many years before
this—had laid sacrilegious hands on a High Court of Justice,
giving rise to what came to be known as the " Black Assizes,"
all that had happened on that occasion was in a fair way of business; good, straightforward, old-fashioned contagion. If prison-
warders did not sterilise persons who had been awaiting their
trial for weeks in Houses of Detention—Pest-houses of Detention—you could not expect a putrid fever to adopt new rules
merely to accommodate legal prejudice. And in the same way
if Cavendish Square came sniffing up pestilential effluvia in Drury
Lane, it was The Square's look out, not Typhus's.

Nevertheless, the Lares and Penates of The Square, who varied
as individuals but remained the same as inherent principles—
its Policeman, its Milk, its Wash, its Crossing-Sweeper—even

after the germ of contagion had been identified beyond a doubt
as a resident in Drury Lane, held fast to a belief that Typhus had
been dormant at the corner house since the days of the Regency,
and had seized an opportunity when nothing antiseptic was looking, to break out and send temperatures up to 106° F. For, said
they, when was the windows of that house opened last? Just
you keep your house shut up—said they—the best part of a century, and see if something don't happen! But the person addressed always admitted everything, and never entered on the
suggested experiment.

Persons of Condition—all the real Residents, that is—did not
allow themselves to be needlessly alarmed, and refused to rush
away into the country. There was no occasion for panic, but
they would take every reasonable precaution, and give the children a little citrate of magnesia, as it was just as well to be on
the safe side. And they had the drains properly seen to. Also
they would be very careful not to let themselves down. That
was most important. They felt quite reassured when Sir Polgey
Bobson, for instance, told them that there was no risk whatever
three feet from the bedside of the patient. "And upwards, I
presume?" said a Wag. But Sir Polgey did not see the Wag's
point. He was one of your—and other people's—solemn men.

Said Dr. Dalrymple—he whose name Dave Wardle had mis-
remembered as Damned Tinker—to Lady Gwen, arriving at Cavendish Square in the early hours of the morning—still early, though
she had been nearly four hours on the road:—"I wish now I had
told you positively *not* to come. . . . But stop a minute!—you
can't have got my letter?"

"Never mind that now. How is she?"

"Impossible to say anything yet, except that it is unmistakable
typhus, and that there is nothing specially unfavourable. The
fever won't be at its height for the best part of a week. We can
say nothing about a case of this sort till the fever subsides. But
you *can't* have got my letter—there has been no time."

"Exactly. It may have arrived by now. Sometimes the post
comes at eight. I came because she telegraphed. Here's the
paper."

The doctor read it. "I see," said he. "She said don't come,
so you came. Creditable to your ladyship, but—excuse me!—quite
mad. You are better out of the way."

"She has no friend with her."

"Well—no—she hasn't! At least—yes—she has! I shall not
leave her except for special cases. They can do very well with-

out me at the Hospital. There are plenty of young fellows at the Hospital."

Gwen appeared to apprehend something suddenly. "I see," she said. "I quite understand. I had never guessed."

He replied:—"How did you guess? I *said* nothing. However, I won't contradict you. Only understand right. This is all on my side. Miss Grahame knows nothing about it—isn't in it."

"Oh!" said Gwen incredulously. "Now suppose you tell me what your letter said!"

"You are *sure* you understand?"

"Oh dear, yes! It doesn't want much understanding. What did your letter say?"

Dr. Dalrymple's reply was substantially that it said what Gwen had anticipated. The patient was in no danger whatever, at present, and with reasonable precautions would infect nobody. He knew that her ladyship's impulse to come to her friend would be very strong, but she could do no good by coming. The wisest course would be for her to keep away, and rely on his seeing to it that the patient received the utmost care that skill and experience could provide. "I knew that if I said I should not allow you to see her, you would come by the next train. Excuse my having taken the liberty to interpret your character on a very slight acquaintance."

"Quite correct. Your interpretation did you credit. I should have come immediately. The letter you did write *might* have made me hesitate. *Now* I want to see her."

The doctor acquiesced in the inevitable. "It's rash," he said, "and unnecessary. But I suppose it's no use remonstrating?"

"Not the slightest!" said Gwen. And, indeed, the supposition was a forlorn hope, and a very spiritless one. Also, other agencies were at work. A tap at the door, that was told to come in, revealed itself as an obliging nurse whose upper front tooth was lifting her lip to look out under it at the public. Her mission was to say that Miss Grahame had heard the visitor's voice and she might speak to her through the door, but on no account come into the room. A little more nonsense of this sort, and Gwen was talking with her cousin at a respectful distance, to comply with existing prejudices; but without the slightest belief that her doing so would make any difference, one way or the other. The dreadful flavour of fever was in everything, and lemons and hot-house grapes were making believe they were cooling, and bottles that they contained sedatives, and disinfectants that they were purifying the atmosphere. It was all their gammon, and the fiend

Typhus, invisible, was chuckling over their preposterous claims, and looking forward to a happy fortnight, with a favourable outcome from his point of view; or, at least, the consolation of *sequelæ*, and a retarded convalescence.

There is a stage of fever when lassitude and uncertainty of movement and eyesight have prostrated the patient and compelled him to surrender at discretion to his nurses and medical advisers, but before the Valkyrie of Delirium are scouring the fields of his understanding, to pounce on the corpses of ideas their Odin had slain. That time was not due for many hours yet, when Gwen got speech of her cousin. She immediately appreciated that the patient was anxious to impress bystanders that this illness was all in the way of business. Also, that she was watching the development of her own symptoms as from a height apart, in the interest of Science.

" I knew I should catch it. But somebody had to, and I thought it might as well be me. I caught it from a child. A mild case. That would not make much difference. Being a woman is good. More men die than women. It's only within the last few years that typhus has been distinguished from typhoid. . . ." After a few more useful particulars, she said:—" It was very bad of you to come. I telegraphed to you not to come, last week. . . . Wasn't it last week? . . . Well then—yesterday. . . . They ought never to have let you in. . . . There!—I get muddled when I talk. . . ." She did, but it did not amount to wandering.

Gwen made very fair essays towards the correct thing to say; the usual exhortations to the patient to rely upon everything; acquiesce in periodical doses; absorb nourishment, however distasteful it might be on the palate, and place blind faith in everyone else, especially nurses. It was very good for a beginner; indeed, her experience of this sort of thing was almost *nil*. But all she got for it was:—" Don't be irritating, Gwen dear! Sit down there, where you are. Yes, that far off, because I've something to say I want to say. . . . No—more in front, so that I needn't move my head to see you. . . . Oh no—my *head's* all right in itself; only, when I move it, the pain won't move with it, and it drags. . . . Suppose I shuffle off this mortal coil? "

Gwen immediately felt it her duty to point out the improbability of anyone dying, but was a little handicapped by the circumstances attendant on Typhus Fever. She had to be concise in unreason. " Don't talk nonsense, Clo dear." The patient ignored the interruption. " Oh dear!—give me another grape to suck without having to open my eyes. . . . Ta!—now I can talk a little more." The obliging nurse headed Gwen off to a proper distance, and herself supplied the grape. In doing this she smiled so hard that the tooth got a good long look at Gwen, who looked another way. The patient resumed, speaking very much from her lofty position of lecturer by her own bedside.

"You see, a percentage of cases recovers, but this one may not be in it. However, the constitution is good. . . . No, Gwen dear, you know perfectly well I may die, so where *is* the use of pretending?" Whereupon Gwen conceded the possibility of Death, and the patient seemed to be easier in her mind; saying, as one who leaves trivialities, to settle down to matters of business:— "I want to talk to you about my small boy, Dave Wardle."

"Shall I go and see him at Sapps Court?"

"Yes—that's what I want. And then come back here and tell me . . . promise!" She was getting very indeterminate in speech, and the nurse was signalling for the interview to close. So Gwen cut it short. But she felt she had made a binding promise. She must go to Sapps Court.

Said Gwen to Dr. Dalrymple, a few minutes later, in the sitting-room:—"I hope she hasn't talked too much." The doctor appeared to have taken temporary possession, and to have several letters to write.

"It makes very little difference," he said. "At present the decks are only being cleared for action. In a few days we shall be in the thick of it—pulse over a hundred—temperature a hundred and four—then a crisis. When it's all over, we shall be able to see how many ships are sunk."

Sapps Court had resumed its tranquil routine of everyday life, and the accident had nearly become a thing of the past. Not entirely, for Mrs. Prichard's portion of No. 7 still remained unoccupied, even Susan Burr remaining absent at her married niece's at Clapham. Aunt M'riar had charge, and kept a bit of fire going in the front-room, so the plaster should get a chance to dry out. Also she stood the front and back windows wide to let through a good draught of air, except, of course, it was pouring rain, and then it was no good. The front-room was a great convenience to Aunt M'riar, who now and then was embarrassed with linen to dry, relieving her from the necessity of rendering the kitchen impassable with it in the morning till she came down and took it off of the lines ready for ironing, and removed the cords on which she had hung it overnight.

Dave and Dolly were allowed upstairs during operations, on

stringent conditions; or, rather, it should be said, on a stringent
condition. They were to leave things be. This was honourably
observed, especially by Dave, who was the soul of honour when
once he gave his word. As for Dolly, she was still young, and if
she did claw hold of a chemise and bring down the whole line, why,
it was only that once, and we was children once ourselves. This
was Uncle Mo, of course; he was that easy-going.

But whenever Aunt M'riar was not handicapping the desicca-
tion of the walls by overcharging the atmosphere with moisture
of the very wettest possible sort, Dolly and Dave could have the
room to themselves, so long as they kep' their hands off the clean
wallpaper; which was included in leaving be, obviously—not an
intrusion of a new stipulation. They would then, being alone, go
great lengths in picturing to themselves and each other the pending reappearance of Mrs. Picture and Mrs. Burr, and the delights
of resuming halcyon days of old. For this strangely compounded
clay, Man, scarcely waits to be quite sure he is landed in existence, before he inaugurates a glorious fiction, the golden Past,
which never has been; between which and its resurrection into
an equally golden Future—which never will be—he san'dwiches the
pewter Present, which always is, and which it is idle to pretend
is worth twopence, by comparison.

" When old Mrs. Spicture comes back "—thus Dolly—" she shall
set in her own chair wiv scushions, and she shall set in her own
chair wiv a 'igh hup bact, and she shall set in her own chair
wiv . . ." Here came a pause, due to inanition of distinctive
features. Dolly's style was disfigured by vain repetitions, beyond
a doubt.

" When old Mrs. Spicture comes back "—thus Dave, accepting
the offered formula, somewhat in the spirit of the true ballad
writer—" she's a-going to set in her own chair with cushions,
just *here!* " He sat down with violence on a spot immediately
below the proposed centre of gravity of the chair. " And then oy
shall bring her her tea."

" No, you *s'arn't!* Mrs. Spicture shall set in her chair wiv
scushions, and me and dolly shall tite her her tea."

Dave sat on the floor fixing two intelligent blue eyes on dolly
junior's unintelligent violet ones, and holding his toes. " Dorly
carn't! " said he contemptuously. " Her legs gives. Besides, she's
no inside, only brand." This was a new dolly, who had replaced
Struvvel Peter, who perished in the accident. His legs had been
wooden, and swung several ways. This one's calves were wax,
and one had come off, like a shoe. But the legs only bent one way.

Dolly the mother did not reply to Dave's insinuations against his niece, preferring the refrain of her thesis:—"When Mrs. Spicture comes back and sets in her chair wiv scushions and an Aunt-Emma-Care-Saw, Mrs. Burr she'll paw out the tea with only one lump of shoogy, and me and dolly shall cally it acrost wivout a jop spilt, and me and dolly shall stand it down on the little mognytoyble, and Mrs. Spicture she'll set in her chair wiv scushions, and dolly hand her up the stoast."

"Let me kitch her at it!" said Dave, with offensive male assumption. "Oy shall see to Mrs. Spicture's toast, and see she gets it hot. And Mrs. Burr she'll give leave to butter it, and say how much, and the soyde edge trimmed round toydy with a knoyf." All these details, safely based on items of past experience, were practically historical.

Dolly always accepted Dave's masculine airisomeness with meek equanimity, but invariably took no notice of it. This is nearly common form in well-organized households. She went on to refer to other gratifying revivals that would come about on Mrs. Picture's return. The sofy should be stood back against the wall, for dolly to be put to sleep on. And Queen Victoria she should go up on one nail, and Prince Halbert on the other. These were beautiful coloured prints, smiling fixedly across a full complement of stars and garters. The red piece of carpet would go down against the fender, and the blue piece near the window, as of yore. Dave looked forward with interest to the resurrection of Mrs. Picture's wroyting toyble with a ployce for her Boyble to lie on, and to the letters to his Granny Marrowbone in the country which would certainly be wrote at it, directly or by dictation, in the blessed revival of the past which was to come. Mrs. Burr's cat, who had travelled by request in a hamper to her married niece's at Clapham, in charge of Michael Ragstroar, would return and would then promptly have kittens in spite of doubtful sex-qualifications suggested by the name of Tommy; which kittens would belong to Dave and Dolly respectively, choice being made as soon as ever it was seen what colour they meant to be.

These speculations, which had made pleasant material for castles-in-the-air in the undisturbed hours when the children were in sole possession of the apartment, seemed to be within a measurable distance of realisation when Aunt M'riar, acting on a communication from Mrs. Burr at Clapham, proceeded to unearth the hidden furniture from the bedroom where Mr. Bartlett's careful men had interred it, and where it hadn't been getting any good, you might be sure. At least, so said Mrs. Ragstroar, who was so obliging as to lend a hand getting the things back in their places, and giving them a dust over to get the worst of the mess off. And Uncle Mo he was able to make himself useful, with a screw here and a tack there, and a glue-pot with quite a professional smell to it, so that you might easy have took him for a carpenter and joiner. For Mr. Bartlett's men, while doubtless justifying their reputation for handling everything with care due to casualties with compound fractures, had stultified their own efforts by shoving the heavy goods right atop of the light ones, and lying things down on their sides that should have been stood upright, and committing other errors of judgment. It was a singular and unaccountable thing that these men seemed to share the mantle of their employer and somehow to claim forgiveness, and get it, on the score of the inner excellence of their hearts and purity of their motives.

So that within a day or two after her young ladyship's sudden appearance at the fever-stricken mansion in Cavendish Square, Mrs. Burr put in her first appearance at Sapps Court since she went away to the Hospital. She was able to walk upon her foot, while convinced that a more rapid recovery would have taken place but for the backward state of surgical knowledge. She was confident they might have given her something at the Hospital to bring it forward, and make some local application—" put something on " was the expression. She seemed to have based an unreasonable faith in bread poultices on their successful employment in entirely different cases.

" Now what, you, got, to, lay out for, the way I look at it, ma'am,"—thus Mrs. Ragstroar, departing and bearing away the hand she had lent, to get supper ready for her own inmates—" is to do no more than you can 'elp, and eat as much as you can get." The good woman then vanished, leaving the united company's chorus to her remarks still unfinished when she reached her own door at the top of the Court. For Uncle Mo, Mr. Alibone, Aunt M'riar, and Dolly and Dave as *claqueurs,* were unanimous that Mrs. Burr should lie still for six months or so, relying on her capital, if any; if none, on manna from Heaven.

However, there was little likelihood of Mrs. Burr being in want of a crust, which is the theoretical minimum needed to sustain life, so long as Sapps Court recognised its liabilities when any component portion of it, considered as a residential district, fell on and crushed one of its residents' insteps. If Mr. Bartlett's repairs had come down on Mrs. Burr in the fullest sense of the expression, she would certainly—unless she outlived the impact of two hundred new stocks and three thousand old bats and closures, deceptively arranged to seem like a wall—have had the advantage, whatever it is, of decent burial, even if she had not had a married niece at Clapham, or any other relative elsewhere. So she was able to abstain without imprudence from immediate efforts to reinstate her dressmaking connection; and was able, without overtaxing her instep, to give substantial assistance to Aunt M'riar, who would have had to refuse a good deal of work just at that time except for her opportune assistance.

It was a natural corollary of this that Mrs. Prichard's tenancy should be utilised as a workshop, as Mrs. Burr was now its only occupant; and that she herself should take her meals below, with Aunt M'riar and the family. So the red and the blue carpet were not put down just yet a while, and Uncle Mo he did what he could with the screw here and the tack there, while Aunt M'riar and Mrs. Burr exercised mysterious functions, with tucks and frills and gimpings and pinkings and gaufferings, which it is beyond the powers of this story to describe accurately.

One mishap had occurred with the furniture which did not come within the scope of Uncle Mo's skill to remedy. The treasured mahogany writing-table that had so faithfully accompanied old Mrs. Picture through all her misfortunes had lost a leg. A leg, but not a foot. For the brass foot, which belonged, was found shoved away in the chest of drawers, which was enough, and more than enough, to contain the whole of the owner's scanty wardrobe. It was a cabinet-maker's job, and rather a nice one at that, to provide a new and suitable leg and attach it securely in the place of the old one. And it would come to nineteen-and-sixpence to make a job of it. The exactness of this sum will suggest the facts, that a young man in the trade, an acquaintance of Uncle Mo at The Sun, he come round to oblige, and undertook to give in a price as soon as he had the opportunity to mention it to his governor. The opportunity occurred immediately he went back to the shop. The sum was for a new leg, involving superhuman ingenuity in connecting it firmly with the pelvis; but a reg'lar sound job. Of course, there was another way of doing it, by tonguing on a new limb below the knee, and inserting a dowell for to stiffen it up. But that would come to every penny of fifteen shillings, and would be a reg'lar poor job, and would show. Nothing like doing a thing while you were about it! It saved expense in the end, and it was a fine old bit of furniture. Bit of old Gillow's!

But there was a point to be considered. The things must be

took out of the drawers and the attached desk, or the governor he'd never have it at the shop. He was a person of the most delicate sensibility, who shrank from making himself responsible for anything whatever. Them drawers must be emptied out, or nothing could be done. Why—you'd only got to shake the table to hear there was papers inside!

This was a serious difficulty. It would, of course, be easy enough to write to Mrs. Prichard for the key; which, said testimony, was very small and always lived in her purse. But then all the milk would be out of the cocoanut; that metaphorical fruit being, in this case, the pleasure of surprising Mrs. Prichard with a writing-table as good as new. Open it, of course, you could! It was a locksmith's job, but the governor would send the shop's locksmith, who would do that for you while you counted half-a-dozen. The counting was optional, and in no sense necessary, nor even contributory, to the operation.

The real crux of the difficulty was not one of mechanism, but of responsibility. Who was qualified to decide on opening the desk and drawers? Who would be answerable for the safety of those papers? The only person who volunteered was Dolly, and Dolly's idea of taking care of things was to carry them about with her everywhere, and if they were in a parcel, to unpack it frequently at short intervals to make sure the contents were still in evidence. Her offer was declined.

The young man in the trade had numerous and absorbing engagements to plead as a reason for his inability to 'ang about all day for parties to make up their minds—the usurper's plea, by-the-by, for a *coup d'état*—so perhaps some emissary might be found, to drop round to the shop to leave word. This young man was anxious to oblige, but altruism had its limits. Just then a knock at the door below led to Dave receiving instructions to sift it and make sure it wasn't a mistake, before a senior should descend to take it up seriously. It was not a mistake, but a lady, reported by Dave, returning out of breath, to be "one of Our Ladies,"—making the Church of Rome seem ill-off by comparison. He was seeking for an intelligent distinction between Sister Nora and Gwen, in reply to the question "Which?", when the dazzling appearance of the latter answered it for him.

"I thought I might come up without waiting to ask," said the vision—which is what she seemed, for a moment, to Sapps Court. "So I didn't ask. Is that Mrs. Picture's writing-table where Dave gets his letters written?"

Never was a more unhesitating plunge made *in medias res.*

It had a magical effect in setting Sapps Court at its ease, and everyone saw a way to contribute to an answer, the substance of which was that the table was Mrs. Prichard's, *but* had lost its leg. The exact force of the *but* was not so clear as it might have been; this, however, was unimportant. Gwen was immediately interested in the repair of the table. Why shouldn't it be done while Mrs. Picture was away, before she came back?

A momentary frenzy of irrelevance seized Sapps Court, and a feverish desire to fix the exact date when the table-leg was disintegrated. "It wasn't broke, when it came from Skillicks," said Mrs. Burr. "That's all I know! And if you was to promise me a guinea I could say no more." Said Aunt M'riar:—"It's been stood up against the wall ever since I remembered it, and Mr. Bartlett's men assured me every care was took in moving." A murmur of testimony to Mr. Bartlett's unvarying sobriety and that of his men threatened to undermine the coherency of the conversation, but the position was saved by Uncle Mo, who seemed less infatuated than others about them. "Bartlett's ain't neither here or there," said he. "What I look at's like this,—the leg's off, and we've got to clap on a new un. Here's a young man'll see to that, and it'll come to nineteen-and-sixpence. Only who's going to take care of the letters and odd belongings of the old lady the whilst? That's a point to consider. I'd rather not, myself, if you ask me. Not without she sends the key, and that won't work, as I see it."

"I see," said Gwen. "You want to make Mrs. Picture a new table-leg, and you can't do it without opening her desk. And you can't get the key from her without saying why you want it. Isn't that it?" Universal assent. "Very well, then! You get the lock opened, and I'll take everything out with my own hands, and keep it safe for Mrs. Picture when she comes back."

This proposal was welcomed with only one reservation. None but a real live locksmith could open a lock, any more than one who is not born a turncock can release the waters that are under the earth through an unexplained hole in the road. It was, however, all within the province of the young man in the trade, who had not vanished when the vision appeared, in spite of those pressing appointments. He would go back to the shop, and send, or bring, a properly qualified operative.

Pending which, an adjournment to the little parlour below, out of all this mess, seemed desirable. Dave and Dolly were, of course, part of this, but Mrs. Burr remained upstairs after answering

inquiries about her own health, and Mr. Alibone went away with
the young man in search of the locksmith.

Gwen had to account for her sudden appearance. "I'm sorry
to have bad news to tell you about my cousin, Miss Grahame,"
said she, so seriously that both her grown-up hearers spoke under
their breaths to begin asking:—"She's not . . . ?"—the rest
being easily understood. Gwen replied:—"Oh no, she's not *dead*.
But she's in the doctor's hands." Uncle Mo looked as though
he thought this was nearly as bad, and Aunt M'riar was so
expressive in sympathy without words that both the children became appalled, and Dolly looked inclined to cry. Gwen continued:—"She has caught a horrible fever in a dreadful place
where she went to see poor people, and nobody can say yet a while
what will happen. It *is* Typhus Fever, I'm afraid."

As Gwen uttered the deadly syllables, Uncle Mo turned away
to the window, leaving some exclamation truncated. Aunt M'riar's
voice became tremulous on the beginning of an unfinished sentence, and Dolly concealed a disposition to weep, because she was
afraid of what Dave would say after. That young man remained
stoical, but did not speak.

Presently Uncle Mo turned from the window, and said, somewhat huskily:—"I wish some of these here *poor people,* as they
call themselves, would either go away to Aymericay, or keep their
premises a bit cleaner; nobody wants 'em here that ever I've heard
tell of, only Phlarnthropists."

Aunt M'riar's unfinished sentence had begun with "Gracious
mercy! . . ." Its sequel:—"Well now—to think of a lady like
that! My word! And Typhus Fever, too!"—was dependent on
it, and contained an element of resignation to Destiny.

Dave struck in with irrelevant matter; as he frequently did,
to throw side-lights on obscurities. "The boy at the School had
fever, and came out sported all over with sports he was. You
couldn't have told him from any other boy." That the other boy
would be similarly spotted was, of course, understood.

Having broken the news, Gwen went on to minimise its seriousness; a time-honoured method, perhaps the best one. "Dr.
Dalrymple is cheerful enough about her at present, so we mustn't
be frightened. He says only very old persons never recover, and
that a young woman like my cousin is quite as likely to live as to
die. . . ."

Uncle Mo caught her up with sudden shrewdness. "Then she's
quite as likely to die as to live?" said he.

"Oh, Mo—Mo—don't ye say the word! Please God, Sister

Nora may live for many a long day yet!" Thus Aunt M'riar, true to the traditional attitude of Life towards Death—denial of the Arch-fear to the very threshold of the tomb.

"So she may, M'riar, and many another on to that. But there's a good plenty o' things would please us that don't please God, and He's got it all His own way."

Uncle Mo, after moving about the room in an unsettled fashion, as though weighed upon by the news he had just heard, had come to an anchor at the table opposite Gwen—obsessed by Dolly, but acquiescent. As he sat there, she saw in his grizzled head against the light; in the strong hand resting on the table, moving now and then as though keeping time to some slow tune; in the other, motionless upon his knee, an image that made her ask herself the question:—"What would Samuel Johnson have been as a prizefighter?" She was not properly shocked, but perhaps that was because she was quick-witted enough to perceive that Uncle Mo had only said, in the blunt tongue of the secular world, what would have sounded an impressive utterance, in another form, from the lips of the sage of whom he had reminded her. She felt she *ought* to say that the Lord would assuredly—a solemn word that!—do what He liked with His own, supplying capitals. She gave it up as out of her line, and went on to business.

"Any of us may die, at any minute, Mr. Wardle," said she. "But my cousin is twenty times as likely to die as you or I, because she's got Typhus Fever, and half the cases are fatal, more or less. . . . They told me how many; I've forgotten. . . . What's that?—is it the locksmith man?" For a knock had come at the street-door, and the sound was as the sound of an operative who had to be back in half an hour or his Governor would cut up rough. He was therefore directed to go upstairs and cast his eye on the job, and the lady would come up in five minutes to see the things took out of the drawer.

"Stop a minute, Aunt M'riar," said the lady. "He mustn't make a mistake and open it, till I come. Please tell him, to make sure!" And Aunt M'riar would have started on her errand if she had not been stopped by what followed. "Or—look here! Let Dave go. You go up, Dave, and say he mustn't touch the lock till I come. Run along, and stop there to see that he does as you tell him." Whereupon, off went Dave, shouting his instructions as soon as he got to the second landing. He felt like a Police-Inspector, or a Warden of the Marches.

As soon as Dave had left tranquillity behind, Gwen set herself to anticipate an anxiety she saw Aunt M'riar wanted to express, but was hanging fire over. "You needn't be afraid about this chick, Aunt M'riar," she said. "It isn't really infectious, only contagious. You can only get it from the patient. Dr. Dalrymple says so. Like the thing you can only buy of the maker. Besides, I've hardly been in the room; they make such a fuss, and won't allow me. And I'm not living in the house at all, but at my father's in Park Lane. And I've been there to-day since Cavendish Square, so anyhow, if I give it to Dolly, my father and mother will have it too. . . . Oh no—she's not rumpling me at all! I like it." It was satisfactory to know that an Earl and Countess were pledged to have Typhus if Dolly caught it. Dolly evidently thought the combination of circumstances as good as a play, and a sprightly one.

Gwen was not sorry when the young ambassador came rushing back, shouting:—"The Man says—the Man says—the Man says it wouldn't take above half a minute to do, and is the loydy a-coming up? Because—because—because if the loydy *oyn't* a-coming up *he—has—to*—get back to the shop." This last was so draconically delivered that Gwen exclaimed:—" Come along, Dolly, we've got our orders!" And she actually carried that great child up all those stairs, and she going to be four next birthday!

Upstairs, the lock-expert was apologetic. "Ye see, miss," he explained, "our governor he's the sort of man it don't do to disappynt him, not however small the job may be. I don't reckon he can wait above a half an hour for anything, 'cos it gets on his narves. So we studies not puttin' of him out, at our shop." At which Gwen interrupted him, sacrificing her own interest in the well-marked character of this governor, to the business in hand; and the prospect, for him, of an early release from his anxiety.

As for the achievement which had been postponed, it really seemed a'most ridiculous when you come to think of it. Such a fuss, and those two men standing about the best part of an hour! At least, so Mrs. Burr said afterwards.

For the operation, all told, was merely this—that the young man inserted a bent wire into the lock, thereby becoming aware of its vitals. Withdrawing it, he slightly modified the prejudices of its tip; after which its reinsertion caused the lock to spring open as by magic. He wished to know, on receipt of a consideration from Gwen, whether she hadn't anything smaller, because it only came to eighteenpence for his time and his mate's, and he had no change in his pocket. Gwen explained that none was needed owing to the proximity of Christmas, and obtained thereby the good opinion of both.   They expressed their feelings and departed.

And then—there was old Mrs. Picture's writing-table drawer, stood open! But only a little way, to show.   For the lady's hands alone were to open it clear out, to remove the contents.   Gwen felt that perhaps she had undertaken this responsibility rashly. It is rather a ticklish matter to tamper unbidden with locks.

So confident was she that old Mrs. Picture would forgive her anything, that she made no scruple of examining and reading whatever was visible.   There was little beyond pens and writing-paper in the drawer, but in a desk which formed part of the table were some warrants held by the old lady as a life-annuitant, and two or three packets of letters, one carefully tied and apparently of considerable age.   There was also a packet marked " Hair," and a small cardboard box.   Little enough to take charge of, and soon made into a neat parcel by Mrs. Burr for Gwen to carry away in her reticule, a receptacle which in those days was almost invariably a portion of every lady's paraphernalia, high and low, rich and poor.   •

The desk opened with the drawer—or rather unrolled itself—a flexible wood-flap running back when it was opened, and releasing a lid that made one-half of the writing-pad when turned back. The letters were under the other half, the old packet being in a small drawer with the parcel marked " Hair."   These were evidently precious.   Never mind! Gwen would keep them safe.

Dave and Dolly were so delighted with the performance of opening and shutting the drawer, and seeing the cylindrical sheath slip backwards and forwards in its grooves, that they could scarcely drag themselves away to accompany their Lady to the carriage that, it appeared, was waiting for her in the beyond, outside Sapps Court.

CHAPTER XI

AN INTERVIEW AT THE TOP OF A HOUSE IN PARK LANE. THE COLOSSEUM.
PACTOLUS. KENSINGTON, AS NINEVEH. DERRY'S. TOMS'S. HELEN
OF TROY. THE PELLEWS. RECONSIDERATION, AND JILTING. GWEN'S
LOVE OF METHOD, AND HOW SHE WOULD GO TO VIENNA. A STAR-
TLING LETTER. HOW HER FATHER READ IT ALOUD. MRS. THRALE'S
REPORT OF A BRAIN CASE. HER DOG. HOW REASON REELED BEFORE
THE OLD LADY'S ACCURACIES. GWEN'S GREAT-AUNT EILEEN AND THE
LORD CHANCELLOR. HOW THE EARL STRUCK THE SCENT. HIS BIG
EBONY CABINET. MR. NORBURY'S STORY. HOW AN EARL CAN DO
A MEAN ACTION, WITH A GOOD MOTIVE. THE FORGED LETTER SEES
THE LIGHT. HOW THE COUNTESS WOKE UP, AND THE EARL GOT TO
BED AT LAST

WHEN the Earl and Countess came to Park Lane, especially if
their visit was a short one, and unless it was supposed to be
known to themselves and their Maker only, they were on their
P's and Q's. Why the new identity that came over them on
those occasions was so described by her ladyship remained a
secret; and, so far as we know, remains a secret still. But that
was the expression she made use of more than once in conversation with her daughter.

If her statements about herself were worthy of credence, her
tastes were Arcadian, and the satisfactions incidental to her position as a Countess—wealth and position, with all the world at
her feet, and a most docile husband, ready to make any reasonable,
and many unreasonable, sacrifices to idols of her selection—were
the merest drops on the surface of Life's crucible. What her
soul really longed for was a modest competence of two or three
thousand a year, with a not too ostentatious house in town, say
in Portland Place; or even in one of those terraces near the Colosseum in Regent's Park, with a sweet little place in Devonshire
to go to and get away from the noise, concocted from specifications
from the poets, with a special clause about clotted cream and new-
laid eggs. Something of that sort! Then she would be able to
turn her mind to some elevating employment which it would be
premature to dwell on in detail to furnish a mere castle-in-the-
air, but of which particulars would be forthcoming in due course.
Or rather, would have been forthcoming. For now the die was

cast, and a soul that could have been pastorally satisfied with a lot of the humble type indicated, had been caught in a whirl, or entangled in a mesh, or involved in a complication—whichever you like—of Extravagance, or Worldliness, or Society, or Mammon-worship, or Plutocracy, or Pactolus—or all the lot—and there was an end of the matter!

"All I can say is that I wonder you do it. I do indeed, mamma!" Thus Gwen, a week later in the story, in her bedroom at the very top of the house, which had once been a smoking-room and which it was her young ladyship's caprice to inhabit, because it looked straight over the Park towards the Palace, which still in those days was close to Kensington, its godmother. The Palace is there still, but Kensington is gone. Look about for it in the neighbourhood, if you have the heart to do so, and see if this is a lie. You will find residential flats, and you will find Barker's, and you will find Derry's, and you will find Toms's. But you will *not* find Kensington.

"You may wonder, Gwen! But if ever you are a married woman with an unmarried grown-up daughter in England and a married one at Vienna, and a position to keep up—I suppose that is the right expression—you will find how impossible everything is, and you will find something else to wonder about. Why—only look at that dress you are trying on!" The grown-up daughter was Gwen's elder sister, Lady Philippa, the wife of Sir Theseus Brandon, the English Ambassador at the Court of Austria. Otherwise, her ladyship was rather enigmatical.

Gwen seemed to attach a meaning to her words. "I don't think we shall ever have a daughter married to an Ambassador at Vienna. It would be too odd a coincidence for anything." This was said in the most unconcerned way, as a natural chat-sequel. What a mirror was saying about the dress, a wonderful Oriental fabric that gleamed like green diamonds, was absorbing the speaker's attention. The *modiste* who was fitting it had left the room to seek for pins, of which she had run dry. A low-class dressmaker would have been able to produce them from her mouth.

The Countess assumed a freezing import. It appeared to await explanation of something that had shocked and surprised her. "*We!*" said her ladyship, picking out the gravamen of this something. "Who are 'We' in this case? . . . Perhaps I did not understand what you said? . . ." And went on awaiting explanation, which any correct-minded British Matron will see was imperatively called for. Young ladies are expected not to refer too freely to Human Nature at any time, and to talk of "having a daughter" was sailing near the wind.

"Who are the 'We'? Why—me and Adrian, of course! At least, Adrian and I!—because of grammar. Whom did you suppose?"

The Countess underwent a sort of well-bred collapse. Her daughter did not observe it, as she was glancing at what she mentioned to herself as "The usual tight armhole, I suppose!" beneath an outstretched arm Helen might have stabbed her for in Troy. Neither did she notice the shoulder-shrug that came with the rally from this collapse, conveying an intimation to Space that one could be surprised at nothing nowadays. But the thing she ought not to have been surprised at was past discussion. Decent interment was the only course. "Who? I? *I* supposed nothing. No doubt it's all right!"

Gwen turned a puzzled face to her mother; then, after a moment came illumination. "Oh—I see-ee!" said she. "It's the children—*our* children! Dear me—one has such innocent parents, it's really quite embarrassing! Of course I shouldn't talk about them to papa, because he's supposed to know nothing about such things. But really—one's own mother!"

"Well—at least don't talk so before the person. . . . She's coming back—*sh!*"

"My dear mamma, she's got six children of her own, so how could it matter? Besides, she's French." That is to say, an Anglo-Grundy would have no jurisdiction.

The dazzling ball-dress, which the Countess had professedly climbed all those stairs to see tried on, having been disposed of satisfactorily, and carried away for finishing touches, her ladyship showed a disposition to remain and talk to her daughter. These two were on very good terms, in spite of the occasional strain which was put upon their relations by the audacity of the daughter's flights in the face of her old-fashioned mother's code of proprieties.

As soon as normal conditions had been re-established, and Miss Lutwyche, an essential to the trying on, had died respectfully away, her ladyship settled down to a chat.

"I've really hardly seen you, child, since you came tearing up from Rocester in that frantic way in the middle of the night. It's always the same in town, an absolute rush. And the way one has to mind one's *P*'s and *Q*'s is trying to the last degree. If it was only Society, one could see one's way. One can deal with Society, because there are rules. But People are quite another thing. . . . Well, my dear, you may say they are not, but look at Clotilda—there's a case in point! I assure you, hardly a minute of the day passes but I feel I ought to do something. But what? One may say it's her own fault, and so it no doubt is, in a sense. No one is under any sort of obligation to go into these horrible places, which the Authorities ought not to allow to exist. There ought to be proper people to do this kind of thing, inoculated or something, to be safe from infection. . . . But she *is* going on all right?"

"They wouldn't let me see her this morning. But Dr. Dalrymple said there was no complication, so far . . ."

"Oh, well, so long as there's no complication, that's all we can expect." The Countess jumped at an excuse to breathe freely. But there were other formidable contingencies. How about Constance and Cousin Percy? "Yes—they've got to be got married, somehow," said her ladyship. "It's impossible to shut one's eyes to it. I've been talking to Constance about it, and what she says is certainly true. When one's father has chronic gout, and one's stepmother severe nervous depression, one knows without further particulars how difficult it would be to be married from home. She says she simply won't be married from her Porchhammer sister's, because she gushes, and it isn't fair to Percy. Her other sister—the one with a name like Rattrap—doesn't gush, but her husband's going to stand for Stockport."

"I suppose," said Gwen, "those are both good reasons. Anyhow, you'll have to accommodate the happy couple. I see that. I suppose papa will have to give her away. If she allows Madame Pontet to groom her, she'll look eighteen. I wonder whether they couldn't manage to . . ."

"Couldn't manage to . . . ?"

"Oh no, I see it would be out of the question, because of the time. I was going to say—wait for *us*. And then we could all have been married together." Gwen had remembered the Self-denying Ordinance, which was to last six months, and was not even inaugurated. She looked up at her mother. "Come, dear mother of mine, there's nothing to be shocked at in that!"

The Countess had risen from her seat, as though to depart. She stood looking across the wintry expanse of Hyde Park, seen through a bow-window across a balcony, with shrubs in boxes getting the full benefit of a seasonable nor'easter; and when at length she spoke, gave no direct reply. "I came up here to talk to you about it," she said. "But I see it would not be of any use. I may as well go. Did Dr. Dalrymple say when Clotilda would be out of danger? Supposing that all goes well, I mean."

"How can he tell? I'm glad I'm not a doctor with a critical case, and everyone trying to make me prophesy favourable results. It's worse for him than it is for us, anyhow, poor man!"

"Why? He's not a relation, is he?"

"No. Oh no! Perhaps if he were one. . . . Well—perhaps if he were, he wouldn't look so miserable. . . . No—they are only very old friends." The Countess had not asked; this was all brainwave, helped by shades of expression. "I'm not supposed to *know* anything, you know," added Gwen, to adjust matters.

"Well—I suppose we must hope for the best," said her mother, with an implied recognition of Providence in the background; a mere civility! "Now I'm going."

"Very well then—go!" was what Gwen did *not* say in reply. She only thought that, if she *had* said it, it would have served mamma right. What she did say was:—"I know what you meant to say when you came upstairs, and you had better say it. Only I shall do nothing of the sort."

"I wish, my dear, you would be less positive. How can you know what I meant to say? Of *what* sort?"

"Reconsidering Adrian. Jilting him, in fact!"

"How can you know that?"

"Because you said it would not be any use talking to me about it. Just before you stopped looking out of the window, and said you might as well go."

Driven to bay, the Countess had a sudden *accès* of argumentative power. "Is there nothing it would be no use to talk to you about except this mad love-affair of yours?"

"Nothing so big. This is the big one. Besides, you know you did mean Adrian." As her ladyship did, she held her tongue.

Presently, having in the meantime resumed her seat, thereby admitting that her daughter was substantially right, she went on to what might be considered official publication.

"Your father and I, my dear, have had a good deal of talk about this unfortunate affair. . . ."

"What unfortunate affair?"

"This unfortunate . . . love-affair."

"Cousin Percy and Aunt Constance?"

"My dear! How can you be so ridiculous? Of course I am referring to you and Mr. Torrens."

"To me and Adrian. Precisely what I said, mamma dear! So now we can go on." The young lady managed somehow to

express, by seating herself negligently on a chair with its back to
her mother, that she meant to pay no attention whatever to any
maternal precept. She could look at her over it, to comply with
her duties as a respectful listener. But not to overdo them, she
could play the treble of Haydn's Gipsy Rondo on the chair back
with fingers that would have put a finishing touch on the exasperation of Helen of Troy.

Her ladyship continued:—" We are speaking of the same thing.
Your father and I have had several conversations about it. As I
was saying when you interrupted me—pray do not do so again!—
he agrees with me *entirely*. In fact, he told me of his own accord
that he wished you to come away with me for six months. . . .
Yes—six! Three's ridiculous. . . . And that it should be quite
distinctly understood that no binding engagement exists between
Mr. Torrens and yourself."

" All right. I've no objection to anything being distinctly understood, so long as it is also distinctly understood that it doesn't
make a particle of difference to either of us. . . . Yes—come in!
Put them on the writing-table." This was to Miss Lutwyche, who
came in, bearing letters.

" To either of you! You answer for Mr. Torrens, my dear,
with a good deal of confidence. Now, do consider that the circumstances are peculiar. Suppose he were to recover his eyesight!"

" You mean he wouldn't be able to bear the shock of finding
out what he'd got to marry. . . ." She was interrupted by her
mother exhibiting consciousness of the presence of Lutwyche,
whose exit was overdue. A very trustworthy young woman, no
doubt; but a line had to be drawn. " What are you fiddling
with my letters for, Lutwyche?" said Gwen. " Do please get done
and go!"

" Yes, my lady." Discreet retirement of Miss Lutwyche.

" She didn't hear, mamma. You needn't fuss."

" I was not fussing, my dear, but it's as well to. . . . Yes, go
on with what you were saying." Because Lutwyche, being extinct, might be forgotten.

Gwen was looking round at the mirror. If Helen of Troy had
seen herself in a mirror, all else being alike, what would her verdict have been? Gwen seemed fairly satisfied. " You meant
Adrian might be disgusted?" said she.

The mother could not resist the pleasure of a satisfied glance
at her daughter's reflection, which was not looking at *her*. " I
meant nothing of the sort," she said. " But your father agreed

with me—indeed, I am repeating his own words—that Mr. Torrens may have a false impression, having only really seen you once, under very peculiar circumstances. It is only human nature, and one has to make allowance for human nature. Now all that I am saying, and all that your father is saying, is that the circumstances *are* peculiar. Without some sort of reasonable guarantee that Mr. Torrens cannot recover his eyesight, I do contend that it would be in the highest degree rash to take an irrevocable step, and to condemn one—perhaps both, for I assure you I am thinking of Mr. Torrens's welfare as well as your own—to a lifetime of repentance."

" Mamma dear, don't be a humbug! You are only putting in Adrian's welfare for the sake of appearances. Much better let it alone!"

" My dear, it is not the point. If you choose to think me inhumane, you must do so. Only I must say this, that apart from the fact that I have nothing whatever against Mr. Torrens personally—except his religious views, which are lamentable—that his parents . . ."

" I thought you said you never knew his mother."

" No—perhaps not his mother." Her ladyship intensified the parenthetical character of this lady by putting her into smaller type and omitting punctuation:—" I can't say I ever really knew his mother and indeed hardly anything about her except that she was a Miss Abercrombie and goes plaguing on about negroes. But "—here she became normal again—" as for his father . . ."

" As for his father?"

" He was a constant visitor at my mother's, and I remember him very well. So there is no feeling on my part against him or his family." Her ladyship felt she had come very cleverly out of a bramble-bush she had got entangled in unawares, but she wanted to leave it behind on the road, and pushed on, speaking more earnestly:—" Indeed, my dearest child, it is of you and your happiness that I am thinking—although I know you won't believe me, and it's no use my saying anything. . . ." At this point feelings were threatened; and Gwen, between whom and her mother there was plenty of affection, of a sort, hastened to allay—or perhaps avert—them. She shifted her seat to the sofa beside her mother, which made daughterliness more possible. A short episode of mutual extenuations followed; for had not a flavour of battle—not tigerish, but contentious—pervaded the interview?

" Very well, then, dear mother of mine," said Gwen, when this

episode had come to an end. " Suppose we consider it settled
that way! I'm to be tractability itself, on the distinct understanding that it commits me to nothing whatever. As for the six
months' penal servitude, you and papa shall have it your own way.
Only play fair—make a fair start, I mean! I like method. You
have only to say when—any time after Christmas—and Adrian
and I will tear ourselves asunder for six months. And then I'll
accompany my mamma to Vienna, because I know that's what she
wants. Only mind—honour bright!—as soon as I have dutifully
forgotten Adrian for six whole months, there's to be an end of
the nonsense, and I'm to marry Adrian . . . and *vice versa*, of
course! Oh no—he shan't be a cipher—I won't allow it. . . ."

" My dear Gwendolen, I wish I could persuade you to be more
serious." But her ladyship, as she rose to depart, was congratulating herself on having scored. The idea of any young lady's
love-fancies surviving six months of Viennese life! She knew that
fascinating capital well, and she knew also what a powerful ally
she would find in her elder daughter, the Ambassadress, who was
glittering there all this while as a distinct constellation.

She might just as well have retired satisfied with this brilliant
prospect; only that she had, like so many of us, the postscript vice.
This is the one that never will allow a conversation to be at an
end. She turned to Gwen, who was already opening a letter to
read, to say:—" You used the expressions ' reconsidering ' and
' jilting ' just now, my dear, as if they were synonymous. I think
you were forgetting that it is impossible to ' jilt '—if I understand
that term rightly—any man until after you have become formally
engaged to him, and therefore. . . . However, if your letter is so
very important, I can go. We can talk another time." This rather
stiffly, Gwen having opened the letter, and been caught and held,
apparently, by something in a legible handwriting. Whatever it
was, Gwen put it down with reluctance, that she might show her
sense of the importance of her mother's departure, whom she kissed
and olive-branched, beyond what she accounted her lawful claims,
in order to wind her up. She went with her as far as the landing,
where cramped stairs ended and gradients became indulgent, and
then got back as fast as she could to the reading of that letter.

It *was* an important letter, there could be no doubt of that,
as a thick one from Irene—practically from Adrian—lay unopened
on the table while she read through something on many pages
that made her face go paler at each new paragraph. On its late
envelope, lying opened by Irene's, was the postmark " Chorlton-
under-Bradbury." But it was in a handwriting Gwen was un-

familiar with. It was *not* old Mrs. Picture's, which she knew quite well. For which reasons the thought had crossed her mind, when she first saw the envelope, that the old lady was seriously ill—perhaps suddenly dead. It was so very possible. Think of those delicate transparent hands, that frame whose old tenant had outstayed so many a notice to quit. Gwen's cousin, Percy Pellew, had said to her when he carried it upstairs in Cavendish Square, that it weighed absolutely nothing.

But this letter said nothing of death, nor of illness with danger of death. And yet Gwen was so disturbed by it that there was scarcely a brilliant visitor to her mother's that afternoon but said to some other brilliant visitor:—" What can be the matter with Gwen? She's not herself!" And then each corrected the other's false impression that it was the dangerous condition of her most intimate cousin and friend, Miss Clotilda Grahame; or screws loose and jammed bearings in the machinery of her love-affair, already the property of Rumour. And as each brilliant visitor was fain to seem better informed than his or her neighbour, a very large allowance of inaccuracy and misapprehension was added to the usual stock-in-trade of tittle-tattle on both these points.

There was only a short interregnum between the last departures of this brilliant throng, and the arrival of a quiet half-dozen to dinner; not a party, only a soothing half-dozen after all that noise and turmoil. So that Gwen got no chance of a talk with her father, which was what she felt very much in need of. That interregnum was only just enough to allow of a few minutes' rest before dressing for dinner. But the quiet half-dozen came, dined, and went away early; perhaps the earlier that their hostess's confessions of fatigue amounted to an appeal *ad misericordiam;* and Gwen was reserved and silent. When the last of the half-dozen had departed, Gwen got her opportunity. " Don't keep your father up too long, child," said the Countess, over the stair-rail. " It makes him sleep in the day, and it's bad for him." And vanished, with a well-bred yawn-noise, a trochee, the short syllable being the apology for the long one.

The Earl had allowed the quiet three, who remained with him at the dinner-table after their three quiet better-halves had retired with his wife and daughter, to do all the smoking, and had saved up for his own cigar by himself. It was his way. So Gwen knew she need not hurry through preliminaries. Of course he wanted to know about the Typhus patient, and she gave a good report, without stint. " *That's* all right," said he, in the tone

of rejoicing which implies a double satisfaction, one for the patient's sake, one for one's own, as it is no longer a duty to be
anxious.

"Why are you glaring at me so, papa darling?" said his daughter. It was a most placid glare. She should have said "looking."

"Your mamma tells me," said he, without modifying the glare,
"that she has persuaded you to go with her to Vienna for six
months."

"She said you wished me to go."

"She wishes you to go herself, and I wish what she wishes."
This was not mere submissiveness. It was just as much loyalty
and chivalry. "Is it a very terrible trial, the Self-denying
Ordinance?"

Gwen answered rather stonily. "It isn't pleasant, but if you
and my mother think it necessary—why, what must be, must!
I'm ready to go any time. Only I must go and wind up with
Adrian first . . . just to console him a little! It's worse for him
than for me! Just fancy him left alone for six months and never
seeing me! . . . Oh dear!—you know what I mean." For she
had made the slip that was so usual. She brushed it aside as a
thing that could not be helped, and would even be sure to happen
again, and continued:—"Irene has just written to me. I got her
letter to-day."

"Well?"

"She makes what I think a very good suggestion—for me to
go to Pensham to stay a week after Christmas, and then go in
for . . . What do you call it? . . . the Self-denying Ordinance in
earnest afterwards. You don't mind?"

"Not in the least, as long as your mother agrees. Is that Miss
Torrens's—Irene's—letter?"

"No. It's another one I want to speak to you about. Wait
with patience! . . . I was going to say what exasperating parents I have inherited . . . from somewhere!"

"From your grandparents, I suppose! But why?"

"Because when I say, may I do this or may I say that, you always
say, 'Yes if your mother,' etcetera, and then mamma quotes you
to squash me. I don't think it's playing the game."

"I think I gather from your statement, which is a little obscure, that your mamma and I are like the two proctors in Dickens's novel. Well!—it's a time-honoured arrangement as between
parents, though I admit it may be exasperating to their young.
What's the other letter?"

"I want to tell you about it first," said Gwen. She then told,

without obscurity this time, the events which had followed the
Earl's departure from the Towers a week since. " And then comes
this letter," she concluded. " Isn't it terrible? "

" Let's see the letter," said the Earl. She handed it to him;
and then, going behind his high chair, looked over him as he
read. No one ever waits really patiently for another to read what
he or she has already read. So Gwen did not. She changed the
elbow she leaned on, restlessly; bit her lips, turn and turn about;
pulled her bracelets round and round, and watched keenly for
any chance of interposing an abbreviated *précis* of the text, to
expedite the reading. Her father preferred to understand the letter, rather than to get through it in a hurry and try back; so
he went deliberately on with it, reading it half aloud, with
comments:

" AT STRIDES COTTAGE,
" CHORLTON-UNDER-BRADBURY,
"*November* 22, 1854.

" MY LADY,

" I have followed your instructions, and brought the old Mrs.
Prichard here to stay until you may please to make another arrangement. My mother will gladly remain at my daughter's at her
husband's farm, near Dessington, till such time as may be suitable
for Mrs. Prichard to return. This I do not wish to say because I
want to lose this old lady, for if your ladyship will pardon the
liberty I take in saying so, she is a dear old person, and I do in
truth love her, and am glad to have charge of her."

" She seems always to make conquests," said the Earl. " I acknowledge to having been *épris* myself."

" Yes, she really is an old darling. But go on and don't talk.
It's what comes next." She pointed out the place over his shoulder, and he took the opportunity to rub his cheek against her
arm, which she requited by kissing the top of his head. He
read on:

" Nor yet would my mother's return make any difference, for we
could accommodate, and I would take no other children just yet a
while. Toby goes home to-morrow. But I will tell you there is
something, and it is this, only your ladyship may be aware of it,
that the old lady has delusions and a strange turn to them, in which
Dr. Nash agrees with me it is more than old age, and recommends
my mother, being old too, not to come back till she goes, for it
would not be good for her, for anything of this sort is most trying
to the nerves, and my mother is eighty-one this Christmas, just old
Mrs. Prichard's own age."

"I think that's the end of the sentence," said the Earl. "I take it that Nash, who's a very sharp fellow in his own line, is quite alive to the influence of insanity on some temperaments, and knows old Mrs. Marrable well enough to say she ought not to be in the way of a lunatic. . . . What's that?"

"A lunatic!" For Gwen had started and shuddered at the word.

"I see no use in mincing matters. That's what the good woman is driving at. What comes next?" He read on:

"I will tell all what happened, my lady, from when she first entered the house, asking pardon for my length. It began when I was showing the toy water-mill on our mantel-shelf, which your ladyship saw with Miss Grahame. I noticed she was very agitated, but did not put it down to the sight of this toy till she said how ever could it have been *my* grandfather's mill, and then I only took it for so many words, and got her away to bed, and would have thought it only an upset, but for next morning, when I found her out of bed before six, no one else being up but me, measuring over the toy with her hands where it stood on the shelf, and I should not have seen her only for our dog calling attention, though a dumb animal, being as I was in the yard outside."

"I think I follow that," said the Earl. "The dog pulled her skirts, and had a lot to say and couldn't say it."

"That was it," said Gwen. "Just like Adrian's Achilles. I don't mean he's like Achilles personally. The most awful bulldog, to look at, with turn-up tusks and a nose like a cup. But go on and you'll see. 'Yard outside.'"

"I would have thought her sleep-walking, but she saw me and spoke clear, saying she could not sleep for thinking of a model of her father's mill in Essex as like this as two peas, and thought it must be the same model, only now she had laid her hands on it again she could see how small it was. She seemed so reasonable that I was in a fright directly, particularly it frightened me she should say Essex, because my grandfather's mill was in Essex, showing it was all an idea of her own. . . ."

"I can't exactly follow that," said the Earl, and re-read the words deliberately.

"Oh, can't you see?" said Gwen. "*I* see. If she had said the other mill was in Lancashire, it would have seemed *possible*. But —both in Essex!"

"I suppose that's it. Two models of mills exactly alike, and both in Essex, is too great a tax on human credulity. On we go again! Where are we? Oh—'idea of her own.'"

"But I got her back to bed, and got her some breakfast an hour later, begging she would not talk, and she was very good and said no more. After this I moved the model out of the way, that nothing might remind her, and she was quiet and happy. So I did not send for Dr. Nash then. But when it came to afternoon, I saw it coming back. She got restless to see the model I had put by out of sight, saying she could not make out this and that, particular the two little girls. And then it was she gave me a great fright, for when I told her the two little girls was my mother and my aunt, being children under ten, over seventy years ago, and twins, she had quite a bad attack, such as I have never seen, shaking all over, and crying out, 'What is it?—What is it?' So then I sent Elizabeth next door for Dr. Nash, who came and was most kind, and Mrs. Nash after. He gave her a sedative, and said not to let her talk. He said, too, not to write to you just yet, for she might get quite right in a little while, and then he would tell you himself."

"Poor darling old Mrs. Picture!" said Gwen. "Fancy her going off like this! But I think I can see what has done it. You know, she has told me how she was one of twins, and how her father had a flour-mill in Essex."
"Did she say the name?"
"No—she's very odd about that. She never tells any names, except that her sister was Phœbe. She told me *that*. . . . Oh yes—she told me her little girl's name was Ruth." Gwen did not know the christened name of either Granny Marrable or Widow Thrale, when she said this.
"Phœbe and Ruth," said the Earl. "Pretty names! But *what* has done it? What can you see? . . . You said just now? . . ."
"Oh, I understand. Of course, it's the twins and the flour-mill in Essex. Such a coincidence! Enough to upset anybody's reason, let alone an old woman of eighty! Poor dear old Mrs. Picture!—she's as sane as you or I."
"Suppose we finish the letter. Where were we? 'Tell you himself'—is that it? All right!"

"Then she was quiet again, quite a long time. But when we was sitting together in the firelight after supper, she had it come on again, and I fear by my own fault, for Dr. Nash says I was in the wrong to say a word to her of any bygones. And yet it was but to clear her mind of the mixing together of Darenth Mill and this mill she remembers. For I had but just said the name of ours, and that my grandfather's name was Isaac Runciman when I saw it was coming on, she shaking and trembling and crying out like before, 'Oh, what *is* it? Only tell me what it *is!*' And then 'Our mill was Darenth Mill," and 'Isaac Runciman was my father.' And other things she could not have known that had been no word of mine, only Dr. Nash found out why, all these things having been told to little Dave Wardle last year, and doubtless repeated childlike. And yet, my lady, though I know well where the dear old soul has gotten all these histories, seeing there is no other way possible, it is I do assure you enough to turn my own reason to hear her go on telling and telling of one thing and another all what our little boy we had here has made into tales for his amusement, suchlike as Mr. Pitt and Mr. Fox our horses, and she had just remembered the foreman's name Muggeridge when she saw the model; it makes my head fairly spin to hear. Only I take this for my comfort, that I can see behind her words to know the tale is not of her making, but only Dave, like when she said Dave must have meant Muggeridge in his last letter, and would I find it to show her, only I could not. And like when she talked of her old piano at her father's, there I could see was our old piano my mother bought at a sale, now stood in a corner here where I had talked of it the evening I had the old lady here first. I am naming all these things that your ladyship may see I do right to keep my mother away from Strides till Mrs. Prichard goes. But I do wish to say again that that day when it comes will be a sad one for me, for I do love her dearly and that is the truth, though it is but a week and a day, and Dr. Nash does not wonder at this."

"If I remember right," said the Earl, stopping, "Nash has made some study of Insanity—written about it. He knows how very charming lunatics can be. You know your Great-Aunt Eileen fairly bewitched the Lord Chancellor when he interviewed her. . . ."

"Did he see the lunatics himself? . . ."

"When they were fascinating and female—yes! . . . Well, what happened was that she waited to be sure he had refused to issue the Commission, and then went straight for Lady Lostwithiel's throat—her sister-in-law, you know. . . ."

"Did that show she was mad?"

"Let us keep to the point. What does 'Muggeridge' mean?"

"I was thinking. 'Muggeridge'! But *I've* got Dave's last letter. I'll get it." And she was off before the Earl could say that to-morrow would do as well.

He went on smoking the bitter—and bitten—end of his cigar,

which had gone slowly, owing to the reading. Instead of finishing up the letter, he went back, carefully re-reading the whole with absorbed attention. So absorbed, that Gwen, coming in quietly with a fresh handful of letters, was behind his chair unobserved, and had said:—"Well, and what do you make of it?" before he looked up at her.

"Verdict in accordance with the medical opinion, I *think*. But let's see Dave's letter." He took and read to himself. "*I* see," said he. "The cross stood for Dolly's love. A mere proxy. But *he* sends the real article. I like the 'homliburst,' too. Why did Dolly's lady want to *towel* Mrs. Spicture? . . . Oh, I see, it's the name of our house . . . h'm—h'm—h'm! . . . Now where do we come to Muggeridge? . . . Oh, here we are! I've got it. Well—that's plain enough. Muggeridge. M, U, one G, E, R, I, J for D, G, E. That's quite plain. Can't see what you want more."

"Oh yes, it's all very easy for you, now you've been told. *I* couldn't make head or tail of it. And I don't wonder dear old Mrs. Picture couldn't. . . ."

The Earl looked up suddenly. "Stop a bit!" said he. "Now where was it in Mrs. Thrale's letter. I had it just now . . . here it is! 'The old lady had just remembered the foreman's name when she saw the model.' Got that?"

"Yes—but I don't see. . . ."

"No—but listen! Dr. Nash found out that all these particulars were of Dave's communicating. Got *that?*"

"Yes—but still I don't see. . . ."

"Don't chatterbox! Listen to your father. Keep those two points in mind, and then consider that when you read her Dave's letter she could not identify his misspelt name, which seems perfectly obvious and easy to me, now I know it. How *could* she forget it so as not to be reminded of it by a misspelt version? Can you conceive that she should fail, if she had heard the name from the child so clearly as to have it on the tip of her tongue the moment she saw the mill she only knew from Dave's description?"

"No—it certainly does seem very funny!"

"Very funny. Now let's see what the rest of the letter says." He went on reading:

"I know your ladyship will pardon the liberty I take to write at such length, seeing the cause of it, and also if I may suggest that your ladyship might send for Mrs. Bird, who lives with Mrs. Prichard, or for the parents of the little Dave Wardle, to inquire of them has she been subject to attacks or is this new. I should tell you that she has now been free from any aberration of mind, so Dr. Nash says, for nearly two days, mostly knitting quietly to herself, without talk, and sometimes laying down the needles like to think. Dr. Nash says to talk to her when she talks, but to keep her off of bygones, and the like. She has asked for things to write you a letter herself, and I have promised as soon as this is done. But I will not wait for hers to post this, as Dr. Nash says the sooner you know the better. I will now stop, again asking pardon for so long a letter, and remain, my lady, your obedient and faithful servant.

"R. Thrale."

"How very like what everyone else does!" said the Earl. "This good woman writes so close to economize paper that she leaves no room for her signature and goes in for her initial. I was wanting to know her Christian name. Do you know it? And see—she has to take more paper after all! Here's a postscript."

"P.S.—There is another reason why it is better not to have my mother back till Mrs. Prichard goes, she herself having been much upset by a man who said he was Mrs. Prichard's son, and was looking for his mother. My son-in-law, John Costrell, came over to tell me. This man had startled and alarmed my mother *very much*. I should be sorry he should come here to make Mrs. Prichard worse, but my mother is no doubt best away. I am not afraid of him myself, because of our dog."

"That dog is a treasure," said the Earl, re-enveloping the letter. "What are those other letters? Irene's? . . . And what?"

"I was trying to think of Mrs. Thrale's Christian name. I don't think I know it. . . . Yes—Irene's, and some papers I want you to lock up, for me." Gwen went on to tell of the inroad on Mrs. Prichard's *secrétaire,* and explained that she was absolutely certain of forgiveness. "Only you will keep them safer than I shall, in your big ebony cabinet. I think I can trust you to give them back." She laid them on the table, gave her father an affectionate double-barrelled kiss, and went away to bed. It was very late indeed.

Mr. Norbury, in London, always outlived everyone else at night. The Earl rather found a satisfaction, at the Towers, in being the last to leave port, on a voyage over the Ocean of Sleep. In London it was otherwise, but not explicably. The genesis of usage in households is a very interesting subject, but the mere chronicler can only accept facts, not inquire into causes. Mr. Norbury always *did* give the Earl a send-off towards Dreamland, and saw the house deserted, before he vanished to a secret den in the basement.

"Norbury," said the Earl, sending the pilot off, metaphorically. "You know the two widows, mother and daughter, at Chorlton-under-Bradbury? Strides Cottage."

"Yes, indeed, my lord! All my life. I knew the old lady when she came from Darenth, in Essex, to marry her second husband, Marrable." Norbury gave other particulars which the story knows.

"Then Widow Thrale is not Granny Marrable's daughter, though she calls her mother?"

"That is the case, my lord. She was a pretty little girl—maybe eleven years old—and was her mother's bridesmaid. . . . I should say her aunt's."

"Who was her mother?"

"I have understood it was a twin sister."

"Who was her father?"

Mr. Norbury hesitated. "If your lordship would excuse, I would prefer not to say. The story came to me through two persons. My own informant had it from Thrale. But it's near twenty years ago, and I could not charge my memory, to a certainty."

"Something you don't like to tell?"

"Not except I could speak to a certainty." Mr. Norbury, evidently embarrassed, wavered respectfully.

"Was there a convict in it, certain or uncertain?"

"There was, my lord. Certain, I fear. But I am uncertain about his name. Peverell, or Deverell."

"What was he convicted of? What offence?"

"I rather think it was forgery, my lord, but I may be wrong about that. The story said his wife followed him to Van Diemen's Land, and died there?"

"That was Thrale's story?"

"Thrale's story."

"He must have known."

"Oh, he knew!"

"What is old Mrs. Marrable's Christian name?"

"I believe she was always called Phœbe. Her first married name was a very unusual one, Cropredy."

"And Widow Thrale's?"

"Ruth—Keziah Solmes calls her, I think."

His lordship made no reply; and, indeed, said never a word until he released Mr. Norbury in his dressing-room ten minutes later, being then as it were wound up for a good night's rest, and safe to go till morning. Even then the current of serious thought into which he seemed to have plunged seemed too engrossing to allow of his making a start. He remained sitting in the easy-chair before the fire, with intently knitted brows and a gaze divided between the vigorous flare to which Mr. Norbury's final benediction had incited it, and the packet of letters Gwen had given him, which he had placed on the table beside him. Behind him was what Gwen had spoken of as his big ebony cabinet. If a ghost that could not speak was then and there haunting that chamber, its tongue must have itched to remind his lordship what a satisfaction it would be to a disembodied bystander to get a peep into the cinquecento recesses of that complicated storehouse of ancient documents, which was never opened in the presence of anyone but its owner.

Gradually Gwen's packet absorbed more than its fair share of the Earl's attention; finally, seemed to engross it completely. He ended by cutting the outer string, taking the contents out, and placing them before him on the table, assorting them in groups, like with like.

There were the printed formal warrants, variously signed and attested, of some assignments or transfers—things of no interest or moment. Put them by! There were one or two new sheets covered with a child's printed efforts towards a handwriting manifestly the same as the one recently under discussion, even without the signature, " dAve wARdLe." There was a substantial accumulation of folded missives in an educated man's hand, and another in a woman's; of which last the outermost—being a folded sheet that made its own envelope—showed a receipt postmark " Macquarie. June 24, 1807," and a less visible despatch-stamp " Darenth. Nov. 30, 1806," telling its tale of over six months on the road. Then one, directed in another hand, a man's, but with the same postmarks, both of 1808, with the months undecipherable. This last seemed the most important, being tied with tape. It was the elder Daverill's successful forgery, treasured by old Maisie as the last letter from her family in England, telling of her sister Phœbe's death. All the letters were addressed to " Mrs. Thornton Daverill," the directions being only partly visible, owing to the folding.

Lest the reader should be inclined to blame the accidental possessor of these letters for doing what this story must perforce put on record, and to say that his action disgraced the Earldom of Ancester, let it remind him what the facts were that were already in his lordship's possession, and ask him whether he himself, so circumstanced, might not have felt as the Earl did—that the case was one for a sacrifice of punctilios in the face of the issues that turned upon their maintenance. Had he any right to connive at the procrastination of some wicked secret—for he had the clue—when a trivial sacrifice of self-respect might bring it to light? He could see that Mrs. Prichard *must* be the twin sister, somehow. But he did not see how, as yet; and he wanted confirmation and elucidation. These letters would contain both, or correction and guidance. Was he to bewilder Gwen with his own partial insights, or take on himself to sift the grist clean before he milled it for her consumption? He was not long in deciding.

Two or three slippered turns up and down the room, very cautious lest they should wake her ladyship in the adjoining one, were all the case required. Then he resumed his seat, and, deliberately taking up the taped letter, opened it and read:

" MY DEAR DAUGHTER MAISIE,
" It is with great pain that I take up my pen to acquaint you of the fatal calamity which has befallen your sister Phœbe and her husband, as well as I grieve to say of your own child Ruth, my granddaughter, all three of whom there is every reason to fear have lost their lives at sea on the sailing-packet *Scheldt,* from Antwerp to London, which is believed to have gone down with every soul on board in the great gale of September 30, now nearly two months since.

" You will be surprised that your sister and little girl should be on the seas, but that this should be so was doubtless the Will of God, and in compliance with His ordinances, though directly contrary to my own advice. Had due attention been paid to my wishes this might have been avoided. Here is the account of how it happened, from which you may judge for yourself:

" Your brother-in-law Cropredy's imprudence is no doubt to answer for it, he having run the risk of travelling abroad to put himself in personal communication with a house of business at Malines, a most unwholesome place for an Englishman, though no doubt healthy for foreigners. As I had forewarned him, he contracted fever in the heat of August, when ill-fed on a foreign diet, which, however suitable to them, is fatal to an English stomach, and little better than in France. The news of this illness coming to your sister, she would not be resigned to the Will of Providence, to which we should all bow rather than rashly endanger our lives, but took upon herself to decide, contrary to my remonstrance, to cross the Channel with the little girl, of whom I could have taken charge here at my own home. Merciful to say, the fever left him, having a good constitution from English living, and all was promise of a safe return, seeing the weather was favourable when the ship left the quay, and a fair wind. But of that ship no further is known, only she has not been heard of since, and doubtless is gone to the bottom in the great gale which sprung up in mid-channel, for so many have done the like. Even as the ships of Jehosaphat were broken that they were not able to go to Tarshish (Chron. II. xx. 37).

"There is, I fear, no room for hope that, short of a miracle, for the sea will not give up its dead (Rev. xx. 13), any remains should be recovered, but you may rest assured that if any come to the surface and are identified they shall be interred in the family grave where your sainted mother was laid, and reposes in the Lord, in a sure and certain hope of a joyful resurrection (Acts xxiii. 6).

"Believe me, my dear daughter, to remain your affectionate father

"ISAAC RUNCIMAN.

"I have no message for my son-in-law, nor do I retain any resentment towards him, forgiving him as I wish to be forgiven (Luke vi. 37).

"DARENTH MILL,
   Oct. 16, 1807."

The Earl read this letter through twice—three times—and apparently his bewilderment only increased as he re-read it. At last he refolded it, as though no more light could come from more reading, and sat a moment still, thinking intently. Then he suddenly exclaimed aloud:—"Amazing," adding under his voice:—"But perfectly inexplicable!" Then, going on even less audibly:—"I must see what Hawtrey can make of this. . . ." At which point he was taken aback by a voice through the door from the next room:—"What *are* you talking to yourself so for? Can't you get to bed?" Palpably the voice of an awakened Countess! He replied in a conciliatory spirit, and accepted the suggestion, first putting the letters safely away in the ebony cabinet.

Anyone who reads this forged letter with a full knowledge of all the circumstances will see that it was at best, from the literary and dramatic point of view, a bungling composition. But style was not called for so long as the statements were coherent. For what did the forger's wife know of what her father's style would be under these or any abnormal circumstances? Had she ever had a letter at all from him before? Even that is doubtful. The shock, moreover, was enough to unbalance the most critical judgment.

Two things are very noticeable in the letter. One that it fights shy of stron gexpressions of feeling, as though its fabricator had felt that danger lay that way; the other that he manifestly enjoyed his Scripture references, familiar to him by his long experience of gaol-chaplains, and warranted by his knowledge of his father-in-law. We—who write this—have referred to the passages indicated, and found the connection of ideas to be about an average sample, as coherency goes when quotation from Scripture is afoot. No doubt Maisie's husband found their selection entertaining.

CHAPTER XII

THE LEGAL ACUMEN OF THOTHMES. OF COURSE IT WAS ISAAC RUNCIMAN'S SIGNATURE. THE ANTIPODEAN INK. HOW LINCOLN'S INN FIELDS WAS MADE OF WOOD. HOW GWEN AND HER FATHER CAME OFF THEIR P'S AND Q'S. THE RIDDLE AS GOOD AS SOLVED. HOW GWEN GOT A LIFT TO CAVENDISH SQUARE AND HER MOTHER WENT ON TO HELP TO ABOLISH SOUTH CAROLINA. ANOTHER LIFT, IN A PILL-BOX. SAPPS COURT'S VIEWS OF THE WAR. MICHAEL RAGSTROAR'S HALF-SISTER'S BROTHER-IN-LAW. LIVE EELS. BALL'S POND. MRS. RILEY'S ELEVEN RELATIVES. MRS. TAPPING'S NAVAL CONNECTIONS. OLD BILLY. RUM SHRUB. LOUIS NAPOLEON AND KING SOLOMON. A PARTY IN THE BAR. WHICH WAY DID HE GO?

SAID his lordship next morning to Mr. Norbury, bringing him preliminary tea at eight o'clock:—"I want to catch Mr. Hawtrey before he goes to Lincoln's Inn. Send round to say. . . . No—give me one of my cards and a pencil. . . . There!—send that round at once, because he goes early."

The result was that Mr. Hawtrey was announced while the Earl was having real breakfast with Gwen and her mother at ten, and was shown into the library. Also that the real breakfast was hurried and frustrated, that Mr. Hawtrey should not be kept waiting. For the Earl counter-ordered his last cup of tea, and went away with his fast half broken. So her ladyship sent the cup after him to the library. He sent a message back to Gwen. Would her ladyship be sure not to go out without seeing him? She would.

Mr. Hawtrey was known to Gwen as the Earl's solicitor, a man of perfectly incredible weight and importance. He was deep in the Lord Chancellor's confidence, and had boxes in tiers in his

office, to read the names on which was a Whig and Tory education. If all the acres of land that had made Mr. Hawtrey's acquaintance, somehow or other, had been totalled on condition that
it was fair to count twice over, the total total would have been
as large as Asia, at a rough guess. His clerks—or his firm's,
Humphrey and Hawtrey's—had witnessed leases, wills, transfers,
and powers of attorney, numerous enough to fill the Rolls Office,
but so far as was known none of them had ever been called on to
attest his own signature. Personally, Mr. Hawtrey had always
seemed to Gwen very like an Egyptian God or King, and she
would speak of him as Thothmes and Rameses freely. Her father
admitted the likeness, but protested against her levity, as this gentleman was his most trusted adviser, inherited with his title and
estates. The Earldom of Ancester had always been in the habit
of consulting Mr. Hawtrey about all sorts of things, not necessarily legal.

So when Gwen was sent for to her father's sanctum, and went,
she was not surprised to hear that he had given Mr. Hawtrey all
the particulars she had told him of Mrs. Prichard's history, and
a clear outline of the incidents up to that date, ending with the
seeming insanity of the old lady.. "But," said the Earl, who
appeared very serious, "I have given no names. I have sent for
you now, Gwen, to get your consent to my making no reserves
with Mr. Hawtrey, in whose advice I have great confidence." Mr.
Hawtrey acknowledged this testimony, and Gwen acknowledged
that gentleman's desert; each by a bow, but Gwen's was the more
flexible performance.

She just hung back perceptibly over giving the *carte blanche*
asked for. "I suppose no harm can come of it—to anybody?"
said she. None whatever, apparently; so she assented.

"Very good," said the Earl. "And now, my dear, I want you,
before I show it to Mr. Hawtrey, to read this letter, which I have
opened on my own responsibility—nobody to blame but me! I
found it among your old lady's letters you gave me to take
care of."

"Oh dear!" said Gwen.

"I shall not show it to Mr. Hawtrey, unless you like. Take
it and read it. No hurry." Gwen was conscious that the solicitor
sat as still as his prototype Thothmes at the British Museum, and
with as immovable a countenance.

She took the letter, glancing at the cover. "Who is Mrs. Thornton Daverill?" said she, quite in the dark.

"Go on and read," said the Earl.

Gwen read half to herself:—"'My dear daughter Maisie,'" and then said aloud:—"But that is Mrs. Prichard's name!"

"Read through to the end," said the Earl. And Gwen, with a painful feeling of bewilderment, obeyed orders, puzzling over phrases and sentences to find the thing she was to read for, and staggered a moment by the name "Cropredy," which she thought she must have misread. There was no clue in the letter itself, as she did not know who "Phœbe" and "Ruth" were.

Her father's observation of her face quickened as she visibly neared the end. She was quite taken aback by the signature, the moment it caught her eye. "Isaac Runciman!" she exclaimed. "Why—that's—that's . . ."

"That's the name of Mrs. Marrable's father that old Mrs. Prichard lays claim to for hers," said the Earl quietly. "And this letter is written to his daughter, Mrs. Thornton Daverill, whose name is Maisie. . . . And old Mrs. Prichard's name is Maisie. . . . And this letter is in the keeping of old Mrs. Prichard." He left gaps, for his hearer to understand.

"Good God!" exclaimed Gwen. "Then old Mrs. Prichard is *not* mad." She could only see that much for the moment—no details. "Oh, be quiet a moment and let me think." She dropped the letter, and sat with her face in her hands, as though to shut thought in and work the puzzle out. Her father remained silent, watching her.

Presently he said, quietly still, as though to help her:—"Norbury told me last night what we did not know, that old Mrs. Marrable's name is Phœbe, and that Widow Thrale's is Ruth. . . ."

"That old Mrs. Marrable is Phœbe and her daughter is Ruth." Gwen repeated his words, as though learning a lesson, still with her fingers crushing her eyes.

"And that Ruth is not really Phœbe's daughter but her niece. And, according to Norbury, she is the daughter of a twin sister, whose husband was transported for forgery, and who followed him to Van Diemen's Land, and died there." He raised his voice slightly to say this.

A more amazed face than Gwen's when she withdrew her fingers to fix her startled eyes upon her father, would have been almost as hard to find as a more beautiful one.

"But that *is* Mrs. Prichard, papa dear," she gasped. "Don't you *know?* The story I told you!"

"Exactly!" said the Earl.

"But the letter—the letter! Phœbe and Ruth in the letter *cannot* be drowned, if they are Granny Marrable and Widow

Thrale." A rapid phantasmagoria of possibilities and impossibilities shot through her mind. How could order come of such a chaos?

"Excuse me," said Thothmes, speaking for the first time. "Do I understand—I assume I am admitted to confidence—do I understand that the letter states that these two women were drowned?"

"Crossing from Antwerp. Yes!"

"Then the letter is a falsehood, probably written with a bad motive."

"But by their father—their father! Impossible!"

"How does your ladyship know it was written by their father?"

"It is signed by their father—at Darenth Mill in Essex. Both say Isaac Runciman was their father."

"It is signed with Isaac Runciman's name—so I understand. Is it certain that it was signed by Isaac Runciman? May I now see the letter? *And* the envelope, please!—oh, the direction is on the back, of course." He held the letter in front of him, but apparently took very little notice of it. "As if," thought Gwen to herself, "he was thinking about his Dynasty."

"What do you make of it, Hawtrey?" said the Earl, but, getting no answer, waited. Silence ensued.

"*Yes,*" said the lawyer, breaking it suddenly. He seemed to have seen his way. "Now may I ask whether we have any means of knowing what the forgery was for which this man was transported?"

"Oh yes!" said Gwen. "Old Mrs. Prichard told me what he was accused of, at least. Forging an acceptance—if that's right? I think that was it."

"But whose signature? Did she say?"

"Oh yes—I made her tell me, her father's." Then Gwen fitted the name, just heard, into its place in old Mrs. Prichard's tale, and was illuminated. "I see what you think, Mr. Hawtrey," said she, interrupting herself. The lawyer was examining the direction on the letter-sheet.

"I think I did right to pry into the letter, Gwennie," said her father; seeking, nevertheless, a salve for conscience.

"Of course you did, you darling old thing! . . . What, Mr. Hawtrey? You were going to say? . . ."

"I was going to say had you seen an odd thing in the direction. Have you noticed that the word *Hobart* has kept black, and all the rest has faded to the colour of the writing inside?" So it had, without a doubt, inexplicably. Mr. Hawtrey's impression was that the word was written in a different hand, perhaps filled in by someone who had been able to supply the name correctly, having been entrusted the letter to forward.

" But," said he, " the person who wrote Hobart must have been in England, and the forger of the letter was certainly in Van Diemen's Land."

" Why ' must have been in England ' ? "

" Bless the girl ! " said the girl's father. " Why—*I* can see that ! Of course, an Australian convict, who could do such a fine piece of forgery, would never ask another person to spell the name of an Australian town. Do you suppose he sent it to England to get an accomplice to spell ' Hobart ' right for him ? No—no, Hawtrey, your theory won't hold water."

" That is the case," said Thothmes, more immovably than ever. " I see I was mistaken. That point must wait. Or . . . stop one minute ! . . . may we examine the other letters ? "

" I had thought," said the Earl, " of leaving them unopened. We have got what we want."

" Very proper. But I only wish to read the directions." No harm in this, anyhow. A second packet was opened. It was the one in the woman's hand, all postmarked " Darenth Mill " and " Macquarie." Then it was that Thothmes, with impassive shrewdness, made up for his blunder, with interest. He saw why the ink of one word of the forged direction was black. It was the same ink as the English directions, and, on close examination, the same hand. This had not been clear at first, as the word was mixed with the English postmark, " Darenth Mill "—so much so as not to clash with the pale hand of the forgery. " That word," said Thothmes, " was never written in Van Diemen's Land. The English stamp is on the top of it."

Gwen took it from him, and saw that this was true. " But then the rest of the direction was written in Australia," said she, " if this man wrote it at all ! Oh dear, I am so puzzled." And indeed she was at her wit's end.

" I won't say another word," said Mr. Hawtrey. " I have made one blunder, and won't run any further risks. I must think about this. If you will trust me with the letter, you shall have it back to-morrow morning. I dare say your lordship will now excuse me. I have an appointment at the High Court at eleven, and it's now a quarter past. . . . Oh no—it's not a hanging matter. . . . I shall make my man drive fast. . . . So I will wish your ladyship a very good morning. I wish those two old ladies could have known this earlier. But better late than never ! "

The Earl accompanied his legal adviser to the head of the stairs to give him a civil send off, while his daughter, white with tension of excitement and impatience, awaited his return. Coming back, he was not the least surprised that she should fall into his arms with a tempest of tears, crying out:—" Oh, papa dearest —fifty years!—think of it! All their lives! Oh, my darling old Mrs. Prichard! and Granny Marrable too—it's the same for both! Oh, think, that they were girls—yes, nearly girls, only a few years older than me, when they parted! And the *horrible* wickedness of the trick—the horrible, horrible wickedness! And then the dear old darling's own daughter, who has almost never seen her, thinks her *mad! . . .* No, papa dear, don't shish me down, because cry I *must!* Let me have a good cry over it, and I shall be better. Sit down by me, and don't let go—there!—here on the sofa, like that. . . . Oh dear, I wish I was made of wood, like some people, and could say better late than never!" This was the wind-up of a good deal more, and similar, expression of feeling. For tears and speech come easily to a generous impulsive nature like Gwen's, when strong sympathy and sorrow for others bid them come, though its own affliction might have made it stupefied and dumb.

Her father soothed and calmed her as he would a child; for was she not a child to him—in the nursery only the other day? I'm not made of wood, darling, am I?" said he. And Gwen replied, refitting spars in calmer water:—"No, dear, that you are not, but Lincoln's Inn Fields is. Sitting there like an Egyptian God, with his hands on his knees!" She repacked a stray flood of gold that had escaped from its restraints—the most conspicuous record of the recent gale—and reassured her father with a liberal kiss. Then she thawed towards the legal mind. "I'm sure he's very good and kind and all that—Lincoln's Inn Fields, I mean, is—because people *are.* Only it's at heart they are, and I want it to come out like a rash." No doubt an interview with Dr. Dalrymple yesterday was answerable for this, having reference to the Typhus Fever patient. The eruption, he said, was subsiding favourably, and he was hourly expecting a fall in the temperature. But he had made a stand against her seeing the patient.

"If Hawtrey came out in a rash over all his clients' botherations," said the Earl, "he would very soon be in a state of confluent smallpox. What he's wanted for now is his brains. You'll see we shall have a letter from him, clearing it all up. . . ."

"And you know what he'll say, I suppose? That is, if he's as clever as you think him!"

"I can't say that I feel absolutely certain. What do you suppose?"

Then Gwen gave a very fair conjectural review of the facts as this story knows them; saying, whenever she felt the ground insecure beneath her feet, that of course it was this way and not the other. A blessed expression that, to reinforce one's convictions!

However, she was not far wrong on any point, if the letter her father received next day from "Lincoln's Inn Fields" was right. It came by messenger, just as the family were sitting down to lunch with two or three friends, and his lordship said, "Will you excuse me?" without waiting for an answer, though one of his guests was a Rajah. Then he read the letter through, intently, while his Countess looked thunderclouds at him. "'Fore God, they are both of a tale!" said he, quoting. Then he sent it to Gwen by Norbury, who was embarrassed by her ladyship the Countess saying stiffly:—"Surely afterwards would do." But Gwen cut in with:—"No—I can't wait. Give it to me, Norbury!" And took it and read it as intently as her father had done. Having finished, she telegraphed to him, all the length of the table:—"Isn't that just what I said?" And then things went on as before. Only the Earl and his daughter had come off their P's and Q's, most lawlessly.

Here is the letter each had read, when off them:

"MY DEAR LORD ANCESTER,

"I have thoroughly considered the letter, and return it herewith. I am satisfied that it is a forgery by the hand of the convict Daverill, but it is difficult to see what his object can have been, malice apart. It is clear, however, that it was to influence his wife, to what end it is impossible to say.

"The only theory I can have about the black ink is far-fetched. It is that a letter from England of that date was erased to make way for the forgery, these few black letters having been allowed to remain, not to disturb the English postmark, which partly-obscures them. You may notice some compromise or accommodation in the handwriting of the direction, evidently to slur over the difference. I suggest that the letter should be referred to some specialist in palimpsests, who may be able to detect some of the underlying original, which is absolutely invisible to me.

"If you meet with any other letter written by this ingenious penman, I suspect it will be in the pale ink of the forgery, which no doubt was as black as the English ink, when new.

"Believe me, my lord, your very faithful and obedient servant,
"JAMES HAWTREY."

"There can't be another letter of the ingenious penman's in the lot we left tied up, because he and his wife were living together, and not writing each other letters." So said Gwen afterwards, deprecating a suggestion of her father's that the packet should be opened and examined. But he replied:—"It is only to look at the colour of the ink. We won't read old Mrs. Prichard's love-letters." However, nothing was found, all these letters having been written in England except the one from Sydney inviting her to come out, which was referred to early in this story. The Sydney ink had been different—that was all.

So all the letters were tied up again and placed *pro tem.* in the cinquecento cabinet, to be quite safe. They had been just about to vanish therein when the Earl made his suggestion. Nothing having come of it, the documents were put away, honourably unread, and Gwen hurried off to be given a lift to Cavendish Square by her mother. Her father exacted a promise from her that she would not force her way past Dr. Dalrymple into the patient's presence, come what might! She accompanied her mother in the carriage as far as her own destination. The Countess was on a card-leaving mission in Harley Street, and devoutly hoped that Lady Blank would not be at home. In that case she might take advantage of her liberty to go to a meeting at the Duchess of Sutherland's to abolish this horrible negro slavery in America, so as not to be exceptional, which was odious; and your father— Gwen's to wit—never would exert himself about anything, and was simply wrapped up in old violins and majolica. Of course it was right to put an end to slavery, and people *ought* to exert themselves. Her ladyship waited in the carriage at the door till Gwen could supply an intensely authentic report—not what the servants were told to say to everybody; that was no use—of the precise condition of the patient, including the figures of the pulse and temperature, and whether she had had a good night. Gwen came back with a report from the nurse, to find Dr. Dalrymple conversing with her mother at the carriage door, and to be exhorted by him to follow her maternal example in matters of prudence. For the good lady had furnished herself with a smelling-bottle and was inhaling it religiously, as a prophylactic.

When she had departed, leaving Gwen wondering why on earth she was seized with such a desire just now to abolish negro slavery, Gwen returned into the house to await the doctor's last word about her friend. Waiting for him in the sitting-room, she read the *Times,* and naturally turned to the news from the Seat of War— it was then at its height—and became engrossed in the details

of the Balaklava charge, a month since. The tragedy of the
Crimea—every war is a tragedy—was at this time the all-engross-
ing topic in London and Paris, and men hung eagerly on every
word that passed current as news. The reason it has so little
place in this story is obvious—none of the essential events intersect. All our narrative has to tell relates to occurrences prede-
termined by a past that was forgotten long before Sebastopol was
anticipated.

Gwen read the story of the great historical charge with a breathless interest certainly, but only as part of the playbill of a terrible drama, where the curtain was to fall on fireworks and a triumph for her own nationality; and, of course, its ally—*ça se vit*.
Dr. Dalrymple reappeared, looking hopeful, with a good report,
but too engrossed in his case to be moved even by the Charge of
the Light Brigade, or the state of the hospitals at Scutari. Where
was Gwen going? To Sapps Court—where was that? Oh yes,
just beyond his own destination, so he could give her a lift. And
the carriage could take her on to hers and wait for her, just as
easily as go home and come back for him. He might be detained
a long time at the Hospital. Gwen accepted his offer gratefully,
as a private brougham and a coachman made a sort of convoy.
In those days young ladies were not so much at their ease without an escort, as they have been of late years. According to some
authorities, the new régime is entirely due to the bicycle.

Sapps Court had not been itself since the exciting event of the
accident; at least, so said Aunt M'riar, referring to the disappearance of Mrs. Prichard chiefly. For the identity of Sapps depended a good deal on the identity of its inhabitants, and its interests penetrated very little into the great world without. It was
very little affected even by the news of the War, favourable or
the reverse: its patriotism was too great for that. This must
be taken to mean that its confidence in its country's power of
routing its foes was so deep-seated that an equally firm belief
that its armies were starving and stricken with epidemics, and
armed with guns that would not go off, and commanded by the
lame, halt, and blind in their second childhood, did not in the
least interfere with its stability. Whatever happened, the indomitable courage of Tommy Atkins and Jack would triumph over
foes, who, when all was said and done, were only foreigners. Sapps
Court's faith in Jack was so great that his position was even
above Tommy's. When Jack was reported to have gone ashore
at Balaklava to help Tommy to get his effete and useless artillery

to bear on the walls of Sebastopol, Sapps Court drew a long breath of relief. Misgivings were germinating in its bosom as to whether cholera patients *could* take fortresses on an empty stomach. But it would be all right now!

No doubt the Court's philosophical endurance of its share of the anxiety about the War was partly due to the fact that it hadn't got no relations there; or, at least, none to speak of. Michael Ragstroar's 'arf-sister's brother-in-law had certainly took the shilling, but Michael's father had expressed the opinion that this young man wouldn't do no good soldiering, and would only be in the way. Which had led Michael to say that this connection of his by marriage would ultimately get himself cashiered by Court Martial, for 'inderin'. Much better have stuck to chopping up live heels and makin' of 'em into pies at Ball's Pond, than go seeking glory at the cannon's mouth! Michael had not reflected on the comparative freedom of his own life, contrasted with the monotonous lot of this ill-starred young man; if, indeed, we may safely accept Micky's description of it as accurate. Sapps Court did so, and went on in the belief that the Ball's Pond recruit would prove a *gêne* upon the movements of the allied troops in the Crimea.

The interest of the Court, therefore, in the contemporary events which were thrilling the remainder of Europe, was ethical or strategical, and one had to go outside its limits to be brought into touch with personal connecting links. But they were to be met with near at hand, for Mrs. Riley had ilivin relatives at the Sate of War, sivin of her own name, thray Donnigans, and one O'Rourke, a swate boy, though indade only a fosther-brother of her nayce Kathleen McDermott. Mrs. Tapping was unable to enumerate any near relations serving Her Majesty, but laid claim to consanguinity with distinguished officers, Generals of Division and Captains of three-deckers, all of whom had an exalted opinion of her own branch of the Family.

In the main, Sapps regarded the War as a mere Thing in the Newspapers, of which Uncle Mo heard more accurate details, at The Sun. There is nothing more unaccountable than the alacrity with which the human mind receives any statement in print, unless it is its readiness to surrender its belief on hearing a positive contradiction from a person who cannot possibly know anything about the matter. One sometimes feels forced to the conclusion that an absolute disqualification to speak on any subject is a condition precedent of procuring belief. Certainly a claim to inspiration enlists disciples quicker than the most subtle argument; acts, so to speak, as an aperient to the mind—a sort of intellectual Epsom Salts. Uncle Mo, in the simplicity of his heart, went every day for an hour to The Sun parlour, taking with him a profound belief in the latest news from the Seat of War, to have it shattered for him by the positive statements of persons who had probably not read the papers at all, and sometimes couldn't. For in those happy days there were still people who were unable to read or write.

Perhaps the only other customer in the parlour at The Sun, when Uncle Mo was smoking his pipe there, on the afternoon which saw the Countess interest herself in negro slavery, *was* able to read and write, unknown to his friends, who had never seen him do either. They, however, knew, or professed to feel assured, that old Billy—for that was his only ascertainable name—knew everything. This may have been their vulgar fun; but if it was, old Billy's own convictions of his omniscience were not shaken by it, any more than a creed he professed, that small doses of rum shrub, took reg'lar, kept off old age. In a certain sense he took them regularly, counting the same number in every bar, with nearly the same pauses between each dose. Whether they were really helping him against Time and Decay or not, they were making him pink and dropsical, and had not prevented, if they had not helped to produce, a baldness as of an eggshell. This he would cover in, to counteract the draughty character which he ascribed to all bar parlours alike, with a cloth cap having ear-flaps, as soon as ever he had hung up a beaver hat which he might have inherited from a coaching ancestor.

This afternoon he was eloquent on foreign policy. Closing one eye to accentuate the shrewd vision of the other, and shaking his head continuously to express the steadiness and persistency of his convictions, he indicted Louis Napoleon as the *bête noire* of European politics. "Don't you let yourself be took in, Mr. Moses," he said, "by any of these here noospapers. They're a bad lot. This here Nicholas, he's a Rooshian—so him I say nothin' about. Nor yet these here Turkeys—them and their Constant Eye No Pulls!"—this with great scorn. "None of 'em no better, I lay, than Goard A'mighty see fit to make 'em, so it ain't, so as you might say, their own fault, not in a manner of speaking. But this Louis Sneapoleum, *he's* your sly customer. He's as bad as the whole lot, all boiled up together in a stoo! Don't you be took in by him, Mr. Moses. Calls hisself a Coodytar! *I* call him . . ." etcetera *de rigueur*, as some of old Billy's comparisons were unsavoury.

"Can't foller you all the way down the lane, Willy-um," said Uncle Mo, who could hardly be expected to identify Billy's variant of *Coup d'Etat.* "Ain't he our ally?" .

"That's the p'int, Mr. Moses, the very p'int to not lose sight on, or where are we? He's got hisself made our ally for to get between him and the Rooshians. What he's a-drivin' at is to get us to fight his battles for him, and him to sit snug and accoomulate cucumbers like King Solomons."

Uncle Moses felt he ought to interpose on this revision of the Authorised Version of Scripture. "You haven't hit the word in the middle, mate," said he, and supplied it, correctly enough. "You can keep it in mind by thinking of them spiky beggars at the So-logical Gardens—porky pines—them as get their backs up when wexed and bristle."

"Well—corkupines, then! Have it your own way, old Mo! My back'd get up and bristle, if I was some of them! Only when it's womankind, the likes of us can't jedge, especially when French. All I can say is, him and them's got to settle it between 'em, and if *they* can stand his blooming moostarsh, why, it's no affair of mine." Which was so obviously true that old Billy need not have gone on muttering to himself to the same effect. One would have thought that the Tuileries had applied to him to accept an appointment as *Censor Morum.*

"What's old Billy grizzlin' on about?" said Mr. Jeffcoat, the host of The Sun, bringing in another go of the shrub, and a modest small pewter of mild for Uncle Mo, who was welcome at this hostelry even when, as sometimes happened, he drank nothing; so powerful was his moral influence on its status. In fact, the Sporting World, which drank freely, frequented its parlour merely to touch the hand of the great heavyweight of other days, however much he was faded and all his glories past. Then would Uncle Mo give a sketch of his celebrated scrap with Bob Brettle, which ended in neither coming to Time, simultaneously. Mo would complain of an absurd newspaper report of the fight, which said the Umpires stopped the fight. "No such a thing!" said Uncle Mo. "I stopped Bob and he stopped me, fair and square. And there we was, come to grass, and stopping there." Perhaps the old boy was dreaming back on something of this sort, rather than listening to boozy old Billy's reflections on Imperial Morality, that Mr. Jeffcoat should have repeated again:—"What's old Billy grizzling about? You pay for both, Mr. Moses? Fourpence half-penny, thank you!"

"He's letting out at the Emperor of the French, is Billy. He'd do his dags for him, Billy would, if he could get at him. Wouldn't you, Billy? I say, Tim, whose voice was that I heard in the Bar just now, naming me by name?"

"Ah, I was just on telling you. He walks in and he says to me, when does Moses Wardle come in here, he says, and how long does he stop, mostly? And I says to him . . ."

"What sort of a feller to look at?" said Uncle Mo, interrupting. "Old or young? Long? Short? Anything about him to go by?"

This called for consideration. "Not what you would call an average party. His gills was too much slewed to one side." This was illustrated by a finger hooking down the corner of the mouth. "Looked as if his best clothes was being took care of for him."

"What did he want o' me?" Uncle Mo's interest seemed roused.

"I was telling of you. When did you come and how long did you stop? Best part of an hour, I says, and you was here now. You'll find him in the parlour, I says. Go in and see, I says. And I thought to find him in here, having took my eyes off him for the moment."

"He's not been in here," said Uncle Mo, emptying his pipe prematurely, and apparently hurrying off without taking his half of mild. "Which way did he go?"

"Which way did the party go, Soozann?" said the host to his wife in the bar. Who replied:—"Couldn't say. Said he'd be back in half an hour, and went. Fancy he went to the right, but couldn't say."

"He won't be back in half an hour," said Uncle Mo. "Not if he's the man I take him for. You see, he's one of these here chaps that tells lies. You've heard o' them; seen one, p'r'aps?"

Mr. Jeffcoat testified that he had, in his youth, and that rumours of their existence still reached him at odd times. Those who listen about in the byways of London will hear endless conversation on this model, always conducted with the most solemn gravity, with a perfect understanding of its inversions and perversions.

Uncle Mo hurried away, leaving instructions that his half-pint should be bestowed on any person whose tastes lay in that direction. Mr. Jeffcoat might meet with such a one. You never could tell. He hastened home as fast as his enemy Gout permitted, and saw when he turned into the short street at the end of which Sapps lay hidden, that something abnormal was afoot. There stood Dr. Dalrymple's pill-box, wondering, no doubt, why it had carried a segment of an upper circle to such a Court as this. If it had been the Doctor himself, it would not have given a thought to the matter, for it used to bear its owner to all sorts of places, from St. James's Palace to Seven Dials.

CHAPTER XIII

HOW UNCLE MO WAS JUST TOO LATE. THE SHINY LADY. THE TURN
THE MAN HAD GIVEN AUNT M'RIAR, AND HER APOLOGIES. DOLLY'S
INTENDED HOSPITALITY TO MRS. PRICHARD ON HER RETURN. DOLLY'S
DOLLY'S NEW NAME. AN ARRANGEMENT, COMMITTING NEITHER
PARTY. GUINEVERE, LANCELOT, AND THE CAKE. MRS. PRICHARD
INSANE?—THE IDEA! HOW GWEN READ THE LETTER ALL BUT THE
POSTSCRIPT. NOTHING FOR IT BUT TO TELL! BUT HOW? FUN,
TELLING THE CHILDREN. ANOTHER RECHRISTENING OF DOLLY.
GWEN'S LAST EXIT FROM MRS. PRICHARD'S APARTMENTS. JOAN OF
ARC'S SWORD'S SOUL. THE POSTSCRIPT. WIDOW THRALE'S DOG.
WHAT THE CONVICT HAD SAID. HOW LONG DOES BONA-FIDE OM-
NIPOTENCE TAKE OVER A JOB?

GWEN, leaving her convoy to wait for her in the antechamber of Sapps Court, and approach No. 7 alone, heard as she knocked at the door an altercation within; Aunt M'riar's voice and a strange one, with terror in the former and threat in the latter. Had all sounded peaceful, she might have held back, to allow the interview to terminate. But catching the sound of fear in the woman's voice, and having none in her own composition, she immediately delivered a double-knock of the most unflinching sort, and followed it by pushing open the door.

She could hear Dave above, at the top window, recognising her as "The Lady." As she entered, a man who was coming out flinched before her meanly for a moment, then brushed past brutally. Aunt M'riar's face was visible where she stood back near the staircase; it was white with terror. She gasped out:—"Let him go; I'll come directly!" and ran upstairs. Gwen heard her call to the children, more collectedly, to come down, as the lady was there, and then apparently retreat into her room, shutting the door. Thereon the children came rushing down, and before she could get attention to her inquiry as to who that hideous man was, Uncle Mo had pushed the door open. He had not asked that pill-box to explain itself, but had gone straight on to No. 7. Dave met him on the threshold, in a tempest of excitement, exclaim-

ing:—" Oy say, Uncle Mo!—the lady's here. The shoyny one.
And oy say, Uncle Mo, the Man's been." The last words were
in a tone to themselves, quite unlike what came before. It was as
though Dave had said:—" The millennium has come, but the crops
are spoiled." He added:—" Oy saw the Man, out of the top window, going away."

Uncle Mo let the millennium stand over. " Which man, old
Peppermint Drops? " said he, improvising a name to express an
aroma he had detected in his nephew, when he stooped to make
sure he was getting his last words right.

" Whoy, the Man," Dave continued, in an undertone that might
have related to the Man with the Iron Mask, " the Man me and
Micky we sore in Hoyde Park, and said he was a-going to rip
Micky up, and Micky he said he should call the Police-Orficers,
and the gentleman said . . ."

" That'll do prime! " said Uncle Mo. For Dave's torrent of
identification was superfluous. " I would have laid a guinea I
knew his game," added he to himself. Then to Gwen, inside the
house with Dolly on her knee:—" You'll excuse me, miss, my
lady, these young customers they do insert theirselves—it's none
so easy to find a way round 'em, as I say to M'riar. . . . M'riar
gone out? " For it was a surprise to find the children alone entertaining company—and such company!

" There, Dolly, you hear? " said Gwen. " You're not to insert
yourself between me and your uncle. Suppose we sit quiet for
five minutes! " Dolly subsided. " How do you do, Mr. Wardle! . . . No, Aunt Maria isn't here, and I'm afraid that man
coming worried her. Dave's man. . . . Oh yes—I saw him. He
came out as I came in, three minutes ago. What *is* the man?
Didn't I hear Dave telling how Micky said he should give him
to the Police? I wish Micky had, and the Police had found out
who he's murdered. Because he's murdered somebody, that man!
I saw it in his eyes."

" He's a bad character," said Mo. " If he don't get locked up,
it won't be any fault of mine. On'y that'll be after I've squared
a little account I have against him—private affair of my own. If
you'll excuse me half a minute, I'll go up and see what's got
M'riar." But Uncle Mo was stopped at the stair-foot by the reappearance of Aunt M'riar at the stair-top. As they met halfway
up, both paused, and Gwen heard what it was easy to guess was
Aunt M'riar's tale of " the Man's " visit, and Uncle Mo's indignation. They must have conversed thus in earnest undertones for
full five minutes, before Aunt M'riar said audibly:—" Now we

mustn't keep the lady waiting no longer, Mo"; and both returned, making profuse apologies. The interval of their absence had been successfully and profitably filled in by an account of how Mrs. Picture had been taken to see Jones's Bull, with a rough sketch of the Bull's demeanour in her company.

Aunt M'riar made amends to the best of her abilities for her desertion. Perhaps the young lady knew what she meant when she said she had been giv' rather a turn? The young lady did indeed. Aunt M'riar hoped she had not been alarmed by her exit. Nor by the person who had gone out? No—Gwen's nerves had survived both, though certainly the person wasn't a beauty. She went on to hope that the effects of the turn he had given Aunt M'riar would not be permanent. These being pooh-poohed by both Uncle Mo and Aunt M'riar, became negligible and lapsed.

"The children came running down directly after you went, Aunt Maria," said Gwen. "So I can assure you I didn't lose my temper at being left alone. I wasn't alone two minutes!" Then she gave, in reply to a general inquiry after the fever patient, inaugurated by Dave with:—"Oy say, how's Sister Nora?"—the very favourable report she had just received from Dr. Dalrymple.

Then Mrs. Prichard was rushed into the conversation by a sudden inexplicable statement of Dolly's. "When Mrs. Spicture comes back," said she, "Granny Marrowbone is to pour out Mrs. Spicture's tea. And real Cake. And stoast cut in sloyces wiv real butter."

"Don't get excited, Dolly dear," said Gwen, protesting against the amount of leg-action that accompanied this ukase. "Tell us again! *Why* is Granny Marrable to make tea? Granny Marrable's at her house in the country. She's not coming here with Mrs. Spicture."

"There, now, Dolly!" said Aunt M'riar. "Why don't you tell clear, a bit at a time, and get yourself understood? Granny Marrowbone's the new name, my lady, she's christened her doll, Dolly. So she should be known apart, Dolly being, as you might say, Dolly herself. Because her uncle he pointed out to her, 'Dolly,' he said, 'you're in for thinkin' out some new name for this here baby of yours, to say which is which. Or 'us you'll get that mixed up, nobody'll know!'"

"I put my oar in," said Uncle Mo, "for to avoid what they call coarmplications nowadays." He never lost an opportunity of hinting at the fallings off of the Age. "So she and Dave they

turns to and thinks one out. I should have felt more like Sally
or Sooky or Martilda myself. Or Queen Wictoria." The last
was a gracious concession to Her Majesty; who, in the eyes of
Uncle Mo, had recently come to the throne.
"No!" said Dolly firmly. "Gwanny Mawwowbone!" This
was very articulately delivered, the previous, or slipshod, pronunciation having been more nearly Granny Mallowbone.
"Certainly!" said Gwen, assenting. "Dolly's dolly Dolly shall
be Granny Marrowbone. Only it makes Dolly out rather old."
Dolly seemed to take exception to this. "I *was* four on my
birfday," said she. "I shan't be five not till my *next* birfday, such
a long, long, long, long time."
"And you'll stop four till you're five," said Gwen. "Won't
you, Dolly dear? What very blue eyes the little person has!"
They were fixed on the speaker with all the solemnity the contemplation of a geological period of Time inspires. The little person nodded gravely—about the Time, not about her eyes—and
said:—"Ass!"
Dave thrust himself forward as an interpreter of Dolly's secret
wishes, saying, to the astonishment of his aunt and uncle:—
"Dorly wants to take *her* upstairs to show *her* where the
tea's to be set out when Mrs. Spicture comes back."
Remonstrance was absolutely necessary, but what form could
it take? Aunt M'riar was forced back on her usual resource,
her lack of previous experience of a similar enormity:—"Well,
I'm sure, a big boy like you to call a lady *her!* I never did, in
all my born days!" Uncle Mo meanly threw the responsibility of
the terms of an absolutely necessary amendment on the culprit
himself, saying:—"You're a nice young monkey! Where's your
manners? Is that what they larn you to say at school? What's
a lady's name when you speak to her?" He had no one but himself to thank for the consequences. Dave, who, jointly with Dolly,
was just then on the most intimate footing with the young lady,
responded point-blank:—"Well—*Gwen*, then! *She* said so. Sister Gwen."
Her young ladyship's laugh rang out with such musical cordiality that the two horror-stricken faces relaxed, and Uncle Mo's
got so far as the beginning of a smile. "It's all quite right,"
said Gwen. "I told Dave I was Gwen just this minute when you
were upstairs. He's made it 'sister'—so we shan't be compromised, either of us." Whereupon Dave, quite in the dark, assented from sheer courtesy.
Aunt M'riar seemed to think it a reasonable arrangement, and

Uncle Mo, with a twinkle in his eye, said:—"It's better than hol- lerin' out 'she' and 'her,' like a porter at a railway-station."

But her ladyship had not come solely to have a symposium with Dave and Dolly. So she suggested that both should go upstairs and rehearse the slaughter of the fatted calf; that is to say, dis- tribute the apparatus of the banquet that was to welcome Mrs. Picture back. Dave demurred at first, on the score of his ma- turity, but gave way when an appeal was made to some equivalent of patriotism whose existence was taken for granted; and con- sented, as it were, to act on the Committee.

"Now, don't you come running down to say it's ready, not till I give leave," said Aunt M'riar, having misgivings that the ap- paratus might not be sufficiently—suppose we affect a knowl- edge of Horace, and say "Persian"—to keep the Committee employed.

"They'll be quiet enough for a bit," said Uncle Mo. Who showed insight by adding:—"They won't agree about where the things are to be put, nor what's to be the cake." For a proxy had to be found, to represent the cake. Even so Lancelot stood at the altar with Guinevere, as Arthur's understudy for the part of bridegroom.

"Do please now all sit down and be comfortable," said Gwen, as soon as tranquillity reigned. "Because I want to talk a great deal. . . . Yes—about Mrs. Prichard. I really should be com- fortabler if you sat down. . . . Well—Mr. Wardle can sit on the table if he likes." So that compromise was made, and Gwen got to business. "I really hardly know how to begin telling you," she said. "What has happened is so very *odd*. . . . Oh no—I have seen to *that*. The woman she is with will take every care of her. . . . You know—Widow Thrale, Dave's Granny's daugh- ter, who had charge of Dave—Strides Cottage, of course! I'm sure she'll all right as far as that goes. But the whole thing is so *odd*. . . . Stop a minute!—perhaps the best way would be for me to read you Mrs. Thrale's letter that she has written me. She must be very nice." This throwing of the burden of disclosure on her correspondent seemed to Gwen to be on the line of least resistance. She was feeling bewildered already as to how on earth the two old sisters could be revealed to one another, and her mind was casting about for any and every guidance from any quarter that could lead her to the revelation naturally. There *was* no quarter but Sapps Court. So try it, at least!

She read straight on without interruption, except for expressions of approval or concurrence from her hearers when they heard the writer's declaration of how *impressionnée* she had been by the old lady, until she came to the first reference to the gist of the letter, her mental soundness. Then both broke into protest. "Delusions!" they exclaimed at once. Old Mrs. Prichard subject to delusions? Not she! Never was a saner woman, of her years, than old Mrs. Prichard!

"I only wish," said Uncle Mo, "that I may never be no madder than Goody Prichard. Why, it's enough to convince you she's in her senses only to hear her say good-arternoon!" This meant that Uncle Mo's visits upstairs had always been late in the day, and that her greeting to him would have impressed him with her sanity, had it ever been called in question.

"On'y fancy!" said Aunt M'riar indignantly. "To say Mrs. Prichard's deluded, and her living upstairs with Mrs. Burr this three years past, and Skillicks for more than that, afore ever she come here!" This only wanted the addition that Mrs. Burr had seen no sign of insanity in all these years, to be logical and intelligible.

Gwen found no fault, because she saw what was meant. But there was need for a caution. "You won't say anything of this till I tell you," said she. "Not even to Mrs. Burr. It would only make her uncomfortable." For why should all the old lady's belongings be put on the alert to discover flaws in her understanding? Uncle Mo and Aunt M'riar gave the pledge asked for, and Gwen went on reading. They just recognised the water-mill as an acquaintance of last year—not as a subject of frequent conversation with Dave. Aunt M'riar seemed greatly impressed with the old lady's excursion out of bed to get at the mill-model, especially at its having occurred before six in the morning. Also by the dog.

Uncle Mo was more practically observant. When the reading came to the two mills in Essex, he turned to Aunt M'riar, saying:—"She said summat about Essex—you told me." Aunt M'riar said:—"Well, now, I couldn't say!" in the true manner of a disappointing witness. But when, some sentences later, the reference came to the two little girl twins, Uncle Mo suddenly broke in with:—"Hullo! . . . Never mind!—go on"; as apologizing for his interruption. Later still, unable to constrain himself any longer:—"Didn't—you—tell—me, M'riar, that Mrs. P. she told you her father lived at Darenth in Essex?"

"No, Mo, that's not the name. *Durrant* was the name she said." Aunt M'riar was straining at a gnat. However, solemn bigwigs have done that before now.

"Nigh enough for most folks," said Uncle Mo. "Just you think a bit and see what she said her father's name was."

"She never said his name, Mo. She never said a single name to me, not that I can call to mind, not except it was Durrant."

"Very well, then, M'riar! Now I come to my point. Didn't —you—tell—me—a'most the very first time you did anything— didn't you tell me Mrs. P. she said she was a *twin*. And Dave he made enquiries."

"She *was* a twin."

"I'm stumped," said Uncle Mo. "I was always groggy over the guessing of co-nundrums. Now, miss—my lady—what does your ladyship make of it?"

"Let me read to the end," said Gwen. "It's not very long now. Then I'll tell you." She read on and finished the letter, all but the postscript. She was saying to herself:—"If I stick so over telling these good people now, what will it be when the crisis comes?" It would be good practice, anyhow, to drive it home to Aunt M'riar. When she had quite finished what she meant to read, she went straight on, as she had promised, ignoring obstacles:—"The explanation is that Mrs. Marrable and Mrs. Prichard are twin sisters, who parted fifty years ago. About five years later Mrs. Prichard was deceived by a forged letter, telling her that her sister was drowned. My father and I found it among her papers, and read it. This Mrs. Thrale who writes to me is her own daughter, whom she left in England nearly fifty years since—a baby! . . . And now she thinks her mother mad—her own mother! . . . Oh dear!—how will they ever know? Who will tell them?"

A low whistle and a gasp respectively were all that Uncle Mo and Aunt M'riar were good for. A reissue of the gasp might have become "Merciful Gracious!" or some equivalent, if Uncle Mo had not nipped it in the bud, thereby to provide a fulcrum for his own speech. "'Arf a minute, M'riar! Your turn next. I want to be clear, miss—my lady—that I've got the record ack-rate. These here two ladies have been twins all their lives, unbe- known. . . ." Uncle Mo was so bewildered that this amount of confusion was excusable.

Gwen took his meaning, instead of criticizing his form. "Not *all* their lives," she said. "Fifty years ago they were thirty, and it's all happened since then." She went over the ground again, not letting her hearers off even the most incredible of the facts. She was surprised and relieved to find that they seemed able to receive them, only noticing that they appeared to lean on her superior judgment. They were dumfoundered, of course; but they *could* believe, with such a helper for their unbelief. Were not the deep-rooted faiths of maturity, once, the child's readiness to believe its parents infallible, and would not any other indoctrination have held as firmly? Even so the rather childish minds of Dave's guardians made no question of the credibility of the tale, coming as it did from such an informant—one without a shadow of interest in the fabrication of it.

Aunt M'riar made no attempt at anything beyond mere exclamation; until, after the second detailed review of the facts, Gwen was taken aback by her saying suddenly:—" Won't it be a'most cruel, when you come to think of it? . . ."

" Won't what be cruel, Aunt M'riar? "

" For to tell 'em. Two such very elderly parties, and all the time gone by! *I* say, let the rest go! I should think twice about it. But it ain't for me to say." She seemed to have a sudden inspiration towards decision of opinion, a thing rare with her. It was due, no doubt, to her own recent experience of an unwelcome resurrection from the Past.

" 'Tain't any consarn of ours to choose, M'riar. Just you go over to their side o' the hedge for a minute. Suppose you was Goody Prichard, and Goody Prichard was you! "

" Well! Suppose! "

" Which would you like? Her to bottle up, or tell? " Aunt M'riar wavered. A momentary hope of Gwen's, that perhaps Aunt M'riar's way out of the difficulty might hold good, died at its birth, killed by Uncle Mo's question.

Which *would* Gwen have liked, herself, in Mrs. Prichard's place? Aunt M'riar was evidently looking to her for an answer.

" I'm afraid there's no help for it, Aunt Maria," said she. " She *must* be told. But don't be afraid I shall leave the telling to you. I shall go back and tell her myself in a day or two."

" Will she come back here? " This question raised a new doubt. Would either of the two old twins care to leave the other, after that formidable disclosure had been achieved? It was looking too far ahead. Gwen felt that the evil of the hour was sufficient for the day, or indeed the next three weeks for that matter, and evaded the question with an answer to that effect.

Then, as no more was to be gained by talking, seeing that she could not give all her proofs in detail, she suggested that she should go up to Mrs. Prichard's room to say good-bye to Dave and Dolly. Promises could not be ignored between hon-

ourable people. Uncle Mo and Aunt M'riar quite concurred.
"But," said they, almost in the same breath, "are the children to
know?"

Gwen had not considered the point. "No—yes—no!" she said,
and then revoked. "Really, though, I don't know, after all, why
they shouldn't! What harm *can* it do?"

What harm indeed? Mo and M'riar looked the question at each
other, and neither looked a negative reply. Very good, then!
Dave and Dolly were to know, but who was to tell?

Gwen considered again. Then it flashed across her mind that
the disclosure of the relationship of his two Grannies could have
no distressing effect on Dave. Time and Change and Death are
only names, to a chick not eight years old, and nothing need be
told of the means by which the sisters' lives had been cut apart.
As for Dolly, she would either weep or laugh at a piece of news,
according to the suggestions of her informant. Passionless narrative would leave her unaffected either way. Told as good news,
this would be accepted as good, and it would be a pleasure to tell
it to those babies.

"I'll tell them myself," said she. "Don't you come up. Is
Mrs. Burr there?" No—Mrs. Burr was at Mrs. Ragstroar's, attending to a little job for her. Gwen vanished up the stairs, and
her welcome was audible below.

She did not mince matters, and the two young folks were soon
crowing with delight at her statement, made with equanimity, that
she knew that Granny Marrowbone was really old Mrs. Picture's
sister. She saw no reason for making the announcement thrilling.
It was enough to say that each of them had been told wicked
lies about the other, and been deceived by bad people, such as
there was every reason to hope were not to be found in Sapps
Court, or the neighbourhood. "And each of them," she added,
"thought the other was dead and buried, a long time ago!" Inexplicably, she felt it easier to say dead and buried, than merely
dead.

Dolly, having been recently in collision with Time, saw her way
to profitable comparison. "A long, long, long time, like my birfday!" she said, suggestively but unstructurally.

"Heaps longer," said Gwen. "Heaps and heaps!" Dolly was
impressed, almost cowed. She could not be even with these æons
and eras and epochs, at her time of life.

Dave burst into a shout of unrestrained glee at the discovery
that his London and country Grannies were sisters. "Oy shall
wroyte to say me and Dolly are glad. Ever such long letters to

bofe." A moment later his face had clouded over. " Oy say! " said he, " will they be glad or sorry? "

" Glad," said Gwen venturesomely. " Why should they be sorry? You must write them very, very long letters." The mine would be sprung, she thought, before even a short letter was finished. But it was as well to be on the safe side.

Dave was feeling the germination in his mind of hitherto unexperienced thoughts about Death and Time, and he remained speechless. He shook his head with closed lips and puzzled blue eyes fixed on his questioner. She saw a little way into his mind as he looked up at her, and pinched his cheek slightly, for sympathy, with the hand that was round his neck, but said nothing. Children are so funny!

" I fink," said Dolly, " old Mrs. Spicture shall bring old Granny Marrowbone back wiv her when she comes back and sets in her harm-chair wiv scushions, and Mrs. Burr cuts the reel cake, wiv splums, in sloyces, in big sloyces and little sloyces, and Mrs. Burr pawses milluck in my little jug, and Mrs. Burr pawses tea in my little pot—ass, hot tea!—and ven Doyvy shall cally round the scups and sources, but me to paw it out "—this clause was merely to assert the supremacy of Woman in household matters—" and ven all ve persons to help veirself to shoogy . . ." etc., etc. Which might have run on musically for ever, but that a difficulty arose about the names of the guests and their entertainer. It was most unfortunate that the latter should have been rechristened lately after one of the former. Her owner interpreted her to express readiness to accept another name, and that of Gweng was selected, as a compliment to the visitor.

Then it really became time for that young lady to depart. Think of that doctor's pill-box waiting all this while round the corner! So she ended what she did not suspect was her last look at old Mrs. Picture's apartment, with the fire's last spasmodic flicker helping the gas-lamp below in the Court to show Dolly, unable to tear herself away from the glorious array of preparation on the floor. There it stood, just under the empty chair with cushions, still waiting—waiting for its occupant to come again; and meanwhile a Godsend to the cat, who resumed her place the moment the intruder rose from it, with an implication that her forbearance had been great indeed to endure exclusion for so long. There was no more misgiving on the face of that little maid, putting the fiftieth touch on the perfection of her tea-cup arrangements, that her ideal entertainment would never compass realisation, than there was on the faces of the Royal Pair in their robes and decorations, gazing firmly across at Joan of Arc and St. George, in plaster, but done over bronze so you couldn't tell; precious possessions of Mrs. Burr, who was always inquiring what it would cost to repair Joan's sword—which had disintegrated and laid bare the wire in its soul—and never getting an estimate. Nor on the face of Mrs. Burr herself, coming upstairs from her job out at Mrs. Ragstroar's, and beaming—prosaically, but still beaming—on the young lady that had come to see her at the Hospital.

"Oh, I remember, by-the-by," said that young lady, three minutes later, having really said adieu all round to the family; including Dolly, who had suddenly awakened to the position, and overtaken her at the foot of the stairs. "I remember there *was* something else I wanted to ask you, Aunt Maria. Did Mrs. Prichard ever talk to you about her son?"

Was it wonderful that Aunt M'riar should start and flinch from speech, and that Uncle Mo should look preoccupied about everything outside the conversation? Can you imagine the sort of feeling an intensely truthful person like Aunt M'riar would have under such circumstances? How could she, without feeling like duplicity itself, talk about this son as though he were unknown to her, when his foul presence still hung about the room he had quitted less than an hour since? That fact, and that she had seen him, then and there, face to face with her beautiful questioner, weighed heavier on her at that moment than her own terrible relation to him, a discarded wife oppressed by an uncancelled marriage.

She had got to answer that question. "Mrs. Prichard *has* a son," she said. "But *he's* no good." This came with a jerk—perhaps with a weak hope that it might eject him from the conversation.

"She hasn't set eyes on him, didn't she say, for years past?" said old Mo, seeing that M'riar wanted help. Also with a hope of eliminating the convict. "Didn't even know whether he was living or dead, did she?"

The reply, after consideration, was:—"No-o! She said that."

And then Gwen looked from one to the other. "Oh-h!" said she. "Then probably the man *was* her son. . . . Look here! I must read you the postscript I left out." She reopened Mrs. Thrale's letter, and read that the writer's mother had been much upset by a man who laid claim to being Mrs. Prichard's son. As her eyes were on the letter, she did not see the glance of reciprocal intelligence that passed between her two listeners. But she looked up after the last word of the postscript in time to see the effect of the dog at Strides Cottage. Even as her father had been influenced, so was Uncle Mo. He appeared to breathe freer for that dog. It struck Gwen that Aunt M'riar seemed a little unenquiring and uncommunicative about this son of Mrs. Prichard's, considering all the circumstances.

When Gwen had departed, Aunt M'riar, seeing perhaps interrogation in Mo's eyes, stopped it by saying:—"Don't you ask me no more questions, not till these children are clear off to bed. I'll tell after supper." And then, just that moment, Mr. Alibone looked in, and was greatly impressed by Dave and Dolly's dramatic account of their visitor. "I've seen her, don't you know?" he said. "When you was put about to get that lock open t'other day. She's one among a million. If I was a blooming young Marquish, I should just knock at her door till she had me moved on. That's what, Mo. So might you, old man." To which Uncle Mo replied:—"They've stood us over too long, Jerry. If they don't look alive, they won't get a chance to make either of us a Marquish. I expect they're just marking time." Which Dave listened to with silent, large-eyed gravity. Some time after he expressed curiosity about the prospects of these Marquisates, and made inquiry touching the relation "marking time" had to them. Uncle Mo responded that it wouldn't be so very long now, and described the ceremonies that would accompany it—something like Lord Mayor's Show, with a flavour of Guy Fawkes Day.

However, Dave and Dolly went to bed this evening without even that inaccurate enlightenment. And presently Mr. Alibone, detecting his friend's meaning when he said he was deadly sleepy somehow to-night, took his leave and went away to finish his last pipe at The Sun.

And then Mo and M'riar were left to resume the day, and make out its meaning. "How long had the feller been here?" he asked, in order to begin somewhere.

Aunt M'riar took the question too much to heart, and embarked on an intensely accurate answer. "I couldn't say not to a minute," she said. "But if you was to put it at ten minutes, I'd have felt it safer at seven. The nearer seven the better, I should say."

"Anyhow—not a twelvemonth!" said Mo. "And there he was skearing you out of your wits, when the lady came in and di-verted of him off. Where was the two young scaramouches all the while?"

"Them I'd sent upstairs when I see who it was outside. Dave he never see him, not to look at!"

"He see him out of the top window, and knew him again. What had the beggar got to say for hisself?" This was the gist of the matter, and Uncle Mo settled down to hear it.

"He'd been to look after his mother in the country, at the place I told him—and the more fool me for telling—and he thought he spotted her, but it was some other old woman, and while he was talking to her, there to be sure and if he didn't see a police-officer after him!"

"What did he do on that?"

"Oh, he run for it, and was all but took. But he got away to the railway, and the officer followed him. And when he saw him coming up, he jumped in the wrong train, that was just start-ing, and got carried to Manchester. And he got back to London by the night train."

"And then he come on here, and found I was in the parlour—round at Joe Jeffcoat's. He thought he see his way to another half-a-sovereign out of you, M'riar, and that's what he come for. He thought I was safe for just the du-ration of a pipe or two."

"What brought you back, Mo?"

"Well, ye see, I heard his ugly voice out in the front bar, askin' for me. And I only thought he was a sporting c'rackter come to see what the old scrapper looked like in his old age. Then I couldn't think for a minute or two because of old Billy's clapper going, but when I did, his face came back to me atop of his voice. More by token when he never showed up! Ye see?" Aunt M'riar nodded an exact understanding of what had happened. "And then I take it he come sneaking down here to see for some cash, if he could get it. He'll come again, old girl, he'll come again! And Simeon Rowe shall put on a man in plain clothes, to watch for him when I'm away."

"Oh, Mo, don'tee say that! It was only his make-believe to frighten me. Anyone could tell that only to see him flourishin' out his knife."

"Hay—what's that?—his knife? You never told me o' that."

"Why, Mo, don't ye see, I only took it for bounce."

"What was it about his knife?"

"Just this, Mo dear! Now, don't you be excited. He says to me again:—'What are you good for, Polly Daverill?' And then I see he was handling a big knife with a buckhorn handle." M'riar was tremulous and tearful. "Oh, Mo!" she said. "Do consider! He wasn't that earnest, to be took at a chance word. He ain't so bad as you think of him. He was only showin' off like, to get the most he could."

"That's a queer way of showin' off—with a knife! P'r'aps it warn't open, though?" But it was, by M'riar's silence. "Anyways," Mo continued, "he won't come back so long as he thinks I'm here. To-morrow morning first thing I shall just drop round to the Station, and tip 'em a wink. Can't have this sort o' thing goin' on!"

M'riar's lighting of a candle seemed to hang fire. Said she:— "You'd think it a queer thing to say, if I was to say it, Mo!" And then, in reply to the natural question:—"Think what?" she continued:—"A woman's husband ain't like any other man. She's never quite done with him, as if he was nobody. It don't make any odds how bad he's been, nor yet how long ago it was . . . It makes one creep to think. . . ." She stopped abruptly, and shuddered.

"What he'll catch if he gets his deserts." Mo supplied an end for the sentence, gravely.

"Ah!—he might be. . . . What would it be, Mo, if he was tried and found guilty?"

"Without a recommendation to mercy? It was a capital offence. I never told it ye. Shall I tell it?"

"No—for God's sake!" Aunt M'riar stopped her ears tight as she had done before. "Don't you tell me nothing, Mo, more than I know already. That's plenty." Uncle Mo nodded, pointed to tightly closed lips to express assent, and she resumed speech with hearing. "Capital offence means . . . means? . . ."

"Means he would go to the scragging-post, arter breakfast one morning. There's no steering out o' that fix, M'riar. He's just got to, one day, and there's an end of it!"

"And how ever could I be off knowing it at the time? Oh, but it makes me sick to think of! The night before—the night before, Mo! Supposin' I wake in the night, and think of him, and hear the clocks strike! He'll hear them too, Mo."

"Can't be off it, M'riar! But what of that? He won't be a penny the worse, and he'll know what o'clock it is." Remember that Uncle Mo had some particulars of Daverill's career that Aunt M'riar had not. For all she knew, the criminal's capital offence might have been an innocent murder—a miscarriage in the redistribution of some property—a too zealous garrotting of some fat old stockjobber. "I'm thinkin' a bit of the other party, M'riar," said Mo. He might have said more, but he was brought up short by his pledge to say nothing of the convict's last atrocity. How could he speak the thought in his mind, of the mother of the victim in a madhouse? For that had made part of the tale, as it had reached him through the police-sergeant. So he ended his speech by saying:—"What I do lies at my own door, M'riar. You're out of it. So I shan't say another word of what I will do or won't do. Only I tell you this, that if I could get a quiet half an hour with the gentleman, I'd . . . *What* would I do! . . . Well!— I'd save him from the gallows—I *would!* Ah!—and old as I am, I'd let him keep a hold on his knife. . . . There—there, old lass! I do wrong to frighten ye, givin' way to bad temper. Easy does it!"

For a double terror of the woman's position was bred of that mysterious, inextinguishable love that never turns to hate, however hateful its object may become; and her dread that if this good, unwieldy giant—that was what Mo seemed—crossed his path, that jack-knife might add another to her husband's many crimes. This dread and counter-dread had sent all Aunt M'riar's blood to her heart, and she might have fallen, but that Mo's strong hand caught her in time, and landed her in a chair. "I was wrong—I was wrong!" said he gently. All the fires had died down before the pallor of her face, and his only thought was how could *she* be spared if the destroyer of her life was brought to justice.

They said no more; what more was there to be said? Aunt M'riar came round, refusing restoratives. Oh no, she would be all right! It was only a turn she got—that common event! They adjourned, respectively, to where Dolly and Dave were sleeping balmily, profoundly.

But Uncle Mo was discontented with the handiwork of Creation. Why should a cruel, two-edged torture be invented for, and inflicted on, an inoffensive person like M'riar? There didn't seem any sense in it. "If only," said he to his inner soul, "they'd a-let *me* be God A'mighty for five minutes at the first go-off, I'd a-seen to it no such a thing shouldn't happen." Less than five minutes would have been necessary, if a full and unreserved concession of omnipotence had been made.

Dave was a man of his word, though a very young one. He seized the earliest opportunity to indite two letters of congratulation to his honorary grandmothers, including Dolly in his rejoicing at the discovery of their relationship. He wrote as though such discoveries were an everyday occurrence.

His mistakes in spelling were few, the principal one arising from an old habit of thought connecting the words sister and cistern, which had survived Aunt M'riar's frequent attempts at correction. When he exhibited his Identical Notes to the Powers for their sanction and approval, this was pointed out to him, and an allegation that he was acting up to previous instructions disallowed *nem. con.* He endeavoured to lay to heart that for the future *cistern* was to be spelt *sister*, except out on the leads. A holographic adjustment of the *c*, and erasure of the *n*, was scarcely a great success, but the Powers supposed it would do. Uncle Mo opposed Aunt M'riar's suggestion that the two letters should go in one cover to Strides Cottage, for economy, as mean-spirited and parsimonious, although he had quite understood that the two Grannies were under one roof; otherwise Dave would have directed to Mrs. Picture at the Towers. So to Strides Cottage they went, some three days later.

CHAPTER XIV

HOW THE COUNTESS AND HER DAUGHTER WENT BACK TO THE TOWERS, AND GWEN READ HER LETTERS IN THE TRAIN. THE TORPEYS, THE RECTOR, AND THE BISHOP. HOW THE COUNTESS SHUT HER EYES, AND GWEN HARANGUED. WHO WAS LINCOLN'S INN FIELDS? THE UP-EXPRESS, AND ITS VIRUS. HOW GWEN RESOLVED TO RUSH THE POSITION. AT STRIDES COTTAGE. HOW GWEN BECAME MORE AND MORE ALIVE TO HER DIFFICULTIES. HOW SHE WENT TO SEE DR. NASH. HIS INCREDULITY. AND HIS CONVERSION. HOW HE WOULD SEE GRANNY MARRABLE, BY ALL MEANS. BUT! HOWEVER, BY GOOD LUCK, MUGGERIDGE HAD FORGOTTEN HIS MARRIAGE VOWS, HALF A CENTURY AGO AND MORE

IT was written in the Book of Fate, and printed in the *Morning Post*, that the Countess of Ancester was leaving for Rocestershire, and would remain over Christmas. After which she would probably pay a visit to her daughter, Lady Philippa Brandon, at Vienna. The Earl would join her at the Towers after a short stay at Bath, according to his lordship's annual custom. The *Post* did not commit itself as to his lordship's future movements, because Fate had not allowed the Editor to look in her Book.

And the Countess herself seemed to know no more than the *Post*. For when her daughter, in the railway-carriage on the way to the Towers, looked up from a letter she was reading over and over again, to say:—"I suppose it's no use trying to persuade papa to come to Vienna, after all?" her mother's answer was:—"You can try, my dear. *You* may have some influence with him. *I* have none. I suppose when we're gone, he'll just get wrapped up in his fiddles and books and old gim-cracks, as he always does the minute my eyes are off him." Gwen made no comment upon inconsistencies, becoming reabsorbed in her letter. But surely a Countess whose eyes prevent an Earl getting wrapped up in fiddles is not absolutely without influence over him.

Gwen's absorbing letter was from Irene, incorporating dicta-tion from Adrian. The writer had found the accepted Official form:—" I am to say," convenient in practice. Thus, for instance, " I am to say that he is not counting the hours till your return, as it seems to him that the total, when reached, will be of no use to him or anyone else. He prefers to accept our estimate of the interval as authentic, and to deduct each hour as it passes. He is at eighty-six now, and expects to be at sixty-two at this time to-morrow, assuming that he can trust the clock while he's asleep." Gwen inferred that the amanuensis had protested, to go on to a more interesting point, as the letter continued:—" Adrian and I have been talking over what do you think, Gwen dear? Try and guess before you turn over this page I'm just at the end of. . . ." Dots ended the page, and the next began:—" Give it up? Well— only, if I tell you, you must throw this letter in the fire when you have read it—I'm more than half convinced that there was once a *tendresse*, to put it mildly, between our respective papa and mamma—that is, our respective papa and your respective mamma —not the other way, that's ridiculous! And Adrian is coming to my way of thinking, after what happened yesterday. It was at dessert, and papa was quite loquacious, for him—in his best form, saying:—' Niggers, niggers, niggers! What does that blessed Duchess of Sutherland want to liberate niggers for? Much better wollop 'em!" The Duchess was, he said, an hysterical female. Mamma was unmoved and superior. Perhaps papa would call Lady Ancester hysterical, too. *She* was at Stafford House, and was *most enthusiastic*. She had promised to drive over as soon as she came back, to talk about Negro slavery, and see if something could not be done in the neighbourhood. Mamma hoped she would interest the Torpeys and the Rector and the Bishop. Only the point was that the moment *our* mamma mentioned *yours*, papa shut up with a snap, and never said another word. It struck me exactly as it struck Adrian. And when we came to talk it over we agreed that, if it were, it would account for our having been such strangers till last year."

Gwen was roused from weighing the possibilities of the truth of this surmise by the voice of one of its subjects. " How very engrossing our letters seem to be this morning! " said the Countess, with a certain air of courteous toleration, as of seniority on Olympus. " But perhaps I have no right to inquire." This with *empressement*.

" Don't be so civil, mamma dear, please! " said Gwen. " I do hate civility. . . . No, there's nothing of interest. Yes—there is. Lady Torrens says she hopes you won't forget your promise to come and talk about abolishing negroes. I didn't know you were going to."

The Countess skipped details. " Let me see the letter," said she, forsaking her detached superiority. She began to polish a double eyeglass prematurely.

" Can't show the letter," said Gwen equably, as one secure in her rights. " That's all—what I've told you! Says you promised to drive over and talk, and she hoped to interest you—oh no!— it's not you, it's the Torpeys are to be interested."

" Oh—the Torpeys," said the Countess freezingly. Because it was humiliating to have to put away those double eyeglasses. " Perhaps if there is anything else of interest you will tell me. Do not trouble to read the whole."

" But *did* you promise to drive over to Pensham? Because, if you did, we may just as well go together. With all those men at the Towers, I shall have to bespeak Tom Kettering and the mare."

" I think something *was* said about my going over. But I certainly made no promise." Her ladyship reflected a moment, and then said:—" I think we had better be free lances. I am most uncertain. It's a long drive. If I do go, I shall lunch at the Parysforts, which is more than half-way, and go on in the afternoon to your aunt at Poynders. Then I need not come back till the day after. I could call at Pensham by the way."

" I won't go to old Goody Parysforts—so that settles the matter! When shall I tell Adrian's mamma you are coming? "

" Are you going there at once? "

" Yes—to-morrow. I must see Adrian to talk to him about my old ladies, before I talk to either of them." Thereupon the Countess became prodigiously interested in the story of the twins, a subject about which she had been languid hitherto, and her daughter was not sorry, because she did not want to be asked again what Irene had said, which might have involved her in reading that young lady's text aloud, with extemporised emendations, possibly complex. She put that letter away, to re-read another time.

and took out another one. " I've had *this*," she said, "from old Mrs. Prichard. But there's nothing in it! "

" Nothing in it? "

" Nothing about what Widow Thrale told us in hers. Nothing about Mrs. Thrale thinking she had gone dotty."

The Countess, with a passing rebuke of her daughter's phraseology, asked to be reminded of the story. Gwen, embarking on a *résumé,* was interrupted by a tunnel, and then had hardly begun again when the train rushed into a second section of it, which had slipped or been blown further along the line. However, Peace ensued, in a land where, to all appearance, notice-boards were dictating slow speeds from interested motives, as there was no reason in life against quick ones. Gwen took advantage of it to read Mrs. Prichard's letter aloud, with comments. This was the letter :—

" ' My dear Lady,

" ' I am looking forward to your return, and longing for it, for I have much to tell you. I cannot tell of it all now, but I can tell you what is such a happiness to tell, of the sweet kindness of this dear young woman who takes such care of me. A many have been very very kind to me, and what return have I to make, since my dear husband died?' . . .

" Her dear husband, don't you see, mamma, was the infamous monster that wrote the forged letter that did it all. . . . Papa read it to you, didn't he? "

" My dear, it's no use asking me what your father read or did not read to me, for really the last few days have been such a whirl. It always is, in London. However, go on! I know the letter you mean—what you were telling me about. Only I can't say I made head or tail of it at the time. Go on! " Her ladyship composed herself to listen with her eyes shut, and Gwen read on :—

" ' But never, no never, was such patient kindness to a tiresome old woman, because that is what I am, and I know, my dear. I know, my dear, that I owe this to you, and it is for your sake, but it ought to be, and that is right. I do not say things always like I want to. She says her own mother is no use to her, because she is so strong and never ill, and I am good to nurse. But she is coming back very soon, and I shall see her. She is my Davy's other Granny, you know, and I am sure she must be good. I cannot write more, but oh, how good you have been to me!

" ' Your loving and dutiful
" ' Maisie Prichard.

"'I must say this to you, that she lets me call her her name Ruth. That was my child's I left at our Dolly's age, who was drowned.'

"Now are you sure, mamma," said Gwen, not without severity, "that you quite understand that it's *the same Ruth?* That this Widow Thrale *is* the little girl that old Mrs. Prichard has gone on believing drowned, all these years? Are you quite clear that old Granny Marrable actually *is* the twin sister she has not seen for fifty years? Are you certain . . . ?"

"My dear Gwen, I beg you won't harangue. Besides, I can't hear you because the train's going quick again. It always does, just here. . . . No—I understand perfectly. These two old persons have not seen each other for fifty years, and it's very interesting. Only I don't see what they have to complain of. They have only got to be told, and made to understand how the mistake came about. I think they *ought* to be told, you know."

"Oh dear, what funny things maternal parents are! Mamma dear, you are just like Thothmes, who said:—'Better late than never'!"

"Who is 'Thothmes'?" Her ladyship knew perfectly well.

"Well—Lincoln's Inn Fields—if you prefer it! Mr. Hawtrey. He's like a cork that won't come out. I cannot understand people like you and Mr. Hawtrey. I suppose you will say that you and he are not in it, and I am?"

"I shall say *nothing,* my dear. I never do." The Countess retired to the Zenith, meekly. The train was picking up its spirits, audibly, but cautiously. The flank fire of hints about speed had subsided, and it had all the world before it, subject to keeping on the line and screeching when called on to do so by the Company.

"I wonder," said Gwen, "whether you have realised that that dear old soul is calling her own daughter Ruth 'Ruth,' without knowing who she is."

"Oh dear yes—perfectly! But suppose she is—what does it matter?" The conversation was cut short by the more than hysterical violence of the up-express, which was probably the thing that passed, invisible owing to its speed, before its victims could do more than quail and shiver. When it had shrieked and rattled itself out of hearing, it was evident that it had bitten Gwen's engine and poisoned its disposition, for madness set in, and it dragged her train over oily lines and clicketty lines alike at a speed that made conversation impossible.

Gwen was panting to start upon the bewildering task she had before her, but only to put it to the proof, and end the tension. It was *impossible* to keep the two old twins in the dark, and it seemed to her that delay might make matters worse. As for ingenious schemes to reveal the strange story gradually, some did occur to her, but none bore reconsideration. Probably disaster lay in ambush behind over-ingenuity. Go gently but firmly to the point—that seemed to her a safe rule for guidance. If she could only anchor her dear old fairy godmother in a haven of calm knowledge of the facts, she was less distressingly concerned about the sister and daughter. The former of these was the more prickly thorn of anxiety. Still, she was a wonderfully strong old lady—not like old Mrs. Picture, a semi-invalid. As for the latter, she scarcely deserved to be thought a thorn at all. She might even be relied on to put her feelings in her pocket and help.

Yes—that was an idea! How would it be to make Widow Thrale know the truth first, and then simply tell her that help she *must,* and there an end! Gwen acted on the impulse produced in her mind during the last twenty minutes of her journey, in which conversation with her mother continued a discomfort, owing to the strong effect which the poisoned tooth or bad example of the down-train express had produced on her own hitherto temperate and reasonable engine. On arriving at Grantley Thorpe she changed her mind about seeing Adrian before visiting Strides Cottage, and petitioned Mr. Sandys, the Station-master, for writing materials, and asked him to send the letter she then and there wrote, by bearer, to Widow Thrale at Chorlton; not because the distance of Strides Cottage from the main road was a serious obstacle to its personal delivery on the way home, but because she wished to avoid seeing any of its occupants until a full interview was possible. Also, she wanted Widow Thrale to be prepared for something unusual. Her letter was:—" I am coming to you to-morrow. I want to talk about dear old Mrs. Prichard, but do not show her this or say anything till I see you. And do not be uneasy or alarmed." She half fancied when she had written it that the last words were too soothing. But this was a mistake. Nothing rouses alarm alike reassurance.

It was a relief to her, between this and an early start for Chorlton next day, to be dragged forcibly away from her dominant anxiety. The Colonel's shooting-party was still in possession at the Towers, though its numbers were dwindling daily. It had never had its full complement, as so many who might have gone to swell it were fighting in the ranks before Sebastopol, or in hospital at Balaklava, cholera-stricken perhaps; or, nominally, waiting till resurrection-time in the cemetery there, or by the Alma, for the grass of a new year to cover them in; but maybe actually—and likelier too—in some strange inconceivable Hades; poor cold ghosts in the dark, marvelling at the crass stupidity of Cain, and even throwing doubts on "glory."

The Colonel's party, belonging to the class that is ready to send all its sons that can bag game or ride to hounds, to be food for powder themselves in any dispute made and provided, was sadly denuded of the young man element, and he himself was fretting with impatience at the medical verdict that had disqualified him for rejoining his regiment with a half-healed lung. But the middle-aged majority, and the civilian juniors—including a shooting parson—could talk of nothing but the War.

Some of us who are old enough will recall easily their own consciousness of the universal war-cloud at this time, when reminded that the details of Inkerman were only lately to hand, and that Florence Nightingale had not long begun to work in the hospital at Scutari. But the immediate excitement of the moment, when the two ladies joined the dinner-party that evening at the Towers, was the frightful storm of which Gwen had already had the first news, which had strewn the coast of the Chersonese with over thirty English wrecks, and sent stores and war material costing millions to the bottom of the Black Sea. She was glad, however, to hear that it was certain that the Agamemnon had been got off the rocks at Balaklava, as she had understood that Granny Marrable had a grandson on the ship.

The time was close at hand, within an hour, when Gwen would have to find words to tell her strange impossible story, if not to that dear old silver hair—to those grave peaceful eyes,—at least to one whose measure of her whole life must perforce be changed by it. What would it mean, to Widow Thrale, to have such a subversive fact suddenly sprung upon her?

More than once in her ride to Chorlton it needed all her courage to crush the impulse to tell Tom Kettering to turn the mare round and drive back to the Towers. It would have been so easy to forge some excuse to save her face, and postpone the embarrassing hour till to-morrow. But to what end? It would be absolutely out of the question to leave the sisters in ignorance of each other, even supposing the circumstances made continued ignorance possible. The risks to the health or brain-power of either would surely be greater if the *éclaircissement* were left to haphazard, than if she were controlling it with a previous knowledge of all the facts. Perhaps Gwen was not aware how much her inborn temperament had to do with her conclusions. Had she been a soldier, she would have volunteered to go on every forlorn hope, on principle. No doubt an "hysterical" temperament, as it is so common among women! But it is a form of hysteria that exists also among men.

Whether or no, here she was at the gate of Strides Cottage, and it was now too late to think of going back. Tom Kettering was requesting the mare, in stable language, not to kick *terra firma*, or otherwise object to standing, till he had assisted the lady down. She was down without assistance before the mare was convinced of sin, so Tom touched his hat vaguely, but committed himself to nothing. He appeared to understand—as he didn't say he didn't, when instructed—that he was to wait five minutes; and then, if nothing appeared to the contrary, employ himself and the mare in any way they could agree upon, for an hour; and then return to pick her up.

The cat, the only inmate visible at Strides, rose from the threshold to welcome the visitor, with explanations perfectly clear to Gwen—who understood cats—that if it had been within her power to reach the door-latch, she would have opened the door, entirely to accommodate her ladyship. She had no mixture of motives, arising from having been shut out. Gwen threw doubt on this; as, having rung the bell, she waited. She might have rung again but for Elizabeth-next-door; who, coming out with advisory powers, said that Mrs. Thrale was probably engaged with the old lady, but that she herself would go straight in if she was her ladyship. Not being able to reach the latch herself over the privet-hedge between them, the good woman was coming round to open the door, but went back when Gwen anticipated her, and entering the empty front-room, heard the voices in the bedroom behind. How strange it seemed to her, to wait there, overhearing them, and knowing that the old voice was that of a mother speaking to her unknown daughter, and that each was unsuspicious of the other.

The dog who trotted in from the passage between the rooms or beyond it, was no doubt the one Gwen had heard of. He examined her slightly, seemed satisfied, and disappeared as he had come. The cat chose the most comfortable corner by the fire, and went to sleep in it without hesitation. The fire crackled with new dry wood, and exploded a chance wet billet into jets of steam, under a kettle whose lid was tremulous from intermittent stress below.

Otherwise, nothing interfered with the two voices in the room beyond; the mother's, weak with age, but cheerful enough, no unhappy sound about it; the daughter's, cheerful, robust, and musical, rallying and encouraging her as a child, perhaps about some dress obstacle or mystery. The effect on Gwen of listening to them was painful. To hear them, knowing the truth, made that knowledge almost unendurable. Could she possess her soul in peace until what she supposed to be the old lady's toilette was complete?

The question was decided by the dog, who was applying for admission at the door beyond the passage, somewhat diffidently and cautiously. Gwen could just see him, exploring along the door-crack with his nose. Presently, remaining unnoticed from within, he made his voice audible—barely audible, not to create alarm needlessly. It was only to oblige; he had no misgivings about the visitor.

Then Gwen, conceiving that a change in the voices implied that his application had been heard, helped the applicant, by a word or two to identify herself; adding that she was in no hurry, and would wait. Then followed more change in the voices; the mother's exclamation of pleasure; the daughter's recognition of her visitor's dues of courtesy and deference, and their claim for a prompt discharge. Then an opened door, and Widow Thrale herself, not too much overpowered by her obligations to leave the dog's explanations and apologies unacknowledged. The utter unconsciousness this showed of the thing that was to come almost made Gwen feel that the strain on her powers of self-control might become greater than she could bear, and that she might break out with some premature disclosure which would only seem sheer madness to her unprepared hearer.

She could hold out a little yet, though. . . . Well!—she had got to manage it, by hook or by crook. So—courage! Five minutes of normal *causeries,* mere currencies of speech, and then the match to the train!

She evolved, with some difficulty, the manner which would be correct in their relative positions; accepted the curtsey before stretching out a hand, guaranteed Olympian, to the plains below. " My dear Mrs. Thrale," said she, choking back excitement to chat-point, " I really am more grateful to you than I can say for taking charge of this dear old lady. I was quite at my wits' end what to do with her. You see, I had to go up to London, because of my cousin's illness—Sister Nora, you know—and it was in the middle of the night, and I was afraid the dear old soul would be uncomfortable at the Towers." She made some pretence of languid indifference to conventional precisions, and of complete superiority to scruples about confessing an error, by adding:—" Most likely I was wrong. One is, usually. But it never seems to matter. . . . Let's see—what was I saying? Oh—how very kind it was of you to solve the difficulty for me. . . . Well—to help me out of the scrape!" For Mrs. Thrale had looked the doubt in her mind—*could* Gurth the Swineherd "solve a difficulty" for Cœur de Lion? She could only do Anglo-Saxon things, legitimately. The point was, however, covered by Gwen's amendment.

Mrs. Thrale had begun a smile of approbation at the phrase " dear old lady," and had felt bound to suspend it for Sister Nora's illness. That was a parenthesis, soon disposed of. The revival of the smile was easy, on the words "dear old soul." She was that, there was no doubt of it, said Mrs. Thrale, adding:—" 'Tis for me to be grateful to your ladyship for allowing me the charge of her. I hope your ladyship may not be thinking of taking her away, just yet-a-while?"

"I think not, just at present. . . . We shall be able to talk of that. . . . Tell me—how has she been? Because of your letter."

" There now!—when I got your ladyship's note last night I felt a'most ashamed of writing that I had been uneasy or alarmed." Gwen saw that her yesterday's attempt at premonition had missed fire, and Mrs. Thrale added:—" Because—*not a word!* "

"How do you mean? I don't quite understand."

" She's never said a word since. Not that sort of word! She's just never spoke of the mill, nor Muggeridge, nor my grandfather. And I have said nothing to her, by reason of Dr. Nash's advice. 'Never you talk to a mental patient about their delusions!'—that's what Dr. Nash says. So I never said one word."

Gwen felt sorry she had not made her note of alarm more definite. For the absolute faith of the speaker in her own belief and Dr. Nash's professional infallibility, that a dropped voice and confidential manner seemed to erect as a barrier to enlightenment, made her feel more at a loss than ever how to act. Would it not, after all, be easiest to risk the whole, and speak at once to the old lady herself? She prefigured in her mind the greater ease of telling her story when she could make her own love a palliative to the shock of the revelation, could take on her bosom the old head, stunned and dumfoundered; could soothe the weakness of the poor old hand with the strength and youth of her own. But into that image came a disturbing whim—call it so!—a question from without, not bred of her own mind:—" Is not this the daughter's right?—the prerogative of the flesh and blood that stands before you?" Perhaps Gwen *was* whimsical sometimes.

If Widow Thrale had said one word to pave the way—had spoken, for instance, of the unaccountableness of the old lady's memories—Gwen might have seen daylight through the wood. But this placid immovable ascription of the whole of them to brain-disorder was an Ituri forest of preconceptions, shutting out every gleam of suggested truth.

A sudden idea occurred to her. Her father had spoken well of Dr. Nash—of his abilities, at least—and he seemed very much in Mrs. Thrale's good books. Could she not get *him* to help, or at least to take his measure as a confidant in her difficulty before condemning him as impossible?

So quickly did all this pass through her mind that the words " I think I should like to see Dr. Nash" seemed to follow naturally. Mrs. Thrale welcomed the idea.

" But he'll be gone," said she. " He goes to see his patient at Dessington Manor at eleven. And if he was sent for it is very like he could not come, even for your ladyship. Because his sick folk he sees at the surgery they will have their money's worth. Indeed, I think the poor man's worked off his legs."

" I see," said Gwen. " I shall go and see him myself, at once." She breathed freer for the respite, and the prospect of help. " But there's plenty of time if I look sharp. Would you tell Tom outside that he's not to run away. I shall want him? May I go through to see her? Is she getting up?"

She was up, apparently, in the accepted sense of the word; though she had collapsed with the effort of becoming so; and was now down, in the literal sense, lying on the bed under contract not to move till Mrs. Thrale returned with a cup of supplementary arrowroot. She had had a very poor breakfast. Certainly, her ladyship might go in.

" Oh, my dear, my dear, I am so glad you are come!" It was the voice of a great relief that came from the figure on the bed; the voice of one who had waited long, of a traveller who sees his haven, a castaway adrift who spies a sail.

" Now, dear Mrs. Picture, you are not to get up, but lie still till I come back. I'm going to try to catch Dr. Nash, and must hurry off. But I *am* coming back."

" Oh—all right!" There was disappointment in her tone, but it was docility itself. She added, however, with the barest trace

of remonstrance:—" I'm quite .well, you know. I don't *want* the
doctor."

Gwen laughed. " Oh no—it's not for you! I've . . . I've a
message for him. I shall soon be back." An excusable fiction,
she thought, under the circumstances.

She was only just in time to catch Dr. Nash, whose gig was
already in possession of him at his garden-gate with a palpably
medical lamp over it, and a " surgery bell " whose polish seemed
to guarantee its owner's prescriptions. " Get down and talk to
me in the house," said her young ladyship. " Who is it you were
going to? Anyone serious? "

" Only Sir Cropton Fuller."

" He can wait. . . . Can't he? "

" He'll have to. No hurry! " The doctor found time to add,
between the gate and the house:—" I go to see him every day
to prevent his taking medicine. He's extremely well. I don't
get many cases of illness, among my patients." He turned round
to look at Gwen, on the doorstep. " Your ladyship doesn't look
very bad," said he.

Gwen shook her head. " It's nothing to do with me," she
said. " Nor with illness! It's old Mrs. Prichafrd at Strides
Cottage."

The doctor stood a moment, latchkey in hand. " The old lady
whose mind is giving way? " said he. He had knitted his brows
a little; and, having spoken, he knitted his lips a little.

" We are speaking of the same person," said Gwen. She followed the doctor into his parlour, and accepted the seat he offered.
He stood facing her, not relaxing his expression, which worked
out as a sort of mild grimness, tempered by a tune which his
thumbs in the armpits of his waistcoat enabled him to play on its
top-pockets. It was a slow tune. Gwen continued:—" But her
mind is *not* giving way."

The doctor let that expression subside into mere seriousness.
He took a chair, to say:—" Your ladyship has, perhaps, not heard
all particulars of the case."

" Every word."

" You surprise me. Are you aware that this poor old person
is under a delusion about her own parentage? She fancies herself
the daughter of Isaac Runciman, the father of old Mrs. Marrable,
the mother of Widow Thrale."

" She *is* his daughter."

The doctor nearly sprang out of his chair with surprise, but
an insecure foothold made the chair jump instead.

"But it's impossible—it's *impossible!*" he cried. "How could Mrs. Marrable have a sister alive and not know it?"

"That is what I am going to explain to you, Dr. Nash. And Sir Cropton Fuller will have to wait, as you said."

"But the thing's impossible in *itself*. Only look at this! . . ."

"Please consider Sir Cropton Fuller. You won't think it so impossible when you know it has happened." The doctor listened for the symptoms with perceptibly less than his normal appearance of knowing it all beforehand. Gwen proceeded, and told with creditable brevity and clearness, the succession of events the story has given, for its own reasons, by fits and starts.

It could not be accepted as it stood, consistently with male dignity. The superior judicial powers of that estimable sex called for assertion. First, suspension of opinion—no hasty judgments! "A most extraordinary story! A *most* extraordinary story! But scarcely to be accepted. . . . You'll excuse my plain speech? . . ."

"Please don't use any other! The matter's too serious."

"Scarcely to be accepted without a close examination of the evidence."

"Unquestionably. Does any point occur to you?"

Now Dr. Nash had nothing ready. "Well," he said, dubiously, "in such a very difficult matter it might be rash. . . ." Then he thought of something to say, suddenly. "Well—*yes!* It certainly does occur to me that . . . No—perhaps not—perhaps not! . . ."

"What were you going to say?"

"That there is no direct proof that the forged letter was ever sent to Australia." This sounded well, and appeared like a tribute to correctness and caution. It meant nothing whatever.

"Only the Australian postmark," said Gwen. "I have got it here, but it's rather alarming—the responsibility."

"If it was written, as you say, over an effaced original, it might have been done just as easily in England." The doctor was reading the direction, not opening the letter.

"Not by a forger at the Antipodes!" said Gwen.

"I meant afterwards—when—when Mrs. Prichard was in England?"

"She brought the letter with her when she came. It couldn't have been forged afterwards."

The doctor gave it up. Masculine superiority would have to stand over. But he couldn't see his way, on human grounds, profundity apart. "What is so horribly staggering," said he, "is that after fifty years these two should actually see each other and still be in the dark. And the way it came about! The amazing coincidences!" The doctor spoke as if such unblushing coincidences ought to be ashamed of themselves.

Gwen took this to be his meaning, apparently. "*I* can't help it, Dr. Nash," she said. "If they had told me they were going to happen, I might have been able to do something. Besides, there was only one, if you come to think of it—the little boy being sent to Widow Thrale's to convalesce. It was my cousin, Miss Grahame, who did it. . . . Yes, thank you!—she is going on very well, and Dr. Dalrymple hopes she will make a very good recovery. He fussed a good deal about her lungs, but they seem all right. . . ." The conversation fluctuated to Typhus Fever for a moment, but was soon recalled by the young lady, whose visit had a definite purpose. "Now, Dr. Nash, I have a favour to ask of you, which is what I came for. It occurred to me when I heard that you would be going to Dessington Manor this morning." The doctor professed his readiness, or eagerness, to do anything in his power to oblige Lady Gwendolen Rivers, but evidently had no idea what it could possibly be. "You will be close to Costrell's farm, where the other old lady is staying with her granddaughter?"

"I shall. But what can I do?"

"You can, perhaps, help me in the very difficult job of making the truth known to her and her sister. I say perhaps, because you may find you can do nothing. I shall not blame you if you fail. But you can at least try."

It would have been difficult to refuse anything to the animated beauty of his petitioner, even if she had been the humblest of his village patients. The doctor pledged himself to make the attempt, without hesitation, saying to himself as he did so that this would be a wonderful woman some day, with a little more experience and maturity. "But," said he, "I never promised to do anything with a vaguer idea of what I was to do, nor how I was to set about it."

Gwen's earnestness had no pause for a smile. "It is easier than you think," she said, "if you only make up your mind to it. It is easy for you, because your medical interest in old Mrs. Prichard's case makes it possible for you to *entamer* the conversation. You see what I mean?"

"Perfectly—I *think*. But I don't see how that will *entamer* old Mrs. Marrable. Won't the conversation end where it began?"

"I think not—not necessarily. I will forgive you if it does. Consider that the apparent proof of delusion in my old lady's mind is that she has told things about her childhood which are either *bona-fide* recollections, or have been derived from the little boy. . . ."

"Dave Wardle. So I understood from Widow Thrale. She has told me all the things as they happened. In fact, I have been able to call in every day. The case seemed very interesting as a case of delusion, because some of the common characteristics were wanting. It loses that interest now, certainly, but . . . However, you were saying, when I interrupted? . . ."

"I was saying that unless these ideas could be traced to Dave Wardle, they must have come out of Mrs. Prichard's own head. Is it not natural that you should want to hear from Granny Marrable what she recollects having said to the child?"

The doctor cogitated a moment, then gave a short staccato nod. "I see," said he, in a short staccato manner. "*Yes.* That might do something for us. At any rate, I can try it. . . . I beg your pardon."

Gwen had just begun again, but paused as the doctor looked at his watch. She continued:—"I cannot find anything that she might not have easily said to a small boy. I wish I could. Her recollection of *not* having said anything won't be certainty. But even inquiring about what she *doesn't* recollect would give an opening. Did Mrs. Prichard say nothing to you about her early life at the mill?"

"She said a good deal, because I encouraged her to talk, to convince myself of her delusion. . . . Could I recollect some of it? I think so. Or stay—I have my notes of the case." He produced a book. "Here we are. 'Mrs. Maisie Prichard, eighty-one. Has delusions. Thinks mill was her father's. It was Widow Thrale's grandfather's. Knows horses Pitt and Fox. Knows Muggeridge waggoner. Has names correct. Qy.:—from child Wardle last year? M. was dismissed soon after. Asked try recollect what for.' I am giving your ladyship the abbreviations as written."

"Quite right. Is there more?" For evidently there was. Gwen could see the page.

"She remembered that he was dismissed for . . . irregularity."

Gwen suspected suppression. "What sort? Did he drink? Let me see the book. I won't read the other cases." And so all-powerful was beauty, or the traces of Feudalism, that this middle-aged M.R.C.S. actually surrendered his private notes of cases into these most unprofessional hands. Gwen pointed to the unread sequel, triumphantly. "There!" she exclaimed. "The very thing we want! You may be sure that neither Granny Marrable nor her daughter ever told a chick of seven years old of *that* defect in Mr. Muggeridge's character." For what Gwen had *not* read aloud was:—"*Mug. broke 7th: Comm:*"

The doctor was perhaps feeling that masculine profundity had not shone, and that he ought to do something to redeem its credit. For his comment, rather judicial in tone, was:—" Yes—but Widow Thrale was not able to confirm this . . . blemish on Mr. Muggeridge's reputation."

" Now, my dear Dr. Nash, why *should* she be able to confirm a thing that happened when her mother was ten years old? "

The doctor surrendered at discretion—perhaps resolved not to repeat the attempt to reinstate the male intellect. " Of course not! " said he. " Perfectly correct. Very good! I'll try, then, to make use of that. I understand your object to be that old Granny Marrable shall come to know that she and Mrs. Prichard are sisters, as gradually as possible. I may not succeed, but I'll do my best. Ticklish job, rather! Now I suppose I ought to look after Sir Cropton Fuller."

Five minutes after saying which the doctor's gig was doing its best to arrive in time to prevent that valetudinarian swallowing five grains of calomel, or something of the sort, on his own responsibility.

Gwen had felt a misgiving that her expedition to Dr. Nash had really been a cowardly undertaking, because she had flinched from her task at the critical moment. Well—suppose she had! It might turn out a fortunate piece of poltroonery, if Dr. Nash contrived to break the ice for her with the other old sister. But the cowardice was beginning again, now that every stride of the mare was taking her nearer to her formidable task. Desperation was taking the place of mere Resolve, thrusting her aside as too weak for service in the field, useless outside the ramparts. Oh, but if only some happy accident would pave the way for speech, would enable her to say to herself:—" I have said the first word! I cannot go back now, if I would! "

On the way to Strides Cottage again! Nearer and nearer now, that moment that must come, and put an end to all this puling hesitation. She could not help the thought that rose in her mind:—" This that I do—this reuniting of two souls long parted by a living death—may it not be what Death does every day for many a world-worn survivor of a half-forgotten parting in a remote past? " For, indeed, it seemed to her that these two had risen from the dead, and that for all she knew each might say

of the other:—"It is not she." For what is Death but the withdrawal from sight and touch and hearing of the evidence of Some
One Else? What less had come to pass for old Maisie and Phœbe,
fifty years ago? How is it with us all in that mysterious Beyond,
that for the want of a better name we call a Hereafter, when
ghost meets ghost, and either lacks the means of recognition?
She knew the trick of that latch now, and went in.

The room was empty of all but the cat, who seemed self-
absorbed; silent but for a singing kettle and a chirping cricket.
Probably Widow Thrale was in the bedroom. Gwen crossed the
passage, and gently opening the door, looked in. Only the old
lady herself was there, upon the bed, so still that Gwen half feared
at first she had died in her sleep. No—all was well! She wondered a moment at the silver hair, the motionless hands, alabaster
but for the blue veins, the frailty of the whole, and its long past
of eighty years, those years of strange vicissitude. And through
them all no one thing so strange as what she was to know on
waking!

CHAPTER XV

HOW GWEN HEARD WIDOW THRALE'S REPORT AND HOW SHE ROSE TO
THE OCCASION. HOW WIDOW THRALE WAS IN FAVOUR OF SILENCE.
HOW GWEN HAD TO SHOW THE FORGED LETTER. THE LINSTOCK AT
THE BREECH. BUT *MY* NAME WAS RUTH DAVERILL! THE GUN GOES
OFF. GWEN'S COOLNESS IN ACTION. BUT WHY IN MRS. PRICHARD'S
LETTER? A CRISIS AND AN AWAKENING. WHO WILL TELL MOTHER?
HOW GWEN GOT FIRST SPEECH OF MRS. PRICHARD. THE DELUSION
CASE'S REPORT OF ITSELF. ANOTHER IMPENETRABLE FORTRESS. THE
STAGE METHOD, AS A LAST RESOURCE. AN *IMPASSE.* "BAS AN AIR
EACHIN." HOW MRS. PRICHARD WANTED TO TELL MRS. MARRABLE
ABOUT HER DEAD SISTER, STILL ALIVE. GWEN'S FORCES SCATTERED,
AND A RALLY. ANOTHER CRISIS, AND SUCCESS. WHO FORGED THAT
LETTER?

THAT had been a quick interview with Dr. Nash in spite of its
importance. For the church clock had been striking eleven when
the mare, four minutes after leaving Dr. Nash, reached Strides
Cottage. A great deal of talk may be got through in a very little
time, as the playwright knows to his cost.

Widow Thrale had been talking with Elizabeth-next-door when
the mare stopped, disappointed at the short run. She heard the

arrival, and came out to find that her ladyship had preceded her into the house. Tom Kettering, having communicated this, stooped down from his elevation to add in confidence:—" Her lady-ship's not looking her best, this short while past. You have an eye to her, mistress. Asking pardon! " It was a concession to speech, on Tom's part, and he seemed determined it should go no farther, for he made a whip-flick tell the mare to walk up and down, and forget the grass rim she had noticed on the footpath. Mrs. Thrale hurried into the house. She, too, had seen how white Gwen was looking, before she started to go to Dr. Nash.

She met her coming from the bedroom, whiter still this time. Her exclamation:—" Dearie me, my lady, how! . . ." was stopped by:—" It is not illness, Mrs. Thrale. I am perfectly well," said with self-command, though with a visible effort to achieve it. But it was clear that the thing that was not illness was a serious thing.

" I was afraid for your ladyship," said Mrs. Thrale. And she remained uneasy visibly.

" I see she is very sound asleep. Will she remain so for awhile? . . . Has not been sleeping at night, did you say? That explains it. . . . No, I won't take anything, thank you! . . . Yes, I will. I'll have some water. I see it on the dresser. That's plenty—thanks! " Thus Gwen's part of what followed. She moistened her lips, and speech was easier to her. They had been so dry and hot. She continued, feeling that the moment had come:—" I want your help, Mrs. Thrale. I have something I must tell you about Mrs. Prichard."

The convict, nearly forgotten since last year, and of course never revived for Widow Thrale, suddenly leaped into her mind out of the past, and menaced evil to her ideal of Mrs. Prichard. She was on her defence directly. " Nay, then—if it is bad, 'tis no fault of the dear old soul's. That I be mortal sure of! "

" Fault of *hers*. No, indeed! It is something I have to tell her. And to tell you." This was the first real attempt to hint at her hearer's personal concern in the something. Would it reach her mind?

Scarcely. To judge by her puzzled eyes fixed on Gwen, and the grave concern of her face, her heart was rich with ready sympathy for whoever should suffer by this unknown thing, but without a clue to its near connection with herself. " Will it be a great sorrow to her to be told it? " said she uneasily. But all on her old guest's account—none on her own.

Gwen felt that her first attempt to breach the fortress of unconsciousness had failed. She must lay a new sap, at another angle; a slower approach, but a surer.

"Not a great sorrow so much as a great shock. You can help me to tell it her so as to spare her." Gwen felt at this point the advantages of the Feudal System. This good woman would never presume to hurry disclosure. "You can help me, Mrs. Thrale, and I will tell you the whole. But I want to know one or two things about what she said." Gwen produced Mrs. Thrale's own letter from a dainty gilded wallet, and opened it. "I understand that the very first appearance of these delusions—or whatever they were—was when she saw the mill-model. Quite the very first?"

"That was, like, the beginning of it," said Mrs. Thrale, recollecting. "She asks me, was little Dave in the right about the wheel-sacks and the water-cart, and I say to her the child is right, but should have said wheat-sacks and water-mill. And then I get it down. . . . Yes, I get it down and show it to her "—this slowly and reminiscently. "And then, my lady, I look round, and there's the poor old soul, all of a twitter!" This was accelerated, for dramatic force.

"You did not put it down to her seeing the mill?"

"No, my lady; I took it she was upset and tired, at her age. I've seen the like before. Not my mother, but old Mrs. Dunage at the Rectory. 'Twas when the news came her mother was killed on the railway. She went quite unconscious, and I helped to nurse her round. She was gone of seventy-seven at the time."

"That was a shock, then?" Gwen felt, although Widow Thrale did not seem to have connected the two things together, that the mill had been the agency that upset Mrs. Prichard.

But she had underestimated the strength of the fortress again. Mrs. Thrale took it as a discrimination between the two cases. "Yes, my lady," said she quietly. "That was a shock. But so you might say, this was a shock, too. By reason of an idea, got on the mind. Dr. Nash said, next day, certainly!"

"Very likely," said Gwen. "But what came next?"

"Well, now—how was it? I was seeing her to bed, unconscious like, and she says to me, on the sudden:—'Whose mill was it?' And then, of course, I say grandfather's. For indeed, my lady, that is so! Mother has had this model all her life, from when grandfather died, and it could be no one else's mill." The irresistible amusement at the absurdity that spread over Ruth's face, and the undercurrent of laughter in her voice, were secret miseries to Gwen, so explicit were they in their tale of the unconsciousness that allowed them. She was relieved when the speaker's voice went back to its tone of serious concern. "And there, now—if the dear old soul didn't say to me, ' How came this mill to be your grandfather's mill?'!"

"And after that?"

"Oh—then I saw plain! But I thought—best say nothing! So I got her off to bed, and she went nicely to sleep, and no more trouble. But next morning early there she was out of bed, hunt-ing for the mill, and feeling round it on the mantelshelf."

"And you still thought it was a delusion?" Gwen said this believing that it *must* excite suspicion of her object. But again unconsciousness, perfectly placid and immovable, had the best of it, where scepticism would have been alert in its defence.

"Well, I did hope next day, talking it over with Dr. Nash, that it was just some confusion of hers with another's mill, a bit like ours; and at her age, no wonder! Because of what she said her-self."

"Said herself?"

"Yes—touching the size of her mill being double. That is, the model. But ah—dear me! It was all gone next day, and she talking quite wild like!" A note of fresh distress in her voice ended in a sigh. Then came a resurrection of hopefulness. "But she has not gone back to it now for some while, and Dr. Nash is hopeful it may pass off."

Gwen began to fear for her own sanity if this was to go on long. To sit there, facing this calm, sweet assurance of that dear old woman's flesh and blood, her own daughter, thick-panoplied in im-penetrable ignorance; to hear her unfaltering condemnation of what she must soon inevitably know to be true; to note above all the tender solicitude and affection her every word was showing for this unknown mother—all this made Gwen's brain reel. Unless some natural resolution of the discord came, Heaven help her, and keep her from some sudden cruel open operation on the heart of Truth, some unconvincing vivisection of a soul! For belief in the incredible, however true, flies from forced nurture in the hothouse of impatience.

Gwen felt for a new opportunity. "When you say that next day she began to talk wildly. . . . What sort of wildly? Are you sure it was so wild?"

Mrs. Thrale lowered her voice to an intense assurance, a heart-felt certainty. "Oh yes, my lady—yes, *indeed!* There was no doubt *possible.* When she was looking at the mill model she had got sight of two little figures—just dollies—that were meant for mother, and her sister who died in Australia—my real mother, you know, only I was but four years old—and the dear old soul went quite mazed about it, saying that was herself and *her* sister that died in England, and they were twins the same as mother and *her* sister. And it was not till she said names Dr. Nash found out how it was all made up of what we told little Davy last year. . . ."

"And you made sure," said Gwen, interrupting, "that you remembered telling little Davy all these things last year?" It took all Gwen's self-command to say this. She was glad to reach the last word.

Widow Thrale looked hurt, almost indignant. "Why, my lady," said she, "we *must* have! Else how could she have known them?" Do not censure her line of argument. Probably at this very hour it is being uttered by a hundred mouths, even as—so says a claimant to knowledge—thirteen earthquakes are always busy, somewhere in the world, at every moment of the day.

Gwen could never give up the attempt, having got thus far. But she could see that hints were useless. "I think I can tell you," said she. And then she pitied the dawn of bewilderment on the unconscious face before her, even while she tried to fortify herself with the thought that what she had to tell was not bad in itself—only a revelation of a lost past. . . . Well—why not let it go? Dust and ashes, dead and done with! . . . But this vacillation was short-lived.

Mrs. Thrale's bewilderment found words. "You can . . . *tell* me!" she said, not much above a whisper. How could she hint at calling her ladyship's words in question, above her breath?

Gwen, very pale but collected, rose to the occasion. "I can tell you what has come to my knowledge about Mrs. Prichard's history. I cannot doubt its correctness." It crossed her mind then that the telling of it would come easier if she ignored what knowledge she had of the other twin sister. So far as Widow Thrale knew, there was nothing outside what had come to light through this incident. She went steadily on, not daring to look at her hearer. "Mrs. Prichard was one of two sisters, whose father owned a flour-mill near London. She married, and her husband committed forgery and was transported. He was sent to Van Diemen's Land—the penal settlement." Gwen looked up furtively. No sign on the unconscious face yet of anything beyond mere perplexity! She resumed after the slightest pause:—"His young wife followed him out there"—she wanted to say that a child of four was left behind, but her courage failed her—"and lived with him. He was out of prison on what is called ticket-of-leave."

She looked up again. Still no sign! But then—consider! Ruth Thrale had always been kept in the dark about the convict. Gwen could not know this, and was puzzled. Was there, after all, some other solution to the problem? Anyhow, there was nothing for it now but to get on. "She lived with him many years, and then, for some reason or other, we can't tell what, he forged a letter from her father in England, saying that her sister and her husband and her own child that she had left behind were all drowned at sea."

At this point Gwen was quite taken aback by Mrs. Thrale saying:—"But they were *not* drowned?" It stirred up a wasps' nest of perplexities. A moment later, she saw that it was a question, not a statement. She herself had only said the letter was forged, not that it contained a lie. How could she vouch for the falsehood of the letter without claiming knowledge prematurely, and rushing into her disclosure too quickly? An additional embarrassment was that, when again she looked up at her hearer, she saw no sign of a clue caught—not even additional bewilderment; rather the reverse.

She could, however, reply to a question:—"Mrs. Prichard believed that they were, and continued to believe it. My father, whom I have told all about it—all that I know—is of opinion that her husband managed to prevent her receiving letters from her sister, and destroyed those that came, which would have shown that she was still alive."

"Oh, God be good to us!" cried Widow Thrale. "That such wickedness should be!"

"He was a monster—a human devil! And *why* he did it Heaven only knows. My father can think of nothing but that his wife wanted to return to her family, and he wanted her to stay. Now, Widow Thrale, you will see why I want you to help me. I think you will agree with me that it would be right that the dear old lady should be undeceived."

Mrs. Thrale fidgeted uneasily. "Your ladyship knows best," she said.

"You think, perhaps," said Gwen, "that it would only give her needless pain to know it now, when she has nothing to gain by it?"

"Yes—that is right." That was said as though Gwen's question had worded a thought the speaker herself had found hard to express.

"*Has* she nothing to gain by it? I do so want you to think over this quietly. . . . I wish you would sit down. . . ." Mrs. Thrale did so. "Thank you!—that *is* comfortabler. Now, just consider this! There is no evidence at all that the young daughter whom she left behind with her sister is not still living, though of course the chances are that the sister herself is dead. This daughter may be. . . . What's that?"

"I thought I heard her waking up. Will your ladyship excuse me one moment? . . ." She rose and went to the bedroom. But the old lady was, it seemed, still sleeping soundly, and she came back and resumed her seat.

Of all the clues Gwen had thrown out to arouse suspicion of the truth, and make full announcement possible, not one had entered the unreceptive mind. Was this to go on until the sleeper really waked? Gwen felt, during that one moment alone, how painfully this would add to the embarrassment, and resolved on an act of desperation.

"I think," said she, speaking very slowly, and fighting hard to hide the effort speech cost her. "I think I should like you to see this horrible forged letter. I brought it on purpose. . . . Oh—here it is! . . . By-the-by, I ought to have told you. Prichard is not her real name." A look like disappointment came on Widow Thrale's face. An *alias* is always an uncomfortable thing. Gwen interpreted this look rightly. "It's no blame to her, you know," she said hastily. "Remember that her proper name—that on the direction there—belonged to a convict! You or I might have done the same."

And then, as the eyes of the daughter turned unsuspicious to her mother's name—forged by her father, to imitate the handwriting of her grandfather—Gwen sat and waited as he who has fired a train that leads to a mine awaits the crash of the rifted rock and its pillar of dust and smoke against the heavens.

"But *my* name was Daverill—Ruth Daverill!" Was the train ill-laid then, that this woman should be able to sit quite still, content to fix a puzzled look upon the wicked penmanship of fifty years ago?

"And your mother's, Ruth Daverill? What was hers?"

"Maisie Daverill." She answered mechanically, with an implication of "And why not?" unspoken. She was still dwelling on the direction, the first name in which was not over-legible, no doubt owing to the accommodation due to the non-erasure of the first syllable by the falsifier. Gwen saw this, and said, quietly but distinctly:—"Thornton."

The end was gained, for better, for worse. Ruth Thrale gave a sudden start and cry, uttering almost her mother's words at first sight of the mill:—"What can this be? What can this be? Tell me, oh, tell me!"

Gwen, hard put to it during suspense, now cool and self-possessed at the first gunshot, rose and stood by the panic-stricken woman. Nothing could soften the shock of her amazement now. Pull her through!—that was the only chance. And the sooner she knew the whole now, the better!

It might have been cruelty to a bad end that made such beauty so pale and resolute as Gwen's, as she said without faltering:— "The name is your mother's name—Mrs. Thornton Daverill. Your father's name was Thornton. Now open the letter and read!"

"Oh—my lady—it makes me afraid! . . . What can it be?"

"Open the letter and read!" But Ruth Thrale *could* not; her hand was too tremulous; her heart was beating too fast. Gwen took the letter from her, quietly, firmly; opened it before her eyes; stood by her, pointing to the words. "Now read!"—she said.

And then Ruth Thrale read as a child reads a lesson:— "My . . . dear . . . daughter . . . Maisie . . ." and a few words more, her voice shaking badly, then suddenly stopped. "But my mother's name was Maisie," she said. She had wavered on some false scent caused by the married name.

"Read on!" said Gwen remorselessly. Social relation said that her ladyship *must* be obeyed first; madness fought against after. Ruth Thrale read on, for the moment quite mechanically. The story of the shipwreck did not seem to assume its meaning. She read on, trembling, clinging to the hand that Gwen had given her to hold.

Suddenly came an exclamation—a cry. "But what is this about Mrs. Prichard? This is *not* Mrs. Prichard. Why is mother's old name in this letter?" She was pointing to the word Cropredy, Phœbe's first married name; a name staggering in the force of its identity. She had not yet seen the signature.

Gwen turned the page and pointed to it:—"Isaac Runciman," clear and unmistakable. Incisiveness was a duty now. Said she, deliberately:—"Why is this forged letter signed with your grand-father's name?" A pause, with only a sort of puzzled moan in answer. "I will tell you, and you will have to hear it. Because it was forged by your father, fifty years ago." Again a pause;

not so much as a moan to break the silence! Gwen made her voice even clearer, even more deliberate, to say:—" Because he forged it to deceive your mother, and it deceived her, and she believed you dead. For years she believed you and her sister dead. And when she returned to Enlgand . . ."

She was interrupted by a poor dumfoundered effort at speech, more seen in the face she was intently watching than heard. She waited for it, and it came at last, in gasps:—" But it is to Mrs. Prichard—the letter—Mrs. Prichard's letter—oh, why?—oh, why? . . ." And Ruth Thrale caught at her head with her hands, as though she felt it near to bursting.

The surgeon's knife is most merciful when most resolutely used.

" Because old Mrs. Prichard *is* your mother," said Gwen, all her heart so given to the task before her that she quite forgot, in a sense, her own existence. " Because she *is* your mother, whom you have always thought dead, and who has always thought you dead. Because she *is* your mother, who has been living here in England—oh, for so many years past!—and never found you out! "

Ruth Thrale's hands fell helpless in her lap, and she sat on, dumb, looking straight in front of her. Gwen would have been frightened at her look, but she caught sight of a tear running down her face, and felt that this was, for the moment, the best that might be. That tear reassured her. She might safely leave the convulsion that had caused it to subside. If only the sleeper in the next room would remain asleep a little longer!

She did right to be silent and wait. Presently the two motionless hands began moving uneasily; and, surely, those were sighs, long drawn out? That had the sound of tension relieved. Then Ruth Thrale turned her eyes full on the beautiful face that was watching hers so anxiously, and spoke suddenly.

" I must go to her at once."

" But think!—is it well to do so? She knows nothing."

" My lady—is there need she should? Nor I cannot tell her now, for I barely know, myself. But I *want* her—oh, I want her! Oh, all these cruel years! Poor Mrs. Prichard! But who will tell mother?" She was stopped by a new bewilderment, perhaps a worse one.

" *I* will tell mother." Gwen took the task upon herself, recklessly. Well!—it had to be gone through with, by someone. And she would do anything to spare this poor mother and daughter. *She* would tell Granny Marrable! She did, however, hope that Dr. Nash had broken the ice for her.

A sound came from the other room. The old lady had awaked and was moving. Mrs. Thrale said in a frightened whisper:—" She will come in here. She always does. She likes to move about a little by herself. But she is soon tired."

Said Gwen:—" Will she come in here? Let me see her alone! Do! It will only be for a few minutes. Run in next door, and leave me to talk to her. I have a reason for asking you." She heard the bedroom door open, beyond the passage.

" When shall I come back, my lady?" This reluctance to go seemed passing strange to Gwen. But it yielded to persuasion, or to feudal inheritance. Gwen watched her vanish slowly into Elizabeth-next-door's; and then, perceiving that the mare had sighted the transaction, and was bearing down towards her, she delayed a moment to say:—" Not yet, Tom! Wait!"—and returned into the house.

" My dear, God has been good to let you come. Oh, how I have prayed to see your face again, and hear your dear voice!" Thus old Mrs. Picture, crying with joy. She could not cling close enough to that beautiful hand, nor kiss it quite to her heart's content.

Gwen left her in possession of it. " But, dear Mrs. Picture," she said, " I thought your letter said you were so comfortable, and that Mrs. Thrale was so kind?"

" What, my Ruth!—that is how I've got to call her—my Ruth is more than kind. No daughter could be kinder to a mother. You know—I told you—my child was Ruth. Long ago—long, long ago! She was asleep when I kissed her. I can feel it still." Gwen fancied her speech sounded wandering, as she sat down in Granny Marrable's vacant chair.

This story often feels that the pen that writes it must resent the improbabilities it is called on to chronicle. That old Maisie should call her own child by the name she gave her, and think her someone else!

" Tell me, dear, what it was—all about it!" Thus Gwen, getting the old lady comfortably settled, and finding a footstool for herself, as in Francis Quarles at the Towers. She had made up her mind to tell all if she possibly could. But it had to be all or nothing. It would be better not to speak till she saw her way. Let Mrs. Picture tell her own tale first!

" I want to tell you." She possessed herself again of the precious hand, surrendered to assist in resettling a strayed head-cushion. " Only, tell me first—did you know . . . ?"—She paused

and dropped her voice—". . . Did you know that they thought
me . . . ? "

" Thought you what? "

" Did you know that they thought me *mad?* "

" They were wrong if they did. But Mrs. Thrale does not think
you mad now. I know she does not."

" Oh, I am glad." Gwen's white and strained look then caught
her attention, and she paused for reassurance. It was nothing,
Gwen was tired. It was the jolting of a quick drive, and so on.
Mrs. Prichard got back to her topic. " They *did* think me mad,
though. Do you know, my dear "—she dropped her voice almost
to a whisper—" I went near to thinking myself mad. It was so
strange! It was the mill-model. I wish she had let me see it
again. That might have set it all to rights. But thinking like
she did, maybe she was in the right. For see what it is when the
head goes wrong! I was calling to mind, all next day, when I
found out what they thought . . ."

" But they did not tell you they thought you mad. How did
you know? "

" It came out by little things—odd talk at times. . . . It got
in the air, and then I saw the word on their lips. . . . I never
heard it, you know. . . . What was I saying? "

" You were calling something to mind, all next day, you said.
What was that? "

" A man my husband would talk about, in Macquarie Gaol,
whose head would be all right so long as no cat came anigh him.
So the others would find a cat to start him off. Only my Ruth
thought to take away what upset *me.* 'Tis the same thing, turned
about like."

Gwen allowed the illustration. " But why *did* Mrs. Thrale think
you mad, over the mill-model? "

" My dear, because to her I must have *seemed* mad, to say that
was my father's mill, and not her grandfather's."

Gwen kept a lock on her tongue. How easy to have said:—
" Your father *was* her grandfather! " She said nothing.

" And yet, you know, how could I be off the thought it was so,
with it there before me, seeming like it did? I do assure you,
there it seemed to be—the very mill! There was my father, only
small, ánd not much to know him by, smoking. And there was
our man, Muggeridge, that saw to the waggon. And there was Mr.
Pitt and Mr. Fox, our horses. And there was the great wheel
the water shot below, to turn it, and the still water above where
Phœbe saw the heron, and called me—but it was gone! " Tears

were filling the old eyes, as the old lips recalled that long-forgotten past. Then, as she went on, her voice broke to a sob, and failed of utterance. But it came. "And there—and there—were I and my darling, my Phœbe, that died in the cruel sea! Oh, my dear —that I might have seen her once again! But once again! . . ." She stopped to recover calm speech; and did it, bravely. "It was all in the seeming of it, my dear, but all the same hard for me to understand. Very like, my dear Ruth here was right and wise to keep it away from me. It might have set me off again. I'm not what I was, and things get on my mind. . . . There now— my dear. See how I've made you cry!"

Gwen felt that this could not go on much longer without producing some premature outbreak of her overtaxed patience; but she could sit still and say nothing; for a little time yet, certainly. "I'm not crying, dear Mrs. Picture," said she. "It was riding against the cold wind. Go on and tell me more." Then a thought occurred to her—a means to an end. "Tell me about your father. You have never told me about him. When did he die?"

"My father? That I could not tell you, my dear, for certain. For no letter reached me when he died, nor yet any letter since his own, that told me of Phœbe's death. Oh, but it is a place for letters to go astray! Why, before they gave my husband charge over the posts, and made him responsible, the carrier would leave letters for the farm on a tree-stump two miles away, and we were bound to send for them there—no other way! And there was none I knew to write to, for news, when Phœbe was gone, and our little Ruth, and Uncle Nick. Such an odd name he had. I never told it you. Nicholas Cropredy."

"I knew it," said Gwen heedlessly. Then, to recover her foothold:—"Somehow or other! You *must* have told it me. Else how could I have known?"

"I *must* have. . . . No, I never knew when my father died. But I should have known. For I stood by his grave when I came back. Such a many years ago now—even that! But I read it wrong. 'May, 1808. . . .' How did I know it was wrong, what I read? Because I looked at his own letter, telling me of the wreck, and it was that very year—but June, not May. And my son was with me then, and he looked at the letter, too, and said it must have been 1818—eighteen, not eight."

Gwen saw the way of this. Phœbe's letter, effaced to make way for the forgery, was to announce Isaac Runciman's death, and was probably written during the first week of June, and posted even later. The English postmark showed two figures for the date; indistinct, as a postmark usually is. Could she utilise this date in any way to sow the seeds of doubt of the authenticity of the letter? She saw no way open. The letter was a thing familiar to Mrs. Prichard, but a sudden thunderbolt to Ruth Thrale. Had Gwen been in possession of Daverill's letter announcing Maisie's own death, she might have shown it to her. But *could* such old eyes have read it, or would she have understood it?

No—it was impossible to do anything but speak. The next opportunity *must* be seized, for talk seemed only to erect new obstacles to action. The perplexities close at hand, there in Strides Cottage, were the things to dwell on. Better go back to them! "But Mrs. Thrale did not think you mad only because you thought that about the mill," Gwen said this to coax the conversation back.

"No, my dear! I think, for all I found to say that night, she might have thought it no more than a touch of fever. And little wonder, too, for her to hear me doubt her grandfather's mill being his own. But what put me past was to see how the bare truth I told of my father's name, and my sister's, and the name of the mill my father would say was older than the church-tower itself— just that and no more—to make her "—here the old lady lowered her voice, and glanced round as though to be sure they were alone —" to make her turn and run from me, quite in a maze, as though I was a ghost to frighten her, that was what unsettled me!" She fixed her eyes on Gwen, and her hands were restless with her distressing eagerness to get some clue to a solution of her perplexity.

Gwen could say nothing, short of everything. She simply dared not try to tell the whole truth, with a rush, to a hearer so frail and delicate. It seemed that any shock must kill. The musical voice went on, its appealing tone becoming harder and harder for her hearer to bear. "Why—oh why—when I was telling just the truth, that my father's name was Isaac Runciman, and my sister was Phœbe, and our mill was Darenth Mill, why should she not have heard me through to the end, to make it all clear? Indeed, my dear, she put me on thinking I was not saying the words I thought, and I was all awake and clear the whole time. Was I not?"

Gwen's response:—"I will ask her what it was," contained, as a temporary palliative, as much falsehood as she dared to use; just to soothe back the tears that were beginning to get the better of speech. She felt vaguely about for a straw to catch at—something that might soften the revelation that had to come. "Did you tell her your sister was Phœbe?"

"I told her Phœbe—only Phœbe. I never said her married name."

"Did you tell her you and your sister were twins?"

"Oh yes—I told her that. And I think she understood. But she did not say."

"I think, dear Mrs. Picture, I can tell you why she was astonished. It was because *her* mother had a twin sister."

The old lady's pathetic look of perplexity remained unchanged. "Was that enough?" she said. The mere coincidence of the twinship did not seem to her to have warranted the effect it produced.

"I am not sure that it was not. There are other things. Did she ever tell you her mother's story? I suppose she told you she is only her mother by adoption? You know what I mean?"

"Oh yes, perfectly! No—Ruth has not told me that. We have not talked much of old Mrs. Marrable, but I shall see her before I go back to Sapps Court. Shall I not? My Davy's other Granny in the country!" It did her good to think and speak of Dave.

"You shall go back to Davy," said Gwen. "Or Davy shall come to you. You may like to stay on longer with Mrs. Thrale."

"Oh, indeed I should . . . if only . . . if only . . ."

"If only she hadn't thought you had delusions!—isn't that it? . . . Well, let me go on and tell you some more about her mother—or aunt, really. It is quite true that she was one of twin sisters, and the sister married and went abroad."

Mrs. Prichard was immensely relieved—almost laughed. "There now!—if she had told me *that,* instead of running away with ideas! We would have found it all out, by now."

Gwen felt quite despairing. She had actually lost ground. Was it conceivable that the whole tale should become known to Mrs. Prichard—or to both sisters, for that matter—and be discredited on its merits, with applause for its achievements in coincidence? It looked like it! Despair bred an idea in her mind; a mad one, perhaps, a stagey one certainly. How would it be to tell Maisie Phœbe's story, seen from Phœbe's point of view?

Whenever an exciting time comes back to us in after-life, the incident most vividly revived is usually one of its lesser ones. Years after, when Gwen's thoughts went back to this trying hour at Strides Cottage, this moment would outstep its importance by reminding her how, in spite of the pressure and complexity of her embarrassment, an absurd memory *would* intrude itself of an operatic tenor singing to the soprano the story of how she was changed at birth, and so forth, the *diva* listening operatically the while. It went so far with her now, for all this tension, as to make a comment waver about her innermost thought, concerning the strange susceptibility of that soprano to conviction on insufficient evidence. Then she felt a fear that her own power of serious effort might be waning, and she concentrated again on her problem. But no solution presented itself better than the stagey one. Is the stage right, after all?

" The sister married and went abroad. Her husband was a bad man, whom she had married against the consent of her family." Gwen looked to see if these words had had any effect. But nothing came of them. She continued:—" Poor girl! her head was turned, I suppose.

" My dear—'twas the like case with me! 'Tis not for me, at least, to sit in judgment."

" No, dear Mrs. Picture, nor any of us. But if she had been as bad as the worst, she could hardly have deserved what came about. I told you she had married a bad man, and I am going to tell you how bad he was." It was as well that Gwen should rouse her hearer's attention by a sure and effective expedient, for it was flagging slightly. Dave's other Granny's sister's misadventures seemed to have so little to do with the recent mystery of the mill-model. But a genuine bad man enthrals us all.

" What did he do? " said his unconscious widow.

" He forged a letter to his own wife, saying that her sister was dead, and she believed it."

" But did her sister never write, to say she was alive? "

" Old Mrs. Marrable? No—because she received a letter at the same time saying that *her* sister . . . You see which I mean? . . ."

" Oh yes—the bad man's wife, who was abroad."

". . . Was also dead. Do you think you see how it was? He told each sister the other was dead."

" Oh, I see *that!* But did they both believe it? "

" Both believed it."

" Then did Mrs. Marrable's sister die without knowing? "

Gwen had it on her lips to say:—" She is not dead," before she had had time to foresee the consequences. She had almost said it when an apprehension struck across her speech and cut it short. How could she account to Mrs. Prichard for this knowledge of Mrs. Marrable's sister without narrowing the issue to the simple question:—" Who and where is she? " And if those grave old eyes, at rest now that the topic had become so impersonal to them, were fixed upon her waiting for the answer, how could she find it in her heart to make the only answer possible, futile fiction apart:—" It is *you* I am speaking of—*you* are Mrs. Marrable's sister, and each has falsely thought the other dead for a life-time " ? All her elaborate preparation had ended in an *impasse,* blocked by a dead wall whose removal was only possible to the bluntest declaration of the truth, almost more cruel now than it would have been before this factitious abatement of the agita-tion in which Gwen had found her.

And then the long tension that had kept Gwen on the rack, more or less, since the revelation of the letter, keenly in this last hour or so, began to tell upon her, and her soul came through into her words. " Oh no—oh no! Mrs. Marrable's sister did not die without knowing—at least, I mean . . . I mean she has not died. . . . She may . . ." She was stopped by the danger of inexplicable tears, in time as she thought.

But old Mrs. Prichard, always on the alert for her Guardian Angel, caught the slight modulation of her voice, and was alive with ready sympathy. " Why—oh why—why this? . . ." she be-gan, wanting to say:—" Why such concern on Mrs. Marrable's account? " and finding herself at fault for words, came to a dead stop.

" You mean, why should *I* fret because of Mrs. Marrable's sis-ter? Is it not that? "

" Ye-es. I think . . . I think that is what I meant to say."

Gwen nerved herself for a great effort. She took both the old hands in hers, and all her beauty was in the eyes that looked up at the old face, as she said:—" I will tell you. It is because—*I*— have to tell *her* to-day . . . that she is . . . that she is . . . Mrs. Marrable's sister ! " The last words might have been a cry for pity.

Could old Maisie fail to catch a gleam of the truth? She did. She only saw that her sweet Guardian Angel was in trouble, and thought to herself:—" Can I not help her? " She immediately said, quite quietly and clearly:—" My dear—my dear! But it will give you such pain. Why not let *me* tell her? I am old, and my time is at hand. It would be nothing to me. For see what trouble I have had myself. And I could say to her . . ."

" What could you say to her? " Desperation was in Gwen's voice. How could this awful barrier be passed? Could it be past at all—ever?

" I could tell her of all the trouble of my own life, long ago. I do think, if I told her and said, ' See—it might have been me,' that might make it easy." The suggestion was based on a perfectly reasonable idea. Gwen felt that her own task would have been more achievable had her own record been one of sorrow and defeat. Old Maisie took her silence—which was helplessness against new difficulties—for an encouragement to her proposal, and continued:—"Why, my dear, look at it this way! If my dear sister Phœbe had lived, anyone bad enough out there in the Colony, might have written a lie that I was dead, and who would have known?... But, my dear, you are ill? You are shaking."

It was a climax. The perfect serenity, the absolute unconsciousness, of the speaker had told the tale of Gwen's failure more plainly than any previous rebuff. And here was the old lady trying to get up from her chair to summon Widow Thrale! Gwen detained her gently; as, having risen from the stool at her feet, she kneeled beside her.

"No, no—I am not ill. . . . I will tell you directly."

Moments passed that, to Gwen's impatience for speech she could neither frame nor utter, might have been hours. Old Maisie's growing wonderment was bringing back the look she had had over that mill-model. But she said nothing.

Gwen's voice came at last, audibly to herself, scarcely more. "I want you—I want you to tell me something. . . ."

"What, my dear? . . . Oh—to tell you something! Yes—what is it?"

Was the moment at hand, at last? Gwen managed to raise her voice. "I want you to tell me this:—Has Mrs. Thrale ever told you her mother's name—I mean her aunt's—Granny Marrable's?"

"Her christened name?—her own name?"

"Yes!"

"No!"

"Shall I tell it you?"

"Why not? . . . Oh, I am frightened to see you so white. My dear!"

"Listen, dear Mrs. Picture, and try to understand. Mrs. Thrale's aunt's name is Phœbe."

"*Is Phœbe!*"

"Is Phœbe." Gwen repeated it again, looking fixedly at the old face, now rapidly resuming its former utter bewilderment.

"Is . . . Phœbe!" Old Maisie sat on, after echoing back the word, and Gwen left her to the mercy of its suggestion. She had done her best, and could do no more.

She saw that some new thought was at work. But it had to plough its way through stony ground. Give it time! Watching her intently, she could see the critical moment when the new light broke. A moment later the hand she held clutched at hers beyond its strength, and its owner's voice was forcing its way through gasps. "But . . . but . . . but . . . Widow Thrale's name is *Ruth!*"

"Is Ruth." Yes—leave the fact there, and wait! That was Gwen's decision.

A moment later what she waited for had come. Old Maisie started, crying out aloud:—"Oh, what is this—what *is* it?" as she had done when she first saw the mill-model. Then on a sudden a paroxysm seized on the frail body, so terrifying to Gwen that her heart fairly stood still to see it.

It did not kill. It seemed to pass, and leave a chance for speech. But not just yet. Only a long-drawn breath or two, ending always in a moan!

Then, with a sudden vehemence:—"Who was it—who was it—that forged the letter that came—*that came to my husband and me?*" Her voice rose to a shriek under the sting of that terrible new knowledge. But she had missed a main point in Gwen's tale. Her mind had received the forgery, but not its authorship.

Gwen saw nothing to wonder at in this. The thing was done, and that was enough. "It was your husband himself," said she, and would have gone on to ask forgiveness for her own half-distortion of the facts, and told how she came to the knowledge. But the look on her hearer's face showed her that this must be told later, if indeed it were ever told at all. She was but just in time to prevent old Maisie falling forward from her chair in a dead swoon. She could not leave her, and called aloud for help.

She did not need to call twice. For Widow Thrale, unable to keep out of hearing through an interview so much longer than her anticipation of it, had come into the house from the back, and was already in the passage; had, indeed, been waiting in feverish anxiety for leave to enter.

"Take her—take her!" cried Gwen. "No—never mind me!" And then she saw, almost as in a dream, how the daughter's strong arms clasped her mother, and raising the slight unconscious figure, that lay as if dead, bore it away towards the door. "Yes," said she, "that is right! Lay her on the bed!"

What followed she scarcely knew, except that she caught at a chair to save herself from falling. For a reaction came upon her with the knowledge that her task was done, and she felt dizzy and

sick. Probably she was, for a minute or more, practically unconscious; then recovered herself; and, though feeling very insecure
on her feet, followed those two strange victims of a sin half a
century old. Not quite without a sense of self-reproach for weakness; for see how bravely the daughter was bearing herself, and
how immeasurably worse it was for her!

She could not but falter between the doors, still standing open.
How could she dare to enter the room where she might find the
mother dead? That was her fear. And a more skilful, a gentler
revelation, might have left her a few years with the other little
twin of the mill-model, still perhaps with a decade of life to
come.

She heard the undertones of the daughter's voice, using the
name of mother. What was she saying?

"My mother—my mother—my mother!" And then, with a
strange acceptance of the name in another sense:—"But when
will mother know?"

Gwen entered noiselessly, and stood by the bedside. She began
to speak, but shrank from her last word:—"She is not . . . ?"

Widow Thrale looked up from the inanimate form she was clasping so closely in her arms, to say, quite firmly:—"No, she is not
dead." Then back again, repeating the words:—"My mother!"
as though they were to be the first the unconscious ears should
hear on their revival. Then once more to Gwen, as in discharge
of a duty omitted:—"God bless you, my lady, for your goodness
to us!"

Gwen's irresistible vice of anticlimax nearly made her say:—
"Oh bother!" It was stopped by a sound she thought she heard.
"Is she not speaking?" she said.

Both listened, and Widow Thrale heard, being the nearer, "Who
called you her mother?" she repeated. "*I* did." And then Gwen
said, clearly and fearlessly:—"Your daughter Ruth!"

CHAPTER XVI

SIR CROPTON FULLER'S LUNCH. LAZARUS'S FAMILY. HOW HIS GREAT-
GRANNY CATECHIZED A TOOTHLESS HUMAN PUPPY THIRTEEN MONTHS
OLD. HOW DR. NASH DRAGGED MRS. PRICHARD IN. A VERY TAKING
OLD PERSON, BUT QUITE CRACKED. GOD'S MERCY IN LEAVING US
OUR NATURAL FACULTIES. THAT WAS A SEVERE CASE AMONG THE
TOMBS. HOW DR. NASH HAD ALL THE MODEL STORY OUT AGAIN,
AND ABOUT MUGGERIDGE'S DON GIOVANITIES. MRS. PRICHARD HAD
KNOWN MAISIE, CLEARLY. EVERYTHING EXPLAINED. THE FUTILITY
OF HYPOTHESES. HOW A MEMORY OF HER MADMAN-CONVICT MADE
OLD PHŒBE FEEL BEWITCHED. OBSTINATE PATERNITY. THE MEAS-
UREMENT OF THAT MODEL. WHY ARM-MEASUREMENT? KID'S JAR-
GON. MR. BARLOW. DAVE'S LETTER DELIVERED. A SORT OF FAINT.
VINEGAR. DR. NASH PURSUED AND BROUGHT BACK. HOW OLD PHŒBE
CAME TO KNOW THE TRUTH THROUGH A CHILD'S DIRECT SPEECH.
HER PRESENCE OF MIND. AND HOW SHE WENT STRAIGHT HOME, TO
LOOK BACK ON FIFTY LOST YEARS

The madman who had claimed as his mother the old woman at
Strides Cottage, whom Granny Marrable had not yet seen, had
certainly no statutory powers to impose an oath. But this did
not stand in the way of her keeping hers, religiously. That is to
say, she kept her tongue silent on every point that she could reasonably suppose to call for secrecy, whether from his point of view
or this old Mrs. Prichard's.

She felt at liberty to repeat what she remembered of his shocking ravings about his prison life, and to dwell on the fact that
he appeared to have mistaken her for his mother. But this could
be told without connecting him with any person in or near the
village. He was a returned convict who had not seen his mother
for twenty years, and meeting an old woman who closely resembled her, or his idea of what she must have become, had made a
decisive mistake in identity.

As to the name he had written down for her, she simply shrank
from it; and destroyed it promptly, as soon as she collected her
faculties after the shock it gave her. She framed a satisfactory
theory to account for it, out of materials collected by foraging
among her memories of fifty years ago. It turned on these facts:—
That the name Ralph Thornton Daverill was the baptismal name

of her sister's little boy that died in England, and that Maisie
had repeated to her what her husband had said after the child's
death, that the name would do over again if ever she had another son; but had added that she herself would never consent
to its adoption. Granny Marrable was sure on both these points,
but so uncertain about what she had heard of the christenings of
her nephews born in Van Diemen's Land, that she had no scruple
in deciding that her sister had dissuaded her brother-in-law from
his intention. For this madman was clearly not Maisie's son, if
Mrs. Prichard was his mother. But what would be more natural
and probable than that if Daverill married again, he should make
use of the name a second time? He might have married again
more than once, for anything Granny Marrable knew. So might
his widow—might have married a man named Prichard. Why
not? Those were considerations she need not weigh or speculate
about.

Nevertheless, though she had destroyed the signed name, it was
a cobweb in her memory she would have gladly brushed away altogether. How she would have liked to tell the whole to Ruth,
when—as once or twice happened—she walked over from Chorlton
to get a report of progress, leaving old Mrs. Prichard in charge
of that loyal dog, supported by Elizabeth-next-door, if need were.
But she was sworn to silence on matters she dared not provoke
inquiry about. So her tale of her meeting with the convict was
minimised.

On the other hand, Ruth was scrupulously uncommunicative
of everything connected with Mrs. Prichard's supposed delusions.
So was Dr. Nash, on the one or two occasions when he looked in
at Costrell's Farm, prophylactically. Where was the use of upsetting Juno Lucina by telling her that her daughter had taken
a lunatic inmate? All the circumstances considered, he would
have much preferred that Mrs. Maisie's mother should take charge
of her. But this young woman liked to have her own way.

The doctor was almost sorry, after Gwen drove away, that he
had not pointed out what an unpropitious moment it was for an
upsetting revelation, and suggested postponement. It was too
late to do anything, by the time he thought of it. He shrugged
his shoulders about it, and perceived that what was done couldn't
be undone. Then he drove as fast as he could to Sir Cropton
Fuller, who asked him to stay to lunch. This meant a long un-
employed delay, but he compromised. He would see another patient, and return to lunch, after which he would go to Costrell's
Farm. It was only a short drive from the Manor House, but if

he had gone there direct, he knew the mid-day meal at the Farm would cut across what might prove a long conversation with Granny Marrable. Suppose circumstances should favour a full communication of the extraordinary disclosure he had it in his power to make to her, he would not feel any hesitation about making it. In fact, he hoped that might prove the natural order of events, although he was quite prepared to act on Lady Gwendolen's suggestion that he should merely lay the train, not fire it, if that should prove possible. But, said he to himself, that will be neither fish nor flesh. Mysterious hints—so ran his reflections—will only terrify the old body out of her seven senses and gain no end. Get the job over!—that was the sacramental word. It took him all the period of his drive to Sir Cropton's, and all the blank bars betwixt prescription and prescription, to get—as it were—to this phrase in the music.

But by the time Sir Cropton had given him lunch, it had become the dominant theme of his reflections. Get the job done—if possible! More especially because he did not want Juno Lucina's nerves to be upset at a critical moment, and that was exactly what might happen if the revelation were delayed too long. If she were told now, and disabled by the shock, there would at least be time to make sure of a capable substitute.

However, he must be guided by his prognosis on arriving at Costrell's. It is just possible, too, that the doctor was alive to the interest of the case on its own account, and not being himself personally involved, felt a sort of scientific curiosity in the issue— What would the old lady say or do, in face of such an extraordinary revelation? What were the feelings of the family of Lazarus when he was raised from the tomb? Or rather, what would they have been, had he been dead half a century?

The males at the farm would be away at this time of day; that was satisfactory. He wanted to talk to Granny Marrable alone, if possible. He could easily get his patient out of the way— that was a trifle. But it would be a bore to have that young brother hanging round. In that case he would have to negotiate a private conversation with Juno Lucina, as such, and to use the opportunity professional mystery would give.

However, events smiled upon his purpose. Only Mrs. Maisie, a perfect image of roseate health, was there alone with Granny; the two of them appreciating last year's output, unconscious in his cradle, enjoying the fourteenth month of his career in this world, having postponed teething almost beyond precedent. His young mother derided her doctor's advice to go and lie down and rest, but ultimately gave way to it, backed as it was by public opinion.

"We seem to be going on very well, Mrs. Marrable," said the doctor, when this end was achieved. The doctor shared a first person plural with each of his patients. "*And* yourself? You're not *looking* amiss."

"No, thank God! And for all that I be eighty-one this Christmas, if I live to see the New Year in, I might be twenty-eight." She then very absurdly referred to the baby, who had waked up and made his presence felt, as to whether this was, or was not, an exaggeration, suggesting that he had roused himself to confirm it. Did he, she asked, want to say his great-Granny was as young as the best, and was he a blessed little cherub? She accommodated her pronunciation to the powers of understanding she imputed to him, calling him, *e.g.*, a bessed ickle chezub. He seemed impatient of personalities; but accepted, as a pipe of peace, an elastic tube that yielded milk. Whereupon Granny Marrable made no more attempts to father opinions on him. "Indeed, doctor," said she, speaking English again, "I wish every soul over fifty felt as young as I do. We shouldn't hear such a many complaints."

"Very bad for the profession, Mrs. Marrable! This isn't a good part of the world for my trade, as it is, and if everyone was like you, I should have to put the shutters up. Well!—you see how it is? Look at Miss Grahame—Sister Nora! Goes up to London the picture of health, and gets fever! Old lady from some nasty unwholesome corner by Tottenham Court Road comes down to Chorlton, and gets younger every day!"

"I was going to ask about Sister Nora, doctor—what the latest news was saying."

"She'll make a good recovery, as things go. But that means she won't be herself again for a twelvemonth, if then!" Granny Marrable looked so unhappy over this, that the doctor took in a reef. "Less if we're lucky—less if we're lucky!" said he. "She's being very well looked after. Dalrymple's a good man."

"I'm glad you should know him to speak well of, for the lady's sake. She's a good lady, and kind. It was through her the little boy Davy came to the Cottage. My little Davy, I always call him."

"So does t'other old lady—she your daughter's got there now. You'll scratch each other's eyes out over that young monkey when you come to meet, Mrs. Marrable."

"There now, doctor, you will always have your joke. Ruth—

my daughter—is quite beside her judgment about the old soul.
What like is she, doctor, to your thinking?"

"Well—your daughter's right about her." He paused a moment, and then added, meaningly:—"So far as being a very—
very *taking* sort of old person goes."

Granny Marrable, rather absorbed in her descendant's relations
with his bottle, found in due course an opportunity to answer,
looking up at the doctor:—"A very taking old person? But what,
then, is to seek in her? Unless she be bad of heart or dishonest."
Her old misgivings about Dave's home influences, revived, had
more share in the earnestness of her tone than any misgivings
about her daughter. And was not there the awful background of
the convict?

"Not a bit of it—not a bit of it! Right as a trivet, I should
say, as far as that goes! But . . ." He stopped and touched his
forehead, portentously.

"Ah—the poor soul! Now is that true?"

"I think you may take it of me that is so." The doctor threw
his professional manner into this. After a moment he added,
as a mere human creature:—"Off her chump! Loose in the top
story!" A moment after, for professional reassurance:—"But
quite harmless—quite harmless!"

Granny Marrable was grave and oppressed by this news. "The
poor old soul!—think of it!" said she. "Oh, but how many's the
time I've thanked God in His mercy for sparing me my senses!
To think we might any of us be no better off, but for Him, than
the man our Lord found naked in the tombs, in the country
of the Gadarenes! But she is not bad like that, this Mrs. Prichard?"

"Oh no!—that was a severe case, with complications. Not
a legion of devils, this time! One or two little ones. Just simple
delusions. Might have yielded to Treatment, taken younger. Too
late, now, altogether. Wastage of the brain, no doubt! She's
quite happy, you know."

Although Dr. Nash had not shone as a reasoner forming square
to resist evidence, he had shrewd compartments in his mind, and
in one of them a clear idea that he would do ill to thrust forward
the details of the supposed simple delusions. This old lady must
not be led to infer that he was interested in *them*—mere scientific
curiosities! She was sure to ask for them in time; he knew that.
And it was much better that he should seem to attach no weight
whatever to them.

Granny Marrable seemed to entertain doubts of the patient's

happiness. "I could never be happy," she said, "if I had been in a delusion."

"Not if you came to know it was a delusion. Very likely not!"

"But does not—does not—poor old Mrs. Prichard ever come to know she has been in a delusion?"

"Not she! What she fancies she just goes on fancying. Sticks to it like grim death."

"What sort of things now, doctor?"

This was a bite. But the doctor would play his fish. No hurry. "*Perfectly* crazy things! Oh—crack-brained! Has not your daughter told you? . . . Oh, by-the-by!—yes!—I did tell her she had better not. . . . I don't think it matters, though."

"But not if you would rather not, doctor!" This clearly meant the reverse.

"Well now—there was the first thing that happened, about that little model thing that stands on your mantelshelf at the cottage."

"What—my father's mill? Davy's mill, we call it now, because the child took to it so, and would have me tell him again and again about Muggeridge and the horses. . . ."

"Ah—you told him about Muggeridge and the horses!"

"Yes, sure! And I lay, now, he'd told Mrs. Prichard all about *that!*"

"Trust him! Anyhow, he *did*. And she knew all about it before ever she came to Chorlton. But her mind got a queer twist over it, and she forgot it was all Master Dave's telling, and thought it had happened to herself."

"Thought what had?"

"I mean, thought *she* had been one of those two little kiddies in violet frocks. . . ."

"Ah, dear me—my dear sister that died out in Australia—my darling Maisie!"

"Hay—what's that? Your darling what? What name did you say?"

"Maisie."

"There we have it—Maisie!" The doctor threw his forefinger to Granny Marrable, in theory; it remained attached to his hand in practice. "That's *her* name. That's what it was all cooked up out of. Maisie!" He was so satisfied with this little piece of shrewd detective insight that he forgot for the moment how thoroughly he knew the contrary.

Granny Marrable seemed to demur a little, but was brought to order by the drastic argument that it *must* have been that, *because* it could not have been anything else. By this time the doctor had recollected that he was not in a position to indulge in the luxury of incredulity.

"At least," said he, "I should have said so, only it doesn't do to be rash. One has to look at a thing of this sort all round." He paused a moment with his eyes on the ceiling, while his fingers played on the arm of his chair the tune, possibly, of a Hymn to Circumspection. Then he looked suddenly at the old lady. "You must have told the small boy a great deal about the mill-model. *You* told him about Muggeridge, didn't you say, and the horses? Not your daughter, I mean?"

"Sure! Mr. Pitt and Mr. Fox."

"Tell him anything else about Muggeridge?"

"Well, now—did I? . . . No—I should say not. . . . I was trying to think what I would have remembered to tell. For you must bear in mind, doctor, we were but young children when Muggeridge went away, and Axtell came, after that. . . . No. I could *not* speak to having said a word about Muggeridge, beyond his bare name. That I could not."

The doctor did not interrupt his witness's browsings in the pastures of memory; but when she deserted them, saying she had found nothing to crop, said suddenly:—"Didn't tell him about Muggeridge and the other lady, who wasn't Mrs. Muggeridge?"

"Now Lard a mercy, doctor, whatever do ye take me for? And all these years you've known me! Only the *idea* of it!—to tell a young child that story! Why—what would the baby have thought I meant? Fie for shame of yourself, that's what *I* say!" A very small amount of indignation leavened a good deal of hilarity in this. The old lady enjoyed the joke immensely. That she, at eighty, should tell a child of seven a tale of nuptial infidelity! She took her great-grandson into her confidence about it, asking him:—"Did they say his great-grandmother told shocking stories to innocent little boys?"—and so forth.

The doctor had to interpose upon this utter unconsciousness, and the task was not altogether an easy one; indeed, its difficulties seemed to him to grow. He let her have her laugh out, and then said quietly:—"But where did Mrs. Prichard get the story?"

Granny Marrable had lost sight of this, and was disconcerted. "What—why—yes—where *did* she get it? Mrs. Prichard, of course! Now, wherever could Mrs. Prichard have got it? . . ." It called for thought.

Dr. Nash's idea was to give facts gradually, and let them work their own way. "Perhaps she knew Mr. Muggeridge herself," said he. "When did he die?"

"Mercy me, doctor, where's the use of asking *me?* Before *you* were born, anyhow! That's him, a man of forty, with the horses and me a child under ten! Seventy years ago, and a little to spare!"

"*That* cock won't fight, then. As I make out, old Mrs. Prichard didn't come from Van Diemen's Land above five-and-twenty years ago."

"*Where* did Mrs. Prichard come from?"

"From Van Diemen's Land. In Australia. Where the convicts go."

"There now! Only to think of that! Why—I see it all!" Granny Marrable seemed pleased.

"What do you see, Mrs. Marrable?" The doctor was puzzled. He had quite expected that at this point suspicion of the facts *must* dawn, however dimly.

"Because that is where my dear sister was, that died. Oh, so many long years ago!" Whenever old Phœbe mentioned Maisie, the same note of pathos came in her voice. The doctor felt he was operating for the patient's sake; but it would be the knife, without an anæsthetic. He had not indefinite time to spare for this operation.

"I am going to ask what will seem a very absurd question," said he, in the dry, professional manner in which he was wont to intrude upon his patients' private internal affairs. "But you must remember I am an outsider—quite in the dark."

A slight puzzled look on the strong old face before him, with —yes—a faint suspicion of alarm! But oh, how faint! Perhaps he was mistaken, though. For Granny Marrable let no sign of alarm come in her voice, if she felt any. "What were ye wishing to be told, doctor?" she cheerfully said. "If it's a secret, I won't tell it ye. You may take my word for that."

He fixed his eyes attentively on her face. "You are absolutely certain," said he, "that the news of your sister's death was . . ." He was going to say "authentic," but was arrested by an ebullition of unparalleled fury in the baby, who became fairly crumpled up with indignation, presumably at being unable to hold more than a definite amount of milk. It was a case that called for the promptest and humblest apologies from the human race, represented by his great-grandmother. She had assuaged the natural exasperation of two previous generations, and had the trick of it. He subsided, accepting as his birthright a heavenly sleep, with dreams of further milk.

Then Granny Marrable, released, looked the doctor in the face, saying:—"'That the news of my sister's death was? . . .'" and stopped for him to finish the sentence.

"Authentic," said he. He did not know whether her look meant that she did not understand the word, and added:—"Trustworthy."

"I know what you mean," she said. "Go on and say why?"

The doctor was fairly frightened at his own temerity. Probably the difficulties of his task had never fully dawned upon him. Would it not be safer to back out of it now, leaving what he had suggested to fructify? He would have fulfilled his promise to Lady Gwendolen, and made it easier for her to word the actual disclosure of the facts. "I was merely trying to think what anyone would say who wanted to make out that this old Mrs. Prichard was not under a delusion."

"The poor old soul! What would they say, indeed?" This was no help. Commiseration of Mrs. Prichard was not the doctor's object. But the position was improved when she added:—"But there's ne'er a one *wants* to make it out."

He thought of saying:—"But suppose there were!" and gave it up, knowing that his hearer, though fairly educated, would regard hypotheses as intense intellectual luxuries, prized academically, but without a place in the sane world without. He decided on saying:—"Of course, you would have documentary evidence." Then he felt that his tone had been ill-chosen—a curfew of the day's discussions, a last will and testament of the one in hand.

So it was, for the moment. Granny Marrable wanted the subject to drop. On whatever pretext it was revived, the story of her sister's life and death was still painful to her. But "documentary evidence" was too sesquipedalian to submit to without a protest. "I should have her husband's letter," said she, "telling of her death."

"Yes, you would have his letters."

"There was but two." Her intense truthfulness could not let that plural pass. "He was a strange man—and a bad one, doctor, if ye want to know—and he never wrote to me again, not after answering my letter I wrote to tell him of my father's death. But I've a long letter from him, saying how Maisie died, and her message to me, giving me—like you might say—her girl for my own. That is my Ruth, you know, at Strides Cottage, this little man's own granny. But I've never heard his name since . . . not till . . . not till . . ."

"What's the matter? Anything wrong?" For Granny Marrable had stopped with a jerk, and her look was one of the greatest bewilderment. The memory of the name the madman who said he was Mrs. Prichard's son had given her as his own had come upon her with a sudden shock, having—strangely enough—been dormant throughout this interview. She was confronted with a host of perplexities, which—mark you!—had no possible solution except the one her mind could not receive, and which therefore never presented itself at all.

"Indeed, doctor, I think I be bewitched outright," said she. "I never was so put to it, all the days of my life. . . . No, don't ye ask me no questions! I haven't the liberty to tell above half of it, and maybe better say nothing at all."

"I see—matter of confidence! Well—I mustn't ask questions." This was really because he was certain the answer would come without asking. Granny Marrable would never let the matter drop, with that look on her face.

So it turned out. In a moment she looked up from the baby, whom she had been redistributing, to his advantage. "I'll tell ye this much, doctor," she said. "There was a crazy man in yonder field near by, when I was coming back from Jane Naunton's—just a few days since. . . ."

"I've heard of him."

"What do they say of him?"

"I only heard the police were after him. Go on."

"Well—the name he called himself by was my sister's husband's, and he said he came from Australia."

"That might be, and no witchcraft. When did your sister die?"

"Five-and-forty—six-and-forty—years ago!"

"Any children left? Boys?"

"Boys?—Lord, no! At least, yes—two boys! What I mean is, not by this name."

"What were the boys' names?"

"One, I call to mind, was Isaac. For Maisie wrote me what work she had to persuade her husband to the name. . . ." She had meant to say more, giving reasons why, but changed her speech abruptly. "The youngest boy's name I let slip. But I know it was never this name that man gave me."

"You remember it near enough for that?"

Granny Marrable's intense truthfulness would not allow margins. "No—it's clean slipped my memory, and I could not make oath I never knew it. It was all out of reach, beyond the seas."

"That seems reasonable. Five-and-forty years! Now, can I

remember anything as long back as that? . . . However, I was two, so that doesn't count."

"Maisie's son never bore this name. That's out of doubt!"

"Why?"

"Because her first was christened by it, and died at Darenth Mill, after . . . after his father went away."

"Roger Trufitt's son is Roger. But both his brothers who died before he was born were named Roger. There's no law against it. You know old Trufitt, the landlord at the Five Bells? He says that if this son died, he would marry again to have another and call him Roger. He's a very obstinate man, old Trufitt."

Granny Marrable sat silent while the doctor chatted, watching her changes of countenance. Her conscience was vacillating. Could she interpret her oath of silence as leaving her free to speak of the convict's claim to Mrs. Prichard as a parent? The extenuation of bad faith would lie in the purely exceptional nature of the depository of her secret. Could a disclosure to a professional ear, which secrets entered every day, be accounted "splitting"? She thought she saw her way to a limited revelation, which would meet the case without breach of confidence.

"Maybe!" said she, putting old Trufitt out of court. "But I can tell ye another reason why he's no son of my sister's. Though he might be, mind you, a son of her husband. My brother-in-law, most like, married again. How should I know?"

"What's the other reason?"

"He told me his mother's name. But I am not free to tell it, by reason I promised not to."

This struck the doctor as odd. "How came you to be talking to a stray tramp about his mother, Granny Marrable?" he asked shrewdly.

"Because he took me for his mother, and would have it I should know him." This was no doubt included in what she had promised not to tell, but the question had taken her by surprise.

A light broke on Dr. Nash. All through the interview he had been wondering at himself for never having before observed the likeness between the two old women, which he now saw plainly by the light of the information Gwen had given him. He might have seen it before, had he heard of the gipsy's mistake, but Ruth Thrale had never mentioned this. He remembered, too, in Gwen's story, some slight reference to a son of Mrs. Prichard who was a *mauvais sujet*. He determined on a daring *coup*. "Are you sure Mrs. Prichard is not the mother he was looking for?" said he.

Granny Marrable was struck with his cleverness. " Now, how *ever* did you come to find *that* out, doctor? " said she. " We're a clever lot, us doctors! We've got to be clever. . . . Let's see, now—where are we? Mrs. Prichard has a son who is called by your brother-in-law's name, but who is *not* your sister's son. Because if he were, Mrs. Prichard would be your sister. Which is impossible. But Mrs. Prichard has got muddled about her own identity, and thinks she is. What can we do to cure such a delusion? I've seen a great deal of this sort of thing—I've had charge of lunatics—and the only thing I know of for the case is to stimulate memory of the patient's actual past life. But we know nothing about Mrs. Prichard. Who the dickens *is* Mrs. Prichard? "

Granny Marrable had looked really pleased at the *reductio ad absurdum*—always exhilarating when one knows what's impossible—but looked perplexed over Mrs. Prichard's real identity. " No, indeed, poor dear soul! " she said. " 'Tisn't as if there was any would tell us about her."

" I have found, and so has your daughter, that she goes back and back in these dreams of her own childhood, which no doubt are made up of . . . which no doubt may have been told her by . . ." He stopped intentionally. He wanted to stagger her immobility by making her recite the nonsense about Mrs. Prichard's informants.

She was quite amenable. " By little Davy," said she contentedly.

" And what she had from your sister in Australia, years ago," said the doctor, and saw her content waver. He had his clue, and resolved to act on it. " For instance, Mr. Muggeridge's gallivantings. You're sure you never told the child? "

" Sure? . . . Merciful gracious me! *That* baby? "

" And how you and she measured the mill-model? That *must* have come from your sister."

She started. " What was that? " she said. " You never told me."

He did not look at her—only at his watch. He really had to be off, he said, but would tell her about the measurements. Thought she knew it before. He went on to narrate the incident referred to, which is already familiar to the story. Then he got up from his chair as though to take leave. If this did not land the suspicion of the truth in her unreceptive mind, it could only be done by a sort of point-blank directness that he shrank from employing, and that he had made it difficult to adopt by his implied pretence of unconcern. He would sooner, if that was to be the

way of it, come to her at the outset as the herald of something
serious, and ask her to prepare herself for a great shock. His
manner had not pointed to an open operation, and such a variation of it would be the sudden production of the knife. Perhaps
the dentist is sometimes right who brings his pliers from behind
his back when the patient fancies he is only scouting; but he runs
a risk, always. Dr. Nash was not at all confident in this case.

But he could venture a little farther with mere suggestion.
" Certainly," said he, " it is a very curious phase of delusion,
that this old lady should go back on a statement of your sister's,
made a lifetime ago, to no apparent end. But the whole subject
of the action of the brain is a mystery." He looked up at his
hearer's face.

She was sitting motionless, with a sort of fixed look. Had he
injured her—struck at the heart of her understanding? Well, it
had got to come, for better, for worse. Moreover, the look implied
self-command. No, he need not be frightened.

" What strikes me about this arm-measurement," said he, " is
the strength of her conviction. If she had only *spoken* of it,
well! But to get up, at six in the morning, the day after she
saw it ! "

The old lady's eyes met his. " Why arm-measurement ? " she
asked, speaking quite steadily and clearly.

" Because that was the way it was done. I don't know if I described it right. Look here—it was like this. . . ." He took her
right wrist, as he stood facing her, with his left hand. " You
stretch out your fingers straight," said he, and brought the tip
of the middle finger of his own right hand to meet hers. " Now,
what Mrs. Prichard fancies she remembers—what your sister told
her in Australia, you know—is that you and she, being girls, tried
the length of your two arms together on the top of the mill-case,
from the elbow down. Just like ours now." He determined to
make the most of this incident, for his impression was that her
mind was already in revolt against the gross improbability of her
sister having dwelt on it to a new acquaintance in the Colony.
He had made Mrs. Prichard linger over the telling of it; it was
such a strange phase of delusion. In fact, he had said to himself
that it must be a genuine memory, ascribed to the wrong persons.
He went on to a cold-blooded use of her minutest details, still
keeping the hand he held in his. " You see, Mrs. Prichard's point
was this—don't take your hand away; I haven't quite done with
it—her point was that your arm and your sister's were exactly
of a size . . ."

" We were twins."

" Precisely. And your two little paws, being young kids, or youngish. . . ."

" We were just children. I mind it well. 'Twas a sort of game, to see how our hands grew. But . . ."

" Let me finish. This old woman, when she went touring about to have a look at the model that had given her such a turn over-night, found that her own arm was well two-thirds the length of it, and something over. She was cocksure the two small arms only just covered it, because unless one cheated and pushed her elbow over the edge, your middle fingers wouldn't jam and go cleck—like this. . . . That's why I wanted your hand for—that'll do! . . . There was such a funny name she called it by—the finger-tips jamming, I mean. . . ."

Granny Marrable was pressing the released hand on her eyes and forehead. " You fairly make my head spin, doctor, digging up of old-time memories. But whatever was the funny name? Can't ye recollect? "

" It was sheer gibberish, you know . . ."

" Can't ye call the gibberish to mind? " This was asked ear-nestly, and made Dr. Nash feel he was on the right tack.

" One can't speak positively to gibberish. The nearest I can go to the word Mrs. Prichard used is "—the doctor paused under the weight of his responsibility for accuracy—" the, nearest, I, can, go is . . . *spud-clicket.*" He waited, really anxiously. If, rather than admit a suspicion of the truth, she could believe that such a piece of infant jargon could dwell correctly for dec-ades in the mind of a chance hearer, she could believe anything.

He was utterly taken aback when equable and easy speech, with a sound of relief in every word, came from lips which he thought must at least be tremulous. " Well—there now! Doesn't that show? Only Maisie *could* have told her that word. It's all right. But I'm none so sure, mind you, that I could have remembered it right, myself."

It seemed perfectly hopeless. So said the doctor to himself. Surely, in this long interview, he had tried all that suggestion could do to get a fulcrum to raise the dead weight of conviction that years of an accepted error had built up undisturbed. How easy it would have been had the tale of Daverill's audacious fraud been a few months old; or a few years, for that matter! It was that appalling lapse of time.

What could the doctor do to carry out his rash promise to Lady Gwendolen, more than what he had done? He was already over-

due at the house of another patient, three miles off. The alterna-
tives before him were:—To rush the position, saying, " Look here,
Granny Marrable, neither you nor your sister are dead, but you
were each told of the other's death by the worst scoundrel God
ever made." To do this or to throw up the sponge and hurry off
to his waiting patient! He chose the latter. After all, he had
striven hard to fulfil his promise to her young ladyship, and only
been repulsed from an impregnable fortress. But he would have
a parting shot.

" You must be very curious to see this queer old Mrs. Prichard,
Mrs. Marrable ? " said he.

The old lady did not warm up to this at all. " Indeed, doctor,
if I tell the truth, I could not say I am. For to hear the poor old
soul fancy herself my sister, dead now five-and-forty years and
more! Not for the pain to myself, but for the great pity for a
poor demented soul, and no blessed Saviour near to bid the evil
spirit begone. No, indeed—I will hope she may be well on her
way home before ever I return to Strides. But my daughter
says she'll be loath to part with her, so I'm not bound to hurry
back."

" Well—I rather hope she'll stop on long enough for you to
get a sight of her. You would be interested. . . . There's the
postman." For they were standing at the farm-gate by this time,
leading into the lane.

" Yes, it be John Barlow on his new mail-cart. He's brought
something for the farm, or he wouldn't come this way. . . . Good-
evening to you, John Barlow! . . . What—three letters! And one
of them for the old 'oman. . . So 'tis!—'tis a letter from my little man Davy, bless his heart! "

" One fower th' ma'aster," said Mr. Barlow's strong rustic accent. " One fower th' mistress. And one fower the granny. It
be directed Strides, but Widow Thrale she says, ' Ta'ak it along,
to moother at Costrell's.' And now ye've gotten it, Granny
Marrable."

" There's no denying that, Master John. I'll say good-bye, doctor." But what the letter-carrier was saying caught her ear, and
she paused before re-entering the house, holding the letters in her
hand.

" There was anoother letter for th' Cottage, the vairy fetch of
yowern, Granny, all but th' neam. Th' neam on't was Mrs. Picture, and on yowern Mrs. Marrowbone, and if th' neam had been
sa'am on both, 'twould have ta'aken Loondon Town to tell 'em
apart."

"And you left one at the Cottage, and brought the other on here? Was that it? Sharp man!" The doctor was pulling on his thick driving-gloves, to depart. Granny Marrable was opening her letter already. "Bless the boy," said she, "he's writing to both his Grannies with the same pen, so they may not be jealous!"

"You may call me a sha'arp ma'an for soomat else, doctor," said Mr. Barlow, locking his undelivered letters into the inner core of the new mail-cart. "This time I be no cleverer than my letters. 'Twas Joe Kerridge's wife, next dower the cottage, said, 'Ta'ak it on to the Granny at Dessington.' And says I to her, 'They'm gotten the sa'am yoong ma'an to write 'em love-letters,' I says. 'You couldn't tell they two letters apart, but for the neams on 'em.' And then Mrs. Lisbeth she says to me, 'Some do say they have to keep their eyes open to tell the old la'adies apart,' she says. 'But I'm anoother way o' thinking mysen,' she says, 'by reason of this Mrs. Prichard's white head o' hair.' And then I handed all the letters to Lisbeth for Strides, as well as her own, seeing ne'er one came out at door for knocking, and brought yowern on with Farmer Costrell's." Mr. Barlow had been spoken of in the village more than once as a woundy chatterbox.

The doctor glanced at Granny Marrable to see how she had taken the reference to her resemblance to Mrs. Prichard, but was just too late to see her face. She had turned to go into the house, and the only evidence he had that it had perturbed her at all was that she said good-night to no one. He felt that he had more than fulfilled his promise to Lady Gwendolen, having done everything short of forcing the pace. His other patient was no doubt already execrating him for not coming to time, so he drove off briskly; at least, so his pony flattered himself. Ideas of speed differ.

The horse whose quick step the doctor heard overhauling him, about a mile on his road, had another ideal, evidently. It did not concern him; so he ignored it until, as its nearer approach caused him to edge close to the margin of the narrow road, the voice of its driver shouted to him, and he pulled up to see why. Perhaps Mr. Barlow, the shouter, had lighted on an overlooked letter for him, and had preferred this method of delivery.

"They're asking for ye ba'ack at t' hoose—ba'ack to Costrell's Varm . . . Noa, noa, doctor—'tis the old Granny, not the yoong wench. She's gone off in a sowart of fayunt."

Dr. Nash turned his pony's head without a word, nodded and started. Mr. Barlow called out, as Parthian information, as many particulars as he thought would be audible, and sped on his course, to stand and deliver at every cottage on the route susceptible to correspondence.

"She was looking queer," said the doctor to himself, stimulating his pony's concept of a maximum velocity. "But I never thought of this. The Devil fly away with the Australian twin! Why couldn't she wait six weeks?"

He was immensely relieved to find the old lady sitting up, with her granddaughter applying vinegar to her forehead. She was discountenancing this remedy, or any remedy, as needless, in an unconvincingly weak voice. She would come round if left to herself. She rallied her forces at sight of the doctor, rather resenting him as superfluous. However, his knowledge of the cause of her upset made him an ally, a fact she probably became aware of. He suggested, after exhibiting two or three drops of hartshorn in a wineglass of water, that she should be taken at her word.

While she came round, left to herself in the big armchair, with her eyes shut and a pillow to lean back on, Maisie the granddaughter told her tale—the occurrence as she had seen it. Hearing the doctor's sounds of departure, she had discontinued a fiction of repose—not admitted as fiction, however—to come down and see what on earth Granny and he had been talking their tongues off for. Granny was reading her letter from Dave Wardle, and just the moment she saw her, gave a cry and fell back in her chair; whereon Maisie, running out, told Mr. Barlow to catch the doctor and send him back, then returned to her grandmother. She herself did not seem seriously upset, though much puzzled and surprised.

The doctor saw something. "Where's the letter?" said he.

"Here on the baby," said Mrs. Maisie. And there on the baby, enjoying, in a holy sleep, deep draughts of imaginary milk, was Dave's large round-hand epistle.

The doctor glanced at it, and had the presence of mind to say:—"Ho!—letter from a kid!" and suppress it. "Your Granny wants something," said he, diverting Mrs. Costrell's attention from it. The old lady was rallying visibly. She was, in fact, making an heroic struggle against a sudden overwhelming shock.

Recent theories of a double consciousness—an inner self—that have been worked hard of late years to account for everything Psychology is at a loss about, might be appealed to to throw light on the changes in Granny Marrable's state of mind in this past hour. Although to all appearance the whole of Dr. Nash's efforts to put it on the track had been thrown away, some of the forces his suggestions had set in motion had told upon it; and, just as a swift, mysterious impatience in the few clouds of a blue sky, and a muttered omen from Heaven-knows-what horizon, precedes the thunder-clap that makes us run for shelter, so this underself of hers may have vibrated in response to the strange hints he had thrown out, and become susceptible to an impression from Mr. Barlow's reference to her likeness to Mrs. Prichard, which otherwise would have slipped off it like water off a duck's back. We have to consider how in those happy years of her youth this almost indistinguishable twinship of the sisters had been a daily topic with all their near surroundings. To hear herself spoken of as a duplicate again, after fifty years, carried with it an inexplicable thrill. Oh, how the hours came trooping back from those long-forgotten days of old, each with its appeal to that underself alone; which she, the old Phœbe of this living world, suspected only to disallow! How she might have let the memories of the old mill and the ever-running wheels; of the still backwater where she failed to see the heron she could even now hear her sister's sweet voice calling to her to come—come quickly to!—or she would miss it; of that dear vanished sister's sweet beauty she could dwell upon, forgetful that it also was her own,—how she might have let these memories run riot in her heart, and break it, but that the very thing that provoked them was also their profanation—Mrs. Prichard at Strides Cottage! Who or what was Mrs. Prichard? A poor old crazypate, a victim of delusions . . .

Yes, but *what* delusions? That was the question her inner self could not ignore, however much her living mind might cancel it. She could run for shelter from it, but the storm would come. She flinched from hearing another word of Mr. Barlow's woundy chatter, and fled into the house, actually bearing in her hand the lightning-flash whose thunder-clap was in a moment to shake the foundations of her soul.

It came with a terrible suddenness when she read Dave's large, roundhand script. "MY DEAR GRANEY MAROBONE—Me and Dolly are so Glad because Gweng has been here To say Mrs. Picture is reely Your Cistern." This is as written first. Old Phœbe deciphered the corrections without illumination; sheltered, perhaps, by some bias of her inner soul to an idea that Mrs. Prichard was a second wife of her convict brother-in-law—a sort of washed-out sister-in-law. The child might have cooked it up out of that. It would explain many things.

Then came the thunderclap. "Gweng says Bad people told you

bofe Lies heaps longer ago than dolly's birfday, so you bofe thort you was dead and buried." Straight to the heart of the subject, as perhaps none but a child could have phrased it. Granny Marrable's sight grew dim as she read:—"Gweng says you will be glad, not sory." Then she felt quite sick, and heard her granddaughter coming downstairs. How to tell her nothing of all this, how to pretend nothing was happening—that was what had to be done! But the world vanished as she fell back in her chair beside the cradle.

*	*	*	*	*	*	*

"Yes, Granny dear, what is it? . . . The letter?—oh, the doctor's got the letter. Does it matter? . . . Never mind the letter! You sit still! I must get you something. What shall I get for her, doctor?"

"Get me nothing, Maisie. I shall be all right directly. . . ." And it really seemed as if she would. Indeed, her revival was amazingly sudden. "I tell you what I should *like*," said she, quite firmly. "I should like a little air. Is not John come in?" John was Mr. Costrell, her grandson-in-law—the farmer.

"I think I just heard him, outside." Maisie had heard him drive up to the door, a familiar sound.

"Then let him drive me over to the Cottage."

"*Yes*," said the doctor, with emphasis. "Good idea!" And Maisie left the room to speak to her husband.

Then old Phœbe, on her feet now, and speaking clearly, with a strange ring of determination in her voice, said to him:—"Have you the young child's letter?" He drew it from his pocket. "If what that letter says is true, this is my sister Maisie, risen from the grave."

He marvelled at her strength. There was no need for reserve; he could speak plainly now. "The letter is all true, Mrs. Marrable," said he. "Mrs. Prichard is your sister Maisie, but she is not risen from the grave. She is ill, and probably knows by now what you know, but for all the shock she has had, she may have years of life before her. You cannot do better than go to her at once. And remember that she will need all your strength to help her. For she is not strong, like you."

The old face relaxed from its tension, and a gleam of happiness was in the life of it. But she only said:—"Maisie": said it twice, as for the pleasure in the name. Then she held out her hand, to take the letter from the doctor.

He handed it to her. "I have been telling fibs, Mrs. Marrable," said he, "or using them, which is the same thing, in trying to tell you this. You will forgive that, I know?" She nodded assent. "Shall I tell you the facts, as far as they are known to me?"

"Please!" She seemed well able to understand.

"Her husband was a damnable scoundrel. . . ."

"He was."

". . . And for some motive we can throw no light on, wrote two letters, one a forgery with your father's signature—a letter to his wife—saying that you, with your own husband and her child were drowned at sea. The other to yourself, telling you that she was dead in Australia."

The blank horror on old Phœbe's face remained in the doctor's memory, long after that. She just found voice to say:—"God help us all!" But there was no sign of another collapse, though he was watching for it.

He continued:—"He must have had some means of suppressing your letters to one another, to be safe in this deception. . . ."

"He was the postmaster."

"Oh—was that it? Mrs. Costrell is coming back, and I shall have to stop. . . . But I must just tell you this. The whole story has come out through Lady Gwendolen Rivers, who is keenly interested in your sister." Old Phœbe gave a visible start at this first mention of Mrs. Prichard's relationship as a certainty. It was like the bather's gasp when the cold water comes level with his heart. "Lady Gwendolen seems to have taken charge of the old lady's writing-desk in London, and his lordship, her father, it appears, opened and read them, having his suspicions. . . ."

"Oh, but his lordship had the right. . . ."

"Surely! No one would question his lordship's actions. . . . Here comes your granddaughter back. I must stop. But that is really the whole." Mrs. Costrell came back to say that John was mending a buckle in the harness, but would be ready to drive Granny in a few minutes. How much better Granny was looking! What was it, doctor? It wasn't like Granny.

"Stomach, probably," said the doctor, resorting to a time-honoured subterfuge. "I'll send her something to take directly after meals."

"No, Maisie," said the old lady, somewhat to the doctor's surprise. "You shall not be told any stories, with my consent. I've had a piece of news—a blessed piece of news as ever came to an old woman!—and it gave me a jump. But I shan't tell ye a word of it yet a while. Ye may just be busy over guessing what it is till I come back." The doctor was obliged to confess to himself that this was a wonderful stroke of policy on the old lady's part, and resolved to back it up through thick and thin.

But although the young wife's good-humoured face showed every sign of rebellion against her arbitrary exclusion from the enjoyment of this mystery, her protest had to stand over. For baby waked up suddenly in a storm of rage, and called Heaven and Earth to witness the grievous injury and neglect of his family in not being ready with a prompt bottle. The doctor hurried away to that patient, and what sort of reception he got the story can only imagine. It hopes the case was not urgent.

The last he saw that day of Granny Marrable was her back, almost as upright at eighty as the young farmer's beside her at thirty, just starting on the short journey that was to end in such an amazing interview. His thought for a moment was how he would like to be there to see it! Reconsideration made him say to himself:—" Well, now, should I ? "

CHAPTER XVII

HOW LADY ANCESTER CALLED ON LADY TORRENS, WHO WAS KEEPING
HER ROOM. BUT SHE SAW THE BART. A QUEER AND TICKLISH IN-
TERVIEW. MAURICE AND KATHLEEN TYRAWLEY. NO NEED FOR HUM-
BUG BETWEEN *US!* THE COUNTESS'S GROUNDS FOR OPPOSING THE
MARRIAGE. HOW ADRIAN, WITH EYES IN HIS HEAD, WOULD HAVE
BEEN MOST ACCEPTABLE. BUT HOW ABOUT JEPHTHA'S DAUGHTER ?
OUGHT WE, THOUGH, TO MEDDLE BETWEEN YOUNG LOVERS ? AN
AWKWARD TOPIC. HOW ROMEO *DIDN'T* FEEL, ABOUT *HIS* EX-JULIET !
HOW COUNTY PARIS MIGHT HAVE WASHED, AND ROSALINE MIGHT
HAVE MARRIED A POPULAR PREACHER. THE SAME LIPS. THE
COUNTESS'S COURAGE. A GOOD SHAKE AND NO FLINCHING. CHRIS-
TIAN-NAMING UNDER TUTELAGE. HOW SIR HAMILTON INDULGED IN
A FIRESIDE REVERIE OVER HIS PAST, AND HIS SON AND DAUGHTER
CAME BACK. HOW MISS SCATCHERD HAD BEEN SEEN BY BOTH. A
FLASH OF EYESIGHT, AND HOPE. HOW THE SQUIRE TOOK THE NEXT
OPPORTUNITY THAT EVENING. CUPID'S NAME NOT DANIEL. WHAT
AN IMAGE OF THE COUNTESS SAID TO ADRIAN

SIR HAMILTON TORRENS is at home, because when a messenger rode from the Towers in the morning with a note from the Countess to say that her ladyship was driving over to Poynders in the afternoon, and could manage a previous visit at Pensham by coming an hour earlier, his wife instructed him that it would never do for him to be absent, seeing that there was no knowing how indisposed she herself might be. There never is, with nerve cases, and she was a nerve case. So Sir Hamilton really must arrange to stay at home just this one afternoon, that Lady Ancester's visit should not be absolutely sterile. If the nerve case's plight and Sir Hamilton's isolation were communicated to her on her arrival, she could choose for herself whether to come in or go on to Poynders. She chose to come in and interview Sir Hamilton. So consider that the lady of the house is indisposed, and is keeping her room, and that the blind man and his sister, and Achilles, have gone to visit a neighbour.

The Countess was acting on her resolution made in the train to be a free lance. She had been scheming an interview with Adrian's father before the next meeting of the lovers, if possible; and now she had caught at the opportunity afforded by her daughter's absence at Chorlton. Hers was a resolution that deserved the name, in view of its special object—the organizing and conduct of what might be a most embarrassing negotiation, or effort of diplomacy.

These two, three decades back, had behaved when they met like lovers on the stage who are carried away by their parts and forget the audience. Unless indeed *they* had an audience, in which case they had to wait, and did it with a parade of indifference which deceived no one.

And now! Here was the gentleman making believe that the lady was bitterly disappointed at not seeing his amiable wife, who was, after all, only the Miss Abercrombie he married at about the same time that she herself became a Countess. And here was she adding to an insincere acceptance of the position of chief mourner a groundless pretext that the two or three decades were four or five—or anything you please outside King Memory's Statutes of Limitations!—and those endearments too long ago to count. And that the nerve case upstairs, if you please, had no existence for her ladyship as the Miss Abercrombie she heard Hamilton was engaged to marry, and felt rather curious about at the time, but was a most interesting individuality, saturated with public spirit, whose enthusiasm about the Abolition of Slavery had stirred her sympathetic soul to the quick.

Endless speculation is possible over the feelings of a man and woman so related, coming together under such changed circumstances, without the lubricant to easy intercourse of the presence of others. The Countess would not have faced the possible embarrassments, but would have driven on to her cousin's house, Poynders, if she had not had a specific purpose. As it was, it was the very thing she wanted, and she welcomed it. She had the stronger position, and was prepared for all contingencies.

Sir Hamilton had very few demeanours open to him. The most obvious one was that of the courteous host, flattered to receive such a visitor on any terms, especially proud and cordial in view of the prospect of a connection between the families. He maintained a penitential attitude under the depressing shadow of the absence of his better half, which certainly was made the most of by both; somewhat artificially, a perceptive visitor might have said, if one had been there to see. The jeremiads over this unfortunate misadventure must have lasted fully ten minutes before a lull came; for the gentleman could catch no other wind in his sails, and had to let out every reef to move at all.

Lady Ancester was not inclined to lose time. "I am particularly sorry not to see Lady Torrens," she said, "because I really wanted to have a serious talk with her. . . . Yes, about the boy and girl—your boy and my girl." A curious consciousness almost made her wince. Think how easily either of the young lovers might have been a joint possession! If one, then both, surely, minus their identities and the *status quo?* It was like sudden unexpected lemon in a made dish.

The worst of it was—not that each thought the same thing at the same moment; that was inevitable—but that each knew the other's thought. The Baronet fell back on mere self-subordination. Automatically non-existent, he would be safe. "Same thing—same thing—Lady Torrens and myself! Comes to the same thing whether you say it to me or to her. Repeat every word! . . . Of course—easier to talk to her! But comes to the same thing." He abated himself to a go-between, and was entrenched.

The Countess affected an easy languor to say:—"I really don't feel able to say what I want straight off. You know I never used to be able"—she laughed a deprecatory laugh—"in the old Clarges Street days. Besides, your man is coming in and out with tea and things. When he's done, I'll go on."

The sudden reference to the time-when of that old passionate relation contained an implication that it was not unspeakable *per se*—although its threat had been that it would do its worst as a cupboard-skeleton—but only owing to the childish silliness of a mere calf-love, a reciprocal misapprehension soon forgotten. Treated with contempt, its pretensions to skeletonhood fell through. Moreover, that pending tea had helped to a pause; showing the speaker to be quite collected, and mistress of the situation.

The little episode had put the Baronet more at his ease. He thought he might endeavour to contribute to general lubrication on the same lines. By-the-by, he had met Maurice Tyrawley last week in London—just back from India—been away much longer than our men usually—Lady Ancester would remember Maurice Tyrawley—man with a slight stammer—sister ran away with her father's groom? Her ladyship remembered Maurice very well. And was that really true about Kathleen Tyrawley? Well—that was interesting! Was she alive? Oh dear yes—living in Tavistock Square—fellah made money, somehow. That was *very* interesting. If the Countess had Kathleen's address, she would try to call on her, some time. What was her name? Hopkins. Oh—Hopkins! She felt discouraged, and not at all sure she should call on her, any time. But she did not say so. An entry of Mrs. Hopkins's address and full name followed, on some painfully minute ivory tablets. The Countess was sure to find the place, owing to her coachman's phenomenal bump of locality. Was Colonel Tyrawley married? . . . Oh—Major Tyrawley! Yes, he was married, and had some rumpus with his wife. Etcetera, etcetera.

This sort of thing served its turn, as did the tea. But both became things of the past, and left the course clear. Provided always that the servant did not recrudesce! " Is he gone? " said the Countess. " If he isn't, I can wait."

" He won't come back now."

" Very well. Then I can go on. I want to talk about our girl and boy. . . . I don't think there need be any nonsense between Us, Sir Hamilton? "

" About our boy and girl? Why should there? " Best not to add:—" Or anything else," on the whole!

" I am speaking of his eyesight only. Please understand that I should not oppose my daughter's wishes on any other ground."

" But I am to understand that you *do* oppose them? "

The Countess held back her answer a few seconds, to take a last look at it before sending it to press. Then she said decisively:—" Yes." She made no softening reservation. She had already said why.

He considered it his duty to soften it for her. " On the ground of his eyesight. . . . This is a sad business. . . . I gather that you empower me to repeat to my wife that you are—quite naturally, I admit—are unreconciled. . . . Or, at least, only partly reconciled to——"

"Unreconciled. I won't make any pretences, Sir Hamilton. I do *not* think there need be any nonsense between us. I am the girl's mother, and it is my duty to speak plain, for her sake."

"My wife will entirely agree with you."

"I hope so. But I am not sorry that I should have an opportunity of speaking freely to you. This is the first I have had. I wish you to know without disguise exactly how this marriage of Gwen and your Adrian—if it ever comes off—will present itself to me, as the girl's mother."

Sir Hamilton inclined his head slightly, which may have meant:—"I am prepared to listen to you as the boy's father, and his mother's proxy."

"As the girl's mother," repeated the lady. "I shall continue to think, as I think now, that there is an *unreal* element in my daughter's . . . a . . . regard for your son."

"An unreal element! Very often is, in young ladies' predilections for young gentlemen."

The Countess rushed on to avoid a complex abstract subject, with pitfalls galore. "Which may very well endanger her future. . . . Well!—may endanger the happiness of both. . . . I don't mean that she isn't in love with him—whatever the word means, and sometimes one hardly knows. I mean now that she is under an influence which may last, or may not, but which might never have existed but for . . . but for the accident."

"My wife has said the same thing, more than once." Her ladyship could have dispensed with this constant reference to the late Miss Abercrombie. She felt that it put her at a disadvantage.

"And the Earl entirely agrees with me," said she. For why should her ladyship not play a card of the same suit? "There is something I want to say, and I don't know how to say it. But *he* said it the other day, and I felt exactly as he did. He said, as near as I recollect:—'If I had twenty daughters to give away, I would not grudge one to poor Adrian, if I thought it would do something to make up for the wrong I have done him. . . .'"

Sir Hamilton interrupted warmly. "No, Lady Ancester, no! I cannot allow that to be said! We have never thought of it that way. We do not think of it that way. We never shall think of it that way. It was an accident, pure and simple. It might have happened to *his* son, on my bit of preserved land. All the owners about shoot stray dogs."

"But if it had, and you had had a mad daughter—because Gwen is a mad girl, if ever there was one—who got a Quixotic idea like this in her head, you would have felt exactly as my husband does."

" Should I? Well—I suppose I should. No, I don't think I should. . . . Well—at least . . . ! "

" At least, what? "

" At least, if I had supposed that . . . that Irene, for instance "—Sir Hamilton's mind required a tangible reality to rest upon—" that Irene was head over ears in love with some man. . . ." He did not seem to have his conclusion ready.

" And you are convinced that my daughter is head over ears in love with your son? Is that it? " The Countess spoke rather coldly, and Sir Hamilton felt uncomfortable. " It seems to me that the whole thing turns on that. Are you certain that you have not allowed yourself to be convinced? "

" Allowed myself—I'm not sure I understand."

" With less proof, I mean, than her parents have a right to ask for—less than you would have asked yourself in the reverse case? "

Sir Hamilton felt more uncomfortable. He ought to have answered that he was very far from certain. But an Englishman is nothing if not a prevaricator; he calls it being scrupulously truthful. " I have no right to catechize Lady Gwendolen," said he.

" And her parents have, of course. I see. But if her parents are convinced—as I certainly am in this case, and I think my husband is, almost—that there is an unreal element on Gwen's side, it ought to . . . to carry weight with you."

" It would carry weight. It does carry weight. But . . . However, I must talk to Lady Torrens about this." He appeared very uncomfortable indeed, and was visibly flushed. But that may have been the red glow of a dying fire in the half-light, or half-darkness, striking his face as he rested his elbow on the chimney-piece, while its hand wandered from his brow to his chin, expressing irresolute perplexity. Until, as she sat silent, as though satisfied that he could have now no doubt about her wishes, he spoke again, abruptly. " I wish you would tell me exactly what you suppose to be the case."

She addressed herself to explicit statement. " I believe Gwen is acting under an unselfish impulse, and I do not believe in unselfish impulses. If a girl is to run counter to the wishes of her parents, and to obvious common sense, at least let her impulse be a selfish one. Let her act entirely for her own sake. Gwen made your son's acquaintance under peculiar circumstances—romantic circumstances—and, as I know, instantly saw that his eyesight might be destroyed and that the blame would rest with her family. . . ."

" No, L-Lady Ancester "—he stumbled somehow over the name, for no apparent reason—" I deny that. I protest against it. . . ."

" We need not settle that point. Your feeling is a generous one. But do let us keep to Gwen and Adrian." Her ladyship went on to develop her view of the case, not at all illogically. Her objection to the marriage turned entirely on Adrian's blindness—had not a particle of personal feeling in it. On the contrary, she and her husband saw every reason to believe that the young man, with eyes in his head, would have met with a most affectionate welcome as a son-in-law. This applied especially to the Earl, who, of course, had seen more of Adrian than herself. He had, in fact, conceived an extraordinary *entichement* for him; so much so that he would sooner, for his own sake purely, that the marriage should come off, as the blindness would affect him very little. But his duty to his daughter remained exactly the same. If there was the slightest reason to suppose that Gwen was immolating herself as a sacrifice—something was implied of an analogy in the case of Jephtha's daughter, but not pressed home owing to obvious weak points—he had no choice, and she had no choice, but to protect the victim from herself. If they did not do so, what was there to prevent an irrevocable step being taken which might easily lead to disastrous consequences for both?

" You must see," said Gwen's mother very earnestly, " that if my daughter is acting, as my husband and I suppose, from a Quixotic desire to make up to your son for the terrible injury we have done him . . . No protests, please! . . . it is our business to protect her from the consequences of her own rashness—to stand between her and a possible lifelong unhappiness! "

" But what," said the perplexed Baronet, " can *I* do? " A reasonable question!

" If you can do nothing, no one can. The Earl and myself are so handicapped by our sense of the fearful injury that we have —however unintentionally—inflicted on your son, that we are really tied hand and foot. But you can at least place the case before Adrian as I have placed it before you, and I appeal to you to do so. I am sure you will see that it is impossible for my husband or myself to say the same thing to him."

" But to what end? What do you suppose will come of it? What . . . a . . . what difference will it make? "

" It *will* make a difference. It *must* make a difference, if your son is made fully aware—he is not, now—of the motives that may be influencing Gwen." The Countess was not at all confident of her case, in respect of any definite change it would produce in the bearing of Adrian towards his *fiancée,* and still less of any effect such change would produce upon that headstrong young lady, if once she suspected its cause. But she had confidence in her memories of the rather stupid middle-aged gentleman of whom, as a young dragoon, she had had such very intimate experience. He was still sensitively honourable, as in those old days —she was sure of that. Unless, indeed, he had changed very much morally, as he had certainly done physically. He would shrink from the idea of his son profiting by an heroic self-devotion of the daughter of a man who was no more to blame for his son's mishap than he himself would have been in the counter-case he had supposed. And he would impress her view of the position on his son. It would have no visible and immediate result now, but how about the six months at Vienna? Might it not be utilised to undermine that position during those six months of fascinating change? She pictured to herself an abatement of what her mind thought of as "the heroics" in the first six weeks.

At least, she could see, at this moment, that she had gained her immediate end. The uneasiness of the Baronet was visible in all that can show uneasiness in a not very expressive exterior— restlessness of hand and lips, and the fixed brow of perplexity. "Very good—very good!" he was saying, " I will talk to my wife about it. You may depend on me to do what I can. Only—if you are mistaken . . ."

"About Gwen? If I am, things must take their own course. But I think it will turn out that I am right. . . . That is all, is it not? I am truly sorry not to have seen Lady Torrens. I hope she will be better. . . . Oh yes—it's all right about the time. They know I am coming, at Poynders. And I should have time to dress for dinner, anyhow. Good-bye!" Her ladyship held out a decisive hand, that said:—" Curtain."

But Sir Hamilton did not seem so sure the performance was over. "Half a minute more, L-Lady Ancester," said he; and he again half-stumbled over her name. "I am rather slow in expressing myself, but I have something I want to say."

"I am not in a hurry."

"I can only do exactly what you have asked me to do—place the case before my son as you have placed it before me."

"I have not asked for anything else."

"Well, then, I can do that, after I have talked over it with his mother. But I can't . . . I can't undertake to *influence* him."

"Is he so intractable? . . . However, young men *are*."

"I did not mean that. I . . . I don't exactly know how to say it . . ."

"Why should you hesitate to say what you were going to say? . . . Do you suppose I don't know what it was?" For he had begun to anticipate it with some weakening reservation. "I could tell you exactly. You were going to say, was it right to influence young people's futures and so on, and wasn't it taking a great responsibility, and so on? Now, were you not?"

"I had some such thought."

"Exactly. You mean you thought what I said you thought."

"And you think me mistaken?"

"Not always. In the present case, yes—if you consider that it would be influencing. I don't. It would only be refraining from keeping silence about—about something it may never occur to your son to think possible." It may have struck her hearer that to call shouting a fact on the house-tops "refraining from keeping silence" about it was straining phraseology; but it was not easy to formulate the idea, offhand. It was easier to hold his tongue. The Countess might have done better to hold hers, at this point. But she must needs be discriminating, to show how clear-sighted she was. "Of course, it is quite a different thing to try to bring about a marriage. That is certainly taking a grave responsibility." She stopped with a jerk, for she caught herself denouncing the very course of action which well-meaning friends had adopted successfully in the case of herself and her husband. If it had not been for the jerk, Sir Hamilton would not have known the comparison that was passing in her mind. She recovered herself to continue:—"Of course, trying to bring about a marriage is a grave responsibility, but mere testing of the strength of links that bind may be no more than bare prudence. A breaking strain on lovers' vows may be acknowledged by them as an untold blessing in after-years." Here she began to feel she was not improving matters, and continued, with misgivings:—"I am scarcely asking you to do even that. I am only appealing to you to suggest to your son a fact that is obvious to myself and my husband, because it is almost impossible for us, under the circumstances, to make such an appeal to him ourselves."

"Are you so confident of the grounds of your suspicions . . . about . . . about the motives that are influencing your daughter?"

"They are not suspicions. They are certainties. At least, I am convinced—and I am her mother—that her chief motive in accepting your son was vitiated—yes, vitiated!—by a mistaken zeal for—suppose we call it poetical justice. I am not going to say the girl does not fancy herself in love." She laughed a maternal sort of laugh—the laugh that seniority, undeceived by life's realities, laughs at the crazy dawn of passion in infatuated children. "Of course she does. But knowing what I do, am I not right to make an attempt at least to protect her from herself?" She lowered her voice to an increase of earnestness, as though she had found a way to go nearer to the heart of her subject. "Does any woman know—*can* any woman know—better than I do, the value of a girl's first love?"

It was a daring recognition of their old relation, and the veil of the thin pretence that it could be successfully ignored had fallen from between them.

The Baronet was a Man of the World. "Women do not take these things to heart as men do." And then, the moment after, was in a cold perspiration to think in what a delicate position it would have landed him. Just think!—with the Miss Abercrombie he had married cherishing her nervous system upstairs, and the pending reappearance of a son and daughter who were very liable to amusement with a parent whom they scarcely took seriously—for *him* to be hinting at the remains of an undying passion for this lady! He could only accept her estimate of girls by stammering:—" P-possibly! Young people—yes! "

But his embarrassment and hesitation were so visible that the Countess had little choice between flinching or charging bravely up to the guns.

She chose the courageous course, influenced perhaps by the thought that if the marriage came off, there would be a long perspective of reciprocal consciousnesses in the future for herself and this man, who had an unfortunate knack of transparency. Could not she nip the first in the bud, and sterilise the rest? It was worth the attempt.

"Listen to me, Hamilton," said she; and she was perfectly cool and collected. "Did I not say to you that there need be no nonsense between *us?* . . . How funny men are! Why should you jump because I called you by name? Do you know that twice since we have been talking here you have all but called me the name you used to me as a girl? . . . Yes—you began saying 'Lip,' and made it Lady Ancester. Please say it all another time. I shall not bite you. . . . Look here!—I want you to help me to laugh at the mistake we made when we were young folks; not to look solemn at it. We were ridiculous. . . . You were going to say, 'Why?' Well—I don't exactly know. Young folks always *are*." The fact is, the Countess was beginning to feel comfortably detached, and could treat the subject in a free and easy manner.

The Baronet could not bring himself to allow that he had ever been ridiculous, without protest. The Man within him rose in rebellion against such an admission. He felt a little indignant at her unceremonious pooh-poohing of their early infatuation. He would have accorded it respectful obsequies at least. But what protest could he enter that would not lay him open to suspicions of that undying passion? It appeared to him absolutely impossible to say anything, either way. So he looked as dignified as he could, consistently with being glad the room was half dark, because he knew he was red.

His uncomfortable silence, instead of the response in kind her ladyship had hoped for, interfered a little with the development of her detachment. She judged it better to wind up the interview, and did it with spirit. " There, now, Hamilton, *don't talk* —because I know exactly what you are going to say. Shake hands upon it—a good shake, you know!—don't throw it away!"

How very different are those two ways of offering a hand, the tender one and the graspy one. The Countess's stopped out of its glove to emphasize the latter, and did it so frankly and effectually that it cleared the air, in which the smell of fire had been perceptible, as in a room where a match has gone out.

He had, as she said, twice very nearly called her by her old familiar name of the Romeo and Juliet days. Nevertheless, when he gave her his hand, saying:—" Perfectly right—perfectly right, Lip! That's the way to look at it," he threw in the name stiffly. It was under tutelage, not spontaneously uttered. Letting it come before would have given him a better position. But then, how if she had disallowed it? There was no end to the ticklishness of their relation.

A *modus vivendi* was, however, established. She could recapitulate without endangering it. " You *will* try to make Adrian see Gwen's motives as I see them. It is quite possible that it will make no difference in the end. If so, we must bow to the decrees of Providence, I suppose. But I am sure you agree with me that he ought not to remain in the dark. As I dare say you know, I am taking Gwen to Vienna for a time. If they are both of a mind at the end of that time—well, I suppose it can't be helped! But you must not be—I see you are not—surprised at my view of the case."

Sir Hamilton assented to everything, promised everything, saw the lady into her carriage, and returned, uncomfortable, to review his position before the drawing-room fire in solitude. He did not go upstairs to the nerve case. He would let his visitor die down before he discharged that liability. He broke a large coal, and made a flare, and rang the bell for lights, to show how little the late interview had thrown him out of gear. But it *had* done so. In spite of the fact that Lady Ancester was well over five-and-forty, and that he himself was four or five years older, and that she had all but hinted that the sight of him would have disillusioned her if the Earl had not—for that was what he read between her lines—she had left something indefinable behind, which he was pleased to condemn as sentimental nonsense. No doubt it was, but it was *there,* for all that.

Just one little tender squeeze of that beautiful hand, instead of that candid, overwhelming wrestler's grip and double-knock handshake, would have been so delightful.

He caught himself thinking more of his handsome visitor and her easy self-mastery, compared with his own awkwardness and embarrassment, than of her errand and the troublesome task she had devolved on him of illuminating his son's mind about the possible self-sacrificial motives of her daughter. His thoughts *would* wander back to their Romeo and Juliet period, and make comparisons between this *now* of worldly-wise maturities and the days when he would have been the glove upon that hand, that he might touch that cheek. He recalled his first meeting with the fascinating young beauty in her first season, at a moonlight dance on a lawn dangerously flanked with lonely sheltered avenues and whispering trees; and the soft rose-laden air of a dawn that broke on tired musicians and unexhausted dissipation, and his headlong reckless surrender to her irresistible intoxication; and, to say the truth, the Juliet-like acknowledgment it met with. He would have been better pleased, with the world as it was now, if less of that Juliet had been recognisable in this mature dame. The thought made him bite his lip. He exclaimed against his recognition perforce, and compelled himself to think of the question before the house.

Yes—he could quite understand why the girl's parents should find it difficult to say to his son:—"We know that Gwen is giving her love to make amends for a wrong, as she thinks, done by ourselves; and whatever personal sacrifice we should be glad to make as compensation for it, we have no right to allow our daughter to imperil her happiness." But he had a hazy recollection of

Adrian's telling him something of the Earl himself having mooted this view of the subject at the outset of the engagement; and, hearing no more of it, had supposed the point to be disposed of. Why did Lady Ancester wish to impress it on him now?

Then it gradually became clearer, as he thought it out, that it would have been impossible to form conclusions at once. The Earl had no doubt expressed a suspicion at first. But his daughter would never have confessed her motives to *him*. What more likely than that her mother should gradually command her confidence, and see that Adrian could not arrive at a full appreciation of them without an ungracious persistence on the part of herself and her husband, unless it were impressed on him by some member of the young man's family? His father, naturally.

He felt perceptibly gratified that Gwen's mother should take it for granted that he would feel as she did about the injustice to her daughter of allowing her to sacrifice herself to make amends for a fault of her parents. It was a question of sensitive honour, and she had credited him rightly with possessing it. At least, he hoped so. And though he was certainly not a clever man, the Squire of Pensham was the very soul of fair play. His division of the County knew both facts. Now, it seemed to him that it would be fairer play on his part to throw his influence into the scale on the side of the Countess, and protest against the marriage unless some guarantee could be found that there was no heroic taint in the bride's motives. In this he was consciously influenced by the thought that *his* side would suffer by his own action, so his own motives were tainted. A chivalric instinct, unbalanced by reasoning power, is so very apt to decide—on principle—against its owner's interests. Behind this there may have been a saving clause, to the effect that the young people might be relied on to pay no attention to their seniors' wishes, or anything else. Gwen was on her way to twenty-one, and then parental authority would expire. Meanwhile a little delay would do no harm. For the present, he could only rub the facts into his son, and leave them to do their worst. He would speak to him at the next opportunity.

Home came Adrian and Irene, and filled the silence of the house with voices. Something was afoot, clearly; something not unpleasant, to judge by the laugh of the latter. The room-door, whose hasp never bit properly—causing Adrian to perpetrate an atrocious joke about a disappointed Cleopatra—swung wide with an unseen cause, which was revealed by a soft nose, a dog's, in contact with Sir Hamilton's hand. He acknowledged Achilles, who trotted away satisfied, to complete an examination of all the other inmates of the house, his invariable custom after an outing. He would ratify or sanction them, and drop asleep with a clear conscience.

"Hay? What's all that? What's all the rumpus?" says the Baronet, outside at the stair-top. The sounds of the voices are pleasant and welcome to him, and he courts their banishment of the past his old fiancée had dragged from its sepulchre. Bury it again and forget it! "What's all the noise about? What's all the chatterboxing?" For the good gentleman always imputes to his offspring a volubility and a plethora of language far in excess of any meaning it conveys. His own attitude, he implies, is one of weighty consideration and temperate but forcible judgment.

"What's the chatterboxing?" says the beautiful daughter, who kisses him on both sides—and she and her skirts and her voice fill the discreet country-house to the brim, and make its owner insignificant. "What's the chatterboxing, indeed? Why,—it's good news for a silly old daddy! That's what it is. Now come in and I'll sit on his knee and tell him." And by the time Adrian has felt his way to the drawing-room, the good news has been sprung upon his father by a Mœnad who has dragged off her head-gear—so as not to scratch—and flung it on the sofa. And a tide of released black hair has burst loose about him. And—oh dear!—how that garden of auld lang syne has vanished!

It behoves a Baronet and a J.P., however, to bring all this excitement down to the level of mature consideration. "Well—well—well—well!" says he. "Now let's have it all over again. Begin at the beginning. You and your brother were walking up Pratchet's Lane. What were you doing in Pratchet's Lane?"

"Walking up it. You can only walk up it or down it. Very well. We were just by the big holly-tree . . ."

"Which big holly-tree? One—thing—at—a time!"

"Don't interrupt! There is only one big holly-tree. Now you know! Well! Ply ran on in front because he caught sight of Miss Scatcherd . . ."

"Easy—easy—easy! Where was Miss Scatcherd?"

"In front, of course! Ply dotes on Miss Scatcherd, although she's forty-seven."

"I don't know about the ' of course,'" says Adrian, leaning on his father's arm-chair. "Because I don't dote on Miss Scatcherd. Miss Scatcherd might have been coming up behind. In which case, if I had been Ply, I should have run on in front."

"Don't be spiteful! However, I know she's bony. Well—am I to get on with my story, or not? . . . Very good! Where did I leave off? Oh—at Miss Scatcherd! Now, papa dear, be good, and don't be solemn."

"Well—fire away!"

"Indeed, it really happened just as I told you: as we were going to the Rectory, Ply ran on in front, and I went on to rescue Miss Scatcherd, because she doesn't like being knocked down by a dog, however affectionate. And it was just then that I heard Adrian speak. . . ."

"Did I speak?"

"Perhaps I ought to say gasp. I heard Adrian gasp. And when I turned round to see why, he was rubbing his eyes. Because he had *seen* Miss Scatcherd."

"How did you know?" The interest of this has made Sir Hamilton lapse his disciplines for the moment. He takes advantage of a pause, due to his son and daughter beginning to answer both at once, and each stopping for the other, to say:— "This would be the second time—the second time! Something might come of this."

"You go on!" says Irene, nodding to her brother. "Say what you said."

Adrian accepts the prolocutorship. "To the best of my recollection I said:—'Stop Ply knocking Miss Scatcherd down again!' Because he did it before, you know. . . . Oh yes, entirely from love, no doubt! Then I heard you say:—'How do you know it's Miss Scatcherd?' And I told you."

"Yes—yes—yes—yes! But how *did* you? . . . How much did you see?" The Baronet is excited and roused.

"Quite as much as I wished. I think I mentioned that I did *not* dote on Miss Scatcherd." For, the moment a piece of perversity is possible, this young man jumps at it.

"Oh, Adrian dear, don't be paradoxical and capricious when papa's so anxious. Do say what you saw!" Thus urged by his sister, the blind man describes the occurrence from his point of view, carefully and conscientiously. The care and conscience are chiefly needed to limit and circumscribe a sudden image of a lady of irreproachable demeanour besieged by an unexpected dog. So sudden that it merely appeared as a fact in space, without a background or a foothold. It came and went in a flash, Adrian said, leaving him far more puzzled to account for its disappearance than its sudden reasonless intrusion on his darkness.

As soon as the narrative ended, perversity set in. It was gratifying, said Adrian, to listen while Hope told flattering'tales, but was it not as well to be on our guard against rash conclusions? Even a partial restoration of eyesight was a thing to look forward to, but would not the extent of the benefits it conferred vary according to the nature of its own limitations? For instance, it might enable him to see everything in a mist, without outlines; or, for that matter, upside down. That, however, would not signify, so long as everything else was upside down. Indeed, who could say for certain that anything ever was, or ever had been, right side up? It all turned on which side "up" was, and on whether there was a wrong side at all.

"All nonsense!" said Irene.

"Shut up, 'Re," said Adrian. "These things want thinking out. A limited vision might be restricted in other ways than by mere stupid opaque fog, and bald, insipid position in Space. Consider how much more aggravating it would be—from the point of view of Providence—to limit the vision to the selection of peculiar objects which would give offence to the Taste or Religious Convictions of its owner! Suppose that Miss Scatcherd's eyes, for instance, could only distinguish gentlemen of Unsound opinions, and couldn't see a Curate if it was ever so! And, *per contra*, suppose that it should only prove possible to me to receive an image of Miss Scatcherd, or her congeners . . ."

"Is that eels?" said Irene, who wasn't listening, but getting out writing-materials. "You may go on talking, but don't expect me to answer, because I shan't. I'm going to write to Gwen all about it."

Her brother started, and became suddenly serious. "No, 'Re!" he exclaimed. "At least, not yet. I don't want Gwen to know anything about it. Don't let's have any more false hopes than we can help. Ten to one it's only a flash in the pan! . . . Don't cry about it, ducky darling! If it was real, it won't stop there, and we shall have something worth telling."

So Irene did not write her letter.

That evening the Squire was very silent, saying nothing about the long conversation he had had with Gwen's mother. His good lady did not come down to dinner, and if she asked him any questions about it, it was when he went up to dress; not in the hearing of his son or daughter. They only knew that their mother had not seen Lady Ancester when she called, and curiosity about the visitor had merged in the absorbing interest of Miss Scatcherd's sudden visibility.

But no sooner had Irene—who was the ladies, this time—departed to alleviate the lot of her excellent mamma, who may have been very ill, for anything the story knows, than Sir Hamilton told the pervading attendant-in-chief to look alive with the coffee, and get that door shut, and keep it shut, conveying his desire for undisturbed seclusion. Then he was observed by his son to be humming and hawing, somewhat in the manner of ourselves when asked to say a few words at a public dinner. This was Adrian's report to Irene later.

"Had a visitor to-day—s'pose they told you—Lady Ancester. Sorry your mother wasn't up to seeing her."

"I know. We passed her coming away. Said how-d'ye-do in a hurry. What had her ladyship got to say for herself?" Thus far was mere recognition of a self-assertion of the Baronet's, as against female triviality. He always treated any topic mooted in the presence of womankind as mere froth, and resumed it as a male interest, as though it had never been mentioned, as soon as the opposite sex had died down.

"We had some talk. Did you know she was coming?"

"Well—yes—after a fashion. Gwen's last letter said we might expect a descent from her mamma. But I had no idea she was going to be so prompt."

"She sent over to tell us, this morning. They took the letter up to your mother. I had gone over to the Hanger, to prevent Akers cutting down a tree. Man's a fool! I rather got let in for seeing her ladyship. Your mother arranged it."

"I didn't hear of it. I should have stopped. So would 'Re."

"Yes—it rather let me in for a . . . tête-à-tête." Why did Sir Hamilton feel that this expression was an edged tool, that might cut his fingers? He did.

"I should have been in the way."

Another time this might have procured a rebuke for levity. Sir Hamilton perceived in it a stepping-stone to his text. "Perhaps you might," he said. But he wavered, lest that stone should not bear; adding, indecisively:—"Well—we had some talk!"

"About?" said his son. But he knew perfectly well what about.

"About Gwen and yourself. That conversation of yours with the Earl. You remember it? You told me."

"I remember it, certainly. He was perfectly right—the Earl. He's the sort of man that is right. I was horribly ashamed of myself. But Gwen set me up in my own conceit again."

His father persevered. "I understood his view to be that Gwen was under the influence of . . . was influenced by . . . a distorted view . . . a mistaken imagination. . . ."

" Not a doubt of it, I should think. My *amour propre* keeps on suggesting to me that Gwen may be of sound mind. My strong common sense replies that my *amour propre* may be blowed ! "

" Adrian, I wish to talk to you seriously. What did you suppose I was referring to ? "

" To Gwen's distorted view of your humble servant—a clear case of mistaken imagination. That, however, is a condition precedent of the position. Dan Cupid would be hard up, otherwise."

" Dan Who ? "

" The little God of Love . . . not Daniel Anybody ! Wasn't that what the Earl meant ? "

" Not at all ! I was referring to his view of . . . a . . . his daughter's view . . . of the accident . . . some idea of her making up to you for . . ." No wonder he hesitated. It *was* difficult to talk to his son about it.

Adrian cleared the air with a ringing laugh. " I know ! What Gwen calls the Self-Denying Ordinance !—her daddy's expression, I believe." He settled down to a more restrained and serious tone. " The subject has not been mentioned, since Lord Ancester's first conversation with me—in the consulship of Mrs. Bailey, at the Towers—not mentioned by anyone. And though the thought of it won't accept any suggestions towards its extinction, from myself, I don't see my way to . . . to making it a subject of general conversation. In fact, I cannot do anything but hold my tongue. I am sure you would not wish me to say to Gwen:—' Hence ! Begone ! I forbid you to sacrifice yourself at My Shrine.' Now, would you ? "

The Squire was at liberty to ignore poetry. He took no notice of the question, but proceeded to his second head. " Lady Ancester has a strong opinion on the subject." He never said much at a time, and this being difficult conversation, his part of it came in short lengths.

" To the effect that her daughter is throwing herself away. Quite right ! It is so. She *is* throwing herself away."

" Lady Ancester expressed no opinion to that effect. She considers that Gwen is not acting under the influence of . . . under the usual motives. That's all she said. Spoke very well of you, my boy !—I must say that."

" But . . . ? "

664 WHEN GHOST MEETS GHOST

" But thought Gwen ought to act only for her own sake."

" Of course she ought. Of course she ought. I see the whole
turn out. Her mother considers, quite rightly, that Jephtha,
Judge of Israel, ought to have been jolly well ashamed of himself.
Perhaps he was. But that's neither here nor there. What does
Gwen's mammy think I ought to do—ought to say—ought to
pretend? That's what it comes to. Am I to refuse to accompany
Gwen to the altar till she can give sureties that she is really in
love, and plead the highest Spartan principles to justify my conduct? Am I to make believe that I cannot, cannot love a woman
unless she produces certificates of affection based solely on the
desirability of my inestimable self? I should never make anyone
believe *that*. Why—if I thought Gwen hated me worse than
poison, but was marrying me on high moral grounds to square
accounts, I don't think I could humbug successfully, to that
extent."

" Well, my dear boy, I am bound to confess that I do not see
what you can *do*. I can only repeat to you her ladyship's conviction, and tell you that I believe it to be—what she says it is.
I mean that she speaks because she is certain Gwen is under the
influence of this—of this Quixotic motive. I can only tell you
so, at her wish, and—and leave it to you. I tell you frankly that
if I were in her place, I should oppose the marriage, under the
circumstances."

" Why doesn't she tackle me about it herself? "

" H'm—well—h'm! I think if you look at it from her point of
view . . . from her point of view, you'll see there would be many
difficulties . . . many difficulties. Done your cigar? I suppose
we ought to go and pay your mother a visit."

Yes—Adrian saw the difficulties! On his way upstairs a vivid
scene passed through his head, in which an image of the Countess
addressed him thus:—" My dear Mr. Torrens, Gwen does not
really love you. She is only pretending, because she considers
her family are responsible for your blindness. All her assurances
of affection for you are untrustworthy—just her fibs! She could
not play her part without them. I appeal to yòu as an honourable
man to disbelieve every word she says, and to respect the true
instinct of a maternal parent. No one grieves more sincerely
than I do for your great misfortune, or is more contrite than
my husband and myself because it was our keeper that shot you,
but there are limits! We must draw the line at our daughter
marrying a scribbler with his eyes out, on high principles." At
this point the image may be said to have got the bit in its teeth,

for it added:—"If Gwen squinted and had a wooden leg, nothing would please us better. But . . . !"
How did the growing hope of a revival of sight bear on the question? Well—both ways! May not Gwen's pity for his calamity
have had *something* to do with her feelings towards him, without
any motive that the most stodgy prose could call Quixotic?

CHAPTER XVIII

A DABBLER IN IMMORTALITY. *ALL* THEIR LIVES! WILL PHŒBE KNOW
ME? STAY TO TELL HER THIS IS ME. THAT POOR OLD PERSON. HOW
GWEN MET GRANNY MARRABLE ON HER WAY HOME. HER DREAD
OF MORE DISCLOSINGS, AND A GREAT RELIEF. *MACTE VIRTUTE*, DR.
NASH! GRANNY MARRABLE'S FORTITUDE. HOW GWEN NOTICED THE
LIKENESS TOO, FOR THE FIRST TIME! A SHORT CHAT THE COUNTESS
HAD HAD WITH SIR HAMILTON. HOW SHE WAS UNFEELING ABOUT THE
OLD TWINS. WHY NOT SETTLE DOWN AND TALK IT OVER? NO AU-
THENTICATED GHOST APPEARS TO A PERFECT STRANGER. A DANIEL
COME TO JUDGMENT. SIR SPENCER DERRICK AND THE OPENSHAWS.
GWEN'S LETTER TO HER FATHER. HOW SHE DID NOT GO TO PEN-
SHAM, BUT BACK TO STRIDES COTTAGE

WHEN Gwen's task came to an end, she had to think of herself.
The day had been more trying even than her worst anticipations
of it. But now at last she had stormed that citadel of Impossible
Belief in the mind of both mother and daughter, and nothing she
could do could bring them, strained and distracted by the incredible revelation, nearer to a haven of repose. She had spoken
the word: the rest lay with the powers of Nature. Probably she
felt what far different circumstances have caused many of us
to feel, on whom the unwelcome task has devolved of bringing
the news of a death. How consciously helpless we were—was it
not so?—when the tale was told, and we had to leave the heart
of our hearer to its lonely struggle in the dark!
This that Gwen had told was not news of death, but news of
life; nevertheless, it might kill. She had little fear for the daughter or the sister; much for this new-found object of her affection
who had survived so many troubles. For Gwen had to acknowledge that "old Mrs. Picture" had acquired a mysteriously strong
hold upon her—its strangeness lying in its sudden development.

She could, however, do nothing now to help the old tempest-tossed bark into smooth water, that would not be done as well or better by her equally storm-beaten consort, whose rigging and spars had been in such much better trim than hers when the galé struck both alike. Gwen felt, too, a great faith that the daughter's love would be, as it were, the beacon of the mother's salvation; the pilot to a sheltered haven where the seas would be at rest. She herself could do no more.

After the old lady's consciousness returned, it was long before she spoke, and Gwen had felt half afraid her speech might be gone. But then—could she herself speak? Scarcely! And Ruth Thrale, the daughter, seemed in like plight, sitting beside her mother on the bed, her usually rosy cheeks gone ashy white, her eyes fixed on the old face before her with a look that seemed to Gwen one of wonder even more than love. The stress of the hour, surely! For all the tenderness of her heart was in the hand that wandered caressingly about the mass of silver hair on the pillow, and smoothed it away from the eyes that turned from the one to the other half questioningly, but content without reply. The mother seemed physically overwhelmed by the shock, and ready to accept absolute collapse, if not indeed incapable of movement. She made no attempt to speak till later.

During the hour or half-hour that followed, Gwen and Ruth Thrale spoke but once or twice, beneath their breath. Neither could have said why. Who can say why the dwellers in a house where Death is pending speak in undertones? Not from fear of disturbance to the dying man, whose sight and hearing are waning fast. This was a silence of a like sort, though it was rather resurrection than death that imposed it.

The great clock in the kitchen, which had struck twelve when Gwen was showing the forged letter to Widow Thrale, had followed on to one and two, unnoticed. And now, when it struck three, she doubted it, and looked at her watch. "Yes," said she, bewildered. "It's right! It's actually three o'clock. I must go. I wish I could stay." She stooped over the old face on the pillow, and kissed it lovingly. "You know, dear, what has happened. Phœbe is coming—your sister Phœbe." She had a strange feeling, as she said this, of dabbling in immortality—of tampering with the grave.

Then old Maisie spoke for the first time; slowly, but clearly enough, though softly. "I think—I know—what has happened. . . . *All* our lives? . . . But Phœbe will come. My Ruth will fetch her. Will you not, dear?"

"Mother will come, very soon."

"That is it. She is mother—my Ruth's mother! . . . But I am your mother, too, dear!"

"Indeed yes—my mother—my mother—my mother!"

"I kissed you in your crib, asleep, and was not ashamed to go and leave you. I went away in the moonlight, with the little red bag that was *my* mother's—Phœbe's and mine! I was not ashamed to go, for the love of your father, on the cruel sea! Fifty years agone, my darling!" Gwen saw that she was speaking of her husband, and her heart stirred with anger that such undying love should still be his, the miscreant's, the cause of all. She afterwards thought that old Maisie's mind had somehow refused to receive the story of the forgery. Could she, else, have spoken thus, and gone on, as she did, to say to Gwen:—"Come here, my dear! God bless you!"? She held her hand, pressing it close to her. "I want to say to you what it is that is fretting me. Will Phœbe know me, for the girl that went away? Oh, see how I am changed!"

The last thing Gwen had expected was that the old woman should master the facts. It made her hesitate to accept this seeming ability to look them in the face as genuine. It would break down, she was convinced, and the coming of a working recognition of them would be a slow affair. But she could not say so. She could only make believe. "Why should she not know you?" she said. "She has changed, herself."

"When will she come?" said old Maisie restlessly. "She will come when you are gone. Oh, how I wish you could stay, to tell her that this is me!"

"Do you think she will doubt it? She will not, when she hears you talk of the—of your old time. I am sorry I must go, but I must." And indeed she thought so, for she did not know that her own mother had gone away from the Towers, and fancied that that good lady would resent her desertion. This affair had lasted longer than her anticipation of it.

Then old Maisie showed how partial the illumination of her mind had been. "Oh yes, my dear," she said, "I know. You have to go, of course, because of that poor old person. The old person you told me of—whom you have to tell—to tell of her sister she thought dead—what was it?" She had recovered consciousness so far as to know that Phœbe was somehow to reappear risen from the dead; and that this Ruth whom she had taken so much to heart was somehow entitled to call her mother; but what that *how* was, and why, was becoming a mystery as her vigour fell away and an inevitable reaction began to tell upon her.

Gwen heard it in the dazed sound of her voice; and, to her thought, assent was best to whatever the dumfoundered mind dwelt upon most readily. " Yes," said she, " I must go and tell her. She must know." Then she beckoned Widow Thrale away from the bedside. " It was her own sister I told her of," said she in an undertone. " I thought she would see quickest that way. . . . Do you quite understand ? " A quick nod showed that her hearer had quite understood. Gwen thanked Heaven that at least she had no lack of faculties to deal with there. " Listen ! " said she. " You must get her food now. You must *make* her eat, whether she likes it or no." She saw that for Ruth herself the kindest thing was the immediate imposition of duties, and was glad to find her so alive to the needs of the case.

Two voices of women in the kitchen without. One, Elizabeth-next-door; the other, surely, Keziah Solmes from the Towers. So much the better ! " I may tell it them, my lady ? " said Widow Thrale. Gwen had to think a moment, before saying :—" Yes— but they must not talk of it in the village—not yet ! Go out and tell them. I will remain with your mother." It was the first time Ruth Thrale had had the fact she had succeeded in knowing in theory forced roughly upon her in practice. She started, but recovered herself to do her ladyship's bidding.

The utter amazement of Keziah and Elizabeth-next-door, as Gwen heard it, was a thing to be remembered. But she paid little attention to it. She was bidding farewell to old Mrs. Picture. The last speech she heard from her seemed to be :—" Tell my little boy and Dolly. Say I will come back to them." Then she appeared to fall asleep.

" You must get some food down her throat, somehow, Mrs. Thrale, or we shall have her sinking from exhaustion. You will stop to help, Keziah ? Stop till to-morrow. I will look in at the Lodge to tell your husband. I must go now. Is Tom Kettering there ? " Gwen felt she would like an affectionate farewell of Ruth Thrale, but a slight recrudescence of the Norman Conquest came in the way, due to the presence of Keziah and Elizabeth-next-door; so she had to give it up.

Tom Kettering was not there, but was reproducible at pleasure by whistles, evolved from some agent close at hand and willing to assist. Tom and the mare appeared unchanged by their long vigil, and showed neither joy nor sorrow at its coming to an end. A violent shake the latter indulged in was a mere report of progress, and Tom only touched his hat as a convention from time immemorial. There was not a trace of irony in his " Home, my lady?" though a sarcastic Jehu might have seemed to be expressing a doubt whether her ladyship meant ever to go home at all. The road to Costrell's turned off Gwen's line of route, the main road to the Towers. A cart was just coming in sight, at the corner. Farmer Costrell's cart, driven by himself. An old woman by his side—Granny Marrable, surely?

Gwen was simply frightened. She felt absolutely unfit for another high-tension interview. Her head might give way and she might do something foolish. But it was impossible to turn and run. It was, however, easy enough to go quickly by, with ordinary salutations. Still, it was repugnant to her to do so. But, then, what else could she do? It was settled for her.

Said Granny Marrable to her grandson-in-law:—"'Tis Gwen o' th' Towers, John, in Tom Kettering's gig. Bide here till they come up, that I may get speech of her ladyship."

"Will she stand still on th' high roo-ad, to talk to we?"

"She'll never pass me by if she sees me wishful to speak with her. Her ladyship has too good a heart."

"Vairy well, Gra-anny." John Costrell reined in his horse, and the cart and gig came abreast.

Granny Marrable spoke at once. Her voice was firm, but her face was pale and hard set. "I have been told strange news, my lady, but it *must* be true. It cannot be else."

"It *is* true. Dr. Nash told you."

"That is so. Our Dr. Nash."

"But how much? Has he told you all?"

"I will tell your ladyship." The old woman's firmness and strength were marvellous to Gwen. "He has told me that my sister that was dead is risen from the grave. . . ."

"God's my life, Granny, what will ye be for saying next to her ladyship?" John Costrell had heard none of the story.

"It's all quite right, Mr. Costrell," said Gwen. "Granny Marrable doesn't mean really dead. She *thought* her dead—her sister. . . . Go on, Granny! That is quite right. And has Dr. Nash told you where your sister is now?"

"At my own home at Chorlton, my lady. And I am on my way there now, and will see her once more, God willing, before we die."

"Go to her—go to her! The sooner the better! . . . I must tell you one thing, though. She is not strong—not like you and your daughter Ruth. But you will see." The old lady began with something about her gratitude to Gwen and to her father, but Gwen cut her short. What did that matter, now? Then she assured her that old Maisie had been told everything, and was only uneasy lest her sister should not know her again, and would even doubt her identity. "But that is impossible," said Gwen. "Because she *is* your sister, and remembers all your childhood together."

After they had parted company, and Gwen was on her way again, relieved beyond measure to find that Dr. Nash had contrived to carry out his mission so well—though how he had done it was a mystery to her as yet—she had a misgiving that she ought to have produced the forged letter to show to Granny Marrable. Perhaps, however, she had done no harm by keeping it; as if the conviction of the two sisters of each other's identity was to turn on what is called "evidence," what would be its value to either? They would either know each other, or not; and if they did *not,* enough "evidence" to hang a dozen men would not stand against the deep-rooted belief in each other's death through those long years.

Besides, like Dr. Nash, she had just been quite taken aback to see—now that she came to look for it, mind you!—the amazing likeness between the old twin sisters. How came it that she had not seen it before?—for instance, when they were face to face in her presence at the door of Strides Cottage, but two or three weeks since. She dismissed the forged letter, to dwell on the enormous relief of not having another disclosure problem before her; and also on the satisfaction she would have in telling her father what a successful outcome had followed his venial transgression of opening and reading it. Altogether, her feelings were those of triumph, trampling underfoot the recollection that she had had nothing to eat since breakfast, and making a good stand against brain-whirl caused by the almost unbearable strangeness of the story.

On arriving at the Towers, she was disconcerted to find that all her solicitude about her mother's loneliness in her absence had been thrown away. She whispered to herself that it served her right for fidgeting about other people. Adrian had been perfectly justified when he said that interest in one's relations was the worst investment possible for opulent Altruism.

Well—she was better off now than she had been in the early morning, when there was all that terrible disclosure ahead. It was *done*—ended; for better, for worse! She might indulge now in a cowardice that shrank from seeing the two old sisters again until they were familiarised with the position. If only she might find them, on her next visit, habituated to a new *modus vivendi,* with the possibility of peaceful years together, to live down the long separation into nothingness! If only that might be! But was it possible? Was it conceivable even?

Anyhow, she deserved a well-earned rest from tension. And

presently she would tell the whole strange story to Adrian, and show him that clever forgery. . . . No!—thought stopped with a cruel jerk, and her heart said:—" Shall I ever *show* him anything! Never! Never!"

" You went to Pensham, mamma?" said Gwen to her mother, the next day, as soon as an opportunity came for quiet talk.

" On my way to Poynders," said the Countess yawnfully. " But it was unlucky. Lady Torrens was keeping her room. Some sort of nervous attack. I didn't get any particulars."

Gwen suspected reticence. " You didn't see her, then?"

" Oh dear no! How should I? She was in bed, I believe."

" You saw *somebody?* "

" Only Sir Hamilton, for a few minutes. He doesn't seem uneasy. I don't suppose it's anything serious."

" Did you see 'Re?"

" Miss Torrens and her brother were out. Didn't come back." Her ladyship here perceived that reticence, overdone, would excite suspicion, and provoke exhaustive inquiry. " I had a short chat with Sir Hamilton. Who gave me a very good cup of tea." The excellence of the tea was, so to speak, a red herring.

Gwen refused to be thrown off the scent. " He's an old friend of yours, isn't he?" said she suggestively.

" Oh dear yes! Ages ago. He told me about some people I haven't heard of for years. I must try and call on that Mrs. What's-her-name. Do you know where Tavistock Square is?"

" Of course I do. Everybody does. Who is it lives there?"

The Countess had consulted the undersized tablets, and was re-pocketing them. " Mrs. Enniscorthy Hopkins," said she, in the most collateral way possible to humanity. " *You* wouldn't know anything about her."

" This tea has been standing," said Gwen. She refused to rise to Mrs. Enniscorthy Hopkins, whom she suspected of red-herringhood.

The Countess was compelled to be less collateral. " She was Kathleen Tyrawley," said she. " But I quite lost sight of her. One does."

" Was she interesting?"

" Ye-es. . . . N-no . . . not very. Pretty—of that sort!"

" What sort?"

" Well—very fond of horses."

" So am I—the darlings!"

" Yes—but a girl may be very fond of horses, and yet not marry a . . . Don't put milk in—only cream. . . ."

" Marry a what ? "

" Marry her riding-master." Her ladyship softened down Miss Tyrawley's groom to presentability. " But it was before you were born, child. However, no doubt it is the same, in principle."

" Hope so! Is that tea right ? "

" The tea? Oh yes, the tea . . . will do. No, I only saw Sir Hamilton. The son and daughter were away."

" Now, mamma, that is being unkind, and you know it. ' The son and daughter!' As if they were people!' "

" Well—and what are they ? "

" You know perfectly well what I mean."

As the Countess did, she averted discussion. " We won't rake the subject up, my dear Gwendolen," she said, in a manner which embodied moderation, while asserting dignity. " You know my feelings on the matter, which would, I am sure, be those of any parent—of any *mother*, certainly. And I may mention to you— only, *please* no discussion!—that Sir Hamilton *entirely shares* my views. He expressed himself quite clearly on the subject yesterday."

" You must have seen him for more than a few minutes to get as far as *that*." This was a shell in the enemy's powder-magazine.

The Countess had to adopt retrocessive strategy. " I think, my dear," she said, with dignity at a maximum, " that I have made it sufficiently clear that I do not wish to rediscuss your engagement, as your father persists in calling it. We must retain our opinions. If at the end of six months—*if*—it turns out that I am entirely mistaken, why, then you and your father must just settle it your own way. Now let us talk no more about it."

This conversation took place in the late afternoon of the day following Gwen's visit to Strides Cottage, and the Countess's to Pensham. All through the morning of that day her young ladyship had been feeling the effects of the strain of the previous one, followed by a night of despairing sleeplessness due to excitement. An afternoon nap, a most unusual thing with her, had rallied her to the point of sending a special invitation to her mother to join her at tea in her own private apartment; which was reasonable, as all the guests were away killing innocent birds, or hares. The Countess was aware of her daughter's fatigue and upset, but persisted in regarding its cause as over-estimated—a great deal too much made of a very simple matter. " Then that is satisfactorily settled, and there need be no further fuss." These were her words of comment on her daughter's detailed account of her day's adventures, which made themselves of use to keep hostilities in abeyance.

"I think you are unfeeling, mamma; that's flat!" was Gwen's unceremonious rejoinder.

The Countess repeated the last word impassively. It was rather as though she said to Space:—"Here is an expression. If you are by way of containing any Intelligences capable of supplying an explanation, I will hear them impartially." Receiving no reply from any Point of the Compass, she continued:—"I really cannot see what these two old . . . persons have to complain of. They have every reason to be thankful that they have been spared so long. The death of either would have made all your exertions on their behalf useless. Why they cannot settle down on each side of that big fireplace at Strides Cottage, and talk it all over, I cannot imagine. It has been engraved in the *Illustrated London News*." This was marginal, not in the text. "They will have plenty to tell each other after such a long time."

"Mamma dear, you are hopeless!"

"Well, my dear, ask any sensible person. They have had the narrowest escape of finding it all out after each other's death, and then I suppose we should never have heard the end of it. . . . Yes, perhaps the way I put it *was* a little confused. But really the subject is so complex." Gwen complicated it still more by introducing its relations to Immortality; to which her mother took exception:—"If they were both ghosts, we should probably know nothing of them. No ghost appears to a perfect stranger—no authenticated ghost! Besides, one hopes they would be at peace in their graves."

"Oh, ah, yes, by-the-by!" said Gwen, "there wasn't to be anything till the Day of Judgment."

"I wish you wouldn't drag in Religion," said her mother. "You pick up these dreadful Freethinking ways of speech from . . . ."

"From Adrian? Of course I do. But *you* began it, by talking about Death and Ghosts."

"My dear, neither Death nor Ghosts are Religion, but the Day of Judgment is. Ask anybody!"

"Very well, then! Cut the Day of Judgment out, and go on with Death and Ghosts."

"We will talk," said the Countess coldly, "of something else. I do not like the tone of the conversation. What are your plans for to-morrow?"

"I don't think I shall go to Chorlton to-morrow. I shall leave the old ladies alone for a while. I think it's the best way. Don't you?"

"I don't think it can matter much, either way." The Countess was not going to come down from Olympus, for trifles. "But what *are* you going to do to-morrow? Go to church, I *suppose?*"

"Is it necessary to settle?"

"By no means. Perhaps I was wrong in taking it for granted. No doubt I should have done well—in your case—to ask for information. *Are* you going to church?"

"Possibly. I can settle when the time comes." Her mother made no reply, but she made it so ostentatiously that to skip off to another subject would have been to accept a wager of battle. Gwen was prepared to be conciliatory. "Is anything coming off?" she asked irreverently. "Any Bishop or anything?"

Her mother replied, with a Pacific Ocean of endurance in her voice:—"Dr. Tuxford Somers is preaching at the Abbey. If you come, pray do not be late. The carriage will be ready at a quarter to ten."

"Well—I shall have to go once or twice, so I suppose now will do for once. There's Christmas Day, of course—I don't mind that. I shall go to Chorlton, and look at the two old ladies in church. I hope Mrs. Picture will be well enough by then."

"I am sure I hope so. A whole week!" The Countess's *parti pris,* that the experience of the old twins was nothing to make such a fuss over, showed itself plainly in this. She passed on to a more important subject. "I understand," said she, "that you intend to go to Pensham on Monday—and stay!"

"I do," said Gwen uncompromisingly. But her mother's expression became so stony that Gwen anticipated her spoken protest, saying:—"Now, mamma dear, you know I've agreed, and we are to go abroad for six whole months. So don't look like a martyr!"

"When will you be back?" said the martyr. The fact is, she was well aware that this was a case of *quid pro quo;* and that Gwen was entitled, by treaty, to a perfect Saturnalia of sweet-hearting till after Christmas, in exchange for the six months of penal servitude to follow. But she preferred to indicate that the terms of the treaty had disappointed her.

"Quite uncertain," said Gwen. "I shall stop till Thursday, anyhow. And Adrian and Irene are to come here on Christmas Eve. I suppose they'll have to share the paternal plum-pudding on Christmas Day. That can't be helped. And I shall have to be here. *That* can't be helped either. *I* think it a pity the whole clanjamfray shouldn't come here for Christmas."

"That is out of the question. Sir Hamilton has his own social obligations. Besides, it would look as if you and Mr. Torrens were definitely engaged. Which you are not."

" Suppose we talk of something else."

" Suppose we do." Her ladyship could only assent; for had she not, Shylockwise, taught her daughter that word?

The agreement that another topic should be resorted to was sufficiently complied with by a short pause before resuming the antecedent one. Gwen did this by saying:—" You will be all right without me for a few days, because Sir Spencer Derrick and his wife are due to-night, and the Openshaws, and the Pellews will be here on Monday."

" Gwendolen! " In a shocked tone of voice.

" Well—Aunt C. and Cousin Percy, then. If they are not the Pellews, they very soon will be. They are coming on Monday, anyhow."

" But not by the same train! "

" I should come by the same train, if I were they. And in the same carriage. And tip the guard to keep everybody else out. Much better do it candidly than pretend they've met by accident. I should.

The Countess thought she really had better change to another subject. She dropped this one as far off as possible. " When do you expect to see your two old interesting twins again? said she conciliatorily. For she felt that reasoning with her beautiful but irregular daughter was hopeless. The young lady explained that her next visit to Chorlton would be by way of an expedition from Pensham. Adrian and Irene would drive her over. It was not morally much farther from Pensham than from the Towers, although some arithmetical appearances were against it. And she particularly wanted Adrian to see old Mrs. Picture. And then, like a sudden sad cadence in music, came the thought: —" But he cannot see old Mrs. Picture."

Keziah Solmes did not come back till quite late in the evening. Her report of the state of things at Strides Cottage was manifestly vitiated by an unrestrained optimism. If she was to be believed, the sudden revelation to each other of the old twin sisters had had no specially perturbing effect on either. Gwen spent much of the evening writing a long letter to her father at Bath, giving a full account of her day's work, and ending:—" I do hope the dear old soul will bear it. Mrs. Solmes has just given me a most promising report of her. I cannot suppose her constant references to the Benevolence of Providence to be altogether euphemisms in the interest of the Almighty. I am borrowing Adrian's language—you will see that. I think Keziah is convinced that Mrs. Prichard will rally, and that the twins may live to be nonagenarians together. I must confess to being very anxious about her myself. She looked to me as if a breath of air might blow her away. I shall not see her again for a day or two, but I know they will send for me if I am wanted. Dr. Nash is to see to that. What a serviceable man he is!" She went on to say, after a few more particulars of Keziah's report, that she was going to Pensham on Monday, and should not come back before the Earl's own return to the Towers. Mamma would do perfectly well without her, and it was only fair, considering her own concessions.

But Gwen did not go to church next day.

Dr. Nash had been sent for to Strides Cottage at a very early hour, having been prevented from fulfilling a promise to go overnight. He must have seen some new cause for uneasiness, although he disclaimed any grounds of alarm. For he wrote off at once to her young ladyship, after a careful examination of his patient:—"Mrs. Prichard certainly is very feeble. I think it only right that you should know this at once. But you need not be frightened. Probably it is no more than was to be expected." That was the wording of his letter, received by Gwen as she sat at breakfast with some new arrivals and the Colonel, and the dregs of the shooting-party. She was not at all sorry to get a complete change of ideas and associations, although the subjects of conversation were painful enough, turning on the reports of mixed disaster and success in the Crimea that were making the close of '54 lurid and memorable for future history. Gwen glanced at Dr. Nash's letter, gave hurried directions to the servant to tell Tom Kettering to be in readiness to drive her at once to Chorlton, and made short work of breakfast and her *adieux* to the assembled company.

If events would only pay attention to the convenience of storytellers, they would never happen at the same time. It would make consecutive narrative much more practicable. It would have been better—some may say—for this story to follow Granny Marrable to Strides Cottage, and to leave Gwen to come to Dr. Nash's summons next day. It might then have harked back to the foregoing chat between her and her mother, or omitted it altogether. Its author prefers the course it has taken.

CHAPTER XIX

WHAT DID GRANNY MARRABLE THINK ON THE ROAD? HER ARRIVAL, AND
HOW KEZIAH TOLD JOHN COSTRELL, WHO WHISTLED. THE MEETING,
WHICH NONE SAW. HOW COULD THIS BE MAISIE? GRANNY MARRA-
BLE'S SHAKEN FAITH. RUTH'S MIXED FILIALITIES. HOW OLD MAISIE
AWOKE AND FELT CHILLY. HOW SHE SLEPT TEN SECONDS MORE AND
DREAMED FOR HOURS. HOW OLD PHŒBE HAD DRAWN A VERY SMALL
TOOTH OF MAISIE'S, OVER SIXTY YEARS AGO

KEZIAH SOLMES was literal, not imaginative. She was able to describe any outward seeming of old Phœbe, or of Ruth. But what
could she know, or guess, of the stunned bewilderment of their
minds? When asked by Gwen what each of the old twins had said
at sight of the other—for she had been present, if not at their meeting, a few moments later—she seemed at a loss for a report of definite speech. But, oh yes!—in reply to a suggestion from Gwen—
they had called each other by name, that for sure they did! "But
'twas a wonderment to me, my lady, that neither one should cry out
loud, for the sorrow of all that long time ago." So said old Keziah,
sounding a true note in this reference to the sadness inherent in
mere lapse of years. Gwen could and did endorse Keziah, on that
score; but there was no wonderment in *her* mind at their silence.
Rather, she was at a loss to conceive or invent a single phrase that
either could or would have spoken.

Least of all could independent thought imagine the anticipations
of old Phœbe during that strange ride through the falling twilight
of the short winter's day. Did she articulate to herself that each
minute on the road was bringing her nearer to a strange mystery
that was in truth—that *must* be—the very selfsame·sister that her
eyes last saw now fifty years ago, even the very same that had
called her, a mere baby, to see the heron that flew away? Yes—the
same Maisie as much·as she herself was the same Phœbe! Did
her brain reel to think of the days when she took her own image in
an unexpected mirror for her sister—kissed the cold glass with a
shudder of horror before she found her mistake? Did she wonder
now if this Mrs. Prichard could seem to her another self, as Maisie
had wondered would *she* seem to *her?* Would all be changed and
chill, and the old music of their past be silence, or at best the jan-
gle of a broken chord? Would this latter end of Life, for both, be

nothing but a joint anticipation of the grave? Gwen tried to sound the plummet of thought in an inconceivable surrounding, to guess at something she herself might think were she impossibly conditioned thus, and failed.

The story, too, must be content to fail. All it can guarantee is facts; and speculation recoils from the attempt to see into old Phœbe's soul as she dismounts from the farmer's cart, at the door beyond which was the thing to baffle all belief; to stultify all those bygone years, and stamp them as delusions.

Whatever she thought, her words were clear and free from trepidation, and John Costrell repeated them after her, making them the equivalent of printed instructions. " If yow are ba-adly wanted, Granny, I'm to coom for ye with ne'er a minute's loss o' time. That wull I. And for what I be to tell the missus, I bean't to say owt."

No—that would not do! The early return of the cart, without the Granny, had to be somehow accounted for. Nothing had been said to Maisie junior, by her, of not returning to supper. " Bide there a minute till I tell ye, John," said she, and went towards the door.

Keziah Solmes was coming out, having heard the cart. She started, with the exclamation:—" Why, God-a-mercy, 'tis the Granny herself! " and made as though to beat a retreat into the house, no doubt thinking to warn Widow Thrale within. Old Phœbe stopped her, saying, quite firmly:—" I know, Cousin Keziah. Tell me, how is Mrs. Prichard? "

Keziah, taken aback, lost presence of mind. " What can ye know o' Mrs. Prichard, Granny? " said she sillily. She said this because she could not see how the information had travelled.

" How is she? " old Phœbe repeated. And something in her voice said:—" Answer straight! " At least, so Keziah thought, and replied:—" The worser by the bad shake she's had, I lay." Neither made any reference to Mrs. Prichard's newly discovered identity. For though, as we have seen, Keziah knew all about it, she felt that the time had not yet come for free speech. Granny Marrable turned to John Costrell, saying in the same clear, unhesitating way:—" You may say to Maisie that her mother wants a helping hand with old Mrs. Prichard, but I'll come in the morning. You'll say no further than that, John; "—and passed on into the house.

John replied:—" I'll see to it, Granny," and grasped the situation, evidently. Keziah remained, and as soon as the old lady was out of hearing, said to him:—" This be a stra-ange stary coom to light, Master Costrell. Only to think of it! The Gra-anny's twin, thought dead now, fowerty years agone!"

"Thou'lt be knowing mower o' the stary than I, belike, Mrs. Solmes," said John. "I'm only the better by a bare word or so, so far, from speech o' the Gra-anny with her yoong la-adyship o' the Towers, but now, on the roo-ad. The Gra-anny she was main silent, coom'n' along."

"There's nowt to wonder at in that, Master Costrell. For there's th' stary, as I tell it ye. Fowerty years agone and more, she was dead by all accounts, out in the Colonies, and counted her sister dead as well. And twenty years past she's been living in London town, and ne'er a one known it. And now she's come by a chance to this very house!"

"She'd never coom anigh to this place?"

"Sakes alive, no! 'Twas all afower Gra-anny Marrable come here to marry Farmer Marrable—he was her second, ye know. I was a bit of a chit then. And Ruth Thrale was fower or five years yoonger. She was all one as if she was the Gra-anny's own child. But she was noa such a thing."

Then it became clear that the word or so had been very bare indeed. "She was an orphan, I ta-ak it," said John indifferently.

"There, now!" said Keziah. "I was ma-akin' a'most sure you didn't see the right of it, Master Costrell. And I wasn't far wrong, that once!"

"Maybe I'm out, but I do-an't see rightly where. A girl's an orphan, with ne'er a fa-ather nor a moother. Maybe one o' them was living? Will that square it?"

"One o' them's living still. And none so vairy far from where we stand. Can ye ma-ak nowt o' that, Master Costrell?"

John *was* a little slow; it was his bucolic mind. "None so vairy far from where we stand?" he repeated, in the dark.

"Hearken to me tell ye, man alive! She's in yander cottage, in the bedroom out across th' pa-assage. And the two o' them they've met by now. Are ye any nearer, Master Costrell?"

For a moment no idea fructified. Then astonishment caught and held him. "Not unless," he exclaimed, "not unless you are meaning that this old la-ady is Widow Thrale's mother!"

"You've gotten hold of it now, Master Costrell."

"But 'tis impossible—'tis *impossible!* If she were she would be my wife's grandmother!—her grandmother that died in Australia. . . . Well, Keziah Solmes, ye may nod and look wise—but . . ."

"But that is th' vairy thing she is, safe and sure, John Costrell. I told ye—Australia. Australia be the Colonies."

John gave the longest whistle a single breath would support. Why he was ready to accept the relation of old Phœbe and Maisie, and revolt against his wife's inevitable granddaughtership, Heaven only knows! "But I'm not to say a word of it to the mistress," said he, meaning his wife.

"The Gra-anny said so, and she'll be right. . . . Was that her voice? . . ." A sound had come from the cottage. Keziah might be wanted. She wished the farmer good-night; and he drove off, no longer mystified, but dumfounded with what had removed his mystification.

Old Phœbe had passed on into the house. She was satisfied that her message would account quite reasonably for the vacant seat in the returning cart. Besides, medical sanction—Dr. Nash's—had been given for her absence.

Now that the moment was close, a great terror came upon her, and she trembled. She knew that Ruth, her daughter for so long, was beyond that closed door across the passage, with . . . With whom? With what?

Who can say except he be a twin that has lost a twin, what more of soul-stress had to be borne by these two than would have been his lot, or ours, in their place? And the severance of Death itself could not have been more complete than theirs for forty-odd years past; nor the reunion beyond the grave, that Gwen had likened theirs to, be stranger. Indeed, one is tempted to imagine that inconceivable palliations may attend conditions of which our ignorance can form no image. On this side one only knows that such a meeting is all the sadder for the shadow of Decay.

She could hardly believe herself the same as when, so few days since, she quitted this old room, that still remained unchanged; so intensely the same as when she, and her memories in it were left alone with a Past that seemed unchangeable, but for the ever-growing cloud of Time. There was the old clock, ticking by the dresser, not missing its record of the short life of every second that would never come again. There on the hearth was the log that might seem cold, but always treasured a spark to be rekindled; and the indomitable bellows, time-defying, that never failed to find it out and make it grow to flame. There was the old iron kettle, all blackness without and crystal purity within, singing the same song that it began a long lifetime since, and showing the same impatience under neglect. There on the dresser was the same dinner-service that had survived till breakage and neglect of its brethren had made it a rarity; and on the wall that persevering naval battle her husband's great-grandmother's needle had immortalised a century and a half ago. The only change she saw was the beadwork tablecloth wrapped over the mill-model, in its place above the hearth. Otherwise there was no change.

And here was she, face to face with resurrection—that was how she thought of it—all her brain in a whirl, unfit to allot its proper place to the most insignificant fact; all her heart stunned by a cataclysm she had no wits to give a name to. She had come with a rare courage and endurance to be at close quarters with this mystery, whatever it was, at once. On the very verge of full knowledge of it, this terror had come upon her, and she stood trembling, sick with dread undefined, glad she need not speak or call out. It would pass, and then she would call to Ruth, whose voice she could hear in the room beyond. There was another voice, too, a musical one, and low. Whose could it be? Not her lost sister's—not Maisie's! Her voice was never like that.

The cat came purring round her to welcome her back. The great bulldog trotted in from the yard behind, considered her a moment, and passed out to the front, attracted by the voices of Keziah and John Costrell. Having weighed them, duly and carefully, he trotted back past Granny Marrable, to give one short bark at the bedroom door, and return to the yard behind, his usual headquarters. Then Ruth came from the bedroom, hearing the movement and speech without.

She was terribly taken aback. "Oh, mother dearest," she said, betrayed into speaking her inner thought, "you have come too soon. You cannot know."

"*I* know," said Granny Marrable. "I will tell you presently. Now take me to her."

Ruth saw she meant that she could not trust her feet. What wonder at that? If she really knew the truth, what wonder at anything? She gave the support of her arm to the door, across the passage. Then the need for it seemed to cease, and the Granny, becoming her strong old self again, said with her own voice:— "That will do, dear child! Leave me to go on." She seemed to mean:—"Go on alone." That was what Ruth took her speech for. She herself held back; so none saw the first meeting between the twins.

Presently, as she stood there in suspense, she heard the words:— "Who is it outside, Ruth?" in Mrs. Prichard's voice, weak but controlled. Then the reply, through a breath that caught:—"Ruth

is outside." Then the weaker voice, questioning:—" Then who?
. . . then who? . . ." But no answer was given.

For, to Ruth's great wonderment, Granny Marrable came back
in extreme trepidation, crying out through sobs:—" Oh, how can
this be Maisie? Oh, how can this be Maisie?" To which Ruth's
reply was:—" Oh, mother dear, who can she be if she is not my
mother?" And though the wording was at fault, it is hard to see
how she could have framed her question otherwise.

But old Phœbe had cried out loud enough to be heard by Keziah,
speaking with John Costrell out in front, and it was quite audible
in the room she had just left. That was easy to understand. But
it was less so that old Maisie should have risen unassisted from the
bed where she had lain since morning, and followed her.

" Oh, Phœbe, Phœbe darling, do not say that! Do not look at
me to deny me, dearest. I know that this is you, and that we are
here, together. Wait—wait and *it will come!*" This was what
Keziah remembered hearing as she came back into the house. She
crossed the kitchen, and saw, beyond Widow Thrale in the passage,
that the two old sisters were in each other's arms.

Old Phœbe, strong in self-command and moral fortitude, and at
the same time unable to stand against the overwhelming evidence
of an almost incredible fact, had nevertheless been unprepared, by
any distinct image of what the beautiful young creature of fifty
years ago had become, to accept the reality that encountered her
when at last she met it face to face.

Old Maisie's position was different. She had already fought
and won her battle against the changes Time had brought about,
and her mind no longer recoiled from the ruinous discolorations of
decay. She had been helped in this battle by a strong ally, the
love engendered for her own daughter while she was still ignorant
of her identity. She had found her outward seeming a stepping-
stone to a true conception of the octogenarian, last seen in the
early summer of a glorious womanhood. Ruth Thrale's autumn,
however much she still retained of a comely maturity, had been in
those days the budding springtime of a child of four. Come what
come might of the ravages of Time and Change, old Maisie was prepared for it, after accepting such a change as that. Did she know,
and acknowledge to herself the advantage this had been to her, that
time when she had said to Gwen:—" How I wish you could stay, to
tell her that this is me!"

But the momentary unexpected strength that had enabled old
Maisie to rise from the bed could not last. She had only just
power left to say:—" I *am* Maisie! I *am* Maisie!" before speech

failed; and her daughter had to be prompt, close at hand though she was, to prevent her falling. They got her back to the bed, frightened by what seemed unconsciousness, but relieved a moment after by her saying:—" I was only dizzy. Is this Phœbe's hand?" They were not seriously alarmed about her then.

She remained very still, a hand of her sister and daughter in each of hers, and the twilight grew, but none spoke a word. Keziah, at a hint from Ruth, attended to the preparation of supper in the front-room. This living unfed through hours of tension had to come to an end sometime. They knew that *her* silence was by choice, from a pressure of the hand of either from time to time. It seemed to repeat her last words:—" I *am* Maisie. I *am* Maisie." That silence was welcome to them, for neither would have said a word by choice. They could but sit speechless, stunned by the Past. Would they ever be able to talk of it at all? A short parting gives those who travel together on the road through Life a good spell of cheerful chat, and each is overbrimming with the tale of adventure, grave or gay, of the folk they have chanced upon, the inns they have slept at, a many trifles with a leaven of seriousness not too weighty for speech. How is it when the ways divided half a century ago, and no tidings came to hand of either for the most part of a lifetime? How when either has believed the other dead, through all those years? Neither old Phœbe nor Ruth could possibly have felt the thing otherwise. But, that apart, silence was easiest.

Presently, it was evident that she was sleeping, peacefully enough, still holding her sister and daughter by the hand. As soon as Ruth felt the fingers slacken, she spoke, under her breath: " How came you to know of it?"

" Dr. Nash. I spoke with her ladyship on the way, and she said it was true."

" What did she say was true?"

Granny Marrable had to think. What was it Gwen had said? She continued, feeling for her memories:—" I said to Gwen o' the Towers 'twas my dead sister come from the grave, and Dr. Nash had spoken to it. And John Costrell would have me unsay my word, but her ladyship bore me out, though 'twas but a way of speech." She paused a moment; then, before Ruth could frame an inquiry as to how much she knew of the story from either Dr. Nash or Gwen, went on, her eyes fixed, with a look that had terror in it, on the figure on the bed:—" If this be Maisie, was she not dead to me—my sister? Oh, how can this be Maisie?" Her mind was still in a turmoil of bewilderment and doubt.

Then Ruth's speech was again at fault, and yet she saw nothing strange in it. "Oh, mother dearest, this *must* be my mother. How else could she know? Had you but heard her talk as I did, of the old mill!—and there she was a-knowing of it all, and I could think her mad! Oh, mother dear, the fool that I was not to see she *must* be my mother!"

"It comes and goes, child," said Granny Marrable tremulously, "that she is your mother, not dead as I have known her. But it is all your life. I mind how the letter came that told it. After your grandfather's death. And all a lie!"

"Her ladyship will tell you that, mother, as she told it to me. I have not the heart to think it, but it was my father's work. God have mercy on him!"

"God have mercy on him, for his sin! But how had he the cruelty? What wrong had I done him?"

"Mother, I pray that I may one day see the light upon it. God spare us a while, just for to know the meaning of it all." It was a confession of the hopelessness of any attempt to grapple with it then.

Keziah Solmes, while preparing some supper, looked in once, twice, at the watchers beside the still sleeping figure on the bed. They were not speaking, and never took their eyes from the placid, colourless face and snow-white hair loose on the pillow; but they gave her the idea of dazed bewilderment, waiting for the mists to clear and let them dare to move again. The fog-bound steamer on the ocean stands still, or barely cuts the water. It is known, on board, that the path will reopen—but when?

The third time Keziah looked in at them, the room being all dark but for a wood-flicker from an unreplenished grate, she gathered courage to say that supper was ready. Ruth Thrale started up from where she half sat, half lay, beside the sleeper, exclaiming:— "She's eaten nothing since the morning. Mother, she'll sink for want of food."

"Now, the Lord forgive me!" said Granny Marrable. "To think I've had my dinner to-day, and she's been starving!" For, of course, the midday meal was all over at Costrell's, in normal peace, when Dr. Nash came in laden with the strange news, and at a loss to tell it.

The withdrawal of her daughter's hand waked the sleeper with a start. "I was dreaming so nicely," said she. "But I'm cold. Oh dear—what is it? . . . I thought I was in Sapps Court, with my little Dave and Dolly. . . ." She seemed slow to catch again the thread of the life she had fallen asleep on. Vitality was very

low, evidently, and she met an admonition that she must eat something with:—" Nothing but milk, please!" It refreshed her, for
though she fell back on the pillow with her eyes closed, she spoke
again a moment after.

The thing happened thus. Keziah, authoritatively, insistent,
would have Ruth eat, or try to eat, some supper. Old Phœbe was
in no need of it, and sat on beside old Maisie, who must have
dreamed again—one of those sudden long experiences a few seconds will give to a momentary sleep. For she opened her eyes to
say, with a much greater strength in her voice:—" I was dreaming
of Dolly again, but Dolly wasn't Dolly this time . . . only, she
was Dolly, somehow! . . ." Then it was clear that she was quite
in the dark, for the time being, about the events of the past few
hours. For she continued:—" She was Dolly and my sister Phœbe
—both at once—when Phœbe was a little girl—my Phœbe that was
drowned. But Phœbe was older than that when she drew my tooth,
as Dolly did in my dream."

Old Phœbe, it must be borne in mind, although intellectually
convinced that this could be none other than her sister, had never
experienced the conviction that only the revival of joint memories
could bring. This reference to an incident only known to themselves, long forgotten by her and now flashed suddenly on her out
of the past, made her faith that this was Maisie, in very truth, a
reality. But she could not speak.

The dream-gods kept their hold on the half-awakened mind, too
old for any alacrity in shaking them off. The old voice wandered
on, every word telling on its hearer and rousing a memory. " We
must have been eight then. Phœbe tied a thread of silk round the
tooth, and the other end to the drawer-knob . . . it was such a
little tooth . . . long and long before you were born, my dear.
. . ." Her knowledge of the present was on its way back, and
she thought the hand that held hers was her new-found daughter's.
" It was the drawer where the knitting-wool was kept."

If you who read this are old, can you not remember among the
surroundings of your childhood things too trivial for the maturities
of that date to give a passing thought to, that nevertheless bulked
large to you then, and have never quite lost their impressiveness
since? Such a one, to old Phœbe, was " the drawer where the knitting-wool was kept." Some trifle of the sort was sure to strike
home its proof of her sister's identity. Chance lighted on this one,
and it served its turn.

Ruth heard her cry out—a cry cut short by her mother's:—" Oh,
Phœbe, Phœbe, I know it all now, and you'll know me." She started

up from a hurried compliance with her Cousin Keziah's wish that she should eat, and went back quickly to the bedroom, to see the two old sisters again locked in each other's arms.

They may have been but dimly alive to how it all had come about, but they knew themselves and each other—twins wrenched asunder half a century since, each of whom had thought the other dead for over forty years.

CHAPTER XX

HOW GRANNY MARRABLE THOUGHT SHE OUGHT NOT TO GO TO SLEEP, BUT DID. HOW A CRICKET WAS STILL AT IT, WHEN SHE WAKED. HOW MAISIE WAKED TOO. HOW THEY REMEMBERED THINGS TOGETHER, IN THE NIGHT. A SKULL TWENTY-SEVEN INCHES ROUND. HOW PHŒBE COULD NOT FORGIVE HER BROTHER-IN-LAW, GOD OR NO! HOW IT HAD ALL BEEN MAISIE'S FAULT. THE OTHER LETTER, IN THE WORKBOX, BEHIND THE SCISSORS. THE STORY OF THE SCORPION. ALL TRUE! ONLY IT WAS MRS. STENNIS, WHO DIED IN AGONY. ELIZABETH-NEXT-DOOR'S IMMOVABLE HUSBAND. HOW GRANNY MARRABLE WAS RELIEVED ABOUT THAT SCORPION. HOW MAISIE'S HUSBAND HAD REALLY HAD A DEVIL—A BLACK MAN'S—WHICH MAISIE'S SON HAD INHERITED. A NEW INFECTION IN THINE EYE. HOW RUTH WENT ·FOR THE DOCTOR. HOW HE RECOMMENDED GWEN, AS WELL AS THE MIXTURE

THE two old twins knew it all now, so far as it would ever be a matter of knowledge. They had got at the heart of each other's identity, before either really understood the cruel machination that had cancelled the life of either for the other.

Ruth Thrale left them alone together, and went back to force herself to eat. Keziah wanted to get back to her old man, and how could she go, unless Ruth kept in trim to attend to her two charges? Who could say that old Phœbe, at eighty, would not give in under the strain? Ruth had always a happy faculty of self-forgetfulness; and now, badly as she had felt the shock, she so completely lost sight of herself in the thought of the greater trouble of the principal actors, as to be fully alive to the one great need ahead, that of guarding and preserving what was left of the old life, the tending of which had come so strangely upon her. She refused Keziah's offer to remain on. Elizabeth-next-door, she said, was always at hand for emergencies.

Keziah stayed late enough to see all arranged for the night, ending with a more or less successful effort to get old Maisie to swallow arrowroot. She helped Ruth to establish the Granny in her own high-backed chair beside her sister—for neither would relinquish the other's hand—and took advantage of a very late return of Brantock, the carrier, to convey her home, where she arrived after midnight.

All know the feeling that surely must have been that of at least one of the old sisters, that sleep ought to be for some mysterious reason combated, or nonsuited rather, when the mind is at odds with grave events. One rises rebellious against its power, when it steals a march on wakefulness, catching the keenest vigilance unawares. There was no reason why Granny Marrable should not sleep in her own arm-chair—which she would say was every bit as good as bed, and used accordingly—except that yielding meant surrender of the faculties to unconsciousness of a problem not yet understood, with the sickening prospect of finding it unanswered on awakening. That seemed to be reason enough for many resentful recoils from the very portals of sleep; serving no end, as Maisie had been overcome without a contest, and lay still as an effigy on a tomb. A vague fear that she might die unwatched, looking so like Death already, may have touched Phœbe's mind. But fears and unsolved riddles alike melted away and vanished in the end; and when Ruth Thrale, an hour later, starting restless from her own couch near by, looked in to satisfy herself that all was well, both might have been leagues away in a dream-world, for any consciousness they showed of her presence.

That was on the stroke of one; and for two full hours after all was silence, but for the records of the clock at its intervals, and the cricket dwelling on the same theme our forefathers heard and gave no heed to, a thousand years ago. Then old Phœbe woke to wonder, for a blank moment, what had happened that she should be sitting there alone, with the lazy flicker of a charred faggot helping out a dim, industrious rushlight in a shade. But only till she saw that she was *not* alone. It all came back then. The figure on the bed!—not *dead, surely?*

No—for the hand she held was warm enough to reassure her. It had been the terror of a moment, that this changed creature, with memories that none but Maisie could have known, had flashed into her life to vanish from it, and leave her bewildered, almost without a word of that inexplicable past. Only of a moment, for the hand she held tightened on hers, and the still face that was, and was not, her dead sister's turned to her, looked at her open-eyed, and spoke.

"I think I am not dreaming now, but I was . . . . I was dreaming of Phœbe, years ago. . . . But *you* are Phœbe. Say that I am Maisie, that I may hear you. Say it!"

"Oh, my darling!—I know you are Maisie. But it is so hard to know."

"Yes—it is all so hard to know—so hard to think! But I know it is true. . . . Oh, Phœbe, where do you think I was but now, in my dream? . . . Yes, where?—What place? . . . Guess!"

"I cannot tell . . . back in the old time?"

"Back in the old time—back in the old place. I was shelling peas to help old Keturah—old Keturah that had had three husbands, and her old husband then was the sexton, and he had buried them all three! We were there, under her porch . . . with the honeysuckle all in flower—and, oh, the smell of it in the heat!—it was all there in my dream! And you were there. Oh, Phœbe darling, how beautiful you were! We were seventeen."

"Ah, my dear, I know when that was. 'Twas the day *they* came —came first. Oh, God be good to us!"

"Oh, Phœbe dear, why be so heartbroken? It was a merry time. Thank God for it with me, darling! . . . Ay, I know—all over now! . . ."

"I mind it well, dear. They came up on their horses."

"Thornton and Ralph. And made a pretext they would like to see inside the Church. Because old Keturah had the key."

"But 'twas an untruth! Little care they had for inside the Church! 'Twas ourselves, and they knew it."

"Oh, Phœbe!—but *we* knew it too! I had no chance to dream how we showed them the Church and the crypt, for I woke up. Ah, but 'tis long ago now!—sixty-two—sixty-three years! I wonder, is the stack of bones in the crypt now that was then? There was a big skull that measured twenty-seven inches."

"That it was! Twenty-seven. Now, to think of us young creatures handling those old bones!"

"Then it was not long but they came again on their horses, and this time it was that their father the Squire would see father righted in his lawsuit about the upper waters of the millstream. That was how Thornton made a friend of father. And then it was we played them our trick, to say which was which. We changed our frocks, and they were none the wiser."

A recollection stirred in old Phœbe's mind, that could almost bring a smile to her lips, even now. "Ralph never was any the wiser. He went away to the Indies, and died there. . . . But not afore he told to my husband how Thornton came to tell us apart. . . . How did he? Why, darling, 'twas the way you would give him all your hand, and I stinted him of mine."

" You never loved him, Phœbe."

" Was I not in the right of it, Maisie? " She then felt the words were hasty, and would have been glad to recall them. She waited for an answer, but none came. The fire was all but out, and the morning chill was in the air. She rose from the bedside and crossed the room to help it from extinction. But she felt very shaky on her feet.

A little rearrangement convinced the fire that it had been premature; and an outlying faggot, brought into hotchpot, decided as an after-thought that it could flare. " I am coming back," said Granny Marrable. She was afraid her sister would think she was going to be left alone. But there was no need, for when she reached her chair again—and she was glad to do so—old Maisie was just as she had left her, quite tranquil and seeming collected, but with her eyes open, watching the welcome light of the new flicker. One strange thing in this interview was that her weakness seemed better able to endure the strain of the position than her sister's strength.

She picked up the thread of the conversation where that interlude of the fire had left it. " You never loved Thornton, Phœbe dearest. But he was mine, for my love. He was kind and good to me, all those days out there in the bush, till I lost him. He was a lawbreaker, I know, but he paid his penalty. And was I not to forgive, when I loved him? God forgives, Phœbe." Half of what she had come to know had slipped away from her already; and, though she was accepting her sister as a living reality, the forged letter, the cause of all, was forgotten.

Granny Marrable, on the contrary, kept in all her bewilderment a firm hold on the wickedness of Daverill the father. It was he that had done it all, and no other. Conceivably, her having set eyes on Daverill the son had made this hold the firmer. To her the name meant treachery and cruelty. Even in this worst plight of a mind in Chaos, she could not bear to see the rugged edges of a truth trimmed off, to soften judgment of a wicked deed. But had she been at her best, she might have borne it this time to spare her sister the pain of sharing her knowledge, if such ignorance was possible. As it was, she could not help saying:—" God forgives, Maisie, and I would have forgiven, if I could have had you back when he was past the need of you. Oh, to think of the long years we might still have had, but for his deception! "

"My dear, it may be you are right. But all my head is gone for thinking. You are there, and that is all I know. How could I? . . . What *is* it all?"

The despair in her voice did not unnerve her sister more. Rather, if anything, it strengthened her, as did anything that drew her own mind out of itself to think only of her fellow-sufferer. She could but answer, hesitatingly:—"My dear, was I not here all the while you thought me dead? . . . If you had known . . . oh, if you had known! . . . you might have come." She could not keep back the sound of her despair in her own voice.

Maisie started spasmodically from her pillow.

"Oh, God have mercy on me! Save me, Phœbe, save me!" she cried. She clung with both hands to her sister, and gasped for breath. Then the paroxysm of her excitement passed, and she sank back, whispering aloud in broken speech:—"I mean . . . it came back to me . . . the tale . . . the letter. . . . Oh, but it cannot be true! . . . Tell it me again—tell me what you know."

Phœbe's response flagged. What could her old brain be said to *know*, yet, in such a whirl? "I'll try, my dear, to say it out right, for you to hear. But 'tis a hard thing to know, and 'tis hard to have to know it. Dr. Nash said it to me, that it was Thornton, your husband. And our young lady of the Towers—she, my dear, you know, that is Lady Gwendolen Rivers—said it to me again." Old Maisie clung closer to the hand she held, and trembled so that Phœbe stopped, saying:—"Ought I to tell?"

"Yes—go on! You know, dear, I know it all—half know it—but I cannot hold it for long—it goes. Go on!"

"He wrote to me—he wrote to you—saying, we were dead. O God, forgive him for his cruelty! Why, oh why?" She fixed her eyes on her sister, and seemed to wait for an answer to the question.

And yet she wondered in her heart when the answer came. It came with a light that broke through the speaker's face, a sound of relief in her words:—"It was his love for me, Phœbe dearest—it was his love for me! He would not have me go from him to my sister in England, even for the time I would have wanted, to see her again. The fault was mine, dear, the fault was mine! I was ever on at him—plaguing—plaguing him to spare me for the time. Oh—'twas I that did it!"

Let her believe it! Let her see a merit in it for the man she loved! That was Phœbe's thought.

"He was always good to me," Maisie continued. "He never thought of what might come of it. All his desire was I should not

leave him.   Oh, Phœbe, Phœbe, if only I might have died there and
then, out in the Colony!"
    "To see me no more? Not this once? I thank God that has
spared ye to me, Maisie, just but to hear your voice and hold your
hand and kiss your face.   If I be dreaming, I be dreaming.   Only
I would not wake, not I.   But I can scarce bear myself for the
wonderment of it all.   How could you come back alone—my
Maisie, alone and old!—back again to England—in a ship—
through the storms?"   For all the mind that Granny Marrable had
left after the bewildering shock was aching to know more.
    Old Maisie was almost too weak for anything like curiosity
about the past; she simply submitted—acquiesced.   This was her
sister, not dead by some miracle.   When in dreams we see again
the departed, do we speak of the interim?   Surely never?   Neither
did Maisie.   She could not even look forward to knowing more.
She could talk on, with no difficulty of speech—indeed, seemed
talkative.   She could reply now to Phœbe's question:—" But, my
dear, I was not alone, nor old.   I was not much older than my
Ruth that I have found. . . .   Where is she?—she is not gone?"
She looked round, frightened, trying to raise herself.
    "She is gone away to sleep.   It is night, you know.   There goes
the clock.   Four.   She will come again. . . .   But, oh, Maisie,
was it as long ago as that?   'Tis but a very little while back Ruth
turned fifty."
    "Is my girl turned of fifty, then?—yes! it must be so.   Fifty
years past I landed ashore in Hobart Town, and it was a babe of
four I had to leave behind.   Well—I was a bit older.   I was fifty-
seven when I lost my son."   This seemed to mean the death of
some son unknown to Granny Marrable.   The convict was never
farther from her mind.   " 'Tis twenty-five years I have been in
England—all of twenty-five years, Phœbe."
    "Oh, God have pity on us all!   Twenty-five years!"   It was
a cry of pain turned into words.   Had she had to say what stung
her most, she would probably have said the thought that Maisie
might have seen her daughter's wedding, or at least the babyhood
of her children.   So much there was to tell!—would she live to
hear it?   And so much to hear!—would she live to tell it?   She
could not understand her sister's words that followed:—" All of
twenty years alone," referring to the period since her son's transportation.   It was really longer.   But memory of figures is insecure in hours of trial.
    Maisie continued:—" When I came back, I went straight to our
old home, long ago—to Darenth Mill, to hear what I might, and

old Keturah was dead, and her husband was dead, and ne'er a soul knew aught to tell me. And there was father's grave in the churchyard, and no other. So what could I think but what the letter said, that all were drowned in the cruel sea, your husband Nicholas, and my little one, all three?"

"And the letter said that—the letter he made up?"

"The letter said that, and I read it. It had black seals, and I broke them and read it. And it was from father, and said you were drowned . . . drowned . . . Yes!—Phœbe drowned . . . and my little Ruth, and . . . . Oh, Phœbe, how can this be you?" The panic came again in her voice, and again she clutched spasmodically at the hand she held. But it passed, leaving her only able to speak faintly. "I kept it in my table-drawer. . . . It must be there still." She had only half got the truth.

Granny Marrable tried to make it clear, so far as she could. "You forget, dear. Her ladyship has the letter, and Dr. Nash knows. Lady Gwendolen who brought you here. . . ."

It was a happy reference. A light broke over the old face on the pillow, and there was ease in the voice that said:—"She is one of God's Angels. I knew it by her golden hair. When will she come?"

"Very soon. To-morrow, perhaps. 'Twas her ladyship told you —was it not? Oh, you remember?"

"My dear, she told it me like a story, and her face was white. But it was all clear to me then, for I could not know who the bad man was—the bad man who made two sisters each think the other dead. And I was for helping her to tell them. Oh, may God bless her for her beautiful face—so pale it was! And then she told me 'twas written by my husband." Some new puzzle confronted her, and she repeated, haltingly:—"By . . . my . . . husband!" Then quite suddenly, struck by a new idea:—"But was it? How could she know?"

"My dear, she showed it to her father, the Earl, and they were of one mind. His lordship read the letter. Dr. Nash told me. But it was Thornton's own letter to me that said *you* were dead. I have got it still." She was stopped by the return of Ruth Thrale, who had been half waked by her mother's raised voice five minutes since, and had struggled to complete consciousness under the sense of some burden of duty awaiting her outside the happy oblivion of her stinted sleep. "How has she been?" was her question on entering.

Granny Marrable could not give any clear account of the past hour of talk; it was growing hazy to her, as reaction after excitement told, more and more. Ruth asked no further questions, and urged her to go and lie down—was ready to force her to do it, but she conceded the point, and was just going, when her sister stopped her, speaking clearly, without moving on the pillow.

" What was the letter ? "

" What letter is she speaking of ? " said Ruth.

Granny Marrable said with an effort:—" The letter that said she was dead."

" Show it to me—show it me now, with the light! You have got it."

" Yes. I said to her that I had got it. But it is put away." This was under Granny Marrable's breath, that old Maisie should not hear.

But she heard, and turned her head. " Oh, Phœbe, let me see it! Can it not be got? Cannot Ruth get it ? " She seemed feverishly alive, for the moment, to all that was passing.

Ruth, thinking it would be better to satisfy her if possible, said: —" Is it hard to find ? Could I not get it ? " To which old Phœbe replied:—" I know where it is to lay hands on at once. But I grudge setting eyes on it now, and that's the truth." Ruth wondered at this—it made her mother's eagerness to see it seem stranger. The story is always on the edge of calling old Maisie Ruth's " new mother." Her mind was reeling under the consciousness of two mothers with a like claim—a bewildering thought! She wavered between them, and was relieved when the speaker continued:—" You may unlock my old workbox over yonder. The letter be inside the lid, behind the scissors. I'll begone to lie down a bit on your bed, child! " Was old Phœbe running away from that letter ?

Ruth knew the trick of that workbox of old. It brought back her early childhood to find the key concealed in a little slot beneath it; hidden behind a corner of green cloth beyond suspicion; that opened, for all that, when the edge was coaxed with a fingernail. It had been her first experience of a secret, and a fascination hung about it still. That confused image of a second mother, growing dimmer year by year in spite of a perfunctory system of messages maintained in the correspondence of the parted twins, had never utterly vanished; and it had clung about this workbox, a present from Maisie to Phœbe, even into these later years. It crossed Ruth's mind as she found the key, how, a year ago, when the interior of this box was shown to Dave Wardle by his country Granny, his delight in it, and its smell of otto of roses that never failed, had stirred forgotten memories; and this recollection, with the mystery of that vanished mother still on earth—close at hand, there in the room!—made her almost dread to raise the box-lid. But she dared it, and found the letter, though her brain whirled at the entanglements of life and time, and she winced at the past as though scorched by a spiritual flame. It took her breath away to think what she had sought and found; the hideous instrument of a wickedness almost inconceivable—her own father's!

"Oh, how I hope it is that! Bring it—bring it, my dear, my Ruth—my Ruth for me, now! Yes—show it me with the light, like that." Thus old Maisie, struggling to raise herself on the bed, but with a dangerous spot of colour on her cheek, lately so pale, that said fever. Ruth trembled to admit the word to her mind; for, think of her mother's age, and the strain upon her, worse than her own!

Nevertheless, it was best to indulge this strong wish; might, indeed, be dangerous to oppose it. Ruth bolstered up the weak old frame with pillows, and lit two candles to give the letter its best chance to be read. She found her mother's spectacles, though in doubt whether they could enable her to read the dim writing, written with a vanishing ink, even paler than the forged letter Gwen and her father had unearthed. Possibly the ink had run short, and was diluted.

Old Maisie strove to read the writing, gasping with an eagerness her daughter found it hard to understand; but failed to decipher anything beyond, "My dear Sister-in-law." She dropped the letter, saying feebly:—"Read—you read!"

Then Ruth read:—

"'I take up my pen to write you fuller particulars of the great calamity that has befallen me. For I am, as my previous letter will have told you, if it has reached you ere this, a widower. I am endeavouring to bear with resignation the lot it has pleased God to visit upon me, but in the first agonies of my grief at the loss of my beloved helpmeet I was so overwhelmed as to be scarce able to put pen to paper. I am now more calm and resigned to His will, and will endeavour to supply the omission.

"'My dear Maisie was in perfect health and spirits when she went to visit a friend, Mary Ann Stennis, the wife of a sheep-farmer, less than thirty miles from where I now write, on the Upper Derwent, one of the few women in this wild country that was a fit associate for her. She was to have started home in a few days' time, but the horse that should have carried her, the only one she could ride, being a timid horsewoman, went lame and made a delay, but for which delay it may be God would have spared her to me. But

His will be done! It seems she was playing with the baby of a native black, there being a camp or tribe of them near at hand, she being greatly diverted with the little monster, when its sister, but little older than itself, found a scorpion beneath a stone, and set it to bite its little brother. Thereupon Maisie, always courageous and kindhearted, must needs snatch at this most dangerous vermin, to throw it at a distance from the children. . . .'"

Old Maisie interrupted the reader. Her face was intent, and her eyes gleamed with an unhealthy, feverish light. " Stop, my dear," said she. " This is all true."

" All true! " Surely her mind was giving way. So thought Ruth, and shuddered at the gruesome thought. " Mother—mother —how *can* it be true? "

" All quite true, my dear, but for one thing! All true but for who it was! It was not I—it was Mary Ann was at play with little Saku. And the scorpion bit *her* hand, and she died of the bite. . . . Yes—go on! Read it all! " For Ruth had begun:—" Shall I—*must I?* " as though the reading it was unendurable.

She resumed, with an effort:—

" ' But got bitten in the arm. At first she made light of the wound, for the reptile was so small. But it became badly inflamed, and no doctor was at hand. The black mother of Saku, the baby, prayed to be allowed to summon the conjurer doctor of the tribe, who would suck the wound. But Maisie would not have this, so only external applications were made . . .'"

Old Maisie interrupted:—" That is not so," she said. " Roo-moro, the doctor, sucked hard at the bite, and spat out the poison in a hole in the ground, to bury the evil spirit. But it was no good. Poor Mary Ann Stennis died a week after. I mind it well."

Ruth thought to herself:—" Is this a feverish dream? " and wavered on the answer. The tale her mother told of the black medicine-man was nightmare-like. All this, fifty years ago! Her head swam too much for speech, reading apart. She could con-tinue, mechanically:—

" ' . . . Only external applications were made, which proved use-less, as is almost invariably the case with poisonous bites. Next day it became evident that the poison was spreading up the arm, and a black runner was despatched to summon me, but he could not cover the ground in less than three hours, and when he arrived I was on my way to Bothwell, some twenty miles in another direc-tion, so he did not overtake me until the evening. I was then de-tained a day, so that it was over forty-eight hours before I arrived at Stennis's. It was then too late for effectual remedy, and my dear wife died in my arms within a week of the scorpion bite . . .'"

"That is not true—it was over a week." Was Maisie really alive to the facts, to be caught by so small a point? She had seen a simple thing that could be said. That is all the story can think. Ruth said:—"Here is more—only a little!" and continued:—

"'I am thankful to say that, considering the nature of the case, her sufferings were slight, and she passed away peacefully, desiring with her last breath that I should convey to you the assurance of her unchanged affection.'

"It is untrue—it is untrue!" moaned Maisie. "Mary Ann died in great pain, from the poison of the bite working in the blood." She seemed to grasp very little of the facts, for she added:—"But was he not good, to hide the pain for Phœbe's sake?" Her mind was catching at fragments, to understand, and failed.

There was another letter, which Ruth opened, of an earlier date. It was a merely formal announcement of the death. She put back the letters in the workbox-lid, behind the scissors; replaced the workbox on its table as before, and returned to her mother. She was glad to find her still, with her eyes closed; but with that red spot on her cheek, unchanged. It was best to favour every approach of sleep, and this might be one. Ruth sat silent, all her faculties crippled, and every feeling stunned, by what she had gone through since Gwen's first arrival yesterday.

This terrible night had worn itself out, and she knew that that clock-warning meant six, when the stroke should come. But there was no daylight yet. Those movements in the kitchen must be Elizabeth-next-door, come according to promise. That was what the guardian-dog from without meant, pushing his way through the bedroom-door, reporting an incomer whom he knew, and had sanctioned. He communicated the fact to his satisfaction, and returned to his post, leaving his mistress the better for his human sympathy, which seemed to claim knowledge of passing event. It comforted her to feel that the day was in hand, and that its light would come. Who could say but its ending might find her convinced that this was all true? Blank, sickening doubts of the meaning of everything flitted across her mind, and she longed to settle down to realities, to be able to love this new mother without flinching. For that was what she felt, that the mystery of this resurrection seared or burnt her. One thing only soothed her—that this was dear old Mrs. Prichard whom she had learned to love before its bewilderments were sprung upon her. That made it easier to bear.

Presently she roused herself, for, was not this morning? A grey twilight, not over-misty for the time of year, was what a raised window-curtain showed her, and she let it fall to deal with it in earnest, and relieve the blind from duty. Then she made sure, by the new light, that all was well with old Maisie—mere silence, no insensibility—and went out to speak with Elizabeth-next-door, and get more wood for the fire. But first she blew out the candles and the rushlight, already dying spasmodically.

Elizabeth-next-door was a strengthening influence, able to look facts in the face. She almost elided forewords and inquiries, to come to her strong point, the way she had used the strange story to produce surprise in her husband; a worthy man, but imperturbable . by anything short of earthquakes or thunderbolts. " Ye may sa-ay your vairy worst to Sam," said Elizabeth, " and he'll just sa-ay back, ' Think a doan't knaw that,' he'll say, ' afower ever yow were born?' and just gwarn with his sooper. And I give ye my word, Widow Thrale, I no swooner told it him than there he sat ! An' if he come down on our ta-able wi' th' fla-at of his ha-and once, that he did thrice and mower, afower he could sa-ay one word. He did, and went nigh to break it, but it be o-ak two-inch thick a'mo-ast. Then a said, 'twas enough to wa-aken oop a ma-an all through the night, he did ! " He seemed, however, not to have suffered in this way, for his wife added:—" Wa-aken him oop? Not Sam, I lay ! Ta-akes a souse o' cold pig to wa-aken up Sam afower t' marnin ! " Ruth felt braced by this bringing of the event within human possibilities. Improbable possibilities surprise. Impossible events stun.

She co-operated in domesticities with her useful neighbour, glancing once or twice at the figure on the bed, and reinforced in the belief that all was safe there, for the time. For she saw what seemed slight natural movement, for ease. Presently she went to hear how it fared with her other mother, her normal one. The cross purposes of her relations to the two old sisters were an entanglement of perplexities.

Granny Marrable, asleep when Ruth looked stealthily in at her, was waked by a creak with which the door just contrived to disappoint hopes of a noiseless escape. She called after her:—" Yes, who's that? " Whereupon Ruth returned. It was their first real word alone since the disclosure.

" Oh, mother, have you slept? " She kissed the old worn-out face tenderly; feeling somehow the reserve of strength behind the response she met. "Oh, can you—*can* you—make it out? . . . Yes, she is lying still. She has seen that letter." She dropped her voice, and shuddered to name it.

"My dear," said Granny Marrable, answering her question, "I cannot say truly yet that I can make it out. But I thank God for letting me be able to know that this must be Maisie. For I know her for Maisie, when she talks of the bygone time. And that letter—God is good, for that! For it was that told of how she died —that wicked poison-bite! My child, it has never gone quite out of my heart to think your mother died so far away in such pain— never in all these years! And now I know it for an untruth. I thank God for that, at least!"

"*She* says," said Ruth, checkmated in an attempt to use any name she could call her real mother by, without some self-blame for the utterance, "*she* says the story is one-half true, but 'twas her best friend died of the bite—not she! But she died in great suffering."

"Ah—the poor thing! Mary Ann Stennis."

"That was the name."

"Will she be able to tell more? Will she tell us who her husband was?"

"Her husband!" Ruth thought this was new trouble—that the Granny's head had given way under the strain. "Her husband was my father, mother," said she. "Think!"

But old Phœbe was quite clear. "I am all right, child," said she reassuringly. "Her *second* husband. Marrable was *my* second, you know, else I would still have been Cropredy. Why is she not Daverill?"

Ruth was really the less clear of the two. "Oh yes!" said she wonderingly. "She is Mrs. Prichard, still."

"Please God we shall know all! . . . What was that?"

"I must go to her. . . . Come!" For old Maisie had called out. Her daughter went back to her quickly, and Granny Marrable followed, not far behind.

"Come, dear, come . . . I called for you to know. . . . Come, Phœbe, come near, and let me tell you. . . . He was not so wicked. . . . Oh no, oh no—it was none of his own doing—I shall be able . . . directly. . . ." Thus old Maisie, gasping for breath, and falling back on the pillow from which she had part risen. The hectic flush in her face was greater, and her eyes were wild under her tangle of beautiful silver hair. Both were afraid for her, for each knew what fever might mean. They might lose her, almost without a renewal of life together.

Still, it might be no more than the agitation of a moment, a passing phase. They tried to pacify her. How *could* the letter be none
of Daverill's own doing? But she would not be soothed—would
say the thing she had set her mind to say, but failed to find the
words or breath for. What was it she was trying to say? Was it
about the letter?

Elizabeth-next-door came into the room, tentatively. Ostensible
reason, inquiry about breakfast; actual reason, curiosity. Sounds
of speech under stress had aroused, and a glance at old Maisie intensified it. Widow Thrale would come directly, but for the moment was intent on hearing what Mrs. Prichard was saying. To
Elizabeth, Maisie continued Mrs. Prichard.

She would not leave unsaid this thing she was bent on:—" No,
dear! No, dear! It does not hurt me to talk, but I want time.
. . . I will tell you . . . I must tell you. . . . I know it. . . . It
was not his own doing. . . . He was set on to do it by a devil that
possessed him. . . . There are devils loose among the blacks. . . ."

The pulse in the hand Ruth held was easy to find. Yes, that
was fever! Ruth left her to speak with Elizabeth, and the hand
went over to its fellow, in Granny Marrable's.

" Phœbe, dearest, that is so—and in those days there were a many
blacks. But they were fewer and fewer after that, and none in our
part when we came away, my son and I. . . . Phœbe!"

" What, dearest?"

" You must say nothing of *him* to Ruth. He was her brother."

" Say nothing of him to Ruth—why not?" She had lost sight
of her adventure with the convict, and did not identify him. She
may have fancied some other son accompanied her sister home.

" Yes—yes—nothing to *her!* He is not fit to speak of—not fit
to think of. . . . Do not ask about him. Forget him! I do not
know if he be alive or dead."

Then an image of the convict, or madman, flashed across Phœbe's
mind. She dared not talk of him now, with that wild light and
hectic flush in her sister's face; it would only make bad worse.
But a recollection of her first association of him with the maniac
in the Gadarene tombs was quick on the heels of this image, and
prompted her to say:—" Had no evil spirit power over *him*, then,
as well as his father?"

The wild expression on old Maisie's face died down, and gave
place to one that was peace itself by comparison. " I see it all
now," said she. " Yes—you are right! It was after his father's
death he became so wicked." It was the devil that possessed his
father, driven out to seek a home, and finding it in the son. That

was apparently what her words implied, but there was too much of delirium in her speech and seeming to justify their being taken as expressing a serious thought.

Old Phœbe sat beside her, trying now and again with quiet voice and manner to soothe and hush away the terrible memories of the audacious deception to which each owed a lifelong loss of the other. But when fever seizes on the blood, it will not relax its hold for words.

One effect of this was good, in a sense. It *is* true, as the poet said, that one fire burns out another's burning—or at any rate that one pain is deadened by another anguish—and it was a Godsend to Granny Marrable and Ruth Thrale that an acupression of immediate anxiety should come to counteract their bewilderment, and to extinguish for the time the conflagration of a thousand questions —whys, whens, and wherefores innumerable—in their overburdened minds. Visible fever in the delicate frame, to which it seemed the slightest shock might mean death, was a summons to them to put aside every possible thought but that of preserving what Time had spared so long, though Chance had been so cruel an oppressor. It would be the cruellest stroke of all that she should be thus strangely restored to them, only to be snatched away in an hour.

Presently she seemed quieter; the fever came in gusts, and rose and fell. She had once or twice seemed almost incoherent, but it passed away. Meanwhile Granny Marrable's memory of that madman or criminal, who had at least known the woman he claimed as his mother well enough to be mystified by her twin sister, rankled in her mind, and made it harder and harder for her to postpone speech about him. She would not tell the incident—she was clear of *that*—but would it harm Maisie to talk of him? She asked herself the question the next time her sister referred to him, and could not refrain from letting her speech about him finish.

It came of her mind drifting back to that crazy notion of an evil spirit wandering to seek a home; as the hermit-crab, dispossessed of one shell, goes in search of another. After a lull which had looked for a moment like coming sleep, she said with an astonishing calmness:—" But do you not see, Phœbe dear, do you not see how good his father must have been, to do no worse than he did? See what the devil that possessed him could do with Ralph—my youngest, he was; Isaac died—a good boy, quite a good boy, till I lost his father! Oh—see what he came to do!"

" He . . . he was sent to prison, was he not? " After saying it, old Phœbe was afraid she might have to tell the whole tale of how

she knew it. But she need not have feared. Old Maisie was in a
kind of dreamland, only half-cognisant of what was going on about
her.

Her faint voice wandered on. "I was not thinking of that.
That was nothing! He stole some money, and it cost him dear.
. . . No!—it was worse than that—a bad thing! . . . It was *not*
the girl's fault . . . Emma was a good girl. . . ."

Granny Marrable was injudicious. But it was an automatic
want of judgment, bred of mind-strain. She could not help saying:—"Was that Emma Drax?" For the name, which she had
heard from the convict, had hung on her mind, always setting her
to work to fashion some horrible story for its owner.

"Yes—Emma Drax. . . . They found her guilty. . . . I do
not mean that. . . . What is it I mean? . . . I mean they laid
it all at her door. . . . Men do!" This seemed half wandering,
and Granny Marrable hoped it meant a return of sleep. She was
disappointed. For old Maisie became more restless and hot, starting convulsively, catching at her hand, and exclaiming:—"But
how came you to know?—how came you to know? You were not
there then. Oh, Phœbe dearest, you were not there *then.*" She
kept on saying this, and Granny Marrable despaired of finding
words to explain, under such circumstances. The tale of her
meeting with the convict was too complex. She thought to herself
that she might say that Maisie had spoken the name as a dream-
word, waking. But that would have been a fib, and fibs were not
her line.

"I went myself to get him," said Ruth, reappearing after a
longer absence than old Phœbe had anticipated. She was removing an out-of-door cloak, and an extempore headwrap, when she
entered the room. "How is she?" she asked.

Old Phœbe shook her head doubtfully. "Whom did you go for,
child? The doctor? I'm glad."

"I thought it better. . . . Mother darling!—how are you?"
She knelt by the bed, held the burning hands, looked into the wild
eyes. "Yes—I did quite right," she said.

Dr. Nash came, not many minutes later. Whether the mixture,
to be taken every two hours, fifty years ago, was the same as would
have been given now, does not concern the story. It, or the reassurance of the doctor's visit, had a sedative effect; and old Maisie
seemed to sleep, to the great satisfaction of her nurses. What
really did credit to his professional skill was that he perceived that

a visit from Lady Gwendolen would be beneficial. A message was sent at once to John Costrell, saying that an accompanying letter was to be taken promptly to the Towers, to catch her ladyship before she went out. We have seen that it reached her in time.

"You found that all I told you was true, Granny Marrable," said the doctor, after promising to return in time to catch her ladyship.

"I shall live to believe it true, doctor, please God!"

"Tut tut! You see that it *is* true."

"Yes, indeed, and I know that yonder is Maisie, come back to life. I know it by thinking; but 'tis all I can do, not to think her still dead."

"She can talk, I suppose—recollects things? Things when you were kids?"

"God 'a' mercy, yes, doctor! Why—hasn't she told me how she drew my tooth, with a bit of silk and a candle, and knew which drawer-knob it was, and the days she saw her husband first, a-horseback? . . . Oh, merciful Heavens, how had he the heart?"

"Some chaps have the Devil in 'em, and that's the truth!"

"That's what she says. She just made my flesh creep, a-telling how the devils come out of the black savages, to seize on Christians!"

But the doctor was not prepared to be taken at his word, in this way. Devils are good toys for speech, but they are not to be real. "Lot of rum superstitions in those parts!" said he. "Now look you here, ma'am! When I come back, I shall expect to hear that you and your daughter. . . Oh ah!—she's not your daughter! What the deuce is she?"

"Ruth has always been my niece, but we have gone near to forget it, times and again. 'Tis so many a long year!"

"Well—I shall expect to hear that you and your niece have had a substantial breakfast. You understand—*substantial!* And you must make *her* take milk, or gruel. You'll find she won't eat."

"Beef-tea?"

"No—at least, have some ready, in case. But her temperature is too high. Especially at her time of life!" The doctor walked briskly away. He had not had the gig out, for such a short distance.

CHAPTER XXI

CHRISTMAS AND THE GREEK KALENDS. O NOBIS PRAETERITOS! THE
WRITING-TABLE BACK. AN INFLEXIBLE GOVERNOR. HOW MR. JERRY
DID NOT GO TO THE WORKHOUSE. BUT HOW CAME M'RIAR TO BE
SO SHORT? THE EMPEROR OF RUSSIA. UNCLE MO'S COLDBATH
FIELDS FRIEND, AND HIS ALLOWANCE. UNCLE MO ON KEEPING ONE'S
WORD. AND KEEPING ITS MEANING. JERRY'S CONSCIENTIOUS TREACH-
ERY, AND HIS INTERVIEW WITH MR. ROWE. HOW M'RIAR HAD PROM-
ISED LOVE, HONOUR, AND OBEDIENCE TO A THING A DEVIL HAD TAKEN
A LONG LEASE OF. HOW SHE SENT A NOTE TO IT, BY MICHAEL
RAGSTROAR. WHO REALISED THREE-HALFPENCE. HOW MISS HAWKINS,
JEALOUSY MAD, TINKERED AUNT M'RIAR'S NOTE. EVE'S CIVILITY TO
THE SERPENT. MUCH ABOUT NORFOLK ISLAND. DAVERILL'S SECOND
VISIT TO ENGLAND, AND ITS CAUSES

SAPPS COURT was looking forward to Christmas with mixed feelings, considered as a Court. The feelings of each resident were in
some cases quite defined or definable; as for instance Dave's and
Dolly's. The children had required from their seniors a trustworthy assurance of the date of Mrs. Prichard's return, and had
only succeeded in obtaining from Aunt M'riar a vague statement.
Mrs. Prichard was a-coming some day, and that was plenty for
children to know at their time of life. They might have remained
humbly contented with their ignorance, if Uncle Mo had not
added:—" So's Christmas!" meaning thereby the metaphorical
Christmas used as an equivalent of the Greek Kalends. He overlooked, for rhetorical purposes, the near approach of the actual
festival; and Dave and Dolly accepted this as fixing the date of
Mrs. Prichard's return, to a nicety. The event was looked forward
to as millennial; as a restoration of a golden age before her departure. For no child is so young as not to *laudare* a *tempus
actum;* indeed, it is a fiction that almost begins with speech, that
the restoration of the Past is the first duty of the Future.

Dolly never tired of recasting the arrangement of the tea-
festivity that was to celebrate the event, discovering in each new
disposition of the insufficient cups and unstable teapot a fresh
satisfaction to gloat over, and imputing feelings in sympathy with
her own to her offspring Gweng. It was fortunate for Gweng that
her mamma understood her so thoroughly, as otherwise her fixed

expression of a maximum of joy at all things in Heaven and Earth gave no clue to any emotions due to events of the moment. Even when her eyes were closed by manipulation of her spinal cord, and opened suddenly on a new and brilliant combination, any candid spectator must have admitted her stoicism—rapturous perhaps, but still stoicism. It was alleged—by her mamma—that she shed tears when Dave selfishly obstructed her line of sight. This was disputed by Dave, whom contact with an unfeeling World was hardening to a cruel literalism.

Dave, when he was not scheming a display of recent Academical acquirements to Mrs. Prichard, dwelt a good deal on the bad faith of the postman, who had not brought him the two letters he certainly had a right to expect, one from each of his Grannies. He had treasured the anticipation of reading their respective expressions of joyful gratitude at their discovery of their relationship, and no letter had come! Small blame to Dave that he laid this at the door of the postman; others have done the self-same thing, on the other side of their teens! The only adverse possibility that crossed his infant mind was that his Grannies were sorry, not glad; because really grown-up people were so queer, you never could be even with them. The laceration of a lost half-century was a thing that could not enter into the calculations of a septennarian. He had not tried Time, and Time had not tried him. He had odd misgivings, now and again, that there might be in this matter something outside his experience. But he did not indulge in useless speculation. The proximity of Christmas made it unnecessary.

Mrs. Burr and Aunt M'riar accepted the season as one beneficial to trade; production taking the form of a profusion of little muslin dresses for small girls at Christmas Trees and parties with a Conjurer—dresses in which the fullest possibilities of the human flounce became accomplished facts, and the last word was said about bows of coloured ribbons. To look at them was to breathe an involuntary prayer for eiderdown enclosures that would keep the poppet inside warm without disparagement to her glorious finery. Sapps Court under their influence became eloquent of quadrilles; "Les Rats" and the Lancers, jangled by four hands eternally on pianos no powers of sleep could outwit, and no execration do justice to. They murmured tales of crackers with mottoes; also of too much rich cake and trifle and lemonade, and consequences. So much space was needed to preserve them unsoiled and uncrushed until consigned to their purchasers, that Mrs. Burr and Aunt M'riar felt grateful for the unrestricted run of

Mrs. Prichard's apartment, although both also felt anxious to
see her at home again.

Mrs. Prichard's writing-table came back, done beautiful. Only
the young man he refused to leave it without the money. He
was compelled to this course by the idiosyncrasies of his employer.
"You see," said he to Uncle Mo, with an appearance of concentrating accuracy by a shrewd insight, "it's like this it is, just
like I tell you. Our Governor he's as good a feller—in *hisself* mind
you!—as you'll come across this side o' Whitechapel. Only he's
just got this one pecooliarity—like a bee has in his bonnet, as the
sayin' is—he won't give no credit, not so much as to his own
wife; or his medical adwiser, if you come to that. 'Cash across
invoice'—that's his motter. And as for moving of him, you
might just as easy move Mongblong." It is not impossible that
this young man's familiarity with Mont Blanc was more apparent
than real; perhaps founded on Albert Smith's entertainment of
that name, which was popular at that time in London. The young
man went on to say that he himself was trustful to a fault, and
that if it depended on him, a'most any arrangement could be
come to. But you had to take a party as you found him, and
there it was!

Uncle Mo said:—"If you'd said you was a-coming with it, mate,
I'd have made a p'int of having the cash ready. My salary's
doo to-morrow." He was looking rather ruefully at an insufficient
sum in the palm of his hand, the scrapings of more than one
pocket.

The young man said:—"It's the Governor, Mr. Moses. But if
you'll square the 'ire of the trolley, I'll run it back to the shop,
and you can say when you're ready for it."

Uncle Mo seemed very reluctant to allow the bird to go back
into the bush. He went to the stairfoot, and called to Aunt M'riar,
upstairs, making ribbons into rosettes, and giving Dolly the snip-
pings. He never took his eye off the coins in his palm, as though
to maintain them as integral factors of the business in hand.
"Got any small change, M'riar?" said he.

"How much do you want, Mo?"

"Six. *And* three. Can you do six-and-three?"

"Stop till I see, Mo." Aunt M'riar descended from above, and
went into her bedroom. But she did not find six-and-three. For
she came out saying:—"I can't only do five-and-nine, Mo. Can't
you make out with that?"

Uncle Mo still looked at the twelve-and-nine he already had in
hand, as though it was a peculiar twelve-and-nine, that might

consent for once to make nineteen shillings, the sum required, when added to Aunt M'riar's contribution; but he was obliged to yield to the inflexible nature of Arithmetic. " Sixpence short, I make it," said he. Then to the young man whose employer was like Mont Blanc:—" You'll have to fetch it round again to-morrow, any time after two o'clock." This was, however, rendered unnecessary by the appearance of Mr. Jerry, who was able to contribute the six-and-three, without, as he said, going to the workhouse. So Mrs. Prichard's old table, with a new leg so nobody could ever have told, and a touch of fresh polish as good as new, was restored to its old place, to join in the general anticipation of its owner's return.

But however M'riar come to be so short of cash Uncle Mo, smoking an afternoon pipe as of old with Mr. Jerry, could not say, not if the Emperor of Roosher was to ask him. Not that shortness of cash was unusual in Sapps Court, but that he had supposed that M'riar was rather better off than usual, owing to recent liquidations by the firm for whom she and Mrs. Burr were at work upstairs. Mr. Jerry urged him on no account to fret his kidneys about mundane trifles of this sort. Everything, without exception, came to the same thing in the end, and weak concessions to monetary anxiety only provided food for Repentance.

Uncle Mo explained that his uneasiness was not due to ways and means, or the want of them, but to a misgiving that Aunt M'riar's money was " got from her."

Now in his frequent confabs with Mr. Jerry, Uncle Mo had let fall many suggestions of the sinister influence at work on Aunt M'riar; and Mr. Jerry, being a shrewd observer, and collating these suggestions with what had come to him otherwise, had formed his own opinions about the nature of this influence. So it was no wonder that in answer to Uncle Mo he nodded his head very frequently, as one who not only assents to a fact, but rather lays claim to having been its first discoverer. " What did I tell you, Mo ? " said he.

" Concernuating ? Of ? What ? " said Uncle Mo in three separate sentences, each one accompanied by a tap of his pipe-bowl on the wooden table at The Sun parlour. The third qualified it for refilling. You will see, if you are attentive and observant, that this was Mo's first pipe that afternoon; as, if the ashes had been hot, he would not have emptied them on that table, but rather on the hob, or in the brazen spittoon.

" Him," said Mr. Jerry, too briefly. For he felt bound to add:—
" Coldbath Fields. Anyone giving information that will lead to

apprehension of, will receive the above reward. Your friend, you know!"

"My friend's the man, Jerry. Supposin'—just for argewment— I fist that friend o' mine Monday morning, I'll make him an allowance'll last him over Sunday. You wouldn't think it of me, Jerry, but I'm a bad-tempered man, underneath the skin. And when I see our old girl M'riar run away with like by an infernal scoundrel. . . . Well, Jerry, I lose my temper! That I do." And Uncle Mo seemed to need the pipe he was lighting, to calm him.

"He's where her money goes, Mo—that's it, ain't it?"

"That's about it, sir. So p'hraps when I say I don't know how M'riar come to be so short of cash, I ought to say I *do* know. Because I *do* know, as flat as ever so much Gospel." So the Emperor of Russia might not have remained unenlightened.

Mr. Jerry reflected. "You say he hasn't been near the Court again, Mo?"

"Not since that last time I told you about. What M'riar told me of. When he showed his knife to frighten her. I couldn't be off telling Sim Rowe, at the Station, about it, because of the children; and he's keeping an eye. But the beggar's not been anigh the Court since. Nor I don't suppose he'll come.'

"But when ever does he see M'riar, to get at her savings?— that's what I'd like to know. Eh, Mo?"

"M'riar ain't tied to the house.- She's free to come and go. I don't take kindly to prying and spying on her."

A long chat which followed evolved a clear view of the position. After Mo's interview with Aunt M'riar just before Gwen's visit, he had applied to his friend the Police-Inspector, with the result that the Court had been the subject of a continuous veiled vigilance. He had, however, been so far swayed by the distress of Aunt M'riar at the possibility that she might actually witness the capture of her criminal husband, that he never revealed to Simeon Rowe that she had an interest in defeating his enterprise. The consequence was that every plain-clothes emissary put himself into direct personal communication with her, thereby ensuring the absence of Daverill from Sapps Court. She was of course guilty of a certain amount of duplicity in all this, and it weighed heavily on her conscience. But there was something to be said by way of excuse. He was—or had been—her husband, and she did *not* know the worst of his crimes. Had she done so, she might possibly have been ready to give him up to justice. But as Mo had told her this much, that his last achievement might lead him to the condemned cell, and its sequel, and she nevertheless shrank from betraying him, probably nothing short of the knowledge of the age and sex of his last victim would have caused her to do so. She had in her mind an image of a good, honest, old-fashioned murder; a strained episode in some burglary; perhaps not premeditated, but brought about by an indiscreet interruption of a fussy householder. There are felonies and felonies.

Mr. Jerry's conversation with Uncle Mo in the Sun parlour gave him an insight into this. "Look'ee here, Mo," said he. "So long as the Court's watched, so long this here gentleman won't come anigh it. He's dodged the London police long enough to be too clever for that. But so long as he keeps touch with M'riar, you've got touch of him."

Uncle Mo seemed to consider this profoundly. "Not if I keep square with M'riar," said he at last.

"How do you make that out, Mo?"

"I've as good as promised the old girl that she shan't have any hand in it. She's out of it."

"Then keep her out of it. But only you give the tip to Sim Rowe that M'riar's in with him, and that he's putting the screw on her, and Sim he'll do the rest. Twig?" Conscious casuistry always closes one eye, and Mr. Jerry closed his.

"That's one idea of keeping square, Jerry, but it ain't mine."

"What's wrong with it, Mo?" Mr. Jerry's confidence in his suggestion had flagged, and his eye had reopened slowly.

"M'riar's not to have *any* hand in it—that's her stipulation. According-ly to my ideas, Jerry, either you take advantage, or you don't. *Don't's* the word, this time. If I bring M'riar in *at all*, it's all one which of two ways I do it. She's out of it."

Mr. Jerry began, feebly:—"You can't do more than keep your word, Mo. . . ."

"Yes, you can, Jerry. You can keep your meanin'. And you can do more than that. You can keep to what the other party thought you meant, when you know. *I* know, this time. I ain't in a Court o' Justice, Jerry, dodgin' about, and I know when I'm square, by the feel. M'riar's out of it, and she shall stop out." Uncle Mo was not referring only to the evasions of witnesses on oath, which he regarded as natural, but to a general habit of untruth, and subtle perversion of obvious meanings, which he ascribed not only to counsel learned in the Law, but to the Bench itself.

"Don't you want this chap to dance the Newgate hornpipe, Mo?"

"Don't I, neither?" Uncle Mo smoked peacefully, gazing on the fire. The silhouette of a hanged man, kicking, floated before his mind's eye, and soothed him. But he made a reservation. "After him and me have had a quiet half-an-hour together!"

Mr. Jerry was suddenly conscious of a new danger. "I say, Mo," said he. "None of that, if *you* please!"

"None o' what?"

"This customer's not your sort. He's a bad kind. Bad before he was first lagged, and none the better for the company he's kept since! You're an elderly man now, Mo, and I'll go bail you haven't so much as put on the gloves for ten years past. And suppose you had, ever so! Who's to know he hasn't got a Colt in his pocket, or a bowie-knife?" Those of us who remember the fifties will recall how tightly revolvers clung to the name of their patentee, and the sort of moral turpitude that attached to their use. They were regarded as giving a mean advantage to murderers; who otherwise, if they murdered fair, and were respectably hanged, merely filled *rôles* necessary to History and the Drama.

"Couldn't say about the barking-iron," said Uncle Mo. "He's got a nasty sort of a knife, because he was flourishing of it out once to frighten M'riar. I'll give him that." Meaning—the advantage of the weapon. A trivial concession from a survivor of the best days of the Fancy! "Ye see, Jerry," he continued, "he'll have to come within arm's length, to use it. *I'll* see to him! Him and his carving-knives!"

But Mr. Jerry was far from easy about his friend, who seemed to him over-confident. He had passed his life in sporting circles, and though he himself had seen more of jockeys than prize-fighters, their respective circumferences intersected; and more than one case had come to his knowledge of a veteran of the Ring unconscious of his decadence, who had boastfully defied a junior, and made the painful discovery of the degree to which youth can outclass age. This was scarcely a case of youth or extreme age, but the twenty years that parted them were all-sufficient.

He began to seek in his inner conscience excuses for a course of action which would—he was quite candid with himself—have a close resemblance to treachery. But would not a little straightforward treachery be not only very expedient, but rather moral? Were high principles a *sine qua non* to such a humble individual as himself, a "bookmaker" on race-courses, a billiard-marker elsewhere in their breathing-times? Though indeed Mr. Jerry in his chequered life had seen many other phases of employment—chiefly, whenever he had the choice, within the zone of horsiness.

For he had a mysterious sympathetic knowledge of the horse. If pressed to give an account of himself, he was often compelled to admit that he was doing nothing particular, but was on the look-out. He might indicate that he was getting sick of this sort of thing, and would take the next chance that turned up; would, as it were, close with Fate. There had never been a moment in his sixty odd years of life—for he was very little Uncle Mo's junior—when he had not been on the eve of a lucrative per-manency. It had never come; and never could, in the nature of things. Nevertheless, the evanescencies that came and went and chequered his career were not quite unremunerative, though they were hardly lucrative. If he was ever hard up, he certainly never confessed to it.

He, however, looking back on his own antecedents to determine from them how straitlaced a morality conscience called for, de-cided, in view of the possibility of a collision between his friend and this ex-convict, that he would be quite justified in treating Aunt M'riar's feelings as negligible, set against the risk incurred by deferring to them as his friend had done. No doubt Mo's con-fidence had been reposed in him under the seal of an honourable secrecy, but to honour it under the circumstances seemed to him to be " cutting it rather fine." He resolved to sacrifice his in-tegrity on the altar of friendship, and sought out Mr. Simeon Rowe, who will be remembered as the Thames Policeman who was rowing stroke at Hammersmith that day when his chief, Ibbetson, lost his life in the attempt to capture Daverill; and who had more recently been identified by Mo as the son of an old friend. Jerry made a full communication of the case as known to him; giving as his own motive for doing so, the wish to shield Mo from the possible consequences of his own rash over-confidence.

" I collect from what you tell me," said the Police-Inspector, " that my men have been going on the wrong tack. That's about it, Mr. Alibone, isn't it ? "

" That's one way of putting it, Mr. Rowe. Anyhow, they were bound to be let in. Why, who was to guess Aunt M'riar? And the reason ! "

" They'll have to look a little sharper, that's all." It suited the Inspector to lay the blame of failure on his subordinates. This is a prerogative of seniors in office. Successes are officially credited to the foresight of headquarters—failures debited to the incompetence of subordinates. Mr. Rowe's attitude was merely human. He expressed as much acknowledgment of indebtedness to Mr. Jerry as was consistent with official dignity, adding without emotion:—"I've been suspecting some game of the kind." However, he unbent so far as to admit that this culprit had given a sight of trouble; and, as Mr. Jerry was an old acquaintance, resumed some incidents of the convict's career, not without admiration. But it was admiration of a purely professional sort, consistent with strong moral loathing of its object. "He's a born devil, if ever there was one," said he. "I must say I like him. Why—look how he slipped through their fingers at Clerkenwell! That was after we caught him at Hammersmith. That was genius, sir, nothing short of genius!"

"Dressed himself in his own warder's clothes, didn't he, and just walked over the course? What's become of your man he knocked on the head with his leg-iron?"

"Oh—him? He's got his pension, you know. But he's not good for any sort of work. He's alive—that's all! Yes—when Mr. Wix pays his next visit at the Old Bailey, there'll be several charges against him. He'll make a good show. I'll give him three months." By which he meant that, with all allowances made for detention and trial, Mr. Wix would end his career at the time stated. He went on to refer to other incidents of which the story has cognisance. He had been inclined to be down on his old chief Ibbetson, who was drowned in his attempt to capture Wix, because he had availed himself of a helping hand held out to him to drag its owner into custody. Well—he would think so still if it had not been for some delicate shades of character Mr. Wix had revealed since. How did he, Simeon Rowe, know what Ibbetson knew against the ex-convict? Some Walthamstow business, as like as not! It was wonderful what a faculty this man had for slipping through your fingers. He had been all but caught by one of our men, in the country, only the other day. He was at the railway-station waiting for the up-train, due in a quarter of an hour, and he saw our man driving up in a gig. At this point Mr. Rowe stopped, looking amused.

"Did he run?" said Mr. Jerry.

"Not he! He made a mistake in his train. Jumped into the Manchester express that was just leaving, and got carried off before our man reached the station. At Manchester he explained his mistake, and used his return ticket without extra charge to come back to London. Our man knew he would do that, and waited for him at Euston. But *he* knew one better. Missed his train again at Harrow—just got out for a minute, you know, when it stopped—and walked the rest of the way!'

Ralph Daverill must have had a curious insight into human

nature, to know by the amount of his inspection of that police-officer—the one who had ridden after him from Grantley Thorpe —whether he would pursue him to Manchester or try to capture him at Euston. How could he tell that the officer was not clever enough to know exactly how clever his quarry would decide he was?

Aunt M'riar, haunted always by a nightmare—by the terrible dream of a scaffold, and on it the man who had been her husband, with all the attendant horrors familiar to an age when public executions still gratified its human, or inhuman interest—was unable to get relief by confiding her trouble to others. She dared to say no more than what she had already said to Uncle Mo, as she knew he was in communication with his friend the police-officer and she wanted only just as much to be disclosed about the convict as would safeguard Sapps Court from another of his visits, but at the same time would not lead to his capture. If she had thought his suggestions of intimidation serious, no doubt she would have put aside her scruples, and made it her first object that he should be brought to justice. But she regarded them as empty threats, uttered solely to extort money.

She knew she could rely on Mo's kindness of heart to stretch many points to meet her feelings, but she felt very uncertain whether even his kind-heartedness would go the length of her demand for it. He might consider that a wife's feelings for a husband—and *such* a husband!—might be carried too far, might even be classified as superstition, that last infirmity of incorrect minds. If she could only make sure that the convict should never show his face again in Sapps Court, she would sacrifice her small remainders of money, earned in runs of luck, to keep him at a distance. An attitude of compromise between complete repudiation of him, and misleading his pursuers, was at least possible. But it involved a slight amount of duplicity in dealing with Mo, and this made Aunt M'riar supremely uncomfortable. She was perfectly miserable about it. But there!—had she not committed herself to an impracticable constancy, with a real altar and a real parson? That was it. She had promised, five-and-twenty years ago, to love, honour, and obey a self-engrossed pleasure-seeker, and time and crime and the canker of a gaol had developed a devil in him, who was by now a fine representative sample—a " record devil " our modern advanced speech might have called him—who had fairly stamped out whatever uncongenial trace of good may have existed originally in the premises he had secured on an indefinite lease. It *was* super-stition on Aunt M'riar's part, but of a sort that is aided and abetted by a system that has served the purposes of the priest-hoods all the world over since the world began, and means to last your time and mine—the more's the pity!

It was the day after her conversation with Mo about the con-vict—the day, that is, after Gwen's last visit to Sapps Court—that Aunt M'riar said to Dave, just departing to absorb erudition at his School, that if he should see Michael Ragstroar he might tell him she had a note for his, Michael's, aunt at Hammersmith; and if he was a-going there Sunday, he might just every bit as well make himself useful, and carry it and save the postage. Dave said:—" Whoy shouldn't oy carry it? " An aspiration crushed by Aunt M'riar with:—" Because you're seven! " So Dave, whose nature was as docile as his eyes were blue, undertook to deliver the message; and Michael presented himself in conse-quence, just after Uncle Mo had took a turn out to see for a newspaper, for to know some more of what was going on in the Crimaera. It was just as well Uncle Mo had, because when it's two, you don't have to consider. If this is obscure, Aunt M'riar, who used the phrase, is responsible, not the story. Its opinion is, that she meant that the absence of a third person left her freer to speak. Perhaps if Mo had been present she would merely have handed Micky the letter directed to his aunt, which would have been palpably no concern of Uncle Mo's, inquirin' and askin' questions.

As it was, she accompanied it with verbal instructions:— " Now you know what you've got to do, young Micky. You've just got to give this letter to your great-aunt Treadwell. And when she sees inside of it, she'll find it ain't for her, but a party."

" What sort of a party, that's the p'int? Don't b'leeve my great-aunt knows no parties. Them she knows is inside of her farmily. Nevoos, sim'lar to myself as you might say. Or hequal value." An Academical degree would have qualified Micky to say " or its equivalent." The expression he used had its source in ex-change transactions of turnips and carrots and greens, anticipat-ing varied calls for each in different markets.

" She may know the address of the lady she'll find in this envelope. And if she don't, all *you* got to do is to bring the letter back."

" Suppose she don't know the address and I do, am I to tell her, or 'old my tongue? "

" Now which do you think? I do declare you boys I never!

Nor yet anyone else! Why, if she don't know the address and you do, all you got to do then is take the letter and leave it."

"Without any address wrote? Wery good! 'Ave it your own way, missis. 'And it over."

Aunt M'riar handed it over. But before Micky was half-way up the Court, she called him back. " Maybe you know the party's name? Miss Julia Hawkins—on the waterside, Hammersmith."

" Her! Not know her! Juliarawkins. Why, she's next door! "

" But do you know her—to speak to? "

" Rarther! We're on torkin terms, me and Juliar. Werry often stop I do, to pass the time of day with Jooliar." An intensification in the accent on the name seemed to add to his claim to familiarity with its owner. " Keeps the little tiddley-wink next door. Licensed 'ouse. That's where they took Wix—him as got out of quod—him as come down the Court to look up a widder."

Aunt M'riar considered a moment whether it would not be better to instruct Micky to find out Daverill and deliver her letter to him in person. She decided on adhering to the convict's instructions. If she had understood his past relations with Miss Hawkins she might have decided otherwise. She affected not to hear Micky's allusion to him, merely enjoining the boy to hand her letter in over the bar to its Egeria. " You won't have any call for to trouble your aunt," said she. For she felt that the fewer the cooks, the better the broth. Questioned as to when he would deliver the letter, Micky appeared to turn over in his mind a voluminous register of appointments. But he could stand them all over, to oblige, and would see if he couldn't make it convenient to go over Sunday morning. Nothing was impossible to a good business head.

As the appointments had absolutely no existence except in his imagination—though perhaps costermonging, at its lowest ebb, still claimed his services—he was able to make it very convenient indeed to visit his Aunt Elizabeth. History repeats itself, and the incident of the half-and-half happened again, point for point, until settlement-time came, and then a variation crept in.

" I got a letter for you, missis," said Micky.

" Sure it ain't for somebody else? Let's have a look at it."

" No 'urry! Tork it over first—that's my marxim! Look ye here, Miss Juliar, this is my way of putting of it. Here's three-halfpence, over the beer. Here's the corner of the letter, stickin' out of my porket. Now which'll you have, the letter or the three-halfpence? Make your ch'ice. All square and no deception! "

"Well—the impidence of the child! Who's to know the letter's for me onlest I see the direction? Who gave it you to give me?" "Miss Wardle down our Court. Same I told you of—where the old widder-woman hangs out. Him the police are after's mother!" Micky was so confident of the success of this communication that he began picking up the three-halfpence to restore them to his pocket, and stood holding the corner of the letter to draw it out as soon as his terms were accepted. The acceptance came unconditionally, with a nod; and Micky departed with his jug.

What were the contents of this letter to Mr. Wix, care of Miss Julia Hawkins, at The Pigeons? That was all the direction on the envelope, originally covered by another, addressed to Micky's great-aunt. It was worded as Daverill had worded it in a hurried parting word to Aunt M'riar, given when Gwen's knock had cut his visit short. This letter, in an uneducated woman's hand, excited Miss Hawkins's curiosity. Of course it might only be from the old woman he supposed to be his mother. If so, there did not seem to be any reasonable objection to her reading it. If otherwise, she felt that there were many reasonable objections to leaving it unread. Anyhow there was a kettle steaming on the fire in the bar, and if she held the letter over the spout to see if it would open easy, she would be still in a position to shut it up again and deliver it with a guiltless conscience. Eve, no doubt, felt that she could handle the apple and go on resisting temptation, so as not to seem rude to the Serpent. The steam was not wanted for long, the envelope flap curling up in a most obliging manner, and leaving all clear for investigation. Miss Hawkins laid the letter down to dry quite dry, before fingering it. Remember to bear this in mind in opening other people's letters this way. The slightest touch on paper moistened by steam may remain as a tell-tale.

This woman was so cautious that she left the paper untouched where she had laid it on the table while she conferred with a recently installed potboy on points of commercial economy. When she returned it was dry beyond suspicion, and she drew the letter out to see if it contained anything she need hesitate to read. She felt that she was keeping in view what is due to the sensitive conscience of an honourable person.

The note she read was short, written so that the lines fell thus:—

"RALPH DAVERILL—The police are
on the look out for you and it is now not

safe to come to the Court—This is written
by your wife to say you will run
great risk of being took if you come—
For you to know who I am I write my name—
POLLY DAVERILL.
Sapps Court Dec 9 1854."

The lines were ill-spaced, so that blanks were left as shown. At the end of the second, a crowded line, the word *not* was blurred on the paper-edge, and looked like a repetition of the previous word.

One does not see without thought, why this letter sent its reader's heart beating furiously. Why should she turn scarlet with anger and all but draw blood from a bitten lip? She knew perfectly well that this gutter Don Juan's depravity could boast as many victims as his enforced prison life had left possible to him. But no particular one had ever become concrete to her, and jealousy of a multitude, no one better off than herself, had never rankled. Jealousy of Heaven-knows-who is a wishy-washy passion. Supply a definite object, and it may become vitriolic. Polly Daverill, whoever she was, was definite, and might be the wife the convict had acknowledged—or rather claimed—when he first made Miss Julia's acquaintance, over twenty years ago.

The lip was perhaps saved from bloodletting by an idea which crossed the mind of the biter. A look of satisfaction grew and grew as she contemplated the letter; not for its meaning—that was soon clear. It was something in the handwriting; something that made her hide half-words with a finger-point, and vary her angle of inspection. Then she said, aloud to herself:—"Yes!" as though she had come to a decision.

She examined an inkstand that the dried ink of ages had encrusted, beyond redemption, in a sunken cavity of restraint in an inktray overstocked with extinct and senile pens. Its residuum of black fluid had been glutinous ever since Miss Julia had known it; ever since she had written, as a student, that Bounty Commanded Esteem all down one page of a copybook. The pens were quill pens past mending, or overwhelmed by too heartfelt nibs; or magnum bonums whose upstrokes were morally as wide as Portland Place, or parvum malums that perforated syllables and spluttered. The penwiper was non-absorbent, and generally contrived to return the drop it refused to partake of on the hands of incautious scribes, who rarely obtained soap and hot water time enough to do any good.

Miss Julia first remedied the ink. A memory of breakfast unremoved still hung about the parlour table—a teapot and a

slop basin. The former supplied a diluent, the latter a haven
for the indisputably used-up quill whose feather served to in-
corporate it with the black coagulum. With the resultant fluid
you could make a mark about the same blackness as what the
letter was, using by preference the newest magnum bonum pen,
which was all right in itself, only stuck on an old wooden handle
that scribes of recent years had gnawed.

What this woman's jealous violence was prompting her to do
was to alter this letter so as to encourage its recipient to put
himself in danger of capture. It was an easy task, as the only
words she had to insert could be copies from what was already
written. The first line required the word *not* at the end, the
fourth the word *no*. The only other change needed was the
erasure of the word *not,* in the second line, which already looked
like an accidental repetition of *now*. Was an erasure advisable?
she decided against it, cleverly. She merely drew her pen through
the *not,* leaving the first two letters intentionally visible, and blur-
ring the last. She then re-enveloped the letter, much pleased
with the result, and wrote a short note in pencil to acompany it;
then hunted up an envelope large enough to take both, and directed
it to W. at the Post Office, East Croydon. This was the last address
the convict had given. Where he was actually living she did not
know.

Her own letter to him was:—"The enclosed has come for you.
I write this in pencil because I cannot find any ink." It was a
little stroke of genius worthy of her correspondent's father.
Nothing but clairvoyance could have bred suspicion in him.
Micky reappeared that evening in Sapps Court, and found an
opportunity to convey to Aunt M'riar that he had obeyed his
instructions. He did so with an air of mystery and an undertone
of intelligence, saying briefly:—"That party, missis! She's got
the letter."

"Did you give it her?" said Aunt M'riar.

"I see to it that she got it," said Micky with reserve. "You'll
find it all correct, just as I say." This attitude was more important than the bald, unqualified statement that he had left
the letter when he fetched the beer, and Micky enjoyed himself
over it proportionately.

Aunt M'riar was easier in her mind, as she felt pretty confident
that the letter would reach its destination. She had killed two
birds with one stone—so she believed. She had saved Daverill from
the police, so far at least as their watchfulness of Sapps Court

was concerned, and had also saved Uncle Mo from possible collision with him, an event she dreaded even more than a repetition
of those hideous interviews with a creature that neither was nor
was not her husband; a thing with a spurious identity; a horrible
outgrowth from a stem on which her own life had once been
grafted. Could woman think a worse thought of man than hers
of him, when she thanked God that at least the only fruit of
that graft had been nipped in the bud? And yet no such thought
had crossed her mind in all these years in which he had been
to her no more than a memory. A memory of a dissolute, imperfect creature—yes! but lovable enough for all that. Not indeed
without a sort of charm for any passing friend, quite short of
any spell akin to love. How could this monstrous personality
have grown upon him, yet left him indisputably the same man?
The dreadful change in the identity of the maniac—the maniac
proper, the victim of brain-disease—is at least complete; so complete often as to force the idea of possession on minds reluctant
to receive it. This man remained himself, but it was as though
this identity had been saturated with evil—had soaked it up as
the sponge soaks water. There was nothing in the old self
M'riar remembered to make her glad his child was not born alive.
There was everything in his seeming of to-day to make her shudder
at the thought that it might have lived.

The cause of the change is not far to seek. He had lived for
twenty years in Norfolk Island as a convict; for fourteen years
certainly as an inmate of the prisons, even if a period of qualified
liberty preceded his discharge and return to Sydney. He was
by that time practically damned beyond redemption, and his brilliant career as a bushranger followed as a matter of course.

Those who have read anything of the story of the penal settlements in the early part of last century may—even *must*—remember
the tale told by the Catholic priest who went to give absolution to
a whole gang of convicts who were to be hanged for mutiny.
He carried with him a boon—a message of mercy—for half the
number; for they had been *pardoned;* that is to say, had permission now to live on as denizens of a hell on earth. As it
turned out, the only message of mercy he had to give was the
one contained or implied in an official absolution from sin, and
it is possible that belief in its validity occasioned the outburst
of rejoicing that greeted its announcement. For there was no
rejoicing among the recipients of His Majesty's clemency—heart-
broken silence alone, and chill despair! For they were to remain
on the rack, while their more fortunate fellows could look for-

ward to a joyous gallows, with possibilities beyond, from which Hell had been officially excluded. It is but right to add that the Reverend Father did *not* ascribe the exultant satisfaction of his clients—if that is the word—to anything but the anticipation of escape from torture. He was too truthful.

If the nearest dates the story has obtained are trustworthy, Daverill's actual term in Norfolk Island may have been fourteen years; it certainly came to an end in the early forties. But he must have been there at the time of the above incident, as it happened *circa* 1836-37. The powers of the sea-girt tropical Paradise to sterilise every Divine impulse must have been at their best in his time, and he seems to have been a favourable subject for the *virus* of diabolism, which was got by Good Intentions out of Expediency. The latter must have been carrying on with Cowardice, though, to account for Respectability's choice, for her convicts, of an excruciating life rather than a painless death. Possibly the Cowardice of the whole Christian world, which accounts Death the greatest of possible evils.

The life of a bushranger in New South Wales, which fills in the end of his Australian career, did not tend to the development of any stray germ of a soul that the prison-fires had not scorched out of old Maisie's son. Small wonder it was so! Conceive the glorious freedom of wickedness unrestrained, after the stived-up atmosphere of the gaol, with its maddening Sunday chapel and its hideous possibilities of public torture for any revolt against the unendurable routine. We, nowadays, read with a shudder of the enormities that were common in the prisons of past times —we, who only know of their modern substitutes. For the last traces of torture, such as was common long after the *moyen âge,* as generally understood, have vanished from the administration of our gaols before a vivified spirit of Christianity, and the enlightenment consequent on the Advance of Science.* After fourteen years of such a life, how glorious must have been the opportunities the freedom of the Bush afforded to an instinctive miscreant, still in the prime of life, and artificially debarred for so long from the indulgence of a natural bent for wickedness; not yet *ennuyé* by the monotony of crime in practice, which often leads to a reaction, occasionally accompanied by worldly success. There was, however, about Daverill a redeeming point. He was incorrigibly bad. He never played false to his father the Devil, and the lusts of his father he did do, to the very last, never disgracing himself by the slightest wavering towards repentance.

* This appears to have been written about 1910.

Probably his return from Sydney to England was as much an escape from his own associates in crime, with whom some dishonourable transactions had made him unpopular, as a flight from the officers of Justice. A story is told, too intricate to follow out, of a close resemblance between himself and a friend in his line of business. This was utilised ingeniously for the establishment of alibi's, the name of Wix being adopted by both. Daverill had, however, really behaved in a very shady way, having achieved this man's execution for a capital crime of his own. Ibbetson, the Thames police-sergeant whose death he occasioned later, was no doubt in Sydney at this time, and may have identified him from having been present at the hanging of his counterpart, whose protestations that he was the wrong man of course received no attention, and whose attempt to prove an alibi failed miserably. Daverill had supplied the defence with a perfectly fictitious account of himself and his whereabouts at the time of the commission of the crime, which of course fell to pieces on the testimony of witnesses implicated, who knew nothing whatever of the events described.

There is no reason whatever to suppose that a desire to see his mother again had anything to do with his return. The probability is that he never gave her a thought until the money he had brought with him ran out—or, more accurately, the money he got by selling, at a great sacrifice, the jewels he brought from Australia sewed into the belt he wore in lieu of braces. The most valuable diamond ring should have brought him thousands, but he had to be content with hundreds. He had drawn it off an amputated finger, whose owner he left to bleed to death in the bush. It had already been stolen twice, and in each case had brought ill-luck to its new possessor.

All this of Daverill is irrelevant to the story, except in so far as it absolves Aunt M'riar of the slightest selfish motive in her conduct throughout. The man, as he stood, could only be an object of horror and aversion to her. The memory of what he had once been remained; and crystallized, as it were, into a fixed idea of a sacramental obligation towards a man whose sole claim upon her was his gratification at her expense. She had been instructed that marriage was God's ordinance, and so forth; and was *per se* reciprocal. She had sacrificed herself to him; *therefore* he had sacrificed himself to her. A halo of mysterious sanctity hung about her obligations to him, and seemed to forbid too close an analysis of their nature. An old conjugation of the indicative mood, present tense, backed by the third person singular's capital, floated justifications from Holy Writ of the worst stereotyped iniquity of civilisation.

CHAPTER XXII

HOW GWEN STAYED AWAY FROM CHURCH, BUT SENT HER LOVE TO LADY
MILLICENT ANSTIE-DUNCOMBE. HOW TOM MIGHT COME AGAIN AT
FIVE, AND GAVE MRS. LAMPREY A LIFT. NOT EXACTLY DELIRIUM.
THE BLACK WITCH-DOCTOR. WERE DAVE AND DOLLY ALL TRUE?
WHAT GWEN HAD TO PRETEND. DAVE'S OTHER LETTER. STARING
FACTS IN THE FACE. GWEN'S COMPARISON OF THE TWINS. MIGHT
GWEN SEE THE AUSTRALIAN LETTER? OLD KETURAH'S HUSBAND THE
SEXTON. HOW GRANNY MARRABLE AND RUTH WENT TO CHURCH,
BY REQUEST, AND HOW RUTH SAW THE LIKENESS. HOW OLD MAISIE
COULD NOT BE EVEN WITH UNCLE NICHOLAS. CHAOS. HOW OLD
MRS. PICTURE RECEIVED DAVE'S INVITATION TO TEA. JONES'S BULL

"You'll have to attend divine service without your daughter, mamma," said Gwen, speaking through the door of her mother's apartment, *en passant*. It was a compliance with a rule of domestic courtesy which was always observed by this singular couple. A sort of affection seemed to maintain itself between them as a legitimate basis for dissension, a luxury which they could not otherwise have enjoyed. "I'm called away to my old lady."

"Is she ill?"

"Well—Dr. Nash has written to say that I need not be frightened.'

"But then—why go? If he says you need not be frightened?"

"That's exactly why I'm going. As if I didn't understand doctors!"

"I knew you wouldn't come to Church. Am I to give your love to Lady Millicent Anstie-Duncombe if I see her, or not? She's sure to ask after you."

"Some of it. Not too much. Give the rest to Dr. Tuxford Somers." The Countess's suggestion of entire despair at this daughter was almost imperceptible, but entirely conclusive.

"Well—he's married! Why shouldn't I?"

"As you please, my dear!"

The Countess appeared to decline further discussion. She said:—"Don't be very late—you are coming back to lunch, of course?"

"If I can. It depends."

"My dear! With Sir Spencer Derrick here, and the Open-shaws!"

"I'll be back if I can. Can't say more than that! Good-bye!" And the Countess had to be content. The story is rather sorry for her, for it *is* a bore to have a lot of guests on one's hands, without due family support.

The grey mare's long stride left John Costrell's fat cob a mile behind, in less than two. Her hoofs made music on the hard road for another two, and then were *assourdi* by a swansdown coverlid of large snowflakes that disappointed the day's hopes of being fine, and made her sulky with the sun, extinguishing his light. The gig drew up at Strides Cottage in a whitening world, and Tom Kettering had to button up the seats under their oilskin passenger-cases, in anticipation of a long wait.

But Tom had not a long wait, for in a quarter of an hour after her young ladyship had vanished into Strides Cottage, she re-turned, telling him she was going to be late, and should not want him. He might drive back to the Towers, and—stop a min-ute!—might give this card to her mother. She scribbled on one of her own cards that she would not be back to lunch, and told Tom he might come again about five. Tom touched his hat as a warrior might have touched his sword-hilt.

Widow Thrale, who had accompanied Gwen, and returned with her into the house, was the very ghost of her past self of yesterday morning. Twenty-four hours ago she looked less than her real age by ten years; now she had overpassed it by half that time at least. So said to Tom Kettering a young woman with a sharp manner, whom he picked up and gave a lift to on his way back. Tom's taciturnity abated in conversation with Mrs. Lamprey, and he really seemed to come out of his Trappist seclusion to hear what she had to tell about this mystery at the Cottage. She had plenty, founded on conversations between the doctor and his sister, whose housekeeper you will remember she was.

"Why—I'd only just left Widow Thrale when you drove past. Your aunt she stayed till ever so late last night,"—Tom was Mrs. Solmes's nephew—"and went home with Carrier Brantock. Didn't you see her?"

"Just for a word, this morning. She hadn't so much to tell as you'd think. But it come to this—that this old Goody Prichard's own sister to Granny Marrable. Got lost in Australia somehow. Anyhow, she's there now, at the Cottage. No getting out o' that!

Only what bothers me is—how ever she came to turn up in her sister's house, and ne'er a one of 'em to know the other from Queen Anne!"

"We've got to take that in the lump, Thomas. I expect your Aunt Keziah she'll say it was Providence. I say it was just a, chance, and Dr. Nash he says the same. You ask him!"

Tom considered thoughtfully, and decided. "I expect it was just a chance," said he. "Things happen of theirselves, if you let 'em alone. Anyhow, it hasn't happened above this once." That was a great relief, and Tom seemed to breathe the freer for it.

"I haven't a word to say against Providence," said Mrs. Lamprey. "On the contrary I go to Church every Sunday, and no one can find fault. So does Dr. Nash, to please Miss Euphemia. But one has to consider what's reasonable. What I say is:—if it was Providence, what was to prevent its happening twenty years ago? Nothing stood in the way, that I see."

Tom shook his head, to show that neither did he see what stood in the way of a more sensible and practical Divine ordination of events. "Might have took place any time ago, in reason," said he. "Anyhow, it hasn't. It's happened now." Tom seemed always to be seeking relief from oppressive problems, and looking facts in the face. "I'm not so sure," he continued, abating the mare slightly to favour conversation, "that I've got all the scoring right. This old lady she went out to Australia?"

"Yes—fifty years ago." Mrs. Lamprey told what she knew, but not nearly all the facts as the story knows them. She had not got the convict incidents correctly from the conversation of Dr. Nash with his sister. Remember that he had only known it since yesterday morning. Mrs. Lamprey's version did not take long to tell.

"What I look at is this," said Tom, seeming to stroke with his whiplash the thing he looked at, on the mare's back. "Won't it turn old Granny Marrable wrong-side-up, seeing her time of life. Not the other old Goody—she's been all the way to Australia and back!" This only meant that nothing could surprise one who had such an experience. As to the effect on Granny Marrable, Mrs. Lamprey said no—quite the reverse. Once it was Providence, there you stuck, and there was no moving you! There was some obscurity about this saying; but no doubt its esoteric meaning was, that once you accounted for anything by direct Divine interposition, you stood committed to a controversial attitude which would render you an obstructive to liberal thought.

This little conversation was presently cut short by Mrs. Lamprey's arrival at her destination, a roadside inn where she had an aunt by marriage.

Ruth Thrale had a bad report to give as she and her young ladyship recrossed the kitchen. It was summed up in the word Fever, restrained by "Not exactly delirium." Granny Marrable came out to meet them, and threw in a word or two of additional restraint. What they had at first thought delirium had turned out quite temperate and sane on closer examination.

"A deal about Australia, and the black witch-doctor," said Granny Marrable. "Now, if one could turn her mind off that, it might be best for her, and she would drop off, quiet." Perhaps her ladyship coming would do her good. The old lady ended with concession about the fever—was not quite sure Maisie had known her just now when she spoke to her.

"Poor old darling!" said Gwen. "You know, Granny, we must expect a little of this sort of thing. We couldn't hope to get off scot-free. Have you had some sleep, yourself? Has she slept, Ruth?"

"Oh yes. Mother got some sleep in the chair beside—beside *her*, till four o'clock. Then she lay down, and had a good sleep, lying down. Didn't you, mother?"

"You may be easy about me, child. I've done very well."

"And yourself, Ruth?" By now, Gwen always called Widow Thrale "Ruth."

"Who—I? I had quite a long sleep, while mother sat by—by *her*." This dreadful difficulty of what to call old Maisie! Her daughter was always at odds with it.

Gwen passed on into the bedroom. Just at the door she paused. "You wait outside, and hear," said she. They held back, in the passage, silent.

Old Maisie's voice, on the pillow; audible, not articulate. Two frail hands stretched out in welcome. Two grave eyes, made wild by the surrounding tangle of loose white hair. Those were Gwen's impressions as she approached the bed.

The voice grew articulate. "Oh, my darling, I knew you would come. I want you close, to tell me. . . ."

"Yes, dear!—to tell you what?"

"I want you to tell me whether one of the things is a dream."

"One of which things, dear?" One has to be a hard old stager not to feel his flesh creep at delirium. Gwen had to fight against a shudder.

"There are so many, you know, now that they all come back

at once. Tell me, darling, were my little boy and girl real, who came up into my room and played and gave me tea out of small cups? I called them Dave and Dolly. Dolly was very small. Oh, Dolly!" Dolly's size, and her tenderness on one's knee, were, so to speak, audible in the voice that became tender to apostrophise her.

"Dave and Dolly Wardle? Of course they are real! As real as you or me! There they are in Sapps Court, with Uncle Mo and Aunt M'riar. And Susan Burr." Then such a nice scheme crossed Gwen's mind.

But old Maisie seemed adrift, not able to be sure of any memory; past and present at war in her mind, either intolerant of the other. "Then tell me, dear," said she. "Is the other real too? Is it not a thing I have dreamed, a thing I have dreamed in the night, here in Widow Thrale's cottage . . . where I came in the cart . . . where I came from the great house where the sweet old gentleman was, that was your father . . . where I could see out over the tree lands . . . where my Ruth came to me? . . ." The affection for her daughter, that had struck root firmly in her heart, remained a solid fact, whether she was thinking of her as before or after the revelation of her identity.

Gwen sat beside her on the bed-edge, her arm round her head on its pillow, her free hand soothing the restless fingers that would not be still. "What is it you think you have dreamed, Mrs. Picture dear?" said she.

"It was all a dream, I think. Just a mad dream—but then— but then—did not my Ruth think I was mad? . . ."

"But what was it? Tell it to me, now, quietly."

"It was that my Phœbe—my sister—oh, my dear sister!—dead so many years ago—sat by me here, as you sit now—and we talked and talked of the old time—and our young Squire, so beautiful, upon his horse. . . . Oh, but then—but then! . . ." She checked herself suddenly, and a look of horror came in her face; then went on:—"No, listen! There was an awful thing in the dream—a bad thing—about a letter. . . . Oh, how can I tell it? . . ."

Gwen caught at the pause to speak, saying gently but firmly:— "Dear Mrs. Picture, it was no dream, but all true. Believe me, I know. When you are quite well and strong, I will tell you all over again about the letter, and how my dear old father found it all out for you. And I tell you what! You shall come and live here with your sister and daughter, instead of Sapps Court. . . . Oh no—you shall have Dave and Dolly. They shall come too." This was Gwen's scheme, but it was no older than the mention just made of it. "I can do these things," she added. "Papa lets me do what I choose."

Old Maisie lay back, looking at the beautiful face in a kind of wonderment. The feeling it gave her that she was in the hands of some superior power was the most favourable one possible in a case where fever was the result of mental disquiet. Presently the strain on the face abated, and the wild look in the eyes. The lids drooped, then closed over them. Something like sleep followed, leaving Gwen free to rejoin old Phœbe and Ruth, outside. They were still close at hand.

"Did you hear all that?" said Gwen. It appeared that they had, or the greater part. The account of how the night had passed was postponed, owing to the arrival of Dr. Nash.

"I would sooner give her no drugs of any sort," said he, when he had taken a good look at the patient. "I will leave something for her to take if she doesn't get sleep naturally. Otherwise the choice is between giving her something harmless to make her believe she is taking medicine, and telling her she has nothing whatever the matter with her. I incline to the last. Get her to take food whenever you can. Always have something ready for her whenever's there a chance. I expect you to see to that, Widow Thrale. And, Lady Gwendolen, *you* are good for her—remember that! You've got to pretend you're God Almighty—do you understand?" It goes without saying that by this time no one else was within hearing.

"I understand perfectly," said Gwen. "That little doze she had just now was because I pledged myself and my father to the reality of the whole thing. She had got to think it was all a dream."

She suppressed, as the sort of thing for London, a thought that came into her head at this moment, that it was the first time the family coronet had been of the slightest use to any living creature! Not here, with the hush of the Feudal System still on the land, and the old church at Chorlton's monotonous belfry calling its flock to celebrate the Third Sunday in Advent. For next Sunday was Christmas Eve, and old Maisie's eighty-first birthday. Next Monday was old Phœbe's, with just the stroke of midnight between them.

Gwen seized the opportunity to get from Dr. Nash a fuller account of his disclosure to old Phœbe. He told her what we know already.

"Only I'm due at the other end of the village," said he, ending up. He looked at his watch. "I've got five minutes. . . . Yes—

it was the small boy's letter that did the job. I had been hammer-
ing away at the old lady to get the thin of the wedge in, and I
assure you it was useless. Worse than useless! So I gave it up.
But I suspect that some shot of mine hit the mark, without my
seeing it. Something had made her susceptible. And when the
kid's letter came, that did it. I wasn't there."

"Oh—then you only heard. . . ."

"I was called back. I found the old body gone off in a faint,
and the letter on the floor—at least, on the baby. I've got it in
my pocket, I do believe. . . . No, I haven't!"

"What's this on the window-ledge? This is Dave's hand."
But Gwen saw that it was directed to "Old Mrs. Picture Strides
Cotage Chorlton under bradBury." She opened it without remorse,
and the doctor said:—"Of course! He wrote two. That one's to
t'other old lady. Just the same, I expect."

It was, word for word. But it had a short postscript:—"When
you come bacK me and Dolly shall give you tea it is stood ready
and grany maroBone too."

"Poor little people!" said Gwen. "How they will feel it! But
I mustn't keep you, doctor."

And then, after a word or two to Widow Thrale, Dr. Nash
drove off through the snow, now thickening.

Gwen, you see, was quite alive to the situation; perhaps indeed
she was ready to put a worse construction on it than the doctor.
He had seen so many a spark of life, far nearer extinction than
old Maisie's, flicker up and grow and grow, and end by steady
burning through its appointed time, that no amount of mere attenuation frightened him. Gwen, on the other hand, could not
bring herself to believe that any creature so frail would stand the
strain of such an earthquake of sensibilities. Unless indeed some
change for the better showed itself in a few hours, she *must* succumb. Probably she was only relieving the tension of her own
feelings by looking facts fiercely in the face. It is a common attitude of inexperience, under like circumstances. Dr. Nash certainly
had said to her that "the strength was well maintained." But do
we not all of us accept that phrase as an ill-omen—a vulture in the
desert? No—no! Look the facts in the face! Glare at them!

Returning to the bedside, where Granny Marrable was sitting
in her arm-chair beside her sister, who was quiet—possibly sleeping—she took the opportunity to note the changes that Time had
wrought in each twin. The moment she came to look for them,
she began to marvel that she had never seen the similarities; for
instance, scarcely a month since, when the two were face to face

outside this house, and each looked at the other, and neither said
or thought:—"How like myself!" Was it possible that they were
really *more* unlike then?—that the storm which had passed over
both had told more, relatively, on the healthy village dame, kept
blooming by a life whose cares were little more than healthy
excitements, than on the mere derelict of so many storms, any
one enough to send it to the bottom? There was little work left
for Time or Calamity to do on that old face on the pillow; while
even this four-and-twenty-hours of overwrought excitement had
left·its mark upon old Phœbe. Gwen saw that the faces *were* the
same, past dispute, as soon as she compared them point by point.
  Once seen, the thing grew, and became strange and unearthly,
almost a discomfort. Gwen went back into the kitchen, where
she found Ruth, affecting some housework but without much
heart in it. She too was showing the effects of the night and day
just passed, her heavy eyelids fighting with their weight, not
successfully; her restless hands protesting against yawns; trying
to curb rebellious lips, in vain.
  "I can see the likeness now," said Gwen, thinking it best to talk.
  "Between mother and—my mother?" was Ruth's reply. How
else could she have said it, without beginning to call old Phœbe
her aunt?
  Gwen saw the embarrassment, and skipped explanation. "Why
not call her Mrs. Picture—little Dave's name?" Then she felt
this was a mistake, and added:—"No, I suppose that wouldn't do!"
  "Something will come, to say, in time. One's head goes, now."
Ruth went on to speak of her childish recollection of the news of
her mother's death—quite a vivid memory—when she was nearly
nine years old. "I was quite a big little maid when the letter
came. We got it out, you know, just now. And, oh, how sick
it made me!"
  "I should like so much to see it," said Gwen. Her young
ladyship's lightest wish was law, and Ruth nearly went to seek
the letter. Gwen had to be very emphatic that another time
would do, to stop her.
  "Then I will get it out presently, and give it to your ladyship
to take away and read," said Ruth, and went back to what she
was saying. "That is how I came to be able to call her my
mother, at once. I mean the moment I knew she was not Mrs.
Prichard. Now that I know it, I keep looking at her dear old
face to make it out the same face that I kept on thinking my
mother in Australia had, all the time I thought she was living
there away from us. And if I had never known she died—I mean

had we never thought her dead—I would have gone on thinking the same face. Oh, such a beautiful young face! Exactly like what mother's was then!—the same face for her that it was when I last saw it. . . ."

"I see. And when you look at your—your aunt's face, you naturally do not look for what she was forty years ago."

"That is it, your ladyship. Because I have had mother to go by, all the time. She has always been the same she was last week—last month—last year—any time. What must it be to *her,* to see me what I am!"

"I don't believe it is harder for her to think about than it is for you. She is feverish now, and that makes her wander. People are always worse in the morning. Dr. Nash says so. I thought yesterday she seemed so clear—almost understood it all." Thus Gwen, not over-sure of her facts.

"She was worse," said Ruth, thinking back into the recent events, "that evening I showed her the mill. That was her bad time. Who knows but that has made it easier for her now? I shouldn't wonder. . . . And to think that I thought her mad, and never guessed who I was, myself, all that time."

"Was that the model?" said Gwen, thinking that anything the mind could rest on might make the thing more real for Ruth. "Do you know I have only half seen it? I should so like to see it again. Why have you covered it up?" A few words explained this, and the mill was again put on the table. If the little dolly figures had only possessed faculties, they would have wondered why, after all these years, they were awakening such an interest among the big movable creatures outside the glass. How they would have wondered at Gwen's next words:—"And those two have lived to be eighty years old and are in the next room!"

Then she was not sure she had not made matters worse. "Oh dear!" said Widow Thrale, "it is all impossible—*impossible!* This was old when I was a child."

Gwen was not prepared to submit to Time's tyranny. "What does it matter?" said she intrepidly. "There is no need for *possibility,* that I can see. She *is* here, and the thing to think of now is—how can we keep her? It will all seem natural in three weeks. See now, how they know one another, and talk of old times already. She may live another five—ten—fifteen years. Who can say?"

"She *is* talking to mother now, I think," said Widow Thrale, listening. For the voices of the twins came from the bedroom. "Suppose we go back!"

"Yes—and you look at the two faces together, this time."
"I will look," was the reply, with a shade of doubt in it that added:—"I may not see the resemblance."

Gwen went first. The two old faces were close together as they entered, and she could see, more plainly than she had ever seen it yet, their amazing similarity. She could see how much thinner old Maisie was of the two. It was very visible in the hand that touched her sister's, which was strong and substantial by comparison.

The monotonous bells at Chorlton Church had said all they could to convince its congregation that the time had come for praise and prayer; and had broken into impatient thrills and jerks that seemed to say:—"If you don't come for this, nothing will fetch you!" The wicked man who had been waiting to go for a brisk walk as soon as the others had turned away from their wickedness, and were safe in their pews making the responses, was getting on his thickest overcoat and choosing which stick he would have, or had already decided that the coast was clear, and had started. Old Maisie's face on the pillow was attentive to the bells. She looked less feverish, and they were giving her pleasure.

What was that she was saying, about some bells? "Old Keturah's husband the sexton used to ring them. You remember him, Phœbe darling?—him and his wart. We thought it would slice off with a knife, like the topnoddy on a new loaf if one was greedy. . . . And you remember how we went up his ladder into the belfry, and I was frightened because it jumped?"

Old Phœbe remembered. "Yes, indeed! And old Jacob saying if he could clamber up at ninety-four, we could at fourteen. Then we pulled the bells. After that he would let us ring the curfew."

Just at that moment the last jerk cut off the last thrill of the chimes at Chorlton ,and the big bell started thoughtfully to say it was eleven o'clock. Old Maisie seemed suddenly disquieted. "Phœbe darling!" she said. And then, touching her sister's hand, with a frightened voice:—"This is Phœbe, is it not? . . . No, it is not my eyes—it is my head goes!" For Gwen had said:—"Yes, this is your sister. Do you not see her?" She then went on:— "My dear—my dear!—I am keeping you from church. I want not to. I want *not* to."

"Never mind church for one day, dear," said Granny Marrable. "Parson he won't blame me, stopping away this once. More by token, if he does miss seeing me, he'll just think I'm at Denby's."

"But, Phœbe—Phœbe!—think of long ago, how I would try to persuade you to stop away just once, to please me—just only once! And now . . ." She seemed to have set her heart on her sister's going; a sort of not very explicable tribute to "auld lang syne."

Gwen caught what seemed a clue to her meaning. "I see," said she. "You want to make up for it now. Isn't that it?"

"Yes—yes—yes! And Ruth must go with her to take care of her. . . . Oh, Phœbe, why should you be so much stronger than me?" She meant perhaps, why should her sister's strength be taken for granted?

Gwen looked at Granny Marrable, who was hesitating. Her look meant:—"Yes—go! Why not?" A nod thrown in meant:— "Better go!" She looked round for Ruth, to get her sanction or support, but Ruth was no longer in the room. "What has become of Mrs. Thrale?" said Gwen.

Ruth had vanished into the front? room, and there Gwen found her, looking white. "I saw it," said she. "And it frightened me. I am a fool—why have I not seen it before?"

Gwen said:—"Oh, I see! You mean the likeness? Yes—it's —it's startling!" Then she told of old Maisie's sudden whim about the service at Chorlton Church. "As your ladyship thinks best!" said Ruth. Her ladyship did think it best, on the whole. It would be best to comply with every whim—could only have a sedative effect. She herself would remain beside "your mother" while the two were away. Would they not be very late? Oh, that didn't matter! Besides, everyone was late. Granny Marrable and Ruth were soon in trim for a hasty departure. But as they went away Ruth slipped into Lady Gwen's hand the accursed letter, as promised. She had brought it out into the daylight again, unwillingly enough.

That was how it came about that Gwen found herself alone with old Maisie that morning.

"My dear—my dear!" said the old lady, as soon as Gwen was settled down beside her, "if it had not been for you, I should have died and never seen them—my sister and my Ruth. . . . I think I am sure that it is they, come back. . . . It is—oh, it is —my Phœbe and my little girl. . . . Oh, say it is. I like you to say it." She caught Gwen by the arm, speaking low and quickly, almost whispering.

"Of course it is And they have gone to church. They will be back to dinner at one. Perhaps you will be strong enough to sit up at table. . . . Oh no!—that certainly is not them back again. I think it is Elizabeth—from next door; I don't know her name— putting the meat down to roast. . . . Yes—she has her own Sunday dinner to attend to, but she says she can be in both houses at once.

I heard her say so to your sister." Gwen felt it desirable to dwell on the relationship, when chances occurred.

"Elizabeth-next-door. I remember her when Ruth was Widow Thrale—it seems so long ago now! . . . Yes—I wished Phœbe to go to church, because she always wished to go. Besides, it made it like *then*."

"'Made it like then?'" Gwenn was not sure she followed this.

"Yes—like then, when the mill was, and our father. Only before I married and went away he made us go with him, always. He was very strict. It was after that I would persuade Phœbe to leave me behind when she went on Sunday. It was when she was married to Uncle Nicholas who was drowned. We always called him Uncle Nicholas, because of my little Ruth."

Gwen thought a moment whether anything would be gained by clearing up this confusion. Old Maisie's belief in "Uncle Nicholas's" death by drowning, fifty years ago, clung to her mind, as a portion of a chaotic past no visible surrounding challenged. It was quite negligible—that was Gwen's decision. She held her tongue.

But nothing of the Chaos was negligible. Every memory was entangled with another. A sort of affright seemed to seize upon old Maisie, making her hand tighten suddenly on Gwen's arm. "Oh, how was that—how was that?" she cried. "They were to-gether—all together!"

"It was only what the letter said," answered Gwen. "It was all a made-up story. Uncle Nicholas was not drowned, any more than your sister, or your child."

"Oh dear!" Old Maisie's hand went to her forehead, as though it stunned her to think.

"They will tell you when he died, soon, when you have got more settled. *I* don't know."

"He must be dead, because Phœbe is a widow."

"She is the widow of the husband she married after his death. That is why her name is Marrable, not . . . Cropworthy—was it?"

"Not Cropworthy—Cropredy. Such a funny name we thought it. . . . But then—Phœbe must think. . . ."

"Think what?"

"Must think *I* married again. Because I am Mrs. Prichard."

"Perhaps she does think so. Why are you Mrs. Prichard? Don't tell me now if it tires you to talk."

"It does not tire me. It is easier to talk than to think. I took the name of Prichard because I wanted it all forgotten."

"About your husband having been—in prison?"

"Oh no, no! I was not ashamed about that. He was wrong, but it was only money. It was my son. . . . Oh yes—he was transported too—but that was after. . . . It was only a theft. I cannot talk about my son." Gwen felt that she shuddered, and that danger lay that way. The fever might return. She cast about for anything that would divert the conversation from that terrible son. Dave and Dolly, naturally.

"Stop a minute," said she. "You have never seen Dave's letter that he wrote to say he knew all about it." And she went away to the front room to get it.

A peaceful joint was turning both ways at the right speed by itself. The cat, uninterested, was consulting her own comfort, and the cricket was persevering for ever in his original statement. Saucepans were simmering in conformity, with perfect faith in the reappearance of the human disposer of their events, in due course. Dave's letter lay where Gwen had left it, between the flower-pots on the window-shelf. She picked it up and went back with it to the bedside.

"You must have your spectacles and read it yourself. Can you? Where shall I find them?"

"I think my Ruth has put them in the watch-pocket with my watch, over my head here." She could make no effort to reach them, but Gwen drew out both watch and glasses. "What a pretty old watch!" said she.

It pleased the old lady to hear her watch admired. "I had it when I went out to my husband." She added inexplicably:—"The man brought it back to me for the reward. He had not sold it." Then she told, clearly enough, the tale you may remember her telling to Aunt M'riar; about the convict at Chatham, who brought her a letter from her husband on the river hulk. "Over fifty years ago now, and it still goes. Only it loses—and gains. . . . But show me my boy's letter." She got her glasses on, with Gwen's help, and read. The word "cistern" was obscure. She quite understood what followed, saying:—"Oh, yes—so much longer ago than Dolly's birthday! And we did—we did—think we were dead and buried. The darling boy!"

"He means each thought the other was. I told him." Gwen saw that the old face looked happy, and was pleased. She began to think she would be easy in her mind at Pensham, to-morrow, about old Mrs. Picture, and able to tell the story to her blind lover with a light heart.

Old Maisie had come to the postscript. "What is this at the end?" said she. "'The tea is stood ready' for me. And for

Granny Marrowbone too." Gwen saw the old face looking happier than she had seen it yet, and was glad to answer:—"Yes—I
saw the tea 'stood ready' by your chair. All but the real sugar
and milk. Dolly sits beside it on the floor—all her leisure time
I believe—and dreams of bliss to come. Dave sympathizes at
heart, but affects superiority. It's his manhood." Old Maisie said
again:—"The darling children!" and kept on looking at the letter.

Gwen's satisfaction at this was to be dashed slightly. For she
found herself asked, to her surprise, "Who is Granny Marrowbone?" She replied:—"Of course Dave wants his other Granny,
from the country." She waited for an assent, but none came.
Instead, old Maisie said reflectively, as though recalling an incident of some interest:—"Oh yes!—Granny Marrowbone was his
other Granny in the country, where he went to stay, and saw
Jones's Bull. I think she must be a nice old lady." Gwen said
nothing. Better pass this by; it would be forgotten.

But the strong individuality of that Bull came in the way.
Had not they visited him together only the other day? He struck
confusion into memory and oblivion alike. The face Gwen saw,
when the letter that hid it fell on the coverlid, was almost terrified.
"Oh, see the things I say!" cried old Maisie, in great distress of
mind. "How am I ever to know it right?" She clung to Gwen's
hand in a sort of panic. In a few moments she said, in an awed
sort of voice:—"Was that Phœbe, then, that I saw when we
stopped at the Cottage, in the carriage, after the Bull?"

"Yes, dear! And you are in the Cottage now. And Phœbe is
coming back soon. And Ruth."

CHAPTER XXIII

CATHERINE WHEELS. CENTIPEDES. CENTENARIANS. BACKGAMMON.
IT. HEREAFTER CORNER. LADY KATHERINE STUARTLAVEROCK.
BISHOP BERKELEY. THE COUNTESS'S VISIT REVIEWED. A CODEX OF
HUMAN WEAKNESS. AN EXPOSITION OF SELFISHNESS. HOW ADRIAN
WOULD HOLD ON LIKE GRIM DEATH. A BELDAM, CRONE, HAG, OR
DOWDY. SUICIDE. THE LITTLE BOTTLE OF INDIAN POISON. MORE
SEPTIMIUS SEVERUS. GWEN'S DAILY BULLETINS. ONESIMUS. TURTLE
SOUP AND CHAMPAGNE. FOXBOURNE. HOW THEY WENT TO CHORL-
TON, AND ANOTHER DOG SMELT ACHILLES.

As he who has godfathered a Catherine Wheel stands at a respectful distance while it spits and fizzes, so may the story that

reunites lovers who have been more than a week apart. The parallel, however, does not hold good throughout, for the Catherine Wheel usually gets stuck after ignition, and has to be stimulated judiciously, while lovers—if worth the name—go off at sight. In many cases—oh, so many!—the behaviour of the Catherine Wheel is painfully true to life. Its fire-spin flags and dies and perishes, and nothing is left of it but a pitiful black core that gives a last spasmodic jump and is for ever still!

Fireworks are only referred to here in connection with the former property. When Gwen reappeared at Pensham, Miss Torrens—this is her own expression—" cleared out " until her brother and her visitor " came to their senses." The Catherine Wheel, in their case, had by that time settled down from a tempest of flame-spray to a steady lamplight, endurable by bystanders. The story need not wait quite so long, but may avail itself of the first return of sanity.

" Dearest—are you really going to stop till Saturday? "

" If you think we shan't quarrel. Four whole days and a bit at each end! *I* think it's tempting Providence."

" Why not stop over Sunday, and make an honourable week of it and no stinting? "

" Because I have a papa coming back to his ancestral home, on Saturday evening, and he will come back boiled and low from Bath waters, inside and out, and he'll want a daughter to give him tone. He gets rid of the gout, but . . ."

" But. Exactly! It's the insoluble residuum that comes back. However, you *will* be here till Friday night."

" Can't even promise that! I may be sent for."

" Why? . . . Oh, I know—the old lady. How is she? Tell me more about her. Tell me lots about her."

Whereupon Gwen, who had been looking forward to doing so, started on an exhaustive narrative of her visit to Strides Cottage. She had not got far when Irene thought it safe to return—hearing probably the narrative tone of voice—and then she had to tell it all over again.

" When I left the Cottage yesterday at about three o'clock," said Gwen, in conclusion, " she was so much better that I felt quite hopeful about her."

" Quite hopeful about her? " Irene repeated. " But if she has nothing the matter with her, except old age, why be anything but hopeful? "

" You would see if you saw her. She looks as if a puff of wind would blow her away like thistledown."

"That," Adrian said, "is a good sign. There is no guarantee of a long life like attenuation. Bloated people die shortly after you make their acquaintance. No, no—for true vitality, give me your skeleton! A healthy old age really sets in as soon as one is spoken of as still living."

"Oh dear, yes!" said Irene. "I'm sure Gwen's description sounds exactly like this old lady becoming a . . . There!—I've forgotten the word! Something between a centipede and a Unitarian. . . ."

"Centenarian?"

"Exactly. See what a good thing it is to have a brother that knows things. A person a hundred years old. I tell you, Gwen dear, my own belief is these two old ladies mean to be centenarians, and if we live long enough we shall read about them in the newspapers. And they will have a letter from Royalty!"

In the evening Gwen got Adrian, whose sanguine expressions were not serious, on a more sane and responsible line of thought. His lady-mother, with whom this story is destined never to become acquainted, retired early, after shedding a lurid radiance of symptoms on the family circle; and it, as a dutiful circle, had given her its blessing and dropped a tear by implication over her early departure from it. Sir Hamilton had involved his daughter in a vortex of backgammon, a game draught-players detest, and *vice versa*, because the two games are even as Box and Cox, in homes possessing only one board. So Gwen and Adrian had themselves to themselves, and wanted nothing more. Her eyes rested now and then with a new curiosity on the Baronet, deep in his game at the far end of the room. She was looking at him by the light of his handsome daughter's saucy speculation about that romantic passage in the lives of himself and her mamma. Suppose—she was saying to herself, with monstrous logic—he had been *my* papa, and *I* had had to play backgammon with him!

She was recalled from one such excursion of fancy by Adrian saying:—"Are you sure it would not have been better for the old twins—or one of them—to die and the other never be any the wiser?"

Said Gwen:—"I am not sure. How can I be? But it was absolutely impossible to leave them there, knowing it, unconscious of each other's existence."

Adrian replied:—"It *was* impossible. I see that. But suppose they *had* remained in ignorance—in the natural order of events I mean—and the London one had died unknown to her sister, would it not have been better than this reunion, with all its tempest of pain and raking up of old memories, and quite possibly an early separation by death?"

"I think not, on the whole. Because, suppose one had died, and the other had come to know of her death afterwards!"

"I am supposing the contrary. Suppose both had continued in ignorance! How then?"

It was not a question to answer off-hand. Gwen pondered; then said abruptly:—"It depends on whether we go on or stop. Now doesn't it?"

"As bogys? That question always crops up. If we stop I don't see how there can be any doubt on the matter. Much better they should have died in ignorance. The old Australian goody was quite contented, as I understand, at Scraps Court, with her little boy and girl to make tea for her. And the old body at Chorlton and her daughter would have gone on quite happily. They didn't want to be excoriated by a discovery."

"Yes—that is what it has been. Excoriation by a discovery. I'm not at all sure you're right—but I'll make you a present of it. Let's consider it settled that death in ignorance would have been the best thing for them."

"Very well!—what next?"

"What next? Why, of course, suppose we don't stop, but go on! You often say it is ten to one against it."

"So it is. I can't say I'm sorry, on the whole."

"That's neither here nor there. Ten to one against is one to ten for. Any man on the turf will tell you that."

"And any Senior Wrangler will confirm it."

"Very well, then! There we are. Suppose my dear old Mrs. Picture and Granny Marrable had turned up as ghosts, on the other side. . . ."

"I see. You've got me in Hereafter Corner, and you don't intend to let me out."

"Not till you tell me whether they would have been happy or miserable about it, those two ghosts. In your opinion, of course! Don't run away with the idea that I think you infallible."

"There are occasions on which I do not think myself infallible. For instance, when I have to decide an apparently insoluble problem without data of any sort. Your expression 'turned up as ghosts, on the other side,' immediately suggests one."

"You can say whether you think they would have been happy or miserable about having been in England together over twenty years, and never known it. *That's* simple enough!"

"Don't be in a hurry! There are complications. If they

knew they were ghosts, they might become interested in the novelty of their position, and be inclined to accept accomplished facts. Recrimination would be waste of time. If they didn't know . . ."

" Goose!—they would be sure to know."

" The only information I have goes to prove the contrary. When Voltaire's ghost came and spirit-rapped, or whatever you call it . . ."

" I know. One turns tables, and it's very silly."

" . . . they said triumphantly that they supposed, now he was dead, he was convinced of another existence. And he—or it— rapped out:—' There is only one existence. I am not dead.' So he didn't know he was a ghost."

Gwen seemed tolerant of Voltaire, as a *pourparler.* " Perhaps," she said thoughtfully, " he found he jammed up against the other ghosts instead of coinciding with them. . . . You know Lady Katherine Stuartlaverock tried to kiss her lover's ghost, and he gave, and she went through."

" A very interesting incident," said Adrian. " If she had been a ghost, too, she would, as you say, have jammed. If Dr. Johnson had known that story, he would have been more reasonable about Bishop Berkeley. . . . What did he say about *him?* Why, he kicked a cask, and said if the Bishop could do that, and not be convinced of the reality of matter, he would be a fool, Sir. I wonder if one said ' Sir,' as often as Dr. Johnson, one would be allowed to talk as much nonsense."

" Boswell must have made that story."

" Very likely. But Boswell made Sam Johnson. Just as we only know of the existence of Matter through our senses, so we only know of Sam's existence through Bozzy. I am conscious that I am becoming prosy. Let's get back to the old ladies."

" Well—it was you that doddered away from them, to talk about Voltaire's bogy. If they *didn't* know they were ghosts, what then?"

" If they didn't know they were ghosts, the discovery would have been just as excoriating as it has been here. Possibly worse, because—what does one know? Now your full-blown disembodied spirit . . . Mind you, this is only my idea, and may be quite groundless! . . ."

" Now you've apologized, go on! ' Your full-blown disembodied spirit ' . . ."

" . . . may be so absorbed in the sudden and strange surprise of the change—Browning—as to be quite unable to partake of excruciation, even with a twin sister. . . . It is very disagreeable to think of, I admit. But so is nearly every concrete form in which one clothes an imaginary other-worldliness."

" Why is it disagreeable to think of being able to shake off one's troubles, and forget all about them. *I* like it."

" Well, I admit that I was beginning to say that I thought these two venerable ladies, meeting as ghosts—not spectres you know, in which case each would frighten t'other and both would run away—would probably be as superior to painful memories on this side as the emancipated butterfly is to its forgotten wiggles as a chrysalis. But it has dawned upon me that Perfect Beings won't wash, and that the Blessed have drawbacks, and that their Choir would pall. I am inclined to back out, and decide that the two of them would have been more miserable if the discovery had come upon them post mortem than they will be now—in a little time at least. At first of course it must be maddening to think of the twenty odd years they have been cheated out of. Really the Divine Disposer of Events might have had a little consideration for the Dramatis Personæ." He jumped to another topic. " You know your mamma paid our papa a visit last— last Thursday, wasn't it?—yes, Thursday! "

" Oh yes—I heard all about it. She had a short chat with him, and he gave her a very good cup of tea. He told her about some very old acquaintances whom she hadn't heard of for years who live in Tavistock Square."

" Was that all? "

" No. The lady very-old acquaintance had been a Miss Tyrawley, and had married her riding-master."

" Was *that* all? "

" No. She called you and 'Re 'the son and daughter.' Then she talked of our 'engagement as your father persists in calling it.' My blood boiled for quite five minutes."

" All that sounds—very usual! Was there nothing else? That was very little for such a long visit."

" How long was the visit? "

" Much too long for what you've told me. Think of something else! "

Now Gwen had been keeping something back. Under pressure she let it out. " Well—mamma thought fit to say that your father entirely shared her views! Was that true? "

" Which of her views? . . . I suppose I know, though! I should say it was half-true—truish, suppose we call it! " Then Adrian began to feel he had been rash. How was he to explain to Gwen that his father thought she was perhaps—to borrow his own phrase—"sacrificing herself on his shrine"? It would be like calling on her to attest her passion for *him*. Now a young lady is at liberty to make any quantity of ardent protestations *off her own bat,* as the cricketers say; but a lover cannot solicit testimonials, to be produced if called for by parents or guardians. However, Gwen had no intention of leaving explanation to him. She continued:—

"When my mother said that your father entirely shared her views, I know which she meant, perfectly well. She has got a foolish idea into her head—and so has my dear old papa, so she's not alone—that I am marrying you to make up to you for . . . for the accident." She found it harder and harder to speak of the nature of the accident. This once, she must do it, *coûte que coûte.* She went on, speaking low that nothing should reach the back-gammon-players. "They say it was *our* fault that old Stephen shot you. . . . Well!—it *was.* . . ."

"My darling, I have frequently pointed out the large share the Primum Mobile had in the matter, to say nothing of the un-doubted influence of Destiny. . . ."

"Silly man—I am talking seriously. I don't know that it really matters whether it was or wasn't—wasn't our fault, I mean—so long as they think I think it was. That's the point. Now, the question is, did or did not my superior mmama descend on your *comme-il-faut* parent to drum this idea into him, and get him on her side?"

"Am I supposed to know?"

"Yes."

"Then I will be frank with you. Always be frank with mad bulls who butt you into corners and won't let you out. Your mamma's communications with my papa had the effect you in-dicate, and he took me into his confidence the same evening. He too questions the purity of your motives in marrying me, alleging that they are vitiated by a spirit of self-sacrifice, tainted by the baneful influence of unselfishness. He is alive to the possibility that you hate me cordially, but are pretending."

"Oh, my dearest, I wish I *did* hate you. . . . Why?—why of course then it would really *be* a sacrifice, and something to boast of. As it is . . . Well—I'm consulting my own convenience, and I . . . I am the best judge of my own affairs. It suits me to . . . to lead you to the altar, and I shall do it. As for what other people think, all I can say is, I will thank Europe to mind its own business."

Then Adrian said:—"I am conscious of the purity of my own

motives. I believe it would be impossible to discover a case of
a Selfishness more unalloyed than mine, if all the records of
Human Weakness were carefully re-read by experts at the British
Museum. I am assuming the existence of some Digest or Codex
of the rather extensive material. . . ."

" Don't go off to that. I always have such difficulty in keeping
you to the point. How selfish are you, and why? "

" I doubt if I can succeed in telling you how selfish I am, but
there's no harm in trying." Speech hung fire for a moment, to
seek for words; then found them. " I am a thing in the dark,
with an object, and I call it Gwen. I am an atom adrift in a
huge black silence, and it crushes my soul, and I am misery itself.
Then I hear the voice that I call Gwen's, and forthwith I am
happy beyond the wildest dreams of the Poets—though really
that isn't saying much, because their wildest dreams are usually
unintelligible, and frequently ungrammatical. . . ."

" Never mind them! Go on with how selfish you are."

" Can't you let a poor beggar get to the end of his parenthesis?
I was endeavouring to sketch the situation, as a preliminary to
going on with how selfish I am. I was remarking that however
dissatisfied I feel with the Most High, however sulky I am with
the want of foresight in the Primum Mobile—or his indifference
to my interests; it comes to the same thing—however inclined to
cry out against the darkness, the darkness that once was light,
I no sooner hear that voice that I call Gwen's than I am at least
in the seven-hundredth heaven of happiness. When I hear that
voice, I am all Christian forgiveness towards my Maker. When
it goes, my heart is dumb and the darkness gains upon me. That
I beg to state, is a simple prosaic statement of an everyday fact.
When I have added that the powers that I ascribe to the
voice that I know to be Gwen's are also inherent in the hand
that I believe to be Gwen's . . . Don't pull it away! "

" I only wanted to look at it. Just to see why you shouldn't
know it was mine, as well as the voice."

" I *know* I couldn't be mistaken about the voice. I don't *think*
I could be wrong about the hand, but I don't know that I couldn't."

" Well—now you've got it again! Now go on. Go on to how
selfish you are—that's what I want! "

" I will endeavour to do so. I hope my imperfect indication
of my view of my own position , . ."

" Don't be prosy. It is not fair to expect any girl to keep a
popular lecturer's head in her lap. . . ."

" I agree—I agree. It was my desire to be strictly practical.

I will come to the point . I want to make it perfectly clear that you *are* my life. . . ."

" Don't get too loud! "

" All right! . . . that you are my life—my life—my glorious life! I want you to see and know that but for you I am nothing —a wisp of straw blown about by all the winds of Heaven—a mere unit of consciousness in a blank, black void. See what comes of it! Here was I, before this unfortunate result of what is from my point of view a lamentable miscarriage of Destiny, a tolerably well-informed . . . English male! . . . Well—what else am I? . . . Sonneteer, suppose we say. . . ."

" Goose—suppose we say—or gander! "

" All right! Here was I, before this mishap, not a scrap more brutally self-indulgent and inconsiderate of everybody else than the ruck of my fellow-ganders, and now look at me! "

" Well—I'm looking at you! "

" Am I showing the slightest consideration for you? Am I not showing the most cynical disregard of your welfare in life? "

" How? "

" By allowing you to throw yourself away upon me."

" It is no concern of yours what I do with myself. I do not intend you to have any voice in the matter. Besides—just be good enough to tell me, please!—suppose you made up your mind *not* to allow me, how would you set about it? "

This was a poser, and the gentleman was practically obliged to acknowledge it. " I couldn't say off-hand," said he. " I should have to consult materfamiliases in Good Society, and look up precedents. Several will occur at once to the student of Lemprière, some of which might be more to the point than anything Holy Writ offers in illustration. But all the cases I can recall at a moment's notice are vitiated by the motives of their male actors. These motives were pure—they were pure self-indulgence. In fact, their attitude towards their would-be charmers had the character of a *sauve-qui-peut*. It was founded on strong personal dislike, and has lent itself to Composition in the hands of the Old Masters. . . ."

" Now I don't know what you are talking about. Answer my question and don't prevaricate. How would you set about it? "

" How indeed? " There was a note of seriousness in Adrian's voice, and Gwen welcomed it, saying:—" That's right!—stop talking nonsense and tell me." It became more audible as he continued:—" You are only asking me because you know I cannot answer. Was ever a case known of a man who cried off because the lady's relatives thought she didn't care about him? What did he do? Did he write her a letter, asking her to consider everything at an end between them until she could produce satisfactory evidence of an unequivocal *sehnsucht* of the exactly right quality—*premier crû*—when her restatement of the case would receive careful consideration? Rubbish! "

" Not rubbish at all! He wrote her that letter and she wrote back requesting him to look out for another young woman at his earliest convenience, because she wasn't his sort. She did, indeed! But she certainly was rather an unfortunate young woman, to be trothplight to such a very good and conscientious young man."

" *Rem tetigisti acu,*" said Adrian. " Never mind what that means. It's Latin. . . . Well then!—it means you've hit it. The whole gist of the matter lies in my being neither good nor conscientious. I am a mass of double-dyed selfishness. I would not give you up—it's very sad, but it's true!—even for your own sake. I would not lose a word from your lips, a touch of your hand, an hour of your presence, to have back my eyesight and with it all else the world has to give, all else than this dear self that I may never see. . . ."

" I'm glad you said *may.*"

" Yes, of course it's *may.* We mustn't forget that. But, dearest, I tell you this, that if I were to get my sight again, and your august mammy's impression were to turn out true after all, and you come to be aware that, pity apart, your humble servant was not such a very . . ."

" What should you do if I did? "

" Shall I tell you? I should show the cloven foot. I should betray the unreasoning greed of my soul. I should never let you go, even if I had to resort to the brutality of keeping you to your word. I should simply hold on like grim death. Would you hate me for it? "

" N-no! I'm not sure that I should. We should see." Certainly the beautiful face that looked down at the eyes that could not see it showed no visible displeasure—quite the reverse. " But suppose I did! *Suppose* is a game that two can play at."

" Very proper, and shows you understand the nature of an hypothesis. What should I do? . . . What *should* I do? "

Gwen offered help to his perplexity. " And suppose that when *you* came to see *your* bargain you had found out your mistake! Suppose that Arthur's Bridge turned out all an Arabian Night! Suppose that the . . . well—satisfactory *personnel* your imagination has concocted turned out to be that of a beldam, crone, hag, or dowdy! How then?"

Instead of replying, Adrian drew his hands gently over the face above him, caressingly over the glorious mass of golden hair and round the columnar throat Bronzino would have left reluctantly alone. Said Irene, from the other end of the room:— "Are you trying Mesmeric experiments, you two?"

"He's only doing it to make sure I'm not a beldam," said Gwen innocently. But to Adrian she added under her breath:— "It's only Irene, so it doesn't matter. Only it shows how cautious one has to be." The Baronet, attracted for one moment from his fascinating dice, contributed a fragment to the conversation, and died away into backgammon. "Hey—eh!—what's that?" said he. "Mesmerism—Mesmerism—why, you don't mean to say you believe in *that* nonsense!" After which Gwen and Adrian were free to go on wherever they left off, if they could find the place.

She found it first. "Yes—I know. 'Beldam, crone, hag, or dowdy!' Of course. What I mean is—if it dawned on you that you were mistaken about my identity . . . I want you to be serious, because the thing is possible . . . what would you do?"

"There are so many *supposes*. Suppose you hated me and I thought you a beldam! Practice would seem to suggest fresh fields and pastures new. . . . But oh, the muddy, damp fields and the desolate, barren pastures. . . . I know one thing I should do. I should wish myself back here in the dark, with my feet spoiling the sofa cushion, and my head in the lap of my dear delusion—my heavenly delusion. God avert my disillusionment! I would not have my eyesight back at the price."

"Don't get excited! Remember we are only pretending."

"Not at all! I am being serious, because the thing is possible. Do you know I can imagine nothing worse than waking from a dream such as I have dreamt. It would be really *the worst*— worse than if *you* were to die, or change. . . ."

"I can't see that."

"Clearly. I should not have the one great resource."

"What resource? . . . Oh, I see!—you are working round to suicide. I thought we should come to that."

"Naturally, one who is not alive to fhe purely imaginary evil of non-existence turns to his *felo de se* as his sheet-anchor. Persons who conceive that the large number of non-existent persons have a legitimate grievance, on the score of never having been created at all, will think otherwise. We must agree to differ."

"But how very unreasonable of you not to kill yourself!—I mean in the case of my not—not visualising well. . . ."

"Quite the reverse. Most reasonable. We are supposing three courses open to Destiny. One, to kill you, lawlessly—Destiny being notoriously lawless. Another to make you change your mind. A third to make me change mine. The reasonableness of suicide in the first case is obvious, if Death is not annihilation. I should catch you up. In the second, all the Hereafters in the Universe would be no worse for me than Life in the dark, without you, here and now. In the third case I should have no one but myself to thank for a weak concession to Destiny, and it would be most unfair to kill myself without your consent, freely given. And I am by no means sure that by giving that consent you would not be legally an accomplice in my *felo de se*. Themis is a colossal Meddlesome Matty with her fingers in every pie."

"Bother Themis! What a lot of nonsense! However, there was one gleam of reason. You are alive to the fact that I should not consent to your suicide. Or anyone else's. *I* think it's wrong to kill oneself."

"So do I. But it might be a luxury I should not deny myself under some circumstances. I don't know that Hamlet would influence me. A certain amount of nervousness about Eternity is inseparable from our want of authentic information. I should hope for a healthy and effectual extinction. Failing that, I should disclaim all responsibility. I should point out that it lay, not with me, but my Maker. I should dwell on the fact that Creators that make Hereafters are alone answerable for the consequences; that I had never been consulted as to my own wishes about birth and parentage; and that I should be equally contented to be annulled, and, as Mrs. Bailey would have said, ill-convenience nobody. . . ."

"Do you know why I am letting you go on?"

"Because of my Religious Tone? Because of my Good Taste? Or why?"

"Because I sometimes suspect you of being in earnest about suicide."

"I am quite in earnest."

"Very well, then. Now attend to me. I'm going to insist on your making me a promise."

"Then I shall have to make it. But I don't know till I hear it whether I shall promise to keep it."

"That's included."

"But no promise to keep my promise to keep it's included."

"Yes it is. If you keep on, I shall keep on. So you had better stop. What you've got to promise is not to commit suicide under any circumstances whatever."

"Not under any circumstances whatever? That seems to me rather harsh and arbitrary."

"Not at all. Give me your promise."

"H'm—well!—I'm an amiable, tractable sort of cove. . . . But I think I am entitled to one little reservation."

"It must be a very little one."

"Anything one gives one's *fiancée* is returned when she breaks one off. When you break me off I shall consider the promise given back—cancelled."

"Ye-es! Perhaps that *is* fair, on the whole. Only I think I deserve a small consideration for allowing it."

"I can't refuse to hear what it is."

"Give me that little bottle of Indian poison. To take care of for you, you know. I'll give it back if I break you off. Honour bright!"

"I shouldn't want it till then, probably. And if I did, I could afford sixpence for Prussic acid. Fancy being able to kill one-self, or one's friends, for sixpence! It must have come to a lot more than that in the Middle Ages. We have every reason to be thankful we are Modern. . . ."

"Don't go from the point. Will you give up the little bottle of Indian poison, or not?"

"Not. At least, not now! If I hand it to you at the altar, when you have led me there won't that do?"

Gwen considered, judicially, and appeared to be in favour of accepting the compromise. "Only remember!" said she, "if you don't produce that bottle at the altar—with the poison in it still; no cheating!—I shall cry off, in the very jaws of matrimony." She paused a moment, lest she should have left a flaw in the contract, then added:—"Whether I have led you there or not, you know! Very likely you will walk up the aisle by yourself."

If Adrian had really determined to conceal the Miss Scatcherd incident from Gwen, so as not to foster false hopes, he should have worded his reply differently. For no sooner had he said:—"Well—we are all hoping so," than Gwen exclaimed:—"*Then* there has been more Septimius Severus." Adrian accepted this without protest, as ordinary human speech; and the story feels confident that if its reader will be on the watch, he will very soon chance across something quite as unlike book-talk in Nature. Adrian merely said:—"How on earth did you guess that?"

Gwen replied:—" Because you said, 'We are all hoping so '—not 'We hope so.' Can't you see the difference?"

Anyway, Gwen's guess was an accomplished fact, and it was no use pretending it was wrong. Said Adrian therefore:—" Yes— there *was* a little more Septimius Severus. I had rather made up my mind not to talk about it, in case you should think too much of it." He then narrated the Miss Scatcherd incident, checked and corrected by Irene from afar. The narrator minimised the points in favour of his flash of vision, while his commentator's corrections showed an opposite bias.

Gwen was, strange to say, really uneasy about that little bottle of Indian poison. Whether there was anything prophetic in this uneasiness, it is difficult to determine. The decision of common sense will probably be that she knew that Poets were not to be trusted, and she wished to be on the safe side. By " common sense " we mean the faculty which instinctively selects the common prejudices of its age as oriflammes to follow on Life's battle-field. Hopkins the witch-finder's common sense suggested pricking all over to find an insensible flesh-patch, in which case the prickee was a witch. We prefer to keep an open mind about Lady Gwendolen Rivers' foreboding anent that little bottle of Indian poison, until vivisection has shown us, more plainly than at present, how brain secretes Man's soul. We are aware that this language is Browning's.

Gwen remained at Pensham until the end of the week. Events occurred, no doubt, but, with one exception, they are outside the story. That exception was a visit to Chorlton, in order that Adrian should not remain a stranger to the interesting old twins. His interest would have been stronger no doubt could he have really seen them. Even as it was he was keenly alive to the way in which old Mrs. Prichard seemed to have fascinated Gwen, and was eager to make as much acquaintance with her as his limitations left possible to him.

Gwen contrived to arrange that she should receive every day from Chorlton not only a line from Ruth Thrale, but an official bulletin from Dr. Nash.

The first of these despatches arrived on the Tuesday afternoon, she having told her correspondents that that would be soon enough. It disappointed her. She had left the old lady so much revived by the small quantity of provisions that did duty for a Sunday dinner, that she had jumped to the conclusion that another day would see her sitting up before the fire as she had seen her in the celebrated chair with cushions at Sapps Court. It was therefore rather a damper to be told by Dr. Nash that he had felt that absolute rest continued necessary, and that he had not been able to sanction any attempt to get Mrs. Prichard up for any length of time.

Gwen turned for consolation to Widow Thrale's letter. It was a model of reserve—would not say too much. "My mother" had talked a good deal with herself and "mother" till late, but had slept fairly well, and if she was tired this morning it was no more than Dr. Nash said we were to expect. She had had a "peaceful day" yesterday, talking constantly with "mother" of their childhood, but never referring to "my father" nor Australia. Dr. Nash had said the improvement would be slow. No reference was made to any possibility of getting her into her clothes and a return to normal life.

Gwen recognised the bearer of the letters, a young native of Chorlton, when she gave him the reply she had written, with a special letter she had ready for "dear old Mrs. Picture." "I know you," said she. "How's your Bull? I hope he won't kill Farmer Jones or anyone while you're not there to whistle to him." To which the youth answered:—"Who-ap not! Sarve they roi-ut, if they dwoan't let un bid in a's stall. A penned un in afower a coomed away." Gwen thought to herself that life at Jones's farm must be painfully volcanic, and despatched the Bull's guardian genius on his cob with the largest sum of money in his pocket that he had ever possessed in his life, after learning his name, which was Onesimus.

When Onesimus reappeared with a second despatch on the afternoon of the next day, Wednesday, Gwen opened it with a beating heart in a hurry for its contents. She did as one does with letters containing news, reading persistently through to the end and taking no notice at all of Irene's interrogatory "Well?" which of course was uttered long before the quickest reader could master the shortest letter's contents. When the end came, she said with evident relief:—"Oh yes, *that's* all *right!* Now if we drive over to-morrow, she will probably be up."

"Is that what the letter says?" Adrian spoke, and Gwen, saying:—"He won't believe my report, you see! You read it!"—threw the letter over to Irene, who read it aloud to her brother, while Gwen looked at the other letter, from Widow Thrale.

What Irene read did not seem so very conclusive. Mrs. Prichard had had a better night, having slept six hours without a break. But the great weakness continued. If she could take a very little stimulant it would be an assistance, as it might enable her to eat more. But she had an unconquerable aversion to wine and spirits in any form, and Dr. Nash was very reluctant to force her against her will.

So said Adrian:—"What she wants is real turtle soup and champagne. *I* know." Whereupon his father, who was behind the *Times*—meaning, not the Age, but the "Jupiter" of our boyhood, looked over its title, and said:—"Champagne—champagne? There's plenty in the bin—end of the cellar—Tweedie knows. You'll find my keys on the desk there"—and went back to an absorbing leader, denouncing the defective Commissariat in the Crimea. A moment later, he remembered a thing he had forgotten—his son's blindness. "Stop a minute," he said. "I have to go, myself, later, and I may as well go now." And presently was heard discussing cellar-economics, afar, with Tweedie the butler.

The lady of the house wanted the carriage and pair next day to drive over to Foxbourne in the afternoon and wait to bring her back after the meeting. The story merely gives the bold wording used to notify the fact: it does not know what Foxbourne was, nor why there was a meeting. Its only reason for referring to them is that the party for Chorlton had to change its plans and go by the up-train from St. Everall's to Grantley Thorpe, and make it stop there specially. St. Everall's, you may remember, is the horrible new place about two miles from Pensham. The carriage could take them there and be back in plenty of time, and there was always a groggy old concern to be had at the Crown at Grantley that would run them over to Strides Cottage in half an hour. If it had been favourable weather, no doubt the long drive would have been much pleasanter; but with the chance of a heavy downfall of snow making the roads difficult, the short drives and short railway journey had advantages.

Therefore when the groggy old concern, which had seen better days—early Georgian days, probably—pulled up at Strides Cottage in the afternoon, with a black pall of cloud, whose white heralds were already coming thick and fast ahead of it, hanging over Chorlton Down, two at least of the travellers who alighted from it had misgivings that if their visit was a prolonged one, its grogginess and antiquity might stand in its way on a thick-snowed track in the dark, and might end in their being late for the down-train at six. The third of their number saw nothing, and only said:—"Hullo—snowing!" when on getting free of the concern one of the heralds aforesaid perished to convince him of its veracity; gave up the ghost between his shirt-collar and his epidermis. "Yes," he continued, addressing the first inhabitant of the cottage who greeted him. "You are quite right. I am the owner of a dog, and you do perfectly right to inquire about him. His nose is singularly unlike yours. He will detect your flavour when I return, and I shall have to allay his jealousy. It is his fault. We are none of us perfect." The dog gave a short bark which might have meant that Adrian had better hold his tongue, as anything he said might be used against him.

"Now you are in the kitchen and sitting-room I've told you of, because it's both," said Gwen. "And here is Granny Marrable herself."

"Give me hold of your hand, Granny. Because I can't see you, more's the pity! I shall hope to see you some day—like people when they want you not to call. At present my looks don't flatter me. People think I'm humbugging when I say I can't see them. I *can't!*"

"'Tis a small wonder, sir," said Granny Marrable, "people should be hard of belief. I would not have thought you could not, myself. But being your eyes are spared, by God's mercy, they be ready for the sight to return, when His will is."

"That's all, Granny. It's only the sight that's wanting. The eyes are as good as any in the kingdom, in themselves." This made Gwen feel dreadfully afraid Granny Marrable would think the gentleman was laughing at her. But Adrian had taken a better measure of the Granny's childlike simplicity and directness than hers. He ran on, as though it was all quite right. "Anyhow, don't run away from us to Kingdom Come just yet a while, Granny, and see if I don't come to see you and your sister—real eyesight, you know; not this make-believe! I hope she's picking up."

"She's better—because Dr. Nash says she's better. Only I wish it would come out so we might see it. But it may be I'm a bit impatient. 'Tis the time of life does it, no doubt."

Ruth Thrale returned from the inner room. "She would like her ladyship to go to her," said she. Gwen could not help noticing that somehow—Heaven knows how, but quite perceptibly—the next room seemed to claim for itself the status of an invalid chamber. She accompanied Widow Thrale, who closed the room-door behind her, apparently to secure unheard speech in the passage. "She isn't any *worse,* you know," said Ruth, in a reassuring manner, which made her hearer look scared, and start. "Only when she gets away to thinking of beyond the seas—that place where she was—that *is* bad for her, say how we may! Not that she minds talking of my father, nor my brother that died, nor any tale of the land and the people; but 'tis the coming back to make it all fit."

Gwen quite understood this, and re-worded it, for elucidation. "Of course everything clashes, and the poor old dear can't make head or tail of it! Has there been any particular thing, lately?" The reply was:—"Yes—early this morning. She woke up talking about Mrs. Skillick, the name sounded like, and how kind she was to bring her the fresh lettuces. And then she found me by her and knew I was Ruth, but was all in a maze why! Then it all seemed to come on her again, and she was in a bad upset for a while. But I did not tell mother of that. I am glad you have come, my lady. It will make her better."

"Skillick wasn't Australia," said Gwen. "It was some person she lived with here in England—not so long ago. Somewhere near London. What did you do to quiet her?"

"I talked to her about Dave and Dolly. That is always good for her—it seems to steady her. Shall we go in, my lady? I think she heard you." Again Gwen had an impression that concession had been made to the inexorable, and that whereas four days ago it was taken for granted that old Mrs. Picture's collapse was only to be temporary, a permanency of invalidism was now accepted as a working hypothesis. Only a temporary permanency, of course, to last till further notice!

CHAPTER XXIV

HOW GWEN INTRODUCED MR. TORRENS, AND MRS. PICTURE TOOK HOLD OF HIS HAND. OF MR. TORRENS'S FIRM FAITH IN DEVILS, AND OLD MAISIE'S HAPPINESS THEREAT. THE DOCTOR'S MEMORY OF ADRIAN'S FIRST APPEARANCE AS A CORPSE. THE LAXITY OF GENERAL PRACTITIONERS. HIS WISH TO INTOXICATE MRS. PRICHARD. HOW GWEN SANG GLUCK TO ADRIAN, AND ONESIMUS BROUGHT HER A LETTER. QUITE A GOOD REPORT. HOW GWEN WASN'T ANXIOUS. OF ADRIAN'S INVISIBLE MOTHER. HER SELECTNESS, AND HIGH BREEDING. ADRIAN'S VIEWS ABOUT SUICIDES. SURVIVORS' SELFISHNESS TOWARDS THEM. HOW HE TALKED ABOUT THAT DEVIL, AND LET OUT THAT THE OLD LADY HAD FLASHED ACROSS HIS RETINA. HOW HE HAD CLOTHED EACH TWIN'S HEAD WITH THE OTHER'S HAIR

HAS it not been the experience of all of us, many a time, that a few days' clear absence from an invalid has been needed, to dis-

tinguish a slow change, invisible to the watchers by the bedside?
And all the while, have not the daily bulletins made out a case
for indefinable slight improvements, negligible gains scarcely worth
naming, whose total some mysterious flaw of calculation persistently calls loss?

There may have been very little actual change; there was room
for so little. But Gwen had been building up hopes of an improvement. And now she had to see her house of cards tremble
and portend collapse. She saved the structure—as one has done
in real card-life—by gingerly removing a top storey, in terror of
a cataclysm. She would not hope so much—indeed, indeed!—
if Fate would only leave some of her structure standing. But
she was at fault for a greeting, all but a disjointed word or
two, when Ruth, falling back, left her to enter the bedroom
alone.

It was a consolation to hear the old lady's voice. "My dear—
my dear—I knew you would come. I woke in the night, and
thought to myself—she will come, my lady. Then I rang, and my
Ruth came. She comes so quick."

"And then that was just as good as me," said Gwen.
"Wasn't it?"

"She is my child—my Ruth. And Phœbe is my Phœbe—years
ago! But I have to think so much, to make it all fit. You are
not like that.'

"What am I like?"

"You are the same all through. You came upstairs to me
in my room—did you not?—where my little Dave and Dolly
were. . . ."

"Yes—I fetched Dolly."

"And then you put Dolly down? And I said for shame!—
what a big girl to be carried!'

"Yes—and Dolly was carrying little dolly, with her eyes wide
open. And when I put her down on the floor, she repeated what
you said all over again, to little dolly:—'For same, what a bid
dirl to be tallied!'"

A gleam came on old Maisie's face as she lay there letting the
idea of Dolly soak into her heart. Presently she said, without
opening her eyes:—"I wonder, if Dolly lives to be eighty, will
she remember old Mrs. Picture. I should like her to. Only she *is*
small."

"Dear Mrs. Picture, you are talking as if you were not to have
Dolly again. Don't you remember what I told you on Sunday?
I'm going to get both the children down here, and Aunt M'riar.

Unless, when you are better, you like to go back to Sapps Court.
You shall, you know!"

Another memory attacked old Maisie. "Oh dear," said she,
"I thought our Court was all tumbled down. Was it not?"
"Yes—the day I came. And then I carried you off to Cavendish Square. Don't you remember?—where Miss Grahame was
—Sister Nora." She went on to tell of the promptitude and effi-
ciency with which the repairs had been carried out. For, strange
to say, the power Mr. Bartlett possessed of impressing Europe with
his integrity and professional ability had extended itself to Gwen,
a perfect stranger, during that short visit to the Court, and she was
mysteriously ready to vouch for his sobriety and good faith.
Presently old Maisie grew curious about the voices in the next
room.

"Is that a gentleman's voice, through the door, talking? It
isn't Dr. Nash. Dr. Nash doesn't laugh like that."

"No—that is my blind man I have brought to see you. I told
you about him, you know. But he must not tire you too much."

"But *can* he see me?"

"I didn't mean *see,* that way. I meant see to talk to. Some
day he will *really* see you—with his eyes. We are sure of it, now.
He shall come and sit by you, and talk."

"Yes—and I may hold his hand. And may I speak to him
about . . . about . . ."

"About his blindness and the accident? Oh dear yes! *You*
won't *see* that he's blind, you know."

"His eyes look like eyes?'

"Like beautiful eyes. I shall go and fetch him." She knew
she was straining facts in her prediction of their recovery of sight,
but she liked the sound of her own voice as she said it, though she
knew she would not have gone so far except to give her hearer
pleasure.

Said old Maisie to Adrian, whom Gwen brought back to sit by her,
giving him the chair she had occupied beside the bed:—"You, sir,
are very happy! But oh, how I grieve for your eyes!"

"Is Lady Gwendolen here in the room still?" said Adrian.

"She has just gone away, to the other room," said old Maisie.
For Gwen had withdrawn. One at a time was the rule.

"Very well, dear Mrs. Picture. Then I'll tell you. There never
was a better bargain driven than mine. I would not have my eyesight back, to lose what I have got. No—not for fifty pairs of
eyes." And he evidently meant it.

"May I hold your hand?"

"Do. Here it is. I am sure you are a dear old lady, and can see what she is. When I had eyes, I never saw anything worth looking at, till I saw Gwen."

"But is it a rule?"

Adrian was perplexed for a moment. "Oh, I see what you mean," said he. "No—of course not! I may have my eyesight back." Then he seemed to speak more to himself than to her. "Men *have* been as fortunate, even as that, before now."

"But tell me—is that what the doctor says? Or only guessing?"

"It's what the doctor says, and guessing too. Doctors only guess. He's guessing."

"But don't they guess right, oftener than people?"

"A little oftener. If they didn't, what use would they be?"

"But you have seen *her?*"

"Yes—once! Only once. And now I know she is there, as I saw her. . . . But I want to know about you, Mrs. Picture dear. Because I'm so sorry for you."

"There is no need for sorrow for me, I am so happy to know my sister was not drowned. And my little girl I left behind when I went away over the great sea, and the wind blew, and I saw the stars change each night, till they were all new. And then I found my dear husband, and lived with him many, many happy years. God has been good to me, for I have had much happiness." There was nothing but contentment and rest in her voice; but then some of the tranquillity may have been due to exhaustion.

Adrian made the mistake of saying:—"And all the while you thought your sister dead."

He felt a thrill in her hand as it tightened on his, and heard it in her voice. "Oh, could it have been?" she said. "But I was told so—in a letter."

It was useless for Adrian to affect ignorance of the story; and, indeed, that would have made matters worse, for it would have put it on her to attempt the retelling of it.

Perhaps he did his best to say:—"Lady Gwendolen has told me the whole story. So I know. Don't think about it! . . . Well—that's nonsense! One can't help thinking. I mean—think as little as possible!" It did not mend matters much.

Her mind had got back to the letter, and could not leave it. "I have to think of it," she said, "because it was my husband that wrote that letter. I know why he wrote it. It was not himself. It was a devil. It came out of Roomoro the black witch-doctor and got a place inside my husband. *He* did not write that letter to Phœbe. *It* wrote it. For see how it had learned all the story when Roomoro sucked the little scorpion's poison out of Mary Ann Stennis's arm!"

To Adrian all this was half-feverish wandering; the limited delirium of extreme weakness. No doubt these were real persons —Roomoro and Mary Ann Stennis. It was their drama that was fictitious. He saw one thing plainly. It was to be humoured, not reasoned with. So whatever was the cause of a slight start and disconcertment of his manner when she stopped to ask suddenly:— " But you do not believe in devils, perhaps? "—it was not the one she had ascribed it to. In fact he was quite ready with a semi-conscientious affirmative. " Indeed I do. Tell me exactly how you suppose it happened, again. Roomoro was a native conjurer or medicine-man, I suppose? "

Then old Maisie recapitulated the tale her imagination had constructed to whitewash the husband who had ruined her whole life, adding some details, not without an interest for students of folklore, about the devil that had come from Roomoro. She connected it with the fact that Roomoro had eaten the flesh of the little black Dasyurus, christened the " Native Devil " by the first Tasmanian colonists, from the excessive shortness of its temper. The soul of this devil had been driven from the witch-doctor by the poison of the scorpion, and had made for the nearest human organisation. Adrian listened with as courteous a gravity as either of us would show to a Reincarnationist's extremest doctrines.

It was an immense consolation to old Maisie, evidently, to be taken in such good faith. Having made up his mind that his conscience should not stand between him and any fiction that would benefit this dear old lady, Adrian was not going to do the thing by halves. He launched out into reminiscences of his own experiences on the Essequibo and elsewhere, and was able without straining points to' dwell on the remarkable similarities of the Magians of all primitive races. As he afterwards told Gwen, he was surprised at the way in which the actual facts smoothed the way for misrepresentation. He stuck at nothing in professions of belief in unseen agencies, good and bad; apologizing afterwards to Gwen for doing so by representing the ease of believing in them just for a short time, to square matters. Optional belief was no invention of his own, he said, but an ancient and honourable resource of priesthoods all the world over.

It was the only little contribution he was able to make towards the peace of mind without which it seemed almost impossible so old a constitution could rally against such a shock. And it was of real value, for old Maisie sorely needed help against her most awful discovery of all, the hideous guilt of the man whom she had loved ungrudgingly throughout. Nor was it only this. It palliated her son's crimes. But then there was a differnece between the son and the father. The latter had apparently done nothing to arouse his wife's detestation. Forgery is a delinquency—not a diabolism!

They talked more—talked a good deal in fact—but only of what we know. Then Gwen came back, bringing Irene to make acquaintance. This young lady behaved very nicely, but admitted afterwards that she had once or twice been a little at a loss what to say.

As when for instance the old lady, with her tender, sad, grey eyes fixed on Miss Torrens, said:—" Come near, my dear, that I may see you close." And drew her old hand, tremulously, over the mass of rich black hair which the almost nominal bonnet of that day left uncovered, with the reticular arrangement that confined it, and went on speaking, dreamily:—" It is very beautiful, but *my* lady's hair is golden, and shines like the sun." Thereon Gwen to lubricate matters:—" Yes—look here! But I know which I like best." She managed to collate a handful of her own glory of gold and her friend's rich black, in one hand. " I know which *I* like best," said Irene. And Gwen laughed her musical laugh that filled the place. " No head of hair is a prophet in its own country," said she.

Old Maisie was trying to speak, but her voice had gone low with fatigue. " Phœbe and I," she was saying, " long ago, when we were girls . . . It was a trick, you know, a game . . . we would mix our hair like that, and make little Jacky Wetherall guess whose hair he had hold of. When he guessed right he had sugar. He was three. His mother used to lend him to us when she went out to scrub, and he never cried. . . ." She went on like this, dwelling on scraps of her girlhood, for some time; then her voice went very faint to say:—" Phœbe was there then. Phœbe is back now—somehow—how is it? " Gwen saw she had talked enough, and took Irene away; and then Ruth Thrale went to sit with her mother.

Dr. Nash, who arrived during their absence, had been greeted by Adrian after his " first appearance as a corpse," last summer. He would have known the doctor's voice anywhere. " You never *were* a corpse," said that gentleman. To which Mr. Torrens replied:—" You *thought* I was a corpse, doctor, you know you did! " Dr. Nash, being unable to deny it, shifted the responsibility.

"Well," said he, "Sir Coupland thought so too. The fact is, we had quite given you up. When he came out and said to me:— 'Come back. I want you to see something,' I said to him:—'Is that why the dog barked?' Because your dog had given a sudden queer sort of a bark. And he said to me:—'It isn't only the dog. It's Lady Gwen Rivers.'"

"What did he mean by that?" said Gwen.

"He meant that your ladyship's strong impression that the body . . . Excuse my referring to you, Mr. Torrens, as . . ."

"As 'the body'? Not at all! I mean, don't apologize."

"The—a—subject, say, still retained vitality. No doubt we *might* have found out—probably *should* . . ."

"Stuff and nonsense!" said Gwen remorselessly. "You would have buried him alive if it hadn't been for me. You doctors are the most careless, casual creatures. It was me and the dog—so now Mr. Torrens knows what he has to be thankful for!"

"Well—as a matter of fact, it was the strong impression of your ladyship that did the job. We doctors are, as your ladyship says, an incautious, irresponsible lot. I hope you found Mrs. Prichard going on well."

Gwen hesitated. "I wish she looked a little—thicker," said she.

Dr. Nash looked serious. "We mustn't be in too great a hurry. Remember her age, and the fact that she is eating almost nothing. She won't take regular meals again—or what she calls regular meals—till the tension of this excitement subsides. . . ."

Said Adrian:—"It's perfectly extraordinary to me, not seeing her, to hear her talk as she does. Because it doesn't give the impression of such weakness as that. Her hands feel very thin, of course."

Said the doctor:—"I wish I could get her to take some stimulant; then she would begin eating again. If she could only be slightly intoxicated! But she's very obdurate on that point—I told you?—and refuses even Sir Cropton Fuller's old tawny port. I talked about her to him, and he sent me half a dozen the same evening. A good-natured old chap!—wants to make everyone else as dyspeptic as himself. . . ."

"That reminds me!" said Gwen. "We forgot the champagne."

"No, we didn't," said Irene. "It was put in the carriage, I know. In a basket. Two bottles lying down. And it was taken out, because I saw it."

"But *was* it put in the railway carriage?"

"I meant the railway carriage."

"I believe it's in the old Noah's Ark we came here in, all the while."

Granny Marrable said:—"I am sure there has nothing been brought into the Cottage. Because we should have seen. There is only the door through, to go in and out."

"You see, Dr. Nash," said Gwen, "when you said that in your letter, about her wanting stimulant, champagne immediately occurred to Sir Hamilton. So we brought a couple of bottles of the King of Prussia's favourite Clicquot, and a little screwy thing to milk the bottles with, like a cow, a glass at a time. Miss Torrens and I are quite agreed that very often one can get quite pleasantly and healthily drunk on champagne when other intoxicants only give one a headache and make one ill. Isn't it so, 'Re?'" Miss Torrens and her brother both testified that this was their experience, and Dr. Nash assented, saying that there would at least be no harm in trying the experiment.

As for dear old Granny Marrable, her opinion was simply that whatever her ladyship from the Towers, and the young lady from Pensham and her brother, were agreed upon, was beyond question right; and even if medical sanction had not been forthcoming she would have supported them. "I am sure," said she, "my dear sister will drink some when she knows your ladyship brought it for her."

The reappearance of the Noah's Ark, when due, confirmed Gwen's view as to the whereabouts of the basket, and was followed by a hasty departure of the gentlefolks to catch the downtrain from London. As Granny Marrable watched it lurching away into the fast-increasing snow, it looked, she thought, as if it could not catch anything. But if old Pirbright, who had been on the road since last century, did not know, nobody did.

The day after this visit, when Gwen was singing to Adrian airs from Gluck's "Alceste," Irene and her father being both absent on Christmas business, social or charitable, the butler brought in a letter from Ruth Thrale in the very middle of a *sostenuto* note,— for when did any servant, however intelligent, allow music to stop before proceeding to extremities?—and said, respectfully but firmly, that it was the same boy, and he would wait. He seemed to imply that the boy's quality of identity was a sort of guarantee of his waiting—a good previous character for permanency. Gwen left "Alceste" in C minor, and opened her letter, thanking Mr. Tweedie cordially, but not able to say he might go, because he was another family's butler. Adrian said:—"Is that from the old

lady?" And when Gwen said:—"Yes—it's Onesimus. I wonder
he was able to get there, over the snow,"—he dismissed Mr. Tweedie
with the instruction that he should see that Onesimus got plenty
to eat. The butler ignored this instruction as superfluous, and
died away.

Then Gwen spun round on the music-stool to read aloud.
"'Honoured lady';—Oh dear, I wish she could say 'dear Gwen';
but I suppose it wouldn't do.—'I am thankful to be able to write
a really good report of my mother' . . . You'll see in a minute
she'll have to speak of Granny Marrable and she'll call her
'mother' without the 'my.' See if she doesn't! . . . 'Dr. Nash
said she might have some champagne, and we said she really must
when you so kindly brought it. So she said indeed yes, and we
gave it her up to the cuts.' That means," said Gwen, "the cuts
of the wineglass." She glanced on in the letter, and when Adrian
said:—"Well—that's not all!"—apologized with:—"I was looking on ahead, to see that she got some more later. It's all right.
'. . . up to the cuts, and presently, as Dr. Nash said, was minded
to eat something. So I got her the sweetbread she would not have
for dinner, which warmed up well. Then we persuaded her to take
a little more champagne, but Dr. Nash said be careful for fear of
reaction. Then she was very chatty and cheerful, and would go
back a great deal on old times with mother . . .' I told you she
would," said Gwen, breaking off abruptly.

"Of course she will always go back on old times," said Adrian.

"I didn't mean that. I meant call her aunt 'mother' without
the 'my.' Let me go on. Don't interrupt! '. . . old times with
mother, and one thing in particular, their hair. Mother pleased
her, because she could remember a little child Jacky they would
puzzle to tell which hair was which, saying if she held them like
that Jacky could tell, and have sugar. For their hair now is quite
strong white and grey instead of both the same. . . .' She was
telling us about Jacky—me and Irene—yesterday, and I suppose
that was what set her off. . . . 'She slept very sound and talked,
and then slept well at night. So we are in good spirits about her,
and thank God she may be better and get stronger. That is all
I have to tell now and remain dutifully yours. . . .' Isn't that delightful? Quite a good report!" Instructions followed to Onesimus not to bring any further news to Pensham, but to take his
next instalment to the Towers.

These things occurred on the Friday, the day after the visit to
Chorlton. Certainly that letter of Widow Thrale's justified Lady
Gwendolen in feeling at ease about Mrs. Picture during the re-

mainder of her visit to Pensham, and the blame she apportioned to herself for an imagined neglect afterwards was quite undeserved.

Adrian Torrens ought to have been in the seventh heaven during the remainder of an almost uninterrupted afternoon. Not that it was absolutely uninterrupted, because evidences of a chaperon in abeyance were not wanting. A mysterious voice, of unparalleled selectness, or *bon-ton,* or gentility, emanated from a neighbouring retreat with an accidentally open door, where the lady of the house was corresponding with philanthropists in spite of interruptions. It said:—"What *is* that? I know it *so* well," or, "That air is very familiar to me," or, "I cannot help thinking Catalani would have taken that slower." To all of which Gwen returned suitable replies, tending to encourage a belief in her questioner's mind that its early youth had been passed in a German principality with Kapellmeisters and Conservatoriums and a Court Opera Company. This excellent lady was in the habit of implying that she had been fostered in various *anciens régimes,* and that the parentage of anything so outlandish and radical as her son and daughter was quite out of her line, and a freak of Fate at the suggestion of her husband.

Intermittent emanations from Superiority-in-the-Bush were small drawbacks to what might perhaps prove the last unalloyed interview of these two lovers before their six months' separation —that terrible Self-Denying Ordinance—to which they had assented with a true prevision of how very unwelcome it would be when the time came. It was impossible to go back on their consent now. Gwen might have hoisted a standard of revolt against her mother. But she could not look her father in the face and cry off from the fulfilment of a condition-precedent of his consent to the perfect freedom of association of which she and Adrian had availed themselves to the uttermost, always under the plea that the terms of the contract were going to be honourably observed. As for Adrian, he was even more strongly bound. That appeal from the Countess that his father had repeated and confirmed was made direct to his honour; and while he could say unanswerably:—"What would you have me do?" nothing in the world could justify his rebelling against so reasonable a condition as that their sentiments should continue reciprocal after six months of separation.

His own mind was made up. For his views about suicide, however much he spoke of them with levity, were perfectly serious. If he lost Gwen, he would be virtually non-existent already. The end would have come, and the thing left to put an end to would no longer be a Life. It would only be a sensibility to pain, with an ample supply of it. A bare bodkin would do the business, but did not recommend itself. The right proportion of Prussic Acid had much to say on its own behalf. It was cheap, clean, certain, and the taste of ratafia was far from unpleasant. But he had a lingering favourable impression of the Warroo medicine-man, whose faith in the efficacy and painlessness of his nostrum was evident, however much was uncertain in his version of its *provenance*.

As to any misgivings about awakening in another world, if any occurred to Adrian he had but one answer—he had *been dead*, and had found death unattended with any sort of inconvenience. Resuscitation had certainly been painful, but he did not propose to leave any possibility of it, this time. His death, *that* time, had been a sudden shock, followed instantly by the voice of Gwen herself, which he had recognised as the last his ears had heard. If Death could be so easily negotiated, why fuss? The only serious objection to suicide was its unpopularity with survivors. But were they not sometimes a little selfish? Was this selfishness not shown to demonstration by the gratitude—felt, beyond a doubt—to the suicide who weights his pockets when he jumps into mid-ocean, contrasted with the dissatisfaction, to say the least of it, which the proprietor of a respectable first-class hotel feels when a visitor poisons himself with the door locked, and engages the attention of the Coroner. There was Irene certainly—and others —but after all it would be a great gain to them, when the first grief was over, to have got rid of a terrible encumbrance.

Therefore Adrian was quite at his ease about the Self-Denying Ordinance; at least, if a clear resolve and a mind made up can give ease. He said not a word of his views and intentions beyond what the story has already recorded. What right had he to say anything to Gwen that would put pressure on her inclinations? Had he not really said too much already? At any rate, no more!

Nevertheless, the foregoing made up the background of his reflections as he listened to more "Alceste," resumed after a short note had been written for Onesimus to carry back over the frost-bound roads to Chorlton. And he was able to trace the revival in his mind of suicide by poison to Mrs. Picture's narration of the Dasyurus and the witch-doctor who had cooked and eaten its body. This fiction of her fever-ridden thoughts had set him a-thinking again of the Warroo conjurer. He had not repeated any of it to Gwen, lest she should be alarmed on old Maisie's behalf. For it had a very insane sound.

But after such a prosperous report of her condition, above all,

of the magical effect of that champagne, it seemed overnice to be
making a to-do about what was probably a mere effect of over-
heated fancy, such as the circumstances might have produced in
many a younger and stronger person. So when Alceste had provided her last soprano song, and the singer was looking for
"Ifigenia in Aulide," Adrian felt at liberty to say that old Mrs.
Picture's ideas about possession were very funny and interesting.

"Isn't it curious?" said Gwen. "She really believes it all, you
know, like Gospel. All that about the devil that had possession of
her husband! And how when he died, he passed his devil on to
his son, who was worse than himself."

"That's good, though," said Adrian. "Only she never told me
about the son. I had it all about the witch-doctor whose devil
came out because he couldn't fancy the little scorpion's flavour.
And all about the original devil—a sort of opossum they call a
devil. . . ."

"She didn't tell me about him."

"They've got one at the Zoological Gardens. He's an ugly customer. The keeper said he was a limb, if ever there was one.
The old lady evidently thought her idea that the doctor's devil was
this little beggar's soul, eaten up with his flesh, was indisputable.
I told her I thought it had every intrinsic possibility, and I'm
sure she was pleased. But the horror of her face when she spoke
of him was really . . ."

"Adrian!"

"What, dearest? Anything the matter?"

"Only the way you put it. It was so odd. 'The horror of
her face'! Just as if you had *seen* it!" Indeed, Gwen was looking quite disconcerted and taken aback.

"There now!" said Adrian. "See what a fool I am! I never
meant to tell of that. Because I thought it threw a doubt on
Scatcherd. I've been wanting to make the most of Scatcherd. I
never thought much of Septimius Severus. Anyone might have
said in my hearing that the bust was moved, and it was just as
I was waking. But I'll swear no one said anything about Scatcherd. Why—there *was* only Irene!"

Gwen went and sat by him on the sofa. "Listen, darling!"
said she. "I want to know what you are talking about. What
was it happened, and why did it throw a doubt on Miss Scatcherd?"

"It wasn't anything, either way, you know."

"I know. But what was it, that wasn't anything, either way?"

"It was only an impression. You mustn't attach any weight
to it."

"Are you going to tell what it was, or *not?*"

"Going to. Plenty of time! It was when the old lady began telling me about the devil. Her tone of conviction gave me a strong impression what she was looking like, and made an image of her flash across my retina. By which I mean, flash across the hole I used to see through when I had a retina. It was almost as strong and life-like as real seeing. But I knew it *wasn't.*"

"But how—how—how?" cried Gwen, excited. "*How* did you know that it wasn't?"

"Because of the very white hair. It was snow-white—the image's. I suppose I had forgotten which was which, of the two old ladies—had put the saddle on the wrong horse."

Gwen looked for a moment completely bewildered. "What on, earth, can, he, mean?" said she, addressing Space very slowly. Then, speaking as one who has to show patience with a stiff problem:—"Dearest man—dearest incoherency!—do try and explain. Which of the old ladies do you suppose has white hair, and which grey?"

"Old Granny Marrable, I thought."

"Yes—but which *hair?* Which? Which? Which?"

"White, I thought, not grey." Whereupon Gwen, seeing how much hung upon the impression her lover had been under hitherto about these two tints of hair, kept down a growing excitement to ask him quietly for an exact, undisjointed statement, and got this for answer:—"I have always thought of Granny Marrable's as snow-white, and the old Australian's as grey. Was that wrong?"

"Quite wrong! It's the other way round. The Granny's is grey and old Mrs. Picture's is silvery white."

Adrian gave a long whistle, for astonishment, and was silent. So was Gwen. For this was the third incident of the sort, and what might not happen? Presently he broke the silence, to say:—"At any rate, that leaves Scatcherd a chance. I thought if this was a make-up of my own, it smashed *her.*"

"Foolish man! There is more in it than that. You *saw* old Mrs. Picture. It was no make-up. . . . Well?" She paused for his reply.

It came after a studied silence, a dumbness of set purpose. "Oh why—why—is it always Mrs. Picture, or Scatcherd, or Septimius Severus? Why can it never be Gwen—Gwen—Gwen?"

The attenuated *chaperonage* of the lady of the house may have been moved by a certain demonstrativeness of her son's at this point, to say from afar:—"I *hope* we are going to have some 'Ifigenia in Aulide.' Because I *should* have enjoyed *that.*" Which carried an implication that the musical world had been palming off an inferior article on a public deeply impressible by the higher aspects of Opera.

CHAPTER XXV

HOW THE EARL ASKED AFTER THE OLD TWINS. MERENESS. RECUPERA
TIVE POWER. HOW THE HOUSEHOLD HAD ITS ANNUAL DANCE. HOW
THE COUNTESS HAD A CRACKED LIP. HOW WAS DR. TUXFORD SOMERS?
SIR SPENCER DERRICK. GENERAL RAWNSLEY. HE AND GWEN'S INTENDED
GREAT GRANDMOTHER-IN-LAW. GWEN HAD NEVER HAD TWINS BEFORE
THE FRENCH REVOLUTION. THE GENERAL'S BROTHER PHILIP. SUPER
ANNUATED COCKS AND HENS. HOW GWEN HAD DREAMED SHE WAS
TO MARRY A KETTLE-HOLDER. HOW MRS. LAMPREY HAD A LETTER
FOR GWEN, WHICH TOOK GWEN OFF TO CHORLTON AT MIDNIGHT

WHEN the Earl of Ancester came back to the Towers next day he certainly did look a little boiled down; otherwise, cheerful and collected. "I am quite prepared to endure another Christmas," said he resignedly to Gwen. "But a little seclusion and meditation is good to prepare one for the ordeal, and Bath certainly deserves the character everybody gives it, that you never meet anybody else there. I suppose Coventry and Jericho have something in common with Bath. I wonder if outcasts can be identified in either. Nothing distinguishes them in Bath from the favourites of Fortune. How are the old ladies?"

This was in the study, where the Earl and his daughter got a quiet ten minutes to recapitulate the story of each during the other's absence. It was late in the afternoon, two hours after his arrival from London. He had been there a day or two to make a show of fulfilling his obligations towards politics; had sat through a debate or two, and had taken part in a division or two, much to the satisfaction of his conscience. "But," said he to Gwen, "if you ask me which I have felt most interest in, your old ladies or the Foreign Enlistment Act, I should certainly say the old ladies." So it was no wonder his inquiry about them came early in this recapitulation.

Gwen found herself, to her surprise, committed to an apologetic tone about old Mrs. Picture's health, and maintaining that she was *really* better intrinsically, although evidently some person or persons unnamed must have said she was worse. She started on her report with every good-will to make it a prosperous one, and got entangled in some trivialities that told against her purpose. Perhaps her last letter to her father, written from Pensham on the night of her arrival there, had given too rose-coloured an account of her visit to Chorlton, and had caused the rather serious head-shake which greeted her admission that old Maisie was still a quasi-invalid, on her back from the merest—quite the merest—weakness. The Earl admitted that, as a general rule, weakness might be mere enough to be negligible; but then it should be the weakness of young and strong people, possessed of that delightful property "recuperative power," which does such wonders when it comes to the scratch. Never be without it, if you can help.

The episode of the champagne was reassuring, and gave Hope a helping hand. Moreover, Gwen had just got another letter from Ruth Thrale, brought by Onesimus the bull-cajoler, which gave a very good account on the whole, though one phrase had a damping effect. We were not "to rely on the champagne," as it was "not nourishment, but stimulus." She *must* be got to take food regularly, said Dr. Nash, however small the quantity. This seemed to suggest that she had fallen back on that vicious practice of starvation. But "my mother" was constantly talking with "mother" about old times, and it was giving "mother" pleasure.

"I wish," said Gwen, as her father went back to "Honoured Lady" for second reading, and possibly second impressions, "I wish that Dr. Nash had written separately. I want to know what he thinks, and I want to know what Ruth thinks. I can mix them up for myself."

The Earl read to the end, and suspended judgment, visibly. "Eighty-one!" said he. "And how did Granny Marrable take it? You never said in your letters."

"Because I did not see her. Dr. Nash told—at least, he tried to. But I told you about the little boy's letter. She knew it from that."

"I remember. . . . Well!—we must hope." And then they spoke of matters nearer home; the impending journey to Vienna; a perplexity created by a promise rashly given to Aunt Constance that she should be married from the Ancester town-residence—two things which clashed, for how could this wedding wait till the Countess's return?—and ultimately of Gwen's own prospects. Then she told her father the incident of Adrian's apparent vision of old Mrs. Picture, and both pretended that it was too slight to build upon; but both used it for a superstructure of private imaginings. Neither encouraged the other.

Adrian and his sister were to have returned with Gwen to the Towers to stay till Monday, which was Christmas Day, when their own plum-pudding and mistletoe would claim them at Pensham. This arrangement was not carried out, possibly in deference to the Countess, who was anxious to reduce to a minimum everything that tended to focus the public gaze on the lovers. Gwen was under a social obligation, inherited perhaps from Feudalism, to be present at the Servants' Ball, which would have been on Christmas Eve had that day not fallen on a Sunday. Hence the necessity for her return on the Saturday, and the interview with her father just recorded. The quiet ten minutes filled the half-hour between tea and dressing for a dinner which might prove a scratch meal in itself, but was distinguished by its sequel. A general adjournment was to follow to the great ball-room, which was given over without reserve on this occasion to the revellers and their friends from the environs; for at the Towers nothing was done by halves in those days. There the august heads of the household were expected to walk solemnly through a quadrille with the housekeeper and head butler. Mrs. Masham's and Mr. Norbury's sense of responsibility on these occasions can neither be imagined nor described. This great event made conscientious dressing for dinner more than usually necessary, however defective the excitement of the household might make the preparation and service thereof.

These exigencies were what limited Gwen's quiet ten minutes with her father within the narrow bounds of half an hour, leaving no margin at all for more than three words with her mother on her way to her own interview with Miss Lutwyche. She exceeded her estimate almost before her ladyship's dressing-room door had swung to behind her.

"Well, mamma dear, I hope you're satisfied."

"I am, my dear. At least, I am not dissatisfied. . . . Don't kiss me in front, please, because I have a little crack on the corner of my lip." The Countess accepted her daughter's *accolade* on an unsympathetic cheek-bone. "What are you referring to?"

"Why—Adrian not coming till to-morrow, of course. What did you suppose I meant?"

"I did not suppose. Some day you will live to acknowledge— I am convinced of it—that what your father and I thought best was dictated by simple common sense and prudence. I am sure Sir Hamilton will not misinterpret our motives. Nor Lady Torrens."

"He's a nice old Bart, the Bart. We are great friends. He likes it. He gets all the kissing for nothing. . . . What?"

The Countess may have contemplated some protest against the

pronounced ratification implied of fatherdom-in-law. She gave it up, and said:—"I was not going to say anything. Go on!"

The way in which these two guessed each other's thoughts was phenomenal. Gwen knew all about it. "Come, mamma!" said she. "You know the Bart would not have liked it half so much if I had been a dowdy."

"I cannot pretend to have thought upon the subject." If her ladyship threw a greater severity into her manner than the occasion seemed to call for, it was not merely because she disapproved of her beautiful daughter's want of *retenue*, or questionable style, or doubtful taste, or defective breeding. You must bear all the circumstances in mind as they presented themselves to her. Conceive what the "nice old Bart" had been to her over five-and-twenty years ago, when she herself was a dazzling young beauty of another generation! Think how strange it must have been, to hear the audacities of this new creature, undreamed of then, spoken so placidly through an amused smile, as she watched the firelight serenely from the arm-chair she had subsided on—an anchorage "three words" would never have warranted, even the most unbridled polysyllables. "Do you not think"—her dignified mamma continued—"you had better be getting ready for dinner? You are always longer than me."

"I'm going directly. Lutwyche is never ready. I suppose I ought to go, though. . . . You are not asking after my old lady, and I think you might."

"Oh yes," said her ladyship negligently. "I haven't seen you since you didn't go to church with me. How *is* your old lady?"

"You don't care, so it doesn't matter. How was Dr. Tuxford Somers?"

"My dear—don't be nonsensical! How can you expect me to gush over about an old person I have not so much as seen?" She added as an afterthought:—"However worthy she may be!"

"You could have seen her quite well, when she was here. Papa did. Besides, one can show a human interest, without gushing over."

"My dear, I hope I am never wanting in human interest. How is Mrs. . . . Mrs. . . . ?"

"Mrs. Prichard?"

"Yes—how is she? Is she coming back here?"

"Is it likely? Besides, she can't be moved."

"Oh—it's as bad as that!"

"My dear mamma, haven't I told you fifty times?" This was

not exactly the case; but it passed, in conversation. "The darling old thing was all but killed by being told . . ."

"By being told? . . . Oh yes, I remember! They were sisters, in Van Diemen's Land. . . . But she's better again now?"

"Yes—better. Oh, here's Starfield, and there's papa in his room. I can hear him. I must go."

At dinner that evening nobody was in any way new or remarkable, unless indeed Sir Spencer and Lady Derrick, who had been in Canada, counted. There was one guest, not new, but of interest to Gwen. Do you happen to remember General Rawnsley, who was at the Towers in July, when Adrian had his gunshot accident? It was he who was nearly killed by a Mahratta, at Assaye, when he was a young lieutenant. Gwen had issued orders that he should take her in to dinner, when she heard on her arrival that he had accepted her mother's invitation for Christmas.

Consider dinner despatched—the word is suitable, for an approach to haste was countenanced or tolerated, in consideration of the household's festivity elsewhere—and so much talking going on that the old General could say to Gwen without fear of being overheard:—"Now tell me some more about your fellow. . . . Adrian, isn't he? . . . He *is* your fellow, isn't he?—no compliments necessary?"

"He's my fellow, General, to you and all my *dear* friends. You saw him in July, I think?"

"Just saw him—just saw him! Hardly spoke to him—only a word or two. Your father took me in to see him, because I was in love with his great-grandmother, once upon a time."

"His *great*-grandmother, General? You must mean his grandmother."

"Not a bit of it, my dear! It's all quite right. I was a boy of eighteen. I'm eighty-four. Sixty-six years ago. If Mary Tracy was alive now, she'd make up to eighty-six. Nothing out of the way in that. She was a girl of twenty then."

"Was it serious, General?"

"God bless me, my dear, serious? I should rather think it was! Why—we ran away together, and went capering over the country looking for a parson to marry us! Serious? Rather! At least, it might have been."

"Oh, General, do tell me what came of it. Did you find the parson?"

"That was just it. We found the Rector of Threckingham—it was in Lincolnshire—and he promised to marry us in a week if he could find someone to give the bride away. He took possession of the young lady. Then a day or two after down comes Sir Marmaduke and Lady Tracy, black in the face with rage, and we were torn asunder, threatening suicide as soon as there was a chance. I was such a jolly innocent boy that I never suspected the Rector of treachery. Never guessed it at all! He told me thirty years after—a little more. Saw him when the Allied Sovereigns were in London—before Waterloo."

"And that young thing was Adrian's *great*-grandmother!" said Gwen. Then she felt bound in honour to add:—"She was old enough to know better."

"She didn't," said the General. "What's so mighty funny to me now is to think that all that happened about the time of the Revolution in Paris. Rather before."

Gwen's imagination felt the vertigo of such a rough grapple with the Past. These things make brains reel. "When my old twins were two little girls in lilac frocks," said she.

"Your *what?*" Perhaps it was no wonder—so Gwen said afterwards—that the General was a little taken aback. She would have been so very old to have had twins before the French Revolution. She was able to assign a reasonable meaning to her words, and the old boy became deeply interested in the story of the sisters. So much so that when the ladies rose to go, she said calmly to her mother:—"I'm not coming this time. You can all go, and I'll come when we have to start the dancing. I want to talk to General Rawnsley." And the Countess had to surrender, with an implication that it was the only course open in dealing with a lunatic. She could, however, palliate the position by a reference to the abnormal circumstances. "We are quite in a state of chaos to-day," said she to her chief lady-guest. And then to the Earl:— "Don't be more than five minutes. . . . Well!—no longer than you can help."

The moment the last lady had been carefully shut out by the young gentleman nearest the door, Gwen drove a nail in up to the head, *more suo*. Suppose General Rawnsley had lost a twin brother fifty years ago, and she, Gwen, had come to him and told him it had all been a mistake, and the brother was still living! What would that feel like? What would he have done?

"Asked for it all over again," said the General, after consideration. "Should have liked being told, you see! Shouldn't have cared so very much about the brother."

"No—do be serious! Try to think what it would have felt like. To oblige me!"

The General tried. But without much success. For he only

shook his head over an undisclosed result. He could, however, be serious. " I suppose," said he, " the twinnery—twinship—whatever you call it . . ."

" Isn't *de rigueur?* " Gwen struck in. " Of course it isn't! Any real fraternity would do as well. Now try! "

" That makes a difference. But I'm still in a fix. Your old ladies were grown up when one went off—and then she wrote letters? . . ."

" Can't you manage a grown-up brother? "

" Nothing over fourteen. Poor Phil was fourteen when he was drowned. Under the ice on the Serpentine. He had just been licking me for boning a strap of his skate. I was doing the best way I could without it . . . to get mine on, you see . . . when I heard a stop in the grinding noise—what goes on all day, you know—and a sort of clicky slooshing, and I looked up, and there were a hundred people under the ice, all at once. There was a f'ler who couldn't stop or turn, and I saw him follow the rest of 'em under. Bad sort of job altogether! " The General seemed to be enjoying his port, all the same.

Said Gwen:—" But he used to lick you, so you couldn't love him."

" Couldn't I? I was awfully fond of Phil. So was he of me. I expect Cain was very fond of Abel. They loved each other like brothers. Not like other people! "

" But Phil isn't a fair instance. Can't you do any better than Phil? Never mind Cain and Abel."

" H'm—no, I can't! Phil's not a bad instance. It's longer ago—but the same thing in principle. If I were to hear that Phil was really resuscitated, and some other boy was buried by mistake for him, I should . . . I should . . ." The General hung fire.

" What should you do? That's what I want to know. . . . Come now, confess—it's not so easy to say, after all! "

" No—it's not easy. But it would depend on the way how. If it was like the Day of Judgement, and he rose from the grave, as we are taught in the Bible, just the same as he was buried. . . . Well—you know—it wouldn't be fair play! *I* should know *him,* though I expect I should think him jolly small."

" But he wouldn't know you? "

" No. He would be saying to himself, who the dooce is this superannuated old cock? And it would be no use my saying I was his little brother, or he was my big one."

" But suppose it wasn't like the Day of Judgement at all, but

real, like my old ladies. Suppose he was another superannuated old
cock! My old ladies are superannuated old hens, I suppose."
" I suppose so. But I understand from what you tell me that
they *have* come to know one another again. They talk together
and recall old times? Isn't that so?"
" Oh dear yes, and each knows the other quite well by now.
Only I believe they are still quite bewildered about what has
happened."
" Then I suppose it would be the same with me and my redi-
vivus brother—on the superannuated-old-cock theory, not the Day
of Judgement one."
" Yes—but I want you not to draw inferences from *them,* but to
say what you would feel . . . of yourself . . . out of your own
head."
The General wanted time to think. The question required thought,
and he was taking it seriously. The Earl, seeing him thinking, and
Gwen waiting for the outcome, came round from his end of the
table, and took the seat the Countess had vacated. He ought to
have been there before, but it seemed as though Gwen's *escapade*
had thrown all formalities out of gear. He was just in time for the
General's conclusion:—" Give it up! Heaven only knows what I
should do! Or anyone else!"
Gwen restated the problem, for her father's benefit. " I am with
you, General," said he. " I cannot speculate on what I should do.
I am inclined to think that the twinship has had something to do
with the comparative rapidity of the . . . recohesion. . . ."
" Very good word, papa! Quite suits the case."
" . . . recohesion of these two old ladies. When we consider
how very early in life they took their meals together . . ." The
General murmured *sotto voce:*—" Before they were born." " . . . we
must admit that their case is absolutely exceptional—absolutely!"
" You mean," said Gwen, " that if they had not been twins they
would not have swallowed each other down, as they have done."
" Exactly," said the Earl.
" And yet," Gwen continued, " they never remember things as
they happened. In fact, they are still in a sort of fog about what
has happened. But they are quite sure they are Maisie and Phœbe.
I do think, though, there is only one thing about Maisie's Australian life that Granny Marrable believes, and that is the devil
that got possession of the convict husband. . . . *Why* does she?
Because devils are in the Bible, of course." Here the devil story
was retold for the benefit of the General, who did not know it.
The Earl did, so he did not listen. He employed himself think-

ing over practicable answers to the question before the house, and
was just in time to avert a polemic about the authenticity of the
Bible, a subject on which the General held strong views. "What
helps me to an idea of a possible attitude of mind before a resurrection of this sort," he said, "is what sometimes happens when
you wake up from a dream years long, a dream as long as a lifetime. Just the first moment of all, you can hardly believe yourself
free of the horrid entanglement you had got involved in. . . ."

"I know," said Gwen. "The other night I dreamed I was going
to be married to a young gentleman I had known from childhood.
Only he was a kettle-holder with a parrot on it."

"Didn't I object?" said the Earl.

"You were upstairs. Don't ask explanations. That was all
there was in the dream. You were upstairs. And the dream had
been all my life. Don't fidget about particulars."

"I won't. That's the sort of dream I mean. It seems all perfectly right and sound until your waking life comes back, and
then vanishes. You only regret your friends in the dream for a
few seconds, and then—they are nobody!"

"Don't quite see the parallel, yet. These old ladies haven't
waked from a dream, that I see." Thus the General, and Gwen
told him he was a military martinet, and lacking in insight.

Her father continued:—"Each of them has dreamed the other
was dead, for half a century. *Now* they are awake. But I suspect,
from what Gwen says, that the discovery of the dream has thrown
a doubt on all the rest of the fifty years."

"That's it," said Gwen. "If the whole story of the two deaths
is false, why should Van Diemen's Land be true? Why should the
convict and the forgery be true?"

"Husbands and families are hard nuts to crack," said the General. "Can't be forgotten or disbelieved in, try 'em any side up!"

At this point a remonstrance from the drawing-room at the delay of the appearance of the males caused a stampede and ended
the discussion. Gwen rejoined her own sex unabashed, and the
company adjourned to the scene of the household festivity. It is
not certain that the presence of his lordship and his Countess, and
the remainder of the party *in esse* at the Towers really added to the
hilarity of the occasion. But it was an ancient usage, and the
sky might have fallen if it had been rashly discontinued. The
compromise in use at this date under which the magnates, after
walking through a quadrille, melted away imperceptibly to their
normal quarters, was no doubt the result of a belief on their part
that the household would begin to enjoy itself as soon as formali-

ties had been complied with, and it was left to do so at its own free-will and pleasure. Nevertheless, a hint at abolition would have been blasphemy, and however eager the rank and file of the establishment may have been for the disappearance of the bigwigs, not one of them—and still more not one of their many invited neighbours—ever breathed a hint of it to another.

Shortly after ten Gwen and some of the younger members of the party wound up a fairly successful attempt to make the materials at their disposal dance the Lancers, and got away without advertising their departure. It was a great satisfaction to overhear the outbreak of unchecked roystering that followed. Said Gwen to Miss Dickenson and Mr. Pellew, who had entered into the spirit of the thing and co-operated with her efforts to the last:—" They will be at bear-garden point in half an hour. Poor respectable Masham!" To which Aunt Constance replied:—" I suppose they won't go on into Sunday?" The answer was:—" Oh no—not till Sunday! But Sunday is a *day*, after all, not a night." Mr. Pellew said:—" Sunrise at eight," and Gwen said:—" I think Masham will make it Sunday about two o'clock. We shan't have breakfast till eleven. You'll see!"

They were in the great gallery with the Van Dycks when Gwen stopped, as one stops who thinks suddenly of an omission, and said, as to herself, more than to her hearers:—" I wonder whether she meant me."

" Whether who meant you?" said both, sharing the question.

" Nothing . . . Very likely I was mistaken. . . . No—it was this. You saw that rather *piquante*, dry young woman? You know which I mean?"

" Danced with that good-looking young groom? . . ."

" Yes—my Tom—Tom Kettering. It was what I heard her say to Lutwyche . . . some time ago. . . . ' Remember she's not to have it till to-morrow morning.' It just crossed my mind, did she mean me? I dare say it was nothing."

" I heard that. It was a letter." Mr. Pellew said this.

" Had you any impression about it?"

" I thought it was some joke among the servants."

Gwen was disquieted, evidently. " I wish I hadn't heard it," said she, " if it isn't to be delivered till to-morrow. That young woman is Dr. Nash's housekeeper—Dr. Nash at Chorlton." She was speaking to ears that had heard all about the twin sisters. She interrupted any answer that meant to follow " Oh!" and " H'm!" by saying abruptly:—" I must see Lutwyche and find out."

They turned with her, and retraced their steps, remarking that no doubt it was nothing, but these things made one uncomfortable. Much better to find out, and know!

A casual just entering to rejoin the revels stood aside to allow them to pass, but was captured and utilised. " Go in and tell Miss Lutwyche I want to speak to her out here." Gwen knew all about local class distinctions, and was aware her maid would not be "Lutwyche" to a village baker's daughter. The girl, awed into some qualification of mere assent, which might have been presumptuous, said:—" Yes, my lady, if you please."

Lutwyche was captured and came out. " What was it I was not to have till to-morrow morning, Lutwyche? You know quite well what I mean. What was the letter?"

The waiting-woman had a blank stare in preparation, to prevaricate with, but had to give up using it. " Oh yes—there was a note," she said. " It was only a note. Mrs. Lamprey brought it from Dr. Nash. He wished your ladyship to have it to-morrow."

" I will have it at once, thank you! Have you got it there? Just get it, and bring it to me at once."

" I hope your ladyship does not blame me. I was only obeying orders."

" Get it, please, and don't talk." Her ladyship was rather incensed with the young woman, but not for obeying orders. It was because of the attempt to minimise the letter. It was just like Lutwyche. Nothing would make that woman *really* truthful!

Lutwyche caught up the party, which had not stopped for the finding of the letter, at the drawing-room door. Gwen opened it as she entered the room, saying, to anyone within hearing:— " Excuse my reading this." She dropped on a sofa at hand, close to a chandelier rich with wax lights in the lampless drawing-room. Percy Pellew and his *fiancée* stood waiting to share the letter's contents, if permitted.

The world, engaged with its own affairs, took no notice. The Earl and the General were listening to tales of Canada from Sir Spencer Derrick. The Countess was pretending to listen to other versions of the same tales from that gentleman's wife. The others were talking about the war, or Louis Napoleon, or Florence Nightingale, or hoping the frost would continue, because nothing was more odious than a thaw in the country. One guest became very unpopular by maintaining that a thaw had already set in, alleging infallible instincts needing no confirmation from thermometers.

The Countess had said, speaking at her daughter across the room:—" I hope we are going to have some music; " and the Colonel had said:—" Ah, give us a song, Gwen; " without eliciting any notice from their beautiful hearer, before anyone but Miss Dickenson and Mr. Pellew noticed the effect this letter was producing. Then the Earl, glancing at the reader's face, saw even from where he sat, how white it had become, and how tense was its expression. He caught Mr. Pellew's attention. "Do you know what it is, Percy?" said he. Mr. Pellew crossed the room quickly, to reply under his breath:—"I am afraid it is some bad news of her old lady at Chorlton. . . . Oh no—not *that*"—for the Earl had made the syllable *dead* with his lips, inaudibly—"but an alarm of some sort. The doctor's housekeeper there brought the letter."

The Earl left Mr. Pellew, reiterating what he had said to the General, and went over to his daughter. "Let me have it to see," said he, and took the letter from her. He read little scraps, half-aloud, "'Was much better all yesterday, but improvement has not continued.' . . . 'Am taking advantage of my housekeeper's visit to the Towers to send this.' . . . 'Not to have it till to-morrow.' . . . How was that?" Gwen explained briefly, and he said:— "Looks as if the doctor took it for granted you would come at once."

"Yes," said Gwen, "on receipt of the letter."

The Countess said, as one whose patience is sorely and unde-servedly tried:—"What *is* it all about? I suppose we are to know." The war and Louis Napoleon and Florence Nightingale lulled, and each asked his neighbour what it was, and was answered:—"Don't know." The Colonel, a man of the fewest possible words, said to the General:—"Rum! Not young Torrens, I suppose?" And the General replied:—"No, no! Old lady of eighty." Which the Colonel seemed to think was all right, and didn't matter.

"I think, if I were you, I should see the woman who brought it," said the Earl, after reading the letter twice; once quickly and once slowly. Gwen answered:—"Yes, I think so,"—and left the room abruptly. Her father took the letter, which he had retained, to show to her mother, who read it once and handed it back to him. "I cannot advise," said she, speaking a little from Olympus. She came down the mountain, however, to say:—"See that she doesn't do anything mad. You have some influence with her," and left the case—one of *dementia*—to her husband.

"I think," said he, "if you will excuse me, my dear, I will speak to this woman myself."

Her ladyship demurred. "Isn't it almost making the matter of too much importance?" said she, looking at her finger-diamonds as though to protest against any idea that she was giving her mind to the case of *dementia*.

"I think not, my dear," said the Earl, meekly but firmly, and followed his daughter out of the room.

Very late that night, or rather very early next day, in the smoking-room to which such males as it pleased to do so retired for a last cigar, sundry of the younger members of the vanishing shooting-party, and one or two unexplained nondescripts, came to the knowledge of a fact that made one of them say—"Hookey!"; another—"Crikey!"; and a third and fourth that they were blowed. All considered, more or less, that Mr. Norbury, their informant, who had come to see the lights out, didn't mean to say what he had said. He, however, adhered to his statement, which was that Lady Gwendolen had had alarming news about an old lady whom she was much interested in, and had been driven away in the closed brougham by Tom Kettering to Chorlton, more than two hours ago. "I thought it looked queer, when she didn't come back," said one of the gentlemen who was blowed.

CHAPTER XXVI

HOW GWEN AND MRS. LAMPREY RODE TO STRIDES COTTAGE, AND FOUND DR. NASH THERE. OF A LETTER FROM MAISIE'S SON, AND HOW IT HAD THROWN HER BACK. AN ANXIOUS NIGHT WATCH. IMAGINATIONS OF SAPPS COURT. PETER JACKSON'S NAMESAKE. HOW GWEN DREAMED OF DOLLY ON GENERAL RAWNSLEY'S KNEE, AND WAS WAKED BY A SCREAM. READ ME ALOUD WHAT MY SON SAYS! WHAT IS CALLED SNEERING. A MAG. A FLIMSY. HOW GWEN WAS GOT TO BED, HALF ASLEEP. OLD MAISIE'S WILL. NOT UPSTAIRS OUT OF A CARRIAGE, DOWNSTAIRS INTO A CARRIAGE. TWO STEPS BACK AND ONE FORWARD. BEFORE THAT CLOCK STRIKES. *THEIR* DAUGHTER

WHOEVER detected a thaw outside the house, by instinct at work within, was an accurate weather-gauge. A wet, despairing moon was watching a soaking world from a misty heaven; and chilly avalanches of undisguised slush, that had been snow when the sun went down, were slipping on acclivities and roofs, and clinging in vain to overhanging boughs, to vanish utterly in pools and gutters and increasing rivulets. The carriage-lamps of Gwen's conveyance, a closed brougham her father had made a *sine qua non* of her departure, shone on a highway that had seen little traffic since the thaw set in, and that still had on it a memory of fallen snow, and on either side of it the yielding shroud that had made the land so white and would soon leave it so black. Never mind!—the road was a better road, for all that it was heavier. No risk now of a stumble on the ice, with the contingencies of a broken knee for the horse, and an hour's tramp for its quorum!

The yew-tree in the little churchyard at Chorlton had still some *coagulum* of thaw-frost on it when the brougham plashed past the closed lichgate, and left its ingrained melancholy to make the most of its loneliness. Strides Cottage was just on ahead—five minutes at the most, even on such a road. "They will be sure to be up, I suppose—one of them at least," said Gwen to the woman in the carriage with her. It was Mrs. Lamprey, whom Tom Kettering was to have driven back in any case, but not in the brougham. Gwen had overruled her attempt to ride on the box, and was sorry when she had done so. For she could not say afterwards:—" I'm sure you would rather be up there, with Tom."

" I doubt they'll have gone to bed, my lady, either of them. Nor yet I won't be quite sure we shan't find the doctor there." Thus Mrs. Lamprey, making Gwen's heart sink. For what but very critical circumstances could have kept Dr. Nash at the Cottage till past one in the morning? But then, these circumstances must be recent. Else he could never have wished the letter kept back till to-morrow. She said something to this effect to her companion, who replied:—" No doubt your ladyship knows!"

There was a light in the front-room, and someone was moving about. The arrival of the carriage caused the dog to bark, once but not more, as though for recognition or warning; not as a dog who resented it—merely as a janitor, officially. The doorbell, in response to a temperate pull, grated on the silence of the night, overdoing its duty and suggesting that the puller's want of restraint was to blame. Then came a footstep, but no noise of bolt or bar withdrawn. Then Ruth Thrale's voice, wondering who this could be. And then her surprise when she saw her visitor, whose words to her were:—" I thought it best to come at once!"

" Oh, but she is better! Indeed we think she is better. Dr. Nash was to write and tell you, so you should know—not to hurry to come too soon." Thus Ruth, much distressed at this result of the doctor's despatch.

" Never mind me! You are sure she *is* better? Is that Dr. Nash's voice?" Yes—it was. He had been there since eleven, and was just going.

Ruth went in to tell Granny Marrable it was her ladyship, as

Dr. Nash came out. "I'm to blame, Lady Gwendolen," said he. "I'm to blame for being in too great a hurry. It was a blunder. But I can't pretend to be sorry I made it—that's the truth!"

"You mean that she isn't out of the wood?"

"That kind of thing. She *isn't.*"

"Oh dear!" Gwen sank into a chair, looking white. Hope had flared up, to be damped down. How often the stokers—nurses or doctors—have to pile wet ashes on a too eager blaze! How seldom they dare to add fresh fuel!

"I will tell you," said the doctor. "She was very much better all Friday, taking some nourishment. And there is no doubt the champagne did her good—just a spoonful at a time, you know, not more. She isn't halfway through the bottle yet. I thought she was on her way to pull through, triumphantly. Then something upset her."

"Well, but—*what?*" For the doctor had paused at some obstacle, unexplained.

"That I can't tell you. You must ask Granny Marrable about that. Not her daughter—niece—whatever she is. Don't say anything to *her.* She is not to know."

Granny Marrable was audible in the passage without. "Can't you tell me what *sort* of thing?" said Gwen, under her voice.

"It was in a letter that came to her from Snaps—Sapps Court. The Granny wouldn't tell me what was in it, and begged I would say nothing of it to Widow Thrale. But the old soul was badly upset by it, shaking all over and asking for you. . . ."

"Was she asking for me? Then I'm so glad you sent for me. I would not have been away on any account."

"It had nothing to do with my writing. I should have written for you to come to-morrow anyhow. . . . Here comes Granny Marrable." They had been talking alone, as Mrs. Lamprey had gone outside to speak to Tom.

"Still asleep, Granny?" said the doctor. Yes—she was, said the old lady; nicely asleep. "Then I'll be off, as it's late." Gwen suggested that Tom might drive him home, with Mrs. Lamprey, and call back for instructions.

Said Granny Marrable then, not as one under any new stress:—"My lady, God bless you for coming, though I would have been glad it had been daylight. To think of your ladyship out in the cold and damp, for our sakes!"

"Never mind me, Granny! I'll go to bed to-morrow night. Now tell me about this letter. . . . Is Ruth safe in there?" Yes, she was; and would stay there by her dear mother. Gwen continued:—"Dr. Nash has just told me there was some letter. But he did not know what was in it."

"He was not to know. But *you* were, my lady. This is it. Can you see with the candle?"

Gwen took the letter, and turned to the signature before reading it. It was from "Ralph Thornton Daverill, *alias* Rix," which she read quite easily, for the handwriting was educated enough, and clear. "I see no date," said she. "Why did Dr. Nash say it had come from Sapps Court?"

"Because, my lady, he saw the envelope. Perhaps your ladyship knows of 'Aunt Maria.' She is little Dave's aunt, in London."

"Oh yes—I know 'Aunt M'riar.' I know her, herself. Why does she write her name on a letter from this man?"

"I do not know. There is all we know, in the letter, as you have it."

"Whom do you suppose Ralph Thornton Daverill to be, Granny?"

"I know, unhappily. He is her son."

"*The* son. . . . Oh yes—I knew of him. She has told me of *him*. Besides, I knew her name was Daverill, from the letters." Granny Marrable was going on to say something, but Gwen stopped her, saying:—"First let me read this." Then the Granny was silent, while the young lady read, half aloud and half to herself, this following letter:—

"Mother—You will be surprised to get this letter from me. Are you sorry I am not dead? Can't say I'm glad. I have been His Majesty's guest for one long spell, and Her Majesty's for another, since you saw the last of me. I'm none so sure I wasn't better off then, but I couldn't trust H.M.'s hospitality again. It might run to a rope's end. Dodging blood-hounds is my lay now, and I lead the life of a cat in hell. But I'm proud—proud I am. You read the newspaper scrap I send along with this, and you'll be proud of your son. I'm a chip of the old block, and when my Newgate-frisk comes, I'll die game. Do you long to see your loving son? If you don't, send him a quid or two—or put it at a fiver. Just for to enable him to lead an honest life, which is my ambition. You can come to a fiver. Or would you rather have your loving son come and ask for it? How would you like it, if you were an honest man without a mag in his pocket, and screwpulls of conscience? You send on a flimsy to M'riar. She'll see I get it. I'll come for more when I want it—you be easy. So no more at present from your dutiful son:—

RALPH THORNTON DAVERILL, *alias* RIX."

"P.S.—You can do it—or ask *a kind friend* to help."

"What a perfectly intolerable letter!" said Gwen. "What does he mean by a newspaper scrap? . . . Oh, is that it?" She took from the old lady a printed cutting, and read it aloud. "Fancy his being *that* man," said she. "It made quite a talk last winter—was in all the papers." It was the paragraph Uncle Mo had come upon in the *Star*.

"I have seen that man," said Granny Marrable. And so sharp was Gwen in linking up clues, that she exclaimed at once:—"What—the madman? Dr. Nash told me of *him*. Didn't he come to hunt her up?"

"That was it, my lady. And he was all but caught. But I have never spoken of my meeting him, and she has barely spoken of him, till this letter came yesterday. And then we could speak of him together. But not Ruth. She was to know nothing. She was not here, by good luck, just the moment that it came."

"And my dear old Mrs. Picture? Oh, Granny—what a letter for her to get!"

"Indeed, my lady, she was very badly shaken by it. I would have been glad if I might have read it myself first, to tell her of it gently." Granny Marrable was entirely mistaken. "Break it gently," sounds so well! What is it worth in practice?

"Could she understand the letter. *I* couldn't, at first."

"She understood it better than I did. But it set her in a trembling, and then she got lost-like, and we thought it best to go for Dr. Nash. . . . No—Ruth never knew anything of the letter, not a word. And her mother said never a word to her. For he was her brother."

"I cannot understand some things in the letter now, but I see he is thoroughly vile. One thing is good, though! What he wants is money."

"Will that . . . ?"

"Keep him quiet and out of the way? Yes—of course it will. Let me take the letter to show to my father. He will know what to do." She knew that her father's first thought might be to use the clue to catch the man, but she also knew he would not act upon it if his doing so was likely to shorten the span of life still left to old Maisie. "What was he like?" said she to Granny Marrable.

"Some might call him good-looking," was the cautious answer.

"You think *I* shouldn't, evidently?" Evidently.

"It is not the face itself. It is in the shape of it. A twist. I took him for mad, but he is not."

"How came you to know him for your sister's son?"

"Ah, my lady, how could I? For Maisie was still dead then, for me. I could know he was Mrs. Prichard's son, for he said so." "I see. It was before. But you talk about him to her now?" "She cannot talk of much else, when Ruth is away. She will talk of him to you, when she wakes. . . . Hush—I think Ruth is coming!" Gwen slipped the letter in her pocket, to be out of the way.

No change in her mother—that was Ruth's report. She had not stirred in her sleep. You could hardly hear her breathe. This was to show that you *could* hear her breathe, by listening. It covered any possible alarm about the nature of so moveless a sleep, without granting discussion of the point.

Gwen had told Tom Kettering to return shortly, but only for orders. Her own mind was quite made up—not to leave the old lady until alarms had died down. If the clouds cleared, she would think about it. Tom must drive back at once to the Towers; and if anyone was still out of bed whose concern it was to know, he might explain that she was not coming back at present. Or stop a minute!—she would write a short line to her father. Ruth and Granny Marrable lodged a formal protest. But how glad they were to have her there, on any terms!

She had really come prepared to stay the night; but until she could hear how the land lay had not disclosed her valise. Tom, returning for orders, deposited it in the front-room, and departed, leaving it to be carefully examined by the dog, who could not disguise his interest in leather.

The only obstacle to an arrangement for one of the three to be always close at hand when the sleeper waked was the usual one. In such cases everyone wants to be the sentinel on the first watch, and not on any account to sleep. A dictator is needed, and Gwen assumed the office. Her will was not to be disputed. She told Granny Marrable and Ruth to go to bed or at least to go and lie down, and she would call one of them if it was necessary. They looked at each other and obeyed. She herself could lie down and sleep, if she chose, on the big bed beside the old lady, and she might choose. The end would be gained. There would then be no fear of old Maisie awakening alone in the dark, a prey to horrible memories and apprehensions, this last one worst of all—this nightmare son with his hideous gaol-bird past and his veiled threats for the future. That was more important than the meat-jelly, beef-tea, stimulants, what not? They would probably be refused. Still they were to be reckoned with, and Ruth was within call to supply them.

In the darkness and the silence of the night, a solitary, discouraged candle in a shade protesting feebly against the one, and every chance sound that day would have ignored emphasizing the other, the stillness of the figure on the bed became a mystery and an oppression. How Gwen would have welcomed a recurrence of the faintest breath, to keep alive her confidence that this was only sleep—sleep to be welcomed as the surest herald of life and strength! How she longed to touch the blue-veined wrist upon the coverlid, but once, just for a certainty of a beating pulse, however faint! She dared not, even when a heavy avalanche of melted snow from the eaves without, that made her start, left the sleeper undisturbed; even when a sudden faggot in the fireplace, responsive to the snowfall, broke and fell into the smouldering red below, and crackled into flame without awakening her. For Gwen knew the shrewd powers of a finger-touch to rouse the deepest sleeper. But she was grateful for that illumination, for it showed her a silver thread of hair near enough to the nostril to be stirred to and fro by the breath that went and came. And by its light the delicate transparency of the wrist showed the regular pulsation of the heart. All was well.

She had plenty to occupy her thoughts. She could sit and think of the strangeness of her own life, and its extraordinary inequalities. What could clash more discordantly than this moment and a memory of a month ago that rushed into her mind for no apparent reason but to make a parade of its own incongruity. Do you remember that brilliant dress of Madame Pontet that she tried on at Park Lane, with "the usual tight armhole"? That dress had figured as a notable achievement of the *modiste's* art, worthy of its wearer's surpassing beauty, in a dazzling crowd of Stars and Garters and flashing diamonds, and loveliness that was old enough for Society, and valour that was too old for the field of battle; and much of the wit of the time and a little of the learning, trappings of well-mounted *dramatis personæ* on the World's stage. That dress and its contents had made many a woman jealous, and been tenacious of many a man's memory, young and old, for weeks after. Here was the wearer, watching in the night beside a convict's relict, a worse convict's mother, a waif and stray picked up in a London Court off Tottenham Court Road! And the heart of the watcher was praying for only one little act of grace in Destiny, to grant a short span yet of life, were it no more than a year, to this frail survivor of a long and cruel separation from one whose youth had been another self to her own.

And as for that other affair, what *did* she really recollect of it?

Well—she could remember that tight armhole, certainly, and was far from sure she should ever forget it. The chance that had brought the sisters back to each other was so strange that the story of their deception and the loss of every clue to its remedy seemed credible by comparison—a negligible improbability. Would they necessarily have recognised one another at all if that letter had not come into the hands of her father? She herself would never have dared to open it; or, if she had, would she have understood its contents? Without that letter, what would the course of events have been? Go back and think of it! Imagine old Mrs. Picture in charge of Widow Thrale, groundedly suspected of lunacy, miserable under the fear that the suspicion might be true—for who can gauge his own sanity? Imagine Granny Marrable, kept away at Denby by her daughter, that her old age should not be afflicted by a lunatic. Imagine the longing of Sapps Court to have Mrs. Picture back, and the chair with cushions, in the top garret, that yawned for her. Imagine these, and remember that probably old Maisie, to seem sane at any cost, would have gone on indefinitely keeping silence about her own past life, whatever temptation she may have been under to speak again of the mill-model, invisible in its carpet-roll above the fireplace. Remember that what Dr. Nash elicited from her, as an interesting case of *dementia*, was not necessarily repeated to Mrs. Thrale, and would have been a dead letter in the columns of the *Lancet* later on. Certainly the chances of an *éclaircissement* were at a minimum when Gwen returned from London, her own newly acquired knowledge of its materials apart. But then, how about the poor crazy old soul's daughter's new-born love for her unrecognised mother, and her mysteriously heart-whole return for it?

That *might* have brought the end about. But to Gwen it seemed speculative and uncertain, and to point to no more than a possible return to London of the mother, accompanied by her unknown and unknowing daughter. A curious vision flashed across her mind of Ruth Thrale, entertained at Sapps by old Mrs. Picture; and there, by the window, the table with the new leg; and, in the drawer of it . . . what? A letter written five-and-forty years ago, that had changed the lives of both! Gwen's imagination restored the unread letter to its place, with rigid honesty. But—how strange!

Then her imagination came downstairs, and glanced in on the way at the room where the mysterious fireman, who came from the sky, had deposited the half-insensible old lady, after the cataclysm. It was Uncle Mo's room, on the safe side of the house;

and the walls were enriched with prints of heroes of the Ring in old time; Figg and Broughton, Belcher and Bendigo, sparring for ever in close-fitting pants· by themselves on a very fine day. She recalled how the unmoved fireman, departing, had shown a human interest in one of these, remarking that it was a namesake of his. Suppose that fireman had not been at hand, how would old Maisie have been got downstairs? Suppose that she herself had been flattened under the ruins, would all things now have been quite otherwise? See how much had turned on that visit to Cavendish Square! No—a hundred things had happened, the absence of any one of which might have changed the current of events, and left old Maisie to end her days undeceived; and perhaps the whole tale of her lonely life and poverty to come to light afterwards, and cast a gloom without a chance of solace over the last hours of her surviving twin. . . .

Was that the movement of a long-drawn breath, the precursor of an unspoken farewell to the land of dreams? Scarcely! Nothing but a fancy, this time, bred of watching too closely in the silence! Wait for the clear signs of awakening, sure to come, in time!

It was so still, Gwen could hear the swift tick-tick-tick in the watch-pocket at the bed's head; and, when she listened to it, her consciousness that the big clock in the kitchen was at odds with the hearth-cricket, rebuking his speed solemnly, grew less and less. For the sound we look to hear comes out of the silence, when no other sound has in it the force to speak on its own behalf. Two closed doors made the kitchen-chorus dim. The new faggot had said its say, and given in to mere red heat, with a stray flicker at the end. Drip and trickle were without, and now and then a plash that said:—"Keep in doors, because of me!" Gwen closed her eyes, as, since she was so wakeful, she could do so with perfect safety; and listened to that industrious little watch.

It had become Dolly reciting the days of the week, before she knew her vigilance was in danger. Gwen was certainly not asleep long, because Dolly had only got to the second Tundy, when a scream awoke her, close at hand to where Dolly was seated on General Rawnsley's knee. But it was quick work, to think out where she was, and to throw her arms round the frail, trembling form that was starting up from some terror of dreamland unexplained, on the bed beside her.

"What is it, dear, what is it? Don't be frightened. See, I'm Gwen! I brought you here, you know. There—there! Now it's all right." She spoke as one speaks to a frightened child.

Old Maisie was trembling all over, and did not know where she was, at first. "Don't let him come—don't let him come!" was what she kept saying, over and over again. This passed off, and she knew Gwen, but was far from clear about time and place. Questioned as to who it was that was not to come, she had forgotten, but was aware she had been asleep and dreaming. "Did I make a great noise and shout out?" said she.

Ruth Thrale appeared, waked by the cry. It had not added to her uneasiness. "She was like this, all yesterday," said she. "All on the jar. Dr. Nash hopes it will pass off." Ruth, of course, knew nothing of the coming of the son's letter, and regarded her mother's state as only a fluctuation. She had a quiet self-command that refused to be panic-struck. In fact, she had held back from coming, long enough to make sure that Granny Marrable had slept through the scream. That was all right. Gwen urged her to go back to bed, and prevailed over her by adopting a positive tone. She agreed to go when she had made "her mother" swallow something to sustain life. Gwen asked if the champagne had continued in favour. "She doesn't fancy it alone," said Ruth. "But I put it in milk, and she takes it down without knowing it." Probably nurses are the most fraudulent people in the world.

Old Maisie kept silence resolutely about the letter until Ruth had gone back; which she only did unwillingly, as concession to a *force majeure*. Then the old lady said:—"Is she gone? I would not have her see her brother's letter. But I would be glad you should see it, my dear." She was exploring feebly under her pillow and bolster, to find it. Gwen understood. "It's not there," said she. "I have it here. Granny Marrable got at it to show to me." She hoped the old lady was not going to insist on having that letter re-read. It made the foulness of the criminal world, unknown to her except as material for the legitimate drama, a horrible reality, and bred misgivings that the things in the newspapers were really true.

Old Maisie disappointed her. "Read me aloud what my son says," said she. Then Gwen understood what Granny Marrable had meant when she said that, of the two, her sister had understood it the better. For as she uttered the letter's repulsive expressions, reluctantly enough, a side-glance showed her old Maisie's listening face and closed eyes, nowise disturbed at her son's rather telling description of his hunted life. At the reference to the "newspaper scrap" she said:—"Yes, Phœbe read me that with her glasses. He got away." Gwen felt that that strange past life, in a land where almost every settler had the prison taint on him, had left old Maisie abler to endure the flavour of the gaol-bird's speech about himself. It was as though an Angel who had been in Hell might know all its ways, and yet remain unsullied by the knowledge.

But at the words:—"Do you long to see your loving son?" she moved and spoke uneasily. "What does he mean? Oh, what does he mean? Was it all his devil?" She seemed ill able to find words for her meaning, but Gwen took it that she was trying to express some hint of a better self in this son, perhaps latent behind the evil spirit that possessed him.

Her comment was:—"Oh dear no! What he means is that he will come and frighten you to death if you don't send him money. It is only a threat to get money. Dear Mrs. Picture, don't you fret about him. Leave him to me and my father. . . . What does he mean by a quid? A hundred pounds, I suppose? And a fiver, five hundred? . . . is that it?"

"Oh no—he would never ask me for all that money! A quid is a guinea—only there are no guineas now. He means a five-pound-note by a fiver." Her voice died from weakness. The "Please go on!" that followed, was barely audible.

Gwen read on:—"'Just for to enable him to lead an honest life.' Dear Mrs. Picture, I must tell you I think this is what is called *sneering*. You know what that means? He is not in earnest."

"Oh yes—I know. I am afraid you are right. But is it *himself*?" That idea of the devil again!

Gwen evaded the devil. "We must hope not," said she. She went on, learning by the way what a "mag" was, and a "flimsy." She paused on Aunt M'riar. Why was "M'riar" to act as this man's agent? She wished Thothmes was there, with his legal acumen. But old Maisie might be able to tell *something*. She questioned her gently. How did she suppose Aunt Maria came to know anything of her son? She had to wait for the answer.

It came in time. "Not Aunt M'riar. Someone else."

"No—Aunt Maria. She wrote her name on the envelope; to show where it came from, I suppose." The perplexity suggested silenced old Maisie. Gwen compared the handwritings of the letter and direction. They were the same—a man's hand, clearly. "From Aunt Maria" was in a woman's hand. Gwen did not attempt to clear up the mystery. She was too anxious about the old lady, and, indeed, was feeling the strain of this irregular night. For, strong as she was, she was human.

Her anxiety kept the irresistible powers of Sleep at bay for a while; and then, when it was clear that old Maisie was slumbering again, with evil dreams in abeyance, she surrendered at discretion. All the world became dim, and when the clock struck four, ten seconds later, she did not hear the last stroke.

When Gwen awoke six hours after, she had the haziest recollections of the night. How it had come about that she found herself in another room, warmly covered up, and pillowed on luxury itself, with a smell of lavender in it that alone was bliss, she could infer from Ruth Thrale's report. This went to show that when Ruth and Granny Marrable came into the room at about six, they found her ladyship undisguisedly asleep beside old Maisie; and when she half woke, persuaded her away to more comfortable quarters. She had no distinct memory of details, but found them easy of belief, told by eyewitnesses.

How was the dear old soul herself? Had she slept sound, or been roused again by nightmares? Well—she had certainly done better than on the previous afternoon and evening, after the receipt of that letter. Thus Granny Marrable, in conference with her ladyship at the isolated breakfast of the latter. Ruth, to whom the contents of the letter were still unknown, was keeping guard by her mother.

"We put it all down to your ladyship," said the Granny, with grave truthfulness—not a trace of flattery. "She can never tire of telling the good it does her to see you." This was the nearest she could go, without personality, to a hint at the effect the sheer beauty of her hearer had on the common object of their anxiety.

Gwen knew perfectly well what she meant. She was used to this sort of thing. "She likes my hair," said she, to lubricate the talk; and gave the mass of unparalleled gold an illustrative shake. Then, to steer the ship into less perilous, more impersonal waters:—"I must have another of those delightful little hot rolls, if I die for it. Mr. Torrens's mother—him I brought here, you know; he's got a mother—says new bread at breakfast is sudden death. *I* don't care!"

The Granny was fain to soften any implied doubt of a County Magnate's infallibility, even when uttered by one still greater. "A many," said she, "do not find them unwholesome." This left the question pleasantly open. But she was at a loss to express something she wanted to say. It *is* difficult to tell your guest, however surpassingly beautiful, that she has been mistaken for an Angel, even when the mistake has been made by failing powers or delirium, or both together. Yet that was what Granny Marrable's perfect truthfulness and literal thought were hanging fire over. Old Maisie had said to her, in speech as passionate as her weakness allowed:—"Phœbe, dearest Phœbe, my lady is God's Angel, come from Heaven to drive the fiend out of the heart of my poor son." And Phœbe, to whom everything like concealment was hateful, wanted sorely to repeat to her ladyship the conversation which ended in this climax. Otherwise, how could the young lady come to know what was passing in Maisie's mind?

She approached the subject with caution. "My dear sister's mind," said she, "has been greatly tried. So we must think the less of exciting fancies. But I would not say her nay in anything she would have me think."

Gwen's attention was caught. "What sort of things?" said she. "Yes—some more coffee, please, and a great deal of sugar!"

"Strange, odd things. Stories, about Van Diemen's Land."

Gwen had a clue, from her tone. "Has she been telling you about the witch-doctor, and the devil, and the scorpion, and the little beast?"

"They were in her story. It made my flesh creep to hear so outlandish a tale. And she told your ladyship?"

"Oh dear yes! She has told me all about it! And not only me, but Mr. Torrens. The old darling! Did she tell you of the little polecat beast the doctor ate, who was called a devil, and how he possessed the doctor—no getting rid of him?"

"She told me something like that."

"And what did you say to her?"

"I said that Our Lord cast out devils that possessed the swine, and had He cast them again out of the swine, they might have possessed Christians. For I thought, to please Maisie, I might be forgiven such speech."

"Why not? That was all right." Gwen could not understand why Scripture should be inadmissible, or prohibited.

Granny Marrable seemed to think it might be the latter. "I would not be thought," she said, "to compare what we are taught in the Bible with . . . with *things*. Our Lord was in Galilee, and we are taught what came to pass. This was in The Colonies, where any one of us might be, to-day or to-morrow."

Gwen appreciated the distinction. It would clearly be irreverent to mention a nowadays-devil, close at hand, in the same breath as the remoter Gadarenes. She said nothing about Galilee being there still, with perhaps the identical breed of swine, and even madmen. The Granny's inner vision of Scripture history was unsullied by realisms—a true history, of course, but clear of vulgar actualities. Still, something was on her mind that she was bound to speak about to her ladyship, and she was forced to use the Gospel account of an incident "we were taught" to' believe no longer possible, as a means of communicating to Gwen what she herself held to be no more than a feverish dream of her sister's weakness. Gwen detected in her tone its protest against the confusion of vulgar occurrences, in all their coarse authenticity, with the events of Holy Writ, and forthwith launched out in an attempt to find the underlying cause of it. "Did the old darling," said she, "tell you how Rookaroo, or whatever his name was, passed his devil on to her husband and son?"

"I think, my lady, she has that idea."

"It seems to me a very reasonable idea," said Gwen. "Once you have a devil at all, why not? And it was to be like the madman in the tombs in the land of the Gadarenes! Poor old darling Mrs. Picture!"

Old Phœbe felt very uncomfortable, for Gwen was not taking the devil seriously. Although scarcely prepared to have Scripture used to substantiate a vulgar Colonial sample, the old lady was even less ready to have such a one doubted, if the doubt was to recoil on his prototype. "Maisie is of the mind to fancy this evil spirit might even now be driven from her son's heart, and bring him to repentance. But I told her a many things might be, in the days of our blessed Lord, in the Holy Land, that were forbidden now. It was just his own wickedness, I told her, and no devil to be cast out. But she was so bent on the idea, that I could not find it in me to say this man might not repent and turn to Godliness yet, by your ladyship's influence, or Parson Dunage's." This introduction of the incumbent of Chorlton was an afterthought. The fact is, Granny Marrable was endeavouring to suggest a rationalistic interpretation of her sister's undisguised mysticism; fever-bred, no doubt, but scarcely to be condemned as delusion outright without impugning devils, who are standard institutions. Good influences, brought to bear on perverted human hearts, are quite correct and modern.

Granny Marrable's words left Gwen unsuspicious that powers of exorcism had been imputed to her. The ascription of them might be—certainly was—nothing but an outcome of the overstrain and tension of the last few days, but the repetition of it in cold blood to its subject might have been taken to mean that it was a symptom of insanity. Gwen did not press her to tell more, as Dr. Nash made his appearance. The frequency of his visits was a source of uneasiness to her. She would have liked to hear him say there was now no need for him to come again till he was sent for.

"Any fresh developments?" said he, as Granny Marrable left the room to herald his arrival. He heard Gwen's account of her own experience in the night, and seemed disquieted. "I wish," said he abruptly, "that people would keep their letters to themselves. I am not to be told what was in the letter, I understand?" For Gwen had skipped the contents of it, merely saying that Mrs. Picture had asked to hear her letter read through again.

Then Widow Thrale came in, saying her mother was ready to see the doctor. Mother was with her mother, she said. The doctor departed into the bedroom.

"How long has your mother been awake?" asked Gwen under no drawback about the designation.

"Quite half an hour. I told her your ladyship was having a little breakfast. She always asks for you."

"I heard that she was talking, through the door. What has she been talking about?"

Ruth's memory went back conscientiously, for a starting-point. "About her annuity," she said, "first. Then about the young children—little Dave and Dolly. That's mother's little Dave, only it's all so strange to think of. And then she talked about the accident."

"What about her annuity? I'm curious about that. I wonder who sends it to her?"

"She says it comes from the Office, because they know her address. She says Susan Burr took them the new address, when they left Skillick's. She says she writes her name on the back. . . ."

"It's a cheque, I suppose?"

"Your ladyship would know. Susan Burr takes it to the Bank and brings back the money." Ruth hesitated over saying:— "I would be happier my mother should not fret so about herself . . . she was for making her will, and I told her there would be time for that."

"Oh yes—plenty!" Gwen thought to herself that old Mrs. Picture's testamentary arrangements were of less importance than tranquillity, as matters stood at present. "What did she say of Dave and Dolly?"

"She was put about to think how they would be told, if she died."

"How would they be told? . . . I can't think." Gwen asked herself the question, and parried it.

Ruth Thrale escaped in a commonplace. The dear children

would have to be told, but they would not grieve for long. Children didn't.

Gwen hoped she was right—always a good thing to do. But what had her mother said about the accident? Oh—the accident! Well—she remembered very little of it. She did not know why she should have become half unconscious. The last thing she could be clear about was that Dave was shouting for joy, and Dolly frightened and crying. Then a gentleman carried her upstairs out of a carriage.

" No! " said Gwen. " Carried her downstairs into a carriage. . . . Oh no!—I know what she meant. It was my cousin Percy, not the fireman."

At this point Dr. Nash returned from the bedroom. Gwen began hoping that he had found his patient really better, but something stopped her speech, and she said:—" Oh! " Ruth Thrale was outside the room by then, far enough to miss the disappointment in her voice.

Dr. Nash glanced round to make sure she was out of hearing, and closed the door. " I don't like to say much, either way," said he.

Gwen turned pale. " You need not be afraid to tell me," she said.

" I see you know what I mean," said he, reading into her thoughts. " Miracle apart, one knows what to expect. I don't believe in any miracle, though certainly she has everything in her favour for it, in one sense."

" Meaning? " said Gwen interrogatively.

" Meaning that she has absolutely nothing the matter with her. If she has any active disorder, all I can say is it has baffled me to find it out."

" But, then, why? . . ."

" Why be frightened? Listen, and I'll tell you. . . . We gain nothing, you know, by not looking the facts in the face."

" I know. Go on." Gwen sat down, and waited. Some faces lose under stress of emotion. It was a peculiarity of this young lady's that every fresh tension added to the surpassing beauty of hers.

" I want you," said the doctor, speaking in a dry, businesslike way—" I want you to go back to when you brought her down here from London. Think of her then."

" I am thinking of her. I can remember her then, perfectly." And Gwen, thinking of that journey, saw her old companion plainly enough. A very old delicate woman, in need of consideration and care. No bedridden invalid!

"When did the change show itself?" The doctor took the image in her mind for granted, successfully.

Then Gwen cast about to find an answer. "I think it must have been . . ." said she, and stopped.

"When did you *see* it?"

"When I came back, first. After I told her, still more."

"After that?"

"I thought she was improving, every day."

"I thought you thought so."

"And you mean that it was a mistake. Oh dear!"

The doctor shook his head, slowly and sadly. "Yesterday, at this time," said he, "she could sit up in bed. With an exertion, you know! To-day she can't do it at all." Both remained silent, and seemed to accept a conclusion that did not need words. Then the doctor resumed, speaking very quietly:—"It is always like this. Two steps back and one forward—two steps back and one forward. We see the one step on because we want to. We don't want to see what's unwelcome. So we don't discount the losses."

Then Gwen, with that quiet resolution which he had known to be part of her character, or he would scarcely have been so explicit, said:—"What will she die of?"

"Old age, accelerated by mental perturbation."

"Can you at all guess when?"

"If she had any definite malady, I could guess better. She may linger on for weeks. It won't go to months, in any case. Or she may pop off before that clock strikes."

"Shall we tell them?"

"I say no. *No.* They will probably have her the longer for not knowing. And, mind you, she is keeping her faculties. She's wonderfully bright, and is suffering absolutely nothing."

"You are sure of that?"

"Absolutely sure. Go in and talk to her now. You'll find her quite herself, but for a little fancifulness at times. It really is no more than that. . . . By-the-by! . . ."

"What?"

"Do *you* know what was in the letter that upset her so? The old Granny did not say what was in it, and charged me to say nothing to her daughter." The doctor had all but said:—"To *their* daughter!"

"I know what was in the letter." Gwen paused a moment to consider how much she should tell, and then took the doctor into her confidence; not exhaustively, but sufficiently. "You are supposed to know nothing about it," said she. "But I don't think it much matters, so long as Ruth—Widow Thrale—does not know. That is her mother's wish. I don't suppose she really minds, about you."

"All I can say is, I wish to God this infernal scoundrel's devil would fly away with him. Good-morning. I shall be round again about six o'clock."

CHAPTER XXVII

HOW SPARROWS GORMANDISE. DAVE'S CISTERN. DOLLY AND JONES'S BULL. THE LETTER HAD DONE IT. HOW TOM KETTERING DROVE WIDOW THRALE TO DENBY'S FARM, AND MAISIE WOKE UP. HOW DAVE ATE TOO MANY MULBERRIES. OLD JASPER. OLD GOSSET AND CULLODEN. HIS TOES. HOW MAISIE ASKED TO SEE THE OLD MODEL AGAIN, AND HAD IT OUT BESIDE THE BED. DID IT GO ROUND, OR WAS DAVE MISTAKEN? THE GLASS WATER, AND HOW MAISIE HAD BROKEN A PIECE OFF, SEVENTY YEARS AGO. HOW A RATCHET-SPRING STRUCK WORK. WAS IT TOBY OR TOFT? BARNABY. BRAINTREE. ST. PAUL'S. BARNABY'S CO-RESPONDENCE. OLD CHIPSTONE. HOW PHOEBE NEARLY LOST HER EYE. OLD MARTHA PRICHARD. A REVERIE OF GWEN'S, ENDING IN LAZARUS. MAISIE'S PURSE

HAS it ever been your lot—you who read this—to be told that Life is ebbing, slowly, slowly, every clock-tick telling on the hours that are left before the end—the end of all that has made your fellow in the flesh more than an image and a name? In so many hours, so many minutes, that image as it was will be vanishing, that name will be a memory. All that made either of them ours to love or hate, to be thought of as friend or foe, will have ceased for all time—for all the time we anticipate; more, or less as may be, than Oblivion's period, named in her pact with Destiny. In so many hours, so many minutes, that unseen mystery, the thing we call our friend's, our foe's, own *self* will make no sign to show that this is he. And we shall determine that he is no more, or agree that he has departed, much as we have been taught to think, but little as we have learned to know.

If you yourself have outlived other lives, and yet borne the foreknowledge of Death unmoved, you will not understand why Gwen's heart within her, when she heard Dr. Nash's words and took their meaning, should be likened to a great stifled sob, nor why she had to summon all her powers afield to bear arms against her tears. They came at her call, and fought so well that the enemy had fled before she had to show dry eyes, and speak with normal voice, to Ruth Thrale, who came in to say that her mother was asking for her ladyship. Come what might, she must keep her gloomy knowledge from Ruth.

"What a fuss about old me!" says the voice from the pillow, speaking low, but with happy contentment. "Would not anyone think I was dying?"

Now, if only Dr. Nash would have kept those prophecies to himself, Gwen would have thought her better. She could have discounted the weakness, or laid it down to imperfect nourishment. She could not trust herself to much speech, saying only:—"We shall have you walking about soon, and what will the doctor say then?"

She looked across at the old sister, grave and silent, whom she had supposed unoppressed, so far, by medical verdicts. But the invitation of a smile she achieved, mechanically, to help towards incredulity of Death, only met a half-response. "Indeed, my lady," said Granny Marrable, "we shall have some time to wait for that, if she will still eat nothing. A sparrow could not live upon the little food she takes."

What was old Maisie saying? She could live on less than a sparrow's food—that was the upshot. The sparrow was a greedy little bird, and she had seen him gormandise in Sapps Court. "My darling Dave and Dolly," she said, "would feed them, on the leads at the back, out of my bedroom window, where the cistern is." Gwen perceived the source of a misapprehension of Dave's.

"He's to come here," said she. "Him and Dolly. And then they can feed the cocks and hens."

"When I'm up," said old Maisie. She had no misgivings.

"When you're up."

"And Dave may go and see Farmer Jones's Bull?"

"And Dave may go and see Farmer Jones's Bull."

"But not Dolly, because she would be frightened."

"Not Dolly, then. Dolly is small, to see Bulls." Old Maisie closed her eyes upon this, and enjoyed the thought of Dave's rapture at that appalling Bull.

Granny Marrable indicated by two glances, one at Gwen, the other at the white face on the pillow, that her sister might sleep, given silence. Gwen watched for the slackening of the hand that held hers, to get gently free. Old Phœbe did the same, and drew the bed-curtain noiselessly, to hide the window-light. Both stole away, leaving what might have been an alabaster image, scarcely breathing, on the bed.

"It is the letter that has done it. Oh, *how* unfortunate!" So
Gwen spoke, to the Granny, in the kitchen: for Ruth, though attending to the Sunday dinner, was for the moment absent. So
the letter could be referred to.

"I fear what your ladyship says is true."

"But at least we know what it is that has done it. That is
something." Granny Marrable seemed slow to understand. "I
mean, if it had not been for the letter, she certainly need not have
been any worse than she was last Sunday. She was getting on so
well, Ruth said, on Friday, after the champagne. Oh dear!"

"It will be as God wills, my lady. If my dear sister is again to
be taken from me . . ."

"Oh, Granny, do not let us talk like that!" But Gwen could
put little heart into her protest. The doctor had taken all the
wind out of her sails.

Old Phœbe let the interruption pass. "If Maisie dies . . ."
said she, and stopped.

"If Maisie dies . . . ?" said Gwen, and waited.

The answer came, but not at once. "It is the second time."

"I don't think I quite understand, Granny," said Gwen gently.
Which was meant, that this made it easier to bear, or harder?

"I am slow to speak what I think, my lady. I would like to
find words to say it. . . . I lost Maisie forty-five—yes!—forty-
six years ago, and the grief of her loss is with me still. Had
she died here, near at hand, so I might have known where they
laid her, I would have kept fresh flowers on her grave till now.
But she was dead, far away across the sea. I am too old now for
what has come of it. But I can see what-like it all is. Maisie is
with me again, from the tomb—for a little while, and then to go.
She will go first, and I shall soon follow; it cannot be long. No
—it cannot be long! The light will come. And God be praised
for His goodness! We shall lie in one grave, Maisie and I. We
shall not be parted in Death." These last words Gwen accepted
as conventional. She listened, somewhat as in a dream, to Granny
Marrable's voice, going quietly on, with no very audible undertone of pain in it:—"It is not of myself I am thinking, but
my child. She has found her mother, and loved her, before she
knew it was herself, risen from the grave. . . . Oh no—no—no,
my lady, I know it all well. My head is right. Maisie has been
at hand these long years past, all unknown to me—oh, how cruelly
unknown!" Here her words broke a little, with audible pain.
"Her coming to us has been a resurrection from the tomb. It is
little to me now, I am so near the end. But my heart goes out

to my child, who will lose her mother. . . . Hush, she is coming back!"

The thought in Gwen's heart was:—"Pity me too, Granny, for I too—I, with all the wealth of the world at my feet!—shall feel a heartstring snap when this frail old waif and stray, so strangely found by me in a London slum, so strangely brought back by me into your life again, has passed away into the unknown." For she had scarcely been alive till now to the whole of her mysterious affection for dear old Mrs. Picture.

Ruth Thrale came back, and the day went on. Old Maisie remained asleep, sleeping as the effigy sleeps upon a tomb, but always with regular breath, barely sensible, and the same slow pulse. Now and again it might have seemed that breath had ceased. But it was not so. If the powers of life were on the wane, it was very slowly.

Tom Kettering returned at the appointed time, to a minute, and took no notice of his own arrival beyond socketing his whip in its stall, in token of its abdication. He had been told to come and wait, and he proceeded to wait, *sine die*. Gwen interrupted him in this employment, by coming out to tell him that she was stopping on, and that he was to go back to the Towers and say so. He looked so depressed at this that she bethought her of a compensation. She knew that Ruth Thrale had cause for anxiety about her own daughter; and, so far as could be seen, her immediate presence was not necessary, for no change appeared imminent. So she persuaded, or half-commanded, Ruth to be driven over to Denby's Farm by Tom Kettering, to remain there two or three hours, and be brought back by him or otherwise, as might be convenient. Her son-in-law might drive her back, and Tom might return to the Towers. It would make her mind easier to see Maisie junior, and get a forecast of probabilities at the farm. Ruth was not hard to prevail upon to do this, and was driven away by Tom over slushy roads, through the irresolute Winter's unseasonable Christmas Eve, after delegating some of her functions to Elizabeth-next-door.

Old Maisie still remained asleep, and almost motionless. With some help from Elizabeth-next-door the perfunctory midday meal had been served, very little more than looked at, and cleared away; then the motionless figure on the bed stirred visibly, breathed almost audibly. At this time of the day vitality is at its best, with most of us. Gwen, standing by the bedside, saw the lips move, and, bending forward, heard speech.

When she said, a moment after:—"I think I must have been asleep. I'm awake now,"—she uttered the words much as Gwen had always heard her speak. Yet another moment, and she said:—"I was dreaming, Phœbe dear, dreaming of our mill. And I was asking for you in my dream. Because Dave was up in our mulberry-tree, and wouldn't come down." She showed how perfectly clear her head was, by saying to Gwen:—"My dear, if I could have kept asleep, I would have seen Phœbe young again. You would never think how young she was then."

Gwen felt that she was nowise bound to dwell on the futility of dreams, and said, as she caressed the old hand's weak hold on her own:—"Was Dave eating too many mulberries in that tree?"

Old Maisie smiled happily at the thought of Dave. "His hands were quite purple with the juice," she said. "But he wouldn't come down, and went on eating the mulberries. It was the tree by itself behind the house, near the big hole where the sunflowers grew."

Granny Marrable's memory spanned the chasm—seventy years or so! "The biggest mulberry," she said, "was Old Jasper, in the front garden, near the wall. . . . It was always called Old Jasper." This replied to a look of Gwen's. Why *should* a mulberry-tree be called Old Jasper? Well—why should anything be called anything?

"I can smell the honeysuckle," said old Mrs. Picture. And her face looked quite serene and happy. "But the pigeons used to get all the mulberries on that tree, because they were close by."

"It stood by itself," said Granny Marrable. "And all the fruit-trees were in the orchard. So old Gosset with the wooden leg was always on that side with his clapper, never out in front."

"Old Gosset—who lost his leg at the battle of Culloden! I remember him so well. He said he could feel his toes all the same as if they was ten. He said it broke his heart to see the many cherries the birds got, for all the noise he made. He said they got bold, when they found he had a wooden leg. . . ." She paused, hesitating, and then asked for Ruth.

Gwen told her how Ruth had gone to her own daughter, who was married, and how a second grandchild was overdue. In telling this, she feared she might not be understood. So she was pleased to hear old Mrs. Picture say quite clearly:—"Oh, but I know. A long while ago—my child—my Ruth—when she was Widow Thrale . . . told me all that. . . ."

"Yes, yes!" Gwen struck in. "*I* know. When you were here at the cottage, before . . ." she hesitated.

"Yes, before," said old Mrs. Picture. "When she showed me

our old model, and did not know. That was the time she thought
me mad. Phœbe—I want you . . . I want you. . . ." Her voice
was getting weaker; as it would do, after much talking.

"What?—I wonder!" said Granny Marrable, and waited.

Gwen guessed. "You want to see the old model again? Is that
it?" Yes, she did. That was a good guess.

"Maisie dearest, I will fetch you the model to the bedside, and
light candles, so you shall see it. Only you will eat something first
—to please me—to please my lady—will you not? Then you may
be able to sit up, you know, and look at it." Granny Marrable
jumped at the opportunity to get some food—ever so little—down
her sister's throat. *She* had not given up hope of her reviving,
if only for a while. Bear in mind that she was still in the dark
about the doctor's real opinion.

The attempt at refection had a poor show of success, its only
triumph worth mentioning being the exhibition of a driblet of
champagne in milk. Almost before the patient had swallowed it,
she had fallen back on her pillow in a drowsy half-sleep, with
what seemed an increased colour, to eyes that were on the watch
for it. She remained so until after the doctor's visit at six o'clock.

The doctor admitted that she *had* picked up a very little, and
when she awoke would probably have another spell of brightness.
But. . . . Speaking with Gwen alone on his way out, he ended
on this monosyllable.

"What does that 'but' mean, doctor?"

"Means that you mustn't expect too much. I suppose you know
that the mildest stimulant means reaction."

"I don't know that I ever thought about it, but I'll take your
word for it."

"Well—you may. And you may take my word for this. When
the vital powers are near their end—without disease, you know,
without disease. . . ."

"I know. She has nothing the matter with her."

"You can intensify vitality for a moment. But the reaction
will come, and must hasten the end. You might halve the out-
standing time of Life by doubling the vitality. If you employ any
artificial stimulant, you only use up the heart-beats that are left.
The upshot of it is—don't go beyond a tablespoonful twice a day
with that liquor."

"I don't suppose she has had so much."

"Well—don't go beyond it. There is always the possibility
—the bare possibility, even at eighty—of a definite revival.
But. . . ."

"*But,* again, doctor!"

"But again! Let it stop at that. I shall do no better by saying more. If I foresaw . . . anything—within the next twelve
hours, I would stay on to see your ladyship through. But there
is nothing to go by. Quite impossible to predict!"

"Why do you say 'to see me through'? Why not her sister
and daughter?"

"Because they *are* her sister and daughter. It's all in their day's
work. Good-night, Lady Gwendolen." Gwen watched the doctor's gig down the road into the darkness, and saw that a man
riding stopped him, as though to give a message. After which
she thought he whipped up his pony, which also felt the influence
of the rider's cob alongside, and threw off its usual apathy.

Old Maisie must have waked up just as the doctor departed,
for there were voices in the bedroom, and Granny Marrable was
coming out. The old lady had an end in view. She was bent on
getting down the mill-model from over the fireplace. "My dear
sister has a great fancy to see it once more," she said. "And
I would be loth to say nay to her." Gwen said:—"Anything to
keep her mind off that brute of a son!" And then between them
they got the model down, and unwrapped the cloth from it. Elizabeth-next-door, coming in at this moment, left Gwen free to go
back to old Maisie in the bedroom, who seemed roused to expectation. The doctor was clearly wrong, and all was going to be well.
Mrs. Picture was not quite herself again, perhaps; but was
mending.

"My dear, I am giving a world of trouble," she said. "But
Phœbe is so kind, to take every little word I say."

"She likes doing it, Mrs. Picture dear. We've got down the
mill to show you, and she will get it in here by the bed, so that you
shall see without getting up. Elizabeth from next door is there
to help her." So the mill-model, that had so much to answer for,
was got out from behind its glass, and placed on the little table
beside the bed.

Old Maisie's voice had rallied so much that surely her power of
movement should have done so too. But no!—she could not raise
herself in bed. It was an easy task to place her to the best advantage, but the sense of her helplessness was painful to Gwen,
who raised her like a child with scarcely an effort, while Granny
Marrable multiplied pillows to support her. The slightest attempt
on her part towards movement would have been reassuring, but
none came.

"I wonder now," she said vaguely. "Was it only Dave?"
"What about Dave, dear? What did Dave say?"
"Was it Dave who said it went round? I had the thought it
went round. Which was it?"

"I showed it to Dave," said Granny Marrable, "and then it
went, the same as new. I could try it again, only then I must
take out the glass water, and put in real. And wind it up."

Old Mrs. Picture almost laughed, and the pleasure in her voice
was good to hear. "Why, now I have it all back!" she said.
"And there is father! Oh, Phœbe, do you remember how angry
father was with me for breaking a piece off the glass water?"

Granny Marrable was looking for something, in the penetralia
of the model. "Oh, I know," said she. "It's in behind the glass
water. . . . I was looking for the piece. . . . I'll take the glass
water out." She did so, and its missing fraction was found,
stowed away behind the main cataract, a portion of which appeared to have stopped dead in mid-air.

"Oh, Phœbe darling," said old Maisie, "we can have it mended."
"Of course we can," said Gwen. "Do let us make it go round.
I want to make it go round, too." Her heart was rejoicing at
what seemed so like revival.

Granny Marrable poured water into what stood for "the sleepy
pool above the dam," and found the key to wind up the clock-
work. "I remember," said old Maisie, "the water first, and then
the key!" Her face was as happy as Dave's had been, watching it.

But alas for the uncertainty of all things human!—machinery
particularly. The key ran back as fast as it was wound up, and
the water slept on above the dam. What a disappointment! "Oh
dear," said Gwen, "it's gone wrong. Couldn't we find a man in
the village who could set it right, though it *is* Sunday?" No—
certainly not at eight o'clock in the evening.

"I fear, my lady," said Granny Marrable, "that it was injured
when the little boy Toby aimed a chestnut at it. And had I known
of the damage done, I should have allowed him no sugar in his
tea. But it may have been Toft, when he repaired the glass, for
indeed he is little better than a heathen." She examined it and
tried the key again. It was hopeless.

"Never mind, Phœbe dearest! I would have loved to see the
millwheel turn again, as it did in the old days. Now we must
wait for it to be put to rights. I shall see it one day." If she
felt that she was sinking, she did not show it. She went on speaking at intervals. "Let me lie here and look at it. . . . Yes, put
the candle near. . . . That was the deep hole, below the wheel,

where the fish leapt. . . . Father would not allow us near it, for the danger. . . . There were steps up, and so many nettles. . . . Then above we got to the big pool where the alders were . . . where the herons came. . . ." A pause; then:—" Phœbe dearest! . . ."
" What, darling ? "
" I was not mad. . . . You were not here, or you would have known me. . . . Would you not ? "
" I would have known you, Maisie dearest—I would have known you, in time. Not at the first. But when I came to think of it, would I have dared to say the word ? "

Gwen remembered this answer of old Phœbe's later, and saw its reasonableness. She only saw the practical side at the moment. " Why, Granny," she said—" if it hadn't been the mill, it would have been something else."

" But I was not mad," Maisie continued. " Only I must have frightened my Ruth. . . . I went up *there* once, Phœbe. Barnaby took me up one day. . . ."

" Up where, Mrs. Picture dear ? " Gwen left the old right hand free to show her meaning, but it fell back after a languid effort. The strength was near zero, though no one would have guessed it from the voice.

" Up *there*—in the roof—where the trap comes out. . . . Phœbe would not come, because of the dust. . . . It was so hot too. . . . Barnaby pulled up a flour-sack, to show me, and would have let me out on the trap, only I was frightened, it was so high ! I could see all the way over to Braintree. . . . And Barnaby said on a clear day you could see St. Paul's. . . . I liked Barnaby—I disliked old Muggeridge. . . . Do you know, Phœbe dear, I used to think Barnaby's wife was old Muggeridge's sister, because her name had been Muggeridge ? "

Old Phœbe threw light on the affair. Barnaby's wife was young Mrs. Muggeridge, who had exchanged into another regiment—was not really Barnaby's wife ! that is to say, not his legal wife.

" But there now ! " said old Phœbe, when she had ended this, " if that was not the very first of it all with me, when Dr. Nash he set me a-thinking, by telling of Muggeridge ! For how would I ever have said a word of that old sinner to our little Dave ? "

Old Maisie's attention was still on the mill-model. " You would not come up into the corn-loft, Phœbe," said she, " because of all the white dust. It was on everything, up there. When I went up with Barnaby the mill was not going, because the stones were out for old Chipstone to dress their faces. His real name was not Chipstone, but Chepstow. He could do two stones in one day, he worked so quick. So both were got out when he came, and the mill was stopped. Oh, Phœbe, do you remember when a chip flew in your eye, you were so bad?"

"Now, to think of that!" said Granny Marrable. "And me clean forgot it all these years! Old Chipstone, with glasses to shelter his eyesight; like blinkers on a horse. 'Tis all come back to me now, like last week. And I might have been a one-eyed girl all my days, the doctor said, only the chip just came a little out of true. To think that all these years I have forgotten it, and never thanked God once!"

"'Tis the sight of the mill brings it all back," said old Maisie. "I mind it so well, and the guy you looked, dear Phœbe, with a bandage to keep out the light. It was wolfsbane did it good, beat up in water quite fine."

"Be sure. Only 'twas none of Dr. Adlam's remedies, I lay. . . . Wasn't it Martha's—our old Martha? . . . There, now!— I've let go her name. . . . 'Twas on the tip of my tongue to say it. . . ."

Old Maisie's voice was getting faint as she said:—"Old Martha Prichard . . . the name I go by now, Phœbe darling. . . . I took it to . . . to keep a memory . . ."

She was speaking in such a dying voice that Gwen struck in to put an end to her exerting it. "I see what you mean," she said. "You mean you took the name to bring back old times. Now be quiet and rest, dear! You are talking more than is good for you. Indeed you are!"

Thereon Granny Marrable, though she had never felt clear about the reason of this change of name, and now thought she saw enlightenment ahead, followed in compliance with what she conceived to be Lady Gwendolen's wishes. "Now you rest quiet, Maisie dearest, as her ladyship says. What would Dr. Nash think of such a talking?"

Ruth might not be back till very late, and as she had not reappeared it might be taken for granted she had stayed to sup with her daughter. Gwen suggested rather timidly—for it was going outside her beat—that the grandchild might have chosen its birthday. The Granny said, with a curious certainty, that there was no likelihood of that for a day or two yet, and went to summon Elizabeth from next door, to help with their own supper. She herself was rather old and slow, she said, in matters of house-service.

Gwen was not sorry to be left for a while to her own reflections before the smouldering red log on the kitchen fire.

The great bulldog from the lobby without, as though his courtesy could not tolerate such a distinguished guest being left alone, paid her a visit in her hostess's absence. He showed his consciousness of her identity by licking her hand at once. He would have smelt a stranger carefully all round before bestowing such an honour. Gwen addressed a few words to him of appreciation, and expressed her confidence in his integrity. He seemed pleased, and discovered a suitable attitude at her feet, after consideration of several. He looked up from his forepaws, on which his chin rested, with an expression that might have meant anything respectful, from civility to adoration. The cat, with her usual hypocrisy, came outside her fender to profess that she had been on Gwen's side all along, whatever the issue. Her method of explaining this was the sort that trips you up—that curls round your ankles and purrs. The cricket was too preoccupied to enter into the affairs of fussy, uncontinuous mortals, and the kettle was cool and detached, but ready to act when called on. The steady purpose of the clock, from which nothing but its own key could turn it, was to strike nine next, and the cloth was laid for supper. Supper was ready for incarnation, somewhere, and smelt of something that would have appealed to Dave, but had no charm for Gwen.

For she was sick at heart, and the moment that a pause left her free to admit it, heavy-eyed from an outcrop of head-oppression on the lids. It might have come away in tears, but her tissues grudged an outlet. She saw no balm in Gilead, but she could sit on a little in the silence, for rest. She could hear the voices of the two old sisters through the doors, and knew that Mrs. Picture was again awake, and talking. That was well!—leave them to each other, for all the time that might still be theirs, this side the grave.

What a whirl of strange unprecedented excitements had been hers since . . . since when? Thought stopped to ask the question. Could she name the beginning of it all? Yes, plainly enough. It all began, for her, at the end of that long rainy day in July, when the sunset flamed upon the Towers, and she saw a trespasser in the Park, with a dog. She could feel again the unscrupulous paws of Achilles on her bosom, could hear his master's indignant voice calling him off, and then could see those beautiful dark eyes fixed on what their owner could not dream was his for ever, but which those eyes might never see again. She could watch the retiring figure, striding away through the bracken, and wonder that she should have stood there without a thought of the future. Why could she not have seized him and held him in her arms, and baffled all the cruelty of Fate? For was he not, even then, hers—hers—hers beyond a doubt? Could she not see now that her heart had said "I love you" even as he looked up from that peccant dog-collar, the source of all the mischief?

That was what began it. It was that which led her to stay with her cousin in Cavendish Square, and to a certain impatience with conventional "social duties," making her welcome as a change in excitements an excursion or two into unexplored regions, of which Sapps Court was to be the introductory sample. It was that which had brought into her life this sweet old woman with the glorious hair. No wonder she loved her! She never thought of her engrossing affection as strange or to be wondered at. That it should have been bestowed on the twin sister of an old villager in her father's little kingdom in Rocestershire was where the miracle came in.

And such a strange story as the one she had disinterred and brought to a climax! And then, when all might have gone so well—when a very few years of peace might have done so much to heal the lifelong wounds of the two souls so cruelly wrenched apart half a century ago, that the frail earthly tenement of the one should be too dilapidated to give its tenant shelter! So small an extension of the lease of life would have made such a difference.

But if it was hard for her to bear, what would it be to the survivor, the old sister who had borne so bravely and well what seemed to Gwen almost harder to endure than a loss; a resurrection from the tomb, or its equivalent? She had often shuddered to think what the family of Lazarus must have felt; and found no ease from the reflection that they were in the Bible and it was quite a different thing. *They* did not know they were in the Bible.

She helped the parallel a little farther, while the cricket chirped unmoved. Suppose that Lazarus had died again in earnest from the shock—and suppose, too, please, that he was deeply beloved, which may not have been the case! How would the wife, mother, sisters, who had said one farewell to him, have borne to see him die a second time? Of course, Gwen was alive to the fact that it would be bad religious form to suggest that this contingency was not covered by some special arrangement. But put it as an hypothesis, like the lady she had ascribed Adrian's ring to!

She could hear Granny Marrable's voice and Elizabeth's afar, in conference. That was satisfactory. It made her certain that the slightest sound from old Maisie, so much nearer, would reach her. Her door stood wide, and the other door was just ajar.

But she did not hear the slightest sound. The dog did, for he flashed into sudden vitality and attention, and was out of the room in an instant. He was unable to say to Granny Marrable:— " I heard your invalid move in the bedroom, and I think you had better go and see if she wants you," but he must have gone very near it. For Gwen heard the old lady's step come quicker than her wont along the passage, and she reached the kitchen-door just in time to see her pass into the room opposite. " Is she all right?" she said.

" I hope she is still asleep, my lady," said old Phœbe.

But she was not asleep, and said so. Her voice was clear, and the hand Gwen took—so she thought—closed on hers with a greater strength than before. If only she had stirred in bed, it would have seemed a return of living power. But this slight vitality in the hands alone seemed to count for so little. She wanted something, evidently, and both her nurses tried to get a clue to it. It was not food; though, to please them, she promised to take some. Gwen's thought that possibly she had something for her ear alone—which she had hesitated to communicate to old Phœbe—was confirmed when the latter left the room to get the beef-tea, and so forth, which was always within reach if needed. For old Maisie said plainly:—" Now I can tell you—my dear! "

" What about, dear Mrs. Picture?" said Gwen, caressing the hand she held, and smoothing back the silver locks from the grave grey eyes so earnestly fixed on hers. " Tell me what."

" My son," said old Maisie. " I have a son, have I not?"— this in a frightened way, as though again in doubt of her own sanity—" and he is bad, is he not, and has written me a letter?"

" That's all right. I've got the letter, to show to my father."

" Oh yes—do show it—to the old gentleman I saw. He is your father. . . ."

" You would like to say something about your son, dear Mrs. Picture—something we can do for you. Now try and tell me just what you would like."

" I want you, my dear, to find me my purse out of the other watch-pocket. I asked my Ruth to put it there. . . . She is Widow Thrale . . . is she not?" Every effort at thought of her surroundings was a strain to her mind, plainly enough.

" There it is!" said Gwen. " Soon found! . . . Now, am I to see how much money you've got in it?"

" Yes, please!" It was an old knitted silk purse with a slip-ring. In the early fifties the leather purses with snaps, that leak at the seam and let half-sovereigns through before you find it out, were rare in the pockets of old people.

"Six new pounds, and one, two, three, four shillings in silver, and two sixpences, and one fourpence, and a halfpenny! Shall I keep it for you, to be safe?"

"No, dear! I want—I want . . ."

"I hope," thought Gwen to herself, "she's not going to have it sent to her execrable son. Yes, dear, what is it you want done with it?"

"I want three of the pounds to go to Susan Burr, for her to pay eight weeks of the rent. It's seven-and-sixpence a week."

"And the rest—shall I keep it?"

"Tell me—my son Ralph's letter. . . . Did it not say that he wanted money?"

"Yes, it did. But I'm going to see about that—I and my father."

Old Maisie's voice became beseeching, gaining strength from earnestness. "Oh my dear—do let me! And, after all, is it not his money? For I had nothing of my own when I came back. I might have gone to the workhouse, but for him." What followed, disjointedly, was an attempt to tell the portion of her story that related to the miscarriage of her husband's will.

"Very well, dear! It shall all be done as you wish it. I'll see to that. The money shall be sent to Aunt M'riar, at Sapps Court, to give to him."

"Why is it Aunt M'riar, at Sapps Court? I know Aunt M'riar." Do what she would, she could not grapple with these relativities. And, indeed, this one was a mystery she could not have solved in any case.

CHAPTER XXVIII

"Has she not talked at all about Australia, Granny? . . . No, thanks! I'm sure it's a beautiful ham—but I shall do very nicely with this. One very big lump of sugar, please, and plenty of milk, or I shall lie awake." Thus Gwen, and the influence of Strides Cottage is visible in her speech.

Old Maisie was again asleep, and they had left her and gone into the front-room; as much to speak together without disturbing her as to get their own suppers. They were doing this last, however, in a grudging sort of fashion; for the pleasures of the table are no match for a heartache. Gwen found it a solace to make her own toast with a long toasting-fork, an experience which her career as an Earl's daughter had denied to her.

"Maisie has talked many times of Australia, my lady. She talks on, so I could not repeat much."

"You mean she jumps from one thing to another?"

"Yes, so I cannot always follow her. But she has told me a many things of her life there. How at first she would never see a soul at the farm from week's end to week's end, and her husband got to own all the land about."

"Do you think she is really alive to her husband's villainy? *I* sometimes think she forgets all about it."

"Please God she does so! 'Tis better for her she should. I

would have felt happier if she could have known me, and Ruth, and never had the tale of his wickedness."

"But that was impossible, Granny. She *must* have known, in the end."

"That is so, I know, my lady. But when I hear her forget it all, it makes my heart glad. When she gets to telling of the old time, on the farm, her mind is off it, and I thank God that it should be so, for her sake! Friday last she was talking so happy, you could not have known her for the same."

"About the farm and the convicts? Do recollect some of the things she told you!"

"There was a creature they hunt with dogs, that leaps on its hind-legs to any height."

"Oh yes—the Kangaroo."

"She called it something else—something like 'Boomer.'" This did not matter. Granny Marrable went on to repeat how a "boomer," chased by the dogs, had made straight for her sister's husband, whose gun, missing fire, had killed his best dog; while the quarry, unterrified by the report, sprang at a bound over his head and got away scathless. This, and other incidents of the convict's after-life in Van Diemen's Land, told without leading to the crime of the forged letter, had shown how completely separate in Maisie's mind were the memories of her not unhappy life with her husband in the past, and that of the recent revelation of his iniquity. She somehow dissociated the two images of him, and her mind could dwell easily on *his* identity as it had appeared to her during her thirty years of widowhood, without losing the new-found consciousness of Phœbe's.

But Granny Marrable had taken special note of the fact that her sister never referred to the son who had come with her from Australia, and had herself been scrupulously careful not to do so. She did not really know whether Maisie was alive to the possibility of his reappearance at any moment; and, indeed, could not have said positively whether allusion had or had not been made to her own alarming experience of him. Her own shock and confusion had been too great for accurate recollection. Silence about him was to her thought the wisest course, and she had remained silent.

She seemed to Gwen a wonderful old woman, this Granny Marrable. Her untiring patience and strength, at her great age; her simple theism, constantly in evidence; her resolute calmness in facing a second time the harrowing grief of a twin sister's death—for that she saw it at hand, Gwen was convinced—were surely the material of which heroism is made, when heroism is in the making. To Gwen's thought, the miraculous news that had been broken to her so suddenly might easily have prostrated many a younger person, even without that mysterious unknown factor, the twinship, the force of which could only be estimated by the two concerned. As the old lady sat there at the supper-table, breaking her resumptions of her sister's Australian tales by gaps of listening to catch any sound from the bedroom, she seemed to Gwen a duplicate of the old Mrs. Prichard of Sapps Court, spared by time or with some reserve of constitutional energy, grey rather than white, resolute rather than resigned. The different inflexion of voice helped Gwen against that perplexing sense of her likeness to her twin, which would assert itself whenever she became silent.

It was to fend this off, in such a pause, that she said:—" You are both just eighty this year, Granny, are you not?"

" Eighty-one, my lady. When our clock strikes midnight Maisie will have been eighty-one years in the world, and myself with but a few minutes to make up the tale. My mother told me so when I was still too young to understand, but I bore her words in mind. She was dead a year when my brother dressed those little dolly figures in the mill. I mind that he put it off, so we should not be in black for our mother. He died himself, none so long after that."

The foolish lines of keeping up hope mechanically to the last did not recommend themselves to Gwen. But she could trust herself to say, seeing the strength on the old face before her:—" Oh, Granny, do not let us despair too soon!" The phrase acknowledged Death, and did not choke her like the sham.

" My lady, have you felt her feet?"

" No—are they so cold?"

Instead of replying, Granny Marrable rose and passed into the bedroom. Gwen, whose own speech had stopped her from hearing old Maisie's half-utterance on waking, followed, and stood beside the bed. Granny Marrable said:—" She is not awake yet, but I heard her." As she said this, Gwen slipped her warm hand between the sheets, and touched the motionless extremities; cold marble now, rather than flesh. A stone bottle of hot water, just in contact with the feet, had heated a spot on each, making its cold surrounding colder to the touch, and laying stress upon its iciness. " Oh, Granny," said Gwen, trying in vain to make the living warmth of her own hand of service, " can nothing be done? Surely—her feet in hot water?"

But old Phœbe only shook her head. *She* knew. It would only be to no purpose! Better let her rest! Moreover, Gwen could not fail to notice that the feet remained passive to her touch, never shrinking. That is not the way of feet. Was ever foot that did not shrink from mysterious unexpected fingers, coming from the beyond in the purlieus of a private couch?

And yet old Maisie was alive there still, and her speech was clear, however low. If anything, its sound savoured of revival. But she was not clear about her whereabouts and whom she was speaking to. She seemed to think it was Susan Burr, who " would find her thimble if she looked underneath." Thus much and no more had come articulate from the land of dreams. The moment after she was quite collected. Was that Phœbe, and her Lady? This was not the conventional phrase " My lady." She was evidently in possession of a Lady she had been guided to find by some Guardian Angel, if, indeed, the Lady were not a Guardian Angel herself. She went on to ask:—Where was her Ruth? When would she come?

She was coming, Ruth was, very soon. Both vouched for it. Gwen added:—" She's gone to see her daughter, who has a little boy."

Then Granny Marrable lost her head for the first time. " She's gone to my granddaughter," said she. " And I'm looking to have another great-grandchild there soon, before a many days are over."

For a moment Gwen was afraid the confusion of Ruth's daughtership might make old Maisie's head whirl, and set her fretting. She began to explain, but explanation was not necessary. The old hand she held was withdrawn from hers, that it might make common cause with its fellow that old Phœbe already held. " My darling," said she, " did I not give her to you when I ran away to the great ship? Fifty years ago, Phœbe—fifty years ago! " There was no trace of any tear in the eye that Gwen could still see, though it looked no longer into her own. The voice was not failing, and the words still came, clear as ever. " I kissed her in her crib, and I would have kissed her yet once more, but I dared not. So I said to myself:—" She will wake and never see me! But Phœbe will be there, to kiss her when she wakes. She will kiss her for me, just on the place we used to say was good to kiss.' Tell me, Phœbe, did my child cry much? . . ."

Granny Marrable's words:—" I cannot—I cannot—my darling! " caught in her voice, as she bent over the face that, but for its frail attenuation, was her own face over again, touching it ten-

derly with her own old lips—the same, thought Gwen, that had
inherited that place it was so good to kiss, on that baby face of
half a century ago, now a grandmother's. She rose noiselessly
from where she half sat, half leaned, beside the figure on the bed,
and stole a little way apart; not so far as to be unable to hear
what that musical voice kept on saying, though she could not catch
the replies.

"I said to myself:—'Phœbe will be her mother when I am
miles away across the sea, and she will be as good a mother as
I. . . .' Was it not best, dearest, I should go alone, rather than
carry my child away and leave all the loneliness for you? . . .
Yes—but my heart ached for my little one on the great ship. . . .
I would watch the stars—the very stars you saw too, Phœbe—
and they were like friends for many a long week, till they sank
down in the sea behind us, and it was thirty years before I saw
them again. . . . Yes—then I knew it would be England soon
and I would know if Phœbe had any other grave than the cold
sea. . . . Yes, my darling, that was my first thought—to go to
the little church by Darenth Mill, and look in the south corner.
. . . I did, and there was mother's grave, and father's name cut
on the stone, but none other. So I thought:—They are all gone—
all gone! . . . Oh, if I had known that you were here! . . ."

The sound of lamentation barely grew in her voice, but it was
there. To turn her mind from the recollection that provoked it,
Granny Marrable thought it well to say that Nicholas Cropredy,
her first husband, whom the forged letter had drowned at sea,
had not been buried at Darenth Mill, but at Ingatestone, with
his kindred and ancestors. "Did they find his body?" said old
Maisie. She knew that he was dead long years back, but had not
received any new impression of the cause of his death.

She did not even now seem to find its proper place in her mind
for this correction of its mistaken record. It could not deal with
all the facts, but held fast to the identities of her sister and child.
Probably the established memory of the false news of her brother-
in-law's death continued in possession. She only looked puzzled;
then drifted on the current of her thought. "If I had known that
you were here! . . . Oh, Phœbe!—such a many times my boy
made me think of his sister he would never see now. . . . That
was before the coming of the news. . . . Oh yes, I always had
a thought till then the time might come before they would be
grown up, so they should be children together. . . . That was my
elder boy Isaac, after father—in those days little Ralph was in his
cradle. . . . But the time never came—only the time to think it

might have been. . . . And all those years I thought you dead, you were here! . . . Oh, Phœbe—you were here! . . . Oh, why —why—*why* could I not be told that you were here?"

"It was the Lord's will, darling. His ways are not for us to understand." Gwen could not for the life of her help recalling some irreverence of Adrian's about Resignation and Fatalism. But though she almost smiled over his reprehensible impiety— "No connection with the shop opposite"—she could and did pay a mental tribute to the Granny's quiet earnestness. She would have done the same by "Kismet" to an old Sheikh in the shadow of the Pyramids.

"Why—oh, why?—when my dear husband was gone could I not have found you then, even if I had died of joy in the finding? Had I not known enough pain? Oh, Phœbe—when I came back —when I came back . . . it would have been so much then! . . . I had some great new trouble after that. . . . Oh, tell me— what was it?"

What could old Phœbe do but answer, seeing that she knew? "It was the wickedness of your son, Maisie darling. We have talked of him, have we not?" She feared to say much, as she shrank from reference to her own knowledge of the convict. She tried to get away from him. "And it was then you took old Martha's name, not to be known by your own, and went to Sapps Court?" This succeeded.

"Not Sapps Court, not yet for a long time. But I did go, and I was happy there. . . . I had my little Dave and Dolly, and when the window stood open in the summer, I heard the piano outside, across the way . . . and Aunt M'riar came, and sometimes Mr. Wardle—he was so big he filled the room. . . . But tell me—was it a horrible dream, or was it true, that a letter came to me? . . ." Her powers of speech flagged.

Gwen took upon herself to answer, to spare Granny Marrable. "Yes, Mrs. Picture dear, it came from your son, and I've got it here. You're not to fret about him. I'm to show his letter to my father, don't you know?—you've seen him—and you know what he does will be all right."

"What he does will be all right." Old Maisie repeated it mechanically, and lay quiet, holding a hand on either side, as before; then after a short time rallied, and turned to Gwen, saying—"My Lady—my dear—I want you to promise me one thing. . . . I want you to promise me . . ."

"To promise you? Is it something I can do?"

The answer came with an extraordinary clearness. "That you

will not let them get him. Read his letter, that I may hear. . . .
Yes—like that!" She fixed her eyes eagerly on it, as Gwen drew
it from her pocket. Granny Marrable snuffed the candles, and
moved them to give a better light.

Gwen read aloud as best she might, for the handwriting was
none too visible. When she came to the writer's picturesque suggestion of his life of constant dodging and evasion of his pursuers, she softened nothing of his brutal phraseology. Maisie only
said:—"That is it. That is what I want." Phœbe was restless
under its utterance, and murmured some protest. That such words
should pass her ladyship's lips—such lips! Gwen merely commented:—"Like a fox before the pack! That's what he means.
He's got to say it somehow, you know! Yes, tell me, what is it
about that?"

"I want you . . . to save him from them. I want you to tell
him . . . to tell him . . ."

"Something from you?—yes!"

"To tell him his mother forgave him. For I know now—I
know it, my dear—that his wicked work was none of his own doing,
but the evil spirit that had possession of him. Was it not?"

Why should Gwen stand between Mrs. Picture, dying, and
something that gave her happiness, just for the sake of a little
pitiful veracity? She was all the readier to endorse a draft on
her credulity, from the knowledge that Granny Marrable would,
if applied to, be ready with a covering security. She said quietly:
—"I think it very far from impossible."

"Then you will tell him for me, and save him—save him from
the officers?"

It seemed a large promise to make, but would its fulfilment ever
be called for? "I promise," said Gwen, "and I will tell him
you forgave him, if ever I see him. . . . There's Ruth back—I
hear her. Now, dear, you must lie quiet, and not talk any more.
You know you don't want her to know anything at all about her
brother." Whereon Maisie lay silent with closed eyes, her hand
in Gwen's just acknowledging its chance pressures, while Granny
Marrable rose and went to the door; and then Gwen heard her
in an earnest undertone of conversation with Ruth, just alighted
from a vehicle whose horse, considered as a sound, she would
have sworn to. It was the grey mare.

Ruth's visit to her daughter was the first since the extraordinary
discovery of Mrs. Prichard's identity, and she had been very
anxious about her. Nevertheless, its object appeared equable,
blooming, and prosperous on her arrival; very curious to hear

details of her new-found grandmother, and indignant with Dr. Nash for telling her husband that he was not, on peril of becoming a widower, to allow his wife to travel over to Strides Cottage to see her. She mixed with this a sort of resentment against the defection from her post of her real grandmother—to wit, the one she had grown up under. For the young woman's wish for her presence had been one of those strong predispositions very common under her circumstances, and far less unreasonable than many such. "Granny" had been all-wise and all-powerful with her from her cradle!

But, in spite of young Maisie's confidence on the subject, her mother could not resist the misgiving that her expected grandchild was girding up its insignificant loins to make a dash for existence. Consider its feelings if it had inherited its great-grandmother's scrupulous punctuality! Widow Thrale was between two fires—duty to a mother and duty to a daughter. An instinct led her to choose the former. Her son-in-law affected to think her nervous; but, after whistling the halves of several tunes to himself, put his horse in the gig and went off to fetch the doctor. The story has seen how he caught him just coming away from Strides.

Ruth had not yet done quite all she could. She could summon someone to take her place beside her daughter in her absence. Preferably her cousin Keziah from the Towers. But she must see her and know that she was available. Tom Kettering, just departing for the Towers, was caught in time for Ruth to accompany him. On her arrival, finding that Keziah *was* available, she arranged to walk with her to Denby's Farm, and then on to the Cottage. Under six miles, all told!—that was nothing.

But there was no need for this. Tom Kettering, going up to the house to report her young ladyship's decision to remain on another day, was told he must wait for a letter her ladyship the Countess would write, to take to Strides Cottage, and bring back an answer. He could easily go a few inches out of his way to leave his Aunt Keziah at Denby's, and take Ruth Thrale home to Strides. But he put up the closed brougham, and harnessed the grey mare in the dogcart, as she wanted a run. He knew that Gwen meant what she said, and would *not* come back.

It was about nine o'clock when they reached the Cottage, and Tom waited for the answer to the Countess's letter. Ruth came in, to be told that her mother had talked too much, and must lie quiet. But she *had* been talking—that was something! The comment was Ruth's, and the reply to it was hopeful and consolatory. Oh yes—a great deal! And she must be better, to be able to talk

so much. However, Ruth saw no change in the appearance of
the still, white figure on the bed.

Gwen sat in the front-room and read her mother's remonstrance
with her for absenting herself in this way and leaving her ladyship
alone to contend with the arduous duty of entertaining her guests.
" I think," it ran, " that you might at least remember that you
are your father's daughter, even if you forget that Sir Spencer and
Lady Derrick have come all the way from Nettisham in Shrop-
shire." What followed was a good deal emphasized. " Understand, my dear, that what I say is *not intended to hold good* if
this old lady is *actually dying,* but *for anything short of that* it
does appear to me that your behaviour is *at least inconsiderate.*
Do let me entreat you to fix *a reasonable hour* for your return
to-morrow, if you *adhere to your resolution* not to come to-night.
Pray tell Kettering when he is to call for you *before twelve to-
morrow, so that you may be in time for lunch."* This last was a
three-lined whip.

In order that Gwen should not suppose that there had been too
flattering a *hiatus* owing to her absence, the letter wound up:—
" We have had some *very nice music.* It turns out that Emily
and Fanny sing ' *I would that my love'* quite charmingly."
Gwen's remark to herself:—" Of course ! " may be intelligible to
old stagers who remember the fifties, and the popularity of this
Mendelssohn duet at that time—notably the intrepidity of the
singers over the soft word the merry breezes wafted away in sport.
Emily and Fanny were two *ingénues,* come of a remote poor relation, who were destined never to forget the week they were spending at the Towers in Rocestershire. The letter was scribbled
across to the effect that General Rawnsley had said he should
ride over to Chorlton to-morrow to see if he could be of any use.
" The dear old man," said Gwen to herself. " And eighty-four
years old ! Oh, why—why—could not my old darling Mrs. Picture live only three years more ? . . . Only three years ! "

*   *   *   *   *   *   *

Ten o'clock. The time was again at hand for those last arrangements we all know so well, when one watcher is chosen to
remain by the sick man's couch, that others may sleep; each one
to be roused from forgetfulness and peace to the sickening foreknowledge of the hour of release for all, when the life he has it
at heart to prolong, if only for a day, shall have become a memory
to perish in its turn, as one by one its survivors grow few and
fewer and follow in its track.

A night comes always when Oblivion becomes a terror, and we dare not sleep, from fear of what our ears may hear on waking. It had come at Strides Cottage for Granny Marrable and Gwen, and even Ruth was conscious of a creeping dread of Death at hand, waiting on the threshold. But she imagined herself alone in her anticipations—fancied that "mother" and her ladyship were cherishing false hopes. She would not allow her own to die lest she should betray fears that might after all be just as false. Why should her mother—her new-found real mother—be sinking, because her limbs were cold, when her speech was still articulate, and her soft grey eyes so full of tenderness and light?

Gwen held a little aloof, not to take more than her fair share of what she feared was an ebbing life, although it kept so strangely its powers of communion with the world it was leaving behind. She could hear all the old voice said, as she had heard it before. What was that she was saying now?

"When the baby comes you will bring it here to show to me? I may not be up by then, to go and see it."

"The minute my daughter is strong enough to bring it, mother dear."

"She must take her time. . . . Is there not a little boy already?"

"Yes. He's Peter. He's a year old. He's very strong and wilful, and gets very angry when things are not given to him."

"Ruth darling—fetch him to me to-morrow. Is it far to bring him?" There was hunger for the baby in her beseeching voice. She might enjoy him a little before the end, surely! Just a brief extension of a year or so—a month or so even.

"I will bring him to-morrow, mother. He's too heavy to carry, but John will drive us."

Old Maisie seemed quite happy in this prospect of a great-grandson. "They are so nice at that age," said she. Why was the child's name Peter?—she asked, and was told that he was so called after his grandfather, Ruth's husband. "He is dead now, is he not?" was her puzzled inquiry, and Ruth replied:—"I buried his grandfather thirteen years ago." To which her mother said:—"Tell me all his name, that I may know," and was told "Peter Thrale." Whereupon she made an odd comment:—"Oh yes—I was told. But that was when Ruth was Widow Thrale."

She never came to any real clearness about the lost history of her sister and daughter. Having once grasped their identities, her mind flinched from the effort to master the forty-odd blank years of ignorance.

But out of the cloud there was to come a grandchild a year old, and in time its mother with another smaller still, newer still. To overhear this talk made Gwen discredit the doctor's unfavourable auguries. How was it possible that old Mrs. Picture should be dying, when she could look forward to a baby in the flesh with such a zest?

The prospect of this visitor had set the old mind thinking of her own babies in the days gone by, apparently. There was her eldest, dead and buried in England while Ruth was still too young to put by memories of her elder brother. Then her second, who died in his boyhood in Australia. No mother ever loses count of her children, even when her mind fails at the last: and old Maisie's memory was still green over the loss of these two. But the third —how about the one who survived his childhood? When she spoke of him, his image was that of an innocent mischievous youngster, full of mad pranks, his father's favourite, not a trace in him of the vices that had made his manhood a curse to himself and his mother. In some still feebler stage of her failing powers the happier phase of his career might have remained isolated. Now, her mind was still too active to avoid the recollection of its sequel.

" What is it, mother dearest? " So Gwen heard her daughter speaking to her, trying for a clue to the cause of some symptom of a concealed distress. Then Granny Marrable:—" Yes, Maisie darling, what is it. Tell us." Some answer came, which caused Ruth to say:—" Shall I ask her ladyship to come? "

Gwen immediately returned to the bedside. " Is she asking for me? " said she. And Granny Marrable replied:—" I think she has it on her mind to speak to you, my lady."

Not too many at once was the rule. Ruth made a pretence of something to be done in another room, but the Granny kept near at hand.

" My dear—my Lady—I am so afraid. . . ."

" Afraid of what, Mrs. Picture dear? Don't be frightened! We are all here."

" Afraid about my son—afraid Ruth may know. . . ."

" No one has told Ruth of him, dear. No one shall tell Ruth. I promise you."

" It is not that. It is what I may say myself." Gwen had not heard her speak so clearly for a long time. " It was on my lips to speak of him—but just now. Because—is he not the same? "

" The same as what, dear? Try and tell me! "

" The same as the son that came with me in the ship. The

same as the baby I suckled the last of four, out there on the farm. It was he that I was telling of before, and I was glad to tell my child—my Ruth—of the brother she never set eyes on. And then it came upon me, the thought of what he was, and what he had come to be. . . . Oh, my dear—my dear! . . ."

Gwen could not think of any stereotyped salve for a wounded heart. She could only say:—"Don't think of it, dear. Don't think of it! Lie still and get better now, and then I will make Aunt M'riar fetch Dave and Dolly, and Dave shall see Jones's Bull, and Dolly shall see the new baby."

"Suppose, my dear, I don't get better, will Dave and Dolly come all the same; for Phœbe and my Ruth, the same as if I was here?"

It was a sore tax on the steadiness of Gwen's voice, but she managed her assent. Yes—even in the improbable event of old Maisie's non-recovery, Dave and Dolly should visit Granny Marrable. And so consolatory had the assurance proved more than once before, that she repeated her undertaking about the visit to Farmer Jones's; for Dave, not for Dolly. "But there will be plenty for Dolly to see," Gwen said. "She won't be frightened of lambs—at least, I think not. Because she has never been in the country."

"No—but she has been in the Regent's Park, and is to go to Hampstead Heath some day with Uncle Mo. She is not frightened of the sheep in the Park, only in . . ."

"Only in where?" said Gwen. "Where is Dolly frightened of sheep?"

"In the street, because they run on the pavement, and the dog runs over their backs. . . . There are very few sheep here, compared to what we had in the colony. . . . Our shepherds were very good men, but all had their numbers from the Governor . . . they had all been convicted . . . but not of doing anything wrong. . . ."

Oh dear!—what a mistake Gwen had made about those sheep! But how could she have known? She knew so little about the colony—had even asked General Rawnsley, when they were talking of Van Diemen's Land, if he knew where "Tasmania" was! She tried to head off the pastoral convicts—the cancelled men, who had become numbers. "When Dolly comes, she will see the mill too. And it will go round and round by then." She clung in a sort of desperation to Dolly and Dave, having tested their power as talismans to drive away the black spectres that hung about.

But the mill was as Scylla to their Charybidis. "Phœbe dearest!" said old Maisie suddenly, "when did father die?"

"When did our father die?" said Granny Marrable. "Nigh upon forty-six years ago. Yes—forty-six."

"How can that be?—forty-six—forty-six!" The words were shadowily spoken, as by a speaker too weary to question them, yet dissatisfied. "How can my father have died then? That was when my sister died, and my little girl I left behind."

"Oh, *how* I wish she could sleep!" Gwen exclaimed under her breath. Granny Marrable said:—"She will sleep, my lady, before very long." She said it with such a quiet self-command, that Gwen accepted the obvious meaning that the sleeper would sleep again, as before. Perhaps nothing else was meant.

There had been a time, just after she first came to the strange truth of her surroundings, when she could follow and connect the sequence of events. Now the Past and the Present fell away by turns, either looming large and excluding the view of the other alternately. But, that Phœbe and Ruth were there, beside her, was the fact that kept the strongest hold of her mind.

Eleven o'clock. Granny Marrable had been right, and old Maisie had slept again, or seemed to sleep, after some dutiful useless attempts to head off Death by trivialities of nourishment. The clock-hand, intent upon its second, oblivious of its predecessors, incredulous of those to come, was near halfway to midnight when Ruth Thrale, rising from beside her mother, came to her fellow-watchers in the front-room and said:—"I think she moved."

Both came to the bedside. Yes—she had moved a little, and was trying to speak. Gwen, half seated, half leaning on the pillow as before, took a hand that barely closed on hers, and spoke. "What is it, Mrs. Picture dear? Say it again."

"Is it all true?"

What could Gwen have said but what she did say? "Yes, dear Mrs. Picture, quite true. It is your own sister Phœbe beside you here, and your child Ruth, grown up."

"Maisie darling, I am Phœbe—Phœbe herself." It was all Granny Marrable could find voice for, and Ruth was hard put to it to say:—"You are my mother." And as each of these women spoke she bent over the white face of the dying woman, and kissed it through the speechlessness their words had left upon their lips.

It was not quite old Mrs. Picture's last word of all. A few minutes later she seemed to make weak efforts towards speech. If Gwen, listening close, heard rightly, she was saying, or trying to say:—"You are my Lady, that came with the accident, are you not?"

"Is there anything you want me to do for you?" For Gwen thought she was trying to say more. "It is about someone. Who?"

"Susan Burr. . . ."

"Yes—you want me to give her some message?"

"Susan . . . to have my furniture . . . for her own."

"Yes—I will see to that. . . . And—and what?"

"Kiss Dave and Dolly for me."

They watched the scarcely breathing, motionless figure on the bed for the best part of an hour, and could mark no change that told of death, nor any sign that told of life. Then Granny Marrable said:—"What was that?" And Gwen answered, as she really thought:—"It was the clock." For she took it for the warning on the stroke of midnight. But old Phœbe said, with a strangely unfaltering voice:—"No—it is the change!" and the sob that broke the silence was not hers, but Ruth's. Old Mrs. Picture had just lived to complete her eighty-first year.

There came a sound of wheels in the road without. Not the doctor, surely, at this time of night! No—for the wheels were not those of his gig. Ruth, going out to the front-door, was met by a broad provincial accent—her son-in-law's. Gwen heard it fall to a whisper before the news of Death; then earnest conversation in an undertone. Gwen was aware that old Phœbe rose from her knees at the bedside, and went to listen through the door. Then she heard her say with a quiet self-restraint that seemed marvellous:—"Tell him—tell John that I will come. . . . Come back here and speak to me." She thought she caught the words as Ruth returned:—"I must not leave her alone." And she knew they referred to herself.

Then it came home to her that possibly her own youth and her difference of antecedents might somehow encumber arrangements that she knew would have to be carried out. They would be easiest in her absence. At her own suggestion she went away to lie down in the bedroom she had occupied.

Granny Marrable followed her. She had something to say.

"Dear Lady, I have to go. God bless you for all your goodness to my darling sister and to me! You gave her back to me. . . ." That stopped her.

"Oh, Granny, Granny, we have lost her—we have lost her!" She could feel that old Phœbe's tears were running down the hand she had taken to kiss, and she drew it away to fold the old woman fairly in her arms, and kiss the face whose likeness to old

Mrs. Picture's she could almost identify by touch. "We have lost her," she repeated, "and you might have had her for so long!"

Said Granny Marrable:—"I shall follow Maisie soon, if the Lord's will is. She might have died, my lady, but for you, unknown to me in London. And who would have told me where they had laid her?"

"Where are you going?"

"I am going to my granddaughter—Ruth's daughter. It is her ′ancy to have me rather than another. There might be harm to her did I stop away. Why should I delay here, when all is over?"

Why indeed? Still, Gwen could not but reverence and love the old lady for her unflinching fortitude and resolute sense of duty. She saw her driven away through the cold night, and went back to her room, leaving Ruth and Elizabeth the neighbour to make an end in the chamber of Death.

Sleep came, and waking came too soon, in a cold, dark Christmas morning. Oppression and pain for something not known at once came first, like a black cloud; then consciousness of what was in the heart of the cloud.

She wrapped herself in a warm dressing-gown, and went out through the silent house. It was still early, and it might be Ruth was still sleeping. Once asleep, why not remain so, when waking could only bring cold and darkness, and the memory of yesterday? Besides, it was not unlikely Ruth had watched half through the night. Gwen opened the door of the death-chamber with noiseless caution, and felt as soon as she saw that the daylight was still excluded, that it was empty of any living occupant. Dread was in her curiosity to see the thing beneath the white sheet on the bed—but see it she must!

The great bulldog, the only creature moving, came shambling along the passage to greet her, and—so she rendered his subdued dog-sounds that came short of speech—concerned that something was amiss he was excluded from knowing. She said a word to comfort him, but kept him outside the room, to wait for her return.

What had been till so lately old Mrs. Picture, whom she had chanced upon in Sapps Court, and found so strange a truth about, lay under that face-cloth on the bed. She moved the window-curtain for a stronger light, and uncovered the marble stillness of the face. The kerchief tied beneath the chin ran counter to her preconceptions, but no doubt it was all right. Ruth would know.

She did not look long. An odd sense of something that was not sacrilege, but akin to it, associated itself with this gazing on the empty tenement. Even so one shrinks from the emptiness of what was his home once, and will never know another dweller, but be carted off to the nearest dry-rubbish shoot. She laid the sheet back in its place, and went into the front-room.

Suddenly the dog growled and barked, then went smelling along the door into the front-garden. There was someone outside. She was conscious of a man on the gravel, through the window. A stranger, or he would enter without leave, or at least find the bell to ring. She glanced at the clock. It was half-past eight already, though it had seemed so early.

How about the dog, if she opened the door? His repute was great for ferocity towards doubtful characters, but he was credited with discrimination. Was this invariable? She preferred to take down his chain from its hook by the window, and to use it to hold him by.

"What is it? Who are you?" She had opened the door without reserve, feeling sure that the dog would be excited by a gap. As it was he growled intolerantly, and had to be reproved.

"You'll excuse me—I was inquiring . . . Is your dog safe? I ain't fond of dogs, and they ain't fond of me." He was a man with a side-lurch, and an ungracious manner.

"The dog is safe—unless I let him go." Gwen was not sorry to have a strong ally in a leash, at will. "You were inquiring—you said?"

"Concerning of an old lady by the name of Prichard. The address given was Strides Cottage, and I see this little domicile here goes by that name. Next we come to the old lady of the name of Prichard. Can you do her, or anything near about?"

"Yes—Mrs. Prichard is here, but you can't see her now. What do you want with Mrs. Prichard? Who are you?"

The man kept looking uneasily up and down the road. "I'm a bad hand at talking, mostly. Standing about don't suit me—not for conversation. If you was to happen to have such a thing as a chair inside, and you was to make the offer, I might see about telling you what I want of old Goody Prichard."

Gwen looked at him and recognised him. She would have done so at once had his clothes been the same as when she saw him before, in the doorway at Sapps Court. He was that man, of course! Only with this difference, that while on that occasion his get-up was nearest that of a horse-keeper, his present one was a carter's. He might have been taken for one, if you had not seen his face. Gwen said to him:—" You can pass the dog. Don't do anything to irritate him." He entered and sat down. " Where have you got the old woman? " said he.

" First tell me what you want with her."

" To introduce myself to her. I wrote her a letter nigh a fortnight since. What did I say to her in that letter? Told her I was looking forward to re-newing her acquaintance. You tell the old lady that, from me. You might go so far as to say it's Ralph, back again." An idea seemed to intensify his gaze of admiration, or rather avidity, narrowing it to her face. " This ain't my first sight of you, allowance made for toggery."

Gwen merely lifted her eyebrows. But seeing his offensive eyes waiting, she conceded:—" Possibly not," and remained silent.

He chose to interpret this as invitation to continue, although it was barely permission. " I set eyes on you first, as I was coming out of a door. You were coming in at that door. You looked at me to recollect me, for I saw you take notice. Ah!— you've no call to blaze at me on that account. You may just as well come down off of the high ropes."

For Gwen's face had shown what she thought of him, as he sat there, half wincing before her, half defiant. She was not in the habit of concealing her thoughts. " I see you are a reptile," said she explicitly. And then, not noticing his snigger of satisfaction at having, as it were, *drawn* her:—" What were you doing at Mr. Wardle's? "

" Ah—what was I a-doing at Moses Wardle's? I suppose you know what *he* was? Or maybe you don't? "

" What was he? "

The convict's ugly grin, going to the twisted side of his face, made it monstrous. " Mayhap you don't know what they call a *scrapper?* " said he.

" I don't. What did he scrap? " She felt that Uncle Mo did it honourably, whatever it was.

" He was one of the crack heavyweights, in my time."

" I know what that means. I should recommend you not to show yourself at his house, unless. . . ."

The man sniggered again. " Don't you lie awake about me," said he. " Old Mo had seen his fighting-days when I had the honour of meeting him five-and-twenty years ago at The Tun, which is out of your line, I take it. Besides, my best friend's in my pocket, ready at a pinch. Shall I show him to you? " He showed a knife with a black horn handle. "I don't open him, not to alarm a lady. So you've no call for hysterics."

"I am not afraid of you or your knife, if that is what you mean." Indeed, absolute fearlessness was one of Gwen's characteristics. "What did you go to Mr. Wardle's for?"

"On a visit to my wife."

Gwen started. "Who is your wife?" said she. Susan Burr flashed into her mind first. But then, how about "Aunt Maria" on the envelope, and her readiness to act as this man's agent?

"Polly Daverill's my wife—my lawful wife! That's more than my father could say of my mother."

"I know that you are lying, but I do not care why. Do you want to see your mother?"

"If sootable and convenient. No great hurry!"

"She is in bed. I will get her ready for you to see her. Do not go near the dog. They say he has killed a man."

"A man'll kill *him* if he gives occasion. Make him fast, for his own sake. There's money there—he's a tike o' some value. Maybe forty pound. You tie him up!" Gwen hooked his chain round the table-leg, starting him on a series of growls—low thunder in short lengths. He had been very quiet.

She passed into the bedroom, and opening the shutters, threw light full on the bed. Then she drew back the sheet she had replaced. Oh, the beauty of that white marble face, and the stillness!

"You can come in, quietly."

"Is she having a snooze?"

"You will not wake her."

"This is one of your games." The sort was defined by an adjective, omitted. "What's your game? What the Hell are you at?" He said this as to himself.

"Go in. You will find your mother." Gwen took back the dog's chain from the table-leg, and the low thunder died down.

She hardly analysed her own motives. One may have been to touch the heart of the brute, if he had one; another to convince him, without a long parley, of his mother's death. He might have disputed it, and in any case she could not have refused him the sight of his own mother's body.

She could not have restrained that dog had he acted on his obvious impulse to strangle, rapidly and thoroughly, this vermin intruder. But he was an orderly and law-abiding dog, who would not have strangled a rat without permission.

Gwen did not catch the convict's exclamation at sight of his

mother, beyond the "What the . . .!" that began it. Then he
was silent. She saw him go nearer without fear of ill-demeanour
on his part, and touch the cold white hand, not roughly or without a sort of respect. As well, perhaps, for him; for Gwen was
quite capable of loosing that dog on him, under sufficient provocation. She thought he seemed to examine the fingers of the left
hand. Then he came back, and they returned to the front-room.
She was the first to speak.

"Are you satisfied?"

"I couldn't have sworn to her myself, not from her face, but
I made sure." Probably he had looked for the cut finger, his own
handiwork of thirty-odd years ago. He said abruptly, after a
moment's pause:—"I don't see nothing to gain by hanging about
here."

"Nothing whatever."

He said not a word more, his only sign of emotion or excitement having been his exclamation at first sight of the corpse.
He walked away towards the village, and had just reached the
point where the road turns out of sight, when Gwen, watching
his slow one-sided footsteps, saw him turn and come quickly
back. She went back into the Cottage and closed the door, resolved not to admit him a second time.

But he passed by, going away by the road towards Denby's
and the Towers, never even glancing at the Cottage. He was
scarcely out of sight when a tax-cart with two men in it came
quickly from the village and stopped.

"You will excuse me, madam. I am Police-Inspector Thomp-
son, from Grantley Thorpe. A man whom I am looking for has
been traced here. . . ." The speaker had alighted.

"A man with a limp? He came here and went away. He
has only just gone."

"Which way?"

"He went away in that direction. . . ."

"What I said!" struck in the second man on the driver's seat.
"He's for getting back to the Railway. He'll cut across by More-
ton Spinney. Jump up, Joe!"

Gwen could easily have added that he had come back, and was
going the other way. But her promise to old Mrs. Picture, lying
there dead, kept her silent. If the officers chose to jump to a
false conclusion, let them! She had misled them by a literal
truth. She would much rather have told a lie, honourably. But
she could not remedy that now, without risk.

Another trot sounded from the opposite direction. It was

Farmer Costrell's cart, and Ruth was in it, driven by her son-in-law. She was bringing some evergreens to place upon the body. Too anxious to remain in ignorance about her daughter, she had walked over to Denby's while it was still almost dark, and had found a new granddaughter and its mother, both doing well.

"And ne'er a soul would I have seen either way," said she, "if it had not been for a tramp a few steps down the road, who set me thinking it was as well I was not alone, by the looks of him. Yes—thank your ladyship—I got some sleep, till after five o'clock. Then I could not be easy till I knew about my child. But all has gone well, God be thanked!"

It was the only time she ever saw that brother, and she never knew it was he.

CHAPTER XXIX

HOW MICKY BECAME A LINKBOY. HIS IDEAS ON INVESTMENTS. DOG FOUND. NO SAFETY LIKE A THICK FOG. OLD MR. NIXON. HIS SELF-RESTRAINT. WIX'S MESSAGE. JULIA'S DILEMMA. HER VIEWS ON MARRIAGE LINES. DAMN LAWFUL POLLY! HOW MICKY'S MOTHER HELPED HIM TO DELIVER HIS MESSAGE. OUR OLD LADY—GONE! WHO WILL TELL DAVE AND DOLLY? HOW PUSSY WAS THE OTHERS. HOW MO DID NOT STOP AT THE SUN. A VISITOR IN HIS ABSENCE. THE END

THE irresolute winter only wavered some forty-eight hours, setting to work in earnest on the second day after Christmas Day, following on suggestions of seasonableness on Boxing Day. London awoke to a dense fog and a hard frost, and its spirits went up. Its citizens became possessed with an unnatural cheerfulness, as is their wont when they cannot breathe without choking, when the gas has to be lighted at what should be the hour of day-break, when the vapour lies thick in places, and will not move from contact; though now and again the darkness, where the sky was once, seems at odds with a languid something that may be light, beyond. Then, fires within, heaped with fresh coal, regardless of expense, to keep the fog at bay, contribute more and more through chimney-pots without to the unspeakable opacities overhead, and each seeming ultimatum of blackness is followed by another blacker still. Then, while timid persons think the last day has come, the linkboys don't care whether it has or not, and enjoy themselves intensely.

A good example of the former class was Mrs. Treadwell, Michael Ragstroar's great-aunt at Hammersmith; of the latter, Michael himself. On the afternoon of that Wednesday in Christmas week he had conducted an old bloke of enormous wealth, on foot, from the said bloke's residence in Russell Square to his son-in-law's less pretentious one at Chiswick, and had earned liberal refreshments, golden opinions, and silver coin by his intrepidity and perception of London localities in Egyptian darkness. And he had never so much as once asked the name of a blooming street! So ran his communication to his great-aunt, on whom he called afterwards; being, as he said, handy.

"Now you do like I tell you, Micky, and bank it with the Savings Bank, and you'll live to be thankful." This referred to Micky's harphacrownd, just earned. That was his exact pronunciation, delivered *ore rotundissimo,* to do full justice to so large an amount.

Micky's reply was:—"Ketch me at it! I don't put no faith in any of these here Banks, like you see at street corners. *The* Bank, where you go on the green bus, is another pair o' stockin's. . . . No—I ain't going to put it on a 'orse. You carn't never say they ain't doctored." He went on to express an astute mistrust of investments, owing to the bad faith of Man, and wound up:—"The money won't run away of itself, so long as you don't let it out of your porket." Into which receptacle Micky returned it, slapping the same in ratification of its security.

"Then you button it in, Micky, and see you don't talk about it to no one. Only I should have said it would be safer put by, or giv' to some responsible person to take charge of." But Michael shook his head, assuming a farsighted expression. He was immovable. Mrs. Treadwell continued:—"Bein' here, I do declare you might be a useful boy, and write *Dog Found* large on a sheet of paper, and ask Miss Hawkins to put it up in her window for to find the owner."

"Wot's the dog?"

"Well now, he was here a minute back! Or he run out when you come in." Fog-retarded search discovered a woebegone refugee under the stairs; who had been fetched in, said Mrs. Treadwell, by her puppy in the early morning, and whom she had not had the heart to drive away.

Michael was proud to show his skill as a penman, and with his aunt's assistance composed an intelligible announcement that

the owner of a black-and-tan terrier with one eye might recover
the same on production of some proof of ownership. Michael
devised one, suggesting that any applicant might be told to say
what name was wrote on the collar.

"But there now, Micky," said the old charwoman. "He
hasn't *got* no collar!"

"Werry good, then," said her nephew. "When he tells you
what's wrote on the collar, you'll know he's a liar, and don't
you give him up the dog."

"But shan't I be a story," said Mrs. Treadwell, "for to tell
him the collar's wrote upon, when it's no such a thing?"

"Not you, Arnty! Don't you say anything's wrote. Just you
ask him what, and cotch him out!"

The puppy wanted to help, and nearly blotted the composition.
But this was avoided, and Micky went out into the fog bearing
the placard, of which he was rather proud.

A typical sot was the only occupant of the bar, who was so
far from sober that he imagined he was addressing a public meeting. Micky distinguished that he was referring to his second
wife, and had some fault to find with the chairman. Voices in
the little parlour behind the bar caught the boy's ear, and took his
attention off. He was not bound to stop his ears. If parties
hollered, it was their own lookout. Parties hollered, in this case,
and Micky could hear, without listening. He was not sure,
though, when he heard one of the voices, that he would not have
listened, if he had any call to do so. For it was the voice of his
old acquaintance the convict.

"No safety like a thick fog, Juliar! I'll pay her a visit this
very afternoon, so soon as ever you've given me some belly-
timber. Sapps Court'll be as black as an inch-thick of ink for
twelve hours yet. Don't you let that steak burn!"

Michael heard the steak rescued—the hiss of its cookery intercepted. Then he heard Miss Julia say with alarm in her voice:—
"You're never going there, Wix! Not to Sapps Court?"

"And why the Hell shouldn't I go to Sapps Court? One place
is as safe as another, a day like this." Insert if you will an adjective before "place," here.

Michael, sharp as he was, could not tell why the woman's answer
sounded embarrassed, even through a half-closed door. The story
knows. She had betrayed the knowledge she had acquired from
the letter she had tampered with, that Sapps was being specially
watched by the Police. How could she account for this knowledge, without full confession? And would not absolution be im-

possible? She could only fence with the cause of her confusion. "I got the idea on my mind, I expect," said she uneasily. "Didn't you say she had a man hanging round?"

"Old Mo, sure enough. Yes, there's old Mo. But *he* won't be there. He'll be swiping, round at The Sun. I can reckon *him* up! He don't train for fighting, like he did thirty years ago. One sight of him would easy your mind—an old dot-and-go-one image!"

"I got the idea the officers would look to catch you there. I *did*, Wix."

"And I got the idea no such a thing!" Omission again before this last word. "Why in thunder do you suppose? . . . Shut to that door!"

"There's no one there—only old Nixon."

"Who's he talking to?"

"Nobody. Empty space!"

"Tell you he is! Look and see." Thereupon Miss Julia, looking through a transparent square in a glass chessboard into the bar, saw that the typical sot was certainly under the impression that he had an audience. He was, in fact, addressing a homily to Michael on the advantages of Temperance. See, he said—substantially—the reward of self-restraint! He was no mere bigoted doctrinaire, wedded to the absurd and exaggerated theories of the Teatolers. He had not a word to say in favour of Toalabshnensh. It was against Human Naysh. But Manshknewwhairtshtop, like himself, was always on the safe side. He charged Micky to be on his guard against Temptation, who lay in wait for inexperience without his first syllable, which had been absorbed in a hiccup. Micky was not grateful to Mr. Nixon for this, as it interfered with his hearing of the conversation within.

"Who are you, in behind that handle?" asked Miss Hawkins. "Come out and show us your face. . . . What's this? 'Dog Found'? Yes—very happy to oblige your aunt. . . . Stick it up against the front-glass yourself. . . . 'Won't stick of itself,' won't it? Wait till I see for a wafer." She returned into the small parlour, and foraged in the drawer of her inkstand, which had probably done no service since her experiment in *faussure*, till it supplied Mr. Wix with a simile for the fog, ten minutes since.

"That's young Ikey," said the convict. "I can tell him by his lip. Fetch him inside. I've a message for him to carry." Miss Julia had found red wafers; and, after instructing Michael how to use them—to suck them in earnest, as they had got dry await-

ing their mission in life—induced him into Mr. Wix's presence.
Micky's instinctive hatred of this man was subdued by the
recollection of the *douceurs* he had received from him. But do
what he would, he was only equal to a nod, as greeting. He
hardly received so much himself.

The convict eyed him sleepily from the window-seat, his usual
anchorage at The Pigeons, and said nothing for some seconds.
Then he roused himself to say:—"Well, young shaver, what the
office for you?—that's the point! Look you now—are you going
home?"

"Quite as like as not. That don't commit me to nothing,
neither way. Spit it out, guv'nor!"

Mr. Wix was filling a pipe, and did it to his satisfaction before
he answered:—"You've to carry a message. A message to Aunt
M'riar. Got that? You know Aunt M'riar."

"Knew Aunt M'riar afore ever you did."

Mr. Wix looked through his first puff of smoke, amused.
"About right you are, that time!" said he. Not that this was
untrue enough to be worth telling as a falsehood. Polly the barmaid had no niece or nephew that he knew of, in the early days.
"But you could carry a message to her, if you didn't. Just you
tell her old Goody Prichard's gone off her hooks."

"The widder two pair up at Number Seven? What hooks?"

"She's slipped her wind, handed in her chips."

"Mean she's dead? Carn't you say so, mister?"

"Sharp boy! That's what *she* is. Dead."

"That won't soote Aunt M'riar." Micky had only known old
Maisie by repute, but he knew the Court's love for her. A wish
for some confirmation of the convict's statement arose in his mind.
"How's she to know it's not a lie?" said he.

"*She'll* know, fast enough! Say I told you. Say who I am.
She'll twig, when you tell her. . . . Stop a bit!" He was thinking how to authenticate the death without telling the boy overmuch about himself. "Look here—I'll tell you what you've got
to say. Say her son—old mother Prichard's son—was just up
from Rocestershire, and he'd seen her dead, with his own eyes.
Dead as a boiled lobster. That's your message."

If Micky had known that this man was speaking of himself
and his own mother! Perhaps it was some instinctive inward-
ness that made him glad he had got his message and could be
gone. He made short work of his exit, saying:—"All right,
mister, I'm your man"—and departed after a word in the bar
to Miss Julia:—"Right you are, missis! Don't you let him

have another half-a-quartern." For Mr. Nixon being a penny
short, her anxiety that he should observe his own rules of life
had been reinforced by commercialism. She drew the line of
encouraging drunkenness at integers—halves not counting as fractions, by tacit consent. They are not hard enough.

Miss Hawkins had placed herself in a difficulty by that indiscreet tampering with Aunt M'riar's letter. She had done it in
a fit of furious exasperation with Daverill, immediately the result of an interview with him on his reappearance at The Pigeons
some weeks ago. Some whim had inclined him towards the exhibition of a better selfhood than the one in daily use; perhaps
merely to assert the power he still possessed over the woman;
more probably to enable him to follow it up with renewed suggestions that she should turn the freehold Pigeons into solid
cash, and begin with him a new life in America. She had kept
her head in spite of kisses and cajolery, which appealed with
some success to her memories of twenty years ago, and had refused to entertain any scheme in which lawful marriage was
postponed till after the sale of her property. The parson was to
precede the auctioneer.

But an escaped convict with the police inquiring for him cannot put up the banns. Had Daverill seen his way to doing so he
would have made light of bigamy. Besides, *was* it likely his first
wife would claim him? He preferred to suppress his real reason
for refusing to "make an honest woman" of Miss Julia, and
to take advantage of the fact that his "real wife" Polly was
still living.

Then Miss Hawkins had made a proposal which showed a
curious frame of mind about marriage law. Her idea may be
not unknown in the class she belonged to, still. It certainly
existed in the fifties of last century. If Aunt M'riar could be deprived of her "marriage lines" her teeth would be drawn, not
merely practically by making proof of a marriage difficult, but
definitely by the removal of a mysterious influence—most to be
likened to the key of a driving-pulley, whose absence from its
slot would leave the machinery of Matrimony at a deadlock. Let
Mr. Wix, by force or fraud, get possession of this charter of respectability, and he and his lawful wife would come apart, like
a steamed postage-stamp and its envelope. Nothing would be
lacking then but a little fresh gum, and reattachment. This ex-
presses Miss Julia's idea, however faulty the simile may be in
itself.

"She's got her lines to show"—So the lady had been saying,

shortly before Michael came into the bar.—" But she won't have them long, if you put your mind on making her give 'em up. *You* can do it, Wix." She seemed to have a strong faith in the convict's cunning.

He appeared to ponder over it, saying finally:—" Right you are, Juliar! I see my way."

" What are you going to do ? "

" That's tellings. I'll get the dockyment out of her. That's enough for you, without your coming behind to see. I'll make you a New Year's present of it, gratish. What'll you do with it ? "

" Tear it up—burn it. That'll quiet *her* off. Lawful Polly! Damn her ! " Really Miss Hawkins made a better figure in a rage, than when merely vegetating. And yet her angry flush was inartistic, through so much pearl powder. It made streaks.

It had its effect on Daverill, soothing his complaisant mood, making him even more cunning than before. " I'll get it out of her, Juliar," said he, " and you shall have it to tear up, to your heart's content. It don't make one farthing's worth of difference, that I see. But have it your own choice. A woman's a woman ! " There seems no place in this for Mr. Wix's favourite adjective; but it called for omission before " farthing's worth," for all that!

" Not a penny of mine shall go your way, Wix, till I've put it on the fire, and seen it burn." Miss Hawkins dropped her voice to say:—" Only keep safe, just the little while left."

After Micky's exit one or two customers called for attention, and subsided into conversation over one or two quarts. One had a grievance that rumbled on continuously, barely pausing for intermittent sympathy from the other or others. Their quarts having been conceded and paid for, Miss Julia returned. That steak—which you may have felt anxious about—was being kept hot, and Mr. Wix was tapping the ashes out of his finished pipe. " There! " said he. " You run your eye through that, and you'll see there's no more cause to shy off Sapps than any other place." His exact words suggested recent carnage in Sapps Court, but only for rhetoric's sake.

Miss Hawkins picked up the letter he threw across the table, and recognised the one she had stealthily converted to an assurance of the disappearance of extra police from Sapps Court. She felt very uncomfortable indeed—but what could she do ?

Ill news is said to travel fast, always. It had not done so in this case, and Sapps Court was still in ignorance of old Maisie's death when Michael passed under its archway, to experience for

the first time the feelings that beset the bearer of fatal tidings
to those it will wound to hear them far worse than himself. To
a not inhuman creature, in such a case, a title to sorrow, that
will lessen the distance between his own heart and the one he
has to lacerate, is almost a relief.

He himself was not to blame for delay in delivering his message. On the contrary, his sympathetic perception of its unwel-
comeness to its recipients took the strange form of a determination not to lose a second in fulfilling his instructions. So deeply
bent was he on doing this that he never questioned the reasonableness of his own alacrity until he had passed the iron post
Dave fell off—you remember?—and was opposite to his own family
residence at the head of the Court. His intention had been to
pass it, and go straight on to No. 7. Something made him
change his mind; perhaps the painfulness of his task dawned on
him. His mother was surprised to see him. " There now," said
she. " I thought you was going to be out all day, and your
father he'll want all the supper there is for hisself."

" So I *was* a-going to be out all day. I'm out now, in a manner
o' speaking. Going out again. Nobody's going to suffer from
an empty stummick along o' me." He had subsided on a rocking-
chair, dropping his old cloth cap between his feet.

" Whereabouts have you been to, Micky? " said his mother
conciliatorily, to soothe her son's proud independent spirit.

He recited his morning's work rapidly. " Linked an old cock
down to Chiswick Mawl what was frightened to ride in a hansom,
till half-past eleven, 'cos he could only go . slow. Got an early
dinner off of his cook by reason of roomuneration. Cold beef
and pickles as much as I choose. Slice o' plum pudding hotted
up a purpose, only no beer for to encourage wice in youth. Bein'
clost handy, dropped round on a wisit to Arnty Lisbeth. Arnty
Lisbeth she's makin' inquiry concerning a young tike's owner.
Wrote Arnty Lisbeth out a notice-card. Got Miss Horkings next
door to allow it up in her window on the street. That's how I
came by this here intelligence I got to pass on to Wardle's. Time
I was going! "

Mrs. Ragstroar stopped scraping the brown outer skin off a
very large potato, and looked reproachfully at Micky. " You've
never said nothing of *that*," said she.

" Who ever went to say I said anything of it? " was the reply.
In this family all communications took the form of contradictions
or indictments, more or less defiant in character. " I never said
not one word. I'd no call to say anything, and I didn't."

" Then how can you ever expect anyone to know unless you
say ? " She went on peeling.

" Who's ever said I expected anyone to know ? " But in
spite of his controversial method, he did *not* go away to give
this message; and evidently wanted a helping hand, or at least
sympathy.

His mother perceived the fact, and said magnanimously:—
" You might just as well up and tell, Micky." Then she nearly
undid the effect of her concession by saying:—" Because you know
you want to ! "

What saved the situation was that Micky *did* want to. He
blurted out the news that was oppressing him, to his own great
relief. " Old Mother Prichard, Wardleses Widder upstairs, she's
dead."   \

" Sakes alive ! They was expecting her back."

" Well—she's dead, like I tell you ! "

" For sure ? "

" That's what her son says. If *he* don't know, nobody don't."

" Was it him told you ? I never heard tell she had a son—
not Mrs. Prichard."

Micky's family pugnacity preferred to accept this as a censure,
or at least a challenge. He raised his voice, and fired off his
speech in platoons, to say:—" Never see her son ! Shouldn't know
him if I *was* to see him. Wot—I'm telling—you—that's—wot—
her—son said to the party what commoonicated it to me. Miss
Wardle she'll reco'nise the party, by particklars giv'." This embodied the impression received from the convict's words, which
had made no claim to old Maisie as his mother.

" Whatever shall you say to Mrs. Wardle ? "

Micky picked up his cap from the ground, and used it as a
nose-polisher—after slapping it on his knee to sterilise it, a use
which seemed to act in relief of perplexity. " If I know, I'm
blest," said he. " Couldn't tell you if you was to arsk me ! "

It was impossible to resist the implied appeal for help. Mrs.
Ragstroar put a large fresh potato on the table to enjoy its skin
yet a little longer, and wiped the memory of its predecessors off
on her apron. " Come along, Micky," she said. " I got to see
Aunt M'riar; you come along after me. I'll just say a word
aforehand." Micky welcomed this, and saying merely:—" Ah !—
like a tip ! " followed his mother down the Court to No. 7.

Someone, somewhere, must have known, clocks apart, that a
day was drawing to a close; a short winter's day, and a dark and
cold one at the best. But the someone was not in the Thames

Valley, and the somewhere surely was not Sapps Court. There Day and Night alike had been robbed of their birthright by sheer Opacity, and humankind had to choose between submission to Egyptian darkness and an irksome leisure, or a crippled activity by candlelight, on the one hand, and ruin, on the other. Not that tallow candles were really much good—they got that yellow and streaky. Why—the very gaslamps out of doors you couldn't hardly see them, not unless you went quite up close! If it had not been that, as Micky followed his mother down the Court, a ladder-bearer had dawned suddenly, and died away after laying claim to lighting you up a bit down here, no one would never have so much as guessed illumination was afoot. But then the one gaslamp was on a bracket a great heicth up, on the wall at the end of Druitt's garden, so called. And Mrs. Ragstroar and her son had followed along the wood-palings in front of the houses, on the left.

Micky's flinching from his mission had grown on him so by the time they reached the end house, that he hung back and allowed his mother to enter first. He wanted the tip to exhaust the subject of Death, and to leave him only the task of authentication. He did not hear what his mother said in a quick undertone to Aunt M'riar, within, manifestly ironing. But he heard its effect on her hearer—a cry of pain, kept under, and an appeal to Uncle Mo, in some dark recess beyond. "Oh, Mo!—only hark at that! Our old lady—gone!" Then Uncle Mo, emerging probably from pitch darkness in the little parlour, and joining in the undertones on inquiry and information mixed—mixed soon enough with sobs. Then the struggle against them in Mo's own voice of would-be reassurance:—"Poor old M'riar! Don't ye take on so! We'll all die one day." Then more undertones. Then Aunt M'riar's broken voice:—"Yes—I *know* she was eighty"—and her complete collapse over:—"It's the children I'm thinking of! Our children, Mo, our children!"

Old Mo saw that point. You could hear it in his voice. "Ah—the children!" But he tried for a forlorn hope. Was it possibly a false report? Make sure about that, anyhow, before giving way to grief! "Was it only that young shaver of yours brought the news, Mrs. Ragstroar? Maybe he's put the saddle on the wrong horse!"

"He's handy to tell his own tale, Mr. Wardle. Here, young Micky! Come along in and speak for yourself." Whereupon the boy came in. He had been secretly hoping he might escape being called into council altogether.

"You're sure you got the right of it, Michael," said Uncle Mo. "Tell it us all over again from the beginning."

Whereupon Micky, braced by having a member of his own noble sex as catechist, but sadly handicapped by inability to employ contentious formulas, gave a detailed account of his visit to The Pigeons. He identified the convict by short lengths of speech, addressed to Mr. Wardle's ear alone, suggestive of higher understandings of the affairs of men than aunts and mothers could expect to share. "Party that's givin' trouble to the Police. . . . Party I mentioned seeing in Hy' Park. . . . Party that come down the Court inquirin' for widder lady . . ." came at intervals. Micky's respectful and subdued reference to Mrs. Prichard was a tribute to Death.

"And did he say her son told him, to his own hearing? . . . All right, M'riar, I know what I'm talking about." This was to stop Aunt M'riar's interposing with a revelation of old Maisie's relation to the party. It would have encumbered cross-examination; which, even if it served no particular end, would seem profound and weighty.

"That's how I took it from him," said Micky.

"Didn't he say who her son was?" Aunt M'riar persisted, with unflinching simplicity.

Micky, instantly illuminated, replied:—"Not he! He never so much as said he wasn't her son, hisself." This did not mean that affirmation was usually approached by denial of every possible negation. It was only the involuntary echo of a notion Aunt M'riar's manner had clothed her words with.

"That was tellings, M'riar," said Uncle Mo. "But it don't make any odds, that I can see. Look ye here, young Micky! What was it this charackter said about coming here this afternoon?"

"Werry first words I heard him say! 'No safety like a thick fog,' he says. 'And I'll pay her a visit this very arternoon,' he says. Only he won't! You may take that off me, like Gospel."

"How do you make sure of that, young master?"

"'Cos he's got nothing to come for, now I've took his message for him. If he hadn't had reliance, he'd not have arxed me to carry it. He knows me for safe, by now, Mr. Wardle."

"Don't you see, Mo," said Aunt M'riar. "He'd no call to come here, exceptin'. It was only to oblige-like, and let know. Once Micky gave his word, what call had he to come four mile through such a fog?"

"That's the whole tale, then?" said Uncle Mo, after reflection.

"Onlest you can call to mind something you've forgot, Master Micky."

"Not a half a word, Mr. Moses. If there had a been, I'd have made you acquainted, and no lies. And all I said's ackerate, and to rely on." Which was perfectly true, so far as reporter's good faith went. Had Micky overheard the conversation two minutes sooner, he would have gathered that Mr. Wix had other reasons for coming to Sapps Court than to give the news of Mrs. Prichard's death. Indeed, it is not clear why, intending to go there for another purpose, Wix thought it necessary to employ Michael at all as an ambassador. But a story has to be content with facts.

Uncle Mo and Aunt M'riar were alone with the shadow of their trouble, and the knowledge that the children must be told. The boy and his mother, their painful message delivered, had vanished through the fog to their own home. The voices of Dave and Dolly came from the room above through the silence that followed. Mo and M'riar were at no loss to guess what was the burden of that earnest debate that rose and fell, and paused and was renewed, but never died outright. It was the endless arrangement and rearrangement of the preparations for the great event to come, the feast that was to welcome old Mrs. Picture back to her fireside, and its chair with cushions.

"Oh, Mo—Mo! I haven't the heart—I haven't the heart to do it."

"Poor old M'riar—poor old M'riar!" The old prizefighter's voice was tender with its sorrow for his old comrade, who shrank from the task that faced them, one or both; even sorrow—though less oppressive—for the loss of the old lady who had become the children's idol.

"No, Mo, I haven't the heart. Only this very day . . . if it hadn't been for the fog . . . Dave would have got the last half-penny out of his rabbit to buy a sugar-basin on the stall in the road . . . and he's saving it for a surprise for Dolly . . . when the fog goes. . . ."

"Is Susan Burr upstairs with them?"

"No—she's gone out to Yardley's for some thread. She's all right. She's walking a lot better."

They sat silent for a while, the unconscious voices overhead reaching their hearts, and rousing the question they would have been so glad to ignore. How should they bring it to the children's knowledge that the chair with cushions was waiting for its occupant in vain? Which of their unwilling hands should be the first to draw aside the veil that still sheltered those two babies' lives from the sight of the face of Death.

The man was the first to speak. "Young Mick, he saw his way pretty sharp, M'riar—about who was . . . her son." His voice dropped on the reference to old Maisie herself, and he avoided her name.

"Did he understand?"

"Oh yes—he twigged, fast enough. . . . There's a p'int to consider, M'riar. This man's her son—but it don't follow he knows whether she's dead or living, any better than you or me. Who's to say he's not lying? Besides, we should have had a letter to tell. . . . Who from? . . . H'm—well—from. . . ." But Mo found the completion of this sentence difficult.

No wonder! How could he reply:—"Her ladyship?" He may have been convinced that Gwen would write, but how could he say so? The sister and daughter, neither of whom were more than names to him, seemed out of the question. Sister Nora would be sure to come with the news, some time. But was she back from Scotland, where they knew she had gone to convalesce?

Aunt M'riar looked the fact in the face. "No—we shouldn't have had no letter, Mo. Not yet a while, at least. Daverill's a bad man, and lies. But not when there's no advantage in it. He'd not go about to send me word she was dead, except he knew."

"How should he know, more than we?"

"Don't you ask me about when I see him, not yet where, nor yet how, and I'll tell you, Mo." She waited, as for a safe-conduct.

"Poor old M'riar!" said Mo pitifully. "I'll not witness-box you. Catch me! No—no!—you shan't tell me nothing you don't like."

"He told me he should try to see his mother again. And I said to him if he went there he would be taken, safe and certain. And he said not he, because the Police were too sharp by half, and would take for granted he would be afraid to go anigh the place again. He said he could always see round them."

"I see what he was driving at. And you think he went."

"None so long ago, I should say. He never see her—not alive. I couldn't say why, only I feel that was the way of it."

"When did you see him last? . . . No—old girl! I won't do that. It's mean—after sayin' I wouldn't witness-box! Don't you tell me nothing."

"I won't grudge telling you that much, Mo. It's a tidy long time back now. I couldn't say to a day. It was afore I wrote to him to keep away from the Court for fear of the Police. . . .

Yes—I did! Just after Mr. Rowe came round that time, asking inquiries. . . . I *am* his wife, Mo—nothing can't alter it."

" I ain't blaming you, old girl."

" Well—it was then he said he'd go to Chorlton again. And he's been."

Silence again, and the sound of the children above. Then a footstep without, recognised as Susan Burr's by its limp.

" She'll have to be told, Mo," said Aunt M'riar. " We've never had a thought for poor Susan."

A commonplace face came white as ashes from the fog without, and a suffocating voice, gasping against sobs. " Oh, M'riar!— Oh, Mr. Wardle!—*Is* it true she's gone?"

Aunt M'riar could not tighten her lips against their instability and speak, at the same time, so she nodded assent. Uncle Mo said, steadily enough:—" I'm afraid it's true, Mrs. Burr. We can't make it out no otherwise." Then M'riar got self-command to say:—" Yes—she's taken from us. It's the Lord's will." And then they could claim their birthright of tears, the last privilege left to hearts encompassed with the darkness of the grave.

The three were standing, some short while later, at the stair-foot, each looking at the other. Which was to go first?

Aunt M'riar made a hesitating suggestion. " Supposin' you was to step up first, and look back to say . . . !"

" That's one idear," said Uncle Mo. " Suppose you do!"

Susan Burr, referred to by both, accepted the commission, limping slowly up the stairs while the others waited below, listening. They heard that the door above was opened, when the children's voices came clearer, suddenly. But Susan Burr had only cautiously pushed the door ajar, making no noise, to listen herself before going in. There was a flare from a gas-birth in the fire as she got a sight of the group within, through the opening. It illuminated Dolly, Dave, and the newly christened wax doll; the Persian apparatus on the floor—a mere rehearsal, whose cake had to be pretence cake, and whose tea lacked its vegetable constituent—and the portraits of robed and sceptred Royalty on the wall. Some point in stage-management seemed to be under discussion, and to threaten a dissolution of partnership. For Dave was saying:—" Then oy shall go and play with The Boys, because the fog's a-stopping. You look out at the winder!"

Dolly met this with a firm, though gentle, prohibition. " No, you *s'arn't*. You *is* to be Gwanny Mawwowbone vis time, and set on the sofa. And me to be old Mrs. Spicture vis time, and set in the chair wiv scushions. And Pussy to be ve uvvers. And

Gweng to paw out all veir teas. Only vey take veir sugar veir-
selves." Dolly may have had it in view to reduce Dave to im-
potence by assigning to him the position of a guest. His manhood revolted against a subordinate part. Superhuman tact is
needed—an old story!—in the casting of the parts of any new
play, and Dolly, although kissable to a degree, and with an iron
will, was absolutely lacking in tact.

"Then oy shall go and play with The Boys, because the forg's
a-stoarping." But this was an empty threat, as Dave knew perfectly well that Uncle Mo would not allow him to go out of doors
so late, even if the fog melted, since its immediate cessation would
have left London in the dark, for it was past the Official hour
of sunset.

Dolly said again:—"No, you sarn't!" and went on with the
arrangements. "You take *tite* hold of Pussy, and stop her off
doin' on ve scushions. Gweng to paw out the tea, only to wait
faw the hot water! Ven I shall go in the chair with scushions,
and be Mrs. Spicture. And ven you to leave hold of Pussy, and
be Gwanny Mawwowbone on the sofa." The supernumeraries
were *intransigeant* and troublesome; that is to say, their representative the Cat was.

Dave, whose enjoyment of these games was beginning to be
marred by his coming manhood—for see how old he was getting!
—utilised magnanimity as an excuse for concession. He kept
the supers in check while Dolly suggested an attitude to Gweng.
Gweng had only to wait for hot water, so it was easy to find one.
Dolly then scrambled into the chair with cushions, and the supernumeraries wedged themselves round her and purred, in the person of the Cat. But having made this much concession, Dave
struck.

Instead of accepting his part, he went to the window. "Oy
can see across the way," said he. "Oy don't call it a forg when
you can see the gairslamp all the way across the Court. That
hoyn't a forg! Oy say, Dolly, oy'm a-going for to see Uncle
Mo round to The Sun parlour, and boy a hoypny sorcer coming
back. Oy *am!*"

Dolly shook a mass of rough gold that cried aloud for a comb,
and said with sweet gravity:—"You tarn't!"

"Why not?" Dave's indignation at this statement made him
shout. "Why carn't oy, same as another boy?"

"Because you're Gwanny Mawwowbone, all ve time. You
tarn't *help* it." Dolly's solemn nods, and a pathos that seemed
to grieve over the inevitable, left Dave speechless, struggling in

vain against the identity he had so rashly undertaken to assume. Susan Burr missed a great deal of this, and marked what she heard but little. She only knew that the children were happy, and that their happiness must end. Even her own grief—for think what old Maisie's death meant to her!—was hushed at the thought of how these babies could be told, could have their first great grief burst upon them. She felt sick, and only knew that she herself could not speak the word.

Aunt M'riar stole up after her stealthily—not Uncle Mo; his weight on the old stairs would have made a noise. They stood side by side on the landing, just catching sight of the little poppet in the armchair, all unkempt gold and blue eyes, quite content with her personation of the beloved old presence it would never know again. Aunt M'riar could just follow Susan Burr's stifled whisper:—" She's being old Mrs. Picture, in her chair."

It was confirmed by Dave's speech from the window, unseen. " You *ain't* old Mrs. Picture. When Mrs. Picture comes, oy shall tell her you said you was her, and then you'll see what Mrs. Picture'll say! " He spoke with a deep earnestness—a champion of Truth against an insidious and ungrounded fiction, that pretence was reality.

Then Dolly's voice, immovable in conviction, sweet and clear in correction of mere error:—" I *is* Mrs. Spicture, and when she comes she'll *say* I was Mrs. Spicture. She'll set in her chair wiv scushions, and *say* I was Mrs. Spicture."

The two listeners without did not wait to hear Dave's indignant rejoinder. They could not bear the tranquil ignorance of the children, and their unconsciousness of the black cloud closing in on them. They turned and went noiselessly down the stairs, choking back the grief they dared not grant indulgence to, by so much as a word or sound. The chronic discussion that they had left behind went on—on—always the same controversy, as it seemed; the same placid assurance of Dolly, the same indignant protest of Dave.

At the stairfoot, Uncle Mo, silent, looking inquiry, mistrusting speech. Aunt M'riar used a touch on his arm, and a nod towards the door of the little parlour, to get safe out of the children's hearing before risking speech, with that suffocation in her throat. Then when the door was closed, it came.

" We c-c-couldn't do it, Mo, we c-couldn't do it." Her sobs became a suppressed wail of despair, which seemed to give relief. Susan Burr had no other tale to tell, and was inarticulate to the same effect. They *could* not break through the panoply of the children's ignorance of Death, there in the very home of the departed, in the face of every harbinger of her return.

"Poor old M'riar! You shan't have the telling of 'em." Uncle Mo's pitying tones were husky in the darkened room; not quite dark, as the fog was lifting, and the Court's one gas-lamp was perceptible again through its remains. "Poor old M'riar! You shan't tell 'em—nor yet Susan Burr. *I'll* tell 'em, myself." But his heart sank at the prospect of his task, and he was fain to get a little respite—of only a few hours. "Look ye here, M'riar, I don't see no harm to come of standing of 'em over till we know. Maybe, as like as not, we'll have a letter in the morning."

But Uncle Mo was not to have the telling of the children.

Once it was clearly understood that the news was to be kept back, it became easier to exist, provisionally. Grief, demanding expression, gnaws less when silence becomes a duty. It was almost a relief to Susan Burr to have to be dry-eyed, on compulsion; far, far easier than to have to explain her tears to the young people. She went upstairs to them, mustering, as she went, a demeanour that would not be hypocritical, yet would safeguard her from suspicion of a hidden secret. She had been a long way, and was feeling her foot. That covered the position. Further, the children might stop upstairs a bit longer, if good. Dave was not to go out. Uncle Mo had said so. If Uncle Mo did go round to The Sun to-day, it would be after little boys and girls were abed and asleep. Mrs. Burr made her attitude easier to herself by affecting a Draconic demeanour. It was due to her foot, Dave and Dolly decided.

The unconscious children accepted the fog as all-sufficient to account for the household's gloom, and never knew how heavily the hours went by for its older members. Bedtime came, and the fog did not go, or, at least, went no further than to leave the gaslamp as Dave had seen it, just visible across the Court, or discernible from the archway at a favourable fluctuation. Susan Burr stepped round to Mrs. Ragstroar's, alleging anxiety to hear Michael's story again, and some hopes of further particulars. She may have felt indisposed for the loneliness of her own room, with that empty chair; and yet that a company of three would bear reduction, all that called for saying having been said twice and again.

This was soon after supper; when little boys and girls are abed and asleep. The little boy in this case was half asleep. He heard his Aunt's and Uncle's voices get fainter as his own dream-voices came to take their place, and then came suddenly awake with a start to find Uncle Mo looming large beside him in the half-dark room. "Made you jump, did I, old man?" said Uncle Mo, kissing him. "Go to sleep again." Dave did so, but not before receiving a dim impression that his uncle went into the neighbouring room to Dolly, and kissed the sleeping child, too; gently, so as not to wake her. That was the impression, gleaned somehow, under which he went to sleep. Uncle Mo often looked in at Dave and Dolly, so this visit was no surprise to Dave.

Aunt M'riar awaited him at the stairfoot, on his return. "They'll be happy for a bit yet," said she. "Now, if only Jerry would come and smoke with you, Mo, I wouldn't be sorry to get to bed myself."

"May be he'll come!" said Mo. "Anyways, M'riar, don't you stop up on account of me. I'll have my pipe and a quiet think, and turn in presently. . . . Or look here!—tell you what! I'll just go round easy towards Jeff's, and if I meet Jerry by the way, I meet him; and if I don't, I don't. I shan't stop there above five minutes if he's not there, and I shan't stop all night if he is. Good-bye, M'riar."

"Good-night's plenty, Mo; you're coming back."

"Ay, surely! What did I say? Good-bye? Good-night, I should have made it." But he *had* said "Good-bye!"

Has it ever occurred to you—you who read this—to feel it cross your mind when walking that you have just passed a something of which you took no notice? If you have, you will recognise this description. Did Uncle Mo, when he wavered at the arch, fancy he had half-seen a figure in the shadow, near the dustbin, and had automatically taken no notice of it? If so, he decided that he was mistaken, for he passed on after glancing back down the Court. But very likely his pause was only due to the fact that he was pulling on his overcoat. It was one he had purchased long ago, before the filling out had set in which awaits all athletes when they relapse into a sedentary life. Mo hated the coat, and the difficulties he met with when getting it on and off.

He was as good as his word about not stopping long at The Sun. Although he found his friend awaiting him, he did not remain in his company above half an hour, including his seven-minutes' walk back to the Court, to which Jerry accompanied him, saying farewell at the archway. He didn't go on to No. 7 at once, remembering that M'riar had said she wouldn't be sorry to go to bed.

Seeing lights and hearing voices in at Ragstroar's, he turned in for a chat, more particularly for a repetition of Micky's tale of his Hammersmith visit. Finding the boy there, he accepted his mother's suggestion that he should sit down and be comfortable. He did the former, having first pulled off the obnoxious coat to favour the latter.

He may have spent twenty minutes there, chiefly cross-examining Micky on particulars, before he got up to go. He forgot the odious coat, for Susan Burr called him back, and tried to persuade him to put it on. He resisted all entreaties. Such a little distance!—was it worth the trouble? He threw it over his arm, and again departed. The two women saw him from the door, and then, as they were exchanging a final word in the passage, were startled by a loud screaming, and, running out, saw Mo fling away the coat on his arm, and make such speed as he might towards a struggling group not over visible in the shadow of the lamp immediately above their heads.

This was within an hour of Mo's good-night, or good-bye, to M'riar at his own doorway.

Aunt M'riar had wavered yet a little before the fire, and had then given way to the thought of Dolly asleep. Dolly would be so unconscious of all things that it would now be no pain to know that she knew nothing of Death. Dolly asleep was always a solace to Aunt M'riar, even when she kicked or made sudden incoherent dream-remarks in the dark.

So, after placing Mo's candlestick conspicuously, that Susan Burr, who was pretty sure to come first, should see that he was still out, and not put up the chain nor shoot to the bolt, M'riar made her way upstairs to bed, very quietly, so as not to wake the children.

She was less than halfway to bed when she heard, as she thought, Susan Burr's return. It could not be Mo, so soon. Besides, he would have struck a match at once. He always did.

She listened for Susan's limping footstep on the stairs. Why did it not come? Something wrong there, or at least unusual! Leaving her candle, she wrapped herself hurriedly in a flannel garment she called her dressing-gown, and went downstairs to the landing. All was dark below, and the door was shut, to the street. She called in a loud whisper:—"Is that Susan?" and no answer came:—"Who is that?" and still no answer.

She went back quickly for her candle, and descended the stairs, holding it high up to see all round. No one in the kitchen itself, certainly. The little parlour-door stood open. She thought she had shut it. Could she be sure? She looked in, and could

see no one—advanced into the room, still seeing no one—and
started suddenly forward as the door swung to behind her.
She turned terrified, and found herself alone with the m‿n she
most dreaded—her husband. He had waited behind the door
till she entered, and had then pushed it to, and was leaning
against it.

"Didn't expect to see me, Polly Daverill, did you now? It's
me." He pulled a chair up, and, placing it against the door, sat
back in it slouchingly, with a kind of lazy enjoyment of her
terror that was worse than any form of intimidation. "What do
you want to be scared for? I'm a lamb. You might stroke me!
This here's a civility call. For to thank you for your letter,
Polly Daverill."

She had edged away, so as to place the table between them.
She could only suppose his words sardonically spoken, seeing
what she had said in her letter. "I wrote it for your own sake,
Daverill," said she deprecatingly, timidly. "What I said about
the Police was true."

"Can't foller that. .Say it again!"

"They *had* put on a couple of men, to keep an eye. They may
be there now. But I'd made my mind up you should not be
taken along of me, so I wrote the letter."

"Then what the Hell . . . !" His face set angrily, as he
searched a pocket. The sunken line that followed that twist in
his jaw grew deeper, and the scar on his knitted forehead told
out smooth and white, against its reddening furrows. He found
what he sought—her letter, which she recognised—and opened it
before he finished his spech. "What the Hell," he repeated, "is
the meaning of *this?*" He read it in a vicious undertone, biting
off each word savagely and throwing it at her.

She had rallied a little, but again looked more frightened than
ever. It cost her a gasping effort to say:—"You are reading
it wrong! Do give an eye to the words, Daverill."

"Read it yourself," he retorted, and threw the letter across
the table.

She read it through and remained gazing at it with a fixed
stare, rigid with astonishment. "I never wrote it so," said she
at last.

"Then how to God Almighty did it come as it is? Answer
me to that, Polly Daverill."

Her bewilderment was absolute, and her distress proportionate.
"I never wrote it like that, Daverill. I declare it true and solemn
I never did. What I wrote was for you to keep away, and I

made the words according. I can't say no other, if I was to die for it."

"None of your snivelling! How came it like it is?—that's the point! Nobody's touched the letter." He used his ill-chosen adjective for the letter as he pointed at it, so that one might have thought he was calling attention to a stain upon it. He dropped his finger slowly, maintaining his reproachful glare. Then suddenly:—"Did you invellop the damned thing yourself?"

She answered tremulously:—"I wrote it in this room at this table, where you sit, and put it in its invellop, and stuck it to, firm. And I put back the blotting-book where I took it from, not to tell-tale. . . ."

He interrupted her roughly. "Got the cursed thing there? *Where* did you take it from? . . . Oh—*that's* your blotting-book, is it? Hand it over!" She had produced it from the table-drawer close at hand, and gave it to him without knowing why he asked for it.

There is no need to connect his promptness to catch a clue to a forgery with his parentage. The clue is too simple—the spelling-book lore of the spy's infancy. The convict pulled out the top sheet of blotting-paper, and reversed it against the light. The second line of the letter was clear, and ended "now not." The "not" might, however, have been erased independently—probably would have been. But how about the end of the fourth line, also clear, with the word "run" on an oasis of clean paper, and nothing after it. That "no" in the letter was not the work of its writer.

"I put it in its invellop, Daverill, and not a soul see inside that letter from me till you. . . ."

"How do you know that?" He paused, reflecting. "It wasn't Juliar. She'd got no ink." This man was clever enough to outwit Scotland Yard, with an offer of fifty pounds for his capture, but fell easily to the cunning of a woman, roused by jealousy. It wasn't Julia, clearly? "Who had hold of the letter, between you and her?" said he, quite off the right scent.

"Only young Micky Ragstroar. . . ."

"There we've got it!" The man pounced. "Only that young offender and the Police. That was good for half a sov. for him. . . . Don't see what I mean? I'll tell you. *He* delivered your letter all right, after they'd run their eyes over it. I'll remember *him,* one day!" A word in this is not the one Daverill used, and his adjective is twice omitted. Aunt M'riar's puzzled face produced a more temperate explanation, to the effect that

Micky had carried the letter to a "tec," or detective, who had "got at him," and that the letter had been tampered with at the police-station.

"I wouldn't believe it of Micky, and I don't," said Aunt M'riar. "The boy's a good boy at heart, and no tale-bearer." She ventured, as an indirect appeal on Micky's behalf, to add:—"I'm shielding you, Daverill, and a many wouldn't."

He affected to recognise his indebtedness, but only grudgingly. "You're what they call a good wife, Polly Daverill. Partner of a cove's joys and sorrows! Got your marriage lines to show! That's your style. You stick to that!"

Something in his tone made M'riar say:—"Why do you speak like that? You know that I have." Her speech did not seem to arise from his words. She had detected a sneer in them.

"You've got 'em to show. . . . Ah! But I shouldn't show 'em, if I were you."

"Am I likely?"

"That's not what I was driving at."

"What do you mean?"

"Shall I tell you, Polly, my angel? Shall I tell you, respectable married woman?"

"Don't werrit me, Daverill. I don't deserve it of you!"

"Right you are, old Polly! And told you shall be! . . . Sure you want to know? . . . There, there—easy does it! I'm a-telling of you." He suddenly changed his manner, and spoke quickly, collectedly, drily. "The name on your stifficate ain't the correct name. *I* saw to that. Only you needn't fret your kidneys about it, that I see. You're an immoral woman, you are! Poor Polly! Feel any different?"

Anyone who knows the superstitious reverence for the "sacred" marriage tie that obtains among women of M'riar's class and type will understand her horror and indignation. And all the more if he knows the extraordinary importance they attach to a certificate which is, after all, only a guarantee that the marriage-bond is recorded elsewhere, not the attested record itself. For a moment she was unable to speak, and when words did come, they were neither protest nor contradiction, but:—"Let me out! Let me out!"

The convict shifted his chair without rising, and held the door back for her exit. "Ah," said he, "go and have a look at it!" He had taken her measure exactly. She went straight upstairs, carrying her candle to the wardrobe by Dolly's bed, where her few private possessions were hidden away. Dolly would not wake. If she did, what did it matter? Aunt M'riar heard a small melodious dream-voice in the pillow say tenderly:—" One cup wiv soody." It was the rehearsal of that banquet that the great Censorship had disallowed.

A lock in a drawer, refractory at first, brought to terms at last. A box found far back, amenable to its key at sight. A still clean document, found and read by the light of a hurriedly snuffed candle. Then an exclamation of relief from the reader:— " There now! As if I could have been mistook! " It was such a relief that she fairly gasped to feel it.

No doubt a prudent, judicious person, all self-control and guiding maxims, would have refolded and replaced that document, locked the drawer, hidden the key, and met the cunning expectancy of the evil face that awaited her with:—" You are entirely mistaken, and I was absolutely right."

But M'riar was another sort. Only one idea was present in the whirlwind of her release from that hideous anxiety—the idea of striking home her confutation of the lie that had caused it in the face of its originator. She did the very thing his subtlety had anticipated. As he heard her returning footsteps, and the rustle of the paper in her hand, he chuckled with delight at his easy triumph, and perhaps his joy added a nail in the coffin of his soul.

The snicker had gone from his face before she returned, marriage certificate in hand, and held it before his eyes. " There now! " said she. " What did I tell you? "

He looked at it apathetically, reading it, but not offering to take it from her. " 'Taint reg'lar! " said he. " Name spelt wrong, for one thing. My name."

" Oh, Daverill, how can you say that? It's spelt right."

" Let's have a look! " He stretched out his hand for it in the same idle way. Aunt M'riar's nature might have been far less simple than it was, and yet she might have been deceived by his manner. That he was aiming at possession of the paper was the last thing it seemed to imply. But he knew his part well, and whom he had to deal with.

Absolutely unsuspicious, she let his fingers close upon it. Even then, so sure did he feel of landing his fish, that he played it on the very edge of the net. " Well," said he. " Just you look at it again," and relinquished it to her. Then, instead of putting his hand back in his pocket, he stretched it out again, saying:— " Stop a bit! Let's have another look at it."

She instantly restored it, saying:—" Only look with your eyes, and you'll see the name's all right." And then in a startled voice:—"But what?—but why?" provoked by the unaccountable decision with which he folded it, never looking at it.

He slipped it inside the breast-pocket of his coat, and buttoned it over. "That was my game, you see!" said he, equably enjoying the dumb panic of his victim.

As for her, she was literally speechless, for the moment. At last she just found voice to gasp out:—"Oh, Daverill, you can't mean it! Give it me back—oh, give it me back! Will you give it me back for money? . . . Oh, how can you have the heart? . . ."

"Let's see the money. How much have you got? Put it down on this here table." He seemed to imply that he was open to negotiation.

With a trembling hand M'riar got at her purse, and emptied it on the table. "That is every penny," she said—"every penny I have in the house. Now give it me!"

"Half a bean, six bob, and a mag." He picked up and pocketed the sixteen shillings and a halfpenny, so described.

"Now you *will* give it back to me?" cried poor Aunt M'riar, with a wail in her voice that must have reached Dolly, for a pathetic cry answered her from the room above.

"Some o' these days," was all his answer, imperturbably. "There's your kid squealing. Time I was off. . . . What's that?"

Was it a new terror, or a thing to thank God for? Uncle Mo's big voice at the end of the court.

The convict made for the street-door—peeped out furtively. "He's turned in at young Ikey's," said he. Then to M'riar, using an epithet to her that cannot be repeated:—"Down on your knees and pray that your bully may stick there till I'm clear, or . . . Ah!—smell that!" It was his knife-point, open, close to her face. In a moment he was out in the Court, now so far clear of fog that the arch was visible, beyond the light that shone out of Ragstroar's open door.

Another moment, and M'riar knew what to do. Save Mo, or die attempting it! If the chances seemed to point to the convict passing the house unobserved she would do nothing.

That was not to be the way of it. He was still some twenty paces short of Ragstroar's when old Mo was coming out at the door with the light in it.

Aunt M'riar, quick on the heels of the convict, who was rather bent on noiselessness than speed, had flung herself upon him—so little had he foreseen such an attack—before he could turn to repel it. She clung to him from behind with all her dead-weight, encumbering that hand with the knife as best she might. She screamed loud with all the voice she had:—" Mo—Mo—he has a knife—he has a knife!" Mo flung away the coat on his arm, and ran shouting. "Leave hold of him, M'riar—keep *off* him—leave *hold!*" His big voice echoed down the Court, resonant with sudden terror on her behalf.

But her ears were deaf to any voice but that of her heart, crying almost audibly:—" Save *him!* Never give that murderous right hand its freedom! In spite of the brutal clutch that is dragging the hair it has captured from the living scalp—in spite of the brutal foot below kicking hard to reach and break a bone—cling hard to it! And if, power failing you against its wicked strength, it should get free, be you the first to meet its weapon, even though the penalty be death." That was her thought, for what had Mo done that he should suffer by this man—this nightmare for whose obsession of her own life she had herself alone to blame?

The struggle was not a long one. Before Mo, whose weak point was his speed, had covered half the intervening distance, a kick of the convict's heavy boot-heel, steel-shod, had found its bone, and broken it, just above the ankle. The shock was irresistible, and the check on the knife-hand perforce flagged for an instant—long enough to leave it free. Another blow followed, a strange one that M'riar could not localise, and then all the Court swam about, and vanished.

What Mo saw by the light of the lamp above as he turned out of Ragstroar's front-gate was M'riar, dressing-gowned and dishevelled, clinging madly to the man he could recognise as her convict husband. He heard her cry about the knife, saw that her hold relaxed, saw the blade flash as it struck back at her. He saw her fall, and believed the blow a mortal one. He heard the voice of Dolly wailing in the house beyond, crying out for the missing bedfellow she would never dream beside again. At least, that was his thought. And there before him was her slayer, with his wife's blood fresh upon his hands.

All the anger man can feel against the crimes of man blazed in his heart, all the resolution he can summon to avenge them knit the muscles of his face and set closer the grip upon his lip. And yet, had he been asked what was his strongest feeling at this moment, he would have answered:—" Fear!"—fear, that is, that his man, more active than himself and younger, should give him the slip, to right or to left, and get away unharmed.

But that was not the convict's thought, with that knife open in his hand. Indeed, the small space at command might have thwarted him. If, for but two seconds, he could employ those powerful fists that were on the watch for him on either side of the formidable bulk whose slow movement was his only hope, then he might pass and be safe. It would have to be quick work, with young Ikey despatched by the screaming women at Ragstroar's to call in help; either his father's from the nearest pot-house, or any police-officer, whichever came first.

Quick work it was! A gasp or two, and the man's natural flinching before the great prizefighter and his terrible reputation had to yield to the counsels of despair. It had to be done, somehow. He led with his left—so an expert tells us we should phrase it—and hoped that his greater alacrity would land a face-blow, and cause an involuntary movement of the fists to lay the body open. Then his knife, and a rip, and the thing would be done.

It might have been so, easily, had it been a turn-to with the gloves, for diversion. Then, twenty years of disuse would have had their say, and the slow paralysing powers of old age asserted themselves, quenching the swift activity of hand and eye, and making their responsive energy, that had given him victory in so many a hard-fought field, a memory of the past. But it was not so now. The tremendous tension of his heartfelt anger, when he found himself face to face with its dastardly object, made him again, for one short moment, the man that he had been in the plenitude of his early glory. Or, short of that, a near approach to it.

For never was a movement swifter than old Mo's duck to the left, which allowed his opponent's "lead off" to pass harmless over his right shoulder. Never was a cross-counter more deadly, more telling, than the blow with his right, which had never moved till that moment, landing full on the convict's jaw, and stretching him, insensible or dead, upon the ground. The sound of it reached the men who came running in through the arch, and made more than one regret he had not been there a moment sooner, to see it.

Speechless and white with excitement, all crowded down to where Mo was kneeling by the woman who lay stretched upon the ground beyond. Not dead, for she was moving, and speaking. And he was answering, but not in his old voice.

"I'm all as right as a trivet, M'riar. It's you I'm a-thinkin' of. . . . Some of you young men run for the doctor."

One appeared, out of space. Things happen so, in events of this sort, in London. No—she is not to be lifted about, till he sees what harm's done. Keep your hands off, all!

By some unaccountable common consent, the man on the ground, motionless, may wait his turn. Two or three inspect him, and one tentatively prods at the inanimate body to make it show signs of life, but is checked by public opinion. Then comes a medical verdict, a provisional one, marred by reservations, about the work that knife has done. A nasty cut, but no danger. Probably stunned by the fall. Bring her indoors. Ragstroar's house is chosen, because of the children.

Uncle Mo never took his eyes off M'riar till after a stretcher had come suddenly from Heaven knows where, and borne his late opponent away, with a crowd following, to some appointed place. He thought he heard an inquiry answered in the words:—"Doctor says he can do nothing for *him*," and may have drawn his inferences. Probably it was the frightened voices and crying of the children that made him move away slowly towards his own house. For he had asked the boy Micky "Had anyone gone to see to them?" and been answered that Mrs. Burr was with them. It was then that Micky noticed that his voice had fallen to little more than a whisper, and that his face was grey. What Micky said was that his chops looked awful blue, and you couldn't ketch not a word he said.

But he was able to walk slowly into the house, very slowly up the stairs. Dave, in the room above, hearing the well-known staircreak under his heavy tread, rushed down to find him lying on the bed in his clothes. Mo drew the child's face to his own as he lay, saying:—"Here's a kiss for you, old man, and one to take to Dolly."

" Am oy to toyk it up to her now this very minute?" said Dave.

" Now this very minute!" said Uncle Mo. And Dave rushed off to fulfil his mission.

When Susan Burr, a little later, tapped at his door, doubting if all was well with him, no answer came. Looking in and seeing him motionless, she advanced to the bed, and touched his hand. It never moved, and she listened for a breath, but in vain. Heart-failure, after intense excitement, had ended this life for Uncle Mo.

THE END

A BELATED PENDRIFT

"I CAN tell you exactly when it was, stupid!" said a middle-aged lady at the Zoological Gardens to a contented elderly husband, some eighteen years after the foregoing story ended. "It was before we were married."

"That does not convey the precise date, my dear, but no doubt it is true," said the gentleman unpoetically. At least, we may suppose so, as the lady said:—"Don't be prosy, Percy."

A little Macacao monkey in the cage they were inspecting withdrew his left hand from a search for something on his person to accept a nut sadly from the lady, but said nothing. The gentleman seemed unoffended, and carefully stripped a brand-label from a new cigar. "I presume," said he, "that 'before we were married' means 'immediately before?'"

"What would you have it mean?" said the lady.

The gentleman let the issue go, and made no reply. After he had used a penknife on the cigar-end to his satisfaction, he said:— "Exactly when was it?"

"Suppose we go outside and find my chair, if you are going to smoke," said the lady. "You mustn't smoke in here, and quite right, because these little darlings hate it, and I want to see the Hippopotamus."

"Out we go!" said the gentleman. And out they went. It was not until they had recovered the lady's wheeled chair, and were on their way towards the Hippopotamus, that she resumed the lost thread of their conversation, as though nothing had interrupted it.

"It was just about that time we came here, and Dr. Sir Thingummybob came up when we were looking at the Kinkajou—over there! ... No, I don't want to go there now. Go on through the tunnel." This was to the chairman, who had shown a tendency to go off down a side-track, like one of his class at a public meeting. "I suppose you remember that?"

"Rather!" said the gentleman, enjoying his first whiff.

"Well—it was just about then. A little after the accident—don't you remember?—the house that tumbled down?"

"I remember all about it. The old lady I carried upstairs.
853

Well—didn't you believe *then* it was all up with Sir Adrian's eye-sight? *I* did."

"My dear!—how you do overstate things! Shall I ever per-suade you to be accurate? We were all much alarmed about him, and with reason. But I for one always did believe, and always shall believe, that there was immense exaggeration. People do get so excited over these things, and make mountains out of mole-hills."

The gentleman said:—"H'm!"

"Well!" said the lady convincingly. "All I say is—see how well his eyes are now!"

The gentleman seemed only half convinced, at best. "There was something *rum* about it," said he. "You'll admit that?"

"It depends entirely on what you mean by 'rum.' Of course, there was something a little singular about so sudden a recovery, if that is what you mean."

"Suppose we make it 'a little singular!' I've no objection."

The interest of the main topic must have superseded the purely academical issue. For the lady appeared disposed towards a reca-pitulation in detail of the incidents referred to. "Gwen went away to Vienna with her mother in the middle of January," said she. "And . . . No—I'm not mistaken. I'm sure I'm right! Be-cause when we came back from Languedoc in June there was not a word of any such thing. And Lord Ancester never breathed as much as a hint. And he certainly *would* have, under the circum-stances. Why don't you speak and agree with me, or contradict me, instead of puffing?"

"Well, my love," said the gentleman apologetically, "you see, my interpretation of your meaning has to be—as it were—con-structive. However, I believe it to be accurate this time. If I understand you rightly . . ."

"And you have no excuse for not doing so. For I am sure that what I did say was as clear as daylight."

"Exactly. It is perfectly true that, when we went to Grosvenor Square in June, Tim said nothing about recovery. In fact, as I remember it—only eighteen years is a longish time, you know, to recollect things—he was regularly down in the mouth about the whole concern. I always believed, myself, that he would sooner have had Adrian for Gwen, on any terms, by that time—sooner than she should marry the Hapsburg, certainly. Not that he be-lieved that Gwen was going to cave out!"

"You never said he said that!"

"Because he didn't. He only cautioned me particularly against believing the rubbish that got into the newspapers. I am sure that if he had said anything *then* about recovery, I should remember it now."

" I suppose you would."

" And then six weeks after that Gwen came tearing home by herself from Vienna. Then the next thing we heard was that he had recovered his eyesight, and they were to be married in the autumn."

This was at the entrance to the tunnel, on the way to the Hippopotamus. One's voice echoes in this tunnel, and that may have been the reason the conversation paused. Or it may have been that resonance suggests publicity, and this was a private story. Or possibly, no more than mere cogitative silence of the parties. Anyhow, they had emerged into the upper world before either spoke again.

Then said the lady:—" It seems that it comes to the same thing, whichever way we put it. Something happened."

" My dear," replied the gentleman, " you ought to have been on the Bench. You have the summing-up faculty in the highest degree. Something happened that did not, as the phrase is, come out. But what was it?—that's the point! I believe we shall die without knowing."

" We certainly shall," said Mrs. Percival Pellew—for why should the story conceal her identity? " We certainly shall, if we go over and over and over it, and never get an inch nearer. You know, my dear, if we have talked it over once, we have talked it over five hundred times, and no one is a penny the wiser. You are so vague. What was it I began by saying?"

" That that sort of flash-in-the-pan he had . . . when he saw the bust, you know . . ."

" I know. Septimius Severus."

". . . Was just about the time Sir Coupland Merridew met us at the Kinkajou, and asked for the address in Cavendish Square. That was the end of September. Gwen told you all about it that same evening, and you told me when I came next day."

" I know. The time you spilt the coffee over my poplinette."

" I don't deny it. Well—what was it you meant to say?"

" What about? . . . Oh, I know—the Septimius Severus business! Nothing came of it. I mean it never happened again."

" I'm—not—so—sure! I fancy Tim thought something of the sort did. But I couldn't say. It's too long ago now to remember anything fresh. That's a Koodoo. If I had horns, I should like that sort."

"Never mind the Koodoo. Go on about Gwen and the blind story. You know we both thought she *was* going to marry the Hapsburg, and then she turned up quite suddenly and unexpectedly in Cavendish Square, and told Clo Dalrymple she had come back to order her *trousseau*. Then the Earl said that to you about the six months' trial."

"Ye-es. He said she had come home in a fine state of mind, because her mother hadn't played fair. He didn't give particulars, but I could see. Of course, that story in the papers *may* have been her mamma's doing. Very bad policy if it was, with a daughter like that. However, he said it was very near the end of the six months, and after all the whole thing was rather a farce. Besides, Gwen *had* played fair. So he had let her off three weeks, and she was going down to the Towers at once—which meant, of course, Pensham Steynes."

"And nothing else?"

"Only that he thought on the whole he had better go with her. Can't recall another word, 'pon my honour!"

"I recollect. But he didn't go, because Gwen waited for her mother to come with her. Undoubtedly that was the proper course." This was spoken in a Grundy tone. "But she was very indignant with Philippa about something."

"Philippa was backing the Hapsburg. All that is intelligible. What I want to understand—only we never shall—is how Adrian's eyes came right just at that very moment. Because, when we met him with his sister in London, he was as blind as a bat. And that was at Whitsuntide. You remember?—when his sister begged we wouldn't speak to him about Gwen. *We* thought it was the Hapsburg."

"Yes—they were just going back to Pensham after a month in London. She just missed them by a few hours. There was not a word of his being any better then."

"Not a word. Quite the other way. And then in a fortnight, or less, he saw as well as he had ever seen in his life. I don't see any use in putting it down to previous exaggeration, because a man can't see less than nothing, and that's exactly what he did see. Nothing! He told me so himself. Said he couldn't see me, and rather hoped he never should. Because he had formed a satisfactory image of me in his mind, and didn't want it disturbed by reality."

"He had that curious paradoxical way of talking. I always ascribed the odd things he said to that, more than to any lack of good taste."

"To what?"

"My dear, my meaning is perfectly obvious, so you needn't pretend you don't understand it. I am referring to his very marked individuality, which shows itself in speech, and which no person with any discernment could for one moment suppose to imply defective taste or feeling. He did say odd things, and he does say odd things."

"I can't see anything particularly odd in what he said about me. If a fillah forms a good opinion of another fillah whom he's never seen, obviously the less he sees of him the better. Let well alone, don't you know!"

"That is because you are as paradoxical as he is. All men are. But you might be sensible for once, and talk reasonably."

"Well, then—suppose we do, my dear!" said the gentleman, conciliatorily. "Let me see—what was I going to say just now—at the Koodoo? Awfully sensible thing, only something put it out of my head."

"You must recollect it for yourself," said the lady, with some severity. "I certainly cannot help you."

The gentleman never seemed to resent what was apparently the habitual manner of his lady wife. He walked on beside her, puffing contentedly, and apparently recollecting abortively; until, to stimulate his memory, she said rather crisply:—"Well?" He then resumed:—"Not so sensible as I thought it was, but somethin' in it for all that! Don't you know, sometimes, when you don't speak on the nail, sometimes, you lose your chance, and then you can't get on the job again, sometimes? You get struck. See what I mean?"

"Perhaps I shall, if you explain it more clearly," said his wife, with civility and forbearance, both of the controversial variety.

"I mean that if I had told Adrian then and there that he was an unreasonable chap to expect anyone to believe that his eyesight came back with a jump, of itself—because that was the tale they told, you know——"

"That was the tale."

"Then very likely he would have told me the whole story. But I was rather an ass, and let the thing slip at the time—and then I couldn't pick it up again. Never got a chance!"

"Precisely. Just like a man! Men are so absurdly secretive with one another. They won't this and they won't that, until one is surprised at nothing. I quite see that you couldn't rake it up now, seventeen years afterwards."

"Seventeen years! Come—I say!"

"Cecily is sixteen in August."

" Well—yes—well!—I suppose she is. I say, Con, that's a queer thing to think of! "

" What is? "

" That we should have a girl of sixteen! "

" What can you expect? "

" Oh—it's all right, you know, as far as that goes. But she'll be a grown-up young woman before we know it."

" Well? "

" What the dooce shall we do with her, then? "

" All parents," said the lady, somewhat didactically, " are similarly situated, and have identical responsibilities."

" Yes—but it's gettin' serious. I want her to stop a little girl."

" Fathers do. But we need not begin to fuss about her yet, thank Heaven! "

" 'Spose not. I say, I wonder what's become of those two young monkeys? "

" Now, you needn't begin to fidget about *them*. They can't fall into the canal."

" They might lose sight of each other, and go huntin' about."

" Well—suppose they do! It won't hurt you. But *they* won't lose sight of one another."

" How do you know that? "

" Dave is not a boy now. He is a responsible man of five-and-twenty. I told him not to let her go out of his sight."

" Oh well—I suppose it's all right. You're responsible, you know. *You* manage these things."

" My dear!—how can you be so ridiculous? See how young she is. Besides, he's known her from childhood."   .

The story does not take upon itself to interpret any portion whatever of this conversation. It merely records it.

The last speech has to continue on reminiscent lines, apparently suggested by the reference to the childhood of the speaker's daughter; one of the young monkeys, no doubt. " It does seem so strange to think that he was that little boy with the black grubby face that Clo's carriage stopped for in the street. Just eighteen years ago, dear! "

" The best years of my life, Constantia, the best years of my life! Well—they think a good deal of that boy at the Foreign Office, and it isn't only because he's a *protégé* of Tim's. He'll make his mark in the world. You'll see if he doesn't. Do you know?—that boy . . ."

" Suppose you give these crumbs to the Hippopotamus! I've been saving them for him."

The gentleman looked disparagingly in the bag the lady handed
to him. "Wouldn't he prefer something more tangible?" said he.
"Less subdivided, I should say."
"My dear, he's grateful for absolutely anything. Look at him
standing there with his mouth wide open. He's been there for
hours, and I know he expects something from me, and I've got
nothing else. Throw them well into his mouth, and don't waste
any getting them through the railings."
"Easier said than done! However, there's nothing like trying."
The gentleman contrived a favourable arrangement of sundry
scoriæ of buns and biscuits in his palms, arranged cupwise, and
cautiously approaching the most favourable interstice of the iron
railings, took aim at the powerful yawn beyond them.
"Good shot!" said he. "Only the best bit's hit his nose and
fallen in the mud!"
"There now, Percy, you've choked him, poor darling! How
awkward you are!" It was, alas, true! For the indiscriminate
shower of crumbs made straight, as is the instinct of crumbs, for
the larynx as well as the œsophagus of the hippo, and some of them
probably reached his windpipe. At any rate, he coughed violently,
and when the larger mammals cough it's a serious matter. The
earth shook. He turned away, hurt, and went deliberately into his
puddle, reappearing a moment after as an island, but evidently disgusted with Man, and over for the day. "You may as well go on
with what you were saying," said Mrs. Pellew.
"Wonder what it was! That fillah's mouth's put it all out of
my head. What was I saying?"
"Something about David Wardle."
"Yes. Him and that old uncle of his—the fighting man. The
boy can hardly talk about him now, and he wasn't eight when the
old chap died. Touchin' story! He has told me all he recollects—
more than once—but it only upsets the poor boy. I've never mentioned it, not for years now. The old chap must have been a fine
old chap. But I've told you all the boy told me, at the time."
"Ye-es. I remember the particulars, generally. You said the
row wasn't his fault."
"His fault?—no, indeed! The fellow drew a knife upon him.
You know he was that awful miscreant, Daverill. There wasn't a
crime he hadn't committed. But old Moses killed him—splendidly!
By Jove, I should like to have seen that!"
"Really, Percy, if you talk in that dreadful way, I won't listen
to you."
"Can't help it, my dear, can't help it! Fancy being able to kill

such a damnable beast at a single blow!" The undertone in which Mr. Pellew went on speaking to his wife may have contained some particulars of Daverill's career, for she said:—"Well—I can understand your feeling. But we won't talk about it any more, please!"

Whereto the reply was:—"All right, my dear. I'll bottle up. Suppose we turn round. It's high time to be getting home." So the chairman put energies into a return towards the tunnel. But for all that, the lady went back to the subject, or its neighbourhood. "Wasn't he somehow mixed up with that old Mrs. Alibone at Chorlton—Dave's aunt she is, I believe. At least, he always calls her so."

"Aunt Maria? Of course. She *is* his Aunt Maria. He was—or had been—Aunt Maria's husband. But people said as little about that as they could. He had been an absentee at Norfolk Island—a convict. That old chap she married—old Alibone—he's the great authority on horseflesh. Tim found it out when they came to Chorlton to stay at the very old lady's—what's her name?"

"Mrs. Marrable." Here Mrs. Pellew suddenly became luminous about the facts, owing to a connecting link. "Of course! Mrs. Marrable was the twin sister."

"A—oh yes!—the twin sister. . . . I remember . . . at least, I don't. Not sure that I do, anyhow!"

"Foolish man! Can't you remember the lovely old lady at Clo Dalrymple's? . . ."

"She *was* the one I carried upstairs. I should rather think I did recollect her. She weighed nothing."

"Oh yes—*you* remember all about it. Mrs. Marrable's twin sister from Australia."

"Of course! Of course! Only I'd forgotten for the moment what it was I didn't remember. Cut along!"

"I was not saying anything."

"No—but you were just going to."

"Well—I was. It was *her* grave in Chorlton Churchyard."

"That what?"

"That Gwen and our girl went to put the flowers on, three weeks ago."

"By-the-by, when are the honeymooners coming back?"

"The Crespignys? Very soon now, I should think. They were still at Siena when Gwen heard from Dorothy last, and it was unbearably hot, even there."

"I thought Cis wrote to Dolly in Florence."

"Not the last letter. They were at the Montequattrinis' in May.

That's what you're thinking of. Cis wrote to her there, then. It was another letter."

" 'Spose I'm wrong! I meant the letter where she told how the very old lady walked with them to the grave."

" Old Mrs. Marrable. Yes—and old Mrs. Alibone had to go in the carriage, because of her foot, or something. She has a bad foot. That was in the middle of June. *That* letter *was* to Fiesole. You do get so mixed up."

" Expect I do. Fancy that old lady, though, at ninety-eight!"

" Yes—fancy! Gwen said she was just as strong this year as last. She'll live to be a hundred, I do believe. Why—the other old woman at Chorlton is over seventy! Her daughter—or is it niece? I never know. . . ."

" Didn't Cis say she spoke of her as ' my mother '?"

" No—that was the twin sister that died. But she always spoke *to* her as ' mother.' "

" Oh ah—that was what Cis couldn't make head or tail of. Rather a puzzling turn out! But I say. . . ."

" What? . . . Wait till we get out of the noise. What were you going to say?"

" Isn't her head rather . . . I mean, doesn't she show signs of . . ."

" Senile decay? No. What makes you think that?"

" Of course, *I* don't know. I only go by what our girl said. Of course, Gwen Torrens is still one of the most beautiful women in London—or anywhere, for that matter! And it may have been nothing but that."

" Oh, I know what you mean now. ' Glorious Angel.' I don't think anything of that. . . . Isn't that the children there—by the Pelicans?"

It was, apparently. A very handsome young man and a very pretty girl, who must have been only sixteen—as her parents could not be mistaken—but she looked more. Both were evidently enjoying both, extremely; and nothing seemed to be further from their thoughts than losing sight of one another.

Says Mrs. Pellew from her chariot:—" My dear, what an endless time you have been away! I wish you wouldn't. It makes your father so fidgety." Whereupon each of these two young people says:—" It wasn't me." And either glances furtively at the other. No doubt it was both.

" Never mind which it was now, but tell me about old Mrs. Marrable at Chorlton. I want to know what it was she called your Aunt Gwen."

" Yes—tell about Granny Marrowbone," says the young man.

The girl testifies:—" Her Glorious Angel. When we first went into the Cottage. What she said was:—' Here comes my Glorious Angel!' Well!—why shouldn't she?"

" She *always* calls her that," says the young man.

" You see, my dear! It has not struck anyone but yourself as anything the least out of the way." Mrs. Pellew then explains to her daughter, not without toleration for an erratic judgment—to wit, her husband's—that that gentleman has got a nonsensical idea into his head that old Mrs. Marrable is not quite . . . Oh no—not that she is *failing,* you know—not at all! . . . Only, perhaps, not so clear as . . . Of course, very old people sometimes do. . . .

The girl looks at the young man for his opinion. He gives it with a cheerful laugh. " What!—Granny Marrowbone off her chump? As sound as you or I! She's called Lady Torrens her Glorious Angel ever since I can recollect. Oh no—*she's* all right." Whereupon Mr. Pellew says:—" I see—sort of expression. Very applicable, as things go. Oh no—no reason for alarm! Certainly not!"

" You know," says the girl, Cis—who is new, and naturally knows things, and can tell her parents,—" you know there is never the slightest reason for apprehension as long as there is no delusion. Even then we have to discriminate carefully between fixed or permanent delusions and. . ."

" Shut up, mouse!" says her father. " What's that striking?"

The young man looks at his watch—is afraid it must be seven. The elder supposes that some of the party don't want to be late for dinner. The young lady says:—" Well—I got it all out of a book." And her mother says:—" Now, please don't dawdle any more. Go the short way, and see for the carriage." Whereupon the young people make off at speed up the steps to the terrace, and a brown bear on the top of his pole thinks they are hurrying to give him a bun, and is disillusioned. Mr. Pellew accompanies his wife, but as they go quick they do not talk, and the story hears no further disconnected chat. Nor does it hear any more when the turnstiles are passed and the carriage is reached.

Soon out of sight—that carriage! And with it vanishes the last chance of knowing any more of Dave and Dolly and their country Granny. And when the present writer went to look for Sapps Court, he found—as he has told you—only a tea-shop, and the tea was bad.

But if ever you go to Chorlton-under-Bradbury, go to the churchyard and hunt up the graves of old Mrs. Picture and Granny Marrowbone.

www.ingramcontent.com/pod-product-compliance
Lightning Source LLC
Chambersburg PA
CBHW030916020726
47498CB00001B/3

* 9 7 8 1 4 3 4 4 2 5 6 3 8 *